★★★★THE★★★★
DOMINATION

★★★★THE★★★★
DOMINATION

S.M. STIRLING

BAEN

THE DOMINATION

This is a work of fiction. All the characters and events portrayed in this book are fictional, and any resemblance to real people or incidents is purely coincidental.

Copyright © 1999 by S.M. Stirling. Abridged and revised by the author from the previously published titles *Marching Through Georgia, Under the Yoke* and *The Stone Dogs*.

A Baen Books Original

Baen Publishing Enterprises
P.O. Box 1403
Riverdale, NY 10471

ISBN: 0-671-57794-8

Cover art by Stephen Hickman

First printing, May 1999

Library of Congress Cataloging-in-Publication Data
Stirling, S. ·M.
    The domination / S.M. Stirling.
       p.   cm.
    ISBN 0-671-57794-8 (hc)
    I. Title.
  PS3569.T543D66   1999   99-18561
  813'.54—DC21   CIP

Distributed by Simon & Schuster
1230 Avenue of the Americas
New York, NY 10020

Typeset by Windhaven Press, Auburn, NH
Printed in the United States of America

★★★★THE★★★★
DOMINATION

Prologue

LOW EARTH ORBIT
JULY 1ST, 2014
INGOLFSSON INCURSION TIMELINE
EARTH/2B

The richest man in the world liked eating pastrami sandwiches in orbit; he also liked conducting certain sensitive interviews there, where it was easier to be really sure nobody was listening in. He and the researcher were sitting and watching the sun set beyond the curve of earth, the planet turning like a great white-and-blue shield below him. The yacht's forward reentry plates were retracted, leaving the nose three-quarters transparent. Beyond earth, stars burned in airless clarity. Bright dots moved across their sight, ships and orbital habitats.

"Damn, I'm still not used to zero G," Henry Carmaggio said, snagging a scrap of pastrami that was floating away. The airscrubber system would get it eventually, but it was a little embarrassing.

The researcher was Japanese. Nomura Takashi by name, an up-and-coming young physicist who had been working for IngolfTech's Basic Research Division for a year now. He waited politely, occasionally straying up against the restraining harness of his seat.

"You're wondering why I brought you here," Carmaggio said, his voice still carrying more than a trace of blue-collar New York. He was a thick-shouldered man in his sixties, with short-cut grizzled hair. Trimly built, like virtually everyone these days—metaboline had been on the market since the turn of the millennium, and obesity was one with Nineveh, Tyre and cancer. The muscle showed the results of effort, though. His face was craggy and big-nosed, with a pleasant lived-in look.

"Yes, sir," Nomura said.

"It's because you've been asking questions," Carmaggio said easily. He chuckled at the sight of the younger man's alarm. "Oh, no problem. You were bound to do that sometime. Essentially, you've gotten through our cover story."

"Cover story?"

1

"The pretense that IngolfTech has actually been inventing the stuff we've been selling since 1999," Carmaggio said easily. "Not surprising. The horseshit about how the curve had to start rising exponentially in the late 90s and we just happened to be riding it—it doesn't make sense, when you think about it, despite what that SF writer—what's his name, Winge?—is always on about. People just accept it because all this"—he waved a hand at the spacecraft—"is here, after all. Something had to cause it."

Nomura ducked his head. "Yes, Carmaggio-san. But . . . you will pardon me . . . the more deeply I became involved in the company's research effort, the more it seemed . . . somehow . . . that we were trying to determine the physical-law basis of the technology, rather than developing technology from established theory. And even then, many of the theoretical breakthroughs were . . . far too convenient! The researchers who claimed them didn't have the information trail that would lead one to expect them to make such startling breakthroughs."

Carmaggio chuckled. *Smart boy*, he thought. *Now let's see how he handles something really weird.*

"Yeah," he said aloud. "In fact, there's just no way we could have gone from the stuff available in 1999—chemical rockets, coal-burning power stations, gasoline-powered cars—to what we've got now. Hell, IngolfTech and Sony just launched the first interstellar probe toward Alpha C! We've got Alfven-drive spaceships all over the solar system, direct-conversion fusion reactors, plasma beam weapons, computers a thousand times quicker and more powerful than at the turn of the century, hundreds of other things that've been tying the world economy in knots. We've eliminated pretty well every disease except old age, and we're working on that. Things nobody else can duplicate until we license. Tell me how we've done all that in fifteen years."

Nomura blinked. He'd have been wearing coke-bottle glasses in the old days, Carmaggio thought.

"Sir . . . the only logical conclusion I can reach is that somehow . . . somehow IngolfTech was *handed* the information it has been releasing. That it comes from outside the sphere of our civilization and its scientific tradition entirely. But that itself is not logical."

Carmaggio nodded. "You're right. We were handed it—captured it, to be blunt."

"Aliens," Nomura breathed. His hands were trembling; the older man judged that was excitement, more than fear. "Or . . . time travel? There are hints, beyond Tipler's work—"

"Not exactly," Carmaggio said. "It's a long story—and it starts more than two centuries ago, in a history that wasn't ours. Thank God for that! It runs up to four centuries in the future, and then loops over to New York, when I was a cop there fifteen years ago. Settle down and disconnect your critical faculties, Dr. Nomura. This shit is so strange you're going to *have* to believe it."

His face went grim. "The human race had a real close brush with disaster," he said. "Something worse than extinction."

"Carmaggio-san . . . what is worse than extinction?"

The young scientist was looking a bit green under his natural amber color, and the American didn't think it was space-sickness.

"Domestication. On our line of history, the Nazis and Communists and control freaks in general eventually lost . . . but on that other one, they won, a particularly nasty bunch of 'em. They thought they were the Master Race, you see."

"But that is a . . . a fatuous concept!" Nomura said, with stiff virtue. Fatuous or not, the Children of Amaterasu hadn't been immune to it; you just had to ask the Koreans or the *ita* to get an earful, even now. "Surely any culture possessed by a concept so illogical would be defeated, as the Nazis were."

"Son, don't generalize from a small sample." Carmaggio smiled bleakly. "Until recently, that's all we had—a sample of one history. Now we've got access to two, and . . . some things look less certain than they did. Nazis? Here's what happened *there* in that other history. . . ."

BOOK ONE

Chapter One

The shattering roar of six giant radial engines filled the hold of the Hippo-class transport aircraft, as tightly as the troopers of Century A, 1st Airborne Legion. They leaned stolidly against the bucking, vibrating walls of the riveted metal box, packed in their cocoons of parasail and body harness, strapped about with personal equipment and weapons like so many deadly slate-gray Christmas trees. The thin, cold air was full of a smell of oil and iron, brass and sweat and the black greasepaint that striped the soldiers' faces; the smell of tools, of a trade, of war. High at the front of the hold, above the rams that led to the crew compartment, a dim red light began to flash.

Centurion Eric von Shrakenberg clicked off the pocket flashlight, folded the map back into his case and sighed. *0400*, he thought. *Ten minutes to drop.* Eighty soldiers here in the transport; as many again in the one behind, and each pulled a Helot-class glider loaded with heavy equipment and twenty more troopers.

He was a tall young man, a hundred and eighty centimeters even without the heavy-soled paratrooper's boots, hard smooth athlete's muscle rolling on the long bones. Yellow hair and mustache were cropped close in the Draka military style; new lines scored down his face on either side of the beak nose, making him look older than his twenty-four years. He sighed again, recognizing the futility of worry and the impossibility of calm.

Some of the old sweats seemed to have it, the ones who'd earned the banners of the Domination of the Draka from Suez to Constantinople and east to Samarkand and the borderlands of China in the last war. And then spent the next twenty years hammering Turks and Kurds and Arabs into serfs as meek as the folk of the old African provinces. Senior Decurion McWhirter there, for instance, with the Constantinople Medal and the Afghan ribbon pinned to his combat fatigues, bald head shining in the dim lights . . .

7

He looked at the watch again: 0405. Time was creeping by. Only two hours since liftoff, if you could believe it.

I'll fret, he thought. *Staying calm would drive me crazy. Christ, I could use a smoke.* It would take the edge off; skydiving was the greatest thing since sex was invented, but combat was something you never really got used to. You were nervous the first time; then you met the reality, and it was worse than you'd feared. And every time after that, the waiting was harder . . .

Eric had come to believe he would not survive this war many months ago; his mind believed it, at least. The body never believed in death, and always feared it. It was odd; he hated the war and its purposes, but during the fighting, that conflict could be put aside. Garrison duty was the worst—

In search of peace, he returned to The Dream. It had come to him often, these last few years. Sometimes he would be walking through orchards, on a cool and misty spring morning; cherry blossoms arched above his head, heavy with scent, over grass starred with droplets of fog. There was a dog with him, a setter. Or it might be a study with a fire of applewood, lined with books with stamped leather spines, windows closed against slow rain . . . He had always loved books; loved even the smell and texture of them, their weight. There was a woman, too, walking beside him or sitting with her red hair spilling over his knees. A dream built of memories, things that might have been, things that could never be.

Abruptly he shook himself free of it. War was full of times with nothing to do but dream, but this was not one of them.

Most of the others were waiting quietly, with less tension than he remembered from the first combat drop last summer—blank-faced, lost in their own thoughts. Occasional pairs of lovers gripped hands. *The old Spartans were right about that,* he thought. *It does make for better fighters . . . although they'd probably not have approved of a heterosexual application.*

A few felt his gaze, nodded or smiled back. They had been together a long time, he and they; he had been private, NCO and officer-candidate in this unit. If this had been a legion of the Regular Line, they would all have been from the same area, too; it was High Command policy to keep familiar personnel together, on the theory that while you might enlist for your country, you died for your friends. And to keep your pride in their eyes.

The biggest drop of the war. Two full legions, 1st and 2nd Airborne, jumping at night into mountain country. Twice the size of the surprise assault in Sicily last summer, when the Domination had come into the war. Half again the size of the lightning strike that had given Fritz the Maikop oil fields intact last October, right after Moscow fell. Twenty-four thousand of the Domination's best, leaping into the night, "fangs out and hair on fire."

He grimaced. He'd been a tetrarch in Sicily, with only thirty-three troopers to command. *A soldier's battle,* they'd called it. Which meant bloody chaos, and relying on the troops and the regimental officers to pull it out of the can. Still, it had succeeded, and the parachute *chiliarchoi* had been built up to legion size, a tripling of numbers. Lots of promotions, if you made it at all. And a merciful transfer out once Italy was conquered and the "pacification" began; there would be nothing but butcher's work there now, best left to the Security Directorate and the Janissaries.

Sofie Nixon, his comtech, lit two cigarettes and handed him one at arm's length, as close as she could lean, padded out with the double burden of parasail and backpack radio.

"No wrinkles, Cap," she shouted cheerfully, in the clipped tones of Capetown and the Western Province. Listening to her made *him* feel nineteen again, sometimes. And sometimes older than the hills—slang changed so *fast*. That was a new one for "no problems."

"All this new equipment: to listen to the briefing papers, hell, it'll be like the old days. We can be heroes on the cheap, like our great-granddads were, shootin' down black spear-chuckers," she continued. With no change of expression, she added, "And I'm the Empress of Siam; would I lie?"

He smiled back at the cheerful cynical face. There was little formality of rank in the Draka armies, less in the field, least of all among the volunteer elite of the airborne corps. Conformists did not enlist for a radical experiment; jumping out of airplanes into battle was still new enough to repel the conservatives.

Satisfied, Sofie dragged the harsh, comforting bite of the tobacco into her lungs. The Centurion was a good sort, but he tended to . . . *worry* too much. That was part of being an officer, of course, and one of the reasons she was satisfied to stay at monitor, stick-commander. But he overdid it; you could wreck yourself up that way. And he was very much of the Old Domination, a scion of the planter aristocracy and their iron creed of duty; she was city-bred, her grandfather a Scottish mercenary immigrant, her father a dock-loading foreman.

Me, I'm going to relax while I can, she thought. There was a lot of waiting in the Army, that was about the worst thing . . . apart from the crowding and the monotonous food, and good Christ but being under fire was scary. Not nice-scary like being on a board when the surf was hot or a practice jump; plain *bad*. You really felt good afterward, though, when your body realized it was alive . . .

She pushed the thought out of her head. The sitreps had said this was going to be much worse than Sicily, and that had been deep-shit enough. Still, there had been good parts. The Italians really had some pretty things, and the paratroops got the first pick. That jewelry from the bishop's palace in Palermo was absolutely divine! And the tapestry . . . she sighed and smiled, in reminiscence. There had been leave, too—empty space on transport airships heading south, if you knew the right people. It was good to be able to peacock a little—do some partying, with a new campaign ribbon and the glamour of victory, and some pretties to show off.

Her smile grew smug. She had been *very* popular, with all the sexes and their permutations; a change from ugly-duckling adolescence. *Men are nice, definitely,* she thought. *Pity I had to wait till I reported to boot camp to start in on 'em.*

That was the other thing about the Army; it was better than school. Draka schooling was sex-segregated, on the theory that youth should not be distracted from learning and their premilitary training. Either that or sheer conservatism. Eight months of the year spent isolated in the countryside: from five to eighteen it had been her life, and the last few years had been growing harder to take. She was glad to be out of it, the endless round of gymnastics and classes and petty feuds and crushes; the Army was tougher, paratroop school more so, but what you did off duty was your own business. It was good to be an adult, free.

Even the winter in Mosul had been all right. The town was a hole, of course—provincial, and all new since the Draka conquest in 1916. Nothing like the mellow beauty of Capetown, with its theaters and concerts and famous nightspots . . . Mosul—well, what could you expect of a place whose main claim to fame was petrochemical plants? They'd been up in the mountains most of the time, training hard. She flexed her shoulders and neck complacently. She'd thought herself fit before, but four months of climbing under full load and wrestling equipment over boulders had taken the last traces of puppy fat off and left her with what her people considered the ideal feminine figure—sleek, compactly curved, strong, and quick.

Sofie glanced sidelong at her commander; she thought he'd been noticing, since she qualified for comtech. Couldn't tell, though; he was one for keeping to himself. Just visited the officer's Rest Center every week or so. But a man like that wouldn't be satisfied with serf girls; he'd want someone he could *talk* to . . .

Or maybe it's my face? she thought worriedly, absently stripping the clip out of the pistol-grip well of her machine pistol and inserting it again. Her face was still obstinately round and snub-nosed; freckles were all very well, enough men had described it as *cute*, but it obstinately refused to mature into the cold, aquiline regularity that was most admired. She sighed, lit another cigarette, started running the latest costume drama over again in her head. *Tragic Destiny:* Signy Anders and Derek Wallis as doomed Loyalist lovers fighting the American rebels, with Carey Plesance playing the satanic traitor George Washington . . .

God, it must have been uncomfortable wearing those petticoats, she thought. *No wonder they couldn't do anything but look pretty and faint; how could you fight while wearing a bloody tent? Good thing Africa cured them of those notions.*

0410, Eric thought. *Time.* The voice of the pilot spoke in his earphones, tinny and remote.

"Coming up on the drop zone, Centurion," she said. "Wind direction and strength as per briefing. Scattered cloud, bright moonlight." A pause. "Good luck."

He nodded, touching his tongue to his lip. The microphone was smooth and heavy in his hand. Beside him the American war correspondent, Bill Dreiser, looked up from his pad and then continued jotting in shorthand.

✧　　✧　　✧

Dreiser finished the paragraph and forced his mind to consider it critically, scanning word by word with the pinhead light on the other end of the pen. Useful, when you had to consult a map or instrument without a conspicuous light; the Domination issued them to all its officers, and he had been quick to pick one up. The device was typical of that whole bewildering civilization; he turned it in his hands, feeling the smooth careful machining of its duralumin parts, admiring the compact powerful batteries, the six different colors of ink, the moving segments that made it a slide rule as well.

Typical indeed, he thought wryly. Turned out on specialized machine tools, by illiterate factory serfs who thought the world was flat and that the Combine that owned their contracts ruled the universe.

He licked dry lips, recognizing the thought for what it was: a distraction from fear. He had been through jump training, of course— an abbreviated version tailored to the limitations of a sedentary American in early middle age. And he had seen enough accidents to the youngsters about him to give him well-justified nightmares; if those magnificent young animals could suffer their quota of broken bones and wrenched backs, so could he. And they would be jumping into the arms of Hitler's Wehrmacht; his years reporting from Berlin had not endeared him to the National Socialists . . .

He glanced across the echoing gloom of the cargo hold to where Eric sat, smoking a last cigarette. His face was impassive, showing no more emotion than it had at briefings around the sand table in Mosul. A strange young man. The eagle-faced blond good looks were almost a caricature of what a landed aristocrat of the Domination of the Draka was expected to be; so was his manner, most of the time. Easy enough to suppose there was nothing there but the bleakly efficient, intellectual killing machine of legend, the amoral and ruthless superman driven by the Will to Power whom Nietzsche had proclaimed.

He had mentioned that to Eric, once. "A useful myth," had been the Draka's reply. That had led them to a discussion of the German thinker's role in developing the Domination's beliefs; and of how Nietzsche's philosophy had been modified by the welcoming environment he found among the Draka, so different from the incomprehension and contempt of his countrymen.

"The Domination was founded by losers," Eric had said, letting an underlying bitterness show through. "Ex-masters like the Loyalists and all those displaced European aristocrats and Confederate southerners; prophets without followers like Carlyle and Gobineau and Nietzsche. The outcasts of Western civilization, not the 'huddled masses' you Yankees got. My ancestors were the ones who wouldn't give up their grudges. Now they're coming back for their revenge."

Dreiser shrugged and brought his mind back to the present, tugging at the straps of his harness one more time. Times like this he could understand the isolationists; he had been born in Illinois and raised in Iowa himself, and knew the breed. A lot of them were decent enough, not fascist sympathizers like the German-American Bund, or dupes like Lindberg. Just decent people, and it was so tempting to think the oceans could guard American wholesomeness and decency from the iron insanities and corruptions of Europe . . .

Not that he had ever subscribed to that habit of thought; it led too easily to white sheets and hatred, destroying a tradition to protect it. Dreiser ground his teeth, remembering the pictures from Pearl Harbor—oily smoke pouring to the sky from Battleship Row, the aircraft carrier *Enterprise* exploding in a huge globe of orange fire as the Japanese dive-bombers caught her in the harbor mouth . . . The United States had paid a heavy price for the illusion of isolation, and now it was fighting on its own soil, full-fledged states like Hawaii and the Philippines under enemy occupation. His prewar warnings of the Nazi menace had not been heeded; now his reports might serve to keep the public aware that Japan was not the only enemy, or the most dangerous of the Axis.

"Jumpmasters to your stations!" Eric's amplified voice overrode even the engines, there was a glisten of eyes, a hundredfold rattle as hands reflexively sought the ripcords. *"Prepare to open hatch doors."*

"And step into the shit," came the traditional chorus in reply.

Far to the south in Castle Tarleton, overlooking the Draka capital of Archona, a man stood leaning on the railing of a gallery, staring moodily at the projacmap that filled the huge room below. He was an Arch-Strategos, a general of the Supreme General Staff. The floor of the room was glass, twenty meters by thirty; the relief map was eerily three dimensional and underlit to put contrast against contour marks and unit counters. The mountains of Armenia extended in an infinity of scored rock, littered with the symbols of legions, equipment, airstrips, and roads; the red dots of aircraft crawled north toward Mount Elbruz and the passes of the Caucasus. Stale tobacco scented the air and the click-hum of the equipment echoed oddly in the unpeopled spaces.

"Risky," he said, nodding toward the map.

"War is risk," the officer beside him replied. The cat-pupiled eye of Intelligence was on her collar, she had the same air of well-kept middle age as he, and a scholar's bearing. "Breaking the Ankara Line was a risk, too; but it gave us Anatolia, back in '17."

The general laughed, rubbing at his leg. The fragments from the Austrian antiairship burst had severed tendons and cut nerves; the pain was a constant backdrop to his life, and worse on these cold nights. *Pain does not hurt*, he reminded himself. *Only another sensation. The Will is Master.* "Then I was an optimistic young centurion, out at the sharp end, sure I could pull it out of the kaak even if the high command fucked it up," he said. "Now the new generation's out there, and probably expecting to have to scoop up *my* mistakes."

"I was driving a field ambulance in '16; all you male lords of creation thought us fit for, then."

He laughed. "We weren't quite so stretched for reliable personnel, then." The woman snorted and poked a finger into his ribs.

"Hai, that was a *joke*, Cohortarch," he complained with a smile.

"So was that, you shameless reactionary bastard," she retorted. "If you're going to insult me, do it when we're on-duty and I can't object . . ."

He nodded, and grew grim. "Well, we're committed to this attack; the Domination wasn't built by playing safe. There'll never be another chance like this. Thank the White Christ that Hitler attacked the Soviets after he finished off the French. If they'd stayed in Europe, we'd never have been able to touch them."

She nodded, hesitated, spoke: "Your boy's in the first wave, isn't he, Karl?"

The man nodded, turning away from the railing and leaning his weight against the ebony cane at his side. "Eric's got a Century in the First Airborne," he said quietly, looking out over the city. "And my daughter's flying an Eagle out of Kars." The outer wall was window from floor to ceiling; Castle Tarleton stood on a height that gave a fine view of the Domination's capital. The fort had been built in 1791, when the Crown Colony of Drakia was new. The hilltop placement had been for practical reasons, once: cavalry had been based here, rounding up labor for the sugar plantations of Natal, where the ancestors of the Draka were settling into their African home.

Those had been American loyalists, mostly southerners, driven from their homes by vengeful neighbors after the triumph of the Revolution. The British had found it cheap enough to pay their supporters with the stolen goods of colonial empire.

"Strange," Karl von Shrakenberg continued, softly enough to make her lean toward the craggy face. "I can command a legion handily enough—by Gobineau's ghost, I wish they'd give me a field command—run my estate; I even get along well with my daughters. But my son . . . Where do the children go? I remember taking him from the midwife, I remember setting him on my shoulders and naming the stars for him, putting him on his first pony. And now? We hardly speak, except to argue. About absurdities: politics, books . . . When did we become strangers? When he left, there was nothing. I wanted to tell him . . . everything: to come back alive, that I loved him. Did he know it?"

His companion laid a hand on his shoulder. "Why didn't you say it?" she asked softly. "If you can tell me?"

He sighed wearily. "Never was very good with words, not that sort. And there are things you can say to a friend that you can't to your blood; perhaps, if Mary were still alive . . ." He straightened, his eyes focusing on the world beyond the glass. "Well. This view was always a favorite of mine. It's seen a lot."

Together they looked down across the basin, conscious of the winds hooting off the high plateau at their backs, cold and dry with winter. The first small fort of native fieldstone had grown over the years; grown with the colony of Drakia, named for Francis Drake and heir to that ruthless freebooter's spirit. It was a frontier post guarding the ranches and diamond mines, at first. Railways had snaked by to the great gold fields of the Whiteridge; local coal and iron had proved more valuable still, and this was a convenient post for a garrison to watch the teeming compounds of serf factory hands that grew beside the steel

mills and machineworks. Then the Crown Colony became the autono-
mous Dominion of Draka and needed a capital, a centrum for a realm
that stretched from Senegal to Aden, from the Cape to Algeria.

Lights starred the slopes beneath them, fading the true stars above;
mansions with roofs of red tile, set in acres of garden. A monorail
looped past, a train swinging through silently toward the airship haven
and airport to the west, windows yellow against the darkness. A tracery
of streets, sprawling over ridge and valley to the edge of sight, interrupted by the darker squares of parkland . . . eight million souls in
Archona. Through the center slashed the broad Way of the Armies,
lined with flowering jacaranda trees, framed between six-story office
blocks, their marble and tile washed snow-pale in moonlight. The
Assembly building, with its great two hundred meter dome of iridescent stained glass; the Palace where Archon Gunnarson had brought
law into conformity with fact and proclaimed the Domination a sovereign state, back in 1919.

Karl's mouth quirked; he had been here in the Castle on that
memorable day. The staff officers had raised a loyal glass of Paarl brandy,
then gone back to their planning for the pacification of the New
Territories and the *next* war. None of them had expected the Versailles
peace to last more than a generation, whatever the American president might say of a "war to end war." Unconsciously, his lip curled
in contempt; only a Yankee could believe something that obviously
fatuous.

"You grew up here, didn't you, Sannie?" he said, shaking off the
mood of gloom.

"*Ja,*" she replied. "Born over there." She pointed past the block of
government buildings, to where the scattered colonnades of the University clustered. "In the house where Thomas Carlyle lived. Nietzsche
visited my father there, seemed to think it was some sort of shrine.
That was a little while after he moved to the Domination. Anthony
Trollope stopped by as well, they tell me. While he was researching
that book, *Prussia in the Antipodes*, back in the 1870s. He was the
one the English didn't pay any attention to, and then wished they had."

Their gaze lifted, to the glow that lit the northern horizon—the
furnaces and factories of the Ferrous Metals Combine, stamping and
grinding out the engines of war. "Well," he said, offering her an arm
with a courtesy old-fashioned even in their generation of Draka. "Shall
we see if, somewhere in this bureaucrat's paradise of a city, two ancient
and off-duty warriors can find a drink?"

He would face the waiting as he would any other trial; as befitted
a von Shrakenberg of Oakenwald. *Even if I'm the last,* he thought,
as his halting boot echoed through the empty halls of the fortress.

Thump! Eric's parachute unfolded, a rectangle of blackness against
the paling stars of dawn. He blinked. Starlight and moonlight were
almost painfully bright after the crowded gloom of the transport; silence
caressed his mind.

Straps caught at crotch and waist and armpits, then cradled him
in their padding. Above him the night was full of thunder, as hundreds

of the huge transports spilled their cargos of troops and equipment into the thin air. Above, a flight of Falcon III fighters banked, their line stretching into an arc, moonlight glinting on the bubble canopies, sharks of the sky.

This is the best time, Eric thought, as the flight of transports vanished, climbing and turning for height and home, southward to their bases. Silence, except for the fading machines and the hiss of the wind through the silk. Silence over a great scattered cloudscape, castles and billows of silver under a huge cool moon, air like crisp white wine in the lungs, aloneness. A feeling beyond the self: peace, joy, freedom—in a life bound on the iron cross of duty, in the service of repression and death. There had been a few other times like this, making love with Tyansha, or single-handing a ketch through monsoon storms. But always here, alone in the sky.

The rest of the Century were forming up behind, wheeling like a flight of birds of prey; he saw with relief that the gliders were following with their cargo of heavy weapons and specialists. The 2nd Cohort was the northernmost unit, and Century A was the point formation of 2nd Cohort. They would take the shock of whatever reaction force the Fritz could muster to relieve their cut-off comrades south of the mountains. Two hundred of them, to blunt the enemy spearheads; they were going to *need* that special equipment. Badly.

Now . . . The cloud cover was patchy, light and shadow. Southward, the main peaks of the Caucasus shone snow white. Below was a black-purple immensity of scree, talus-slope, dark forests of beech and holm oak, sloping down to a valley and a thread of road winding up into the mountains. On a map it was nothing, a narrow sliver of highland between the Black and Caspian Seas. . . .

Over it all loomed the great mass of Mount Elbruz. Beyond it was the south slope, ex-Soviet Georgia; beyond that the Draka armored legions massing in the valleys of Armenia. The symbolism of it struck him—all Europe was in shadow, in a sense. From the Elbe to the Urals, there was a killing under way great enough to leave even the cold hearts at Castle Tarleton shaken . . . Eric had been a student of history, among other things; his mouth quirked at the supreme irony that the Draka should come as deliverers.

He stooped, a giddy exhilarating slide across the sky, a breathless joy. For a moment he was a bird, a hunting bird, an eagle. Stooping on the world, feeling the air rushing past his wings . . . *Be practical, Eric,* he reminded himself severely. Once they grounded they would have only their feet, and the south slope of the mountains was German-held.

But lightly; and now they were a *very* long way from home—thousands of miles of mud trail, torn-up railway, scorched earth.

The ground was coming up fast; he could smell it, a wet green scent of trees and spring meadow-grass and rock. This area had been swarming with Draka reconnaissance planes for months; the contours were springing out at him, familiar from hundreds of hours poring over photomaps. He banked to get a straight run at the oblong meadow.

Carefully now, don't get caught in that fucking treeline. . . . Branches
went by three meters below. He hauled back on the lines, turning up
the forward edge of the parasail; it climbed, spilled air, slowed. With
the loss of momentum it turned from a wing to a simple parachute
once more, and good timing landed him softly on his feet, boots vanishing in knee-high grass starred with white flowers.

Landing was a plunge from morning into darkness and shadow, as
the sun dropped below the mountains to the southeast. And always,
there was a sense of sadness, of loss; lightness turning to earthbound
reality. *Not an eagle any more,* went through him. *More like a hyena,*
a mordant part of his mind prompted. *Come to squabble over the carcass
of Russia with the rival pack.*

Swiftly, he hit the quick-release catches and the synthsilk billowed
out, white against the dark grass. He turned, clicking on the shielded
red flashlight, waving it in slow arcs above his head. The first troopers of his Century were only seconds behind him, gray rectangles against
the stars. They landed past him, a chorus of soft grunts and thuds,
a curse and a clatter as somebody rolled. A quick check: mapcase,
handradio, binoculars, Holbars T-6 assault rifle, three 75-round drums
of 5mm for it, medikit, iron rations, fighting dagger in his boot, bush
knife across his back . . . that was an affectation—the machete-sword
was more a tradition than anything else, but . . .

Dropping their chutes and jogging back by stick and section, rallying to the shouts of their decurions and tetrarchs, platoon commanders,
the troopers hurried to form in the shadows of the trees. Sofie jogged
over to her position with the headquarters communication *lochos,* the
antennae waving over her shoulder; she had the headset on already,
tufts of bright tow hair ruffling out between the straps. As usual, she
had clipped her helmet to her harness on touchdown; also as usual,
she had just lit a cigarette. The match went *scrit* against the magazine well of her machine pistol; she flicked it away and held out the
handset.

For Dreiser, leaving the airplane had been a whirling, chaotic rush.
For a moment he tumbled, then remembered instructions. *Arms and
legs straight.* That brought the sickening spiral to a stop; he was flying forward, down toward silver clouds and the dark holes between
them.

"Flying, hell, I'm *falling,*" he said into the rush of cold wind. His
teeth chattered as he gripped the release toggle and gave the single
firm jerk the Draka instructors had taught. For a heart-stopping moment
there was nothing and then the pilot chute unfolded, dragging out the
main sail. It bloomed above him, the reduction in speed seeming to
drag him backward out of his fall. Air gusted past him, more slowly
now that the parachute was holding. He glanced up to the rectangle
above him, a box of dozens of long cloth tubes fastened together side
by side, held taut by the rush of air. " 'The parasail functions as both
a parachute and a wing,' " he quoted to himself. " 'To acquire forward
speed, lean forward. Steer by hauling on left or right cords, or by shifting
the center of gravity' . . ."

God it's working. Blinking his eyes behind the goggles that held his glasses to his face, he peered about for the recognition light. The aircraft had vanished, nothing more than a thrum of engine noise somewhere in the distance. There it was, a weak red blinking: he shifted his weight forward, increasing the angle of glide. Cautiously; you could nose down in these things and he doubted he could right it again before he hit.

The meadow rose up to strike; he flung himself back, too soon, lost directional control, and barely avoided landing boot-first in another chute at a hundred feet up. Ground slammed into his soles and he collapsed, dragging.

"Watch where you puttin' y'feet. Yankee pigfuckah," an incongruously young and feminine voice snarled as he skidded through tall grass and sharp-edged gravel on his behind, scrabbling at the release straps until the billowing mass of fabric peeled away to join the others flapping on the ground. He stood, turned, flung himself down again as the dark bulk of a glider went by a foot above his head, followed by a second.

"Jesus!" he swore, as they landed behind him and collided with a brief crunch of splintering plywood and balsa. Boots hurdled him, voices called in throttled shouts, the clearing filling with a shadowy ordered chaos.

Dreiser walked toward the spot where the Draka commanders would be gathering, feeling strength return to his rubbery legs and a strange exhilaration building.

Did it, by God! he thought. So much for being an old man at thirty-eight. . . . Now, about the article, let's see: *The landing showed once again the value of careful preparation and training. Modern warfare, with its complex coordination of different arms, is something new on this earth. Our devotion to the "minuteman" tradition of the amateur citizen-soldier is a critical handicap . . .*

Eric took the handset, silent for a moment as the gliders came in. The sailplanes slewed to a halt, the wing of one catching the other's tail with a crunch of plywood. A sigh gusted up as the detachable nose sections fell away and figures began unloading.

Sofie gently tapped his hand. "Set's workin' fine, Centurion," she said. "Got the Cohort Sparks already, green-beepers from all the hand-radios in the Century . . . want a smoke?"

"Trying to give it up," he grunted, lifting the phone to his ear and clicking the pressure button in his call sign. "You should too." He glanced at his watch: 0420 almost exactly. Forty-five minutes to dawn.

"Hey, Centurions, do I complain about your sheep?" she replied, grinning. The rest of the headquarters tetrarchy were falling in around him: Senior Decurion McWhirter, two five-trooper rifle "sticks" who would double as runners, two rocket-gun teams and a heavy machine gun.

They both fell silent as the hissing of static gave way to voices, coded sequences and barked instructions. Unconsciously, Eric nodded several times before speaking.

"Yes? Yes, sir. No, sir; just coming in, but it looks good." Reception

was excellent; he could hear a blast of small-arms fire in the background, the rapid snarl of Draka assault rifles, the slower thump and
chatter of German carbines and MG 34s.

"Ah, good." Then he and the comtech winced in unison. "The armor
landed *where?* Sorry, sir, I know you didn't design this terrain . . .
Right, proceed according to plan, hold them hard as long as I can.
Any chance of extra antitank . . . Yes, Cohortarch, I appreciate everybody
wants more firepower, but we *are* the farthest north . . . Yes, sir, we
can do it. Over and out, status report when Phase A is complete. Thank
you, sir, and good luck to you, too."

"Because we're both going to need it," he added under his breath
as he released the send button. The Legion had had a Cohort of light
tanks, Cheetahs with 75mm guns in oscillating turrets. Those had
apparently come down neatly in a gully . . .

The gliders were emptying, stacks of crates and heavy weapons being
lifted onto their wheeled carts. And already the trunks of the birches
were showing pale in the light of dawn.

A sudden sense of the . . . *unlikeliness* of it all struck Eric. He
had been born in the heartlands of the Domination, fourteen thousand kilometers away in southern Africa. And here he stood, on soil
that had seen . . . how many armies? Indoeuropeans moving south
to become Hittites, Cimmerians, Scythians, Sarmatians, Persians, Greeks,
Romans, Byzantines, Armenians, Arabs, Turks, Tzarist Russians, Bol-
sheviks . . . and now a Century of Draka, commanded by a descen-
dant of Hessian mercenaries, come to kill Germans who might be remote
cousins, and who had marched two thousand kilometers east to meet
him . . .

What am I doing here? Where did it start? he thought. Such a long
way to journey, to die among angry strangers. A journey that had lasted
all his life . . . The start? Oakenwald Plantation, of course. In the year
of his birth; and last year, six months ago. But that was the past, and
the battle was here and now, an ending awaiting him. An end to pain,
weariness; an end to the conflict within, and to loneliness. One could
forget a great deal in combat.

Eric von Shrakenberg took a deep breath and stepped forward, into
the war.

Chapter Two

ARCHONA TO OAKENWALD PLANTATION
OCTOBER 1941

The airdrop on Sicily had earned Eric von Shrakenberg a number of things: a long scar on one thigh, certain memories, and a field promotion to Centurion's rank. When the 1st Airborne Chiliarchy was pulled back into reserve after the fall of Milan, the promotion was confirmed; a rare honor for a man barely twenty-four. With it came fourteen-day leave passes to run from October 1, 1941, and unlike most of his comrades, he had not disappeared into the pleasure quarter of Alexandria; it was well for a man to visit the earth that had borne him, before he died.

He spent the last half-hour in the airship's control gallery, for the view; they were coming in to Archona from the north, and it was a side of the capital free citizens seldom saw, unless business took them there. For a citizen, Archona was the marble-and-tile public buildings and low-rise office blocks, parks and broad avenues, the University campus, and pleasant, leafy suburbs with the gardens for which the city was famed.

Beyond the basin that held the freemen's city lay the world of the industrial combines, hectare upon hectare, eating ever deeper into the bush country of the middleveld. A spiderweb of roads, rail sidings, monorails, landing platforms for freight airships. The sky was falling into night, but there was no sleep below, only an unrestfulness full of the light of arc lamps and the bellowing flares of the blast furnaces; factory windows carpeted the low hills, shifts working round the clock. Only the serf compounds were dark, the flesh-and-blood robots of the State exhausted on their pallets, a brief escape from a lockstep existence spent in that wilderness of metal and concrete.

Eric watched it with a fascination tinged with horror as the crew guided the great bulk of the lighter-than-air ship in, until light spots danced before his eyes. And remembered.

In the center of Archona, where the Avenue of Triumph met the Way of the Armies, there was a square with a victory monument. A hundred summers had turned the bronze green and faded the marble plinth; about it were gardens of unearthly loveliness, where children played between the flowerbanks. The statue showed a group of Draka soldiers on horseback; their weapons were the Ferguson rifle-muskets and double-barreled dragoon pistols of the eighteenth century. Their leader stood dismounted, reins in one hand, bush knife in the other. A black warrior knelt before him, and the Draka's boot rested on the man's neck.

Below, in letters of gold, were words: To the Victors. That was *their* monument; northern Archona was a monument to the vanquished, and so were the other industrial cities that stretched north a thousand kilometers to Katanga; so were mines and plantations and ranches from the Cape to Shensi.

In the morning the transport clerk was apologetic; also harried. Private autocars were up on blocks for the duration mostly; in the end, all she could offer was a van taking two Janissaries south to pick up recruits from the plantations. Eric shrugged indifferently, to the clerk's surprise. The city-bred might be prickly in their insistence on the privileges of the master caste, but a von Shrakenberg was raised to ignore such trivia. Also . . . he remembered the rows of Janissary dead outside Palermo, where they had broken the enemy lines to relieve the encircled paratroops.

The roadvan turned out to be a big six-wheeled Kellerman steamer twenty years old, a round-edged metal box with running boards chest-high and wheels taller than he. It had been requisitioned from the Transportation Directorate, and still had eyebolts in the floor for the leg shackles of the work gangs. The Janissaries rose from their kitbags as Eric approached, flicking away cigarettes and giving him a respectful but unservile salute; the driver in her grimy coverall of unbleached cotton bowed low, hands before eyes.

"Carry on," Eric said, returning the salute. The serf soldiers were big men, as tall as he, their snug uniforms of dove gray and silver making his plain Citizen Force walking-out blacks seem almost drab. Both soldiers were in their late thirties and Master Sergeants, the highest rank subject-race personnel could aspire to. They were much alike— hard-faced and thick-muscled; unarmed, here within the Police Zone, but carrying steel-tipped swagger sticks in white-gloved hands. One was ebony black, the other green-eyed and tanned olive, and might have passed for a freeman save for the shaven skull and serf identity-number tattooed on his neck. The vehicle pulled out of the loading bay with the smooth silence of steam power, into the crowded streets; he brought out a book of poetry, Rimbaud, and lost himself in the fire-bright imagery.

When he looked up in midmorning they were south of the city. Crossing the Whiteridge and the scatter of mining and manufacturing settlements along it, past the huge, man-made heaps of spoilage from the gold mines. Some were still rawly yellow with the cyanide compounds used to extract the precious metal; others were in every stage of reclamation, down to forested mounds that might have been natural.

This ground had yielded more gold in its century and a half than all the rest of the earth in all the years of humankind; four thousand meters beneath the road, men still clawed at rock hot enough to raise blisters on naked skin. Then they were past, into the farmlands of the high plateau; it was a relief to smell the goddess breath of spring overtaking the carrion stink of industrial-age war. The four-lane asphalt surface of the road stretched dead straight to meet the horizon that lay around them like a bowl; waist-high fields of young corn flicked by, each giving an instant's glimpse down long, leafy tunnels floored with brown, plowed earth. Air that smelled of dust and heat and green poured in, and the sea of corn shimmered as the leaves rippled.

It would be no easier to meet his father again if he delayed arrival until nightfall. Restlessly, he reopened the book; anticipation warred with . . . yes, fear: he had been afraid at that last interview with his father. Karl von Shrakenberg was not a man to be taken lightly.

It was still day when they turned in under the tall stone arch of the gates, the six wheels of the Kellerman crunching on the smooth crushed rock, beneath the sign that read OAKENWALD PLANTATION, EST. 1788. K. VON SHRAKENBERG, LANDHOLDER. But the sun was sinking behind them. Ahead, the jagged crags of the Maluti Mountains were outlined in the Prussian blue of shadow and sandstone gold. This valley was higher than the plateau plains west of the Caledon River; rocky, flat-topped hills reared out of the rolling fields. The narrow plantation road was lined with oaks, huge branches meeting twenty meters over their heads; the lower slopes of the hills were planted to the king trees as well.

Beyond were the hedged fields, divided by rows of Lombardy poplar: wheat and barley still green with a hint of gold as they began to head out, contour-ploughed cornfields, pastures dotted with white-fleeced sheep, spring lambs, horses, yellow-coated cattle. The fieldworkers were heading in, hoes and tools slanted over their shoulders, mules hanging their heads as they wearily trudged back toward the stables. A few paused to look up in curiosity as the vehicle passed; Eric could hear the low, rhythmic song of a work team as they walked homeward, a sad sweet memory from childhood.

Despite himself he smiled, glancing about. It had been, by the White Christ and almighty Thor, two years now since his last visit. "You can't go home again," he said softly to himself. "The problem is, you can't ever really leave it, either." Memory turned in on itself and the past colored the present; he could remember his first pony, and his father's hands lifting him into the saddle, how his fingers smelled of tobacco and leather and strong soap. And the first time he had been invited into his father's study to talk with the adults after a dinner party. Ruefully, he smiled as he remembered holding the brandy snifter in an authoritative pose anyone but himself must have recognized as copied from Pa's . . . And yet it was all tinged with sorrow and anger; impossible to forget, hurtful to remember, a turning and itching in his mind.

He looked downslope; beyond that screen of pines was a stock dam where the children of the house had gone swimming sometimes, gods

alone knew why, except that they were *supposed* to use the pool up
by the manor. There, one memorable day, he had knocked Frikkie
Thyssen flat for sneering at his poetry. The memory brought a grin;
it had been the sort of epic you'd expect a twelve-year-old in love
with Chapman's Homer to do, but that little bastard Thyssen wouldn't
have known if it had been a work of genius . . . And over there in
the cherry orchard he had lost his virginity under a harvest moon one
week after his thirteenth birthday, to a giggling field wench twice his
age and weight . . .

And then there had been Tyansha, the Circassian girl. Pa had given
her to him on his fourteenth birthday. The dealer had called her something more pronounceable, but that was the name she had taught him,
along with her mother tongue. She had been . . . perhaps four years
older than he; nobody had been keeping records in eastern Turkey during
those years of blood and chaos. There were vague memories of a father,
she had said, and a veiled woman who held her close, then lay in a
ditch by a burning house and did not move. Then the bayonets of
the Janissaries herding her and a mob of terrified children into trucks.
Thirst, darkness, hunger; then the training creche. Learning reading
and writing, the soft blurred Draka dialect of English; household duties,
dancing, the arts of pleasing. Friends, who vanished one by one into
the world beyond the walls. And him.

Her eyes had been what he had noticed first—huge, a deep pale
blue, like a wild thing seen in the forest. Dark-red hair falling to her
waist, past a smooth, pale, high-cheeked face. She had worn a silver-
link collar that emphasized the slender neck and the serf-number
tattooed on it, and a wrapped white sheath-dress to show off her long
legs and high, small breasts. Hands linked before her, she had stood
between his smiling father and the impassive dealer, who slapped her
riding crop against one boot, anxious to be gone.

"Well, boy, does she please?" Pa had asked. Eric remembered a
wordless stutter until his voice broke humiliatingly in a squeak; his
elder brother John had roared laughter and slapped him on the back,
urging him forward as he led her from the room by the hand. Hers
had been small and cool; his own hands and feet felt enormous, clumsy;
he was hideously aware of a pimple beside his nose.

She had been afraid—not showing it much, but he could tell. He
had not touched her; not then, or in the month that followed. Not
even at the first shyly beautiful smile . . .

Gods, but I was callow, Eric thought in sadly affectionate embarrassment. They had talked; rather, he had, while she replied in tense,
polite monosyllables, until she began to shed the fear. He had showed
her things—his battle prints, his butterfly collection—that had disgusted
her—and the secret place in the pine grove, where he came to dream
the vast vague glories of youth . . . A month, before she crept in beside
him one night. A friend, one of the overseer's sons, had asked casually to borrow her; he had beaten the older boy bloody. Not wildly,
in the manner of puppy fights, but with the *pankration* disciplines,
in a cold ferocity that ended only when he was pulled off.

There had been little constraint between them, in private. She even came to use his first name without the "master," eventually. He had allowed her his books, and she had devoured them with a hunger that astonished him; so did her questions, sometimes disconcertingly sharp. Making love with a lover was . . . different. Better; she had been more knowledgeable than he, if less experienced, and they had learned together. Once in a haystack, he remembered; prickly, it had made him sneeze. Afterward they had lain holding hands, and he had shown her the southern sky's constellations.

She died in childbirth three years later, bearing his daughter. The child had lived, but that was small consolation. That had been the last time he wept in public; the first time since his mother had died when he was ten. And it had also been the last time his father had beaten him: for weakness. Casual fornication aside, it was well enough for a boy to have a serf girl of his own. Even for him to care for her, since it helped keep him from the temptations that all-male boarding schools were prone to. But the public tears allowable for blood-kin were unseemly for a concubine.

Eric had caught the thong of the riding crop in one hand and jerked it free. *"Hit me again, and I'll kill you,"* he had said, in a tone flat as gunmetal. He'd seen his father's face change as the scales of parental blindness fell away, and the elder von Shrakenberg realized that he was facing a very dangerous man, not a boy. And that it is not well to taunt an unbearable grief.

He shook his head and looked out again at the familiar fields; it was a sadness in itself, that time healed. Grief faded into nostalgia, and it was a sickness to try and hold it. That mood stayed with him as they swung into the steep drive and through the gardens below Oakenwald's Great House. The manor had been built into the slope of a hill—for defense, in the early days—and it still gave a memorable view. The rocky slope had been terraced for lawns, flowerbanks, ornamental trees, and fountains; forest grew over the steepening slope behind, and then a great table of rock reared two hundred meters into the darkening sky.

The manor itself was ashlar blocks of honey-colored local sandstone, a central three-story block fronted with white marble columns and topped with a low-pitched roof of rose tile; there were lower wings to each side—arched colonnades supporting second-story balconies. There was a crowd waiting beneath the pillars, and a parked gray-painted staff car with a *strategos'* red-and-black checkerboard pennant fixed to one bumper; the tall figure of his father stood amidst the household leaning on his cane. Eric took a deep breath and opened the door of the van, pitching his baggage to the ground and jumping down to the surface of the drive.

Air washed over him cool and clean, smelling of roses and falling water, dusty crushed rock and hot metal from the van; bread was baking somewhere, and there was woodsmoke from the chimneys. The globe lights came on over the main doors, and he saw who awaited: his father, of course; his younger sister Johanna in undress uniform; the overseers, and some of the house servants behind . . .

He waved, then turned back to the van for a moment, pulling a half-empty bottle out of his kit and leaning in for a parting salute to the Janissaries.

They looked up, and their faces lit with surprised gratitude as he tossed the long-necked glass bulb; it was Oakenwald Kijaffa, cherry brandy in the same sense that Dom Perignon was sparkling wine, and beyond the pockets of most freemen.

"Tanks be to yaz, Centurion, sar," the black said, his teeth shining white. "Sergeants Miller and Assad at yar s'rvice, sar."

"For Palermo," he said, and turned his head to the driver. "Back, and take the turning to the left, half a kilometer to the Quarters. Ask for the headman; he'll put you all up."

A young houseboy had run forward to take Eric's baggage; he craned his head to see into the long cabin of the van after making his bow, his face an O of surprise at the bright Janissary uniforms. And he kept glancing back as he bore the valise and bag away. Eric stopped him to take a few parcels out of the bag, reflecting that they probably had another volunteer there. Then he was striding up the broad black-stone steps, the hard soles of his high boots clattering. The servants bowed like a rippling field, and there were genuine smiles of welcome. Eric had always been popular with the staff, as such things went.

He clicked heels and saluted. His father returned it, and they stood for a wordless moment eye to eye; they were of a height. Alike in color and cast of face as well; the resemblance was stronger now that pain had graven lines in the younger man's face to match his sire's.

"Recovered from your wound, I see." The strategos paused, searching for words. "I read the report. You were a credit to the service and the family, Eric."

"Thank you, sir," he replied neutrally, fighting down an irrational surge of anger. *I didn't want the Academy,* a part of him thought savagely. *The first von Shrakenberg in seven generations not to, and a would-be artist to boot. Does that make me an incompetent, or a coward?*

And that was unjust. Pa had not really been surprised that he had the makings of a good officer; he had too much confidence in the von Shrakenberg blood for that. *What was it that makes me draw back?* he thought. Alone, he could wish so strongly to be at peace with his father again. Those gray eyes, more accustomed to cold mastery, shared his own baffled hurt; he could see it. But together . . . they fought, or coexisted with an icy politeness that was worse.

Or *usually* worse. Two years ago he had sent Tyansha's daughter out of the country. To America, where there was a Quaker group that specialized in helping the tiny trickle of escaped serfs who managed to flee. They must have been surprised to receive a tow-haired girlchild from an aristocrat of the Domination, together with an annuity to pay for her upkeep and education. Not that he had been fond of the girl; he had handed her to the women of the servant's quarters, and as she grew her looks were an intolerable reminder. But she was Tyansha's . . . It had required a good deal of money, and several illegalities.

To Arch-Strategos Karl von Shrakenberg, that had been a matter touching on honor, and on the interests of the Race and the nation.

His father had threatened to abandon him to the Security Directorate; that could have meant a one-way trip to a cold cellar with instruments of metal, a trip that ended with a pistol bullet in the back of the head. Eric suspected that if his brother John had still been alive to carry on the family name, it might have come to that. As it was, he had been forbidden the house, until service in Italy had changed the general's mind.

I saved my daugh—a little girl, he thought. *For that I was a criminal and will always be watched. But by helping to destroy a city and killing hundreds who've never done me harm, I'm a hero and all is forgiven.* Tyansha had once told him that she had given up expecting sense from the world long ago; more and more he saw her point.

He forced his mind back to the older man's words. "And the Janissaries won't have any problems in the Quarters?"

"Not unless someone's foolish enough to provoke them. They're Master Sergeants, steady types; the headman will find them beds and a couple of willing girls."

There was another awkward pause, and the strategos turned to go. "Well. I'll see you when we dine, then."

Johanna had been waiting impatiently, but in this household the proprieties were observed. As Eric turned to face her, she straightened and threw a crackling salute, then winked broadly and pointed her thumb upward at the collar of her uniform jacket.

He returned the salute and followed her digit. "Well, well. *Pilot Officer* Johanna von Shrakenberg, now!" He spread his arms and she gave him a swift fierce hug. She was four years younger than he; on her the bony family looks and the regulations that cropped her fair hair close produced an effect halfway between elegance and adolescent homeliness.

"That was quick—fighters? And what's this I hear about Tom? You two are still an 'item'?" With a stage magician's gesture he produced a flat package.

"They're turning us out quick, these days—cutting out nonessentials like sleep. Yes, fighters: Eagles, interceptors." The wrapping crumpled under strong, tanned fingers. "And no, Tom and I aren't an item; we're *engaged.*" She paused to roll her eyes. "Wouldn't you know it, guess where his lochos's been sent? *Xian!* Shensi, to watch the Japanese!"

The package opened. Within were twin eardrops, cabochon-cut rubies the size of a thumbnail, set in chased silver. Johanna whistled and held them up to the light as Eric shook hands with the overseers, inquired after their children in the Forces, handed out minor gifts among the house servants and hugged old Nanny Sukie, the family child-nurse. Arms linked, Eric and Johanna strolled into the house.

"Loot?" she inquired, holding up the jewels. "Sort of Draka-looking . . ."

"*Made* from loot," he said affectionately. It was a rare Draka who doubted the morality of conquest. To deny that the property of the vanquished was proper booty would go beyond eccentricity to madness. "You think I'm buying rubies like that on a Centurion's pay?

They're from an Italian bishop's crozier—he won't be needing it in the labor camp, after all." The man had smiled under the gun muzzles, actually, and signed a cross in the air as they prodded him away. Eric pushed the memory aside.

"I had the setting done up in Alexandria . . ."

Chapter Three

OAKENWALD PLANTATION
OCTOBER 1941

Eric woke in mid-morning. It was his old room at the corner of the west wing, a big, airy chamber five meters by fifteen with two walls giving on to the second-story balcony through doors of sliding glass. The air was sharp with spring, with a little of the dew smell yet, full of scents from the garden and a wilder smell from the forest and wet rock that stretched beyond the manor: the breath of his childhood years, the smell of home.

He lay for a moment, enjoying the crisp smooth feel of the linen sheets, feeling rested enough but a little heavy with the wine and liqueurs from last night. It was like being sick, when he was a child. Not too ill, just feverish, allowed to lie abed and read. Ma would be there, to see that he drank the soup . . .

Dinner had been better than he expected; Pa had avoided topics which might set them off (which meant platitudes and silence, mostly), and everyone had admired Johanna's eardrops, which led naturally to the hilarious story of the near-mutiny in Rome, when the troops arrived to find Security units guarding the Vatican and preventing a sack. Florence had been much better; he had picked up a number of interesting items, including a Cellini, two Raphaels and a couple of *really* interesting illuminated manuscripts. Better than jewelry, far too precious to sell.

Illegal, of course, he mused, throwing a loose kaftan over his nakedness and tossing down a glass of the fresh-squeezed orange juice from the jug by the bedside. *Still, why let the Cultural Directorate stick the books in a warehouse for a generation while the museums and the universities quarreled over 'em?*

The baths were as he remembered them—magnificent, in a fashion forty years out of date, like much of the manor. That had been the last major renovation, in the expansive and self-confident years just before the Great War, when the African territories were well pacified

27

and the Draka were pleasantly engaged in dreaming of further conquests, rather than performing the hard, actual work. There was a
waterfall springing from dragon heads cast in aluminum bronze, steam
rooms and soaking tubs and a swimming pool of red and violet
Northmark marble. The walls were lined with mosaics from the Klimt
workshops, done on white Carrara in gilded copper, silver, coral, semi-
precious stones, gold and colored faience; his great-grandmother's taste
had run to wildlife, landscapes (the dreamlike cone of Kilimanjaro rising
above the Serengeti was a favorite), dancing maidens of eerily elongated shapes . . .

Soaking, massage, and a dozen laps chased the last stiffness from
his muscles; he lazed naked against a couch on the terrace, toying
with a breakfast of iced mango, hot breads, and Kenya coffee with
thick mountain cream. Potted fruit trees laid dappled patterns of sun
and shade across his body; a last spray of peach blossom cast petals
and scent on long, taut-muscled arms and deep runner's chest. The
angry purple scar on his thigh had faded toward dusty white. He was
conscious of an immense well-being as wind stroked silk-gentle across
cleansed skin.

The serving girl padded up to collect the dishes. Lazily, he stretched
out a hand as she bent and laid it on the small of her back. She froze,
controlled a shrinking and looked back at him over her shoulder.

"Please, masta, no?" she said in a small breathless voice.

Eric shrugged, smiling, and withdrew his touch. . .

Too young, anyway, he mused. He preferred women about his own
years or a little older. *Hmmmm, I could take a rifle up into the hills
and try for that leopard Pa mentioned before it takes any more sheep.
No, too much like work. And curse it, Johanna will already be out
hawking; she said "early tomorrow"* . . . A ride with a falcon on his
wrist was something that had been lacking these last few years.

He looked down and grinned; the body had its own priorities. *No,
first thoughts are best: a woman.* That was a minor problem; he had
been away from the estate for years now. There had been a few serf
girls he'd been having, after his period of mourning for Tyansha ended,
but they would be married now. Not that a serf wedding had any legal
standing, but the underfolk took their unions seriously; more seriously
than the masters did, these days. It would cause distress, if he called
one of them to his bed.

He snapped his fingers. Rahksan—Johanna's maid. She'd have
mentioned it in her letters if the wench had taken a lasting mate. Uncle
Everard had brought her back from Afghanistan, one small girl found
miraculously alive in a village bombed with phosgene gas for supporting
the *badmash* rebels. He had given her to Johanna for her sixth birthday,
much as he might have a puppy or a kitten. They had all run tame
together, and she had seldom said no, in the old days . . .

*Let's see, Johanna's out with her hawk; Rahksan'd probably be in
her rooms, tidying up.*

The corridor gave onto Johanna's study; the door was ajar, and he
padded through on quiet feet, leaning his head around the entrance

into the bedroom. Rahksan was there, but so was Johanna, and they were very much occupied. Eric pursed his mouth thoughtfully, lifted one eyebrow and withdrew to the study unnoticed. There was a good selection of reading material, he picked up a news magazine with a profile of Wendel Wilkie, the new Yankee President. The speech he had given opening the new lock at Montreal in the State of Quebec was considered quite important, bearing on the new administration's attitude to the war . . .

Rahksan came through the door with her shoes in one hand, buttoning the linen blouse with the other. She was a short woman, full in breast and hip, with a mane of curling blue-black hair and skin a pale creamy olive that reminded him of Italians he had seen. Her face was roundly pretty, eyes heavy-lidded above a dreamy smile.

He stood: the serf squeaked and jumped in startlement, then relaxed into a broad grin as she recognized him.

"Why, masta Eric, good t'see yaz egin," she said, tilting her head on one side and glancing up at him; she came barely to his shoulder.

He laughed and pulled her close; she flowed into his arm, warm, soft skin damp and carrying a faint pleasant scent of woman.

"I was looking for you, Rahksan," he said.

"Why, what*evah* fo'?" she asked slyly, snuggling. They had always been friendly, as far as different stations allowed, and occasional bedmates in the years since Tyansha died.

" . . . unless you're too tired?" he finished politely.

"Well . . . ah *do* have wuk t'do, masta. 'Sides all this bedwenchin', that is." she paused, with a show of considering. "Tonaaht? Pr'bly feel laahk it agin bah then."

He nodded, and she jumped up with an arm around his neck; he tasted musk on her lips as they kissed, and then she was gone with a flash of bare feet, giggling as she gave him a swift intimate caress in passing. Eric shook his head, grinning.

Another thing that hasn't changed about Oakenwald, he thought. Rahksan had always had a sunny disposition, and an uncomplicated outlook on life. It was restful, for a man given to introspective brooding.

His sister's voice interrupted his musing. "Well, brother dear, if you're *quite* finished making assignations with my serf wench, come on in."

Johanna was lying comfortably sprawled across her bed amid the rumpled black satin of the sheets, sipping at pale yellow wine in a bell goblet and toe-wrestling with a long-haired persian cat. She was, he noted with amusement, still wearing his gift of eardrops, if nothing else; she had the grayhound build of the von Shrakenbergs, but was thicker through the neck and shoulders than when he had seen her last, a year ago. Wrestling a two-engined pursuit plane through the sky took strength as well as skill.

He seated himself and took up the second glass, pouring from the straw-covered flask in its bed of ice. "Glad to see you're not wasting *your* leave," he said. "A little . . . schoolgirlish, though, isn't it?"

"Now, listen to me, Eric—" She sank back into the pillows at his smile. "Freya, but it's always a surprise when that solemness of yours breaks down." Johanna paused to pick a black hair from her lip with thumb and forefinger.

"Glad you knew I was joking; Pa might not be, though. He's a stickler for dignity," Eric said.

Johanna snorted. "I'm old enough to fight for the Domination, I'm old enough to choose my own pleasures," she said. More slowly: "For that matter, it's *like* school around here, these days: no men. Not between eighteen and forty, at least. Draka men, that is; plenty of likely-looking serf bucks . . . just joking brother, just joking. I know the Race Purity laws as well as anyone, and I've no wish to do my last dance on the end of a rope. Actually, the only man I'm interested in is six thousand kilometers away in Mongolia, while celibacy interests me not at all."

She sighed. "And . . . the lochos's going operational in another month, once we've finished shaking down on ground support. Ever noticed how war puts a hand on your shoulder and says 'hurry'?"

"Yes indeed," he said, refilling her glass. "Confidentially . . . Johanna, the Germans are getting pretty close to the Caucasus. They've taken Rostov-on-Don already, and it looks like Moscow will fall within the month. Then they'll push on to the Caspian, which will put them right on our northern border. Three guesses as to where the next round of fighting begins."

She nodded, thoughtful. The Domination had never really been at peace in all the centuries of its existence; a citizen was reared to the knowledge that death in combat was as likely a way to go as cancer in bed. This would be different: a *gotterdammerung*, where whole nations were beaten into dust. . . .

Too big, she mused. Impossible to think about in any meaningful sense; you could only see it in personal terms. And seeing it that way, Armageddon itself couldn't kill you deader than a skirmish. It was the personal that was *real*, anyhow. You lived and died in person-time, not history-time.

"Funny," she said. "Back when we were children, we couldn't wait to grow up . . . Do you remember when Uncle Everard gave Rahksan to me? I was around six, so you must have been going on ten."

Eric nodded, reminiscing. "Yes: you'd play at giving orders, until she got tired of it; then she'd plump down and cross her arms and say, 'This is a stupid game and I'm not going to play anymore,' and we'd all roll around laughing."

"Hmmm, well, it was a change to give anybody orders. At that age, nurse and all the house serfs tell you what to do, and wallop your bottom if you don't . . . Did you know she'd have nightmares?"

Surprised, he shook his head. "Always seemed a happy little wench."

"At night, she'd wake up sometimes on the pallet down at the foot of the bed, thinking she couldn't breathe. Damn what the vet said, I think she got some lung damage when they gassed her village. I'd let her crawl in with me and hold her until she went to sleep; then later, when we were both older, well . . ." She paused and frowned. "You know, I never did go in for the schoolgirl stuff, the real thing, roses and fruit left at the window, bad poetry under the door, meetings in the pergola at midnight . . . Always seemed silly, as if this was seventy years ago and you could get in real trouble. So did what happened in the summer months off, everyone rushing out and falling on the nearest boy like ravening leopardesses on a goat."

He laughed. She had always been able to draw him out of himself, even if that humor was a little barbed at times.

"Rahksan . . . that's just fun and exuberance, and release from need, with more affection than you can get in barracks. I really like her, you know, and she me." She paused to sip the cool tart wine. "And I miss Tom."

"I always thought you two were in love," Eric said lightly. "From the way you quarrelled: you'd ride ten miles just to have a fight with him."

Johanna smiled ruefully. "True enough. And I do love him . . ." She paused, set down the empty glass and linked her fingers about one knee. "Not the way you felt about that Circassian wench," she continued softly. "Don't think I didn't notice. I'll never love anyone with that . . . crazy single-mindedness, never, and I thank the nonexistent gods for it."

He glanced away. "There has to be one sensible person in this family," he said. He thought of his other sisters, twins three years younger than Johanna. "Besides the Terrible Two, of course."

"Yes; they were threatening me bodily harm if I won the war before they could get into it . . . Eric, you know the problem with you and Pa? You think and feel exactly alike."

"We haven't agreed on a goddamned thing in ten years!"

"I didn't say the *contents* of your thoughts were alike, but the *way* you think is no-shit identical, big brother. You feel things . . . too much: duty, love, hate, whatever. Everything's a matter of principle; everything counts too much. You both *want* too much—things that aren't possible to us mortals."

"Possibly; but even if that's true, it's no solution to our problems."

"Shit, you always did want *solutions*, didn't you? Most of the things that bother you two *aren't* problems, and they don't *have* solutions: they're the conditions of life and you have to *live* with them." She sighed at the tightening of his lips. "It's like talking to a rock, with either of you. Mind you, Pa's more often right on some things, to my way of thinking. Politics, certainly."

"You don't think I should have gotten Tyansha's child out of the Domination?"

"Oh, that—that was your business. And she was yours, after all. You could have done it more . . . discreetly. The law is intended to discourage *escape*, not a man sending his own property out. I can even see *why* you did it, not that I would have, myself; with her looks that one was going to have trouble once she was into her teens. Tyansha was very lucky to end up belonging to you. No, I meant the other stuff, real politics."

"Hmmm," he said. "I can't remember you ever taking much interest in party matters."

"Well," she said, sitting up and stretching. "I'm a voter now. I mean, how long has it been since the Draka League party lost an election, even locally? Sixty years, seventy? Regular as clockwork, seventy percent of the vote. The Liberals—'free enterprise'—doesn't it occur to them that three-quarters of the electorate are employees of the State and the Combines? They could all be underbid by serf labor if the restrictions were lifted, then there'd be revolution and we'd all be dead. That the Liberals get as much as three percent is a monument to human stupidity. Then there's the Rationalists. I suppose you support them because they want a pacific foreign policy and an end to expansion. Same thing, only slower; we're just not *compatible* with the existence of another social system. And we're unique . . . ."

"The government line, and very convenient; but this war might kill us both," he said grimly. "The way our precious social system already killed our brother. I wouldn't be much loss to anyone, even myself, but you would, and I miss John."

They turned their eyes to the portrait beside Johanna's bed. It showed their elder brother in uniform, field kit; a Century of Janissaries had stood grouped around him. It was policy that those earmarked for advancement hold commands in both the serf army and the Citizen Force. John was smiling; that was how most remembered him. Alone of the von Shrakenberg children of this generation he had taken after their mother's kindred, a stocky broad-faced man with seal-brown hair and eyes and big capable hands.

He had died in the Ituri, the great jungle north of the Congo bend. That was part of the Police Zone, the area of civil government, but there was little settlement—a few rubber plantations near navigable water, timber concessions, and gold mines in the Ituri that were supplied by airship. The rest was half a million square kilometers of National Park, where nothing human lived but a few bands of pygmies left to their Old Stone Age existence, looking up in wonder as the silvery shapes of Draka dirigibles glided past.

The mines were conveniently isolated. They were run by the Security Directorate, and used as a sink for serf convicts, the incorrigibles, the sweepings of the labor camps. The Draka technicians and overseers were those too incompetent to hold a post elsewhere, or who had mortally offended the powers that were. There had been an uprising below ground, brief and desperate and hopeless. The usual procedure would have been to turn off the drainage, or dump the tunnels full of poison gas. But the rebels had taken Draka hostages, and John's unit had been doing jungle-combat training nearby. There was no time to summon Security's Intervention Squads, specialists in such work. Their brother had volunteered to lead his troops below; they had volunteered to follow, to a man.

Eric had never wanted to imagine what it had been like, he had always disliked confined spaces. The fighting had been at close quarters, machine pistols and grenades, knives and boots and picks and lengths of tubing stuffed full of blasting explosive. The power lines had been cut early on; at the last they had been struggling in water waist high, in absolute blackness. . . . Incredibly, they had rescued most of the prisoners; John had been covering the withdrawal when an improvised bomb went off at his feet. His Janissaries had carried him out on their backs at risk of their lives, but it had been far too late.

They had been able to keep his last words, spoken in delirium. "I tried, Daddy, honest. I tried real hard."

"I'm not surprised they brought him out," Eric said into the silence. "He was an easy man to love."

"Unlike you and Pa," Johanna said drily. "Rahksan was head-over-heels for him; Pa . . . took it hard, you'll remember. I thought he was going to cry at the funeral. That shook me; I can't imagine Pa crying."

"I can," Eric said, surprising her. "You were too young, but I remember when Mother died. Not at the funeral, but afterwards I went looking for him, found him in the study. He'd forgotten to lock the door. He was sitting there at the desk with his head in his hands." The sobs had been harsh, racking, the weeping of a man unaccustomed to it.

They looked at each other uncomfortably and shifted. "Time to go," Johanna said at last. "Pa wanted us down in the Quarters when the recruits get selected."

They had taken horses, this being too nearly a formal occasion to walk. The path led down the slope of the hill between cut-stone walls, through the oak wood their ancestors had planted and patches of native scrub where the soil was too thin over rock to grow the big trees. The gravel crunched beneath hooves, and light came down in bright flickering shafts as the leaf canopy stirred, lancing into the cool wet-smelling green air of spring. Ferns carpeted the rocky ground, with flowers of blue and yellow and white. The trunks about them were thick and twisted, massive moss-grown shapes sinking their roots deep into the fractured rock of the hill.

Like the von Shrakenbergs, Eric thought idly, as they clattered over a small stone bridge, well-kept but ancient; the little stream beneath had been channeled to power a gristmill, in the early days.

They passed through a belt of hybrid poplar trees, coppiced for fuel, and into the working quarters of the plantation on the flat ground. The old mill bulked square, now the smithy and machine shop, about it were the laundry, bake house, carpenter's workshop, garage—all the intricate fabric of maintenance an estate needed. The great barns were off to one side, with the creamery and cheese house and cooling sheds where cherries and peaches from the orchards were stored. Woolsheds and round granaries of red brick bulked beyond; holding paddocks, stables for the working stock . . . then a row of trees before the Quarters proper.

Four hundred serfs worked the fields of Oakenwald; their homes were grouped about a village green. Square, four-roomed cottages of field-stone with tile roofs stood along a grid of brick-paved lanes, each with its patch of garden to supplement the ration of meat and flour and roots. Pruned fruit trees were planted along the streets; privies stood behind the cottages, with chicken coops and rabbit hutches. Today was Saturday, a half-holiday save during harvest; only essential tasks with the stock would be seen to. Families sat on their porches, smoking their pipes, sewing, mending pieces of household gear; they rose to bow as Eric and Johanna cantered through on their big crop-maned hunters, children and dogs scattering before the hooves.

The central green was four hundred meters on a side, fringed with tall poplars. The south flank held the slightly larger homes of the headman and the elite of the Quarters gang—foremen, stockmen, skilled workers. The others were public buildings—a storehouse for cloth and rations, the communal bathhouse, an infirmary, a chapel where the serf minister preached a Christian faith the masters had largely abandoned. Beside it was the most recent addition—a school where he taught basic letters to a few of the most promising children; there were more tasks that needed such skills, these last few generations.

The green itself was mostly shaggy lawn, with a pair of goal posts where the younger field hands sometimes played soccer in their scant leisure time; the water fountain was no longer needed now that the cottages had their own taps, but it still played merrily. Dances were held here of an evening; there was a barbecue pit, where whole oxen and pigs might be roasted at harvest and planting and Christmas festivals, or when a wedding or a birth in the Great House brought celebration.

And on one side was a covered dais of stone, with a bell beside it; also stocks, and the seldom-used whipping post. Here the work assignments were given out, and the master sat to make judgments. The son and daughter of the House drew rein beside it, leaning on their saddle pommels to watch and nodding to their father, seated in his wooden chair.

The two Janissaries were there, with a crowd of the younger serfs standing about them. They were stripped to shorts and barefoot, practicing stick-fighting with their swagger canes, moving and feinting and slashing with no sound but the stamp of feet and grunting of breath. But for color they were much alike, heavy muscle rolling over thick bone, moving cat-graceful; scarred and quick and deadly. A smack of wood on flesh marked the end, they drew themselves up, saluted each other with their canes, and repeated the gesture to the Draka before trotting off to wash and change back into their uniforms.

Eric dismounted and tossed his reins to a serf. "Formidable," he murmured to his sister as they mounted the dais and assumed their seats. "Wouldn't care to take on either of them, hand to hand."

She smiled agreement; the elder von Shrakenberg nodded to the crowd of young field hands before them. "Not without its effect there," he said, and raised his voice. "Headman, summon the people." That elderly worthy bowed and swung the clapper of the bell. Almost at once the serfs began to assemble, by ones and twos and family groups, to stand in an irregular fan about the place of judgment. Eric spent the time musing. This was, he supposed, the best side of the Domination. Certainly, he had seen worse in Italy; much worse, among the peasants of Sicily and Calabria—sickness, hunger, and rags. All the von Shrakenberg serfs looked well-fed, tended, clothed; there had been callous men and women among his ancestors, even cruel ones, but few fools who expected work from starvelings. A drab existence, though: labor, a few simple pleasures, the consolations of their religion, old age spent rocking on the porch. So that the von Shrakenbergs might have power and wealth and leisure; so that the Domination might have armies for its fear-driven aggression.

There would always be enough willing recruits for the Janissaries. In theory they were conscripts, but there were a million plantations such as this, not counting the inhabitants of the Combines' labor compounds. And that was well for the Domination, for it was the Janissary legions that made the Draka a Great Power, able to wage offensive war. The Citizen Force was a delicate precision instrument, a rapier; it destroyed armies not by destroying their equipment and personnel, but by shock and psychological dislocation. Its aim was not to kill men, but to break their hearts and make them *run*. Draka were trained to war from childhood, and none but cripples escaped the Forces. But by the same token, their casualties were expenditure from capital, not income; too many expensive victories could ruin their nation.

And the Janissaries . . . they were the Domination's battle-ax, their function to gore and crush and utterly destroy. Half a million had died breaking the Ankara line in Anatolia, in 1917, and as many more in the grinding campaigns of pacification in the Asian territories after the war. Where there were no elegant solutions, where there could be no escaping the brutal arithmetic of attrition, the Janissaries would be used—street fighting, positional defense, frontal assault.

Eric was startled to hear his father speak. "Economical," he murmured, and continued at his son's glance.

"Conquest makes serfs, serfs make soldiers, soldiers make conquest . . . empire feeds on itself."

Eric made a noncommittal sound and looked out over his family's human chattel; he could name most of them, and the younger adults had been the playmates of his childhood, before age imposed an increasing distance. They stood quietly, hats in hand, their voices quiet *shusshps* running under the sound of the wind. Most were descendants of the tribes who had dwelt here before the Draka came, some of imports since then—Tamil, Arab, Berber, Egyptian. None spoke the old language; that had been extinct for a century or more, leaving only loan words and place names. And few were of unmixed blood; seven generations of von Shrakenberg males and their overseers taking their pleasure in the Quarters had left light-brown the predominant skin color. Not a few yellow heads and gray eyes were scattered through the crowd, and he reflected ruefully that most of his blood-kin were probably standing before him.

It occurred to him suddenly that these people had only to rush in a body to destroy their owners. *Only three of us,* he mused. *Sidearms, but no automatic weapons. We couldn't kill more than half a dozen.*

It would not happen, could not, because they could not think it. . . . There had been serf revolts, in the early days. His great-great-great-grandfather had commanded the levies that impaled four thousand rebels along the road from Virconium to Shahnapur, down in the sugar country of the coast; there was a mural of it in the

Great House. Oakenwald serfs had worked the fields in chains, in his day. Past, long past . . .

The two NCO's returned, spruce and glittering in the noonday sun, each bearing a brace of file folders; these they stacked neatly on a camp table set up before the dais. They turned to salute the dais, and his father rose to speak. A ripple of bows greeted him, like wind on corn.

"Folk of Oakenwald," he said, leaning on his cane. "The Domination is at war. The Archon, who commands me as I command you, has called for a new levy of soldiers. Six among your young men will be accorded the high honor of becoming arms bearers in the service of the State, and for the welfare of our common home. Pray for their souls."

There was another long-drawn murmur. The news was no surprise; a regular grapevine ran from manor to manor, spread by the servants of guests, serfs sent to town on errands, even by telephone in these times. The young men shuffled their feet and glanced at each other with uneasy grins as the black Janissary rose to his feet and called out a roster of names. More than two score came raggedly forward.

"Yaz awl tinkin' how lucky yaz bein'," he began, the thick dialect and harsh tone a shock after the master's words. "T' be Janissary— faahn uniforms, t' best a' food an' likker, usin' t' whip 'stead a' feelin' it, an' plunder 'n girls in captured towns. Live laahk a fightin'-cock, walk praawd."

His glance passed across them with scorn. There was more to it, of course: to give a salute rather than the serf's low bow before the masters; excitement; travel beyond the narrow horizons of village or compound. Education, for those who could use it; training in difficult skills; respect. And the mystery of arms, the mark of the masters; for any but the Janissaries, it would be death to hold a weapon. A Janissary held nearly as many privileges over the serf population as a master, with fewer restraints. The chance to discharge a lifetime's repressed anger . . .

His voice cracked out like a lash. *"Yaz tink t' be Janissary? Yaz should live s'long!"* He came forward to walk down the ragged line, the hunting-cat grace of his gait a contrast to their ploughboy awkwardness. They were all young, between seventeen and nineteen, all in good health and over the minimum height. Draka law required exact records, and he had studied them with care. The swagger stick poked out suddenly, taking one lad under the ribs. He doubled over with a startled *oofff!* and fell to his knees.

"Soft! Yaz soft! Tink cauz yaz c'n stare all day up t' arse end of a plough mule, yaz woan' drop dead onna force-march. Shit yaz pants when a' mortar shells star' a' droppin.' Whicha yaz momma's darlin's, whicha yaz houseserf bumboys tink they got it?"

He drew a line in the sparse grass with his swagger stick and waited, rising and falling slowly on the balls of his feet and tapping the stick in the palm of one gloved hand, a walking advertisement.

The serf youths looked at him, at his comrade lolling lordly-wise at the table with a file folder in his hands, back at the humdrum village of all their days. Visibly, they weighed the alternatives: danger against boredom; safety against the highest advancement a serf could achieve. Two dozen crowded forward over the line, and the Master Sergeant grinned, suddenly jovial. His stick pointed out one, another, up to the six required; he had been watching carefully, sounding them out without seeming to, and the records were exhaustive. Their friends milled about, slapping the dazed recruits on the back and shoulder while in the background Eric could hear a sudden weeping, quickly hushed.

Probably a mother, he thought, rising with his father. Janissaries were not discouraged from keeping up contacts with their families, but they had their own camps and towns when not in the field, a world to itself. The plantation preacher would hold a service for their leaving, and it would be the one for the dead. Silence fell anew. "In honor of these young men," the general called, smiling, "I declare a feast tonight. Headman, see to issuing the stores. Tell the House steward that I authorize two kegs of wine, and open the vats at the brewery."

That brought a roar of applause, as the family of the master descended from the dais to shake the hands of the six chosen, a signal honor. They stood, grinning, in a haze of glory, as the preparations for the evening's entertainment began; tomorrow they would travel with the two soldiers to the estates round about, there would be more feasts, admiration . . . and the master had called them "young men," not bucks . . .

Eric hoped that the memories would help them when they reached the training camps. The roster of formed units in the Janissary arm was complete, but the *ersatz* Cohorts, the training and replacement units, were being expanded. Infantry numbers eroded quickly in intensive operations; the legions would need riflemen by the hundred thousand, soon.

As he swung back into the saddle, he wondered idly how many would survive to wear the uniforms of Master Sergeants themselves. Not many, probably. The training camps themselves would kill some; the regimen was harsh to the point of brutality, deliberately so. A few would die, more would wash out into secondary arms, the Security Directorate could always use more executioners and camp-guard "bulls." The survivors would learn; learn that they were the elite, that they had no family but their squad mates, no father but their officer, no country or nation but their legions. Learn loyalty, *kadaversobedienz*— the ability to obey like a corpse.

His father's quiet words jarred him out of his thoughts as they rode slowly through the crowd and then heeled their mounts into a canter through the deserted village beyond.

"Eric, I have a favor to ask of you."

"Sir?" He looked up, startled.

"A . . . command matter. It's the Yankees. They're the only major Power left uncommitted, and we need them to counterbalance the Japanese. We *don't* need another war in East Asia while we fight the Germans, and if it does come we'll have to cooperate with the U.S. Certainly if we expect them to do most of the fighting, and help out in Europe besides."

Eric nodded, baffled. More reluctantly, his father continued. "As part of keeping them sweet, we're allowing in a war correspondent."

"I should think, sir, knowing the Yankees, allowing a newspaperman into the Domination would be likely to turn them against us, once he started reporting."

"Not if he's allowed to see only the proper sights, then assigned to a combat unit and, ah, overseen by the proper officer."

"I see. Sir." Eric said. *Now, that's an insult, if you like,* he thought. The implication being that he was a weak-livered milksop, unlikely to arouse the notorious Yankee squeamishness. The younger man's lips tightened. "As you command, sir. I will see you at dinner, then."

Karl von Shrakenberg stared after the diminishing thunder of his son's horse, a brief flush rising to his weathered cheeks. He had suggested the assignment; pushed for it, in fact, as a way to prove Eric's loyalty beyond doubt, restore his career prospects. The Security case officer had objected, but not too strongly; Karl suspected he looked at it as a baited trap, luring Eric into indiscretions that not even an Arch-Strategos' influence could protect him from. And this was his reward . . .

Behind him, Johanna raised her eyes to heaven and sighed. *Maybe Rahksan can ease him up for tomorrow,* she thought glumly. *Home sweet home, bullshit.*

Chapter Four

OAKENWALD PLANTATION
OCTOBER 1941

The car pulled into Oakenwald's drive three hours past midnight. With a start, William Dreiser jerked himself awake; he was a mild-faced man in his thirties, balding, with thick black-rimmed glasses and a battered pipe tucked into the pocket of his trench coat. Sandy-eyed, he rubbed at his mustache and glanced across at the Draka woman who was his escort-guard. The car was a steam-sedan, four-doored, with two sets of seats facing each other in the rear compartment. Rather like a Stanley Raccoon, in fact.

It had been two weeks' travel from New York. By rail south to New Orleans, then ferryboat to Havana. The Caribbean was safe enough, rimmed with American territory from Florida through the Gulf and on through the States carved out of Mexico and Central America a century before; there were U-boats in the South Atlantic, though, and even neutral shipping was in danger. Pan American flying-boat south to Recife, then Brazilian Airways dirigible to Apollonaris, just long enough to transfer to a Draka airship headed south. That was where he had acquired his Security Directorate shadow; they were treating the American reporter as if he carried a highly contagious disease.

And so I do, he thought. *Freedom.*

They had hustled him into the car in Archona, right at the airship haven. The Security decurion went into the compartment with him; in front were a driver in the grubby coverall which seemed to be the uniform of the urban working class and an armed guard with a shaven head; both had serf-tattoos on their necks. The American felt a small queasy sensation each time he glanced through the glass panels and saw the orange seven-digit code, a column below the right ear: letter-number-number-letter-number-number-number.

Seeing was not the same as reading, not at all. He had done his homework thoroughly: histories, geographies, statistics. And the Draka basics, Carlyle's *Philosophy of Mastery*, Nietzsche's *The Will to Power*, Fitzhugh's *Imperial Destiny*, even Gobineau's turgid *Inequality of Human*

Races, and the eerie and chilling *Meditations of Elvira Naldorssen.* The Domination's own publications had a gruesome forthrightness that he suspected was equal portions of indifference and a sadistic desire to shock. None of it had prepared him adequately for the reality.

Archona had been glimpses: alien magnificence. A broad shallow bowl in the edge of the plateau. Ringroads cut across with wide avenues, lined with flowering trees that were a mist of gold and purple. Statues, fountains, frescoes, mosaics: things beautiful, incomprehensible, obscene. Six-story buildings set back in gardens; some walls sheets of colored glass, others honeycomb marble, one entirely covered with tiles in the shape of a giant flowering vine. Then suburbs that might almost have been parts of California, whitewashed walls and tile roofs, courtyards . . .

The secret police officer opened her eyes, pale blue slits in the darkness. She was a squat woman with broad spatulate hands, black hair in a cut just long enough to comb, like the Eton crop of the flappers in the '20s. But there was nothing frivolous in her high-collared uniform of dark green, or the ceremonial whip that hung coiled at her belt. One hand rested on her sidearm, he could see the house lights wink on the gold and emeralds of a heavy thumbring.

"We're here," she said. His mind heard it as *we-ahz heah,* like a Southern accent, Alabama or Cuba, but with an undertone clipped and guttural.

The silence of the halt was loud, after the long singing of tires on asphalt, wind-rush and the *chuff-chuff-chuff* of the engine. Metal pinged, cooling. The driver climbed out and opened the front-mounted trunk to unload the luggage. The policewoman nodded to the dimly seen building.

"Oakenwald Plantation. Centurion von Shrakenberg's here; Strategos von Shrakenberg, too. Old family; very old, very prominent. *Strategoi,* Senators, landholders, athletes; probably behind the decision to let you in, Yankee. Political considerations, they're influential in the Army and the Foreign Affairs Directorate . . . You're safe enough with them. A guest's sacred, and it'd be 'neath their dignity to care what a foreign scribbler says."

He nodded warily and climbed out stiffly, muscles protesting. She reached through the window to tap his shoulder. He turned, and squawked as her hand shot out to grab the collar of his coat. The speed was startling, and so was the strength of fingers and wrist and shoulder; she dragged his face down level with hers, and the square bulldog countenance filled his vision, full lips pulling back from strong white teeth.

"Well, it isn't 'neath, mine, rebel pig!" The concentrated venom in the tone was as shocking as a bucketful of cold water in the face. "You start causin' trouble, one word wrong to a serf, *one word,* and then by your slave-loving Christ, you're *mine,* Yankee. *Understood?"* She twisted the fabric until he croaked agreement, then shoved him staggering back.

He stood shaking as the green-painted car crunched its way back down the graveled path. *I should never have come,* he thought. It had not been necessary, either; he was too senior for war-correspondent work in the field. His *Berlin Journal* was selling well, fruit of several years observation while he managed the Central European section of ABS' new radio-broadcasting service. The print pieces on the fall of France were probably going to get him a Pulitzer. He had Ingrid and a new daughter to look after . . .

And this was the opportunity of a lifetime. . . . The United States was going to have to hold its nose and cooperate with the Draka if Germany was to be stopped, and a newsman could do his bit. His meek-and-mild appearance had been useful before; people tended to underestimate a man with wire-framed glasses and a double chin.

He glanced about. The gardens stretched below him, a darkness full of scents, washed pale by moonlight; he caught glints on polished stone, the moving water of fountain and pool. The house bulked, its shadow falling across him cold and remote; behind loomed the hill, a smell of oak and wet rock, above wheeled a brightness of stars undimmed by men's lights. It was cold, the thin air full of a high-altitude chill like spring in the Rockies.

The tall doors opened; he blinked against the sudden glow of electric light from a cluster of globes above the brass-studded mahogany. He moved forward as dark hands lifted the battered suitcases.

Dreiser found Oakenwald a little daunting. Not as much so as Hermann Goering's weekend parties had been at his hunting lodge in East Prussia, but strange. So had waking been, in the huge four-poster bed with its disturbing, water-filled mattress; silent smiling brown-skinned girls had brought coffee and juice and drawn back the curtains, laying out slippers of red Moorish leather and a gray silk kaftan. He felt foolish in it; more so as they tied the sash about his waist.

The breakfast room was large and high-ceilinged and sparsely furnished. One wall was a mural of reeds and flamingos with a snow-capped volcano in the background, another was covered with screens of black-lacquered Coromandel sandalwood, inlaid with ivory and mother-of-pearl. Tall glass doors had been folded back, and the checkerboard stone tiles of the floor ran out onto a second-story roof terrace where a table had been set. He walked toward it past man-high vases of green marble; vines spilled down their sides in sprays of green leaf and scarlet blossom.

Irritated, Dreiser began stuffing his pipe, taking comfort from its disreputable solidity. There were three Draka seated at the table: a middle-aged man in the familiar black uniform of boots, loose trousers, belted jacket and roll-topped shirt, and two younger figures in silk robes.

Good, he thought. It made him feel a little less in fancy dress. All three had a family resemblance—lean bodies and strong-boned faces, wheat-colored hair and pale gray eyes against skin tanned dark. It took him a moment to realize that the youngest was a woman. That was irritating, and had happened more than once since he had entered the Domination. It wasn't just the cut of the hair or the prevalence of uniforms, he decided, or even the fact that both sexes wore personal jewelry. There was something about the way they stood and moved; it deprived his eye of unconscious clues, so that he had to deliberately *look*, to examine wrists and necks or check for the swell of breast and hip. Baffling, that something so basic could be obscured by mere differences of custom . . .

The elder man clicked heels and extended a hand. It closed on his, unexpectedly callused and very strong.

"William Dreiser," the American said, remembering what he had read of Draka etiquette. Name, rank and occupation, that was the drill. "Syndicated columnist for the Washington *Chronicle-Herald* and New York *Times*, among others. Bureau chief for the American Broadcasting Service."

"Arch-Strategos Karl von Shrakenberg," the Draka replied. "Director of the Strategic Planning Section, Supreme General Staff. My son, Centurion Eric von Shrakenberg, 1st Airborne Chiliarchy; my daughter, Pilot Officer Johanna von Shrakenberg, 211th Pursuit Lochos." He paused. "Welcome to Oakenwald, Mr. Dreiser."

They sat, and the inevitable servants presented the luncheon: biscuits and scones, fruits, grilled meats on wooden platters, salads, juices.

"I understand that I have you to thank for my visa, General," Dreiser said, buttering a scone. It was excellent, as usual; he had not had a bad meal since Dakar. The meat dishes were a little too highly spiced, as always. It was a sort of Scottish-Austrian-Indonesian cuisine, with a touch of Louisiana thrown in.

The strategos nodded and raised his cup slightly. Hands appeared to fill it, add cream and sugar. "Myself and others," he said. "The strategic situation makes cooperation between the Domination and North America necessary; given your system of government and social organization, that means a press policy as well. You have influence with ABS, an audience, and are suitably anti-German. There was opposition, but the Strategic section and the Archon agreed that it was advisable." He smiled thinly.

Dreiser nodded. "It's reassuring that your Leader realizes the need for friendship between our countries at this critical juncture," he said, cursing himself for the unction he heard in his own voice. *This is a scary old bastard, but you've seen worse,* he told himself.

Johanna hid a chuckle behind a cough. The elder von Shrakenberg grinned openly. "Back when our good Archon was merely Director of Foreign Affairs, I once overheard her express a fervent desire to separate your President from his testicles and make him eat them. Presumably a metaphor, but with Edwina Palme, you never know. That was in . . . ah, '38. She's a mean bitch, but not stupid, and she can recognize a strategic necessity when we point it out."

He crumbled a scone and added meditatively: "Personally, I would have preferred McClintock, or better still Terreblanche, particularly in wartime; he could have made the General Staff if he'd stayed in uniform. Just not on, though; the Party wouldn't have him."

Dreiser laid down his knife. "To be frank, General, if you hope to convert me, this is scarcely the way to go about it."

"Oh, not in the least. How did Oscar Wilde put it, after he settled in the Domination? The rest of the Anglo-Saxon world is convinced that the Draka are brutal, licentious, and depraved, the Draka are convinced that outlanders are prigs, hypocritical prudes, and weaklings, and *both parties are right. . . .*"

Dreiser blinked again, overcome by a slight feeling of unreality. "The problem," he said, "will be to convince the American public that Nazi Germany is more dangerous than your Domination."

"It isn't," the Draka general said cheerfully. "We're far more dangerous to you, in the long run. But the National Socialists are more dangerous right now; the Domination is patient, we never bite off more than we can chew and digest. Hitler is a parvenu, and he's in a hurry; wants to build a thousand-year Reich in a decade. As I said, the strategic situation—"

Dreiser leaned forward. "What is the strategic situation?" he asked.

"Ah." Karl von Shrakenberg steepled his fingers. "Well, in general the world situation is approaching what we in Strategic Planning call an *endgame.* Analogous to the Hellenistic period during the Roman-Carthaginian wars. The game is played out between the Great Powers, and ends when only one is left. To be a Great Power—or World Power—requires certain assets: size, population, food and raw materials, administrative and military skills, industrial production.

"The West Europeans are out of the running; they're too small. That leaves two actual World Powers—the Domination, and the United States. We have more territory, population, and resource base; you have a slightly larger industrial machine."

He wiped his fingers on a napkin of drawn-thread linen. "And there are two *potential* World Powers: Germany and Japan. Germany holds all of Europe, and is in the process of taking European Russia; Japan has most of China, and is gobbling up the former European possessions in Southeast Asia and Indonesia. In both cases, if given a generation to digest, develop and organize their conquests, they would be powers of the first rank. Germany is more immediately dangerous because of her already strong industrial production and high degree of military skill. This *present* war is to settle the question of whether the two potential powers will survive to enter the next generation of the game. I suggest it is strongly in the American interest that they not be allowed to do so."

"Why?" Dreiser said bluntly, overcoming distaste. This brutal honesty was one of the reasons for the widespread hatred of the Domination. Hypocrisy was the tribute vice paid to virtue, and the Draka refused to render it, refused to even *pretend* to virtues that they rejected and despised.

The Draka grinned like a wolf. "Ideology, demographics . . . If National Socialism and the Japanese Empire consolidate their gains, we'll have to come to an accommodation with them. In both, the master-race population is several times larger than ours. We're expansionists by inclination, they by necessity. *Lebensraum,* you see. The only basis for an accommodation would be an alliance against the Western Hemisphere, the more so as all three of us find your worldview subversive and repugnant in the extreme. Of course, two of the victors would then ally to destroy the third, and then fall out with each other. Endgame."

"And if Hitler and the Japanese *are* stopped?" the American said softly.

"Why, the U.S.A. and the Domination would divide the spoils between them," the Draka said jovially. "You'd have a generation of peace, at least: it would take us that long to digest our gains, build up our own numbers, break the conquered peoples to the yoke. Then . . . who knows? We have superior numbers, patience, continuity of purpose. You have more flexibility and ingenuity. It'll be interesting, at least."

The American considered his hands. "You may be impossible to live with in the long run," he said. "I've seen Hitler at first hand; he's impossible in the *short* run . . . but an American audience isn't going to be moved by considerations of *realpolitik:* as far as the voters are concerned, munitions merchants got us into the last one, with nothing more to show than unpaid debts from the Europeans and more serfs for the Draka."

The general shrugged, blotted his lips and rose. "Ah yes, the notorious Yankee moralism; it makes your electorate even less inclined to rational behavior than ours. I won't say *tell it to the Mexicans . . .*" He leaned forward across the table, resting his weight on his palms. "If your *audience* needs a pin in the bum of their moral indignation to work up a fighting spirit, consider this. You've heard the rumors about what's happening to the Jews in Europe?"

Dreiser nodded, mouth dry. "From the Friends Service Committee," he said. "I believed them; most of my compatriots didn't. They're . . . unbelievable. Even some of those who admit they're true won't believe them." Out of the corner of his eye he saw the younger von Shrakenbergs start at the name of the Quaker humanitarian group.

The general nodded. "They *are* true, and you can have the Intelligence reports to prove it. And if the Yankee in the street isn't moved by love of the Jews, the Fritz—the Germans—plan to stuff the Poles and Russians into the incinerators next." He straightened. "As a guest, of course my house is yours—ask the steward for anything you wish in the way of entertainment or women. Good day."

Dreiser stared blankly as the tall figure limped from the terrace. He looked about. The table faced south, over a courtyard surrounded by a colonnade. Cloud-shadow rolled down the naked rock of the hill behind, over the dappled oak forest, past fenced pasture and stables, smelling of turned earth and rock and the huge wild mountains to the east. The courtyard fountain bent before the wind, throwing a mist of spray across tiles blue as lapis. The two young Draka leaned back in their chairs, smiling in a not unkindly scorn.

"Pa—Strategos von Shrakenberg—can be a little . . . alarming at times," Eric said, offering his hand. "Very much the *grand seigneur.* An able man, very, but hard."

Johanna laughed. "I think Mr. Dreiser was a bit alarmed by Pa's offer of hospitality in the form of a wench," she drawled. "Visions of weeping captive maidens dragged to his bed in chains, no doubt."

"Ah," Eric said, pouring himself another cup of coffee. "Well, don't concern yourself; the steward never has any trouble finding volunteers."

"Eh, Rahksan?" Johanna said jokingly, turning to a serf girl who sat behind her on a stool, knitting. She did not look like the locals, the American noticed; she was lighter, like a south European. And looking him over with cool detachment.

"*Noo*, thank yaz kahndly, mistis," Rahksan said. The Draka woman laughed, and put a segment of tangerine between the serf's lips.

"I'm married," the American said, flushing. The two Draka and the serf looked at him a moment in incomprehension.

"Mind you," Eric continued in a tactful change of subject, "if this was Grandfather Alexander's time, we could have shown you some more spectacular entertainment. *He* kept a private troupe of serf wenches trained in the ballet, among other things. Used to perform nude at private parties."

With a monumental effort, Dreiser regained his balance. "Well, what did your grandmother think of that?" he asked.

"Enjoyed herself thoroughly, from what she used to cackle to me," Johanna said, rising. "I'll leave you two to business; see you at dinner, Mr. Dreiser. Come on, Rahksan; I'm for a swim."

"This . . . isn't quite what I expected," Dreiser said, relighting his pipe. Eric yawned and stretched, the yellow silk of his robe falling back from a tanned and muscular forearm.

"Well, probably the High Command thought you might as well see the Draka at home before you reported on our military. This," he waved a hand, "is less likely to jar on Yankee sensibilities than a good many other places in the Domination."

"It is?" Dreiser shook his head. He had hated Berlin—the whole iron apparatus of lies and cruelty and hatred; hated it the more since he had been in the city in the '20s, when it had been the most exciting place in Europe. Doubly exciting to an American expatriate, fleeing the stifling conformity of the Coolidge years. *Be honest,* he told himself. *This isn't more evil. Less so, if anything. Just more . . . alien. Longer established and more self-confident.*

"Also, out here and then on a military installation, *you* are less likely to jar on *Security's* sensibilities." Eric paused, making a small production of dismembering a pomegranate and wiping his hands. "I read your book *Berlin Journal*," he said in a neutral tone. "You mentioned helping Jews and dissidents escape, with the help of that Quaker group. You interest yourself in their activities?"

"Yes," the American replied, sitting up. A newsman's instincts awakened.

The Draka tapped a finger. "This is confidential?" At Dreiser's nod, he continued. "There was a young wench . . . small girl, about two years ago. Age seven, blond, blue eyes. Named Anna, number C22D178." The young officer's voice stayed flat, his face expressionless; a combination of menace and appeal behind the harsh gray eyes.

"Why, yes," Dreiser said. "It created quite a sensation at the time, but the Committee kept it out of the press. She was adopted by a Philadelphia family; old Quaker stock, but childless. That was the last

I heard. Why?" It *had* created a sensation: almost all escapees were adults, mainly from the North African and Middle Eastern provinces. For a serf from the heart of the Police Zone there was nowhere to go and an unaccompanied child was unprecedented.

Eric's eyes closed for a moment. "No reason that should be mentioned by either of us," he said. His hand reached out and gripped the other's forearm. "It wouldn't be *safe*. For either of us. Understood?"

Dreiser nodded. The Draka continued: "And if you're going to be attached to a paratroop unit, I strongly advise you to start getting into shape. Even if it's several months before the next action."

Chapter Five

"Both love and hatred can be frustrating emotions, when their object is not present. My father had sent me away. Not that I missed him overmuch; it was not he who had raised me, after all. But he had sent me away from the only home I had ever known from those who had loved and cared for me. How could I not hate him? But I was a precocious child, and of an age to begin thinking. In Philadelphia I was a stranger, and lonely, but I was free. Schooling, books, later university and the play of minds; all these he had given me, at the risk of his own life; there was nothing for me in the Domination. And he was my father: how could I not love him?

"And he was not there: I could not scream my anger at him, or embrace him and say the words of love. And so I created a father in my head, as other children had imaginary playmates: daydreams of things we would do together—trips to the zoo or Atlantic City, conversations, arguments . . . an inner life that helped to train the growth of my being, as a vine was shaped by its trellis. Good training for a novelist. A poor substitute for a home."

Daughter to Darkness: A Life, by Anna von Shrakenberg
Houghton & Stewart, New York, 1964

OAKENWALD PLANTATION
OCTOBER 1941

Arch-Strategos Karl von Shrakenberg sipped carefully from the snifter, cradling it in his hands while looking down from the study window, southwest across the gardens and the valley, green fields and poplars and the golden hue of sandstone from the hills . . .

One more, he thought, turning and pouring a careful half-ounce into the wide-mouthed goblet. One more, and another when Eric came; he had to be careful with brandy, as with any drug that could numb the pain of his leg. The surgeons had done their best, but that had been

1917, and technique was less advanced; also, they were busy. More cutting might lessen the pain, but it would also chance losing more control of the muscle, and that he would not risk.

He leaned weight on the windowsill and sighed; sun rippled through the branches of the tree outside, with a cool wind that hinted of the night's chill. He would be glad of a fire.

Ach, well, life is a wounding, he thought. *An accumulation of pains and maimings and grief. We heal as we can, bear them as we must, until the weight grows too much to bear and we go down into the earth.*

"I wish I could tell Eric that," he whispered. But what use? He was young, and full of youth's rebellion against the world. He would simply hear a command to bow to the wisdom of age, to accept the unacceptable and endure the unendurable. His tongue rolled the brandy about his mouth. *Would I have stood for that sort of advice when I was his age?*

Well, outwardly, as least. My ambitions were always more concrete. He rubbed thumb and forefinger against the bridge of his nose, wearily considering the stacks of reports on his desk; many of them were marked with a stylized terrestrial globe in a saurian claw: top secret. *I wanted command, accomplishment, a warrior's name—and what am I?* A glorified clerk, reading and annotating reports: Intelligence reports, survey reports, reports on steel production and machine-tool output, ammunition stockpile reports . . .

Old men sitting in a basement, playing war games on sand tables and sending our sons and daughters out to die on the strength of it, he thought. *You succeeded, won your dreams, and that was not the finish of it.* Not like those novels Eric was so fond of, where the ends could be tied up and kept from unravelling. Life went on . . . how dry and horrible that would have seemed once!

Stop grumbling, old man, he told himself. There had been good times enough, girls and glory and power, more than enough if you thought how most humans had to live out their lives. Limping, he walked down one wall, running his fingers lovingly along the leather-bound spines of the books. The study was as old as the manor, and had changed less; a place for the head of the family, a working room, it had escaped the great redecoration his mother had overseen as a young bride. His eyes paused as he came to his wife's portrait. It showed her as she had been when they had pledged themselves, in that hospital on Crete, looking young and self-consciously stern in her Medical Corps uniform, doctor's stethoscope neatly buttoned over her breast and her long brown hair drawn back in a workmanlike bun.

Mary would have helped, he thought, raising his glass to her memory. She had been better than he at . . . feelings? No, at talking about them when it was needful. She would have known what to do when Eric became too infatuated with that damned Circassian wench.

No, he thought grudgingly. *Tyansha understood—better than Eric. She never tried to get him to go beyond propriety in public.*

He had tried to talk to his son, but it had been useless. Maybe Mary could have got at him through the girl. Mary had been like that—

always dignified, but even the housegirls and fieldhands had talked freely with her. Tyansha had frozen into silence whenever the Old Master looked at her. Tempting just to send her away, but that would have been punishing her for Eric's fault, and a von Shrakenberg did not treat a family serf that way; honor forbade. He had been relieved when she had died naturally in childbirth, until. . .

Mary could be hard when she had to be, Karl thought. *It was a tool with her, something she brought out when it was needed. Me . . . I'm beginning to think it's like armor that I can't take off even if I wanted to.*

The Draka had made more of the differences between the sexes in his generation, although less than other peoples did. The change had been necessary—there was the work of the world to do, and never enough trustworthy hands—but there were times when he felt his people had lost something by banishing softness from their lives.

Well, I'll just have to do my best, he thought. His hand fell on a rude-carved image on a shelf—a figurine of Thor, product of the failed attempt to revive the Old Faith back in the last century. "Even you couldn't lift the Midgard Serpent or outwrestle the Crone Age, eh, Redbeard?"

A knock sounded. That would be his son.

Haven't seen the inside of this very often, since I was a boy, Eric thought, looking about his father's study. *And not often under happy circumstances then. Usually a thrashing.* There was nothing of that sort to await today, of course; merely a farewell. *Damned if I'm going to kneel and ask his blessing, tradition or not.*

The room was big and dim, smelling of leather and tobacco, open windows overshadowed by trees. Eric remembered climbing them to peer within as a boy.

Walls held books, old and leather-bound; plantation accounts running back to the founding; family records; volumes on agriculture, stockbreeding, strategy, hunting. Among them were keepsakes accumulated through generations: a pair of baSotho throwing spears nearly two centuries old, crossed over a battle-ax—relics from the land-taking. A Chokwe spirit mask from Angola, a Tuareg broadsword, a Moroccan *jezail* musket, an Armenian fighting-knife with a hilt of lacy silver filigree . . .

And the family portraits, back to *Freiherr* Augustus von Shrakenberg himself, who had led a regiment of Mecklenberg dragoons in British service in the American Revolution, and taken this estate in payment. Title to it, at least; the natives had had other ideas, until he persuaded them. Six generations of Landholders since, in uniform, mostly: proud narrow faces full of wolfish energy and cold, intelligent ferocity. Conquerors . . .

At least those were the faces they chose to show the world, he thought. *A man's mind is a forest at night. We don't know our own inwardness, much less each other's.*

His father was standing by the cabinet, filling two brandy snifters. The study's only trophy was above it, a black-maned Cape lion. Karl von Shrakenberg had killed it himself, with a lance.

Eric took the balloon glass and swirled it carefully to release the scent before lifting it to touch his father's. The smell was rich but slightly spicy, complementing the room's odors of books, old, well-kept furniture, and polished wood.

"A bad harvest or a bloody war," the elder von Shrakenberg said, using the ancient toast.

"Prosit," Eric replied. There was a silence, as they avoided each other's eyes. Karl limped heavily to the great desk and sank into the armchair amid a sigh of cushions. Eric felt himself vaguely uneasy with childhood memories of standing to receive rebuke, and forced himself to sit, leaning back with negligent elegance. The brandy bit his tongue like a caress; it was the forty-year Thieuniskraal, for special occasions.

"Not too bloody, I hope," he continued. Suddenly, there was a wetness on his brow, a feeling of things coiling beneath the surface of his mind, like snakes in black water. *I should never have come back. It all seemed safely distant while I was away.*

Karl nodded, searching for words. They were Draka and there was no need to skirt the subject of death. "Yes." A pause. "A pity that it came before you could marry. Long life to you, Eric, but it would have been good to see grandchildren here at Oakenwald before you went into harm's way. Children are your immortality, as much as your deeds." He saw his son flinch, swore inwardly. *He's a man, isn't he? It's been six years since the wench died!*

Eric set the glass down on the arm of his seat with immense care. "Well, you rather foreclosed that option, didn't you, Father?"

The time-scored eagle's face reared back. "I did nothing of the kind. Did nothing."

"You let her die." Eric heard the words speak themselves; he felt perfectly lucid but floating, beyond himself. Calm, a spectator. *Odd, I've felt that sentence waiting for six years and never dared,* some detached portion of himself observed.

"The first I knew of it was when they told me she was dead!"

"Which was why you buried her before I got back. Burned her things. Left me nothing!" Suddenly he was on his feet, breath rasping through his mouth.

"That was for your own good. You were a child—you were obsessed!" Karl was on his feet as well, his fist smashing down on the teakwood of the desk top, a drumbeat sound. They had never spoken of this before, and it was like the breaking of a cyst. "It was unworthy of you. I was trying to bring you back to your senses!"

"Unworthy of *your blood,* you mean; unworthy of that tin image of what a von Shrakenberg should be. It killed John, and it's hounded me all my life. When it's killed Johanna and me, will that satisfy your pride?" He saw his father's face pale and then flush at the mention of his elder brother's name, saw for a moment the secret fear that visited him in darkness; knew that he had scored, felt a miserable joy. The torrent of words continued.

"Obsessed? *I loved her!* As you've never loved anything in your reptile-blooded life! And you let me go a month at school without a word, if my favorite *horse* had died, you would have done more."

The shout bounced off the walls, startling him back to awareness of self. There was a tinkling, a stab of pain in his right hand; he looked down to see the snifter shattered in his grasp, blood trickling about glass shards. He brought his focus back to his father. "I hold you responsible," he finished softly.

Karl's eyes held his. *Love? What do you know about it—you're a child. It's something to be done, not talked about.* Aloud: "God's curse on you, boy, pregnancy isn't an illness—she had the same midwife who delivered you!" He fought down anger, forced gentleness into his voice. "It happens, Eric; don't blame it on me because you can't shout at fate." Sternly: "Or did you think I told them to hold a pillow over her face? She knew your interests, boy, better than you did; she never stepped beyond her station. Are you saying that I'd kill a von Shrakenberg serf who was blameless, to punish my own child?"

"I say—" Eric began, and stopped. His father's face was an iron mask, but it had gone white about the nostrils. Something inside him prompted *sayitsayitsayit,* a hunger to deliver the wound that would hurt beyond bearing, and he closed his lips by sheer force of will. Blood-kin or not, no one called Karl von Shrakenberg a liar to his face. Ever.

"I say that I had better leave. Sir." He saluted, his fist leaving a smear of blood on the left breast of his uniform tunic, clicked his heels, marched to the door.

Karl felt the rage-strength leave him as the door sighed closed. He sagged back into the chair, leaning on the desk, the old wound sending a lance of agony from hip to spine.

"What happened?" he asked dully. His eyes sought out a framed photograph on the desk—his wife's black-bordered. "Oh, Mary, you could have told me what to say, what to do . . . Why did you leave me, my heart? This may be the last time I see him alive—John and—" His head dropped into his hands. *"My son, my son!"*

Chapter Six

Eric stood, the steel folding stock of his rifle resting on one hip, looking downslope. The forest was mostly below eye level from the plateau where the paratroops had landed. Black tree limbs twisted in the paling moonlight, glistening with frost granules, the first mist of green from opening buds like a tender illusion trembling before the eyes. Breath smoked white before him; the thin cold air poured into his lungs like a taste of home. Yet these mountains were not his; they were huger, wilder, sharper. To the east across the trough of the pass the peaks caught rosy light, their snowcaps turning blood red before his eyes.

"Right," he said. The tetrarchy leaders and their seconds were grouped around him, squatting and leaning on their assault rifles. It had taken only a few minutes to uncrate the equipment and form the Century: training, and a common knowledge that defeat and death were one and the same.

"First, two minor miracles. We hit our drop zone right on; so did Cohort, chiliarchy, and legion." Southward, higher up the slope of the pass, man-made thunder rolled back from the stony walls. "So, they're engaging the main Fritz units farther up. Should go well, complete strategic surprise. Also, the communications are all working right for once."

There were appreciative murmurs. Vacuum tubes and parachutes simply went ill together, and fragile radios had cost the experimental paratroop arm dearly earlier in the war. Experience was beginning to pay off.

"Which is all to the good; we aren't fighting Italians anymore. In fact, there seem to be complete formed units up there, not just the communications and engineering personnel we were hoping for. Now for the rest of it. The gliders with the light armor came down perfectly—right into a ravine. Chiliarchy HQ says they may be able to

52

put a rubble ramp down for some of it; take a day, at least." There was a collective wince. He went on: "No help for it. Right."

He pointed downslope; they were high enough to catch glimpses of the road over treetops still black in the false dawn. Morning had brought out the birds, and a trilling chorus was starting up. The troopers waited quietly below, a few smoking or talking softly, most silent.

"That track, believe it or not, is the Ossetian Military Highway, half the road net over the mountains." He gestured southward with his mapboard. "The rest of the legion is up there, fighting their way into Kutaisi and points back toward us."

His hand cut the air to the north. "Down there, the Fritz armor is regrouping around Pyatigorsk. We're not sure exactly what units—the Intelligence network is shot to hell since the Fritz got here and started liquidating anything that moves—but definitely tank units in strength. If they're up to form, we should be getting a reaction force pretty damn quick."

The Centurion's next gesture was due east, to the unseen S-curve of the two-lane "highway" that hugged the mountain slope on which they stood. "And a kilometer that way is Village One. Dense forest nearly to the road. Stone houses, and a switchback starts there. Our objective. Tom?"

"I head up the road, cross above the village, spread 1st Tetrarchy as a stop force."

"And *don't* let them get past you into the woods. Marie?"

"15mm's and the 120mm recoilless along the treeline; mortars back; flamethrower and demolition teams to key off you and move forward in support. "

"Einar, Lisa, John?"

"Left-right concentric, work our way in house-to-house. You coordinate on the rough spots."

"Correct. Any questions?"

Tetrarch Lisa Telford shifted on her haunches. "What about locals?"

"Ignore them if they're quiet. Otherwise, expend 'em. Synch watches: 0500 at . . . *mark!* Go in at 0530, white flare. Nothing more? Good, let's *do* it, people, let's *go!*"

The Germans in the Circassian village were wary—enough to set sentries hundreds of meters in the woods beyond the fields. Eric stooped over the body, noted the mottled camouflage jacket, glanced at the collar tabs, up at the trooper who stood smiling fondly and wiping his knife on the seat of his trousers.

"Got his paybook?" he snapped.

"Heah y'are, suh."

Eric riffled through it. "Shit! Waffen-SS, Liebstandarte Adolf Hitler! I was hoping for a logistics unit, or at least line infantry." The soldier had been nineteen, and an Austrian; for a brief instant the Draka officer wondered if the Caucasus had reminded him of the Tyrol. On impulse, he reached down and closed the staring brown eyes.

With luck, there were ten minutes before the Fritz noticed; they were probably expecting attack from the south. The noise there was peaking, the narrow walls of the pass channeling a rapid chatter of automatic-weapons fire as well as the boom of heavy weapons; that would be the rest of first and second Cohorts . . . or even the legion. Heavy fighting riveted the attention. Even so, the Fritz in the village had an all-around perimeter, for anti-partisan defense, if nothing else.

Their CO is probably getting screams for help. They might pull out . . . No, too chancy.

Ducking through thickening underbrush of wild pistachio, he made his way toward the treeline. The sun was well up now, but the mountain beeches wove a canopy fifteen meters above, turning the air to a cool olive gloom. Nearer the edge of the woods, sunlight allowed more growth and the thicker timber had been logged off; there were thickets of saplings laced together with wild grapevines and witch hazel and huge clumps of wild rhododendron.

He dropped to his belly and leopard-crawled forward. The support teams were setting up, manhandling the tripod mounts of the heavy 15mm machine guns into position, the long, slender, fluted barrels snaking out of improvised nests of rock and bush. The heavy *snick* of oiled metal sounded as the bolts were pulled back. The three 120mm recoilless rifles were close behind, wrestled through by sheer strength and awkwardness; working parties clearing the way with bush knives, others following, bent under loads of the heavy perforated-shell ammunition. The infantry spread out, shedding their marching packs for combat load.

Carefully, Eric nudged his rifle through the last screen of tall grass and sighted through the x4 integral scope. The view leaped out at him. Half a thousand meters of cleared fields stretched around the village, more downslope to the north, bare and brown in the spring, still sodden from melting snow. The fields themselves were uneven, steeply sloped, studded with low terraces, heaps of fieldstone, walls of piled rock: much of it would be dead ground from the town. Closer to the tumbled huddle of stone houses were orchards, apple and plum, and walled paddocks for sheep.

Distantly he was aware of his body's reaction, sweat staining the field jacket down from his armpits, blood loud in his ears, a dryness in his mouth. He had seen enough combat to know what explosive and flying metal did to human bodies. The fears were standard, every soldier felt them—of death, of pain even more. Stomach wounds particularly, even with sulfiomide and antibiotics. Castration, blinding, burns; a life as a cripple, a thing women would puke to see . . . Draka officers were expected to delegate freely and lead from the front; a Centurion had a shorter life expectancy than a private. Almost without effort, training overrode fear, and his hands were steady as he switched to field glasses.

Standard, he thought. The village might have been any of a thousand thousand others in High Asia, anywhere from Anatolia to Sinkiang: flat-topped structures of rough stone with mud mortar, some plastered and whitewashed, others raw, sheds and narrow twisted lanes. The military "highway" went straight through, with the burnt-out wreckage of a Russian T-34 standing by the verge on the northern outskirts, the blackened barrel of its cannon pointing in silent futility down toward the plains. There was a square, and a building with onion domes that looked to have been a mosque, before the Revolution, then until last fall a Soviet "House of Culture." There were a few other modernish-looking structures, two nondescript trucks in German army paint, more horse-drawn vehicles parked outside.

Movement; chickens, an old woman in the head-to-toe swathing of Islamic modesty . . . and *yes*, figures in Fritz field gray. He switched his view to the outskirts, almost hidden in greenery: spider holes, wire, the houses with firing slits knocked into their walls . . . it wasn't going to be a walkover.

He reached a hand behind him and Sofie thrust the handset into his grasp. Senior Decurion McWhirter and the five troopers waited behind her. He clicked code into the pressure button and spoke: "Marie."

"Targets ranged, teams ready." Along the firing line, hands clutched the grips and lanyards; a hundred meters behind, she stood with her eyes pressed to the visor of a split-view rangefinder. The automortar crews waited, hands on the elevating screws, loaders ready with fresh five-round clips.

"Tetrarchy commanders."

"In position."

Eric forced himself to half a dozen slow, deep breaths. *Hell*, he thought. *Why don't I just tell them I'm going for a look-see and start walking to China?* Because it would be silly, of course. Because these were his friends.

"Well, then." He cased the binoculars, hooked the assault sling of his rifle over his head, watched his wrist as the second hand swept inexorably around to 0530. When he spoke, his voice was quiet, conversational.

"Flare."

It went up from the observation post with a quiet pop and burst two hundred meters up. Magnesium flame blossomed against the innocent blue of the sky, white and harsh. *Plop-whine*, the first mortar shells went by overhead, plunging downward into the pink froth of apple blossom along the edge of the village: *thump-crash* fountains of black earth and shattered branches, steel and rock fragments equally deadly whirling through the air. *Crash-crash-crash-crash*, without stopping; the new automortars were heavier, on their wheeled carriages, but while the ammunition lasted, they could spray the 100mm bombs the way a submachine gun did pistol bullets. Century A's teams had been practicing for a long time, and their hands moved reloads in with steady, metronomic regularity.

From either side the heavy machine guns erupted, controlled four-second bursts arching toward the smoke and shattered wood on the town's edge. Red tracer flicked out, blurring from the muzzles, seeming to float as it approached the roiling dust of the target zone. The firing positions here at the treeline overlooked the thin net of German defensive posts, commanded the roofs and streets beyond. They raked the windows and firing slits, and already figures in SS jackets were falling.

"Storm storm!" the officers' shouts rang out. The Draka infantry rose; they had shed their marching loads and the lead sticks were crouched and ready. Now they sprinted forward, running full-tilt, bobbing and jinking and weaving as they advanced. A hundred meters and they threw themselves down in firing positions; the assault rifles opened up, and the light rifle-calibre machine guns. The second-string lochoi were already leapfrogging their positions, moving with smooth athlete's grace. The operation would be repeated at the same speed, as many times as was necessary to reach the objective. This was where thousands of hours of training paid off—training that began for Draka children at the age of six to produce soldiers enormously strong and fit. Troops that could keep up this pace for hours.

And the covering fire would be *accurate*—sniper accurate, with soldiers who could use optical scopes as quickly as those of other nations did iron sights.

"BuLala! BuLala!" The battle cry roared out, as old as the Draka, in a language of the Bantu extinct for more than a century: *Kill! Kill!*

The return fire was shaky and wild—the slow banging of the German Kar 98 bolt-action rifles, then the long *brrrrrtttt* of a MG 34. The line of machine-gun bullets stabbed out from a farmhouse on the outer edge of the village. Draka were falling. Seconds later one of the 120mm recoilless rifles fired.

There was a huge sound, a crash at once very loud and yet muffled. Behind the stubby weapon a great cloud of incandescent gas flared— the backblast that balanced the recoil. Saplings slapped to the ground and leaf litter caught fire, and the ammunition squad leaped to beat out the flames with curses and spades. But it was the effect on the German machine-gun nest that mattered, and that was shattering. The shells were low-velocity, but they were heavy and filled with *plastique*, confined by thin steel mesh. The warhead struck directly below the muzzle of the German gun, spreading instantly into a great flat pancake of explosive; milliseconds later, the fuse in its base detonated.

Those shells had been designed for use against armor, or ferroconcrete bunkers. The loose stone of the farmhouse wall disintegrated, collapsing inward as if at the blow of an invisible fist. Beyond, the opposite wall blew outward even before the first stones reached it, destroyed by air driven to the density of steel in the confined space of the house. The roof and upper floor hung for a moment, as if suspended against gravity. Then they fell, to be buried in their turn by the inward topple of the end walls. Moments before, there had been a house, squalid enough, but solid. Now there was only a heap of shattered ashlar blocks.

"Now!" Eric threw himself forward. The headquarters lochos followed. Ahead the mortar barrage "walked" into the town proper, then back to its original position. But now the shells carried smoke, thick and white, veiling all sight; bullets stabbed out of it blindly. The 120s crashed again and again, two working along the edge of the village, another elevating slightly to shell the larger buildings in the square.

With cold detachment, Tetrarch Marie Kaine watched the shellfire crumble the buildings, flicked a hand to silence the firing line as the rifle Tetrarchies reached the barrier of smoke. It thinned rapidly; she could hear the crackling bang of snake charges blasting pathways through the German wire. The small-arms fire died away for a brief moment as the first enemy fire positions were blasted out of existence, over-run, silenced. The medics and their stretcher bearers were running forward to attend to the Draka wounded.

"Combat pioneers forward!" she said crisply. The teams launched themselves downhill, as enthusiastically as the rifle infantry had done; being weighed down with twenty kilos of napalm tank for a flame-thrower, or an equal weight of demolition explosive, was as good an incentive for finding cover as she knew.

"All right," she continued crisply. "Machine-gun sections cease fire. Resume on targets of opportunity or fire requests."

The smoke had blown quickly; a dozen houses were rubble, and fires had started already from beams shattered over charcoal braziers. The fighting was moving into the town; she could see figures in Draka uniforms swarming over rooftops, the stitching lines of tracer. They were as tiny as dolls, the town spread out below like a map . . .

But then, I always did like dolls, she thought. *And maps.* Her father was something of a traditionalist; he had been quite pleased about the dolls, until she started making her own . . . and organizing the oth-ers into work parties.

The maps, too: she had loved those. Drawing her own lines on them, making her own continents for the elaborate imagined worlds of her daydreams. Then she discovered that you could do that in the real world: school trips to the great projects, the tunnel from the Orange River to the Fish, the huge dams along the Zambezi. *Horses and engineering magazines,* she thought wryly. *The twin pillars of my teenage years.*

It had been the newsreels, finally. There wasn't much left to be done south of the Zambezi, or anywhere in Africa—just execution of projects long planned, touching up, factory extensions. But the New Territo-ries, the lands conquered in 1914–1919 . . . ah! She could still shiver at the memory of watching the final breakthrough on the Dead Sea-Mediterranean Canal, the frothing silver water forcing its way through the great turbines, the hum, the *power.* The school texts said the Will to Power was the master force. True enough . . . but anyone could have power over serfs, all you needed was to be born a Citizen. The power to make cultivated land out of a desert, to channel a river, build a city where nothing but a wretched collection of hovels stood—*that* was power! Father had had a future mapped out for her, or so he thought: the Army, of course; an Arts B.A.; then she could marry, and satisfy herself with laying out gardens around the manor. Or if she must, follow some genteel, feminine profession, like architecture . . .

But no, I was going to build, she thought. And here I am, destined to spend the best years of my life laying out tank traps, clearing minefields and blowing things up. Oh, well, the war won't last for-ever. Russia, Europe . . . we'll have that, and there's room for projects with real *scale,* there.

A trained eye told her that it was time. "Forward," she called. "Wallis, stop fiddling with that radio and bring the spare set. New firing line at the first row of houses." *Or rubble*, her mind added. That was the worst of war—you were adding to entropy rather than fighting it. *Just clearing the way for something better,* she mused, dodging forward. *Hovels, not a decent drain in the place.*

Chapter Seven

"*. . . saw little of my father. Home was the servants' quarters of Oakenwald, where I was happy, much of the time. Tantie Sannie fed me and loved me, there were the other children of the House and Quarters to play with, the gardens and the mountainside to explore. Memory is fragmentary before six: it slips away, the consciousness which bore it too alien for the adult mind to reexperience. Images remain only—the great kitchens' and Tantie baking biscuits, watching from behind a rosebush as guests arrived for a dance, fascinating and beautiful and mysterious, with their jewels and gowns and uniforms.*

"*A chid can know, without the knowledge having meaning. We had numbers on our necks; that was natural. The Masters did not. There were things said among ourselves, never to the Masters. I remember watching Tantie Sannie talk to one of the overseers, and suddenly realizing she's afraid . . . The Young Master was my father, and came to give me presents once a year. I thought that he must dislike me, because his face went hard and fixed when he looked at me, and I wondered what I had done to anger him. A terrible thought—my Mother had died bearing me. Had I killed her? Now I know it was just her looks showing in me, but the memory of that grief is with me always. And then he came one night to take me away from all I had known and loved, telling me that it was for the best. Movement, cars and boats, strangers; America, voices I could hardly understand . . .*"

Daughter to Darkness: A Life, by Anna von Shrakenberg
Houghton & Stewart, New York, 1964

VILLAGE ONE, OSSETIAN MILITARY HIGHWAY
APRIL 14, 1942: 0530 HOURS

Eric cleared the low stone fence with a raking stride. Noise was all around them as they ran: stutter of weapons, explosion blast, screams;

the harsh stink of cordite filled his nose, and he felt his mouth open and join in the shout. The rifle stuttered in his hands, three-round bursts from the hip. Behind him he heard Sofie shrieking, a high exultant sound; even the stolid McWhirter was yelling. They plunged among the apple trees, gnarled little things barely twice man height, some shattered to stumps; the Fritz wire was ahead, laneways blasted through it with snake charges. Fire stabbed at them; he flicked a stick grenade out of his belt, yanked the pin, tossed it.

Automatically, they dove for the dirt. Sofie *ooffed* as the weight of the radio drove her ribs into the ground, then opened up with her light machine pistol. A round went *crack-whhhit* off a stone in front of his face, knocking splinters into his cheek. Eric swore, then called over his shoulder.

"Neal! Rocket gun!"

The trooper grunted and crawled to one side. The tube of the weapon cradled against her cheek, the rear venturi carefully pointed away from her comrades; her hands tightened on the twin pistol grips, a finger stroked the trigger. *Thump* and the light recoilless charge kicked the round out of the short smooth-bore barrel. It blurred forward as the fins unfolded, there was a bright streak as the sustainer rocket motor boosted the round up to terminal velocity: *crash* as it struck and exploded. Her partner reached to work the bolt and open the breech, slid in a fresh shell and slapped her on the helmet.

"Fire in the hole!" he called.

Forward again, through the thinning white mist of the smoke barrage, over the rubble of the blasted house. That put them on a level with the housetops, where the village sloped down to the road. He reached for the handset.

"Marie, report."

"Acknowledged. Activity in the mosque, runners going out. Want me to knock it down?"

"Radio?"

"Nothing on the direction finder since I hit the room with the antennae."

"Hold on the mosque, they'd just put their HQ somewhere else, and we're going to need the 120 ammo later. Bring two of the heavies forward, I'll take them over; keep the road north under observation. And send in the Ronsons and satchelmen—we're going to have to burn and blast some of them out." A different series of clicks. "Tom, close in. Tetrarchy commanders, report."

"Einar here. Lisa's hit, 3rd Tetrarchy's senior decurion's taken over. Working our way in southwest to southeast, then behind the mosque."

Damn! He hoped she wasn't dead; she'd been first in line if he "inherited the plantation."

"John here. Same, northwest and hook."

"John, pull in a little and go straight—Tom's going to hit the northeast anyway. We'll split them. I'll be on your left flank. Everybody remember, this is three-dimensional. Work your way down from the roofs as well as up; I'll establish fire positions on commanding locations, move 'em forward as needed. Over."

Eric raised his head over the crest of the rubble. The peculiar smell of fresh destruction was in the air, old dust and dirt and soiled laundry. Ruins needed time to achieve majesty, or even pathos; right after they had been fought over there was nothing but . . . seediness, and mess. Ahead was a narrow alleyway: nothing moved in it but a starved-looking mongrel, and an overturned basket of clothes that had barely stopped rocking. The locals were going to earth, the crust of posts in the orchard had been overrun, and the bulk of the Fritz were probably bivouacked around the town square: it was the only place in town with anything approaching a European standard of building. Therefore, they would be fanning out toward the noise of combat. Therefore . . .

"Follow me," he said. McWhirter flicked out the bipod of his Holbars, settled it on the ridge and prepared for covering fire. Eric rose and leaped down the shifting slope, loose stone crunching and moving beneath his boots. They went forward, alleys and doors, every window a hole with the fear of death behind it, leapfrogging into support positions. Two waves of potential violence, expanding toward their meeting place like quantum electron shells, waiting for an observer to make them real.

They panted forward, bellies tightening for the expected hammer of a Fritz machine pistol that did not come. Then they were across the lane, slamming themselves into the rough wall, plastered flat. That put them out of the line of fire from the windows, but not from something explosive, tossed out. One of the troopers whirled out, slammed his boot into the door, passed on; another tossed a short-fuse grenade through as the rough planks jarred inward.

Blast and fragments vomited out; Eric and Sofie plunged through, fingers ready on the trigger, bu tnot firing: nobody courted a ricochet without need. But the room beyond was bare, except for a few sticks of shattered furniture, a rough pole-ladder to the upper story . . . and a wooden trapdoor in the floor.

That raised a fraction of an inch; out poked a wooden stick with a rag that might once have beenwhite. A face followed it, wrinkled, gray bearded, emaciated and looking as old as time. Somewhere below a child whimpered, and a woman's voice hushed it, in a language he recognized.

"*Nix Schiessen!*" the ancient quavered in pidgin-German. "*Stalino kaputt—Hitler kaputt urra Drakanski!*"

Despite himself, Eric almost grinned; he could hear a snuffle of laughter from Sofie. The locals seemed to have learned something about street fighting; also, their place in the scheme of things. The smile faded quickly. There was a bleak squalor to the room; it smelled sourly of privation, ancient poverty, fear. For a moment his mind was daunted by the thought of a life lived in a place such as this—at best, endless struggle with a grudging earth wearing you down into an ox, with the fruits kept for others. Scuttling aside from the iron hooves of the armies as they went trampling and smashing through the shattered garden of their lives, incomprehensible giants, warriors from nowhere. *The lesson being,* he thought grimly, *that this is defeat, so avoid it.*

"Lochos upstairs," he snapped. "Roof, then wait for me." He motioned the graybeard up with the muzzle of his assault rifle, switching to fluent Circassian.

"You, old man, come here. The rest get down and *stay* down."

The man came forward, shuffling and wavering, in fear and hunger both, to judge from the look of the hands and neck and the way his ragged kaftan hung on his bones. But he had been a tall man once, and the sound of his own tongue straightened his back a little.

"Spare our children, honored sir," he began. The honorific he used meant "Lord," and could be used as an endearment in other circumstances. "In the name of Allah the Merciful, the Compassionate—"

The Draka cut him off with a chopping hand, ignoring memories that twisted under his lungs. "If you want mercy, old one, you must earn it. This is the *Dar al Harb*, the House of War. *Where are the Germanski?*"

The instructions were valuable—clear, concise, flawed only by a peasant's assumption that every stone in his village was known from birth. Dismissed, he climbed back to his family, into the cellar of their hopes. McWhirter paused above the trapdoor, hefted a grenade and glanced a question. At the Centurion's headshake he turned to the ladder, disappointment obvious in the set of his shoulders.

"McWhirter doesn't like ragheads much, does he, Centurion?" Sofie said as she ran antenna line out the window; the intelligence would have to be spread while it was fresh. Not that she was going to say much—the old bastard was always going on about how women were too soft for front-line formations.

With a grunt of relief, she turned and rested the weight of the radio on a lip of rock. The Centurion was facing her; that way they could cover each other's backs. She looked at his face, thoughtful and relaxed now, and remembered the hot metal flying past them with a curious warm feeling low in her stomach. It would be . . . unbearable if that taut perfection were ruined into ugliness, and she had seen that happen to human bodies too often. And . . .

What if he was wounded? Not serious, just a leg wound, and I was the one to carry him out. Images flashed though her mind—gratitude in the cool gray eyes as she lifted his head to her canteen, and—

Oh, shut the fuck up, she told her mind, then started slightly; had she spoken aloud? Good, no. *Almighty Thor, woman, are you still sixteen or what? The last time you had daydreams like that it was about pulling the captain of the field-hockey team out of a burning building. What you really wanted was bed.* That was cheering, since she *had* gotten to bed with *her*.

Eric stood, lost in thought. His mind was translating raw information into tactics and possibilities, while another layer answered the comtech's question about McWhirter: "Well, he *was* in Afghanistan," he said. "Bad fighting. We had to hill three-quarters to get the rest to give up. McWhirter was there eight years, lost a lot of friends."

Sofie shrugged. She was six months past her nineteenth birthday, and that war had been over before her tenth. "How come you understand the local jabber, then?" And to the radio: "Testing, acknowledge."

"Oh, my first concubine was a Circassian; Father gave her to me as a fourteenth birthday present. I was the envy of the county—she cost three hundred aurics." He thrust the memory from him. There was the work of the day to attend to. "Next . . ."

Standartenführer Felix Hoth awoke, mumbling, fighting a strangling enemy that he only gradually realized was a mass of sweat-soaked bedclothes. Panting, he swung his feet to the floor and hung his head in his hands, the palm heels pressed against his eyes. *Lieber Herr Gott,* but he'd thought the dreams had stopped. Perhaps it was the vodka last night; he hadn't done that in a while, not since the first month after Moscow. He was back in the tunnels, in the dark, but alone; he could hear their breathing as they closed in on him and *he could not even scream* . . .

"Herr Standartenführer?" The question was repeated twice before it penetrated. It was one of his Slav girls—Valentina, or Tina, whatever; holding out a bottle of Stolichnaya and a glass. The smell of the liquor seized him with a sudden fierce longing, then combined with the odors of sweat and stale semen to make his stomach twist.

"No!" he shouted. His hand sent it crashing to the floor. She stood, cringing, to receive the backhanded slap. "You stupid Russki bitch, how many times do I have to tell you not in the morning! Fetch coffee and food. *Schnell!*"

The effort of rage exhausted him; he fought the temptation of a collapse back onto the four-poster bed. Instead, he forced his muscles into movement walking to the dresser and splashing himself with water from the jug, pouring more from the spirit-heater and beginning to shave. Sometimes he thought she was more trouble than she was worth, that he should find a good orderly, and only send for her when he needed a woman. You expected an *untermensch* to be stupid, but it was what, five months now since he had grabbed her out of that burning schoolhouse in Tula, and she still couldn't speak more than a few words of German. His Russian was better. And she was supposed to have been a teacher!

It showed that Reichsfuhrer Himmler was right: intellectual training had nothing to do with real intelligence—that was in the blood. Or . . . sometimes he wondered if she was as dull as she seemed. Perhaps it would be better just to liquidate her. Two were enough, surely, or there were thousands more . . .

No. That was how Kube had gotten it, up around Minsk: one of them had smuggled an antipersonnel mine under the bed and blown them both to bits. Frightened but not completely desperate, that was the ticket.

Breakfast repaired his spirits; the ration situation was definitely picking up, not like last winter when they'd all been gnawing black bread in the freezing dark. Real coffee, now that the U-boats were keeping the English too busy for blockades; good bacon and eggs and butter and cream. He glanced around the room with satisfaction as he ate; it was furnished with baroque elegance. Pyatigorsk had been a health resort for Tzarist nobles with a taste for medicinal springs at the foot of the Caucasus, and the Commissars had not let it run down. Not bad for a Silesian peasant's son, brought up to touch the cap to the *Herr Rittermeister;* the Waffen-SS offered a career open to the talents, all right. No social distinctions at the Bad Tolz Junkerschul, the officer's training academy. No limits to how high a sound Aryan could rise; in the Wehrmacht he'd have been lucky to make Unteroffizier, with some traitorous monocled "gentleman" telling him what to do.

Well, piss on the regular Army and their opinion of Felix Hoth. Felix Hoth now commanded a regiment of SS-Division "Liebstandarte Adolf Hitler." The Leader's own Guards, the victors of Minsk, Smolensk, Moscow, Kharkov, Astrakhan. The elite of the New Order . . . and just finishing its conversion from a motorized infantry brigade to a Panzer division. He glanced at the mantel clock with its plump cupids— 0530. Good, another half hour and he'd roust the second Panzergrenadier battalion out—surprise inspection and a four-kilometer run. Good lads, but the new recruits needed stiffening. Not many left of the men who had jumped off from Poland a year ago. And as soon as they finished refitting they'd be back in the line—real fighting out on the Sverdlosk front instead of this chickenshit anti-partisan work.

The situation reports had come up with breakfast; they were a real pleasure. The trickle of equipment from the captured Russian factories was turning into a steady flow, not like the old days when the Wehrmacht had grudged the SS every bayonet, and they'd had to make do with Czech and French booty. The SS could improvise; if the supply lines to the Fatherland were long, seize local potential! Ivan equipment: their armor and artillery were first-rate. He winced at the memory of trying to stop that first Russian T-34 with a 37mm antitank gun.

Burning pine forest, the smell like a mockery of Christmas fires. Burning trucks and human flesh, the human wave of Russian troops in their mustard-yellow uniforms, arms linked. *Urra! Urra!* The machine guns scythed them down, artillery firing point-blank, blasting huge gaps in their line, bits and pieces of human flung through the forest and hanging from the trees . . . and the tank, low, massive, unstoppable, its broad tracks grinding through the swamp.

Aim, range 800, pull the lanyard . . . *crack-whang!* He'd frozen for a moment in sheer disbelief, the reload in his hand. A clean hit, and the thick-sloped plate had shed it into the trees like . . . like a tennis ball. Left only a shallow gouge, crackling and red as it cooled. Coming on, shot after shot rebounding, grinding over the gun, cutting Friedrich in half. He'd lain there looking up and not even bleeding for a second, then it had all come out . . .

Hoth looked down at his right hand; half the little finger was missing. He had been very lucky; jumping on the deck of a tank and ramming a grenade down the muzzle of its cannon was not something you did with any great hope of survival. Automatic, really; not thinking of living, or of the Knight's Cross and the promotion . . .

With a smile on his thick-boned, stolid face he strode to the window and pulled open the drapes. There they were, spread out in leagues three stories below, across the tread-chewed lawns of what had once been a nobleman's park. Dawn was just breaking, reaching beams to gild the squat, gray-steel shapes, throw shadows from the hulls and long cannon. Tanks in the outer ring, then the assault guns, infantry carriers (praise Providence, all the motorized infantry on tracks at last!), soft transport. Russian designs, much of it. Improved, brought into line with German practice, pouring out of Kharkov and Stalingrad and Kirovy Rog, with technicians from Krupp and Daimler-Benz to organize, and overseers from the SS Totenkopf squads with stock whips, to see that the Russian workers did not flag at their eighteen-hour days.

Not really necessary to pull into a hedgehog like this, but it was good practice and the partisans seemed damnably well informed. Suicide parties with explosive charges had infiltrated more than once. *Perhaps more hostages,* he thought, turning to the east and taking a deep breath of fresh, crisp spring air with a pleasant undertang of diesel oil.

The aircraft were difficult to spot, coming in low out of the dawning sun. He squinted, his first thought that it was a training flight . . .

The smile slid slowly off his face. Too many, too fast, too low; at least 450 km/h, hedgehopping over poplars and orchards. Two engines, huge radials; low-wing monoplanes, their noses bristling with muzzles, long teardrop canopies . . . *One 40 mm autocannon, six 25mm,* the Luftwaffe intelligence report ran through his head. *Five tonnes of bombs, rockets, jellied petrol* . . . Draka ground-attack aircraft, P-12 Rhino class. The nominal belligerence of the Domination had suddenly become very real.

There was no time to react; the first flight came in for its strafing run even as the alarm klaxon began to warble. He could hear the heavy *dumpa-dumpa-dumpa* of the 50mm's, see the massive frames of the Rhinos shudder in the air with recoil. Crater lines stitched through the mud, meaty *smacks* as the tungsten-cored solid shot rammed into wet earth, then the heavy *chunk* as they struck his tanks, into the thinner side and deck armor. The lighter autocannon were a continuous orange flicker, stabbing into the soft-skinned transport. Something blew up with a muffled *thump*, a soft soughing noise and flash; petrol tanker, spraying burning liquid for meters in every direction. Vehicles were flaming all over the fields about the house, fuel and ammunition exploding, early-morning fireworks as tracer and incendiary rounds shot through the sky trailing smoke. The crews were pouring out of hutments, racing through the rain of metal to their tanks and carriers, and falling, their bodies jerking in the grotesque dance of human flesh caught in automatic-weapons fire. The attackers were past; then another wave, and the first returning, looping for a second pass.

"*Totentanz,*" he murmured. *Dance of death.* The telephone rang: he picked it up and began the ritual of questions and orders, because there was nothing else to do. And nothing of use *to* do; this was a quiet sector, and he had been stripped of most of his antiaircraft for the east, where the enemy still had some planes. The rest were *flackpanzers,* out there with the rest . . .

Engine rumble added to the din of blast and shouts; some of the Liebstandarte troopers were reaching their machines, and a percentage of crews were always on duty. A four-barreled 20mm opened up, one of the new self-propelled models. The ball turret traversed, hosing shells into the air, a Draka airplane took that across a belly whose skin was machined from armorplate, shrugged it off in a shower of sparks. Another was not so lucky, the canopy shattering as the gun caught it banking into a turn. Unguided, it cartwheeled into a barracks, building and wreck vanished in a huge, orange-black ball of flame as its load of destruction detonated. The blast blew the diamond-pane windows back on either side of him, shattering against the stone walls. He could feel the heat of it on his face, like a summer sun after too long at the swimming baths, when the skin has begun to burn, taut and prickling. Another Rhino wheeled and fired a salvo of rockets from its underwing racks into the flackpanzer that had killed its wingmate. Twisted metal burned when the cloud of powdered soil cleared, and now the others were dropping napalm, cannisters tumbling to leave trails of inextinguishable flame in their wake, yellow surf-walls that buried everything in their path . . .

Standartenführer Hoth had been a young fanatic a year ago. Only a year ago, but no man could be young again who had walked those long miles from Germany to the Kremlin; who had stood to break the death ride of the Siberian armor as it drove for encircled Moscow; who had survived the final nightmare battles through the burning streets, flushing NKVD holdout battalions from the prison-cellars of the Lubyanka . . . That year had taken his youth; his fanaticism it had honed, tempered with caution, sharpened with realism. His face was sweat-sheened, but it might have been carved from ivory as he held the field telephone in a white-fingered grip.

"Shut up. They are not attacking the barracks because they are at the limit of operational range and must concentrate on priority targets," he said tonelessly. "Get me Schmidt."

The line buzzed and clicked for a moment, but the switchboard in the basement was secure. *Probably overloaded, to be sure,* came a mordant thought. One part of his mind was raging, longing to run screaming into the open, firing his pistol at the black-gray vulture shapes. He could see the squadron markings as some of them flew by the manor at scarcely more than rooftop height; see the winged flame-lizard that was the enemy's national emblem, with the symbolic sword of death and the slave-chain of mastery in its claws.

Fafnir, he thought. *The reptile cunning, patience to wait until all the enemies are weakened . . .*

And another part wished simply to weep, for grief of loss at the destruction of his work, his love, the beautiful and deadly instrument he had helped to forge . . .

"Sch-Schmidt here," a voice at the other end of the line gasped. "Standartenführer, air raid—"

"And Stalin is dead, is this news?" he used the sarcasm deliberately, as a whip of ice.

"No—sir, Divisional HQ in Krasnodar, too, and, and—reports from the Gross Deutschland in Grozny, the Luftwaffe . . ."

"Silence." His voice was flat, but it produced a quiet that echoed. The sound of aircraft engines was fading; the raid was already history. One did not fight history, one used it. He looked south, to the pass.

"You will attempt to contact Hauptsturmfuhrer Keilig in the village. There will be no reply, but keep trying."

"*Ja wohl*, Herr Standartenführer."

"Call Division. Inform them that the Ossetian Military Highway is under attack by air-assault troops."

"But, Standartenführer, how—"

"Silence." An instant. "You will find Hauptman Schtackel, or his immediate subordinate if he is dead or incapacitated. Tell him to prepare a reconnaissance squadron of Puma armored cars; also my command car, or a vehicle with equivalent communications equipment. By exactly—" he looked at the clock, still ticking serenely between its pink-cheeked plaster godlets "—0600 hours, I wish to be under way. He is also to begin formation of a *Kampfgruppe* of at least battalion size from intact formations, jump-off time to be no later than 1440 today. I will have returned and will be in command of the kampfgruppe. Should I fail to return, Obersturmbannfuhrer Keistmann is to exercise his discretion until orders arrive from HQ. " His voice lost its metronomic quality. "*Is that clear?*"

"Zum Befehl, Herr Standartenführer!"

He replaced the receiver with a soft click and turned from the scene of devastation his eyes had never left for an instant during the conversation. He saw that the girl Tina had returned. "Leave the tray, I will be finishing it," he said. A soldier ate when he could, in the field. "Fetch my camouflage fatigues and kit. Have them ready here within ten minutes."

He paused in the doorway, to give the fires smoking beyond one last glance. "My loyalty is my honor," he quoted to himself the SS oath. "If nothing else, there is always that."

Valentina Fedorova made very sure that the footsteps were not returning before she crossed to the folder and began to leaf through it with steady, systematic speed. Her fluent German she had learned in the Institute, almost as a hobby; she had a gift for languages. The memory that made a quick scan almost as effective as the impossible camera was a gift as well, one that had been very useful these past few months. Not that she had expected much besides a little, little revenge before she was inevitably found out, before the drum was beaten in the town square for another flogging to the death. She raised the lid of the coffeepot, worked her mouth, spat copiously. Then she crossed to the window, allowing herself the luxury of one long, joyous look before laying out the uniform. She smiled.

It was the first genuine smile in a long time.

"Burn," she whispered. "Burn."

Sofie's eyes had widened. The muzzle of her machine pistol had come up, straight at him; time froze, the burst cracked past his ears, powder grains burnt his cheek. He wheeled to watch the Fritz tumble down the steps dropping his carbine, clutching at a belly ripped open by the soft-nosed 10mm slugs.

The wounded man's mouth worked. "*Mutti,*" he whispered, eyes staring disbelief at the life leaking out between his fingers. "*Mutti, hilfe, mutti—*"

A three-round burst from Eric's rifle hammered him back into silence.

Eric looked up, met Sophie's gaze. She was smiling, but not the usual cocksure urchin grin; a softer expression, almost tremulous. Quickly, she glanced aside.

Well, well, he thought. Then: *Oh, not now.* Aloud, he murmured, "Thanks; good thing you've got steady hands."

"Ya, ah, c'mon, let's get up those stairs, hey?" she muttered, leading the way with a smooth steady stride that took her up the board steps noiselessly, even under the heavy load of the backpack radio.

The 15mm had hammered beside his ear; for a moment part of him wondered how much combat it would take to damage his hearing. This was worse than working in a drop-forging plant. His mouth was dry, filled with a thick saliva no swallowing could clear; there was water in his canteen, but no time for it. The rifles of his lochos took up the firing, hammering at the narrow slit window twenty meters away, keeping the Fritz machine-gunner from manning his post. The light high-velocity 5mm rounds skittered off in spark trails; heavy 15mm bullets chewed at the stone, tattering it with craters.

"Damn hovels are built like forts!" one of the troopers snarled, as the ammunition drum of his Holbars emptied and automatically ejected. He scrabbled at his belt for the last replacement, slapped the guide lips into the magazine well, and jacked the cocking lever.

"They *are* forts," McWhirter grunted. "Sand coons are treacherous. Don't sleep easy without bunkers and firing slits 'tween them and the neighbors."

Serfdom was too easy on them, he thought viciously. It was the smells that brought it back—rancid mutton fat and spices, sweaty wool and kohl. You could never trust ragheads—Afghans or Circassians or Turks or whatever; they kept coming back at you. Better to herd them all into their mosque and turn the Ronsons on them. He remembered that, from the Panjir Valley in Afghanistan; reprisals for an ambush by the *badmash*, the guerillas.

The Draka had found the drivers of the burnt-out trucks with their testicles stuffed into their mouths. . . Ten villages for that; he'd pulled the plunger on the flamer himself. The women had tried to push their children out the slit windows when the roof caught, flaming bundles on hands dissolving into flame as he washed the jet of napalm across them, limestone subliming and burning in the heat. He saw that often, waking and asleep.

One hand snuggled the butt of his Holbars into his shoulder while the other held the pistol grip; he was trying for deflection shots, aiming at the windowframe to bounce rounds inside. Tracer flicked out; he clenched his teeth and tasted sweat running down the taut-trembling muscles of his face. "Kill them all," he muttered, not conscious of the whisper. Figures writhed in his mind, Germans melting into burning villagers into shadowed figures in robes and turbans with long knives into prisoners sewn into raw pigskins and left in the desert sun. "Kill them all."

"Sven, *short bursts*, unless you've got a personal ammo store about you," he added with flat normality. The trooper beside him nodded, turned to look at the noncom, turned back sweating to the sight-picture through the x4 of his assault rifle. It was considerably more reassuring than a human voice coming out of the thing McWhirter's face had momentarily become. Below them two paratroopers crawled down in the mud and sheep dung of the alley. One had a smooth oblong box strapped to her back; a hose was connected to the thing she pushed ahead—an object like a thick-barreled weapon with twin grips. Four meters from the window and she was in the dead ground below it, below the angle the gunner could reach without leaning out . . . and in more danger from the supporting fire than the enemy.

"Cease fire!" McWhirter and Eric called, in perfect unison; gave each other gaunt smiles as silence fell for an instant. Then the flamethrower spoke, a silibant roar in the narrow street. Hot orange at the core, flame yellow, bordered by smoke that curled black and filthy, the tongue of burning napalm stretched for the blackened hole. Dropped through it, spattering: most of a flamer's load was still liquid when it hit the target. And it would burn on contact with air and cling, impossible to quench.

Flame belched back out of the window. A pause, then screams— screams that went on and on. Wreathed in fire, a human figure fell out over the sill to writhe and crackle for an instant, then slump still. A door burst open and two more men ran shrieking into the street, their uniforms and hair burning, the gunner at the 15mm cut them down with a single merciful burst.

Senior Decurion McWhirter turned to curse the waste of ammunition, closed his mouth at her silent glare, shrugged, and followed the rest as they jogged down the lane and waited while the pointman dropped to the ground and peered around the corner.

"Love those Ronsons," he said using the affectionate cigarette-lighter nickname. "Damn having women in a combat zone anyway," he grumbled more quietly. "Too fucking sentimental if you ask me." He grunted again. "Meier, Huff, follow me."

Sofie stuck out her tongue at his departing back. "Old fart," she muttered.

The last pocket had fallen around 0600. The water in Eric's canteen was incredibly sweet; he swilled the first mouthful about, spat it out, drank. His body seemed less to drink than to absorb, leaving him conscious of every vein, down to his toes. He was abruptly aware of his own sweat, itching and stinking; of the black smudges of soot on hands and face, the irritating sting of a minor splinter-wound on his leg. The helmet was a monstrous burden. He shed it, and the clean mountain wind made a benediction through the dense tawny cap of his cropped hair. Suddenly he felt light, happy, tension fading out of the muscles of neck and shoulders.

"Report to Cohort," he said. "Phase A complete. Then get me the tetrarchy commanders." They reported in, routine until the Sapper tetrarch's.

"Yo?"

"Seems the Fritz were using the place as some sort of supply dump," Marie Kaine said.

"What did we get?"

"Well, about three thousand board-feet of lumber, for a start. Had a truck rigged to an improvised circular saw—nice piece of work. Then there's a couple of hundred two-meter lengths of angle-iron, a shitload of barbed wire . . . and some prisoners in a wire pen, most of them in sad shape." A pause. "Also about a tonne of explosives."

"Loki on a jumping jack, I'm glad they didn't remember to blow *that* bundle of Father Christmas' store."

"Exactly: it's about half loose stuff and the rest is ammunition— 105mm howitzer shells, propellant and bursting charges both. Lots of wire and detonators, too. Must have been planning some construction through here. And blankets, about a week's worth of rations for a Cohort, medical supplies . . ."

Eric turned to the south, studying the valley as it narrowed toward the village in which he stood. It was a great, steep-sided funnel, whose densely wooded slopes crowded closer and closer to the single road. His mind was turning over smoothly, almost with delight. His hand bore down on the send button.

"Is McWhirter with you? Look, Marie, see you in front of the mosque in ten. Tell McWhirter to meet us there, with the old raghead; he'll know who I mean. Tell him *absolutely* no damage. Tetrarchy commanders' conference, main square, ten minutes. Oh, and throw some supplies into that holding cage." He looked up to see Sofie regarding him quizzically.

"Another brilliant flash, Centurion?" she said. He was looking very, well, *alive* now. Some men's faces got that way in combat, but the Centurion's just went more ice-mask when they were fighting. It was when he came up with something tricky that it lighted up, a half-smile and lights dancing behind the gray eyes. *Damn, but you're pretty when you think,* she reflected wryly. Not something you could say out loud.

"Maybe. See if you can get me through to Logistics at division." He waited for a moment for the patch relay; the first sound through the receiver was a blast of gunfire. Whoever held the speaker was firing one-handed as he acknowledged the call.

"Centurion von Shrakenberg here. Problems?"

"No," the voice came back. "Not unless you count a goddamned Fritz counterattack and a third of my people shot up before they hit the fuckin' ground—" The voice broke off: more faintly Eric could hear screams, a rocket-gun shell exploding, a shouted instruction, *They're behind that bloody tank hulk—*

The quartermaster's voice returned, slightly breathless: "But apart from that, all fine. What do you need, besides the assigned load?"

"Engineering supplies, if you have any—wire, explosives, hand tools, sandbags. More Broadsword directional mines if you can spare them, and any Fritz material available." He paused. "Petrol—again, if there is any. We're the farthest element south; unless we stop them, you're going to be getting it right up the ass. Can do?"

"What are you going to do with all . . . never mind." The Draka had a tradition of decentralized command, which meant trusting an officer to accomplish the assigned tasks in his own fashion. "Will if we can—as soon as the tactical situation here is under control. It depends on how much Fritz stuff gets captured intact . . ."

Chapter Eight

VILLAGE ONE, OSSETIAN MILITARY HIGHWAY
APRIL 14, 1942: 0700 HOURS

CRACK went the bullet, then *spang-winnng* off the stone.

Reflexively, Dreiser froze as spalled-off microfragments of stone drove into his forehead. A hand grabbed him by the back of his webbing harness and yanked him down behind the ruined wall. He controlled his shaking with an effort, drawing in deep drafts of air that smelled of wet rock and barnyard, blinking sunlight out of his eyes. The closest he had come to the sharp end before was reporting on the German blitzkrieg through western Europe in 1940, but that had been done from the rear. Comfortable war reporting, with a car and an officer from the Propaganda section; interviews with generals, watching heavy artillery pounding away and ambulances bringing casualties back to the clearing stations. For that matter, it might be some of the same men shooting at him. He had followed the German Sixth Army through Belgium, and here he was meeting them again in Russia.

"Thanks," he said shakily to the NCO.

"You was drawin' fire," the Draka decurion replied absently, crawling to a gap and cautiously glancing around, head down at knee-level, squinting against the young sun in the east.

Panting, the American put his back to the stones of the wall and watched the Draka. There were six: the other four members of the decurion's stick and a rocket-gun team of two. They lay motionless on the slope of rubble—motionless except for their eyes, flicking ceaselessly over the buildings before them. Mottled uniforms and helmet covers blended into the mud-covered wreck of the ruined building. He had picked this stick as typical, to do a few human-interest stories. It was typical, near enough: four men and three women, average age nineteen and three-quarters. Average height and weight five-eleven and 175 pounds for the males, five-six and 140 for the females. A red-head, two blonds, the rest varying shades of brown.

He had spent much of the winter getting to know Century A: not easy, since Draka were xenophobes by habit and detested the United

72

States and all its works in particular by hereditary tradition. It had helped that Eric and he got along well—the Centurion was a popular officer. Trying his best to keep up did more.

Although my best wasn't very good, he admitted ruefully to himself, even though he was in the best condition he could remember. It was all a matter of priorities; the wealth and leisure to produce these soldiers had been wrung out of whole continents. He focused on one trooper . . .

Cindy, his mind prompted him. *Cindy McAlistair.* Although nobody called her anything but Tee-Hee.

Fox-colored hair, green eyes, a narrow, sharp-featured face—Scots-Irish, via the Carolina piedmont. Her grandfather had been a Confederate refugee in 1866, had escaped from Charleston in one of the last Draka blockade runners, those lean craft that had smuggled in so many repeating rifles and steam warcars. He had established a plantation in the rich lands north of Luanda, just being opened by railways and steam coaches for coffee and cotton.

His granddaughter rested easily, one knee crooked and a hand beneath her; it might have looked awkward, if Dreiser had not seen her do six hundred one-hand pushups in barracks once, on a bet. Sweat streaked the black war paint on her face, dark except for a slight gleam of teeth. The Holbars rested beside her, the assault sling over her neck; her hand held the pistol grip, resting amid a scatter of empty aluminum cartridge cases and pieces of belt link.

The dimpled bone hilt of a throwing knife showed behind her neck, from a sheath sewn into the field jacket, and she was wearing warsaps—fingerless leather gloves with black-metal insets over knuckles and palm edge—secured by straps up the forearms. For the rest, standard gear: lace-up boots with composition soles; thick tough cotton pants and jacket, with leather patches at knee and elbow and plenty of pockets; helmet with cloth cover; a harness of laced panels around the waist that reached nearly to the ribs, and supported padded loops over the shoulders. A half-dozen grenades, blast and fragmentation. Canteen, with messkit, entrenching tool, three conical drum magazines of ammunition, field dressing, ration bars, folding toolkit for maintenance, and a few oddments. Always including spare tampons: "If you don't have 'em, sure as fate you gonna need 'em, then things get plain disgustin'."

The whole outfit had the savage, stripped-down practicality he had come to associate with the Draka. This was an inhumanly functional civilization, not militarist in the sense of strutting, bemedaled generals and parades, but with a skilled appreciation of the business of conquest, honed by generations of experience and coldly unsentimental analysis.

The decurion completed his survey and withdrew his head with slow care; rapid movement attracted the eye.

"Snipah," he said. "Bill-boy, Tee-Hee, McThing—"

The three troopers looked up. "You see him?"

Cindy giggled, the sound that had given her the nickname. "Cross t' street, over that-there first building row a' windows?"

"*Ya.* We're gonna winkel him. You three, light out soon's we lay down fire. *Jo!*" The rocket gunner raised his head. "Center window, can do?"

The man eased his eye to the scope sight and scanned. There was a laneway, then a cleared field of sorts, scrap-built hutments for odds and ends, blocks of stone and rubble. Then square-built stone houses, on the rubble pile; the second row of houses stood atop those but set back, leaving a terrace of rooftop. Distance about two hundred meters, and the windows were slits . . .

"No problem hittin' roundabouts, can't say's I'll get it in. Hey, dec, maybe more of 'em?"

"Na," the NCO snapped. "Would've opened up on us 'fore we got to this-here wall. Just one, movin' from window t' window. Wants us to get close. Jenny, ready with t' SAW. *Now!*"

The rocket gun went off, *whump-ssssssst-crash.* The decurion and the trooper with the light machine gun came to their knees, slapped the bipods of their weapons onto the low parapet of the stone wall, and began working automatic fire along the line of slit windows.

And the three troopers *moved.* Lying with his back to the wall, Dreiser had a perfect view; they *bounced* forward, not bothering to come to their feet, flinging themselves up with a flexing of arm and legs, hurdled the wall without pausing, hit the other side with legs pumping and bodies almost horizontal, moving like broken-field runners. Dreiser twisted to follow them, blinking back surprise. No matter how often it was demonstrated, it was always a shock to realize how *strong* these people were, how fast and flexible and coordinated. It was not the ox-muscled bull massiveness of the Janissaries he'd seen, but leopard strength. Twenty years, he reminded himself. Twenty years of scientific diet and a carefully graduated exercise program; they had been running assault courses since before puberty.

And—he had been holding his hands over his ears against the grinding rattle of automatic-weapons fire. The rocket gun fired again; the whole frontage along the row of windows was shedding sparks and dust and stone fragments.

He must have tripped, was the American's first thought. So quickly, in a single instant that slipped by before his attention could focus, the center Draka was down.

Dreiser could see him stop, as if his headlong dash had run into a stone wall; he could even see the exit wound, red and ragged-edged in his back. Two more shots struck him, and the trooper fell bonelessly, twitched once and lay still.

No dramatic spinning around, he thought dazedly. *Just . . . dead.*

Beside him, the machine gunner grunted as if struck in the stomach; the American remembered she had been the fallen trooper's lover. Her hand went out to grip the bipod and her legs tensed to charge, until the decurion's voice cracked out.

"None of that-there shit, he *dead.*" He nodded grimly at her white-mouthed obedience, then added: "Cease fire. Tee-Hee 'n McThing there by now."

Dreiser jerked his head back up; the other two Draka had vanished.

The sudden silence rang impossibly loud in his ears, along with the beat of blood; there was a distant chatter of fire from elsewhere in the village. It had been so *quick*—alive one second, dead the next. And it was only the second time in his life he had seen violent death; the first had been . . . yes, 1934, the rioting outside the Chamber of Deputies in Paris, when the *Camelots du Roi* had tried to storm the government buildings. A bystander had been hit in the head by a police bullet and fallen dead at his feet, and he had looked down and thought, *That could have been me.* Less random here, but the same sense of *inconsequentialness.* You never really imagined death could happen to you; something like this made you realize it could, not in some comfortably distant future, but right *now*, right *here*, at any moment. That no amount of skill or precaution could prevent it . . .

Beside him, the decurion was muttering. "If that-there snipah knows his business, he outa there by now. Maybe not; maybe he just sharp-eyed and don't scare easy. Then he stay, try So' anothah . . ."

Seconds crawled. Dreiser mopped at the sweat soaking into his mustache, and started to relax; it was less than an hour since the attack began, and already he felt bone-weary. Fumes of cordite and rocket propellant clawed at the lining of his nose and throat. *Adrenaline exhaustion*, he thought. Draka claimed to be able to control it, with breathing exercises and meditation and such; it had all sounded too Yoga-like, too much a product of the warrior-mystic syndrome for his taste. *Maybe I should have—*

There was a grenade blast; dust puffed out of the narrow windows of the house from which the sniper had fired. Almost instantly two blasts of assault-rifle fire stuttered within; the Draka tensed. A trap-door flipped open on the roof and one of the troopers vaulted out, doing a quick four-way scan-and-cover. Then she crawled to the edge and called:

"Got the snipah! What about Bill-boy?"

The decurion cupped a hand around his mouth, rising to one knee. "Bill-boy is expended," he shouted. "Hold and cover."

Expended. Dreiser's mind translated automatically: dead. More precisely, killed in action; if you died by accident or sickness you *skipped*.

Jenny, the machine gunner, rolled over the wall and crouched, covering the roofs behind them. The other Draka rose and scrambled forward, moving at a fast trot, well spread out; at the body two of them stooped, grabbed the straps of the dead man's harness and half-carried, half-dragged him to the shelter of the wall. Dreiser noted with half-queasy fascination how the body moved, head and limbs and torso still following the pathways of muscle and sinew with a disgusting naturalness. The back of his uniform glistened dark and wet; when they turned him over and removed the helmed Dreiser noted for the first time how loss of blood and the relaxation of sudden death seemed to take off years of age. Alive, he had seemed an adult, a man—a hard and dangerous man at that, a killer. Dead, there was only a sudden vast surprise in the drying eyes; his head rolled into his shoulder, as a child nuzzles into the pillow.

The others of the stick were stripping his weapons and ammunition with quick efficiency. Jenny paused to close his eyes and mouth and kiss his lips, then touched her fingers to his blood and drew a line between her brows with an abrupt, savage gesture.

This was not a good man, Dreiser thought. And he had been fighting for a bad cause; not the worst, but the Domination was horror enough in its own right. Yet someone had carried him nine months below her heart; others had spent years diapering him, telling him bedtime stories, teaching him the alphabet . . . He remembered an evening two months ago in Mosul; they had just come in from a field problem, out of the cold mud and the rain and back to the barracks. There had been an impromptu party—coffee and brandy and astonishingly fine singing. Dreiser had sat with his back in a corner, nursing a hot cup and his blisters and staying out of the way, forgotten and fascinated.

This one, the one they called Bill-boy, had started a dance—a folk dance of sorts. It looked vaguely Afro-Celtic to Dreiser, done with a bush knife in each hand, two-foot chopping blades, heavy and razor sharp. He had danced naked to the waist, the steel glittering in the harsh, bare-bulb lights, the others had formed a circle around him, clapping and cheering while the fiddler scraped his bow across the strings and another slapped palms on a zebra-hide drum held between his knees. The dancer had whirled, the edges cutting closer and closer to his body; had started to improvise to the applause, a series of pirouettes and handsprings, backflips and cartwheels, laughing as sweat spun off his glistening skin in jewelled drops. Laughing with pleasure in strength and skill and . . . well, it was a Draka way of looking at it, but yes, beauty.

How am I supposed to make "human interest" out of this? ran through him. *How the* fuck *am I supposed to do that? How am I supposed to make this real to the newspaper readers in their bungalows? Should I?* If there was some way of showing them war directly, unfiltered, right in their living rooms, they'd *never* support a war. And it *is* necessary. They *must* support the war, or afterwards we'll be left alone on a planet run by Nazis or the Domination, and nothing to fight them with . . .

Shaking his head wearily, he followed the Draka into the building.

Chapter Nine

The impromptu war council met by an undamaged section of the town hall's outer wall; the cobbles there were a welcome contrast to the mud, dung, and scattered rocks of the main square. It was a mild spring day, sunny, the sky clear save for a scattering of high, wispy cloud; the air was a silky benediction on the skin. Clear weather was doubly welcome: it promised to dry the soil which heavy movement was churning into a glutinous mass the color and consistency of porridge, and it gave the troopers a ringside view of the events above, now that there was a moment to spare. Contrails covered the sky in a huge arc from east to west, stark against the pale blue all along the northern front of the Caucasus; it was only when you counted the tiny moving dots that the numbers struck home.

"Christ," the field-promoted senior decurion of the late Lisa Telford's tetrarchy said, swiveling his binoculars along the front. "There must be hundreds of them. Thousands . . . That's the biggest air battle in history, right over our heads." He recognized the shapes from familiarization lectures: Draka Falcons and twin-engine Eagles, Fritz 'schmidts and Wulfes, wheeling and diving and firing. As they watched, one dot shed a long trail of black that ended in an orange globe; they heard the *boom*, saw a parachute blossom.

"So much for 'uncontested air superiority,'" said Marie Kaine dryly as she shaded her eyes with a palm. A Wulfe dove, rolled, and drove down the valley overhead with two Draka Eagles on its tail, jinking and weaving, trying to use its superior agility to shake the heavier, faster interceptors. The Eagles were staying well-spaced, and the inevitable happened—the German fighter strayed into the fire cone of one while avoiding the other. A brief hammering of the Eagle's nose battery of 25mm cannon sent it in burning tatters to explode on the mountainside; the Eagle victory-rolled, and both turned to climb back to the melee above. The air was full of the whining snarl of turbocharged engines, and spent brass from the guns glittered and tinkled as it fell to the rocky slopes.

The officers of Century A were considerably less spruce than they had been that morning: the black streak-paint had run with sweat; their mottled uniforms were smeared with the liquid gray clay of the village streets, most had superficial wounds at least.

So much for the glory of war, Eric thought wryly. Once the nations had sent out their champions dressed in finery of scarlet and feathers and polished brass. Now slaughter had been industrialized, and all the uniforms were the color of mud.

A stretcher party was bearing the last of the Draka hurt into the building. Eric had made the rounds inside—a commander's obligation, and one he did not relish. In action, you could ignore the wounded, the pain and sudden ugly wrecking of bodies, but not in an aid station. There was a medical section, with all the latest field gear—plasma and antibiotics and morphine; most of the wounded still conscious were making pathetic attempts at cheerfulness. One trooper who had lost an eye told him she was applying for a job with the Navy as soon as a patch was fitted, "to fit in with the decor, and they'll assign me a parrot." And they all wanted to hear the words, that they had done well, that their parents and lovers could know their honor was safe.

Children, Eric thought, shaking his head slightly as he finished his charcoal sketch map of the village on a section of plastered stone. *I'm surrounded by homicidal children who believe in fairy stories, even with their legs ripped off and their faces ground to sausage meat.*

The commanders lounged, resting, smoking, gnawing on soya-meal crackers or raisins from their iron rations, swigging down tepid water from their canteens. There was little sound—an occasional grunt of pain from the aid station within, shouts and boot-tramp from the victors, the eternal background of the mountain winds. The town's civilians had gone to ground.

The Circassian patriarch stood to one side, McWhirter near him, leaning back with his shoulders and one foot against the building, casually stropping his bush knife on a pocket hone. The native glanced about at pale-eyed deadliness and seemed to shrink a little into himself; they were predator and prey.

"Nice of the Air Corps to provide the show," Eric began. "But business calls. As I see it—"

Sofie tapped his shoulder.

"Yes?"

"Report, Centurion; vehicles coming down the road from the pass. Ours . . . sort of."

The convoy hove into sight on the switchback above the town, the diesel growl of its engines loud in the hush after battle, a pair of light armored cars first, their turrets traversing to keep the roadside verges covered with their twin machine guns, pennants snapping from their aerials. Behind them came a dozen steam trucks in Wehrmacht colors. The machines themselves were a fantastic motley—German, Soviet, French, even a lone Bedford that must have been captured from the English at Dunkirk or slipped in through Murmansk before the Russian collapse; two were pulling field guns of unfamiliar make. Bringing up the rear were a trio of cross-country bakkies, light six-wheeled vehicles mounting a bristle of machine guns. All were travelling at danger speed, slewing around the steep curves in spatters of mud and dust.

"Quick work," Eric commented, as the vehicles roared down the final slope, where the military road cut through the huddle of stone buildings. "I wonder who—"

The daunting hoot of a fox-hunter's horn echoed from the lead warcar, and an ironic cheer went up from the paratroopers.

"Need I have asked," the Centurion sighed. "Cohortarch Dale Jackson Smythe Thompson III."

The lead warcar skidded to a halt, and a jaunty figure in pressed fatigues rose from the hatch, a swagger stick in one gloved hand. He nodded to the assembled commanders. "Now, I suppose you'd like to know how the war's going . . ." He assumed a grave expression. "Well, according to the radio, the Americans claim that resistance is still going on in the hills of Hawaii three months after the Japanese landings, and promise that McArthur's troops in Panama will throw the invader back into the Pacific—"

"Dale, you're impossible!" Marie burst out, with a rare chuckle.

"No, just a Thompson. . . . Actually, we had a bit of a surprise."

"We heard about the tanks," Eric said.

"That was the *least* of it. Have you ever heard of a Waffen-SS unit, *Liebstandarte Adolf Hitler*? Perhaps met a few of them?" He smiled beatifically at their nods. "Well, it seems that the good old Fritz were so anxious to get those field fortifications at the southern end of the pass finished that they moved our friends of the lightning bolts up to help the engineers and forced-labor brigades we were expecting. Still stringing wire and laying mines when we dropped in right on their heads. Not on their infantry—praise god—on their HQ, signals, combat engineers, vehicle park, artillery . . .

"Luckily, not all of them were there; still a fair number down in Pyatigorsk, from what the prisoners say. And we had complete surprise, which was just as well, seeing as we lost about a fifth of our strength to their flak before we hit the ground."

There was a general wince; that was twice the total casualties of a month's fighting in Sicily.

"The rest of us are in hedgehogs down the length of the pass; the Fritz within our lines don't have heavy weapons, but they are making life difficult for our communications, and a secure perimeter is out of the question. So, I'm afraid, are those two Centuries you were supposed to get."

There was a stony silence, as the leaders of Century A realized that they had just been condemned to death, then a sigh of acceptance. The warcar commander looked slightly abashed.

" 'The first casualty of war is always the battle plan,' " Eric quoted.

"Well!" the cohortarch concluded cheerfully. "Now to the good news. That air strike on your friends down the road in Pyatigorsk came off splendidly, according to the reports; also, they seeded a good few butterfly mines between thence and this, to muddy the waters, as it were. What's more, we captured just about everything in the Lieb-standarte divisional stores intact, apart from their armor—hence the two antitank pieces. Russian originally, but quite good. And all the other stuff you requested, blessed if I know what that food and so forth is for, but . . .

"Also, they're putting in a battery of our 107 howitzers just up the way a piece, so you should have artillery support soon, and some Fritz stuff—150s. I brought along the observer. As to ammunition, there's plenty of 5mm and 15mm, but I'm afraid we're running a bit short of 85 and 120; we've already had an attack in brigade strength with armored support. They're desperate, you know."

Aren't we all, Eric thought, and turned to the trucks, absently slapping one fist into his palm as he watched the unloading. It went quickly, aided by the two laborers in the rear of each vehicle; they were of the same breed as the drivers handcuffed to the steering wheels—sullen, flat-faced men in the rags of yellow-brown uniforms.

"Ivans?" he asked.

"Oh, yes; we, hmmm, inherited them from the Fritz." A snort of laughter. "Perhaps, if we're to do this often, they and we could set up a common pool?"

Even then, there was a chuckle at the witticism. Eric's eyes were narrowed in thought. "Surprised you got them to drive that fast," he said.

"Oh, I made sure that they saw explosives being loaded," Dale said. He grinned wolfishly: his family might be from the Egyptian provinces, where a veneer of Anglicism was fashionable, but he was Draka to the core. "It probably occurred to them what could happen if we stayed under fire long. 'Where there's a whip, there's a way.'"

"And there's more ways of killing a cat than choking it to death with cream," Eric replied and turned, pointing to the combat engineer. "Marie, what do you think of this place as a defensive position?"

"With only Century A?" She paused "Bad. These houses, they're fine against small arms, but not worth jack shit against blast—no structural strength." Another pause. "Against anybody with artillery, it's a deathtrap."

"My sentiments exactly. What about field fortifications?"

"Well, that's the answer, of course. But we just don't have the people to do much . . ."

He chopped a hand through the air, his voice growing staccato with excitement. "What if you had a thousand or so laborers?"

"Oh, completely different, then we could . . . you mean the natives? Doubt we could get much out of them in time to be worthwhile."

"Wait a second. And stick around, Dale. I need that devious brain of yours. All *right.*" Eric turned from his officers. His finger stabbed at the Circassian. "Old one, how many are your people? Are they hungry?"

The native straightened, met gray eyes colder than the snows of Elbruz, and did not flinch. "We are two thousand, where once there were many. Lord, kill us if you must, but do not mock us! Hungry?

We have been hungry since the infidel Georgian pig Stalin—" he spat "—took our land, our sheep, our cattle, for the *Kholkohz*, the collective; sent our bread and meat and fruit to feed cities we never saw." The dead voice of exhaustion swelled, took on passion. "Then the Germanski war began. He took our seed corn, and our young men—those that did not flee to the mountain. This they called desertion, the NKVD, the Chekists, they killed many, many. What is it to us if the infidels slay one another? Should we love the Russki, that in the days of the White Tzar they did to us what the Germanski would do to them? Should we love the godless dog Stalin, who took from us even what the Tzars left us—freedom to worship Allah?"

He shook a fist. "When the Germanski came, many thought we would be free at last; the soldiers of the gray coats gave us back our mosque, that the Chekists had made a place of abomination. I hoped that God had sent us better masters, at least. Then the Germanski of the lightning came and took power over us—" he drew the runic symbol of the SS, and spat again "—and where the Russki had beaten us with whips, they were a knout of steel. They are mad! They would kill and kill until they dwell *alone* in the earth!"

He crossed his arms. "We are not hungry, lord. We are starving; our children die. And now we have not enough to live until the harvest, even if we make soup of bark—not unless we eat each other. What is my life to me, if I will not live to see my grandson become a man? Kill us if you will; thus we may gain Paradise. We have already seen hell—it is home to us."

Eric smiled like a wolf, but when he spoke his voice was almost gentle. "Old man, l will not slay your people; I will feed them. Not from any love, but from my own need. Listen well. We and the Germanski will do battle here; we and they are the mill, and your people will be as the grain between us. Of this village, not one stone will stand upon another. Hear me. If all those of your people who can dig and lift will work for one day, the others and the children may leave, with as much food as they can carry.

"If they labor well, and if twenty young men who are hunters and know the paths and secret places of the wood stay to guide my soldiers, then by my father's name and my God, if I have the victory, I will leave enough food for all your people until the winter—also cloth, and tools."

Much good may they do you once the Security Directorate arrives, his mind added silently. Still the offer was honest as far as it went. The Domination of the Draka demanded obedience; its serfs' religion was a matter of total indifference, and a dead body was useful only for fertilizer, for which guano was much cheaper.

The Circassian patriarch had not wept under threat of death; now he nodded and hid his face in a fold of the ragged kaftan.

"Plan," Eric snapped. The tetrarchy commanders and the visiting cohortarch had their notebooks ready. There was silence, except for the scrunch of the commander's soft-treaded boots on the gritty stone of the square.

"We have to hold this town to hold the road, but it's a deathtrap.

Look at how we took it. Marie, I just secured you about 1,500 willing laborers; also some guides who know the way through that temperate-zone jungle out on the slopes. Over to you."

She stood, thoughtful, then looked at the crude map of the village, around at the houses. She picked up a piece of charcoal, walked to the wall and began to sketch.

"The houses're fine protection from small arms, as I said, but too vulnerable to blast. So. We *use* that."

She began drawing on a stucco wall. "Look, here at the north end, where the highway enters the town. A lane at right angles to it on both sides, then a row of houses butting wall to wall. We'll take the timber from the Fritz stores, some of it, whatever else we can find—corrugated iron would be perfect—and build a shelter right *through* on both sides, and knock out the connecting walls. Then we blow the houses down on both; knock firing ports out to command the highway. Those Fritz-Ivan 76.2mm antitank, they can be manhandled—you can switch firing positions under cover, with four feet of rock for protection. Couple of the 15mm's in there, too."

The charcoal revealed, in diagrams, a schematic of the village. Her voice raced, jumping, ideas coalescing into reality.

"Time, that's the factor. So, that antitank stuff first. With three thousand *very* willing pairs of hands though . . . Listen. This whole village, it's underlain by arched-roof cellars. They don't connect, but there's damn-all between them but curtain walls. Break through, here, here, here put up timber pillars"—her hands drew a vertical shaft through the air— "pop-up positions; we blow the houses around them, perfect camouflage, let the Fritz get past you and hit them from *behind*.

"Then, we can't let them flank us. Get that angle iron, and the wire; wire in like this"—she sketched a blunt *V* from the woods to the edge of town—"downslope of these two stone terraces and trenches just above them. Only two hundred meters to the woods on the east, three hundred to the west. Mine the ground in front, random pattern. State those fields are in, a thousand badgers could dig for a week and you couldn't tell.

"If the Patriarch Abraham here is going to have hunters show us the forest tracks, we'll mine the forest edge, then the paths—put a few machine gun nests in there, channel things into killing fields—cohortarch, I'm going to need more of the Broadsword directional mines, can you get them? Good. Also more radio detonators, and any Fritz mines you can scavenge.

"And I can rig impromptu from that Fritz ammunition," she murmured, almost an aside to herself. That would be tricky; she'd better handle it herself.

"We'll need a surprise for their armor. We've got that clutch of plastic antitank mines, lovely stuff. *Very* good, they can't be swept. Those for the road. That blasting explosive, with the radio detonators, by the verge . . . and there, there, where the turnoff points are. And we—"

"All right," Eric broke in with a grim smile. Marie was brilliant in anything to do with construction. He could see a glow of pure happiness spreading over her face—the joy of an artist allowed to practice her craft. The problem would be keeping her from trying to put up the Great Wall of China.

"We need immediate antitank while this is going up," he continued briskly. "Tom, you take two of the 120s." His hand indicated where the tips of the V met the woods. "Emplace 'em there. Spider pits for the crews, with overhead protection, close enough to jump to. Marie, push the third down the road, down past the bend—somewhere where it can get one flank shot off where it'll do the most good, and the crew can run like hell. We don't have enough 120 ammunition to use three barrels. Booby traps along the trail, if you've got time. Better ask for volunteers. Take half the rocket-gun teams, start familiarizing them with the woods up both sides of the valley, for if—when—the Fritz break through. And I want minefields *behind* us as well. Don't get trapped thinking linearly." He paused. "Booby traps, there, as well. Everywhere."

He turned to the comtech. "Sofie, we're going to need secure communications. If we ran the Fritz field telephone wire all over the place, underground too, stripped, would it carry radio?"

She frowned. "Ought . . . *Ya*, Centurion."

"Coordinate with Sparks in Marie's tetrarchy. And set up the stationary radio; I'm going to need a steady link to cohort and up. Run more lines out to the woods, tack it up. A cellar, somewhere as far from the square as possible. Those buildings are going to draw a lot of fire." He paused. "Anything impossible?"

"All that demolition," the sapper Legate said. "Chancy. Very. Especially if we use nonstandard explosives. I can estimate, some of my NCOs . . . "

" 'It has to be done, it can be,' " Eric quoted with a shrug. "If we're going to be sacrificial lambs, at least we can break a few teeth. There'll be a lot of details; solve 'em if you can, ask me or Marie if you can't.

"Now," he said, turning to the cohortarch. "Dale?"

"It's all a little, well, *static*, isn't it?'' The ex-cavalryman paused. "Besides your skulkers in the woods, I'd say you need a mobile reaction force to maneuver in the rear, once they're fixed against your fieldworks."

Eric nodded. "Good, but we don't have any reserve left for that . . ."

Dale examined his fingertips. "Well, old man, I could run a spot down the road, conceal my vehicles, then—"

Eric shook his head. "Nice of you to offer, Dale, but you're needed back above. That's going to be a deathride, and . . . I've got an idea." He looked around the circle of faces. "Tell you later if it works out. No—let's *do* it, people; let's *move*."

There was a moment of silence, of solemnity almost. Then the scene dissolved in action.

Eric turned to the old man. "Hadj, those prisoners the Germanski were holding behind the hall—they are not of your people?"

The Circassian came to himself, blew his nose in the sleeve of his kaftan and shook his head.

"They are Russki—partisans, godless youths of the *komsomol* from the great city of Pyatigorsk that the Tzars built, when they took the hot springs of the Seven Hills from my people. Even so, we would not have betrayed them to the Germanski with the lightning, if they had not demanded food of us that we did not have. There are more of them westward in the hills; many more. The garrison came here to hunt them." He bowed. "Lord, may I go to tell my people what you require of them?"

Eric nodded absently, tugging at his lower lip, then smiled and turned for the alley leading past the town hall.

Sofie trotted at his side, a quizzical interest in her eyes; her tasks would not be needed immediately and a matter puzzled her. Eric was moving with a bounce in his stride; his eyes seemed to glow, his skin to crackle with renewed vitality. She remembered him at the loading zone, quiet, reserved; in the fighting that morning, moving with the bleakly impersonal efficiency of a well-designed machine. Now . . . he looked like a man in love. Not with her, her head told her. But it was interesting to see how that affected him; definitely interesting.

"Centurion," she said. "Remember Palermo?"

"What part?"

"Afterward, when we stood down. That terrace? We were talking, and you told me you didn't like soldiering. Seems to me you like it well enough now, or I've never seen a man happy."

He rubbed the side of his nose. "I like . . . solving problems. Important ones, real ones; doing it quickly, getting people to do their best. And understanding what makes them tick, getting inside their heads. Knowing what they'll do if *I* do this or that . . . I've even thought of writing novels, because of that. After the war, of course." He stopped, with an uncharacteristic flush. Sofie was easy to talk to, but that was not an ambition he had told many. Hurriedly, he continued: "Marie's a crackerjack sapper. I had some of the same ideas, but not in nearly so much detail. And I couldn't organize so well to get them done."

"But you could organize her, and the ragheads, and whatever these 'Russki partisans' are good for." She smiled at his raised brow. "Hell, Centurion, I may not talk their jabber, but I know the word when I hear it. I can see all that's part of war." She frowned. "And the fighting?" Draka were supposed to like to fight; more theory than fact. She didn't, much; if she wanted to have a fun risk, she'd surf. Yet there was a certain addiction to it. She could see how the combat junkies felt, and certainly the Draka produced more of them than most people, but on the whole, no thanks. This had been hairier than anything before, and she had an uneasy feeling it was going to get worse.

"We're of the Race: we have our obligations."

There was no answer to that, not unless she wished to give offense. For that matter, there were many who would have stood on rank already.

"Think we'll have time to get all this stuff ready?"

"I don't know, Sofie," he said simply. "I hope so. Before the real attack, anyway. We'll probably get a probe quite soon. With luck . . ."

Senior Decurion McWhirter cleared his throat. "Say, sir, what was it you used on the old raghead? Thought he was a tough old bastard but he caved in real easy."

"I used the lowest, vilest means I could," Eric said softly. The NCO's eyes widened in surprise. "I gave him hope."

Chapter Ten

VILLAGE ONE, OSSETIAN MILITARY HIGHWAY
APRIL 14, 1942: 0700 HOURS

The partisans were being held in what looked to be a stock pen—
new barbed wire on ancient piled stone. A walking-wounded Draka
trooper stood guard; the German formerly assigned to that duty was
lying on his back across the wall, his belly opened by a drawing slash
from a bush knife and the cavity buzzing black with flies. The prisoners ignored him; even with Eric's arrival, few looked up from their
frenzied attack on the loaves of stale black bread that had been thrown
to them. One vomited noisily, seized another chunk and began to eat
again. There were thirty of them, and they stank worse than the rest
of the village. They were standing in their own excrement, and half
a dozen had wounds gone pus-rotten with gas gangrene.

They were Slavs, mostly: stockier than the Circassian natives, flatter faced and more often blond, in peasant blouses or the remnants
of Soviet uniform. Young men, if you could look past the months of
chronic malnutrition, sickness, and overstrain. A few had been tortured,
and all bore the marks of rifle butts, whips, rubber truncheons. Eric
shook his head in disgust; in the Domination, this display would have
been considered disgraceful even for convicts on their way to the prison
mines of the Ituri jungles or the saltworks of Kashgar, the last sink-
holes for incorrigibles. Anybody would torture for information in war,
of course, and the Security Directorate was not notable for mercy toward
rebels. Still, this was petty meanness. If they were dangerous, kill them;
if not, put them to some use.

One thick-set prisoner straightened, brushed his hands down a torn
and filth-spattered uniform tunic and came to the edge of the wire.
His eyes flickered to the guard, noted how she came erect at the officer's
approach.

"Uvaha hchloptsi, to yeehchniy kommandyr," he cast back over his
shoulder, and waited, looking the Draka steadily in the eye.

Eric considered him appraisingly and nodded. *This one,* he thought,
is a brave man. Pity we'd probably have to kill him if the Fritz don't

do us the favor. Aloud: *"Sprechen zie Deutsch? Parlez-vous Français? Circassian?"*

A shake of the head; the Draka commander paused in thought, almost started in surprise to hear Sofie's voice.

"I speak Russian, Centurion," Sofie said. He raised a brow; everybody had to do one foreign language, but that was not a common choice. "Not in school. My pa, he with Henderson when the Fourth took Krasnovodsk, back in 1918. He brought back a Russki wench, Katie. She was my nursemaid, an' I learned it from her. Still talk it pretty good. He just said: 'Watch out, boys, that's the commander.'"

Sofie turned to the captives and spoke, slowly at first and then with gathering assurance. The Russian frowned and waved his companions to silence, then replied. The ghost of a smile touched his face, despite the massive bruise that puffed the left side of his mouth.

Grinning, she switched back into English. "*Ya,* he understands. Says I've got an old-fashioned Moscow accent, like a *boyar,* a noble. Hey, Katie always said she was a countess; maybe it was true." A shake of the head. "S'true she was never much good at housework, wouldn't do it. Screwing the Master was all right, looking after children was fine, but show her a mop and she'd sulk for days. Ma gave up on trying . . ."

Actually, the whole Nixon household had been fond of Ekaterina Ilyichmanova; with her moods and flightiness and disdain for detail, she had fitted in perfectly with the general atmosphere of cheerfully sloppy anarchy. Sophie's father had always considered her his best war souvenir and had treated her with casual indulgence; she was something of an extravagance for a man of his modest social standing, and her slender, great-eyed good looks were not at all his usual taste. Sophie and her brothers had gone to some trouble to find their nursemaid the Christian priest she wanted during her last illness, and had been surprised at how empty a space she left in the rambling house below Lion's Head.

Eric nodded thoughtfully. "Good thinking, Sofie. All right . . . ask him if there are more like him in the woods, and the villages down in the plains."

The Russian listened carefully to the translation, spoke a short sentence and spat at the Draka officer's feet. Eric waved back the guard's bayonet impatiently.

"Ahhh—" Sofie hesitated. "Ah, Centurion, he sort of asked why the fuck he should tell a *neimetsky*-son-of-a-bitch anything, and invited you to take up where the fornicating Fritzes left off." She frowned. "I think he's got a pretty thick country-boy accent. Don't know what a *neimetsky* is, but it's not nohow complimentary. And he says it's our fault they're in this mess anyway."

Eric smiled thinly, hands linked behind his back, rising and falling thoughtfully on the balls of his feet. There was an element of truth in that; the *Stavka,* the Soviet high command, had never been able to throw all its reserves against the Germans with the standing menace of the Domination on thousands of kilometers of southern front. And the Draka had taken two million square miles of central Asia in the Great War, while Russia was helpless with revolution and civil strife, all the way north to the foothills of the Urals, and east to Baikal.

Fairly perceptive, the Draka officer thought. *Especially for a peasant like this. He must have been a Party member.* The flat Slav face stared back at him, watchful but not at all afraid.

Can't be a fool, Eric's musing continued. *Not and have survived the winter and spring. He's not nervous with an automatic weapon pointed at him, either.* Or at the bayonet, for that matter; the damn things were usually still useful for crowd control, if nothing else.

"Stupid," he said meditatively.

"Sir?" Sofie asked.

"Oh, not him, the Fritz. Talking about a thousand-year Reich, then acting as if it all had to be done tomorrow . . ." His tone grew crisper. "Ask his name. Ask him how he'd like to be released with all his men—with all the food they can carry, a brand-new Fritz rifle and a hundred rounds each."

Shocked, Sophie raised her eyebrows shrugged and spoke. This time the Russian laughed. "He says he's called Ivan Desonovich Yuhnkov, and he'd prefer MP40 submachine guns and grenades. While we're at it, could we please give him some tanks and a ticket to New York, and Hitler's head, and what sort of fool do you think he is? Sorry, sir."

Eric reached out a hand for the microphone, spoke. Minutes stretched; he waited without movement, then extended a hand to Sofie. "Cigarette?" he asked.

Carefully expressionless, she lit a second from her own and placed it between his lips. *Well, the iron man is nervous, too,* she thought. Sometimes she got the feeling that Eric could take calculated risks on pure intellect, simply from analysis of what was necessary. It was reassuring that he could need the soothing effect of the nicotine.

The other partisans had finished the bread. They crowded in behind their leader, silent, the hale supporting the wounded. A mountain wind soughed, louder than their breath and the slight sucking noises of their rag-wrapped feet in the mud and filth of the pen. The eyes in the stubbled faces . . . Covertly, Eric studied them. Some were those of brutalized animals, the ones who had stopped thinking because thought brought nothing that was good; now they live from one day . . . no, from one meal to the next, or one night's sleep. He recognized that look; it was common enough in the world his caste had built. And he recognized the stare of the others—the men who had fought on long after the death of hope because there was really nothing else to do. *That* he saw in the mirror, every morning.

A stick of troopers came up, shepherding a working party of Circassian villagers and the American war correspondent. The Circassians were carrying rope-handled wooden crates between them; Dreiser's face had a stunned paleness. *Well, he's seen the elephant,* Eric thought with a distant, impersonal sympathy. There were worse things than combat, but the American probably wasn't in a mood to be reminded of that right now. The crates were not large, but the villagers bore them with grunts and care, and they made a convincing splat in the wet earth.

"Bill," the Draka said. "What's your government's policy on Russian refugees?"

Dreiser gathered himself with a visible effort, watching as Eric reached up over his left shoulder and drew his bush knife. The metal was covered in a soft matte-black finish, only the honed edge reflecting mirror bright. He drove it under one of the boards of a crate and pried the wood back with a screech of nails.

"Refugees? Ah . . ." Bill forced his thoughts into order. "Well, better, now that we're in the war." He shrugged distaste. "Especially since there isn't any prospect of substantial numbers arriving." Relations with Timoshenko's Soviet rump junta in west Siberia were good, but with the Japanese holding Vladivostok and running rampant through the Pacific, the only contact was through the Domination. Which visibly regarded the Soviet remnant as a caretaker keeping things in order until the Germans were disposed of and the Draka arrived. Attempts to ship Lend-Lease supplies through had met with polite refusals.

A few wounded and children had been flown out, over the pole in long-range dirigibles, to be received in Alaska by Eleanor Roosevelt with much fanfare.

"Back before Pearl Harbor, they wouldn't even let a few thousand Jews in. Well, the isolationists were against it, and the Mexican states, they're influenced by the Catholic anti-Semites like Father Coughlin."

"*Ya.*" Eric rose, with a German machine pistol and bandolier in his hands. "Those there are Russian partisans there in the pen, Bill. The Fritz captured 'em, but hadn't gotten around to expending them. Take a look."

Eric heard the American suck in his breath in shock, as he stripped open the action of the Schmeisser. Not bad, he thought, as he inserted a 32-round magazine of 9mm into the well and freed the bolt to drive forward and chamber a bullet. Not as handy as the Draka equivalent; the magazine well was forward of the pistol grip instead of running up through it; it had a shorter barrel, so less range, and the bolt had to be behind the chamber rather than overhanging it. Still, a sound design and honestly made. He took a deep breath and tossed the weapon into the pen.

The partisan leader snatched it out of the air with the quick, snapping motion of a trout rising to a fly. The flat slapping of his hand on the pressed steel of the Schmeisser's receiver was louder than the rustling murmur among his men; much louder than the tensing among the Draka. Eric saw the Russian's eyes flicker past him; he could imagine what the man was seeing. The rifles would be swinging around, assault slings made that easy, with the gun carried at waist level and the grip ready to hand. The troopers would be shocked, and Draka responded to shock aggressively. Especially to the sight of an armed serf, the very *thought* of which was shocking. Technically the Russians were not serfs, of course, but the reflex was conditioned on a deeper level than consciousness.

One did not arm serfs. Even Janissaries carried weapons only on operations or training, under supervision, and were issued ammunition only in combat zones or firing ranges. Draka carried arms; they

S.M. Stirling 90

were as much the badge of the Citizen caste as neck tattoos were for serfs: a symbolic dirk in a wrist sheath or a shoulder-holster pistol in the secure cities of the Police Zone; the planter's customary side- arm; or the automatic weapons and battle shotguns that were still as necessary as boots in parts of the New Territories. A Citizen bore weap- ons as symbol of caste, as a sign that he or she was an arm of the State, with the right to instant and absolute obedience from all who were not, and power of life and death to enforce it. There was no place on earth where free Draka were a majority: no province, no district, no city. They were born and lived and slept and died among serfs.

They lived because they were warriors, because of the accumulated deadly aura of generations of victory and merciless repression. Folk- memory nearly as deep as instinct saw a serf with a weapon in his hands and prompted: *kill.*

Training held their trigger fingers, but the Russian saw their faces. Sweat sheened Eric's face, and he kept the machine pistol's muzzle trained carefully at the ground. And yet, the weight in his hands straight- ened his back and seemed to add inches to his height.

"Khrpikj djavol," he muttered, staring at Eric.

"Ummm, he says you one crazy devil, Centurion," Sophie translated. "Maybe crazy enough to do what you promise." She gave him a hard glance, before continuing on her own: "You might just consider it's other folks' life you risking too, *sir*. I mean, he might've been some sorta crazy amokker."

Startled, Eric ran a hand over the cropped yellow surface of his hair. "You know, I never thought of that . . . you're right." More briskly: "Tell him that I promise to kill a lot of Germans, and that he can kill even more, with my help. After that I promise nothing, absolutely nothing." He pointed to Dreiser, standing beside him. "This man is not a Draka, or a soldier: he is an American journalist. About what happens after this fight, talk to him."

"Hey, wait a minute, Eric—" Dreiser began.

Eric chopped down a hand. "Bill, it's your ass on the line, too. Even if the Fritz roll right over us, the Legion will probably be able to hold the next fallback position well enough; we'll delay them, and the maximum risk is from the south, from the Germans in the pocket there trying to break out to the north. But that won't do *us* any good. Besides . . . what am I supposed to promise them, a merry life digging phosphates in the Aozou mines in the Sahara, with Security flogging them on? Soldiers don't get sold as ordinary serfs, even: too dangerous."

"You want me to promise to get them out? How can I?" Dreiser's eyes flinched away from the Russians, from the painful hope in their faces.

"Say you'll use your influence. True enough, hey? Write them up; your stuff is going through Forces censorship, not Security. They don't give a shit about anything that doesn't compromise military secrecy."

Dreiser looked back into the pen and swallowed, remembering. He had been in Vienna during the *Anschluss. Memories—the woman had been Jewish, middle class.* In her forties, but well kept, in the rag of a good dress, her hands soft and manicured. The SS men had had her down scrubbing the sidewalk in front of the building they had taken over as temporary headquarters; they stood about laughing and prodding her with their rifle butts as others strode in and out through the doors, with prisoners or files or armfuls of looted silverware and paintings from the Rothschild palace.

"Not clean enough, filthy Jewish sow-whore!" The SS man had been giggling-drunk, like his comrades. The woman's face was tear-streaked, a mask of uncomprehending bewilderment: the sort of bourgeois *hausfrau* you could see anywhere in Vienna, walking her children in the Zoo, at the Opera, fussing about the family on an excursion to the little inns of the *Viennerwald*; self-consciously cultured in the tradition of the Jewish middle class that had made Vienna a center of the arts. A life of comfort and neatness, spotless parlors and pastries arranged on silver trays. Now this . . .

"Sir . . ." she began tremulously, raising a hand that was bleeding around the nails.

"Silence! Scrub!" A thought seemed to strike him, and he slung his rifle. "Here's some scrubbing water, whore!" he said, with a shout of laughter, unbuttoning his trousers. The thick yellow stream of urine spattered on the stones before her face, steaming in the cold night air and smelling of staleness and beer. She had recoiled in horror; one of the men behind her planted a boot on her buttocks and shoved, sending her skidding flat into the pool of wetness. That had brought a roar of mirth; the others had crowded close, opening their trousers, too, drenching her as she lay sobbing and retching on the streaming pavement . . .

Dreiser had turned away. There had been nothing he could do, not under their guns. A few ordinary civilians had been watching, some laughing and applauding, others merely disgusted at the vulgarity. And some with the same expression as his. Shame, the taste of helplessness like vomit in the mouth.

They were pissing on the dignity of every human being on earth, Dreiser thought as his mind returned to the present. He shivered, despite the mild warmth of the mountain spring and the thick fabric of his uniform jacket, and looked at the partisans. The Domination might not have quite the nihilistic lunacy of the Nazis, but it was as remorseless as a machine. *I just might be able to bring it off,* he thought. Just maybe; the Draka were not going to make any substantial concessions to American public opinion, but they very well might allow a minor one of no particular importance. The military might; at least, they didn't have quite the same pathological reluctance to see a single human soul escape their clutches that the Security Directorate felt. And here . . . here, he could *do* something.

"I could talk it up in my articles, they're already doing quite well," he said thoughtfully. "Russians are quite popular now anyway since Marxism is deader than a day-old fish." He looked up at Eric. "You have any pull?"

"Not on the political side, I'm under suspicion. Some on the military,

and more—much more—if we win." He paused. "Won't be more than
a few of them, anyway."

Dreiser frowned, puzzled. "I thought you said there'd be more than
these, still at large."

"Oh, there are probably hundreds, from the precautions the Fritz were
taking. I certainly hope so. There won't be many *left*." The Draka turned
to Sofie. "Ahhh . . . let's see. Sue Knudsen and her brother. Their family
has a plantation near Orenburg, don't they?" That was in northwest
Kazakhstan—steppe country and the population mostly Slav. "They probably talk some Russian. Have one of them report here so Bill will have
a translator. Get the tetrarchy commanders, hunt up anybody else who
does. We're going to need them. Make it snappy," he glanced up at the
sun, "because things are going to get interesting soon."

The pair of Puma armored cars nosed cautiously toward the tumbled
ruins of the village in the pass, turrets traversing with a low whine
of hydraulics to cover the verges. The roadway was ten meters wide
here, curving slightly southwest through steep-sided fields. Those were
small and hedged with rough stone walls and scrub brush, isolated
trees left standing for shade or fodder or because they housed spirits. Even the cleared zones were rich in cover—perfect country for
partisans with mines and Molotov cocktails. Beyond the village the road
wound into the high mountains, forest almost to the edge of the
pavement; the beginning of "ambush alley," dangerous partisan country
even before the Draka attack. The Puma was eight-wheeled, well-armored
for its size and heavily armed with a 20mm autocannon and a machine
gun, but the close country made the drivers nervous.

Too many of their comrades had roasted alive in burning armor for
them to feel invincible.

Standartenführer Hoth propped his elbows against the sides of the
turret hatch and brought up his field glasses. Bright morning sunlight
picked detail clear and sharp, the clean mountain air like extra lenses
to enhance his vision. The command car had halted half a thousand
meters behind the two scout vehicles; from here, the terrain rolled
upslope to the village. The military highway cut through it, and he
could catch glimpses of the mosque and town hall around the central square, more glimpses than he remembered; a number of houses
had been demolished, including the whole first row on the north side
of town. There was an eerie stillness about the scene; there should
have been locals moving in the fields and streets, smoke from cooking fires . . . and activity by the SS garrison. He focused on the patch
of square visible to him. Bodies, blast holes, firescorch . . . And there
had been nothing on the radio since the single garbled screech at 0500.
He glanced at his watch, a fine Swiss model he had taken from the
wrist of a wounded British staff officer in Belgium: 0835—they had
made good time from Pyatigorsk.

Raising a hand, he keyed the throat mike and spoke. "Schliemann,
stay where you are and provide cover. Berger, the road looks clear
through to the main square. Push in, take a quick look, then pull back.
Continuous contact."

"Acknowledged, Standartenführer," the Scharfuhrer in the lead car replied. The second vehicle halted; for a moment Hoth felt he could sense the tension in its turret, a trembling like a mastiff quivering on the leash.

Nonsense, he thought. *Engine vibration.* A humming through arms and shoulders, up from the commander's seat beneath his boots. The air was full of the comforting diesel stink of armor, metal and cordite and gun oil; even through the muffling headset, the grating throb of the Tatra 12-cylinder filled his head. The two cars ahead were buttoned tight; he could see the gravel spurting from the tires of the lead Puma, the quiver of the second's autocannon muzzle as the weapon quivered in response to the gunner's clench on the controls. Fiercely, he wished he was in the lead vehicle himself, up at the cutting edge of violence . . .

"Wait for it, wait for it," Eric breathed into the microphone. He was perched on the lip of the shattered minaret; the trench periscope gave him a beautiful view of the SS officer in the command vehicle, enough to see the teeth showing in an unconscious snarl below his field glasses. Yes, it had to be the command vehicle from the miniature forest of antennae the turret sprouted. Details sprang at him: fresh paint in a dark-green mottle pattern, unscarred armor, tires still sharp-treaded . . . it must be fresh equipment, just out from Germany. His fingers turned the aiming wheels to track the other two cars, one in a covering position, another edging forward down the single clear lane into the village.

"Let him get into the square," he said. "Anyone opens fire without orders, I'll blast them a new asshole." The positions on the north edge were complete, the first priority, but there was no need to reveal them to deal with light armor like this, and much need to make the enemy commander underestimate the position. Silently, he thanked a God in which he had not believed since childhood for the ten minutes warning the advantage of height and the position northward beside the road had given. Enough to get the Century and the Circassians under cover. It helped that most of them had been in the cellars, of course.

He could hear the Fritz car now as it entered the village: whine of heavy tires on the gravel, the popping crunch as stones spurted out under the pressure of ten tonnes of armorplate. Below, in the square, the bodies waited—the thirty dead SS men gunned down in a neat line, and as many others hurriedly stuffed in the jackets of Draka casualties. *Got to let him get a look at it,* Eric thought. He wanted the German commander overestimating the Draka casualties; easy enough to make him think his comrades had taken a heavy blood-price. Not too good a look at those corpses, though—the rest of their uniform was still Fritz, and besides, they were all male. But the view from inside a closed-down turret was not that good.

"Centurion." Marie's voice. "That second car is only two hundred meters out. We could get him with a rocket gun, or even one of the 15mm's."

"After we blast the lead car," Eric said. His voice was tight with excitement; this was better even than catsticking, hunting lion on horseback with lances. And these were enemies you could really *enjoy* fighting. The Italians . . . that had been unpleasant. Far less danger-ous, but how could you respect men who wouldn't fight even at the doorsteps of their own homes, for their families? It made you feel greasy, somehow. This . . . if it weren't for the danger to the Century, he would have preferred it; he had long ago come to peace with the knowledge that he would not survive this war. *At least I won't have to live with the aftermath of it, either,* ran through him with an undercurrent of sadness.

The lead car was in the square. "Position one! Five seconds . . . *Now!*"

Below, the trooper snuggled the rocket gun into his shoulder. This was a good position, clear to the back with a good ledge of rubble for the monopod in front of the forward pistol grip. Fifteen kilos of steel and plastic was not an easy load to shoulder-fire; still, better than the tube launchers the more compact recoilless hybrids had replaced. The armored car was clear in the optical sight; no need for much rang-ing at less than a hundred meters, just lay the crosshairs on the front fender. He squeezed the trigger, twisted and dove back into the safe darkness of the foxhole without bothering to stay and watch the results. He had seen too many armored vehicles blow up to risk his life for a tourist's-eye view.

The 84mm shell kicked free of the meter-long tube with a *whump-fuff* as the backblast stirred a cloud of dust behind the gun. At eighty meters there was barely time for the rocket motor to ignite before the detonator probe struck armor. The shell was slow, low-velocity; even the light steel sheathing of a Puma would have absorbed its kinetic energy with ease. But the explosive within was hollow-charge, a cone with its widest part turned out and lined with copper. Exploding, the shaped charge blew out a narrow rod of superheated gas and vapor-ized metal at thousands of meters per second; it struck the armorplate before it with the impact of a red-hot poker on thin cellophane. Angling up, the jet seared a coin-sized hole through the plate, sending a shower of molten steel into the fighting compartment. The driver had barely enough time to notice the lance of fire that seared off his body at the waist; fragments of a second later, it struck the fuel and ammu-nition. Shattered from within, the Puma's hull unfolded along the seams of its welds; to watching eyes it seemed for an instant like a flower in stop-motion film, blossoming with petals of white-orange fire and gray metal. Then the enormous *fumph* of the explosion struck, a pressure on skin and eyeballs more than a noise, and a *bang* echoing back from the buildings, an echo from the sides of the mountains above. Steel clanged off stone, pattering down from a sky where a fresh column of oily black smoke reached for the thin scatter of white cirrus above.

The twisted remains burned, thick fumes from the spilling diesel oil. Eric nodded satisfaction. "One 15mm only on the second car!" he barked into the microphone. "See the third off but don't kill him."

✧   ✧   ✧

Standartenführer Hoth had been listening to the lead car's commentary in a state of almost-trance, his mind filing every nuance of data while he poised for instant action.

" . . . bodies everywhere, Draka and ours. No sign of movement. More in the central square; heavy battle damage . . . Standartenführer, there are thirty of our men here in front of the mosque, lined up and shot! This . . . this is a violation of the Geneva Convention!"

For a moment Hoth wondered if he was hearing some bizarre attempt at humor. Geneva Convention? In *Russia*? On the *Eastern Front*? But there was genuine indignation in the young NCO's voice; what were they *teaching* the replacements these days? Thunder rolled back from the mountains, as the all-too-familiar pillar of smoke and fire erupted from a corner of the square out of his sight.

Schliemann in the second car was a veteran, and so was the Standartenführer's own crew. They reacted with identical speed, reversing from idle in less than a second with a stamp of clutches and crash of gears. The turrets walked back and forth along the line of rubble that had been the northern edge of the village, 20mm shells exploding in white flashes, machine gun rounds flicking off stone with sparks and sharp *pings* that carried even through the crash of autocannon fire. Brass cascaded from the breeches into the turret as the hull filled with the nose-biting acridness of fresh cordite fumes. Speed built; Pumas were reconnaissance cars, designed to be driven rearward in just this sort of situation. And they had come for information, not to fight; the luckless Berger had been a sacrificial decoy duck to draw fire and reveal the enemy positions.

No accident that he had been sent forward, of course. Most of the casualties in any unit were newbies—mostly because of their own inexperience, partly because their comrades, when forced to choose, usually preferred that it was a new face which disappeared. It was nothing personal; you might like a recruit and detest someone you'd fought beside for a year. It was just a matter of who you wanted at your back when the blast and fragments flew.

Hoth kept his glasses up, flickering back and forth to spot the next burst. It came, machine-gun fire directed at Schliemann's car. He kicked the gunner lightly on the shoulder: "Covering fire!" he barked.

There was a flash from the rubble, a cloud of dust from the tumbled stones above the machine gun's position. A brief rasping flare of rocket fire, and a shell took Schliemann's car low on the wheel well. The jet of the shaped charge seared across the bottom of the vehicle's hull, cut two axles and blew a wheel away to bounce and skitter across the road before it slammed itself into a tree hard enough to embed the steel rim. The cut axles collapsed and the heavy car pinwheeled, caught between momentum and the sudden drag as its bow dug into the packed stone of the road with a shower of sparks. Other sparks were flying as the 15mm hosed hull and turret with fire; even the incendiary tracer rounds were hard-tipped, and the car's armor was thin. Some rounds bounced from the sloped surfaces; others punched through, to flatten and ricochet inside the Puma's fighting compartment, slapping through flesh and equipment like so many whining lead-alloy bees.

The radio survived. Hoth could hear the shouting and clanging clearly, someone's voice shouting *"Gottgottgott—"* and Schliemann cursing and hammering at the commander's hatch of the car. The impact had sprung the frames, probably, jamming the hatches shut. That often happened. He could see the first puff of smoke as fuel from the ruptured tanks ran into the compartment and caught fire; hear the frenzied screaming as the crew burned alive in their coffin of twisted metal. It went on as the Standartenführer's command car reversed out of sight of the village, into dead ground farther down the pass. Reaching down, he switched the radio off with a savage jerk and keyed in the intercom.

"Back to Pyatigorsk!" Schliemann had been a good soldier, transferred from the Totenkopf units: a Party man from the street-fighting days, an *alte kampfer*. And his death had bought what they came for— some knowledge of what they faced. Of course, once they overran the Draka in the village there would be more positions farther up. It depended on how many from the division's motorized infantry brigades had been killed, and what sort of counterattack the units to the south were staging. A thought came to him, and his face smiled under its sheen of sweat; the gunner looked around at him, shivered, turned his gaze back to the sighting periscope as the car did a three-point turn and headed down the road.

I must take prisoners for intelligence about the Draka fallback positions, the SS officer thought. *I will enjoy that. I will enjoy that very much.*

Eric sighed and lowered his eyes from the trench periscope. That rocket gunner had been a little impulsive, but the result suited well enough. No way of concealing their presence from the Germans, but he could hope to make them underestimate the position. Whoever the man in that command car was, time was his enemy. The paratroopers only had to hold until the main Draka force broke through to win; the Fritz had to overrun them and all the rest of the legion, in time to pull their forces back and bring up replacements to block the pass. With only a little luck the German would try to take them on the run with whatever he could round up.

"Von Shrakenberg to all units: back to work, people. *Move!*" He handed the receiver to Sofie and rolled over on his back; he would be needed to coordinate, to interpret when the Circassians and the Draka reached the limits of their mutually sketchy German. But not immediately; these were Citizen troops, after all, not Janissaries. They were expected to think, and to do their jobs without someone looking over their shoulders.

The mid-morning sky was blue, with a thickening scatter of clouds; they looked closer here in high mountain country than down in the plains about Mosul, where they had spent the winter.

"Hey, Centurion?" Sofie held out the lighted cigarette, and this time Eric accepted it. "More ideas?"

He shook his head. "Just thinking about home," he said. "And about a Greek philosopher."

"Come again?"

"Heraklitos. He said: 'No man steps twice into the same river.' The home I was remembering doesn't exist anymore, because the boy who lived there is dead, even if I wear his name and remember being him."

"Ah, well, my dad always said: 'Home is where the heart is.' Of course, he was a section chief for the railways, so we moved around a lot."

Eric laughed and turned to look over his shoulder at the noncom. "Sofie, you're . . . a natural antidote to my tendency to gloom."

Sofie's eyes crinkled in an answering grin; she felt a soft lurch in the bottom of her stomach. Jauntily, she touched the barrel of her machine pistol to her helmet. "Hey, any time, Centurion."

The Centurion's gaze had returned to the village and the burning Puma. "While this war does exactly the opposite," he whispered.

The comtech frowned. "Hell, I'd rather be on the beach, surfin' and fooling around on a blanket, myself."

"That wasn't exactly what I was thinking of," he said softly. Unwise to speak, perhaps, but . . . *I'm damned if I'm going to start governing my actions by fear at this late date.* "If we lose, we'll be destroyed. If we win . . . what's going to happen, when we get to Europe?"

"The usual?"

Eric shook his head. "Sofie, how many serfs can read?"

She blinked. "Oh, a fair number—'bout one in five, I'd say. Why?"

"Which ratio worries the hell out of a lot of highly placed people. Most of the places we've taken over have been like this"—he nodded at the village—"peasants, primitives. If they're really fierce, like the Afghans, we have to kill a lot of them before the others submit. Usually, it's only necessary to wipe out a thin crust of chiefs or intelligentsia; the rest obey because they're used to obeying, because they're afraid, and because the changes are mostly for the better. Enough to eat, at least, and no more plagues. No prospect of anything better, but then, they never *did* have any prospect of anything better. Sofie, what are we going to *do* with the Europeans? We've never conquered a country where everybody can read, is used to thinking. Security—" He shook his head. "Security operates preventively. They're going to go berserk; it's going to be monumentally ugly. And I'm not even sure it will *work*."

The comtech puffed meditatively, trickling smoke from her nostrils. "Never did have much use for the Headhunters," she said. "Keep actin' as if they wished we all had neck numbers."

He nodded. "And it's not just that." His hands tightened on the Holbars. "Killing . . . it's natural enough; part of being human, I suppose. But too much of it does things. To us, that will hurt us in the long run." He sighed. "Well, at least I won't be there to see it."

"How so?" Sofie's voice was sharper.

Eric snorted weary laughter. "Well, what are the odds on a paratrooper surviving the whole war?"

"Hell," Sofie said, shocked. *This has to stop, and quick,* she thought. It was far too easy to die, even when you wanted to live. When you didn't . . .

Surprised, Eric turned: she was standing with her hands on her hips, lips compressed.

"Hell of a thing t'say, Centurion. *I* do my job, but I intend to die in bed."

"Sorry—" he began.

"Not finished. Now, that was interestin', what you had to say. Food for thought. You're *not* the only one who does that. Thinkin', I mean. So: you don't like what you see happenin'; what're you going to do about it?"

"What can I do—"

"How the fuck should I know? Sir. You're the one from the political family; I'm just a track foreman's daughter. Not even sure I'd agree with anything you wanted to do, but it'd be a damn sight more comfortin' to have you callin' shots than some of the *kill-kill-kill-rape-what's-left* brigade. If it's your responsibility—an' who appointed you guardian of the human race?—then start thinkin' on what you can *do*, even if it isn't much. Can't do more than we can, hey? Waste an' shame to do less, though. Never figured you for a coward or a quitter or a member of the Church'a Self-Pity. Sir. And if the future of the State and the Race *isn't* your lookout, an' I can't no-how see how the fuck it should be, then acting as if 'tis is pretty goddamn arrogant. Unless it's really something personal?

"Meanwhile," she said, pausing for breath, "this-here Century *is* your responsibility; we're your people and your blood."

Stunned, Eric stared at her, aware that his mouth was hanging slightly open. *I shouldn't underestimate people, I really shouldn't* . . . his mind began. Then, stung, he fell back on pride: "You could do better, Monitor Nixon?"

Sofie glanced away. "Oh, hell no, sir. Ah . . ."

He brushed past her, movements brisk. Their boots clattered on the stairs of the shattered mosque.

Sofie stubbed out her butt and flicked it out a slit window, watching the arch of its failing with a vast content. There was a time to soothe, and a time for a medicinal kick in the butt. It was a beautiful day for a battle, and there was no better way of . . . getting close.

Who knows, she thought, watching the energy in his stride. *We might even both live through it, with him to supply the ideas, and me to keep his starry-eyed head from disappearin' completely up his own asshole.* Shrewdly, she guessed it had been too long since he'd had to listen to anyone. And it promised to be a nice long war, so none of them were going anywhere. . . .

Chapter Eleven

VILLAGE ONE, OSSETIAN MILITARY HIGHWAY
APRIL 14, 1942: 1400 HOURS

The village waited quietly; at least, its shell did, for a village is a human thing, even a village starving under the heel of a foreign conqueror. The heap of stone was no longer a place where peasants lived and grew food; it was a fortress, where strangers intricately trained and armed would kill each other, thousands of kilometers from their homes. The last of the Circassians had left for the forest, bent under their sacks of food; all except for the aged *hadji*, who remained in the cellar beneath the mosque, praying in the darkness over a Koran long since committed to memory. Half the houses had been demolished, and the remainder were carefully prepared traps; the cellars below were a spiderweb network that the Draka could use to shift their personnel under cover, or to bring down death on anyone who followed them into the booby-trapped tunnels. Two hundred soldiers had labored six hours beside the natives, sledgehammer and pick, shovel and blasting charge. The troops were working for their lives and the hope of victory.

The villagers had motivation at least as strong; their numbers had dropped by half since the *Liebstandarte* moved in, and every shovelful was a measure of revenge. Two hours past noon, and the defenses were ready. The paratroopers rested at their weapons, taking the opportunity for food, water, sleep, or a crap—veterans knew you never had time later.

Eric sat back against the thick rough timbers of the passageway, unbending his fingers with an effort. Beside him, Sofie swore softly and broke out a tube of astringent wound ointment. The Centurion looked aside as she began smearing the viscous liquid on the tattered blisters that covered his hands, ignoring the sharp pain. It had a thin, acrid petroleum smell, cutting through the dry rock dust and the heavy scent of sweat from meat-fed bodies. They were at the northernmost edge of the village, where the military road entered the built-up area. Two long heaps of rubble flanked it now, where there had been rows of houses; rubble providing cover for two long timber-framed bunkers. The Draka commander was on the left, the western flank; gray eyes flicked south and east, to the forest where the people of the village had gone.

"I hope you can see it, Tyansha," he murmured softly in her language. "And for once, there is mercy."

Five meters away an improvised crew sprawled about their Soviet/German 76.2mm antitank gun, ready to manhandle it to any of the four firing positions in the long bunker. A pile of shells was stacked near it; a ladder poked out of the floor nearby, and more ammunition waited below with strong arms to pitch it up. The sleek, long-barreled solidity of the gun was reassuring; so was the knowledge that its twin was waiting in the other bunker, across the street. One of the gunners was singing, an old, old tune with the feel of Africa in it; Eric remembered it murmured over his cradle, as smooth brown arms rocked:

"A shadow in the bright bazaar
A glimpse of eyes where none should shine
A glimpse of eyes translucent gold
And slitted against the sun . . ."

His palms were sticky; strips of skin pulled free as he opened and closed them absently. There was very little to do, until the action started. A fixed defensive position with secure flanks was the simplest tactical problem a commander could have; the only real decision-making was when and where to commit reserves, and since he didn't have any, to speak of . . .

" . . . faster than a thought she flees
And seeks the jungle's sheltering trees
But he is steady on the track
And half a breath behind . . ."

Sofie was speaking; he swiveled his attention back. "—cking soul of the White Christ, Centurion, you trying to punish yourself or something? And don't give me any of that leading-by-example crap!" The tone was a hissed whisper, but there was genuine anger in it.

He smiled at her, flexing the hands under the bandage pads; she maintained the scowl for a moment, then grinned shyly back. *You are really getting quite perceptive, Sofie,* he thought. *And you glow when you're angry.*

"She tastes his scent upon the breeze,
And looking past her shoulder sees
He treads upon her shadow—
She fears the hunter's mind."

"The Fritz will take care of any punishment needed for my sins," he said. "Good, I can fight with these." A pause. "Thank you." She blushed. "I was just thinking about the war again, and didn't notice, actually."

"Oh," she replied, hunting for something to say in a mind gone blank. "You . . . think we're going to win?"

"Probably. Depends what you mean by win."

"In woman form, in leopard hide
Fording, leaping, side to side
She doubles back upon her track
And sees her efforts fail."

She frowned, reached up to free the package of cigarettes tucked into the camouflage cover of her helmet, tapped one free and snapped her Ronson lighter. "Ahh . . . well, the Archon said we were fighting for survival. I guess, we come out alive and we've won?"

Eric laughed with soft bitterness. "Not bad. Did you hear what our esteemed leader said, after we attacked the Italians and they complained that we'd promised not to? 'You were expecting truth from a politician? Christ, you'll be looking for charity from a banker, next.' One thing I always liked about her, she doesn't mealymouth." He let his head fall back against the timbers. "Actually, she's right . . . it all goes back to the serfs."

" . . . her gold flanks heaving in distress,
Half woman and half leopardess
To either side, nowhere to hide
It's time to fight or die."

She looked at him blankly, retaining one of the bandaged hands; he made no objection. "The serfs?" she said.

"Yes . . look, our ancestors were soldiers mostly, right? They fought for the British, they lost, and the British very kindly gave them a big chunk of African wilderness . . . inhabited wilderness, which they then had to conquer. And they made serfs of the conquered—there were too many of them to exterminate the way the Yanks did to their aborigines—so, serfdom. Slavery, near as no matter, but prettied up a little to keep the abolitionists in England happy. Or less unhappy." He sighed. "Can you spare one of those cancer sticks?"

She lit another from hers. "What's that got to do with the war?" The song tugged at her attention.

"A sight none will forget
Who once have seen them, near or far,
In sunlight or where shadows are
As, side by side they hunt and hide
No one has caught them yet."

"I'm coming to that. Look, what do you think would happen if we eased up on the serfs?"

"Eased up?"

"Let them move off their masters' estates or factory compounds, gave them education, that sort of thing."

"Oh." Sofie's face cleared; that was simple. "They'd rise up and exterminate us," she answered. "Not all of them; some'd stick by us. Some house servants, straw bosses 'n foremen, Janissaries, technicians, that sort. They'd get their throats cut, too."

"Damn straight, they would. And there would go civilization, until outsiders moved in and ate the pieces. So, once we'd settled in, we were committed to the serf-and-plantation system, took it with us wherever we went. We had the wolf by the ears: hard to hang on, deadly to let go. Did you know there were mass escapes, in the early years? Rebellions, too." His eyes grew distant. "My great-great-great-grandfather put one down, in 1828. Impaled four thousand rebels through the sugar country, from Virconium to Shanapur. He had a painting made of it, still hanging in the hallway at home." Tyansha had refused to look at it; he had wondered why, at the time. "Well, one of the main reasons for all that was the border country with the wild tribes: a place to escape to, hope for overthrowing us. So we had to expand. Also, you run through a lot of territory when every one of a landholder's sons expects an estate."

The comtech leaned forward, interested despite herself. Not that it was much different from the history she had been taught, but the emphasis and shading was something else entirely.

"Then, by the 1870s, we'd grown all the way up to Egypt, no borders but the sea and the deserts, and we'd started to industrialize, so we had modern communications and weapons."

"Hmm," Sophie said. "Why didn't we stop there?"

He grunted laughter and dragged smoke down his throat. "Because we'd gotten just strong enough to terrify people. Not afraid enough to leave us alone, though. People with real power, in Europe. And we were different—so different that when they realized what was going on, they were hostile by reflex. Demanding reforms we couldn't make without committing suicide." Eric gestured with the cigarette, tracing red ember-glow through the gloom. "So, there were murmurs about boycotts; propaganda, too. And we couldn't keep the city serfs completely illiterate, not if they were going to operate a modern economy for us. That's when the Security Directorate was set up, and it's been getting more and more power every decade since. Which means power over Citizens, too."

Caught up in his words, he failed to notice the comtech's worried glance from side to side. Unheeding, he continued. "Well, the Great War was a godsend; we took on the weakest of the Central Powers, and grabbed off Persia and Russian central Asia and western China too. And the War shattered Europe, which gave us time to consolidate; then we were a Great Power in our own right."

He grinned, showing teeth. "Stroke of genius, no? Only now, we had thousands of kilometers of land frontier, with a hostile Great Power! See, liberal democrat, Communist, even Fascist, any different social system is a deadly menace to us, if it's close. And they're all different. All close, too; with modern technology the world's getting to be a pretty small place. The boffins say that after the war, radios will be as small and cheap as teakettles were, before. Imagine every serf village out in West Bumfuck having a receiver; we can jam, but . . . So, on to the war. Another heaven-sent stroke of luck, although we were counting on something like that. Divide and rule, let others wear themselves out and the Domination steps in—our traditional strategy. If we win, we'll have the earth, the whole of North Asia, and most of Europe besides what we took last time."

"Think we can do it?" Sofie asked in a neutral tone.

"Oh, sure. The problem will be holding it. Remember that cartoon in the Alexandria *Gazette*?"

She nodded. The chief opposition newspaper had shown a python with scales in the Draka colors that had just throttled a hippo. It lay, bleeding and bruised, muttering: "Sweet Christ, now do I have to *eat* the bloody thing?"

"But that won't be enough," Eric continued.

"What will?"

"In the end . . . we'll have to conquer the earth. The Archon was right, you see? To survive, we've got to make sure nobody else does, except as serfs." Eric, who had long since come to an acceptance of what his people and nation were, ground the cigarette out with short, savage motions of his hand. "We're like a virus, really: we'll never be safe with uninfected tissue still able to manufacture antibodies against us."

Sofie folded the hand in hers. "You don't sound . . . too enthusiastic about it, Centurion."

"It could be worse. That's the analysis the Academy will give you, anyway; they just think it's a wonderful situation."

She hesitated, then decided on bluntness. "What are you doing in a fighting unit, then?" she asked quietly.

He looked up, his mouth quirking; even then, she noticed how a lock of butter-yellow hair fell over the tanned skin of his forehead. "I love my people. Not like, sometimes, but . . . That's enough to fight and die for, isn't it?" And very softly, "But is it enough to live for?"

Their eyes met. And the comset hissed, clicking with Eric's code. Efficiency settled over him like a mask as he reached for the receiver.

"Ah," said Eric, watching the German column winding up the road toward the village. "There you see the results of Fritz ingenuity." A glance at his wrist. "1610—good time."

"Oh?" Marie Kaine asked, not taking her eyes from the trench periscope. She had always had doubts about the cost-effectiveness of tanks. So delicate, under their thick hides, so complex and highly stressed and failure prone . . . Still, it was daunting to have them coming at you.

The Fritz convoy had been dipping in and out of sight with the twists of the road from the north: six tanks, two heavy assault guns, tracked infantry carriers in the rear. The optics brought them near, foreshortened images trembling as slight vibrations in the tube were translated to wavering over the kilometer of distance. She could see the long cannon of the tanks swinging, the heads of infantrymen through

the open hatches of the APCs, imagine the creaking, groaning, clanging rattle that only armor makes. They were still over two thousand
meters out when a brace of self-propelled antiaircraft guns peeled off
to take up stations upslope of the road. The sun had baked what
moisture remained out of the rocky surface, and the heavy tracks were
raising dust plumes as they ground through the crushed-rock surface
of the military highway.

Military highway, she snorted to herself. Of course, the Soviets hadn't
had much wheeled traffic. Even so, for a strategic road, this was a
disgrace.

"Mmm. You know the Wehrmacht-SS situation?" the Centurion
continued.

Marie nodded wordlessly. Sofie spoke, without looking up from the
circuit board she was working on. "Elite units, aren't they? Volunteers.
Like us, or Boss' Brass Knucks?" That was the Archonal Guard Legion;
their insignia was a mailed fist.

"Yes, but they're not part of the regular army; they're organs of
the Nationalsozialistiche Deutsche Arbeiterpartei. And they're always
fighting with the regulars over recruits and equipment. So their
organization took over the Russian factories to get an independent
supply base." He nodded to the squat combat machines grinding their
way up the road. "Those are Ivan KV-1 heavy tanks, with a new
turret and the Fritz 88mm/L56 gun; cursed good weapon, plenty of
armor and reasonable mobility. Better than their standard-issue
machines. Hmmm . . . the assault guns look like the same chassis, with a 150mm gun-howitzer mounted in the front glacis plate.
The infantry carriers and flakpanzers are on SU-76 bodies; that was
the Ivans' light self-propelled gun. Ingenious; they've actually made
a good thing out of departmental in-fighting."

"Sounds as bad as the pissing matches the Army and Air Corps
and Navy are always getting into at home," Marie Kaine said. She
made a final note on her pad and called instructions to the gun
crew; a round of AP ammunition slid into the breech with a *chunk-
chang* of metallic authority. Range would be no problem; a dozen
inconspicuous objects had been carefully measured, and the guns were
sighted in. First-round fire would be as accurate as the weapons
permitted; Marie was not impressed with the standard of the machining. A sound design, but crude: there was noticeable windage in the
barrel, even with lead driving bands, and the exterior finish was
primitive in the extreme.

Sofie handed the sheet of electronic components back to the artillery observer, a harassed-looking man with thinning sandy hair and
a small clipped mustache. He slid it back into the open body of
his radio, reinserted the six thumb-sized vacuum tubes, and touched
the leads with a testing jack. "Ahhh," he said. "Good work; all
green. Thanks, our spares had a little accident on the way down,
hate to have to run a field-telephone line in."

He rose, dusting off his knees, and peered out a slit. "Hmmm,
our Hond IIIs are better. Not much heavier, twice the speed, better sloping on the armor, a 120mm gun."

"Oh, yes," Eric said. "And all sorts of extras: gyrostabilizers on the gun, shock absorbers on the torsion bars . . . Only one problem." He pointed an imaginary pistol at the SS panzers. "Our armor is a hundred kilometers away; those machines are here. Got the battery on line?"

"Yessir." He handed over the receiver; Sofie's set would have done as well, but it was more efficient to have a dedicated channel.

"Palm One to Fist, over."

"Roge-doge, Palm One. Our 105s're set up, and the captured Fritz 150's. Covering your position and about 4,000 meters out. Going to need a firefall soon?"

"That's negative, Fist; this looks like a probing attack. Later."

"All go, Palm One. But watch it: this is the only decent position in range, so they've got it map-referenced for sure, they don't need observation to key in. And if they've got self-propelled heavies, no way I can win a counterbattery shoot. They're immune to blast and fragments; we're not and we can't move, either. And you know what the odds are on hitting armored vehicles with indirect fire: about the same as flying to the moon by putting your head between your knees and spitting hard."

"Green, Fist; we'll only need you once. What about the Air Corps boys?" Artillery observers doubled as ground-control liaison for strike aircraft.

A sour chuckle. "You should hear the commo channels; everybody from here to Tiflis is screaming that the bogeyman's out of the closet, and will Momma fly in and help, please. At least there aren't any of Hitler's pigeons around shitting on *us* . . . For that matter, I could have used air support an hour ago myself—couple hundred of those-there Fritz holdouts tried to rush my perimeter."

Eric winced. That could cause hard trouble; it was a good thing they had not waited for darkness. "Over and out, Fist."

"Kill a few for us, Palm One."

"Range, one thousand meters," Marie said expressionlessly. Eric leaned a hand on the bunker ceiling and watched. Six heavy AFVs, twelve infantry carriers with eleven men each . . . not counting the flakpanzers, about two lochoi of armor and a century of panzergrenadiers. The enemy was doing about what he'd expected; about what Eric would have done with the same information—trying to bull through with whatever could be scraped up at short notice and moved under skies controlled by the opposition, in the hope that there was nothing much to stop him. And he'd know his opponents were paratroopers, hence lightly equipped. On the battlefields of Europe, that meant negligible antitank capacity; the armed forces of the Domination had a rather different definition of *light*.

"Seven hundred meters," Marie said. "They're probably going to deploy their infantry any time now, Centurion." The diesel growl of the German engines was clearly audible now: Eric gave a hand signal to Sofie, and she relayed the stand-ready command. The bunker was hushed now. Tension breathed thick; it was silent enough to hear the steel-squeal and diesel growl from the enemy armor over the windsough from the forest.

The first of the German tanks was making the final turn, a move that presented his flank; after that it would be a straight path into the village. Eric raised a hand, lips parted slightly, waiting for the first tank to pass by a white-painted stone at the six-hundred-meter mark. Time stretched, vision sharpened; this was like hunting, not the adrenaline rush of close combat. For a moment he could even feel a detached pity for his opponent.

"Now!"

CRACK! and the antitank gun cut loose, a stunning blast of noise in the confined space. The dimness of the bunker went black and rank with dust, and the barrel of the cannon slammed back almost to the far wall; the crew was leaping in with fresh ammunition even as the cradle's hydraulics returned to "rest," and the casing rang on the stones of the floor. Downslope to the north, the lead tank stopped dead as the tungsten-cored shot took it at the junction of turret and hull, smashing through the armor and fighting compartment, burying itself in the engine block. There was a second's pause before the explosion, a flash, and the ten-tonne mass of the turret blew free and into the air, flipping end over end into the sky, landing twenty meters from the burning hulk.

That blocked the road. The German armor wheeled to deploy into the fields; the assault gun in the rear had turned just enough to present its flank when the second antitank gun in the other bunker fired— one round that twisted it askew with a tread knocked loose, a second that struck the side armor with the brutal *chunggg* of high-velocity shot meeting steel. Assault guns are simply steel boxes, with a heavy cannon in a limited-traverse mount in the bow. From the front they are formidable; from the flanks, almost helpless. The hatches flew open, and the crew poured out to throw themselves down in the roadside ditches; one was dragging a man whose legs had contested passage with twenty kilograms of moving metal, and lost badly. The damaged vehicle burned sullenly, occasional explosions jarring the ground and sending tongues of flame through its hatches and around the gun that lay slanting toward the ground, its mantlet slammed free of the surrounding armor. Another pillar of black oil-smoke reached for the mild blue of the afternoon sky.

The bunker crew had time for a single cheer before the response came. All the armored vehicles had opened up with their secondary armament, but the machine-gun fire was little menace to dug-in positions. The second Fritz assault gun was a different matter, and its commander was cool enough to ignore the burning wreckage before and behind him. The two muzzle flashes had given away the position of the gun that killed his comrades, and the third shot howled off the thick frontal armor of his gun. Carefully he traversed, corrected for range, fired. The sound of the six-inch howitzer was thicker and somehow heavier than the high-velocity tank guns, but at this point-blank range there was no appreciable interval between firing and impact. And the shell carried over a hundred pounds of high explosive.

Eric felt the impact as a flexing in the ground, as if the fabric of the bunker had withdrawn and struck him like a huge palm. Dust smoked down from the ceiling, between the heavy timbers; he sneezed. There was another impact, then a thudding to their right: the second bunker was catching it.

"Marie! Get that gun to the end firing position." The crew sprang into action, manhandling the heavy weapon back and turning it; it rumbled off down the curved length of the bunker toward the firing slit at the western end.

"Follow me!" He turned and scuttled toward the eastern end of the bunker; this was not going to be a healthy sector in a few seconds. As they ran he cupped the hand radio to his ear.

"Gun two, gun two, come in. Come in, goddammit!" Then to himself: "Shit!" Even with a 150mm shell, it would have taken a direct hit to disable the other antitank gun. *Luck plays no favorites,* he thought bleakly. Chances were the other gun was out, which meant he was naked of antitank on the eastern side of the road, except for the 120mm recoilless dug in on the edge of the forest, and he had been hoping not to have to use that just yet. Aloud, he continued. "Tom, try to get someone through to gun two's position. Report, and see if the machine gun positions in B bunker are intact." A different code-click. "East wing recoilless, engage any armor your side of the road, but not until within two hundred meters of our front."

The acknowledgments came through as they dropped to a halt beside the machine gun team at the east end of the bunker. Eric rested a hand on their shoulders, leaning forward to peer through the irregular circle of the firing port.

"Yahhh!" he snarled. The bunker shook as another heavy shell impacted; bullets spalled chips of stone from the rubble outside. Light poured through the opening—a yellow beam through the dust motes that hung, suspended, in the column of brightness. The three tanks had fanned out into the fields, swinging to present their frontal armor to the village and accelerating forward, their guns barking at the long heaps of rubble on either side of the road. And . . . yes! One leaped as a white flash erupted under a tread, settled back with a shattered road wheel. Now the Draka machine guns were opening up, hosing over the stranded behemoth. They could not penetrate the armor; not even the antitank gun could without a side shot, not without great good luck. But they could shatter optics, rattle the crew . . .

Eric hammered a fist into the wall in glee; the other two were falling back, unwilling to chance a mine field without engineers or special vehicles to clear it. Accelerating in reverse, they circled the assault guns and climbed back onto the road, retreating until they were hull down in a patch of low ground. Still dangerous, those long 88mm guns had plenty of range, but the bluff of his scant handful of antitank mines had worked.

The German infantry carriers had halted well back; their thin armor offered protection from small arms and shell fragments only. Now they were opening up with the twin machine guns each carried, and the Waffen-SS panzergrenadiers were spilling out of the opened ramp doors at the rear of each vehicle. Eric could see them marshalling, fanning out west of the road. They could see the waiting V-spread of wire and trench that threatened to funnel them into a killing ground as they advanced south; their officers' shouts pushed them toward the sheltering forest, where they could operate under cover and flank the strong frontal positions. Even a few snipers and machine guns upslope from the village could make field trenches untenable.

"Smart, Fritz; by the book," he murmured. The Draka infantry were opening up with their crew-served weapons; a few of the Germans were falling under the flail of the 15mm's, but that was over a thousand meters, extreme range, and the Germans were making skillful use of cover. Happily, he waited for them to reach the protection of the woods. They would do it on the run; even well-trained soldiers threw themselves into cover when under fire. The trees would beckon, and they had already been shaken by what had happened to their armor.

"Now," he whispered. Now it was up to those at the treeline.

"Not yet," the Draka decurion murmured to himself. The Germans had been coming in across the fields well spread out, but they bunched as they approached the treeline, the underbrush was thinner here and they were unconsciously picking the easiest way in. In they came, out of the punishing fire coming from the Draka positions, up the valley to their left. Bunching, speeding up, their attention divided.

The moment stretched. Above him a bird sounded a liquid *di-di-di*, announcing its nesting territory to the world. The Draka soldier waited behind the log, his eyes steady on flickers of movement through a shimmering haze of leaves, confident in the near invisibility of camouflage uniform and motionlessness. His tongue ran over dry lips, tasting forest mold and green dust. Insects buzzed, burrowed, dug.

'*Course, they-all could spot those dumbshit Ivans,* he thought. The Russian partisans were with him, a tetrarchy's worth with captured Fritz weapons. Forget about that, concentrate . . .

Ya . . . Now! His thumb clamped on the safety release of the detonator, and he rapped it sharply three times on the moss-grown trunk of the fallen beech before him. Ahead of him the thick band of undergrowth along the forest edge exploded, erupted into a chaos of flying dust, shedded leaves, wood chips. Louder than the explosion was a humming like a hundred thousand metal bees: Broadsword directional mines, curved plates lined with plastique, the concave inner face tight-packed with razor-edged steel flechettes like miniature arrows. Pointed toward an enemy, mounted at waist-height, they had the effect of titanic shotgun shells. The German infantry went down, scythed down, the first ranks shredded, sliced, spattered back into their comrades' faces.

They halted for an instant, too stunned even to seek cover. The loudest sound was the shrill screaming of the wounded—men lying thrashing with helmets, weapons, harness nailed to their bodies. The decurion rolled to his Holbars, over it, came up into firing position and began picking targets, hammering three-round bursts.

"Ya! Ya! Beautiful, fuckin' *beautiful!*" he shouted. The others of his stick opened up from positions in cover, and a volley of grenades followed.

Grunting in annoyance, the Draka NCO noticed one of the Russian partisans he had been assigned kneeling, staring slackjawed at the chewed bodies in SS uniforms that lay in clumps along a hundred meters of the forest edge. He was shaking his head, mouth moving silently, the Schmeisser dangling limply from his hands.

"*Shoot,* you stupid donkeyfucka!" The Draka dodged over and planted his boot in the Russian's buttocks with a thump. "Useless sonofabitch, *shmert, shmert Fritz!*"

The partisan scarcely seemed to feel the blow. He grinned, showing the blackened jagged stumps of teeth knocked out by a rifle butt; through the rags on his back bruises showed yellow and green and black.

"Da, da," he mumbled, raising the machine pistol. Holding it clamped tight to the hip and loosing off a burst, then another; short bursts, to keep the muzzle from rising too much. He came to his feet, disregarding the return fire that was beginning to whine overhead and drop clipped-off twigs on their heads. His bullets hosed out, across the back of a wounded SS grenadier who was hobbling away with a leg trailing, using his rifle for a crutch.

"*Da! Da!*" he shouted.

The decurion dropped away. The partisans had opened up all along the treeline, thirty of them thickening up his firepower quite nicely. The SS were rallying, crawling forward now; a MG34 machine gun began firing in support, and an 88mm shell from one of the tanks smashed a giant hornbeam into a pillar of splinters and fire. Thick green-wood smoke began to drift past as the first Germans reached the woodland and crashed through the tangled resiliency of the bushes. They were still taking casualties, of course, and still under fire from the village on their left flank. The Draka paused to smack a fresh drum into his Holbars, whistling tunelessly between his teeth. In a moment they would fall back, into the thick woods; the partisans could cover that. Fall back to the *next* ambush position; the trees would channel pursuit nicely. He doubted the Germans would come farther than that, this time.

Beside him, the Russian was laughing.

Eric watched as the SS infantry halted, rallied, began to fight their way into the woods. The armored vehicles had swiveled their weapons to support them; only the assault gun kept the village under fire, the heavy shells going over their heads with a freight-train-at-night rush. And the flakpanzers moving forward and risking their thin plating to hose their quadruple 20mm autocannon over the village, short bursts that hit like horizontal explosive hail-storms. The Draka in the bunker dove for the floor, away from the firing slits. Not that there was much chance of a hit even so; the antiaircraft weapons ate ammo too rapidly to keep up the support fire long enough to saturate an area, but there was no point in risking life for a bystander's view. The action was out of range of their personal weapons, anyway.

Eric continued his scan, forcing the mind's knowledge of probabilities to overcome the hindbrain's cringing. Some of the SS infantry carriers were reversing, ready to reembark their crews; the Fritz commander must be a cool one, prepared to cut his losses.

The Centurion closed his eyes for a moment, struggling to hold the battle whole in his mind without focusing on its component parts. *Know how a man fights and you know what he is and how he thinks:* the words ran through him like an echo. Who . . . Pa, of course; that was one of his favorite maxims. How had the German commander reacted? Well, ruthlessly, to begin with. He had sacrificed that warcar to gain information. Not afraid of casualties, then. Bold, ready to gamble; he'd tried to rush through with no more than two companies, to push as far up the pass as he could before the Draka solidified their defense.

Eric opened slitted eyes, scratched at the itching yellow stubble under his chin. *Damnation, I wish I had more information.* Well, what soldier didn't? And he wished he could have spent more time with the partisan leader, pumped him for details, but it was necessary to send him off to contact the others, if anything valuable was to come of that. After showing him enough dead Germans to put some spirit in him and backbone back into his followers, not to mention what Dreiser had done, that was good work. Escape from the cauldron of death that Russia had become was a fine lure, glittering enough to furnish enthusiasm, but so distant that it was not likely to make them cautious.

But it would have been good to learn a little more about this man Hoth in Pyatigorsk. Still . . . there had been a bull-like quality to the attack. Plenty of energy, reasonable skill, but not the unexpected, the simple after-the-fact novelty that marked a really inspired touch. The *Liebstandarte* had always been a mechanized unit, no doubt the SS commander knew the value of mobility but did he understand it was as much an *attitude* as a technique? Or was he wedded to his tanks and carriers, even when the terrain and circumstances were wrong?

What was that speech of Pa's again? *Don't think in terms of specific problems, think in terms of the task.* A commander who was a tactician and nothing else would look at the Draka position in the village and think of how to crush it; one problem at a time. *I would have tried something different,* he thought. *Hmm, maybe waiting until dark, using the time to bring up reserves, filtering infantry through the woods in the dark and then attacking both sides.* It was impossible to bypass the village completely—it sat here in the pass like a fishbone in a throat—but there were ways to keep to the principle of attacking weakness rather than strength . . .

Ways to manipulate the enemy, as well. Pa again: *If you hurt him, an untrained man will focus on the pain. In rage, if he's brave and a fighter; without realizing that even so he's allowing you to direct his attention, that your Will is master.* Eric had found that true in personal combat; so few could just *accept* a hurt, keep centered, prevent their mind's eye from rushing to the sensory input of the threatened spot. The way some chess players focused on this check rather than the mate five moves into the future. *Discipline, discipline in your soul; you aren't a man until you can command yourself, body as well as mind. Without inner discipline a man is nothing more than a leopard that thinks, and you can rule him with a whip and a chair until he jumps through hoops.*

He reached for the handphone of the radio, brushing aside an old resentment. *So you're a bastard. I'm not so stupid I can't see when you're right,* he thought at the absent form of Karl von Shrakenburg.

Three quick clicks, two slow: recognition signal for the mortars. Focus on the valley below: the German panzergrenadiers falling back from the edge of the woods, dragging their hurt, the SS armor opening up again on the bunker positions, trying to keep the gunners' heads down and cover the retreat. Bright muzzle flashes, the heavy *crack* of high-velocity shot. Flickering wink of automatic weapons, and the sound of the jacketed bullets on rock, like a thousand ball-peen hammers ringing on a girder. Stone rang; raw new-cut timber shifted and creaked as the shells *whumped* against rock and dirt filtered down from above and into his collar. He sneezed, hawked, spat grit out of his mouth, blinking back to the brightness of the vision slit.

Wait for it, wait for it. Now: now they were clustered around their vehicles.

"Firefall," he said.

Thick rock hid the sound of the automortars firing the *fumpfumpfump* as their recoil-operated mechanisms stripped shells out of the hoppers and into the stubby smooth-bore barrels. Eric raised the field glasses to his eyes; he could see a flinching as the veterans among the SS troopers dove for cover or their APC's, whichever was closest. Survivors, who knew what to expect. Rifles and machine guns pin infantrymen, force them to cover, but it is artillery that does the killing, from overhead, where even a foxhole is little help. And all foot soldiers detest mortars even more than other guns; mortar bombs drop out of the sky and spread fragments all around them rather than in the narrow cone of a gun shell. Much less chance to survive a near miss, and there is more explosive in a mortar's round than an artillery shell, which needs a thick steel wall to survive firing stresses.

CRASH! Crashcrashcrash . . . Tiny stick figures running, falling, lifting into the air with flailing limbs. Lightning-wink flashes from the explosions, each with its puff of smoke. Imagination furnished the rest, and memory: raw pink of sliced bone glistening in opened flesh; screaming and the low whimpering that was worse; men in shock staring with unbelief at the wreck of selves that had been whole fractions of a second before; the whirring hum of jagged cast-iron casing fragments flying too fast to see and the cringing helplessness of being under attack with no means of striking back . . .

"Sofie," he said. She started, forcing her attention back from the distant vehicles.

"Ya, sir?"

"Can you break me into the Fritz command circuit?" The SS personnel carriers were buttoning up, the hale dragging wounded up the ramps and doors winching shut. Even thin armor would protect against blast and fragments. The tanks had raised their muzzles, dropping high-explosive rounds in the village on the chance of finding the mortar teams that were punishing their comrades. Brave, since it risked more fire from the antitank guns in the forward positions, but hopeless. More hopeless than the Germans suspected; there were only three of the automortars with the Draka, their rate of fire giving them the impact of a Century of conventional weapons. At that, the shells were falling more slowly, one weapon at a time taking up the bombardment, to save ammunition and spare the other barrels from heat buildup.

Another of TechSec's marvels, another nightmare for the supply officers, a detached portion of Eric's mind thought. Officially, Technical Section's motto was "Nothing But the Best"; to the gun-bunnies who had to hump the results of their research into battle, it was commonly held to be "Firepower at All Costs."

Sofie had unslung the backpack radio, opened an access panel, made adjustments. Draka field radios had a frequency randomizer, to prevent eavesdropping, It was new, experimental, troublesome, but it saved time with codes and ciphers. The Fritz, now, still . . . She put fingers to one earphone and turned a dial, slowly.

"Got 'em," she said cheerfully, raising her voice over the racket of combat. "They don't seem happy, nohow."

Eric brought the handset to his ear, willing distractions to fade until there was only the gabble of static-blurred voices. His own German was good enough to recognize the Silesian accent in the tone that carried command.

"Congratulations," he said, in the language of his ancestors. There was a moment's silence on the other end; he could hear someone cursing a communications officer in the background, and the measured thudding of explosions heard through tank armor.

"Congratulations," he repeated, "on your losses. How many? Fifty? A hundred? I doubt if we lost six!" He laughed, false and full and rich; it was shocking to the watching Draka, hearing that sound coming from a face gone expressionless as an axe. A torrent of obscenities answered him. *A peasant, from the vocabulary,* Eric thought. *Pure barnyard.* And yes, he could be distracted, enraged. Probably the type with cold lasting angers: an obsessive. The German paused for breath, and Eric could imagine a hand reaching for the selector switch of his intercom. With merciless timing, the Draka spoke into the instant. "Any messages for your wives and sisters? We'll be seeing them before you do!

"Our circuit," he continued, and then: "Cease fire."

A pain in one hand startled him. He looked down, saw that the cigarette had burned down to his knuckle, dropped it and ground the butt into the dirt. Two-score men had died since the brief savage encounter began: their bodies lay in the fields, draped over bushes along the western edge of the forested hills, roasting and shriveling in the burning fighting vehicles down below on the road. All in the time it might have taken to smoke a cigarette, and most of them had died without even a glimpse of the hands that killed them.

He snorted. "Someday TecSec will find a way of incinerating the world while sitting in a bunker under a mountain," he muttered. "The apotheosis of civilized warfare."

"Sir?" Sofie asked.

Eric shook himself. There was the work of the day to be done; besides, it had probably been no prettier in mail.

"Right. Get me the medics, I want a report on what happened in Bunker B. Put—Svenson, wasn't it?—down on the treeline. Put him on as soon as he reports in; that was well done, he deserves a pat for it."

"So do you, sir."

Startled, he glanced over at her as she finished rebuckling the straps of the radio and stood with a grunt. Teeth flashed in the gloom as she reached over and ceremoniously patted him on the back; looking about with embarrassment, he saw nods from the other troopers.

"Luck," he said dismissively. Combat was an either-or business: you took information always scanty and usually wrong, made a calculated guess, then stood ready to improvise. Sometimes it worked, and you looked like a hero; sometimes you slipped into the shit headfirst. Nobody did it right every time, not against an opponent less half-hard than the Italians.

"Bullshit, *sir*," Sofie said. "When you stop worryin' and do it, it gets fuckin' *done*." She shrugged at his frown. "Hey, why give the Fritz a call in the middle of things?"

"Because I always fancied myself as a *picador*, Sofie," he said, turning to watch the Germans disappear down the valley, infantry carriers first, the tanks following, reversing from one hull-down position to the next so that they could cover each other. "Let's just hope the bull I goaded isn't too much for our cape."

Chapter Twelve

DRAKA FORCES BASE KARS, PROVINCE OF ANATOLIA
APRIL 14, 1942: 0600 HOURS

The barrage lit the sky to the east, brighter than the false dawn. Forty kilometers, and the guns were a continuous flicker all along the arch of the horizon, as of heat-lightning, the sound a distant rumbling that echoed off the mountains and down the broad open valleys.

Johanna von Shrakenberg stood to watch it from the flat roof of the two-story barracks. She had risen early, even though her lochos was on call today and so spared the usual four-kilometer run; slipped out from between Rahksan and the sleeping cat, and brought her morning coffee and cigarette up here. The cold was bitter under the paling stars, and she was glad of the snug, insulated flight suit and gloves. Steam rose from the thick china mug, warm and rich, soothing in her mouth as she sipped.

The guns had been sounding since the start of the offensive. She tried to imagine what it was like under that shelling: earth and rock churning across square kilometers, thousands of tons of steel and explosive ripping across the sky . . . the artillery of sixty legions, ten thousand guns, everything from the monster 240s and 200s of the Army Corps reserve to field guns and mortars and rocket launchers.

" 'Only the mad inhuman laughter of the guns,' " she quoted softly. Beyond that was the Caucasus, and the passes where the Airborne legions had landed in the German rear. Her brother among them . . . she shook her head. Worry was inevitable and pointless, but Eric's grip on life was not as firm as she would have liked. *The sort of man who needs something or someone to live for,* she thought. *I wish he'd find one, this business is dangerous enough when you're trying.*

Dawn was breaking, rising out of the fire and the thunder. Shadow chased darkness down the huge scored slopes of the mountains, still streaked with old drifts. Rock glowed, salmon-pink; she could see a plume of snow trailing feather-pale from a white peak. Below, clusters of young trees marked the manors the Draka had built, and fields of wheat showed a tender, tentative green. A new landscape, scarcely older than herself.

114

There had been much work done here in the last generation, she thought; it took Draka to organize and plan on such a scale. Terraces like broad steps on the hillsides, walled with stones carted from the fields; canals; orchards and vineyards pruned and black and dusted with green uncoiling buds. All of it somehow raw and new, against this bleakness made by four thousand years of peasant axes and hungry goats.

Well, only a matter of time, she mused. Already the Conservancy Directorate was drawing a mat of young forest across the upper slopes; in another hundred years these foothills would be as lush as nature permitted, and her grandchildren might come here to hunt tiger and mouflon.

The scene about her was also Draka work, but less sightly. Kars was strategic, a meeting of routes through the mountains of eastern Turkey, close to the prewar Russian border. The conquest back in 1916–1917 had been a matter of foot infantry and mule trains and supply drops by dirigibles. Castle Tarleton had enough problems guarding six thousand miles of northern frontier without transportation worries; even before the Great War was over, a million laborers had been rounded up to push through railways and roads and airship yards.

So when the buildup for the German war began there was transport enough; just barely, with careful planning. The air base around her sprawled to the horizon on the south and west, and work teams were still gnawing at scrub and gravel. Others toiled around the clock to maintain the roads pounded by endless streams of motor transport; the air was thick with rock dust and the oily smell of the low-grade distillate the steam trucks burned. Barracks, warehouses, workshops, and hangars sprawled, all built of asbestos-cement panels bolted to prefabricated steel frames: modular, efficient, and ugly. On a nearby slope the skeletal mantis shape of an electrodetector tower whirled tirelessly.

Johanna flicked the cigarette butt over the edge of the roof and drank the last lukewarm mouthful of coffee. "Like living in a bloody construction site," she muttered, turning to the stairwell.

The bulletin board in the ready room held nothing new: final briefing at 0750, wheels-up half an hour later, a routine kill-anything-that-moved sweep north of the mountains to make sure the Fritz air kept its head down. Merarch Anders was going over the maps one more time as she passed through, raising his head to nod at her, his face a patchwork of scars from twenty years of antiaircraft fire and half a dozen forced landings. She waved in response, straightening a little under the cool blue eyes. Anders was the "old man" in truth, forty-two, ancient for a fighter pilot. He had been a *bagbuster* in the Great War, flying one of the pursuit biplanes that ended the reign of the dirigibles. And even in middle age the fastest man she had ever sparred with.

The canteen was filling with her fellow Draka. The food was good; that was one of the advantages of the Air Corps. The ground forces had a motto: "Join the Army and live like a serf," but a pilot could fly out to fight and return to clean beds, showers, and cooked food. This time she took only a roll and some fruit before heading out to the field; combat tension affected everybody a different way, and with her it tightened the gut and killed her appetite and any capacity for small talk.

The planes of her lochos were having a final checkover in their sandbagged revetments, sloping pits along either side of an accessway that led out into the main runway for this section. Technicians were checking the systems, pumps chugged as the fuel tanks filled, armorers coaxed in belts of 25mm cannon shells for the five-barrel nose battery.

Her ground crew paused to smile and wave as Johanna settled herself on the edge of the revetment and sat cross-legged, watching. On excellent advice, her father's among others, she had gone out of her way to learn their names and take an interest in their conditions. They were serfs, except for the team commander; not Janissaries, unarmed auxiliaries owned by the War Directorate, but privileged and highly trained. Their work would be checked by the inspectors, of course, but there was a world of difference between the best and just-good-enough.

She sighed as she watched them work on her aircraft. Even earthbound, with the access panels open, the Eagle was a beautiful sight: as beautiful as a dolphin or a blooded horse, enough to make one's breath catch when it swam in its natural element above the earth. It was a midwing monoplane, the slender fuselage just big enough for pilot, fuel, and the five cannon, slung between two huge H-form 24-cylinder Atlantis Peregrine turbocharged engines in sleek cowlings. Twice the power of a single-engine fighter and far less than twice the weight: not quite as agile in a dogfight, but better armored and more heavily armed, and *much* faster . . .

Like most pilots, she had personalized her machine: a Cupid's bow mouth below the nose, lined with shark's teeth, and a name in cursive script: LOVER'S BITE. There were five swastikas stenciled below the bubble canopy, the marks of her victories.

Johanna's mouth quirked. Flying was . . . flying was like making love after a pipeful of the best rum-soaked Arusha Crown *ganja*; she had always had a talent for it, and the Eagle was a sweet ship. And somewhat to her surprise, she had turned out to be an excellent fighter pilot; she had the vision and the reflexes, and most important of all the nerve to close in, *very* close, right down to 100 meters, while the enemy wings filled the windscreen and her guns hammered bits of metal loose to bounce off the canopy . . .

And frankly, I could do without it, she thought. There were worse ways to spend the war: sweating in the lurching steel coffin of a personnel carrier, or clawing your hands into the dirt and praying under a mortar barrage—but dead was dead, and she had not the slightest desire to die. Nor to spin in trapped in a burning plane, or . . .

She shrugged off the thought. War was the heritage of her people and her caste; it was just that she would have preferred to be lucky. Peacetime duty for her military service, then, hmmm, yes, Capetown for her degree. Nothing fancy; a three-year in Liberal Arts and Estate Management and an aristocratic A- grade. And days spent lying naked on the beaches of the Peninsula, surfing, going to the *palaestra* to run and wrestle, throw the disk and javelin and practice the pankration. Wearing silk and skirts; concerts and theaters and picture galleries, love affairs and long talks and walking under the olives on starlit nights . . .

"Well, on to the work of the day," she murmured. Then: "Got her ticking over?"

One of the technicians looked up, grinning as the last of an ammunition belt ran across the leather pad on her shoulders and into the drums, the aluminum casings dull against the color-coded shells: red for tracer-incendiary, brown for explosive, blue for armor-piercing.

"She-un loaded fo' lion, Mistis," the serf said. Johanna's mind placed the dialect: Police Zone, but not the Old Territories—Katanga or Angola, perhaps . . . serf specialists were given a thorough but narrowly technical education, which did not include master-class speech patterns. "Giv't to tha Fritz, raaht up they ass," she continued.

"I intend to, Lukie-Beth," the Draka said, and considered lighting a cigarette. No, a bad example to break regulations around so much high octane. Instead she threw the package to the crew chief, who tucked one behind his ear and handed the others around. He nodded a salute as she rose, touching the steel hook on the stump of his left wrist to his brow.

" . . . and engage targets of opportunity on the ground," the briefing officer concluded.

Merarch Anders rose and walked to the edge of the dais. "All right, you glory hounds," he said. The harsh voice dampened the slight murmur that had swelled across the ranks of folding chairs.

Here begineth the lecture from the Holy Book of Air Operations, section V, paragraph ii, Johanna thought with resignation.

"A few reminders of the facts of life," the Merarch continued. "The Air Corps does not exist so you can dogfight and rack up kills. It exists to help the Forces win wars. Its most important function is reconnaissance; the second most important is ground support. We have a fighter arm to protect the scouting and ground-support units, and to shoot down any enemy aircraft who try to do the important stuff for the other side.

"Another fact of life: Eagles are *pursuit* craft. They are designed to shoot down *bombers*. The *Falcons* are supposed to shoot down fighters; that's why we have lochoi of the buggers flying cap-cover for us. You will *not* engage enemy fighters except defensively, and then only if you can't run, which should be easy, seeing as the Domination has gone to the trouble of giving you the fastest aircraft on earth. I see anyone glory-hunting"—his seamed face jutted forward, one half a pattern of scars, the other smooth—"I goin' to see that he *suffer*. Understood?"

"Sir, yes *sir!*" the lochos replied.

The cockpit smelled of rubber, oil, and old sweat. Johanna wiggled her shoulders in the straps and folded the seat back into the semi-reclining position that helped you take g-force without blacking out.

Her hand moved the stick, feet pumped the pedals; she glanced back over one shoulder to check the flaps and rudder, and the flipped-up visor of her bonedome went *clack* against the metal rim of the seat. The synthetic of the face mask rested cool and clammy against her cheeks, and sounds came muted through the headphones of her helmet, even the start-up roar of engines. That faded again as she gave a thumbs-up to the ground crew and the bubble canopy slid down over her head.

Training sent hands and eyes in a final check over the instrument panel: gyrosight, fuel, oil pressure, RPM, pitch control. Static buzz and click in her ears, sound-offs as each plane called go-condition, her own voice like a stranger's.

"Green board, von Shrakenberg" she said.

The override call of the control center came through: "Lochos cleared, two and four, Merarch. Next ten minutes."

Her fingers touched the throttles, and the *Lover's Bite* rolled out of the revetment and onto the holding strip. She moistened her lips in the cool, rubber-tasting air flowing from the mask, and touched the shoulder pocket of her flight suit that held Tom's picture. They had exchanged special photographs, cased in plastic with a lock of hair: two "Knights of the Air" going into battle with their lover's favor on their sleeve.

Policy let spouses or fiances serve in the same unit if they chose, but suddenly she was glad they had decided against it; he could spend the next few years in safe boredom, deterring the Japanese in China. There would be no war with Nippon, not now; the Domination would let the Americans pour out blood and treasure to break the island empire's strength, then leave the Yankees holding a few South Sea isles while the Draka snapped up Japan's rich Asian provinces.

She saw him, sharply: broad freckled face and hazel eyes cold with that ironic humor; wide thin-lipped mouth, stocky muscled body fitting so comfortably against hers . . . They had settled the future. A land grant in Italy, Tuscany by preference, Pa could probably swing that, and there were plenty of nice villas that could be renovated easily enough. Children, of course: four, that was enough to do one's duty by the Race. Breeding horses, dabbling in estate-bottled premium wine, snapping up a surplus light transport so they could fly over to Alexandria for big-city amusements now and then.

She smiled more widely and touched the pocket on the other shoulder. Rahksan had presented her with a favor, too: a silk handkerchief, with a lock of her hair and an inked pawprint from Omar, Johanna's cat—"Jist t' get us awl in theyah, Jo' darlin'." Johanna sighed: it was good to have that gentle and undemanding affection to hand, and Rahksan would make a good nursemaid, she was marvelous with children.

Oh, what a happy little Draka I shall be, she thought mordantly. *If I survive—so stop woolgathering, woman!*

The planes of the 211th Lochos taxied in file down the approach lane; an orange-uniformed flight launcher waited with signal paddles in hand to key them on to the takeoff runway. Engine roar rose to a grating howl as the dozen Eagles boosted their craft from idle. Her turn came; she glanced across at her wingman, young de Grange, and gave a clenched-fist salute. He answered with exaggerated decisiveness.

Natural, she thought. A newbie—this was only his second combat mission. In air-to-air combat the minority of veterans did most of the killing, the novices most of the dying. Unfair, like life. The solution was to *win*; and as the old saying went, if you couldn't win, *cheat*.

She pressed the throttles forward, props biting the air at coarse pitch, then released the brakes. Acceleration pushed her back into the padding of the seat; the tailwheel came up; the controls went light as the *Lover's Bite* left the earth, with a tiny slip-sway as her hand firmed on the stick.

Formation came automatically, a tight box of pairs here in the crowded airspace over Kars. The airfields were laid out in circles, neat as a map beneath her as she gained altitude: rings of silver thousand-foot transport dirigibles; rows of six-engined Helot cargo planes, like boxes with great slab wings; rank after rank of Rhino ground-strike craft, shuttling back and forth at low altitude to the front. And the vehicle parks of the armored legions, huge blunt wedges stacked beside the roads, flat beetle shapes of the tanks and infantry carriers, flashes as their heavy self-propelled guns fired, tasked to support the Janissary units in contact with the enemy.

The Eagles climbed, clawing at the thin air with whining turbochargers, through a layer of cirrus clouds into a high brightness under a sky that seemed ready to bleed lapis lazuli as the props sliced it. Four thousand meters altitude, and the front was invisible as they passed, only a ragged pattern of explosions pale in the bright sunlight, lines and clumps that must indicate Fritz strongpoints, fading to scatterings on road junctions behind the lines. Columns of smoke rose, black pillars fraying at their tops, brutal and emphatic in the cool pastels of the upper air. Ahead were the mountains, through the clouds and ringed by them, snow-peaked islands lapped by fleece-surf and patches of darkness where earth showed through.

Johanna waggled her craft and her wingman closed up with a guilty spurt of acceleration. The lochos had spread out into the loose pairs-of-pairs formation that was most effective for combat, and she began a constant all-around scan. That was the reason pilots wore silk scarves, to prevent chafing; not derring-do, but survival. The electrodetectors in the dirigible warning and control craft hovering south of the mountains were supposed to pick up enemy aircraft long before visual contact, but electrodetection was in its infancy. You could still get jumped . . .

Minutes stretched. She concentrated on her breathing, keying into the state of untense alertness that kept you alive. If you let your glands pump adrenaline into the bloodstream you could end up wringing wet and exhausted in minutes, even standing still. They reached cruising altitude at six thousand meters and crossed the mountain peaks; there was less cloud cover north of the Caucasus, a clear view of forested slopes rippling down to an endless steppe, bright-green squares of young grass and coal-black ploughland. And . . .

"Target," the Merarch's voice spoke in her ears. "Three o'clock; Stukas. Follow me."

Christ, he's got good eyes, she thought, tilting her craft to scan down and to the right. Black dots crawling north; they must be hedgehopping to avoid detection, moving up to support the Fritz units trying to clear the passes, or even hoping to cross the mountains. Smoothly, the lochos peeled off and began a power dive toward their prey.

Her hands moved on the controls, and the *Lover's Bite* banked, turned, fell. There was a moment of weightlessness while the world swung about her, then a giant soft hand lifting and pushing. Her own gloved palm rammed the throttles forward, and the engines answered with a banshee shriek. They were diving head-on toward the Germans, a three-thousand-meter swoop that closed at the combined speed of the two formations. Acceleration pushed her back into the padding of the seat; she could feel it stretching the tissues of her face, spreading lips into a death's-head grin beneath her face mask. The airplane began to buck and rattle, the stick quivering and then shuddering in her hand.

Mach limit, she thought, easing back slightly on the throttles until the hammer blows of air driven to solidity died down to a bearable thrumming. Air compression just under the speed of sound could break an aircraft apart or freeze the controls. They were closing fast now, altimeter unreeling in a blur, the Germans turning from specks to shapes. Stuka dive bombers, single-engined craft with the unmistakable "cranked" gull wing and spatted undercarriage. Johanna's thumb flicked back the cover over the firing button on the head of her joystick, and the gyrosight automatically projected a circle on the windscreen ahead of her. *Dream target,* went through her gleefully. Only a single rear-mounted machine gun for defensive armament, slow, unhandy.

Less than a thousand meters, and the Germans spotted the Draka fighters stooping out of the sun and scattered, their formation breaking apart like beads of mercury on glass, diving to hug the ground even more closely. Johanna braced and pulled back on the stick, gray creeping in at the edges of sight as the g-force mounted. The black wings grew, filling the center ring of the gunsight, then overlapping the outer circle. Time slowed; her thumb came down on the firing button as the Stuka's fuselage touched the outer rim. The aircraft were closing at well over seven hundred KPH; the burst was on target for barely four-tenths of a second. Beneath her the revolver-breeches of the cannon whirled, and two hundred shells hosed out as her thumb tapped the button; more than half of them struck.

The Stuka exploded in a globe of orange light, folded in half and tumbled to leave a burning smear on the ground a hundred meters below, all at once. The shock wave slapped the Draka Eagle upwards, even as Johanna pulled back on the stick, rolling up in an Immelman and trading speed for height.

"*Ngi dHa!*" she shouted the old triumph cry her ancestors had borrowed from the tribes they overran: *I have eaten.* The sudden jolt of exultation ran belly-deep, raw and primitive.

"Warning." The voice cut through the static and chatter on the lochos circuit, cool and distant; from the control dirigible south of the mountains. "Hostiles approaching from northeast your position, altitude ten thousand meters. Speed indicates fighters, estimated intercept, two minutes." Johanna could feel the excitement wash out of her in a wave, replaced by a prickling coldness that tasted of copper and salt. She worked pedals and stick, snapped the *Lover's Bite* back level, scanned about. Most of the Stukas were splotches of black smoke and orange flame on the rumpled landscape below, the Eagles were scattered to the limits of visibility and beyond, and her wingman was nowhere to be seen.

"*Shit!*" That was Merarch Anders. She could imagine what was running through his mind; height and speed were interchangeable, and the Fritz had too much. Too much for the Draka to run for it.

"Anders, control. *Where are our Falcons?*"

"Sorry, Merarch: diverted on priority."

The lochos commander wasted no time on complaints. "Form on me, prepare for climb," he said. "One pass through them, then we turn and head south."

Johanna closed in, climbing, and keyed her microphone. "De Grange, close up. *De Grange!*"

"I've almost got him—"

"*Leave the fucking rabbit and close up!*"

"Yessir . . . ah . . . where are you?"

She could imagine his sudden frightened glance around a sky empty of motion. "Look for the *smoke plumes*, de Grange." She switched to lochos frequency. "Merarch, my wingman's got himself out of visual."

"He'll have to find his own way home. Radio silence."

The lochos climbed steeply, clawing for altitude as they drove northeast to meet the approaching Germans. A head-on passing engagement was quick, and would leave the Draka above their opponents, able to turn and head for home. *If we live*, Johanna thought, moistening her lips as she flipped down the sun visor of her helmet and squinted into the brightness ahead: pale blue sky and white haze and the sun like a blinding tic at the corner of her eye. The insides of her gloves were wet, and she worked the fingers limber around the molded grip of the joystick.

"One minute." The voice of the controller sounded, olympian and distant; Johanna felt a moment's fierce resentment that faded into the blank intensity of concentration. Nothing . . . then a line of black dots. Growing, details; single-engine fighters. Large canopies set well back, long cylindrical noses. Focke-Wulf 190s, the best the Germans had.

Oh, joy, she thought sardonically, picking her target. This would be a celestial game of chicken, with whoever banked first vulnerable. The oncoming line seemed to swell more swiftly, speed becoming visible as the range closed. Hands and feet moved on pedals and stick, feedback making the Eagle an extension of her body. Like *another* body: she had seen a barracuda once, spear-fishing along a reef off Ceylon, on a summer's holiday with a schoolfriend; hung entranced in the sapphire water, meeting an eye black and empty and colder than the moon.

A living knife, honed by a million years of evolution. Here she had that, the power and the *purity* of it . . .

The Focke-Wulf was closing. Closing. Toy-model size, normal, huge, filling the windscreen—the crazy fucker's not turning *now*.

Her thumb clamped the firing button just as lights sparkled along the wingroot firing ports of the Focke-Wulf. Fist-blow of recoil, like a sudden headwind for a fractional second, and a multiple *punk-tinggg* as something high-velocity struck the Draka aircraft's armor. Then she was banking right as the German flipped left; they passed belly-to-belly and wings pointing to earth and sky, so close that they would have collided had the landing gear been down.

A quick glimpse into the overhead mirror showed the German going in. Not burning, but half his rudder was missing. Johanna flipped the Eagle back onto the level with a smile that turned to a snarl as a red temperature warning light began to flicker and buzz on the control panel. Her hand reached for the switches, but before she could complete the movement a flare of light caught at the corner of her right eye. A rending *bang* and she felt the *Lover's Bite* shake, pitched on her side and dove for the earth six thousand meters below in a long spiral, trailing smoke from the port engine nacelle; more than smoke, there were flames licking from ruptured fuel lines; a sudden barrage of piston heads and connectors hammered the side of the cockpit as the roar of a functioning engine abruptly changed to the brief shriek of high-tensile steel distorting under intolerable stress.

G-force worse than the pull-out from a power dive pushed Johanna into a corner of the seat, weighing on her chest like a great soft pillow. Will and training forced her hand through air that seemed to have hardened to treacle, feathering the damaged engine and shutting the fuel lines, opening the throttle on the other. *Stamp* on the pedal *left* stick . . . she could almost hear the voice of her instructor, feel the wind rattling the wires of the training biplane: *Recruit, next time you needs three tries to pull out of a spin I'll put us'n into a hill myself to spare the Race the horror of you incompetent genes. . . .*

So you were right, she thought. *You're still a son of a bitch.* The *Lover's Bite* came out of the spin, straight and level. Also horribly slow and sluggish, and she had to keep the stick over . . .

"Mayday." Her voice was a harsh blur in her own ears. "Mayday, engine out, altitude—" She blinked out the cockpit at muddy fields grown horribly close, unbelievably fast. "—three thousand." A glance at the board. "B engine running, losing hydraulics slowly, fuel fast."

"Acknowledged." The Merarch's voice was steady, calming. "Run for it, we'll cover as long as we can." A pause. "And your stray duck de Grange is back."

"Acknowledged," she answered shortly. Mind and body were busy with the limping, shuddering aircraft. For a moment sheer irritation overrode all other feeling; the effortless power and response of the Eagle had become part of her life, and this limping parody was like a rebellion of her own muscles and nerves. Her eyes flicked to the gauges. Hydraulic pressure dropping steadily; that meant multiple ruptures somewhere. The controls were growing soft, mushy; she had to overcorrect and then correct again. A glance at the ruined engine: still burning, fuel must be getting through somehow, and the gauge was dropping as if both engines were running on maximum boost. And—

The Focke-Wulf dove from over her left shoulder. Reflex made her try to snap the Eagle aside, and the unbalanced thrust of the single engine sent the aircraft into the beginnings of another flat spin that carried her six hundred meters closer to the ground. Cannon shells hammered into the rear fuselage; then the *Lover's Bite* pitched forward in the shockwave of an explosion. Pieces of the German fighter pitched groundward, burning; another Draka Eagle swooped by, looped and throttled back to fly wing-to-wing, the pilot giving her a thumbs-up signal. He was as impersonal as a machine in bonedome, dark visor and face mask, but she could imagine the cocky grin on de Grange's freckled face.

"Thanks," she said. "Now get back upstairs."

"Hell—"

"That's an *order*, Galahad! If I want a knight-errant, I'll send to Hollywood."

Reluctantly, he peeled off and climbed. She fought down a feeling of loneliness; an Eagle had the advantage in a diving attack on a Focke-Wulf, but in a low-and-slow dogfight the smaller turning radius of a single-engine fighter made it a dangerous opponent.

Until then emergency had kept her focused, consciousness narrowed down to the bright point of concentration. Now she drew a ragged breath and looked about. More smoke and fire trailed from the right engine, and she could smell somewhere the raw stink of high-octane fuel. That was bad, fuel didn't explode until it mixed with air . . . Ahead and high above shone the peaks of the Caucasus; *very* high, she must be at no more than two thousand meters. A push at the stiff joystick and the plane responded, slowly, oh so slowly. Still losing pressure from the hydraulics; it was a choice between the controls freezing up, midair explosion, and the last of the fuel coughing through the injectors. As for clearing the mountains, even through one of the passes, as much chance of that as of flying to the moon by putting her head between her knees and spitting hard.

But I'm *me*, something gibbered in the back of her mind. I'm only twenty, I can't die, not *yet*. Images flashed through her mind: Tom, Eric, Rahksan, her mother's body laid out in the chapel, Oakenwald . . . her father giving her a switching when she was seven, for sticking one of the housemaids with a pin in a tantrum. "You will use power with restraint and thrift, because your ancestors bought it with blood and pain. The price is high; remember that, when it comes your turn to pay."

"Dying, hell," she said. "Damned if I'm going to do that until I'm fuckin' *dead*." Her hand reached to hammer at the release catch of the canopy. Jammed: she flipped up a cover on the control panel and flicked the switch beneath that should have fired the explosive bolts.

"No joy," she muttered, then looked down sharply. Fuel was seeping into the cockpit, wetting the soles of her boots. *"Shit!"* A touch keyed the microphone. "Merarch, she's a mess, no hope of getting her home."

"Bail out. We've seen those Fritzes off, we'll cover you."

"Can't. Cockpit cover's jammed, I think part of the engine hit it. I'll have to ride her in." There was a moment's silence filled with static buzz and click. "I'll see if I can shoot out the catch, then make it to our lines on foot. Got my 'passport,' anyway." That was the cyanide pill they all carried; Draka did not surrender and were not taken alive.

"Right . . . good-bye."

The other voice murmured a farewell; high above, she could see the silver shapes turning and making for the south. Johanna set her teeth and forced her eyes to the terrain ahead, easing back on the throttle. If the fuel lines were intact it would have been better to fly the *Lover's Bite* empty, less risk of fire, but by then the stuff would be sloshing around her feet. Easy . . . the plain was humping itself up into foothills, isolated swells rising out of the dead-flat squares of cultivation. All the arrangements had been made: updated letters to Tom and Eric and her father, a new home for her cat Omar, a friend who had promised to see Rahksan safely back to Oakenwald, and Pa would see her right. Patches of forest among the fields now, the blackened snags of a ruined village, a rutted road . . . almighty Thor, it was going by fast; speed that had seemed a crawl in the upper air becoming a blurring rush as she dropped below a hundred meters.

Slow down. Throttle back again, flaps down, just above stalling speed. Floating . . . *up* over that damned windbreak, White Christ she's hardly responding at all . . . good, meadow, white-and-black cows scattering . . . floating, nose up and—

Slam, the belly hit, rending scream of duralumin ripping, pinwheeling, body flung forward in the harness, something struck her head . . .

Blackness.

Chapter Thirteen

Archstrategos Karl von Shrakenberg leaned his palms on the railing and stared down at the projacmap of Operations Command. Steel shutters rose noiselessly behind him, covering the glass wall and darkening the room, to increase the contrast of the glass surface that filled the pit beneath them. That white glow underlit the faces of the ten *Archstrategoi* spaced around the map, pale ovals hanging suspended, the flat black of their uniforms fading into the darkness beyond, the more so as few of them wore even the campaign ribbons to which they were entitled. Scattered brightwork glowed in soft gold stars against that background: here a thumb ring, there the three gold earrings that were the sole affectation of the Dominarch, the Chief of the Supreme General Staff.

Ghosts, jeered a mordant shadow at the back of Karl's mind. *Hovering over a world we cannot touch directly.* Below them the unit counters moved, Draka forces crowding against the shrinking German bridgeheads south of the Caucasus, pushing them back toward the blocking positions of the airborne Legions at their rear.

Ghosts and dreams, he thought. *We stand here and think we command the world; we're lords of symbol, masters of numbers, abstractions.* So antiseptic, so cool, so rational . . . and completely out of their hands, unless disaster struck. Twenty years they had planned and trained; worked and argued and sweated; moved millions of lives across the game board of the world. *Or does the world dream us? Are we the wolf-thought-inescapable that puts a face on their fear?*

Karl looked around at the faces: his contemporaries, colleagues—his friends, if shared thoughts and work and belief were what made friendship. Quiet well-kept men in their middle years, the sort who were moderate in their vices, popular with their grandchildren, whose spare time was spent strolling in the park or at rock-meditation. When they killed it was with nod or signature, and a detachment so complete it was as empty of cruelty as of pity.

For a moment he blinked: a fragment of song went through his mind, a popular thing, how did it . . .

"Frightened of this thing that I've become . . ."

And yet we were young men once. Karl looked across at John Erikssen, the Dominarch. His head was turned, talking to his aide, young Carstairs. *Ha. I must be nodding to my end—she's forty and I think of her as "young."* John and he had been junior officers together in the Great War. He remembered . . .

The shell hole. Outside Smyrna: winter, glistening gray mud under gray sky, stinking with month-old bits of corpse. Cold mud closing about him, flowing rancid into his gasping mouth, the huge weight of the Turk on his chest. The curved dagger coming down, straining millimeter by millimeter closer to his face as his grip on the other man's wrist weakened, and he would lie there forever among the scraps of bone and rusty barbed wire . . . There had been a sound like the *thock* of a polo mallet hitting a wooden ball, and the Turk had gone rigid; another crunch, softer, and his eyes had widened and rolled and Karl rose, pushing the corpse aside. John had stood looking at the shattered buttplate of his rifle, murmuring, "Hard head. *Hard* head."

Now, that was real, the elder von Shrakenberg mused. The hands remembered, the *skin* did, as they did the silky feel of his firstborn's hair when he lifted him from the midwife's arms. John had stood godfather, to a son Karl named for him.

But the cobra of ambition had bitten them both deeply, even then. That was back when there was still juice in it, the wine of power, every victory a new birth and every promotion a victory. He had commanded a merarchy of warcars later in the Great War, Mesopotamia and Persia. Clumsy things by modern standards; riveted plates and spoked wheels and steam-powered, as only civilian vehicles and transport were today. Sleek and deadly efficient in their time . . .

Power exercised through others, men and machines as the extensions of his Will; the competition of excellence, showing his skill. Scouting for the Archonal Guard legion, vanguard of Tull's V Army as it snapped at the heels of the retreating enemy. They had caught the Ottoman column by surprise on a plain of blinding-white alkali, swinging around through *erg* and dry wadi beds. For a quarter-hour while the rest of the unit came up they had watched the enemy pass beneath them, dark men in ragged earth-brown uniforms. Ambulance carts piled with the wounded; soldiers dropping to lie with cracked and bleeding lips; the endless weary shuffle of the broken regiments, and the stink of death.

The gatlings had fired until the turrets were ovens, the floors of the warcars covered in spent brass that glittered and shifted underfoot, the crews choking on cordite and scorched metal. That was when he had burnt his hand, reaching down to the gunner who sat slack-faced, hands still gripping the triggers as the pneumatics hissed and drove the empty barrels through their whirring circle. He had not felt the pain, not then, his mind's eye seeing over and over again the ranks dropping in the storm of tracer, tumbled, layered in drifts that moaned and stirred; afterward silence, the sough of wind, bitter dust, and steam.

There had been nothing for John's truck-born infantry to do but collect ears and bayonet the wounded.

The stink, the stink . . . they had gotten very thoroughly drunk that night, with the main body there to relieve the vanguard. Drunk and howling bad poetry and staggering off to vomit in the shadows. A step further, and another.

He had transferred to the Air Corps, valuable experience for one slated for Staff. The last great dirigible raid on Constantinople: Karl von Shrakenberg had been on the bridge of the *Loki* in the third wave, coming in at five thousand meters over the Golden Horn to release her biplane fighters while the bombardment ships passed below. The airship was three hundred meters long, a huge fragile thing of braced alloy sheeting; it had trembled in the volcanic updrafts from the tracks of fire across the city spread out below them like a map, burning from horizon to horizon, the beginnings of the world's firestorm. Traceries of flame over the hills, bending like the heads of desert flowers after spring rain. Streets and rivers of fire, casting ruddy blurs on the underside of soot-black cloud; heat that made the whole huge fabric of the airship creak and pop above him as it expanded. Diesel oil and burning and the acrid smell of men whose bodies sweated out the fear their minds suppressed.

He had been calm, he remembered; yet ready to weep, or to laugh. Almost lightheaded, exalted: a godlike feeling; he was a sky god, a war god. Searchlights like white sabers, cannon fire as bright magenta bursts against the darkening sky where no stars shone, muzzle flashes from the antiairship batteries of the Austrian battlewagons at anchor below. The great dome of the Hagia Sophia shining, then crumbling, Justinian's Church of Holy Wisdom falling into the fire. He had watched with a horror that flowed and mingled with delight at the beauty of that single image, the apotheosis of a thousand years. The ancient words had come of their own volition:

"Who rends the fortified cities
    As the rushing passage of time
    Rends cheap cloth . . ."

Other voices—"Prepare for drop—superheat off—stand by to valve gas!" "Dorsal turret three, fighters two o'clock." A new shuddering hammer as the chin-turret pom-pom cut loose. "Where're the escorts—that's Wotan, she's hit."

The ship ahead of them had staggered in the sky, a long smooth metal-clad teardrop speckled with the flickers of her defensive armament. Then the second salvo of five-inch shells had struck, punched through cloth-thin metal, into the gas cells. Hull plating blew out along the lines of the seams; four huge jets of flame vomited from the main valves along the upper surface, and then enough air mixed with the escaping hydrogen to ignite; or it might have been the bomb load, or both. For a moment there was no night, only a white light that seared through eyelids and upflung hand. The *Loki* had been slammed upright on her tail, pitched forward; he could recall the captain screaming orders, the helmsmen cursing and praying as they wrestled with the man-high rudder wheels . . .

One moment a god, the next a cripple, the general thought, shaking himself back to the present. Men told him he had been the only bridge officer to survive the shellburst that struck in the next instant; that he had stood and conned the crippled airship with one hand holding a pressure bandage to his mangled thigh. He had never been able to recall it; the next conscious memory had been of the hospital in Crete, two heads bending over his leg. A serf nurse, careful brown hands soaking and clipping to remove the field dressing. And the doctor, Mary, looking up with that quick birdlike tilt of the head when his stirring told her he was awake. Fever-blur, and the hand on his forehead.

"You'll live, soldier," she had said. She had smiled, and it wiped the exhaustion from her eyes. "And walk, that's all I promise."

And that too was power, Karl von Shrakenberg thought, looking around at his fellow commanders. *Strange that I never minded being helpless with her.*

He flexed his hands on the smooth wood. He must be getting old, if the past seemed more real than the present. Time to retire, perhaps; he was just sixty, old for active service in the Domination's forces, even at headquarters.

"Well." Karl was almost startled to hear the Chief of Staff speak in a normal voice, overriding the quiet buzz and click of equipment and sigh of ventilators. He nodded at the map. "Seems to be going as well as can be expected."

The German fronts were receding, marked by lines like the tide-wrack of an ocean in retreat from the shore. *And Eric behind to stop an armed tide with his flesh,* Karl thought. *I wish there were gods that I could pray for you, my son. But there is only what we have in ourselves; no father in the sky to pick you up and heal your hurts. I knew, Eric, I knew that someday you would have nothing but yourself; we ask the impossible of ourselves and must demand it of our children.* Harshness was necessary, sometimes, but . . . *Live, my son. Conquer and live.*

The Dominarch turned to his aide. "Appraisal."

That woman frowned meditatively. "Second Legion can't hold until we break through. Their bridgehead is contiguous but shrinking from both ends . . ." A pause. "Basic reason things're goin' so well with First Legion over on the Ossetian Highway is the situation on the north. Century A of 2nd Cohort is savin' it; they're guardin' the back door."

Erikssen nodded. "Accurate, chiliarch. That's your boy, Karl, isn't it?" The elder von Shrakenberg nodded. "*Damned* good job."

Karl felt a sudden, unfamiliar sensation: a filling of the throat, a hot pressure behind the eyelids. *Tears,* he realized with wonder, even as training forced relaxation on the muscles of neck and throat, covered the swallow with a cough. And remembered Eric as a child, struggling with grim competence through tasks he detested, before he escaped back to those damned books and dreams . . .

"Thank you, sir," he muttered. *Tears. Why tears?*

The Chief of the General Staff looked down at the map again.

"*Damned* good," he murmured. "Better to get both passes, but we have to have one or the other, or this option is off. There's always an attack out of Bulgaria, or an amphibious landing in the Crimea, or even a straight push west around the top of the Caspian, but none of them are anything like as favorable . . ."

The *strategoi* nodded in unconscious agreement. It would not be enough to push the Germans back into Europe; to win the war within acceptable parameters of time and losses they had to bring the bulk of the Nazi armies to battle on the frontiers, close to the Draka bases and far from their sources of supply in Central Europe. The sensible thing for the Germans to do would be to withdraw west of the Pirpet marshes, but Hitler might not let them. The Draka *strategoi* had a lively professional respect for their opposite numbers, and a professional's contempt for the sort of gifted amateur who led the Nazis.

"And not just good, unconventional," the Dominarch said. "Daring . . . Where's that report?" He reached around, and one of the aides handed him the file. "Your boy didn't just freeze and wait for the sledgehammer, which too many do in a defensive position. Interesting use of indigenous assets, too—those Circassians and Russki partisans. That shows a creative mind." A narrow-eyed smile. "That American has Centurion von Shrakenberg travellin' all around Robin Hood's barn for tricks . . ." A hand waved. "Lights, please." The shutters sank with a low hum, and they blinked in the glare of noon.

"With respect, Dominarch . . ." Silence fell, as the beginnings of movement rippled out. An officer of the Security Directorate had spoken; the sleeve of his dark-green uniform bore the cobra badge of the Intervention Squads, the anti-guerilla specialists who worked most closely with the military. "Ah've read the report as well. *Unsound* use of indigenous assets, in our . . . mah opinion. Partisans, scum, savin' effort now at the price of more later. The internal enemy is always the one to be feared, eh?"

Karl leaned his weight on one elbow, looking almost imperceptibly down the beaked von Shrakenberg nose. *An overseer's sense of priorities,* he thought. Aloud: "Most will die. This American seems anxious to remove the survivors; if that is inadvisable, we can liquidate them at leisure."

"Strategos von Shrakenberg, mah Directorate's function is to ensure the security of the State, which cannot be done simply by killing men. We have to kill *hope*, which is considerably moah difficult. *Particularly* when sentimental tolerance fo' rebel-dog Yankee—"

The Dominarch broke in sharply. "That is enough, gentlemen!" Institutional rivalry between the two organizations which bore arms for the State was an old story; there was a social element, as well. The old landholder families of scholar-gentry produced more than their share of the upper officer corps, mostly because their tradition inclined them to seek such careers. While Security favored the new bureaucratic elites that industrialization had produced . . .

"Von Shrakenberg, kindly remember that we are all here to further the destiny of the Race. We are not a numerous people, and *nobody* loves us; we are all Draka—all brothers, all sisters. *Including* our comrades from the Security Directorate; we all have our areas of specialization."

Karl nodded stiffly.

The Dominarch turned to the liaison officer from the secret police. "And Strategos Beauregard, will *you* kindly remember that conquest is a necessary precondition for pacification. Consider that we began as a band of refugees with nothing but a rifle each and the holes in our shoes; less than two centuries, and we *own* a quarter of the human race and the habitable globe. Because we never wavered in our aim; because we were flexible; because we were *patient*. As for the Yankee—" he paused for a grim smile "—as long as they serve our purposes, we'll let his reports through. Right now we need the Americans; let this Dreiser's adventure stories keep them enthralled. Their turn will come, or their children's will; then you can move to the source of the infection. Work and satisfaction enough for us all, then . . . along with the rape and pillage!"

There was an obligatory chuckle at the Chief of Staff's witticism. Erikssen's eyes flicked to Karl's for a moment of silent understanding. *And if those reports make your son something of a hero in the Domination as well, no harm there either, eh, old friend?*

The Dominarch glanced at his watch. "And now, gentlemen, ladies: just to convince ourselves that we're not *really* as useful as udders on a bull, shall we proceed to the meeting on the Far Eastern situation? Ten minutes, please."

The corridor gave on to an arcaded passageway, five meters broad, a floor of glossy brown tile clacked beneath boots, under arches of pale granite. Along the inner wall were plinths bearing war trophies: spears, muskets, lances, Spandau machine guns. The other openings overlooked a terraced slope that fell away to a creek lined with silverleaf trees. Karl von Shrakenberg stood for a long moment and leaned his weight on his cane. Taking in a deep breath that was heady with flowers and wet cypress, releasing it, he could feel the tension of mind relaxing as he stretched himself to *see*. Satori, the condition of *just being*. For a moment he accepted what his eyes gave him, without selection or attention, simply *seeing* without letting his consciousness speak to itself. The moment ended.

The eye that does not seek to see itself, the sword that does not seek to cut itself, he quoted to himself. And then: *What jackdaws we are.* The Draka would destroy Japan some day, he supposed; they saw nothing odd in taking what was useful from the thoughts of her Zen warrior-mystics. *The Scandinavian side of our ancestry coming out,* he thought. *A smorgasbord of philosophies.* Although consistency was a debatable virtue; look what that ice-bitch Naldorssen had done by brooding on Nietzche, perched in that crazy aerie in the High Atlas.

Stop evading, he told himself, turning to the Intelligence officer.

"Well, Sannie?"

Cohortarch Sannie van Reenan held up a narrow sheaf of papers. "A friend of a friend, straight from the developer . . . They did the usual search-and-sweep around the last known position, and they found the plane, or what was left of it." She paused to moisten her lips. "It came in even, in a meadow: landed, skidded, and burned." The scored eagle face of the strategos did not alter, but his fingers clutched on the mahogany ferrule of his cane. "Odd thing, Karl . . . there was a Fritz vehicle about twenty meters from the wreckage, a kubelwagon, *and it was burned, too.* At about the same time, as far as it's possible to tell. Very odd; so they're sticking to *Missing in Action,* not *Missing and Presumed Dead."*

He laughed, a light bitter sound. "Which is perhaps better for her, and no relief to me at all. How selfish we humans can be in our loves." It was not discreditable, strictly speaking, for him to inquire about his daughter's fate; it *would* be, if he made too much of it when his duties to the Race were supposedly filling all time and attention.

The sun was bright, this late-fall morning, and the air cool without chill; sheltered, and lower than the plateau to the south, Archona rarely saw frost before May, and snow only once or twice in a generation. The terraces were brilliant with late flowers, roses and hibiscus in soft carpets of reddish gold, white and bright scarlet. Stairways zigzagged down to the lawns along the river bank, lined with cypress trees like candles of dark green fire. Water glittered and flashed from the creek as it tumbled over polished brown stone; the long narrow leaves of the trees flickered brighter still, the dove gray of the upper side alternating with the almost metallic silver sheen of the under.

"Johanna . . ." he began softly. "Johanna always loved gardens. I remember . . . it was '25; she was about three. We were on holiday in Virconium, for the races; we went to Adelaird's, on the Bluff, for lunch. They've got an enclosed garden there, orchids. Johanna got away from her nurse, we found her there walking down a row going: *pilly flower . . . pilly flower,* snapping them off and pushing them into her hair and dress and . . ." He shrugged, nodding toward the terraces.

"Gardens, horses, poetry, airplanes . . . she was better than I at enjoying things; she told me once it was because I thought about what I thought about them too much. Forty years I've tried for *satori,* and she just fell into it."

You're a complicated man by nature, Pa, she had said, that last parting when she left for her squadron. *You tangle up the simplest things, like Eric, which is why you two always fight; issues be damned. I'm not one who feels driven to rebel against the nature of what is, so we're different enough to get along.* She had seemed so cool and adult, a stranger. Then she had seized him in a sudden fierce hug, right there in the transit station; he had blinked in embarrassment before returning the embrace with one awkward arm. *I love you, Daddy,* whispered into his ear. Then a salute; he had returned it.

"I love you too, daughter." That as she was turning; a quick surprised wheel back and a delighted grin.

"I may be an old fool, Johanna, but not so old I can't learn by my mistakes when a snip of a girl points them out to me." He touched a knuckle to her chin. "You'll do your duty, girl, I know." He frowned for unfamiliar words. "Sometimes I think . . . remember that you have a duty to live, too. Because we need you; the earth might grow weary of the Race and cast us off, if we didn't have the odd one like you."

She had walked up the boarding ramp in a crowd of her comrades, smiling.

And if she had wisdom, surely she inherited it from her mother. He mused, returning to the present. *Eric . . . did I show my daughters more love because my heart didn't seek to make them live my life again for me?*

He jerked his chin toward the brown-clad serfs in the gardens below, weeding and watering and pruning.

"D'you know where they come from, Sannie?" he asked more briskly.

She raised a brow. "Probably born here, Karl. Why?"

"Just a thought on the nature of freedom, and power. I'm one of the . . . oh, fifty or so most powerful men in the Domination; therefore one of the freest on earth, by theory. And they are property, powerless; but I'm not free to spend my life in the place I was born, or cultivate my garden, or see my children grow around me."

She snorted. "Jean-Jacques Rousseau has been dead for a long time, my friend; also, other people's lives always look simpler from the outside, because you can't see the complexities. Would you change places?"

"Of course not," he said with a harsh laugh. "Even retirement will probably drive me mad; and she may not be dead, at all. She's strong, and cunning, and she wants to live very much . . ."

He forced impassiveness. It was not often he could be simply a private person—that was another sacrifice you made for the Race. "Speaking of death, for our four ears: I suspect that headhunter in green would like to do at least one von Shrakenberg an injury and the General Staff through him."

Sannie van Reenan nodded decisively. Keeping track of Skull House's activities was one of the Intelligence Section's responsibilities, after all. "They *don't* like that son of yours, at all. Still less now that he's achieving some degree of success, and by . . . unorthodox means. The headhunters never forget, forgive, or give up on a suspicion; well, it's their job, after all."

The master of Oakenwald tapped his cane on the flags. "Sannie, it might be better if that man Dreiser's articles found a slightly wider audience. In *The Warrior* for instance." That was one of the Army newspapers, the one most popular with enlisted personnel and the junior officer corps. "Unorthodox, again. Things that happen to people in the public view provoke questions, and are thus . . . less likely to happen."

The woman nodded happily. "And Security's going to be overinfluential as it is, after the war. Plenty of work to do in Europe; we'll be working on pacification and getting ready to take the Yanks, which is a two-generation job, at least. Better to give them a gentle reminder that there are *some* things they'd be well advised to leave alone."

Karl looked at his watch. "And more ways of killing a cat than choking it to death with cream. Now, let's get on to that meeting. Carstairs keeps underestimating the difficulties of China, in my opinion . . ."

✧   ✧   ✧

"You've assigned a competent operative?"

"Of course, sir." *How has this fussbudget gotten this high?* the Security Directorate Chiliarch thought, behind a face of polite agreement. *Of course, he's getting old.*

"No action on young von Shrakenberg until *after* we break through to the pass. Then, the situation will be usefully fluid for . . . long enough."

The car hissed quietly through the near-empty streets. The secret-police general looked out on their bright comeliness with longing; a nursemaid sat on a bench, holding aloft a tow-haired baby who giggled and kicked. Her uniform was trim and neat, shining against the basalt stone like her teeth against the healthy brown glow of her skin.

Tired, he thought, pulling down the shade and relaxing into the rich leather-and-cologne smell of the seats. *Tired of planning and worrying, tired of boneheaded aristocrats who think a world-state can be run like a paternalist's plantation.* He glanced aside, into the cool, intelligent eyes of his assistant. They met his for an instant before dropping with casual unconcern to the opened attaché case on his lap. *Tired of your hungry eyes and your endless waiting, my protégé. But not dead yet.*

"The son's the one to watch. The old man will die in the course of nature, soon enough; the General Staff aren't the only ones who know how to wait after all. The daughter's missing in action; besides, she's apolitical. Smart, but no ambition."

"Neither has Eric von Shrakenberg, in practical terms."

"Ah," the older man said softly. "Tim, you should look up from those dossiers sometimes; things aren't so cut and dried as you might think. Human beings are not consistent; nor predictable, until they're dead." *And you will never believe that and so will always fall just short of your ambitions, and never know why.* "Black, romantic Byronic despair is a pose of youth. And war is a great realist, a great teacher." A sigh. "Well, the Fritz may take care of it for us." He tapped the partition that separated them from the driver. "Back to Skull House; autumn is depressing, outdoors."

Chapter Fourteen

VILLAGE ONE, OSSETIAN MILITARY HIGHWAY
APRIL 15, 1942: 0230 HOURS

"Sir." A hand on his shoulder. "Sir."

"Mmmph." Eric blinked awake from a dream where cherry blossoms fell into dark-red hair and sat up, probing for grains of sleep-sand until the warning twinge of his palms forbade; grimacing at the taste in his mouth. He glanced at his watch: 0230, five hours' sleep and better than he could expect. The command section was sleeping in the cellar-cum-bunker he had selected as the HQ: a cube four meters on a side, damp and chilly, but marginally less likely to be overburdened with insect life.

The floor was rock because the earth did not reach this deep, five meters beneath the sloping surface. The walls and arched ceiling were cut-stone blocks, larger and older and better-laid than the stones of the houses above, even though the upper rows were visibly different from the lower. This village was *old*, the upper sections had probably been replaced scores of times, after fire or sack or the sheer wasting of the centuries. The cold air smelled of rock, earth, the root vegetables that had been stored here over the years, and already of unwashed soldier. One wall had a rough doorway knocked through it, with a blanket slung across; a dim blue light spread from the battery lamp someone had spiked to one wall.

Shadows and blue light . . . equipment covered much of the floor: radios, a field telephone with twisted bundles of color-coded wires snaking along the floor and looping from nail to nail along lines driven between the stone blocks. The rest was carpeted in groundsheets and sleeping rolls, now that they had had time to recover their marching packs and bring the last of the supplies down from the gliders, with scavenged Fritz blankets for extra padding. Someone had improvised a rack along one wall to hang rifles and personal gear, strings of grenades, spare ammunition, a folding map table. Somebody else had one of the solid-fuel field stoves going in a corner, adding its chemical and hot-metal odor to the bunker, along with a smell of brewing coffee.

"Thanks," Eric muttered as hands pushed a mug into his hands: Neal, the command-section rocket gunner, a dark-haired, round-faced woman from . . . where was it? Taledar Hill, one of those little cow-and-cotton towns up in the Northmark.

"Patrol's in," she said. He remembered she had a habit of brevity, for which Eric was thankful; waking quickly was an acquired and detested skill for him. He sipped; it was hot, at least. Actually not bad, as coffee; a lot closer to the real thing than ration-issue wine.

McWhirter was awake, over in his corner, back to the wall, head bent in concentration over tiny slivers of paper that his fingers creased and folded into the shapes of birds and animals and men . . . not the hobby Eric would have predicted. A muttering at his feet. Sofie lay curled beneath the planks that supported the static set, headphones clenched in one sleeping hand and head cradled on her backpack, machine pistol hanging by its strap from one corner of the table. A foot protruded, its nails painted shocking pink; he grinned, remembering the disreputable and battered stuffed rabbit he had glimpsed at the bottom of her rucksack. She slept restlessly, with small squirming motions; for a moment her nose twitched and she rubbed her cheek into the fabric.

Now, I wonder . . . he thought. *Have I been avoiding Citizen women because I don't think I'm going to live or is that an excuse not to give any more hostages to fortune?*

He shook his head and turned back to Neal. "So what's it like out there—"

A gloved hand swept the blanket-door aside, letting in a draft of colder air from cellars not warmed by body heat as the command bunker had been. The figure behind was stocky, made more so by the dripping rain poncho and hood; her Holbars was slung muzzle-down, and it clicked against the stone as she leaned her weight on one hand and threw back the hood. She had a square face, tanned and short-nosed, pale blue eyes and irregular teeth in a full smiling mouth, sandy-blond hair plastered wetly to her forehead.

"Sir, it's just such a fuckin' *joy* out there, what with bein' dark laak a coal mine, about six degrees C, an' the gods pissin' down our necks an' branches a'slappin' us in the face, we just naturally cannot *contain* our urge to roll nekkid in th' flowers, laak-so it was Saturday night at the Xanadu in Shahnapur. Sir."

She reached behind her and pulled a native forward by his elbow; the Circassian was young, and unlike most of the villagers his sopping rags were what remained of native garb rather than a European-style outfit. One of the hunters they had been promised . . . painfully thin, huge dark eyes hollowed in a face that quivered and chattered its teeth with the cold. Then the eyes bulged at the sight of Sofie Nixon sitting up naked to the waist and lighting a cigarette.

"An' this-here's one of you tame ragheads. Says laak he's heard somethin'."

Eric yawned, stretched, snapped his fingers to attract the man's attention. "You saw the graycoats?" To Neal, in English "I think Monitor Huff could use a cup, too, trooper."

The Circassian swallowed and bowed awkwardly. "Not saw, lord, but heard. Down below, where the trail crosses the third hill, before the hollow: many of the—" a Slavic-sounding word Eric did not recognize. Tyansha had been the child of Circassians settled in Turkey, descendants of refugees from Russian conquest, chieftains and their followers. The tongue she had taught him was more formal and archaic than the Russian-influenced peasant dialect spoken here.

Eric made a guess. "Steam wagons—carts that go of themselves?"

The Circassian nodded eagerly.

"Yes, lord. Many, many, but not of the ones with the belts of metal that go around and around."

Treads, Eric's mind prompted. "They stopped?"

A quick nod. "Yes, and then the engines became quiet, but there was much talking in the tongue of the Germanski. Perhaps three hundreds, perhaps more." A sniff. "Germanski are always talking, very loud; also they make much noise moving in the woods."

"Do they, now," Eric mused. Then: "McWhirter." The NCO looked up, his hand slowly closing to crush the delicate figure of a flying crane. "My compliments to Einar, and 2nd Tetrarchy ready on the double. *Le jeu commence.*"

Sofie had risen, yawning, and was stamping her feet into her boots to the muttered complaints of nearby sleepers.

"No need to go out in the wet," Eric said. "I'm just taking the 2nd. Einar's sparks can handle it."

"Nah, no problem," she replied, with a shrug and a slight sideways jerk of the head. "Wallis c'n handle this end, we'll need somebody listenin' . . ." She prodded a recumbent figure with a toe. "Hey, skinny, arse to the saddle, ready to paddle."

There was a slight, rueful smile on her face as she turned away to check her weapons and strap an extra waterproof cover on the portable set. *And someone has to look after you, hey?*

Einar Labushange's tetrarchy had drawn the ready-reaction straw that night; most of them had been sleeping with their boots on, in a cellar with a ladder to the surface. Several rolled out of their blankets as he ducked into the cellar, assault rifles ready even before full consciousness. The tetrarchy commander smiled without humor; there were merits to sleeping with your rifle, but he hoped nobody was doing it with the safety off and the selector on full-auto.

"On your feet, gun-bunnies!" The rest woke with a minimum of grumbling, shrugging into their equipment, handing around cups from the coffee urn one of them had prepared and using it to wash down caffeine pills and the inevitable ration bars and *choko*, sweet chocolate with nuts for quick high energy. Being a paratrooper was less comfortable than being in a line unit. Most Citizen Force units had attached serf auxiliaries who handled maintenance and support tasks; the air-assault troops had to do for themselves in the field, but nobody grudged taking their turn. A half-second slowness from lowered blood sugar could kill, and a body needed care to perform at full stretch.

"Right, shitcan the 15," Einar said, and the team with the heavy machine gun gratefully let it drop back onto the tripod they had been preparing to disassemble. The soldiers were shadows in the dim gleam of a looted kerosene lamp; the light of the flame was soft, blurring through dusty air full of the muffled metallic clicks and snaps of gear being readied. "Just one of the rocket guns; other team, hump in the mortar. Oh, and this-here is goin' to be close-in work, just us and some satchelmen from Marie's bunch; black up." The soldiers broke out their sticks of greasepaint.

He turned as Eric ducked through the hole in the wall. With him were five of the combat engineers, the Circassian, his signaler and the two sticks of rifle infantry from the HQ tetrarchy. The dripping form of Monitor Huff followed, moving over to rejoin her lochos.

"Also, it rainin'," he added, breaking out his slicker and turning it out to the dark-mottled interior: better camouflage at night than the dirt-and-vegetation side. There was a chorus of groans.

Eric threw up a hand and grinned. "Nice to know y'all happy to see me," he said dryly. "Gather round." McWhirter stepped through the ragged "door" and spoke.

"Go with Cohort. Got a good map ref—good enough for a blind shoot."

The Centurion nodded without turning, crouching and spreading a map on the floor. The helmeted heads leaned around, some sitting or kneeling so that the others could see; there were thirty-three troopers in a Draka tetrarchy at full strength, and 2nd tetrarchy had only had three dead and five too hurt to fight. Eric pulled the L-shaped flashlight from his webbing belt, and the fighting knife from his boot to use as a pointer. "Right. Our trusty native guide—" He pointed back over his shoulder with the knife, glanced back and saw the man shivering, then switched briefly to Circassian: *There is coffee and food in the corner; take it, I need you walking.*"

"Our trusty native guide informs me that he heard vehicles. And Fritz voices." The knife moved. "*Here.* See, this valley we're in is shaped like a V down to here. Then it turns right, to the east, and opens out into rolling hill country. Foothills." The point stabbed down. "Right *here*, right where the valley and road turn east, is a *big* hill, more like a small mountain, with low saddles on either side. The road goes east, then loops back west through this valley—and it passes only two klicks north of the big hill, the loop's like a U on its side with the open end pointing west, so. And *that*"—his knife pointed at the large hill—"is where Ali Baba here heard the Fritz trucks."

"Another attack up the valley?"

Eric shook his head. "On a narrow road, over uncleared minefields, in the dark? Besides, they were transport, not fighting vehicles, stopping and disembarking troops." The blade moved again, tracing a path around the shoulder of the hill, then south up the west side of the valley to the mountainside where the paratroops had landed. "*That's* the way they're going to come, and on foot. The natives say this side of the valley is easier: lower slope, more trails, some of which the

Fritz will know since they've been here six months. Then they'll either try to take us from the rear, or wait until their armor arrives tomorrow morning."

"How many, sir?"

Eric shrugged. "No telling; all they can scrape up, if their commander is as smart as I think. There was a regimental *kampgruppe*, about four cohorts' equivalent, down in Pyatigorsk. The Air Corps reported hitting 'em hard—"

"Probably meanin' they pissed on 'em from a great height," someone muttered. Eric frowned at the interruption.

"—and they've been hit since, besides which we've been dropping butterfly mines. Probably lost more vehicles than men." He shrugged. "Anything up to a cohort of infantry, call it four hundred rifles and supporting weapons. It's"—he looked at his watch—"0245, they jumped off at about 0200, they're 'turtles' so, moving on unfamiliar trails in the dark, they're less than a klick into the forest by now. Woods and scrub all the way . . ."

He looked up, face grim. "They're counting on us not knowing the lie of the land. We have guides who *do*, better than the Fritz. That's worse than Congo jungle out there; so we go straight down the road, then deke left into the woods and onto the trails. We'll split up into sections and sticks, lie up, hit, run, hit them again, then it's 'mind in gear, arse to rear.'"

"Sir?" That was one of the troopers at the back, a gangling, freckled young man with his hands looped up to dangle casually over the light machine gun lying across his neck and shoulders. "Ah . . . this means, you saying, that we're goin' out on account of these Fritz?" Eric nodded, and the soldier grinned beatifically.

"Brothers an' Sisters of the Race!" he cried in mock ecstasy. "These are *great times*. Do you realize what this means?" He paused for effect. "For once—just like we always dreamed in Basic—just this one time in our young nearly-maggot-recruit lives, bros, we gets a chance to *kill* the sumbitch donkeyfuckahs that're roustin' us out of bed in the middle of the fuckin' night!"

The voices of the tetrarchy lifted, something halfway between laughter and a baying cheer. Eric waved his followers to silence, fighting to keep down his own smile; fighting a sudden unexpected prickling in the eyes as well. These were no unblooded amateurs; they knew the sort of blindfolded butchery he was leading them into, and trusted that it was necessary, trusted him to get as many out as could be . . . and god *damn* but nobody could say the Draka were cowards, whatever their other vices!

Behind him, Senior Decurion McWhirter stroked the ceramic honing stick one last time down the edge of his Jamieson semi-bowie and then slid it back into the hilt-down quick-draw sheath on his left shoulder. He remembered cheers like that . . . long ago. So long ago, with his friends. Where were his friends? Where . . . He jerked his mind from the train of thought; he was good at turning his mind away from things. Sometimes it squirmed in his grasp, like a throat or a woman, and he had to squeeze tighter. Someday he would squeeze too tight and kill it, and then . . . think about something else. The Centurion was talking.

Eric jerked his thumb southwards. "Look, no speeches, I'm not going to quote that woo-woo Naldorssen at you. The rest of the Legion and our Eagle are up there across the pass, holding off ten times their number; there is a *world* of hurt coming down there, people. We've gotten off lucky because most of the *Liebstandarte* are south of the mountains, and Century A's given them a bloody nose cheap twice, because we caught them on the hop—well, what're the Airborne for? Tomorrow they'll hit us with everything and keep coming; think how we'd do it if it was our friends trapped behind this pass, eh? These aren't Draka, but they aren't gutless woppos or brainless Abduls, either. They're trying to flank us tonight; if it works we're sausage meat and the rest of our Legion gets it from behind. Hurt them, people; hurt them *bad*, it's our last chance before the crunch. Then come back walking. Bare is back without brother to guard it."

He nodded to Einar. "Now let's *do* it, let's *go*."

The tetrarchy commander hesitated a moment on the pole ladder. "Yo realize, sir, it's not really needful to have the Century commander along. Or, ah, maybe we could make it a two-tetrarchy operation?"

Eric smiled and signed him onward. "You're from Windhaven, eh, Einar?" The other man nodded, seized by a sudden fierce nostalgia for the bleak desert country south of Angola: silver-colored grass, hot wind off sandstone pinnacles, dawn turned rose-red . . .

The Centurion continued: "You've trained in forest; I *grew up* in wet mountains covered with trees. Never sacrifice an edge . . . we're taking one tetrarchy because if we lose it, the village can still hold out long enough to make a difference. Two, and there wouldn't be enough of us here left to slow them even an hour come dawn, and it's hours that'll count. This is a delaying operation, after all. Now, let's go."

Unnoticed in his corner, the Circassian had started and paused for a second in the process of stuffing the undreamed-of luxury of chocolate into his mouth. Stopped and shivered at the sound of the cheer, swallowing dryly. That reminded him, and he swigged down half a mugful of scalding-hot coffee before taking another bite of the bar. These *Drakanski* were fierce ones, that was certain. Good; then they could protect what they had taken. He expected masters to be fierce, to take the land and the girls and swing the knout on any who opposed them, but it was not often that a *hokotl*, a peasant, had the opportunity to eat like a Party man.

Urra Drakanski, he thought, stuffing bars of chocolate into the pockets of the fine rainproof cape he had been given, and hefting the almost-new Germanski rifle. Powerful masters for all that their women were shameless, masters who would feed a useful servant well: better than the Russki, who had been bad in the White Tzar's time and worse under the Bolsheviki, who beat and starved you and made you listen to their godless and senseless speeches as well. The Germanski . . . He grinned as he followed the new lords of Circassia up the rough

ladder, conscious of the rifle and the sharp two-edged kindjal strapped
to his thigh. It would be a *pleasure* to meet the Germanski again.

The cold rain beat steadily on the windscreen of the Opel three-
ton truck, drumming on the roof and the canvas cover of the troop
compartment behind. Standartenführer Felix Hoth braced himself in the
swaying cab and folded the map; the shielded light was too dim for
good vision anyway. For a moment he could imagine himself back in
the kitchen of his father's farm in Silesia: on leave last month, with
his younger sister sitting in his lap and the neighbors gathered around,
eating Mutti's strudel at the table by the fire while sleet hissed against
the windows. His bride-to-be playing with one of her blonde braids
as he described the rich estates in the Kuban Valley that would be
granted after the war. Vati had leaned back in the big chair with his
pipe, beaming with pride at his officer son, he who had been a lowly
feldwebel through the Great War . . .

I could never tell them anything, he thought. How could he talk
to civilians about Russia? Reichsführer Himmler was right: those who
bore the burden of cleansing the Aryan race's future *lebensraum* bore
a heavy burden, one that their families at home could not hope to
understand.

Enough. I defend them now. If Germany was defeated, his family
would be serf plantation hands. Or—he had been in Paris in 1940,
doing some of the roistering expected of a soldier on leave. One of
the *Maisons Tolerees* had had a collection of Draka pornography; it
was a minor export of the Domination, which had no morals censorship to speak of. He felt his mind forming images, placing his fiancée
Ingeborg's face on the bodies of the serf girls in the glossy pictures;
of his sister Rosa naked on an auction block in Rhakotis or Shahnapur,
weeping and trying to cover herself with her hands. Or splayed open
under a huge Negro Janissary, black buttocks pumping in rhythm to
her screams . . .

He opened the window and the lever broke under his hand; cold
wet wind slapped his face with an icewater hand that lashed his mind
back to alertness. The convoy was travelling barely faster than a man
could run, with the vehicles' headlights blacked out except for a narrow
strip along the bottom. Thirty trucks, four hundred *panzergrenadiers*,
half his infantry, but he had left the tracked carriers behind. Too noisy
for this work, and besides that they ate petrol. The supply situation
was serious and getting worse: Draka aircraft were ranging as far north
as the Kuban, meeting weakening resistance from a Luftwaffe whose
fighters had to work from bases outside their enemy's operational range.
The oil fields at Maikop were still burning, and the Domination's armor
had taken Baku in the first rush. . . .

It can still come right. Despite his losses so far, shocking as they
were; if he could get this force up on the flank, they could carry the
village in one rush at first light. It would be a difficult march in the
dark, but his men were fresh, and as for the Draka . . . they had no
mechanical transport, no way to get down from the village in time
even if they knew of the attack, which was unlikely in this night of

black rain. He turned his head to look behind. There was little noise: the low whirring of fans ramming air into the steam engines' flash-tube boilers, the slow *shuusss* of hard-tired wheels through the muddy surface of the road; all were drowned in the drumming of rain on the trees and wet fields. Not very much to see, either, no moon and dense overcast.

I can't even see the ground, he thought. *Good.* Not that it was at all likely the Draka would have any sentries here; it was ten kilometers to Village One, in a straight line. It was tangled ground, mostly heavily wooded, and the invaders were strangers here, while the Liebstandarte had been stationed in the area since the collapse of Soviet resistance in Caucasia back in November of '41.

The armor and self-propelled artillery would be moving up later, now that they had paths cleared through those damnable air-sown plastic mines. Everybody would be with them, down to the clerks and bottle washers, everybody who could carry a rifle, with only the communications personnel and walking wounded left in Pyatigorsk. Everything would be in place by dawn.

"It should be . . ." he muttered, risking a quick flick of his light. "Yes, that's it." A ruined building—the Ivans had put up a stand there last year. Nothing much, no heavy weapons; they had simply driven a tank through the thin walls. A suitable clearing; and the trail over the mountain's shoulder started here. He twisted to thrust his arm past the tilt-covered cab of the truck and blinked the light three times.

The paratroop boots hit the pavement with a steady *ruck-ruck-ruck* as 2nd Tetrarchy ran through the steady downpour of rain. It was flat black, clouds and falling water cutting off any ambient light—dark enough that a hand was barely a whitish blur held before the eyes, invisible at arm's length. Equipment rustled and clinked as the Draka moved in their steady tireless lope, rain capes flapping; Eric heard someone stumble, then recover with a curse: "Shitfire, it dark as Loki's asshole!"

"Shut the fuck up," an NCO hissed.

The tetrarchy was running down the road in a column four abreast, spaced so that each trooper could guide himself by the comrades on either side, with the outside rank holding to the verge of the crushed-rock surface. There was a knockdown handcart at the rear, with extra ammunition and their two native guides, who had collapsed after the first three kilometers; they were hunters who had lived hard, but their bodies were weakened by bad food and they had never had the careful training in breathing discipline and economical movement that the Citizen class of the Domination received. It was hard work running in the dark; moving blind made the muscles tense in subconscious anticipation, waiting to run into something. The ponchos kept out the worst of the rain, but their legs were slick with thin mud cast up from the rutted surface of the road, and bodies sweated under the water-proof fabric until webbing and uniforms clung and chafed; they were carrying twenty kilos of equipment each, as well. Nothing unbearable, since cross-country running in packs had been a daily routine from childhood and the paratroops were picked troops unusually fit even for Draka.

"Lord . . . lord . . ." one of the Circassians wheezed. Eric whistled softly and the tetrarchy halted with only one or two thumps and muffled *oofs* proclaiming collision. The native rolled off the cart, coughed, retched, then wormed through to the Draka commander.

The Centurion crouched and a circle of troopers gathered, their cloaked forms making a downward-pointing light invisible. The sound of his soldiers' breathing was all around him, and the honest smell of their sweat; they had covered the ten klicks of road faster than horse cavalry could have, in a cold and damp that drained strength and heart—after a day with a paradrop, street combat, hours of the hardest sort of labor digging in, then another battle and barely four hours' sleep. Now there would be more ground to travel, narrow trails through unfamiliar bush, with close-quarter fighting at the end of it . . . only Draka could have done it at all, and even they would be at less than their best. Well, this was war, not a field problem in training. The enemy had been rousted out of bed, too, but they had spent the trip from their base in dry comfort in their trucks; not fair, but that was war, too.

He rested on one knee, breath deep but slow, half regretful that the run was over. You could switch off your mind, running; do nothing but concentrate on muscle and lung and the next step . . .

"Here," the panting local said. "Trail—" he coughed rackingly. "Trail here."

White Christ and Heimdal alone knows how he can tell, Eric thought. *Years of poaching and smuggling, no doubt.* He shone the light on his watch, estimated speed and distance, and fitted them over a map in his mind. Yes, this would be where the road turned east.

"Einar. Straight west, split up and cover the trails. If they're moving troops in any number, they'll probably use all three. Everybody: do *not* get lost in the dark, but if you do, head *upslope* and wait for light if the Fritz are between you and the road. Otherwise back to the road and burn boot up to the village."

The lanky tetrarch shrugged, a troll shape in the darkness. "No wrinkles, we'll kill 'em by the shitload and send 'em back screamin' fo' their mommas." To his troops: "Lochoi A an' B with me, and the mortar. Huff, you take C an' the rocket gun. Hughes, run D up to that little trail on th' ridge. *Go.*"

The troopers sorted themselves into sections and moved off the road, the Circassians in the lead, an occasional watery gleam of light from a flashlight: nobody could be expected to walk over scrub and rock-strewn fields in *this*. Rain hid them quickly, and the woods would begin soon after that. *Dense* woods, with thick undergrowth.

Eric waited by the side of the road as the columns filed past, not speaking, simply standing present while they passed, dim bulks in the chill darkness; a few raised a hand to slap palms as they went by, or touched his shoulder. He replied in kind, with the odd word of the sort they would understand and appreciate, the terse cool slang of their trade and generation: "Stay loose, snake." "Stay healthy for the next war."

The gods would weep, he thought. If they didn't laugh. The only time they could be themselves among themselves, show their human faces to each other, was when they were engaged in slaughter. The Army, especially a combat unit up at the sharp end, was the only place a Draka could experience a society without serf or master; where rank was a functional thing devoted to a common purpose; where cooperation based on trust replaced coercion and fear. *And how we shine, then,* he thought. Why couldn't that courage and unselfish devotion be put to some *use*, instead of being set to digging them deeper into the trap history and their ancestors had landed them in?

At the last, he turned to the command tetrarchy and the satchelmen from the combat engineers.

"Follow me," he said.

Felix Hoth watched the last of his grenadiers vanish into the blackness. This close to the trees the rain was louder, a hissing surf-roar of white noise on a million million leaves, static that covered every sound. The trails would be tunnels through the living mass of vegetation, cramped and awkward—like the tunnels under Moscow. *Blackness like cloth on his eyeballs, crawling on knees and elbows through the filthy water, a rope trailing from his waist and a pistol on a lanyard around his neck . . .* He jerked his mind back from the image, consciously forcing his breath to slow from its panting, forcing down the overwhelming longing for a drink that accompanied the dreams. Daydreams, sometimes, the mind returning to them as the tongue would obsessively probe a ragged tooth, until it was swollen and sore. But Moscow, that was more than six months gone, and the men who had fought him were dead. He would kill the dreams, as he had killed *them*—shot, suffocated, gassed, or burned in the sewers and subways of the Russian capital. *This* battle would be fought in the open, as God had meant men to fight.

And this time he would win. The troops he had sent into the woods were heavily burdened, but they were young and fit; they would be in place on the slopes overlooking Village One by dawn, plentifully equipped with mortars and automatic weapons, and the best of his snipers with scope-sighted rifles. The Draka in the village would be pinned down, there were simply not *enough* of them to hold a longer perimeter. The other pass, the Georgian Military Highway, was nearly clear. He had had radio contact with the units over the mountains. They were pressing the Draka paratroops back through the burning ruins of Kutasi; they were taking monstrous casualties, but inflicting hurts, too, on an enemy cut off from reinforcement. The Janissaries were at their rear, but once in the narrow approaches over the mountains, they could hold the Draka forever. Perhaps negotiate a peace; the Domination was known to be cold-bloodedly realistic about cutting its losses.

The trucks had laagered in the clearing, engines silent. The air smelled overwhelmingly of wet earth, a yeasty odor that overrode burnt fuel and metal. Only the drivers remained, mostly huddled in their cabs, a platoon of infantry beneath the vehicles for guards, and the radio operator. The bulk of the regiment would be here in a few hours; pause here to regroup and refuel, then deploy for action. Wehrmacht units were following, hampered by the hammering the road and rail nets were taking, but force-marching nonetheless. He would roll over Village One, and they would stop the Draka serpent.

"We must," he muttered.

"Sir?" That was his regimental chief of staff, Schmidt.

"We must win," Hoth replied. "If we don't, our cities will burn, and our books. A hundred years from now, German will be a tongue for slaves; only scholars will read it—Draka scholars."

"I wonder . . ."

"What?" The SS commander turned his light so that the other's face was visible; the wavering gray light through the wet glass of the torch made it ghastly, but the black circles under the eyes were genuine. There had been little sleep for Schmidt these past twenty hours: too much work, and far too much thought.

"Wonder about Poles having this conversation in 1939, or Russians last year," Schmidt said, exhaustion bringing out the slurred Alsatian vowels. "They had to hold, everything depended on it. But they didn't hold."

"They were our racial inferiors! The Draka are Aryans like us; that is why they are a threat! The Leader himself has said so."

Schmidt looked at him with an odd smile. "The Draka aristocrats are Nordic, yes, Herr Standartenführer. But they are a thin layer; most of the Domination's people are Africans or Asians. Most even of their soldiers and bureaucrats, at the everyday level: blacks, mulattoes, Eastern Jews, Arab Semites, Turks, Chinese. A real *schwarm*. Would that not be an irony? We National Socialists set out to cleanse Europe of *juden* and slavs and gypsies, and it ends with the home of the white race being ruled and mongrelized by chinks and kikes and Congo savages—" He laughed, an unpleasant, reedy sound.

"*Silence!*" Hoth snapped. The other man drew himself up, his eyes losing their glaze. "Schmidt, you have been a comrade in arms, and are under great stress; I will therefore forget this . . . defeatist obscenity. Once! Once more, and I will myself report you to the Security Service!"

Schmidt swallowed and rubbed his hands across his face, turning away. Hoth forced himself back to calm; he would need a clear head.

And after all the man's from Alsace—he's an intellectual, and a Catholic, he thought excusingly. A good fighting soldier, but the long spell of antipartisan work had shaken him, the unpleasant demands of translating Party theory into practice. Combat would bring him back to himself.

He swung back into the radio truck and laced the panel to the outside, clicking on the light. This was going to be tricky; it was all a matter of time.

This is going to be tricky timing, Eric thought as they reached the edge of the clearing. Even trickier than threading their way through the nighted bush; they had followed the Circassian blindly, had dodged aside barely in time and lain motionless in a thicket of witch hazel as a long file of Germans went past. One of them had slipped and staggered; Eric had felt more than seen the boot come down within centimeters of his outstretched hand. He heard a muttered *"Scheisse"* as the SS man paused to resettle his clanking load of mortar-tripod, then nothing but the rain and fading boots sucking free of wet leaf mold. He felt his face throb at the memory of it, like a warm wind; the rich sweet smell of the crushed brush was still with him. Extreme fear was like pain: it fixed memory forever, made the moment instantly accessible to total recall . . .

The native hunter crept up beside him and put his mouth to the Draka's ear; even then Eric wrinkled his nose slightly at the stink of rotten teeth and bad digestion.

"Here, lord." His pointing arm brushed the side of Eric's helmet, and he spoke in a breathy whisper. Probably not needful, the rain covered and muffled sound, but no sense in taking chances. "The road is no more than five hundred meters that way. Shall I go first?"

"No," Eric said, unfastening the clasp of his rain cloak and sliding it to the ground. "You stay here, we'll need you to guide us back. In a hurry! Be ready."

And besides, it isn't your fight. Except that the Draka would let his people live and eat, if they obeyed. He brought the Holbars forward and jacked the slide, easing it through the forward-and-back motion that chambered the first round rather than letting the spring drive it home with the usual loud *chunk*. Safety or no safety, he was not going to walk through unfamiliar woods in the dark with one up the spout . . . Soft *clack-clicks* told of others doing likewise.

Eric's mouth was dry. *How absurd*, he thought. His uniform was heavy with water, mud and leaves plastered on his chest and belly, and his *mouth* was dry.

A brief glimpse of yellow light from downslope to the north. Sofie slapped his ankle; he reached back to touch acknowledgment, and their hands met, touched and clasped. Her hand was small but firm. She gave his hand a brief squeeze that he found himself returning, smiling in the dark.

"Stay tight, Sofie," he whispered.

"You too, Eri—sir," she answered.

"Eric's fine, Sofie," he answered. "This isn't the British army." Slightly louder, coming to his feet: "Ready."

He crouched, eyes probing blindly at the darkness. Still too dark to *see*, but he could sense the absence of the forest canopy above; it was like walking out of a room. And the rain was individual drops, not the dense spattering that came through the leaf cover. Ripping and fumbling sounds, the satchelmen getting out their charges. *Why am I here?* he thought. *I'm a commander, doing goddamn pointman's work. I could be back in the bunker, having a coffee and watching Sofie paint her toenails.* His lips shaped a whistle, and the Draka started forward at a crouching walk. Their feet skimmed the earth, knees bent, ankles loose, using the soles of their feet to detect terrain irregularities.

Nobody's indispensable, another part of his mind answered. His belly tightened, and his testicles tried to draw themselves up in a futile gesture of protection against the hammering fire some layer of his mind expected. *Marie can handle a fixed-front action as well as you can. And you've been expecting to die in battle for a long time now.*

But he didn't want to, the White Christ be his witness.

Eric's step faltered; he recovered, with an expression of stunned amazement that the darkness thankfully covered. He grunted, as if a fist had driven into his belly.

I don't, I truly don't, he thought with wonder. Then, with savage intensity: *There are hundreds within a kilometer who don't want to either.* He was acutely conscious of Sofie following to his right. *You still can, and everyone with you. Careful!*

Chapter Fifteen

VILLAGE ONE, OSSETIAN MILITARY HIGHWAY
APRIL 15, 1942: 0350 HOURS

Trooper Patton wiped the sap from her bush knife and sheathed it over her shoulder; carefully, with both hands. It was *far* too sharp to fling about in the dark. Then she knelt to run her fingers over the product of her ingenuity: a straight sapling, hastily trimmed to a murderous point at both ends. One point was rammed into the packed earth of the trail; the middle of the stake was supported by the crutch of a Y-shaped branch cut to just the right length. The other end slanted up . . . Patton stood against it, measuring the height. Just at her navel, coming up the trail from the north. The briefing paper *did* say that the Fritz SS had a minimum height requirement, so it should hit. . . .

The Draka woman was grinning to herself as she slid back four meters to her firing position to the left of the trail, behind the trunk of a huge fallen beech; laughing, even, an almost soundless quiver. One that Monitor Huff beside her knew well. Lips approached her ear, with crawling noises and a smell of wet uniform.

"What's so fuckin' amusin', swarthy one?" asked Monitor Huff, commander of C lochos, the squad.

Patton was dark for a Draka, short and muscular, olive-skinned and flat-faced; their people had a Franco-Mediterranean strain that cropped out occasionally among the more common north-European types. Huff could imagine the disturbing glint of malicious amusement in the black eyes as she heard the slightly reedy voice describe the trap.

"Belly or balls, Huffie, belly or balls. Noise'll give us a firin' point, eh?"

"You're sick. Ah love it." Their lips brushed, and Huff rolled back to her firing position. *Gonna die, might as well die laughin'*, she thought.

Down the trail, something clanked.

"Clip the stickers," Tetrarchy Commander Einar Labushange said as he crawled past the last of his fire teams. This was the largest trail;

147

half the tetrarchy was with him to cover it, where a ridge crossed the path and forced it to turn left and west below the granite sill. Less cover, of course, but that had its advantages. He touched the bleeding lip he had split running into a branch, tasting salt. "And be careful, if'n I'm goin' to die a hero's death, I don't want to do it with a Draka bayonet up my ass."

He slid his own free and fixed it, unfolding the bipod of his Holbars, worrying. The little slope gave protection, but it also gave room for the Fritz to spread out. And withdrawing would be a cast-iron bitch, down the reverse slope at his back and over the stream and up a near-vertical face two meters high. At least they could all rest for a moment, and there was no danger of anybody dropping off, not with this miserable cold pizzle running down their—

The sound of a boot. A hobnailed boot, grating on stone. The heavy breathing of many men walking upslope under burdens. *Close, I can hear them over the rain. Very close.* He pulled a grenade out of his belt and laid it on the rock beside him, lifting his hips and reaching down to move a sharp-edged stone. He rose on one elbow to point the muzzle of the assault rifle downslope and drew a breath.

Eric could smell the trucks now, lubricants and rubber and burnt distillate, overpowering churned mud and wet vegetation. They must be keeping the boilers fired; he could hear the peculiar hollow drumming of rain on tight-stretched canvas, echoing in the troop compartments it sheltered. Only a few lights, carefully dimmed against aircraft; that was needless in an overcast murk like tonight's, but habit ruled. To his dark-adapted eyes it was almost bright, and he turned his eyes away to keep the pupils dilated. There was an exercise to do that by force of will. Dangerous in a firefight, though; bright flashes could scorch the retina if you were overriding the natural reflex. He counted the trucks by silhouette.

There must be at least some covering force. Adrenaline buzzed in his veins, flogging the sandy feel of weariness out of his brain. He would have to be careful: this was the state of jumping-alert wiredness that led to errors. Some of the trucks would mount automatic weapons, antiaircraft, but they could be trained on ground targets. Eight assault rifles, including his, and the demolitions experts from Marie's tetrarchy—they were going to be grossly out-numbered. Mud sucked at the soles of his boots and packed into the broad treads, making the footing greasy and silence impossible.

Thank god for the rain. Darkness to cover movement, rain to drown out the sounds. That made it impossible for him to coordinate the attack, once launched; well, Draka were supposed to use initiative.

"*Halten Sie!*" A German voice sounded from out of the darkness, only a few meters ahead now: more nervous than afraid, only barely audible over the drumming rain. He forced himself to walk forward, each footfall an eternity.

"Ach, it's just me, Hermann," he replied in the same language. "We got lost. Where's the *Herr Hauptman*?" And knew his own mistake, even before the spear of electric light stabbed out from the truck's cab. *Hauptman* was German for "Captain." At least in their Regular army, of which the Liebstandarte was no part.

The SS don't use the German Army rank system! The night lit with tracer fire, explosions, weird prisms of chemical light refracted into momentary rainbows through the prism of the falling rain. The Germans were shooting wild into a darkness blacker to them than to their opponents.

He flung himself down and fired, tracer flicking out even before his body struck the ground. Grenades went off somewhere, a sharp *brak-brak*; a fuel truck went up with a huge woosh and orange flash in the corner of his eye. A bullet went over his head with the unpleasantly familiar *crack!* of a high-velocity round; the Holbars hammered itself into his shoulder as he walked it down the length of the truck, using the muzzle flash to aim. Stroboscopic vision. Lightflash, blinkblinkblinkblink.

Blink. The driver tumbling down from the open door, rifle falling from his hands. Blink. Metal dimpling and tearing under the ratcheting slugs. Blink. A machine gunner above the cab trying to swing his weapon toward him, jerking and falling as the light slugs from the Holbars struck and tumbled and chewed. Ping-*ting*, ricochet off something solid. Blink. Shots down the canvas tilt, sparks and flashes, antennae clustering on its roof . . .

"Almighty Thor, it's the command truck!" Eric whooped, and ran for the entrance at the rear. His hand was reaching for a grenade as he rounded the rear of the truck, skidding lightly in the torn-up wet earth. The canvas flap was opening at the rear. The Draka tossed the blast grenade in and dove to one side without breaking stride, hit the ground in a forward roll that left him low to the earth in the instant the detonation came, turned and drove back for the truck while it still echoed. You had to get in *fast*, that had been an offensive grenade, blast only, a hard lump of explosive with no fragmentation sleeve. Fast, while anybody alive in there was still stunned . . .

Standartenführer Hoth had been listening on the shortwave set in the back of the radio truck, to the broadcasts from over the mountains. It was all there was to do; as useful as Schmidt's poring over the maps, there by the back of the vehicle. Reception was spotty, and he kept getting fragments. Fragments of the battle south of the passes, in German or the strange slurred Draka dialect of English; his own command of that tongue was spotty and based on the British standard. Evaluations, cool orders, fire-correction data from artillery observation officers, desperate appeals for help. . . . There were four German divisions in the pocket at the south end of the Ossetian Military Highway—the Liebstandarte, split by the Draka paratroops and driving to clear the road from both ends, with three Wehrmacht units trying to hold the perimeter to the south. Trying and failing.

Time, time, he thought. The faint light of dials and meters turned his hands green; the body of the truck was an echoing cavern as the canvas above them drummed under the rain.

"Are you getting anything?" he said to the operator.

The man shook his head, one palm pressed to an earphone and the fingers of the other hand teasing a control. "Nothing new, Standartenführer. Good reception from Pyatigorsk and Grozny, a mishmash from over the mountains—too much altitude and electrical activity tonight. And things skipping the ionosphere from everywhere: a couple of Yank destroyers off Iceland hunting a U-boat, the Imperial Brazilian news service . . ."

The first explosion stunned them into a moment of stillness. Then Schmidt was leaping to his feet, spilling maps and documents. Hoth snatched for his helmet. Firing, the unmistakable sound of Draka automatic rifles, more explosions; only a few seconds, and already orange flame-light was showing through the canvas. The truck rocked, then shook as bullets struck it, a shuddering vibration that racked downward from the unseen cab ahead of them. Slugs tearing through the rank of electronic equipment, toppling boxes, bright sparking flashes and the lightning smell of ozone. The radio operator flew backwards across the truck bed with a line of red splotches across his chest, to slump with the headphones half pulled off and an expression of surprise on his face.

Hoth was turning when the grenade flew through the back of the truck, between the unlaced panels of the covering. It bounced back from the operator's body, landed at Schmidt's feet. There was just light and time enough to recognize the type, machined from a hard plastic explosive. It was safe at thirty feet, but more than enough to kill or cripple them all in the close quarters of the truck. He had enough time to feel a flash of anger: he *could* not die now, there was too much to do. It was futile, but he could feel his body tensing to hurl himself forward and kick the bomb out into the dark, feel the flush of berserker rage at the thought of another disaster.

Eyes locked on the explosive, he was never sure whether Schmidt had thrown himself forward or slipped; only aware of the blocky form plunging down and then being thrown up in a red spray. That barrier of flesh was enough to absorb the blast, although the noise was still enough to set his ears buzzing. The SS commander was a fast heavy man, with a combat veteran's reflexes: in a night firefight, you had to get *out*—this was a deathtrap. There was a motive stronger than survival driving him forward, as well.

The past day had seen his life and his cause go from triumph to the verge of final disaster. He had seen his men cut down without an opportunity to strike back, while he blundered like a bull tangled in the matador's cape. Out there was something he could kill. A thin trickle of saliva ran from one corner of his mouth as he lunged for the beckoning square of darkness.

A step brought Eric back to the rear of the truck. He had just time to wonder why the explosion had sounded so muffled when a German stepped over the body of the comrade who had thrown himself on the Draka grenade and kicked Eric in the face, hard.

The Draka's rifle had been in the way. That saved him from a broken jaw; it did not prevent him from being flung back, stunned. The ground rose up and struck him; arms and legs moved sluggishly, like the fronds of a sea anemone on a coral reef; the strap of his Holbars was wound around his neck.

Self-accusation was bitter. Overconfidence. He had just time enough to think *stupid, stupid* when a huge weight dropped on his back. The darkness lit with fire.

Down. Reflex drove Sofie forward as motion flicked at the corner of her eye, letting the Centurion run on ahead. She landed crouched on toes and left hand, muscle springing back against the weight of body and radio. Shins thudded against her ribs, and the German went over with a yell; she flung out the machine pistol one-handed and fired, using muzzle flash to aim and recoil to walk the burst through the mud and across the prone Fritz's back, hammering cratering impacts as the soft-nosed slugs mushroomed into his back and blew exit wounds the size of fists in his chest. Eric had stopped ahead of her, walking a line of assault-rifle fire down the truck. Explosions; there was light now, enough to seem painful after the long march through the forest. Eric—

Ignore him, *have* to. She twisted and pivoted, flicking herself onto knees and toes, facing back into the vehicle park, its running shouting silhouettes. Her thumb snapped the selector to single-shot and she brought the curved steel buttplate to her shoulder, resting the wooden forestock on her left palm; there was enough light to use the optical sight now, and the submachine gun was deadly accurate under fifty meters. The round sight-picture filled her vision, divided by the translucent plastic finger of the internal pointer, with its illuminated tip. Concentrate: it was just school, just a night-firing exercise, pop-up targets, outline recognition. A jacket with medals, lay the pointer on his chest and stroke the trigger and *crack*. The recoil was a surprise; it always was when the shot felt just right. The Fritz flipped back out of her sight; she did not need to let her eyes follow. More following him, this truck must mean something; quickly, they could see the muzzle flashes if not her. *Crack. Crack. Crack.* The last one spun, twisted, only winged; she slapped two more rounds into him before he hit the ground.

A bullet snapped through the space her stomach would have been in if she had been standing; she felt the passage suck at her helmet. Aimed fire, if she hit the dirt he might still get her, or the centurion in the back. Scan . . . a helmet moving, behind one of the bodies. Difficult . . . Her breath went out, held; her eyes were wide, forcing a vision that saw everything and nothing. The Fritz working the bolt of his Mauser. Blood from a bitten cheek. The pointer of her scope sinking with the precision of a turret lathe, just below the brim of the coal-scuttle helmet. Her finger taking up the infinitesimal slack of the machine pistol's trigger. They fired together; the helmet flipped up into the ruddy-lit darkness with a *kting* that she heard over the rifle bullet buzzing past. A cratered ruin, the SS rifleman's head slipped down behind the comrade he had been using as a firing rest.

Sofie blinked the afterimage of the Mauser's flash out of her eyes, switching to full-auto and spraying the pile of dead: you never knew.

Knee and heel and toe pushed her back upright as her hands slapped a fresh magazine into her weapon, hand finding hand in the dark. Unnoticed, her lips were fixed in a snarl as she loped around the truck Eric had been attacking; her eyes were huge and dark in a face gone rigid as carved bone. He could not be far ahead. She would find him; his back needed guarding. She would.

Plop.

The Fritz flare arched up from behind a boulder. Harsh silver light lit the trees, leeching color and depth, making them seem like flat stage sets in an outdoor theater, turning the falling rain to a streaking argent dazzle. The Draka section hugged the earth and prayed for darkness, but the flare tangled its parachute in the upper branches and hung, sputtering. Einar Labushange laid his head on his hands; the light outlined what was left of the Draka firing line on the ridge with unmerciful clarity. He was safer than most, because when his head dropped, the dead SS trooper in front of him hid him. He could feel the body jerking with pseudo life as bullets struck it, hear the wet sounds they made. Rounds were lashing the whole ridge; the firepower of the Fritz infantry was diffuse, not as many automatic weapons per soldier, but their sheer numbers made it huge now that they were deployed.

Not as many as there had been when the Draka had caught them filing along below. Forgetting, he tried to shift himself with an elbow, froze, and sank back with a sound that only utter will prevented from being a whimper. Briefly, some far-off professional corner of his mind wondered if he had been justified in using an illuminating round, that fifteen-minute eternity ago. Yes, on the whole. The Fritz had been in marching order; he did not need to raise his head to see them piled along the trail, fifty or sixty at least. More hung on the undergrowth behind it, shot in the back as they waded through vine and thicket as dense as barbed wire. *Clumsy*, he thought, conscious even through the rain of the cold sweat of pain on his body, the slow warm leakage from his belly. Open-country soldiers, Draka would have gone through like eels or used their bush knives.

Stones and chips tinked into the air; a shower of cut twigs and branches fell on the soldiers of the Domination, pattering through the rain. They crouched below the improvised parapet; occasionally a marksman would pop up for a quick burst at the muzzle flashes, roll along to another position, snap-shoot again at the answering fire that raked their original shooting stand.

"Fuckahs never learn!" he heard one call out gleefully. There was no attempt at a firing line; the survivors of the two *lochoi* would rise to fire when the next charge came in. Overhead, a shell from 2nd Tetrarchy's 60mm mortar whined. Only one, they were running short. Short of everything; and the Fritz still had more men. Despite the dozens shattered along the trail, the scores more lying in windrows up the slope they had tried to storm, and thank the One-Eyed that the bush was too thick to let them around the flanks easily . . .

Einar did not move. As long as his body stayed very still, the knee that had been shattered by the sniper's bullet did not make him faint. He could feel the blood runneling down his face from the spot where he had bitten through his lip the last time the leg had jerked. It would be the bayonet wound in the stomach that killed him, though.

He struggled not to laugh: it was very bad when he did that. A flare had gone off just as the last Fritz charge crested the ridge, too late for either of them to alter lunges that had the weight of a flung body behind them. Just time enough to see each other's faces with identical expressions of surprise and horror; then, his bayonet had rammed into the German's throat, just as the long blade on the end of the Mauser punched through his uniform tunic right above the belt buckle. It had been cold, very cold; he could *feel* it, feel the skin parting and the muscle and crisp things inside that popped with something like a sound heard through his own bones. Then it had pulled free as the Fritz collapsed, and he had watched it come out of him and had thought, *How odd, I've been killed* as he started to fall. That was very funny, when he thought about it. Unlikely enough to be killed with a bayonet, astronomical chance for a Draka to lose an engagement with cold steel. Of course, he had been very tired . . .

Light-headed and a little sleepy, as he was now. He must not laugh. The stomach wound was death, but slow; just a deep stab wound, worked a little wider when the blade came out. Not the liver or a kidney or the major arteries, or he'd be dead by now. The muscles clamped down, letting the blood pool and pressure inside rather than rush out and bring unconsciousness as the brain starved. But there were things in his gut hanging by strained threads.

It was very bad when he laughed.

And he was *very* sleepy; the sound of the firing was dimming, no louder than the rain drumming on his helmet . . .

He rocked his ruined leg, using the still-responsive muscle above the tourniquet. The scream was probably unheard in the confusion of battle; he was very alert, apart from the singing in his ears, when the second decurion crawled up beside him, the teenaged face white and desperate in the dying light of the flare.

"Sir. Pederssen and de Klerk are expended, the mortar's outa rounds, they're working around the flanks, an' we can't stop the next rush; what'm I supposed to *do*?" The NCO reached out for his shoulder, then drew his hand back as Einar slapped at it.

"Get the fuck out. No! Don't try to move me; I can feel things . . . ready to tear inside. I'd bleed out in thirty seconds. Go on, burn boot; *go* man, *go*."

The sounds died away behind him; the buzzing whine in his ears was getting louder. Nobody could say they hadn't accomplished the mission: the Fritz must have lost a third or better of their strength. They would never push on farther into this wet blackness with another ambush like this waiting for them. A hundred dead, at least . . . Somehow, it did not seem as important now, but it was all that was left.

The flare light was dimming, or maybe that was his eyes. Maybe he was seeing things, the bush downslope stirring. Clarity returned for a moment, although he felt very weak, everything was a monstrous effort. No choice but to see it through now . . . *Oh, White Christ, to see the desert again* . . . It would be the end of the rains, now. A late shower, and the veld would be covered in wildflowers, red and magenta and purple, you could ride through them and the scent rose around you like all the gardens in the world, blowing from the horizon. *No choice, never any choice until it's too late, because you don't know what dying is, you just think you do* . . .

Einar Labushange raised his head to the sights of his rifle as the SS rose to charge.

"Ah. Ah. Ahhhaaaa—"

It was amazing, Trooper Patton thought. The German impaled on the stake still had the strength to moan. Even to scream, occasionally, and to speak, now and then. Muzzle flashes had let her see him, straddling as if the pointed wood his own weight had punched into his crotch was a third leg. Every now and then he tried to move; it was usually then that he screamed. The bodies behind him along the trail were still; she had put in enough precautionary bursts, the trail was covered with them, and a big clump back down the trail about twenty meters. That was where the rocket-gun shell had hit them from behind, nicely bunched up and focused on the fire probing out of the night before them.

"Amazing," she muttered. Her voice sounded distant and tinny in ears that felt hot and flushed with blast; she wished the cold rain would run into them. Amazing that nothing had hit him. There was a pile of spent brass and bits of cartridge belt by her left elbow, some still noticeably hot despite the drizzle, and two empty drums; the barrel of her rifle had stopped sizzling. She thought that there was about half of the third and last ammunition canister left, seven or eight bursts if she was lucky and light on the trigger. Cordite fumes warred with wet earth, gun oil and a fecal stink from the German, who had voided his bowels as he hung on the wood. Uneasily, she strained her battered ears. She and Huff had been reverse-point; the plan was that they would block the trail, the Fritz would pull back to spread out, and then the rest of the lochos would hit them, having let them pass the first time to tempt them to bunch. It had worked fine, only there was no more firing from farther north. Glimpses had been enough to estimate at least a tetrarchy's worth of dead Fritz; the other six troopers of their lochos couldn't have killed all the rest, so . . .

"Huffie."

"Ya?"

"You thinkin' what I—"

They had both risen to hands and knees, when Patton stopped. "Wait," she said, reaching out a hand. "Give me a hand, will you?" She felt in the darkness, grabbed a webbing strap and pulled the other soldier toward the trail. Outstretched, her hand touched something warm and yielding; there was a long, sobbing scream that died away to whimpers.

"What the *fuck* you doin'?"

"Lay him out, lay him out!" Patton exclaimed feverishly. And yes, there was a tinge of light. *Couldn't* be sunlight, the whole action was barely ten minutes old. Something was burning, quite close, close enough for reflected light to bounce in via the leaves. "Easy now, don' kill him. Right, now give me your grenades."

There was a chuckle from the dim shape opposite her. The German was crying now, with sharp intakes of breath as they moved him, propped the stake up to keep the angle of entry constant, placed the primed grenades under his prone body, wedging them securely. The flesh beneath their fingers quivered with a constant thrumming, as if from the cold. Huff paused as they rose, dusting her hands.

"Hey, wait. He still conscious; he might call a warnin'."

Patton looked nervously back up the trail. If the Germans had spread out through the bush to advance in line, rather than down the trail . . . but there was no time to lose. It depended on how many of them were left, how close their morale was to breaking. "Right," she grunted, reaching down and drawing the knife from her boot. The Fritz's mouth was already open as he panted shallowly; a wet fumbling, a quick stab at the base of the tongue, and the SS trooper was forever beyond understandable speech.

The cries behind them were thick and gobbling as the pair cautiously jog-trotted down the trail.

"Fuckah *bit* me," Patton gasped as they stopped at a sharp dip. There was running water at her feet; she rinsed her hands, then cupped them to bring it to her lips. Pure and sweet, tasting of nothing more than rocks and earth, it slid soothingly down a sore and harshened throat.

"Never no mind; this's where we supposed to meet the others." Again, they exchanged worried glances at each other without needing to actually see. The ambush force was supposed to pull out before they did; that was the only explanation for the silence. Or one of only two possible explanations . . .

To the south there was a multiple crash, as of grenades, then screams, and shouts in German.

"*Shit*," said Huff. There had been seven of them in the lochoi assigned to this trail . . . "Like the boss man said, mind in gear—"

"Ass to rear. Let's *go!*"

Silently, the two Draka ran through the exploding chaos of the vehicle park. Eric had tasked the satchelmen in general terms: to destroy the SS trucks, especially fuel or munitions carriers, or block the road, or both, whichever was possible. Most of the satchelmen had run among the trucks with a charge in each hand, thumbs on the time fuses, ready to switch the cap up. *Get* near a truck, *throw* the charge, *dive* out of the way . . .

Trooper McAlistair shoulder-rolled back to elbows and knees, bipod unfolded, covering the demolition expert's back. *Blind-sided chaos*, she thought. Feet ran past on the other side of an intact truck; she snap-shot a three-round burst and was rewarded with a scream. That had not been the only set of feet; without rising she scuttled forward, moving in a leopard crawl nearly as fast as her walking pace, under the truck and over the sprattling form of the Fritz, who was clutching at a leg sawn off at mid-shin. She rolled again, sighting, wishing she was on full-auto as she saw the group rounding the truck. Six. Her finger worked on the trigger, *brap-brap-brap*, tracer snapping green into their backs; one had a machine gun, a MG42. He twisted, hand clamping in dying reflex and sending a cone of light upwards into the gray-black night as the belt of ammunition looped around his shoulders fed through the weapon, then jammed as it tightened around his throat, dropping him backwards into the mud. The overheated barrel hissed as it made contact with the wet soil, like a horseshoe when the farrier plunges it from the forge into the waiting bucket.

The satchelman had not been idle on the other side of the truck. The target had been especially tempting, an articulated tank-transporter with a specialized vehicle aboard; that was a tank with a motorized drum-and-chain flail attached, meant for clearing mine fields before an attack. The charge of plastique flashed, a pancake of white light beneath the transporter's front bogie. All four wheels flew into the night, flipping up, spinning like coins flicked off a thumb. The fuel tank ruptured, spreading the oil in a fine mist as the atomizer on a scent bottle does to perfume. Liquid, the heavy fuel was barely flammable at all without the forced-draft ventilation of a boiler. Divided finely enough, so that all particles are exposed to the oxygen, anything made of carbon is explosive: coal dust, even flour.

The cloud of fuel oil went off with the force of a 15mm shell, and the truck and its cargo disintegrated in an orange globe of fire and fragments that set half a dozen of its neighbors on fire themselves. The *crang* blasted all other sound out of existence for a second, and echoed back from hills and forest. Most of the truck's body was converted into shrapnel; by sheer bad luck a section of axle four feet long speared through the satchelman as a javelin might have, pinning him to the body of another vehicle like a shrike's prey stuck on a thorn. Limbs beat a tattoo on the cab, alive for several seconds after the spine had been severed; there was plenty of light now, more than enough for the Liebstandarte trooper to see the bulge-eyed clown face that hung at his window, spraying bright lung-blood from mouth and nose beneath burning hair. Since the same jagged spear of metal had sliced the thin sheeting of the door like cloth and crunched through the bones of his pelvis, he paid very little attention.

Tee-Hee McAlistair flattened herself; the ground rose up and slapped her back again as the pressure wave of the detonation passed. For an instant, there was nothing but lights and a struggle to breathe. Above her the canvas tilt of the Opel truck swayed toward her, then jounced back onto its wheels as the blast proved not quite enough to topple it past the ballast weight of its cargo. Vaguely, she was conscious of blood running from ears and nose, of a thick buzzing in her skull that was not part of the ratcheting confusion of the night battle. That had been a *much* bigger bang than it was supposed to be. Doggedly, she levered herself back to her feet, ignoring the blurred edges of her sight. The buzzing gave way to a shrilling, as needles seemed to pierce slowly inwards through each ear. The satchelman—

"Shitfire, talk about baaad luck," she muttered in awe, staring for an instant across the hood of the truck at the figure clenched around the impaling steel driven into the door. That drooped slightly, and the corpse slid inch by inch down the length of it, until it seemed to be kneeling with slumped head in a pool that shone red in the light of the fires. Behind, the transporter was a large puddle of fire surrounded by smaller blazes, with the flail tank standing in the middle, sending dribblets of flame up through the vision slits in the armor. As she watched, a segment of track peeled away to fall with a thump, beating a momentary path through the thick orange carpet of burning oil.

A burst crackled out of nowhere her dazzled eyes could see, ripping the thin sheet metal of the truck's hood in a line of runnels that ended just before they reached her.

"Gotta get out of the plane a' fire," she said to herself. It was strange; she could hear the words inside her head, but not with her ears . . . Turning, she put her foot on the fender of the truck and jumped onto the hood, then the cab roof, a left-handed vault onto the fabric cover of the hoops that stretched over the body of the truck. That was much more difficult than it should have been, and she lay panting and fighting down nausea for an instant before looking around.

"Whoo, awesome." The whole cluster of Fritz vehicles was burning; there was a fuzziness to her vision, but only the outermost line near the road was not on fire. There was plenty of light now, refracted through the streaked-crystal lines of the rain; muzzle flashes and tracers spat a horizontal counterpoint to the vertical tulip shapes of explosions and burning vehicles, all soundless as the needles of pain went farther into her head. It occurred to her that the Fritz must be shooting each other up—there were more of them and the Draka had gotten right into the position. That would have made her want to giggle, if her ears had not hurt so much; and there seemed to be something wrong with her head, it was thick and slow. She should *not* be watching this like a fireworks show. She should . . .

One of the trucks pulled out of the line and began to turn back onto the road; its driver executed a flawless three-point and twisted bumping past the guttering ruin of the first to be destroyed; other explosions sounded behind him, nearly as loud. The actions of hands and boots on wheel and throttle were automatic; all the driver could see was the fire, spreading toward him: fire and tracers probing out of the unknowable dark.

Tee-Hee reacted at a level deeper than consciousness as the truck went by. Kneeling, she raked the body of it with a long burst before leaping for the canvas tilt. The reaction almost killed her; it calculated possibilities on a level of performance no longer possible after blast-induced concussion slowed her. Her jump almost failed to reach the moving truck, and it was chance that she did not slide off to land in the deadly fire-raked earth below. She sprawled on the fabric for an instant, letting the wet roughness scratch at her cheek. But her education had included exhaustion drill—training patterns learned while she was deliberately pushed to the verge of blackout, designed to keep her functioning as long as it was physically possible at all. Crawling, she slithered to the roof of the driver's cab and swung down, feet reaching for the running board and left hand for the mirror brace to hold her on the lurching, swaying lip of slick metal.

That seemed to clear her head a little. Enough to see the driver's head turning at last from his fixed concentration on the road and escape; to see the knowledge of death in his widening eyes as she raised the assault rifle one-handed and fired a burst through the door of the cab. His lips shaped a single word: *"Nein."*

The recoil hammered her back, bending her body into an arch and nearly tearing loose the left-hand grip. Then she tossed the weapon through the window and tore the door open, reaching in and heaving the dying German out; pulling herself into the cab with the same motion, hands clamping on the wheel. She took a shaky breath, wrenched the wheel around to avoid a wreck in her path.

"Freya, what's that stink?" the Draka soldier muttered, even as she fumbled with the unfamiliar controls. It was still so hard to think; out to the road, then shoot out the wheels. Grenade down the fuel pipe. Block the road, back to the woods, where was the throttle . . . ? Not totally unfamiliar; after all, the autosteamer had been *invented* in the Domination, the design must be derived . . . there!

Shit, she thought, slewing the truck across the narrow road. There was a steep dropoff on the other side; this should slow them a little once she popped a charge to make the hulk immovable. *Literally. I'm sitting in what the Fritz let out. White Christ have mercy, I'll never live it down!*

At that moment, the SS trooper fired his Kar-98 through the back of the cab. It was not aimed; there was no window, and it was the German's last action before blood loss slumped him back onto the bullet-chewed floorboards. Chance directed it better than any skill; the heavy bullet slapped the Draka between the shoulder blades; she pitched forward against the wheel, bounced back against the back rest, then forward again.

But I won, was her last astonished thought. *I can't die, I won.*

Eric felt the German's impact like a flash of white fire across his lower back and pelvis. Then there *was* white fire, dazzling even though his head was turned away: explosion. Eric's bruised face was driven deeper into the rocky earth; his tongue tasted dirt and the tenderness of grass. Fists pounded him, heavy knobby fists with thick shoulders behind them, driven without science but with huge strength into back and shoulders, ringing his head like a clapper inside the metal bell of helmet that protected neck and skull. His conscious mind was a white haze, disconnected sense-impressions flooding in: the breathy grunts of the man on his back as each blow slammed down; the bellows action of his own ribs, flexing and springing back between knuckles and ground; shouts and shots and some other, metallic noise.

Training made him turn. That was a mistake; there was no strength in his arms; the movements that should have speared bladed fingertips into the other's throat and rammed knuckles under his short ribs turned into feeble pawings that merely slowed and tangled the German's roundhouse swings.

Bad luck, he thought, rolling his head to take the impact on his skull rather than the more vulnerable face; he could hear knuckles pop as they broke. Fists landed on his jaw and cheek, jarring the white lights back before his eyes; he could feel the skin split over one cheekbone, but there was no more pain, only a cold prickling over his whole skin, as if he were trying to slough it as a snake does. One hand still fumbled at the SS officer's waist; it fell on the butt of a pistol; he made a supreme effort of concentration, drew it, pressed it to the other's tunic and pulled the trigger.

Nothing. Safety on, or perhaps his hand was just too weak. He could see the Fritz's face in the ruddy flow of burning petrol and lubricants and rubber: black smudged, bestial, wet running down the chin. The great peasant hands clamped on his throat. The light began to fade.

Felix Hoth was kneeling in the mud behind his radio truck, and yet was not. In his mind the SS man was back in a cellar beneath the Lubyanka, strangling an NKVD holdout he had stalked through the labyrinth and found in a hidden room with a half-eaten German corpse. He did not even turn the first time Sofie rang the steel folding butt of her machine pistol off the back of his head; she could not fire, you do not aim an automatic weapon in the direction of someone you want to live.

Hoth *did* start to move when she kicked him very hard up between the legs where he straddled the Centurion's body. That was too late; she planted herself and hacked downward with both hands on the weapon's forestock, as if she were pounding grain with a mortar and pestle. There was a hollow *thock*, and a shock that jarred her sturdy body right down to the bones in her lower back; the strip steel of the submachine gun's stock deformed slightly under the impact. If the butt had not had a rubber pad, the German's brains would have spattered; as it was, he slumped boneless across the Draka's body. With cold economy she booted the body off her commander's and raised her weapon to fire.

It was empty, the bolt back and the chamber gaping. Not worth the time to reload. The comtech kneeled by Eric's side, her hands moving across his body in an examination quick, expert, fearful. Blood, bruises, no open wounds, no obvious fractures poking bone splinters through flesh . . . So hard to tell in the difficult light, no *time* . . . She reached forward to push back an eyelid and check for concussion. Eric's hand came up and caught her wrist, and the gray eyes opened, red and visibly bloodshot even in the uncertain, flickering light. The sound of firing was dying down.

"Stim," he said hoarsely.

"Sir—Eric—" she began.

"*Stim*, that's an *order*." His head fell back, and he muttered incoherently.

She hesitated, her hands snapping open the case at her belt and taking out the disposable hypodermic. It was filled with a compound of benzedrine and amphetamines, the last reserve against extremity even for a fit man in good condition; for use when a last half hour of energy could mean the difference. Eric was enormously fit, but *not* in good condition, not after that battering; there might be concussion, internal hemorrhage, *anything*.

The sound echoed around the bend of the road below: steel-squeal on metal and rock, treads. Armored vehicles, many of them; she would have heard them before but for the racket of combat and the muffling rain. Their headlights were already touching the tops of the trees below. She looked down. Eric was lying still, only the quick, labored pumping of his chest marking life; his eyes blinked into the rain that dimpled the mud around him and washed the blood in thin runnels from his nose and mouth.

"Oh *shit!*" Sofie blurted, and leaned forward to inject the drug into his neck. There, half dosage, Wotan pop her *eyes* if she'd give him any more.

The effect of the drug was almost instantaneous. The mists at the corners of his eyes receded, and he *hurt*. That was why pain overload could send you into unconsciousness—the messages got redundant. . . . He hurt a *lot*. Then the pain receded; it was still there, but somehow did not matter very much. Now he felt good, very good in fact; full of energy, as if he could bounce to his feet and sweep Sofie up in his arms and *run* all the way back to the village.

He fought down the euphoria and contented himself with coming to his feet, slowly, leaning an arm across Sofie's shoulders. The world swayed about him, then cleared to preternatural clarity. The dying flames of the burning trucks were living sculptures of orange and yellow, dancing fire maidens with black soot-hair and the hissing voices of rain on hot metal. The trees about him were a sea that rippled and shimmered, green-orange; the roasting-pork smell of burning bodies clawed at his empty stomach. Eric swallowed bile and blinked, absently thrusting the German pistol in his hand through a loop in the webbing.

"Back—" he began hoarsely, hawked, spat out phlegm mixed with blood. "Back to the woods, *now*."

McWhirter stepped up, and two of the satchelmen. The Senior Decurion was wiping the blade of his Jamieson on one thigh as he dropped an ear into the bag strapped to his leg. The lunatic clarity of the drug showed Eric a face younger than he recalled, smoother, without the knots of tension that the older man's face usually wore. McWhirter's expression was much like the relaxed, contented look that comes just after orgasm, and his mouth was wet with something that shone black in the firelight.

The Centurion dismissed the brief crawling of skin between his shoulder blades as they turned and ran for the woods. It was much easier than the trip out, there was plenty of light now; enough to pinpoint them easily for a single burst of automatic fire. The feeling of lightness did not last much beyond the first strides. After that each bootfall drove a spike of pain up the line of his spine and into his skull, like a dull brass knife ramming into his head over the left eye; breathing pushed his bruised ribs into efforts that made the darkness swim before his eyes. There was gunfire from ahead and upslope, muffled through the trees, and *there* a flare popping above the leaf canopy. He concentrated on blocking off the pain, forcing it into the sides of his mind. *Relax* the muscles . . . pain did not make you weak, it was just the body's way of forcing you to slow down and recover. Training could suppress it, make the organism function at potential . . .

If this is wanting to be alive, I'm not so sure I want to want it, he thought. *Haven't been this afraid in years*. They crashed through the screen of undergrowth and threw themselves down. The others were joining him, the survivors; more than half. The shock of falling brought another white explosion behind his eyes. Ignore it, reach for the handset. Sofie thrust it into his palm, and he was suddenly conscious of the wetness again, the rain falling in a silvery dazzle through the air lit by the burning Fritz vehicles. Beyond the clearing, beyond the ruined buildings by the road, the SS armor rumbled and clanked, metal sounding under the diesel growl, so different from the smooth silence of steam.

He clicked the handset. The first tank waddled around the buildings, accelerating as it came into the light. Then it braked, as the infantry riding on it leaped down to deploy; the hatches were open, and Eric could see the black silhouette of the commander as he stood in the turret, staring about in disbelief at the clearing. Wrecked trucks littered it, burning or abandoned; one was driving slowly in a circle with the driver's arm swaying limply out the window. Bodies were scattered about— dozens of them; piles of two or three, there a huddle around a wrecked machine gun, there a squad caught by a burst as they ran through darkness to a meeting with death. Wounded lay moaning, or staggered clutching at their hurts; somewhere a man's voice was screaming in pulsing bursts as long as breaths. Thirty, fifty at least, Eric estimated as he spoke.

"Palm One to Fist, do y'read?"

"Acknowledged, Palm One." The calm tones of the battery commander were a shocking contrast to Eric's hoarseness. "Hope you've got a target worth gettin' up this early for."

"*Firefall*." Eric's voice sounded thin and reedy to his own ears. "Fire mission Tloshohene; *firefall*, do it *now*."

He lowered the handset, barked: "Neal!" to the troopers who had remained with the guide in the scrub at the edge of the woods.

The rocket gunner and her loader had been waiting with hunter's patience in a thicket near the trail, belly-down in the sodden leaf mold, with only their eyes showing between helmets and face paint. With smooth economy the dark-haired woman brought the projector up over the rock sill in front of her, resting the forward monopod on the stone. She fired; the backblast stripped wet leaves from the pistachio bushes and scattered them over her comrades. The vomiting-cat scream of the sustainer rocket drew a pencil of fire back to their position, and then the shell struck, high on the turret, just as it began to swing the long 88mm gun toward the woods. The bright flash left a light spot on Eric's retina, lingering as he turned away; the tank did not explode, but it froze in place. Almost at once bullets began hammering the wet earth below them, *smack* into mud, crack-*whinnng* off stone. The rocket gun gave its deep *whap* once more, and there was a sound overhead.

The Draka soldiers flinched. The Circassian guide glanced aside at them, then up at the deep whining rumble overhead, a note that lowered in pitch as it sank toward them. Then he bolted forward in terror as the first shellburst came, seeming to be almost on their heels. Eric hunched his head lower beneath the weight of the steel helmet: no real use in that, but it was psychological necessity. The Draka guns up the valley were firing over their heads at the Fritz: firing blind on the map coordinates he had supplied, at extreme range, using captured guns and ammunition of questionable standard. Only too possible that they would undershoot. Airburst in the branches overhead, shrapnel and wood fragments whirring through the night like circular saws . . .

The first shells burst out of sight, farther down the road and past the ruined buildings, visible only as a *wink-wink-wink-wink* of light, before the noise and overpressure slapped at their faces. The last two of the six landed in the clearing, bright flashes and inverted fans of water and mud and rock, bodies and pieces of wrecked truck. He rose, controlling the dizziness.

"On target, on target, *fire for effect*," he shouted, and tossed the handset back to Sofie. "Burn boot, up the trail, *move*."

It was growing darker as they ran from the clearing, away from the steady metronomic *wham-whamwham* of shells falling among the Fritz column, as the fires burnt out and distance cut them off. A branch slapped him in the face; there was a prickling numbness on his skin that seemed to muffle it. The firefights up ahead were building; no fear of the SS shooting blind into the dark, with their comrades engaged up there. Although they might pursue on foot . . . no, probably not. Not at once, not with that slaughterhouse confusion back by the road, and shells pounding into it. Best leave them a calling card, for later.

"Stop," he gasped. Something oofed into him, and he grabbed at brush to keep himself upright. "Mine it," he continued.

Behind him, one of the satchelmen pulled a last burden out of her pack. Unfolding the tripod beneath the Broadsword mine, she adjusted it to point back the way they had come, downslope, northwards. Then she unclipped a length of fine wire, looped one end through the detonator hook on the side and stepped forward. One step, two . . . around a handy branch, across the trail, tie it off . . .

"Good, can't see it mahself. Now, careful, careful," she muttered to herself as she stepped over the wire that now ran at shin height across the pathway and bent to brush her fingers on the unseen slickness of the mine's casing. The arming switch should be . . . *there*. She twisted it.

"Armed," she said. Now it was deadly, and very sensitive. Not enough for the pattering raindrops to set it off, she had left a little slack, but a brushing foot would detonate it for sure. The trail was lightless enough to register as black to her eyes, with only the lighter patches of hands and equipment catching enough of the reflected glow to hover as suggestions of sight. Still, she was sure she could detect a flinch at the words; mines were another of those things that most soldiers detested with a weary, hopeless hatred; you couldn't do anything much about them, except wait for them to kill you.

The sapper grinned in the dark. People who were nervous around explosives did not volunteer for her line of work; besides that, her training had included working on live munitions blindfolded. And Eddie had not made it back; Eddie had been a good friend of hers. *Hope they-all come up the trail at a run,* she thought vindictively, kissing a finger and touching it to the Broadsword.

Eric stood with his face turned upward to the rain while the mine was set, letting the coolness run over his face and trickle between his lips with tastes of wood and greenness and sweat from his own skin; he had been moving too fast for chill to set in. The scent of the forest was overwhelming in contrast to the fecal-explosive-fire smells of the brief battle—resin and sap and the odd musky-spicy scents of weeds and herbs. *Alive,* he thought. Gunfire to the south, around the slope of the mountain and through the trees, confusing direction. A last salvo of shells dragged their rumble through the invisible sky. Sofie was beside him, an arm around his waist in support that was no less real for being mostly psychological.

"Burn boot, people," he said quietly, just loud enough to be heard over the rain. "Let's go home."

They were nearly back to the village before he collapsed.

Chapter Sixteen

William Dreiser clicked off the tape recorder and patted the pebbled waterproof leather of the casing affectionately. It was the latest thing— only the size of a large suitcase, and much more rugged than the clumsy magnetic-wire models it had replaced—from Williams-Burroughs Electronics in Toronto. The Draka had been amazed at it; it was one field in which the United States was incontestably ahead. And it had been an effective piece: the ambush patrol setting out into the dark and the rain, faces grim and impassive; the others waiting, sleeping or at their posts, a stolid few playing endless games of solitaire. Then the eruption of noise in the dark, giving almost no hint of direction. Imagination had had to fill in then, picturing the confused fighting in absolute darkness. Finally the survivors straggling in, hale and walking wounded and others carried over their comrades' shoulders . . .

He looked up. The command cellar was the warmest place in the warren of basements, and several of the survivors had gathered, to strip and sit huddled in blankets while their uniforms and boots steamed beside the field stove. Some were bandaged, and others were rubbing each other down with an oil that had a sharp scent of pine and bitter herbs. The dim blue-lit air was heavy with it, and the smells of damp wool, blood, bandages, and fear-sweat under the brewing coffee. Eric was sitting in one corner, an unnoticed cigarette burning between his fingers and the blanket let fall to his waist, careless of the chill. The medic snapped off the pencil light he had been using to peer into the Centurion's eyes and nodded.

"Cuts, abrasions an' bruises," he said. "Ribs . . . better tape 'em. Mighta' been a concussion, but pretty mild. More damage from that Freya-damned stim. They shouldn't oughta issue it." He reached into the canvas-and-wire compartments of his carryall. "Get somethin' to eat, get some sleep, take two of these-here placebo's an' call me in the mornin'."

Eric's answering smile was perfunctory. He raised his arms obediently,

164

bringing his torso into the light. Sofie knelt by his side and began slapping on lengths of the broad adhesive from the roll the medic had left. Dreiser sucked in his breath; he had been with the Draka long enough to ignore her casual nudity, even long enough that her body no longer seemed stocky and overmuscled, or her arms too thick and rippling-taut. But the sight of the officer's chest and back was shocking. His face was bad enough, bruises turning dark and lumpy, eyes dark circles where thin flesh had been beaten back against the bone and veins ruptured, dried blood streaking from ears and mouth and turning his mustache a dark-brown clump below a swollen nose blocked with clots. Still, you could see as bad in a Cook County station house any Saturday night, and he had as a cub reporter on the police beat.

The massive bruising around his body was something else again: the whole surface of the tapered wedge was discolored from its normal matte tan to yellow-gray, from the broad shoulders where the deltoids rose in sharp curves to his neck, down to where the scutes of the stomach curved below the ribs. Dreiser had wrestled the young Draka a time or two, enough to know that his muscle was knitted over the ribs like a layer of thick india rubber armor beneath the skin. What it had taken to raise those welts . . . *Christ, he's not going to be so good-looking if this happens a few more times*, the American thought. *And I'm* damn *glad I'm not in this business.* Even then, he felt his mind making a mental note; this would be an effective tailpiece to his story. "Wounded, but still thoroughly in command of the situation, Centurion von Shrakenberg . . ."

Sofie finished the taping, a sheath like a Roman's segmented breastplate running from beneath his armpits to the level of the floating ribs. Eric swung his arms experimentally, then bent. He stopped suddenly, lips thinning back over his teeth, then completed the motion, then he coughed and spat carefully into a cloth.

"No blood," he muttered to himself. "Didn't think doc was wrong, really, but—" He turned his head to give Sofie a rueful smile, stroking one hand down the curve of her back. "Hey, thanks anyway, Sofie."

She blushed down to her breasts, looked down and noticed the goosebumps and stiffened nipples with a slight embarrassment, coughed herself, and drew on a fresh uniform tunic. "*Ya*, no problem," she said. "Ymir-cursed cold in here . . ." She turned to pick up a bowl and dampen a cloth. "*Ag, cis,* Centurio—Eric, we need y' walkin', come dawn."

He sighed and closed his eyes as she began to clean the almost-dried blood from his face, pushing back damp strands of his hair from his forehead. The cigarette dangled from one puffed lip.

"Better at walking than thinking, from the looks of tonight's fuckup," he said bitterly.

"Bullshit." Heads turned; that had been McWhirter, from the place where he sat with the neatly laid-out parts of an assault rifle on a blanket before his knees; he had more than the usual reluctance to let a rifle go without cleaning after being fired. He raised a bolt carrier to the light, pursed his lips and wiped off excess oil. "With respect, sir. From a crapped out bull, at that."

Eric's eyes opened, frosty and pale-gray against the darkening flesh that surrounded them. The NCO grinned; he was stripped to shorts as well, displaying a body roped and knotted and ridged with muscle that was still hard, even if the skin had lost youth's resilience. His body was heavier than the officer's, thicker at the waist, matted with graying yellow hair where the younger man's was smooth, and covered with a pattern of scars, everything from bullet wounds and shrapnel to what looked like the beginning of a sentence in Pushtu script, written with a red-hot knife.

"Yes, Senior Decurion?" Eric said softly.

"Yes, Centurion." The huge hands moved the rifle parts, without needing eyes to guide them. "Look, *sir*. I've been in the Regular Line since, hell, '09. Seen a lot of officers; can't do what they do—the good ones—Mrs. McWhirter didn't raise her kids for that, but I can run a firefight pretty good, and *pick* officers. Some of the bad ones"—he smiled, an unpleasant expression—"they didn't live past their second engagement, you know? Catchin' that Fritz move up the valley was smooth, real smooth. *Had* to do somethin' about it, too. Can't see anything else we could've done. Sir."

He slapped the bolt carrier back into the receiver of the Holbars, drew it back and let the spring drive it forward. The sound of the *snick* had a heavy, metallic authority. "An' we did do something. We blew their transport, knocked out, say, two-three more tanks, killed, oh, maybe two hundred. They turned back; next attack's goin' to come straight up our gunsights. For which we lost maybe fifteen effectives. So please, cut the bullshit, get some rest and let's concentrate on the next trick."

"My *trick* lost us half of 2nd Tetrarchy," Eric said.

The NCO sighed, using the rifle to lever himself erect and sweeping up the rest of his gear with his other hand. "With somewhat *less* respect, sir, y'may have noticed there's a *war* goin' on, and it's mah experience that in wars people tend to get killed. Difference is, is it *gettin' the job done or not?* That's what matters.

"*All* that matters," he added with flat sincerity from the doorway. "'Course, we may all die tomorrow." Another shrug, before he let the curtain drop behind him. "Who gives a flyin' fuck, anyhow?"

Eric blinked and started to purse his lips, stopping with a wince. Sofie dropped the cloth in the bowl and set it aside, staring after the Senior Decurion with a surprised look as she gathered a nest of blanket and bedroll around herself and reached out a hand to check the radio.

"He's got something right, for once," she muttered. Everything green, ready . . . She shivered at the memory of the palm on her shoulder. *Can it. Later. Maybe.*

"Well, *Ah* give a flyin' fuck," said a muffled voice from the center of the room. It was Trooper Huff, lying facedown on the blankets while her friend kneaded pine oil into the muscles of her shoulders and back. The fair skin gleamed and rippled as she arched her back with a sigh of pleasure.

"Centurion? Now, all *Ah* want is to get back—little lower, there, sweetlin'—get back to Rabat province an' the plantation, spend the rest of mah life raisin' horses an' babies. Old Ironbutt the deathfuckah is *still* right. If those Fritz'd gotten on our flank tomorrow they'd have had our ass for *grass*, Centurion." She sighed again, looking up. "Your turn." The dark-haired soldier handed her the bottle and lay down, and Huff rose to her knees and began to oil her palms. Then she paused. "Oh, one last thing. Didn't notice you askin' anyone to do anything you wouldn't do yo'self."

Eric's face stayed expressionless for a moment, and then he shook his head, squeezing his eyelids closed and chuckling ruefully. "Out-voted," he said, suddenly yawning enormously. He grinned down at Sofie, eyes crinkled. "I'm not going to indulge in this-here dangerous sport of plannin' things to do once the war is over," he said in a tone lighter than most she had heard from him. "Bad luck to price the unborn calf. But did you have anything planned for your next leave, Sofie?"

"Hell, no, Eric, *sir!*" she said with quiet happiness grinning back.

"Dinner at Aladdin's?" he said. That was a restaurant built into the side of Mount Meru, in Kenia province. The view of the snowpeak of Kilimanjaro rising over the Serengeti was famous, as were the game dishes.

"Consider it a date, Centurion," she said, snuggling herself into the blankets and closing her eyes.

Tomorrow was going to be a busy day.

Eric looked across at Dreiser. "That's private, Bill, but we could all three get together for some deep-sea fishing off Mombasa afterwards. Owe you something for those articles, anyway; they're going to be . . . use-ful, I think. Better than the trip you had with that writer friend of yours—what was his name, Hemingway?"

Dreiser laughed softly. "Acquaintance; Ernest doesn't have friends, just drinking buddies and sycophants. I'll bet you don't get drunk and try to shoot the seagulls off the back of the boat . . . and you seem to be in a good mood tonight, my friend."

"Because I've got things to do, Bill, things to do. And with that, goodnight." He stubbed out the cigarette, swilled down the last of the lukewarm coffee. *And probably about twenty hours of life to do them with,* he thought. Pushing the sudden chill in his gut away: *White Christ and Wotan One-Eye, what's different about that? The odds haven't changed since yesterday.* But his wants had, he forced himself to admit with bleak honesty, and his vision of his duty—an expanded one, which required his presence, if it could be arranged.

There was one good thing about the whole situation. Whatever happened, he no longer had to face death with an attitude indistin-guishable from Senior Decurion McWhirter's. *That* he had *never* felt comfortable with.

Dreiser waited while the room grew still; half an hour and there were no others awake, save himself and the cadaverous brown-bearded man who had the radio watch. The cold seemed deeper, and he pulled another blanket about himself as he laid down the notebook at last. They were not notes for his articles; those could be left to the tape, flown out with the STOL transports that took out the wounded, given to the world by the great military broadcast stations in Anatolia. These were his private journals, part of the series he had been keeping since his first assignment to Berlin in 1934.

If I'm going to be a fly on the wall of history, something ought to come of it, he thought. Something truer than even the best journalism could be. Get the raw information down now; raw feeling, as well. Safe in silence, where the busy censors of a world at war could not touch it. Safe on paper, fixed, where the gentle invisible editor of memory could not tint and bend with subconscious hindsight.

Later he would write that book: a book that would have the truth of his own observations in it, what he could research as well, written in some quiet lonely place where there would be nothing between him and his thoughts. A truth that would last. Add up the little truths, and the big ones could follow. This action tonight, for example. A Draka tetrarch had given a force twenty times its size a bloody nose, turned back a major attack by the enemy's elite troops and inflicted demoralizing casualties. And it still *felt* like defeat, at least to a civilian observer. Maybe every battle was a defeat for all involved; some just got more badly beaten than others. Soldiers always lost, whichever set of generals won.

Ambition, he mused, looking across the room at the battered face of the Draka officer. *Strange forms it takes.* What was Eric's? Not to be freed from a world of impossible choices, not any longer. And not simply to climb the ladder of the power machine and breed children to do the same in their turn—not if Dreiser knew anything of Eric's truth.

Do we ever? The truth is, we may be enemies. But for now, we *are* friends.

It was late, and he was tired. What was that Draka poet's line? "Darkness *is* a friend of mine . . . Sometimes I have to beat it back, or it would overwhelm me . . ." And sometimes it was well to welcome it. He closed his eyes.

Chapter Seventeen

NORTH CAUCASUS, NEAR PYATIGORSK
APRIL 14, 1942: 0800 HOURS

Johanna blinked. *I'm alive*, she thought. *Fuckin' odd, that*.

There was not much pain, no more than after a fall from a horse or surfboard, apart from a fierce ache in her neck. But there was no desire to move anything, and she was *hot*.

She blinked again, and now things came into focus behind the blue tint of her face shield. The wreck of the *Lover's Bite* was pitched forward, down thirty degrees at the nose over some declivity in the ploughed field. She was hanging limp in the safety harness, only her buttocks and thighs in contact with the seat. Her view showed a strip of canopy with blue sky beyond it, the instrument panel, the joystick flopping loosely between her knees. And her feet, resting in a pool of fuel that was up to her ankles where they rested on the forward bulkhead by the control pedals. The stink of the fuel was overwhelming; she coughed weakly, and felt the beginnings of the savage headache one got from breathing too much of the stuff.

Flames licked at the corner of her vision. She swiveled an eye, to see the port wing fully involved, roaring white and orange flames trailing dirty black smoke backward as a steady south wind whipped at it. The engine was a red-metal glow in the center of it, and . . . yes, the plane was slightly canted down to that direction, that was *lucky*, the fuel would be draining into the flames and not away from it.

Feeling returned; fear. She was sitting *in* a firebomb, in a pool of high-octane, surrounded by an explosive fuel-air mixture. Probably no more than seconds before it went.

Got to get *out*, she thought muzzily. Her left hand fumbled at a panel whose heat she could feel even through her gloves, looped through the carrying strap of the survival package. Her right was at her shoulder, pawing at the release catch of her harness. *Good*, she thought. It opened, and her body fell, head slamming into the instrument panel.

169

✧   ✧   ✧

Consciousness returned with a *slam* against her ear and a draft of incredible coolness. A hand reached down and lifted the helmet from her head.

Voices speaking, as she was lifted from the cockpit; in German, blurred by a fire that roared more loudly as the canopy slid back. She felt disconnected, hearing and thought functioning but slipping away when she tried to focus, as if her mind were a screw with the thread stripped.

"The pilot's alive . . . Mary Mother, it's a girl!" A young man, very young. Bavarian, from the sound of his voice; a thorough knowledge of German was a family tradition among the von Shrakenbergs.

Girl, hell, Johanna thought muzzily. She was new enough to adulthood to be touchy about it. *Two years since I passed eighteen.*

"Quick, get her out, this thing's ready to blow." An older voice, darker somehow, tired. Plattdeutsch accent, she noted no *pf* or *ss* sounds.

"I can't—her hand's tangled in something. A box."

"Bring it, there may be documents." That would be her survival package, rations and map, machine pistol and ammunition.

The cold air brought her back to full awareness, but she let herself fall limp, with eyes closed. The younger man braced a boot on either side of the cockpit, put his hands beneath her armpits, and lifted. She was an awkward burden, and the man on the ground grunted in surprise as his comrade handed her down and he took the weight across his shoulder. She was slim but solid, and muscle is denser than fat. He gave a toss to settle her more comfortably, and she could feel the strength in his back and the arm around her waist, smell the old sweat and cologne scent. Her stomach heaved, and she controlled it with an effort that brought beads of sweat to her forehead. *He might suspect I was conscious if I puked down his back.* She had her "passport" pill, but one could always die.

The German carried her some distance, perhaps two hundred meters; she could see his jackboots through slitted lids, tracking through the field, leaving prints in the sticky brown-black clay. Camouflage jacket, that meant SS. The hobnails went *rutch* on an occasional stone, *slutch* as they pulled free of the earth; the soldier was breathing easily as he laid her down on the muddy ground beside the wheels of some sort of vehicle. Not roughly, but without any particular gentleness; then his boots vanished, and she could hear them climbing into the . . . it must be a field car of some sort; her head had rolled toward it, and she could see the running board dip and sway under the man's weight.

The other soldier hurried up, panting, his rifle in one hand and the sheet-metal box of her survival kit in the other. Johanna could feel him lean the weapon against the vehicle and begin to speak. Then there was a crashing bang, followed by a huge muffled thump and a wave of heat. Light flashed against the side of the scout car, and heat like lying too close to the fireplace, and a piece of flaming wreckage sliced into the dirt in front of the wheels.

"Just made it," the man in the car said. Johanna let her eyes flutter open, wishing they had taken the trouble to find a dry spot; she could feel the thin mud soaking through her flight suit, and the wind was chill when it gusted away from the pyre of her aircraft. Sadness ran through her for a moment. It had been a beautiful ship . . .

It was a tool, and tools can be replaced, she chided herself. The young soldier was kneeling and leaning over her, face still a little pale as he turned back from the blaze to his left. That might have been him . . . Nineteen, she thought. Round freckled face, dark-hazel eyes and brown hair, still a trace of puppy fat. A concerned frown as he raised her head in one hand and brought a canteen to her lips. She groaned realistically and rolled her head before accepting the drink; the water was tepid and stale from the metal container, and tasted wonderful.

That let her see his companion. *Another dish of kebob entirely,* she thought with a slight chill. Stocky and flat-featured, cropped ash-blond hair over a tanned square face, in his mid-twenties but looking older. He was standing in the bed of the car, a little open-topped amphibian with balloon wheels, a *kubelwagon,* keeping an easy all-corners watch. The campaign ribbons he was wearing on the faded and much-laundered field tunic told a good deal; the way he moved and held the Schmeisser across his chest told more. Most of all the eyes, as he glanced incuriously her way: flat, empty, dispassionate. Familiar, veteran's eyes, the thousand-meter stare, she had been seeing it now and again all her life and it always meant someone to watch out for. People to whom killing and dying were neither very important any more. . . .

"Ach," the young SS trooper was saying, "she's just a young maiden—"

Not since I was fifteen, or thirteen if you count girls, she thought, wincing in half-pretended pain and taking inventory. Good, everything moving. She accepted another sip of the water.

"—and of fine Nordic stock, just look at her, even if they've cut that beautiful blond hair so short. And look," he indicated the name tag sewn over her left breast, " '*Johanna von Shrakenberg,*' a German name. What a shame, to be fighting our own stock; and a crime, to expose a potential Aryan mother to danger like this." He clucked his tongue, tsk-tsking.

Why, you son of a bitch, Johanna thought indignantly as the fingers of her right hand curled inconspicuously to check the hard lump at her wrist. Ignore the one holding her . . . the other SS trooper was keeping up his scan of the countryside around them, eyes scanning from far to near, then moving on to a new sector. They flicked down to her for an incurious second, then back to look for danger.

"Don't like von types," he grunted.

Johanna groaned again, and let her eyes come into focus, reaching a hand up to the young Bavarian's shoulder as if to steady herself. He patted it clumsily, and put away the canteen.

Are these people total idiots? she wondered. The way they were acting . . . Almighty Thor, they hadn't even searched her . . .

She smiled at the young soldier, and he blushed and grinned in return.

"Do you speak German?" he asked. "*Chocolaten?*" He began to fumble a package of Swiss bonbons from his breast pocket. Johanna took a deep breath, pushed pain and fear and battering out to the fringes of her mind.

"Perfectly," she whispered in the same language. "And no, thanks." He leaned close to hear, her left hand slid the final centimeter to his throat. Thumb and fingers clamped down on the carotid arteries; the soldier made a single hoarse sound as what felt like slender steel rods drove in on either side of his larynx. She jerked forward savagely and he followed in reflex, falling over her on his elbows; otherwise half his throat would have been torn free. Johanna ignored the ugly, queasy popping and rending sensations beneath her fingers; her hands were strong, but surely not strong enough to punch through the neck muscles. She *hoped* not.

Her right hand flicked. The knife came free of the forearm sheath and slapped into her hand in a single practiced movement, smooth metal over leather rubbed with graphite. Just barely into her palm, her fingers almost dropping the leather-wrapped hilt. She was still groggy; the loss of speed and coordination was frightening.

Damn worse than I thought! went through her as she turned the point in, poised, thrust. The knife was more delicate than the issue model Jamieson tucked into her boot, hand-made by Ildaren of Marrakesh, a slender-edged spike of steel fifteen centimeters long. It slid through the tunic without resistance, through the skin, slanting up under the breastbone and through the diaphragm with a crisp sensation like punching through a drumhead. Up into the heart, razoring it in half, then quarters as she wrenched the weapon back and forth in the wound. The youngster's face was less than the breadth of a hand from hers, close enough for her to smell the mints on his breath. His eyes and mouth jerked open, shut, open again in perfect circles, like a gaffed fish; she could see the pupils dilating. No sound, even though the tongue worked in the pink cavern of his mouth. Her free hand slipped from his throat to his chest to hold the twitching, juddering body off hers as she wrestled with the knife.

For a moment the fierce internal spasm of the German's muscles clamped the blade tight but it was narrow and supernally sharp. The steel slid free. With it came a warm rushing tide that flowed over her breasts and stomach, and the seawater smell of blood. The man's eyes rolled up and glazed as the dropping pressure in his veins starved the brain into unconsciousness. Johanna's knife hand moved, flipping the blade and taking a new hold on the point, three fingers and a thumb. Her arm moved it under the sheltering corpse above her, her face tracking like a gun turret for the next target.

The other SS *panzergrenadier* was intent on his surroundings. You did not survive a year on the Eastern Front by being careless, and there were too many clumps of forest within rifle range. Not that a partisan needed trees; they crept through grass or scrub like lice in the seams of a uniform worn too long, almost impossible to exterminate. Alertness was second nature; he could check for movement and breaks in the pattern while thinking of other things. Women, *schnapps,*

how home leave was a waste of time, the front was home now . . .
He looked down at his partner's body, bent over the prisoner's, giving one last shiver and then going limp. The Draka slut's eyes were
on his over Lothair's shoulder, fixed and glaring, lips rucked back from
her teeth. He frowned. *That* was not like Lothair; little bastard thought
he was Siegfried . . .

He opened his mouth, began to speak. The body was tossed aside,
there was a glint of steel . . .

"Lothair, what're you screwing arou—"

Johanna knew the throw had gone wrong even as she wrenched
the dead German's body aside, using it for leverage as her right arm
snapped across and up. The hilt had been touching her left ear; the
motion ended with her arm extended toward the standing SS man. Even
caught by surprise he was too *fast*, crouching, turning, the muzzle
of his submachine gun coming up in a smooth controlled arc as his
words turned into a formless shout of rage. The Draka could see his
finger tightening on the trigger as the knife turned, room for four
rotations in the five meters between them.

I never trained with a wet knife and gloves! something within her
wailed. The position's wrong, the sun's behind him, my head hurts,
it isn't *fair*. Flick-rolling, ignoring the jagged pain that ripped up between
her shoulders at the sudden motion, curling her feet beneath her, a
no-hold leap with arm outstretched and fingers curled back to strike
with the heel of the hand. Impossible. Too *slow*.

The knife had been aimed at his throat; an eye shot was impossibly risky in the circumstances, the ribs armored the heart, a stab wound
in the gut took too long to kill a gunman whose weapon could rip
you open. Her own error and the German's speed placed it just below
his pelvis, in the meaty part of the upper thigh near his groin. He
twisted; the startled yell of pain and the first *peckapecka-pecka* of the
Schmeisser were simultaneous. The aim was thrown off: craters in the
mud, chopping into the other SS man's body in dimples of red and
tattered cloth, an impact on her foot that flung her sprawling from
the beginnings of her leap. And saved her life; the shots whipcracked
the air over her head as her shoulder thudded into the man's stomach. Pink-*ting* as rounds punctured the thin metal of the vehicle's hood
and struck something solid beneath.

"*Frikken hund!*" the German screamed, in rage fueled by pain. His
wounded leg slammed the dashboard and buckled, and he pitched on
his back, bracing his elbows wide to prevent himself from falling into
the narrow well in front of the seats. The knob of the gearshift struck
him in the lower back, and for a moment his body dissolved in a liquid
flash that seemed to spread through every nerve, a web extending to
his finger tips.

Johanna bounced as her torso struck the trooper and the kubelwagon's door, resilient flesh and metal absorbing her momentum and
throwing her back, tuck-rolling as she fell, curling forward to cast her
weight against the fall. A quarter of a forward roll and it was a crouch,
facing the kubelwagon again and two meters away. No sign of the SS
man; he could be out, she could have time to stop and pick up a

weapon and finish him. Or the Schmeisser might be rising, about to clear the side of the vehicle and kill her. Training deeper and faster than thought made her decision, and the long muscles of her thighs uncoiled like living springs.

Half a second. That was a long time in personal combat. Her body was parallel to the ground for an instant, and her hands slapped down on the top of the scout car's door. She pivoted, legs together swinging wide and high over the windscreen—movements etched into her nerves by ten thousand hours of practice in gymnasium and salle d'armes. Legs *bend*, a quick hard push off her hands, and she was rotating in midair. There was a moment when she seemed to hang suspended, combat adrenaline slowing the instant to a breathless pause, like the endless second at the top of an Immelman or the crest of a roller coaster. She came down on the SS man knees-first as he struggled up on one elbow, eyes wide with shocked surprise.

The breath went out of the soldier with an explosive *whuff!* as one knee rammed home into the pit of his stomach. Her other came down painfully on the receiver of the Schmeisser, slid; then she was on him, the weapon trapped between their bodies, one of his arms immobilized by the strap. They grappled, snarling, the Draka gouging for the nerve clusters; she could feel the man's muscles coiling and bunching, forcing him upward from the awkward slump into the gap between seat and dashboard. Johanna arched herself against the panel behind her and pushed him back; one hand fell on the hilt of the knife in his thigh, and she jerked it free. A harsh gasp broke the struggling rasp of his breath, and he bucked in a convulsive twist that left them lying face to face on their sides across the seats. The SS man's palm slapped onto her wrist as the point of her knife drove for his face.

His *right* hand, the arm stretched across his body; the outer arm was still trapped at the elbow by the sling of his machine pistol. Useless, he kept the left fist flailing at her hip and ribs in short punishing arcs but the seatback protected her vulnerable spine and kidneys. Johanna's right arm was free, and she had solid bracing to push against; the German had leverage against him, and his grip on her wrist was reversed, weak, the thumb carrying the whole weight of her arm and body. The knife hung trembling above and between them, a long spike, motionless save for the quiver of locked muscle, slow red drops spilling down on the German's face. Johanna's was close enough to catch the spatter, close enough to smell the garlic and stale beer on his breath and the harsh musk of male sweat. To see the eyes widen in surprise as the blade jerked forward a fraction, and hear the quiver in his breath as he halted it again.

Never wrestle with a man: the instructors had told her that often enough. They simply had stronger arms. It didn't make much difference in block-and-strike fighting—if a blow landed on the right place just hard enough that was all she needed, and if she missed it didn't matter how hard she punched the air.

She jerked a breath in, clenched down and forced it out with the muscles of the gut, where strength comes from. Felt it flow into her arms, felt her face fill with blood and saw traceries of vein across her eyes.

How many hours at school, swinging the practice bar and the weights, squeezing the hand-spring? Waking stiff and sore despite the saunas and massage, rolling out of bed for the morning set of chinups . . .

Her heart beat in her ears. Her left hand forced its way between their bodies; no chance of getting it free for a strike or eye-claw, but . . . Johanna's thumb forced its way into the sweat-wet warmth of the German's armpit. Into the nerve cluster where the arm meets the shoulder, just above the beginning of the bicep. Pushed.

Her enemy made a sound, something halfway between a yelp and a snarl. The grip on her wrist was weakening, slipping, the German's arm bending back, faster as the angle changed and cast the whole strain on his forearm. Johanna wrapped one leg around the man's and heaved, twisting him onto his back and rising to throw her weight behind the knife. It crept into her sight; first the point, and then the crusted blade itself. Then their hands, his bare and dusted with freckles and sun-bleached hairs like gold wires, her fingers slim and night-black in the thin kidskin gloves; and the pommel of the knife, steel showing through the rawhide binding. She willed force into knife hand and thumb; the German's eyes widened as the steel touched his throat and he began to buck and twist, frantic; screamed once as all the strength left his arm and the knife punched down.

It had the suddenness of pushing at a stuck door and then having it open all at once; the point went through with no more effort than pushing a lump of meat onto a skewer around the fire at a braai-party. Her weight came down on the hilt and the blade sliced through the thick neck, like the upper blade of a pair of scissors; she collapsed forward into a bright spray of arterial blood, breathed it in with her first sobbing inhalation and threw herself back, sitting on her heels astride the still-quivering body and coughing, retching up and spitting out a mouthful of thin bile. And wiping at the blood: blood on her hands, in her eyes, in her hair, running down in sticky sheets over her face and neck and under her flight suit to join the cooling, tacky-thick mass from the younger German. Blood in her mouth, tasting of iodine and iron and salt; she spat repeatedly as she forced her breathing to go slow and deep, suppressing the instinctive but inefficient panting.

There was a sharp hiss, as the bullet-punctured flashcoil of the kubelwagon's boiler released its steam and joined the stink of over-heated metal to the fecal odor of death. With floodgate abruptness feeling returned, overwhelming the combat concentration. Fear first, cold on the skin, and a tight prickling up from the pubis. She looked down at the dead German; he had been so *strong*, quick too. She could never have taken two Draka like this, but this one had had potential, far too much.

His head lolled, opening the great flap of muscle and skin, blood still welling. How much blood there was, and tubes and glands showing . . . she glanced away. Physical sensation next: the ache in her head, a dozen minor scratches and bruises where her body had been ham-mered against projecting metal. They had gone unnoticed in the brief savage fight, but now the abrasions stung with salt sweat and blood, and the bruises ached with a to-the-bone sick feeling that meant they would turn a spectacular green and yellow in a day or two. And one knee was throbbing every time she moved it, where it had come down on the machine pistol when she landed on the Fritz.

Johanna looked down over one shoulder at her foot. *No pain there*, she thought dazedly. Or at least none of the pain that a real wound would cause, just another ache. One heel of her boot had been torn off, left dangling by a shred of composition rubber. "Never bet on the horses again, woman, you've used it all up," she muttered to herself.

A shout brought her head up, and she clutched at the wheel against a wave of dizziness. A line of figures was trotting toward her from the copse of forest to the east, twenty of them. They were still five hundred meters away, but they looked too ragged to be Fritz, and German troops would have come up in a vehicle, anyway. Russians, then; the situation reports had mentioned partisan activity. They might be hostile, or not. The German yoke had lain heavy here, and she had two very dead Fritz for credentials. On the other hand . . . as the saying went, nobody loved the Draka. Russians least of all, after the bite the Domination had taken out of the lands east of the Caspian back in the Great War; and there had been a generation of border clashes since. A Russian young enough to be in the field now had probably been brought up on anti-Draka propaganda and atrocity stories, at least half of which were true.

A heavy, weary annoyance seized her for a moment. "Mother Freya," she said to herself, scrubbing a forearm over her lips again. "I really don't want to be here." Not so much the fear or discomfort, they were bearable, but she definitely did not want to be here in this cold and foreign place, covered in blood and sitting on a corpse. "I want to be *home*." Rahksan giving her a massage and a rubdown with Leopard Balm liniment and a cuddle, twelve hours' sleep, waking up clean and safe in her own bed with her cat on the pillow, with no dangers and nobody telling her what to do . . . " 'Nothing's free, and only the cheaper things can be bought with money'; you never said a truer word, Daddy."

She stood, feeling the raw breeze as her breathing slowed. One hand clenched on the other. Time enough to move when the shaking stopped.

The partisans came up in a wary half-circle as Johanna finished strapping on the gear from her kit, murmuring and pointing as they reconstructed the brief fight. None of them was pointing a weapon at her: she recognized "Drakansky" among the liquid Slavic syllables, and wary sidelong glances. That was reasonable enough; she must look a sight, with drying blood matted in her hair and smeared about her mouth. From the way some of them leaned into the kubelwagon and then glanced back at her, fingering their necks, she imagined they were speculating that she had torn out the second SS trooper's throat with her teeth; it was obvious enough that neither of the Germans had been shot. There was awe in the glances, too, at the woman who had climbed out of a burning plane and killed two armed soldiers of the SS elite with her hands . . .

She ignored them with studied nonchalance as she slipped a magazine into the grip of the machine pistol, clipped the bandolier to her belt and tossed back two pills from one of the bottles; aspirin, for the pounding ache between her eyes and the stiff neck and shoulders. Limping as little as her bruised foot and the missing heel would allow, she walked over to the corpse of the young Fritz on the ground. There were already flies, crawling into the gaping wound in his stomach and across dry eyeballs frozen in a look of eternal surprise. The heavy smell of excrement brought the bile to the back of her throat as she flipped his rifle up with a toe and tossed it to a startled Russian.

They never mention the smell of shit in the old stories, she thought, fighting down the vomit. *Maybe they had tighter assholes in the days of the sagas.* Johanna did not consider herself more squeamish than the average Draka, but there was nothing pleasing about looking at the ruin that had once been a person. Once, with an adolescent's fascination for horrors, she had gone to the public execution ground in Hyancitha, the market town nearest Oakenwald, to see a serf broken on the wheel and impaled for striking an overseer. Once had been enough.

Enough. She had an audience, and upchucking with buck fever was *not* the way to impress them. Not that this was the first time she had killed, but aerial combat was a gentleman's form of killing. You didn't have to see the results of it; they fell out of the sky in a convenient and sanitary fashion and you went home . . . Gritting her teeth, she forced herself to reach out, grasp the ear, make a quick slash. Her blade was still sharp enough to cut gristle with two drawing strokes . . . The grenade in the German's boot went into hers, and she walked grimly over to the scout car and repeated the docking process, a little frightfulness was always good for a first impression, or at least so the textbooks said. Cleaning and sheathing the knife, she looked back once; for an outlander, that Fritz had not been bad at all. It was going to be an expensive war if there were more like him.

The partisans had come a little closer; their weapons held ready but not immediately threatening; there were about twenty of them, incredibly filthy, ragged, armed with a motley collection of Russian and Fritz weaponry, with a lean starved ferocity about them. None of them seemed to have blanched at the ear collection; from the look of it, affection for the Fritz in general and the SS in particular was running low in this part of Russia. They stank, with a smell of unwashed filth and the sour odor of men who have not had a good meal in a very long time. She walked toward them, and suddenly it was all she could do not to laugh and skip.

Alive, suddenly bubbled up within her. She felt a giddy rush of sensation, the blood cooling and drying on her chest, mild spring air, bright morning sunlight and the sweet vanilla-green scent of flowering oaks from the copse at the top of the hill ahead of her. Feelings pushing at her control: tears, affection, incredibly a sudden rush of sexual arousal. *Freya, what a time to feel horny,* she giggled to herself, and then it faded out into a vast well-being. Fighting down the smile that threatened, she walked through the partisan line. Their leader seemed to be a thin man with no front teeth and a long scar where one eye should be; he had been waiting for her to stop and speak, and her steady pace threw him off his mental center, as if he had reached the bottom of a stairwell one tread too soon.

PD, she thought. Psychological dominance, keep 'em off balance. It might not work, but on the other hand . . . *Every moment of my life from now on is a bonus.* She waited until the partisans had walked after her toward the woods for a good ten meters, until she could sense their leader about to reach out and touch her sleeve. Then she turned, pulled the grenade from her boot, yanked the tab and tossed it up in the air, caught it as the Russians dived flat with a chorus of yells and threw it back toward the Fritz scout car.

Perfect. The throw felt right, a smooth heavy arc that her mind drew to the target. Suddenly, she could do no wrong: the stick grenade pinwheeled through the air and dropped neatly into the kubelwagon's front seat. She stayed casually erect, hands on hips, tapping a foot to time the fuse. One . . . two . . . three . . .

Whump! Stamped-steel panels blew out of the German car, and the doors sprang open and stayed that way, sprung on their hinges. The body was flung out of the front seat to land a few yards away; flames began to pool and lick beneath it as the fuel tank ruptured. Johanna glanced from it to the shattered, burning framework of the *Lover's Bite*. Turnabout's fair play, she thought, and looked to the figure at her feet. The partisan leader had been holding his tattered fur cap down around his ears with both hands. Unclenching hands and eyes, he looked up at her with the beginnings of anger. The fragments of casing could have been lethal, if the grenade had not fallen into something that absorbed them.

"*Sprechen sie Deutsch?*" she asked calmly, narrow blonde head tilted to one side, an eyebrow elegantly arched.

"Crazy devil woman!" he began in an understandable pidgin of that language, then continued more slowly. "*Ja, ein wenig.*" *Yes, a little.* Strange things were happening, the partisan thought, since the Draka had attacked the *neimetsky*. Ivan escaping certain death over in the village on the highway, calling them all together . . . Caution was always wise, and at least there was an opportunity to shovel his intimidating whatever-she-was onto somebody *else's* plate. "My name Dmitri Mikhaelovitch Belov."

"Good," Johanna answered, with cool friendliness. "Then take me," she tapped a foot lightly against his shoulder for emphasis, "to your leader."

It took them most of a day to reach the guerilla rendezvous. Hard marching through increasingly rugged hills, always south toward the snowpeaks of the Caucasus. Forest closed in until they were always under cover, diving for thickets when aircraft snarled by overhead; Johanna watched a dogfight far above with a sudden thick longing that was more than fear and aching feet and the strain of keeping up a show of tireless strength for her escort-captors. Tiny silver shapes, wheeling in the sad blue light of early evening. *That* was where she belonged . . .

Or with Tom on the sheepskins in front of a crackling fire, she added to herself as they waded through a stream whose iciness spoke of a source in melting glaciers. Thick woods now, huge moss-grown beeches and oaks, a carpet of leaves and spring wildflowers and occasional meadows where the scent grew dizzying. Simple enough to ignore the blisters in boots never designed for walking; her well-fed fitness made the march easy enough. Surprising that these scarecrows could set a pace that pushed her even a little, even still feeling the mild concussion from the crash. But then, anyone who had stayed alive and under arms in Russia for the last year or so was going to be a real survivor type.

A break in the bird chorus warned them to go to earth just after cautiously crossing a rutted "road," and they laid up in the undergrowth while a column of German half-tracks and armored cars thundered by. There was little chance of discovery, with the speed the Germans were making; also, they seemed to be primarily worried about the sky above them, had probably chosen this trail precisely because it had branches meeting above it.

After that the partisans seemed to relax, an almost subliminal feeling. Their weapons still stayed at the ready, and nobody spoke; the fieldcraft was not up to Draka standards, but far from bad.

Probably the noisy ones all died this last year, she thought. Dmitri tapped her on the shoulder, indicating a cleft in the hill up which they toiled.

"Fritz never come this far," he whispered. "This place."

A sharp hail brought them to a halt, and suspicious figures appeared out of the woods around them. The partisans who had found her engaged the others in a lengthy question-and-answer session; this group seemed marginally less ragged and better armed, and it included several women as tough-looking as any of the men. Johanna could puzzle through a simple Russian sentence, if it was written in Roman script; this rapid conversation left her with no more than the odd word— "Drakansky," "Fritz," "Aeroplane." Pretending boredom, she split the cellophane cover on a package of cigarettes, tapped one out, lit it with her American Ronson.

That brought attention—a circle of faces, bearded and desperate; she handed the package to Dmitri. He seemed to be expanding on the subject of the strange Draka, rather like a man who had brought home some dangerous exotic and called his friends around to see the basilisk, the more so as she sensed him a stranger here. Even the ear-cropping devil woman who tore out Fritz throats was not as interesting as tobacco, though; hands mobbed him, clawing. Dmitri shouted, and then used the butt of the rifle to restore order and hand the cigarettes out in halfs and quarters.

"No smoke for long," he said, puffing happily as they walked toward the steep path up the cliff. "For Fritz only, eh? Always vodka while potatoes is, but no *rhakoria. Dasvedanya!*"

The hollow inside was crowded despite covering several thousand square meters, and Johanna guessed that this was a gathering of several bands, more than its usual population. Bluffs and dense forest surrounded it and the scattering of lean-tos, tents and brush shelters.

Cooking fires were few and carefully smokeless, but otherwise the scene was a cross between the military and the domestic; there were even a few silent children, if no toddlers. Murmurs ran among them, and a steady stream began moving toward the party walking through the entrance. Johanna's eyes moved in on a face whose slight smile remained fixed, noting the dug-in machine guns farther upslope, slit trenches and the absence of stench that told of good latrine discipline, several mortars and stacked ammunition, a knocked-down heliograph set . . .

And one solid log-and-stone hut, the door opening to show a bearlike figure with dramatic crossed cartridge belts across a bulging stomach, belt full of daggers, baggy trousers and black astrakhan-wool cap . . . Dmitri snapped a salute, then continued his animated speech to the gathering crowd, full of hand gestures, swooping like planes, teeth worrying an imaginary neck.

Well, if it isn't Boris the Cossack, Terror of the Steppe, Johanna thought, glancing aside at the hulking figure by the hut. With a slight chill; there was no foolishness in the narrow black eyes. A figure in a patched but recognizable Soviet uniform followed the huge man: pale intelligent face and long thin hands. Green tabs on the collar. NKVD, she thought. Oh, joy.

The big man rumbled a question; his face was round and puffy, but strong with thick red lips. Dmitri answered, then seemed to be arguing; there were murmurs from the crowd around them, until the big man turned on them and roared. That quieted most; when the man with the green tabs spoke, it grew silent enough for Johanna to hear breathing, and the whistling wind through the leaves.

Dmitri turned to her unhappily. "This," he said indicating the man with the bandoliers, "Sergeant Sergei." Another rumble from the hulk. "Pardons, *Comrade Colonel* Sergei Andropovitch Kozin." A frightened glance. "With . . . helpings-man? Ah, *aide,* Comrade Blensikov. Comrade Colonel is being our *leader—*" he used the literal German term, *führer,* with a slight emphasis "—while our commander, Ivan Yuhnkov, was prisoner of SS. Commander Ivan—" using the Russian word *kommandyr* "—is becoming here again in charge soon now, has called all First Partisan Brigade to meet him here."

Johanna pursed her lips, feeling sweat trickle down her flanks from her armpits. Her back crawled with the consciousness of so many about her: wild serfs, strange ones, not domesticated, and armed . . . And these two were not going to be rhinoed that easily. She forced her perceptions into action, to see them as individuals, reading the clues of hands and face and stance. *The tool that speaks can also think,* she reminded herself. *You're supposed to be more intelligent—outthink them!*

It was not comforting. The big one was an animal, and the bug-under-the-rock type a fanatic. From the signs, a smart fanatic. But . . . this was like running down a steep hill. If you kept running, you *might* fall on your ass; if you tried to stop, you *certainly* would.

"Tell them, she said in neutral tones, "that I will speak to this Commander Ivan, when he comes."

Dmitri translated, his ravaged face becoming even unhappier. "They . . . they saying you talking to them, now, in *khutzba*, in hut." He held out his hand. "Gun?"

Too many of them out here, she thought with tight-held control. Brushing him aside, she followed the NKVD officer into the hut, blinking at the contrast between the bright sunlight through the leaves outside and the gloom of the interior. That deepened as the other man filled the door, swung it to behind him with a heavy thud. He did not bother to shoot home the bar.

The interior of the hut smelled rank, like an animal's den, but with an undertone of clean wood. Johanna breathed deep and slow, needing the oxygen and the *prahnu*-trained calmness that the rhythmic flexing of her diaphragm produced. It would all depend on . . .

The thin man seized her, hands on her *upper* arms, thumbs digging into her shoulder blades, trying to make her arch her chest out. She let the muscles go limp under his grip, the shoulders slump. There was no fear now. *Ju*, went through her. *Go with.* The big man stepped close, very fast for someone his size; he must be twice her weight easily, and there was plenty of muscle there. A hand clamped painfully on her breast, kneading and twisting; another behind her head, pulling her mouth up to meet his. The smell of him filled her nostrils, strong, like a mule that has been ploughing in the sun. The two men crowded her between them; they must be expecting her to try to kick shins like a child.

Is everybody *outside the Domination a complete idiot about immobilizing an enemy?* she thought in momentary wonderment. Her arms could not move forward or back to strike . . . and did not need to. Instead her elbows punched *out*, away from her sides. The NKVD officer found his grip slipping; instinctively raising his own stance, he found himself pushing down on her shoulders rather than gripping her upper arms. The Draka's own hands shot down to clasp the fabric of the Cossack trousers; she let her knees go limp, and pulled herself downward with a motion that drew on the strength of back and stomach as much as arms. The thin Russian found the rubbery muscle and slick fabric vanishing from his hands, bent to follow them. His forehead met his comrade's descending kiss with a *thock* of bone on teeth that brought a roar of pain from the giant.

Johanna found herself squatting, her knees between the big Russian's straddled legs, her face level with the long swelling of his erection. There were several means of disabling a large, strong man from that position; she chose the most obvious. Her hand dropped to the ground, clenched into a fist, punched directly up with a twist of hip and shoulder, flexing of legs, *hunnnh* of expelled breath that put weight and impact behind it. The Russian would probably have been able to block a knee to the groin while she was standing; against this, there was no possibility of defense. The first two knuckles of her fist sank into his scrotum, with a snapping twist at the moment of impact that flattened the testicles against the unyielding anvil of his pubic bone. He did not scream; the pain was far too intense for that. His reflex bending was powerful enough to send his comrade crashing into the bunk at the rear of the cabin, and he staggered away clutching his groin and struggling to breathe through a throat locked in spasm.

Johanna flowed erect, turning. The NKVD man turned out to be a fool, after all: he staggered to his feet and threw a punch at her head, rather than going for his gun. She relaxed one knee, swaying out of the fist's path; her right palm slapped onto his wrist, drawing him farther along . . . *pivot* on the heel, *straddle* stance . . . *throw* the weight into it . . . her left elbow drove into his side just below the armpit, with the force of his own momentum behind it. Her left arm went tingling numb, but she heard something snap audibly, felt bone give under her blow. She kept control of the Russian's arm, bent, twisted, heaved. His body left the ground, began a turn, ran into the door three-quarters of the way through it. Something else snapped, and he went limp to the split-log floor.

One down, the Draka thought, turning again. The machine pistol was out of immediate reach on her back . . . and the giant was coming at her again.

She blinked, backing, almost frozen with surprise. He was moving with one hand pressed to his groin, as if he could squeeze out the pain, but the other held a knife, a khidjal, held it as if he knew how to use it. His face worked; he spat out a broken tooth, grinning with a blood-wet mouth in an expression that was nothing *like* a smile. The knifepoint made small circles in the air.

Johanna snapped out her own, hilt low, point angled up. Left hand bladed, palm down, shuffling back in a flat-footed crouch. This was *not* good. The Russian had a full ten centimeters' advantage of reach and there was no room to maneuver, the whole Loki-cursed hut was only four meters on a side, and the knife was *not* a weapon to duel with. It was fine for surprise, good for an ambush in the dark, but in a straight-on knife fight the one who ended up in the hospital was the winner.

What do I do now? she thought. Then: *Kill or die, what else?*

The Cossack straightened a little and came in. The blade moved up, feinting a thrust to the belly, and his left hand reached going for a hold. Stupidity again, still trying to subdue her. She spun, slashing, and the blade sliced up the outside of the other's arm from wrist to elbow. Cloth parted under as the edge touched meat, cutting a long, shallow gash. The giant roared and attacked, thrusting and slashing in deadly earnest this time.

Some far-off portion of her mind wished for a heavier blade; the narrow steel strip she carried in her wrist sheath was a holdout weapon, without the weight for a good cut. There are few places on a human body where a stab is quickly disabling, and none of them is very vulnerable at arm's length to an alert opponent. To kill quickly in a knife fight you must slash, cut every exposed surface to ribbons and rely on blood loss to knock the other out.

That seemed unlikely. A long blade and longer arm were reaching for her life, and she backed, parrying steel-on-steel, the most difficult of all defenses, drawing out the exchange until an opening let her side-slip past the Russian and back into the center of the room. The effort had been brutal; she stood and breathed in deep careful motions, eyes never leaving her opponent's. He waited for an instant, face gone blankly calculating, even the pain in his crotch forgotten. The three-second passage had let them feel each other out; Johanna knew that she was more skilled with the knife, and faster—just enough to compensate for the cramped quarters and her enemy's longer reach and heavier knife—and she would have less margin for error. Desperation surged; could she reach the gun before . . .

Her back was to the door as it opened, forcing the limp body of the NKVD man aside. Light speared in, taking the huge Russian in the eyes, and he squinted, peering. Then his face changed, first to a fresh rage, then sudden fear. Johanna almost had him then, and his recovery cost him a cut across the face. Johanna bored in, knocked his knife wrist aside with a bladed palm, skipped her left foot forward and flick-kicked. The toe of her boot landed solidly under one kneecap, and there was a tearing *pop* as cartilage gave way; she spun back out of reach as he bellowed and tried to grapple. The Russian stayed on his feet, but his face was gray and all the weight on one leg. Now to finish it: she came in low and smooth and fast, and—

—one foot skidded out from underneath her in a patch of blood. The floor slammed into her back, hard enough to knock the breath out of her. She saw lights before her eyes, and knew the knife would come down before she could recover.

"*Shto*," a cool voice from behind her said. "*Ruki verch, Sergei*." Then purling Russian syllables, meaningless. A woman's voice, with crowd-mutter behind her. And a very meaningful metallic click—the safety of a pistol being flicked off. The man before her kept his involuntary crouch, and pain-sweat dripped into his thin black beard; he licked blood off his lips as he dropped the knife and put his open hands above his shoulders, speaking in a wheedling tone. The woman's voice cut him off sharply, a sneer in it.

Johanna rolled out of the line of fire and came erect. She stood, slipping the knife back into its sheath as she took a careful step to the side, slowly, hands well out and empty. Turned slowly also, in a position where she could see her opponent as well as the door. She was not going to turn her back on that sort of strength—not until she knew what the score was.

At first the woman in the doorway was nothing but a silhouette, surrounded by sun-dazzle and haze. Then her pupils adjusted, her body lost the quivering knowledge of steel about to slice into vulnerable flesh. *Tall*, was her first thought; about the Draka's own height. Long straight hair the color of birchwood, gathered in a knot at the side of her head. Open coat, fine soft-tanned sheepskin edged with embroidery and astrakhan, reaching almost to the floor. Pressed-silk blouse, tailored pleated trousers tucked incongruously into muddy German boots a size too large and stuffed with straw. *Young*, was her next impression. Not much more than the Draka's own age. Pale oval face, high-cheeked in the Slav manner, but not flat. High forehead, eyes like clover honey, straight nose, full red lips drawn back slightly from even white teeth. Broad shoulders emphasized by the coat; full high breasts above a narrow waist; hips tapering to long dancer's legs . . .

With a Walther P48 in one elegantly gloved hand, pointed unwaveringly at the other Russian's face.

Interesting, Johanna mused. *That is a seven-hundred-auric item, if I ever saw one.* A thought crossed her mind: if they both came through this alive, it would be almost a charitable act to acquire . . .

The pistol swiveled around to her. Johanna considered the black eye of it, followed up the line of the arm to meet the amber gaze. *Then again, no. Definitely not. This is not someone to whom I can imagine saying "Lie down and play pony for me."* Pity. Lovely mouth, really.

"Valentina Fedorova Budennin," the woman said. "Once of the Linguistic Institute, now of the partisan command, and just out of Pyatigorsk. At your service, although you seem to need less rescuing than Dmitri led me to expect." Astonishingly, she spoke in English, almost without accent except for a crisp British treatment of the vowels. "Air Corps, I see. You may have paid me a very pleasant visit yesterday, then." She smiled, an expression which did not reach her eyes.

"Pilot Officer Johanna von Shrakenberg," the Draka said, keeping the surprise out of her voice. "Believe me, the effort was appreciated. Although," she frowned, "this is the *second* time today I've survived because somebody assumed I was a harmless idiot. Not complainin' about the results, but it's damned odd."

"Ah." The smile grew wider, but remained something of the lips only. "That would be because you are a woman. I have been relying on men underestimating me because of that for some time, the more fools, they." The Russian woman called over her shoulder. "Ivan!" and a sentence in her own language. A stocky Russian walked in with a Fritz machine pistol over his shoulder and . . . a *Draka* field dressing on one side of his face, nobody else used that tint of blue gauze.

To Johanna: "This will seem odd, but I think I have a man here who knows your brother. We should talk." Her gaze went back to Sergei, backed against the wall, eyes flickering in animal wariness. "After we dispose of some business." The pistol turned back and slammed, deafening in the enclosed space. A black dot appeared between the big Russian's eyes, turning to a glistening red. The impact of his falling shook the floor.

It was much later before Ivan and Valentina could talk alone, low-voiced before the fireplace of the hut, ignoring the bodies at their feet.

"Impressive," Ivan said, nodding to the door. Johanna had gone for a tactful walk, while they considered her advice.

"The Draka did not get where they are by accident," Valentina said, seating herself and crossing one leg elegantly over another. "Which leaves the matter of your decision. There are two alternatives: to attack Pyatigorsk while the Germans are occupied, or to strike at the rear of the SS column attempting to clear the pass."

"What do *you* think we should do, Valentina Fedorova?" Ivan asked, feeling with his tongue for the loose tooth. Truly, it was a little better, and the gums had stopped bleeding. Amazing things, these vitamin pills.

The woman shrugged. "Whatever helps that Draka officer you spoke to; it is our best chance. Finding his sister here," she shrugged. "Well, the truly impossible thing would be a world in which the unlikely never happened."

"Best chance for us, but what of the Revolution? The Party? Russia?"

She turned her head and spat, lofting the gobbet across the room to land on the dead NKVD agent.

"The Revolution and the Party are as dead as that dog. Stalin killed them, but the corpse lover kept his mother aboveground until Hitler came with a shovel. Do not delude yourself, Ivan Desonovitch, the way that one did."

The partisan commander looked down, fiddling with the strap of his Schmeisser; it was more comfortable than meeting the woman's eyes. "And our people?"

Valentina sighed, rubbing two fingers over her forehead. "The *narod*, the Russian people . . . we survived Genghis Khan and the Tatar yoke; we endured the tzars, the boyars . . . we can outlive the Draka, too." She smiled coldly. "My grandmother was a serf; a nobleman in St. Petersburg pledged her for a gambling debt, and bought her back for two carriage horses."

"We could fight them!" He laid an encouraging hand on her shoulder, then snatched it back with a muttered apology as she froze in distaste.

Valentina shook her head. "We fought the Nazis, my friend, because they would not only have enslaved us, they would have killed three-quarters of us first whether we fought or not. I did not lie on my back for that mad dog Hoth for six months without learning something of them! If the Draka win, and we try to fight on here, at first there would be partisans, yes." She paused to kick the dead Sergei and spit again, in his face. "Then only bandits like this dead Cossack pig, preying on their own people because it was easier. In the end, hunted animals, eating roots and each other in the woods until the Draka killed the last one; and our peasants would be glad, if it gave them a chance to work and eat and rear their children without the thatch being burnt above their heads."

She turned on him, and he shrank slightly from the intensity of her. "No, Ivan Desonovitch, we shall retreat because that is the way to work and fight for our people; retreat to the Americans, who will fight the Draka someday, because they must. If there is a hope that our people may be free, that is it." She laughed, chillingly. "Free. For the first time. Everything possible must happen in the end, no?"

Chapter Eighteen

"In the end, I was left with nothing but fading memories and the stereotypes of popular culture to build the father in my head. Yet, however tempting, the strutting uniforms and sinister drawls of Hollywood's Draka never seemed enough; cutout shapes against a background of sun-bomb missiles and jets and nuclear submarines prowling the Atlantic. All my life I had been conscious of the layers of consciousness itself: there was the me *I had shown to my schoolmates, the* me *my adoptive parents knew, the surfaces and masks I showed to friends and lovers, the fragments of self that became the characters of my work. There was even a* me *kept for New York editors, almost as deep as the one I saved for my agent. None of them was the* me *to whom I spoke in darkness, the secret self that said 'I am I.' Yet all of these—roles, masks, fragments—were* me *to the people who saw them: all of* me. *And I was* those masks while I wore them; they were . . . partial things, but not lies. The single thing that has always stood in my memory as the bridge between childhood and maturity, the gap between myself-as-I-am and the young alien whose memories I bear, was the realization that was true for others as myself.*

"That was the beginning of all my art and my deepest contact with my father. There was a time when I collected his photograph obsessively: newspaper clippings, from the back-jackets of his books, plastered over the walls of my Manhattan loft. Yet it was a line from one of his works that made him real to me, as the images could not: 'A man's mind is a forest at night.' Was he the man who had owned and used my mother, and discarded me as an inconvenience? Or the father who loved her, and me enough to risk life and reputation to give me freedom? Both, and neither; we cannot know each other, or ourselves; there is no knowing, only an endless self-discovery, 'often as painful as collisions in the dark, truths rough as bark and sharp as thorns. Knowledge is a journey; when it ends, we die.'"

Daughter to Darkness: A Life, by Anna von Shrakenberg
Houghton & Stewart, New York, 1964

VILLAGE ONE, OSSETIAN MILITARY HIGHWAY
APRIL 17, 1942; 1300 HOURS

CRASH. CRASH. CRASH. CRASH—
The shells were falling at three-second intervals. The bunker vibrated with every impact, stone and timber groaning as they readjusted under the stress, ears popping in the momentary overpressure. Dust filtered down in clouds that coated mouth and nose and lungs with a dryness that itched; the blue light of the lamp was lost in the clouds, a vague blur to eyes that streamed water, involuntary tears. The wounded satchelman in the corner was breathing slowly, irregularly, each painful effort bubbling and wheezing through the sucking wound in his chest. Eric sneezed, hawked, spat, wiped his eyes on his sleeve and looked about. There were nearly twenty crowded into the room besides the wounded, mostly squatting and leaning on their weapons; one or two praying, more with their eyes shut and wincing as the hammer blows struck the rubble above. More waited, locked in themselves or holding hands.

Sofie knelt by the communications table, fingers working on the field telephone. "Sir, can't raise bunker four; it's not dead, just no answer."

Eric sneezed again. "Wallis! Take a stick and check it out. If Fritz is in, blow the connector passage."

Five troopers rose and pulled their kerchiefs over mouth and nose, filing over to the door. They moved more slowly than they had earlier. *Exhaustion*, Eric thought. Not surprising; the shelling had started well before first light. An attack at dawn, three more since then, each more desperate than the last. Combat was more exhausting than breaking rock with a sledgehammer; the danger hormones of the fight-flight reflex drained the reserves down to the cellular level.

And when you got tired, you got slow, you made mistakes. The cellars had saved them, let them move through the village under cover and attack where they chose. But there was only so much you could do against numbers and weight of metal; they were killing ten for one, but there was always a Fritz number eleven. The casualties had been a steady drain, and so had the expenditure of fungibles, ammunition, explosives, rocket-gun shells. That last time, the Fritz had come down the holes after them, hand-to-hand in the dark, rifle butt and bayonet, bush knife and boots and teeth . . . if there had been a few more of the SS infantry, it would have been all over. The Draka garrison of Village One was running out—of blood and time and hope.

"Lock and load," Wallis said, and there was a multiple rattle as bolts were drawn back and released. They vanished, heads dipping below the ragged stone lintel, like a sacrificial procession in some ancient rite.

Eric reached for his canteen, trying to think over the noise that hammered like a huge slow heart. The dark closed in; they were listening to that heartbeat from the belly of the beast. The war had become very small, very personal.

Gods and demons, aren't the bastards ever going to run out of ammunition? It was heavy stuff falling —150s and 170s, long-range self-propelled guns. As beyond any countermeasure as weapons mounted on the moon would have been, turning the village above into a kicked-over mound of rubble, raising and tossing and pulverizing the stone. Splinters of steel, splinters of granite, fire and blast; nothing made of flesh could live in it. Just keeping lookouts up there under shelter was costing him, a steady trickle of casualties he could not replace.

There was a stir. Something different, in the private hell they had all come to believe was timeless. It took a moment for the absence to make itself felt; the lungshot sapper had stopped breathing with a final long sigh. After a moment Trooper Patton released her friend's hand and crawled over, to shut the man's eyes and gently remove the canvas sack of explosives that had been propping up his head and shoulders.

Let something happen, he prayed. *Anything.*

"Third Tetrarchy reporting—"

He snatched at the handset, jamming a thumb into his left ear to drown out the noise. Third Tetrarchy was holding the trenchline west of the village, or was supposed to be; the connection had been broken an hour ago. There was as much at the other end, but . . .

" . . . hold, can't hold; we're being overrun, pulling back to the woods. Stopped the infantry but the tanks are through, no antitank left, they're into the village as well—" The line went dead again.

White Christ have mercy, they're sending the armor in alone through their own shellfire, rammed into him. Brutally dangerous, but it might work, the odds against a round actually *hitting* a tank were still vanishingly small . . .

"*Up and at 'em!*" he barked, his finger stabbing out twice. "You two stay, Sofie put it on the wire, all bunkers, everybody *move*." The Fritz could saturate the village, then bring in sappers to pump the bunkers full of jellied gasoline, or lay charges heavy enough to bury them . . .

He went through the doorway with an elbow crooked over his mouth to take the worst of the dust, coughed, and felt the ribs stab pain. He was panting, and the breath didn't seem to be doing any *good*, as if the inside of his lungs had gone hot and stretched and tight, unable to suck the oxygen out of the air. The cellars were dim-dark, full of sharp edges and projections looming up to bruise and cut and snag. Full of running soldiers and the sound of composition-soled boots on gritty stone under the monstrous anger of the guns, sound that shivered in teeth and bone, echoed in the cavity of the lungs. As the survivors of Century A dashed for the remaining pop-up holes, Eric flung himself at the rough timbers of the ladder, running up into the narrow darkness one-handed, the other holding his Holbars by the sling, until . . .

"*Fuck* it!" he screamed, voice raw with dust and frustration. There was a section of wooden-board wall toppled over the carefully concealed entrance and something heavier on that. He let the assault rifle fall to hang by its strap, turned, braced his back against the obstruction and his face against the stones off the wall. Took a deep breath, relaxed, drew into himself. Pushed, pushed until lights flared red behind his closed lids, pushed against the stone and his hatred of the place that held him entrapped.

"God *damn!*" There was a long yielding slither, and a crunch of breaking oak boards.

Then he was blinking in the light that poured through the hole, coughing again, breathing by will power against the greater pain in his chest. Rubble had shifted, and the way was clear into what was left of the ground floor of the house. Still a roof overhead, that was good, and the row across the street was almost intact. *Flash-crash* and he dropped his face into the broken stone, waiting for the last of the shrapnel to *ping-ting* into harmlessness, then leopard-crawled into the interior of the building. Out here the shellbursts sounded harder, the edges of the sound unblurred. Impact bounced at him, lifting his body and dropping it again on hard-edged ruins. Above him the long timbers that upheld the second story creaked and shifted, their unsupported outer ends sagging further, rock and less identifiable objects hitting and bouncing around him with a patter and *snak-snak.*

Sunlight was blinding even with the overcast, after the perpetual night of the cellars. He glanced at his watch as the other six followed him and flowed over the uneven rock to the remnant of the roadside wall; there was enough of it to make a decent firing parapet if nothing killed them from above. 1330 hours. Early afternoon; unbelievable. A flicker of movement from the second-story rooftop opposite; good, the others were in place. Elbows and knees to the low heap of the wall; and—

—the shelling of the long-range heavies stopped. Tank guns still sounded, and the direct-fire assault weapons, the two the Fritz had left. But that was nothing, now; silence rang in his ears, muffled, like cotton wool soaked in warm olive oil. Now he could catch the background: shattered bits of wall and fires burning, mostly, a great pillar of soot-black coming from the next street over. That was where the P-12 had crashed, when the Air Corps came in to give them support against the first wave. The Fritz had 88s and twin 30mm flakpanzers high up the shoulders of the valley; the cloud cover was at five hundred meters, low level attack was suicide. They had come in anyway, with rockets and napalm; one had lost control right above the village, and the explosion had done as much damage as the Fritz shelling. Another fire in the street outside: an SS personnel carrier, simple thing, not much more than a thin steel box on treads; the 15mm slugs from the heavy machine gun had gone through it the long way. It was still burning, in the middle of a round puddle of sooty-orange flame from the ruptured fuel tanks. Probably rendered fat from the crew, too; the screaming had stopped long ago, but he was glad that the dust was cutting off most of the smell. Grit crunched between his teeth and he spat again, black phlegm.

"Too soon," he muttered, as he came up beside Sofie and spread the bipod of his Holbars. From here he could *just* see down a little of the long curve of the street: parts still blocked by houses on either side, others merely a lower patch in a sea of stone lumps, bits of broken timber, bodies, wrecked vehicles. "Too soon to stop the shelling. Why?"

❖   ❖   ❖

"Herr Standartenführer, I just cannot raise them!"

The radioman in the command tank winced in anticipation, but the SS commander's face remained set. Voices were crackling in, demanding to know why the artillery support had ceased. One minute, magenta flashes and cedar-shaped blossoms of dust white and black, walls collapsing, thunder echoing back from the walls of the valley, fire. Now, *nothing*.

How should I know? his mind complained, as hands levered him back into a sitting position in the turret and he turned to look north and west. Futile, the guns were behind the ridge and two kilometers away, but instinct did not work on the scale of modern warfare. He switched circuits.

"Weidner. Take two carriers, get back there and find out what the problem is with those guns!" He paused, considering. "Radioman, get me Pyatigorsk; perhaps *they* have a through connection."

Waiting, he turned to consider the remnants of the Circassian town. That was all that was left, the flanking trenches had been pounded out of existence. Shell holes pocked the uneven surface of the fields, the shattered stumps that had been the orchards around it. Even now that the buildings were mostly battered down he could not see much past the first mounds of broken stone blocks, but columns of smoke pocked it; the sharp rattle of automatic fire, grenade blasts, glimpses of moving vehicles. There were more of those south, up the valley— tanks and carriers moving past the ruins and onto the Ossetian Military Highway once more. Slowly, cautiously; the Draka had taught them that, and the special mine-clearing tanks were burning wreckage in the fields below the village.

Unwillingly, his eyes shifted down. More pillars of smoke from wrecks, far too many. Here a twisted mass after an ammunition explosion in a pierced hull; there a turret flipped forty meters from its tank, still gleaming wetly even though the rain had stopped hours ago. Another that had shed its track and turned helplessly in a circle as the length of flexible metal unreeled behind it; the crew lay where the machine guns had caught them bailing out. Fuel and scorched metal, burnt flesh and explosive, wet dung-smell from the fields. More bodies lying in the glistening chewed-up gray mud, in straggling lines, in bits where the mines had gone off, singly and in clumps where they had been shot off the tanks they rode toward the buildings . . . His infantry had suffered even more than the tanks; many were still slow and exhausted from last night's ambush-fiasco in the woods. He flushed, hammering a hand into the side of the hatch.

"Lieber Herr *Gott*, how am I going to explain this?" Professional reflex ran a tally in his head. A hundred tanks and assault guns yesterday at dawn; barely twenty now, and that was including the damaged ones that were still mobile. The infantry? Four hundred down, dead or with incapacitating wounds, many more who should be in hospital beds still on their feet and carrying weapons. He rammed the side of his hand into the solid steel again. *The transport, you had that shot out from under you last night, don't forget that.* All his painfully accumulated

motor transport, most of his fuel supply, all of the specialized engineering and mine-clearing equipment except for the two machines
burning before his eyes. Two mornings ago he had had a regimental
combat group, a third of the strength of the best Panzer division Greater
Germany could field. Two days of combat had destroyed it, and for
what?

To overrun one single, reinforced company of light infantry, who
even yet held out. "They will stand me up against a wall, and they
will be right," he muttered, putting a hand to his bandaged head. He
did not clearly remember how he had come to be lying unconscious
in the mud, but whatever had hit him had come within a fraction of
cracking his skull. Or might have indeed; the medic had not wanted
to qualify him for duty, but there was no time for weakness. A
benzedrine tablet had brought back alertness enough.

"What sort of trolls am I fighting? Why are they so hard to kill?"
he continued, in the same inaudible murmur that barely moved his
lips; the SS commander was unconscious of making any sound at all.
Then in a sudden snarl: "Shoot!"

Crack and the 88mm gun of his tank cut loose. The long flash dazzled
him for an instant, backblast drying the sweat on his face with an
instant of chill-heat. He could feel the massive armored weight of the
vehicle rock on its treads beneath him with the recoil, an almost sexual
shuddering. Spray and bits of road surface flew up, droplets hissing
on the muzzle brake of the long probing gun. The tank was like a
steel womb, warm and comforting, nothing like the dark clamminess
of earth and stone. A glance skyward; the low cover was holding, a
gift of Providence. With luck—

"Standartenführer, HQ in Pyatigorsk."

"Ja." The voice of the regimental medical officer, with his heavy
Dutch accent, sounded tinny in his ears, like someone from Hanover
with a head cold. HQ had been completely stripped; he was senior
officer, but Felix Hoth did not like it, or the Hollander. It was policy
to accept kindred Nordics in the SS but . . .

"Yes? Any report from the battery?"

"No, Standartenführer."

That was suspicious. Oosterman always said "Sir" unless something
had gone wrong. Unless he had done something wrong. Had the pig
been into the medicinal drugs again? One more offense and it wouldn't
be demotion, he would have him *shot,* and never mind that his sister was married to the head of the Dutch Nazi party. "What is it, man?
Spit it out!"

"Your . . . the *osthilfe* volunteer Valentina, she is missing."

"*What?*" he screamed. Then his voice dropped to a flat tone that
was far more menacing. "You are wasting time on a command circuit with news about subhuman Slavic whores." You decadent cosmopo-
lite pimp masquerading as a National Socialist, his mind added. It was
time to *do* something about Oosterman, even if he did have protection.

"Standartenführer, she left an antipersonnel mine in your quarters
rigged to the door, four men were killed!"

He stopped himself just in time from barking "Impossible." Even

Oosterman would not dare to lie to him so, over an open circuit. "Continue," he said weakly.

"There was a written message."

"But . . . she cannot even *speak* decent German," the SS commander said in bewilderment. This—no, there was no time. "Condense it."

"It . . . Herr Standartenführer, it lists our order of battle for the last six months, and, ah, is signed 'Comrade Lieutenant Valentina Fedorova Budennin, *Politruk* and Military Intelligence Officer, First Caucasian Partisan Brigade.'" There was gloating under the fear in the Dutchman's voice; Hoth the incorruptible would have some trouble explaining *this*.

The gunner of Hoth's tank had been peppering the village with machine-gun fire from the co-axial MG38, on general principle. Even over that ratcheting chatter, gunner and loader both heard the sound their commander made. They exchanged glances, and the loader crossed himself by unconscious reflex. Usually the gunner did not let that pass, being a firm neopagan and believer in Hoerbiger's ice-moon theory, the *Welteislehre*. This time he simply licked his lips in silence and turned back to the episcope, scanning for a target. The antitank weapons in the village frightened him, but he could shoot back at *them*.

"Forward, all reserve units, into the village, *kill* them." Hoth's voice rasped over the command circuit, with a catch and break halfway through the sentence.

"Sir." That was the squadron commander. "Herr Standartenführer, we have lost more than two-thirds of our strength, the enemy is neutralized and time is of the essence; why don't we just pass through the cleared lanes, and leave a blocking force to contain enemy survivors until the Army infantry comes up?"

"That is an order!"

A hesitation. *"Jawohl. Zum befehl."*

Hoth switched to the intercom. "Forward. Schnell!" With a grunting diesel roar, the command tank threaded its way around the huge crater in the road and the circle of overturned fighting vehicles; the driver geared down and began the long climb to the burning town.

Johanna flattened as the Fritz artillery fired, then raised her head again. The noise was overwhelming, as much a blow against the ears as a sound, echoing from the hills and the blank wall of the forested mountain behind her. The guns were spread out along the narrow winding road: a two-lane country track, barely good enough for an internal plantation way in the Domination. The surface was broken, beginning to disintegrate into mud—mud like the soupy mass she was lying in, that coated her from head to foot after the long night march through the rain. It was nearly thirty hours since she had slept. There had been nothing to eat but a heavy bread full of husks; she belched, adding to the medley of stale tastes in her mouth. The branches above were still dripping, adding their load of wet misery to the gray color of the day, and the pain in her neck had never left her since the crash . . . *In the infantry after all*, she thought disgustedly. *Knights of the Sky, bullshit.*

A five-gun battery was firing from the little clearing ahead of her, amid the hulks of burnt-out trucks and a wrecked tank and old-looking roofless farm buildings. The road fell away on the other side, but there were more guns there, from the sound of it. The guns themselves were simple field weapons, long-barreled 170mm's mounted in open-topped boxes atop modified Soviet tanks, nothing like the custom-built models with enclosed turrets and 360-degree traverse her own people used. But they were pumping out death effectively enough, the recoil digging the spades at the rear of the guns deeper into the muck, crews dashing between the supply tractors and the breeches, staggering back in pairs bearing shell and charges in steel-rod carrying frames. The men were stripped to the waist, sweating even in a damp raw chill that let her see their breath as white puffs around their heads. She shivered, and swallowed again, her throat hot and scratchy.

"A cold," she muttered to herself. "Happiness, happiness." They were close, close enough to see liquid earth splash from the running feet of the nearest crew . . .

The partisan, Ivan, crawled in beside her and put his mouth to her companion's ear. He whispered: unnecessarily, between the firing and the engines they could have shouted without much risk of being overheard, and the SS were fiercely concentrating on their tasks. Valentina translated in a normal tone: "Where are their infantry? That is most of the Liebstandarte's Divisional artillery regiment, there should be at least two companies for perimeter defense."

How should I know? I'm a fighter pilot, Johanna answered in her head. Aloud: "Up the valley, attacking."

"If they've done that, Pyatigorsk should be wide open." Valentina translated the remark, then answered it herself before continuing to the Draka: "I said again, there is no use in blowing up fuel depots there if the Fritz come back victorious."

Ivan sighed, raised the flare pistol he had borrowed from her. Johanna tensed, bringing a leg beneath her and raising the machine pistol.

Eric, if you only knew, she thought. There was none of the fear-exhilaration of aerial combat. *Just plain fear,* went through her. She belched again, felt her stomach rumble, tightened her rectum instinctively. *Oh no, not that.* Eyes were on her: the Russians', her father's . . .

The flare went *pop*, pale against the massive muzzle flashes of the cannon. Three hundred partisans rose and threw themselves forward. *Urra! Urra!* Her feet pushed her upright and after them, gaining, in among the wet green-gray hulks, breathing their burnt-oil and propellant stink. Crewmen and gunners turned, snatching for personal weapons and pintle-mounted machine guns. Finger clenching, bucking weight in her hands, *pingpingping* across armorplate, a German falling with red splotches across his hair-matted chest, a silver crucifix winking.

Something struck the weapon in her hand. *Hard:* she spun, feet going out from under her on the slippery rock-strewn mud. A tread came up to meet her face, dun-colored mud on massive linked gray steel flecked with rust. Impact, earth, hands on her collar. Warmth, and a fading . . .

❖   ❖   ❖

"Here they come," Eric said. Engine rumble and steel-squeal from around the curve. He sucked the last drops from the canteen and tossed it behind him. The tanks were visible now. A line of them, turrets traversed alternately to left and right; even as he watched, the first one fired into the base of a building and the walls collapsed, straight down with an earthquake rumble. The tank came on through the cloud of debris, its machine guns winking from turret and ball mount in the glacis plate of the bow. Rounds went *crack* overhead, tracer drawing lines through the air where he would have been if he had stood. Then the second tank in line fired into the ruin on the opposite side of the road, and the others. They were going to repeat that, all the way to the central square. Then back out again, until nothing moved; then they would squat on the ruins, while foot soldiers searched for the entrances. After that, it would be like pouring insecticide down a broken ant heap . . .

"Neal!" he called. "That last round, make it count!" Eight tanks, probably with infantry following up behind. Eight was nearly half of what the Fritz had left; unfortunately, Century A had run out of antitank just slightly before the enemy ran out of tanks.

"Yep."

It might have been marksman's instinct that brought the heavyset rocket gunner to her knees for a better aiming point, or a coldly calculated risk. A mistake, in either case; a machine gun bullet punched her back just as her finger stroked the trigger. The rocket lanced into the already holed personnel carrier five meters before the moving tank, slewing it around and actually clearing the road for the advancing SS armor.

"We'll never stop them now." Eric did not know who had made that statement, but there was no reason to doubt it; heading back into the bunker would be simply a slower form of death. Neal's heels drummed on the clinking rubble for an instant, then were still. The beams overhead had begun to burn, set alight by a stray incendiary round. Long and slim, the barrel of the lead tank's 88 was swinging around to bear on them.

"They'll never stop them," Monitor Huff said. There was nobody else alive on the rooftop across the laneway from Eric's position to hear her. She looked down at Meier's slumped body; if the burst had come up through the floorboards a few centimeters farther right, it would have struck her instead. As it was—she forced herself to look down at the wound in her thigh; there were bone splinters in the pulped red-and-purple wound, and the blood was runneling down past her clenched hands. Shock was keeping out the worst of the pain, but that would come—if the blood loss did not kill her first; she estimated that at no more than two minutes, with unconsciousness in less. The Centurion was across the way, with five others. And Patton.

"Heavy," she muttered, fumbling at the dead trooper's body. She had had an improvised antitank weapon with her, a bundle of unscrewed grenade heads strapped around an intact stick grenade with a bungie cord. *Suicide system,* she thought: that was the nickname for it. "Scarcely applies now, do it?"

The journey to the edge of the roof was endless, her wet fingers fumbling with the tab of the grenade. She imagined that she could hear it sizzling, once she pulled the button. *Up, use it like a crutch, gotta see t' place dang thing . . .*

The second tank had an alert pair of eyes head-and-shoulders out of the hatch, with the pintle-mounted MG38 ready to swing; that was one reason for the in-echelon formation. There is a natural tendency to fire too high when aiming up; still, the first round of the burst took Huff just above the nose, and left with her helmet and much of the top of her skull. The bundle of grenades dropped at her feet, harmless except to corpse and roof; the body twisted off the edge, turned once and landed broken-backed across the hull of the wrecked personnel carrier below. Blood and pink-gray brain dripped into the burning oil, hissing.

"They shot Huff! The dirty bastards shot Huff!" Patton's voice cracked. Then she was moving, fast and very smooth, scooping up the satchel charge, arming it, hurdling the low wall into the street and across it while bullets flicked sparks around her feet. Less a dash than a long leap, screaming, a forward roll *through* the puddle of flame that surrounded the wreck. Still screaming as she vaulted with her uniform and hair burning onto the deck, three steps down it with the plating booming, over the body, diving into the air headfirst toward the SS panzer. A shrieking torch that the green tracer slapped out of the air to fall beneath the treads. The satchel charge detonated.

Tank designers crowd their heaviest plating onto the areas that are likely to need it: the mantlet that holds the gun, the glacis plate at the bow, the frontal arc of the turret. Not much is left for the rear deck . . . or the bottom of the hull. The satchel charge held twenty pounds of plastique, confined between the forty-four-ton weight of the tank and the unyielding ground. Thin plating buckled as the globe of hot gas expanded; there was no *time* for it to go elsewhere. Pieces of it bounced through the fighting compartment, slicing, supersonic. Fire touched the wrenched-open cases of 88mm ammunition on the floor of the panzer, still nearly a combat load.

The first explosion bounced the tank onto its side and threw it across the road, a huge armored plug across the laneway. The second opened the hole in its belly into a splayed-out puncture wound, like a tin can left too long in the fire. Yet the hull barely moved; recoil balanced recoil as the turret and its basket blew out the other side of the vehicle, flying twenty meters down the laneway and demolishing a wall with its ten-ton weight. Surprise froze the Draka for a moment. Eric recovered first.

"Back down, back down, quick, go go *go*," he shouted, slapping shoulders and legs as they went by him, back toward the narrow opening at the rear of the room. Already, figures in camouflage uniforms were trying to edge past the blockage of the wrecked tank, and he snapped a burst at them. They fell; hurt or taking cover was impossible to say even at ten meters' distance as thick metallic-smelling smoke drifted across his eyes. The pain of the Holbars hammering against his raw shoulder brought him back to himself, and he slithered feet first to the opening. Hands caught and assisted him; they half-fell into the welcome gloom, scrambling back beyond a dogleg that kept them safe from a grenade tossed down their bolthole.

"Back to the radio room, this is it, it's over, we've got to tell Legion HQ and then get out. Split up and carry the word, south end and bug out to the woods, *move*, people." They paused for a single instant, dim gleams of teeth in faces black with soot and dirt. "Good work," he added quietly, before spinning and diving through the next ragged gap. "Fuckin' good."

Dreiser felt very lost in the dark tunnel. Everybody else had seemed to know what to do, even when the order went out to scatter; he clutched the precious tapes through the fabric of his jacket and lurched into a bank of stone jags. For a moment pain blinded him in the echoing dark, then hands gripped him and jerked him aside through an L-angle where one cellar joined another through an improvised passage. A palm clapped over his mouth, hard and calloused.

"Shuddup," hissed into his ear, as he was passed through another set of hands and parked against a wall. The American struggled to control his breathing, feeling his heart lurching between his ribs; that might have been a bullet or a dagger. Fighting a feeling of humiliation as well: he was *tired* of being handled like a rag doll. The blackness was absolute, silence broken by dripping water and the distant explosions. Then hobnails rutching on stone, and closer a long, faint *schnnnng*, a bush knife being drawn from its sheath. Dreiser found himself holding his breath without conscious decision.

A light clicked on: only a handlight, but blinding to dark-accustomed eyes. It shone directly into the faces of the two Germans who had turned the corner. They had been keeping close to the right-hand wall, facing forward; the Draka were on the left, across the two-meter width and parallel to their opponents. Nearest to Dreiser was the woman with the bush knife, reaching as the light came on. Her left hand jerked the SS trooper forward by the blouse while the right thrust the two-foot blade forward, tilted up. Dreiser could see the German's face spasm, hear the wet slicing and grating sound as she twisted the broad machete blade and withdrew it in a wrenching motion. The next Draka was a man, tall enough to stoop slightly under the seven-foot roof. He merely slammed a fist forward as the German turned toward him; it connected with the SS man's face, and the Draka was wearing warsaps. Bone crunched under the metal-reinforced glove, and the German's helmet rang as his head bounced backward and rebounded off stone.

The third Draka had been kneeling nearest the L-junction. He dropped the light as his comrades struck, swept up his assault rifle, and fired. Dreiser blinked in puzzlement. The curve was sharp, there was no direct line of fire at the room beyond, and the paratrooper was firing *up*. Then the American followed the line of tracer up to the groined vault of the ceiling: continuous fire, long, ten-second bursts, the roar of the shots in the enclosed space of the cellar almost hiding the whining ping of the ricochets. His mind drew a picture of the narrow stone reach beyond the exit, bullets sawing back and forth . . . There were screams from around the corner now, and the sound of bodies falling, and blind crashing retreat. The morale of the SS men was growing shaky.

And no wonder, Dreiser thought, wiping an arm across his face. The slightest misjudgment or ill luck and those metal wasps could have come bouncing back into this section of tunnel; that risk was why the fighting below was mostly cold steel or cautious grenades. The Draka gunman was shaking the empty drum out of his Holbars, snapping in a fresh one with a contented grin but leaving the bolt back to allow the chamber to cool. Darkness returned as he snapped out the light. There was a moaning, then the sound of a boot stamping on a throat, as unbearable as fingernails on slate.

"C'mon, Yank," one of them said. "We'll drop you at the aid station. Clear path from there to the south end. Less'n' you meets cousin Fritz, a'course."

My morale would be shot, too, the correspondent's musing continued as he coughed raw cordite fumes out of his throat and stumbled along with the retreating troopers. The Draka were nearly as deadly as they thought they were, and they never gave up; hunting them down here would be like going blindfolded and armed only with a spear into a maze full of tigers.

Tigers with the minds of men.

"Nobody in here but the wounded!" Dreiser shouted, in German. The cellar beneath the mosque was the aid station; his post the only place a noncombatant could do any good. The darkness was thick with muffled noise, or the louder shouts of the delirious, but he had heard the SS men talking in the next chamber. And "grenade" was hard to miss. "We surrender!"

A cautious hand and head came through, flicked on a torch, speared Dreiser where he stood plastered against a wall, zigzagged briefly across the rows of bandaged figures.

"*Ja,*" the German barked over his shoulder, and another figure with a Schmeisser followed. Perhaps it was the dim glow, but the American thought he could see the strain of fighting in this warren on their faces, death waiting in cramped blackness like the inside of a closet. They straightened, relaxing.

"*Hande hoche!*" one said to the American, tucking the grenade back into his belt.

"I am an American war correspondent," Dreiser began. The burst of automatic fire caught him almost as much by surprise as it did the two SS troopers it smashed back against the stone.

The flashlight fell, bounced, did not break as it came to rest on the stomach of a staring red-headed corpse, lighting the expression of shocked amazement on her freckled face. The glow diffused quickly in the dusty air, but Dreiser could see a head that was a ball of bandage with a slit for the eyes, and the muzzle of the Holbars poking through the blankets that had concealed it. The head eased back down to its pack-pillow, and the assault rifle dropped out of sight again.

"Keep . . ." A halt, and a grunt. "Keep 'em coming, Yank."

"No answer," Sofie said. She and Eric were alone now in what had been the command bunker, except for the corpse of the sapper in one corner. It *felt* abandoned, colder somehow, darker despite the constant blue glow and the flicker of lights from the radio at which the comtech labored. A burst of assault-rifle fire echoed on the stone, bringing their heads up.

"Scan the cohort and tetrarchy frequencies, then," he said, laying down his Holbars to load the bandoliers with extra drums. "Quick."

Her fingers turned the dials; static, German voices, then snatches: "Sir, sir, come in, *please*." A young voice, tight-held. "Sir, the centurion went out half an hour ago and didn't come back, I can hear them talking in Fritz outside the door, what'm I supposed to—" Shots, static.

"Fall back to the green line an' regroup, fall back—"

"This is Palm One, Palm One, I've got Fritz armor coming at me from north'n' south both, I'm spikin' mah guns and pullin' out, over." A decisive click.

Sofie abandoned the radio, tearing off the headset and throwing it at the communications gear, turning to him with a snarl.

"That's *it*?" she said, her voice shrill. "That's *it*? It was all fo' *nothin'*?"

"It's never for nothin', Sofie," he said gently, "We fight for each other; the job is what we do together." Sharply: "Now *move*, soldier!"

"*Shit!*" The obstacle was soft, and might once have lived. Eric tripped, and his hand came down into something yielding and wet. "Light, Sofie." They had to risk that; information was worth a brief stop. A click, and he was blinking down into the turned-up face of the old Circassian, the *hadj*. Something had sliced halfway through his skull, something curved that pulled out raggedly and spilled the brain that had seen Mecca and spent fifty years in a losing fight to protect his people. The Draka recognized the signs: a sharpened entrenching tool swung like an axe, not popular among the Domination's forces, who preferred the ancestral bush knife. He hoped it was not one of his who had killed the old man, in a moment of fear or frustration. Grunting, he knelt up and turned to look at Sofie.

And froze. The shovel gleamed beyond her head, held like a spear in a two-handed grip, point down and ready to chop into her back. *No firing angle* went through him, as he watched the reflected light glint on the honed edges. But the weapon was trembling, and it had not fallen. Sofie saw the fear in his eyes, checked her turning motion before it began at his lips' silent command. He could see her face glisten, but the hand with the torch did not shake, or even move.

Slowly, slowly, Erie came to his feet. *No aggressive movement*, he thought, with a sudden huge calm. He could not afford to fail, and therefore he would not. Not now, or ever. Up, half-crouch, erect. There was a German behind her, standing rigid as a statue save for the trembling of the hands clenched on the haft of the spade. The underlit face quivered as well, lumps of muscle jerking under the skin, tears pouring down through dirt and soot, cutting clear tracks down from the wide-held eyes, a swath of bandage covering the back of his head. White all around the iris, pupils enormous, staring through time and space. It was eerie to hear words coming from that face; it was as if a statue had spoken, or a beast.

"You . . . killed them," he said. "You. You."

Standartenführer, Eric thought, reading the tabs. Meeting the eyes was more of a strain than he would have believed possible; like peering inside one of the locked, red-glowing tombs of Dante's hell. The Draka spoke very softly, in the other's language, as much to himself as to his enemy.

"Yes. *We* killed them, all of them, both of us." The other's face seemed to change, and the uplifted spade wavered. Eric extended his left hand to Sofie; hers joined, the palm warm and dry against the wet chill of his. She turned, facing the German.

"Inge—Ingeborg?" he asked. It was a different voice, a boy's. "What are you doing here? This is Moscow—this is no place for you." The shovel came down to the stone with a light *clink*, and something went out of the man. Eric and Sofie took a step backward, and another; there was nothing to prevent the Centurion from using the Holbars hanging at waist level in its assault sling. Nothing physical, at least. The SS man faded out of their circle of light.

"I am not afraid," he said, in a conversational tone. "Not afraid of the dark, Ingeborg. Not any more. Not any more."

The panzer rumbled toward them as they turned the corner at the south end of the village; the steel helmets of infantry riders showed behind its massive turret. There was no escape, not even back to the tunnels.

Sofie cursed and scrabbled for her weapon, feeling even more naked now that the familiar weight of the backpack radio was gone. Eric controlled his impulse to dive for cover; what point, now?

So tired, he thought, raising the Holbars. One of the soldiers stood, black face dull gray in the overcast afternoon light.

"*Black* face?" Eric said, as the man shed his German helmet and stood, waving a rifle that was twin to the one in the Draka's arms. A vast white grin split his face as he leaped to earth. The rest of his lochos followed, spreading out and deploying past the two Draka, toward the ruins and the sound of the guns.

The turret of the tank popped open, and another man stiff-armed himself out of the hatch. A Draka, thin, sandy-haired, with twin gold earrings and the falconer's-glove shoulderflash worn by Citizen officers commanding the Domination's serf soldiers.

"Hey, point thayt-there somewheres else," he called. "This here a *ruse*, my man. A plot, a wile, a *stratagem* y'know." There were more vehicles behind the tank with its Liebstandarte markings, light eight-wheeled personnel carriers Peltast-class.

"The Janissaries," Sofie said, in a voice thick with tears. "Oh, how

I love the sight of their jungleboy faces." A warm presence at his side, and an arm about his waist. "And you, Eric."

"Me too, Sofie, me too," he said. The Holbars fell to earth with a clatter. "And, oh, gods, I want to sleep."

Shapes were coming down the road to the south, low broad tanks whose armor was all smooth acute slopes. A huge wedge-shaped turret pivoted, the long 120mm gun drooping until he could almost see the grooves spiraling up it; he could make out the unit blazon on the side of the turret, an armored gauntlet crushing a terrestrial globe in its fist: the Archonal Guard. A flash, the crack of the cannon a moment later. Clatter as the split halves of the light-metal sabot that had enfolded the APDS round fell to earth five meters beyond the muzzle; from down range a fractional second later the heavy *chunnnk!* of a tungsten-carbide penetrator slapping into armor.

We won, Eric thought, more conscious of the warm strong shoulders in the circle of his arm. It might be years, this was a big war, but nothing could stop them now. Victory.

Victory had the taste of tears.

There were fifty members of Century A left, when the medics had taken the last of the seriously wounded; enough casualties were coming in from the direction of Pyatigorsk that walking wounded would be left until there was spare transport to evacuate them all to the rear. The Ossetian Military Highway was bearing a highway's load, an unending stream of Hond III tanks and Hoplite APCs, ammunition carriers and field ambulances and harried traffic coordinators. The peculiar burbling throb of turbocompound engines filled the air, and bulldozers were already working, piling rubble from the ruins of the village to be used for road repair when time permitted.

The noise was deafening, even inside the shattered remnants of the mosque, where walls still rose on three sides. Especially when the multiple rocket launchers of the Archonal Guard Legion cut loose from their positions in the fields just to the south, ripple-firing on their tracked carriages, painting the clouds above with streaks of violet fire like a silk curtain across the sky. The explosions of their 200mm warheads on the Fritz positions eight kilometers to the north echoed back, grumbling, from mountains shrouded in cloud like a surf of fire, glittering like sun on tropical spray, each shell paced with a score of submunitions, bomblets. Behind them came the deeper bark of the self-propelled 155mm gun-howitzers.

"I—" Eric began, looking around the circle of faces. There was no one there but his own people; they had taken the medical help and the rations and nobody had cared to intrude further. Or to object to Dreiser's presence.

"I—" he rubbed a hand over his face, rasping on the stubble, feeling an obscure shame at the grins that answered him. "Oh, shit, people, congratulations. We made it." A cheer, that he shouted down. "Shut up, I got the most of us killed!"

"Bullshit again, sir. That was the Fritz, near as I recall," said McWhirter, a splinted leg stretched out before him, leaning on his crutch.

"You saw the job got done." More laughter, and he shook his head, turning away and wiping at his eyes.

"I'm turning into a fuckin' sentimentalist, Bill," Eric said. The American shut his notebook with a snap and stood.

"Not likely, Eric," he said, and extended his hand. "And my thanks, too. For what will be the story of a *lifetime* if I'm lucky!" More seriously: "It's time I went home, I think. I have things to do; but I won't forget, even if we have to be enemies someday."

"We may," said Eric quietly, gripping his hand. "But I won't forget either. If only because this is the place where I learned I have things to do, as well." He glanced over at Sofie, smoking a cigarette and leaning against the scrap of wall. She met his eye, winked, blew a kiss. "Other reasons as well, but that mainly."

"Things to do?" Dreiser said, carefully controlling eagerness. He had more than a reporter's curiosity, he admitted to himself. Eric's face was different; not softer but . . . more animated, somehow.

"I'm going to write those books we talked about, Bill. Got a more definite idea of them now. Also . . ." he drew on his own cigarette " . . . I've about decided to go into politics, after the war."

"Good!" Dreiser clapped him on the shoulder. "With someone like you in charge, there could be some much-needed *changes* in this Domination of yours."

Eric stared at him for a moment, then burst into laughter, fisting him lightly on the shoulder. "Don't look so astonished, my friend; I was just reflecting on how . . . how *American* that was. How American you are, under that reporter's cynicism you put on."

Slightly nettled, the correspondent raised a brow.

"How much of a believer in Progress," Eric amplified, his face growing more serious. "An individualist, a meliorist, an optimist, a moralist; someone who doesn't really believe that History can happen to them. . . ." Another flight of rockets went overhead, cutting off all conversation for the ninety seconds the salvo took to launch. Eric von Shrakenberg propped a foot on the tumbled stone of the mosque and leaned on his knee, watching the armored fist of the Domination punching northward; the turrets of the tanks turning with a blind, mechanical eagerness, infantry standing in the open hatches of their carriers. The noise sank back to bearable levels.

"Which shows me how much of a Draka *I* am. A believer in the ultimate importance of what you Will; that what life is about is the achievement of honor through the fulfillment of duty." He smiled again, affection rather than amusement, the expression turned slightly sinister by the yellowing green of his bruises. "I always loved my people, Bill; enough to die for them. Now, well, I've found more to *like* about them. Enough to work and live for them, if I can.

"Bill—" his hand tightened on his knee, "*nothing* is inevitable. The Draka have always been a hard people; we're a nation of masters, oppressors, if you will. But it's a human evil, limited by what human beings can do. I've tried to look into our future, Bill; I've seen . . . possibilities that even *Security's* headhunters would puke at, if they had the imagination. Read Naldorssen again someday, only imagine a science that could make her ravings something close to reality." He made a grimace of distaste. "It doesn't *have* to be that way."

Dreiser frowned. "Like I said, Eric: changes."

"Oh, Bill." The Draka crushed his cigarette out underfoot. " 'To desire the end is to desire the means: if you are not prepared to do what is necessary to achieve it, you never wanted it at all.' *That's* a Draka philosophy I believe in. To have any chance at prominence at all, I'll have to gain my people's respect in the way they understand. Doin' . . . questionable things." His face went hard, and a hand chopped out over the village, to a fragment of wall that stood forlornly upright. *"This!* It isn't enough to be willing to die for my people, I have to be willing to *kill* for them. It's what they know an' respect.

"And changes? At best, with a lifetime's effort, if I'm *very* smart and *very* lucky, I can hope to . . . lay the beginnings of the foundations for others to build on. Delusions of omnipotence is one national vice I haven't fallen prey to. For a beginning, for the Draka to change they'd have to stop bein' afraid, which means all their external enemies are defeated. Then maybe they could face the internal one with something besides a *sjambok*. I know—" more softly "—I know it can be done on an individual scale. Then, perhaps in a hundred or a thousand years—"

Reliable operative, the Security Directorate Chiliarch thought. *You want reliable, do it yourself.*

He was surprised at how . . . alarming the offensive was, at close range. Especially now that they were passing the forward artillery parks; even inside the scout car's armor, the noise was deafening. Still, it all ought to be over soon. Then back to Archona, back to the center of things. With a kudo on his dossier that the ultimate masters would note.

The old fool's past it, he thought with satisfaction, then cursed as the car lurched. They were driving well off the shoulder of the road, away from the priority traffic pouring down from the heights of Caucasus.

Did he really expect I'd let him have the credit for this?

Eric looked up as the three ragged figures limped into the ruined mosque. *Ivan the partisan, by almighty Thor!* he thought, looking around for Dreiser. The American was deep in his notebooks; time enough to roust him out later. It would be tricky to get the Russian survivors out, but not impossible; he had heard the awe in the voices of the relieving troops, and the legend would grow. Such myths were useful to the Domination. *And to me, in this case.*

There were two others with the Russian—women, one in muddied finery that could not disguise an almost startling loveliness, the other in the wreck of an Air Corps flight suit, cut away for the bandages that covered right arm and leg and that side of her face. She was tall, hair yellow-blonde, visible eye gray . . .

Sofie let out a squawk as his grip on her hand grew crushing; then he was running as if his fatigue had vanished, nimble over the uncertain ground.

"Johanna!" he shouted. At the last moment he checked his embrace, careful of her wounds; hers was one-armed, tentative. Held close her body felt somehow more fragile, the familiar odor of her sweat mixed with a sharp medicinal smell.

"How bad is it?" he asked, holding her at arm's length.

"Goddamn wonderful, I'm *alive*," she said, reaching out to grasp him by the torn lapels of his tunic. "And so are you." She pushed her hands gently against his chest. "I'm glad, my brother." More briskly: "They told me I'd probably keep the eye, know in a year or two, fly a desk until then. Who's this glarin' at me?"

Sofie saluted. "Monitor Tech-Two Nixon . . ." She peered more closely at the other Draka's name tag. "Oh, you're his *sister*. Hell, I'm Sofie." She grinned, and rattled off a sentence in Russian to the two partisans.

Eric opened his mouth to speak, closed it again slowly as he looked over their shoulders. Two vehicles were bouncing through the uneven surface where the entrance of the mosque had been: not large, simple flattened wedges of steel plate with four soft pillow-tires, but green painted, with the Security Directorate's badge on their flanks. They halted, and metal pinged and cooled. The rear doors opened, and three figures disembarked. The drivers' heads showed through the hatches: serfs, carefully disinterested. The others . . . two Intervention Squad troopers, and an officer. Not any type of field man; the uniform was far too neat, the boots polished, ceremonial whip at his belt and an attaché case in one hand.

Politician Section, Police Zone Division, Eric thought. *A Chiliarch, they're doing me proud.*

The others looked around. "Headhunters," Sofie said.

"Shit," Johanna added. "Metaphorically an' descriptively."

"Well, well, well," McWhirter said. The survivors of Century A had closed in a semicircle about the secret police vehicles. "Aren't you people a *lot* closer to the sharp end a' things than you like?"

"Right." That was Marie Kaine. "Of course, so far back from the front, the brain tends to be ninety percent asshole, anyway; maybe they got lost."

Eric raised a hand, a quiet gesture that stilled the muttering. "Let me guess—" he began.

"No need for guessing here, von Shrakenberg," the secret policeman said. "We've been watching; we always are. Ah am requirin' you to accompany me for investigations under Section IV of the Internal Security Act of 1907, which provides for detention by administrative procedure, for—"

"'—actions or thoughts deemed prejudicial to the security of the State'—yes, Chiliarch, I'm familiar with it." *Nearly having been its victim once before.* "I also recall legislation statin' that members of the Citizen Force on active service in a war zone may only be arrested by the military police, for arraignment or trial before a duly constituted court-martial."

The Chiliarch was a thin man, with a redhead's complexion despite his dark hair and pencil mustache. "Don't try to play the lawyer with me, von Shrakenberg! You'd be well advised to take a cooperative attitude—*well* advised. Now, come along; this isn't an arrest, merely a detention for investigation. Yes, and the American too. And—" his eyes noticed Valentina Budennin, and his mouth smiled "—yes, this Russian too. I'll interrogate at our field headquarters in Kars. We'll round up the rest of these 'partisans' in due course."

Eric was silent for a long moment. The sounds in the background seemed to recede, dying down into a murmur no louder than the blood in his ears. *Well,* he thought.

"Y'know, Chiliarch," he said conversationally. "I think you'd be surprised at the direction those subversive thoughts of mine have been taking. I *learned* something here."

The police agent snorted. "What, pray tell?" They might have to restrain him after all.

Eric indicated the ring of soldiers. "That these are my people. Killers? Yes. But they have courage, and honor, and love and loyalty to each other. Those are real virtues, and on that something can be built, something can grow."

He drew the Walther P-38 that was still thrust into the waistband of his battle harness.

The two Security troopers had come expecting an arrest, not combat. Yet they were Draka, too; their rifles came up with smooth speed to cover Eric. Policemen's reflex, that let them ignore the two-score paratroopers within arm's reach, and a fatal mistake. One managed to get a burst off, cracking the air over the security Chiliarch's head. There was a moment of scuffling, a meaty *thud*, a wet *schunk* sound; the secret policeman wheeled to see the Security troopers going down, and the bayonets flashing again and again. Two of Century A's survivors were staggering away, one clutching white-faced at a broken arm, the other squeezing at a stab wound in his thigh; the Century's own medics were moving forward.

"The drivers, too," Eric called coolly. "No noise." He averted his eyes slightly as the two serfs were dragged from their hatches and their throats slit. They submitted in stunned silence, one jerking and bleating as the steel went home.

"Where was I?" Eric continued to the secret policeman. "Sayin' that the 'convenient accident' in a moment of confusion can work both ways? Pity about your party runnin' into those Fritz holdouts. Or, extending my analysis. Ah, yes. From *them* something can be built, in time. What you are is a disease, and the only thing you'll ever produce is rot."

The Security agent turned back again; his face was even paler now, about the lips, but his voice was steady.

"I *know* you, it's all in the dossier! You don't have the guts—"

Eric shot him, low through the stomach. He dropped, unbelieving eyes fixed on the red leak between his fingers, legs limp from a shattered spine. The Centurion felt Sofie's arm go about his waist. His left arm looped over her shoulders. "Thanks, Sofie," he said, and looked up at the rest of them. "Thanks, all of you."

"Hell," Marie Kaine said. "It's a long way to the Atlantic Coast and the end of the war, Eric. We all want you in charge till then."

Suffering eyes turned up to him, over a gaping mouth that soon would scream.

Make an end, do it clean, he thought. "And there's one thing you should never have forgotten," he said to the man who had come to arrest him. "Whatever *else* I may be, I'm still a von Shrakenberg."

The pistol barked.

LOW EARTH ORBIT
JULY 1, 2014
INGOLFSSON INCURSION TIMELINE
EARTH/2B

Nomura shivered. "Not entirely mad," he said. "But . . ."

"Yeah, that makes it worse, not better," Carmaggio said. "If your enemies are all drooling lunatics, cowards and blackhats, everything gets real easy. The problem is that people with admirable qualities can end up using them for distinctly unadmirable purposes."

"What . . . happened next?"

"Nothing good," Carmaggio said. "Correction—brave men and women did their best. Here—"

BOOK TWO

Chapter One

LYON, PROVINCE OF BURGUNDIA
REGIONAL HQ, SECURITY DIRECTORATE
DETENTION CENTER XVII
APRIL 1947

"Pater Noster, qui est in caelis . . ."

"Shut up, slut-bitch!" The guard raked her hard-rubber truncheon along the bars in frustration, then stalked off down the corridor

Sister Marya Sokolowska lowered her head and fought to recapture the Presence; a futile effort, it could not be forced. *Enough, prayer is more than feelings,* she chided herself, while habit droned the sonorous Latin words and told the beads of her rosary. The words were a discipline in themselves; faith was a matter of the intellectual will more than subjective sentiment. And the others relied on her: even Chantal Lefarge, the communist over in the corner, was joining in; it helped remind them they were human beings and not animals-with-numbers, that they were a Community, linked one with the other. Something easy to forget in the ten-by-twelve brick cube of cell 10-27, under the Domination of the Draka. Though she was the only Pole here, and the only religious.

Covertly, her eyes followed the guard as far as the grill-door would allow. The building had not been designed as a prison; the Draka had taken it over when Lyon fell, back in '45. Before then . . . a school, perhaps, or some sort of offices. Then the Security Directorate had come, and cordoned off as many square blocks of the city as need dictated; blocked doors and built walkways between buildings, surrounded the whole with razor wire and machine-gun towers, put in bars and control doors. It was a warren now, brick and concrete, burlap and straw ticking, the ever-present ammonia stink of disinfectant. Lights that were never dimmed, endless noise. The tramp-tramp-clank of chain gangs driven in lockstep to mess halls or to their work maintaining and extending the prison complex. Far-off shouts and screams, or someone in the cell across the corridor waking shrieking from a nightmare. Mornings were worst. That was the hour for executions, in the courtyard below their cell. The metal grille blocked vision but not sound; they could hear the footsteps, sometimes pleading or whimpering, once or twice cracked voices attempting the "Marseillaise," then the rapid chuttering of automatic weapons and rounds thumping into the earth berm piled against their block's wall . . .

The nun finished the prayer and came to her feet, putting solemnity aside and smiling at the others. Together they rolled the thin straw-stuffed pallets up against the walls, each folding her single cotton blanket on top and placing the cup and pan in the regulation positions. There was nothing else to do; it was forbidden to sleep or sit after the morning siren. Conversation was possible, if you were careful and very quiet, a matter of gesture and brief elliptical phrases, and it helped break the terrible sameness of each day. Newcomers brought in fresh tidings from the world outside, and bits of gossip passed from hand to hand on work details or at the mess hall . . . not as elaborate as she had expected, there were too many informers and turnover was too high. This was a holding and processing center, not a real prison; a place to sit and wait until they took you away. Terrible rumors about what lay beyond: factories, labor camps, bordellos, medical experiments such as the Germans had done during the Nazi years . . . but no real information. For herself, it was not so bad, she had much time to meditate, and the others to help, and what came after would be the will of God, Who would give her strength enough to meet it, if no more.

Marya crossed herself and moved a careful half-pace closer to the bars. Good. The guard had gone around the corner. She was just a trusty, a prisoner like the rest of them, with no key to open cell doors. She *could* mark an individual or a whole cell down and inform the real guards, the Security bulls and retired Janissaries who ran Block D, Female Section. That could mean flogging or electroshock or sweatbox for all of them, you never knew. But the guard would be reluctant to do that; it was unwise to have more contact with the bulls than you had to. A prayer was not enough provocation; a real racket might be, because then she would be in danger of losing her position and being thrown back into a holding pen, which meant being quietly strangled one night. Seven to one was bad odds.

God forgive them all, Marya thought. *For them too the Savior died.* She herself would probably get nothing more than a whack across the kidneys with the rubber truncheon at mess call.

Not for the first time, she reflected that Central Detention was like being inside a machine. Not a particularly efficient one, more like an early steam engine that gasped and wheezed and leaked around its gaskets, shuddering with loose fittings and friction. But it used the Domination's cheapest fuel—human life—and it was simple and rugged and did its work with a minimum of attention; she had been here six months and rarely even saw the serf guards and clerks who did the routine management, much less one of the Citizen-caste aristocracy of the Domination. . . .

There was an iron *chung-chang* from the landing down at the south end of the corridor, the main door to Block D, two stories up the open stairwell. A sudden hush caught the cells along the narrow passageway, an absence of noise too faint for conscious attention, then a rustle as the inmates sprang to stand by their bedrolls. The nun moved to her own and assumed the proper posture, feet together, head bowed, hands by sides. She could feel the sweat prickle out on her palms, wiped them hurriedly down the coarse cotton sack dress that prisoners were issued. Suddenly the familiar roughness itched against her skin, and she forced her toes to stop their anxious writhing in the sisal-and-wood clogs.

A whimper. Therese; she had never been strong or quite right in the head since they brought her and Chantal in. A slight girl, dark and too thin, who never spoke and slept badly. The nun had had medical training, but it was nothing physical; the abuse that had made the elder Lefarge sister strong with hate had broken something in Therese. Perhaps it could never be healed, and certainly not here. Eyes met across the cell, and someone coughed to cover the quick squeeze of the shoulder and whisper of comfort that was all they had to offer.

Pauvre petite, Marya thought; then with desperation: *much too early for the bulls to be down looking for amusement. And they had never picked cell 10-27. Holy Mary, mother of God*, please . . .

The guard pelted down the corridor and dropped to her knees by the stairs from the landing. Marya's bedroll was nearest the door; she could see boots descending the pierced-steel treads. Three sets, composition-soled leather with quick-release hooks rather than eyes for the lacings. Draka military issue, the forward pair black and the other two camouflage-mottled. Quickly, she flicked her eyes back to toes. A Citizen! Could they have found out? Silently she willed the boots to pace by, on down the corridor. Not praying, because this could only mean bad trouble and the only words her heart would speak would be: somebody else, anyone but me.

Marya swallowed convulsively, thick saliva blocking her throat. *Even Our Lord asked that the cup pass from him.* But he had not wished it on anyone *else*. Nor would she.

The lock made its smooth metal sound of oiled steel and the cell door swung open. She could feel the breeze of it, smell leather and cloth, gun oil and a man's cologne.

"Bow, you sluts!" the guard barked, hovering nervously in the corridor. The eight inmates of cell 10-27 put palms to eyes and bent at the waist.

"Up, stand up." A man's voice, cool and amused, speaking French with a soft slurred accent. "Present, wenches."

Marya jerked erect and bent her head back to show the serf identity code tattooed behind her left ear, one hand holding back the long ash-blond hair that might have covered it.

The position gave her a good look at the three men. Their armed presence crowded the cell, even though there was room in plenty with the inmates braced to attention. Two were common soldiers, Janissaries from the Domination's subject race legions with shaven skulls and serf-numbers on their own necks. Big men, young, thick heavy-muscled shoulders and necks and arms under their mottled uniforms. Both carried automatic rifles; ugly, squared-off things with folding stocks and snail-shaped drum magazines; there were heavy fighting knives in their boots, stick-grenades clipped to their harness, long machetelike bush knives slung over their backs. Dark men, with blunt features and tight-curled hair and skins the color of old oiled wood; Africans, from the heartlands of the continent where the Domination began. Their people had been under the Yoke for generations, and the Draka favored them for such work; they looked at the women with indifferent contempt and casual desire.

The third was an officer, a Citizen. In the black tunic and trousers of garrison uniform, with a peaked cap folded and thrust through his shoulder strap; Marya understood just enough of the Domination's military insignia to know he was a Merarch, roughly a colonel. A tall man, leopard to the Janissaries' bull strength. Tanned aquiline features, pale gray eyes, brown hair streaked with a lighter color, a single gold hoop earring. No more than thirty, with white scar lines on his hands and face, one deep enough to leave a V in his left cheekbone. A machine pistol rested in an elaborate holster along his thigh, but it was the weapon in his hand that drew her eye. A steel rod as thick as a man's thumb with a rubber-bound hilt, tapering along its meter length to the brass button on its tip; cable ran from hilt to the battery casing at his belt. An electroprod.

The tip came towards her face. Sweat prickled out along her upper lip as she fought against the need to flinch. Marya knew what it could do; the prod was worse than a whip, as bad as the sweatbox. The Draka used it to control crowds; the threat was usually as effective as an automatic weapon, and less wasteful. Too many times and you could start having fits. Applied to the head it could cause convulsions, loss of memory, change you inside . . . She closed her eyes.

Metal touched her chin. Nothing. Not activated. She opened her eyes, and the Draka nodded with approval.

"Spirited," he said. "Sound off, wench."

"Marya seven-three-E-S-four-two-two, Master," she recited, fighting off a flush of hatred that left her knees weak, on the verge of trembling. She would not show it, not when it might be mistaken for fear.

The man in black flipped open a small leather-bound notebook with his left hand. "Sssa, thirty-four, literate, languages French, German, English, Polish . . ." He raised an eyebrow. "Quite a scholar . . . advanced accounting . . . ah, category 3m73, religious cadre, that would account for it." The electroprod clicked against the crucifix and rosary that hung through the cloth tie of her sack dress. Made from scraps of wood, silently at night beneath her blanket. "Nun?"

"I am a Sister of the order of St. Cyril, Master."

The Draka flicked the steel rod against her hip, hard enough to sting. "You were. Now you're 73ES422, wench." He read further, pursed a lip. "Suspicion of unauthorized education? Ah, that was six months ago; Security must have been dithering whether to pop you off or send you to the Yanks with the Pope and the rest." He shook his head and made a *tsk* sound between his teeth. "Headhunters, typical."

Marya felt herself pale. "The . . . the Holy Father has been exiled?"

Two more cuts with the rod, harder this time. "Master," she added.

He turned without answering, scanning the others. "You," he pointed.

"Chantal nine-seven-E-F-five-seven-eight, Master." Marya could see the film of sweat on the other woman's face, and knew it was rage, not terror.

Calm, keep calm, she thought. *Suicide is a mortal sin.*

The Draka stepped over and looked her up and down, smiling slightly. She had dark Mediterranean good looks, long black hair and a heart-shaped face, a full-curved body under the coarse issue gown. "At ease," he said, and the inmates straightened and dropped their eyes again; the officer chuckled as he watched the dark woman glaring at his boots and consulted the notebook.

"Twenty years, literate, numerate, French and English . . . ex-book-keeper, member of the Communist Party . . ." He caught the hem of her gown on the end of the electroprod and raised it to waist height, and murmured in his own tongue: "Not bad haunches, but these Latins run to fat young."

Marya understood him, with difficulty; the English her Order had taught her was the standard British form, not the Domination's mutation of an archaic eighteenth-century southern dialect. He paused, let the cloth fall, tapped the steel rod thoughtfully against one boot.

"Shuck down, wenches," he said after a moment.

There was a quick rustle of cloth as the inmates stripped; the prison gowns simple cotton sacks with holes for arms and legs. Marya undid her belt, pulled the garment over her head, folded it atop her bed-roll, slipped off the briefs that were the only undergarment and folded them in turn, stepped out of the clogs and stood in the inspection posture, hands linked behind the head and eyes forward. The dank chill of the place seemed suddenly greater, raising the gooseflesh on shoulders and thighs, making her wish she could hug herself and run her palms over her arms.

When she had been arrested, it was only chance that the secret school was not in session and the children gone. All unauthorized education was forbidden, under penalty of death; they would have penned her and the children together in the room and tossed in a grenade. Alone, she would have died there and then had any evidence been found. As it was, two of the mothers had been with her, and there was no room in the police van; the green-uniformed Security Directorate officer had drawn her pistol and shot them both through the head as they knelt, to save the trouble of calling in for a larger vehicle. And inside Central Detention there had been no interrogation, no torture; only the cell and the endless monotony spiced by fear, until she realized that her gesture of defiance was not even worth investigating.

There had been a speech for her batch of new inmates. Very brief: "This is a bad place, serfs, but it can always be worse. We ask little from the living, only obedience; from the dead, nothing."

Beside her Therese was weeping silently, slow fat tears squeezing out from under closed lids and running down her face, dripping from her chin onto her breasts. Most of the others were expressionless, a few preening under the dispassionate gaze; the Draka nodded and turned to the guard.

"This one and that one," he said, flicking the prod toward Marya and Chantal. "Put the restraints on them."

Marya's stomach lurched as the guard's rough hands turned her around and pulled her arms behind her back. The ring-and-chain bonds clanked, fastening thumbs and wrists and elbows in a straining posture that forced the shoulders back; you could walk in them if you were careful, but they were as effective as a hobble when it came to running. Not that there was anywhere to run; and anything at all might be waiting beyond the iron door. Cell 10-27 was a bad place, of cold and fear and a monotony that was worse than either, grinding down your mind and spirit. Now it seemed a haven . . . The one thing you could be certain of in the Domination was that there was always someplace worse.

The guard shoved the two women roughly toward the door of the cell. Marya staggered, turned and bowed awkwardly.

"Master," she said. "Our things?"

"You won't be back, wench," the Draka said, stretching. The Janissaries chuckled; one reached out and grabbed the weeping Therese by the breast, pinching and twisting. She folded about the grip in a futile shrimp curl of protection, mouth quivering as she sobbed.

"You be needin' us'n, suh?" he said. "Mebbeso weuns stay here fo' whaal?"

The officer laughed, and Marya could feel Chantal quivering behind her. Therese was her younger sister; they had been swept up together for curfew violation. Distributing leaflets, probably, but they had been clean when the patrol caught them and might have gotten off with a light flogging if Chantal had not attacked the squad leader when he started to rape Therese . . . The nun forced herself between the other woman and the soldiers, pushing her back against the bars, hearing the quick panting breath of adrenaline overload in her ear and a low guttural sound that was almost a growl. Madness to attack three armed men with hands bound, but a berserker does not count the odds. Even worse madness if by some freak chance she could hurt one of their captors; that would mean impalement, a slow day's dying standing astride a sharpened stake rammed up the anus. And not just for her; the Draka believed in collective punishment, to give everyone a motive for restraining the wilder spirits. Innocents would die beside her.

The Draka laughed again, reaching out and playfully rapping the Janissary across the knuckles with the electroprod. "Na, no rough work with Security's property," he said. "Besides, I know you lads; once you had your pants down you wouldn't notice even if one of the others pulled the pin on a grenade and shoved it where the sun don't shine. *Then* think of the paperwork I'd have to do."

The dark soldier released the woman and saluted. His officer returned the gesture, then grinned and clapped him on the shoulder. "But no reason you shouldn't hit the Rest Center until we're due; consider yourselves off-duty until . . ." He looked at his watch. " . . . 2000 hours. Report to the depot then. Off you go; I think I can handle the wild French wenches alone."

"Yaz, *suh!*" the serf soldiers chorused. Their clenched right fists snapped smartly to their chests before they wheeled and left.

It had been half a year since Marya last saw the main door of Block D; not since the night of her arrest, when she had been kicked through, still bruised and dazed from the standard working-over with rubber hoses that all new inmates received. And she was nearly the oldest inhabitant; the others came and went, swept in off the streets for some offense too petty to merit an immediate bullet, processed through and vanishing to places unknown. A few found the courage to call farewell as they climbed the pierced steel treads . . . Behind them came Therese's voice, thin and reedy: "Chantal, don't leave me, come back, please—"

Then the welded panels clanged shut, and they were outside. A serf clerk at a desk kiosk, a saffron-skinned slant-eyed woman in neat coveralls who bowed as she took the papers the Draka handed her.

More corridors, more cells, the electroprod tapped hard on the shoulder, left, right, pointing to crossings. A harder jab to Chantal's lower back, just over the kidneys. She gasped, stumbled, would have turned her head to glare if the aching strain of the restraints had not prevented.

"Walk more humbly, wench," the Draka said softly. "Through there, I think."

A men's section, hairy faces crowding close to the bars, eyes glittering, silent and intent, others who looked at her with pity, or away. The nun felt herself flushing under that hopeless hunger, forced herself not to shrink back towards the sound of the Draka's bootheels. Courtyards, and she began to shiver as a thin drizzle of cold rain fell slick on her skin. Cobblestones, a brief glimpse of a road outside as a convoy of steam trucks chuffed in with a new load of detainees, ragged figures clutching bundles and children as the guards chivied them into ranks for processing. Overhead, huge and silent, a dirigible was passing, its lights disappearing northward . . .

Then they were in an office complex. Soft diffused lighting instead of the harsh naked bulbs, warmth, rain beating against sound windows of frosted glass. Incredulous, her feet felt carpet beneath, soft and deep; somewhere a teleprinter was chuttering, and the homey familiarity of the office sound brought sudden inexplicable tears prickling under her lids. She was conscious of her nakedness again; not in shame or modesty, but as vulnerability. Most of those she saw were serfs as well, but they were neatly clad in pressed overalls and good shoes, clipboards and files in their hands as they strode purposefully down the aisles or sat at desks working, typing, filling the air with a clatter of abacuses and adding machines. Their eyes flicked over her and away, and she could see herself in them: nude and wet and muddy-footed, rat tails of wet hair clinging to her shoulders, arms locked behind her. Livestock, beneath contempt to these born-serf bureaucrats, the selected elite who occupied the management positions just below the Draka aristocracy.

"Hope these'un're house broken," a voice said, and others chuckled.

Her ears burned, and Chantal beside her stiffened and glared. The man
behind them evoked more interest: deferential bows, and curiosity. Marya
saw a few other Citizens, through the open doors of offices or walking in their bubbles of social space, crowds parting for them; but those
men and women were in the olive green of the Security Directorate,
not War Directorate black. The free folk grew more numerous as they
climbed stairs and at the last an elevator to the upper level. There
was no bustle here; empty corridor with wide-spaced doors, wood
paneling replacing the institutional-bile paint of the lower levels. Names
and mysterious number-letter codes on brass plates: MORRISON: INFL.77A
RELIG.delation, CARRUTHERS: ALLOC.10F LABOR. A larger door still, unmarked,
at the end of a hallway.

"Through," the Draka said, tapping them again on the backs of their
necks with the prod. Hesitantly, Marya stepped closer. The dark oak
panel slid aside with a soft *shusssh*, and she stepped through, blinking with astonishment. She had been six months in prison; before that
six years in war-crippled cities, on the roads of Europe, in refugee centers
and tenements. . . . For a moment she lost herself in wonder.

The room was large, a lounge-office fifteen meters by twenty. Two
walls were floor-to-ceiling tinted glass, a view over the tumbled rooftops of Lyon down to the choppy surface of the Rhône, iron gray under
a sky the color of a wet knife blade. The other walls were murals in
the Draka style: hot tawny savannah and herds of zebra beneath a
copper sun. A huge desk of some unfamiliar glossy-russet wood occupied
one corner with a sparse scattering of files, intercom, telephone, closed-
circuit television monitor. The floor was covered in Isfahan carpets,
the furniture soft chairs around a cluster of low brass tables on filigree stands, Arab work. The remains of a light meal were scattered
on one, meats and cheeses, fruit and bread, coffee warming over a
spirit lamp with little pots of sugar and cream.

Marya felt her nostrils flaring and mouth filling. The prison fodder
was abundant and adequate; porridge laced with fish and soya meal,
hardtack, raw vegetables. Bland, bland; after months of it, years on
scrimping wartime rations, the smell of the good food was intolerable.
She was used to austerity, would not have chosen a religious vocation if comfort were essential to her, but she could feel her skin drinking
in the softness and warmth, eyes flooding with the color and brightness. To feel something besides harsh cloth and stone, to see something that pleased the eye and was not ugly and hurtful . . .

The Draka officer's hand rested on her shoulder, forcing her to her
knees beside Chantal. Inwardly, she shook herself as she bowed her
head and glanced upward through the lashes; a prisoner could not afford
the luxury of distraction. *Focus on the people,* she thought. *Study them.
Know those with power.* Knowledge was the only defense of the weak.

There were five others in the room. A man behind the desk; Security
uniform, high rank. In his forties but athletic, short, with dark curly
hair, blue eyes, tanned pug face and a cigarette in an ivory holder.
In the lounger . . . Marya blinked. The woman lolling there was the
first Draka she had ever seen not in some type of uniform; she was
wearing low tooled boots, loose burgundy trousers, a long blouse over

a stomach that showed the seventh month of pregnancy. Somehow that seemed unnatural, shocking . . . of course Draka had to be born like other folk, but . . . Tall, hawk-faced, hair a mixture of brown and gold that gave the effect of burnished bronze, one hand holding a cup. A massive thumb ring, long fingers . . . And beside her a girl of perhaps ten years in a thick silk tunic, playing with a long needle-pointed knife.

The nun frowned, glanced covertly from one face to another. There were two servants, in dark elegant liveries; one knelt in a corner and played softly on a stringed instrument, the other was a middle-aged black woman standing by the child, probably a nurse. Forget them for a moment; there was something about the Draka . . . All the Citizens she had seen had a certain look, of course: hard sculpted faces, gymnast's physique, the studied grace that came of long training. Even the girl had none of the coltish awkwardness usual on the verge of adolescence; her hands moved the blade with relaxed precision, spinning it up and snapping it closed again around the hilt without looking down. But there was something more . . .

Ah, a family likeness. Pale eyes and long limbs and sharp-featured eagle-nosed high-cheeked faces; the pregnant woman might be the sister of the officer who had fetched Marya from the cell. She licked her lips, waiting.

"Gudrun, you said you were old enough to carry a weapon: don't fiddle with it." The woman's voice. Soft, rather husky. The child pouted, flushed and pulled up the hem of her tunic to slide the blade into a sheath on her leg. The blush was very evident under pale freckled skin; there were dark circles under her eyes.

The pregnant woman worked her fingers and spoke to the man behind the desk. "And yes, Strategos Vashon, I've been known to do outlines for mural work; the Klimt workshops have a few in their standard offer book. Not takin' commissions right now, though, what with everythin'." She transferred her attention to the two prisoners.

"So, Andrew, these two are the best you could do?"

The voice stirred a memory, elusive; darkness and pain, dust and the hot-metal stink of engines . . . It slipped away as she tried to grasp at it.

The Draka who had brought the women from their cell snapped his fingers for coffee, sinking into one of the chairs with a grateful sigh and hooking the electroprod onto his belt. "More difficult than the manual workers, sister dear, you wanted them spirited and intelligent . . . troublemakers, in other words. That, these are; healthy sound stock, as well."

The woman shifted, sighed, rested one hand on her belly and held out the other.

"The tag," she said, and her brother tossed a strip of metal; her hand picked it out of the air with a hard fast slap. "Yasmin." The girl in the corner laid down her mandolin and rose to take the key. "Take the restraints off'n them."

Marya kept her head bent as the serf approached, knelt behind the two inmates. A crisp sound of linen and silk, a smell of scented soap, a soft hand on her arm.

"These-heah on way too tight." The girl's voice was harder to understand than the Draka's had been, the same soft drawl but a more extreme dialect. "It goin' hurt." Metal clicked. Agony lanced through muscles and tendons, throbbing as circulation returned. Then relief through the fading pain, almost as hard to bear; involuntary tears starred her lashes, breaking the light into rainbows that flickered like kaleidoscopes as she blinked, as her hands fell trembling to the rough surface of the carpet. She heard Chantal's hoarse grunt, and the metal of the restraints clanking as the serf girl folded them. When the dark woman spoke it was in a whisper, barely audible and spoken downward into the rug so as not to carry.

"Be brave, mah sistahs. Things bettah soon." Yasmin rose, laid the restraints on a table with a bow and returned to her instrument, strumming a faint wandering tune.

Endless moments passed, and Marya became aware of the Draka speaking among themselves.

" . . . nice pair of Danes, but I thought you still had that Jewish wench, what was her name . . ." the woman was saying.

"Leja." The officer in black worked his shoulders into the cushions and sipped his coffee. "I do, but I'm out of Helsinki in the field, most of the time. No company while I'm gone, too much work for one when I'm back. Besides, she's pregnant again."

"Why not have her fixed, for God's sake?"

Andrew sighed. "And spoil years of work? She just might not *like* that, you know; even gratitude has its limits. Why do you think I pulled her out of that Treblinka place when we overran it back in . . . yes '42. *Don't* roll your eyes, I'm *not* going to start another boring war story."

"You don't have to, I remember the pictures you sent. Fuckin' sick picking her out too, she couldn't have weighed more than thirty kilos." A grimace. "What happened to the rest of them, anyway?'

"Ask our good friend Strategos Vashon here."

The squat secret police officer looked up from his desk and leaned back in the swivel chair, picking up a ball of hard india rubber. "Nursed them back to health, every one we could," he said; the ball flexed under the rhythmic squeezing of his hand. "Most enthusiastic collaborators we've got, particularly in Germany."

Andrew nodded. "And Leja was well worth the trouble, to me; six months an' bounciest wench you could want. Saw she had good bones from the start, an' spirit, too." He grinned without opening his eyes, as if savoring a memory, a gaunt expression. "Gave her a knife and she went down a row of SS guards we had tied up, slittin' throats. The two I picked up in Copenhagen, Margrethe and Dagmar, they're just nice little bourgeois muffins, pathetically happy to be out of the ruck and terrified of goin' back."

"Why not Finns?"

Andrew snorted. "Almighty Thor, no! When I want to commit suicide, I'll do it decent, with a pistol." He opened his eyes and extended a finger at Chantal. "Those Finns're most-all like Leja, or her; hearts of fire. *Sisu*, they call it. Place won't be safe for a decade. You can tell it by the eyes."

He waved his cup toward Chantal. "Speakin' of which, look at that one, sister dear. I didn't save her from a gas chamber. Sure you want her round about the place?"

The pregnant woman rested her elbows on the arms of the lounger, placed her palms together, tapped fingers, addressed the inmates.

"Look at me, wenches." Gray eyes, impassive. Appraising. "My name is Tanya von Shrakenberg," she said. "You will address me as 'Mistress Tanya'; we pronounce it 'Mistis.' This is my daughter Gudrun; you will call her 'Young Mistis Gudrun.' I have bought you out of Central Detention." A smile. "It may interest you to know that your price was roughly the same as a record player's; the tort bond I had to put up was considerably larger, because you two're classified as potential troublemakers."

Her head went to one side. "This is a bad place . . . Freya's truth, and you've probably heard rumors 'bout what might happen when you leave; most of them are true . . . breaking rock and shoveling rubble in a chain gang until you died, most likely. Or worse. You've been very lucky indeed; now you're going to be part of the *familia rustica* on the plantation my family is establishing west of here. Household serfs; interpreters, bookkeepers. Possibly in positions of responsibility, eventually. Well fed and clothed, not punished unless you break my rules. Which are simple and plainly stated, by the way." She pointed at Chantal, turned the hand palm-up, crooked a finger. "Come and kneel here by me, Chantal."

The Frenchwoman shuffled forward on hands and knees, wise enough in the Domination's etiquette not to rise without permission. Tanya cupped a hand beneath her chin, forcing the head up. "I've read your dossier, wench. You were picked up for curfew-breaking by an Order Police *lochos*; you then tried to brain the monitor with a piece of pavin' stone. Why?" A tighter squeeze. "The truth, Chantal, not what you think I want to hear."

"He—" A pause. "He tried to rape my sister, she's a child, she's only fourteen, *Mistis.*" The last word was a hiss.

Tanya used her grip on the other's chin to wag her head back and forth. "With the result that you were both raped, repeatedly, then beaten bloody and ended up here, rather than in the factory compound where your family was sent." Another pause. "Have you enjoyed it here? From the report, she's simple-minded now; 'post-traumatic shock syndrome.' How do you think she's going to do without you to look after her, here in Central Detention?"

Marya could see the hands clenched by Chantal's sides, quivering. The Draka's voice continued: "Have you leaned anything from this, Chantal? Besides the fact that the Draka are not humanitarians, that is.

"Hearken to the voice of experience, wench. Where are we?"

"In—in prison, Mistress."

"Beyond that."

"France, Mistress."

The hand shook her head again. "Wrong. We are in the Province of Burgundia, under the Domination; *I* am at home, *you* are an immigrant, ignorant of the laws and customs of the land." A smile. "And a serf, who is new to being a serf. *I* am a serf owner, born of seven generations of serf owners; consider who will have the advantage of knowing all the tricks, here.

"Now, here's what I'll do. I will buy your sister Therese, as well as you. She will have a room, light work; nobody will hurt her, and I'll even tell the overseers that she's hands off." Chantal jerked and made a muffled sound. "Or, if you wish, I will have you sent back to her cell and pick someone else. Your choice. Shall I send you back, or not? *Now*, wench."

A whisper. "No, Mistress."

"Louder. I can't hear you."

"No, Mistress, please."

Tanya chuckled and leaned closer. "Now, that's what you should have learned from the incident that brought you here: the difference between courage and recklessness. Not at all the same thing. Tell me, Chantal, do you know what *in loco parentis* means? Yes? Good; you will be *in loco parentis* for your sister. Only, for you a special rule will be made; when the parent sins, the child is punished. Understand?"

She removed the restraining hand, but Chantal did not move.

"Yes, Mistress," she said, in a quiet, conversational tone.

"Oh, ho, what a look," Tanya said, keeping her eyes locked with Chantal's. "Andrew was right; a heart of fire, this one. Maybe we'll continue this conversation at greater length, someday." She brought up finger and thumb and flicked the other's nose. "Back."

Marya let her breath out in a long shudder, only then conscious of holding it, averting her eyes as the other woman crawled back and sank on her heels by the nun's side, panting as if from a sprint. The sight was disquieting; the nun felt a flush of shame rising from breasts to cheeks and bent her head, letting the pale curtain of her hair hide her face and silently cursing the milk-pale skin her Slavic ancestors had left her. The war, the Soviet and Nazi occupations, the long flight westward before the Draka had been chaos, random death, hunger, sickness, running through the cold wet squalor of the refugee centers. Soldiers and police, prison and camps she understood; even the Draka occupation had been merely a harsher version.

This was not a matter of armies and bureaucracies, however brutal; it was a ritual of submission rawly personal, as much a matter of calm everyday routine to her new owners as eating a meal. *Oh, I understand the psychology of it,* she thought; hers had been a teaching Order, and a progressive one. It was still something out of the ancient world, come to impossible life around her.

Tanya turned to her daughter, stroking her hair. "You've been patient, darlin'; now tell me, what do *you* think of these two."

"Well . . ." the child frowned and wrinkled her nose. "They seem sort of, well, uppish. Sort of . . . um, shouldn't you punish them, Mother?"

Tanya laughed, and tousled the girl's hair. "Gudrun, sweetlin', school can teach any number of useful things. But handlin' serfs is like . . ." She pursed her lips and tapped one thumb on her chin. "Like dancing;

has to be passed on, one practitioner to the next. There's never a set answer, not on an individual scale. What did the Romans call their slaves?"

Gudrun's frown relaxed; that was much easier. "*Instrumentum vocale,* Mother. The tool that speaks."

"A wise people. But always remember, the tool that speaks is also the tool that thinks, and believes. Watch." She turned her attention back to the two kneeling figures. Fascinated, Marya observed the change sweep over her face; less a matter of expression than of some indefinable shadow behind the eyes, warmth vanishing until frosted silver looked out at her human chattel.

"You, you were a nun, eh?"

"Yes, I am, Mistress."

"Were. Now, if'n I told you to sweep the floor, would you do it?"

"Yes, Mistress."

"If I gave you Gudrun's knife an' told you to cut Chantal's throat, would you?" There was a silent pause. "The truth, wench: don't try lyin' to me."

Marya moistened her lips."No, Mistress."

"Ah." The Draka smiled. "And if I told you to jump out the window?"

"No, Mistress." At the Draka's arched brows: "Suicide is a mortal sin."

The Draka woman laughed softly. "And if I told you that if you didn't, I'd kill Chantal here?"

Marya opened her mouth, hesitated, shook her head.

"More difficult, eh?" Tanya chuckled and nodded to her daughter. "Remember this; there is always some order that won't be obeyed. Either don't give it, or be prepared to kill. Human bein's are like horses, born wild but with a capacity fo' domestication. These are old fo' breaking so it'll be difficult." She turned to the serf girl with the mandolin.

"Yasmin," she continued, writing and tearing a leaf from a pocket notebook. "Here. There's a Stevenson & de Verre office on the ground level. Take them down and see to them, there's a good wench. Light cuffs, clothing, tell them the basics. We'll come down when you're finished."

Yasmin covered her instrument in a velvet case and pattered over to them, signaling them to rise. Tanya levered herself to her feet and approached also, stopping them for a moment with a lifted finger, paused.

"You two are mine now," she continued. Neither of the women lifted their eyes from the carpet. "All your choices are gone, except one. Obedience, life. Disobedience, death. That one we can never take from you." Another pause. "But you've already made it, no?" She shrugged. "I am your fate, then. You've decided to spend life under the Yoke; so remember, there's no point kickin' and buckin'. Be good serfs, an' my family will be good masters. Resist, and you suffer."

Chapter Two

Echoing, thundering, the darkness of the B-30's cargo pod shook around Captain Fred Kustaa, toning through muscle and bone with subsonic disharmonies. He was strapped almost flat in the crashcouch, imprisoned in the pressure suit and helmet, packed about with gel-filled bags to absorb the bruising punishment of the experimental craft's passage through the upper atmosphere. Outside the titanium-alloy skin would be glowing, the edges of the huge square ramjet intakes turning cherry red as air compressed toward the density of steel.

It was the helpless feeling that was hardest to take, he decided, not the physical danger. He had been a combat soldier in the Pacific before he transferred to the OSS in '44, and God knew liaison work with the Draka in Europe in the last year of the War had been no picnic, but this . . .

Experimental, he thought. *Everything's too fucking experimental for my taste. Donovan should have tried the submarines first.* Hell, Murmansk wasn't more than a few weeks on foot through the forest to Finland, although it would be a bit difficult to carry the contents of the cargo pod on his back.

The aircraft lurched and banked, and his stomach surged again; he concentrated on dragging in another breath through the rubber-tasting face mask. Vomiting inside it would be highly unpleasant and possibly fatal. *About as maneuverable as a locomotive*, had been the test pilot's words; too little was known about airflow at these speeds. Kustaa did not understand the B-30—he would not have been risked over enemy territory if he did—but even just looking at it from the outside was enough to know it was leading-edge work. It didn't even *look* like an airplane, it looked like a flattened dart pasted on top of two rectangular boxes. . . .

"*Merde.*" The pilot's voice, Emile Chretien; Kustaa recognized the thick Quebec French accent. He spoke a little of the *patois* himself, there were plenty of *habitants* scattered among the Finnish-Americans of his home in the Upper Peninsula. "Electrodetection, high-powered scanners."

222

Kustaa winced. Well, that had been one reason for this mission, to find out for sure just how good the Domination's new Northern Lights Chain was. The dark pressed against his eyes, and he used it to paint maps; their course from the Greenland base, over the Arctic toward darkened Europe. His imagination refused to stop, and he saw more; saw the alert going out below, to bases in Sweden and Norway, alarm klaxons ringing out over concrete and barracks, flight-suited pilots scrambling to their stations. The blue flare of jets lighting the predawn as the stubby delta shapes of the Draka Shark-class fighters rolled onto the launch paths. . . .

The B-30 was supposed to be immune to interception; the Domination had the physical plant of the German ramjet research projects, but the U.S. had managed to smuggle out most of the actual scientists and the crucial liquid hydrogen results. The aircraft lurched again, shook as if the wings were going to peel away at the roots, stooped. One of the Pacific Aircraft researchers had said something about eventually flying right into outer space if they could lick the problem of combustion in a supersonic airstream; damned long-hairs had no sense of need-to-know, shouldn't have been talking like that in a canteen.

"*Tabernac!* Another ray . . . guidance beam, something's coming up after us!"

Of course, he reminded himself, the U.S. hadn't gotten *all* the German scientists; some had stayed, captives or those who had taken the Domination's offer of Citizen status for themselves and their immediate families. And the Draka army's Technical Section had good ideas too, sometimes; it was propaganda that they stole all their inventions.

"Positive detection . . . *fille d'un patain*, three of them; not manned, not at those speeds. They're closing on us, they must be riding the beam. Hold on, Captain, I'm dropping chaff and taking evasive action."

You mean this battering about wasn't evasive action? Kustaa thought plaintively.

This was as bad as going down the tunnels after the Nips, back on Sumatra in '43, pushing the flamethrower ahead into the cramped mud-smelling blackness. *Japanese, Captain, Japanese,* he reminded himself. Part of the Alliance for Democracy now, they'd be associate signatories to the Rio Pact as soon as Halleck and the Army of Occupation got through restructuring . . . Couldn't call the little yellow bastards monkey-men anymore.

His mind skipped, nerves jumping in obedience to a fight-flight reflex that was pumping him full of adrenaline. *And all I can do is sweat,* he thought wryly. He could feel it trickling down his flanks, smell the rankness and taste salt on his upper lip. *Think,* he commanded himself. *You're not an animal driven by instinct, think.*

Unmanned antiaircraft missiles, a typical Draka brute-force solution. Crude engines would be enough, if they were intended to burn out after a single use. The U.S.—he corrected himself mentally—the Alliance didn't have guidance systems small and rugged enough for a missile like that, although they would soon—so the Domination wouldn't either; they were years behind in electronics. But they could put the tracking and electrodetection on the ground, just a passive receptor-steering system on the missile itself, that and a big simple two-stage drive and a warhead.

Christ have mercy, I hope it isn't an atomic, he thought. Probably not—they were still rare and mostly reserved for strategic use—but the Draka would be willing to explode one over a populated area. Populated by serfs, that is.

Jets and atomic bombs built by slaves, he thought. *Insane.* The Domination was madness come to earth; he shivered, remembering his liaison work with the Draka army, during the misbegotten period of joint action against Hitler. *Gray faces of the Belgian farmers as they prepared to drive their tractors out over the minefields . . .* and the sick wet noises of the one who had refused, seated on an impaling stake cut out of the little forest, his feet had scuffed around and around as he tried to rise off the rough wood sunk a foot deep into his gut, and blood and shit dribbled down the bark. Some of the Draka dug in at the treeline had laughed, at him or at the explosions and screams in the plowed field ahead.

The B-30 went *thump*, absurdly like an autosteamer going over a bump at speed, and the sensation was repeated. That would be the strips of foil being ejected, hopefully to baffle the Draka electrodetectors. Acceleration slammed him down and to the side; they were climbing and banking, and metal groaned around him as the big aircraft was stressed to ten-tenths of its capacity.

"Still locked on. *Merde.* Coming up on target. Prepare for ejection, Captain." The pilot's voice was full of a tense calm; Air Force tradition, can-do, wild blue yonder . . .

Kustaa's heart lurched, and his mind refused to believe the time had gone so fast, so fast; it was like the wait between boarding the landing craft and the moment the ramp went down on the beach. Kustaa wished he could spit out the gummy saliva filling his mouth, as he had running waist-deep through the surf in a landing zone. Some men did that, some were silent and some shrieked wordlessly, a few shouted the traditional *gung-ho* and a surprising number pissed their pants or shat themselves; you never saw *that* in the papers, but only a recruit was surprised at it.

Damn, start out a Gyrene and end up a paratrooper, he thought. "Acknowledged." His circuit was locked open, had to be with his hands strapped down, but there was no point in distracting Emile.

"Ten seconds from . . . *mark.*" There was no point in bracing himself, the harness was as like a womb as the technicians could make it.

Nine, he counted to himself. He had married in '41, right after the Nips had attacked Hawaii; they had planned to wait until he finished the engineering course, but being a Marine private was a high-risk occupation. Aino had spent the war years in San Diego working in a shipyard. They had bought one of the new suburban ranch-style bungalows that started springing up around L.A. right after the Armistice. . . .

Eight. The sweating dreams had been bad, waking screaming as the bunker door opened and the calcinated body of the Japanese soldier dropped out onto him, knocking him down in an obscene embrace with their faces an inch apart; Aino had held him and asked no questions.

Seven. She hadn't wanted him to continue with the OSS, especially not when it meant moving back East to New York; the capital was no place to raise a family. She had seen to the sale of the home where she had expected to live the rest of her life, doggedly settled into the Long Island brownstone, entertained his co-workers on awkward evenings when nobody could talk shop and long silences fell.

Six. They had been out to a movie, a Civil War epic called *President Douglas*. The newsreel had been a political piece, film of a serf auction in Archona. The usual sensational stuff lifted from the Domination's news services, no routine shots of black factory hands here, ABS-Pathway knew their audience found injustice more titillating spiced with sex and inflicted on white people. A showing of high-cost European concubines in heels and jewelry and nothing else, parading down an elevated walkway; the American film editors had inserted black rectangles to keep the Catholic Decency League happy. The shabby refugee beside Aino had stood and begun screaming, pointing at the screen. *"Mein Gott, Christina, Christina!"* Still screaming, climbing over the seats with clawed hands outstretched towards the smiling blond image standing hand-on-hip. He was screaming as the attendants carried him away.

Five. Kustaa's wife had not objected to his volunteering for secret duty after that. He dreamed of the bunker less, now; but sometimes it was the refugee who stumbled through the steel-plate door in the nightmare, and the face was his own.

Four. It was not getting agents into Europe that was the trouble, it was moving them around, harder each month as more and more of the population vanished into pens and compounds. The Domination had leaned on its "allies" to reveal their Resistance contacts during the War, and had been politely refused. Some of the networks still survived, incredibly, but they were useful mostly for small stuff— escape conduits and microfilm. Virtually impossible to move in equipment, except a few microscopic loads by submarine on wilderness coasts.

Three. His tongue touched the false tooth at the back of his mouth; melodrama, bad Hollywood, but he knew too much. It was lousy tradecraft, sending him in multiply tasked. There were too many contact names and dates and codes in his head, but what was the alternative? Besides, they needed a survey, an overview of what was going on. If only they could get deep-cover agents into the Security Directorate! It was easy enough to slip in agents posing as Europeans or Chinese, it would be years before a billion individuals could be necked and registered, but every Citizen's identity was established from birth and there were only forty million of them.

Two. Of course, the Draka had probably slipped hundreds through with the vast flood of refugees that had poured across the English channel in the last days of the War, when the Domination's armies were driving for the Atlantic. More would come through with every boatload of escapees, probably many sleepers under deep cover. It was long-term planning and the Draka thought that way, but what could you do?

One. He had seen his daughter take her first steps on his last leave; Aino had looked up, and as their eyes met—

Impact. Blackness.

Kustaa was unconscious as the pod fell, the flexing snap of deceleration striking like a horse's hoof. It needed no guidance, a ton-weight egg of soft curves and dull, nonreflective coating that would make any but the most sophisticated electrodetector underestimate its size. Plummeting, tumbling, then turning to present its broadest end to the earth as weight and drag stabilized it. The shards of the cover that had held it to the B-30's belly tumbled away; *their* inside surfaces were shiny, polished reflectors to draw the invisible microwave eyes that probed through the low clouds. Unpowered, the pod was arching to earth as might a rock dropped by a bird. The bird had been high and fast, and the curve would be a long one.

If there had been a conscious observer aboard, and a port to see, the sky would have darkened as the sun dropped below the horizon and the pod fell from the fringes of space. Below, the gray waters of the Gulf of Finland were hidden by a white frothed-cream curtain of cloud; there were gaps to the east, swelling views of forest and lakes and overgrown fields, a land of dark trees and water reflecting back the moon like a thousand thousand eyes. Lights moved slowly across the land, Draka dirigibles with massive electrodetectors whirling soundlessly inside their gasbags. Then a humming whine, and lean shapes lifted through the clouds, twin-engine Sharks with the moonlight bright on the polished metal of their stub wings; bubble canopies and painted teeth and cannon ports.

Helmeted heads moved in the fighter cockpits, visual scan added to the short-range detectors in the interceptors' noses, hungry eyes linked to thumbs ready on the firing buttons. But the Alliance designers had done their work well, the vision of humans and machines slipping from the dark shin and smooth curves of the capsule. Kustaa hung in his cocoon of straps and padding, while pressure sensors clicked softly under the whistle of parted air. The pod dropped through cloud with a long thrumming shudder, and unliving relays determined a preset altitude; for a moment a tiny proximity detector adapted from a shell fuse pulsed at the ground and calculated distances.

The pod split at its upper point, jerking as the chute deployed; it was barely a thousand feet from the ground, and still traveling fast. The larger canopy followed with a thunder *crack* that echoed over the dark silence of the forest below; the rending crackle of branches bending and breaking followed almost at once. Lines and shrouds and camouflage-patterned cloth caught and tangled, snapping and yielding, but each absorbed a little more of the pod's momentum, until it halted and spun and beat a slow diminishing tattoo against the strong old trunk of a hundred-foot pine, and was still. Night returned, with its small sounds of animal and bird, liquid ripple from a stream falling over a sill of granite below, wind through branches and wind through synthsilk cords and a gentle snap and flutter of cloth.

Kustaa slept.

"He's concussed. Not too badly." A thumb was peeling back his eyelids, and a flashlight shone painfully in the darkness. Kustaa tensed, then relaxed; Finnish, his parents' first language. The guerrillas had found him.

Another voice, deeper. "Get him down, and those crates."

Hands unstrapped him and lifted, passing him downward to damp mud-smelling earth. The world heaved and turned, he twisted his head to one side and emptied the contents of his stomach in an acid-tasting rush. A canteen came to his lips, and the American rinsed and spat. There was a clatter from above, as the cargo pod emptied.

"Careful . . . with those fuses . . . delicate," he mumbled. Pain swelled behind his eyes, a hot tightness that threatened to open the bones of his skull. Nausea twisted his stomach again, and he *hurt*, right down to his bones. It was a familiar sensation, this was not the first time he had been knocked out. After the *Robert Adams* was hit by the kamikaze off Surabaya, he had woken up in sickbay, puking and with a head just like this. Absurdly, among the shrilling along his nerves, he remembered a movie . . . a Western, *Steamcoach*, where the hero took a chair leg across the side of the head and woke up in a few hours fit enough to outdraw the villain.

So Jason Waggen is a better man than me, ran through him as the Finns lifted him onto a stretcher. *Of course, he had the scriptwriter on his side.* The guerrillas were dark shapes against darker trees, only the occasional low glow of a hooded light showing as they quickly stripped the ton weight of crates from the pod. Someone put a pill between his lips, offered the canteen, and he swallowed. The pain faded, and the nighted forest turned warm and comfortable. Before the dark closed around him he heard a rising scream of turbines, howling across the sky from south to north, horizon to horizon. A blue-red flare of tailpipes streaked by above, close enough that the treetops bowed in the hot wind.

"No' much longer," he mumbled.

Waking was slow. He lay for minutes beyond counting with his eyes closed, watching the dull glow that shone pink through the skin. Soup was cooking somewhere near, and there was a background of voices, movement, tapping of tools; the air was close and smoky with a feeling of being indoors or underground and an odor of raw cedarwood. He was naked, in a hard bed laid with coarse woolen blankets. There was a foul taste in his mouth, his teeth felt furred, and legs and arms were heavy as lead . . . but the pain behind his eyes was mostly gone, and the smell of cooking food made his mouth water instead of turning his stomach.

I'm recovering, he thought, as he blinked crusted eyelids open. Not as well or as quickly as the time when his troopship had been hit, but then he wasn't a new-minted lieutenant fresh from his first battle and field promotion any more. *Thirty is too old for this shit,* he mused. *Sergeant McAllister was right: in this business it's easy enough to end up with your ass in a crack without volunteering for it.*

The room was windowless, log-walled, a twenty-by-ten rectangle with a curtained doorway at one end. Both walls were lined with bunks made from rough spruce poles and pallets; there was a small stove made from a welded oil drum in a corner, and a long trestle table down the center. Light came from a single dim lantern overhead, showing the blanketed mounds of sleepers in the other beds. Rifles, machine pistols, what looked like a breakdown rocket launcher were clipped to frames beside the bunks, a dozen or so guerrillas sat at the table, spooning broth from bowls, chewing on crusts of hard black bread, working on their weapons, or simply sitting and staring before them. One man looked up from his task and caught Kustaa's eye, then returned to his methodical oiling of his rifle's bolt carrier; the other parts lay spread before him on a cloth.

Kustaa frowned; he had spent a good part of the last decade in barracks of one sort or another, and this one disturbed him. For one thing, nobody was *talking.* Granted these were Finns, and the average man of that breed made the most taciturn north-country Swede look like a chatterbox, but even so . . .

The American sat up cautiously, ducking his head to avoid the edge of the bunk above him. The blanket slipped down from his shoulders, but he ignored the damp chill, cleared his throat.

"I'm awake," he said.

The man who had glanced at him earlier looked up, nodded, went back to his work on the weapon. It slid together with a series of oiled metallic clicks and ratcheting sounds; a Jyvaskyia semiautomatic, the soldier's corner of his mind noticed. The Finn thumbed ten rounds into a magazine, snicked it home in the rifle, and rose to lay it on the pegs above an empty bunk.

"We have to talk," Kustaa continued. The other man nodded again, coming to sit on a corner of bench nearer the American.

"Talvio," he said to one of the fighters sitting on the bench, a woman. She rose, filled a bowl of soup and a mug of what smelled like herb tea, set them down on the bed beside Kustaa, and returned to sorting through a pile of blasting detonators.

"Arvid Kyosti," the Finn continued. "Regional commander," and held out his hand. It had a workingman's calluses, the form behind it was blocky beneath the shapeless field jacket and woolen pants, the face broad and snub-nosed, high-cheeked, with slanted blue eyes and shaggy black hair.

Not more than my age, but he looks older, the American thought. *I'm not surprised.*

"Fred Kustaa," he replied aloud, conscious of the other's slow, considering stare. *At least I've kept in shape.* Kustaa was a big man, two inches over six feet, broad-shouldered and long in the limbs. A farm boy originally, and a light-heavyweight of some promise at St. Paul Institute, before the War; the slight kink of a broken nose still showed it. The Marines worked a man hard, too, and after the War he had spent some time on Okinawa and joined a dojo; the OSS had encouraged him to keep it up. . . . A ragged pattern of old white scars showed along one flank and up under the thatch of yellow hair on his chest, legacy of a Japanese grenade.

"The equipment came through all right?" he said, to break the silence.

"As far as we can tell," Arvid replied. "My people are studying the manuals." He nodded toward a sealed packet. The hint of a smile. "Fortunate you survived to explain that. Hard landing. Too close to the firebase. The snakes would have had you, in another couple of hours."

"There's a Draka base near here?" he said, with an inward wince at the thought of being taken prisoner.

A nod. "Regiment of Janissaries, two batteries and an airstrip. Use it as a patrol base, so the complement fluctuates."

Kustaa took up the bowl of soup and sipped. It was thin and watery, a few bits of potato and rubbery fish, but it was hot and filled the hollowness behind his stomach. The Finns looked hungry too; not starved, but without the thin padding of fat beneath the skin that a really healthy body shows.

"Good intelligence," he said.

Arvid shrugged. "They built it over a year ago," he said. "Used local forced labor; they've learned better since, but we got the layout. Keep it under observation, as much as we can. Managed to make them think we're farther away, so far."

"Well, that's one reason they sent me. We need to know the general situation, and how the Alliance can best help you."

A few of the others looked up; their eyes were as coldly flat as Arvid's. "General situation is that we're being slowly wiped out. Help? Declare war on the snakes and invade," he said coldly.

Kustaa forced a smile. "Personally, I'm inclined to agree we should," he said. "But they've got atomics as well, now." True enough . . . he forced down memory of what Osaka had looked like, when the Air Force teams went in to study the consequences of a nuclear strike on a populated area. The photographs had been classified, to prevent general panic, and New York was *the* target. His mind showed him Aino's skin peeling away with radiation sickness, gums bleeding, blind and rotting alive; little Maila sitting in a burning house screaming for her mother with melted eyes running down a charred face.

"An amphibious task force is a big target, and their submarines are good enough to take out some of the coastal cities, at least. The plan is to deter them, and make them choke on what they've taken. You've been bleeding them here; if we can help you, and help others match your performance, who knows?"

Arvid's face went white around the mouth, with rage, Kustaa realized with a start. Behind him, one of the guerrillas half-raised her weapon, before two others seized her; she hung between their hands, her face working, before regaining enough control to tear herself free and stumble through the cloth door-cover. The guerrilla commander mastered himself and spoke again.

"That was a stupid thing to say, American." He looked down at his hands. "You know how many troops the snakes have in Finland?" Kustaa shook his head silently. "Sixty thousand: three legions of Janissaries, a brigade of their Citizen troops. Lots, no? Want to know why so many?"

Arvid rummaged under the table, brought out Kustaa's kit and tossed him his pipe and matches. While the American's hands made the comforting ritual of filling, tamping and lighting, Arvid continued, in an emotionless monotone.

"Snakes made a mistake with us. Bypassed us in '43, to deal with the Germans. We had two years, to watch what Draka conquest meant, and to prepare. No point trying to hold the cities or borders. We'd been mobilized since the Winter War with the Russians, in '40 . . . put everyone to work. Making weapons, explosives, supplies. Digging bunkers and tunnel complexes like this, stockpiling, training everyone who could fight. Then they demanded we surrender."

"And you didn't," Kustaa said softly.

"The cities did . . . so the snakes thought. All the ones who could were out in the forests. We destroyed our machinery, fuel, everything useful; burnt the crops, and all the livestock was already salted down. Some stayed behind in the towns for sabotage; many of the ones who couldn't fight took poison." He paused. "My wife, and our children." Another pause. "After a while, the snakes got sick of time bombs and ambushes in the cities, so they deported everyone they could catch. The younger children to training creches, the rest to destructive-labor camps. We've heard . . . we've heard they sterilize the camp inmates, and lobotomize the troublemakers." Arvid grinned like a death's-head. "And we Finns are all born troublemakers, no?"

There was a silence that echoed. "I doubt there are half a million people left in the whole of Finland," the guerrilla finished softly. "Most of those Swedes and Danes and Germans the snakes brought in for labor. The documents we've captured say they aren't going to ever try and settle more than a few hundred plantations on the south coast. The rest of the country will be a nature preserve and timber farm. Right now it's a hunting preserve, and we're the game."

Kustaa looked around the long room, at the men and women sitting at the table, at others lying wakeful on their bunks, at the eyes empty alike of hope and fear.

"Damned dangerous game," he said. "Damned dangerous. More so now that I've brought the new radio, and our little surprises for their Air Force." He nodded to the sealed package. "The codes, and directions on how to fit the deciphering wheel."

Some of the cold hostility faded from the faces turned to him. "What if they'd captured you?" Arvid said.

"There's a sequence of four randomly selected sentences you have to use on the first four contacts. One word wrong, and they cut off contact permanently, and then the codes are useless." He shrugged. "Don . . . Donovan . . . the OSS trusted me enough to hold out convincingly long, then give them the wrong word group. Not necessary, as it turned out; and with luck, we can set up a permanent supply route."

Arvid nodded. "This is bad country for armor, and they don't have enough infantry to spare to really comb us out. We've got plenty of weapons and ammunition, enough food. Their aircraft, though, and the damned helicopters—with an answer to *that* we can cause them even more grief, before we die." Thoughtfully: "There are outposts east of here, in Karelia and Ingria, almost as far as the White Sea; if we could set up a supply line through submarines, then . . .

"The doctor says you'll be ready for action in a day or two. Come along and see your toys in action."

"I'm supposed to make Helsinki as soon as possible," Kustaa said carefully. Then a broad grin split the weathered tan of his face. "Obviously, it'll be impossible to leave before we stomp a few snakes, hey?"

Chapter Three

Tanya von Shrakenberg eased herself to her feet, leaving the half-empty cup of coffee on the table and gently uncurling the small solid weight of her daughter. Not so small anymore, either; arms and legs just starting to lengthen out, she would have the rangy height of the von Shrakenberg line, even if her coloring took after her father's maternal ancestors. Tanya looked down at the fine-featured oval face, already losing its puppy fat and firming towards adulthood, and stroked one cheek.

I wonder if I could catch that? she mused, in painter's reflex. Difficult, when so much of an image like this was your own response to it; that was the weakness and strength of representational art, that it relied on a common set of visual codes . . . *Oh, shut up*, Tanya told herself. *Critics theorize, you're a painter.*

The girl murmured without opening her eyes, turning towards her waiting nurse and nuzzling her face into Beth's wide soft chest. Tanya felt a slow warmth below her heart, and reached out to draw a light finger down her cheek. *Mother, painter, soldier, Landholder*, she mused. *All true, but which is really me, the me I talk to inside my head?* Knowledge was a thing of words, but you could never really reduce a human being to description. Still less a child, whose self was still potential, before the narrowing of choice. She felt a moment's sadness; children changed so fast, the one she knew and loved reshaping into someone else as she watched.

"Shall Ah wakes her, Mistis?" Beth asked.

"Let her rest," Tanya replied. Not enough sleep last night, and then the long drive down, the family gathering in Paris had been enjoyable but strenuous for all of them, a good thirty adults and more children. The first opportunity since the War, now that travel was getting back to normal and demobilization nearly complete, and most of those still in the Forces able to get leave. A good deal of useful work, besides

232

the socializing; plans had been made, political and otherwise, and the dozen or so younger members who were settling in Europe had compared notes.

Damnation, Tanya thought, catching herself on the back of the chair. *Balance going again.* Pregnancy always did that to her.

She looked around the office, eager to be gone but reluctant to face the bother of the trip; the air smelled of coffee and food from the buffet and the peculiarly North European odor of very old damp stone, so different from the dry dust-scent of her birth province, Syria. At Evendim, her parents' plantation in the Bekaa Valley, the days would already be hot. From her old room in the east wing she could watch the sun set over the Lebanon mountains to the west, down from the snowpeaks and the slopes green with the forests of young cedar her people had planted; over the terraced vineyards in patterns of curving shadow; slanted golden sheets between the tall dark cypress that fringed the lawns behind the manor.

They tossed in the evening cool, the wind down from the mountains faintly chill against your skin while the stone of the window ledge was still blood-warm from the day's sun. Sweetness from the mown lawns, delicate and elusive from the long acres of cherry orchard blossoming between the greathouse and the main water channel; sometimes the sound of a housegirl singing at her work, or faint snatches of the muezzin calling his flock to prayer, down in the Quarters.

No use getting homesick, she chided herself. It was probably just this damned depressing city. . . . Tanya had been a Cohortarch in the Archonal Guard Legion when she saw Lyon last, back in '45; burntout rubble, and the natives sick and hungry enough to eat each other. Things had improved a little, but not enough.

Or it could just be pregnancy, the aches and itches and the continual humiliating need to pee. It was unfair: some women went into the sixth month hardly showing at all . . . Thank Freya this was the third; one more and she could count that particular duty to the Race done. Or no more if it was twins again; her family ran to them. Children were delightful and no particular bother; if anything, between the servants and the eight months a year at boarding school required of all young Draka, you scarcely saw them enough. She glanced over at Gudrun, the bright copper hair resting against Beth's dark breast. Sleep was the only time you saw her still; where all that energy came from was a mystery. But *having* them was something she would rather have skipped, the whole process was stupid and barbaric, like incubating and then shitting a pumpkin.

"Thank you for your time," she said. "It'll help; stonemasons and electricians and bookkeepers are in demand. I expect you'll be glad when the other Directorates and the labor agencies get set up proper an' things normalize.

"It'll be good to get back home," she said more quietly, to Andrew. Her brother looked up, unhooking the borrowed electroprod from his waist and smiling.

"The new place is home already?" he asked, lifting one eyebrow.

The movement pulled at the scar on his cheek, exaggerating the quizzical gesture.

"Of course. Chateau Retour's mine, and Edward's"—she laid a hand on her stomach—"an' our next will be born there. Evendim stopped being home a long time ago, it's Willie's." Draka law and custom demanded a single heir for an estate, usually the eldest. "We can visit, but that isn't the same. . . . I worry about you, brother mine; where's the place you can call home? Officers' quarters in Helsinki? We fought the War, let the next generation do their share. There's still some good landholdings ready for settlement, down in the Loire valley. You should get yourself a mate, stop wastin' all your seed on the wenches, make a place for y'self. The Race has to build, or what's the conquerin' for?"

"Maybe after my next hitch," he said absently, pulling the folded cap from under his shoulder strap and settling it on his head. "Loki's hooves, I'm barely thirty-odd; still plenty of time, unless I stop a bullet, and good Janissary officers are scarce. An' Finland will be a while bein' tamed. A while, surely." He blinked, and she could see his consciousness returning, pulled back from the forests and snowfields of the Baltic. "Meanwhile, leave the motherin' to Ma, she's been bombardin' me with the same advice since we reached the Channel."

"An' the young fogey should shut up about it, eh?" Tanya reached to stroke her daughter's forehead. "Wake up, sweetlin', time to go down to the cars." To her brother: "Well, don't forget to visit, before they post you back east. Some good hunting a little up valley; boar and deer, at least. And we've still got crates of that stuff you picked up, in the attics. Should get it cataloged soon."

Her brother laughed and took the yawning Gudrun from her nurse, tossing her and holding her up easily with his hands beneath her arms; she smothered a smile and responded with an adult glower. "Not too old to play with y'uncle, I hope?" he said, and continued over his shoulder to his sister: "It took a two-ton car to drag the lot you got out of Paris, as I recall."

He turned to the Security officer. "Thanks again, Strategos Vashon."

The secret policeman closed a folder, rose and circled the desk to take the offered hand, give a chuck under the chin to Gudrun as she sat on her uncle's shoulder. "No trouble," he said. "A relief from my other problems, frankly; and I knew your granduncle Karl, we worked together after the last war." Unstated was the fact that Karl von Shrakenberg was now an Arch-Strategos of the Supreme General Staff; there was always an undercurrent of tension between the Directorates of War and Security, the Domination's two armed services. It never hurt to have a favor due. "Nothin' *but* problems; sometimes I'd be glad to be back home, promotion or no."

Tanya nodded to the murals of rocky hills and plains covered in long lion-colored grass. "There, Strategos?"

He shook his head, fitting another cigarette into the ivory holder. "That's North Katanga, where I was born; I meant Bulgaria. Sofia's home; I worked out of there from 1920 until the Eurasian war started. Probably why they sent me here, similar problems."

Tanya shrugged. "Ah, Sofia; pretty town, had a leave there durin' the War . . . '43, I think." A grin. "Gudrun here'll take care of the Yanks, eh, chile?"

Brother and sister nodded approvingly as her hand made an unconscious check of the knife in its leg sheath.

Vashon laughed dutifully. "Maybe our grandchildren," he said with sour pessimism. "If then."

"That ol' stretched-thin feelin'?" Andrew said, swinging the girl to the ground.

Vashon shrugged. "Ah, well, it's only two years since the War ended . . . so much gained, and at relatively negligible cost."

"Didn't seem quite so negligible in the Guard," Tanya said dryly, hitching up the elastic waistband of her trousers. "An' the Fritz didn't seem so exhausted, not when they damn near shot my tank out from under me, half a dozen times."

Vashon spread his hands in an apologetic gesture. "Negligible in relation to the booty," he said. "Half the earth, an' half mankind; two-thirds, with what we had before. It's *assimilatin'* it that's going to be the problem. We aren't a—"

"—numerous people, and nobody loves us," Tanya said, completing the proverb as she crossed to the windows, leaned her palms against the strong armor glass. "Doin' my best about that, Strategos. Perceptible improvement here, since I saw it last."

The Security officer scowled. "Partly because so many of the labor force don't have anything to do but shift rubble." He stubbed his cigarette out with a savage gesture. "*Damn* that sack! Waste: waste of raw materials, waste of skilled workers, waste of machinery. We could have used it, the Police Zone is still run-down from lack of maintenance durin' the War an' having trouble retooling."

"What's the point of victory, without looting?" she said lightly. The clouds were thinning, a good augury for the trip home.

"To take what they make and grow—for which we need them *alive*, and their tools. More important than stealin' their jewelry, no?"

Andrew snorted. "My Legion was in on that sack, Strategos. We took twenty, thirty percent casualties between the Rhine crossin's an' here. Janissaries aren't field hands or houseserfs; you need to give them proof positive of a victory. Lettin' them loose in a town, drinkin' themselves wild, pickin' up pretties and riding the wenches bloody is the best way I know. Does wonders for morale, sir; wish there was somethin' equivalent on antipartisan duty."

Vashon composed himself and donned a smile. "At least with you settlers gettin' agriculture in order, we won't have to sell much more oil to the Yanks for wheat to feed Europe with. . . . How's it going, over there along the Loire, Cohortarch?"

She stretched. "Jus' Tanya, Strategos; I'm in the Reserve now. Well as can be expected, all in all; the French were good farmers, but they pushed the land too hard durin' the War. Shortages of fertilizer and livestock, equipment, horses . . . Lovely country, fine climate, grow anything well kept . . . but Frey and Freya, the way things are cut up! Fields the size of handkerchiefs, little hamlets 'n' villages all over the place, goin' take a generation or two to get things in order."

He nodded. "Same on the industrial front, or so the people from the Combines tell me. Overall output about equivalent to ours, or nearly, but the *methods* are so bloody different, it's a mess. Had a fellah in from the Ferrous Metals Combine, actually broke down an' *cried* after doin' a survey; said the Poodles had thirty-six times the number of different machine tools we did, all of 'em needin' a skilled operator, all split up in tiny little factories."

Andrew raised a brow. "You're beginnin' to sound like my distressingly liberal cousin Eric. *He* thinks we should hold off on modernizin' the Europeans, at least the Western provinces, supervise 'n' tax them instead." A laugh. Maybe-so I should report you to Security, sir?"

Vashon forced himself to echo the laugh. Eric von Shrakenberg was a sore point with the Security Directorate, but after all, he was Arch-Stategos Karl von Shrakenberg's *son*. And he had never quite qualified for a Section-IV detention, "by administrative procedure." Not quite. He sighed, clicked heels.

"Service to the State," he said in formal farewell as the von Shrakenbergs turned to leave.

"Glory to the Race," they replied; the adults, at least. Gudrun put her head back through the door for a brief instant, stuck out her tongue and fled giggling.

Below was an internal alleyway, a narrow street closed off when the Security complex was established. Tanya looked up at the gaps of blue sky between the long tatters of cloud and breathed deeply; the chill was leaving the wet air, and some hopeful soul had hung pots of flowering impatiens from the eaves on either side, slashes of hot pink, coral and magenta against the browns and grays of the stone. The alley was lined on both sides with agency showrooms, the Settlement and Agriculture Directorate liaison office, a few restaurants, outfitters. It was crowded to the point of chaos, not least with construction crews making alterations; civil settlement in France was just getting under way and receiving priority as a matter of State policy. Every settler needed labor, even if it was only a few household servants. Planters in soft working leathers, bureaucrats in the four-pocket khaki working dress of the civil service, Combine execs in suits of white linen and Shantung silk . . . Serfs of every race and kind and degree pushed through.

Sort of irregular, she thought as she stopped before the Stevenson & de Verre office, a converted house. That was the largest agency in the Domination, with hundreds of branches. Back—she stopped herself—back near the *old* home, even in a small provincial town like Baalbeck, it would have been much larger. Showrooms and auction pits, holding pens, workshops, medical facilities; in a major city like Alexandria or Shahnapur, a complex of creches and training centers . . . Here there were only the offices and catalogs and a simple fitting-out room, with the serfs in the Security cells.

"Well," she said, stopping on the worn stone steps of the shop. "Take care, brother mine; y'all remember the door's always open."

"An' you've *got* to see my new white Caramague horse, she's a beauty, Uncle," Gudrun said. "Pa gave me a real Portuguese bullfighter's saddle, with silver studs."

"So you've been tellin' me for the last week, sweetlin'," he said stooping for her hug. "Maybe-so I will; been a while since I done any riding."

Tanya embraced him as he straightened, feeling the huge and gentle strength of his arms as they closed around her, the slight rasp of his mustache on her neck, smelling cologne and soap and leather. She dug her fingers fiercely into the hard rubbery muscle of his neck.

"I love you, brother," she whispered.

"An' I you, sister," replied quietly; stepped back, saluted and strode away into the crowd.

She looked down, to find Gudrun scowling at the unseemly adult display of emotion, took her hand despite an effort at evasion, pushed through the swinging doors. *While I can*, she thought, giving it a quick squeeze. *They grow so quick.*

Chapter Four

Therese had been crying when the guard thrust her through the side door of the serf dealers' office, into the holding bay.

"Anybody goan' sign for thissere piece a' shitbitch?" he said, giving a final flat-palmed shove between her shoulder blades that sent her sprawling on the floor; she was unbound, but the guard was a hulking man, muscle under fat, a baton in one hand and lead-backed brass knuckles on the other. His green coverall was faded, and there was no weapon on his webbing belt.

The room was a four-meter cube with wooden benches along the walls, dusty and empty and dim, silent save for Therese's sobs as she crawled toward her sister. Chantal broke forward and hugged the slight girl to her; Marya sat trembling on the brink of action, suddenly acutely conscious of the slats digging into her naked flesh. Beside her, she heard Yasmin take a long breath and then rise; the serf girl had only just come in from the main section of the shop.

"I's the one," she said calmly, striding forward, trim in her jacket and shirt. The guard saw her, straightened slightly at the clothes and manner; only slightly, and his smile was insolent as he transferred his gaze back to the nude prisoners and extended the sheaf of documents. Yasmin took it, read, signed, pivoted on one heel and slammed the pasteboard flat across the side of the man's face with a full-armed swing.

Crack. The sound seemed loud as a gunshot in the musty stillness, and the nun felt time slow in gelid coldness as her stomach clenched; the green-uniformed man loomed a head higher than the dark serf girl, and Marya saw the tension in her back. None of it showed in her voice as she spoke, even when the fist with its glove of spiked and weighted metal pulled back.

"Is that how you treats you momma? You sistah? Tings not hard enough fo' the po' little wench, you big, strong man gotsta make 'em worse?" Marya could make out the angry red right-angled mark of the

238

clipboard as the man paled in rage; it had not done any great harm, but a blow like that carried an unmistakable significance in the world of the Domination.

"Yo cain' talk to me like that-there, wench! I's Security; you blind?" He jerked his chin at the skull markings on his collar.

"Ohhh, dearie *me*," Yasmin drawled, and Marya could suddenly see the expression of mock fear even though the girl's back was turned. "Whut *have* I gone an' done? I's jes' *pissin'* mahselfs with fear, watch me throw mahself on mah back 'n' spread outa tremblin' respec' fo' you awesomeness, chain-dog."

Her other hand dipped inside her jacket and came out with a palm-sized leather folder, snapped it open and held it at eye level for the man, above her own head.

"Cain you read, hmm? See this? This whut *I* is; I gots *Category I* papahs, chain-dog. I's gotta thousand-auric bond posted on me, I's private property—an ol' family servant, and mah mistis trusts me, an' she a von Shrakenberg, *an'* she a Landholder, *an'* my pa a soldier under *her* pa. *Citizens* doan' lay hand to me without they got permission or provocation." She raised the clipboard and slapped him across the other cheek.

His fist snapped up again. Yasmin laughed; a little breathless, but loudly.

"Go 'head, chain-dog. All I has t'do is *say* you hits me, an' they trice you to the frame an' uses a whip to show the world you backbone." The fist relaxed; the man's eyes dropped from the intimidating identity-card, past Yasmin's glare.

"Jes' doin' my job," he grumbled.

"You job was to brings her heah," Yasmin snapped. "Not to slap her 'round. These wenches is all bought-out now, belongs to the von Shrakenbergs same's me. An' if'n they didn't, 's that any cause to be treatin' 'em rough? Is they fightin', disobeyin'?" She tore the top sheet from the clipboard and threw the remainder into the guard's face. "Ain't tings bad enough fo' us, withouten we makes it worse fo' each othah? Git outta my sight; you makes me sick."

Yasmin turned as the door closed, drew her hands across her face and then clenched them together while she struggled to control her breathing; looked up with a smile as Chantal brought her sister to her feet.

"Jes' fo' now," Yasmin said cheerfully, fitting the light padded handcuffs to their wrists. Therese shrank back with a sound of protest; the dark girl immediately laid the cuffs down and sat beside her, laying an arm around her shoulders.

"It's all right, Therese," Yasmin said, in her accented French. "S'all right, really. Just for the rules, understand; just for a little while. I'm here, nobody will hurt you . . ." Coaxing, she stroked the younger girl's arm until it relaxed, then slid the metal circlet around the wrist. "See? It don't hurt . . ."

Chantal jerked her hands apart to the full twenty-centimeter length of the chain, ignoring the pain in wrists still bruised by the overtight restraints, and again. The serf girl frowned, concern on her face. Marya stepped close and shook the Frenchwoman by the shoulder.

"Chantal! Save your energy for something useful, and your anger. See to your sister, she needs you."

The communist took a deep breath and turned to Therese, who sat wide-eyed and on the verge of tears again, shrinking from her sister's tension. They were in the dealer's fitting room, space leased from the Security Directorate by a labor agency and used to process serfs bought out of Central Detention into private ownership; racks of clothes and undergarments and shoes . . . Yasmin had sneered at the quality, but the drab-colored skirt and jacket, blouse and scarf and flat-soled brogans felt solid and warm. Good-quality cotton and wool and leather, with metal snaps and fasteners; better than had been available to ordinary people in Europe since before the War started. Marya smoothed her hair back and tied the scarf tightly; there was ample slack in the handcuffs for that if she was careful. It was a relief to have her hair covered again; the full habit of her Order was a physical impossibility, but even this little felt good.

"You've been very kind," Marya said, fighting down a sudden irrational surge of optimism and vague friendliness; that was merely the effect of comfort, clothing and privacy and the remembered benevolence of hot water cleansing her skin.

All good things are good as they reflect God, she reminded herself. Nothing was evil in itself, only as it turned away from the Source of all good; evil was a negative quality, an absence rather than a presence. *I must see the Divine in every thing and person,* she reflected; then she could love God through them. To love any thing for itself was to erect an idol, and destroy the good one saw in it.

The door swung open.

Yasmin moved smoothly to her feet, bowing with fingertips to forehead. Tanya van Shrakenberg leaned her head through the fitting-room door, smiled at Yasmin, ran her eyes over the others as they repeated the servant's bow more clumsily.

"Here," she said, tossing something underhand at Marya's head, turning and leaving without another word.

The nun snatched it out of the air, found herself gripping the scrapwood crucifix and rosary. She remembered working on it after lights-out under her blanket carefully, by feel, month after month. Not that it was forbidden, except that everything was forbidden that was not compulsory, in Central Detention. She had named each bead to herself, a private remembrance of her Sisters. The Order of St. Cyril had not been large or wealthy, but it had taught children and cared for the sick and given so many bright and pious girls a window on the life of the mind. . . .

One. Mother Superior Jadwiga. Old enough to remember teaching secret classes in Polish in Poznan, in Bismarck's time. She had stopped once to show a novice named Marya how to bunch the skirt of her habit under her knees when scrubbing floors.

Nineteen thirty-nine, when the Bolsheviki divided Poland with Hitler. The day in the little village in Malopolska, mist and gray mud and the hating eyes of the Ukrainian villagers who had betrayed them to the Red cavalry. Mother Superior had told the Sisters to forgive them, they were simple peasants and had no reason to love Poles, who had forbidden their language and Orthodox church, which was a heresy but must be combated with truth, not guns—

"*Spit!*" the Soviet officer had said to the Mother Superior. "Spit on the cross!"

Marya remembered the thin pockmarked face, the cap with the red star above. Torn mustard-yellow uniform, a smell of old sweat and cheap perfume, a Russian smell. Gaping dull faces of the soldiers, and the long triangular bayonets on their rifles glinting in the rain. His hand slapped the Mother Superior's head back, forth; the wimple of her habit came loose, exposing her cropped gray hair; there was blood on her cheeks, but she signed herself. He struck again and again, until she fell and crawled to kiss the carved rood they had carried from the abbey in Lwow, embracing it where it lay in the slick churned-up clay and sheep dung of the street. The officer stepped back; signalling to one of his men; the Cossack grinned, heeled his shaggy pony forward, drew the long guardless saber and leaned far over.

The honed steel gleamed wetly, a shimmering arc that ended in flesh. . . .

Two. Sister Kazimiera. Slight and nervous and dark, a lawyer's daughter from Znin, always ill with something.

Nineteen forty-one, in German-occupied Mazovia, north of Warsaw; Modlin, that was the name of the town. Some of the Sisters had objected to hiding the Jewish children, in the root cellar below the stable that was their only shelter; there were Christian youngsters whose need was almost as great. Sister Kazimiera had looked at them and quoted, "Insofar as ye do it unto the least of these my little ones . . ."

Marya remembered the bored impassive faces of the SS *Einsatzkommandos* as they hammered with boots and rifle butts on the floors and walls, thrust bayonets into the heaps of straw and bedding. The nuns had gone down on their knees and begun to pray. Marya remembered fighting a sneeze as ancient hay dust flew up from the boards of the walkway; it was an old stable, brick and battered wooden stalls and bright sunlight streaming through small broken windows and the cracks in the doors.

All of them kneeling, except Sister Kazimiera in the cellar, keeping the children quiet. But there were a dozen of them, some only five or six years old; they must have heard the shouting in German and been frightened. One cried, a thin reedy sound through the boards, then the others. The *Rottenführer* had laughed, going down on one knee and probing amid the straw and dirt for the lifting ring of the trapdoor. Marya had screamed as he lifted it and pulled the stick grenade from his belt, and he had laughed again with the Schmeisser bouncing against his chest as she lunged forward and froze with a trooper's bayonet before her face. Then more of the nuns were shrieking, as the heavy timber of the trapdoor lifted and the sound of the children weeping became louder; Marya could see the thin black-clad bodies and sidelocks and yarmulkes, the girls' kerchiefs, the huge staring eyes.

Sister Kazimiera's were closed as she crouched protectively over them; the SS man yanked the tab on the grenade, tossed it in and let the door drop. . . .

Marya squeezed the wood of her rosary until her nails showed white.

Three. Sister Zofia. Fat, so long as they had any food at all. A peasant's daughter, her father had beaten her when she claimed a vocation until the village priest shamed him with valuing a pair of hands more than God's will.

Nineteen forty-four, Marya and the others had been looking north, toward Brussels, when it happened. A high whistling in the sky: one of the new reaction-jet airplanes, a thin thread of contrail against the aching blue of a morning sky. Draka; there were almost no European aircraft left. A flash of . . . not fire; light, intolerable, brighter than the sun, a single moment of light so intense that the shadow of a single leaf before the face could be *felt* against the skin. Then hot darkness, absolute, not even the flickers that come beneath closed lids.

Blind, she had thought. *I am blind.* The earth shook, rose up and struck her amid a noise like the laughter of Satan, louder than the world's ending, and the heat; there were screams, and the sound of buildings breaking. Sister Zofia had been inside; she pushed her way out of the rubble and stood looking at the mushroom cloud climbing above the horizon like the wrath of the angry God who turned His eyes on Sodom; had led them stumbling in a line to the intact cellar and sealed it, and bandaged their eyes, and nursed them through the weeks that followed, and gone out to find sealed food and water. Nursed them through the fever and the bleeding gums and falling out of hair, and had said when they heard her vomiting in a corner that it was bad food. Marya's eyes had recovered first; the vision was blurry but she had been glad of that, it would have been unbearable to vomit herself at what Sister Zofia's face had become, or shrink from the oozing, ulcerated hands that had saved her life. God had been good; Sister Zofia died quickly, with none of the raving that brain lesions brought to some of the others. Her dosage had been too extreme.

Marya's mind skittered sideways, the focus of remembrance darting away as the hand does from a fire, instinctively. *"No,"* she whispered fiercely, in Polish. "No, I *will* remember. I will remember all of you; always, I will remember."

You do not need a rosary or cross to be near to God, she reminded herself severely as the breath caught in her throat and she stuffed the thing of wood and string into the pocket of her skirt. They walked out behind Yasmin, behind Tanya and the beautiful evil-eyed child in the silk dress, through the outer rooms of the shop that sold people, into the corridors of Central Detention. The guards and clerks looked at her differently. As if they *saw* her now, as if the clothes and the company of the Draka made all the difference, and she had been invisible naked. Part of the process, she judged; strip everything away, then give it back in another pattern.

I am afraid, she thought, as they came out into a courtyard. The rain had stopped, and the clouds were breaking up; the courtyard had been a road, the walls that closed it off on three sides were new concrete blocks topped with razor wire; the gate was tall panels of perforated steel. There was a work group sweeping rain and mud into the gutters.

Two cars and a truck with a torn canvas tilt were parked by the gate, the draft fans of their boilers making a gentle hissing; a coffle of serfs in neck collars linked to a central chain waited by it, twenty or so. Mostly men, working-class Lyonnaise by their looks, with the dulled skin of people who have not eaten properly in years, dressed in new drab issue clothing of the same sort she was wearing.

The two cars were large six-wheelers with sides of stamped steel panels colored olive drab.

Two Draka waited by the lead car, a man and a woman in soft black leather trousers and armless cotton singlets, passing the time throwing a heavy medicine ball back and forth. They had the Draka look, long swelling muscle moving under skin with no padding of fat, blurring-quick speed and a bouncy, tensile physical presence. The ball arched up a final time and landed through the roof hatch of one car with a *thunk*.

I am afraid, ran through her again, as the two looked at her and Chantal and Therese. The sensations were familiar, dry mouth and nausea and a lightness behind the eyes. Cold light eyes examined her. Not with hostility, not even the deadly indifference of the Security officer who had arrested her those six long months ago. She was a servant, not an enemy; they were looking at her and wondering whether she would work well or badly, how much trouble she would be to direct.

Odwaga, she thought: courage, in her own language. I am afraid but I will not show it. I am a Pole, we are a small people and poor and backward, we have no frontiers and everyone on earth has taken it in turn to crush us, but even when we must hitch ourselves to the plough so that our men may ride the horse to fight tanks we have never lacked *odwaga*. Common sense, yes; luck, yes, but never courage. I am a Pole and a religious and a Sister of the Order of St. Cyril and these I will be until I die, and if this is the sin of pride I cannot ask God's forgiveness because I do not repent it.

Perhaps there would be a priest, though, wherever they were going. It would be good to confess again, and receive the sacraments.

Chantal Lefarge looked away from the Draka. Her eyes fell on the green-uniformed Order Police by the gate, caught the glitter of the chain-slung gorgets around their necks; she turned away, shaking as her mind turned back the months, her mouth dry, hearing—

"Hold her, Achmed." Therese screaming through the muffling of her dress that the *Orpos* had pulled up over her head, thin rabbit-shrieking, running blindly into the wall, dress a blot of dark in the night-dim alley and her body thin and white . . . The fist struck her and filled her mouth with the taste of salt. Again, and the world blurred.

Jean-Paul had said that leaflets were essential, to show the workers that the Party still existed. In Lyon the Party was Jean-Paul, who had been a minor cell leader before the war, and a dozen others. More had survived the War and the Gestapo, but the Draka found them somehow;

impaled them all. Jean-Paul said he was still getting orders from Paris, but she had seen him once writing the letters from "headquarters" himself, sitting alone with the papers and a bottle of absinthe, writing and drinking and weeping slow tears. She had backed out and said nothing.

The serf policeman stepped closer and rammed his fist into her again, into the belly, and she doubled over with an anguished *whoop* of air, silver dazzles before her eyes, weakness like water running through her arms and legs. A foot kicked her behind the leg and she was down on hands and knees on the garbage-slimed cobbles of the alley. One of them squatted and ripped open her blouse, grabbed at her breasts and squeezed first one and then the other; a milking gesture, saying that she was nothing, a cow. Another knelt behind her and hit her again, a hard ringing cuff to the back of her head. Threw up her skirts and tore her underwear down one seam and let it fall along that thigh. Night air cold on her buttocks, raising gooseflesh.

"Changed my mind, Achmed, you kin have that othah little thing," the voice said. Hands gripping her hips, another pain through the dazzle. Then—

No. She shivered back to the present. The coffle were looking at her and the nun. Marya was a good sort despite her absurd superstitions and that air of passive meekness . . . Most of the coffle were just staring, dazed; some with curiosity, others with a sullen burning hostility broad enough to lap over from the Draka onto her and anyone standing near them, all overlaid with a heavy numb fear. Those were her people, she had grown up among them in the shrilling garlic-smelling brick tenements between the two rivers, ancient noisy factories and little frowsy shops and cafes . . . the run-down overcrowded schools which taught her nothing but reading and writing and how to be an obedient drudge for the rich, the Party libraries that had opened a world.

The Draka woman was walking forward; the two who had waited by the car as well, shrugging on jackets of the same soft black leather as their trousers, buckling on gunbelts, slinging assault rifles and the machetelike bush knives; the long whips they swung in their hands. Blacksnake whips, *sjamboks* they called them; the lashes trailed on the wet pavement, the metal tips making dull chinking sounds on the cracks. The coffle struggled to their feet, bowed, jostling one another in their clumsiness. Chantal watched and felt a taste at the back of her throat, sour, like vomitus after too much cheap Languedoc red wine; it was odd that hatred had a physical taste. The *sjamboks* cracked suddenly, a volley like gunshots; birds flew up protesting from the walls of the courtyard, and a fine mist blew from the wet leather.

"Good." The Draka woman speaking, French this time; nodding as she saw the eyes fix on her. "It is too early for the whip, serfs." A thumb directed towards herself. "I am Mistis Tanya von Shrakenberg; my husband and I are your new owners." She paused.

"You are stonemasons, builders, electricians; we have bought you for our estate, because we need more skilled labor."

Another pause, and she rested her hands on her hips. "Now, being plantation serfs is about the best thing that could happen to you all, here in the Domination; you've got the added advantage of belonging to the von Shrakenbergs, who do not believe in unnecessary cruelty to underlings." Another smile. this one like a shark's. *"Unnecessary."*

"You have a chance," she concluded. "Use it."

Oh, I will, Chantal thought fiercely. *I will, Mistress.*

Tanya turned her back as the overseers chivied the coffle into the truck; there was a creaking of springs, a metallic clatter as the ends of their chain were reeved through stout eyebolts and padlocked closed. It was difficult, dealing with Europeans. They certainly had weaker stomachs than born-serfs; you could terrify them with even the mildest physical punishment; on the other hand, anything could set them off, something as routine as a cuff over the ear. She shook her head. Then there were others who just collapsed completely, more totally pliable than any but the best house-bred servants in the Police Zone.

Hope these two work out, she thought wearily. "Good work, Yasmin," Tanya said, running a critical eye over Marya and the Frenchwomen. "No trouble?"

"No, Mistis. 'Cept that-there greencoat who brought Therese up from th' cells. I had a few words wit' him, he bein' rough." A sniff. "They pigs, beggin' you pahdon, Mistis."

"No argument, Yasmin," Tanya said. The serf girl glanced about, leaned closer.

"Ah, Mistis, 'bout Therese, might be good idea, if'n—"

Tanya nodded. "Already gave the orders." A sigh. "There are times when I wish I were still in uniform," she said.

Yasmin smiled, with a small chuckle. "Not what yous sayin' right after the War, Mistis, when yous come home." A sly glance from under demurely lowered lashes.

"Mmm, true enough, too busy celebrating."

Her gaze turned towards the airship haven; Andrew's flight would be leaving that afternoon; officers returning from leave did not rate heavier-than-air transport priorities. *At least I'm not heading into a combat zone,* she thought. *Luck go with you into the north, brother.*

Chapter Five

CENTRAL FINLAND, 22,000 FEET
NEAR FIREBASE ALPHA
2ND MERARCHY, XIX JANISSARY LEGION
DISTRICT 3, EAST BALTIC COMMAND
JUNE 16, 1947

Strategos Sannie van Reenan glanced down through the porthole at her elbow as the transport's engines changed their droning note, signalling descent. Soundproofing could only do so much, and after a while the vibration became like her heartbeat; not something she heard consciously, but a change was instantly apparent. The smudged glass of the window showed the same endless dark green coniferous forest they had been flying over since Moscow, hours ago, but the lakes and rivers had been growing steadily more numerous. Cultivated fields, too, or the weed-grown spaces that *had* been fields, before the Draka came. Yawning, she rubbed at her face. She had worked and catnapped through the night, cleaning up details of her notes from the Ukrainian and Russian sectors. She made a slight face.

"I hope this is a little less grim," she said to her aide.

He looked up from a file folder on the table between their recliner seats, closing it neatly and tapping it between palms to align the contents. The interior of the transport was fitted as an office with microfiche racks, files, copier and a hot plate: bunks could be folded down from the walls. The aide signed for coffee and one of the serf auxiliaries brought the pot; he gave her a smile and thanks before she returned to her typewriter and the headphones of the dictorec machine. These were skilled specialists, part of a team that had worked together for years, not to be spoiled by mistreatment.

"Well, from the sitreps and digests, near like as bad, even if the reasons are different."

His superior yawned again, patting her mouth with the back of her hand. She was a small woman with an air of well-kept middle age, neatly made, trim despite twenty hours without change of uniform.

246

Looking very much what she was, an Archona-born career Intelligence officer of an old professorial family.

"Reasons give mere fact human significance, Ivar," she said. "Russia left a bad taste in m'mouth, to be frank."

The aide shrugged. "We underestimated the Germans," he said; his voice had the precise, rather hard-edged accent of Alexandria and the Egyptian province. "It took a year longer to muscle them back into Central Europe than we anticipated." Another shrug. "We couldn't be expected to spare transport to feed the cities, now could we?" North Russia's industrial centers had been fed from the Ukraine, before the war, and the black-earth zone yielded little grain while the Domination's armies fought their way west across burning fields.

"Hmm. Necessary I know." It was an old precept of Draka ethics that to desire the goal was to approve the means needed to achieve it. "Still, technically, they were Draka cattle as soon as the Fritz pulled out. For all we know, good cattle, obedient an' unresistin'. We made a mistake, thirty million of them died for it."

Her finger flicked open a report. "With regard to MilRef 7:20a, demographic projections indicate nonpositive . . . Sweet soul of the White Christ, an' to think I once had pretensions to a passable prose style. Why not 'They're all dead'?" she muttered. "Must be some internal dynamic a' large organizations." To her assistant: "Not to mention the waste a' skilled labor; those that didn't eat each other are too demoralized t' do much good."

"Well, at least the bloody survivors aren't giving us much partisan trouble."

She shrugged in her turn. "Patchwork way of doin' things, Ivar: serfs're supposed to get an implicit promise of work, bread an' protection in return for submission, you know. Despair's as like to produce rebellion as obedience, in the long run; let 'em think we're like to slaughter whole populations just 'cause they're inconvenient. . . . That famine may be savin' trouble now and causin' us problems for two generations. Patchwork, short-term way a' doin' things."

Sannie closed her eyes, touched fingertips to the lids. "Sometimes I get to feelin' we don't do anything else but run around all our lives thinkin' up short-term solutions t' problems created by the last set of short-term . . . Nevah mind."

Ivar took another sip of his coffee, then chuckled. "One humorous aspect, though, dear Chief." At her raised brow he continued: "Well, most of the machinery is intact, now that transport and power are functional again. We're drafting in industrial labor in job lots, besides landworkers. And where are they coming from?" he asked rhetorically. "Germany, mostly. They started the war for *Lebensraum*, living room, and now they're certainly getting it."

Strategos van Reenan smiled dutifully before returning her attention to the porthole. . . . It *was* ironic. Also Ivar was bright and capable, possibly even a successor on that distant but eagerly awaited day when she retired. *I'll be glad to get back to the capital*, she thought.

For a moment homesickness squeezed her with a sudden fierce longing. Archona: the time-mellowed marble colonnades of the

University, gardens, fountains, broad quiet streets, cleanliness and order. *Damnation, I could be sitting under a pergola at the Amphitheater.* An original Gerraldson concerto this week, his new *Fireborne Resurrection* opus . . . or visiting the galleries, or her nieces and nephews. Gardening in the half-hectare about the house that had been her parents', or just sitting with a good book and Mamba curled purring in her lap.

Enough, she told herself. Work to be done, and not all of it could be accomplished from a desk in Castle Tarleton. The Eurasian War had left the Domination doubled in size, tripled in population; civil administration, economics, military, all the decision-making branches had critical choices to make by the score, all of them needed information. Not raw data, Archona was inundated with it; they needed *knowledge* more than facts, and knowledge had to proceed from understanding. *We are so few, so few,* went through her, with weariness and fear. *So few, and so much to be done.* The State to be safeguarded, built up, made more efficient, wealthy, powerful. Not as an end in itself, but because it was the instrument of the Race, people and blood and her own descendants.

Still, it would be good to be home. *I'm tired of it,* she realized. Tired of mud and flies and filth, the shattered empty cities. Memories flitted by. Goblin-faced children tearing the rotting meat from a dead horse, not even looking up as the cars splashed them in passing. Janissaries kicking heaps of black bread from a moving flatbed, laughing at the struggling piles of bodies that tore at each other for the loaves; there was enough, more than enough for all, but not much resembling a human mind left in the survivors. The peculiar wet stink of cholera, bodies piled high on the steam trucks: rag-clad stick figures lining up for inoculation and neck numbering, staring at her with dull apathy and a sick, brutalized hatred.

Yes, it will be very good to be home. All the nonexistent gods know we're not a squeamish people, but this is getting beyond enough. Sannie sighed. One day there would be an end to it. When all the world was under the Yoke, peaceful; when the Race no longer had to forge each individual into a weapon, or squeeze their underlings so hard for the means of war, and long-tamed peoples gave no cause for fear and the cruelty it made necessary. Then they could rest; scholarship, beauty, simple pleasure, all could become more than something to be fitted into the spare moments . . . She forced herself back to the present; that good day would not come in her lifetime, or her grandchildren's. In the meantime, each day was a brick in the final edifice.

"These Finns are an *immediate* problem, though," Ivar was saying "The number of troops tied down here is ridiculous, considerin' the relative importance."

"That it is, Ivar," she answered. Below, something winked from beneath a stretch of trees. *Quartz,* she thought idly. *Tin can, shell fragment.* Flying was a humbling experience. In an office in Castle Tarleton, you dealt with maps, reports, photographs; the accumulated knowledge of centuries at your fingertips, an unmatched research staff, electronic tendrils reaching out over half the earth. The illusion of control came easily there. Out here, flying hour after hour above the living earth, you realized how big it was, how various, how unknowable.

"Aircraft. Down, everybody *down*."

Kustaa froze in place, crouching, with the other members of the guerrilla patrol that was threading its way through the forest. The noise swelled overhead, coming from the south, their own direction. Two planes; not fighters or strike aircraft, too high, wrong noise . . . medium bombers or transports. Ten thousand feet and coming down.

Ahead of him, one of the guerrillas rolled over on her back and unshipped a pair of binoculars. That was a risk, although a slight one. There was a pine seedling not far from his nose, growing canted beside a cracked slab of granite rock. The brown duff of needles and branches was damp beneath his hands and knees, sparsely starred with small blue flowers and coarse grass. An ant crawled over the back of his hand, tickling; the air smelled coolly of resin, wet spruce needles. Wind soughed through the high branches above, louder than the throb of engines. Light swayed over the patchwork camouflage clothing of his companions, dapple and flicker. . . .

It was unbearably like home. Almost, this might be a hunting trip with Dad back in the '30s, up in the woods north of town. Or that time right after the War, when he and Aino had visited home; everyone sitting down to Mom's blueberry pancakes, then Dad and Sam and he driving out to the lake and canoeing down the Milderak, finding a good spot under the lee of Desireaux Island and throwing their lines out on water so clear you could see the pike gliding by like river wolves twenty feet below.

No, it isn't like home, he thought wryly. *Home is like this.* Which was why so many Suomaliset had settled there around Duluth and the upper Lakes; it reminded them of the home they had been driven by hunger to leave, let them make a living in the ways they were used to. Lake sailors, lumberjacks, miners, hardscrabble back-clearing farmers.

The woman ahead of him lowered her captured Draka binoculars. "Light transports," she said. "Heading into the snake base."

Circling, the aircraft made their approach to Firebase Alpha. It was laid out in a double star pattern, to give overlapping fields of fire on the perimeter: that was standard. The doubled number of heavy machine-gun nests were not. Nor were the dug-in antiaircraft tanks, the snouts of their six-barreled Gatling cannon pointing outward. Sannie's eyes flickered, taking in other details; two batteries of heavy automortars in gun pits near the center of the base, with top covers improvised from welded steel sheet; everything underground except the vehicles, and those in sandbagged revetments.

"Well," the Staff officer's aide said again as they banked and began the steep in descent to the pierced-steel surface of the airstrip. "This *is* a bit out of the ordinary. Firepower, eh?"

The Strategos smiled. "If Andrew's put all this in, I'm sure it's necessary. He was always a boy to take pains."

"You've known him a fair bit?"

"Unofficial aunt," she replied, sliding the Russian reports into the wire rack holder by her elbow for the clerical staff to refile.

"Not one of the Oakenwald von Shrakenbergs, is he?"

Sannie shook her head. Ivar was Alexandria-born, city-bred, and he had spent most of his service in the outer provinces. Nothing wrong with that, of course, that was where the work was, but it was time for him to learn the social background, if he was to operate out of Castle Tarleton. The elite military aristocracy of the Domination were a close-knit group; new names came in on merit but the old ones tended to recur generation after generation.

"No, younger branch. You met Karl an' his son Eric at the reception on Oakenwald, last January, remembah? Andrew's the second son of Everard, Karl's younger brothah; Everard mustered out back in the '20s, took up a land grant in Syria, near Baalbeck. He's got a sister, cohortarch in th' Guard, settled down in France, near Tours. Married to a fourth cousin from Nova Cartago, near Hammamet . . . complex, isn't it?" A pause. "Used to meet Andrew a good deal, when he was down south visitin'. Good boy, bit too serious. Smart, but quiet about it."

The command bunker was three meters down: sandbags for the walls and floor, the ceiling layers of pine logs, earth, and salvaged railway iron. Radios and teleprinters were lined along the walls; short corridors with switchbacks to deflect blast led to other chambers. It was morning, but there was no light here except the overheads, little sound but the click and hum of equipment, the sound of ventilators. It smelled of damp earth, raw timbers, leather and metal and oil, faintly of ozone, in the center was a map of the surrounding area, cobbled together from aerial photographs and scrawled with symbols and arrows in colored greasepaints. The officers around it had talked themselves silent; now they were thinking.

The map was of central Finland, their Legion's area of responsibility. Forest, starred with lakes scattered like a drift of coins from a spendthrift's hand, bog, burnt farmhouses and fields going back to brush. Red marks for ambushes; too many of them. Green for counterambushes, blue for arms caches and guerrilla bases discovered; far too few.

"Suh?" The word was repeated twice before Merarch Andrew von Shrakenberg looked up from the table. It was one of his Janissary NCO's, Mustapha, the Master Sergeant from Headquarters Century. "Suh, the plane come, radio say five minutes." A reliable man, half-Turk, his father some anonymous Draka passing through a Smyrna comfort station, raised in a training creche. Stocky, hugely muscular, square-faced and green-eyed.

Andrew sighed, returned his salute and stretched. "Take over, Vicki," he said. His second grunted without looking up and continued her perusal of the map. "Corey, we'd bettah see to it. Mustapha, attend."

Corey Hartmann grunted in turn, throwing down a cigarette and grinding the butt out on the floor of the command bunker. The two officers snapped their assault rifles from the racks by the exit and pushed past the spring-mounted door, up the rough stairwell and into the communications trench, blinking and adjusting their helmets as they reached surface level. The dank smell of the bunker gave way to the dust-bodies-burnt-distillate stink of a working firebase, and under it a hint of the vast pine forests that stretched eastward ten thousand kilometers to Kamchatka and the Pacific.

Four light utility cars waited, amphibious four-seaters with balloon tires; Andrew swung into the second, standing with a hand on the roll bar, next to the Janissary gunner manning the twin barrel. It was a fine day, warm for Finland. Warm enough to forget the winter, or nearly. He grimaced at the memory, slitting his eyes in the plume of gritty dust thrown up by the lead vehicle. It was a short ride to the airfield, a simple stretch of pierced steel sheet laid on earth and rock laboriously leveled; the light transport was already making its approach run.

Twin-Zebra class, he thought. An oblong fuselage, high-winged, two engines, two slender booms holding the tail. He looked for the national blazon; the Domination's crimson dragon, wings outstretched, talons clutching the slave fetter of mastery and the sword of death. But the shield covering the Snake's midsection was a black checkerboard with a silver Roman numeral II, not the usual green-black-silver sunburst. Supreme General Staff, second section, Strategic Planning. Behind, another dot was circling, another Twin-Zebra. That would be the flunkies, secretaries, comtechs, whatever.

"Well, well," he said. "Staff planes not Transport Section. A panjandrum indeed." An ordinary Staff inspection would be a fairly junior officer, taking his luck with the transportation pool. There were not many who could command this sort of following.

"Sheee-it. Sir." Corey added.

"Know how y'feel," Andrew replied, with a wry smile. "Still, we always complainin' GHQ gives the Citizen Force more 'n its share of attention, can't nohow complain when they take us at ouah word."

"Outposts here, here, here," Arvid said, sketching with his finger in the dirt. The other half-dozen Finnish officers were folding their maps, giving their notebooks final once-overs before they departed to rebrief their subordinates. There was a ridge of frost-shattered granite between them and the road that speared down from the north and turned west in front of them, enough to give a prone man good cover. The wet earth behind it was an excellent sand table.

Kustaa watched, aware that much of the information was added for his benefit. Arvid continued, "Marsh through here, and this approach is blocked by the lake; hard for us to get in, but it limits the routes out for their patrols. The main base is out of mortar range for us, so we pepper the outposts now and then; then they chase us, and we can usually count on taking out a few at least. They patrol the roads and sweep the woods at random intervals. Not much contact for the last six months."

"Why?" Kustaa asked, shrugging his shoulder against the prickling itch of the foliage stuck into loops on his borrowed tunic. *I feel like a bloody Christmas tree,* he thought resentfully; they were all in uniforms sewn with loose strips of cloth colored dull-green and brown to break the outlines of their bodies, stuck all over with bits of grass and branch. Very effective for a stationary ambush.

They had stopped well short of the gravel-surfaced road and the cleared zone that extended twenty meters on either side. The sun was bright enough to set him blinking after the green-gold twilight of the trees, and the tall grass that had grown up around the stumps waved, spicy-smelling, as their feet crushed it, starred with flowering weeds and thistles that clung to their trousers. Nothing remarkable, simply a good two-lane country road through tall pine timber, coming from the north and curving sharply east. There was a whiff of tar—the crushed rock must have been lightly sprayed to lay the dust but not even the Domination's resources extended to putting a hard surface on every back-country lane.

The squads laying the mines were lifting the rock with swift, careful motions of their trowels and entrenching tools. Hands lowered the heavy round bundles of plastique into the earth as carefully as a mother tucks her child into the cradle. Kustaa watched a woman kneel beside the hole, the butt of her knife between her teeth as she peeled apart the strands at the end of a reel of wire. Sinewy brown tanned hands stripped the insulation from the bright copper and twisted the leads to the detonators, pressing the blue painted rods of fulminate into the soft explosive. Others were unreeling the wire as she worked, trenching the surface of the road and then placing the gravel back in reverse order to keep the darker weathered stones on top; Kustaa could hear the rhythmic tinking of their spade handles hammering the surface to the proper consistency. The Draka supply convoy was going to get a warm reception.

Good work, he thought. They weren't putting them all in the roadway either, more along the sides, and homemade directional mines spiked to stumps and concealed by the brush. No trampling that lovely waist-high cover, even though there must be the equivalent of two companies—they'd been joining the march in dribs and drabs. Nobody who didn't absolutely have to be was in view, and those were getting their business done and getting back past the treeline.

"And I'm surprised they don't keep the vegetation down more," he said.

"Not enough manpower," Arvid replied. "Which is the basic reason for the light contact, too. Remember, they're stretched thin, they took thirty million square kilometers in the War. And they're not in any overwhelming hurry; the snakes are like that, long-term thinkers. Cold-blooded."

"Like real snakes," one of the others said with a grimace.

"Finland isn't all that important to them," Arvid continued in a dry, detached tone. "There isn't anything here they need badly enough to make an all-out effort to get. They've swept the civilians out. Just us and the snake military; they're not even trying to run the timber camps anymore. Their aircraft make sure there's no farming going on, and they mostly just wait for us to die, helping when they can. I think the only reason they try to occupy us at all is the resistance we've put up. They're like that too. Aggressive." A sour grin. "Most of our attacks are directed at their supply convoys. Polish hams, Danish butter, French wine . . . it'll be a while before we starve to death."

Kustaa nodded, remembering the storerooms he had seen stacked with cans and boxes, the camouflaged garden plots, night-fishing equipment.

"I think they're afraid, too," the American said. "Right now the Domination's like a lucky gambler, they want to get up from the table with their winnings . . . Sure they're going to send in their air?"

"Oh, yes," a guerilla said. "Policy: they always give a cut-off unit full support. Air strikes, and a rescue column."

Kustaa turned and looked behind him. Two crates of the missiles had come with the guerrillas on this strike. Two units here under camouflage tarpaulins, spidery swivel-mounted tripods with a bicycle-type seat for the gunner, battery clusters, the black-box exotica of the launching system. A pair of rockets for each, one on the rail and a reload, cylinders a little taller than he, a uniform twelve inches through except for the last foot that tapered into a blunt cone. Simple cruci-form control fins at the base, and a single nozzle for the rocket, like an illustration for *Thrilling Planet Stories*, the pulp he had hidden folded inside serious reading in his teens. Except that gaunt female guerrilla in faded overalls was nothing like as photogenic as the brass-braed earth women who had figured on the garish covers, usually menaced by something with tentacles and a lust for mammalian flesh.

"But I'm up against monsters, sure enough," he whispered to himself.

There were no markings, no serial numbers or manufacturer's stamps anywhere inside the apparatus. Kustaa sneered mentally at the security worldview run amok; as if transistors were something the Finns could cobble together in their bunker hideouts. As if the Fifth Cav hadn't paraded a dozen of them past President Marshall's reviewing stand on Fifth Avenue last Inauguration Day, with the Draka embassy's military attaché taking notes and snapping pictures. The hastily-trained crews lay beside the missile launchers, going over the manuals again. Well, the mothering things were *supposed* to be soldier-proof—they were designed for infantry use. Skills built into the machinery, anyone who could walk and breathe at the same time capable of operating them.

At that, these old country Finns had picked up the theory quickly enough, better than a lot of the hill-crackers and ladino peons he'd had to train on much simpler equipment in the Corps during the War. . . .

"Ambush in more senses than one," he said to Arvid. The Finn nodded and settled down behind the jagged granite crenel.

"Not long," he replied. "Mines all ready. First action this close to the base since snowmelt, they'll react quickly."

Damn, you never remember how hard the waiting is, Kustaa thought, as silence settled on the stretch of forest. Silence enough for the wind-rustle through branches and occasional birdsong to fill his ears. His mouth was dry; he brought out a stick of chewing gum, stopped himself from tossing the scrap of silvered wrapping paper aside and tucked it neatly in the front pocket of his fatigues. There was no point in giving the Draka an extra clue, it might be important if they made it away clean. *And you never remember how stupid the reasons for volunteering sound in your head, either.*

"God *damn* you, Donovan," he muttered under his breath, sliding the borrowed Finnish rifle through the fissure in the rock before him. Nice sound design, gas-operated semiauto, not much different from the Springfield-7 he'd used in the Pacific except that it had a detachable box clip, and that was an improvement. He'd managed to persuade them to give him a scope-sighted model, too.

"I've given Uncle my share, I'm too old for this shit," he said, continuing the dialogue with his absent superior. "You and that fucking Mick blarney; you could've made a fortune selling suntan oil to Eskimos." Something tiny burrowed up from the grass beneath him and bit him on the stomach; he crushed the insect and rubbed his palm down a pant leg before tucking the stock of the rifle back against his cheek. It was cool and smooth against beard stubble grown long enough to be silky.

There was a muffled buzz from above, no louder than a dragonfly humming at arm's length. A brief flash off plastic and metal and a scout plane went by overhead toward the south, a twin-boomed bubble fuselage on long slender wings with a shrouded pusher engine. Then it banked and turned north again, flying a zigzag pattern less than a hundred feet above the treetops. His stomach felt sour, the same feeling as too much coffee; Kustaa could feel his eyes jumping back and forth across the scene before him, looking for movement with a reflex much stronger than conscious thought. *Hell, I know where they are and can't see them*, he told himself. *No way a plane's going to spot anything.*

Sounds echoed back and fourth between the trees, motor sounds. Turbo compounds, the Domination's internal-combustion engines of choice for automotive applications. Many, but not really heavy stuff; other noises under that, a vague mechanical hum. This was different from ambushes in Sumatra. The jungle of southeast Asia hid sounds better; the Nips could be right on top of you and walking by before you heard anything. He had always hated having to shoot the pack mules, the way they screamed. At least there wouldn't be any of that, with a mechanized convoy.

Donovan was wrong, this isn't a job for a veteran, he thought. *This is work for a fucking kid who doesn't believe he can* die. His mind was running through everything that *might* happen. Sergeant Hicks, that was the first casualty he'd ever seen. Hicks'd lived for hours after the bullet went widthwise through his face behind the nose; his eyes had popped out like oysters. . . .

They saw the dust plume before the vehicles, spreading brown-white above the road. Now things were clear, very clear, like the sight-picture that firmed up as you turned the focusing screw of a pair of binoculars. His stomach settled with a last rumble. Then the first Draka warcar was in view, keeping to the right of the road. Light armored car, six-wheeled, a smooth welded oval with a hexagonal turret mounting a heavy machine gun and grenade launcher; two more behind it, same class, their weapons traversed to alternate sides of the road. The commanders head-and-shoulders out of the turret hatches: that was good practice, you couldn't see shit buttoned up. He eased his eye forward to the telescopic sight and the first man's head sprang into view. There was not much to be seen, just a line of mouth and square strong hands beneath helmet and dust goggles. Black hands, black face, a Janissary; a camo uniform, with some sort of shoulder rig for an automatic pistol.

Trucks behind the armored cars, a dozen of them, then three armored personnel carriers, Peltast class, eight-wheeled, not the heavy tracked Hoplites the Citizen Force legions used. More trucks, then something military that was hard to make out through dust and engine-induced heat haze. The trucks nagged at him with familiarity . . . yes, German make. *Wehrmacht* Opels, four-ton steamers, but not worn enough to be leftovers from the War. That made sense; it would be easier to keep the production lines going than retool right away, even with the spare-parts problems that would cause. Autosteamers were fairly simple beasts, anyway, low-maintenance. Ten-yard spacing and they were doing thirty-five miles an hour tops.

The lead car slowed; Kustaa could see the figure in the turret put one hand to his ear, pressing the headset home to improve hearing. The American stiffened, his finger touching delicately down on the smooth curve of his rifle's trigger, resting, waiting.

"Wait," Arvid said. "I think . . ." The whining hum of heavy tires sank into a lower note, punctuated by the popping crunch of gravel spitting sideways under the pressure of ten-ton loads of armor plate. The whole convoy was slowing, half a kilometer of it, the warcars and APC's first as the radio message reached them and the cargo vehicles responded jerkily. Trucks halted in the center of the roadway, but the escorts wheeled theirs to face the woods, staggered herringbone fashion in alternate directions. The warcars' engines sank to idle, no louder than the thrumming of the autosteamers' boiler fans, and there were shouts back and forth along the line of vehicles.

Arvid swore viciously under his breath in Finnish, then relaxed as the cab doors of the trucks opened. "Rest stop," he muttered. "All the better." He laid a hand on the Finn waiting with his hand on the plunger of the detonator box. "Wait for it."

The drivers were climbing down, stretching, walking to the ditch and opening the flies of their gray overalls to piss; the strong musky odor of urine and wet earth came clearly across the sixty feet of open space. Kustaa winced, hoping they would be finished before the action started. Shooting a man peeing was like killing him while he picked his nose: the homey human action made the target too much a person. It was more comfortable to keep targets as simply shapes in your mind. You put a shot through the center of mass and move on to the next. Targets did not come back before your eyes while you were sleeping or eating or making love . . .

A file of soldiers came jog-trotting up from the APC's, dropping off pairs every ten yards; the troopers fanned out from the road halfway to the trees with their assault rifles slung across their chests. One soldier with a cardboard carton over his shoulder walked to unpin the back flap of the truck closest to Kustaa. He reached up to help the first of the occupants down, his grin visible even at this distance.

"Christ, women!" the American blurted in a whisper.

Arvid turned his head fractionally, studied the two trucks that were shedding passengers. "Whores," he said flatly. "The snakes rotate twenty or so every two weeks. Must be busy, there's a thousand men in that base."

Kustaa slid his eye to the scope. There were ten from each of the trucks, dressed alike in plain dark skirts and white blouses. All young, mid-teens to mid-twenties (although it was hard to judge through the narrow field of the telescope), wearing handcuffs with two-foot chains. Mostly white, but he could see a tall statuesque Negro girl and a couple of Chinese; they were milling and chattering, a few bringing out combs and taking the kerchiefs from their travel-tousled hair. The Janissary was talking to a girl with reddish-brown braids done up in Gretchen coils on the sides of her head; she was snub-nosed and freckled, a dead ringer for the bobby-soxer daughter of his next-door neighbor back in New York except for the serf-number tattooed on her neck.

She took the carton from the soldier and opened it, began handing rolls of toilet paper to the other women. They walked away from the truck toward the granite outcropping, the soldier beside them; he was still talking to the Gretchen girl, laughing and gesturing with his free hand while the right rested lightly on the pistol grip of his rifle. Closer, closer, Kustaa could feel Arvid tensing beside him, hear that the Janissary and the girl were speaking German to each other. The soldier was young too; the face leaped into close-up in the crosshairs of his sight, shaven-skulled but adorned with a wispy yellow mustache and plentiful acne, the neck tattoo standing out bright orange against his tan.

They halted ten meters from the rocks, and the girl gestured imperiously to the serf trooper. He laughed again, turning his back on the clump of women squatting in the long grass, dropping to a knee. His rifle rested across one thigh as he scanned the edge of the treeline and reached inside his mottled tunic to bring out a package of cigarettes, flicking one half-free of the container and raising it toward his lips. Kustaa saw the pack freeze halfway to the young man's mouth, sink back, then drop from stiffening fingers. Pale blue eyes went wide in alarm, and the face rocketed past his 'scope as the soldier shot to his feet.

"*Now!*" Arvid shouted, and the man with the detonator twirled the crank handle on its side and raised the plunger. For a half-second he paused, an expression of utter pleasure on his face, then slammed it down.

Kustaa's finger stroked the trigger of his rifle, and he felt the recoil as a surprise the way it always was when the aim was right. The blond Janissary pitched back, the *smack* of the bullet punching through his stomach close enough to be heard with the *crack* of the round firing. Then the earth under the lead warcar erupted, a sound so huge it struck the whole face like a giant's invisible hand. Groundshock picked him up and slammed him down again, with the iron-salt taste of blood in his mouth from a cut tongue. Nothing was left of the lead car but a tattered rag of steel crossed by the heavier lines of axles, centered in a circle of burning scraps and fuel.

The second armored car was over on its side, wheels spinning in slow futility. Its crew crawled from their hatches, staggered erect, were caught and shredded in the metallic sleet of fire that raked the column from both sides; another roar and pillar of black smoke came from the rear of the convoy, then half a dozen more along the kilometer length of stalled vehicles, *crash-crash-crash*, ripple-firing in a daisy chain of high explosive that sprouted like malignant black mushrooms. Trucks were burning, and a pattering hail of wood and metal and human body parts came down all about them; the heavy oily smell of distillate burning in the open was all around them, and the throat-rasping fumes of burnt propellant.

All along the treeline off both sides of the road, arcs of tracer swept out to chew at the convoy's edges from concealed machine guns. The heavier *snapsnapsnap* of semiauto rifles joined in, and an anvil chorus of ricochets hornet-buzzing from engine blocks and armor. Kustaa shifted aim, found a Janissary kneeling and firing a light machine gun from the hip, strobing muzzle flashes and his mouth gaping pink against the dark-brown skin as he shouted defiance. The crosshairs dropped over his face and *crack*, the rifle hammered at Kustaa's shoulder. The Janissary snapped backward with a small hole just above his nose and the back of his skull blown away in a spatter of gray-pink brains and white bone; he was still kneeling, his body arched back like a bridge and the kindly grass closing over the shock-bulged eyes.

A whipcrack sound went by overhead, close enough for the wind of it to snatch the cap from Kustaa's head and brush heat across his forehead. Ice crystallized in his stomach as he wrestled the rifle out of the notch in the granite and swung it to the left; the third Draka warcar was coming towards them, the long fluted barrel of its 15mm machine gun spraying rounds and blasted spalls and fragments from the stones before them. The stubby muzzle of the grenade launcher beside it made a duller sound, more like ripping canvas. The two-inch bomblets were low velocity, almost visible as they blurred through the air. Their bursting charges were much louder, a *crang* and vicious hum as the coils of notched steel wire inside dissolved into a cloud of miniature buzz saws; each one cleared a five-meter circle in the long grass, as neat as a lawn mower.

With angry helplessness, Kustaa forced out a long breath as he steadied his aim on the gunner's vision-block; bullets were already sparking and whickering off the sloped plates of the car's armor, leaving lead splashes and gouges but not penetrating the welded-alloy plates. The warcar lurched over the rough ground, its six independently-sprung wheels moving with a horrible semblance of life like the legs of some monstrous insect. A few seconds and that line of fire would walk across his missiles, across *him*. He squeezed gently at the trigger—

—and the shot went wild as a streak of fire dazzled across his vision to impact on the glacis plate of the warcar. *Pazooka*, he thought, with an involuntary snigger of relief. Actually a Finnish copy of the German 88mm *Panzerschreck*, but never mind . . . A globe of magenta fire blossomed against the armor, and the warcar turned flank-on and stopped as if it had run into a wall. The American's mind drew in the picture within, the long jet of plasma and superheated metal from the shaped-charge warhead spearing through like a hot poker through cellophane, searing flesh, igniting fuel and ammunition. A second of hesitation, then the turret of the car blew apart with a sharp rending *crang*; pieces of jagged metal went whirring by overhead, and he dropped back to a prudent knees-and-elbows position.

Now he could see the rocket-launcher team; the backblast had set a grass fire that was a black and orange finger pointing to their position. The gunner rose, letting the sheet-metal tube droop behind him while his partner carefully slid a second round home and slapped his shoulder. They shifted position in a quick scuttling run, moving a hundred yards north towards the rear of the convoy; dug-in guerrillas cheered as they passed.

Kustaa wiped a shaky hand over his forehead; that had been far too close, and he could smell the rank musk of his own sweat, taste the sickly salt of it on his lips. His eye caught the wristwatch. Only four minutes, and the muscles of his shoulders were shaking. He forced them to untense as he rolled back to look for his original targets; dense black smoke was billowing past, obscuring the view, but he could see one of the APC's past the trucks glowing cherry red with interior fires, another nosedown in the roadside ditch, disabled by a contact mine but exchanging fire with the guerrillas. Another lancing shriek of fire from the antitank launcher, striking high on its flank, and the small turret on its deck fell silent.

The women were barely visible through the thickening smoke to his front; milling and screaming, some with their underwear around their ankles. Then the big black woman was running among them, pushing them down into whatever safety there was on fire-beaten ground. The German-speaking girl with the braids had dashed forward; now she was dragging the Janissary Kustaa had shot back toward the road, leaning into it with her hands clenched in the shoulder straps of his web harness. The American could see her face quite clearly, huge-eyed with terror and speckled with blood now as thickly as the freckles, her mouth flared in a rictus of effort and determination.

From the way the man's head lolled Kustaa thought there was probably very little point, but he had done things as pointless himself, in combat. Overload, no way to take it all in, so you focused on something. Your job, or some detail you could make your job, even if it was meaningless and the only sensible thing was to scream and run, it was still something you could *do*. Better than freezing, or cowering, or panic. *At least, that's my preference,* the American thought, scanning the thickening smoke for a target. As for the rights and wrongs of a slave-whore risking her life to save a slave-soldier, he supposed she was operating on the general assumption that the people shooting at her were not friends. He could sympathize with that, too, the equation "someone trying to kill me = enemy" had a certain primitive force. . . .

From their right, from the north beyond the veil of smoke, came a sound like a chainsaw. But far too loud. It would have had to be a Paul Bunyan-sized model. A courier dashed up, fell panting on his knees by Arvid and gasped out a message as he leaned on his rifle, between the breathy gabble and the thick Karelian dialect, Kustaa caught only the English word in the middle of the sentence: "Gatling." Then he heard the engine sound from the same direction, and saw two horizontal lines of white-orange light stab out of the smoke. Where they struck the edge of the uncleared forest, the hundred-foot pines fell, sawn through at knee height in white-flashing explosions that sent splinters flying as lethal as shrapnel.

One smashed down in front of the forward wheels of the Draka flakpanzer, clearing the smoke like a fan for an instant before the burning truck next to it ignited the dry resinous branches. Kustaa recognized the type, Dragon class, two four-wheeled power units at each end and a big boxy turret between them: antiaircraft mounting, originally designed to escort mechanized-infantry columns. The armament was two six-barreled Gatling cannon, 25mm; each was capable of pumping out 6,000 rounds a minute. That was why the vehicle was so large, it had to be to carry enough ammunition for the automatic cannon to be useful. Very effective against ground-attack aircraft coming in low; at short range, against surface targets, whatever came in front of the muzzles simply disappeared.

"Shit," Arvid said, listening to the courier and twisting to keep the attacking flakpanzer in view, then rising to his knees and cupping his hands about his mouth. "Tuuvo! Keikkonnen!" The rocket-launcher team looked up from their new blind. "Circle around and take it out!" he shouted. They rose and went back into the woods at a flat run, wasting no time on acknowledgments. "This had better be worth it, American," he continued in a flat conversational voice.

The Dragon's turret moved again, a 180-degree arc; two seconds of the savage chainsaw roar, and a hundred yards of forest went down like grass before a scythe, the twin lines of fire solid bars through the smoke. Then it lurched forward again, the wedge-shaped bow plowing through burning timber in a shower of sparks. The outside wheel sets were in the ditch to allow the gun truck to ease past the burning wreckage in the center of the road, and the thick cylindrical tubes of the Gatlings were canted up sharply to compensate. Trees were burning half a kilometer back into the woods, ignited by stray incendiary rounds and sparks, and he could hear the pulsing bellow of a full-fledged forest fire beginning.

And the volume of small arms' fire from the area under the iron flail of the flakpanzer's cannon was slacking off noticeably.

Another runner slid into the covered zone, gasping as the shock of landing on her back jarred the crudely bandaged arm bound across her body.

"There were four trucks more of infantry at the rear of the convoy," she gasped, between deep panting breaths.

"Replacements," Arvid rasped. "God damn."

"They've pushed us back into the woods on the west side but everything's on fire, we and the snakes are both breaking contact and trying to circle round, it's spreading fast." She glanced back to where the armored vehicle was systematically clearing *this* side of the road.

"The antitank teams on the west are out of range and the one you sent back up toward us is gone." The runner gestured toward her bound arm. "Nearly got it in the same burst. Eino's going to try and take out that fucker with a—"

Another roar of autocannon fire. Kustaa swiveled his rifle, in time to see three figures in guerrilla uniform bounce to their feet and race forward toward the Dragon with satchel charges in their hands. *The Gatlings can't depress enough to stop them, God damn it, they're going to make it!* he thought with a shock of elation.

The crew of the Dragon reached the same conclusion. Hatches cracked open on the square-wheeled power units at either end of the long vehicle, and the muzzles of machine pistols whickered spitefully.

"Shit, shit, shit," Kustaa cursed under his breath, emptying his magazine at the narrow gap between hatch cover and deck. The machine pistol jerked and ceased firing, lay slumped for a moment before it was pulled back inside with a limp dragging motion that suggested an inert body being manhandled down into the driving compartment. The hatch banged shut again, and the guerrilla was only ten yards away, his arm going back in the beginning of the arc that would throw the cloth bag of explosives under the hull of the Dragon; the other two satchelmen were down. "Go, go, go," the American chanted under his breath, eyes urging the Finn on as his hands felt blindly for a fresh clip and slid it into the loading well of the rifle.

The hatch opened again, this time only for a second, just long enough for a stick grenade to come spinning out. It flew in a flat arc, whirling on its own axis, the sharp bang of its detonation coming while it was still at head height. The Finn stopped and fell with an abrupt finality, as if he were a puppet whose strings had been cut, and the sweep of his arm faltered. Wobbling, the satchel charge fell short, throwing up a plume of rock and soil amid the muffled thump of an open-air explosion. Dust cleared, with a ringing hail of rock on metal; the armored cab of the Dragon was intact, but three of the wheels on the outer flank were shredded ruin, and the fourth was jammed by a twisted steel panel.

"Good," Arvid said. "Runner, get back to Eino; bring some of those trees down on that thing, there're a dozen or so in reach." He looked at her arm. "And then get out to the fallback rendezvous; you're not fit for combat."

A shout from a machine-gun team beside them. "Ah, thought so," Arvid muttered. "They're going to try and peel us back up here while the Dragon keeps the center of our line busy."

Figures were dodging through the smoke of the burning trucks on the road ahead, behind the clump of women prone in the roadside grass. A sudden scream like a retching cat, and a line of fire streaked out toward Kustaa's position, slamming the cluster of rocks ahead of him with an explosion that sent fragments of granite blasting uncomfortably close overhead. The sound was fainter than it should have been; his eardrums were ringing, overstrained and losing their capacity to absorb the battering noise. The Janissary infantry poured out into the cleared zone along the road, into the waist-high grass and stumps.

A score of them, running, some falling as the Finnish positions swept them. Squads throwing themselves down to give covering fire, others leapfrogging their positions. The American picked a target, fired, shifted to another. Lizard-mottled uniforms, drug-magazined assault rifles, machetes slung over their backs. Bucket-shaped helmets with cutouts for the faces; he could see one's mouth move, a curse, as he broke stride to avoid stamping on a hysterical girl who lay face-down, beating her hands into the earth. A sergeant, bare-headed save for a checked bandana around his gleaming dome of skull. Kustaa's bullet struck his thigh, sledged him around in a circle that sent a cone of tracer into the air from the light machine gun in his hand. Then he was up again, kneeling, firing from the hip and waving his men on as blood gouted from the massive flap of torn muscle hanging down his leg.

Kustaa slapped another magazine into his weapon and jacked the slide with his right hand; the metal of the barrel burned his palm, overheating from rapid fire. The volume of fire from the Draka infantry was appalling, and damnably well-aimed. He ducked as he reloaded, thankful of an excuse to get out of the way of the light high-velocity bullets that tinked and spanged off the stones before him. He had seen enough combat to know that a firefight was less dangerous than it sounded, it took thousands of rounds to cause a casualty, but standing up in front of that many automatic weapons was still unhealthy.

"We can't hold them!" he shouted to the man beside him.

"Hell we can't!" Arvid said, reaching for a handclasp solenoid detonator linked to a spreading fan of wires. "This is what I laid the directional mines for."

Kustaa froze. His mind's eye saw the weapons; curved steel plates lined with plastique, faced in turn with hundreds of ball bearings. Like giant shotgun shells, their casings spiked to the stumps and ready to fill the whole space between forest and road with a hail of ricocheting metal. His hand streaked toward the guerrilla's.

"The women—" he shouted. The Finn hacked backward with an elbow, a paralyzing blow into the point of Kustaa's shoulder.

"Fuck them," he said, still not raising his voice. His other hand clenched, and the roar of the fires was cut by explosions and a sound like the whining of a million wasps. "Get your missiles ready, American," he continued. Then he raised his voice to a shout. "Follow me, the rest of you, don't let them rally!"

A leap, and he was over the stones and running toward the road. The others followed him with a deep guttural shout, loud enough to drown out the shrill screaming of the wounded lying among the murdered trees.

The Twin-Zebra slid in, flaps dappling the square wing to shed lift, touched smoothly down with the gentle touch of an expert's hands on the controls, rolled to a stop not twenty meters from the two cars. The ramp dropped, but the first two passengers were down before the further end touched. Bodyguards: Special Tasks Section, General Staff Division.

Ah, Andrew von Shrakenberg mused. *They* did *send someone important.* Standard camo uniforms, but cut away from the arms, customized assault rifles, automatic pistols in quick-draw Buchliner harnesses across the stomach. The eyes slid over him without pausing, flickering in an endless animal wariness. Special training, careful selection, and there weren't very many of them. Even among Draka, few had the aptitude, and fewer still were the Citizens who could be spared for such work.

Two more figures came walking sedately down the ramp in garrison blacks. Silently, he approved; even out here, fairly near the sharp end, it was a little ridiculous for staff types to travel in field kit and armed to the teeth. He drew himself up and saluted, conscious of the other officer doing likewise.

"Merarch Andrew von Shrakenberg," he said. "Cohortarch Corwin Hartmann. Service to the State."

The leading staff officer removed her peaked cap and nodded; small, slight, gray-streaked brown hair, broad face and snub nose . . . She smiled at the slight shock of recognition.

Tantie Sannie, I'll be damned, he thought, slightly dazed. Sannie van Reenan; Uncle Karl's aide. . . . Andrew had been born on Oakenwald, the original von Shrakenberg estate south of Archona; his father a younger brother of Karl, landless until after the Great War. Tantie Sannie had been there often enough when he visited, had taken him under her wing when he was stationed there during his year at the Staff Academy.

"Glory to the Race," she replied formally. "Strategos Sannie van Reenan. Soon to be von Shrakenberg." A laugh; this time his brows had risen appreciably. "Permission to satisfy your curiosity, Andrew. Yes, it's officially Tantie Sannie now, not just by courtesy."

"Uncle Karl?"

"Who else, man?" She patted her stomach. "You're due for another cousin, come eight months, too." She turned to Hartmann, saluted. "Combinin' the tour with a little family business, Centurion." A wave to the other officer. "Cohortarch Ivar Barden Couteaux." A cluster of gray-uniformed auxiliaries were following, secretaries and clerks.

"Ah, mmm, this is rather sudden, Strategos," Andrew muttered, as they walked toward the cars.

"It's breakin' out all over, now the War's—as we jokin'ly put it— over. An' I'm not *that* old, Merarch; bit of a risk, but one can always terminate. About time I did my duty to the Race, anyway."

She stepped into the car, paused standing with one hand on the rollbar, looking about. Andrew stopped beside her, stripping away the veil of familiarity and trying to see it through her eyes. Ugly, of course; vegetation ripped away to leave rutted sand and mud, pavements of gravel and crushed stone. Bunkers, buildings of modular asbestos-cement heaped about with earth berms, a few floating balloon-held aerials. Spider-webbed with communications trenches, skeletal support towers for lookouts and arc lights . . .

"You've got a Century of the Third Airborne Legion here, I understand," she said, nodding to a section of revetments; the long drooping blades of helicopter rotors showed over the sandbagged enclosures.

"*Ya*, it's unorthodox"—Citizen Force troops were rarely brigaded with Janissaries, and it was even rarer for them to come under the command of an officer over a Janissary formation—"but we needed a quick-reaction force pretty bad. Trio of gunboats, too." Nearly three thousand troops inside the wire, counting several hundred unarmed auxiliaries in the maintenance and combat-support units.

"I wondered why Castle Tarleton would send anyone to Finland," he continued, as the driver twisted the utility car's fuel feed. "Back to HQ, Mustapha. We goin' get some organic helicopter transport of our own?"

"Not my department, officially," she said, as the car accelerated with a quiet *chuffchuffchuff* of steam. "Unofficially, no, not fo' a while. Bottlenecks in the turbine plants, they tell me, an' maintenance problems. Still a new technology, aftah all. Also, we're givin' priority to convertin' more Citizen Force units to air cavalry, cuttin' back on the heavy armor."

"An' *we* get the short end of the stick, as usual," he said. Conscious of her questioning look, he added: "Take it this is a general survey?"

"Very general," she replied. "Makin' a swing-through all the way from China to the Atlantic, gettin' an overview, combinin' with the Board's compilation of regular data." She was silent for a moment. "A mess, t' be frank."

"Well, we *did* take a shonuff big bite, this time," he said, absently returning the salute of a Citizen officer as they ate dust down the gravel street.

"Hmmmm, yes. Still, only thing we could do, at the time." A pause. "Long-range strategic situation's what I was talkin' about, though." Sannie reached for her cigarettes, remembered the doctor's advice and settled for a hard candy. "Damn those Fritz, they had to go an' discover tobacco's bad for you. Anyway . . . we're just realizin' down in Archona that the progress of the Race is, ahhh, enterin' a new phase."

"How so?" he said, as they reached the headquarters bunker. "Welcome to our humble home." The Strategos looked around, nodded.

"Good to see the real thing, after spendin' so much time in the Castle . . . Well, it's the blessin' and curse of atomics, for starters." The maps had been cleared from the rough plank table in the center of the bunker and pinned to a board framework on one wall; Sannie van Reenan absently returned the salutes of the HQ staff and poured coffee in a thick chipped mug.

"Gods, I'd forgotten how vile the Field Force brew is . . . Where was I?"

Andrew nodded as they seated themselves at the map table. "Atomic stalemate," he said. "An' a good thing, too, in my opinion."

"Good in the short term; without we had 'em, the Yankees could beat us now. Muscle us out of Europe an' eastern China, at the least." She sighed and rubbed her eyes again, grateful for the cool gloom of the bunker. "Trouble is, the atomics'll still be theah, ten, twenty, forty years from now. Unless the TechSec people pull somethin' completely unexpected, traditional mass warfare is goin' to be, hmmm, completely out of th' question. Not to mention there's considerable ocean 'tween us and them."

Andrew pulled a cheroot from a box on the table, snipped the end and puffed it alight. "See your point. On the one hand, we get time to consolidate, on the othah, when we're ready we can't attack them. An' it's destabilizin' to have a non-Draka society too close to our borders; these days, the whole planet is close."

"Perceptive, younglin', but it's worse than that. We're bein' forced into a new type of competition, an' it's one we're not really suited for." She frowned. "Look at it this way. We started off by conquerin' southern Africa usin' weapons and techniques developed here in Europe; enslaved the natives, applied European organization to their labor, an' used the crops and minerals we sweated out of 'em to buy more weapons and machinery. Well, that wasn't a stable arrangement, so we industrialized to supply our own military, buyin' machine tools and hirin' technicians instead of importing finished goods.

"But all propaganda aside, it's always been a spatchcock modernization, pasted on the surface. *Exemplia gratia*, right up till the Eurasian War most of our exports were agricultural, an' minerals; still are, fo' that matter, oil and chrome and rubber and so on. Mostly we used the resultin' war potential against really backward societies, the rest of Africa, then the Middle East and Asia."

"We beat the Europeans," Andrew protested mildly, drawing on the dark mouth-biting smoke. *It must be nice to have the leisure to think strategy,* he thought wryly. *So much more interesting than tactics, also safer.*

"Hmm, 's much by luck as anythin' they wrecked each other first." A shrug. "Oh, we've got advantages; sheer size, fo' one thing, substituting quantity fo' quality. We do some things very well indeed, bulk production, agriculture, mining, mass-production industry: the sort of thing that organization an' routine labor can handle. Our great weakness is the size of the Citizen population, of course—an aristocracy *has* to be small in relation to the total population—but we compensate by concentratin' it where it counts and by specializing in war, primarily.

"So you might say the Domination's like a lower-order animal, a reptile, that's learned to do some mammal tricks, mimicry. Or a big shamblin' zombie with a smart little bastard sittin' on its shoulder whisperin' orders into its ear."

Andrew raised a brow; of course, there was nobody from Security around . . . that he knew of.

"Fear not, nephew. As I was saying . . . we're going to be fightin' the Yankees and their Alliance fo' a long time. We can't count on them cuttin' their own throats the way Western Europe did. I mean, if there's one thing the Eurasian War showed so's even a Yankee couldn't miss it, it was exactly what the Domination is an' what we intend. The Alliance will hold; we may be able to convince a few useful idiots of our peaceful intent, but not enough to matter. Pity. Likewise buyin' outright traitors with promises of Citizen status; that worked well enough with a few score thousand Europeans, but it's a limited tactic. Our traditional tools of brute force, terror an' violence are out of the question. System as centralized as ours is *more* vulnerable to atomics than theirs.

"Which moves the competition onto other grounds. Production, technology, science, not our strong points." Another frown. "This is a little speculative, but what the hell, the Strategic Planning Board is supposed to be . . . Apart from the fundamental fact that they're a society oriented to dynamism while we're committed to stasis, we an' TechSec are gettin' a very nasty feeling that development is movin' into areas where we're at a *structural* disadvantage. The Domination couldn't have been built without machine technology, but it was the nineteenth-century version. Coal an' iron an' steam; rifle-muskets, railways and hand-cranked Gatlings. Then steel an' petroleum, no problem; we're the perfect Industrial Age empire.

"Only, it looks like the balance is shiftin' toward things based on nuclear physics an' quantum mechanics. Rare alloys, ultra-precision engineerin', electronics. Electronics especially, an' they're already ahead; we can steal their research, but bein' able to *apply* it's a different matter. At least we don't have to try an' compete in general living standards; this isn't a popularity contest, thank the nonexistent gods."

"Bleak picture, Tantie," Andrew said, with a frown of his own. A bit vague, but the Draka had always tried to plan for the unlikely. Living on the edge, being conscious of having no margin for error, at least made you less likely to fall into complacency.

"Not as bleak as all that. We *do* have some serious advantages. For one, the Alliance is a strong coalition but it's still a coalition, an' a coalition of democracies, at that. Which means it'll only make outright war if we push it into a corner, which we'll carefully avoid— unless an' until we can win quick an' final." She unwrapped another candy, began absently folding the paper into a tiny animal shape. "Very democratic democracies; accordin'ly, they have trouble plannin' as much as a year ahead. Some of their agencies can, surely; the OSS are just as smart an' nearly as nasty as our Security Directorate. But the most of 'em are short-term thinkers; we can use that any number of ways. Example, by gettin' them to sell us their technology for profit. Yankee civilization as a *whole* may be smarter than ours but we're better right at the top—leadership's a scarce resource fo' us, so we make better use of it.

"No, it's their society in gen'ral we've got to be wary of. Their dynamism, flexibility, the way they can bend with the wave of change. Army fo' army, bureaucracy fo' bureaucracy, we can beat 'em every time. Accordin'ly what we've decided to do is to keep the military tension ratcheted up as tight as possible, indefinitely." A wolf's grin. "If we can't fight 'em, we can at least force 'em to tax, to regulate, make 'em security conscious an' secretive . . . force 'em onto ground where we've got the advantage, get 'em to waste resources."

Andrew grinned in his turn. "Lovely double bind, Tantie, but . . . not that I don't appreciate your takin' the trouble to fill me in on high strategy. I'm commandin' a Merarchy of Janissaries; what's the relevance to me?"

She leaned forward, resting her chin on her palms. "Well, twofold, nephew. Firstly, I'm afraid our 'armed peace' policy is goin' to make your pacification work even more of a nightmare than 'tis now. Provokes the Alliance to strike back in covert style, an' we can't hardly object too hard, seein's we're stompin' on their toes every chance we get, plus makin' big bad Draka faces at them all the time. Fo' example, we think that alarm a few nights ago was an attempt to get somethin'— agents, weapons, who knows—into Finland." Andrew winced. "It gets worse. You've been havin' troubles enough with the Finns *here*; we've got evidence they've been infiltratin' small parties across the pre-War border, equipped for long-term wilderness survival."

"And there's a *lot* of wilderness east of here," he said.

" 'Zactly, nephew. More joy . . . y'know that scare we had, few days back? Security's sources in the U.S. say that wasn't just a probe at our Northern Lights Chain; they were puttin' in an agent, possible-like with advanced weapons. Might be tryin' to link up with them, set up a long-term supply effort."

"Submarines? No *earthly* way we could guard the whole northern flank of Eurasia in detail."

" 'Specially not with all our other commitments, and seein' as they're ahead in submarine-warfare technique. Hell with it, light me up one of those . . ." She paused to inhale the smoke. "Now, this is confidential, younglin'." She looked around; there was nobody within earshot. "Besides the operational problems all this creates, we're a *little* worried 'bout the way this prolonged pacification situation is reboundin' on the Army-Security balance."

Andrew leaned back, puffed at his own cheroot and grimaced. The Directorates of War and Security were the two armed branches of the State, and their rivalry went back generations; more emphaticly, the higher you went in the command-structure, as well.

"If we're goin' to be spendin' the next two generations sittin' tight and makin' faces at the Yankees, I can see how it would sort of rebound to the headhunters' benefit," he said carefully.

"Mmm-hm. Like, they're agitatin' to have more of the Janissary Corps put under their direction."

That brought the younger Draka sitting bolt upright. "The *hell* you say, Tantie—Strategos," he amended himself hastily. "Fuck the bureaucratic bunfights, those ghouls *spoil* good fightin' men, I won't have any of *us* put—"

He stopped at the quizzical lift of her eyebrow. "Us?" she murmured. There was a certain detached sympathy in her face as she leaned forward to pat the clenched fist of his hand where it rested on the pine board. "Andy, it's inevitable there should be some degree of identification, when you lead men into battle. Inevitable, desirable even, fo' maximum performance. But never, never forget what the Janissary corps was established *for*."

She lifted the cheroot, considered the glowing ember on the end and flicked away ash with a judicious finger. " 'Sides, we in Castle

Tarleton basically agree with your position. The headhun—ah, Security Directorate are gettin' as many recruits fo' their Order Police as they can handle, in our opinion. Janissary units are useful fo' *both* open-field warfare an' pacification, whereas the Order Police are a militarized gendarmerie, not combat soldiers. Limited usefulness, even in guerrilla warfare, not that the Security people look at it that way."

Sannie shrugged. "On the other hand, we *do* have to coordinate more closely; the Archon's made it clear, an' the sentiment in the Assembly's likewise gettin' pretty intolerant of jurisdictional squabbles. Remember, most Citizens just do their three-to-six military service an' leave; they're primarily interested in gettin' the pacification completed in the quickest possible time. Quite rightly, too. 'Service to the State,' hey? Which *we* have to remember, and not confusin' our own particular institution with the State itself—which a certain Directorate I could name but won't is prone to do. We all got spoiled by the Eurasian War an' the run-up to it, bein' free to concentrate on conventional warfare.

"Which brings me to what we have in mind fo' you. Now, you made it to Tetrarch in the Citizen Force originally; transferred to the Janissary Corps as per SOP, excellent record since . . ."

Andrew tensed. "Now wait a minute, I've been with this unit since '42, I know them an' they me, they *need*—"

"Policy, Andy, and you know it. Next step up fo' you is a Chiliarchy or Legion command, and you do *not* get it without rotation back to the Citizen Force." She held up a hand. "Unless yo were thinkin' of commandin' the 2nd Merarchy, of the Nineteenth Janissary fo' the rest of your career? Which *could* happen, you know."

Andrew von Shrakenberg opened his mouth to speak, hesitated. The calm eyes resting on his were affectionate but implacable; loyal to the tradition that put State and Race above any personal tie. Like Pa's, or Uncle Karl's. *How can I leave them?* he thought; braced himself and—

—the radio squawked frantically. "Mayday, Mayday, convoy one niner, undah attack! Come in, Firebase Alpha, come in!"

Sannie van Reenan stepped back to one wall and crossed her arms, withdrawing person and presence; it never paid to hinder experts at their work. An alarm klaxon was wailing across the base; officers and senior NCO's piled into the command bunker, moving with disciplined haste.

One flipped the map back onto the table, smashing the crockery aside. Andrew took the microphone, forcing calm down the transmission by an act of will. It was obviously a Janissary NCO on the other end, and a young one from the voice. *Not* the commander of the convoy due in today.

"This is the Merarch. Quiet now, son, an' give me the facts."

"Ah, Sarn't Dickson, suh; 4th Ersatz Cohort, reportin'."

"The recruit shipment, by God," somebody in the room murmured. "Where's the escort CO?"

As if to answer, the static-laden voice continued, stumbling over itself in haste: "Tetrarch Galdman, he up front, the car jus' blow up, mines suh, front an' rear, we pinned. All thaz warcars done be knocked out, suh. Mast' Sergeant Ngolu take t' Dragon an' his Tetrarchy 'n try goin up t'support, lotsa firin'; jus' me an' the replacements left here back a' the column, suh. Allah, they *close* suh, mus' be near two hundred, I kin hear 'em talkin' bushtalk to each othah in thaz woods, we runnin' short on ammo."

"Report your position, soldier."

"Ahhh—" He could hear the Janissary taking a deep breath. "We 'bout thirty kilometers out from you, suh. Jus' past t'long thin lake, an' turnin' west."

"Right, now listen to me, son. Dig in, an' *hold your position,* understand? Help is on the way, and *soon.* Keep broadcastin' on this frequency, the operator will relay. When you hears us, fire flare—you've still got a flare gun?"

"Yazsuh."

"Good. Recognition code." Red this week, but no need to advertise it to anybody who might be listening; the Finnish guerrillas still had pretty good Elint. "An' stay put, a world of hurt goin' to be comin' down round there."

He handed the microphone back to the operator, turned, orders snapping out as he walked to the map table.

"Sten, get the gridref to the flyboys and they're to boot it, blockin' force behind the ambush, the bushmen will have to retreat through that bottleneck between the lake and the marsh. The gunboats are to give immediate support, and they will *not* cause friendly casualties this time, or I will personally blow their pilots new assholes. Same to the Air Force base, max scramble. See to it.

"Vicki, got the position?"

"Sho do. Here, the dogleg." Her close-chewed fingernail tapped down on a turn in the road, just east of the firebase.

"Joy, joy, just out of automortar range, even with rocket-assist. *Damn,* they haven't gotten this close since spring. Corey, ready?"

"Reaction cohort scrambled an' ready to roll at gate 2, suh," he said; that would be his unit, they were on call today.

"Right. Jimbob, detach two of you SP automortars to follow." Mounted in armored personnel carriers, 100mm weapons would thicken up his firepower nicely. "Tom, get the mineproofs rollin' two of them, to lead off. Vicki, my personal car an' a communications vehicle. You're in charge while I'm gone; maximum alert, it may be a diversion fo' an' attack on the base. Appropriate messages to Legion HQ an the Third Airborne, this is a chance to do some long cullin'; let's *move,* people, let's *go.*"

Andrew took the stairs two at a time, with the other reaction-force officers at his heels. Sannie van Reenan turned to follow, pausing for a moment as the Special Tasks Section bodyguard put a hand on her shoulder.

"I know," she said, to his silent inquiry. "But I wouldn't miss this for the world; nor is any individual immortal or irreplaceable."

"Ma'am, it's our responsibility—"

"—to keep me alive, yes. Now you'll just have to earn your pay, hey? Let's go find a lift."

✧   ✧   ✧

"Twenty minutes," Kustaa said, glancing at his wrist.

"Always seems longer, doesn't it?" the Finn beside him said, running through a last quick check of the missile controls. The American had been a good teacher, but there had been no possibility of a test firing. "They'll be here soon."

"Oh?"

"Well, it's only a half-hour drive from here to the snake base," he said, running a finger approvingly along one of the control boxes beside the bicycle-style gunner's seat. "Such fine workmanship, so precise and light . . . Yes, only half an hour, at high speed. Of course, they can't come barreling down here, that's the oldest trick there is, a relief column lured into another ambush. They'll have to stop short of here, deploy and come in on foot with their armor backing them up. It's roadbound, you see; a lot of small timber just west of here—there was a forest fire a few years ago. More brush, once the tall timber is down."

Sort of fire-prone around here, Kustaa thought sardonically. The wind was from the south, moving the forest fire north along the road in the direction from which the supply convoy had come; even moving away from them the heat and smoke were punishing, backdrafts of ash and tarry-scented breathless air. By now it had spread out into a C-shaped band a mile wide, moving before the wind as fast as a galloping horse, with outliers leaping ahead a thousand yards at a time as burning branches tossed free and whirled aloft.

"Smokey the Badger will hate me," he muttered, and shook his head at the Finn's incomprehending look. *Only YOU can prevent forest fires.*

The remains of the Draka column smoldered, guttering oily flames still bringing the scorch-stink of hot metal to their position beneath the unburnt fringe of trees. A pop-popping of small-arms fire came from the north where the last survivors were holed up, punctuated by bursts of machine gunfire and the occasional grenade. Three trucks came back toward them, singed and bullet-holed but still mobile, jouncing as they left the edge of the road and moved across to the missile position. Arvid Kyosti stood on the running board of the first; it stopped near enough for Kustaa to see the neat row of bullet holes across the door on the driver's side, and the sticky red-brown stain beneath it.

The guerrilla commander waved the other two trucks on, and they disappeared to the southwest as he hopped down, there was blood caked in his mustache, where a near miss with a blast grenade had started his nose bleeding. The truck he had been riding slid ten yards into the cover of the trees and halted; half a dozen guerrillas emerged from the bed, and began rigging planks into a ramp up which equipment could be dragged in a hurry.

"Ready?" Arvid said.

"Ready," the American replied. "Motor transport?" he added, jerking his chin toward the other vehicles disappearing among the tall pine trees.

"A little. Get the heavier supplies and the wounded well into the woods before the snakes get here. A lot of it can be sunk in the swamp and retrieved later, tinned food and sealed boxes. You can go five, ten kilometers easy if you know the way; then we pack it out. This one's for your missile launchers, when we need to move fast."

Another pair of the ex-German, ex-Draka Opels passed them. "We got some useful booty, too. Snake rocket-guns." Kustaa nodded; those were shoulder-fired recoilless weapons, a light charge throwing a rocket shell out twenty meters before the sustainer motor cut in. Very effective antiarmor weapons and good bunker busters. "Good to get *something* out of this."

Arvid offered the American agent a package of cigarettes. Janissary army-issue, in a plain khaki-colored package. Kustaa inhaled gratefully; they were good, nice light mild flavor.

"You killed a fair number of them," he said.

Arvid lit one himself and sat on the running board, heedless of the sticky remains of the driver still pooling there.

"We lost thirty dead, killed maybe that many Janissaries," Arvid said with the flat almost hostility that Kustaa had grown accustomed to. "It takes them, what, six to eight months to train a Janissary, from induction to posting. Replacements with this convoy, they were mostly Europeans. Germans, Czechs, Croats, some Swiss. The Janissaries are volunteers, you know? They get more than they need. We destroyed some equipment, too." He nodded to the Dragon; four trees had fallen across it, and the crew had chosen to burn alive inside rather than emerge to face the guerrilla bullets. The turret had peeled open along the lines of its welds when the ammunition blew, but the armored cabs were outwardly intact save for scorch marks. The screams had stopped long ago.

"They have their own industry and all Europe, all Asia to replace that. As easy for them as replacing the drivers and whores."

"Those are people you're talking about," Kustaa said quietly. "Have you thought of asking them if they want to join you?"

The guerrilla smiled without humor. "The snake secret police would just love that, an opportunity to get agents among us. We've had enough problems with that, American; my family killed themselves so they couldn't be used as levers against me."

Fanatic, Kustaa thought, chilled. Then: *And who's to blame him?* He tried to imagine Aino giving Maila a cyanide pill crushed into her milk, raising one to her mouth with a shaking hand and tears running down her cheeks, pictured them lying together cold and twisted with blue froth on their lips . . .

That's what I'm here to prevent, he thought. The guerrilla was speaking again.

" . . . probably killed one, two Citizens at most. And a couple of Janissary senior NCOs, they're harder to replace than the cannon fodder." He glanced up. "The survivors got a message through to their HQ, the aircraft should be here any minute." Most of the guerrillas were already fading back into the woods, to let the counterstrike fall on empty ground. "It's up to you to make this worthwhile, American."

A faint *thupthupthup* came blatting over the trees from the west, louder than the crackling roar of the forest fire. And a turbine howl, growing. "Helicopters," Arvid said bitterly. "Damnation, I was hoping for jets . . ."

They ducked beneath the chest-high canvas with its load of shoveled pine duff, crowded with the angular metal tubing of the launcher and the half-dozen guerrillas who would help him operate it. Arvid's field glasses went up, and Kustaa followed suit. Three droop-nosed shapes coming in low, two thousand feet, narrow bodies and long canopies tilted down under the blur of the rotors. "Gunboats," Kustaa muttered. He was tired, with the swift adrenaline-flush exhaustion of combat; the sound flogged him back to maximum alertness. The Alliance hadn't put as much effort into helicopters as the Draka, and the Domination had captured most of the German research effort as well. A question of priorities: gunboats and assault transports were more useful for antipartisan work, and the Alliance had little of that, thank God. Their choppers were mostly for casualty evacuation and naval antisubmarine . . .

"Damn, air cavalry as well," Arvid said. A broad wedge of troop transports followed the ground-support craft, but behind and much further up, tiny dark boxy shapes. "Can you take the transports?"

"No. Not unless they come a lot closer and lower. The operational ceiling's four thousand, and—"

The transports broke east and south, sweeping in a long curve that took them away from the missiles waiting crouched by the road. Arvid's eyes followed them. "Must be trying to get behind us at the lake, bottle us up," he said quietly. "Most of us will get through, they don't know that area as well as they think. A pity they're not coming here, ten Draka in every one of them. The gunboats have Citizen pilots too, of course. Don't miss."

"I don't intend to," Kustaa replied, and turned to the crews. The missile launchers were spaced ten yards apart, for safety's sake; the reloads well back, in case of a misfire. "Ready," he said. "Remember, second team *waits* until I've fired. These things track thermally, we don't want them chasing each other. Fire from *behind* the target only, you have to get the exhausts. *Do not fire until the lock-on light comes on and the signal chimes.* Then fire immediately." Repetition, but never wasted. "Now, get the tarps unlaced, and be ready to pull them off *fast.*"

A flare rose from the north end of the convoy, popped into a blossom of red smoke. The gunboats circled over the dug-in Janissaries, then peeled off to run straight down the road at nearly treetop height. *Whapwhapwhapwhap* echoed back from the forest, the blades drove huge circles of smoke and ash billowing into the forest, fanned the embers on charred trunks into new flickers of open flame. Kustaa buried his mouth in the crook of his arm to breathe through the cloth, blinking pain-tears from his eyes and keeping the helicopters in view. They had their chin turrets deployed to either side, firing the Gatlings in brief *brap-brap-brap* bursts; one sawed across the wet ground in front of his position, the sandy mud spattering across the camouflage tarpaulin. Machine guns spat at them from the ground, carefully grouped away from the rockets to attract the Draka gunners' attention.

The firing ceased as helicopters swept south past the head of the
convoy and banked, turning 180 degrees like a roller skater grabbing a lamp post. Kustaa worked his tongue inside a dry mouth and
reflected that even without insignia it would be obvious to anyone
watching that the craft were Draka-crewed, the hard arrogant snap
of the piloting was unmistakable. They were nearly back level with
him—

"Now!" he shouted, sliding into the gunner's seat. Strong hands
flipped the tarp back, pumped at the hydraulic reservoir to maintain
pressure, and the launch rail swung smoothly erect. The helicopters
were going by in line, six hundred feet up; they wouldn't notice, not
with the smoke. . . . Ring-sight up, just a gimbal-mounted concentric wire circle, adjust for range, *there* they were past, lay the wires
on the two exhaust ports of the last gunboat's turbines, *clench* left
hand. The electronics whined and his feet played across the pedals,
keeping the whole frame centered on the blackened circles and heat
shimmer of the exhausts.

Come on, come on, he thought. God, not a vacuum tube failure,
he'd tested every component individually when they assembled them,
when were they going to get everything solid state, the Draka had to
notice any second, even with the launchers behind them—

Ping. Pingpingping—the idiot-savant sensor in the rocket's nose
announced it had seen the thousand-degree heat source moving away
from it. Someday they would have something smaller, more reliable,
but for now . . .

"Clear, firing!" he shouted and his right hand clenched down on
the release. The solid-fuel booster of the missile ignited with a giant
ssssSSHHH and a flare that flash-blinded him even from the side; *that*
they were going to notice for sure. No need to shout for a reload,
the crew were heaving the long cylinder onto the rail. Out of the corner
of his eye he could see that one of them had a jacket shredded and
smoldering. He had *told* them to stand clear of the backblast.

But his focus stayed on the line of white fire streaking away from
him, across the dazzled, spotted field his abused retinas were drawing on the sky. Spear-straight one second, two, and the flight lines
of the helicopter and the rocket intersected. The explosion was an undra-
matic *thump*—the warhead was smaller than a field mortar—but the
result was spectacular enough to satisfy the most demanding taste. The
tail boom of the last gunboat vanished, and the shock wave of the
detonation slapped the rotors from behind. Unbalanced, the helicopter flipped nosedown, and the blades acted like a giant air brake, killing
its forward momentum. Killing more than that. For a fractional second it seemed to hang suspended, and then it slid two hundred yards
straight down into the road.

Vision ended in a hundred-foot fireball, as fuel and munitions burned.
The shock wave struck hard enough to rock the launcher on its outspread pads, drying his eyeballs with a slap from a soft hot invisible
hand.

"Wait, wait!" he barked to the other team, as the orange fire-globe
cleared; the next helicopter was pitching and yawing across the sky

as the pilot fought to regain control. Even as he shouted, the dragon-hiss of the other launcher sounded. Kustaa watched with angry fatalism as the missile arced neatly toward its target, dipped, and crashed itself into the burning wreckage of the one he had downed; that was hotter than the exhausts, and more consistent.

"Ready," the reload team gasped, and he felt a hand slap his boot.

"Keep the pressure up," he rasped, working with heel and toe to control elevation. The second helicopter was travelling straight and level again, impressive piloting to regain control after getting tumbled flying low and fast like that. Extreme range, two thousand yards, dark fuselage against the black smoke of the forest fire. . . .

Ping. This time he scarcely noticed the heat of launch, too focused on slitting his eyes to follow the flare. Four seconds to impact, three, *Christ, I hope they don't have rear-view mirrors,* two—

"Shit," he said. The Draka helicopter waited until the last possible instant, then pulled up in a vertical climb that turned into a soaring loop. Less agile, the missile overshot and began to climb; then the sensor picked up the unvarying heat of the burning trees and began its unliving kamikaze dive. "They learn fast."

The seat almost jerked out from underneath him as the Finns hurled themselves at the frame, ten strong backs lifting it in a bend-snatch-heave that clashed it down on the bed of the truck with a vigor that brought a wince to Kustaa's face; electronics were just too sensitive for that sort of treatment. Suddenly he was conscious of Arvid pounding him on the back, the hard grins of the others.

"Not bad, American!" The Finn's face was black with soot and dried blood, a gargoyle mask for white teeth and the tourmaline blue eyes. "One hit for three shots, a gunboat and two snake Citizens dead!"

Kustaa grinned in reply and fisted the guerrilla on the shoulder. "Where've the other two gone, that's what I'd like to know," he replied. Neither helicopter was in view. *Run away?* he thought. Quite sensible, in the face of a new weapon of unknown qualities, but unlikely. If the Domination's elite warriors had a military fault, it was an excess of personal aggression. Nothing in the smoke-streaked blue of the sky ahead and to either side; he shook his head against the ringing in his ears and concentrated. Yes, the thuttering of helicopter blades and engine noise . . . getting louder, but *where?* The Finnish crew were taut and ready by the four outrigger legs of the second launcher, the snub nose of the missile tracking a little as the gunner's toes touched the pedals.

Not worth the disruption to go and take over, he thought.

Arvid tensed and broke into a sprint. "Behind you!" he called to the missile team, running toward them, pointing frantically back into the forest. Kustaa had just enough time to twist and see the shadow of the gunboat flicker through the trees as it dove toward the ground at a near-vertical angle. It ripple-fired its rocket pods nearly above his head, and the blast as they impacted on the waiting missile was behind him. He felt it as pressure, first on his back and then as if his eyeballs were bulging, pushed from within his skull; the impact as he struck the tailgate of the truck came as a surprise, something distant in the red-shot blackness.

Vision cleared almost at once; Kustaa could see as the Finns hauled him in beside the frame of the launcher. See clearly, as if through the wrong end of a telescope, things small and sharp and far away, too far away to be worth the effort needed to move a body turned warm and liquid. There was a crater, scattered about with bits of twisted metal and softer things, the tree trunks and rocks that had absorbed much of the force, still settling and smoking. And a figure was probably Arvid, that had to be Arvid, though it was difficult to tell since it was burning. The man-thing took a step, two, fell forward; its back was open, and things moved in there, pink and gray-cooked and charred. Then the far-off scene was vanishing, into shadows and movement and somewhere the sound of weeping.

The bodies moved. Both the Special Tasks gunmen had their pistols cleared and slapped three rounds each into the topmost corpse before Andrew could react, swinging in to put themselves between Sannie and the stirring in the jumbled pile of wood and flesh.

"Wait," the Merarch said, the staff Strategos echoed it, and soldiers all along the line of smoldering wrecks that had been a convoy came out of their instinctive crouches. There was still firing from the southeast, an occasional popping and the crackle of Draka assault rifles as the Janissaries mopped up the guerrilla rear guard. Here the loudest sound was the protesting whine of engines as the recovery vehicles dragged wreckage to the side of the road, mine-clearance teams were sweeping the verges with infinite caution, marking their progress with fluttering banners of white tape. The burial details were busy too, an excavator digging a mass trench for the dead drivers and other auxiliaries, prefab coffins for the Janissary casualties.

I hope the ceremonial does them some good, wherever, Andrew thought wryly. Actually, the flags and banners at the Legion's homebase cemetery served the same purpose as any funeral, to comfort the living and remind them that the community lived even when its members died.

He hooked off the top layer of dead partisans with his boot, *their* heads would decorate stakes around the firebase, after somebody collected the ears. There were flies already; he looked up, noticing almost with surprise that the sun was still bright on a summer's afternoon, still high above a horizon that had darkened no further than twilight. A haze of smoke obscured it, and that was the smell; smoke from burning wood, metal, fuel, explosive, rubber, bodies. At least it covered the usual stink of death, stunning his nose so that he could barely smell the liquid feces that streaked the uniforms. There was another stirring; he reached down and grabbed a jacket, heaved.

"Take him," he snapped, and two troopers grabbed the Finn, pinned his arms and searched him with rough efficiency. Andrew resumed his measured pacing along the line of burnt-out trucks and armored vehicles. A cutting torch dropped sparks amid the tangle of alloy plate that had been an APC; melted fat was pooled beneath it, overlaid with the iridescent sheen of petroleum distillate.

Corey Hartmann was walking towards them from the head of the convoy. "That's where the whatever-it-was was located," he said, pointing east to a crater just beyond the cleared fire zone that edged the road. "I've got my people cataloging and bagging the fragments, but the gunboat didn't leave much."

"Can't say's I blame him," Andrew said dryly, taking a look back at the much larger crater where one of the helicopters had crashed.

"There were two of them, we're thinkin'," Hartmann said as they turned through the burnt grass. "Seems they got the othah 'way in a steamtruck."

"Interestin'," Sannie van Reenan mused, narrowing her eyes. "They must've backpacked it in; we didn't think they could build 'em that light an' portable."

"They? The Yankees?" Andrew asked sharply.

"Who else? Fo' sure, the bushmen didn't cobble it together in their caves. We couldn't make somethin' that small an' capable, but the Alliance is ahead of us on miniature stuff."

They came to another line of bodies in the black stubble, scattered women with gunshot wounds or the flesh-tattering multiple punctures of directional mines. One of the females lay sprawled beside a dead Janissary, her hands still gripping his harness. Young, Andrew thought, studying her face. Probably quite attractive too, before her hair burned. Another of the women sat beside her, cradling her head in her lap and rocking back and forth with a low ceaseless moaning; the live girl's hands were swelling with their burns, skin cracked and glistening with lymphatic fluids.

"Medic, we need a medic ovah here!" he called sharply.

"Comin', comin'!" the nearest called, a Citizen doctor, overseeing the auxiliaries who were inserting a plasma drip in a Janissary whose legs were mostly gone below the tourniquets. She stood as they eased him onto a stretcher. "Priorities heah, you knows."

Andrew wheeled sharply, lighting a cigarette with a needlessly aggressive snap of the Ronson. "Corey," he said flatly. "These were the replacements fo' the Comfort Station, weren't they?"

The Cohortarch nodded. "Out of luck, po' bitches," he said, glancing up from a clipboard someone had handed him.

"Well, soon's our wounded're out, have 'em lifted to Legion HQ as well an' tell the duty officer to find somethin' for them to do when they're patched up," he said. The other Draka nodded again.

"Only fittin', seein' as we were supposed to be guardin' them," he said with a grimace.

Andrew flicked the half-smoked cigarette to the ground, lit another. "You . . . Sergeant Dickson, right?"

A young Janissary with junior NCO's stripes made an effort to straighten to attention; it was difficult to see his expression, since half his face was bandaged.

"Suh," he said dully.

"Good work here, son. I'm puttin' you down for a month's furlough, an' a 'recommended' on your promotions record."

"Suh." The reply was almost as dull, then a more enthusiastic *"Suh!"* as the words sank past pain and exhaustion.

"Dismissed," Andrew continued; he saluted, and the Janissary began a snapping reply, winced and completed the gesture slowly but in regulation wise before wheeling and marching off.

"Now," the Draka commander said, turning his attention to the two troopers who held the prisoner. The Finn was reviving, bore no obvious wounds beyond the battering to be expected; an adolescent, with a shock of flax-colored hair and gray eyes. No noticeable difference in dilation, so any concussion would be mild.

"You," he said in Finnish, pidgin but understandable. "Where they go? How many?"

The partisan tried to spit, but his mouth was too dry and his lips still too numb; it dribbled down his own chin, cutting a track through soot-grime.

Andrew lowered his bunched fist, hearing the slight *click* as the metal inserts in his gloves touched each other. Too crude, far too crude. His eyes went to the Janissaries holding the guerrilla: Dieter, yes, one of the new replacements. German, might even have fought on the other side; they had been taking them young, toward the end. Quiet, did his work and kept to himself, very little in his personal file. The other was . . . Ecevit. Turk: there were a lot of volunteers from those provinces; hook-nosed, hairy and thick-bodied, enlisted before the War. Capable but too impulsive for promotion beyond squad leader, and—

"Ecevit," he said musingly.

"Sar!"

"As I recall, you've something of a taste fo' blond boys." The trooper straightened, suppressing a hopeful grin. "This one looks as if he'll wash up nicely. Bring him to Interrogation tomorrow, alive, able to talk, and in a more cooperative frame of mind. Understand, soldier?"

"Yaz, *sar*!" the soldier said. "Many thanks, effendi!"

The Finn must have understood some English too, because he began to scream as the two Janissaries dragged him away.

"Rough an' ready, but effective," Sannie van Reenan said with in a dry murmur. "Perhaps Intelligence work was your calling aftah all."

"I'm"—he paused to look at the wreckage about them—"somewhat annoyed," he finished. "And maybe it is, Strategos, I couldn't fuck it up worse'n I've done this, could I?"

"Spare me the guilt, such a bourgeois emotion," Sannie said, with a snap in her tone. More softly: "Actually, your jungleboys did quite well, heah."

"That *they* did," Andrew said, meeting her eyes. "You know, they really don't care much fo' that particular nickname." A slow drag on the cigarette hollowed his cheeks and cast the harsh planes of his face in outline; for a moment, she could see the skull behind the flesh. "An' frankly, neither do I."

"Point taken," Sannie said with a nod. "Now, about that proposition I was speakin' of, before this little *shauri* started." She waited with hunter's patience while his mind fought back past the last two hours; he was the sort of man who concentrated with his whole being— a valuable trait if controlled. "We're thinkin' of formin', hmmm, specialized *hunter teams*, to deal with . . . certain types of problem. Fo' example, Yankee agents formin' links with bushman groups. We have some information on this particular one, an' expect more. There'll have to be a coordinatin' officer, and a fluctuatin' unit structure; part Intelligence work, part bushman huntin', part liaison. Security will have to cooperate closely, of course."

Or present its behind for the appropriate political shrapnel, went unspoken between them.

"Ahhh, an' this *particular* case would be a trial run?" Andrew asked.

Sannie smiled at the interest in his voice. "Indeed it would, nephew mine. Indeed it would."

Chapter Six

The car was not crowded, even with seven and an assortment of bags and parcels; the interior was open, folding metal seats in the rear and two bucket chairs at the front, a view through the front windows to the coffle of serfs huddled on the floor of the truck ahead. Marya crossed herself and waved to them as she climbed through the clutter to her seat, composing herself neatly out of long habit, feet and knees together, skirt folded about them and hands clasped in her lap. The car smelled of machine oil and leather, wickerwork and a stuffy heat that brought a prickle of sweat to her upper lip.

The driver was a thin-faced Frenchman in overalls, wearing a cap pulled down over his eyes and cuffs with a long chain looped through the steering wheel; the man beside him was uncuffed, with an automatic shotgun across his knees and a leather vest full of loops for the fat shells. A serf, European, a thin strong young man with a dark face and old-looking green eyes; a Jew, Marya thought, Polish or Lithuanian or from the Ukraine. She ventured a smile; he looked her up and down with cold disinterest and turned back to the front, his right hand stroking lightly across the receiver of his weapon.

The women sat in the rear, with the other serf: a big man, even sitting down with his kettle belly spilling into his lap; African-dark, wide-featured and wide-shouldered, the arms below his short-sleeved cotton shirt thick and corded with muscle. Grizzled tight-curled hair and muttonchop whiskers, shrewd black eyes with yellowed whites. A rifle was resting upright by his side. Not the T-6 assault rifles the Domination had used in the Eurasian War; this was a full-bore semi-automatic model, dark wood and blued steel and a look the nun recognized, of machinery that is old but lovingly cared for.

He smiled with strong square yellow teeth as they chuffed into motion, but he did not speak; there was a moment of backing and circling as the convoy lined up for the gate. The engine had the silence of automotive steam, but the heavy vehicle still quivered with the subliminal feeling of life, rocked slightly as a uniformed figure hopped up on the running board. A woman's face leaned in the window, green military-style uniform and cloth-covered steel helmet; a Citizen officer of the Security Directorate's internal-security troops—Order Police. Therese buried her face in her sister's shoulder, and the other serfs covered their eyes and bowed. There was another rocking as she stepped down, a brief sound of boots on pavement.

Marya could hear a murmur of voices, then Tanya's weary drawl: "No, Tetrarch, I *don't* have clearance papers fo' two armed serfs. I'm violatin' the law and armin' *all* my field hands. Didn't we go through this all three hours ago? Or didn't the duty officer log it?"

The nun raised her head and craned to see through one of the windows. The Security officer saluted and returned a file folder through the opened door of the other car. A *lochos* of green-uniformed troopers behind her, shaven-skulled and neck-tattooed; the Domination did not waste elite troops on that sort of duty. The Tetrarch shouted, and one swung up the barrier while two more threw their shoulders against the steel gate. It groaned open, and the light seemed to brighten as the cars accelerated smoothly and turned into the road outside.

Yasmin shivered and shook her shoulders. "Doan' *like* that place," she said. "An I *sho'* doan' like them chain-dogs. They look at you an' they gotta impalin' stake in they eyes."

The middle-aged man beside her brought the rifle across his knees, slapped in a magazine and jacked the action. "Headhunters," he said in agreement, turned and spat out the open window behind him. "Greencoats, *tloshohene* dogs; stay clear of 'em." He looked up at the women across the body of the car, and grinned broadly. "Name's Tom," he said. "Late o' th' 15th Janissary, an' father to this here uppity wench, fo' mah sins. Listen to what-all she say, this time. Usually nohow good for anything but sassin' and bed-wenchin' with her betters."

Marya nodded warily, with a shock of alarm, feeling Chantal stiffen beside her. Therese was paying no attention, eyes dreamy, humming under her breath. Better for her that way.

Janissary, Marya thought with distaste. Serf soldier. Volunteers—she could understand why many would choose such a way out of the dull drudge's life of a Draka factory or plantation hand . . . though not the courage with which they fought. And they had a merited reputation for relentless brutality. She shivered inwardly. They would be confined with him for hours; they were bound and he was armed. Although . . . she glanced at Yasmin. Her father? And even a Janissary could hate the green-coated secret police troopers. *Remember the publicans,* she reminded herself. Roman tax collectors had not been well regarded in Judea in the Lord's time on earth, either. *Hate the sin, love the sinner.*

She nodded in return, swiveling to watch the city go by. Much had changed in the six months of her imprisonment. Central Detention had been a fortress then, wire and firing trenches and dug-in armored vehicles; all that was gone, save for two concrete machine-gun bunkers beside each gate. The road outside the wall had been repaired, and the cleared fire zone beyond was being converted to a park by labor squads and construction machinery; piles of earth and sand, benches of brick and marble, fountains, pavements, a flatbed steamtruck loaded with young trees, springing up from burlap balls of root and earth. The city beyond was changing, too. There had been a fair amount of street fighting when Lyon fell two years ago; more damage after the surrender, when the Domination turned its troops loose for a three-day sack that killed more than the artillery and air bombardments.

Marya forced that out of memory: days spent crouching thigh-deep in a sewer, furnace-hot air roaring overhead as the buildings burned, and the fever the filthy water brought . . . No, consider what this meant. Less Resistance activity, obviously; that was bad, very bad that it should happen so quickly.

Now the ruined buildings and rubble were mostly gone, cleared gaps where they had been and new structures going up, buildings in the low-slung gaudily-decorated Draka style. There were more Citizens walking on the streets or driving little four-wheel runabouts, many in civilian dress; armed, but from what she had heard, Draka always were, even in their homelands. The native French were less numerous than she remembered, fewer of them in rags, more in gray issue overalls or the sort of warm, drab outfit she had been given in the serf dealer's rooms. That might account for much; it had been years since rations were enough to still hunger, even to sustain health.

The man's voice broke in on her thoughts. "Not a bad-lookin' town, pity I's too ol' an' useless to git in on this here war, git me some lootin'."

"Oh, Poppa," Yasmin said in resigned exasperation. "That ain't nohow polite, these folks is from around hereabouts."

She pulled up a wicker basket from under her seat and began to open it. "Who's fo' somethin' to—" The ex-Janissary's hand shot into the basket, came out with a sandwich made from a split loaf of French bread, pink ham and onions and peppers showed around the edges. "—eat," Yasmin finished.

Marya had absorbed the byplay in silence. The food brought an involuntary spurt of saliva to her mouth, and she could feel her ex-cellmates stirring beside her. Yasmin carefully tucked a linen napkin into the high collar of her silk jacket and began unloading the basket; sandwiches and slices of thick crusty bread with real butter, tart cheese, olives and tomatoes, sugar-dusted biscuits and real fruit, a thermos of coffee and a bottle of the violet-scented wine of Bourgueil. The dark girl coaxed a peach into Therese's hand, laughing at the little sound of pleasure she made as she bit; they were a country-orchard variety, small, tart and intensely flavored. Chantal put a hand on her sister's shoulder and leaned back into the padded wall of the vehicle.

"You are a soldier, sir?" she asked slowly in her careful English. "Or do you also belong to the von Shrakenbergs?"

Marya could read the expression of polite interest; Chantal was Gathering Intelligence, in the recesses of her own mind. *Carefully, carefully,* she thought; but it was a sign of something more than rage born of despair, at least. You could come to know someone well, after four months together in a crowded cell. A wave of pity overtook her; at least her own faith was not so tied to the fortunes of war. God promised no victories over material enemies, His Kingdom was not of this fallen earth . . . but poor Chantal had given her heart to a prophet who promised a tangible paradise. The Marxist heresy was sinful and godless, but the Frenchwoman's belief had been deep and sincere, rooted in love of the poor whom Christ also had held dear, her hatred a hatred of injustice as well of the rich.

Be cautious, my friend. It was ironic, here a Pole was being the calculating and rational one, cautioning a Frenchwoman against romantic gestures . . .

"Doan' need to 'sir' me," the man replied, his voice a slow deep rumble. "Yaz 'n no. I's Janissary. Born on Oakenwald, that Mistis Tanya's home, down in th' Old Territories, way south. I go fo' Janissary back in, Allah, that be 1911, '12. Masta Everard, Tanya's pa, he officer in mah legion, th' 15th."

He flipped the rifle up, holding it out by the barrel to show a small ivory inset near the buttplate: the head of a hyena, biting down on a human thighbone.

"We the Devil Dogs, th' *bone-makers*," he said proudly. "This here mah original piece; fight all through th' Great War, beatin' the ragheads; Syria, Persia, Bulgaria. Aftah that, we'se in The Stan." He paused at his audience's blank looks. "Afghanistan. Hoo, deedy; we make our bones heah, sho'ly did." His smile slid away. "Left plenty bones, too. Damn few come out what went in, damn few." More softly: "Damn few, sho'ly."

"Well," he continued brightly. "That where I loses th' foot." He shifted his right leg, knocked it against a strut with a hollow sound. "Step onna land mine, 'n lemme tell yaz—"

"Oh, Poppa, not more of you war stories," Yasmin broke in, rolling her eyes and turning to the others. "They *disgustin'*."

The man grinned slyly and glanced sidelong at his daughter: "Hell, jes' losin' a foot not so bad. I's rememberin' a sergeant, supply sergeant that was, ragheads caught him, and we found him with his—"

"*Poppa!*"

He laughed again, and reached out one huge hand to stroke the knuckles gently down her cheek. "Alright, sweetlin', jes' jokin'."

"So," he continued, taking a meditative bite of the sandwich, "coulda took retirement, laak a twenty-year man. Didn' seem mucha life fo' a young man, though. Done seen too many old Janissary, nothin' to do but drink an' knife each othah over cards 'n whores down at the *caserne*. You can go home, though. Janissary always belong to th' State, cain't never be sold, or whupped 'cept by our own officer, but if'n you volunteer, they rent you back. As guard, foreman, like that-there. Masta Everard, he settin' up Evendim, that his place in Syria; he younger son, 'n Masta Karl gettin' Oakenwald. I go with Masta Everard; he know me, y'see?

"I's settle down nice; get me a wench, Fatima." An affectionate sadness. "She got no sense, but she a good woman, I doan' want no other while she 'live. She die birthin' back befo' this new war come;

mah boys gone fo' Janissary too—they in th' 15th now too, out east flghtin' down the slope-eyes, someplace called *Ko*rea. Yasmin heah mah las' chile, 'n she go with Mistis Tanya, so I comes too. You Frenchies got lotsa book learnin' but you needs us t'learn the Draka. Some folks here is pretty sensible—got me a nice little widow wench 'n cottage—others altogethah useless 'n triflin'."

He shifted his grip on the rifle, holding the heavy weapon by the stock and prodding the driver lightly in the back of the neck. "Like Jacques here, I's got mah eye on you, boy. Doan' forget it." The rough voice went cold for a moment, and then he flicked the rifle upright beside him and relaxed once more. "Issac—th' skinny boy with th' bird gun—he a smart one. Doan' talk much, though."

"Like you, Poppa," Yasmin said dryly as she repacked the basket, handing him a bottle of dark German beer. Her father snorted amusement, flicked the cap off with one horn-hard thumb and turned sideways to watch the passing scene, the rifle cradled in the crook of his arm.

"*I*," the girl continued, fastidiously wiping her hands on her napkin and then using it to clean Therese's chin, "am second indoor servant."

It was said with a slight unconscious preening; the ex-Janissary's glance was fond and proud. *Even slaves must have their accomplishments*, Marya thought. Then: *be careful, this is real power, here and now.*

"If'n you got any questions, come right to me." She sighed and tossed back the loose black mane of hair. "Sometimes doan' know rightly how to start, with you Frenchies. Doan' sass back; doan' sulk or disobey. There's ways 'n ways of gettin' around the Mastahs, but goin' straight up agin' they will ain't accomplishin' nothin' but grief fo' us all. Remembah all us serfs is family; talk as y'wants, *do* as y'wants if'n yous the only one to suffer, but *doan'* do anythin' what gets us all traced up to the whuppin' post or worse. If'n you finds someone's doin' a crazy, like tryin' to hide weapons or sneak off to the bushmen, come tell me an' we'll decide amongst ouahselfs what to do."

Yasmin smiled and nodded toward the cuffs. "Soon's we gets back to Chateau Retour"—she pronounced the French words carefully—"we'll get those-there off. The Big House doan' cuff or hobble on the plantation, 'cept as a punishment. Now," she continued briskly, "the overseers, Masta Donaldson, Mistis Wentworth"—she shrugged—"they overseers, whats cain I say? Not too bad, 'n the Mastah 'n Mistis keep a close eye on 'em. Mistis Tanya, she downright easy going fo' a Draka, long as you doan' cross her. Masta Edward, her man, he pretty much the same 'cept when his head painin' him."

One brown finger tapped an eye. "He gets a head wound in th' War; lose an eye, headaches real bad sometimes; gets pretty testy when one comin' on, you sees it, stay outta his way. Other times, doan' talk to y'much." She giggled. "Not so bad in bed, either, if'n y'likes it, not rough, anyhow. 'cept sometimes he finish too quick, but you be findin' out that fo' youselfs." An ironic eye at their flinch. "Call it work, call it play, doan' make no nevah-mind to them, dearies. Honest, the things you new-caught get upsets about, it beyond me."

Chantal cleared her throat, spoke in genuine wonderment: "Are . . . you content with your life, then?"

There was silence for a moment, a thrumming as the car swung onto the bridge over the Rhône. Light flickered by as they passed through the shadow of the girders, winked back from the surface of the river below; Yasmin wound down a window, and the stream of wet silt-smelling air poured in, ruffling the black curls around her face. She brushed them back with one hand, craning her neck to see a train of coal barges passing below.

"Pretty river," she said quietly, turning back to them. "You thinks there's somethin' wrong with lookin' at it?" She paused, pursed her lips in thought. "My life? It the only life I's got, or is goin' get; if'n I ain't content with it, then I ain't goin' get much contentment, eh?"

A spread of the hands. "Ain't sayin' as everythin's the way I'd put it, were I God, but that-there position's filled, last time I looks. Plenty good things in my life; pretty things"—she touched the buttons of her jacket—"'joyable things, like m'work, which I's good at an' getting better, my music"—she touched the case of her mandolin—"'n my fam'ly an' friends. Someday I's have children of my own, maybe-so a steady man. If'n I doan' take no pleasure from all that-there, who it hurt? Me, that who. Somebody else hurt you, that fate; hurt youself, that plain ignorant; troubles enough in anyone's life, withouten you go courtin' 'em. I ain't hongry, ain't sickenin' to die, never been whopped; plenty folks worse off than me, I saves my pity fo' them, doan' waste it on myself.

"Look," she continued gently, "I knows y'all not born an' raised to this." She touched her identity tattoo. "But this-here the only life *you* has to live, likewise same's me. I's not sayin' nothin' bad doan' happen, but"—she gestured helplessly, as if trying to pluck words out of the air—"not everythin' is bad, unless you makes it so. The Draka?" She shrugged. "They's like the weather, they's jus' there. I's known folks, rather cut off they foot than 'commodate to the mastahs; they-all end up churnin' they guts with hatin'. Hate enough, it make go' hateful; it jus' ain't worth the trouble, to my way a' thinkin'."

Earnestly: "You sees, the Draka can make you obey, but they can't make you miserable. Well," she amended, "not unless they sets out to, which the ones which owns us doan', speakin' general-like." A tap on the head. "They orders, but we can say what goes on in here, eh? I's do my work, takes the days one at a time, doan' hurt nobody, helps those I can; when I's got to do somethin' I doan' like, I does it an' puts it outa my mind, soon's I can."

She smiled, trailing a hand out into the airstream. "Yous looks like sensible wenches, y'all will learn."

For a moment Marya's gaze touched Chantal's, and they knew a rare moment of perfect agreement; an understanding so complete it was almost telepathy—*Never*.

❖ ❖ ❖

> *"Beads of sweat glisten—*
> *Ai!*
> *In the undergroun' lights—*
> *Wo-hum*
> *Where a million lifetimes go—*
> *Wo-hum*
> *All our lives gone,*
> *Wo-hum*
> *Lost down the mineshafts . . ."*

The car lurched and slowed, and Marya jolted out of a dreamy semisleep; the day had turned warm, and she and the Lefarge sisters had dozed, lulled by the comfort and food and even a single glass of wine, after so long without. And the music, strange quiet folksongs in Yasmin's fine husky contralto, rhythmic minor-key laments. *Odd how sad music can make you happy,* she thought, stretching and rubbing at her eyes. She looked up, her ears ringing as the rush of air gave way to a pinging silence.

Wind blew through the opened windows, and the sound of earth-moving equipment, clanks and the sharp *chuff* of steam pistons, a turbine hum and the burbling growl of a heavy internal-combustion engine. The cars had halted before a roadblock, a swinging-pole barrier set across the two-lane road, a pair of armored cars flanked it, light four-wheeled models with twin machine guns in hexagonal turrets. There was a fence along their left, running down the eastern flank of the road, steel mesh on thick reinforced concrete posts three meters high; razor wire on top, and thin bare copper threads held away from it by insulated supports. Electrified, then.

And signs wired onto the mesh: PROHIBITED AREA. ENTRY FORBIDDEN ON PAIN OF DEATH.

Marya glanced the other way, south and east to the direction they had come. That was where the activity was, broad weed-grown fields littered with wrecked and rusted war machines; German models, *Panzergrenadier* half-tracks and Leopard tanks with their long 88mm guns swiveled every direction in silent futility. Broken, peeled open like fruit by the explosions that had wrecked them, still blackened by the dark oily soot of burnt motor-fuel; armor crinkled around the narrow entry-holes of the penetrator-rods, lighter vehicles like soup-cans stamped on by cleated boots.

Workers were swarming over them, cutting torches laying bright trails of sparks; others were winching the carcasses onto flatbed trucks. A recovery vehicle was dragging the most difficult cases out, the ones whose weight had half-buried them in the light volcanic soil. The turretless tank bellowed, its broad tracks raking stones and dry-smelling dust into the air, the hook dangling from the jib of the crane on its deck shaking; black fumes quivered from the slotted exhaust louvres, and she could see the bare head of the driver twisting in the hatch-way as he rocked the treads. Elsewhere gangs ripped out vegetation, leveled and pounded earth, spread crushed rock.

The nun lifted her eyes. They were in a high plain bordered by hills, shaggy fields and copses of trees bright-green with the late spring, the Auvergne mountains beyond blue and hazy in the distance. A glint of metal over them, approaching. It swelled into a circle, then a shape; long slender squared-off wings, a bulbous nose compartment that was all curved transparent panels save for the metal supports of the pilot's seat and the console, a pusher-prop engine in a tubular cowl slung between the twin booms of the tail. It passed overhead; ghost-silent, wheeled and returned: observation plane, muffled engine. Slots and flaps opened on the wings as the undercarriage came down. The little aircraft slid down at an angle, as if hitched to an invisible rope, bounced lightly and rolled to a stop ten meters from contact on a finished section of the landing platform.

Marya dragged her attention back to the road outside, her owner was there, stretching and rubbing her back and talking to an officer as they strolled back from the lead car.

" . . . better than 'copters for scouting," the man was saying. Mottled camouflage uniform, black-edged rank badges, paratrooper wings. Citizen Force, of course, the elite military, and the airmobile arm were picked volunteers within the Citizen Force. Marya looked west, toward the area behind the fence. That would be the town of Le Puy, and there were rumors of what had been done there, during the war and since. Atomics. She shivered, and listened.

"Doan' have anywhere near enough landing grounds," he continued. "Everythin' short, as usual; just got things under control out east and they move us back." He jerked a thumb over his shoulder, towards the fence and the minefields behind it. "We're refitting after China, overseein' this here construction work fo' our permanent base, and doin' antipartisan work in the hills, and watchin' *that.*"

Tanya nodded thoughtfully, looked at the wrecked war machines. "The Guard went down from Paris to Tours, but some of my friends were through here; the Fritz held hard." She shrugged. "Well, not exactly the Fritz; by '45 it was all odds and sods. Spaniards, these were, if'n I remember. Chewed up two Janissary units, and held the Vl Cartago fo' three days; tryin' to keep us off until their atomics got goin'." A shudder. "Wouldn't *that* have been jus' lovely."

The airborne officer nodded, watching the observation plane. The transparent egg had folded open, and a fuel cart had pulled up beside the three-wheeled runabout that was unloading the cameras.

"Natural place fo' it," he added. "Hydro power, lots of water, remote, not too far from their uranium mines; that's why Tech Section took it over: even damaged, the equipment was useful." He grimaced. "Wotan's spear, I's glad they didn't blow the reactor."

"Sho'ly am myself," Tanya said. "Praise be to Hitler's ghost; even after the little bastard died—when was that?"

"December of '42; I's in hospital then."

Tanya nodded. "Poland, myself . . . anyways, his memory kept the other Europeans from unitin' against us until it was too late. Even as it was, we used too many of the atomics breakin' through into Spain. I considered settlin' in Rosillon, down near the Pyrenees, but on second thoughts, no. Not that I doubt Tech Sec's infallible judgment 'bout it bein' safe, but I wanted to stay as far upwind of that hell garbage as possible."

The officer spread his hands. "It was a long war, we-all was tired, everybody wanted to get it over an' go home." He looked into the rear car; Marya averted her eyes, but the man's gaze was on Tom's rifle. "By Frey's cock, a T-5! Couldn't you get him a Holbars?" He slapped the T-6 assault rifle slung across his chest.

"I prefers whut I's trained on, mastah," Tom rumbled respectfully.

Tanya snuffled laughter. "Tom's bein' polite; s'far as he's concerned, a T-6 is a 'girl-gun.' He's damned good with that old big-bore monster, though. Hell, we conquered half of Asia with them; a weapon's never obsolete if'n it'll kill someone." She extended a hand. "Glad to have your assurance the route's safe," she concluded.

He gripped hers. "Pretty well," he answered. "There may be a few bushmen left, but we've been huntin' hard." A sigh. "Most of this mountain country was swept clear by Security—plan is to put it all back into forest—but I wish they'd get the cultivated portions settled an' modernized; hard to keep these little peasant farms from slippin' supplies an' information to the holdouts."

Tanya shrugged. "There's only so many of us, Cohortarch, an' we can't *all* be Landholders." She patted her stomach. "Take a generation or three to get it all covered."

"Oh, sweet Mother of God, let it be food," the guerrilla whispered, flexing his fingers on the grip of the machine gun. The muzzle trembled, shaking the screen of leaves and blurring the view of the winding road in the gorge below; the soft whisper of wheels and engines echoed, but the vehicles were still hidden by the hill shoulder to the left.

"Shut up," his partner hissed savagely, but his mouth filled at the thought. He adjusted the ammunition belt with trembling hands. German ammunition, 7.92mm; there was little of it left, little of anything. He could smell the new-bread scent of starvation on both of them, under the rankness of unwashed bodies and the sap-green of crushed leaves.

"Shut up," he said again, wiping his hand across his mouth, and wincing as it jarred one of his few remaining teeth. The belt was lying smooth, ready to feed; his rifle was by his hand, and the single precious stick grenade.

"Shut up," he repeated. The enemy had stopped convoying all vehicles through the Massif Central a month ago, while the *maquis* were hiding in their winter caves; there were only a dozen men left in their unit, but that should be enough. One of the survivors from Denard's group had told of the single truck they took two months ago. Cans of food, ammunition, medicines. "Of course they will have food."

If nothing else, meat.

The gorge was drowsy with the afternoon heat as the convoy dropped through, down from the plateau into the winding valley the Loire had carved through basalt and limestone. The road was rough, only sketchily repaired; the underbrush had been cut and burned back twenty meters upslope and down, but the angles above the way were steep enough that greenery overhung them as often as not. Young and turbulent with spring, the river bawled and tumbled below them to the left. At two hundred meters Marya could still hear the deep-toned rumble as the water poured oil-smooth over curves and then leapt in manes of white froth from the sharp rocks. It send drafts of coolness buffeting up from the river surface, the smell of wet rock and silt.

Ahead of her Issac's head was bent over a portable chess set, carved wood, with peg holes for the pieces. He moved, slipped the knight he had taken into the inside of the box, snapped it closed and turned to hand it to Tom. He was stretched over the back of his seat when she heard the sound.

Crack. Familiar: rifle bullet. A starred hole in the window ahead. The Jew pitched forward as if slammed by an invisible giant's hand, the thin face liquid with shock and only inches from hers, the chess set dropping from fingers that spasmed open in reflex. He bounced back, and she could see the dark welling crater of the exit wound in his shoulder. Then he slumped between the two seats, left hand pawing feebly at the wound. Blood welled between his fingers, bright primary red in the dusty sunlight. Marya felt herself darting forward, braced her hands under the Jew's armpits, heaved to haul him back into the body of the car. The smell of blood was in her nose and mouth, raw salt and iodine, like the scent of the sea.

He stuck briefly as the shotgun caught in the seat, then slid free. The cab was full of noise and confusion as the driver wrestled with the wheel; the car slid out toward the ravine, turned, skidded sideways with its length perpendicular to the road. The nun's hands were moving automatically, ripping at the wounded man's clothes for pads to block the holes, shifting him to lie flat and applying pressure. She could feel the vehicle sway, pause sickeningly on three wheels, jounce back down on all six and give a brief spurt of forward motion; then they clanged into the boulders on the hillside verge of the road.

Marya lurched, spreading her knees and fighting to keep position beside her patient. One hand was beneath his shoulder, spread flat with the palm up; her other bore down on the exit wound. Boxes and wicker crates swayed about her, buffeted and bruised her. Her fingers grew slippery.

Plasma, she thought. *Clamps, stitching, sulfa powder. More plasma, whole-blood typing, transfusion. Sterile gauze.* The techniques she had been trained for, before the War as a nurse's aide. In the long years since by experience, in true hospitals and tented field-medic camps, hundreds of hours of observation and reading and the sort of personal instruction harried doctors could give, enough to make her an M.D. of sorts herself. Now all she had was the knowledge and her hands and the memory of too many dying as she tried to help.

Not this one, she thought. The flow of blood was slowing; skin gray-tinged but not clammy or cold, unconscious or semiconscious, rapid shallow breathing beginning to slow . . . and the blood *was* tapering off, praise to the Mother of God and His Son and all the saints, not nearly enough lost to kill if shock didn't take him off, but she didn't dare move or the hemorrhaging would start again . . .

Sweat rolled into her eyes. Another rifle shot, and something pinged off metal. She looked left, toward the rear of the car; Chantal crouched, her fingers white on the lip of the window, her head craning to scan up the cliff face above them. Therese on the floor, crying again. Crouched over her protectively was Yasmin, cradling the French girl's head. Tom also at a window, the rifle held easily in one hand below the metal body of the car, binoculars to his eyes. They moved in tiny, precise movements along the slope outside, rock and scrub oak. A ripple of automatic-weapons fire, machine gun; she recognized a German MG38, an experienced gunner tapping off short bursts. Then Draka assault rifles, and the savage hammer of the 15mm twin-barrel on the lead car, echoing around the curve of road that hid it.

A click. She turned her head, looked toward the driver's seat. The driver, Jacques, had not spoken half a dozen words that whole day. Now he lay twisted across the seat, one arm through the wheel to give the other room; the chain stretched taut between his wrists, and she could see blood beneath the cuffs. His right hand reached the shotgun and held it between the bucket seats, pointing back into the cab. Marya's vision was suddenly very clear, the blued steel muzzle of the gun wavering uncertainly, fear-sweat and desperate tension on Jacques's face as it craned over his shoulder in the unnatural posture his bonds and position forced.

"Out of the way, Sister," he hissed. "Let me get a shot at the Janissary, that is the *maquis* out there, the Resistance, move, *please*."

The moment stretched as she felt the slowing ooze of blood past her fingers, as her mind sketched the narrow space behind her. If she flung herself forward and down she might be out of the cone of fire; the muzzle of the shotgun was only a hand's breadth from her face. Then the wounded boy would die, of course. The shotgun would empty its six-round magazine as quickly as Jacques could squeeze the trigger, and recoil would slam the barrel back and forth in his awkward grip, would fill the rear of the cab with the heavy mankiller double-buckshot rounds. Therese huddled wide-eyed on the floor, Yasmin stroking her hair with her body between the French girl and unknown gunmen, Chantal.

And if Marya did not move, and Jacques fired, the first round would tear off her face.

The nun kept her eyes on the driver's as she straightened and leaned forward, as far forward as she could without relaxing her hands on Issac. The cold metal of the gun muzzle millimeters from her throat, she could feel the skin crinkled into gooseflesh at the wind of its passing.

"Do what you must, my son," she said. Her mouth was very dry, her tongue felt coarse, like soft sandpaper. She began to shape the prayers.

"*Please*—" Jacques screamed.

A blur passed her eyes and a clang of metal on metal; the buttplate of Tom's rifle, lashing down on the barrel of the shotgun. Jacques screamed again, in pain this time as the trigger guard dislocated his finger. The shotgun fired once, into a wicker crate full of some dense-packed cloth that absorbed sound and shot both. Marya looked back; saw Tom raise the rifle again, held like a spear at the balance point above the magazine, and all his teeth were showing in a grin that had nothing to do with laughter. Chantal was reaching for him, until Yasmin snatched the chain between the Frenchwoman's wrists and braced a foot against the seat.

"You *stop* that, now," she snapped. The other woman reared back, struggling and shouting; Yasmin straightened her leg and pulled with all her strength, and Chantal went to the floor with a squawk and a flurry of limbs. "*Damn* you hide, wench, I's savin' your worthless *life.*" The serf buried both hands in the other woman's hair, gripped tight and bounced her head on the floor with a hollow booming sound. And turned to her father:

"Doan' kill him, Poppa!"

The rifle stayed poised, but something flickered out in the black eyes. A flat hardness, a total intensity of focus; his attention switched to the nun for an instant.

"Please," she said.

He nodded at her, a brief jerk of the head. "Owes yaz one," he said. "Now duck." The rifle flashed past her ear, to where Jacques lay cradling his wounded hand and moaning, between the front seats. The butt cracked down on the back of his skull and he slumped.

"He woan' die," Tom said grimly. "May wish to, 'fore I's through with him." His eyes were back on the road outside; one hand stroked Yasmin's hair. "Yous too soft-hearted for y'own good, girl. I's promised you momma to look after you . . ." For a moment his voice softened, speaking to a memory: "I is very sorry, Fatima . . ."

The fire from the lead car had died down to an occasional burst, less loud than the screams and pleas and moaning of the coffle chained to the truck in the middle of the convoy. Tom scanned the slope again and laid the binoculars down carefully; he twisted to face the road behind the car and the cliff face above.

"They not shootin' much, pro'bly short of ammo," he said conversationally, half to himself. "Just tryin' to pin the lead car, then . . . haaa, here they comes." Marya could see the huge brown hands close more tightly on the smooth wood of the stock. "Everybody shuts up, hear?"

Yasmin crawled to the nun, rummaged under the driver's seat for the aid box; Marya took the bandages and ointment thankfully, and for moments there was only the work of her hands. Applying the bandages, gauze pads, tape to immobilize the arm, it would do for now. Then the tip of a shadow fell across the window, and she looked up from the wounded man.

Two men stood in the road behind them, armed with Mauser carbines. Wild, bearded figures; their rags might once have been uniforms, but patches and caked mud made it impossible to tell with any certainty. They came toward the car at a trot, spaced across the road and moving in the instinctive half-crouch of men who expect to come under fire. Closer, and she could see the marks of hardship on them; scabs, weeping open sores clumsily bandaged, the slack-skinned gauntness that comes when the body has drawn down all its reserves of fat and begun to cannibalize the muscle beneath. They were strung about with a motley collection of string-tied bundles and sacks; as they came closer, she could see the lice moving in their beards, catch a gagging whiff of their stink.

The guerrilla nearest the river went to one knee and began a nervous scan up and down the road; the other hailed the car.

"Who's there? Answer, or I fire!"

Tom's voice replied, in slow ungrammatical French: "Just us serfs, here. Who yaz an' what you want?"

"This is the Auvergne command of the National Resistance," the man said; he repeated it as if it were a spell, a mantra against reality. "Food; we need food, medicine, weapons, clothing."

His comrade called from the verge of the road. "And ask them if there's any wine."

The first guerrilla turned to the other with a rebuke ready when Tom spoke.

"'Fraid there's nothin' for yaz here," the ex-Janissary said mildly.

"What—why—"

"*Because yaz gonna die, bushman!*" The guerrilla was an experienced soldier, but the bull bellow still checked him for the first fraction of a second.

Tom's rifle cleared the lower sill of the window with smooth economy; he fired from the hip, with the forestock braced against the metal of the windowframe. Even with the muzzle outside the car, the blasts were deafening. Marya's ears rang as she watched the guerrilla slip backward, and the hot brass of an ejected cartridge case bounced unnoticed off her forearm. Tom had fired three shots at less than ten meters range; all of them had struck the guerrilla in a patch over his breastbone no larger than the palm of a hand. They were standard load, 7.5mm jacketed hollowpoint rounds that mushroomed inside a wound; a plate-sized area of the *maquisard's* back fountained out in an eruption of bone chips, spine and shards of flesh. The corpse went back, eyes bulging with hydrostatic shock, then fell limply.

The other *maquis* fighter was up, turning and shouting. His first round went over the car with a vindictive crack, and then he threw himself flat behind a boulder to work the bolt of his carbine.

Tom fired twice more, and the bullets bounced off the sheltering rock in front of the guerrilla with sparking whines.

"Shee-it," he muttered. "Gettin' old an' slow." One broad hand dove into the satchel at his feet, came out with a stick grenade. A quick yank pulled the tab; he brought it up across his chest, counted three and threw it out the window in a flat spinning arc toward the rock. The guerrilla was up and running toward the river edge of the road before it landed. Tom's first two rounds kicked up dust and stone shards at the running man's heels, the third sledgehammered him over the verge of the road an instant before the grenade's blast struck. The guerrilla's rifle pinwheeled free as he toppled over the retaining wall, metal twinkling in the afternoon sun, then clattering on the rocks below.

"Shee-it," Tom said again. "Three rounds, *slow*." He reached up, pulled a lever and swung the roof hatch open, kicked a box over to give himself a platform to stand on. Head and shoulders out of the hatch, he turned to the cliff face above them. "You wenches stay down now, hear?"

Marya drew a long breath and wrenched her attention from the blocky torso filling the center of the car. Chantal was lying with her head in her hands, muttering; Therese lay beside her, eyes wide and frightened. The air smelled of burnt propellant and the sour sweat of fear; the nun started with nervous tension as Yasmin touched her arm.

"I am goin' back to take care of the chile," she whispered, jerking her head toward Therese. Marya nodded. The younger woman's brown skin had gone muddy-pale around mouth and eyes, but there was no quaver in her voice. Yasmin hesitated for a moment, then squeezed the nun's shoulder reassuringly.

"Doan' worry," she said in an obvious attempt to comfort. "Poppa woan' let the bushmen get us."

When the attack came, Tanya von Shrakenberg had been paging through the *Landholder's Gazette*, mildly annoyed that the workstock breeding programs were still behind schedule.

Dammit, they should let us use tractors, at least temporarily, she thought. There were sound reasons for the limits on mechanization, both social and economic, but a little more flexibility . . .

The first burst tore into the thin metal of the car's hood, ripping and dimpling the sheet steel; the second pinged and hammered at the thicker side panels. Instantly her mind snapped back three years, plantation-holder's reflexes yielding to the instincts of a Guards tank commander. The driver had frozen, eyes round as circles and whipping back and forth; he was reliable enough to go unchained, being very fond of his wife and children, but prone to panic. The car was losing power, a swift hiss of high-pressure steam and a mushy slowing-down feeling, but there was a fall of flat rock only twenty meters ahead, right side by the cliff.

"The rocks!" she shouted, wrenching the wheel back and clouting him over the head to break the grip of fear. "Pull us in by the rocks." That in French, it would penetrate better. Her hands were stripping the machine pistol out of its clamps over the dashboard, an elbow to pop out the window beside her and look up the tumbled face of the cliff. Halfway between a cliff and a very steep hill, yes, muzzle flashes—

The twin-barrel cut loose above her head in a continuous blast of noise, double streams of tracer in economical two-second bursts. The familiar bitter chemical stink of burnt propellant, and the sound of the 15mm rounds on stone, like thousands of ball-peen hammers on a boulder. Sparks and splinters and dust from the target, a ledge up near the summit; a bush falling, cut through. That would keep their heads down: the heavy rounds could chew through brick walls and cut down trees . . . The car lurched as it left the road, skidded in the gravel shoulder and fishtailed to a halt in the shadow of the rocks;

they were two meters high, enough to cut the body of the car out of the guerrilla machine gun's sight-picture.

Tanya pushed at the driver's head. "Down, *stay* down," she said, pulling the radio receiver from the dashboard and punching the send button. It was a powerful set, predialed to the Settler Emergency Network.

"Code one, code one: 10-7 von Shrakenberg, main road two kilometers north of Vorey, bushmen. Do you read, ovah."

"This is 1st Airborne, Le Puy. Say again, 10-7?" A young voice, bored; from what the officer at the roadblock had told her, it had been months since there was any activity this close to the air-cavalry base. Ambush on a main road was inconceivable; she recognized the tone of one resisting information because it violated mental habit.

The sloppiness was intolerable. "*Damn you, puppy, I'm bein' shot at!* Three-vehicle convoy, under fire from automatic weapons in the gorge three klicks south of Chamalieres. *Ovah.*"

"Ah . . . code seven, scramblin', maintain tone-transmission fo' location; ETA—" a pause, "16:10."

Tanya glanced at her watch: ten minutes, quick work. "Good work, 1st. I'm stalled on a C-shaped curve, northbound. My car first, a truck right on the bend, other car out of sight to the rear. Steep slope to the river on my left, an' a 80-degree forested cliff to my right. From the volume of fire, I'd judge one MG and possible six-twelve riflemen."

" 'Rodge-dodge, A.K."

"A.K.," she acknowledged grimly, leaning out the window and firing a short burst one-handed over the rock outside, aiming off-hand toward the muzzle flashes that winked out of the sunlit bush. No practical chance of a hit, that was four hundred meters, but it would help keep their heads down.

"An' hurry it. I've got two overseers, two armed serfs, a child an' me; an' I'm not up to much just now."

She pressed a button. "Switchin' to tracer." The signal would broadcast steadily now, for the triangulator stations to produce a guide beam that the reaction-squad aircraft could ride.

She levered herself up and squeezed back between the seats into the open body of the car. *Damn this belly,* she thought. Gudrun was at the rear doors, craning eagerly to see with her knife in one hand; she yanked the girl back by the hem of her tunic.

"Gudrun!" she snapped, swiveling her around to where the terrified nurse was huddling in a corner with one of the French housegirls. "Protect the serfs, and stay out of the line of fire. That's an *order*, understand?"

Damnation, she thought. *I would run into the last holdouts in central France with Gudrun along.* She pushed the anxiety down below consciousness; there was no time for it.

"Ogden," she continued, turning to the overseer at the twin-barrel. "Can you get them?"

As if in reply, a fresh burst from the hillside machine gun hammered at them. It dimpled the roof panels behind her, where the rear and riverward flank of the car extended beyond the cover of the rocks.

Wasp-buzz sounds, and the unpleasant *pink-tinnng* of ricochets: rifle fire. She felt obscenely exposed in this unarmored soup can, after all the years in a Hond battletank, acutely conscious of the quickened infant beneath her heart.

"Na," the overseer said. "Have to be dead lucky, Tanya. Bushmen got a nice firin' slit between two boulders, an' heavy cover. Best I can do is keep they heads down."

"Shit." Tanya looked over at Sarah, the other overseer; she knelt by the rear-door windows with her assault rifle at the ready, scanning the bush along the road with the x4 optical sight. That was where they would come, and soon, the *maquisards* would know as well as the Draka that a reaction force would be headed this way. There was a crackle of rifle shots, the slow banging of bolt-action carbines, a quick blast of semiauto fire, and a grenade from around the curve to the south, where the truck and the other car were stalled on the narrow road. The guerrillas might have assumed the rear of the convoy was soft meat, but Tom was teaching them otherwise.

"Right," she continued. "Ogden, Sarah, get ready to bail out an' tickle 'em. I'll cover you on the twin. When the airborne come in, *get back down*. Fast."

"A.K.," Ogden said, stepping down from the meter height of welded-steel platform beneath the gun and pulling his own Holbars from its clip beside his seat.

Tanya replaced him, blinking in the bright vertical sunlight as she came head-and-shoulders out of the roof hatch. Her hands went to the molded twin spade grips of the weapon, warm from the sun and Ogden's skin. Infinitely familiar, steel and checked *marula* wood against her palms, thumbs falling home on the butterfly pressure trigger. The twin-barrel was swivel-mounted on a ring that surrounded the hatch; she braced her elbows, laid the cross-wires of the sight on the bullet-scarred patch halfway up the cliff, and waited. There was no way they could get out of there without being seen. A very good spot for covering the road, but just a little too low to rake the right-hand verge where the car had run in . . . Yes, right there, a V-shaped slit between the big round grayish rock and the triangular pink one—

"And a very good thing they don't have a mortar," she muttered to herself. The black flared muzzle of the enemy machine gun slipped through the notch, stick-tiny at four hundred meters.

"*Now!*" she shouted, and thrust down on the ridged steel of the trigger. The massive weapon shuddered in her hands, a vibration that pounded into her shoulders and hummed tight-clenched teeth together; it was strongly braced, but the yoke and pin that held it to the ring mount could not completely absorb the recoil. Blasting noise and twin streams of tracer arching away from the muzzles, solid light as they left, seeming to slow and float as sparks before the heavy 15mm rounds dropped home. Spent brass tinkled down across her stomach and into the car, hot enough to sting through the thin fabric of her shirt. Short bursts, push *wait* push. The air over the fluted steel barrels was already quivering with heat; she could feel it on her forearms and face.

Above her the rocks dissolved behind a cloud of dust and chips and sparks. She raked across the top of the two boulders that hid the machine gun, to discourage any idea of standing up and firing down from the hip, then began working the edges of the opening. It was just possible she might be able to bounce a few rounds in, and it did not take many of the thumb-sized slugs to put a machine-gun crew out of action.

Behind her the rear doors of the car slammed open. From the corner of her eye she could see Ogden's squat form catapult out and dive into the roadside bush, a blur of black leather and metal. Sarah followed, a running leap from the back of the passenger compartment that took her three bodylengths out into the road, half the distance to the center truck. Then she backflipped, once, twice, dropped flat behind the truck and spider-crawled beneath it on palms and toes, a quick scuttling movement. A second's pause, and then the rapid *brrrt-brrrt* of a Holbars set for three-round bursts.

That will keep their heads down, she thought, and depressed the muzzles for an instant to rake a burst across the cliff face below the machine-gun nest. Not *too* far below, Ogden would be hunting there . . .

There was a sudden choked scream and a body catapulted from the scrub-covered slope five meters up; it flew through the air with arms and legs windmilling in an arc that ended in a crunching impact on the pavement. Broken, the guerilla lay for a moment and then began to crawl. His comrades in the bush-covered rock of the cliffside were firing at the center truck, trying to silence the automatic rifle beneath it. Bullets pocked the thin metal of the cab and ripped through the canvas tilt; the screaming of the chained serfs within was louder than the gunfire, and their scrambling rocked the vehicle on its springs.

"Come *on*, come *on*," Tanya whispered fiercely as she walked another burst back up the hillside and across the two bullet-scarred boulders. This was *not* good, a blindsided firefight against odds. "Come *on*, you knights of the air."

Chantal retched as she awoke, and Marya's hand pressed her back to the floor of the car. The nun briskly pulled up an eyelid and checked the pupil. "No concussion. You were unconscious for a little; keep quiet and keep down." In a whisper: "And there is nothing we can do except die to no purpose."

Marya kept her eyes resolutely below the level of the windows, down among the tumbled bundles and baskets. It could not have been long since the ambush, the hot metal of the flashtube boiler was still clicking and pinging. Danger stretched time, drew the seconds out, it seemed like hours. The sensation had become familiar in the war years, but the long changelessness of Central Detention had dulled the memory. Blood pounded in her ears, so loud that for long moments, the *thup-thup-thup* outside seemed no more than her own heartbeat. Then Chantal dropped her hand from her eyes and looked up questioningly.

"What *is* that?" she asked. It grew louder, a steady multiple whapping with a rising mechanical whine beneath.

Tom answered, looking down from the roof hatch above them.

"Those-there newfangled helicopters," he said, with satisfaction in his voice. "Not too soon, neither."

Chantal and the nun exchanged glances and crawled cautiously to the outside windows, raising their eyes to the lower edge and peering south. A line of dots was visible through the long gash of the gorge, swelling as they watched. Six of them in staggered line abreast, under the whirling circles of their rotors. Closer, close enough to see the rounded boxy fuselages and long tail booms, then the gaping twin mouths of the turbine intakes. The noise grew, shrilling and pounding; the fire from the hillside increased, no careful conserving of ammunition now, a panic-stricken crackle.

The helicopters rose slightly, to perhaps four hundred meters above the level of the gorge. Marya peered upward, blinking. Their speed was apparent now, as they snapped by with the bright flicker of tracer stabbing out from their flanks. The nun could see the door gunners standing to the grips of their weapons, the troopers crouching behind. The face of the slope above the road erupted in dust and the chittering whine of ricochets; Tom ducked down as gravel and twigs and branches pattered onto the roof of the car. Then the flight passed beyond the cliff edge, the sound of the rotors changing as they came in to land.

"Look." Chantal tugged at her sleeve.

Marya turned west; two more aircraft were approaching from the other side of the river, not more than fifty meters apart. A different type, approaching slowly in a straight line toward the rock face above the road. Helicopters like the others, but slender rather than boxlike, with stub wings and droop noses. Long flat-paned canopies above the nose and she could see the figures of two crewmen in each, one sitting behind and above the other. Both craft had multibarreled Gatling cannon in small domed chin-turrets beneath their prows, and she could make out the pitted cones of rocket pods under their wings.

"Sharkmouth markings," she whispered, mostly to herself. Gaping red-and-white grins painted on the metal, with clutching hands and screaming faces drawn between the teeth. At Chantal's quick glance she continued: "Draka fighters and ground-attack aircraft have them."

The gunboats halted over the middle of the Loire. The nun had seen a few helicopters before—both sides had been using them by the end of the War—but it still seemed somehow unnatural for objects to hang in the sky like that. She swallowed through a dry throat; in the cockpit of a helicopter one of the bulbous helmets moved and the Gatling beneath followed it, tracking with a blind, mechanical malevolence. The noise was overwhelming as the war machines hung above the water, the pulsing wind of the rotors thumping against the side of the car and raising a skidding ground-mist of dust, leaving circles of endless ripples on the surface of the river. A howling like wolves in torment echoed back and forth between the stony walls.

Above, on the cliff, the *maquisard* machine gun spat at the Draka helicopters. A burst sparked off the armor-plate nose of the left-hand vehicle; its neighbor turned slightly, corrected back.

"Down!" Marya cried, dragging the French girl with her as the first dragon-hiss and flash of rocket fire caught her eye. The flare of ten-round pods being ripple-fired stitched a line of smoke between the warcraft and the stone; and where the line met granite, the side of the cliff exploded. She was deafened and dazzled for a moment; the steel beneath her shook, and a section of the cliff face slid free onto the road. Rocks hammered down, starring the high-impact glass of the car and denting its metal; there was a fresh chorus of shrieks from the truck ahead as jagged fragments tore through the bullet-weakened canvas. Marya looked up through the windshield as another piece the size of a piano toppled away, hit a crag and split with a *tock* sound exactly like that of a pebble dropped on flagstone multiplied a thousand times.

One fragment bounced high, hung twirling at the apex of its curve, and dropped straight down to crush the truck's engine compartment with a *crang* of parting metal. Thick distillate fuel spilled down from the ruptured tank, then caught from some edge of hot steel and burned with a sullen orange flicker and trickles of oily black smoke. The other half of the stone was pear-shaped, wobbling through the air toward the car and missing it by a handspan before bounding down the gorge. Silence fell, or so it seemed as the rockslide ended. Shots, screams, the roaring *thutter* of the gunboats' engines as they soared by overhead with slow insolent grace . . . Then true silence as they landed and the fighting ceased.

Draka airborne troopers were dropping down the face of the cliff from rock to rock in an easy bounding scramble; she could hear them calling to each other, yipping hunting cries and laughter that sounded harsh and tinny to her battered ears. She looked at them and blinked the grit out of her watering eyes, turning to Issac and checking the bandages, hoping there would be no prisoners.

"We got about eight of them," the Tetrarch said to Tanya. South along the road there was another hiss as the extinguisher sprayed foam on the smoking hood of the truck; the oily stink of burnt distillate and overheated metal was in the air, the universal scents of machine-age war.

The Tetrarch was Eva von Shrakenberg, a cousin, daughter of Tanya's father's eldest brother. A mild surprise, but their family was old, prominent, and had always produced more than its share of officers. The Draka were not a numerous people, the Landholders even less so; one was always running into familiar faces. Eva's sister Ava was the twin tetrarchy's senior decurion.

"Interrogation?" Tanya asked.

"Oh, we'll keep one or two. Up to the headhunters, really." A lochos of Order Police had flown in with the airborne troops.

They were walking back past the wrecked truck: Ogden and Sarah had unreeved the coffle's common chain from the eyebolts and pulled the serfs out to sit in the vehicle's shade. The Polish nun was working on the wounded, with the Airborne medic standing by. Tanya's nose wrinkled at the familiar smell; the flies were there already, the gods alone knew where they all came from; there were even a few ravens circling overhead or perched waiting in the trees. Chains clanked as the serfs saw her and stirred.

"How many did we lose?" she asked the senior overseer.

Ogden looked up. He was leaning against the tailgate and honing a nick out of a long fighting knife, the ceramic whetstone going *screet-screet* on the steel. There was a nostalgic smile on his face; Ogden had been with her husband during the War, a reconnaissance commando.

"Three kilt daid," he rasped in his nasal north-Angolan accent, and jerked a thumb over his shoulder at the shrouded bodies in the truck. "Two like to die. Woulda been mo', but that tow-haired wench got 'em patched quick. Saved Issac's ass, too."

"Marya?" The nun looked from her work; she had a tourniquet around the man's thigh, and a plasma drip in one arm. "We goin' lose any more?"

Marya nodded toward a still figure. "That man, yes. Shattered spine, multiple perforations of the intestine, spleen and liver. He is in a coma. Even a good surgeon and a hospital could do nothing; I have given him morphine and prayed for him.

"This one—" She looked down. "The bullet entered above the hip and ran the length of the thighbone. Multiple compound fracture." He was unconscious, and better so: blood oozed from the sodden trouser leg, and the exit wound above the knee was cratered, vivid red flesh, white fat, pink shards of bone. "He needs immediate hospital care, and even so I fear the leg must go."

Tanya looked over to the Draka medic; he nodded. Ogden walked over, wiping the long clip-pointed knife on his leather-covered thigh; his jacket hung from one shoulder, and he tested the edge on one of the sparse reddish chest hairs that curled through the cotton mesh of his undershirt.

"That's our plumber," he said. "Not much use, a one-legged plumber. Kill him?"

The nun looked up sharply, her eyes going wide. Tanya looked at her for a moment, and then to the woman who sat cradling the man's head in her lap, stroking his forehead with a slow regular movement that set her wrist shackles chiming. Young, under the cropped hair and gray prison pallor. There was blood on her hands. She must have clamped the leg herself; the wounded serf would have bled out otherwise.

"*Vôtre Marie?*" the Draka asked.

The woman looked up. "*Oui, maîtresse,*" she said. "My Marcel. He is a good man, my Marcel." She blinked, forced a trembling smile. "He will work well for you, *maîtresse.* Always a good worker, Marcel; he never drank his wages, or fought or . . . his skill is in his hands, fix anything, I will help him—"

Tanya signed her to silence. "No," she said to the overseer. "A plantation isn't a prison mine, Ogden; you can't kill 'em offhand like that."

He shrugged. "You're the Landholder." His knife slid into the boot sheath. "Best Ah see to the lead car, might be fixable, anyhows."

She turned to her cousin. "Favor, coz?"

The officer nodded. "*Pas de problème,* as they-uns say hereabouts." She turned and whistled for a stretcher, and Tanya nodded to her other overseer.

"Unshackle me two bearers, here, Miss Wentworth." To the woman beside the wounded man: "They're taking him back to Le Puy; there'll be doctors for him there, and a place on Chateau Retour if he lives." A frown as Marya clung doubtfully. "If I was going to kill him, I'd say so; don't push your luck, wench."

Gudrun had come up while her mother and the others spoke; walking briskly, but pale even by a redhead's standards. Tanya put a hand on her shoulder and steered her a little away. "Your first time under fire and you did right well, daughter." She could feel the girl straighten pridefully into an adult's stance, hand on hip, and gave her a quick squeeze around the shoulders.

"Pity about losing the serfs just after we bought 'em, Ma," she said, returning the pressure with an arm about her mother's waist.

"In more ways than one, younglin'." At the girl's frown she continued. "Gudrun . . . these are cattle, but they're *ours*. Ours to use, an' ours to guard; we domesticated them, an' when you tame somethin' you make it helpless. Like sheep, or dairy cows. Lettin' the wolves at 'em is a failure of responsibility. You understand?"

She nodded slowly. "I think so, Ma . . . Suppose it'll make it harder to tame them proper, if they don't think we can protect them."

"Good," Tanya said. *Well, something of that lecture on the Tool that Thinks sunk in, at least.* "We want these to be good cattle, submissive, hard-workin' an obedient even when they're not bein' watched. They have to fear us, but that isn't enough. You have to make them depend on us; that's one reason we make the world outside the plantation bounds so rough fo' serfs. Reminds them, 'Masterless serf, lost soul.' "

Gudrun smiled. "I know that one, Ma. Carlyle." A laugh. "Why don' we keep some of those-there bushmen around, then?"

Tanya joined the child's chuckle for a moment. "We did, sweetlin', back in the old days, in Africa. A few runnin' wild in the woods or mountains . . . made for good huntin', too. That's too risky here, for a lot of reasons." She looked up at the cliff face, spoke more softly, as much to herself as her daughter. "We'll import leopards, later. Bring back the wolves, give the field hands reason to be afraid of the dark . . . dangerous. That's the blood price of mastery, child; we take the freedom for ourselves, the wealth, the power, the pleasure, the leisure . . . we get the danger and the responsibility, too, all of it."

The guerrilla prisoners came up then, stumbling along with their elbows tied roughly behind their backs, prodded forward by bayonets whose points were dripping dark. Gudrun wrinkled her nose at their stink; green-coated Security troopers slung their rifles and two gripped each *maquisard*.

"Phew, Ma. An' they're so *ugly*."

"I've smelled 'most as bad, sweetlin'; sometimes there's no time to wash, in the field." A quick appraisal. "These look like they've been dyin' by inches fo' a while, too."

A working party came out of the roadside scrub with poles over their shoulders and their bush-knives in hand. Tanya turned and clapped her hands for Yasmin, and the serf scuttled up with her head bowed, glancing nervously over her shoulder at the soldiers.

"Yasmin, take Gudrun and, hmm, what's-her-name, the halfwit wench—Therese—an' walk a ways up past my car. Ahh, on second thoughts, take Tom with you too. Don't get out of Mister Donaldson's sight, but don't come back 'lessn youre called. Understand?"

"Aw, Ma, why can't I stay an' watch?" Gudrun said with a trace of petulance. Tanya gripped her chin firmly and tilted the head up to meet her eyes.

"Because you're too young. This is necessary; it's also an ugly thing. It's not for entertainment—that's a sickness an' I won't tolerate it. Were it possible I'd kill them clean; so would you, I hope. Understood?"

"I reckon, Ma." A glower at the prisoners. "But they tried to *hurt* you, Ma!"

"So they did; an' you, sweetlin', which is worse. But it's 'neath us to hate them for it; we kill 'cause it's needful, not for hate; that hurts you inside. Remember that . . . and scoot!"

Tanya walked over to the coffle. "Look at me, serfs," she said, jerking her chin back at the airborne troopers and their prisoners. "That bushman offal tried to attack the Draka; they ended by attacking you. It's always that way, we've seen it a thousand times. Now watch how we protect our own, and punish rebellion."

The working party were hammering in the stakes by the side of the road, swinging their entrenching tools and wedging the bases with chips of rock. She could feel a shiver and murmur run through the seven *maquisards*, and turned to watch their faces. Fear, but not real belief, not yet; that was familiar, it was not easy to really believe that there would be no rescue, no reprieve. And these were brave men, to have remained starving in the mountains for . . . years, probably. A glance; the squad monitor was walking down the row of waist-high poles, kicking to check their set. He nodded, and the troopers began trimming the points, fresh-cut white wood oozing sap. Their task finished, the airborne soldiers scattered; some standing to watch the serf police at their work, others beginning the climb back to their vehicles.

One of the guerrillas shouted some sort of political slogan. The Security NCO finished wiping his bush knife, slid it over his shoulder into the sheath as he walked back to the man, grinning. A flicking back-fist blow smashed teeth and jaw with a sound like twigs crackling; the impact ran through the watching serfs with a ripple and a sound of breath like wind amid dead grass.

"This one wants to sing," the monitor said. "Him first. Mboya. Scaragoglu."

The two troopers lifted the man easily, each with a hand on shoulder and thigh, carried him out to the first length of sharpened wood. He began to fight then, kicking and twisting wildly; the serf policemen ignored his flailing and lifted him higher as they turned to face him in toward the road. Liquid feces stained his ragged trousers, and urine spread dark on their front. The sudden hard stink carried across the five meters of road, mixing incongruously with the smells of vegetation and river.

"Shit," said the younger of the Order Police.

"Every time," the other grunted, with a frown of effort. Shuffling their feet, they arranged the Frenchman carefully, spreading his legs over the point. "Raaht, let's put a cork in him. Not too far."

They pushed down. The scream came then, long and hoarse and bubbling. The monitor waited until it died down, replaced by a desperate grunt as the guerrilla's feet scrabbled on tiptoe, moving in a splay-legged dance. He strained, trying to drag himself off the six inches of rough timber shoved up through his anus into his gut. Inevitable futility; the rock-tense muscles of his calves could only carry his weight for a few moments. He sank down on his heels, and the scream rose again to a wailing trill as the point went deeper inside. Then a series of tearing grunts; the sound of the wind was louder, and the noisy vomiting of one of the coffle.

Strolling, the monitor paced down the line of prisoners, tapping the knuckles of his right hand against his left. A block-built man with broad Slavic features, he was wearing warsaps, and the steel inserts of the fingerless gloves made a *tink-tink* sound. Then a thumb shot out to prod another guerrilla in the chest.

"You. C'mon, sweetheart, you've gotta date with the Turk."

The troopers dragged him past Tanya; she could see that this one had gone limp, hear him sobbing with a bawling rasp. This one believed now, yes, *knew* that the dirty unspeakable impossible thing was happening to *him.*

Ugly indeed. That's the point, she thought, watching the wide, staring eyes of the coffle. Nobody died well on the stake, or bravely. It had the horror of squalor, death robbed of all dignity, all possibility of honor.

There are so many of them, she thought. *So few of us.* A kick inside her womb; she put a hand to her belly and looked back at the row of stakes with a chilly satisfaction. "So, so, little one," she whispered. There had been times in the War when she felt a detached sympathy for the men she killed. Not here, never here. This was *home.*

Another kick. "I'll keep you safe, doan' worry, child of my blood." Tanya looked at the coffle once more, a sudden fierce anger curling the lips from her teeth, bristling the tiny hairs along her spine. *Remember,* ran through her. *Remember, all of you, make this worth it. Remember this forever, tell your children and your children's children.* It was the ultimate argument. *When you think submission is impossible, remember* this. This *is what raising your hand to one of the Race means.*

The executions continued at a measured pace, until only two of the captured *maquis* were left. The monitor stood before them, tapping a finger on his chin; their eyes were wild, and they trembled in the strong hands that gripped them.

"Well, well. One for Abdul the Turk's lovin', one for the interrogators back in Le Puy." He stretched the moment. "Yaz the one."

His finger stretched out, slowly, to touch the man on the nose. The Frenchman's head reared back, spittle running down his chin, until the touch. His companion was shaking with hysterical relief, giggling and weeping.

Then the first man slumped, boneless, as the serf policeman's fingertip touched his face. Laughing, the monitor pushed back an eyelid.

"Allah, fainted," he said, shaking his head. "Well, no point in takin' a sleepin' man to the Turk." He turned to the other. "You luck's out, sweetheart."

Tanya ignored the last impalement, watching the two women she had bought in Lyon instead. Chantal was standing with her hands pressed over her face, the fingers white as they pressed into her forehead. Marya . . . Marya was glaring at the execution, face pale and rigid, eyes alight with . . . *No, not hatred*, the Draka judged. *Anger.* A huge and blazing fury, held under tight control, and the more furious for all that.

Her cousin touched her shoulder. "Your transport's on its way," she said, then followed Tanya's gaze, blinked. "Got somethin' interestin', there."

"Yes," Tanya said. "But is it an interestin' plow, or a landmine?" She sighed. "Ah, well, the work to its day."

Chapter Seven

CHATEAU RETOUR PLANTATION
TOURAINE PROVINCE
APRIL 1947

It was sunset when the vehicles reached the boundaries of the plantation. They had been driving along the north bank of the Loire, on the road that ran along the embankment of the levee. Tiredness dragged at Marya like water, a band of weariness over the brow weighting her head, and still the scene brought her out of herself.

The river lay to their left as they drove westward past ruined Tours, broad and slow and blue, long islets of yellow sand like teardrops of gold starred with the green of osier willow. It was mild, with the gentle humid freshness of spring in the Val of Touraine; the sun was on the western horizon, throwing the long shadows of cypress and poplar towards them, flickering bars of black against the crushed white limestone of the road. Clouds drifted like cotton puffs in a sky turning dark royal blue above, shading to day-color and the flaming magenta shade of bougainvillea on the horizon.

Down the bank to the river was long grass, intensely green, broken by clumps of lilac in white and purple; on the narrow strip of marshy ground along the base of the embankment were willow trees leaning their long trailing branches into the slow-moving water, over carpets of yellow flag iris.

I am so tired and so afraid, Marya thought, sliding the window down and breathing in. Forty kilometers an hour, and streamers of hair the color of birchwood flicked out from under her kerchief. *But this minute is the gift of God; He is here, so here home is.* The fleeting scent of the lilacs, a delicate sweetness, the heavier scent of a flowering chestnut tree. Country smells, warmer and more spicy than her native Malopolska. She smiled and sighed, ceasing to fight the weariness. How had Homer put it, in the mouths of those fierce bronze-sworded Achaean warriors, so long ago? "It is well to yield unto the night."

✧   ✧   ✧

Chantal raised her head from her hands, breaking the silence that had kept her crouched and swaying with the motion of the vehicle for hours past.

"Are you so happy, then, nun?" she asked. Black circles lay under her eyes, like bruises. She should be hungry, sleepy, but there was only a scratchiness beneath her eyelids and a sour feeling in her gut that left a bitter taste at the back of the mouth. This was her first time so far from Lyon if you did not count one train trip to Paris before the War, when she had marched in a Party youth group delegation for May Day.

The Pole smiled at her. "For a moment, Chantal, for a moment. Life is a distance race, not a sprint. Tomorrow I may be in terror, or in pain, so now I take a minute of joy to strengthen myself." A chuckle. "Or as the kitchen sister used to say when I was a novice, 'You only need to wash one dish at a time.' " Grimly: "God made the world, we humans make its horrors. Let me enjoy a moment where our handiwork has not marred His."

The communist snorted and turned sideways in her seat, looking out her window. *Humility*, she thought. *The opiate of the people.*

Although there would be few people here, few of her sort. The fields were turning dark, and there was a deafening chorus of field crickets, nowhere a light or sign of man. She shuddered; this was the country, and she a child of streets and buildings. Empty, the home of the brutal rurals, the quadrupeds, as the Party men called peasants. Unfamiliar noises echoed; birds, she supposed, and shivered again at the thought of woods and animals and emptiness with no sustenance or hiding place. Insects crawling through everything, dirt, shit from animals lying about. Pigs and cows and horses, sly-faced farmers and beaten beast-of-burden women; all that and the Draka too.

She shivered and hugged her shoulders. *I can face death,* she thought. It was dying, the way of it, that was the problem.

Marya turned back to the window and sighed again. Anger so fierce was like vodka; one glass at the right time could give you the strength of a bear, too much or too often and it ate you out from the inside. Anger demanded a direction, an expression; if you could not turn it on the ones who aroused it, your mind turned it on yourself, turned hatred to self-hatred and self-contempt. *Such is the nature of fallen man,* she thought. Also, anger and hatred gave an enemy too much grip onyou. The emotions locked you to them, and in hatred as in love one took on the lineaments of the mind's focus; only God and His creation, and mankind in general, were safe targets for such feelings. Pity was safer, charity, the unconquerable Christian meekness off which an oppressor's physical strength slid like claws from glass.

Your way is hard, Lord . . .

They turned left and north off the main road, between two tall pillars of new fitted stone, with a chain slung between them at three times head-height. She read:

CHATEAU RETOUR PLANTATION
EST. 1945
EDWARD AND TANYA VON SHRAKENBERG, LANDHOLDERS

Beyond were the remains of a small village, an old Loire riverport of white tufa-stone cottages and shops. It was being . . . not destroyed, disassembled; she could see piles of salvaged windows, doors, piles of stone block chipped clean of mortar, flat farm wagons piled with black Angers roof slates. A few workers were about stacking tools and clearing up for the next day's labor; they paused and bowed as the cars passed. Marya looked questioningly at Yasmin.

"Port Boulet," she said drowsily, straightening up and rubbing her face with a handkerchief dipped in acceder from a thermos. "Ahhh, tha's bettah. Port Boulet; we knockin' it down to build the Quartahs." Seeing the look of puzzlement, she continued: "The field hands' quarters, the village, the mastahs doan' like folks livin' scattered about, wants 'em all near the Great House. And fo' buildin's, smithy and barn and infirmary and suchlike. Even puttin' up a church, bringin' it piece by piece from over t' Chouze-sur-Loire, a bit west of hereabouts."

The nun nodded. It made sense; a pattern of great estates worked from a common center made for concentrated settlement, just as small single-family holdings often meant scattered farmsteads.

"We's not long to home, now," Yasmin said, looking over to her father where he slept stretched out with his rifle by his side and his graying head on a folded coat. "Poppa," she called softly, nudging him cautiously in the foot. "Poppa, almost there. Ten minutes."

He stirred, touched the weapon, then levered himself up, yawning hugely. "Ahh, *gutgenuk*," he said; the nun filed it away, another of the dialect words that sprinkled his English. That one sounded Dutch or German. "Nice t'be backs under m'own roof."

Home, Marya thought, and fought a new shiver of apprehension. A stopping place at least.

She forced her eyes back to the darkening fields outside; they were driving north now, away from the river and into the flat alluvial *vienne* of Bourgueil. There was a line of low hills ahead, five or six kilometers, visible in glimpses between the lines and clumps of trees that cut the horizon. Already those were shapes whose upper branches caught blackly at the light of the three-quarters moon. The open ground was still touched lightly with the last pinkish light; a big field of winter wheat to their left, bluish-green and already calf-high. Her countrywoman's eye found it reassuring; flourishing, this was a fat earth. Potatoes to the right, neat rows well-hoed, about twenty acres. Marya could see the marks of recent field boundaries within the standing crops, lines and dimples brought out by the long shadows of evening.

Smaller fields thrown together, she thought. Then they turned west, onto a narrower lane bordered on both sides by oaks huge and ancient, into a belt of orchard. The convoy switched on its headlights, bringing textures springing out in the narrow cones of blue-white light. Swirling horizontal columns of ground fog rising with the night, rough-mottled oak bark and huge gnarled roots, trefoil leaves above their heads underlit to a flickering glow. The apricot trees beyond with their pruned circular tops, bands of whitewash on their trunks, a starring of blossom and a sudden intoxicating rush of scent. Then through darkened gardens to a gravel way before the looming gables of . . . not a house, not a castle, really—a chateau.

Marya had a confused view of towers round and square, patterned in alternate blocks of white limestone and dull-red brick, before the vehicles swung over a gravel drive that crunched and popped beneath the tires. They halted in a glare of floodlights before the main doors, and the silence rang in ears accustomed to wind-rush. The door of the car opened and she stumbled out onto the drive, staggered slightly with bone-heavy weariness and the stiffness of a body confined far too long. People were bustling about, servants in dark trousers or skirts and white shirts, lifting parcels and bundles with shouts. The coffle was unshackled from the flatbed truck and led away, the vehicle followed, driven down the lane to some garage or storage area.

The nun blinked again beside Chantal, trying to flog her mind into alertness. Stretcher parties were taking Issac and the lightly wounded serfs from the truck. Beside her Tom was stripping the magazine from his rifle, handing weapon and bandolier to another servant; that one joined four more staggering under the dismounted twin-barrel from the front car, all shepherded off by the overseers. To an armory, she supposed, although the ex-Janissary kept the fighting knife in his boot, and two steel-tipped sticks rested in his gear bag. The cars reversed and moved away as the crowd melted into the house with their burdens.

A woman shouldered her way toward them against the movement, waving and calling with a wide smile.

" 'Allo! 'Allo, Tom!" A Frenchwoman in a good plain dark dress, with a baby on her arm and a boy of four or so walking by her side. The child sprinted ahead and leapt at Tom, was caught in the thick arms, swept up laughing and seated on a shoulder. The boy was towhaired, but the six-months babe in the woman's arms was as dark as Yasmin; the Frenchwoman was in her thirties, well-preserved with a robust village look about her, big-breasted and deep-hipped. She embraced Yasmin's father with her free arm, was kissed with surprising gentleness.

" 'Allo, Yasmin," she said, as the younger girl took the baby, who was looking out from a cocoon of blanket with wide dark eyes and a dubious expression.

"How y'all, Annette?" Yasmin replied, cooing and blowing at the infant, who replied with a broad toothless smile, waving pudgy fists and drooling. "And how my little sister? Eh? Eh?"

"I am well," Annette replied in slow, careful English. "Justin is well; little Fleurette is well." She stepped back from Tom and glared.

"I am happy also to see that my husband is well. After an *affaire* of shootings, such as he promised me was behind him, at his age one expects a man to act with some sense, *non?* But of a certainty, no: they are all little boys who must play with their toys, *n'est pas?* One man already I have lost with this soldier's nonsense." She crossed her arms on her broad bosom. "Do I ask too much that the second refrain? Or perhaps consorting with all the courtesans of Paris and Lyon has restored his youth?"

Tom grinned, reached up to tug on the boy Justin's hair and hand up a rock candy, then spread his hands in a placating gesture.

"Sweetlin', it weren't nohows my doin'." He fished in his pocket, came out with a velvet case. "An' Paris, that where I gits this fo' you."

"Hmmmp." She opened it: pearl eardrops. "Hmmp." A sigh. "Ah, well, *d'accord*, there is perhaps a ragout waiting on the stove." She turned to Yasmin, took in the two new house servants with an incline of her head.

"You will join us, daughter?"

Yasmin shook her head, handed the baby back to its mother with unconscious reluctance. "Thanks kindly but I's got things to do; settle Marya and Chantal here down, 'n Mistis may need me. Mebbeso tomorrow 'round lunchtime?" A grin. "'Sides, ain't nice to separate man 'n wife after they's been apart two weeks."

"Sho 'nuff." Tom laughed, and swung a hand that landed on Annette's buttocks with a sharp *crack*. She jumped, squealed, and dug a sharp elbow into his ribs.

"For that, my old, perhaps you sleep on the floor and learn manners." To Marya and Chantal in French: "*Mesdames*, you will be weary from your journey. Another time we will speak: we have a cottage not far from the manor you must visit. I will introduce you to others of us." A smile. "You will find us all very much *en famille* here on Chateau Retour. It is needful."

Yasmin watched as the four moved off, the adults with their arms about each other's waists, boy seated astride Tom's neck. A fond look touched her eyes.

"Annette good fo' Poppa," she said. "After Momma die, he get old faster than needs." Shrewdly: "Good fo' her, too. Her man die in the War, an' there widows aplenty: three wenches for every buck. Annette she kinda *practical* 'bout things, like you French mostly is; do y'all good to listen to her, she talk sense. Set her cap for Poppa, land him a year ago, get things fixed up regular with a preacher an' all." A sigh. "Pretty weddin': Mistis Tanya set store by Poppa. Well, time's a-wastin'."

She put a hand under their elbows and moved them off toward the steps; Marya felt blank, as if her mind was storing information at a rate beyond her exhaustion's capacity to sort it. The family of the master and mistress were still grouped by the doors; the three serf women halted just in earshot and made obeisance, waiting. Marya glanced up under lowered lids, examining the man who also owned her; he and Tanya were standing face to face, both hands linked.

He was tall, even for a Draka. Light khaki trousers and shirt showed a broad-shouldered, taper-waisted silhouette; muscled arms, and a sharp V of deltoid from shoulders to neck. His face had a cousin's similarity to his wife's, a masculine version; dark tan, set off by the wheat-colored hair and gray eyes. Eye, rather: the left socket was covered by a leather patch and thong. Scarring below and above, deep enough to notch the bone; his little finger was missing on that hand, and there were more scars up the back of it and along the arm. A boy of perhaps nine stood beside him, a younger version but with the mother's brown-and-bronze hair.

" . . . worst problem was the baby tryin' to get out and kick the bushmen to death, leastways that's what it felt like," Tanya was saying. She turned her head. "Ahh, here's Yasmin with the two book-keepers. The light-haired wench here's the one I told you about, has medical trainin' as well, saved Issac's life."

"You could always pick them, my love," the man said. Deep voice, slightly hoarse; the three women stepped forward and the new arrivals made the hand-over-eyes bow they had been taught.

"Up, look up," he said to them. "We save that for formal occasions, here in the country."

He rested his right hand on the holster of his automatic pistol as he turned to them; not a menacing gesture, simply habit. The other hand gripped his wife's; he was still smiling from the reunion as he looked them over with swift care, turning Marya's head sideways with a finger.

"Slav?" he said.

"Yes, Master," she answered. "Polish." *At least he isn't looking at our* teeth, she thought. Of course, he had access to dental records.

"That was swift thinkin' and nerve, savin' Issac in the ambush. Good wench." He turned to Yasmin. "These two look exhausted, settle them in." A grin. "You worn down from travelin' too?"

Yasmin smiled back from under her lashes. "Wouldn't say so, Mastah," she murmured.

Tanya laughed outright and tossed a key to Yasmin. "This for the cuffs. And since you're not tired . . . when you're finished unpackin', collect Solange and attend upstairs to help with our celebration; 'bout eleven, or thereabouts." The Landholders turned toward the stairs, and Tanya ruffled her son's hair; he hesitated a moment, watching the two women with his head slightly to one side before following his parents.

"The blond one isn't very pretty," he said, glancing back at his mother. "Her face is square an' her legs are short."

His father smiled, dropped a hand to his shoulder and shook him lightly, chiding. "That was unkind, Timmie, an' she's done good service. Remember what . . ." The doors closed.

"Wake up."

"Mmph," Marya said. A hand shook her shoulder, gently insistent. She blinked awake, then shot bolt upright in shock. No siren, no pallet; the air smelled of cloth and wood and greenery, not the wet stone and disinfectant reek of Central Detention. Warmth, and sunlight on oak floorboards, the bright tender light of early morning in spring-time, and birds singing.

Yasmin stepped back in an alarm that faded quickly. The nun rubbed granular sleep out of her eyes, looking about the room she had not seen when she tumbled into bed last night. Up under the eaves of

the chateau, with a sloped roof and a dormer window, three beds—
for herself, Chantal and Therese—dressers, mirrors, chairs. The furniture was plain but sound; there was a rug on the floor, and the beds
had clean sheets and blankets. She crossed her arms on her shoulders, feeling at the thick flannel nightdress, warm and new. Luxury,
compared to Central Detention; more comfort than the mother house
of the Order, in Lwow before the War.

The serf girl yawned prettily and patted her lips with the back of
one hand; she was wearing a belted satin robe. "Solange," she called
over her shoulder. "Y'all got their stuff?" To the three newcomers: "This
shere Solange, Mistis Tanya's maid."

"Yes, *cherie.* I have it," a voice from the corridor outside answered
Yasmin's question. A woman's voice, soprano, mellow and beautiful.
"*Viens, Pierre,*" it continued.

A man backed into the room, dragging a wooden crate, straightened with a grunt and left. Solange edged past and stood at Yasmin's
side, looping a companionable arm over her shoulders.

Parisian, Marya thought; not just the accent, everything. She managed to make the midnight-blue pajamas look like a chic lounging outfit.
A little past twenty, but she looked younger in the overlarge clothes;
long sleek black hair bound up in a Psyche knot at the side of her
head, big violet-rimmed blue eyes heavy with a tired satiation. Straight
regular features and small-boned grace, a dancer's movements.

"Well, well," she said, gesturing with her free hand. Cigarette smoke
lazed from the tube of dull gold in its ivory holder, a green musky
herbal scent that was not tobacco. "Open your present, there's good
children."

Chantal looked up; she had been beside her sister, who was smiling shyly at the newcomer, warmly at Yasmin. There was no warmth
in Chantal's eyes; Marya could read the thought directed at Solange:
collaborationist bourgeois slut. And Solange's answer: *blowsy, overblown
gutter tart.*

The nun knelt by the box and undid the rope fastenings. A scent
of camphor and sandalwood greeted her. The crate was full of clothes,
carefully packed in thin transparent paper. Silk underwear and stock-
ings, blouses, skirts, dresses. Unconsciously, her hands caressed the
fine cloth. Chantal came and knelt beside her, running an experienced
hand through the stacks; she had not grown up among textile workers and trades for nothing.

"This is beautiful work," Chantal said appraisingly. "Pre-War." She
stiffened. "Clean but not new, a lot of it." She looked up, full lips
compressed. "This is loot!" Her hands wiped at her nightgown, as if
to remove a stain.

Solange drew on the cigarette holder, held the breath for an instant,
exhaled with slow pleasure. "But yes, my child; the plunder of Paris.
I sat in a truck and watched them drag it from shops and apartments.
And sack the Louvre; Renoirs and Manets, mostly, for our owners, the
von Shrakenbergs. The fruits of victory, my old, even as you and I
are."

Yasmin reached up to give a warning squeeze to the hand on her shoulder. "C'mon, darlin', be nice. Why doan' I meets you at breakfast?" After the Frenchwoman had left, she yawned again and set a foot on the edge of the box.

"Should be enough's to get you started," she said. More sharply, to Chantal: "An' no foolishness, hear?" She looked about, an unconscious reflex of caution. "Ahh . . . 'bout Solange. She friendly enough, once you gets to know her; bit snooty, on 'count her poppa a *professor* befo' the War." An aside: "He nicest ol' man y'wants to meet." Pursing her lips. "Solange . . . she an' the Mistis ain' just like *that*"— she held her index and forefinger together horizontally—"they like *that*, too." She crossed the fingers, and sighed at their incomprehension. "She tells the Mistis everythin'. Watch what you talks, 'round her." A shake of the head. "Ain' no harm in likin' yo Mastah, if they merits it. Lovin' 'em"—she shrugged—"bad fo' everybody, in the end."

More briskly: "Anyhows, it six o'clock. Showers down the hall, bottom of the stairs; shower every mornin', that the rule. Those as doan' keep clean gets scrubbed public, with floor brushes. Evenin' bath if'n you wants to. Breakfast in th' kitchen, six-thirty; work starts seven sharp, that the *general* rule fo' House servants. Midday meal at one, half hour. Supper at seven, two hours fo' yoselfs, then lights out." A laugh. " 'Lessen you bed-wenchin', like we was last night. Sees you at table."

The kitchens were abustle, a long stone-floored chamber dimly lit by small high windows; the whole looked to have been part of the Renaissance core of the chateau. The walls were lined with stoves, fireplaces, counters, plain wood, brick, black iron; above hung racks of pots, pans, knives, strings of onions and garlic. About forty serfs were eating at trestle tables that could be taken up later; a makeshift arrangement, Yasmin told Marya, until proper dormitories and refectories could be built. There was an upper table for the chefs and senior House staff.

The servants were wildly mixed. A dozen or so were like Yasmin and her father, from the old African and Asian provinces of the Domination. There were a half-dozen Germans, a scattering from as far east as China, the rest locals, mainly girls in their teens. They chattered, in French and fragments of their native tongues, and here, at the upper tables, for the chefs and senior House staff, mostly in the Draka dialect of English.

Ah, she thought. *Cunning.* The imported serfs would turn to English as their *lingua franca*, and the other house servants gradually pick it up from them, the more so as it was the language of the serf elite, the bookkeepers and foremen. The young girls would spread it in the Quarters, since most of them would marry fieldworkers and move back into the cottages. Of course, it would help that such education as there was in the Domination was in English only; writing in other tongues was forbidden on pain of death. Without a literate class, French would decline into a series of mutually incomprehensible regional *patois* . . . Two generations, and it would be the despised tongue of illiterate fieldhands; a century or so, and there would be a scattering of loan words in a new dialect of Draka English, and dusty books that only scholars could read.

She shivered and turned her attention to the food, crossing herself and murmuring a quick grace. Bowls passed down the tables, eggs and bacon and mushrooms, fresh bread and fruit; the Draka must have imposed their own Anglo-Saxon habit of starting the day with a substantial meal, coffee as well. She was surprised at that for a moment, until she remembered where Europe's sources had been before the War. The Domination's coffee planters would be anxious to restart their markets. Marya ate with slow care, a respect born of a decade of rationing and hunger, remembering grass soup and rock-hard black bread full of bark, the sticky feel of half-rotten horsemeat as she cut it from a carcass already flyblown and home to maggots. Food was life; to despise it was to despise life itself, and the toil of human hands that produced it.

An old man limped in, sitting carefully beside Solange; she gave him a perfunctory peck on the cheek and returned to pushing her eggs around her plate with moody intensity. He nodded to Yasmin and the others addressed Marya and Chantal:

"Ah, my successors." One of the cooks put a plate of softboiled eggs in front of him, and a bowl of bread soaked in hot milk.

"A little cinnamon, perhaps?" he asked the server, and sighed as he sprinkled the bland mush and began to spoon it up. "The infirmities of my digestion," he said to the nun. "One of the reasons you have been purchased to replace me." He extended a hand that trembled slightly. "Jules Lebrun, professor of anthropology late of the Sorbonne, and now bookkeeper for this estate. And my daughter, Solange."

Marya's eyes widened in involuntary surprise; she would have sworn that this man was eighty at least . . . *No, look at the hands and neck,* she thought. The hair was white and there were loose pouches beneath the watery blue eyes, but that could be trauma; the limp and hunched posture due to internal injuries. He chuckled hoarsely. "Yes, yes, not so old as I look." The chuckle turned into a cough, and Solange turned to touch him on the shoulder.

"*Pere?*" she asked anxiously. "Are you well?"

He shook his head, wiped his mouth with a handkerchief, patted her hand. "I am dying, child; but slowly, and it's in the nature of things. You should be more concerned with your own health." To Marya and Chantal, "*Mesdames?*"

They rose; the nun and the communist exchanged a swift glance and stationed themselves on either side, ready to support an elbow. Lebrun rapped his cane on the flags.

"I am not dead *yet,* ladies," he said. A raised eyebrow. "You, I presume, are Sister Marya?" She noticed that he caught the pronunciation, difficult for a French speaker. "And Mademoiselle Lefarge, who I believe was a member of the Party. I find that I need little sleep, these days, and spent some time getting the records in order for you."

They walked through the kitchen doors, into a central section of the house. Workmen's tools lay scattered about; partitions had been pulled down, doors removed; the air smelled of old dust, plaster and wood, and the early morning light streamed in through tall, opened windows. Lebrun waggled his cane to either side and spoke in a dry lecturer's tone.

"You see here the eighteenth-century additions to the chateau. A square block of three stories above the cellars; that was when the moat was filled in. Observe the changes the von Shrakenbergs are making; very much in the Draka taste. Fewer but larger rooms, you will notice. More light; marble floors, eventually. The stonework is sound—local tufa limestone—but structural reinforcements in steel are to be made." He walked slowly, and Marya put a hand beneath his elbow in concern.

"I have some medical training," she said quietly. "Is there—"

Lebrun glanced about, stopped for a moment, continued more quietly. "Your solicitude is appreciated, Sister, but the doctor tells me there is nothing to be done."

"How were you hurt, sir?" Chantal asked; she had the serious, self-improving worker's respect for learning.

He shrugged, a very Parisian gesture. "Cancer," he said. "It started while I was in New Guinea on a field trip, then started spreading more recently. Surgery, remissions, but it is beyond that now. Exacerbated by injuries sustained in the sack of Paris." A mirthless smile. "A tetrarchy of Janissaries were amusing themselves by kicking me to death, while they raped my wife and daughter; this was at my offices in the university, you understand. Mistress von Shrakenberg stopped them, as she was looking for some books at the time and the sight of them burning my library annoyed her. I survived, with some difficulty, as did Solange; my wife did not. It is debatable which of us was luckiest, *n'est-ce pas?*"

He resumed his walk. "Now, ahead of us is the oldest section of the manor: fifteenth century. Most interesting, when you see the outside you will note the checkerboard effect, red brick and white stone. Two round towers of four stories facing south, with conical roofs of black Angers slate; on the eastern side, two square towers, one three stories and one five; and the rear of the house, looking out on the wine cellar and the chapel. The most thoroughly renovated section, begun two years ago when the von Shrakenbergs took up their land grant here; fascinating to watch it change. The master tells me they plan to put a whole new wing in there, on the north side, when the more utilitarian parts of their building program are done. 'Decent baths,' was one of the phrases he used, by which a Draka means something rather Roman. Ah, here we are."

They had passed into a corridor in the family apartments, the area renovated in the Draka style. Smooth glowing-white marble floors under soft indirect lighting, doors in lustrous tropical woods a dark contrast. The walls were mosaic murals, done in iridescent glass, copper, coral, gold; scenes of hunting, harvest and war. A pride of lions at bay amidst tumbled rocks, against a background of thorn trees and scrub grass; horses reared amid a tumult of huge black-coated dogs, and the lances of the shouting riders glittered. They turned a corner and were amidst a landscape of cool hills green with clipped tea-bushes and neat rows of shade trees, with a mansion's red-tiled roof and white walls half-hidden among gardens. Workers in garish cotton garb plucked leaves and dropped them in wicker panniers slung over their backs.

"Ceylon," Lebrun said. "The von Shrakenbergs have relatives there.

The Draka took it from the Dutch in 1786; their ancestors, rather—
they were still a British colony then. And here is one the mistress did
the drawings for herself."

A German farmhouse burning under a bright winter sun, the pillar
of black smoke a dun club in the white and blue arch of the sky.
Dead cattle bloating in the farmyard, torn by ravens, one crushed
into an obscene pancake shape by the treads of a tank. Skeletal trees
about the steading, their branches like strands of black hair frozen
in a tossing moment of agony; a human figure hung by the neck
from a branch, with snow that drifted into his open mouth. Self-
propelled guns were scattered back across the fields, the long barrels elevated, their slim lines broken by the cylindrical bulkiness of
muzzle breaks and bore evacuators, the vehicles half invisible in
mottled white-on-gray camouflage. In the foreground a group of figures,
Draka soldiers bulky in their white parkas and flared bucket helmets.
They were grouped about the bow of a Hond battletank, under the
shadow of its cannon.

The detail was amazing for a medium as coarse as mosaic. The nun
could make out the eagle pommel of a knife, duct tape about the
forestock of a rifle, a loop of fresh ears dangling from a belt—and
recognized faces. Tanya von Shrakenberg rested her palms on a map
spread over the sloping frontal plate; her bulbous tank commander's
communication helmet weighed down one corner. Marya stooped to
peer at the other figure, a man who tapped a finger on the map and
pointed with the drum-magazined assault rifle in his other hand.

"Master Edward?" she asked.

"*Exactement*," Lebrun replied. "Note that there is a caption." The
two women stepped back to view the cursive script below the mural:
THE PROGRESS OF MANKIND. Lebrun laughed with a rattle of phlegm. "Our
owners' sense of humor," he said, and led them into a stairwell that
was old stone and new wood, stained and polished.

"Observe: we are on the ground level, behind the lesser tower of
the east wall. Behind there is Mistress Tanya's bedroom; not to be
entered without permission."

He began climbing the spiral staircase, slowly and with pauses for
breath. "At least I will no longer have to climb these stairs . . . The
second floor, library. Not to be entered unless you have the privilege.
And here—the office."

The door swung open, and they blinked into bright daylight. The
office was a room fifteen feet by thirty, the last ten jutting out onto
the final stage of the square tower that formed the southeast corner
of the manor. It had originally been open between the rectangular roof
and the waisthigh balustrade; the renovations had closed it in with
sliding panels of glass. They had been pushed back, and a pleasant
scent of cut grass and damp earth was blowing in. Bookcases and filing
cabinets lined the walls; two desks flanked the entrance, neatly arrayed
with ledgers, blotters, adding machines, pens, telephones.

"Where you will work," Lebrun said. He walked forward to the tower
section. "The owners' desks. Mistress Tanya uses this as a studio, as
well; she says the light is good." His cane tapped on the smooth brown

tile; he settled himself with a sigh on the cushioned divan that ran beneath the windows.

Marya stepped up to look at the canvases on the walls: landscapes, several portraits of a dark-haired Draka girl in her teens. Two paintings were propped on easels. One was completed; it showed a man standing nude beside a swimming pool in bright sunlight. *Master Edward*, she thought. *But younger.* Younger and without the scars, water beading on brown-tanned skin and outlining a long-legged athlete's body of taut muscle, broad-shouldered and thick armed without being heavy. The other was three-quarters complete, a watercolor of a nude female figure lying on a white blanket beneath a vine trellis of pale mauve wisteria. The treatment was free, the brush strokes almost Impressionist, sensuous contrasts of dappled sunlight, flesh tones, hair.

"My daughter," Lebrun said, pointing with his cane. "I am, I fear, something of a disappointment to her, hard as she wheedled to get me this position. She *will* persist in believing that I will live another twenty years; only natural, in one who has lost so much." He peered shrewdly at Chantal. "Ah, Mademoiselle Lefarge, you are thinking that there is not one of us who has not lost much. Remember, if you please, that each of us has his breaking point, the unendurable thing."

He waved a hand at their expressions, shaking his head and settling his head back into the cushions, eyes closed. Then they opened, rheumy but sharp. "Please, *mesdames*, no pity." Slowly: "I have regrets enough, myself, but no complaints . . . I was born in 1885, did you know? In Paris; ah, Paris before the Great War . . . they do not call it *la belle epoque* for nothing. It was truly a golden age—not that we thought so at the time!" Another shake of the head. "Every generation thinks its own youth was a period like no other; mine had the misfortune to be right." Silence for a moment.

"We were very arrogant . . . we believed in Reason and Democracy, and greatly in Science; together they would abolish war and poverty, unlock the secrets of the Universe, exempt us from history." A dry laugh. "Indeed, history has come to an end, but not as we imagined. Not as we *could* imagine. I was born into the pinnacle of Western civilization, and I have lived to see it fall by its own folly. When I was a young man, the Domination was no more than a cloud on the horizon, an African anachronism that had somehow acquired the knack of machine industry."

His hand tightened on the head of the cane. "Our god Progress would destroy them, we thought. Which it would have done, of a certainty, had we not committed deicide; here in the heartland of enlightenment we made the Great War, and Hitler's war which was nothing but its sequel. *That* was what let the barbarians inside the walls: we were undermined from within, we conquered ourselves, we Europeans. And so I will die a slave, and my child and my grandchildren after her." He paused. "The Draka . . . they are an abominable people, in the mass if not always as individuals. But do not blame them for what has happened; blame us, us old men. *We* deserve our fate although you do not. I have seen a world die, and while watching this new one being born has a certain academic interest"—he rose, his gaze going to the door at the rear of the room—"I can see what it must become, and have no desire to live in it."

Louder, in English: "Good morning, Mistress. I trust you slept well?"

Tanya von Shrakenberg yawned as she padded into the room on silent bare feet, feeling a pleasant early-morning drowsiness. She had never been able to sleep past sunrise, no matter how late the night before. *Six hours is plenty*, she thought, as the two new wenches made awkward attempts at the half bow of informality, and she took another bite of the peach in her right hand.

"Mornin', Jules," she said. "Slept well enough, when I did." Tanya finished the peach and flicked the stone across the room with a snap of her wrist. It struck the metal of the wastebasket with a crack and pattered down to the bottom in fragments; she pulled a kerchief from one sleeve of the loose Moorish-style djellaba she wore to wipe hands and mouth.

What I really want is bacon and hominy, she thought. *And another two cups of coffee. And a cigarette.* That would be against the doctor's orders, though; cut down on the caffeine, no tobacco, restrict the fats and salts, limit the alcohol . . . *Shit, the things I do for the Race*, she thought. *Can't even ball with my husband.* She grinned and rubbed a red mark on the side of her neck: there were some remarkably pleasant alternatives . . .

Tanya walked past the elderly Frenchman and leaned a knee against the divan. There was lawn below, and then low beds of flowers where the ancient moat had been filled in a century before. She squinted against the young sun beyond, as it outlined the beeches and poplars of the gardens that separated the manor from the first belt of orchards; light broke through the leaves with a flickering dazzle, a nimbus about shadow-black trunks and branches, and the birds were loud. She had spent some time learning them: the hollow cry of hoopoes, golden orioles fluffing or giving their distinctive raucous cat-screams. Tanya laid a hand on her stomach. *Someday I will bring you here, little one, and teach you how to read the birds' songs*, she thought.

To work. She turned to the serfs. "Relax," she said. "You're goin' to be livin' under my roof the rest of your days; get used to talkin' to me. Relax."

The nun already had, to a schooled implacable calm that would waste no energy. *Twenty-seven,* Tanya thought. *Probably too old to ever be completely tamed.* A pity; she was brave and intelligent, the most difficult type to train, but the most valuable if you could. Chantal was easier to read and would be easier to handle, in the long run: a fiery type full of hatred. Tight rein and rope, spur her and let her break heart and spirit against it. Tanya considered her more carefully, and called up memories from the inspection at Lyon: sullen pouting mouth, full dark-nippled breasts, tucked-in waist, round buttocks and thighs, and a neatly thatched bush. *Lush little Latin bunch of grapes*, she thought consideringly; at the best age for her type, too—the bloom went quickly. *And just the sort of filly Edward likes to ride. I'll remind him when she's had a few weeks to rest up; a little regular tuppin' and a few babies could be just what's needed to get her tamed down and docile.*

"Well," she said. "Jules here understands the workin's well enough; just doesn't have the energy for it. He'll stay to show you the books for a week or two; an' you can come to me or Mastah Edward with problems. Here."

She walked to one side of the room, where bamboo-framed maps were hinged along one edge to the wall, and began flipping through them like a deck of cards.

"These are overhead maps of the plantation, done up from aerial photographs an' the old French survey maps; shows all the field boundaries, crops, buildin's, an' so forth. An' this"—she swung open the stack to expose one in the middle—"is how it'll look in fifteen years, when we've finished. The ones in between are year-by-year plans for the alterations." They clicked by, movement like a time-exposure photograph. Fields flowed into each other, and new hedgerows ringed them, arranged into a simpler pattern of larger plots. Internal roads snaked out from the manor and its dependencies; watering ponds and stock dams; the scatter of farmsteads and hamlets vanished, consolidated into a large village to the southeast of the Great House, except for a tiny clump at the north end of the map, where low hills marked the boundary of the property.

"Bourgueil," she said. "That's the old winery an' the caves they used for storage. Those hillsides are the best fo' quality vines."

A quick riffle past the maps. "So, with these we can tell what's to be planted, where, at any given time, what buildin' projects are to be completed when, an' so forth. Now, these show the manor, Quarters and outbuildings; as they were when we arrived, then at six-month intervals, up to completion in five years or so. This here is an overall view of the Loire Valley, from Decize to the sea, markin' the boundaries of the plantations and where the towns and cities will be." It was an emptier landscape than the present, the scatter of smaller towns gone, the woods spreading farther.

"Over here," she continued, "are the personnel files. Complete personal records on every serf, updated monthly or as needed. This set with the combination lock contains the passes serfs have t' carry off the property. These are the supply ledgers . . ."

Marya sat and strained to absorb the information; it would be best to be efficient. The accounting system was well organized, easy to understand. Very routinized, designed to function almost automatically once the decision makers had set a policy.

" . . . an' these-here are the inflow-outflow ledgers," Tanya concluded. "Mostly from the Landholders' League—that's the cooperative agency. We send them bulk produce, they process an' market it; we order supplies an' tools, they deliver. Debits an' credits're automatic 'n' itemized, sent round from League regional HQ in Tours. Over time, we'll most likely have other outlets; estate-bottled wine an' fresh produce direct to restaurants an' suchlike." She sketched in the other equipment: the photo reducer to prepare microfilms for storage and the appropriate governmental agencies, the teleprinter, the brand-new photocopier.

"Now," Tanya said, "I, my husband, or one of the overseers will generally be spendin' a few hours a day in here, but you two'll be doin' most of the routine work—I may buy another clerk if it piles up. The headman down in the Quarters has two bookkeepin' staff of his own, an' they'll be coordinatin' with you. Detailed check by one of us once a week, and the League audit is twice yearly. You work eight to seven, half-hour for lunch—it'll be brought up—five days and a half-day Saturday with the usual holidays; as long as the work gets done, we're pretty relaxed."

A smile. "If it *doesn't* get done, there are punishments rangin' from bendin' bare-ass over a chair fo' a few licks with a belt to things you'd really rather not know about." She pointed a finger at Marya. "You're in charge; that makes yo respons'ble for errors by Chantal as well as your own. Chantal, remember your sister; both of you, remember that you could be scullions or fieldhands." A warmer expression. "That's the pain side; if things go well, plenty of, hmm, incentives. Not least, smooth-runnin' plantation easier for everybody, serf an' free alike."

As she turned to go, Marya spoke. "Mistress?"

The Draka stopped and glanced her way.

"What is that?" Marya pointed; a plinth: waisthigh, covered with a white cloth.

"Ah, one of mah attempts at sculpture. 'Bout finished."

The Draka pulled the cloth free. Beneath was the model of a tank, about a meter long. Painted clay, the nun assumed, although it had the authentic dull gray and mottle sheen of armorplate in camouflage markings. A Hond III, a squarish rectangle of sloped plates with a huge oblong cast turret—one of the midwar models, judging by the sawtooth skirting plates protecting the suspension: a commander's craft, from the extra whip antennae bobbing above the turret. A very good model. Detailed down to the individual shells in the ammunition belts of the machine-gun pod over the commander's hatch, cool brass gleams. And it showed combat damage, one of the forward track-guards twisted and torn, gouges, mud and dust spatters on the unit insignia of the Archonal Guard, and . . .

The nun's face went white with the shock of recognition. Tanya's was fluid with surprise for an instant, and then she stepped forward to pull off the Pole's kerchief. Snapping it through the air she held it over Marya's head, imitating the wimple of a nun's habit.

"Almighty Thor," she said wonderingly, shaking her head. Marya stared at her with mute horror. "We've met. Ahhh . . . '43, late summer. That village—"

Chapter Eight

Warsaw was burning. The cone of it was a ruddy glow on the darkening eastern horizon, matching the huge copper disk of the setting sun in the west. Even at this distance the firestorm gave a smoky taste to the wind, a hint of that sulfur-tinged darkness, the taste of death. The flicker and rumble of artillery were faint, no louder than the hiss of grain stalks against the steel flanks of the Draka armor hull-down on the low crest overlooking the village. Four dozen of them, squat massive shapes in mottled green-yellow camouflage paint with the mailed-fist symbol of the Archonal Guard Legion stenciled on their bows. Their engines thrummed, the roar of free-piston gas generators blending with the power turbine's hum. Air quivered over the exhaust baffles on their rear decks, and the whip antennae swayed erratically in the breeze.

Loki take the heat, Cohortarch Tanya von Shrakenberg thought, and rubbed a gloved hand over the wet skin of her neck. She glanced back over the rear of the command tank, through the narrow gap left by the hatch cover poised over her head like a steel mushroom-cap.

Behind them trails stretched two kilometers south to the woodlot where the unit had last paused. Broad parallel stripes where the treads had pulped grain and stalk into the earth, arcs and circles across the rolling plain showing where the fighting vehicles had maneuvered. Ten minutes of combat, and the taste of it was still in her mouth, salt and iron and copper, acid in the stomach, ache in the muscles of neck and back. Training helped, *prahna* breathing and muscle control, the simple knowledge that the job had to be done whatever the state of your emotions . . . and still, every time you knew a little something was gone. A little of whatever it was that kept you functioning while you waited for the armor to buckle under the brute impact of an antitank shell and send spalls flying like supersonic buzzsaws, for the millisecond flame of exploding ammunition, for the slower trickle of

burning fuel as you hammered at a jammed hatch. You survived, and
lost a little of yourself from within, and knew that one day, if you
kept coming, the well would be dry. . . .

The German armor was scattered back there among the ruined corn,
burning with the sullen flicker of diesel oil in circles of blackened straw,
or frozen with only the narrow entry hole of a tungsten-carbide
penetrator rod to show reason for immobility. The *pakfront* of Fritz
antitank guns had been dug in along the crest of this . . . not really
a ridge, more a gentle swelling.

The Cohortarch shook her head; they were expecting to lie low as
their armor pulled back past them to the village, then hit the Draka
tanks as they pursued, no doubt. A good trick, but one she had met
before; the Fritz were like that: fine tacticians but a little inflexible.
Artillery to suppress the antitank, then a slow advance to force the
Fritz armor to engage at ranges where Draka APDS shot would punch
through German tanks the long way. Bodies lay hidden in the tall grain
or draped around shattered half-tracks; her infantry had hunted them
down from the turrets and firing ports of their combat carriers. Two
Draka Hond III's remained, victims of shells fired point-blank through
the thinner armor of flank and rear, the blanket-shrouded corpses of
their crews showing victory could kill you as finally as defeat.

Moisture trickled out of the sodden lining of the communications
helmet as Tanya turned from the wreckage to her rear and made a
slow scan of the wheatfield ahead.

The thick armor of a Hond soaked up heat like a sponge under direct
sunlight. There was a lot of that in the Polish summer, and she would
swear firing the main gun racked up another five degrees with every
round. The ventilation fans continued their losing battle; the *Baalbeck
Belle* had been buttoned up for more than ten hours, in the line for
over a month with scant time for anything but essential maintenance.
The inside of the tank was heavy with the smells: lubricant, burnt
propellant and scorched metal, old sweat; an empty shellcasing off in
one corner of the turret basket was half full of urine with a couple
of used menstrual pads floating in it . . . She ignored it, as she ignored
the salt itch of her unwashed uniform and the furry texture of her
teeth and the ground-glass feeling under eyelids from too little sleep
and too much exposure to abrasive fumes.

It could be worse, she mused, glancing down at the swivel-mounted
map tray on the left arm of her reclining seat, past it into the white-
painted gloom of the tank's interior. There was not much open space;
the huge breech and recoil mechanism of the main cannon cut the
turret's interior nearly in half, flanked on either side by the coaxial
machine gun and grenade launcher. Dials, gauges and armored conduits snaked over every surface. The gunner lay to the right of her
weapon nearly prone on a crashcouch that raised her head just enough
to meet the padded eyepiece of episcope and sights. Behind the gunner's
head was the sliding armorplate door that blocked off the ammunition stored in the turret bustle, ready to the hand of the loader on
his swivel-seat below.

Economy of space was the formal term; it took considerable training to move even in a stationary tank without bruising yourself, and there was barely enough open space to tape snapshots of her husband and children below the vision blocks of the commander's cupola. Still, better than the infantry . . .

Could be much worse; the Fritz could be using nerve gas again. Which would mean everybody into those damned rubber suits, and *that* would mean casualties from heat prostration, even among Draka.

She rapped the heel of one hand against the pressure plate beneath the vision blocks, and the hatch cover snapped upright with a sough of hydraulics. The lift-brace-step motion that left her standing on the turret deck with boots astride the hatch was nearly as unconscious as walking, after two years in the field. Wind blew into her face as she raised the field glasses, warm and dry, dusty and much, much cleaner than the air in the tank; the sodden fabric of her overalls turned cool as the moving air let sweat evaporate.

Still alive, she thought. On a fine summer's day, in the odd alien beauty of the Baltic twilight, like a world seen through amber honey; and it was good to feel the faint living quiver in the sixty-ton bulk beneath the soles of her feet.

Reliable old bitch, she thought affectionately. The *Belle* had carried her a long way since the spring of '42. North from the Caucasus, over the Don, west across the Ukraine, through the murderous seesaw winter battles around Lwow. Wherever the Supreme General Staff thought the Domination's best armored Legion was needed . . . Eighteen months, a long lifetime for a tank, even counting weeks in the Legion repair shops and a complete rebuild; there were scars and gouges on the sloped plates of the armor, two dozen victory rings on the thermal cover of the long 120mm cannon, Fritz skull still wearing its SS helmet on a spike welded to the fume extractor.

The reverse slope to the village was gentle; this part of the Vistula valley was water-smoothed, sandy alluvial loam. Ripe wheat, a big field of it, fifty or sixty hectares, bordered by a row of poplars; more of those lining the country road or serving as field boundaries beyond. The grain was overripe, gold turning brown in spots and the over-burdened stalks falling in swales, and the field was scattered with wildflowers and thistles.

Damned waste, a Landholder's corner of her mind noted. *Lost if it isn't harvested soon.* Three thousand meters to the north a white dirt road crossed the river that wound tree-bordered through the dry summer landscape, and the junction had spawned a straggling farm town. Trees, unpaved streets lined with fences and gardens and whitewashed log homes, barns, a few brick structures around the flamboyantly painted stone church. Past it . . . heat haze and dust cut visibility, so did the long shadows of evening; woodlot, could be a manor house, hedges and gardens. Beyond were more fields, patches of forest, vanishing northward into the dusty horizon.

Hmmmm, question is, was that half-hard feint their idea of a rear guard, or is there more in the village?

Orders were to consolidate once she met solid resistance. Then the Janissary motorized infantry would pass through and establish a perimeter; the serf soldiers were good enough at positional warfare, and the Citizen Force legions were supposed to save themselves for shock and pursuit. It was a big war, too big to be won in a single rush; you got weaker as you advanced away from your bases, and the enemy stronger as they fell back on theirs. The Fritz had been soundly beaten east of the Vistula, but without Hitler to order senseless last stands they had withdrawn in good order, their mechanized forces screening the foot-infantry's retreat; von Mehr, the German commander of Army Group Center, was a master at luring an attacker to over-extend and then catching him with a backhand stroke. It was time to halt, refit, bring up supplies for the next leap.

It never paid to underestimate the Fritz tactically, either; Germans tended to fight by the book, but the one they used was excellent, and there could be anything ahead. Tanya tapped a meditative thumb against her lower lip, then returned attention to the hum and crackle of voices in her ears; habit strained it out, unless her call sign came through. She keyed the intercom circuit: "Call to Bugeye, Sparks," she said. A click, a warble, then the sound of an airplane engine.

"Check, Groundpound to Bugeye, that's negative on movement, over."

"Affirm'tive, Groundpound. Nary nothin' but dead cows an' that-there wrecked convoy I spotted earlier, over."

And the convoy had been moving away from here northwest toward the Fritz hedgehog around Chelmno when the ground-strike aircraft caught them.

Worth it, she decided. Plaster the village with HE, cut in with a pincers movement, then halt. The low ground along the river would make a good stop zone. *Damn I wish I wasn't so tired*, ran through her. Hard to make proper decisions when body and mind and soul together whined for rest; harder still when the lives of friends and comrades depended on it. *No tremendous hurry*, she reminded herself. The village looked deserted, no human movement at all, which meant everyone there had already gone to ground. She blinked again, fasci-nated for a moment by the quality of the light, the wash of a . . . *faded gold?* Bright, but aged somehow, as if the view had been worn down by the impress of too many eyes. Tired light.

Back to the work of the season, she thought. No point in getting too fancy, but just in case . . .

"Command circuit," she said. That would cut into the headphones of all her officers. "Orders, mark." She flicked up the mapboard hanging from her waist, glanced at it, sideways at the turretless observation tank with its forest of antennae and episcopes; they would be in constant touch with the fire-support tetrarchy. "Century A . . ." she began.

The village was thick with smoke. The ground quivered under the bombardment, shook from the hundreds of tons of tread-mounted metal moving through the laneways, cast itself up as dust and fragments; the sounds of lesser weapons were a counterpoint, machine-gun chatter and the ripping canvas sounds of grenade launchers spewing out their belts of 40mm bomblets.

The explosions were continuous overhead, seven rounds a second

from the Flail automortars four kilometers to the south. Their proximity fuses blew them at an even six meters above the ground, the
rending *crang* of explosive and overpressure thumping like a drum
against the sternum. Tanya kept her mouth open to spare her eardrums
and ignored the occasional sandblast rattle of fragments against the
armor of the *Belle*; the odds of something dangerous flicking through
the narrow gap between the turret deck and the hatch cover over her
head were too small to be worth the effort of worry.

Besides, if you let yourself think of danger in a situation where it
was everywhere and inescapable, you froze. And that *was* dangerous.

The Draka fighting vehicles ground down the street in line, tanks
and Hoplite personnel carriers alternating; a fairly wide street, mud
mixed with cobbles—more mud than cobbles, and those disappeared
under the treads with a tooth-grating squeal of metal on stone. Tanya
kept her eyes moving constantly, probing the dense gray-white mist
for movement; anybody waiting with a *Panzerfaust* was going to have
to stay under cover until the last minute, or be scythed down by the
mortar rounds; and at ground level, their visibility would be even worse
than hers. The *Belle* had a round of *wasp* up the spout of the main
gun, like a giant shotgun shell loaded with steel darts, but the twin-
barrel 15mm machine gun in its servo-controlled armored pod beside
her hatch was better for this work.

Flickers, adrenaline-hopping vision, presenting each glimpse as a
separate freeze-frame. Roof collapsing inwards, sparks and floating
burning straw. A crippled pig, shrilling loud enough to hear as a tread
ground it into a waffle of meat and mud. A square of ground lifting
and spilling dirt off the board cover of a concealed foxhole, a man
coming erect, blond hair and gray uniform and white-rimmed eyes stark
against dirt-black face.

And the tube of a rocket launcher over his shoulder. "Target, six
o'clock, *Panzerfaust*," she rasped, her voice too hoarse to carry emotion. Her hand was twisting at the pistol grips on the arms of her
seat, and the twin barrel pivoted whining above her head; she walked
the burst toward him, the heavy 15mm slugs blasting fist-sized craters in the mud. Too slow, too slow, she was close enough to *see* his
hand clenching on the release . . .

CRACK. The main gun fired. The whole weight of the tank rocked
back on its suspension as the trunnions and hydraulics transmitted the
huge muzzle-horsepower of the cannon's recoil through mantlet and
hull. There was a whining buzz as the flechette rounds left the barrel, like their namesake wasp magnified a thousand thousand times.
The Fritz infantryman vanished, caught by sheer chance within the
dispersal cone. Not ten meters from the muzzle, blast alone would have
killed him; the long finned spikes left nothing but chewed stumps of
legs falling in opposite directions, and hardly even a smear on the
riddled wood behind him, a circle of thick log wall turned to a crumbling honeycomb by the passage of the darts.

The *Panzerfaust*'s bomb had already been launched. Deflected, it
caromed off the slope of the sow-snout mantlet that surrounded the
tank's cannon, the long jet of flame and copper reduced to plasma

gouging a crackling red trough along the side of the turret rather than spearing through the armor. The blue-white spike hung in afterimage before her eyes, blinking in front of the sullen red of the wounded metal.

That was a brave man, she thought. The Fritz would make magnificent Janissaries, once they were broken to the yoke. A brave man who had come within half a second of trading five Draka lives for his own. *Odd, fear really does feel like a cold draft.* A flush like fever on the face and shoulders and neck, tightness across the eyes, then cold along the upper spine. Deliberately, she suppressed the memory of burn victims, of calcinated bone showing through charred flesh, and equipment melted onto human skin. No practical thickness of steel could stop a square hit from a shaped-charge warhead.

"Nice," she said over the intercom, forcing an overtight rectum to relax.

"Th' iron was just pointin' fight," the gunner drawled.

"Load—" Tanya began.

"Shit!" The voice was tinny in her earphones, override from Century A's commander back on the ridge. "There's somethin' still firin' from in theah, and whatevah it is, still goin' too fast over my head! Permission to return fire on the muzzle flash."

"—load APDS," she continued on the intercom circuit, and switched to broadcast. "Permission denied." That would be *all* they needed, a hail of armor-piercing shot at extreme range from their own guns. Below her came multiple chunk-clank sounds: she glanced down to see the round slide into the breech, a two-inch core of copper-tipped tungsten carbide, wrapped in the circular aluminum sabot. "Sparks, general override circuit." She heard the radiotech's voice calling for attention, and spoke into the hissing silence.

"Groundpound talkin'. Support battery, *cease fire.*" Silence, as the noise dropped below the level she could hear through ears ringing with blast and muffled by the headset. She looked to either side, at the burning log huts; down the empty curving road that lead to the straggling green along the river and the only substantial buildings in this mudhole of a town. Mist curled, patchy as it caught the gathering evening wind, touched with gold in the long slanting rays of a northern-hemisphere twilight.

"Everyone in the village, back yourselves into some cover. Tetrarch de la Roche," she continued. Tanya had brought a Century of mechanized infantry with her; four Tetrarchies, a little over a hundred troopers at full strength.

"Yo, ma'am?"

"Johnny, un-ass your beasts and scout the square. Look-see only, I think there's somethin' big, mean an' clumsy there."

There was a series of muffled *thungs* as the powered rear ramps of the personnel carriers went down, and she could see helmets bobbing into the fog. Only six from the Hoplite behind the *Belle,* when there should have been eight; every unit in the Cohort was under strength, casualties coming in faster than replacements . . . She reached down and flicked a cigarette out of the carton in the rack beside her seat, lit it, drew the warm comfort into her lungs. There had been very little in the village by way of resistance, probably no time for the Fritz commander to set it up. Whatever was firing at Century A up on the ridge had been left behind, waiting for her to advance downslope, and had been unable to reorient enough to engage the Guard's tanks as they came in from each flank under cover of smoke.

A *Jagdpanzer* then, a limited-traverse antitank gun in the bow of a turretless tank. The Germans used them extensively; they were less flexible than a real tank but well suited to defensive action and much easier to manufacture, a quick cheap way to get a heavy well-protected gun onto the battlefield. This was probably one of the bigger ones, a waddling 70-ton underpowered monster mounting a modified antiairship gun.

A typical Fritz improvisation. She snorted smoke and patted the armor of the *Belle* lovingly; TechSec had taken the time to get this design *right.* Of course, Hitler hadn't come to power until 1932, not much time to prepare for war, and even then had not dared squeeze the German people the way the Domination could the righteous chattel who made up nine-tenths of its population. Occupied Europe could have made the difference, if the National Socialists had waited a generation or so, but no, they had to throw for double or nothing. . . . *At least the Race knows enough not to bite off more than we can chew. I hope.*

"Johnny here," the infantry officer replied.

"Yo." She snapped alert and flicked the cigarette out between hatch and turret. An infantry backpack radio, you could tell because the receiver let through more background noise than the shielded microphone of a commo helmet.

"Got as close's Ah could. There was lookouts, we went in and took 'em out quiet. Three big buildin's in a row, north side over from the church, look-so maybe brick warehouses; rooflines cut off the view of the ridge we jumped off from. Holes in the walls, treadmarks comin' back to a common point from all three; whatever it is, it *heavy.* Big smeared place where the tracks meet."

"Good. Pull back now, meet me here."

Tanya pinched thumb and forefinger to the bridge of her nose, concentrating. An *Elefant* for sure, the only Fritz vehicle with firepower and protection in the same class as a Draka Hond III, but limited by the lack of a rotating turret, painfully slow, even more painfully difficult to turn in tight quarters. The three buildings formed the base of a triangle, covered fire positions commanding the open country south of the village. By backing out to the triangle's apex the *Jagdpanzer* could switch quickly without having to do more than a quarter-turn; her respect for the probably deceased commander of the certainly defunct German battalion increased. He had had the sense to use the *Elefant* as a self-propelled antitank gun, rather than as a fighting vehicle, which its designers had intended it to be and which it most manifestly was not. If she had simply blasted through the first line of antitank guns up on the ridge and come straight down the hill, there would have been a *very* nasty surprise waiting.

Now, what would the *Elefant*'s commander do? *Run away, as Montinesque said any rational army would,* she thought wryly.

That was easier said than done, though, in something that could do maybe forty kph on a good level road; also, their back was to a soft-bottomed river. That was a problem Tanya von Shrakenberg could empathize with wholeheartedly. The Hond III had range, it had speed, it had broad tracks and a good suspension that let it cover any ground firm enough to hold a foot soldier's boots, but the only bridges that could carry it safely were major rail links or the Domination's own Combat-Engineer units. The *Elefant* would be even more of a pain to move any distance, and across a soft-bottomed riverbed . . .

There had been a *lot* of rivers to cross, coming west.

Better to catch him while Century A back on the ridge kept his attention; that *Jagdpanzer* was nothing to meet head-on at point-blank range in one of these laneways. She looked up again, whistling soundlessly between her teeth and wishing she had not thrown away the cigarette, wishing the *Belle* was not best placed, less than two hundred meters from the church. Not that anyone would doubt her courage if she sent someone else; a coward would not have achieved her rank. The Draka had a firm unwritten tradition of seeing that such did not live long enough to breed and weaken the Race. The trouble was that they had an equally firm tradition of leading from the front . . .

The infantry Tetrarch came trotting back up the laneway, keeping to the side beside the fence with his comtech at his heels; he bounced up onto the glacis plate of the *Belle* without breaking stride and vaulted to the turret with a hand on the cannon.

Tanya popped the hatch to vertical and handed him a cigarette. "Don't suppose you could tell which of those three buildin's the *Jagdpanzer*'s in now?"

"Not without we send in a *lochos*'r two, or they move position, Tanya." He puffed meditatively. "Could try an' get a rocket gun team in close; likely to cost, though." A grin. "Prefer to let you turtles butt heads with it. Fuckin' nightmare, eh?"

"Isn't it always," she replied with a sour smile. There was little formality of rank in the Citizen Force, and anyway they were old friends. Both from Landholding families as well—all Citizens were aristocrats, of course, but there was still a certain difference between urban bureaucrats and engineers and schoolteachers and the Old Domination, the planters and their retainers. Many younger gentry favored the Guard for their military service, since it was kept at full strength in peacetime and saw more action. There were five hundred troopers in the Cohort; counting families, that represented a million hectares of land and a hundred thousand serfs.

Tetrarch John de la Roche was two years younger than her twenty-five, but he no longer looked like a young man. It wasn't just the weathering and ground-in oily dirt and caked dust; there was something, a look about the eyes, a weariness that no amount of rest could ever completely erase. A familiar look. She had grown up seeing it in the men of the older generation. *Pa had it, sometimes. Seeing it in the mirror more than I like, lately.* They had met back in the '30s, when he was posted to her *lochos* as a recruit; she had been a Monitor then, sub-squad commander. Her father had known his in the Great War. He was smart and quick and learned well, was handsome in a bony blond way. They had become friends. She had gone to hunt lion on his family's sprawling cattle-and-cotton spread in equatorial Kasai, he had visited her father's plantation under the Lebanon range and chased gazelle in the Syrian desert. They had made love a few times, once in a sandwich with a serf wench—that had been amusing . . . friends, they had all been friends when it started. Comrades now, the ones who were left, and the replacements all looked so *young*.

By the White Christ, were we ever that young? she thought briefly. The infantry officer lit another cigarette from his and handed it back to his radio operator; the comtech followed him to the turret deck, a short dark-haired woman careful to keep the set within arm's reach of her commander.

"Ride me in, Johnny," Tanya said. "As near to the brick buildings as you can"—that would give her a chance to take the *Jagdpanzer* with a flank shot as it backed out—"and I'd like to be inconspicuous." Which was difficult if you knocked down houses. "But don't forget to dodge out when we get there."

He snorted laughter and rang the back of his hand against the turret. "Surely will," he said. "These movin' foxholes attract the eye."

She touched the microphone before her mouth. "Sparks, command circuit." A click. "Noise, everybody; rev the engines and move in place." Another click. "Sammi, you take the western approach to the square behind the buildings. McLean, you're north. We'll all three go in together, that ways somebody should get a good flankin' shot."

"Groundpound to Century A," Tanya whispered, and cursed herself for the tone; nobody was going to hear a voice over the racket. The *Baalbeck Belle* was only one house away from the green, a house whose caved-in thatch was still smoldering; the *Elefant* would be there, under cover, still facing south for its inconclusive duel with the tanks of Century A, hulldown on the ridge . . . Three Draka tanks would advance into the square where they could pound the German vehicle cover or no; hers from the east, two more from north and west, any more and there would be too much chance of a shot going astray. Point-blank range, no place to be on the wrong end of a Hond's 120mm rifle.

"He's in the center buildin'; commence firin', HE," she continued in a normal speaking tone. The Century of tanks back on the ridge to the south opened up, she could hear the whirrrrrrr*crash* of high-explosive shot bursting along the fringe of the village. Her teeth clenched; now she would have to move, out into the open . . . *Almighty Thor, but I don't want to do this*, she thought. Not fear, so much as sheer weariness and distaste. The pictures of her children caught her eye, there down below the vision blocks. Solemn in their school tunics, red-haired Gudrun with a mask of sunbred freckles across her face, Timmie tanned dark under his butter-yellow curls; she had promised them she would come back.

If I have to kill every living thing between here and the Atlantic to do it, she thought grimly, took a long breath and spoke:

"Sammi, McLean. Now!"

The engine howled behind her, and she felt the tank lurch as the driver engaged the gearing, rocking her shoulders back against the padded rear surface of the hatch. The *Belle* accelerated smoothly, then slammed into the thick log wall, the bow rising as the tread cleats bit and tried to climb the vertical surface. Her braced hands kept her from flinging forward as sixty tons of moving steel clawed at the wood, and it gave with a rending, crackling snap. The tank lurched again, rocking from side to side as the torsion bars of the suspension adjusted to the uneven surface. A brief glimpse of tables and beds vanishing beneath tumbled logs, and a shuddering *whump* as the surface caved in a few feet; a clash of epicyclic gearing and the engine snarled again, a deeper sound under the turbine's whine.

The front wall burst out from the *Belle*'s prow in a shower of fragments, and she ducked her head as a last surf of broken wood came tumbling and rattling up the glacis plate and over the turret. Splinters caught on the shoulders of her uniform. The tank pivoted left and south, the turret moving faster than the treads could turn the hull; to the north and west the other two Honds were grinding into the churned mud of the square. The muzzles of their cannon moved like the heads of blind serpents, questing for prey. Tanya scanned the center building: that had to be it. Two stories of brick, square windows, a gaping hole where the main door had to have been. The roof had settled, sagging in the middle; but it was the entrance that mattered, there where the track marks emerged. Nothing, and—

An explosion. Not loud, a sharp cracking from the northern edge. Her head turned. The center tank of the trio had lost a track. It pivoted wildly, the intact loop of metal pushing it in a circle as the broken tread flopped to lie like a giant metal watchband on the mud, curling and settling as gravity and tension unlooped it.

"Shit, mines! McLean, bail out! Sammi, back under cover." *Shit, shit, they must've turned the Jagdpanzer around to face north; the donkey-fuckers outthought me!* Tanya's mind ran through a brief litany of disgust as the *Belle* slammed to a too-swift halt, nosed down and rocked back. The engine bellowed, and the driver reversed along their own tracks with careful haste; it did not take a large charge to snap a tread, and a stationary tank was a deathtrap.

McLean's *Sofia Sweetheart* stopped, and the hatches opened. "Coverin' fire," Tanya rasped. Two dozen automatic weapons opened up on the buildings across the square and the whole facade erupted in dust and chips and sparks, slugs punching holes through the brick and gnawing at the wall, like a time-lapse film of erosion at work. Then the infantry weapons, assault rifles and the white-fire streaks of rocket guns. From the ridge south of town came a multiple whirr*crash* as the reserve Tetrarchy opened up with high-explosive shell, most falling well short. Then a shadow moved within the black openings of the building, a long horizontal shadow tipped with the bulky oblong of a double-baffle muzzle brake.

"Sue, can you take him?" Tanya asked, voice carefully controlled.

Somebody else was trying; she could see the cannon of a Hond moving, then the flare and crack.

"Might ought." McLean's crew were crawling back into the shadow of their crippled vehicle, two of them dragging a third. "Tricky." The main gun moved in its gyro-controlled cradle, a faint humming whine as the mantlet moved, the breech riding up smoothly.

The *Belle*'s commander slitted her eyes against the flash of the main gun. There was a metal-on-metal sparking from the darkness where the *Elefant* waited, a high brief screech of steel deforming under the impact of tungsten traveling at thousands of feet per second.

Tanya opened her mouth to speak, but before the words passed her throat there was another crash, louder than the Draka tank-cannon, less sharp, a lower-velocity weapon. But the German antitank round was still moving fast enough when it struck the *Sofia Sweetheart* at the junction of turret and hull. The Draka tank lurched, and the turret's massive twenty-ton weight flipped backward like a frying pan. Tanya watched with an angry foreknowledge as it dropped straight down on the two crewmen hauling the wounded driver. A leg was left sticking out from under the heavy steel, and it twitched half a dozen times with galvanic lifelessness.

"Century A," she barked. "Target the center building an' knock it down, HE only. Everybody here in the village who's got a vantage, load APDS an' stay under cover." The *Elefant* would have to come out sometime or be buried under rubble. Thick armor on the front, heavily sloped, good protection; too good, as long as it had cover. Out in the open . . .

Just a stay of execution, Fritz, she thought grimly.

Senior Decurion Smythe saluted as she came up to the *Belle*. Tanya had been leaning back against the scarred side-skirts of the tank, looking with sour satisfaction at the burning hulk of the German *Jagdpanzer*; she came erect and returned the salute. Smythe was like that, a long-service regular. Forty, old enough to have started her military service back before women were allowed in combat units; green eyes in a leather-tanned face, a close-cropped cap of gray-shot black hair.

"Ten fatalities altogether since morning roll call, Cohortarch," the NCO said, in a faintly sing song accent. Ceylonese, Tanya remembered; her family were tea planters near Taprobanopolis. "Fifteen wounded seriously enough for evacuation. Three tanks and two APC's are write-offs . . ."

The Cohortarch cursed fluently in the Arabic picked up from serf playmates as a child; there was no better language for swearing. Smythe shrugged.

"We took out better than two hundred of them," she added. "A complete armored battalion."

"The usual odds and sods?" Tanya asked.

"Mixed *Kampfgruppe*, accordin' to the prisoners, SS, Third Panzer, bits and pieces from here and there." Tanya nodded; the battles that broke the Fritz's Army Group Center east of the Vistula had left shattered units scattered over hundreds of kilometers, and far too many had made it back to the German lines through the Domination's overstretched forces.

"Put in to hold us up whiles they pulled they infantry back," Smythe continued. "Oh, Cohortarch, about those prisoners?"

Tanya paused, clenched the fingertips of her right glove between her teeth and stripped the thin leather off. The sun was still throwing implausible veils of salmon pink to the west, and the breeze was cool on the wet skin of her hand. She removed the other glove, slapped them into a palm, looked at the enemy fighting vehicle half-buried in the ruins of the building her guns had brought down on top of it. The saw-toothed welds had come apart along their seams, and the six-inch thickness of armor plate was twisted and ripped like sheet wax. Melted fat had pooled under the shattered chassis, congealing now with a smell like rancid lard.

"How many?" she asked.

"'Bout twenty, mostly wounded."

"Hm." Tanya looked again at the wreck of the *Sofia Sweetheart*. Then again . . . "They fought well, hereabouts. We'll have to keep two or three fo' the headhunters; yo pick 'em. Give the rest a pill, do it quick." Army slang for a bullet in the back of the neck, and utter mercy compared to the attentions of Security's interrogators. She tucked the gloves into her belt, yawned, continued: "Legion HQ's word is to get out of the way, the Guard's to freeze in place; the Seventh Janissary is movin' up into the line north of us, an' the Fritz are still tryin' to break contact."

"We're goin' to let them?" the decurion asked.

"'Bout time. We should've done bettah today; the troops are tired an' they need rest. Remembah, we've got to win the war, not just beat the Fritz. A victory you destroys youself to get is a defeat. Anyways, that fo' Castle Tarleton to decide. Meantime, we set up a perimeter an' wait until they can spare transport to pull us back, minimal support till then. Prob'ly refit 'round Lublin, they've got the rail net workin' that far west by now."

She yawned again, nodded toward the little stream that ran behind the churchyard half a kilometer north. "Call TOE support, get the scissors forward." That was their bridging equipment, a hydraulic folding span on a tank chassis. "We'll laager on that-there clear spot just north of the river, less likely to be unpleasant surprises waitin'. Standard perimeter, no slackin' on the slit trenches."

"Consider it done, Cohortarch. Ahh . . . L&R?" More military slang: Loot and Rape, a parody of the official Rest and Recreation. The troops' right by ancient custom, as soon as military necessity was past.

"Loot? *Here?*" Tanya straightened and glanced about at the straggling village, burning thatch, splintered log walls, tumbled brick. "No pokin' about until it's cleared, nothin' here worth stepping on a mine fo'. No takin' wenches off in a corner, either, same reason; wait till we've got the civilians sorted." She wrinkled her nose slightly; what followed would be rather ugly, and she had never found fear an aphrodisiac. Certainly not from some cringing peasant one couldn't even talk to . . . Still, it was probably the only thing worth taking, for those so inclined.

Smythe nodded. I'll need 'bout four sticks," she said. Twenty troopers. "Church'll be best for the pen, seein's how the walls're still standin', an' solid," she continued, settling her helmet and clipping the chinstrap. Her tone had the same bored competence Tanya remembered from that time back in the Ukraine, when infiltrators had tried to overrun Cohort HQ in the night; Smythe had counterattacked with the communications technicians.

You're an odd one, Tanya thought. You got to know people quickly in combat, *needed* to. Smythe was an exception. Always polite, never a laugh, nothing more than a smile. No close friends, no lover, not even any letters from home, and she had never mentioned her family. The Guard were quartered in Archona in peacetime, in the Archon's Palace when they weren't field training on one of the military preserves. A senior NCO rated a small apartment; Smythe had kept to hers, except for the informally obligatory mess evenings, nobody there but three servants she'd brought with her from Ceylon back in the '20s. *Model noncommissioned officer*, Tanya mused. *Soul of efficiency, but not a martinet. And something like burnt-out slag behind the eyes; wonder if I could capture it . . .*

"Johnny?" she called. The Tetrarch looked up from the circle of his soldiers, rose. The others stayed, kneeling or squatting, leaning on butt-grounded assault rifles.

"Need a detail; decurion an' two sticks from you, get Laxness on the blower an' tell off the same from 2nd Tetrarchy. Pen the locals."

Chapter Nine

CHATEAU RETOUR PLANTATION
TOURAINE PROVINCE
APRIL 1947

"Yes, it's comin' back. The Fritz, that was like a hundred other skirmishes," Tanya said. "But yo, now that's a different matter, not very often somebody hands me two kilos a' plastique under a loaf of rye." Her smile was slow and broad, as she looked the nun up and down. "Y'haven't changed much, would've recognized you earlier, 'cept the penguin suit's missin'. An' the last I saw of you was you rump, goin' away." She laughed, a rich sound full of amusement, bracing her hands in the small of her back. "Who says Fate doesn't have a sense of humor?" The grin turned wolfish. "We really should talk it over, see how our recollections differ. Might be interestin'. If you remembers, that is."

Chantal and Lebrun were glancing from Marya to their owner, bewildered. Tanya was more relaxed than ever, if anything. The Pole's naturally pale complexion had gone a gray-white color; she closed her eyes for a moment, lips moving. Then they opened again, and she planted herself on her feet.

"Yes, I remember," she whispered.

KALOWICE
MAZOVIA
GOVERNMENT-GENERAL OF POLAND
AUGUST 17, 1943

Sister Marya Sokolowska crossed herself with her right hand and held the weeping child closer to her with her left. The cellar beneath the church was deep and wide, lined with brick; bodies crowded it, huddled together in the shuddering dark. Two dim lanterns did little more than catch a gleam on sweat-wet faces, stray metal, the sun-faded white of a child's hair tufting out from beneath a kerchief. Their smell was peasant-rank garlic and onions and the hard dry smell of bodies that had worked long in the sun; the noise of their breathing, prayers, moans ran beneath the throbbing hammer blows of the shells. *Remember their names*, she reminded herself. *Wojak, Jozef, Andrezej, Jolanta.* Her father had been a blacksmith in a little village like this, far to the east.

There was a new burst of shells above, three in quick succession, a bang of impact on the roof, then a *thud-CRASH* as the next two burst in the enclosed space of the nave and on the floor itself. The whole cellar seemed to sway as the lanterns swung crazily, and fresh dust filled the air. The child hugged himself against her side, as if to fold himself inside her; Marya looked down into a wide-eyed face wet with tear tracks and trails of mucus from a running nose, and reached into her sleeve for a handkerchief.

Damn them, she thought with cold hatred, as she wiped him clean and settled down with her back to a wall, setting the child on her lap and rocking gently. *Damn all the generals and dictators, all the ones who sit at tables and make marks on maps and set this loose on the people Christ died for.* These folk were poor, they raised wheat to sell for cash to pay rent and taxes and ate black rye-bread themselves, and lately there had been little enough of that. The church was the grandest building in the village and the best kept, because its people gave freely; Wojak the mason had spent two days on the roof only last month. If their own cottages were bare enough, God's house had light and warmth and beauty, and images of His mother and the holy saints, who stood between them and the awful glory of the Imminence . . .

She shook her head and glanced over at the German soldiers. They were different, controlling their fear with a show of nonchalance; she could smell them too, a musky odor of healthy young meat-fed male bodies. A dozen of them strong enough to walk, a few wounded. Most of their injured too hurt to move had suicided, a custom of the SS if they could not be evacuated.

Poor lost souls, she thought. Self-murder was certain damnation. It was hard, doubly hard for a Pole, to remember Christian charity with the hereditary enemy and oppressor. What was it Pilsudski had said? "Poor Poland: so far from God, so close to Germany and Russia." *They did not ask to be sent here.*

"Politics makes strange bedfellows, Sister," their officer said loudly, more loudly than the artillery demanded. At least, most of them did not, she thought, looking at him with distaste. An SS officer, what was his name? *Hoth*, yes; a *Hauptscharführer*, the equivalent of a captain, born near the frontier in German Silesia and with a borderer's hatred of Poles. There was alcohol on his breath, not enough for drunkenness, but too much. In daylight, his face was ten years older than his true age.

"War makes strange alliances, you mean," she replied in crisp Junker-class Prussian; the Order taught its members well. "So does defeat." *Calmly, calmly*, she told herself. Wrong to take pleasure in another's downfall, even an evil man's. Vengeance was the Lord's, He would judge.

Marya felt the SS man's tremor, rage, not fear. "A setback," he said. "We still hold everything from here to the Atlantic, and Europe is rallying to us."

There was a hard pity in the nun's voice. "Your man-god is dead, and his promises are dust," she said. "Now that you need us, no more *slawen sin sklaven*, no more slavs are slaves, eh?"

That was still a dangerous thing to say. Officially the regime in Berlin was still National Socialist; officially, Hitler's death had been from natural causes. In fact, the generals ruled the Reich now, and German Army Intelligence had killed Hitler—for good military reasons. His attack on the Soviet Union had the left Wehrmacht overextended and his crazed refusal to allow retreat had left whole armies to be encircled and destroyed when the Draka entered the war. Now the SS were barely tolerated, only the hapless and powerless Jews still left at their mercy.

The soldier gripped her shoulder, bruisingly hard. "Is your Jew god going to protect you, sow?"

"No," she said, looking down at the hand until he removed it. "His kingdom is not of this earth. And I am going to protect you, Herr Captain." She turned her head and called sharply, "Tarski!"

A shock-headed peasant came shouldering through the press, with a dozen armed men at his back; there was a German pistol thrust through the belt of his sheepskin jacket. The others drew back, and the man smiled through broken brown teeth and spat on the floor near the SS officer's boot.

"You want me to get rid of this manure, Sister?" he asked.

She shook her head. "You know the new orders from the Home Army," she said: that was the underground command. Not that they were in a position to enforce orders, but Tarski was a good man, devout and well-disciplined. Also tough and resourceful, or he would not have stayed alive in the resistance during the last three years of German occupation.

"Get them out," she continued. "Through the tunnel, then into the woods and northwest to the front lines. Everything is still in motion, it should be possible. Leave a force at the tunnel exit, north of the river, well hidden. I will try and rejoin them there, if God wills."

"Is it really needful to help these swine, Sister?" Tarski said dubiously in Polish. The German soldiers glowered back at him, helpless; without the Pole they would fall into the hands of the Draka, and that meant immediate execution if they were fortunate.

"Yes, it is. Now, the tunnel."

The SS man showed his teeth again as Tarski groped behind the blackened coal-fired heating stove. "So that was where you hid it," he said.

The heavy metal swung back.

"You aren't hunting partisans now, German," she said. He glowered, then turned and led his troops into the dark hole. The man was a killer and a brute, but an experienced soldier, and every one of those was precious. The peoples of the West would not fight for Hitler, even against the Draka; now they were flocking to enlist: even an ending that left a Prussian *junta* in control would be paradise compared to a Draka victory. *And the remnants of the SS will fight for civilization, and the Church*, she thought. *So the Lord God turns the evil that men do to good, though they will it not.* Even this Hoth was a human soul, and no soul was tried beyond what it could bear. Perhaps there was a chance of salvation even for such as him.

It had been so long, this war. So much was wrecked and broken; impossible even to imagine what peace might be like.

She turned to the others, lifting her hands and voice. "Good people," she said, in a clear carrying tone. The murmur and rustle died, leaving the earth-deep *crashcrashcrash* of the shells. *This is work for a priest, it isn't my place*, she thought for a helpless second. Then: *Take up your cross, Marya Sokolowska, and follow Him.* There were too few clergy left in Poland, too few religious of any kind. Nation and Church had always been intertwined in this land where the Madonna was Queen; the Germans knew it, and they had been unmercifully thorough.

"Good people, have courage." *We are all going to need it. Especially those of us who have to make a diversion, risking Polish lives so that those Germans can escape.* "God is with us, God is our strength. Let us pray."

"Out, out, everybody out!" Then, as if realizing the futility of English in this Polish village, the voice switched to rough pidgin German. "*Raus*, out! Against the wall. *Hande hoche*, hands up. Move, move, *move!*"

Marya stood, spat to clear her mouth of the dust, shook her head against the ringing in her battered ears. The shelling had been over for half an hour now, and she had been waiting for something like this since the last crackles of small-arms fire had died down. She blinked up the stairs at the helmeted silhouette and leveled rifle, raised her skirts slightly in both hands, and climbed. "I am coming," she called in German. "Do not shoot."

The Draka soldier backed into the center of the church as the Poles emerged, fanning them against the wall with the eloquent muzzle of her rifle. Another stood closer, prodding air with his bayonet.

"Over against the wall, face to the wall, go, go," he barked, and caught her by one arm. Marya jerked against the hold, felt a prickle of cold at a grip as immovable as a machine's. Coughing, blinking, the surviving villagers climbed the stairs and filed through into the central nave of the church—what had been the nave. There were gaping holes in the ceiling, wisps of smoke from the rafters, more holes in the walls, and the stained-glass windows had been sprayed as glittering fragments over rubble and the splintered wood of rood screen and pews. The hand released her with a shove that sent her staggering, and Sister Marya walked through debris that crunched and moved beneath her feet, toward the cluster of Draka soldiers by the door.

Draka. She had never seen one . . . pictures, of course. A few reliable books, but it had been a long time since anyone with any sense believed what they read in newspapers and magazines. They were standing spread

about the shattered doors, helmeted heads scanning restlessly back and
forth, quartering the ruined interior of the church. Mottled summer-
pattern camouflage uniforms . . . helmets like shallow round-topped
buckets with a flared cutout for the face. Automatic rifles hung across
their chests by assault slings, most with machetelike blades in sheaths
across their backs. She stepped closer, out of the spreading crowd along
the south wall, and the heads moved toward her with a motion like
gun turrets. Marya swallowed dry fear and continued, movements
carefully slow and nonaggressive.

Four of them. One with chevrons on his—no, her—arms.

"*Halte*," the woman said. To her companions: "Check if thissun's
carryin'."

One of the troopers swung behind her. A hand gripped the heavy
fabric between her shoulder blades, lifting her effortlessly into the air.
The nun closed her eyes and forced herself limp as another frisked
her with brisk efficiency.

"Nothin' but penguin meat under here," he said. "Haunches like a
draft horse."

Marya barely had time to stiffen her legs as the soldier released her;
she landed staggering. The Draka decurion had removed her helmet
to reveal a sweat-darkened mop of carrot-colored hair, cropped short
at the sides and back; salt ran in trickles down into the narrow blue
eyes that blinked thoughtfully at her. A pair of dust-caked goggles hung
loose around the soldier's muscled neck; her face was pale and freckled
across the eyes where the rubber and plastic had covered it, coated
with streaked dirt below. A flower had been painted around one eye,
incongruous yellow and green. . . . The nun could see the cords in
her forearms ripple as she flicked a cigarette from a crumpled pack
in the web lining of her helmet.

A finger stabbed out to silence Marya, and the Draka looked up
to the gallery that ran about the interior of the church, four meters
up.

"Y'all finished?" she called to the two troopers.

"*Ya*, nothin', dec," one called.

"Down."

The Draka soldiers walked to the railing of the gallery and casually vaulted over it. One landed facing the Polish villagers along the
wall, rifle ready; the other grunted slightly as the thirty-pound weight
of the rocket gun across his shoulders drove him into a half-crouch.

The NCO turned to Marya, spoke something in a horribly mangled
Slavic that sounded as much Ukrainian as anything else.

"Your pardon, ah, sir," she replied, in precise British-accented English,
keeping her head and eyes down. There was a string of . . . yes, *ears*
hanging from the woman soldier's belt. Dried and withered, some still
fresh enough to show crusts of blood. Danger, hideous danger, and
to her flock as well. Marya had only been in the village a few months.
Most of that in hiding, until it was clear whether the new German
regime's offer of amnesty was genuine, but these villagers were *hers*,
both as the only representative of the Church and agent for the Home
Army.

"It talks," the Draka said in mild wonder, drawing on the cigarette. There was a short high-pitched scream from behind Marya, from the Poles. The NCO looked up sharply, and walked past the nun with a brisk curse as Marya spun on one heel.

The soldier who had landed facing the villagers was pulling a girl out of the line by her hair. Walking out, rather, with one gloved hand locked in the tow-colored mass spilling out of her kerchief; a red-faced toddler ran after her beating small fists on the soldier's leg and yelling. The trooper grinned, scooped up the child and dumped him in another woman's arms.

"Hold the brat," he said.

The mother screamed again as his hand gripped her dress at the neck and pulled, the heavy coarse wool stripping away like gauze as the Draka worried her free of the homespun. There was a growl from the villagers, and the other trooper standing near swung her Holbars back to quiet them. Then the decurion was behind the would-be rapist.

"Goddamit, Horn-dog!" she shouted, and swung her boot in a short arc that ended in a solid *thump* against his buttocks. The man spun, snarling, then straightened as the NCO continued the tongue-lashing.

"We're here to pen this meat, not hump it. Freya's *tits*, Horn-dog, you keep thinkin' with you dick an' we all gonna get *kilt*. Y'wanna ride that pony, come back an' get it after we're stood down."

"Ah, Dec—" The Polish girl scuttled past him, weeping, rags of her dress held over her breasts.

"Shut the fuck up, dickhead!" She shook her head, muttering: "Men, all scrotum an' no brain." To Marya: "All right, penguin"—the nun puzzled at the word, then remembered the black-and-white of her habit—"what's down in the crypt?"

"A few sick and wounded. German soldiers, but they are unarmed and—"

"Good," the Draka grunted. She drew a grenade from her harness, a stick-grenade with a globular blue-painted head, and tossed it spinning underhand to the woman who stood by the door to the cellar. That one caught it out of the air with a quick snapping motion, pulled the tab and dropped it down the stairs. She kicked the heavy trapdoor down with a hollow *boom* that almost hid the thump and hiss of the detonation below.

"Shee-it, be mo' *careful* with them-there things," she added nervously to the section leader.

"It heavier than air," the decurion replied, and continued to Marya: "Nerve gas."

The nun started with shock, and missed the next few words. Her mind was with the helpless men below, the sudden bone-breaking convulsions, death like a thief in the dark.

" . . . find the rest." The decurion stepped closer and slapped her across the face, hard enough to start her nose bleeding. "Wake up, bitch. Ah said, is this lot all of 'em?"

"No . . . no, sir. There are others, many others; they have dug shelters under their houses."

"Sa. Can you talk 'em out? We's sure not goin' down lookin'."
Unspoken: *Otherwise we'll blast or gas anything belowground.*

"Yes! Yes, please, they are harmless people."

"People?" The Draka grinned. "Wild cattle, masterless an' fair game.
Yo! Meatmaker!" The woman who had gassed the cellar raised the
muzzle of her assault rifle in acknowledgment. "Take Horn-dog'n this
wench, check with the Tetrarch, 'n then talk the rest of the meat out
of their holes. She can translate. Get 'em all back here. If'n she starts
fuckin' around, expend her an' the locals both. Speakin' a fuckups,
Horn-dog, remember this is still combat even if they ain't shootin'."

The decurion jabbed Marya in the stomach with her own weapon.
"You hear?" A nod. She gave the nun another slap across the face,
stunning her and wheeling her half around. The gunshot sound echoed through the ruined church, amid a dead silence broken only by
the naked girl's sobbing.

"Yes, sir."

"Bettah. Tell these-here t'sit, facin' the wall. Hands on heads. Anybody
moves, we kill 'em; any resistance we kill 'em all. Do it, bitch."

"What's that?" the one called Horn-dog said.

Marya turned with the basket in her hands, willing the fluttering
in her stomach to quiet. This was the last house, a Jewish merchant's
before the War; the cellar had been crowded. And the stores had been
there, just enough time to get what she needed, passed to her in the
dark and confusion.

O Jesu, O Maria, she thought. *I had to set the timers by touch*, please
let them be right. A mechanical timer, improvised, needing only a strong
shake to start its countdown.

"Food," she answered. "Fresh bread, from this morning. Cheese,
sausage, vodka. For your officer."

"Hmmm," he said, reaching under the cloth and pulling out a small
round loaf of bread, tearing at it with square white teeth. His other
hand closed on her breast, kneading and pinching at the nipple through
the heavy serge cloth. Marya clenched her teeth to endure the pain
passively, the anger like the flush of fever; the man had been putting his hands on her all through the hour it had taken to clear the
village; her thighs and buttocks and breasts would be covered with
bruises tomorrow. And he would have thrown her down and taken
her if the other soldier had not been present to hold him to his work.

Fear seasoned the rage. He was a big man, two inches over six feet
and twice her weight but that was not all; she had seen him open
doors by slamming a fist through solid pine planking, kill a resisting
villager by crushing in his head with the edge of one palm. Stronger
than any man she had ever met, and more than strong, quicker than
a cat and as graceful. She knew that Draka were trained to war virtually from babyhood in military boarding schools, but meeting the
results in the flesh was something else again. Compared to these, the
Nazis were nothing, cheap reproductions from a cut-rate plant, a child's
flattery, a slave's imitation.

The other soldier came back into the kitchen, kicking a splintered chair aside. She sneezed at the dust; the air was heavy with it, murky with the dim twilight. A basket of eggs had smashed in a corner some time ago, adding its tinge of sulfur to the reek.

"Right, all clear," the woman soldier said. Her hand blurred, and came away with half of the bread the man had been eating. "Now we report." She looked at the hand mauling the nun's bosom. "An' no, we cain't take time off until we do. Shitfire, Horn-dog, y'got laid jus' last night, wait half an hour, hey?"

"Some's need it more than others," he said, releasing Marya and shoving her toward the door. "You gets it by killin', Meatmaker."

She shook her head. "You check the basket?"

"Shorely did."

"Well," she continued amiably. "Horn-dog, you're as good a fighting man as any of us in the Tetrarchy—when somebody's shootin' at you—an' you've been in it from the start, an' yous *still* a private. Gotta learn more self-control, my man, if'n you wants to make monitor. Sides, thissun isn't even good-lookin'."

"Never had me a penguin before," he said. They walked through into the gardens, feet sinking into the sandy dirt and sparse grass.

"Just another wench, when you've gotten her stripped an' spread." She kicked Marya lightly in the leg. "Hey, wench. You been tupped any?"

The nun clenched her hands into fists inside the voluminous sleeves of her habit. "No, sir," she ground out.

"So, Horn-dog: mutton this old, still virgin, she'll have a cunt like concrete an' a cherry made a' rhino hide." A section of Draka came trotting down the laneway. Meatmaker hailed them: "Bro's, seen Tetrarch de la Roche?"

"With the Cohortarch, sis. North a ways; past the jungleboys ' bridge a bit, laager. Cain't miss it."

The vehicle park had been established just north of the little stream, in a stretch of green common. A sprawl of more substantial houses lay to the north, probably the homes of the little town's professionals, a few traders, perhaps a doctor and notary; the manor of the local landlord beyond that. The heat of the day had faded to a mild warmth, and the soft pink glow on the tops of the poplars was dying; the wind blew in from the northwest, smelling of green and dust, spicy. The first stars were out, over toward the east; the glow of burning Warsaw was brighter, its smoke a black stain spreading like an inverted triangle against the constellations.

"Odd how long the light lasts after sunset, Johnny," Tanya murmured. After ten, and still not full dark. "Might like to try an' paint it." They had been switched down to Inactive status, ready-reserve and available in a crisis, but otherwise only expected to guard their own perimeter. The High Command would move them back when the transport situation improved.

She called down past her crossed legs into the interior of the tank: "Sue, the camera, hey?" A protesting mutter; the gunner, for reasons of her own, preferred to sleep on the reclining couch beside

the weapon. The heavy Leica was tossed up through the hatch and
Tanya snatched it out of the air, a little resentful of the careless-
ness. Barring some Russian icons, this was the best piece of loot
she had come by in the last year, taken from the corpse of a Fritz
military correspondent.

Sue might be less surly about it . . . Of course, it was a private
matter, and so outside rank. *Ah, well, at least in the Citizen Force I'm
not expected to hold the troops' hands while they get ready for bed.*
Janissaries had to be watched over constantly.

Tanya stood, focused, quartered the horizon in a swift *click click
click* until the roll was finished. Then she laid the instrument aside,
relaxed, tried to open herself to the scene; the record could never be
more than a prompt, to help the heart see again and the fingers
interpret. Even now they itched for the feel of the materials, worn
brushes, smooth nubbliness of canvas, her nose for the smell of lin-
seed oil and turpentine. But first you had to get out of the way, let
the moment just *be*, a perfect thing out of time. It proved difficult,
even once she had let her mind sink out of the iron analytical command-
logic mode.

"Sort of a shimmerin', these summer evenin's," the infantry Tetrarch
said, leaning one elbow back against the barrel of the coaxial grenade
launcher. He twisted his face back up over his shoulder to look at
her, a pale glimmer of blond hair and teeth in what was quickly
becoming full dark. "Good subject . . . Plannin' on another Archon's
Prize?"

How to paint it, ahhh . . . Sunsets had always been a favorite subject of hers; there was an inherent sadness to them, a melancholy. But
this was different, without the harsh-edge sharpness of the Levant where
she had been raised. *A long way from home.* Memories intruded, of other
evenings. Home, Syria Province, sunsets so different, swifter, more . . .

. . . dramatic, yes, that's the word. Images flitting. School, that had
been an old monastery up in the Lebanon range, renovated after the
conquest. That evening with her first lover, Alexandra . . . Freya, was
that a decade ago now? So alien, that creature self of fifteen years.
Just a day like so many others, yet still unbearably vivid with the
intensity that only great happiness or perfect despair can lend to
recollection. Bright dust and sweat in the palaestra, back to the baths
and companionable gossip among their classmates, then a ramble hand-
in-hand through the nature preserve outside the walls, winding tiny
wild hyacinths into each other's hair.

Memory: the room, and the pale blue flowers against a foam of dark
curls, that javelin leaned carelessly by the window ledge, a loose thong
casting a black shadow on the cream silk coverlet. Laughing amber
eyes in the tanned young face, pale rose-colored wine in the cup they
shared, the taste a little too sweet, fingers touching on the cool glass.
Through the window, the huge slope of the mountains in tawny-gold
rock and pine and green-gray olives, falling away beyond to a sea like
a dark-purple carpet, thread-edged with white surf. The sun hovering,
a giant disk of hot gold at the head of a flickering bronze highway
on the water. Smell of lavender and bruised thyme . . .

Damn. She should be thinking of new subjects. And too much nostalgia verged on self-pity, a despicable emotion.

Tanya paused a moment, shook herself back to the present, made a dismissive gesture. "Oh, the Prize," she said. "Baldur knows, all *that* thing does is ruin your reputation with everyone worth listenin' to; you should *see* the crowd a' antiquated fuzzles on the panel of judges." *Long surging roar from the crowd and the hard prickle of the gold laurel wreath—* "I'm thinkin' of givin' up pure landscape anyways. Worked out. Contemplatin' a series on the War; not battle scenes, just ah, things that have the *essence* of it, eh? Direct experience—" She stood and stretched. "Speakin' of which, you bunkin' alone tonight, Johnny?"

"Mmm, 'fraid not. Sorry."

She shrugged; it was no great matter. *Anyway, should be able to wangle a visit with Edward when we're pulled back into Army Corps reserve.*

"I suppose we should push a patrol or two a little north; it's part of the built-up area an' our responsibility." She blew a smoke ring. "On the othah hand, the jungleboys seem to be fresh an' full of beans," she added, looking to the noise and light from the bridging team a thousand meters upstream to the east. They were combat engineers from the Seventh Janissary; the prefabricated steel sections were in place, but the sappers were shoring and reinforcing even as the bulk of the legion pounded across. Welding torches blinked, trailing blue-white sparks; concrete mixers growled; a low tracked shape dug its 'dozer blade into the earth and bellowed. The combat elements were pouring over the river, a metallic stream of headlights snaking up from the south, speed more important than the unlikely chance of a Fritz air raid; there were antiaircraft cannon dug in around the bridge, but that was just doctrine. Six-wheeled *Peltast* APC's full of serf riflemen, or towing heavy mortars and 155mm gun-howitzers with the barrels rotated back and clamped over the trails.

"Bettah them than us," she said. The other officer nodded. Any fighting north of here for the next few weeks would be a toe-to-toe slugging match, absorbing the Fritz counterattack: high-casualty work. Artillery was the greatest killer on any battlefield, and positional warfare made you a fixed target for the howitzers to grind up. Just the sort of thing the serf legions were recruited for . . .

As if to point the thought, the sky growled behind them to the south. Soldier reflex tensed muscles, sent a few of the troopers working on vehicle maintenance or just strolling flat on their bellies. Then training identified it, outgoing fire from the Guard's own heavy-support batteries, keeping the enemy occupied while the Janissaries pushed forward and dug in. Bombardment rocket, a single long streak of white-orange fire across the bowl of the sky and a lightning flicker north-ward where it impacted.

"Ranging round," Johnny said.

A Citizen Force armored legion included fifty mobile launchers, each an eight-tube box on a modified tank chassis firing a 200mm round. One or two to establish the fall of shot, and then . . . The sky above them lit, a rippling magenta curtain that howled like the Wild Hunt, a huge moaning that drowned all other sound and left retinas blinking with streaked afterimages. Thirty seconds of it, as four hundred rockets ripple-fired at quarter-second intervals. Then the northern skyline lit with the impacts, a strobing flicker that threw lurid orange shadows on the smoke plumes, and a bitter chemical scent drifting downward.

"There must be some natural law that war has to smell bad," Tanya said, when the ringing had died a little from her ears. "And damage your hearin'. Those yours, Johnny?"

She nodded toward three figures walking toward them through the parked vehicles. The Tetrarch peered and nodded.

"Must've got the rest of the locals rounded up an' penned," he said. To the troopers, as they came to the scarred skirt-plates of the *Baalbeck Belle*: "All done?"

The woman of the pair nodded. "Ya. Sent those Tetrarchy D types back to they mommas, 'n' corralled the last lot a' the meat ourselves. No problems."

The man prodded the figure in the tattered nun's habit forward. "Thissun got a present fo' you, suh. Somethin' in the way of fresh food."

Tanya puffed a smoke ring, and John de la Roche snorted amusement; these Europeans never seemed to learn that they had nothing to bribe their conquerors *with*, since all they had including themselves belonged to the Draka anyway. Still, it would be welcome. Out here at the sharp edge not even the Domination's armed forces could maintain a luxurious ration scale; there was plenty of transport but the roads imposed an absolute limitation. Ammunition first, then fuel, then food and medical supplies, that was the priority; the food was standardized ration bars mostly, unless they could plug into the local economy.

The nun stepped closer, offering the bundle with a curious archaic gesture, one hand beneath and one in the shadowed basketwork. The infantry officer leaned down to take it, handed it up to Tanya where she lay beside the commander's hatch. "Here, you artists need to keep up your strength."

"Excuse me, please, respected sirs?" The Draka turned to look at the Polish nun, and she braced herself visibly under the cool carnivore eyes. "Please what is to happen to my . . . to the people of this village?"

Well, this one has spirit, at least, Tanya thought. There was a small pivot-mounted searchlight by the hatch; she toed the switch and turned the light down onto the other's face with her foot. The bright acintic light washed the flat square Slav face, and a hand flung up to guard her eyes from the hurtful brilliance. The delicate colors vanished from its cone, left black and white and gray, stark and absolute. *Might as well answer*, the Draka mused. Impertinence to ask, instead of silently awaiting orders, but it would be unfair to expect a Pole to know serf etiquette. Yet.

"That depends, wench," Tanya said. She rummaged in the basket; the nun tensed, then relaxed as a length of sausage emerged. "If the front moves on quick, they'll probably be left to work the land fo' a while; saves on transport space an' such. Until the Security people arrive, an' the serf traders an' settlers, after the war. Does the fightin' last long, the able-bodied'll be rounded up fo' work on 'trenchments and such, the rest culled an' killed, saves feedin' 'em." A bite at the kielbasa. "*They* aren't you concern, wench; put you mind to y'own fate. Life, most like, short of interpreters as we are."

The other's hand dropped as she slitted her eyes against the search-light and glared back at the Draka. Tanya knew the nun could see nothing, nothing but a black outline rimmed in hazed white. And the hulking scarred steel presence of the tank, so much more massive than its mere size, intimidating as few other things on earth were. Yet there was little fear in the slow nod, more as if the Pole were confirming something to herself. The trooper beside her started to call to his officer and then the sky lit again with the whistling howl of dead metal racing to bring death to living men, an agony impersonal and remote, touching everything beneath with a limning outline of orange fire.

"—she's useful, Horn-dog, so doan' do anythin' permanent." The Tetrarch was chuckling when she could hear again.

"Hey, give me a hand, Meatmaker, hey?" the soldier said, an ugly panting rasp in his voice.

The other trooper laughed indulgently. "Well, y'saved mah life just last week, an' I swore I'd pay you back," she said, and gripped the nun, spun her around, tossed her staggering back to the man.

Tanya drew meditatively on her cigarette as she watched the two Draka toss the Polish woman back and forth through the puddle of the searchlight's beam. Another bite of the kielbasa, tough and stringy and heavy with garlic; she dug at a fragment stuck between her teeth with a fingernail. *Still not panicking*, she thought with interest; the nun was openly afraid now, but fighting to stay on her feet and dodging for what she thought were openings, her cries involuntary gasps of effort and not screams. Meatmaker's face, halfway between boredom and a cruel laughter directed as much at her companion as their victim. The man's . . . his mouth caught the light, open and wet, teeth shining liquid. Curling with the same dreadful sidelong desire that left no thought behind his eyes, flat and hot and sick, the eyes of a rutting dog.

Satyriasis, Tanya thought. *Godawful thing to be stuck with.* Although she remembered reading somewhere that most males were like that for the initial year or so after puberty set in, hormones five or six times an adult's level. A few never got over that thirteen-year-old's first wild realization that they were in a world of serf women who could not tell them no, fantasy become reality. Of course, even then, most households wouldn't tolerate this sort of crude field expedient; a certain degree of privacy was expected . . . A scream, short and breathless; the two troopers had the nun's habit up around her neck and over her head in a floppy black bag, pinning her arms; Meatmaker was whirling her like a top, while the other's hands tore at the odd clumsy undergarments with scrabbling haste.

And most wenches back in the Domination didn't kick up this sort of fuss, either; willing to please, or meekly submissive. She remembered walking into her father's study once, looking for a book; it had been a rainy October's morning, the water pattering down the long windows in streaks that blurred the tapping of branches. The housegirl's giggles and sighs scarcely louder than the crackling of the burning cedarwood in the fireplace; they had been standing in front of it, Pa behind her with his face in the angle of her neck and shoulder, and his hands just lifting her breasts out of her blouse. He had not seen her, but the wench had. Smiled at her as she stroked the master's thinning blond hair, and Tanya had backed out soundlessly, humiliatingly conscious of her burning cheeks.

Odd, how the memory seems so shocking, she thought. *Still, I was twelve. Girls get flighty and fanciful around that age.*

Down in the churned dirt by the treads of the tank Horn-dog put his hand between the nun's shoulder blades and pushed. She lurched, stumbled, fell forward and caught herself on her shrouded hands; Meatmaker stepped forward and planted a boot on the bundle of cloth, pinning it to the earth.

"C'mon, wench," she said, and leaned forward. "My friend's got somethin' fo' you." Her hands closed on the other's waist and jerked her forward, leaving the Pole standing bent double with her hands between her feet.

"All right, Horn-dog, can't no friend do better for you than that," she continued jovially, with a slap-pat on Marya's buttocks. "Go to it."

Tanya folded her arms and flicked ash off her cigarette, moving the searchlight with her toe to cover the two soldiers. *Thick legs*, she thought idly. Broad bottomed, as well, peasant build. The genitals were rather pretty, unstretched and neatly formed like a teenager's, nestled in curling dark blond hair.

"Best-lookin' part of the human anatomy," de la Roche said, as if to echo her thought.

Below her she could hear the clink and rustle as the infantryman undid the clasps of his webbing belt, could hear his breathing, hoarse and rapid. *What an absolutely impoverished erotic imagination he must have*, she thought with mild contempt. Pursuing a little dry friction and a few seconds of second-rate pleasure as if it were the Grail . . . *Freya knows, men tend to be creatures of reflex, but this one is a caricature. Thank the nonexistent gods I was born the right gender.*

He stepped up behind the nun and opened her vulva with a brutal drive of paired thumbs; she screamed then, a shrill sound loud enough to hear through the muffling cloth. *An exquisitely uncomfortable ten minutes for you, wench*, Tanya thought. Wasteful way to treat a serf, of course. Raw brutality was a crude tool of domination, only occasionally useful unless you were planning to destroy the individuals in question. Besides . . . how had Pa put it? "The whip is more effective as a threat than a reality; and don't forget, using it changes you, too." She bent to pick up the basket, rummaging for the bottle of vodka; a drink would do no harm, even though they were not far enough into rear echelon to risk getting drunk. A pity; it would be good to completely relax. There was a click and buzz from the radio within as she stooped over the hatch, a ticking—

Ticking?

"Down, down, everybody *down!*" she shouted, as her hand swept the wicker container forward over the north-pointing prow of the tank. Dropped flat as it left her fingers, ignoring the projections that gouged and bit, to hug herself close to the steel, gloved fingers scrabbling. De la Roche shouted as it whipped past his ear, turning fast enough to blur in the beginning of the leap that would take him to the ground, infantry reflex to seek the safety of soft earth. Glaring and helpless, Tanya followed the arching parabola of the bomb; her grip on the handle had been light, no time to firm it up . . . the basket turned slowly as it flew, shedding bread and sausages, wedges of cheese and a square bottle. Hesitated at the top of its arc, dropped. Down, accelerating, dropping below the slope of the *Belle*'s glacis plate and—

WHUMP.

A huge, soft sound, then an invisible hand lifted her and slammed her down again on the unyielding metal, bouncing, the adrenaline rush slowing the involuntary movement of her head until she could feel the movement of her neck swinging up, flexing down again, impact and the sagging pull on muscle and skin as inertia tried to strip them from her skull and spread the soft tissues like a pancake. Watching de la Roche caught in midair by the blast, the pillow of compressed air slapping the precise leopard curve of his jump into a thrashing fall that ended in a landing with one arm bent beneath him at an angle that made her mind wince even then. There was a moment of sliding, as if time were a film that had slipped the sprockets of the projector and now it was catching again.

De la Roche forcing himself to his knees, to his feet, hand clamping an upper arm where bone fragments pushed through his uniform, white about the mouth. Horn-dog rolling on the ground, clutching at genitals his fall had driven into the dirt. The other trooper lying on her back, blood glistening in her hair where skull had met track link. Tanya blinked, and felt particles of grit turning under the lids where the explosion had sandblasted them into her eyeballs. Saw the nun moving north in a desperate blind scrabbling crawl, up on her hands and knees as her head emerged from the cocoon of fabric, then running with the skirts around her waist and white legs twinkling in the dark.

"Alive!" she shouted; the reaction squad was already pounding up, and one had swept his Holbars to his shoulder. "Alive, I want answers, *alive.*" They dashed forward, skirmish-spread, overhauling the fugitive as if she was standing still. Then muzzle flashes low to the ground, the flickers of light showing figures rising from concealed rifle pits, dirt cascading off the covers. One of the Draka infantry stopped as if she had run into an invisible wall, flopped boneless to the ground. The others dove to earth and returned fire, and the turret whirred and began to turn under her.

CRACK as the world broke away from the axis of the main gun, afterimages strobing across her retinas. Her hand stabbed through the hatch, jerked the microphone free of its clamps; she spat blood from tooth-cut lips.

"Two an' three, move forward in support, all other units, *no firin'
except on confirmed targets*." Too many other Draka units moving
around—it would set Loki himself to laughing if they started shooting each other up now. Her thumb pressed the hold button down, and
she raised her head to shout to the infantry. "Wait for support, no
chargin' off into the dark!"

Tanya hawked and spat blood, felt the iodine taste and stream pouring
from her nose. She keyed the mike again: "Senior Decurion Smythe,
report to me immediately."

" . . . dead meat by the time we got 'em," the monitor said, and
kicked the body of the Pole at his feet; bone snapped with a moist
muffled crunching. "Never saw hide'r hair of the penguin."

Tanya grunted; it was less painful than speaking. A starshell went
off overhead with a slight *pop* and bathed the cohort's laager with
its blue-white metallic glare; the Senior Decurion looked away to
preserve her night vision. Tetrarch de la Roche was leaning against
the *Belle* as a medic set the fractured humerus of his arm; his eyes
were closed, face expressionless as fat drops of sweat trickled down
his face.

Meatmaker raised her bandaged head from her knees, where she
sat before the body of her squadmate. "You wants a patrol, search the
houses, maybe-so get a few ears fo' Horn-dog?" she said, in a hope-
fulness muffled by gauze.

Tanya inserted a cigarette between her lips with care and glanced
northward herself, shaking her head. *Pointless*, she thought, forcing
down a sudden rage that left a twist of nausea in her gut. Pointless
to risk Citizen lives in this sort of scuffle. Reprisals pointless; it would
be nothing but killing to soothe her injured self-esteem, and a von
Shrakenberg did not lie to herself that way. Likewise interrogation of
the villagers—the Guard was not trained for it, the only language they
had in common with the remaining peasants was mangled fragments
of German . . . waste. Let the specialists do it. Frustration tasted like
vomit at the back of her throat.

"Senior Decurion," she began, forcing the words clear and crisp
through the pain of torn lips.

"Cohartarch?"

"At first light put in a tetrarchy with support to flush those buildings to the north."

"Yes, Cohortarch."

"Notify all troops: no natives within the perimeter an' nobody but
assigned guards outside durin' darkness. No group smaller than five
in daylight, fully armed."

"At once, Cohortarch."

"An' get on the blower to Legion. To Centurion De Witt. *Security*
Centurion, antipartisan liaison section. My compliments to the Centurion, an' tell him"—she threw the cigarette to the dirt, ground it
out with a savage twist of her bootheel, looked around—"that Sector
VI may now be considered . . . *active*."

❖   ❖   ❖

"Are you all right, Sister?" the partisan whispered anxiously.

Marya nodded, one hand covering her mouth and the other gripping the bark of the tree beside her. She nodded, heaved, stumbled around the tree and fell to her hands and knees. Vomit spattered out of her mouth, thin and sour from an empty stomach; she coughed, spat, wiped her mouth and spat again, clung to the rough surface of the tree as another spasm gripped her. The nun pulled a handkerchief from the sleeve of her habit and wiped at her face, conscious of the sick-sweet stink of the vomitus spattering the ground. Another smell added to the sweat and dirt and fluids ground in from days spent crouching in the cellar and tending the sick . . . The thought of a bath beckoned like salvation.

Seconds, she thought, trying to control the cold shaking in her arms and legs. A few seconds earlier and she would have died, torn to tatters of raw bone and meat by the explosive charge. Fresh pain lanced up from her crotch as she dragged herself erect along the trunk of the pine, and she could feel hot wetness trickling down the insides of her thighs from her ruptured hymen. A few seconds later and she would have died with the Draka pumping inside her, lubricated with blood, bent double and blinded in the stifling tent of her habit.

Marya recalled the man's eyes as he had torn at her clothing, the blank shallowness of them, like chips of blue tile. To die like that, a thing used by a thing, a knothole and an animal . . . her body heaved again. Then she found herself gripping the wood hard enough that blood and feeling left her fingers, glad of the distraction. Hate was a different nausea, shrill-sick and twisting under the ribs, making her head throb. Visions from the *Inferno* and Hieronymus Bosch moved behind her eyelids, eternal torment for the evildoer, burning, flaying, rotted with insects crawling through immortal diseased flesh—

Shuddering, she forced a different picture into the forefront of her mind, the Savior on the cross. *Lord, they flogged you until the ribs showed, beat nails through your hands and feet, stabbed you in the side with a spear, and when you cried out for water they gave you vinegar to drink. As you died you called out to the Father to forgive them.*

"Your way is hard, Lord," she whispered to herself, "I will try." To the guerrilla whose concern she could sense through the near-absolute darkness of the nighted woods: "I can walk, my child, but turn your back for a moment, please."

He obeyed, moving off a few paces with an embarrassed mutter. Marya fumbled up her skirts, improvised a pad from the handkerchief and the rags of her undergarments to absorb the flow of blood. She winced again at the pressure of cloth on the bruised, torn flesh, and distracted herself with the prayers the Rule prescribed when it was necessary to touch the private parts; the words served well enough to take the mind off pain.

"Come," she said, forcing discomfort down into the dark well where she kept fear and loneliness and despair, waiting until there was time to deal with them. She looked up, hunting stars to confirm the map in her mind. "We've got a fair distance to cover and shelter to find before dawn."

Chapter Ten

CHATEAU RETOUR PLANTATION
TOURAINE PROVINCE
JULY 1947

"Must we do it today?" Chantal Lefarge asked, shifting the ledger restlessly from one arm to another.

"It will do you good to get out of doors," Marya Sokolowska said firmly. The other woman had been losing weight and sleep. The nun forced herself not to think of the real reason: it was not something she could alter, and bringing it up would help neither of them. "Besides, we've done as much as we can without instructions. This way."

They turned right from the south-facing main doors between tall beeches that threw dazzling leaf blinks of sunlight in their faces. The gardens to the east of the Great House were warm and softly murmurous with bee hum, drowsing in the early summer afternoon. Further out they grew shaggy, where fields had been enclosed for future care. Labor and time were still too short for much to be spent on adornment, and the von Shrakenbergs had merely transplanted sapling trees where avenues and groves would be. Sheep grazed there, keeping the grass mowed short and starting the process that would end in dense velvet-textured lawns. Lately they were joined by a group of dik-dik, miniature antelopes four inches at the shoulder; by peacocks and red deer and flamingos.

One of the huge black-coated hounds the Draka kept ambled over to the two women, nosing at Marya's hand; she ruffled the beast's ears, which were nearly at the level of her chest. *Lion-dog indeed*, she thought. That was the Draka name for the breed, so called for their size, and the thick manelike ruff the males grew. And because they were used in catsticking, putting lions at bay for mounted hunters with lances. It wagged its tail, sniffed suspiciously at Chantal, who was holding herself rigid with control. Lion-dogs were also used to hunt runaway serfs, and they had both seen the scars on a man who had tried to make the Channel, soon after the plantation was founded; he had been kept alive at considerable trouble, as an example.

"It's only a dog, Chantal," Marya said. "Touch it, go ahead." The younger woman extended a hand, which received a perfunctory sniff; it wagged its tail and trotted away, nails clicking on the bricks. They continued around a screen of bushes, past a dry fountain, its link to the water main not yet finished.

Marya stopped at an open manhole cover; the man sitting on the edge beside a wheeled tray of tools stubbed out his cigarette and made to rise, removing his flat cloth cap.

"No, Marcel," the nun said. "How is the leg? I thought you had permission to rest a while yet." *Although he's making a good recovery,* she thought critically. Still drawn and underweight, but it had been only three months since the ambush in the gorge, and it was excellent progress for such a serious injury, followed by major surgery. Of course, the Domination's medical corps had a matchless fund of experience in dealing with wound trauma.

He laughed with a slightly sheepish expression and slapped the cap against the stainless-steel prosthetic that replaced his left leg above the knee. "A good afternoon, Sister. Don't worry, I'm not walking far on it yet. I sit on the cart and young André here"—an adolescent popped his head out of the hole, nodded to Marya and Chantal, and returned below to the accompaniment of a metallic clanking and banging— "pushes me about. He's a good apprentice, but he needs direction. I only work where I can sit, *vraiment* . . . and I was getting bored, sitting in the cottage and annoying Jacqueline, she has her own work to do. Believe me, Sister, it does a man good to get out in the fresh air and feel he's doing something useful. Very interesting system of piping they've put in here, extruded aluminum where we'd've used cast iron."

He yawned, paused to look down. "No, no, the *number three connector,* imbecile!" To Marya: "And is it true there's to be a holiday, Sister?"

Chantal answered, running her hand through her uncombed hair. "Yes. The next generation of tyrants is a month old."

The air was warm, scented with tea roses and freshly cut grass, but a chill seemed to touch them. "Now, that was a very stupid thing to say, Mademoiselle Lefarge," the plumber replied softly. "Very stupid indeed." Down the hole, where the noises had ceased: "Continue, André, and keep your ears shut."

Chantal glared at him through red-rimmed eyes; the pipefitter had belonged to the Catholic trade union, before the War. *Class-traitor,* she thought: just the sort one would expect to turn out a collaborationist. "You were expecting a song of praise for our owners, perhaps?"

"Chantal!" Marya whispered sharply.

"No, Sister, let me reply."

Marcel picked up a wrench and spun the adjusting screw, but his eyes never left Chantal's. "I heard a great deal of that sort of thing before the War," he said. The nun looked at his hands, broad and battered like any working man's, but also scarred across the knuckles.

"Union jurisdictional disputes" in Lyon had meant more than handing out pamphlets, she suspected.

"In the Army, too, after I was called up; that was in '40, before the Nazis attacked Russia. The Party men were always going on about how it was a war for the rich only; after we lost, they said right out we should collaborate. I know, I spent three years in a German prisoner-of-war camp and they let copies of *L'Humanité* circulate. Then when we were released I fought again as a volunteer against the Draka, in Belgium, and I escaped because a Flemish peasant saw a rosary in my hand when he found me lying wounded in the woods. And it was a Frenchman who shot off my leg.

"So now, *comrade* Lefarge, I have my work, my garden, a child on the way, and a wife whom I do not intend to leave alone again. That is *all* that concerns me. About what used to be, I try not to think at all; I have fought enough. Too much to be pushed by someone like you, the type who lost us everything. Now if Father Adelard, or the good Sister here, tells me to do more, I would consider it . . . As for you, *comrade*, endanger yourself if you must. *But not me or my family!* Or you may suffer an accident. You understand me?"

The Frenchwoman's eyes slid away from his. He nodded to the nun. "A beautiful day, Sister, isn't it? As pretty a place to work as any, as well." A shaky smile. "Better smelling than most a man in my trade gets."

Marya nodded, and decided not to rebuke the man for the threat. Besides which, he was right; it was pure folly to take risks without need or hope of results. Sinful, even; *prudentia* was a virtue, and God had not given the gift of life to be spent recklessly.

"Indeed it is, Marcel," she replied gently; he was sweating, struggling to control his breathing and put on an appearance of calm. There were so many with memories too hurtful to bear, on this wounded earth. She glanced around. "Beautiful, today."

Here, closer to the manor, the changes were more extensive, old plantings with alterations in the Draka taste; French gardens were too formal and close-pruned to suit them. Pathways in tessellated colored bricks salvaged from ruins and towns, ponds and watercourses, a few fine pieces of statuary in bronze or marble, mostly loot as well. And flowerbeds, bush and trellis roses, young hedges of multiflora, banks of purple violets, impatiens in mounds of hot coral and magenta, geraniums nodding in trembling sheets of pale translucent lavender. She had seen Tanya's watercolors of what the grounds would look like when the plans were complete; this was merely a foreshadowing.

Well, at least they use their stolen wealth for something *besides tanks and bombers*, she thought wryly.

"I'm sorry," Chantal said, beside her. "It's just—I—"

"I know," Marya said, putting an arm around her shoulders. She could feel a quiver under her palm. "I understand, child. Do you want to go back? I can give the mistress her summaries myself."

"No, no." Chantal drew herself up. "You do more than your share already."

The pergola was set in the middle of a maze, the young hedges only knee-high as yet, with tall beeches and poplars left standing from the pre-War gardens. Climbing roses twined through wooden trellises between the marble columns, over lacework arches above them, through the verdigrised metal flowers of the dome; for a moment Marya thought of blood drops on a sheet of crumpled green velvet. Music sounded over the quiet plashing of the water.

"Solange," Chantal said. Marya nodded; the instrumental portion was a recording but the voice of Tanya's body servant was unmistakable, a soaring mezzo-soprano, beautifully trained. Solange had spent two years in the *Conservatoire* in Paris, and practiced faithfully since.

"Delibes," Chantal continued. The nun nodded, startled at another flash of the scholarship the girl from Lyons occasionally showed. "Delibes' *Lakme*, the *Fleurette à deux.*

"Quite good," she continued. "Not meant for a solo, but quite good." It was spoken grudgingly: there was bad blood between the two.

The two bookkeepers entered, made their obeisance; Tanya von Shrakenberg signaled them to wait with an upraised palm. Marya looked at her, then transferred a fixed gaze to the edge of the pergola above, blushing furiously. The mistress of Chateau Retour was reclining on a lounger, wearing an undergarment that seemed to be made of nothing but two triangles of silk. *Shameless*, the nun thought. *I should be accustomed to it, but I am not.* She herself was dressed in an ankle-length skirt and a high-collared blouse that buttoned at the wrist; she wiped sweat from her upper lip and suppressed a moment's envy at the cool comfort of the long body resting in the dappled shade. *Indecent.* The Rule of her own Order forbade even bathing without at least a shift.

Of course, it could be worse: at least Tanya was a woman. Draka men were equally careless. Grimly she forced her eyes down again, aware that her ears had turned a bright burning pink and that her owner would see and be amused. The Draka was lying with one arm behind her head, the other resting on a table beside the couch that bore a Carries coffee service and a bowl of strawberries beside a tall glass of clotted cream. Beyond that was a wheeled stroller with her month-old twins; one was looking around with the mild wide-eyed wonder of any infant, the other suckling at the breast of the wet nurse who sat beside the carriage.

That did not embarrass her; it was something you saw every day in a Polish village. *Madonna and child,* she thought with a brief warmth. A real thing, and also the representation of a Mystery, the first icon of compassion; even the heathen in the days before Christ had made the Mother and Babe a symbol of holiness. Marya watched the wet nurse as she smiled and stroked the baby's cheek; remembered hearing that Draka women almost never breast-fed their infants, and wondered how they could bear not to.

" . . . and these are the estimates from the League for the construction crew, Mistress," Marya finished. A team of specialists, hired out for heavy building work, they had left last week, and the nun was glad of it; they had created no end of noise and confusion.

"Hm." Tanya flipped through the last of the account sheets. "Excellent work, Marya, youve got a talent fo' administration . . . ouch." She folded the contractor's bill. "Piracy, even if everybody *does* need them. Oh, well, we can always take out anothah loan. Anythin' else?"

"A circular from the Transportation Directorate. They are moving one of their labor camps into the area, the gauge-standardization project." The Domination's railways ran on a 1.75-meter gauge, wider than the European system, and tens of thousands of kilometers had to be relaid. "They would appreciate any bulk foodstuffs available, to save transport. We have several thousand kilograms of potatoes surplus to projected requirements, Mistress."

"By all means, sell 'em."

"And a cablegram for you in this morning's mail, I think concerning the naming-day celebrations for your children."

Tanya ripped open the flimsy. "Probably Tom and Johanna," she said. To Marya: "Third an' first cousins respectively; they have a place down in Tuscany." A snort of laughter as she read it. "Johanna, all right. Askin' why I've had the infernal bad manners to pup at such an inconvenient time, with grape harvest comin' on. Says can't I count to nine, or have I jus' forgotten what activity results in babies? Hmmm, that's them, their two children an' six staff. Flyin' up in their Cub. How many so far?"

"Thirty-seven Citizens who will be staying at least overnight, Mistress, with about twice that number of servants. Where are we going to put them all, Mistress? The new wing is just a shell."

"Pavilions, of course. We have a couple around *somewheres*. We'll set them up in the cherry orchard just south. Serfs can double up. Then we'll have to find room for the namin' gifts, as well." A sigh. "Just because I *paint* pictures, everyone assumes I *want* pictures, 'sides everyone havin' loot comin' out they ears. I'm goin' to have to open a gallery." She reread the cablegram. "Ahh, no, second thoughts—Tom and Johanna are comin' up in *two* Cubs. They two were in the Air Corps, they've got pull, an' I suspect they're goin' to be giving one to us. We'll have to buy another mechanic. Hmmm, we might be able to pick up an ex-Auxiliary from the Forces."

"I will make a note of it, Mistress." A piece of meadow had been marked off as a grass-strip runway for those guests flying in, but she supposed something more permanent would be needed if the plantation was to have an aircraft of its own. Cubs were small six-seater runabouts, but the waiting list was long. "And I've received a telephone message from Tours; the thousand kilos of oranges you ordered have arrived, the steamtruck will be here Thursday."

Tanya opened her eyes in alarm. "Wait a minute, isn't the cold-storage room out of order?"

"Yes, Mistress; Josef tells me it will take a week to repair once the parts arrive . . . and they are overdue." The Landholder's League had just established a schedule of per-capita citrus consumption, to get the export trade from the Domination's old territories going again. It was more convenient to buy in bulk and issue from storage, but the oranges would not keep without refrigeration.

"Shit. Burn up the wire, try an' get the parts. Issue every household a big sack, an' hunt up mason jars; we'll put up preserves an' marmalade. No use tryin' to send them back—those League bureaucrats would rather eat their children than muss the paperwork. Damn waste."

Tanya rose, yawned, put her hands together back-to-back above her head, linked the fingers and bent backward. She was not bulky, but for an instant the long smooth swellings of muscle jumped out into high definition, like a standing wave beneath her skin. Frowning, she probed at the curve of her stomach where it scalloped in under her ribs. "Damn, bettah put in another couple of hours, today; still too slack. Last thing we need is fo' me to get six months' punitive callup fo' bein' unfit for service."

Solange rose and slid the Draka's white-striped black caftan over her head, tied the belt and knelt to fasten her sandals. The wet nurse had taken the infant from her breast and had it on her shoulder, patting gently at its back until a small, surprised belch indicated success. She wiped up the results and Tanya held out her hands for the wiggling pink form, taking it in an experienced head-and-fundament grip.

"They always look like piglets at this age, don't they?" she asked the air, chuckling and swooping the child around in a circle. It gurgled and waved its arms and legs with a gum-baring smile; Tanya brought it close and fluttered her lips against its stomach. A hand stuck tiny fingers into her nose as wide infant eyes looked down uncertainly, deciding whether to laugh or bawl. They settled on sleep instead; heavy eyelids blinked down, and the Draka settled her child in the stroller beside its twin.

"Hush now," she murmured, pulling up the light coverlet. "You two don' know it, but the whole clan, the neighbors, an' half creation are comin' to give you toys." A smile, soft and amused. "Give you momma and poppa toys in your name, really." The baby gave a small half-cry and then dropped off with the abrupt collapse-in-place finality of infant sleep. "Don' you worry though, little ones. Momma an' Poppa are goin' give yo the whole *world* fo' a toy."

"Come on, Marya," she said as she straightened. "Few mo' things we need to talk about, might as well do it on the way to the palaestra."

Chantal sat staring dully as the Draka left, watching with blank indifference as Solange hopped up onto the lounger and leaned over to pour herself a cup of coffee.

"A cup, Chantal?" she said, using the silver tongs to drop two of the triangular lumps into her own. "Or some of these strawberries? Really, they are very good, just picked. One doesn't appreciate what freshness is until one lives in the country, a shame to waste them." Sighing with contentment, she spooned some of the cream over the fruit and sank back against the rear of the lounger, cross-legged with the bowl in her lap.

The other woman looked up, the blank apathy leaving her narrowing eyes. "You are *disgusting*," she hissed. "A disgusting *whore*."

"Ah." Solange dipped the long slender spoon into the bowl, picked up a berry and considered it a moment before eating. "I will spare you, *cherie*, the obvious retort that far from being disgusting, I am a beautiful and accomplished whore . . . and instead merely point out that nobody is paying money for my favors; one should use words with precision, no? 'Kept woman,' perhaps, or 'concubine.' Furthermore, you have been called to the master's room fairly often of late. In fact, last night—he was with the Mistress, you understand, and I sleep at the foot of her bed—I heard him express great satisfaction with you. Particularly the way you squeeze your—"

The other jumped to her feet with a strangled sound; Solange dropped the spoon and spread her hands in a placatory gesture.

"I am sorry. Truly, that was cruel, and I should not have said it. Accept my apologies, *ma soeur*."

Chantal dropped back to the stool, let her face fall forward into her hands and wept with a grinding sound, hopeless and disconsolate, misery past all thought of privacy or control. Solange turned on one side, busying herself with the cup and saucer in embarrassment until the other woman had command of herself once more.

"I suppose I deserved it," Chantal said at last, blowing her nose and wiping at her eyes with a handkerchief. "I am no better than you, after all."

The serf on the lounger sighed in exasperation and clinked the stoneware down on the marble table slightly harder than necessary. "Lefarge, it is not a matter of better or worse, but of less or more foolish. This grows rapidly more tiresome, my old, this martyred pose of yours. If the von Shrakenbergs took you seriously, there might already have been grave happenings. Some . . . friends have asked me to speak with you." She shook her head at Chantal's quick suspicion. "No, not the masters—Mistress Tanya does not, I fear, think of me in connection with such practical matters—some of the other servants. You are becoming a somewhat dangerous person to be about. Not Sister Marya either . . ." A pause.

"The good Sister is, as one might expect, something of an innocent. She would sympathize, but say you have nothing to reproach yourself for, as one who submits passively to superior force." She kept her eyes on Chantal's, until they dropped again. "Which we both know is not *entirely* the case, *n'est-ce pas?*"

"Say what you have to," Chantal replied in a mumble.

A sigh. "Did you ever see the Bastille Day parade in Paris, Chantal?"

"No," she replied with surprise, startled out of her thoughts. "May Day only."

"A great pity, the spectacle was beautiful. I remember well. I was about six, so this must have been '32 or '33, the first time my father took me. He was just back from a field trip, burned dark as an Arab, with a most dashing beard; he held my hand as we walked to our seats in the reviewing stand where others with the *Croix du Guerre* would sit, and I was very proud of him. Maman—" she continued, smiling dreamily, "Maman had the most lovely hat, with flowers; she put it on my head and it fell right over my eyes and I pushed it off again because it was very important to see everything. Poppa put me on his shoulder when the soldiers went by; there were hussars in red cloaks, and cuirassiers in shiny breastplates, and Foreign Legionnaires in white kepis and epaulets.

"I was a little frightened, they looked so fierce and the horses were so large. But Poppa explained that these were men from all over France, who would fight to keep bad men from coming and hurting me, as he had fought the Germans in the Great War; he showed me the President of the Republic, who I could tell was very important because of his frock-coat and sash, and told me how he would command them. I felt very safe, then, my maman was with me, and Poppa was the strongest and handsomest man in the world, and now there were all these others who would look after me, so there was nothing that could hurt me."

Chantal blinked at her, astonished and sadly envious. Remembered *her* father stumbling home smelling of cheap sour Midi wine, and his fumbling hands; remembered hiding in the closet too frightened to cry while her parents screamed at each other outside and then the slap of a fist on a face and the tinny crash of kitchenware. Wondering, she studied Solange, trying to see the child with the starched pinafore and the ribbons in her hair, perched on the laughing bronzed explorer's shoulder. *Watching the soldiers,* she thought bemusedly. For *her*, soldiers were the men who came and broke strikes, or the way her eldest sister picked up a little extra cash for drink after the bottle got to her.

Solange was frowning slightly in concentration, her lower lip caught between her teeth. *Well, I'll listen,* Chantal thought resignedly. *My god, how did the little princess end up here? Perhaps I was wrong to envy; at least I was never allowed to think I could rely on anyone but myself.*

"There is a point?" she said.

"Well, we're neither of us little girls any more, are we, Chantal? Nor are you the only one to have suffered," Solange said with a shrug. "The past is gone, and everything it held, as well. Why should we fight, you and I? Because of things from before the War, politics, classes? It's absurd; that world is *gone* and this one of ours is all we have.

"I remember the War," she continued. "Better, because I was old enough to understand and be frightened. We stayed in Paris when the government fled to Bordeaux. Maman wanted to go, but Poppa said it would be safer staying than on the roads. When the Germans came, my father went out to watch them parade down the Champs Elysees. Then he came home and got drunk, the first time I can remember that happening. He was already ill and his hands trembled; he just kept raising the glass and wouldn't listen to me, as if Maman and I weren't there—that frightened me even more. Later, we'd be crouching in the cellar of our building with the other families, listening to the English robot bombs overhead like . . . like bees in the sky, waiting for the engine to stop and the bomb to come down and kill us with nerve gas, and he was afraid too, there was nothing he could do."

"Then the Draka came?" Chantal asked gently. A corner of her mind noted how much of a relief it was, to have the arrow of attention dragged around from its unrelenting focus on the pain at the center of herself.

"Yes." Solange looked down at her hands. "You heard?" The other woman nodded. "The Janissaries picked my father up and threw him into the glass shelves with his souvenirs and kicked him and kicked him, and they . . . they were killing me, there were too many. Big men, crazy drunk, stronger than horses. I knew I was dying, could feel my life flowing away, I was only eighteen and *I didn't want to die*—"

She stopped for a moment, dabbed at her cheeks with the back of her hand, took a deep breath. "Then Mistress Tanya came in. I could see a little still. They had guns, they were many; she just told them they were baboons out of . . . order, I think, and to go. Stared at them, and they shuffled their feet and went away. She picked me up and"—a shrug—"I woke up in a hospital, swathed like an Egyptian mummy. It gave me a great deal of time to think. The Mistress came and visited once or twice, but I had a good deal of time, once the pain was less. Time to consider my decisions carefully."

"Decisions?" Chantal asked. "You weren't in a position to make choices, surely?"

"Oh, one always has some choices to make. *Par example*, the Mistress offered to find me another owner, if I would rather not stay with her. My decision . . . I decided to give up, Chantal. To surrender absolutely, to submit, to make the best of whatever came. Which, you must admit, could be much worse. We could be whoring in a Janissary brothel, or spending the rest of our lives between a factory and a concrete barracks. Or anonymous lobotomized lumps of flesh in a labor camp. Instead . . ." She waved a hand at the pergola.

"Actually, I find myself unable to complain even a little," Solange continued more brightly. "Here I am, *safe*, after all. Protected. Unless the Americans drop their atomics on us, or the world ends, of course. Safe, pampered, given every luxury and pleasure, hardly required to work at all, indulged, treated—"

"—like a pet animal!" Chantal snapped.

"No, like a pet human, *cherie*. With affection, valued for my talents and beauty and skills; the Mistress is quite proud of me. I'm not treated as an equal, of course, but then we aren't their equals, are we?"

"Are you so convinced of their superiority, then, this *master race?*" Chantal said quietly, but with an ugly rasp below the surface of her voice.

"Superiority?" Solange made a moue. "Is the wolf superior to the deer? Superior at what, my dear . . . singing, perhaps? By that standard, *I* am the superior one on this estate; except perhaps for Yasmin, and she is stronger on the instrumental side. Mistress can paint in a superior fashion; you are superior to me in mathematics. Master race? They *are* a race of masters, that is plain fact, Chantal. Also that they are stronger than we; that is a better word than 'superior.' Stronger in their armies, of course, stronger in their wills and bodies, as well. They are *here*, are they not?

"That," she continued, lying back and linking her hands behind her head, "is what I meant when I said that I had surrendered, Chantal.

I don't try to fight, or pit my pride against theirs . . . There's a curious freedom to it, really. No more tension, no more struggle or fear. Like stepping off the high diving board, everything's out of your hands and all you have to do is . . . let go. I just let . . ." She paused, quirked her lips. "No, I *helped* them change me, inside." She tapped her temple. "Like surgery in here, you see? The scars still ache a little, now and then, but that is fading. Once you've stepped through that wall you find they're not so bad. Even kind."

"Kind?" Chantal came to her feet. "Leaving aside the War—"

"—which they did not start," Solange interjected.

"—Leaving that *aside*, I said, leaving aside what is happening to *me*, what about the people they *killed*? Here, on this land they call theirs."

Solange sighed. "A pity, but those three attempted armed revolt, Chantal. If you lift your hand to the masters, you die. Everyone knows that."

"What about Bernard, then? In the stables? *They cut off his balls.* And made everyone watch!"

"Chantal, he tried to burn down the house"—she jerked her head back at the towers of the chateau—"at night, with *forty people* inside, most of them locked in their rooms! I would not have been so merciful." She cocked an eyebrow. "We become somewhat abstract, my dear. Let it suffice to say these people suffered because they resisted. Once you have said in your own heart, 'do with me as you will,' the suffering ends, *n'est-ce pas?*" Her tone became dry. "One might add, at least you are not required to learn a whole new set of . . . ah, *habits*, shall we say." Chantal flushed, and Solange giggled again.

"Actually, it's a bit like those revolting-sounding Normandy dishes we ate in Montparnasse when I was a student, you know, tripe cooked in cream with calf's brains. Horrible to think about—you have to close your eyes the first time; quite nice once you're used to them." A smile. "She could see I was trying hard, and was very . . . patient with me, very gentle. Besides, there is a certain enjoyment to be had from making another happy, is there not?" She sat up on the lounger and moved down, closer to the other serf.

"Let's get to the heart of it, Chantal. You feel that you are a person, and are being used like a . . . like a convenience, isn't that it?"

"Yes, that is it," she replied bitterly. "I'm surprised at your insight."

"Now, now." Solange paused and bit her lip. "Look I've slept with him too, you know." At Chantal's surprised glance: "He asked her, she asked me, I agreed . . . why not, after all? He's not a bad man, once you get to know him. Have you tried talking to him?"

"What for?" Chantal said wearily. "What could I say?"

"Because, if you want to be treated as a person, well, people talk, things don't. I talk to the Mistress a good deal, you know: I amuse her, she . . . terrifies me, fascinates . . . What to say to him? 'Isn't it a nice day,' or 'How did you get that scar,' or ask him what he'd like you to do . . . They're perfectly willing to treat you as a person, Chantal, *on their terms*. After all, he doesn't want as much from you as the Mistress does from me, just a certain degree of . . . ah, cheerful complaisance. Why not give it a try?"

"No."

"Why not?"

"*No!*" She looked up; there was no anger in her face, only the translucent blankness of someone looking within themselves for knowledge of their own soul. "I am too afraid."

"Afraid of what?"

"Afraid of becoming like you."

"Well," Solange said, stopped herself and threw up her hands, then leaned forward and patted Chantal on the shoulder. "So was I, before I did it. I'm a different person now, and happy . . . Ah well, I've done my best for you. If your pride means that much to you, well just don't drag anyone else into your suffering." She stood, the violet eyes lidded. "Because you *are* going to suffer, you know, until they break you or you die. Until dinner, *cherie*; I'm supposed to see Father Adelard about the choir."

She bent to strap up the player and walked out into the sunlight past the fountain of the nymph. Her kidskin slippers scuffed across the grass, and already she was singing.

Tanya von Shrakenberg watched the stroller being wheeled off to the main entrance of the manor, her head cocked to one side. It was very quiet, the loudest sound the wind through the chestnut trees above them, somewhere children were playing, an ax sounded on wood; far off and faint came the long mournful hoot of a steam locomotive's whistle.

"Ahh, children," she said. "One of the better things in life. Once you've pupped, that is, as my cousin so elegantly put it: conceivin' them is nice, too. *Bearing* them is an insufferable nuisance, but then, life is like that."

Marya made a noncommittal noise as they walked along the path at the foot of the chateau's east wall. The sun was just behind the high bulk of the towers, leaving a strip of shade for the brick path; outside it, to their right, the gardens shone with the cruelly indifferent beauty of nature.

No, the nun thought. *The pathetic fallacy. Nature is merely indifferent, it is the heart of fallen man that is cruel.*

"I would not know, Mistress," she said in the flat, calm tone she found best for dealing with the masters.

"Yes. Pity you're sterile, shame to lose your heredity." Marya started. "Haven't read y'own file?" the Draka continued, surprised. "Radiation overdose." Her face grew somber for a moment. "I wish t'hell we hadn't invented those things, I surely do."

The Pole blinked aside memory of the intolerable flash and searing heat. "I am sworn to chastity, in any case, Mistress," she went on.

"So?" To the plumber and his apprentice, shifting into French: "*Ça va, Marcel?*"

Marcel smiled cautiously and bowed in place; the younger man rose from the manhole and made a more formal obeisance. "It goes well,

Mâitresse," he said. "The fountains should all be working for the cel-ebrations. Also the standpipes in the Quarters are all completed." He shook his head. "You were right about the total input, *Mâitresse."*

"Water-borne sewage systems are hungry beasts, that's why we put in a twenty percent margin." A smile. "You've been doing good work, Marcel," Tanya said. "Don't overstrain now: I want you healthy. Jacqueline and her baby?"

This time the plumber's smile was more genuine. "Very well, *Mâitresse;* there is some sickness in the mornings, but the women tell me that is to be expected."

Tanya nodded, and patted her own stomach. "Inconvenient process . . . Anyway, I'll be sending the midwife by, and I've told the kitch-ens to send down anything special she recommends. Jacqueline looks like she hasn't been eating as well as she should these past few years, so we don't want to take any chances."

"Thank you, *Mâitresse,"* Marcel said with a worried frown. "She is tired, but will not rest as much as I would wish."

"I'll mention it to the headman. Keep well."

They came to what had been the north side of the chateau, where the new construction began: the old east–west I-shape had been turned into a C by adding a three-story wing to each end. Reinforced con-crete frames, Marya remembered, and prestressed panels for the walls, exterior cladding in a stone-and-brick checkerboard that matched the older part of the chateau without trying to imitate it. Tall windows looked in on echoing empty space, but the ground outside was already comely with fresh sod and transplanted trees; Tanya stopped and nodded to a group transplanting creepers along the base. They were girls in their early teens, mostly, and Chantal's sister Therese. She had been giggling and talking with the others, falling silent than they as the Mistress halted.

"Good work," Tanya said, and patted Therese casually on the head.

"How is she?" the Draka asked Marya as they continued.

"Somewhat better," Marya replied, keeping her eyes carefully for-ward. "She speaks more freely, particularly to young people; she remembers a little, although all from her earlier childhood, mostly before the War. But she is still easily frightened, particularly around men, and the nightmares continue." She frowned in thought. "Essen-tially, she is stabilizing in a regressed state. Very delicate . . ." She hesitated.

"Spit it out," Tanya said.

"Mistress, in Lyon, you, ah, intimated that if Chantal were to misbehave—"

"That Therese would be punished for it?"

"Yes, Mistress. I must advise you that further mistreatment could easily drive her into catatonia, and—"

"—and you're afraid Chantal might do somethin' stupid and Therese would suffer fo' it," Tanya finished.

Marya stopped, wheeled and confronted the Draka; her face was calm, but her hands were clenched and shoulders braced, as if she leaned into a storm.

"Mistress, with all due respect, Chantal is on the verge of a nervous breakdown. The abuse to which she is being subjected—"

"Stop."

Marya jerked slightly, with a prickling consciousness of danger running over her skin like the feet of ants; she forced herself to remember what Chantal's eyes had been like, the last time the summons came. Tanya's were unreadable, the clear pale gray of snow at sunset; her lips were slightly parted, impossible to tell whether in amusement, anger or anticipation.

"Marya," Tanya said softly, taking the long ash-blond braid of the nun's hair and switching her lightly on the cheek with it. "Marya," she continued, with another admonitory tap, "on this plantation we don't starve our serfs, let them get sick, beat them for pleasure, or rape their children. Any of those would be abuse, perfectly within our rights, but grounds fo' complaint. Chantal isn't bein' abused, just used. As a bookkeeper, like you; and fo' pleasure. Fucked, to be blunt, and occasional sexual intercourse is no inherent problem to a healthy wench her age, particularly if she lubricates properly, which I'm told she does. If she chooses to find it unpleasant, that's *her* problem. As fo' you worries about Therese, fo'get them."

"But—"

"I lied." Tanya gave a wolf's grin. "Never had any intention of makin' her a hostage. Now, as fo' a 'breakdown,' breakin' Chantal down is one of the reasons I mentioned her to Edward. Saw it in her background, the way she fought up out of the guttah, got an education, that sort of thing; took spirit, determination an' a strong sense of self. All of which need to be . . . rechanneled. She's just gettin' what you might call a graphic demonstration of her own helplessness, on a level impossible to ignore or deny. All she has to do is *accept* her own weakness, dependence an' so forth. Lucky we didn't decide hunger or physical pain would be mo' efficient."

Another grin. "Mo' fun fo' my husband this way, too." Her head went to one side. "Why, Marya, sometimes I think you disapprove of me." A laugh. "Nice stone face, an' you've got good voice control, but when youre really upset or angry, yore ears turn a brighter shade of red. Wouldn't be a problem if'n you were wearin' a wimple an' coif, of course."

Marya snatched down a hand that had flown to the side of her head from reflex, and spoke in a voice whose steadiness brought her a small guilty spurt of pride, even now.

"It is not my place to approve or disapprove of you, Mistress," she said. To herself: *That is God's prerogative, and be assured that He will, you murderer, blasphemer, and corrupter of innocence.*

"Marya, words cannot *express* mah utter lack of concern fo' you opinions, 's long as you are reasonably polite about expressin' them . . . Just to clarify, though, we are not tormentin' Chantal fo' its own sake, or because we enjoy seein' her suffer. Draka have two professions, basically: we fight wars—beatin' down open, organized opposition an' enforcin' political obedience—an' we manage serfs, doin' the same thing on a *personal* basis. Obedience isn't enough, in the long run; the objective is domestication. Her sufferin' is incidental to what we do enjoy, the feelin' of another's will breakin', leavin' obedience and humility. Pain is just another tool we use fo' the process, like a hammer; we take it out when necessary, then put it away. Analogous to trainin' a horse to the saddle."

"We are, then, not human in your eyes, Mistress? Animals?"

"To the contrary, we never fo'get you're human, that's exactly the point. It'd be mo' accurate to say we don't consider ourselves human in the usual sense; we're higher up the food chain. In terms of culture, if not biology, though the eugenics people are workin' on that. Or to be blunt again, you farm the earth an' we farm you. Domesticated humans are much mo' profitable and rewardin' than plants and animals, although much mo' dangerous and tricky, of course."

A blink, followed by laughter. "And if serfs weren't human, we'd all be guilty of bestiality, no? I'll have to tell Edward that one. Well . . . little Chantal's education is goin' to continue until she learns her lesson, after which it'll be recreation instead. I might take that pretty pony fo' a trot myself, when she's properly tamed down; don't much like it unless there's . . . interaction . . . on a personal level, as well. Men do, of course, but"—she made an offhand gesture—"men, well . . . lovely creatures at their best, very satisfyin' at times, but their nerve endings are a little crude, difficult fo' the poor dears to appreciate the subtleties of the amatory arts. Prisoners of their hormones, really . . ." Another shrug. "If Chantal comes to you fo' advice, consider givin' her Solange as an example of successful adaptation."

Marya coughed to cover the lump in her throat and waited a moment. Curiosity as much as anger drove her to speak. "Mistress, in my opinion—my professional opinion, that is—Solange is mentally ill."

Tanya laughed as she turned to walk on, giving the nun's braid a tug to bring her along. "Marya, Marya, I expected better than that from an intelligent and well-educated person like you. Sanity is always socially defined." She stopped to pick a flower and tuck it behind one ear.

"Among Romans of the late Republic, fo' example, overt sadism was the normal personality type. Mass masturbation in the stands of the Coliseum while they watched people bein' burned alive or torn apart by wolves. I'm familiar with the technical terminology you might apply to Solange, masochism, fo' example, learned helplessness, regression, transferal, identification with the aggressor. All addin' up to a perfectly functional response to this environment, even if it would have been neurosis before the War. Fo' that matter, what was that Viennese fellow, Englestein, we studied him in introductory Psychological Manipulation— claimed women were inherently masochistic. Nonsense among us Draka, of course, but perfectly sensible among outlanders, where females are slaves anyways."

Marya opened her mouth, considered certain doctrines of the Church and closed it again; futile, to try and explain the difference to a Draka. *Yet a woman was Mother of God,* she reminded herself. *Beside that, even being Pope is very little.*

"Actually, Solange—well, she's the finest piece of loot I acquired in the whole War. Beautiful, of course; intelligent, well educated as far as cultural things go, good conversationalist, playful, wonderful singer, first-rate amourist . . . and charmin', simply charmin'. Pleasure just to contemplate, and an inexpressible pleasure to own; like havin' one of those magical jeweled birds in the *Thousand and One Nights*, all fo' myself. Fun just to pet an' pamper, she *enjoys* things so much."

A sigh. "An exotic luxury; I spent five years in that stinkin' tank, figure I deserve it. Also"—she paused for words—"difficult to convey to someone outside the Race—the emotional twining . . . that particular combination of adoration, fear, desire and willing, total submission . . . It does somethin' fo' a Draka. An intoxication like bein' a god, one of the more disreputable Greek ones." She glanced aside at Marya's face. "Ah, shocked you a little, eh?"

Tanya released the nun's hair, and they walked in silence for a moment, the Pole was white-faced, her hands pressed together to control their shaking. "It . . . disarms us too," the Draka mused, almost to herself. "Like a wolf stops fightin' when its enemy rolls over on its back an' shows its belly. Operates below the conscious level, just as pride an' defiance arouse our aggression." She spread her hands. "Practical reasons, as well. Notice that I don't allow Chantal access to the nursery; won't, either, fo' a good long while."

The nun looked up, the breathing exercise learned as part of meditation giving her back control enough; her mind felt detached, washed in a white light of anger and revulsion. "I notice that you place no such restriction on me," she said huskily, the liquid Slavic accent stronger. "Have you some program to break my spirit? Am I so tame, then, Mistress?"

"No, I think you are incapable of harmin' a helpless infant," Tanya said amiably. "Chantal might, in a fit of temper, though she'd probably flail herself with guilt afterwards. Such a grubby bourgeois emotion, guilt . . . Solange wouldn't hurt a child, but she'd quite probably *neglect* one." A shrug. "Marcel back there, still another case of tolerable adaptation. Even better in a few years, nothin' like a family to teach a man caution an' humility."

They had come to the north end of the new wing, a glassed-in shell with a flat second-story roof ringed by a balustrade of red porphyry. Through the windows they could see climbing bars, mats, ropes, wall racks for weights and weapons, suits of padded unarmed-combat armor, machines of springs and balances. Behind would be the steambaths, soaking tubs and massage rooms; not so well equipped or elaborate as it would become but what the von Shrakenbergs considered a good beginning. The outdoor cold-water plunge was an embellishment of nature, a stretch of slough and marsh dredged into several acres of artificial lake; trees, gardens, walkways and lawns bordered it, and an island held a grove and pergola. Not entirely a luxury, since it also served as the main reservoir, with intakes below taking off the filtered water.

Most of the fringes were tawny-gold sand brought up from the Loire, but here near the palaestra was a half-moon beach of gently sloping marble; Marya remembered coming across the indent-order for it while organizing the files, forest-green serpentine stripped from a bank building in Tours. The paved space between building and water held potted trees, stone benches and tables, some shaded by trelliswork, others by ornamental hoods of stained glass on wrought-iron frames. Water quivered under the breeze like ticklish skin, shot fifteen meters skyward from a fountain amid the lake's waters, arching up in a sunlit cloud of spray. The sun turned the flat surface into a sheet of silver-gilt and blue for an instant, making her blink back tears with its eye-hurting brightness.

Father Adelard was sitting at one of the tables with Solange's father, playing chess on a board inlaid into the granite surface. The two old men looked up as Tanya and the nun approached, down again when they halted out of earshot.

This too God made, Marya thought, glancing out at the water and heartening herself to look back at her owner. *Despair is a sin*, she reminded herself. *Hope one of the cardinal virtues*. And still meeting the pale gray gaze made her remember what Dante had said, that one of the worst torments of the damned in Hell was having to look daily on the faces of the infernal Host.

"So, no," Tanya continued, untying her sash. "I'm not under the impression you're tame . . . hold this." She tossed over the cloth belt and began pulling the robe over her head. "And this . . ." adding the caftan and putting a foot up on a bench to unlace the sandal. "Plain to see, your soul belongs to your God, your Churchan' possibly Poland. Irritatin', in the abstract; obviously, there are orders we can't give you, if they conflict with those. You don't have the sense of bein' defeated that, say, Marcel does, either. That turn-the-other-cheek nonsense, it's irritatin' as well, makes dealin' with you like punchin' a pillow.

"On the other hand," a shrug as she kicked her foot out of the leather and began on the right, "we can't give every fieldhand the sort of detailed attention necessary fo' tamin' a wild-caught house serf. Surface obedience has to be enough; find the levers and keep a close eye on 'em.

"Same with you, Marya. After all, we don't want you fo' either a bedwench or a whip-wieldin' bossboy; we want an accountant an' administrator. The medical skills are a bonus, and as fo' actin' as a wailin' wall, buckin' people up an' so forth, just nuts and cream to us. You work hard and conscientiously—if I'd known nuns were so well trained, I'd've bought mo' of them. Christianity's a good religion fo' slaves; of course, it has serious drawbacks, but we'll cure that, in time. Reedit it."

"*Will you! Will you, you—*" Marya shouted, and then stopped, appalled. The priest and Professor Lebrun looked up, shocked. The nun swallowed and braced herself; Tanya straightened up from untying her last sandal and came closer, eyes narrowing slightly.

"Yes, we will," she said softly. "In time, and we have all the time there is. Examine the Koran we allow our Muslim serfs compared with the original, fo' example." A thin smile. "We've had a nice talk, Marya: you've learned somewhat about me, which helps you to serve bettah, and I've learned more about you, which helps me. But that last outburst was a little beyond the line. You realize that?"

Marya nodded. "Yes, Mistress," she whispered. You did *not* shout defiantly in a master's face: Tanya allowed frankness, you could even state opinion fairly openly, but there was an etiquette, forms of respect. And she had broken the forms, before witnesses at that. *Our Lord was scourged*, she told herself. *It can be no worse than that. Thank you, Lord, that I may share Your wounds.*

Tanya smiled and patted her on the cheek. "But I was pushin' you, too. No *sjambok*; pointless to feed your desire to be a martyr, anyways. Finish foldin' my clothes, then come here an' hold still."

Marya laid them neatly on a table: caftan, cloth belt, underwear, sandals with the thongs together in a bow.

"You realize I'm not doin' this because I enjoy hurtin' yo?" Marya nodded; that was true, in a sense. "Believe it or not, Marya, I'd prefer you were happy here. Try acceptin' this in the right spirit, and it might be a first step . . ." A sigh. "No, I suppose not. Speak the proper words, wench."

"This serf is ignorant and insolent. I beg forgiveness, Mistress."

Crack! An open-handed slap across the side of the nun's face, with a hand that felt like a board wrapped in cloth. Hard enough to jar her head around and sting, but not to injure.

"Thank you, Mistress."

Crack.

"Thank you, Mistress."

Crack.

"Thank you, Mistress."

"That's that, then." They walked over to the table, and Tanya leaned over the chess game, studying it in silence for a full minute.

"Knight to queen's pawn four?" she said to Professor Lebrun. He cleared his throat, glanced at Marya, back down at the board.

"Perhaps, Mistress," he said after a moment. "Though perhaps . . . ?" He indicated a complex of strike and counterstrike.

"Hmm. That's the conservative approach; still, you goin' to be down another castle in three moves." She indicated the sequence. "So it's probably worth the risk. Still, suit yourself."

Shifting into French: "Priest." Father Adelard looked up, carefully averting his eyes. "About that request for a school you and Marya made. It's granted." A smile. "Don't look so surprised, priest; we do need mechanics and clerks, after all. You can start this winter; no more than thirty pupils, give us a list of names. Marya, can you get me a list of everything necessary?"

"Ah, that is, yes, Mistress."

"Good: by Monday, then. Oh, and look up Solange on your way back—tell her to attend in the massage room in two hours with my riding clothes."

She nodded in return to the men's bows and walked down to the water's edge; ran the last two steps, sprang, and hit the surface in a clean flat racing dive. The sleek head broke surface ten meters further out, and she began a quick overarm crawl toward the opposite shore. Father Adelard smiled and left then.

"This arrived," Jules Lebrun said to Marya, sliding the folded slip

of rice paper out of his sleeve. It was only a few letter-number com-
binations on a liner from a carton of cigarettes; a cheap mass-produced
brand, issued to semiskilled Class IV serfs in ten thousand canteens
across the Domination. His back was to the lake where the Mistress
of Chateau Retour was methodically swimming her kilometers, and the
paper could be disposed of in an instant.

The nun came to herself with a start. He peered at her through the
upper lens of his bifocals, squinting against the blur and the colored
light that filtered through the glass overhead. *Not hard enough to stun
her*, he thought. As beatings went, it had been mild, more a symbol
of humiliation than real punishment. Something else had struck at her,
a blow on the mind or heart. *Name of a dog, but this fading eye-
sight is inconvenient*, he thought irritably. *One does not realize how
much of a conversation depends on seeing the details of another's face.*

"Thank you," she said, curling her fingers around the scrap of stiff
liner and letting her eyes drop to it without moving her head. Her
face turned, and her hand seemed to brush casually against her mouth;
the Frenchman could see her throat work silently. Overlapping hand-
prints stood out redly on her square firm cheeks, but the animation
was trickling back into her eyes as she turned them to him.

"It's an acknowledgment. They know that Chantal and I have been
moved out of Central Detention in Lyon, and where: you are to be
the conduit." She smiled slightly at his silent nod. "Good, under no
circumstances should I know who."

"Sister, I am not sure who it is," he replied dryly. *One of two drivers
on the regular supply run, but that too shall remain confidential.* "Also,
I did several monographs on secret societies during my academic career."
He inclined his head toward the seat that Father Adelard had occupied. "You do not think we should recruit him?"

Marya frowned. "Forgive me, Professor Lebrun, but I would not
tell you if I did. Nor approach him during a courier drop, in any
case. But no . . ." A hasty gesture with one hand. "Father Adelard
is . . . a holy man, a good priest. My superior in the religious life,
of course."

She crossed herself: "I must risk the stain on my soul and not confess
explicitly what we do, Professor. Understand . . . Father Adelard is a
brave man, one always ready to take the crown of martyrdom for the
Faith. But he thinks mainly of his flock—as is understandable. The
bishop the Draka allow is duly ordained; we must obey his commands
in spiritual matters, but . . . I suspect they selected him carefully. The
Holy Father might feel constrained to agree, for fear of losing all contact
with the faithful here in Europe. Likewise Father Adelard is fearful of
who might be appointed if he were removed. And the people on this
estate *must* have a spiritual shepherd whose first loyalty is to God.
Best he not know of what we do. If we do anything of consequence,"
she added in what was almost a mumble.

Lebrun extended a hand that trembled with the misfiring of his nerves
and rested it on hers; the nun's fingers closed around the professor's
with careful force.

"Tell me, Sister," he said gently. "If you cannot confess to a priest, let me help bear the burden of your doubts. I may not share your faith, but I have faith in you, at least. There was anger in your voice when you shouted—is that what is troubling you?"

"No," she sighed, looking up at him with a smile of gratitude. "She— not boasted, just mentioned, that they intended to . . . geld the Church, I suppose you could say. Over generations, alter its message into one of worship of the Draka, I suppose."

Another sigh. "God moves in history, my friend; if He sends us trials, they are no greater than we can bear. We must do our best, and the Church Militant will survive. Oh, it may fall into corruptions for a space—the Church is the Bride of Christ, but here on earth it is made of men, and all men are fallen. Satan speaks in their hearts, and chausubles and vestments are not enough to bar him entrance; the Borgia Popes, even—" A shrug. "For a moment I believed despite myself that they could do this thing, and my anger was the anger of despair."

"Something else troubles you, though, does it not?" he asked. She bowed her head.

"Another despair; for myself. All this time I have told myself that I had refused compromise beyond the point that my conscience could bear. The Holy Father has said that such religious as remain in Europe must minister to the needs of the people; they may render unto Caesar, so long as no specific action violates faith or morals. What I have done here . . . nothing beyond bookkeeping, and there must be records if people are to be fed, the sick tended, houses built, whether we are free or slave."

"And you have helped whenever you could," he reminded her. "Interceded, often at risk to yourself."

Marya laughed, and he was slightly shocked at the bitterness of the sound. "She . . . that woman, no, that *female Draka* . . . pointed something out to me. That all my work, even my helping of others, makes this *plantation* run more smoothly. They approve! She praised my accomplishments!" Sudden tears starred her eyes and thickened her voice. "So much for my careful distinctions. *This* Caesar demands everything, most certainly including what should be rendered only unto God. Have I become accomplice in abomination?"

The old man felt warm drops spattering on the liver-spotted surfaces of his hands, and forced the faltering muscles to give an emphatic squeeze to the strong work-hardened palms between his.

"Sister." He waited. "Sister Marya Sokolowska!" She looked up at him. "Remember who invented lies, Sister. And that the best lie is a twisted truth."

The nun gave a shaky nod, returned the pressure of his hands and withdrew hers to find a handkerchief in the pocket of her skirt. "It would be simpler," she said with a slight twist of the lips that might have been called a smile, "simpler, if—"

"They were just brutes and monsters?" he replied, and gave a Gallic shrug. "The Domination is an evil that twists and poisons everything it touches, including the better qualities of its leaders. You have nothing of which to be ashamed, Marya Sokolowska." A grin. "Name of a name,

I don't think she would congratulate you on what we've been doing here today."

She returned his smile. "Forgive me for pouring out my doubts and despairs to you, my friend; it seems I'm nothing but a thundercloud today."

"You carry too much of a burden yourself. Chantal was involved in such affairs in Lyon; couldn't you bring her into this?"

Marya frowned and shook her head, once more in command of herself, and her tone had a professional's objectivity. "No, professor, I think not. She was with another organization to begin with—one we felt was compromised. She herself I have no doubt of, as far as her loyalties go. But she is, you must know, under severe stress at the moment."

He nodded quickly to spare her embarrassment, and she looked aside as she continued. "I am afraid for her stability, and this is no business for one who may lose control of herself. In recklessness or otherwise. Besides which—" She paused. "I find myself reluctant to take *anyone* into this matter, the risks are so great, balanced against what we can accomplish, a little information passed along, perhaps a package hidden . . . I feel guilty for endangering you, my friend."

"Allow me to chose my own martyrdoms, my devout one. I am an old man, and will be gone soon enough in any case; let me die as something more than a Draka pensioner, at least in my own mind."

She hesitated, then pursed her lips and spoke: "You do have a daughter, and we may be endangering her as well, through you. Not to mention . . . well, I had hoped you might be the means of her . . . recovery."

It was Lebrun's turn to look aside. "Have no fears on that score, Sister. Or hopes. Solange . . . Solange is safe, whatever befalls me. The Mistress would neither believe her capable of conspiracy, nor allow her to be punished in my stead. She is safe, even happy, regardless if I live or die. So I may operate with no fear except for my own, eminently expendable, life."

He turned his hands palm-up on the stone and concentrated on slowing the shaking. "The Mistress is right, you see. My daughter would report me in a moment, if she knew." Marya made a shocked sound and reached out to touch his arm, knowing the comfort useless against an unbearable grief, but offering it nonetheless.

"I am the false idol, you see," he said quietly, looking off over the roofs of the chateaus. "She loves me still, but I am the god who failed to protect her." His hands clenched into fists, and despite the wasting and shaking they showed a little of the strength that had been his. "I *did* fail her and her mother, I did." He smiled. "I must have failed my daughter long before the War, for things to have happened as they did; I never wanted to be an idol in her sight. Only for her to be happy and secure, and then a woman who would remember her father kindly; one who could stand on her own feet, with no need of a protector-god. She was such a bright child, so full of life—" Jules Lebrun shook his head with slow finality. "I failed her, perhaps by seeking to protect too much. But you I shall not fail, Sister."

Chapter Eleven

Captain Manuel Guzman leaned against the periscope well of the *Benito Juarez* and felt the clammy sweat trickling down under the roll-top collar of his sweater. The control center was underlit by the eerie blue glow of the silent-running lights, and utterly quiet; even the feet of the crewmen were muffled in felt overboots, and when they moved at all it was with an exaggerated care. Natural enough, since their lives depended on it: the *Juarez* was grounded in the soft silt of the estuary and helpless if the Draka searchers found a trace of her. The passive sound-detection gear was in operation, but they could all hear the throbbing of high-speed screws through the hull, resonating in the closed spaces of the submarine.

Twin screws, the captain thought. He was a stocky brown-skinned man with the flat face and hook nose of Yucatan's Maya Indians, old enough to have been a sub commander in the Pacific during the Eurasian war, and there was sympathy behind the impassive brown eyes as he watched the younger members of the bridge crew. This was the hardest part: nothing to do but think, nothing to think about but the crushing weight of water outside the thin plating of the hull, and of drowning in darkness.

Twin screws, going fast, his mind continued. Boosting on peroxide-turbines, much more powerful than the fuel-cell cruise motors but noisy. Over them, fading now. Probably one of the new Direwolf class stalker-killer subs, based on German research the snakes had captured; they had never been much at naval design. His mind drew in the details, long cigar-shaped hull, streamlined conning tower, cruciform control rudders with rear-mounted propellers . . . built to hunt other subs, but the Domination's sensor technology was nothing like as good as the Alliance's.

And the *Juarez* was a fine boat for this clandestine work. Modified from a mid-War cargo sub design, slow but ultraquiet, with a hold capable of shipping a variety of surprises.

"What do we do now?" the man from the OSS asked in a whisper, after the noise faded.

"We wait," Guzman said curtly. He did not like the Ivy League types secret intelligence seemed to attract; this one reeked of old-stock Yankee money and breeding. *Too many of that sort at Annapolis*, he thought resentfully. The kind who had made his first days at the Academy Hell Week in plain truth, back when *indios* were a government-mandated rarity and fiercely resented, when the only other Spanish speakers there had been *criollo* bluebloods, the sort of hacienda-owning *maricones* his father had spent a lifetime working for.

"Consider yourself lucky, amigo, that this isn't one of the old diesel-electric boats," he continued. Fuel cells did not need exterior oxygen, and if necessary they could wait two weeks, with abundant energy to crack fresh atmosphere out of seawater. "Now we wait, run up the antenna every night. When we get the message, you can bring out that fancy folding airplane of yours. If we get the message."

The agent blinked back at him; the captain reminded himself that the look of mournful reproach in the man's deep-set eyes was a trick of his features, not genuine expression. *Face like a horse with a receding chin*, he thought.

"Our man will make it," the OSS man said in his nasal twang. "He's been in there a long time, but he'll make it, and with the job done. He's . . . that sort of fellow."

Guzman nodded. It would take a man with real balls to survive very long among the snakes and make it back to the west. He looked up, imagining the destroyers putting out from Nantes, the patrol aircraft and dirigibles lifting from their runways and docking towers. *It's going to take balls* and *luck to be here alive when he arrives*, he thought wryly, The Alliance and the Domination were not formally at war, hence the *Benito Juarez* was still *officially* in her homeport at Hampton Roads, or out on a training cruise.

That was the necessary fiction. And there would be, could be no action to save the nonexistent *Juarez* here in the Domination's territorial waters. Nothing but a "lost at sea" telegram to their families if they did not return.

His eyes went to the picture taped to the guardrail of the periscope well, a smiling woman with hair the color of cornsilk and a Hawaiian lei around her neck. Bonnie-Lee would wait, and not in vain.

"Secure to holding stations," he told his exec. The man nodded, none of that surface-navy nonsense about bracing to attention in pigboats. "Carry on," Guzman continued, turning to go. There were always letters to write, even if they could not be posted.

Frederick Kustaa braked the Kellerman mini to a halt on the embankment road, steering over to the verge. The sudden quiet struck ears numbed by the rush of air past the open windows, the *pink-ting* of gravel thrown up by the wheels, and the dull roaring of the burner. Metal pinged as it cooled, and the fan sank to a gentle sough as the engine's feedback system signaled reduced demand for steam. He looked back over his shoulder: nothing on the long stretch of road behind him, nothing ahead since the two staff cars had whipped by fifteen minutes ago. Silently, he cursed the chance that had brought them up behind him just before the turnoff; under no circumstances did he want any Draka to see where his car had left the main road.

"We are unobserved?" the man in the backseat said. A thick Austrian-German accent, Professor Ernst Oerbach was a balding man in his late forties, looking incongruous in a servant's livery of dark-brown trousers and high-collared jacket.

More at home in sloppy tweeds, Kustaa thought. the man was almost a caricature of a *Mitteleuropan* Herr Doktor of physics. At a pinch he could pass for a medical man swept up in the conquest and sold cheap to a crippled Draka veteran.

"I hope we are," he said aloud, pushing down the reversing lever and turning the little car in a U. It handled well, very much like an American autosteamer of the same class, say, a Stanley Chipmunk. More of a driver's auto, less in the way of auxiliaries, but it was solidly built and the standard of the machining was beautiful; the Domination had never developed Pittsburgh's liking for planned obsolescence.

The American flogged his mind to keep awake as they drove east once more; his eyes were sandy with fatigue, and his mind and tongue felt thick with it. He looked at his watch: ten to seven in the afternoon. *No, 1850 hours,* he reminded himself doggedly, pulling the ragged edges of his cover personality's protective blanket back up about himself. *You're a Draka, they use the twenty-four-hour system all the time.* The Loire turned gently amid islands of warm gold sand and green willow, a hypnotic glittering as the sun sank behind them, soothing and lulling . . . He jerked his head up and wound down the window, letting the warm air blast at his face. Hot and a little humid, but nothing like a Midwestern summer, and the smells were different, more varied.

The fields beside the road were turning to the harvest; big fields of tasseled corn, sheets of sunflower and chrome-yellow rapeseed, wheat gold-brown and flecked with blue cornflowers and red poppies. Grain rippled in long slow billows, dusty yellow sunlight catching the flowers so that they glowed like jeweled chips afloat on an ocean of molten bronze. Pasture was a faded green, until they passed a hayfield being mowed by half a dozen horse-drawn cutter bars; that was a darker alfalfa color, and thescent struck home with a memory of warm barns and the weight of a pitchfork in his hands. There were orchards, cherries and peaches and others he could not identify, and vineyards, the grapes showing blue-purple among the big forest-green leaves, hanging from the trellis wires along which the vines were trained. The land seemed more wooded than it was, the slow rise to the north hidden by lines of trees high enough to cut the horizon.

"How it has changed," Ernst said, and the American could feel the headshake in his voice.

"You were here before?" Kustaa said, grateful for the conversation; he had not wanted to force it.

"In the '20s; I was doing some work at the Curie Institute, and friends took me on a . . . pilgrimage. Just this time of year, as well." A long silence. "If it was not for the river and the lay of

the land, I would not recognize it. All this"—he waved his hand—
"was small farms, with scattered houses and little barns. Small fields,
vegetables, and the flowers, so beautiful . . . Little inns where we
stopped, and had wine and crayfish soup and hot bread; there was
Madeleine, I remember, and Jules, he was a good friend, and Andre
. . . We were young, the Great War was over and such madness
could never come again. We would make. the world anew with the
power of Science. Jules would tell me that first we must learn how
to design a just and rational society, and I would say that no, first
we must tap the power of the atom to free men from the poverty
of nature so that they could *afford* to be humane."

He laughed. "And now all anyone wants of me is means to destroy,"
he said. "Turn this"—he nodded at the landscape outside the auto—
"into a poisoned wasteland. It is not my world, this place of fire and
ice you young men must inherit."

"Doubts, professor?" Kustaa said lightly. Unseen by the man behind
him, his lips tightened; this was only bare-bones possible with the
civilian willing.

"No. No doubts, my young friend. These Draka," and his lips twisted
at the word, "they have the souls of reptiles and their Domination is
a cancer. That they have atomics is bad enough, but fusion . . . there
is no way to prevent them forever, nobody can declare secret a law
of nature, but yes, I believe your United States, your Alliance, should
have it first. If only because you are less likely to unleash it."

Unfortunately true, Kustaa thought with bitterness. There was a long
pause before the Austrian spoke again. "Yet you also used atomics on
a city of men," he said softly. "Human beings flashed to shadows on
the concrete, children burned alive, cancer, leukemia, sterility. The
warlords of Japan were evil men, but can that justify—"

"You have a better way, Professor?" Kustaa asked sharply.

"No." A sigh. "No, I do not; if I did I would not be here, *ja?*
Ruthlessness drives out restraint, as bad money drives out good, until
we are left using madness against madmen, with the death of all that
lives as a prize; such is this *Totentantz* of a century of ours." Another
pause. "I am glad to be old, my friend, very glad indeed."

Kustaa remembered his family in the primary target zone; remembered the microfilm in his belt, and what rested in the baggage trunk
of the autosteamer. This time he slammed his hand against the pressed-
steel panel of the car door, hard enough to skin a knuckle. The sharp
pain jolted him back into alertness—how long had it been since he
slept?—Christ, two days now. Fear returned with thought, the waiting between his shoulder blades for sirens and shots. He almost stamped
on the throttle when the two figures stepped out into the road to flag
him down by the tall stone gates. The men leaped aside with a yell
as the Kellerman leaped forward witha spurt of dust, then slammed
to a halt.

Kustaa heard Ernst's quick surprised curse in German as he shoved
home the brake and the cylinders exhausted with a quick *hiss-chuff!*
The older man's forehead thumped against the back of the seat, and
his own nearly slammed into the padded surface of the wheel. He sat,

shaken, staring at the sign that hung in chains between the gateposts:

CHATEAU RETOUR PLANTATION
EST. 1945
EDWARD AND TANYA VON SHRAKENBERG, LANDHOLDERS

"That's it, by God," he mumbled. "That's the one." *Now* the problem was gaining entry to the household. The fabled planter hospitality would do him some good, his wounded-veteran status more, but . . . he remembered the notice in the local paper, this christening party or whatever it was. *Maybe they haven't got the last guest, yet.*

The two men with branches came cautiously to the driver's side of the car; French by their looks and dress, serfs certainly by the numbers on their necks.

"Maître," one said, and shifted into barely comprehensible English, obviously picked up from Draka or Domination-born serfs:

"Mastair, pleez to 'company moi, a l'Great House, to be guest?"

Kustaa croaked, and waved a suitably imperious hand at Ernst, who responded with accented but fluent French. The serf's face cleared from its frown of concentration, and he poured out a torrent of response accompanied by hand-waving.

"He says that you are bidden to the house as a guest, for a naming feast, Master," Ernst said.

Kustaa hid his grin; the nearest thing most Draka had to a religion was a belief in the destiny of the Race, but they had as much need for ceremonial as any people. There had been a Nietzsche-and-Gobineau-inspired attempt to revive Nordic paganism back in the 1890s, but it had failed even more dismally than the later Nazi efforts, only a scattering of swearwords surviving to mark it. Customs like this helped fill the gap; he supposed they also built communal solidarity. The Citizen caste was thinly scattered and would need some sort of structure to ensure a minimum of social intercourse. *Which makes them less suspicious of a passing fellow Draka, which I will take* full *advantage of,* he thought.

The other serf suddenly slapped his forehead, pushed the first aside and bowed, presenting a square of cardboard pulled from his pocket. Kustaa took it with a grunt of relief, read the flowing cursive script. It was handwritten, in a neat old-fashioned copperplate penmanship familiar from his study courses:

> *Edward and Tanya von Shrakenberg bid the passer-by to be Wayfarer-guest at the naming feast of their newborn twins, now to be welcomed to the Race. If your duties allow, enter for the sake of the blood we share and join in our celebration of kinship, standing as honored guest for all brothers and sisters of the Dragon breed. Let the bond of past, present and destined Future be renewed!*
> *We expect the feast to last three days from tomorrow morning.*
> *Be welcome; our house is yours.*

"Shit," Kustaa whispered, remembering to turn it to a cough at the last minute. *Our luck is in at last,* he thought with hammering glee. The recognition codes sounded through his head.

The manor house of the plantation was an old French chateau; he glanced indifferently at the bulk of towers, the eighteenth-century additions, more recent construction. There would be time to memorize the floor plan later, he thought, climbing stiffly out of the Kellerman, time when his brain was functioning on something less than reflex. He slung the battle shotgun from the boot beside his seat and looked about. They had halted in a graveled yard in front of the arched entrance that cut between two round towers, and through the bulk of the building; he could see hints of courtyard and garden through the dim recess and the wrought-bronze gates that closed it. His mouth tasted of chalk, and his feet seemed to float over the rock and dry dusty pinkish earth of the drive as he moved to unlock the baggage compartment at the front of the auto.

Ernst's small cardboard case. His own luggage, carefully faked by the OSS; two fold-and-strap bags of ostrich leather and aluminum framing with the gold stamp marks of Foggard of Alexandria. A marula-wood case for the shotgun; he took that himself as servant hands reached for the other luggage.

"*No,*" he croaked as they touched the other piece that filled most of the compartment, a box like a small steamer trunk with handle sat the corners, securely locked, plain steel freshly painted in dark green. His mind saw the markings underneath: TECHNICAL SECTION: WEAPONS RESEARCH DIVISION. DO NOT TOUCH—RADIOACTIVE AND TOXIC. With the purple skull-and-bones symbol to add emphasis.

Even without markings, it would provoke too much curiosity if the serfs tried to lift it; there were a dozen sealed tubes of raw plutonium oxide inside, each slotted into its holder. Plutonium is heavy, and the lead tubes and multiple lead-foil baffles of the shielding were even more so. The sight of it made him sweat, and he slammed down the lid with unnecessary force.

"L'auto a parkin', Mastair?"

He started and wheeled; the Frenchman jumped back with stark terror on his face, mouth working as if he was about to burst into tears. The sight of it turned Kustaa's stomach into a tight knot of nausea, adding to the sour taste at the back of his mouth.

I'm a strange Draka, he reminded himself. *I could blow his head off with this scattergun and get nothing worse than a fine and a tongue-lashing for destroying other's property.* More reluctantly: *No, not exactly. These planters are paternalists, in their way; they'd call out anyone who did that and kill them on the dueling field, the way an American might beat up someone who shot his dog. I'm a special case, with immunity to the usual sanctions.* And he would look wild, dusty and tousled from the drive, unshaven, eyes glaring and red-rimmed from lack of sleep.

The American straightened and forced himself to calm, plastering a smile on his face as he detached the control-locking key and handed it to the man. A garage would be as safe a place as any, for the next little while. He *had* to sleep. And the cargo would be ready to move.

Ernst came to his side. "Horses," he muttered.

Kustaa nodded jerkily, hearing the galloping sound of hooves. Two half-dressed children leaped their mounts over a lane gate on the west side of the chateau and pelted on behind it, yelling. He rubbed his eyes, wondering if he was seeing straight; then two adults followed more sedately, pausing to let a servant dismount and open the white-painted board gate before cantering over to him and dismounting; A man and a woman, he saw, both in planter's countryside garb. The man piratical with an eyepatch and scarred face, about Kustaa's own height, tow-colored streaks through short butter-yellow hair, wedge-shape build from shoulders to hips, the usual Draka combination of startling muscle definition and swift controlled movement. Dangerous-looking, even without the marks.

The woman stood with a hand on the man's shoulder, the riding crop hanging by its thong from her right wrist tapping against one boot. Hard and mannish-looking to American eyes, like most Citizen women, bronze-blond hair cut in a short pageboy; gymnast's figure but long limbs and broad in the hips and shoulders, smaller bust than an American woman with her build would have had. They both wore the standard gun belts with holstered 10mm automatics, pouches, long bowies at their left hips and slender daggers tucked into boot sheaths. The weapons were of the finest quality and customized, inlay and engraving on the pistols, checked hardwood knife handles. But still eminently practical, and they both wore thumb rings also, with surfaces chased to represent the knuckles of a mailed fist: the Archonal Guard.

Don't underestimate them, Kustaa thought, stepping forward. *Nothing to arouse suspicion, nothing.*

"Service to the State." he said, in a rasping croak. *Damn, much more of this and my vocal cords* will *be injured*, he thought with exasperation. His left hand flipped back the crushed-velvet lapel of his jacket, showing a seven-pointed star of turquoise and red gold; his right waved Ernst forward.

"Glory to the Race," the two Draka replied in unison, their eyes dipping to the insignia, then back to his face with respect and sympathy. Kustaa's mind flicked back to his instructor, the Draka defector who had drilled him on basic etiquette.

"Remember most Citizens don't just wear uniforms, they see combat," she had said, waving the cigarette for emphasis. "Auxiliaries do the scutwork. A Category III disability is somethin' we all risk; everyone has a subconscious reason to follow the custom of treatin' you like a tin god. You'll have to beat off the women with a stick, an' men will buy you drinks an' listen to you war stories, or leave you alone if'n you wants. Y'can get away with bein' considerable eccentric, too, 'specially with a headwound."

"Edward von Shrakenberg, Landholder, Tetrarch, Archonal Guard, Reconnaissance," the man said.

Shit, Kustaa thought. *Recon-commando, close-combat specialist, have to watch it.*

"Tanya von Shrakenberg, Landholder, Cohortarch, Archonal Guard, Armor," the woman added.

Oh, goody, an armored-battalion major, he mused. *Well, she* looks *tough enough.*

Ernst spoke for him. "My masters, my owner is Frederick Kenston: traveler in art materials, private, Twentieth Mechanized Infantry Legion, Combat Engineers. He regrets that his injury from blast and gas renders speech difficult, besides damage to balance and hearing. I am his medical attendant as well as his servant."

That had been the best cover available. A Category III veteran got a pension of 5,000 aurics a year, equivalent to a steady middle-class income, enough for a ten-room villa and six servants. "Traveler in art materials" meant loot buyer essentially, a freelance contractor who bought from individuals to resell in the cities of the Police Zone, or to collectors and museums; it was a plausible occupation for a restless man, one not content to sit and vegetate. The injuries enabled him to avoid an accent only years of practice could duplicate exactly; when he *did* have to speak, the croak would cover most of it, and the XX Legion was raised in Alexandria, where the usual Draka slur was more clipped, a legacy of nineteenth-century immigration.

And the balance problems . . . He recalled the defector, "You combat style would be a dead giveaway in any palaestra in the Domination, an' anyhows you cain't fight worth shit." Kustaa had bristled at the time, but a few humiliating sparring sessions had cured him of that. "Mo' to the point, you cain't practice, or do gymnastics, or even dance, and all of them is impo'tant socially. This gets you off, an' nobody will pick fights with you." Impaired hearing would make others more likely to talk around him, and the Combat Engineers accounted for the workman's set of his muscles.

The two Landholders stepped back and saluted him, fist to chest, then gave him the forearm-clasp Draka handshake. "Honor our home," the man said. *Edward, I'll have to remember his name,* Kustaa prompted himself.

"Stay a day, stay a week, stay a month," the woman added. "An' while you do, what's ours is yorn."

Kustaa nodded, failed to repress an enormous yawn. His fingers signed at Ernst.

"My master thanks you, masters," he said. "And begs your pardon, but he is very weary." The Cartwright system, American, but that would arouse no suspicion: the Domination had never evolved a full-fledged sign language. Handicapped serfs went to jobs within their capabilities, Draka born without hearing were sterilized and sent to luxurious institutions calculated to shorten their lives. For the few cases outside those categories, a Yankee invention was tolerable.

"Pas de problème, as they says hereabouts," the mistress of the plantation said, clapping for service. "The guest room is ready; dinner by youself, right away? Good."

Kustaa hardly noticed the stairs. The bed was wide and soft; sleep softer, deeper, more dark.

Chapter Twelve

CHATEAU RETOUR PLANTATION
TOURAINE PROVINCE
AUGUST 2, 1947

"Master, wake up, plait," the voice said.

Kustaa's hand darted under the pillow to touch the butt of his pistol; the Domination's 10mm service-issue, but he had practiced enough to be as much at home with it, he had been with the Concord .44s he carried in Sumatra. Awareness came on the heels of the movement, and he relaxed into his yawn, catching himself in time to stop his natural reflex to cover himself with a woman in the room.

She had stepped prudently back after putting the tray on the table beside the bed, and smiled timidly at him as he sat up with another yawn and a stretch. *God, it's difficult to be nonchalant with a hard-on*, he thought, unconsciously glancing down at a morning erection like nothing he could remember since he was a teenager. *Well, two months of celibacy doesn't help*, he reminded himself wryly. That brought other memories, and he slapped the servant's hand aside with unnecessary violence when she followed his eyes and reached tentatively for him.

"Sorry," he grunted, and saw confusion added to alarm as she jumped back with a cry, cradling her hand. *Christ, what a bastard you can be*, he thought at himself. Bad enough the momentary temptation, but to take his self-disgust out on her in anger . . . *She's just a kid.* Sixteen, he judged; slim, with long russet hair and eyes the honey-brown color of water in a forest pond blinking at him. Dressed in some sort of long knit-silk shirt to just above her knees, and a tied-off cloth belt, with sandals that strapped up her calfs. *She's probably afraid of getting whipped if she doesn't lay you.* The orange number-tattoo was obscenely evident behind her ear.

Kustaa stood and let her put the caftan over his head, sat while she poured him coffee. The smell was almost intoxicating, and it was black and strong, enough to jolt him into higher gear. The room was midway up the taller square tower at the rear of the old chateau

374

building, about ten feet by fifteen. Two tall narrow windows, one looking east over the gardens and the other north along the roofline of the new wing, with its neat black slates and the balustraded terrace at the end. Both windows were open, letting in fresh green smells and early-morning light; it was about six, he estimated.

I could at least have fallen in among decadent *aristocrats who lolled in bed until noon,* he thought grumpily. The ones who owned this estate were probably up already, working at the famous Draka fitness. *No rest for the wicked,* he mused sardonically. *In this case, literally.* The coffee finished, he accepted a glass of orange juice and began prowling about the room; it was paneled in plain dark polished oak to thigh level, then finished in deep-blue tiles with silver-gilt edges. The ceiling looked like translucent glass, probably some indirect-lighting system; the floor was jade-green marble squares, covered by an Oriental-looking rug that felt silky to his bare feet. He stopped by the east window, pointing east to a set of large striped tents half-hidden among trees, a thousand yards away.

"What are those?" he grated. Not quite so exaggeratedly as he had for the Draka—it was unlikely they would compare notes with the French girl.

"*Ces?*" she said, coming to stand beside him. "Pour . . . fo' les guests, maistre. No, how you say, room here fo' all."

A discreet scratching at the door; the girl answered in French and another woman entered, pushing a wheeled tray. This one middle-aged, dressed in blouse and skirt; there were razors, basins and towels on the metal-framed stand before her. With a sigh, Kustaa sank back into the chair, submitting to the routine of hot towels, a trim for hair that was growing a little shaggy by the standards of the Domination's military-style crop, a careful edging with tiny scissors at his mustache, manicure, pedicure, neck, face and scalp massage . . .

The girl kept up a stream of French chatter throughout, handing tools to the older woman in an apprentice-to-master style. Kustaa waited until his face was being rubbed with some astringent cologne before he pointed a finger to the ceiling.

"Up . . . there?" he said.

"Above us, Master, is the armory," the woman replied in accented but fluent English; learned pre-War, he judged. "Above that is the communications room, for telephone and radio." A jolt of excitement ran through him at the news: perfect. There had to be a communications room, every plantation had one; there was a regular schedule of calls required by the Settler Emergency Network, to make sure no uprising went long unreported. But to have it right over his head— frustration followed, here he had an English-speaking informant, a legitimate excuse for curiosity . . . and a cover story which kept him dumb as a post. Nor could he simply say, "Where is Sister Marya Sokolowska?"

I can't count on making it clean away, he thought. With returning vigor the fear was having its usual effect, sharpening wits and sight, making the world clearer and more real. *Nobody can throw sixes on every roll; Lyon was far too close anyway. It's getting tight.* The sub would be in place from tonight, for a full week. Waiting *that* long would be an invitation to disaster.

Patience, patience, he told himself. *One battle in a campaign, one campaign in a very long war. More haste, less speed.*

The plantation was not a very large community; he would have breakfast, and then wander. Sooner or later he would make contact, and he would just have to hope it was soon enough. One of the things the most gung-ho officer had to keep in mind was that men were going to stop to rest, eat and take a crap every so often, whether they had orders to or not. He had slept, and now—

"Thank you," he said to the manicurist.

"It is nothing, Master," she said, packing away her instruments with quick, efficient movements. "My name is Annette—Tom's wife Annette, anyone will direct you—if you require anything. This young wench is Madeline; she will show you the Great House, if directed." A stern glance at Madeline, who looked meekly down at folded hands. "Although her English is not of the best, Master. Breakfast will be served on the terrace for the family for the next two hours: your servant has been directed there. Nothing more? A good morning, then, Master, and may you enjoy your stay on Chateau Retour."

"I—will," he grated. To himself: *But Chateau Retour probably will not.*

The terrace was a section of flat second-story roof at the north end of the new wing. Inside, the recent construction was still mostly empty echoing space, smelling of green concrete and strewn with ducts and wires, no break in the sweep but the occasional structural member. The far wall was stained glass; he gave the design a quick cursory glance, the usual intertwining vines and flowers the Draka were so fond of. Up under the peak of the roof, in what would be the attic crawlspace, he could see the mounts for an extensible aluminum-framed glazed shelter that would run out over the terrace in winter or bad weather. As he pushed through the swinging doors, he noticed the metal rails for more glass panels, running out along the sides; a clear wall, to make the outdoor space a greenhouse-like enclosure.

Now it was open to heaven, a stretch of warm yellow honeycomb marble flooring, the cells separated by strips of darker stone. The edges were fringed with a balustrade of some shiny reddish stone that looked semitransparent, carved into fretwork; the surface was big enough to seat fifty or sixty when tables were set out, not counting the space taken up by potted trees, topiaries and flowers. Six tall cast-iron lampstands held globe lights about the perimeter in tendrils that looked suggestively like tentacles; pots of brown earthenware trailed sprays of impossibly red-purple bougainvillea. *Actually quite pretty*, he thought.

Somewhere within him a puritanic Lutheran was asking where all this came from, and if he would ever find bayonet marks on the furniture from the last moments of the previous occupants. *Shut it off. Show some interest, man: you're a Draka, an aristocrat, aesthetics are half your life.* Plus he was what passed for a lower-class Citizen; mixing with Landholders wouldn't be all that common for him.

He nodded appraisingly and turned in a circle, froze with his back to the north and his face turned to the stained-glass wall. The view from this side was better, much, much better. The vines ran around the border of the arched picture, and wove through the base of it. It depicted a row of crouching figures, naked human forms all enlaced about with thorn vines and flowers no redder than the trickles of their blood; there were chains dangling from collars about their necks as well, down to pitted eyebolts in the ground. The faces . . . every race and age of mankind, male and female, alike only in their expressions of weary despair and endless strain.

Across their backs, supported by shoulders and knotted hands, was the bottom of a terrestrial globe, not a solid sphere, but an openwork projection with outlines for the continents. Overlaying the world, the Dragon.

Drakon, he thought. *I've met you before, oh, yes.* Whoever had done this one was a real artist, of sorts. The vast wings outspread, angled out and up in a flaring gesture; scalloped like a bat's, and colored a dull crimson that experience reminded him was almost exactly the shade of clotting blood. A skeletal ribbing supported the stretched skin, rendered in a glass halfway between black and indigo blue. Taloned feet braced against the outline of the globe, clutching symbols: a slave manacle, the glass somehow suggesting the pebbled black surface of wrought iron, and a sheathed bush knife, the machete-sword of the Domination. The body itself was the same dead-blood red as the wings, with an underlying hint of darker color where the bones would be. Enough to suggest a starved leanness to match the eternal hunger in the yellow eye that caught at his.

The face was a final masterwork, the bony outlines of the reptile visage curved and planed, not with any obvious mimicry of expression, yet still conveying something . . . a mockery that seemed to see within him and laugh at his defiance and his plans, an arrogance and cruelty vaster than worlds. *Power for power's own* sake, he thought, recalling the words of Naldorssen, the Draka philosopher. *Power is an end, not a means.* Power to crush the homes and hopes of men like him to be used as building rubble in this prison they called a Domination. Eternal tyranny.

With an effort that brought sweat to his face he stopped himself from emptying his automatic into the obscene thing. Hatred he had felt before, but it had always left him feeling a little dirty—like masturbation. *This* hatred felt clean, as if the thing on the wall before him was something that it was truly *right* to hate, the thing for which the feeling of hatred had been made.

You've been here too long and seen too much, he thought. *Control, control.* Then: *Come on, you're a Draka, you fucking love the shitty thing.*

He turned with a cheerful smile plastered on his face. *I was not cut out for clandestine ops, I truly was not. If—when—I get back, I'm going to tell Donovan to go fuck a duck, and settle down with Aino so hard I'll grow roots like a barnacle. Reup to Active in the corps, even a line command, go back to university, hell, take the wife and daughter and head for the north woods and farm with Dad.* His false smile turned genuine and wry. *Who am I kidding? Every time I looked at Aino or the kid I'd be seeing these people here in Europe. Waiting for the bomb to drop.*

The family breakfast table was in the far left corner of the terrace, with a good view over the courtyard at the north side of the chateau and the lake beyond. A few serfs were sitting at a smaller table nearby. Personal servants, he supposed, required to be on call at all times. They rose and bowed to him, the hands-over-eyes gesture that always set his teeth on edge. Two caught his eye. One was a pretty colored girl who looked like a mulatto, with a mandolin propped beside her, and a smile that seemed genuine. The other was a Frenchwoman, *her* brief flicker of the lips had all the warmth of February in Minnesota, but her looks were enough to stop him an instant in midstride. *God, what a man trap*, he thought. That brought a chill, as he considered what it probably meant to her life. *No wonder the poor bitch looks depressed.*

He seated himself where the house servant indicated; the table was set for seven, with plenty of room, and he was the first there. Folded newspapers beside five of the plates, with neat stacks of mail on top for four—those must be the resident adults. He unfolded the paper, grateful for its cover, remembered Aino scowling at him while he hid behind it over the breakfast table at home. *Some men like to talk in the morning, some don't,* he'd said. *Me, I like to chew my way through the sports section while I eat.* Hands filled his coffee cup, began piling his plate. Little fluffy omelets stuffed with herbs and cheese, smoke-cured bacon and sausages, grits with butter, hot croissants . . . Kustaa waved them to a halt, propped up the paper and began methodically fueling himself.

The paper was the *New Territories Herald*; about sixty pages, and more like an Army field rag than a civilian newspaper, say, something on the order of the *Star-Spangled Banner* he'd read in the Pacific. Logical: most of the Citizens in the conquered lands would still be military, or on some sort of official business, administrative or economic. He scanned the leading stories:

FAMINE IN RUSSIA OVER

Command sources indicate that the food distribution program has now reached most of the remaining population centers; grain production should reach sufficient levels with two years to discontinue . . .

MEDITERRANEAN PROJECT AUTHORIZED

Energy Combine spokeswoman Marie Kaine today announced that preliminary studies have confirmed the techno-economic feasibility of a large hydroelectric project in the straits of Gibraltar. "It will actually be more on the nature of a huge bridge rather than a dam, an arched structure that will be a virtual city in itself, supported by an openwork lattice descending to great depths. There are currents in both directions at different levels, and modularized power units, large low-speed turbines, will be added in series over a long period. The temperature differentials at various depths will also supply energy, and there are obvious aqua-cultural and industrial applications. The Dardanelles Project is a model, of course, but the Gibraltar complex will be of a new order of magnitude. We estimate a labor force in the 2,000,000–6,000,000 range, and thirty to forty years for the first phase alone. While the general concept is undoubtedly sound, I expect to spend the rest of my career troubleshooting this one."

BUSHMAN ACTIVITIES IN LYON

Kustaa tensed, hid his reaction with a cough. *Two days,* he thought. *I would have expected them to keep it quiet longer.* On the other hand . . . yes, the citizen population was simply too *small* to keep the ordinary sort of secret well. Too stubborn as well: they were disciplined enough but lacked the sort of meekness that obeyed bureaucratic dictates without question. He read quickly; just an acknowledgment that sensitive materials had been attacked in transit, the safe house of a resistance cell raided, and . . .

. . . suspicion of Alliance involvement. "We caught some of them." Strategos Felix Vashon of the Security Directorate assured our reporter. "Right now they're telling us everything they know and some things they didn't know they knew. Soon we'll catch the others—this meddling Yankee, too, if that turns out to be the truth—and they can join their friends. My people are experts; we can keep them all alive, sane and screaming for weeks. By the time we impale them, they'll consider it a mercy."

The editors of the *Herald* wish Strategos Vashon all success in tracking down the last of the Bushmen, and making Europe a place fit for the Race's habitation.

Not as bad as it could have been, he thought with relief. *Thank God for the cell system and Resistance paranoia.* Of course, the ones who had survived this long, first the Gestapo and now the Security Directorate, had to be paranoids. Blinking his way back from his thoughts, he noticed the flavor of the omelet on his fork: superb, a little too spicy but very good. The bacon was not smoked with anything like hickory, and the sausages had a trifle too much garlic, but both would do.

A grim smile: the spy heroes of the films he had seen rarely enjoyed breakfast on enemy territory, they were too busy dodging the invariably stupid machinations of the villains. His experience of clandestine operations was rapidly confirming that espionage fiction bore about the same relationship to reality as the war films he had seen in the Corps. And he fondly remembered joining a mob of enraged Gyrenes at a rest center wrecking a projector and screen after those USO morons tried to show what was left of an assault battalion Jason Waggen in

Hills of New Guinea. Not that they would have appreciated a realistic war film—what they wanted was a nice light comedy with lots of leggy showgirls and music—but the heroic speeches and neatly photogenic casualties had been just too much.

Of course, those fictional heroes could also afford to spit in the interrogator's eye as the hot irons came out, because something always rescued them at the last moment, or their captors would stand cackling and spouting all their secrets before the dashing adventurer grabbed their gun . . . Kustaa took a last bite of buttered croissant, touched his coffee cup for a refill and leaned back with a slight belch. *I must have gained six pounds, even with all the running,* he thought. *Funny, you never see a fat Draka.*

There was a sharp clacking from the courtyard below. *Then again, not so funny.* Two of them were practicing there, stick-fighting on the tiled stretch just in from the colonnade that ran along the inner edge of the building. Not the ones he had been introduced to, so they were probably overseers. A short squat dark-haired man and a taller woman with reddish-brown curls cut close to her head; both stripped to trousers and singlets, the thin fabric clinging to their sweat-slick bodies. Swinging fighting sticks in each hand, meter-long ebony rods with rounded steel tips. Swift flicking strikes, thrusts and darting slashes that blurred the night-colored wood and would have crushed bone and ruptured organs if they had landed.

Fast, God, but they're fast, he thought enviously. Another form dashed out from the exercise room beneath his feet. Anonymous in unarmed-combat armor of brown leather and padding and steel; it dove forward on its forearms and kicked back with both feet. The one following was only a flicker before it flew back out of sight with a crash. He recognized Tanya as she went into a forward roll and twisted back the way she had come, just barely in time, as her husband followed in a huge bounding leap that ended with a side-kick and his heel driven into her midriff. Their feet and hands were thickly padded, the armor over the stomach strong, but Kustaa was still surprised to the edge of shock to hear no more than a *huff!* of exhaled breath as the woman was knocked back half a dozen feet.

She backrolled half a dozen times and came to her feet to meet Edward's attack; for twenty seconds they fought almost in place, hands, feet, knees, elbows, blocking and striking almost too fast for the American's trained attention to follow. *Pankration* was what they called it, the classical Greek term for all-in wrestling-boxing, although it was an outgrowth of Draka contacts with the Far East in the 1880s. He could see the origins of the style in the Oriental schools he had studied, but this level of skill could only be learned by continuous training from babyhood. *And we have better things to do with our lives,* he thought. Furthermore, the Way of the Gun beat the Way of the Empty Hand every time, in his opinion. *Automatic weapons at two hundred paces, that's my preference.*

It was functional, though, he supposed. Serfs rarely confronted their masters with weapons in hand, and on a subconscious level a demonstration of personal deadliness was probably more daunting than weapons, no matter that the firearm was so much more objectively destructive. Just as a rifle with a bayonet could drive back a crowd better than the rifle alone, even though the blade added little to actual combat effectiveness. A fresh clatter broke into his thoughts; the owners of the plantation were down on the ground now, rolling, close-quarter work, driving knuckles at pressure points and trying for choke or breaking holds. Weight and strength told more in grappling style, and Edward called victory with clawed fingers in a position that would have ripped out his wife's windpipe in true combat.

They pulled off their helmets of padding and steel bars and kissed. "Not bad fo' a turtle-minded tanker," he heard the man say.

"Pretty damn good fo' someone who trained to crawl through ditches an' listen at windows," she replied, as they both shoulder-rolled to their feet.

"Mistah Kenston!" she called up to him. "Good mornin'; see you in half an hour!"

The two Draka were shedding their padding and clothes, tossing them aside with the casual unconcern of those raised to expect things to be picked up, cleaned and neatly replaced by ever-attentive hands. Kustaa remembered his own mother's weariness after he and Dad came back from the fields, keeping house for a family of six far from electricity and the sort of money that bought appliances. *Bastards,* he thought. They were trotting down to the marble beach; Edward swept the woman up in his arms and began to run, clearing a stone table with an easy raking stride. At the edge he halted and threw her; Tanya twisted in midair and hit the surface with a clean dive, her blurred form swimming out underwater for a dozen yards.

The overseers joined Kustaa at the table, freshly washed and dressed in long robes. *Any more of this and we'll look like a Southern Baptist's idea of the Last Supper,* Kustaa thought irritably. The man was wearing an earring and bracelets, too, one joined to his thumb ring by a silver chain; it still looked unnatural to see men wearing jewelry. A rueful glance down at his own clothes: loose indigo-blue trousers with gold embroidery down the seams, ruffled shirt, string tie with a jeweled clasp, black silk-velvet jacket with broad lapels edged in silver-gilt, buckled shoes. He had drawn the line at the diamond ear studs the outfitting section back at OSS HQ tried to insist on, but there was no alternative to the floppy-brimmed hat with the side clasp and spray of peacock feathers; the only really comfortable item was the gunbelt. At least he didn't have to wear *that* to breakfast.

I look like the most dangerous goddam pansy in the world, he thought. The overseers were making conversation among themselves, tactfully including him when replies could be limited to yes or no. Making conversation about this party coming up, and the impending harvest; it was late this year, evidently the spring had been cold and the summer delayed. Once he was jarred by a question about Alexandria, his supposed hometown, but the Draka answered it herself after his noncommittal grunt. They were going to have to get more agents trained in Draka speech patterns; the trouble was that the ones who could pass even casually for Citizens were so few. The dialect was

not really all that much like American Southern, either: derived from
the same roots, but a hundred and fifty years made a *lot* of difference. Not to mention the regional variation; he could tell the two
overseers came from separate areas, but . . .

Two of the von Shrakenberg children joined them, a towheaded boy
and a girl of the same age with freckles and red braids; disturbing—
it was easier to think of Draka as adult monsters. Then the master
and mistress themselves. . . .

They halted by the servants' table, Edward only long enough to sign
Ernst over to his "master's" chair; Tanya stopped and spoke to the
French girl. *Girl?* Kustaa thought. She *looked* young, with that clear
porcelain skin, on the other hand . . . The conversation was in French.
His own command of the language was rather good, and he strained
unobtrusively to hear over the sounds of wind and water.

" . . . lonely, Mistress," the serf was saying. "My bad dreams again."

Tanya ruffled her hair. "I do have to sleep with my husband occasionally, you know, my sweet. Tonight, then; the day will be a busy
one."

Does that mean what I think—Kustaa's thought began. Then they
kissed, and he managed to avoid staring. *Jesus, they're french-kissing,*
he thought, halfway between fascination and disgust. Reaching for
another croissant, he used the movement to glance aside at Edward;
the Draka had looked up from his newspaper and smiled, proud and
fond, before glancing down again.

"Glad they've approved that Gibraltar thing," he remarked to his
wife. Then "See you've got yorn mo' enthusiastic about domestic duties
than I've ever managed on mine."

"That's because you're a man and therefore crude, love," she said
with a grin. "But keep tryin', by all means." He laughed and kissed
her fingers, then turned to Kustaa.

"We 'spect to be rather busy, today, Mr. Kenston," he said affably.
"Guests should be arrivin' any minute—"

"Speak of the devil," the male overseer remarked, and jerked his
head to the east.

Two black dots coming in low and fast: twin-engine small planes.
Engine roar grew swiftly, and they flashed by overhead; one began
to circle, while the other drove across the chateau again at barely rooftop
level and began a series of wild-looking acrobatics, looping and turning.

"My cousin Johanna," Tanya said. "Ace pilot durin' the War, an'
never lets you fo'get it." She snapped her fingers and the mulatto girl
came running. "Yasmin, up to the radio room an' have the operator
tell 'em where the landin' field is."

Kustaa signed at Ernst. "My master asks," the Austrian said, "if you
have landing facilities, Masters."

"Why yes," Edward said. " 'bout two kilometers north, there were
some buildin's suitable fo' light hangars. Up near our primary wine-
cellars an' the shelter."

"Shel-ter?" Kustaa asked in his own gravelly "voice."

"Oh, the War Directorate's insistin'," Tanya said with an expression
of distaste. "Good idea, I suppose, but . . . shelter from radioactivity,

in case o' war with the Yankees. Underground, industrial-strength fuel cell, air filters, food an' water, so forth. Jus' fo' the family an' some key serfs to start, eventually fo' everyone. Hopes to God we nevah have to use the damn thing."

"Amen," Edward said. "Though at least we didn't have to put it in ourselves. Public Works Directorate did it, nice neat job, reinforced concrete shell an' doors from an old French cruiser. Pretty well all local materials an' labor, come to that."

Kustaa signed. "My master says you seem to be making rapid progress, Masters," Ernst said.

"Very," Tanya replied, taking a second helping of the grits. "Almighty Thor, but I missed these while I was expectin'. Mo' coffee, Francois. . . . Yes, very rapid. Troublesome, conquerin' an advanced area like Europe, but there are compensations. Got the road net intact, fo' one, that saved us ten years. Local supplies of skilled labor, an electric power grid needin' only a little fixin' . . . well, you know."

Kustaa nodded and accepted a slim brown cigarillo. A nursemaid had pushed out a double stroller with the youngest von Shrakenbergs, to be dandled and appropriately exclaimed over; the American carefully shut his mind to how much the wiggling forms resembled any human children.

"Now," Edward said. "As I was sayin' we're goin' to be ferocious busy, Mr. Kenston. But Tanya has volunteered to give you a quick once-over of our art collection, if you'd like."

The woman sighed, opening a cablegram. "I'm the resident appraiser, fo' my sins. We got a fair bit in Paris; that's another benefit of conquerin' wealthy countries—they have more worth stealin'." That sally brought a general chuckle; Kustaa managed to join in.

"Darlin'!" Tanya exclaimed suddenly, the hard tanned face turning radiant. "It's from Alexandra! They can make it!" Politely, she explained to Kustaa: "You know, the Alexandra from my 'Alexandra Portraits,' my lover in school, the exhibition I won my first Archon's Prize with?"

The American nodded, his grin going fixed. *Christ, these people are strange*, ran through him. And: *I'm supposed to be an art expert!* with a trace of panic. Running into what was evidently a well-known painter was just the sort of lousy break in his luck that was due, by now.

"And she's been pesterin' me ever since the war to do a new portrait, one so people won't think of her stuck at seventeen fo'evah; after all she's older than me an' a responsible official with four children, but we've never had time to do another study." A sigh, and she looked down at the paper with a slightly misty-eyed smile. "Ah, youth, sad an' sweet."

Kustaa coughed, and signed again. "My master says thank you very much," Ernst followed fluently, almost a simultaneous translation. "But he has several crates of selected pictures ready for shipment in Paris. Presently he is rounding off this trip by acquiring antique jewelry."

"Hmmm," Edward said doubtfully. "We're anxious to cash in some of the paintin's fo' want of space. The jewelry, what we're not keepin', takes no space to mention an' can only appreciate; market's glutted right now."

Tanya nodded; they both glanced at Kustaa, concerned to make his visit a productive one.

More signs. "My master says, thank you, a few days relaxation is what he principally needs, he grows tired more easily these days." Nods of sympathy. "If, perhaps, you could show him some of the estate, particularly the winery, my Masters, he would appreciate the kindness?"

"No problem 't'all," Tanya said decisively. "Goin' up there now anyways." She rose, dusting off her hands and chamois breeches. "Glad of you company, Mr. Kenston."

They were almost to the main doors when the stout blond serf stopped the Landholder of Chateau Retour.

"I have those seating plans you wished, Mistress," she said. The accent was unusual, not French or even German, despite the transpositions of "w" and "v": singsong and heavy at the same time. Kustaa's mind struggled to place it, the automatic filing process that kept covert ops personnel alive; languages were his tools as a spy, as much as his rifle had been as a Marine, and he was good with both. He snapped mental fingers. Kowalski had the same accent! The big coal-country Polack, the one who'd gotten the Bronze Star on Bougainville for taking out the Nip machine gun.

Polish. His eyes snapped back to her, in her thirties, about one-fifty pounds, five-three, built like a Slavic draft horse, flat face and ash-pale Baltic hair . . . and something about the eyes that reminded him of Kowalski or Sergeant McAllister, or even himself, sometimes. Longer skirt than any he had seen here, long sleeves, rosary and cross at her belt . . .

"Not now," the Draka was saying, when Kustaa touched her on the arm.

"Ex-cuse," he said, jerking a suitably casual thumb toward the serf woman. "Po-lish?"

Tanya stopped, swung round to nod. "Yes, though we picked her up here. Met her in Poland . . . long story, tell you later, Mr. Kenston. Nun, oddly enough; name's Marya, Sister Marya. Bit set in her ways, but a good hard-workin' wench; my head bookkeeper an' clerk."

Jesus fucking Christ, my contact! ran though Kustaa like a song of exultation. Patience evaporated in a fury of calculation: perhaps his luck had not quite reached the turning point. Radio, airfield, hiding place . . . and his contact, who could put them all together. *Wait a minute.* He rearranged his face, conscious that at least something had shown, they were both looking at him a little oddly. *I've got to talk to her, somehow.* Privately, with no possibility of interruption, so that he could give her the recognition code that *must* be kept secret. The way occurred to him; he almost gagged, but it was necessary. The Sister would have a bad time of it, but only until the door was closed, after all . . .

"Ex-cuse," he said, taking the Pole by the arm. Ernst interpreted his signals, his eyes going wide in surprise.

"My master says . . . ah, excuse—" Kustaa signaled further and the Austrian's eyes narrowed in understanding. "My master says, could he have the use of this wench?"

The nun's arm went rigid under his fingers, and she wheeled around on him with a look of pure hatred in her eyes before they dropped in the worst imitation of meekness he had ever seen. Tanya stared at him, began a peal of laughter and ended it in a cough. "No offense, Mr. Kenston, no offense, you don't know her. Ahhh . . ." She looked at the nun. Kustaa could see her evaluating the stocky figure, graceless in its thickset strength. Not what a Draka looked for in a wench, at all, or comely by the separate standard a Citizen male used for women of his own caste, either.

"No offense, but this'n isn't trained or suited fo' erotic service. Really, if'n you don't like the one sent to attend you this mornin'"—so his guess had been right—"there's a dozen others, prettier an' mo' enthusiastic."

"Pu-lease," he grated. Sweat had started out on his forehead, and his smile was more of a rictus. Perfectly genuine desperation, if the cause was one the Draka could not suspect. "Pu-lease, thu-is one." He put a hand to his throat, as if the effort had strained his damaged vocal cords.

Tanya stepped closer, put a firmly sympathetic hand on his shoulder and steered him a few steps away. He was suddenly surprisingly aware of her scent, a mixture of fresh-washed body and some slight violet-based perfume. "I'm ashamed to admit it," she said with low-voiced sincerity, "but that one won't answer you bridle, sir. Stubborn an' we haven't broken her to it, a work horse an' not a play pony."

"Pu-lease," and a rasping cough.

"Mr. Kenston, suh, if it's a nun you has to have, well, there's one on our neighbor's place down the road a spell. I'll phone over an' borrow. They've got a Carmelite, nice bouncy little thing; they might have her original robes 'round someplace an'—"

He shook his head vehemently; from what he had heard he was straining the limits of hospitality, but a Class III veteran could push pretty far. There was a sickening fascination to it, as well, a realization that this could actually have been happening. Nobody knew but him . . . No need to hide his emotions now, just the opposite.

"Suh, I warn you, she'll have to be subdued, an' even then once you're into her she'll be dry an' refuse to move." A sigh at his obdurate face. "You might need help gettin' her stripped and spread. Do you want her drugged or a couple of hands to help? No?"

Another sigh. "Well, Mr. Kenston, I'm tryin' to be mindful of a host's obligations, but I really can't spare her any time today; in fact she'll be workin' overtime until after dinner. So, if you'd like somethin' in the meantime?" He shook his head again. "Well, if you insist, suh. I must insist that she not be marked or injured. We don't allow anythin' too rough here. I'm givin' you fair warnin' of that. Clear? Then I advise you to tie her legs to the bedstead first thing."

Tanya turned, a puzzled and half-angry frown on her face; she shrugged at Marya, who was standing with her hands clenched at her sides. "Well . . . this mastah seem's determined to have you fo' a mount, Marya. Attend his room aftah you finished work, and serve his pleasure. And no slackin' today. Understood?" The nun continued to glare at the ground before her feet, until her owner barked sharply: *"Is that understood, wench?"*

Marya's head came up slowly. For an instant Kustaa felt an eerie prickle of *deja vu* as the fresh-cropped hairs at the base of his skull struggled to stand upright. Then he remembered where he had felt it before: Java, when the "disabled" pillbox had come back to life, and the turret-mounted cannon lifted its muzzle with a whine of gears. The Polish woman nodded once, with a curt snap, her square pug face held like a fist, then turned and stalked away. Her heels clicked like gunbolts closing on the marble floor of the vestibule, amid the statuary and the downslanting rays of crisply golden summer-morning light.

He became conscious of a hand under his elbow and shook himself loose again, turning to follow her out into the bright sunlight with its smells of garden and dusty gravel and the slightly oily smell of distillate. A six-wheeled car waited at the foot of the stairs, and the driver sprang down to open the doors.

"Well, well, you've turned out to be a man of . . . interestin' interests," Tanya said to him.

"Th-ank you," he said, anxious to choke off curiosity. A shrug. "I'll have restraints an' some oil-cream jelly sent up," she said. "And a silk switch." A snuffle of laughter. "I warn you, though, the last man to get anythin' into that one got scant joy of it. I'll tell you the sad story of Horn-dog on the way up." She rapped on the back of the driver's seat. "The winery, Pierre. An' maybe you could tell me a little 'bout what you saw in Lyon, been a while since I was there."

Lyon? Kustaa mused. *Somehow I don't think so.*

Chapter Thirteen

LYON, PROVINCE OF BURGUNDIA
AIRSHIP HAVEN
JULY 28, 1947
1100 HOURS

The *Issachar* was approaching Lyon from the north. Kustaa let his eyes drop from the pale turquoise haze of the sky to the land droning by six thousand feet below. The Savoie Alps were passing by to the east, dark blue with distance and higher than the airship itself; below, the Rhône trough was widening out, a patchwork of varicolored orchard, vineyard and field and the russet brown of ploughed earth. Vehicles moved insect-small along the long straight roads, trailing dust plumes like the white-gray feathers of sparrows; the river itself was blue-brown, with hammered-silver patches downstream where banks of pebbles broke the low level of the summer waters. An aircraft passed, climbing, a swift flashing of combined velocity, and there were two more dirigibles in sight, long whale shapes laboring north against the backdrop of mountain.

The American took another sip of the single beer he had allowed himself; Danish, excellent, mellow amber with just the right hint of bitterness, biting at the back of his throat. Methodically, he probed at his nerves. *Not bad,* he thought. *Still a little shaky.* Hamburg had been bad, very bad indeed; he was running through cover identities faster than Donovan had planned for. The danger was different from combat strain, more like a night-ambush patrol; less intense, but it didn't *end.* Worse than the danger was the effort of simply *being* a Draka for so long; having them hunt him through the Finnish woods had been simple by comparison.

He'd been skipping a good deal of the multiple tasking Donovan had planned for, as well. It was even worse tradecraft than he had anticipated, endangering the indigenous networks that were all the OSS had to build on, until it could somehow infiltrate the Domination's own organizations.

Shit, endangering me, too. Now I know too much; I've got to get

387

back. Straight to Lyon, but the delays had put him right back on schedule. With any luck, the coded messages had been sent out for the last week. With any luck, there was still someone *there* to pick them up. *With any luck and a day at the races, I'd be rich,* he mused.

"Docking in ten minutes." the voice over the intercom said. "Docking in ten minutes. All passengers please be seated until docking is complete."

Kustaa finished his beer and waved to the stewardess. The airship lurched as she reached across him to pick the glass off the veneered aluminum table, and a half-full bottle on the tray in her other hand toppled, sending a stream of amber-colored Tuborg splashing off the rim of the birchwood platter and into his lap. He began a yell, remembered to turn it to a strangled grunt and sank back into the seat.

The girl was on her knees beside his chair, reaching out with a cloth that trembled in her shaking hands to mop at the stain on the front of his fawn-colored trousers.

"Oh, Master, I'm *sorry*, I'm so *sorry*, please, let me help, please, Master—"

The lilting Swedish accent was raw with fear as he irritably snatched the towel and hastily wiped off the worst of the mess. Looking down he saw huge cornflower-blue eyes starring with tears, and a mouth working with terror.

"A-ll right," he grated, keeping to the strangled grunt that his cover allowed. "G-o."

She righted the bottles on the tray with frantic speed, wiping the floor plates, froze again when she saw who was looking her way, the senior stewardess, a born-serf in her thirties with a hard flat Kazakh face and a leather razor strap on a thong around her wrist. They were both in the same livery, a smart tailored jacket with a long V neck and a pleated skirt of indigo blue, but the older woman did not have the Swede's look of vulnerability. She came over with a brisk stride, her low-heeled shoes clicking on the roughened-metal planking, muffled over the rugs.

The offending woman (*No, girl,* Kustaa decided. *Seventeen, maybe eighteen*) stood and held the tray before her, there was a slight rattling from the glasses and bottles, a quiver she could not suppress.

"You wish punish this slut youself, Mastar?" The Kazakh's English was Draka-learned, with the hint of a barking guttural beneath, Kazakhstan had been the northernmost of the Domination's conquests in the Great War, a generation ago, about when this one had been born, he estimated. Her face held no more than her voice or the posture of her well-kept body: precisely trained deference.

"N-o," Kustaa said, waving a casual hand. "Is nothing." As much as he could say, as much as he could *do. You're here to observe and report,* he reminded himself savagely, behind a mask of detachment as perfect as the serf's. *Follow orders, dammit!*

The Kazakh nodded. "Rest assured, Mastar, she no sit fo' week." A jerk of the head, and the blond girl walked staring past them, through the cloth-curtain door behind the bar. There was a murmur of voices, one pleading it had been too little time since the last strapping.

The American rubbed at his eyes. *I thought I was tough*, he thought wonderingly to himself. *Every little bit pushes you a bit further. Fuck it, I want to be home, away from these people!*

"Not a bad little piece," the man across the table from Kustaa said, idly.

He was an exec from the Dos Santos Aeronautics Combine, up from the Old Territories to oversee conversion of European facilities. A square-faced man in his fifties, conservatively dressed by Draka standards, down to the small plain earrings and Navy thumb ring, smelling of expensive cologne. It mingled with the leather-liquor-polish scent of the long room along the lower edge of the dirigible's gondola; this was a short-range bird, shuttling between the larger European cities, not equipped with overnight cabins. No rows of bus-type seats, as there might have been on an American equivalent, though. Scattered tables for four, and freestanding armchairs, and a long bank of canted windows giving a view of the ground below.

"Not bad at all," he continued, with the air of a bored man making conversation. There was a flat *smack* of leather on flesh from the curtained alcove, thin yelps of suffering giving way to a low broken whimper. "Wonder how she strips."

"Black an' blue, now," the Air Corps officer beside him said. "You'd have to let her get on top."

She laughed at her own joke, more than mildly risque by the Domination's standards, began stuffing files in the flat attache case before her, then frowned. "That's a bit much," she said, and raised a brow at Kustaa. He nodded vigorously.

"Enough, there," she called, and the sound of blows ceased. Yawning, the pilot glanced idly out the window and exclaimed: "Look! *Just* what I was talkin' about, Mr. Sauvage."

The exec followed her pointing finger, and Kustaa's eyes joined his. They were over the military section of the air haven north of the city, the usual tangle of runways, hangars, workshops and revetments. The usual expansion work going on as well, the iron-ordered standardization of the Domination being overlaid on the more haphazard pre-War foundations. Long modular buildings, a chaos of dust as the road net was pushed out. Neat rows of fighters, older prop-driven models and sleek melted-looking jets. Strike aircraft, twin-engine Rhinos mostly, grim and squat and angular with their huge radial engines and mottled paint; they had been known as the "flying tanks" during the Eurasian War, for their ability to absorb punishment. Kustaa's OSS antennae picked up at the sight of the electrodetector towers, but they were basic air-traffic-control, phased-pulse models; no real need for air defense here, he supposed.

And a row of helicopters, gunboats; that was what the Air Corps tetrarch was pointing at. He remembered the smell of burning woods, and the chin turrets' blind seeking . . . There were wings on the breast of the officer's uniform tunic, and the Anti-Partisan Cross below that. Probably she flew the choppers; his ears went into professional mode again. He had convinced them that the cripple did not want to be included in a conversation he could not fully share, convinced them to the point that they ignored the human recording system sitting across the table.

"Look!" she said. "An' tell me those are cost-effective."

The exec cleared his throat. "Precision firepower," he said stolidly. "Entirely new application, an' barely a decade since we turned out our first single-seater scout model. Fo' once, we're completely ahead of the Yankees. We have to concentrate on capital-intensive weapons, we're—"

"—not a numerous people," she finished. "Look again," she continued. "How many of those are on-line, an' how many yanked fo' maintenance? Serious stuff, not jus' cleanin' fuel lines."

Kustaa checked . . . yes, three out of seven with the dismounted assemblies that told of more than routine care. Interested, he glanced back at the Draka woman; she was small for one of her race, thin-featured and dark with a receding chin and big beaked nose pierced for a small turquoise stud. For a moment he wondered what had moved her to emphasize her worst feature. Naivety? Defiance?

"An' that's the problem. Sho' you got them to us fast—too fast. They're the best thing since the hand-held vibrator when they workin', but the whole beast is a collection of prototypes, every subsystem experimental. An' the power train is too highly stressed. An' the servos fo' the weapons systems is temperamental; and either they works *wonderful* or they don't work *at all*."

The man examined his nails. "Technical Section—" he began.

"TechSec doan' end up in the bundu with the bushmen breathin' down they necks an' only those things to save they ass! You should 'a taken another four, five years makin' sure of things, in the meantime produce mo' Rhinos. They can't hover, but they *works*.

"*And* yo should be simplifyin' maintenance. As *is*, we keep the squadrons goin' by keepin' preassembled subsystems on hand, jus' jerkin' anything that doan' work and sendin' them back to the factory." She thrust a thumb at the stewardess, who had emerged ashen-faced from the bar cubicle and was walking stiffly about her tasks. "Look, it *easy* to train the cattle to pour drinks an' fuck, or to dig holes an' break rock. Maintainin' high-speed turbines is anothah matter!"

The exec rubbed his jaw. "Tetrarch," he said, "my own children are pilots; we are doin' the best we can. There are just so many engineers, aftah all, and any number of projects. As fo' maintenance technicians, that's always been tight. I'd've thought with all these Europeans comin' on the market, fully or partly trained already . . ."

"That another thing, we gettin' spoiled by Europe. Richest place we've ever took, an' skills the best part of it. Trouble is, we're livin' off loot; an' consider the social costs of maintainin' that level of trainin' over generations."

The man glanced from side to side in an instinctive gesture of caution and leaned forward, lowering his voice. "Mo' right than you know, Tetrarch. We had some bad trouble in South Katanga, just last month." She duplicated his look and leaned closer herself; that was one of the important industrial subregions of the central Police Zone—mines, hydrodams and a huge complex of electrical-engineering and motor works, mostly owned by the Faraday Electromagnetic Combine.

"Took a lot of the serf cadre out of the plants there fo' the conquered territories, promoted from their understudies, an' shipped in Europeans to do the donkey work."

"Uprisin'?"

"Serious. Citizen casualties, mob of 'em nearly bust out of their compounds into the free zones, turned them back with vehicle-mounted flamethrowers." The pilot winced; there had been nothing like that in the Police Zone in living memory, the sort of measure used in newly-conquered areas. "They had to gas a whole mine. Decided to lobotomize an' ship most of the survivors; three big factory compounds out of order, jus' when demand fo' industrial motor systems is gettin' critical."

The two Draka shook their heads; the woman seemed about to speak when the *Issachar* jolted. Kustaa looked up, and saw that they had docked. The dirigible quivered as her steerable tiltmotors held the nose threaded into the anchor ring of the tower; then there was a long multiple clicking sound as the restraining bolts shot home into the machined recesses. Another quiver as the engines died, the sudden absence of their burbling whine louder than their presence. More clicks and jolts as the anchor ring moved to thread the docking cable through the airship's loops, then cast them loose.

The American looked out the window, saw the horizon sinking as the winches bore the dirigible down below the level of the surrounding buildings, down to the railed tracks. A final quiver as the keel beneath them made contact with the haulers, and a whining of pumps as gas was valved through the connectors into the haven's reservoirs, establishing negative buoyancy. The observation deck was only five meters up, now; he could see the cracked concrete surface, the interlacing rails, the huge silver-gray teardrop shapes of the other dirigibles, most locked at rest, flocks of nose-in circles around their terminals. Groundcrew swarmed about, little electric carts flashed by tugging flatbed trailers loaded with luggage; a train of heavy articulated steam drags was passing under an anchored airship, unloading cargo modules that clipped down on their backs with prefitted precision. The scene moved, creeping by as the haulers dragged the *Issachar* to her resting place, and there was a bustle as the passengers moved to fasten jackets and assemble forward.

Kustaa remained in his seat as the disembodied voice came tinnily through the speakers; just as fast to stay in comfort for a minute as wait standing at the end of the line. "Prepare to disembark. All passengers to Lyon prepare to disembark by the forward ramp, please. Through passengers to Marseilles, Genoa and Florence, please remain seated."

He was alone when the stewardess came by again. Her eyes flicked aside at him, returned to the table she sponged down. Her face was gray, with a bleak pinched look that aged her ten years, or a hundred, and she moved with the arthritic care of an old woman. Against his will, Kustaa felt his hand go out to touch her sleeve. She came to a halt, instantly.

"Sor-ry," he croaked, standing and taking up the heavy leather case that never went out of arm's reach. "Ve-ry sor-ry."

The stewardess's face crumbled for an instant at the words, then she shot a lightning glance around and began to speak, her eyes flickering up to his face as she whispered fiercely and scrubbed at the veneer: "Oh, Master. you look like a kind man, please here's my number"—a slip of paper, palmed and tucked into his jacket pocket in an invisibly swift movement—"please, I can't *stand* it any longer, buy me, please, I know it can be done, someone bought Inge out just last month because their children liked her, I'm a hard worker really I am, I can cook and look after children and type and drive a car and play the piano and I'm good in bed, very very good, buy me and I'll be the best worker you've ever had always, Master, only 75 aurics, *please.*"

She scuttled away to the next table and Kustaa stood for a moment, fingering the slip of paper in his pocket. Then he turned and walked calmly along the gallery, out into the passageway and down to the ramp that dropped from the nose of the airship, forward of the control deck. The last of the passengers were still there, checking out their firearms from the counter clerk, smiling and laughing in unconscious relaxation as they shed the subtle tension Citizens felt when deprived of their weaponry. The American watched his hands strip the clip from the automatic, reinsert it and chamber a round and snap on the safety before holstering it. The battle shotgun was handed to him still in its black-leather scabbard, with the harness wrapped around it. An autoshotgun, basically, with a six-round tube magazine below the barrel, the butt cut down to a heavy pistol grip. He jerked it free, popping the restraining strap, and checked the action: six rounds, alternate slug and double buckshot.

How many could I kill? he thought calmly, estimating the placing of the dozen Draka around him as his fingers caressed the chunky wooden forestock of the weapon. *You for sure, Mr. Concerned-Citizen airplane maker who wonders how little girls looked stripped. Maybe you too, big-nose pilot, you'd be meat just like the two-legged cattle you killed to get that medal.*

More calmly still: *I am going insane.* A few of the Citizens were glancing his way, feeling the prickle of danger without knowing why. *When I get back to my family, will I still be fit for them?*

His hands put the shotgun back in its sheath, slung it over his back with the butt conveniently behind his right ear, buckled the harness around his chest; while his mind painted the varnished metal red and pink and gray with blood and shattered bone and brains. *Not enough,* he decided. Not nearly enough.

"How may I serve you, Mastah? Kellerman two-door? Here keys, yaz sar, Mastah, right this way—"
Where had that been?
"Street St. Jacob? Right that way, suh; my respects to one who gave so much fo' the Race. Nothin' more I cain do? Service to the State!"
What had he replied?

"Drink? Certainment, maistre, you wish perhaps other entertainment—yes, maistre, I go—"

"Yes, this is certainly the place," he said to himself, then started to his feet, the snifter of brandy in his hand. A frantic look at the bottle reassured him: only two drinks. He strode over to the table beside the bed; 25 Rue St. Jacob, Transit Hotel #79, room 221. Precisely right.

"My god, I nearly lost it," he muttered to himself, raising the blinds. An ordinary European street, a little broader than most, five-story brick buildings. A few autosteamers going by; sunset behind the buildings opposite, streetlights winking on, the branches of the chestnut tree outside tapping against his window. Ordinary hotel room—bed with white coverlet, nightstand, desk, carpet, bathroom. "I nearly lost it, my subconscious is a better fucking agent than I am."

He threw up the windowpane, letting in a breeze cooling with evening and fragrant with city smells, coalsmoke, dirty river, acre upon acre of summer-warmed brick and stone, burnt steamer distillate. A few deep breaths and he took up the phone. "Dinner," he rasped. "Standard." Now to wait for contact.

Well, well, fancy being back here so soon, Andrew von Shrakenberg thought, looking around the office of Lyon's Security chief. *Not just shopping, this time, unfortunately.* The room was much as he remembered it, really quite nice murals, the two glass walls with their tinted panes swiveled open like vertical venetian blinds to let in the cooling evening air. Westering sunlight sparkled on the broad surface of the Saone where it swung south and east to join the Rhône, forming the Y shape whose tongue of land had been the original site of Lyon. *Celtic,* he remembered. *Called Lugdunum, originally.* After the Gallic Sun-God; then a Greek settlement, followed by a colony of Roman veterans. Burgundians, later, an East Germanic tribe related to the Goths and Vandals. French, of various types . . . *and then us, which is the end of the story everywhere.*

He took another draw on the cheroot, a sip of the coffee, touched his lips to the Calvados in the goblet in his right hand; he had always enjoyed the scent more than the taste. Strategos Vashon was at his desk, checking through a report and making notes on a yellow pad with his left hand. Ignoring the Security Cohortarch standing at parade-rest in front of his desk, who was probably earnestly willing a suspension of her vital functions behind the blank mask of her face. The bruise that was turning most of its left side an interesting shade of yellow-purple helped, of course. The Strategos continued his methodical labors, with a detachment which was certainly an effective demoralizer for the officer on the carpet before him.

The problem is, does he really want to demoralize his subordinates? Andrew asked himself, laying down the eau-de-vie and fingering the gold hoop in his left ear. *The headhunters were set up to play that sort of mindfucking game; the problem is, they become addicted to it, even with each other.* Which raised the interesting point, frequent at the higher levels of the War Directorate, of whether they were being too paranoid about the paranoids . . . *I wonder what the headhunter is thinking, I really do.*

Strategos Vashon scowled slightly at the report before him, stripped the handwritten notes off the yellow pad and peeled the foil paper off a wax seal to attach it. *The development people are letting their enthusiasm run away with them again,* he decided. Pages of hyperbolic notes on how addiction to pleasure-center stimulation produced complete docility in even the most refractory subjects . . . Of course it did! So did lobotomy! This new treatment degraded performance levels almost as much, and to boot they had to leave a bloody great *electrode* sticking in the subject's skull; most of them developed infections and *died*, and the remainder had to have intensive medical care.

He wrote on the bottom of the paper, "Note: The Race's need is not for a breed of hospitalized idiots to serve them." So far, this new approach was no better than the standard electroshock-sensory-deprivation-pentothal-chemoconditioning methods; a little more sure to stick, but with even more unfortunate effects on their capacities. The Holy Grail of a safe, quick method of ensuring absolute obedience without affecting intelligence or ability would have to remain a dream a while longer; and serf-breaking would have to remain a primitive craft industry, not one conducted on modern conveyor-belt principles.

He closed the folder, wound the cord around the fastener, sealed it with another prepackaged wax disk and tossed it in the OUT box for his assistant to take in the morning. Morning . . . he glanced out the windows. After seven again: perhaps he should go home . . . *No,* he decided. Home was an empty shell; his wife was six years dead in a traffic accident, his children off at school, nothing to do at home but prowl about, reread Psych and Organization texts, mount his concubines . . . dull compared to work. He took a sip at his coffee; decaffeinated, like eating deodorized garlic, but he had to watch the stimulants, the doctor said. *Sometimes I wonder who's the one who works like a slave around here* . . . That was the price of power; the serfs down on the lower levels were the ones with nice regular ten-hour days.

He transferred his gaze to the officer from the . . . research facility—better keep it at that level even mentally—research facility at Le Puy. The medical report said she hadn't been exposed to more radiation than would result in some nausea and purging. *Which was less than the bitch deserved.*

"Well, Cohortarch," he said pleasantly, looking at her for the first time and steepling his fingers. "How do you account fo' yesterday's events in Le Puy? Is it treason on you part, or simple incompetence?"

She did not move her head, but he could feel her attention move to the War Directorate officer in the lounger. "Don't worry, Cohortarch Devlin, our comrade-in-arms here is involved." *Slightly,* his mind added, but he could see another film of sweat break out on her face at the hint of yet higher levels of interest.

"Now, Devlin," he continued, leaving out her rank with deliberate malice, "I'm waiting fo' an explanation."

"Suh." Her eyes were fixed on the window behind his head. "The new link fixtures fo' the reprocessin' of the enriched uranium were shipped from the Kolwezara facility, in the Police Zone, an' checked as adequate because the machinin' matched the older European parts. Incompatible alloys, leadin' to possible corrosion—"

"Shut up." Vashon's voice returned to its even, genial tone. "That's in TechSec's preliminary report, Devlin," he continued. "And TechSec sees the world in terms of engineerin' and physics, but we know better, don't we?" Another bark: *"Don't we?"*

"Yes, suh. Mah own prelim'nary survey indicates that there could have been a manual override on the standard valve shunts, allowin' explosive mixtures of gases in the precipitatin' tanks."

"Oh, very good, very good. An' who would have had the required access?"

"Ah . . . suh, apart from mahself, the personnel with the required access levels are all among the casualties. Suh."

"Buggerin' marvelous!" He leaned forward over the axeblade of his steepled hands. "Devlin, *four hundred dead,* an' twice that injured in this little accident of yorn. I'm not talkin' about field cattle or broom pushers, Devlin, I'm talkin' about the most highly trained scientific an' technical personnel in the Domination, Devlin. A hundred of them Citizens, Devlin; their skills an' heredity lost to the Race, Devlin. Includin' ten European scientists so good we gave them an' their families Citizenship in return fo' workin' fo' us, Devlin. Not to mention we've lost facilities crucial to the . . . new weapon project, which we're runnin' neck-and-neck with the Alliance in even *befo'* this happened—they *may* not take advantage of a one-year lead, *but would you care to bet on it?"*

Vashon smiled and tapped his fingers on the blotter of his desk: tip-tap, tip-tap, and the Cohortarch gave a nearly visible flinch at each sound. "Anythin' mo', Devlin?"

"Suh . . . yes, suh. Nothin' certain, but . . ." She glanced at his eyes, returned hers to the windows over his head and continued hurriedly. "We haven't found some of the bodies . . . well, the acids used fo' refinin' the plutonium out of the spent uranium slugs . . . but Professor Ernst Oerbach was completely missin'. He's over on the . . . new weapons side, but was visitin', some conference on trigger timers an' deuterium processin'. No trace 'tall, an' . . ."

"Tell me the joyful news, Devlin."

"Well . . . twelve cylinders of first-stage plutonium oxide from the recovery process are unaccounted fo' as well. They could have been ruptured an' scattered in the original explosion, but—"

"Joy." Vashon dropped his head, supporting his forehead on the splayed fingers of one hand. "Explain, please, Cohortarch, how a man *supposedly* under twenty-fo'-hour surveillance fo' the rest of his life would get out. If he wasn't just dissolved in a bath of acid an' suspended particles of uranium-238, that is."

"Suh." The Cohortarch came to attention. "Suh, the responsibility is completely mine. The, the explosion released radioactive an' toxic material extensively, suh, and the fires would have released mo'. Extensive contamination outside the restricted area was barely avoided. I authorized all personnel undah my orders to aid in the containment efforts." More softly: "A numbah of them died doin' so, suh."

Vashon was silent for a full minute, then lit a cigarette and considered the glowing tip; it had become dark in the wide office, as the sunset glow faded. "I agree, Cohortarch. And will so note on my report."

The woman in Security Directorate green managed to convey surprise and relief without movement of face or body. Vashon smiled once more, unpleasantly. "Agree *reluctantly*, Devlin. Emphasis on the *reluctantly*. You know the code: there is no excuse fo' failure, you're responsible fo' everythin' you subordinates do, and so am I. Skull House is on my ass about this, so is Castle Tarleton an' the Palace . . . shitfire, every agency of every Directorate is formin' line on the left, tappin' lead pipes into their palms an' smilin' in anticipation!"

He paused. "You know, they're diggin' canals to join the Ob-Yenisey system southward to the Aral Sea? Irrigate Central Asia. Need administrators fo' the labor camps: nice simple work, no technical problems, just plain diggin'. In West Siberia province. Fo' the next thirty years. *If I go there, you join me!* Now get you ass back to Le Puy, and *find out what happened.* I want to *know*, I want the report on my desk by *yesterday*. Is that *clear?*"

"Yes, suh!"

After she left, the two Draka sat in silence while servants came in with a fresh tray of coffee and a cold supper. Vashon moodily buttered a piece of *baguette* and spoke to the younger man:

"Well?"

"Well, I was beginnin' to think you were the sort of commander who keeps his subordinates so scared of failure they're unwillin' to take risks. Glad to see I'm not"—*entirely*, his mind added—"right," Andrew said.

"Thank you kindly," Vashon replied dryly. "Try the anchovy salad, they do it well here. What I *meant*, do you think the Yankee you've been chasin' is involved, Merarch?"

"Hmmm." A moment of impassive chewing. "Not unless he's an amoeba who can split in two; besides Finland"—for a moment a hungry carnivore looked out through the handsome aquiline face—"we're pretty sure he was involved in the Hamburg incident. Sparked it, rather. The local bushmen stuck they heads out to impress him, wanted a Yankee link real bad." A grin. "Foolish of 'em. We chopped a good few off an' turned the prisoners over to you people there. This hunter-team thing Castle Tarleton came up with is workin' out surprisin' well; thought it was a boondoggle, at first, but it's becomin' real interestin', integratin' and gettin' the best out of a mixed force. We got real close to him there."

"Close only counts with fragmentation weapons," Vashon said. "What trail?"

"Damn little. The ones we caught unfortunately doan' seem to know much. Last seen at the airship haven. Which is right next to the port an' the heavier-than-air station; could be anywhere from Archona to Beijing, by now." He pulled over a file. "Got a physical description . . . tall, fair hair, muscular build, blue eyes, mustache."

Andrew laughed, a deep chuckle of unforced mirth. "Oh, wonderful; accordin' to my recollections of the Eugenics Board survey, the average height fo' an adult male Draka is 183 centimeters, and about forty percent are blond. Leaves about six million possibles, 'less'n he's dyed his hair; eighty-three percent have light eyes, that ups it a bit." He snapped his fingers in mock enlightenment, then swiveled his forefinger inward. "I've got it! It's me!"

A sour smile. "Well, at least we know he's travelin' alone." Vashon slapped his hand on the desk. "Loki's balls, we've got to have more checks on Citizen movements."

Andrew shrugged. "Strategos, we already restrict movement of people an' information about as much as practical. We start runnin' that sort of surveillance on each other, there'd be no time fo' Citizens to do anythin' else. 'Sides, Draka don't like bein' gimleted all the time, what's the point of bein' on top, then?"

"True, but . . . anyway, this thing at Le Puy—provided it isn't jus' an industrial accident, the gods know quality-control is always a problem—it's out of character fo' the local bushmen."

"They tamed down?"

"Contrary, sneaky-subtle. Good leadership . . . that's why I smell you Yankee. It's even worse than the Hamburg thing, which is goin' to delay launchin' that aircraft carrier six months to a year."

"Blessin' in disguise." At the secret policeman's raised brow, Andrew continued: "We're never goin' to have a navy to beat the Alliance, not while we're forced to maintain a large army, too." More meditatively. " 'Sides, Strategos, look at the Alliance powers. Yankees, Britain, Japan too now. Island nations, history of naval war an' seaborne trade. We Draka, we could build the Domination because steam technology lowered transport costs and times enough to make it possible to unify and develop the continental interiors. We're a land beast. And finally, aircraft carriers are yesterday's weapons, in my opinion, like-so battleships thirty years ago. A big surface fleet would be a total waste of scarce personnel; should concentrate on subs and coastal defense. We're only launchin' that damned carrier on account the Fritz laid the keel."

Vashon ground out his cigarette. "Maybe. Anyhow, Merarch, I do have one asset inside the local bushman net."

"Ah, good. Impo'tant?"

"They pretty tightly celled, but not bad. I've been usin' him fo' information only, makin' him look good. But this Le Puy thing is crucial, 'specially if the Alliance is involved."

"How'd you turn him?"

Vashon laughed. "Fritz technique; y'put the subject and maybe a close relative—we used his father—in opposin' chairs. Gag the passive subject. Active subject has a switch under his hand. Every time he presses, the current goes through the passive one, an' every time he lets up, it goes through him—in increasin' increments, until the passive subject dies. Great fo' crushin' the will; the subject's convinced right down deep that he'll do anythin' to save his own skin. We've got this one's momma and sister, too, he's quite the family man, an' anxious to avoid their bein' the next passive subjects."

"I can imagine," Andrew said dryly, lifting the goblet. Vashon shot him a quick glance.

"Squeamish, Merarch von Shrakenberg?"

Andrew pursed his lips as he rolled the apple brandy around his mouth. "Fastidious, Strategos, only fastidious. Still, to get the stable clean you has to step in horseshit, as the sayin' goes. 'To desire the end is to desire the means necessary to accomplish it,'" he amplified, quoting Naldorssen. He hesitated, then continued: "Had any subjects refused to push the switch on they nearest and dearest?"

"Some," Vashon admitted with a reminiscent smile. "Which provides us with one corpse an' the valuable datum that that serf would rather die than submit. Neat an' tidy . . ." He pressed a buzzer. "I'm controllin' this particular double myself. A man has to have a hobby, an' it's good to go hands-on sometimes, after spendin' all day readin' reports."

A serf stumbled through, pushed by two Order Police who saluted and left him kneeling on the carpet. He blinked about the darkened office, winced as a light speared down from the ceiling, the chain-and-bar restraints holding his arms behind him clanked. A young man with a thin stubbled olive face and an uncontrollable twitch beneath one eye, in a rough gray overall stained with oil and stenciled with the wheel-and-piston insignia of the Transportation Directorate.

"Why, good evenin', Jean 55EF003," Vashon said in a voice of mellow friendliness. The serf would be effectively blinded, of course; that was the reason for having the focused spotlight in the ceiling. His hand nudged the control up slightly, to keep the two Draka shadows looming in a deeper darkness.

"Master . . . Master, if they suspect I'm being held, please, I won't be trusted any more, I'll be no use—"

"*Do* credit us with some intelligence, Jean," Vashon said, chuckling at his own pun. "But you haven't been much use to us, anyway. How old is you sister, Jean?"

"Nine, Master." The Frenchman jerked as if struck. "Oh, Mary Mother of God, not the chair, not her, please, Master, I'll do anything, *anything!*"

Vashon considered him; the buck was transparently sincere, but also crumbling. *A pity if he goes insane,* the security officer thought. *I was hoping he'd make good in this little bushman network, before we activated him and snapped them up.* "We know you'll do anythin', Jean—" he continued, in the same friendly tone. "Even kill you own father. Tsk tsk." The Frenchman began to sob. "Pull youself together, serf, if'n you don't want to add two more to the list!" A pause. "Nothin' from you but a few times an' places fo' courier drops, an' two names from you own cell."

The ragged breathing slowed. "Master, I tell everything I know, everything! Henri is cell leader, he gets the orders, Ybarra and I just do as we're told, believe me," Jean said with desperate earnestness.

"You know, Jean," Vashon continued, "I'm goin' to do you a favor. Tell you something about me, personal. I don't like seein' little girls fucked by dogs. Have a friend who does, though." He slid a glossy color photograph the size of a placemat from a stack-rack on his desk and flipped it to land faceup in the puddle of light by the serf. The young man looked down, then screwed his eyes tightly shut, so tightly that his face trembled, as if he sought to squeeze the information his optic nerves had absorbed back out through the lids. His throat worked convulsively.

"Puke on my carpet an' you'll regret it, *skepsel*," the secret policeman said with quiet deadliness, using the old word for a two-legged beast. Then in the friendly tone once more: "That isn't you sister, of course, Jean. No, you momma an sister are safe, workin' in a canteen. Jus' washin' dishes, buck, that's all."

The serf was panting, eyes still closed. "Such altruism, from a creature who'd torture his own pa to death. Of course, you family *could* be better off. Maybe a trip to the sunny Western Hemisphere?"

Jean's eyes snapped open. "You . . . you would let us go?"

"Well, I'm not promisin' anythin', but . . . we do need people ovah there as well, you know. Send you an' you sister, maybe, nice cover story and a little nest egg."

"God, Master, thank you, thank you!" The serf's tears were like a dam bursting this time, of relief and gratitude; his face shone with it. Unseen in the darkness, Vashon smiled like a shark.

"But you've got to *earn* it, Jean. You understand that, don't you, Jean?" A frantic nod. "Now, we have othah sources in that pathetic little group you call the Resistance," Vashon continued. "So we know somethin' . . . of unusual size may be a-happenin', soon."

He reached into the desk and tossed a cylinder the size of a single-cigar case toward the serf; it struck him in the chest and fell on the photograph.

"Look at that, Jean." The buck obeyed, although Vashon could see him blurring the focus of his eyes to avoid looking at the picture beneath. "It's a fancy little gadget. Yankee components, actually. Radio, inside the case, with attachments so's you can wire it onto somethin'. If you was to take that along, next time there's a meetin' at higher than cell level, I'd be mighty pleased when it was switched on. Or if you could get me somethin' *really* useful, like-so a Yankee we feel may be comin' through, that would make me very happy. Yo *does* want to make me very happy, Jean, don't you?"

"Oh, yes, Master, of all things I want that most in the whole world, believe me, yes, certainly. Master . . . how shall I carry this?" His voice shook with a crawling eagerness to please.

Vashon laughed again, as he flipped the switch on his desk. "They'll take you down to the clinic an' show you right now, Jean. I'd have thought it was obvious."

The two Order Police troopers came back in, silent helmeted shadows, saluted, picked up the serf and radio with similar lack of effort, left. As the door soughed shut, Andrew rose and stooped to take the print between thumb and forefinger.

"Feh," he said, studying it for a second with a grimace of disgust before sliding it back onto the Strategos's desk. "Strange friends you has, Vashon, no offense."

"None taken," he said, keying the room lights and holding it out at arm's length. "It's a standard print from *Gelight's Erotic Art Sampler*. Minority interest, but *de gustibus*, eh? Actually, I think this is simulated."

Andrew chuckled reluctantly. "Strategos, you are one evil son of a bitch," he said.

"Goes with the job, Merarch. Taken as a compliment . . . Your hunters are here in Lyon, aren't they?"

"Mm-hm. Ready fo' stand-down; experimental unit, aftah all. Castle Tarleton"—*meaning my new aunt*—"wants to do an evaluation, befo' they decide on the program as a whole. I'm goin' to lay over at my sister's plantation; there's a namin' feast fo' her newborns comin' up in a few days." For courtesy's sake: "To which I've been asked to invite you, of course."

"Ah. Why, thanks kindly, I think I could find the time," Vashon replied blandly, hiding his amusement at the other's surprise; it might be interesting to mingle with the Landholders for an evening, and once the full consequences of the disaster at Le Puy avalanched down, there would be little free time in the Lyon office. "Care fo' a little huntin', first?"

"Huntin'? I take it you don't mean wild boar?"

"Another type of swine altogetha. If the local bushmen are involved— still mo' if it's you Yankee—we'll have somethin' from young Jean, and soon. Hell, maybe tonight!"

"Agreed," Andrew said, finishing the Calvados. "I'll alert the watch officer at transit barracks, if you can get us transport fo' insertion in-city." The secret policeman nodded briskly. "We're supposed to be developin' closer liaison, anyhow; it'll be good practice."

He stood, slipping on his gloves and smoothing the thin leather over his fingers. His eyes met the Security officer's, and Vashon felt a slight sudden impact along his nerves, like a cold brush over the face. "And I hope we meet my Yankee. I sho'ly do."

The blindfold was snug, and Kustaa resisted the temptation to tug at it. It was sensible, simply the easiest way to make sure he could say nothing even if he broke under interrogation; the same reason he had torn up the slip of paper the serf stewardess had handed him without looking at the number, and flushed it down the commode with the address he had found under his souffle, during dinner. That he had to remember, of course, but it had simply been the point where whoever-they-were had met him. Since then he had moved on foot and in vehicles, indoors and out; presumably discreetly—an armed Draka Citizen being led blindfolded by serfs was a trifle unusual . . . Once through a sewer, he thought, but a dry one.

"*Arrête*," the voice at his elbow said.

Halt. He stopped obediently, obscurely glad of the knife and pistol at his belt, the battle shotgun across his back. As irrational as the feeling of helplessness the blindfold engendered, but a useful counterweight. He could sense that he was inside a building from the movement of the air, from its smell—factory smell. It reminded him of the summer he had worked at the National Harvester plant in St.

Paul, machine oil and steel and brass, rubber transmission belts and the lingering ozone of industrial-strength electric motors, underlain by a chalky scent like an old school's. Something else as well, sickly-sweet, a hint of decay.

A hand turned him to his left; he could hear a faint sound from that direction, a tiny wheezing and shifting.

"Take off the blindfold, American. But do not turn."

A new voice, an educated man's French, sounding middle-aged. Kustaa obeyed, squinting his eyes against the prospect of light. Even after an hour of blindfold, the interior of the great room was dim. He had been correct: a factory. Dim shapes of lathes and bench presses around him, fading into distance and shadow, a little light from grimy glass shutters far above. Enough light to see what hung on the wall before him. A man standing with his feet on an angle-iron brace bolted to the sooty brick. His weight rested on the steel hooks through ribs and armpits.

Dead, Kustaa thought. *That's the smell of rot.* Then he saw the outstretched fingertips flutter, the whites of eyeballs move.

"Hnng-hnng-hnng," the pinned man said, "hnng-hnnng-hnng."

The quiet, cultured voice came again from somewhere in the room; there was a hint of movement, but Kustaa's eyes remained fixed forward.

"You see this thing," the man said, "and you think, 'Monstrous, inhuman.' Do you not, Mr. American?"

"Yes," Kustaa replied quietly. "At least that."

"Ah, no, my American friend. I will explain why that is an error. To think of this as the act of inhuman monsters is a step toward thinking of it as the work of devils. Toward thinking of the Draka as not human, as devils: which is a step in turn toward thinking of them as gods. That, my old, is what they themselves think, in the madness of their own hearts, that they are gods or devils, perhaps they care little which. This . . . A Citizen supervisor noted that the output of this plant was too low, or more likely the spot-checks showed too many defective parts. He informed a born-serf manager, who passed it on down the line to a gang boss, probably a Frenchman like myself, who picked perhaps the least popular or most insolent of his gang, and the plant's serf drivers came and took him from his machine one shift, and put him on the hooks. Men did this, human men."

Kustaa waited a few moments before replying, in a soft and careful voice. "Why have you brought me here, then, *monsieur?*"

"Did you not wish to make contact with the Resistance of Lyon? *Voila*, we are here." There were rustling noises around him in the darkness. "More of us than have gathered in one place in some time, Mr. American. Ah, to this spot? Because it is as safe as any . . . and for the same reason that our masters put this man on the steel, as an object lesson."

"Which is supposed to teach—?" Kustaa continued. The pinned man's eyes might be open, but the OSS agent did not think there was much mind or consciousness left behind them.

"A different lesson, my old. This man, perhaps he is my brother, perhaps my son, perhaps my closest friend. Here am I, one of the leaders of the best organized Resistance group in all France, perhaps all Europe . . . and what can I do for him? Nothing, not even to end his agony, not unless some means can be found utterly untraceable."

"Why not?" Kustaa said.

"Because then, there would be two men on this wall. You see, Mr. American, Mr. Secret Agent, I think you seek to make contact with us for certain reasons. To call us to valiant action, perhaps? This man here, he was active: now he is less so. There were other groups here, in the beginning, more daring than we. Some of them believed, for example, that we could deny the Draka the fruits of their conquest with the weapons of class struggle. Strikes." There was an ironic wonder in the man's next word: "*Strikes*. Can one believe it? Others thought of sabotage, assassination, very active measures. Now these other groups are corpses, or lobotomized in chain gangs . . . and very much less 'active' than our network. Like the *maquisards* in the countryside, the last of whom are being hunted down like starving animals."

"The Finns—" Kustaa began.

"Ah yes, the heroic Finns. The *extinct* Finns, very shortly. Mr. American, there are always those who would rather die on their feet than live on their knees; if you seek to make contact with such, you had best hurry. If there is one thing under heaven at which our masters are experts, it is for arranging for such to have their wish, and die."

"You are running a very considerable risk by *having* an organization," Kustaa said. "If you don't *do* anything with it, what is the point?"

"Very true . . . Mr. American-whose-family-is-far-away, we *do* take this risk. Because we are not content to live as cattle, between our work and our stalls and our fodder, to be bred and sold as cattle, slaughtered when it suits our owners with as little thought as a chicken is killed and plucked. Why does this organization exist? For memory's sake. To preserve that discontent, not simply as sullen beast-hatred, but as knowledge. That once there was something different, that there may be again. That we are a nation . . . perhaps no longer the nation of France, but still a people.

"Thus we organize, we recruit, we organize . . . in tiny groups, with cutouts at every stage. We pass on information; occasionally we can help individuals who suffer more than the common lot. Simply to tell a kinsman where his family has been sent, that is victory. Very occasionally we take direct action, against a foreman perhaps; even the Draka cannot make massacres at every accident. And we wait. We were conquered by an enemy more patient than we, more far-sighted, more ruthless; by conquering us they offer lessons, and we learn. Do you know how many Draka there are in Europe?"

"We estimate no more than a million."

"Too high, I would say . . . many times that many born-serfs, of course. The great strength of the Draka is that they are skilled at using others; thus they accomplish feats far beyond their own raw power. Their great weakness, exactly the same, that they must use others. These born-serfs, the Draka bring them to teach us obedience. They are just beginning to suspect, I think, that such learning can be a two-way process. Always before they have smashed the societies they conquered, killed their elites and reduced the survivors to isolated human atoms, to be refashioned as they wished. Here as well, to a certain extent, but not completely. *And that is the central purpose of this organization.* To *exist*, simply to exist. So long as we do, their victory is not complete.

"What we have done—are trying to do—is build a brotherhood that they can wound but cannot kill. Strong and hard they are; if we try to match their strength, we will be smashed. Instead we must be as soft as water and as patient. Enduring, that wears away the rock slowly, but, oh, so surely. Perhaps you Americans and your allies will come and liberate us; if that is so, we will welcome you with tears and flowers and as much gratitude as humans can find in their souls to give. But we are those to whom the worst has happened, and we must prepare for the worst, that they destroy you in the end as well. Then our quiet war must last, who knows, perhaps a thousand years, to ensure that their 'Final Society' joins so many lesser tyrannies in the grave."

"That," Kustaa said with a slight chill in his voice, "sounds very much the sort of plan a Draka might conceive."

"If they had the flexibility, my old, which they do not." A laugh. "Perhaps we become like that which we fight."

Perhaps, Kustaa thought, looking at the man on the wall, *if you have to fight an enemy too closely, too long, perhaps that is so.* "You refuse to help me, then?"

"Did I say this?" The same even, almost monotone voice. *Control would be something living at the bottom here would teach*, Kustaa thought.

"No, we will aid you, Mr. American, *on our terms.* Information, yes, provided it can be conveyed without serious risk. The Draka are no fools, but sometimes they forget we have ears . . . and sometimes they are too eager to believe a serf has knelt in his heart and accepted chains upon his soul. Although, God in His mercy knows, that is true often enough. Sometimes, rarely, *very* rarely, we will be prepared to take direct action on your prompting. None of us is essential; they could take everyone in this building, and what we have built will continue. Wounded, but that is the virtue of an organism so simple and diffuse as ours, it regenerates. And endures if need be, generation after generation, until . . . in the end, if nothing else, they will become lazy . . ."

"Information is what I'm mostly after," Kustaa said. *And getting. Not information that will make Donovan or President Marshall particularly happy, but then, just because these people are allies doesn't mean they have identical perspectives or interests.* "Specifically, here, information about the Draka weapons program at Le Puy."

A laugh startled him, full and mellow. "Well, after all my eloquent preaching of the virtues of inaction, I must confess that something along those lines has already been done. The facility at Le Puy was largely destroyed a short time ago."

"Judas Priest!" Kustaa said, grunting as if a fist had driven into his belly. *Donovan will shit his pants.* "You did that?"

Another laugh. "No, no, *au contraire.* It was done by one of the scientists themselves; we merely took advantage of the confusion." More soberly: "And thousands were nearly killed, as well . . . remember that we live here, Mr. American; and our families. And atomics were used on our soil. Our feelings concerning the good professor are, how shall I say, mixed. You may turn, *monsieur*."

Kustaa swiveled, thankful for the opportunity to take his eyes from the thing on the wall. A man was standing close behind him, a tall cadaverous-looking man in middle age, dressed in badly-fitting servant's livery. *Still no sight of the Resistance people,* he thought. *Good.*

"Ernst Oerbach, at your service, *Mein Herr*," the man said, offering his hand and inclining his head with a gesture that somehow suggested a heel click. The face was too expressive for a Prussian's, though, now showing mostly exhaustion and a bone-deep melancholy. "Late of the Imperial University in Vienna, physics department." Kustaa took the Austrian's hand, a dry firm grip.

"I'm going by the name Frederick Kenston, just now," he said in reply. "You were in a position to sabotage the plant? I'm surprised the Draka let a serf that close to critical equipment."

"Ah, Mr. Kenston, I was not a serf, you see. I was given Citizenship after the war, in return for my services. "

"What?" Kustaa managed to restrain himself from jerking back his hand, or wiping it on the side of his jacket.

Ernst Oerbach smiled sadly. "A natural reaction, Mr. Kenston. One I have felt myself, often enough . . . but though my son was dead by then, my daughter-in-law and grandchildren were alive, and included in the offer." His eyes went over the American's shoulder, to the figure on the wall. "You can imagine the alternatives. The Draka considered me valuable enough, for my genes as well as my self." Another of those gently self-deprecating smiles. "I was fencing champion of Lower Austria in my youth, I suppose they decided my descendants would be desirable . . . The children were taken away, of course. Helge and I would be Citizens by courtesy, only: a sort of second-class Citizenship, always closely watched. The children were to be adopted into Draka families who could not bear, and would forget."

Kustaa's eyes narrowed. It fit with what the OSS had been able to learn from European scientists who had made it out in the chaos toward the end; the Draka had contacted some of the ones who decided to chance a try for the Alliance instead. Not many—this would be a one-in-a-million arrangement—but there weren't that many first-rate creative brains. Others could be forced to work by more immediate pressures, but for a few Citizenship made sense. *Hell, it's only a generation since they stopped accepting selected immigrants*, he mused.

"Why did you change your mind?" he asked.

"I could not stomach it any longer," Oerbach said simply. "Even in luxurious isolation, I saw too much of what I was giving the power to destroy the earth."

Kustaa grunted again. *That bad, whatever it is*, he thought. "Your grandchildren?" The man winced, but it was necessary to be quite sure.

"There the Draka made a mistake," he said. "Citizenship would mean nothing if it could be withdrawn. Citizens can be killed, yes . . . but

I have come to believe that a clean death might be preferable, even for little Johann and Adelle. And they will not kill them, because there would be nothing to gain from it once I am out of their power, and two members of the Race to lose." A shake of his head. "I have come to . . . understand them, somewhat."

Kustaa turned his head sharply. The faceless voice spoke confirmation: "A major disaster. Hundreds killed. They have been flying in decontamination teams and doctors around the clock. This is being kept very secret, you understand, Mr. American. But continue, professor, you have not told our friend what other gifts you bring beside yourself."

"Ah, *ja*," he said, patting at his pockets like a movie-version absentminded professor. "*Ja*, the microfilm of my research results on the threshold temperatures for deuterium-lithium fusion."

A spool of translucent tape, and a masked face wheeled a green steel box beside them on a dolly, let the stand-bar come down with a thump that told of considerable weight. "Well, it was not my department, you understand, the plutonium refining. Plutonium for the triggers, you see. But it was there. You must understand I had been thinking of doing *something* for some time, but the opportunity was fleeting." A bleak grin, over in an instant. "You might say Satan whispered in my ear, and I fell. It probably even looks like an accident, and this unprocessed material was there; plutonium is a considerable bottleneck, so . . ."

Kustaa took a half-step back and leaned against a lathe, heedless of metal angles digging into his back. "Judas Priest," he whispered again, this time almost as a wheeze. "Tempted by Satan? More like divine inspiration, Professor Oerbach! Maybe you should have been in *my* line of work."

"No." He looked up at the tone, and saw tears glitter behind the spectacles. "A temptation to mass murder and I fell. Hundreds . . . *thousands* could have been killed, Mr. Kenston. Thousands of innocents, women, children. The earth itself for hundreds of square miles, *that* was what I risked. I am a murderer, Mr. Kenston, I who never harmed a living soul before that day. *That* is what the Draka have done to me!" Softly: "And the alternative was to give them a power for murder beyond conception. What I did will delay it, at least. If I have no part in it, perhaps some of the guilt will wash off me, perhaps . . . that I must believe."

Qualms later, Kustaa thought, and turned to speak to the faceless shadow voice. "*This* you have to help me with, by God," he said.

"We agree. For this, we agree. What do you need?"

"A place within a hundred miles of the Atlantic, where an aircraft can land and take off. A grass field a hundred meters clear would do. Some manpower, if possible."

"You have the means to signal?"

"In that leather case your man took from my car."

"Ah. Tell me no more, I may guess, but . . ." The voice withdrew, and there was a murmur of conversation, footsteps returning. "Mr. American, another will come to stand where I am. Approach closely, but do not attempt to make out a face. A name will be given you, a location, a password. But first . . . do you, by any chance, know the Cartwright system?"

"Sign language? Yes, why?" One of a number of bizarre skills Donovan insisted his field men learn.

The Austrian looked up sharply, shaken from thoughts that his expression said were less than pleasant.

"Excellent, so does the good professor here. With your so-ingenious cover story—do not be disturbed, only two know of it and I am one— it will account for his presence. I suggest you pass him off as your servant in the medical sense as well; we have applied an appropriate tattoo. You will grasp that this is a facility useful to us . . . And now another will impart the information you seek. A place within the distance you specify; about guards and helpers, I will have to think. Perhaps."

Chateau Retour, Kustaa repeated to himself. *Sister Marya Sokolowska. The escargots of Dijon are very fine*. That last brought a slight smile; he supposed food codes were natural in a continent that had been hungry for some time.

"Now, you will be returned to your autosteamer," the voice said. "Please, the blindfold—" A masked man had come to stand beside the dolly with its so-ordinary looking box of green-painted steel; Kustaa sensed he was young from his stance, could smell fear and another odor, fecal. He wrinkled his nose slightly. *What the hell, I hope he hasn't shit his pants*, the American thought. *Oh, well, they've been efficient so far.*

"Shit!" The green-uniformed serf technician ripped the earphones from her head with a violence that set the van rocking slightly on its springs, clutching at her ears.

"Report!" Andrew von Shrakenberg snapped from the map table, and the tech's spine stiffened, shaven head locking in eyes-front despite the pain that crinkled her eyes almost shut in an involuntary grimace. Above on the roof the motors of the directional loop antenna whined, searching.

"Mastah, signal irregular, compatible with movement through built-up areas an' steel-frame buildin's, stable fo' the last five minutes, then, *ah, shit*, sorry Mastah, blast a' static an' lost signal."

The Draka's lips peeled back in a snarl, but his finger stayed steady on the map, resting on the last spot where the lines from the two vans crossed.

"Cause?" he barked.

"Power line, anythin' givin' off strong radio impulse, tha' thing would've shut down to prevent surge burnin' out circuits, Mastah, I doan' *know*."

Specialized training, Andrew thought bitterly. Necessary, but it did not give the sort of broad base of knowledge from which intuitive leaps spring. *Well, the creative intelligence is supposed to be your job!* he told himself as his hand stabbed down on the send button.

"All Strike units, all Strike units, execute Downfall on last position posted. *Now!* Do it people, let's *go!*"

His hand swept the Holbars from the table, and he dove through the open rear doors of the van, rolled, came up running.

"FREEZE! THIS IS SECURITY! DROP YOUR WEAPONS AND PUT YOUR HANDS UP OR YOU DIE!"

Kustaa dropped to the ground in instant combat reflex as the amplified voice roared in their ears, like the shout of an angry god. Hard concrete thumped at him, ignored in a surge of adrenaline that brightened the murk as it flared his pupils wide. Multiple echoes, as if it was sounding throughout a complex of buildings, broadcast from half a dozen sources. The skylights shattered, and round objects fell through, to burst hissing. Tendrils of mist snaked through the gloom, then sprang into brilliant blue-white as searchlights played on the roof and reflected electric-arc glare within.

Voices shouted, there was a rapid thudding of feet, and Kustaa felt a swift tug at his heel as he snaked forward and yanked the Austrian off his feet and behind a lathe. Hands reached out and dragged the man away, and someone called in French, in Lyonnaise dialect: "American! We have him! This—"

A stab of tracer went by above, the light bullets pinging and whining off metal and stone. The OSS agent's hand went over his shoulder and stripped the shotgun free with a surge of cold elation at the thought of targets. A Draka voice, shouting, "You headhuntin' fools! *Take 'em, boys! Bulala! Bulala!*"

Shots were flickering through the half-lit immensity of the factory shed, and Kustaa could see the flash and sparkle of ricochets running across the motionless machines like sun flicker on moving leaves. Men and women dodged, fired, screamed. Boots slammed on concrete, and a shadowy figure loomed, helmet bulking, bulbous-nosed with its gas mask. Kustaa rolled up to one knee, snaked the battle shotgun around the drill press which sheltered him, fired.

Crung. The heavy weapon bucked against the muscles of his wrists and forearms, lost. The solid slug hammered through the fleshy part of the uniformed man's thigh, spinning him around in a circle before he pitched to earth; the last wild burst sent rounds close enough to the American to sting with spalls flicked out of the pavement, nearly killing him by chance where aimed fire was useless. The wounded man thrashed in his small square of open space.

"Ah'se hit, Ah'se hit!" he screamed, the first half of the shout muffled by the mask he ripped off before pressing both hands to his thigh, as if trying to squeeze shock-shattered bone and flesh back together. His blood flashed from red to black in the strobing light, as the searchlights played back and forth above.

Bullets flicked at the prostrate figure, and struck; his second scream was shrill, wordless. Another man followed him, but this one leaped *over* the lathe the soldier had blundered into; headfirst, landing in a perfect forward roll just beyond the writhing casualty. He was masked, but there was no helmet on the bristle-cut red hair, and he had a machine pistol in each hand, firing at muzzle flashes and glimpsed movement.

"Get him out, get him out!" the man shouted through rubber and plastic. *Branggg* and a burst hammered the machine by Kustaa's ear, *brangg*, and a scream as a Resistance fighter pitched back, *brangg* and another dropped without sound. Behind the Draka the thrashing Janissary was being dragged away, as the submachine guns snapped their three-round bursts with killing precision and the hands behind them moved like oiled metronomes.

Kustaa's second round took the man in the stomach. At close range the heavy buckshot did not have room to spread much; it pulped a circle of chest and stomach the size of a small dinner plate. Even then, the muzzles wavered up toward the target that had killed him before the second charge let the Draka's intestines spill forward into his lap. *One*, the American thought, with chilling satisfaction, his mind seeming to move in layers like the leaves of a book. Behind him the voice was shouting in gutter argot.

"Jean, drop that dolly, *drop it*; Ybarra, you two, get that box and out. *American, this way!*"

Kustaa had never felt less like a berserker, or himself. There seemed to be an infinity of time for thought: *They are dying to buy me seconds*. On hands and knees, he followed the voice into the gun-shot dark.

"Well, here's our tracer," Vashon said, nudging the brown-streaked metal casing that was wired to the underside of the overturned dolly.

Andrew grunted in reply, watching as the stretcher with the shrouded bundle passed by. "Always were a little reckless, Corey," he murmured. Around him the factory lights had been reconnected, and Security techs were swarming with their cameras, measuring cords, fingerprint kits. *Busy locking the door on the empty stable*, he thought.

"But why wasn't it functioning?" the Strategos asked the senior technician, who had opened the feces-streaked container with gloved hands.

"Damned if I know," the man replied, frowning at the circuit board with its black transistor beads. "Have to take it to the lab." He spoke loudly to override the wailing scream of a field interrogation going on a few yards distant.

"Don't—don't—don't—"

"Would close contact with a, oh, an X-ray machine've done it?" Andrew asked.

"Yes, even a fairly light dosage; nothin' that would do a human bein' any harm. These-here bitty things is sensitive to any sort a' energetic particles. Scarcely likely here, Merarch."

Andrew locked eyes with Vashon. "Well. Pull in you double?"

The older man ran a hand through the dense sable cap of his hair. "Nnnno, Merarch, I don't think so. No, he'll try really hard; be difficult fo' him to make contact, of course . . . but worth waitin' fo'. They'll go to earth, of course . . ."

"And we'll dig them out." Andrew smiled. "Oh, Mr. Yankee, I'm beginin' to dislike you." His eyes went up to the man pinned to the wall. The Holbars was across his chest on its assault sling; his hand found the pistol grip, squeezed. Two dozen muzzles pivoted toward him, then wavered away in puzzlement or indifference.

Andrew looked up at the slumped corpse with the neat line of holes across its chest, wondering why he had killed the serf. He felt the answer roll through the undersurface of his consciousness; it was there, but his mind refused to analyze it.

"Enough," he said. "Tomorrow, then, Strategos."

Chapter Fourteen

CHATEAU RETOUR PLANTATION
TOURAINE PROVINCE
AUGUST 3, 1947
0200 HOURS

It was the quiet hours after midnight, the time of deepest sleep, the time when old men die and young ones lie awake and shiver with an emptiness glimpsed at the heart of things. The wind had died, and the stars shone soft and huge through the damp clear air; grass gave off its heavy scent as the dew beaded on stems, but the flowers were curled in on themselves, petal folded over petal. Mysterious creaks and rustles sounded through garden and field, stalks rubbing one on the other in the slow cellular swellings of growth and decay. A light went by on the river, drifting downstream silently, then others passed overhead with a quiet throb of engines and a long torpedo shape black against the moon.

Below, a fox crouched and barked shrilly as the dirigible passed, then went about his rounds with swift paws that moved the leaves hardly more than his black questing nose. Green bush crickets sounded, strident bursts of sound fading into the empty spaces, and a midwife toad pipped from the borders of the lake.

In the Great House of the plantation, this passed. . . .

"Non."
Tanya woke at the stirring, from a dream where burning rubble collapsed again over the vision blocks, and ventilators poured smoke. For a moment she was bewildered, expecting first the engine growl and the thunder of the falling building; then she recognized the harsh feel of the sleeping bag, starlight and the bulk of her tank above.

Home, she thought. *I am home.* Smooth silk against her skin, the near-absolute blackness of her own bedroom, underneath her the wavy resilience of a bed whose mattress was water-filled cells. No prickle of dirt or sweat; clean smells of fabric and wood and the garden odors from beyond the curtains. No light except the radium dial of the clock

410

on the table across the room. She sank back into a half-drowse, smiling to herself. It was a pleasure like waking up early on a school holiday as a child, just so you could realize that you were free to go back to sleep. Her own home, bulking solid about her. Edward, the twins, the new-born pair, all near at hand.

"Non."

The bed was big enough that Solange's thrashing had not touched her, but the sound and the flowing transmitted through the liquid mattress brought her fully awake. With a sigh, Tanya slid over until her hand touched the smooth warmth of the serf's back; the Frenchwoman was curled into a fetal ball, and her owner could feel the shudders of nightmare running under her skin. A mumble in her native tongue; pleading, Tanya thought, and she could catch "Poppa" and "Maman" occasionally.

Damn, thought this was tapering off, the Draka mused to herself. Aloud: "Wake up." A firm, arm's-length shake. "Wake up, Solange."

The younger woman convulsed, shot into a sitting position and screamed twice, shatteringly loud; Tanya winced, but kept her hand between the other's shoulder blades. The Draka could imagine it from times when the light had been on, the serf's hands plastered to the sides of her face, eyes owl-wide and unseeing. Her quick shallow panting echoed through the room, slowing gradually as the rigid lock of her muscles relaxed. When her hands sank from her face, Tanya pulled her down and close; Solange pushed her face into the angle of the Draka's neck and clung within the circle of her arms, shivering quietly.

"I was—I was—" she began.

"Shhh, shhh, I know," Tanya whispered into her hair, rocking her gently. "It's all right, all right, you're not there now." There were several places Solange went during her worst dreams, and none of them were pleasant.

They lay together in the darkness for quiet minutes; Tanya could feel the serf's heart beating against hers, fluttering in the cage of her ribs. It slowed, until Solange sighed and moved her face so that their lips touched.

"Thank you, *Maîtresse,*" she whispered.

Well, I know what comes next, Tanya thought. There was a complex wiggling beneath the sheets as Solange slid out of her panties. *Do I want to?* She probed mentally at herself; it was only three days since her period had ended, which was generally a low point in her libido. Also she had only been asleep four hours and . . . *No, I don't,* she thought. *I want to go back to sleep. On the other hand, she'll be hurt, she needs the reassurance, and besides, in a few minutes I will feel like it.*

They kissed, and she could taste the slight salt of fear-sweat on the singer's upper lip; the stronger mint from her toothpaste; and the natural flavor of her mouth which had always reminded Tanya of apples and earth. A pointed tongue flicked at hers, ran lightly along the inside of her lips. The Draka nudged with her knee and Solange welcomed it between hers, gripping with her thighs.

"You wish to make love, Mistress?" Solange asked breathlessly, a small catch in her voice.

Tanya murmured assent, running her fingers through the serf's hair, marveling at the texture, soft as ostrich down, how it was matched in the fine curls pressing against her leg. Solange's mouth was moving across her face to the angle of her jaw, feather-light brushes of petal lips and tongue tip, while her hands stroked at Tanya's neck with only the pads of the fingers touching, just enough to brush the near-invisible hairs. The sensation was an unbearable mixture of caress and tickle; she heard her own breath catch as the pulse speeded in her ears with a long swelling.

Now I want, she thought, smiling silently into the darkness. *Now I want.* Their bodies moved for long minutes in a subtle mutual urging, and then Tanya rose to hands and knees, while the serf slid beneath her and lower. *Her hands are so soft,* the Draka thought, as they slid down over her shoulders to cup her breasts and then trace delicately along her flanks. They moved in slow gliding circles as the kisses floated down her throat. Tanya shivered as her skin grew tingling-tight, even her lips feeling swollen, like buds about to burst.

"Ahhh," she hissed aloud as the mouth closed around a nipple, and made a small convulsive arching of her back when small sharp teeth slid over it, nibbling. *All sweet goddesses, that's hotwired to my crotch,* she thought exultantly. Solange moved to the other breast, stroked her stomach.

"I—want," the Draka said hoarsely.

Solange lay back, wiggling lower, and Tanya could feel hands gliding up the backs of her thighs. The serf's voice was still a whisper. "Then ride this pony."

Tanya reached up with her right arm to touch the ivory plaque that controlled the lights. They flickered once and shone dimly on the lowest setting, reflected through gaps between the frosted glass false ceiling and the wall all around the big room. Shadows remained, hinting at a few large pieces of furniture, desk and armoire and massage table, hiding inlay and rare woods and even the colors of the glowing thousand-knot Isfahan carpet. There was a slightly brighter patch above the big bed, and the crumpled black silk of the sheets had a liquid shine around and across their bodies. The Draka lay back, examining the face in the crook of her left arm: spots of bright red high on her cheeks—that was familiar enough from their more usual times together, afternoons mostly—but not the tears that slid quietly from under her closed eyelids, pooling and beading and then running in slow tracks down the sides of her face. It was a contrast to her usual sleepy-smug-catlike expression of satiation, but common on these rare nights when she woke from the terrible dreams. *Amazing,* Tanya thought. *She looks lovely even when she cries; most people get red and puffy.*

She bent her head to kiss the tears, the salt taste of melancholy and of life, stroked back the drifting wisps of black hair. A kiss, smelling and tasting the warm flavor of sex, her own and the lighter musk of the serf's, mingled on their mouths.

"Why so sad, my pretty pony, my butterfly, kitten?" Tanya said softly, pulling up the sheet and holding her closer. "Didn't I make you happy?"

A sigh, and the long curved lashes fluttered back. "Oh, yes, I felt marvelous."

"Thought so. Do you know, you sing when you come? Anyone awake on this floor is goin' know I did right by you." Solange smiled through the tears and snuggled closer; Tanya could feel the slow dropping warm on her arm, then cooling, a little chill where the serf's breath ran over the wet skin. "Still haven't said why you cryin', though. Happens whenever you get like this."

"I . . . don't know, Mistress. It was my dream, I was . . . alone, everyone had turned away from me. I wanted them to come back to me, because there were . . . things . . . and I called out to them to help me, to save me, but they wouldn't, they walked away without speaking. I ran from one to the other but my hands could not touch them. And then, just before I woke up, they did begin to turn towards me, and I knew suddenly that if I saw their faces it would be too terrible to bear, my heart would burst."

Solange gripped Tanya fiercely, hiding her face in the angle of shoulder and neck. "Isn't that a silly dream to be frightened of?" she said, muffled.

The Draka stroked her back. "No, it isn't," she said, resting her cheek on the other's head. "Not at all."

"And then . . . when I wake up and you are there . . . I want very much to make pleasure with you. Not like other times, but because it makes me feel—" A hesitation. "Real again, not alone. As if I am found, not lost." The tears dripped more slowly onto Tanya's shoulder, and Solange sniffed. A moment later she spoke again, almost too soft to hear. "I love you."

Never promise more than you will give, Tanya reminded herself, as she stroked the serf's hair. She stretched, feeling a delightful lassitude that was not quite sleepiness, as if every muscle had been individually massaged and soaked and returned painlessly at half its original weight. *I feel such tenderness*, she mused, reaching up for a handkerchief and gently pushing Solange's shoulder down to the pillow so that her face was exposed. *Odd. Ah well, it's my feeling, why not?*

"I know you do," she said, wiping the streaks from the other's cheeks and putting the kerchief to her nose. "Here, blow." A tremulous smile, and the Frenchwoman obeyed. "There, isn't that bettah? I know, my sweet. I'm glad you do, and I'm . . . very attached to you. You are wonderful and precious to me, you give me infinite enjoyment in a dozen ways."

Solange reached up and gripped her arms, eyes searching Tanya's. "You will never . . . send me away, Mistress?"

Tanya kissed her firmly. "What a thought! Nevah."

"Not even . . . not even when I am old and ugly?" More quietly: "I am twenty-one this Christmas, mistress."

The Draka chuckled. "Look . . . Solange, honeybee, how old were you the first time I took you?"

"Eighteen, Mistress." An answering smile. "So frightened and ignorant . . . how did you tolerate me?"

"Easily, sweet." Tanya remembered the violet eyes watching her undress, huge and misted with terror and determination. "You were tryin' . . . anyways, that's about as young as I care to go." She gave the serf a peck on the nose. "I don't fuck children, Solange, and I'm ten years older than you, as is. Keep up you dancin', and you'll still be breath-stoppin' beautiful at fifty."

She rolled closer and took the other's face firmly between her hands. "And," she said slowly, "I've said I care fo' you. That means there'll always be a home fo' you here, an' I've made provision in my will. Word of a von Shrakenberg."

Solange sighed again, took one of Tanya's hands and kissed the palm before pressing it against the side of her face. They settled to sleep, curled spoon fashion in a warm tangle of arms and sheets.

"Oh, one thing," Tanya murmured sleepily.

"Yes, Mistress?"

"When we're sleepin' together alone like this, call me by name."

Solange inhaled sharply, knowing the rarity of the privilege, especially for one not estate-born. "Thank you, ma—Tanya," she said.

"You welcome, sweet," the Draka said. Twenty-one, she mused. *Have to get her a present.* Perfume, probably, or more platters for her needle-player. Or another crate of those trashy pre-War romance novels; she devoured them like candy. . . .

Dirigible, Fred Kustaa thought, leaning out the window and looking upward. *The Paris-Alexandria passenger shuttle.* Below, the grounds were washed in moonlight and starlight, only a low seeping of yellow somewhere from a curtain not completely drawn. There was a countryside quietness to the landscape; the sounds of merrymaking from the pavilions had ceased. The Draka were early to bed even in a party mood. The air smelled of dew but not rain, and he could tell that tomorrow would be another day of dry sun and heat. *Good for the crops,* he thought sardonically. The harvest of his plans was prepared, and needed only the cutter to bring it in. With a controlled impatience he turned and strode across the room, kicking angrily at the hem of his caftan.

He passed the bed, which the servants had noiselessly stripped of the usual sheets and relaid with smooth linen, less likely to tear. The posts had soft cloth restraints fitted to them, laced to the wood and with quick-fasten loops suitable for holding an ankle or a wrist; there were other fasteners on a table nearby, hard pillows, a jar of what the label claimed was scented, flavored lubricating oil, a blindfold and a whip with a dozen cords of hard-woven silk. Kustaa looked at them for an instant, then turned to the window, hawked and spat copiously into the night; it was silent enough that he heard the tiny *splat* as it landed on the roof of the shorter tower below.

Childish, he thought. *But sometimes a man's got to . . . say what he thinks.* Then: *Where is she? It must be going on two* A.M. There wasn't much time for what they had to plan; not to mention that the sooner she arrived, the sooner he could tell her the truth. It could not have been a pleasant day for her and the news seemed to have spread rapidly. At least there had been a couple of hard looks from the servants who arranged the room for his "pleasure;" he suspected that Sister Marya had made herself well-liked.

A knock at the door. He cleared his throat, grunted. It opened smoothly, and the nun stumbled through. The male overseer leaned his head in past the jamb for a moment.

"Found this-here wench still ditherin' in her room, 'stead of reportin' to be tupped, Mistah Kenston." He looked her up and down. "No accountin' fo' tastes . . . Anyhows, enjoy youself and maybe-so you can pump some manners into her, too. Uppity inside her head, I kin tell."

Marya shrank back against the door. She was carrying a cloth bundle in her hands, probably tomorrow's morning clothing. Some perverse Draka sense of humor had had her dressed in a short silk peignoir, transparent, that lifted her heavy bare breasts and swept open beneath to show the round belly sagging slightly over her thickset legs. He had started forward to whisper reassurance when he saw that her crouch was not a cower; her eyes had gone to the bed and seen what awaited her, and the sound she made was a low growling as the lips curled away from her teeth. The bundle of clothes she held floated down, and time slowed as he saw what came free of it in her right hand. Knife, fighting knife, long and slender and double-edged with a round hide-wound hilt. Draka knife; she must have palmed it somewhere, an Ildaren wrist blade.

It should have been comical, the fat woman in the obscene silk nightie coming for him with the hilt clutched in a clumsy white-knuckled hatchet grip. It was not, not to a man who had seen and dealt violence as often as Kustaa, not with that face behind the seven inches of edged metal. He backed away behind the corner of the bed, and fear blocked his throat for an instant before he could stutter out words, quietly but in his own voice.

"American, I'm an American!" The woman kept coming, her eyes rimmed all about with white, the point of the knife moving in the gloom. "I'm not a Draka, the Resistance sent me." Even then, the absurd code phrase almost stuck in his throat. "The escargots of Dijon are very fine. Goddammit, Sister, the escargots of Dijon are very fine!"

She stopped, as if a glass wall had come between them. The berserker look faded from her eyes as she began to straighten; it was probably the sound of his undamaged voice that got home, as much as the words and accent. "Not . . . American? Resistance?" The knife slipped from her hand, bounced once on the carpet, lay still with lamplight breaking off the honed edges. He was barely in time to catch her as she began to crumple.

"*Ah,*" Edward von Shrakenberg said. "Ahhh."

He looked down. The wench Chantal had her legs about him as he knelt on the surface of the bed, thrusting steadily. Her back was arched, making her a bow with weight resting on her shoulders and neck. His hands were clamped on her hips, thumbs kneading at the edge of her bush and fingers moving her in rhythm with him; he watched the mingling of their pubic hair at the end of each stroke, dark coarse black and tawny down below the ridged muscles of his belly. Obedient, she gripped tighter with her thighs and pushed up to meet him each time, the full plum-nippled breasts jiggling. The air was heavy with sweat and sex and the fumes of strong Moroccan kif.

They were both sweat-slick; her body seemed to glisten with it, but her face was hidden. He leaned back slightly on his heels and let his head fall back also, looking into the pattern of silvered mirror-tiles on the ceiling. Tanya had laughed at that, calling it a symptom of encroaching vanity. He smiled at the memory, smiled more at the soft warm moistness clenching and unclenching around his penetration of the wench. He could see her face in the mirror, although he doubted her open eyes were seeing much beyond the spray of black hair that lay across them. Her mouth was closed but her lips were wide in a teeth-baring grimace; half from the hard muscular effort that was making her grunt with every straining breath, half fury at this steady, intolerable invasion of her self.

But she's learned not to try that passive-resistance nonsense anymore, he thought with satisfaction. Amazing what a little pain, a few drugs and patiently ruthless will could accomplish. *By Frey,* he mused, in the intervals of lucid thought, *this may not be a serf-taming technique fo' mass employment, but it has a lot to be said for it in individual cases.* Though he doubted the odd Mr. Kenston was having as much luck with his nun; the two thoughts brought him a snort of laughter.

Chantal broke rhythm; his fingers gave her a tweak, and she settled back. *Still, can't keep this up all night,* the master of Chateau Retour decided. *Might get boring.*

He turned his head to Yasmin, who was beside them on the wide bed. She was lying on her stomach with her chin in one hand, the mouthpiece of the water pipe in the other; her feet swayed in time to the rhythm of the act that rocked the fluid-filled mattress beneath her. Edward nodded at her, and she smiled lazily, blew scented kif smoke toward him through pouted lips, rolled closer. One hand went down to where the master's body joined the wench he was riding, caressing them both; the other settled on Chantal's fist where it clenched straining beside her shoulder. The brown girl's mouth went close to the other's ear, whispered. *How to bring him off faster and get it over with,* Edward supposed.

He let slip the control that had kept his thrusts slow for twenty minutes, increased the speed until Chantal's buttocks were slapping against the hard flat muscles of his upper thighs with the violence of their movement. Yasmin's long cool fingers stroked unendurably at him, and he could hear her calling encouragement to the wench, until everything was lost in the long exquisite moment of release and his own triumphant shout.

The Draka came back to himself with a long sigh and worked his hands down under the Frenchwoman, working his fingers into the slackened muscles and feeling the residual tremors deep within. Her head whipped back and forth, a sound halfway between a whimper and a cry of protest escaping her: there were words in it.

"No," he heard. "No, no, no, not with you, no, *never*."

Pity she takes it so hard, Edward thought idly. There was a . . . what was the French word? A certain *frisson* to it, with her so visibly defiant; still, it would be better when her heart broke and she truly submitted. *Tanya was right,* he mused. *This one's hard but brittle. Not the type who can live without hope.*

He released her, and she moved away to the edge of the bed with jerky motions, curling her knees up against herself and reaching blindly for the mouthpiece of the water pipe, drawing on it as if it were air and she drowning. Drawing, coughing, drawing again. The Draka yawned hugely and stretched out his arms, the thick muscles sliding and bunching beneath the damp skin. Yasmin was looking at Chantal's hunched back, shaking her head with a frown; at his movement she shrugged, smiled and picked up the damp and dry cloths from the head of the bed.

"Pleasure you good, Mastah?" she asked politely and began to clean his genitals with gentle deftness.

"Just fine," he said, with another stretch and yawn, conscious of enormous contentment. *And a full bladder. Damn.*

The dark girl had finished and was cradling him in her hands. "Then maybe-so you doan' need Yasmin no mo', Mastah?"

He laughed and ran square strong fingers through her hair as she bent her head to take him in her mouth. "You'll see how much in a little while," he said, using the thick black curls to lift her away from his crotch and kiss her. "Wotan's balls, you do that good. But first I've got an errand. Back in a minute."

Yasmin watched him pad across the darkened room and then moved to touch the other woman's shoulder where she lay in a shuddering ball. Chantal slapped at her without looking around.

"Go away, don't touch me, go *away*," she said, in a hoarse thready wail.

Yasmin caught the hand that struck at her and held it in a grip as soft as her voice. "Chantal, honeybee, it's terrible to see you sufferin' so. Is there anythin' I can do t'help?"

"Help? You help *him*, bitch, slut, whore, go *away*!"

A sigh. "Chantal, we all does what we's told; me an you both, we's serfs, honeybee. I tries not to hurt anybody, I really does. Look, Chantal, it's just fuckin', that don't mattah nothin' at all, really it doan'."

Wide-pupiled black eyes came up to peer at her through matted hair and a face wet with tears and sweat. "So you serve him with a smile, you!"

"Well, I's born 'n raised to service, Chantal. He was m'first man, too . . . sometimes I'm not bothered by it, sometimes I likes it, an' if I could take all this on mahself an' spare you, I would certain-sure. But I *cain'*. Jus' like you cain' say no, or lie still like you tried." She shook her head. "Sometimes they can be pow'ful cruel . . ."

Patting the other's hand, "I knows you doan' want to end up like Solange, givin' them everythin'; well, *I* doan' give everythin', either. Somethin', yes, cain' be helped an' why bothah? It like the wind an' rain; no shame to bend to the wind, let the rain fall on you. Grass an' reeds, they mighty humble, bend right to the ground, but the rain and wind, they come an' go and the grass and reeds still there. Proud strong tree git tumbled ovah, broken."

"I want to die," Chantal whispered, letting her head slump back to the bed. "I want to die."

Yasmin gave an almost-painful tug on her arm, and there was real fear in her voice. "Now that jus' *stupid*, wench! 'Less'n you believes Marya's stories 'bout the place we go when we dies, which is too good t' be true, like-so them tales 'bout the Western Land where everyone free an' happy. You die an' that an end to everythin', good as well as bad. No mo' eatin', drinkin', singin', tellin' stories, playin' with babies—" She stopped, struck by a thought. "Is that it? Chantal, is that it? You quickenin'?"

A mumble almost too low to be heard. "I'm three weeks late. Vomiting in the mornings."

Yasmin's face lit in a smile as she leaned over the other serf. "Why, that wonderful! A chile of you own, an—"

"It's *his*!" The Frenchwoman's face was a gorgon's mask as she reared off the resilient surface, hissing so that a drop of spittle struck Yasmin on the cheek. "*He* put it in me like a *maggot*!" She collapsed as if a string had been cut. "I want to die," she repeated, in the voice of a weary child. "I want to die."

"Oh, honey, doan' feel like that!" Yasmin said softly. "It only a baby, doan' matter whose seed, baby belong to the momma. Be your'n to raise, if'n you wants. Jus' little an' helpless, needin' everythin'. Your'n to love an' to love you; everybody need that. Where we all be, if'n our mommas didn' raise an' care fo' us?" A sigh. "You feeling pretty bad, I knows. Doan' do nothin' foolish . . . but look, Chantal, when they knows, they leave you alone, doan' bed you fo' a year or mo'."

"Truly?"

"Mm-hm, that the rule." A hesitation. "They pro'bly let you get rid of it, if'n you wants, but then you . . ." She patted the surface of the bed. "Say, you go back to the room now. Only, first, go take a *nice* hot shower. I tell mastah you take too much smoke an' puke; ain' no man in creation wants a pukin' woman around while he pleasures hisself. Then I make him feel real good, an' I tells him you bearin', and gets him to say you doan' have to bedwench no mo'. Hey?"

Chantal nodded dully and pulled herself to her feet, groping along the wall in the detached lassitude that *kif* and despair together bring. *To be left alone*, she thought; it was like a vision of . . . of the Revolution. She touched her stomach and thought of the price, and almost doubled over with nausea in truth. *Shower*, she thought. *Shower first, long and hot.*

❖   ❖   ❖

"I'm sorry, Sister," Kustaa said, as she sat hunched and shivering in the chair with the blanket wrapped securely around her, eyes fixed on the knife in her lap.

"I just couldn't see any other safe way of managing it, without blowing my cover."

"I forgive you, Mr. . . . No, don't tell me. 'Need to know.' A day of fear is a little thing, compared with what so many others have suffered. And suffering is a great teacher. How did the Englishman—More, I think—put it? 'God whispers to us in our thoughts, sings to us in our pleasures: but in our pain, He *shouts*.' I forgive you as I hope for forgiveness."

"Forgiveness?" he asked, puzzled. "Given what you thought was in store for you, it was . . . heroic." He glanced at the bed, with the dangling bonds he did not dare remove. "By the way, my first name really *is* Frederick. My friends call me Fred. And considering your, ah, vocation, Sister . . ." He paused delicately.

To his surprise, the nun laughed. "You are a Protestant, are you not, Mr. . . . Frederick? I know Americans use first names easily, but . . ." At his nod she proceeded. "I swore an oath of chastity, Frederick. Renouncing a good for a higher good; but when I became a Bride of Christ, I did not swear to be omnipotent, able always to prevent my body being violated and abused by armed and ruthless men. Chastity is a matter of choice, Frederick."

He blushed, and she returned her gaze to the knife. "So I ask forgiveness for the sins of pride, cowardice, despair." At his startlement, she nodded to the weapon. "I thought all today, as I counted figures and solved problems . . . I thought, why has God let this thing come to me? To strike a blow and die? As I decided in the end, fully expecting to be killed, either tonight or later on the stake. Perhaps that was God's will, His test of me, as He tested Abraham when He commanded the son of his heart be laid upon the altar. I knew that there was purpose in this," she continued, with another of those astonishing smiles. "Vanity is not one of my sins, Frederick: I know why that particular trial has not been mine so far. I am not comely."

A slow shake of the head. "Or perhaps, I thought, God wished me to know—with my heart and soul, not merely my intellect—how it feels to be so compelled and used as the vessel of another's lust, so that I might better comfort others." She sighed. "This very night, on this very estate, others are experiencing that which I only feared. Some with complaisance or even willingness, no doubt, so staining their souls with sin; but sin may be forgiven. Others, more, in fear and pain. How better could I aid such, perhaps even lead them a trifle closer to the Truth, than if I could say: 'Sister in God, I know your anguish, it is my own'? If that was God's purpose, then I have failed Him, who said 'Be ye perfect.' "

A smile. "There are no end to my doubts and weakness, it seems. For I also thought, perhaps God wishes me to preserve my life for some small part in the greater work that you, Frederick, are also helping to accomplish, the overthrow of the Domination."

"Sister, I've wondered why—if there is a God—He permits it to exist.

I was raised Lutheran, don't go to church much anymore, but I guess I still believe . . . but . . ." A wave of his hand. "Ah, hell—sorry—why are we talking about this?"

"Because it is late, and we have neither of us had a chance to talk openly and without fear for very long . . . and I think also because we are friends, is that not so, Frederick?" The smile again, and he wondered how he could have thought her plain. Beautiful, not in any sexual sense, but beautiful still.

"And as to the Domination, that is part of the Problem of Evil, bearing on free will—and I will not burden you with the theology of Aquinas tonight, my friend. Also a Mystery, which we can never completely understand. . . . You see my problem, though? Every day the Domination exists, it causes evils far greater than the mere theft of my body's privacy; which if I truly do not consent is mere suffering, even suffering for the Faith.

"The Domination . . . it feeds on all the seven deadly sins, and engenders them. It robs men of everything. Of the fruit of their labors, making them despise the toil which is Adam's legacy; of the building of their own families and households, the source of right education and morals; of the chance to hear uncorrupted the Good Tidings; menaces Holy Church, crushes the ordered liberty in which men were meant to live . . . Its very existence causes millions to doubt God or His goodness; it is the masterwork of Satan." A long pause. "Not least for what it does to the Draka themselves. I often think of that."

Slowly: "So, if in any way my services could hasten its end, was it not my duty to endure all, even . . ."—she nodded to the bed—"for others' sake? And my reluctance mere pride, desire for death, my being *delicati*, fastidious? Or was that the voice of the Tempter using Scripture for evil's ends, when my duty was resistance unto death and the martyr's crown?"

Kustaa looked at the square face, the pale brows set in a frown of thought. Opened his mouth, closed it, struggled to put a name to an unfamiliar emotion, finally decided: awe. "You don't hate the Draka, then?" he asked.

"I *try* not to—to hate the sin and not the sinner," she said with a wry grimace. "Father, Son, Holy Spirit, Mary Mother and all the Company of Saints know, it isn't easy, the Draka do their vile best to make it impossible." A quick glance up at him. "You know, Frederick, if you think about the implications, the most terrifying thing Our Lord ever said was: 'Judge not, lest ye be judged.' Draka children, at least: no more innocent than other children—we are all fallen—but no less so either. Then think: all their best qualities turned to the service of their worst. Natural love of homeland and family, twisted to idolatrous worship of a 'Race' whose philosophy is about as close as imperfect man can come to pure evil. Bravery and loyalty turned to brutality; every perversion of natural feeling which we are prone to encouraged . . . Socrates, who so often glimpsed doctrines of the Truth, said it was better for one's soul to suffer evil than to do it. Also a counsel of perfection . . ." She threw up her hands. "But on to practical things,

Frederick. Tell me just so much of your plans as is necessary for me to accomplish them."

"Just for starters, Sister, you've increased my morale."

"What, by half-hysterical spoutings of the words of those greater than I? And burdening you with my doubts?"

Kustaa shook his head. "I don't know how or why, Sister, but just listening helped." A nod. "Now, here's what I need—"

She listened in silence, nodding occasionally. When he had finished she propped her chin in her hands and frowned.

"An old man, a scholar from the few words I had with him, and a heavy box," she said. "I think I can guess." A troubled sigh, and she spoke as if to herself. "This is a Just War if ever there was one, yet the Just War must be waged by just and appropriate means. Perhaps it is legitimate to use these weapons as a threat to prevent the Draka from using them, which they would . . . yet to be believed such a threat must be genuine, and no earthly cause whatever could justify . . ." The words sank away. and she stood up briskly.

"Frederick, you Protestants cannot know what a comfort dogmatic authority and the Magisterium of the Holy Father can be in cases of doubt. If all use of these instruments of destruction is evil, the Church will tell me. Until then, I may safely assume it is not.

"Our first item of business is to get this box of yours safely close to the place where your airplane may land; the shelter near the winery and airstrip will be ideal; nobody enters it, and I have the combination. Come." She started toward the door.

"Wait, Sister," he said. "Whoa a minute. Can we be sure nobody's going to stop us?"

Marya looked aside, then down at the blanket and visibly forced herself to unwrap and fold it neatly over one arm. When she spoke, it was to the wall. "It is a warm night, Frederick. Anyone who sees us will assume you—the Draka you pretend to be, rather—is simply taking his, ah, wench elsewhere for his sport. Outside, that is. We can drive to our destination quite openly. The message—that should be sent tomorrow, I think. The confusion of the feast will be at its height, and . . . yes, tomorrow."

Kustaa smothered a grin: the nun could be quite wickedly cunning, it seemed. He bowed her toward the door, then froze as two screams rang out from a window somewhere on the same side of the chateau as his room. A woman's screams, desolate and piercing, full of pain and raw grief.

"What the *hell*—" he began.

Sister Marya touched his arm, her face sorrowful. "There is nothing you can do, my friend. That was Solange, Mistress Tanya's . . . body servant."

He remembered the elfin beauty of the sad-faced girl at the breakfast table, the hard strength of the Draka woman's face, and shuddered. "Poor bit—sorry, poor woman."

The nun looked at him with eyes full of reflected pain and pity; pity for him, he realized, for his innocence. "Poorer than you think, my friend. That was nightmare, not mistreatment." At his raised eyebrow, she continued. "Solange has . . . embraced her chains. With the zeal of a convert, I fear. At least, one of her has."

"One of her?"

"The one that rules her waking soul. I think . . . I think there is another; and sometimes, at night, it remembers what it was, and what it has become."

He recalled the scream and shuddered again. "Let's get going," he said roughly. "Get the hell out." *Of hell*, his mind japed at him.

The driver slowed, easing the long lever of the steam throttle back. The vehicle rattled and whuffled in protest, bolts groaning; it was an ancient Legaree that might have hauled supplies in the Great War, an antique with a riveted frame and steel tires. He dimmed the headlights and peered around: nothing, except a few distant houses showing yellow-soft through the trees, the blinking running lights of a dirigible high overhead.

"Now!" he called back through the window behind him, into the body of the truck. It was brighter tonight than he liked, and the stretch of road beside the Loire looked hideously exposed in the moonlight. A patrol boat had gone by a few minutes ago, and he could still taste the sour fear at the back of his throat from that moment when its searchlight had speared him, hiding the ready muzzle of the Gatling cannon behind it.

There was a series of thumps from the road behind him, and he rammed the throttle back up with a nervous jerk and twisted the fuel and water intakes to the boiler.

A stop in a few kilometers, to lace the canvas tilt back up, and then on to Nantes ahead of schedule. The "feed-pump problem" that kept him from the usual daylight departure time had already earned him ten strokes with the rubber hose from that swine of a foreman.

"Filthy Serb," he muttered, as the bruises shot pain through his back; the man couldn't even speak understandable French. The driver knew nothing of the men who had darted out of an alley into the briefly halted truck, wished to know nothing. It was better that way. An order came through, passed anonymously, and you carried it out. Never anything conspicuous—a driver with night-pass papers was too precious an asset to waste.

I am a highly valued man, me, he thought sardonically. The Transportation Directorate used him on high-priority transport like this load of parts for the naval shipyard at Nantes. Electronics, he speculated, then consciously washed the guess out of his head with a drift of no-thought. That was a habit they were all getting used to. The Frenchman reached down beside the frayed padding of his seat and carefully extracted a cigarette, pinching the end to prevent the loosely packed tobacco from falling out. A7 drivers got a double ration, which opened up interesting trading possibilities, if one was abstemious. The match went *scrit* on the crackle-surfaced metal of the dashboard, a brief smell of sulfur and a glow over the dim bulbs of the dials.

He used the opportunity to study the valve-pressure gauge: dark as usual. He must speak to maintenance about it. *No more cigarettes tonight,* he decided. The docking reception clerk in Nantes was an agreeable Breton widow; for half a carton, he might be able to get a bottle of Calvados as well as a meal in the canteen and a cot.

"Name of a dog, Jean, hurry up!" the team leader hissed, pulling on his own dark knit ski-mask and thrusting the Walther 9mm through the waistband of his overalls. The young machinist was fumbling with his knapsack—that was the bricks of *plastique*; Henri hoped to God the man hadn't forgotten to pack the detonators safely. You had to rely on others to do their jobs while you did yours, but sometimes he wondered about Jean, especially since his father was executed and his mother and sister were sold off in that big sweep this spring. You would think it would have toughened him. . . . Ironic, that the innocent father had been executed and the Resistance-worker son not even detained.

"Ready," came another voice. They crawled out of the ditch where they had lain to let the truck get out of sight, north into the dark, rustling hedgerow of old poplars and new thornrose.

That was Ybarra, the Spaniard; reliable, even if she was a woman and a foreigner and a communist. Their explosives expert, and very good with the long stiletto or the piano-wire garotte; she had learned them all during the war in Spain back in the '30s, when the Reds had taken over and defeated the generals. From what one heard, that had been almost as bloody as the Eurasian War itself, allowing for differences of scale. They were all serfs now, all on the same side, as she was fond of saying.

The three Resistance fighters lay on their stomachs in the shadow of the hedge, relaxing slowly. No sound, except the harsh rasping of the crickets and the slight water-noises from the river a hundred meters south; not even much wind, tonight. More light than he liked, but they were all in dark clothing, their faces covered, nearly invisible from any distance. The smell of sandy earth and green things overbore the traces of tar and oil-drippings from the road. A warm night: sweat gathered in his armpits and on his face, insulated by the wool. He was about to signal them to move when the faint whine of tires on pavement alerted him.

No need for words; they all froze in place. *Coming from the west,* he thought. *No lights.* Both bad. Could they have stopped the truck, found something? Had someone seen it slow to let them off? The Frenchman controlled his breathing with conscious effort, remembering lying in the burning forest of the Ardennes, not moving while the Draka hunted, yipping, through the woods for the survivors of his volunteer company. Not moving as pitch melted out of the trees above his boulder and dripped down around the curve to fall on his back, not moving at the laughter and the screams as they bayonetted the wounded and collected ears. Not moving.

A military auto but not an armored fighting vehicle, silent and steam-powered. Helmeted heads, difficult to tell the color of uniforms in the dark; he peered at the door insignia as it halted. A skull, black in a circle of red chain: Order Police. The doors swung open and four men emerged, stretching. One handed around a canteen, another did a few deep knee-bends; a third walked to the edge of the road and opened the fly of his trousers, and the team-leader smelled the ammonia of urine seconds before the spattering on the leaves at the bottom of the ditch. The talked softly among themselves; there was laughter, and the slap of a hand on a shoulder, then a quick order from their NCO.

Just a rural security patrol, he thought with relief. Out looking for plantation hands off-bounds without a pass, candidates for a working-over and a day in the local police pen until their owners came to take them home for the serious flogging. None of the Resistance fighters moved. They had a mission, and it was not to attack a few serf policemen; not that the odds would be good anyway.

My pistol, Ybarra's knife and Jean's Schmeisser, he thought. One and a half clips for the machine pistol, six rounds for the Walther, against four trained fighting men with automatic rifles. They would fight if discovered, of course. Being found out of their pens at night warranted suspicion, a beating and interrogation. Being caught with weapons meant an immediate hamstringing slash across the back of the legs with a bushknife, torture for days, death on the stake or the hooks.

"Right," he said, after the police steamer had been gone a safe ten minutes. "We're . . ."—he looked up at the stars, down at a pocket-compass flicked open for a moment—". . . about two kilometers from the chateau." They would not go to earth anywhere near the plantation headquarters itself, of course. Far too much chance of a Draka out for a night stroll, and none of them had much illusion about their ability to silently dispose of a Citizen in hand-to-hand combat. Disaster even if they did. A police patrol that did not report in would bring Security and the military swarming about, but a dead Citizen would mean slaughterous reprisals all through the countryside.

"We'll head for Bourgueil," he concluded; safer to stick with the plan, although he had authority to vary according to circumstances. The town was on the fringe of the plantation, and their informants said it was unpeopled, heavily damaged in the fighting back in '44 and mined for building material since; only the winery in use. On the edge of a big forest area, too. "Lie low until daylight, then see about making contact."

It must be important, to risk his whole cell, whatever it was they were to help the American with. He reached over his shoulder to pat the radio set. "You first, madame," he said. "I'll take the rear. Ten-meter intervals."

"Right, comrade."

"And don't call me comrade, Ybarra," he added with a slight smile. Better her insolence than Jean's sweating nerves; if he had known the man was this shaken, he would have left him behind.

"Then don't call me madame."

"*Merde* with that, get going."

She moved past him, less than a ghost presence in the blackness. "*Su madre,* yes, sir."

⋄   ⋄   ⋄

"How's it work?" Kustaa asked, shivering slightly in the damp of the cave. Except for his shielded handlight it was pitch-black, dank, smelling of wet rock and concrete. The surface was rough under his feet, still bearing the marks of pneumatic hammers.

The drive up from the chateau had been uneventful, barely two miles; nothing in the ruins of the town, nothing but piles of stone, the shattered ruins of the Gothic church and arcaded marketplace looking as if they had been desolate two generations instead of three years. Moonlight on tumbled rock and the serried ranks of the vines on the low hills; an open field with a windsock and a strip of darkened landing-lights and three light aircraft tied down with lines and stakes. Not even a watchman. In a countryside under permanent curfew, where the population had no access to money and rarely left the Quarters, there was little danger of theft.

Perhaps it was that which was depressing: the sheer confidence of it. *Arrogant overconfidence,* he reminded himself. *And you're the living proof of it. Or perhaps it was what he and the nun had lifted in short jumps from the compartment of the auto; the thing always gave him the willies.* He looked over at her, and she smiled back at him with serene confidence. *You've got it good, buddy,* he told himself. *You're getting out of here.*

"Well, this is the outer entrance, Frederick," she said, with that trace of dignified old-world formality that was already becoming familiar. She nodded back along the short sloping tunnel cut into the pale limestone of the hill. "You see the niches? Those will be command-detonated mines."

Ahead of them was a blank surface of smooth gray metal; in its center was a naval-type blast door with a dogging wheel inset in the center. "This is from the cruiser *Baboeuf,* sunk in Toulon by the English in '40, after the surrender to the Germans. A section cut out of one of her main turrets, I believe, and slightly modified." There was a ball mounting beside the door on one side, with an armorglass vision block above it, tank style. "That is for a machine gun."

Her hand fell on his wrist and guided the light to the other side. A steel box had been welded to the surface, and she undid the latch to show a mate's combination lock recessed into the metal. "This controls the locking mechanism from the outside, although it can be disabled from within." She began twirling the dial.

"How on earth did you get the combination, Sister?" he asked.

"Oh, it's kept in the office," she said, as the tumblers clicked. "The lock on that cabinet is childishly simple . . . here we are."

Something clicked and whined deep within, and the wheel of the door swung with oiled smoothness as he spun it. The bolts went *chung-chank* and the thick metal swung open, bringing a hint of deeper chill from within, and a stronger smell like stone after rain, of mass concrete poured within the last few months. They wrestled the box through and dropped it, panting, with a dull *chunk.* Kustaa shoved the door home, and heard the nun feeling in the dark for a switch. It ticked, and overhead fluorescent lights hummed, flickered, and shed bright bluish light on a square box of a room ten feet on a side, lined with metal closets. The air smelled stale, with paint and metal and rubber odors, like the basement of a construction site. In the center of the room was something he recognized.

"Periscope!" he said wonderingly.

Marya nodded. "German," she said. "More military salvage. Through there"—she pointed to another ship's watertight door—"are more rooms. A suite for the masters, dormitories for some serf cadre, storerooms, a control room for the power system. There is a fuel cell in a sealed unit, it utilizes exterior air. Water comes from deep wells, there are air filters, room for a year's supply of food, weapons . . ." Her finger pointed to the ceiling. "Five meters of strong rock, not to mention the concrete. Ventilating shafts, but they will be baffled and fitted with filters, later." He noticed the inlets around the room, covered with temporary grilles, steel cap-covers hanging ready to be bolted into place.

"Protection against a fairly close miss, and complete safety from radioactive debris. Only the shell, now; the furnishings and so forth are to be added over the next few years. Eventually a linked system for the rest of the serfs, and even sealed barns for breeding stock."

"So they do plan atomic war," Kustaa said softly, glancing around the bare, well-lit, evil room.

"No," the nun said slowly. "No, I do not think so . . . not without a chance to strike first and suffer little retaliation themselves. I've heard them speak of it and every one has had fear and hatred in their voice. At least at the prospect of the land itself being laid waste; they care for that, more than they do for any number of non-Draka lives. This is . . . a precaution. On the initiative of the State, you understand."

"It'll be safe here?" he said, nudging the box. "And you'd better give me the combination, as well."

"Very safe. Only the Landholders and the overseers have the combination"—she made an impish smile—"officially, and none of them come here unless they must. With the feast and their duties, virtually no chance at all. And we are close to the airfield, relatively far from the Great House. Where better?" She shrugged, then pulled the door of one of the metal cupboards open. "This will be decontamination gear someday . . . in here." They struggled it over to the locker, Kustaa repeating the numbers after the nun as he went.

As they swung the outer door shut, the nun stopped as if struck, then gave a low laugh.

"What is it?" he said. The night outside was still black, but it had the flat depthless quality of the time between moonset and sunrise.

"This place? Frederick, it was designed to keep that poison out. And what is inside it now?"

His own laugh had only begun when a word came from just outside the tunnel.

"Attend."

Kustaa felt his mind click over into another mode, another time and place; his hand moved silently, cautiously through the darkness toward the butt of his pistol.

"Wait," came the voice again. French, male, hoarse. "What are your tastes in cuisine, Monsieur-with-the-American-accent?"

Cuisine? thought the OSS agent blankly. Then: "Okay. Well, the escargots of Dijon are very fine," he continued casually.

A gusty sigh, and the unpleasant metallic sound of an automatic pistol's action being eased back into place by hand. "That is true, *monsieur*, very true. With some fresh bread to mop up the garlic butter, and perhaps a bottle of—"

"Wait, that isn't in the password," Kustaa said.

"No, merely being nostalgic, Monsieur." The man came forward, a knitted mask over his head, dressed in dark stained city-serf overalls; the woman beside him was similarly clad, but tapping the blade of a long slim knife on her knuckles. "Lyon felt," he added, "that it might be important to forward certain items you left behind in your haste." He removed his backpack. "Your radio, for example, my old."

Kustaa took the offered hand, feeling the hard strength of a manual laborer. "Damned nice of you, but as it turns out, Sister—"

"No names, please," the man said, taking in the blanket and the wispy silk beneath with a slightly raised eyebrow. "Our contact, I suppose." He drew her aside and they exchanged codes in voices too low for the others to hear. "And you do not need the radio, you say?"

"She has access to the one in the chateau. It's an authorized transmitter, less likely to attract attention."

"*Merde.* Well, we also brought twenty kilos of *plastique*—"

"*Twenty kilos?*"

A purely Gallic shrug. "It is easier to steal it than hide it. It had to be disposed of in any case; we thought that it might prove useful. As might three helpers—" He looked around, swore, strode out to the entrance.

"Jean!" he called, low but sharp. A figure by the raised hood of Kustaa's Kellerman started erect. "Jean, name of a name, what are you *doing*, imbecile?"

"Nothing, nothing, just looking at this auto," he said.

"You repair the accursed things every day; get inside and under cover!"

To the two beside him: "Even if we are not so essential as we hoped, there has been a great deal of effort to account for our absence for three days. A place of refuge is most essential. . . ."

Kustaa and Sister Marya both began to speak at the same time; the American nodded to the Pole and let her continue.

"I think," she said, "we have a refuge available and one of . . . unique strength."

"And," Kustaa added, his eyes narrowing in the dim starlight, "I've just thought of a possible use for that plastique, boys. Just by way of a fail-safe."

Chantal halted, leaning in the corner of the corridor. Her skin felt raw with the scraping she had given it in the showers, but not clean. *Not clean for weeks,* she thought bitterly. At least the man's smell was off her, but she could still sniff the stink of it . . . She thought again of what was growing beneath her heart, and nearly heaved her empty stomach once more. Voices ahead drew her alert; Marya's, and a man's.

She pressed herself back against the wall, leaned her head around.

It was Marya, wrapped in a blanket. The man with her, the Draka visitor they had sent her to . . . and he was speaking. Low, but without the hoarseness she had been told of. Chantal felt something cold crystallize inside herself as she pulled her head back; the nun was not holding herself like a woman speaking to the man who has just raped her. *I should know,* she thought savagely. And why would he bring her back here, to her own quarters? A master would use her, then dismiss her when he was done with her. The Frenchwoman risked another look: the tall man was handing something to Marya. Something that glittered . . . a knife. Something else as well, from his belt: a cartridge case.

" . . . eggs in one basket," he was saying. "You hold this for a while." *An American accent!* She recognized it from the radio and motion pictures, before the War.

Chantal pulled back again and sank to the floor, hugging her knees to herself, waiting for the closing of the door and the sound of the man's boot heels walking away. *Something* was going on. *Something that sanctimonious bitch hasn't been telling me,* she thought with a wild flare of rage that left spots swimming behind the closed lids of her eyes. *Her with her sympathy and prayers! Resistance work, it must be.* Something to *do,* a way to strike *back.* And the nun had left her out of it, left her in the misery of utter helplessness, a powerless victim, a *thing.*

"You're not leaving me out any longer," she whispered savagely. "Not anymore."

Chapter Fifteen

CHATEAU RETOUR PLANTATION
TOURAINE PROVINCE
AUGUST 3, 1947
1100 HOURS

"Andrew! You made it!" Tanya's eyes widened as the long car with the Security-skull blazon crunched to a stop by the steps. He was in crisp garrison blacks, with nothing nonregulation but a tasteful ruby eardrop. The warmth of her smile and embrace was still on her face as she turned to formally clasp forearms with the Security officer who followed. "And Strategos Vashon," she continued. "You welcome to my House, sir. Make youself free of it." A rueful shrug. "Bit crowded, I'm afraid."

To her brother: "Edward's up by the winery, lookin' over our new Cub with Johanna and her Tom." She turned to the waiting housegirl and took two greeting cups, handing them to the guests while harried-looking servants swarmed down to take their luggage and direct the *Orpo* trooper-driver to the vehicle-park west of the Great House.

They poured ceremonial drops and sipped at the wine, eyes widening slightly in appreciation at the taste.

"Spicy." Vashon said. "Hmmm, hint of . . . flint, maybe? Local?"

"From a friend's place, east of here: Pouilly-Fume. Fo'give me if I don't join you, gentlemen, but I've got to get through the day standin'."

Andrew held out a hand to stop one of the serfs going by with the luggage. "Not those two, boy, they're the gifts."

The serf, a middle-aged fieldhand hurriedly kitted out in house livery for the day, bobbed his head and looked at Tanya questioningly. "*The table with the gifts, Marcel*," she translated into French.

"*Oui, Maîtresse*," he said, and trotted up through the main doors.

"You lookin' good," Andrew said to his sister as she turned back to them. "And considerable less pregnant than last time." Fresh and summery in a crisp white linen suit, with no hint of color but the ebony butt of the little Togren 9mm tucked into its holster inside her belt.

"Never again." She shuddered, linking an arm through his and courteously motioning the Security officer before her. They turned to the high arched gateway that passed like a tunnel through the bulk of the chateau's oldest section. Light showed at the other end, and the soft lilt of a string quartet. "Through here; the main court is out back . . ."

It was a bright noon, almost cloudless; hot and dry, with a fitful breeze from the north. The courtyard along the north side of Chateau Retour was a blaze of color; from banks of flowers, from the silks and jewels, from the dragon's hoard that sprawled along the long cloth-draped trestles where the naming gifts were exhibited, from the tile and stone of the courtyard pavement itself.

A wooden bandstand draped in tapestries from Lyon held musicians in pre-War formal dress, contributed from neighboring estates for the occasion. In the cool shadow of the arcade along the court's eastern flank more trestle tables held food: piles of scarlet lobsters, roasts, salads, fruit, with white-hatted carvers and servers standing ready. Housegirls in brief gauzy costumes circulated with platters of delicacies, dabs of cheese on wafers, brandied truffles, savory morsels of fish or spiced sausage, wine coolers, juices, cigarillos and hashish.

Kustaa leaned against a pillar beside the buffet table and watched the crowd, taking occasional nibbles from a plate held in one hand. He had never seen so many Citizens in one place on a social occasion. Forty adults, he estimated, and nearly as many children, from infants being carried by their nurses to the teams playing water polo down at the lake. Their shouts and splashing echoed back, and he could see their sleek bodies slipping naked through the clear water and flung spray. The guests seemed to fill the great yard without effort, though they were far too few to crowd it, and less noisy than this number of Americans would be.

I wonder what it is, he thought. They were in every combination of attire, formal and informal, from one severely elegant woman in her sixties dressed in a Grecian-style gown of pure white, through uniforms of every rank in the Domination, to a few who had just come up from the lake in nothing but the glistening water on their skins. Sitting on the benches, strolling, talking, one even in a wheelchair. . . . There was a sickness to them, he could feel it, a rot somewhere within, but it had not seemed to weaken them. Instead they fed on it and it made them strong. . . . You could see it in their eyes and movements, a consciousness of power. Power of life and death over other human beings, power held since birth by hereditary right.

They believe, he decided. That was what gave them that air of absolute confidence and cold will. *They believe their own myth of what they are and, believing, confirm it to themselves every day of their lives.* Then: *Don't get spooked; they put their pants on one leg at a time like everybody else.*

When they wore pants, that was. He tried to imagine a similar gathering in the U.S., Social Register types and *haciendasdos,* with one in every ten of them down to the buff. A grin forced its way to his mouth: they probably wouldn't strip half as well. Which reminded him to be careful himself; he was circumcised, and he was getting graphic evidence that Draka men were not. Beside him Ernst waited, in a creditable imitation of a personal servant's combination of attentive waiting and don't-notice-me deference. *Hell with it,* Kustaa thought. *Can't be helped, so why should I feel guilty about it?*

Then the man stiffened, looking over Kustaa's shoulder. His fingers moved: *Send me away. Quickly!*

Why? He was officially nearly dumb without him, and it was a nuisance. Particularly since there were some here who might have valuable information, and they seemed reluctant to offend or directly deny him. He wished everyone in the States were as pleasant to disabled veterans, and that tall fiftyish man was a member of the Domination's Senate, just retired from the Supreme General Staff. A quantum opportunity . . .

Because there's a Security general coming through the gate who's seen me before and probably read my file a hundred times. Even without the beard and in livery he may recognize me.

Kustaa's fingers flew, and he made an imperious wave for audience effect, if somebody should be looking. *Get your ass out of here. The shelter, if you can. Back after dark and be careful.*

"Yes, Master." A low bow and the Austrian hurried away, weaving through the partygoers. Carefully, with left-and-right bobs of the head: Citizens expected to be avoided.

Kustaa turned, feeling his heart surge and slow with the brief rush of adrenaline, then subside into alert wariness. *He* was too conspicuous to run. A Citizen was noticed when he moved, not part of the continuous background flicker of life like a serf. He would have to take his chances; his tongue probed at the capped tooth at the rear of his molars, imagining the swift crunch, a brief bitterness and oblivion. That was a choice he had made his mind up to long ago. Not simply that he accepted that there was too much knowledge in his skull, but they had sent Rutherford *back.* Alive, in a dirigible shipping container to London, with glossy prints of his progress from capture to the thing that had made one of the bomb squad team that had opened the lid faint. With "Thanks for the lovely chat" carved in his forehead, above the lidless eyes.

The container had been correctly addressed to OSS clandestine headquarters in Britain.

For a moment, he thought of Sister Marya. Who would never use the tooth, never even consider it, even knowing what would follow . . . *And there are advantages to being a lapsed Lutheran,* he told himself. Somehow he was smiling as he completed the turn and saw Tanya von Shrakenberg walking through the archway. She waved and guided the two men with her toward him.

One in black, tall, with what Kustaa was coming to think of as the von Shrakenberg face, bony eagle-handsome features and pale eyes. Another, short, black-haired and green-eyed, in a Security Directorate uniform that matched the shade almost exactly. *Jesus, a Strategos.*

"Mr. Kenston, pleased to see you lookin' so well," she was saying; seeming to mean it, too. An odd pang of guilt, quickly suppressed:

This isn't the middle ages, Marine. You don't owe them anything because you've eaten beneath their roof. It isn't theirs, anyway.

"I'd like you to meet my brother Andrew," she continued. "An' Felix Vashon, here. Mr. Kenston," she continued to the two, "is the Wayfarer guest. Art-supply buyer, and a Class III veteran. Throat an' head injuries, unfortunately, but he's got a boy to talk fo' him . . . Where is he, Mr. Kenston?"

"Hel-o." Kustaa grated, exchanging forearm grips with the two men. *Christ, I'm glad I don't have to arm-wrestle for a living here,* he thought. "Se-nt . . ." he waved vaguely. "Er-rand."

"Andrew von Shrakenberg, Merarch. XIX—formerly Nineteenth Janissary. Now on detached duty." Hard arm, direct stare, polite expression, expressionless eyes. . . No. Flat, slightly dead; thousand-yard stare, familiar as the cracked scraps of shaving mirrors on troopship bulkheads during the War. Combat man, and not from a bunker, either.

"Felix Vashon, Strategos, West-Central European district," the secret policeman said. Pleasant smile, well-modulated voice. The sort who made you understand why the standard nickname for Draka was "snake"—or that might just be knowledge of what he did for a living. *Maybe this is the one that cut off Rutherford's eyelids and left him staring into a strobe light for a week,* the American thought.

Tanya was about to continue, halted, beckoned imperiously. Marya came up to the small group of Draka, bowed politely and stood with a clipboard in her hands, eyes meekly downcast.

"Report," her owner said.

"Mistress, all the scheduled guests have arrived. These masters are also to be staying?" She brought up the paper and produced a pen. "Masters, there is camp-style accommodation in the pavilions in the cherry orchard west of the maze, or rooms at the plantations surrounding. Here? Very good, Masters; the last pavilion on the right; your luggage will be laid out." To Tanya: "The final check on provisions indicates more than ample supplies, Mistress. Cook says the suckling pigs are turning out very well. The extra servants and the personal retinues of the guests have all been settled in and familiarized with the floor plan and the events. The transport for the boar hunt tomorrow is on schedule. Refueling arrangements for the aircraft at the landing field are complete, and the tanker-steamer is standing by. Repairs on the dock at Port Boulet are complete and the yacht is at anchor. Yasmin and Solange are completing their rehearsals and Solange says she is satisfied with the musicians"—she inclined her head toward the dais by the old chapel building—"for a provincial group. No serious problems, Mistress."

Tanya patted her on the cheek and spoke to her brother. "Remember pickin' her up fo' me, back this spring? You were kind enough to offer me the run of you pens back there in Lyon, Strategos."

"It's a festive occasion. Felix, please. The wench is satisfactory? I had my doubts, frankly."

"Mo' than satisfactory. Occasionally troublesome, but worth it; real mind fo' organization. New plantation, routines not set. Edward an'

I have to concentrate on plannin' and getting the labor force goin', she's invaluable."

"Hmmm, thought she might be," Andrew said. "You get a feelin'. Type you have to watch, though."

"Yes . . . although she turns out to have unexpected talents as well. Mr. Kenston here"—she gave him a smile and a friendly squeeze on the forearm; her fingers were like slender metal rods, precisely controlled force—"took a sudden hunger fo' her yesterday. To tell the absolute truth," she continued frankly, "if there'd been a way of refusin' him compatible with manners, I would have." A favorite horse or a regular concubine was something only a friend could ask the loan of, as a favor; ordinary household goods like Marya were a guest's to use, of course. "I've gotten to know the wench somewhat, an' I'd've sworn on the soul of the Race and the first von Shrakenberg's grave all her erotic juices were channeled into her superstitions, need a prybar and help to get her knees open. Pro'bly girl-only if she *were* beddable, at that. Instead—"

She put a finger under Marya's chin and lifted her face to the light. "Look at that. You wouldn't notice, but the skin around her eyes is mo' relaxed. Set of the shoulders, too." A rueful shake of the head. "Happy! An' I was afraid she'd be sulkin' and poutin' off her work fo' weeks, at least. Turned out all she needed was a night rider and she's purrin'. Shows, never be too certain about anybody."

To her guest: "Satisfactory fo' you?"

Kustaa smiled, looking at the three; their sleek strong bodies so expensively trained, the beautifully tailored clothes and uniforms, the cold predator eyes that never lost that speck of icy watchfulness. At the woman waiting patiently, dowdy in her long sleeves and the heavy wool that brought a glow of sweat to her face. Waiting with serene patience. *Filth*, he thought at the Draka, behind the mask of his smile. *You're all filth, none of you worth a thousandth the Sister.*

"Go-od," he said, nodding and smiling, knowing his face was flushing—but that was all right, they weren't going to guess it was with the intensity of his need to kill them all. *Out*, he thought. *If the world were ruled by sanity and justice as she believes, I could get her out. Introduce her to Maila. God, I'd send my kid to any school she taught in.*

The Draka's finger freed the nun's chin; her eyes met his for a moment before dropping into the proper downcast position. Level and very calm. *Do nothing foolish, Frederick.* No, he wasn't going to do anything foolish, no, there was an entire lifetime of work ahead of him. Until the last Draka was dead. *Do not let them damage your soul with hatred. You owe your wife and child more than that, and yourself.*

That brought him up cold. "Th-an-k y-o," he said. The Draka woman nodded, taking the gratitude that was not meant for her, as he had intended. And the Sister would say this place was her cross, which she would take up to follow Him.

"Hold youself at this mastah's disposal, when you not workin'," Tanya said. "If you'll forgive me, Mr. Kenston?" He nodded, and the group moved on.

"Uncle Karl," he heard the voice say. "Cousin Eric, you two aren't fightin' again? Sofie, you'd better learn how to keep this pair of bull rhinos—"

"It's the *Boche*," Jean said, when Henri finally called from the other room. He inserted his head through the hood of the vision block beside the door, pressing his face to the padded visor. There was enough light in the short section of tunnel beyond the armorplate for him to see a distorted image of Ernst's face. Peering behind him, so there was only a stretch of neck swollen by the mirrors and thick glass that bent the image through ninety degrees to bring it to him. Turning around, mouth working, he must be talking.

Whunk-whunk-whunk, a stone on the thick steel. So far away. *Like Father's face, when the switch was under my hand and the pain—* Nothought, no thoughtno-thoughtnothought. White sound inside his head, soothing. Forget the shaking, the sweat, they could not trouble him while he whitesound-nothought could not remember the room and the chair and the whitesound-nothought—

"Well, let him in, you young cretin!" Henri's voice. Henri's hands shoving him aside, spinning the wheel. He turned, helped, the heavy door swung open. The *Boche* stepped through, shaking his head, speaking in heavy guttural French even as they strained together to swing it shut again, quietly, quietly. *Shhhh-chung*, and the bolts were sliding home again.

"What took you so long? I might have been *seen*. Ach, there's no possible excuse for my being here."

"Quite correct," Henri replied. "We are supposed to be *hiding* here." Suddenly he turned and gripped Jean by the collar. "*Merde*, what were you waiting for! You know we can't hear anything in the inner—" He turned suddenly, looked at the periscope. Jean felt a sudden stab of fear; it was up again.

Did I do that? Yes, he had; an impulse, in the hope that the masters would see.

Henri's hand came around and hit him, across the face and back again. "Are you *drunk*, you little shit?" he said. Something seemed to snap behind Jean's forehead, and now he was seeing very clearly.

"Are you drunk? Have you been sucking that piss-smoke kif the snakes give us to rot our brains again? Or are you simply fucking insane? That thing's naked to the sky except for some wire mesh, anyone could have seen it move up there!"

Seeing very clearly, the strong jowly face of Henri Maloreaux, who had been like his uncle. His father's (screamingtwistedswitchchair whitenoisenothoughtnothought) best friend, old friend from faded pictures on the mantel before the War, old army friend. *God, how I hate you,* he thought, very clearly, as he smiled with the right degree of shakiness.

"Thank you, Henri," he said. "I've . . . well, I keep remembering little Marie-Claire, and—thank you." The man's eyes softened, not the hard clench of his muscles. Jean knew what he was remembering, he was seeing Marie-Claire in her white First Communion dress. The photo, only it was his sister across the padded block and the dog was—whitenoisenothoughtnothought. The Draka had let him talk to her just last week, her and Maman: hello Jean I love you no we are well the work is hard but nobody hurts us we love you when can you come to us—

"I understand," Henri was saying.

Hate you.

"It must be absolute hell, not knowing where they are." The Maloreaux family was in the same compound, three concrete bunks across the room. "I understand."

The *Boche* was looking sympathetic too. "Ach," he said. "It is always the families that make it worst." *Hate you.* Ybarra was in the room now too, looking at him. Cold eyes, considering. Filthy Red whore, she was the one they had picked to kill the foreman, the one who listened at the doors and asked questions. Got him into her bunk—they could all hear the wet slapping sounds behind the curtain, then the thin whining cry as she put the steel needle in under the hair at the back of his neck; everyone thought it was a heart attack. *Hate you, bitch.*

I will go to America, he thought with the same gleeful clarity. I and Marie-Claire will go to America. I don't know how I will get word to the masters, but I will. Not the chair, not with her or Maman, not their faces bulging around the gag and my hand pressing the switch and pressing and pressing and stopping the pain the pain pressing *whitenoisenothoughtnothought.* The masters will come for me, and we will go to America and Marie-Claire will wear a white dress, and we will sail under the big bridge like the newsreel and never again the compound, she will laugh and clap her hands and not bend over the block with the dog *whitenoisenothoughtnothought.*

"It's that pigdog Vashon; he didn't see me," the German was saying. Jean felt another clear metallic thing go *snap* behind his eyes, because it was all working just right, just as the master called Vashon had said it would, the voice that spoke to him from the darkness beyond the blinding light, it always did and the photo landed at his feet and he looked down, no he didn't.

"Probably just chance he's here, but we've got to be even more careful. Almighty Lord God but he's a cunning devil."

Not chance. The voice from darkness was strong, it was wise, it would lead him into the newsreel and the ship and the tall fountains of water and the thrown streamers and confetti, where Marie-Claire laughed and did not huddle beside him on the concrete bunk listening to the noises in the dark. The voice knew he was its faithful servant and had come to reward him.

"But there's one stroke of luck, as good as Vashon is bad: Jules Lebrun is here. He and I were friends in the old days, and he's in on it with the other, the nun. They've arranged to have him on radio watch during the celebrations tonight, and with him I can 'play chess.' The American will slip away as soon as he can. When the message is received, we will flash the lights *three* times from the upper window. That gives us an hour before the airplane arrives; you must have the diversion ready, to draw all attention from this place. And the landing lights."

Henri smiled, nodded. *How ugly his teeth, why did I not see that before.* "Don't worry," he said, clapping the older man on the shoulder. *Disgusting, a Boche, maybe Henri just boasted of fighting them, he ran away and was a collaborator.* "We'll be employing our little *plastique* surprises, they'll be too busy attending to the transformer and their autos to notice a silenced plane. No killings, even, so it shouldn't mean more than a few sore backs among the locals; we'll all be far away in our different directions, no?" *He's a coward too, a coward.*

Vashon was here. It would be difficult to slip away, they were all watching him. Perhaps when they went to plant the explosives. The voice from darkness would take away all his sins as he knelt and begged forgiveness. It would wash him clean and it would all be clear in his head, like this.

"Sounds too good to be true, comrades." Ybarra's voice came from behind his shoulder.

His own mouth made sounds, and they were clear and good because Henri laughed and nudged him. *Die, bitch. Die.*

"Don't call me comrade," Henri was saying, an arm around Jean's shoulders.

Die.

"I think," the Austrian replied, resting a hand for a moment on Henri's arm, the woman's shoulder, "we can reclaim that word for all of us. It is a good word, *Kamerad.*"

Jean smiled and said the word. *Die. Leave me alone in my head stop talking to me inside, die.*

Tonight.

All of you. Die.

The picture was one of the middle series. Alexandra caught with the discus in her hand, leaning back against the wall with one leg propped up against it. Old stone wall, Mediterranean-white. Strong bare slender foot trailing toes in the white dust, just highlights of the rest, the scratched bronze of the disc, school tunic, metallic-black of hair, face shadowed by the colored dark of the bougainvillea . . .

"I was always too fond of putting flowers in," Tanya said.

"No," Alexandra replied. They were sitting on the solitary couch in an empty echoing room in the new east wing, the picture propped up before them on a wooden chair. Their arms were over each other's shoulders, the free hands holding cooling late-afternoon glasses of beer. Light scattered through the windows, shafts into darkness, slanting hazy pillars of yellow crossed by the slow white flecks of dust motes.

Gods, I'm glad to get away for a while, Tanya thought, and let her head loll against the high scrollwork back of the seat. The tour of the Quarters had been deadly dull . . .

"Still thinkin' 'bout all those old fogies complainin' the serfs would be spoiled with four-room cottages an' runnin' water?" Alexandra said, with a slight teasing note in her voice.

Tanya turned her head. *She's aged well,* was her first thought. *Better than me.* Experience lines beside the eyes that were a blue deeper than indigo, almost black. They kissed, drew back and laughed, turning to the painting.

"No, thinkin' of . . . back then."

"Gods bless, it's like rememberin' another universe. . . . What were we goin' to do?"

"What weren't we? Conquer the world—"

"About half, it turned out."

"Paint the most beautiful pictures ever done, design planes to fly to the moon . . . love like nobody ever had or would."

"Ah, what happened to us?" Alexandra mused.

"What didn't? The war. Life. Love, death, victory, defeat, joy, anguish, children . . . time."

"There it is, captured fo'ever," the dark-haired woman said. "Not many can say that, Tanya. All the fire an' the sweetness and the old familiar pain . . ." A sigh. "While we, we're not those two any longer, are we?"

"No; we're older, sadder, and friends."

A door slammed and a small figure bounced through, cartwheeling, a flash of orange fire as the hair passed like a bar of flame through a patch of light.

"Ma, Ma!" Gudrun said, then stopped politely when she saw her mother had company. "Sorry, Ma, ma'am. I'll come back later."

Alexandra laughed. "Time takes, time gives. I'd best go see to my own, they've probably burned down half the province an' set sail on you yacht to play pirates all the way to Ceylon."

They touched fingers. "See you later, 'Zandra," Tanya said.

"Sho'ly, Tannie."

Tanya held up her arm. "Not too old to snuggle with you momma?" she said.

The child settled into the curve of her shoulder, a wiry-hard bundle whose calm trust finished the task of relaxing the tension out of her back. *Not too old,* she thought. *Not yet.* Gudrun sighed and yawned, curling up, the bouncing energy suddenly flipping over into sleepy thoughtfulness. *How did I feel at her age? How did I think?* The effort to recall was maddening, slipping away from the fingers of the mind. A rage, a rage to do, to live, to be . . . Fragments of memory: holding a dragonfly's wing to the sun and seeing it suddenly as a vast plane of gold ridged with rivers of amber. Lying in her bed alone in the dark and feeling consciousness staggering as she comprehended death for the first time, realized that one day she, herself, the inner "I" would *cease to be.* Enormous unappeasable frustration with all-powerful adults who would not, could not *understand* . . . things that seemed so clear, but that she could never have put into words.

Her daughter was looking at the painting. "Did you love her, Ma?" she asked.

Tanya smiled and put down the glass, used the other arm to hold her daughter close. *Well, she's getting to the age when your parents' love lives are troubling mysteries instead of boring grown-up stuff,* she thought tenderly.

"Yes, very much," she said.

"As . . . as much as you love Pa?" the girl asked.

"Different, child, different . . ." How to explain? "Remember what happened when we said you were old enough to drink you wine unwatered?" Tanya felt the beginnings of an embarrassed squirm.

"No, don't feel bad, baby, everyone takes a great big gulp just to see what it's like. Love's like that, Carrottop, you have to practice, an' the first real try makes you head spin. Makes everythin' wild an' strange-like, because it *is* the first an' the skill isn't there. Flares up like a bonfire, where you freeze and roast. Then you learn how to make the good warm coals that'll last all you life long, the way Pa and I've done. But, ah! Those first tall flames are a lovely sight."

A long pause. She looked down and saw the red brows knitted in thought, then a slow nod.

"Will I ever have a special friend like your Miss 'Zandra?" she asked shyly. "The girls in the senior forms at school, they're always goin' on about who's fallin' fo' who, and it all seems so . . . silly, like a game."

"Sometimes it is, Carrottop, and it'll all seem less silly once you body changes—I know it's hard when we say, 'Wait until you older,' but sometimes it's all we can." She kissed the top of the child's head, feeling the sun-warmth still stored in the coppery hair. "Jus' have to wait, child; doan' ever rush into things 'cause others are doin' it and you want to fit in. When you time comes listen to you heart; maybe in school, maybe later in the Army when you old enough fo' boys, maybe not till University. Maybe everythin' will work perfect right off, or you might have to try an' try again—most folks do."

"If . . . if you love someone like that, and it doesn't . . . work, does it hurt?"

A rueful laugh. "Sweet goddesses, yes, baby, worse than anythin' else in the world."

"Then why does anybody do it, Ma?"

"Can't help themselves, child, no ways."

Another silence. "Pa never had a special friend like Miss 'Zandra, did he, Ma?"

Tanya squeezed a hug. "Freya, Carrottop, you wants to find out everythin' in a hurry." A pause for thought. "No, though some do . . . Men are different from us, baby." A nod: Draka children learned the physical facts of life early, from observation and in their schooling. "Not just the way they're made, but inside."

She tapped her daughter's head. "They . . . come to the need fo' lovin' late, but need the pleasurin' part of it more, 'specially when they're young, and they can keep the two apart more. We're the other way 'round, the lovin' comes first, in general, and then the needin' grows on us. Not everybody's that way, you understand, but most. That's why the boys mostly start with wenches, because at first with them it's just this . . . blind drive to plant their seed."

Gudrun frowned again, and when she spoke it was in a quiet voice. "Ma, doesn't that mean . . . well . . ."

Tanya rocked her, smiling over her head. *That* was a question all Draka children asked, sooner or later; important to give the right answer. "An' you wonderin' if that means he loves you less, with all those wenches' babies he made, makes you less special," she said. A quick nod. "No, never, darlin' of my heart," she went on, letting a note of indulgent amusement into her voice, showing that the fear was understood but not a thing to be taken seriously, feeling the momentary tension relax out of the girl's body. "You see, Pa and I made you together; like he loves me special out of all the world, we love you and Timmie and the twins, because only you children of our blood are really ours. Y'understand, sweetlin'? You the children we raised an' trained, and you our . . . well, when we're gone, you'll be all that's left of us.

"Know how we always say, 'Service to the State,' and 'Glory to the Race'?" A nod: civics classes would have taken care of that. "There's another meanin', and this is real important. *You* are the glory of the Race, darlin'. Because of you and you brothers and sisters, Pa and I are joined to the Race, through the children you'll have some day, and their children and children's children, forever. Just like we join y'all to the ones who went before, right back to the beginnin'."

"Oh. That's sort of scary."

"Mm-*hm*. Big responsibility, Carrottop, but it'll be a while before you has to worry about that. Never be in a rush to grow up, my baby; that's what 'Zandra and I were talkin' about, before you came. Lookin' ahead you see all the things you can do that you can't now; but lookin' back, you see what's lost. Take each year with what it brings, Gudrun."

"Ma . . . "

"What, *mo'* questions?" A laugh. "Go ahead, daughter, go ahead. Just remember, fo' you own when their favorite word is 'why.'"

"Why do Pa and you . . . I mean, I know you love each other, so why, umm—"

"Aha, the wenches. Well, darlin', that's another thing you'll understand better when you're older, but . . . it's like candy and real food. You could live without candy, fairly easy, but on nothin' but candy you'd sicken. Nice to have both, though."

"Why only, well, only wenches, Ma?"

"It isn't," she said frankly. "Fo' men so inclined, there's prettybucks. Remember what I said about the Race?" A nod. "Well, women can't mother as many as a man can father, and it takes a Draka mother to make Draka, child. Especially since we've other things to do, like fightin' and helpin' run the estates and so forth. So we have to save our wombs fo' the Race's seed." *We'll leave aside the vexed question of whether contraception's made the Race Purity laws obsolete, and the even more vexed question of the primitive male confusion between penetration and domination; that's for your generation to deal with.* "Another thing that pro'bly won't trouble you for a good many years yet." More somberly: "When it does, remember, we're like iron, they're glass; be careful touchin' them, you can shatter them without meanin' to."

Gudrun yawned again, snuggled her head down against her mother's bosom, squirming into a more comfortable position. Tanya sat without words for a few minutes, watching the near-invisible lashes flutter lower, the near-transparent redhead's eyelids drooping down.

"But what did you come runnin' in to ask, my sleepy baby?"

Another huge yawn, and a near mumble. "Beth said I had to nap, but I'm too old to take naps in the afternoon, Ma."

"'Course you are, honeybunch. You just lie there a while, and momma'll sing fo' you."

Rocking, she began very softly: "Hush little baby, doan' you cry/ You know the spirit was meant/ To fly—"

" . . . fiasco in Lyon," someone's voice was saying.

Kustaa pricked up his ears, bending over the gift table. It was sunset, and the night's entertainment had begun. He glanced at his watch; Ernst and Jules would be in the radio room at 2130, and for three hours after that. His scheduled transmission time started a half hour later. Plenty of time, and it would be suspicious in the extreme if he absented himself; he could plead sickness but then his hosts would exercise their *damned* consideration and call for medical help, which he could not afford.

He smiled to himself as he edged nearer to the cluster about Tanya's brother and the Security general. The throat story was bad enough, making elaborate explanations impossible; sometimes he felt Donovan had outsmarted himself there. The speech training had worked to *some* extent, a more moderate injury would have been better. The head injuries were even worse, because if he played sick they might over-ride his objections to a doctor's examination.

Ah, well.

"Not quite a fiasco, sho'ly," Vashon was saying.

"Since I was there, and jointly responsible, I think I can speak frankly without givin' offense, Strategos. 'Fiasco' I said and meant," Andrew replied.

Kustaa moved down again, past studbooks showing the pedigree livestock among the presents, past a da Vinci and a Cellini saltshaker. There was no formal organization to the viewing; you went and examined young Karl and Alexandra in their cradles, perfectly ordinary looking examples of two-month-old children, round squashed-looking faces and starfish hands. Then you drifted along, giving each item the grave attention or amusement or comment it merited; the American took his cues from others. A pair of pistols caught his eye, and he lifted one out of the satin lining in the rosewood case.

"We caught a good number of them," Vashon objected.

"Spearchuckers. That bunch is so tightly celled, even they contact men don't know who their opposite numbers are, they just a voice in the dark."

"So they're claimin', to date."

"Strategos, you know as well as I do that it isn't impossible to lie while bein' castrated, blinded and bastinadoed, but it is impossible to lie *well* and *coherently* and *consistently.* We didn't get their leaders, or the American, or the scientist, or the . . . well, you know."

Kustaa turned the weapon over in his hands, hiding savage elation as the old oiled metal sheened in the lamplight. It was a six-shot revolver, but—with a second barrel under the normal one—a massive weapon: the patterned Damascus steel inlaid with elongated leopards and buck, the butt with plaques of turquoise and ivory. He flipped it up to look at the white-metal plate on the end of the grip: LE MATT, VIRCONIUM, 1870. Back, to examine the barrel. There was a slight pattern of randomly-etched pits around the muzzles; these had been used, and fairly frequently. He reached into the case for two of the cartridges— brass centerfire models, no corrosion—so they must be made up to fit the antique. A standard revolver bullet, about .477, and what looked like a miniature shotgun shell. There was a faint smell of gun oil and brass about the weapon, the patina of another's palm on the grip.

"Cobbler to the last, a fightin' man to weapons," a voice said by his ear. He turned, startled; the speaker was a tall gray-haired man in an Arch-Strategos' uniform. *That* was a rarity; there weren't more than a hundred or so in the Domination.

"Karl von Shrakenberg, Landholder, Arch-Strategos, Supreme General Staff, retired," the man said. Kustaa took his hand and gave the strangled grunt expected of him. Another of the eagle faces, but this was an old bird, tired, face scored by years and pain; he moved stiffly, with a limp.

"Sannie von Shrakenberg, Landholder, Strategos, Supreme General Staff, Strategic Plannin', active." Kustaa blinked; the woman looked to be in her forties, a little old for the six-month belly, but it was still disorienting. *Like seeing one of the Joint Chiefs knitting booties,* he thought with a smile. The woman nodded to him again and moved off.

"I knew Charley Stenner, you commander," the retired general said. Kustaa turned his start into an appropriate grimace. "Good man, pity that strafin' got him."

Maybe Donovan was right after all, Kustaa thought thankfully. Following two conversations at once was another skill he had been taught; the secret policeman was still arguing.

" . . . not an irretrievable disaster, in any case. We were a little ahead of the Yankees on that project, now we're a little behind. Bad losin' Oerbach, but the basic research is done an' recorded; the plutonium is really unfortunate, bottleneck fo' us and the Alliance both."

"It's the Yankee that sticks in my gullet," Andrew replied. "Much mo' of that and we'll have them runnin' wild. And Corey Hartmann was a friend of mine."

"Agreed. I want a film of him dyin' on the stake. After we've gotten what he knows, of course . . . still, in the long run, we gain mo' from espionage than they do."

Kustaa put the pistol in the general's outstretched hand. The older man snapped the action open with a practiced motion. "Le Matt," he said. "He did his best work in Virconium after the Yankees ran him out of New Orleans; sugar country must have been homelike to him.

This was his first swing-out cylinder model, and the last black-powder sidearm authorized for regular use. Best close-quarter weapon of its day." He made another adjustment, and the thicker barrel beneath the main one slid forward. "Buckshot barrel, just the thing fo' a cavalry melee."

"One thing, I'm glad we've still got his grandchildren. Nice to have that tricky an' ruthless a set of genes in the Race." Andrew, in a tone of rueful admiration.

"I still say we should hold them ready to use as a lever, should, Loki fo'bid, he surface in Yankeeland." Vashon's voice was neutrally cold.

"No. Primus, he's shown he's ready to sacrifice them fo' principle; secundus, by grantin' Citizenship, we made them part of the Race. With all the protection that my sister's children have, or any other young Draka." Still friendly, but with an icy finality underneath. That would be reassuring to tell Ernst. As far as the OSS knew, the military were still more powerful in the Domination's hierarchy. Of course, the Party was stronger than either of the armed branches . . .

"These were my father's," the old general continued. Kustaa smiled and nodded. "Weddin' present; my mother's parents were Confederates. He carried them in the Northern War." The American racked his brain . . . yes, that was what they called the Anglo-Russian War of 1879–1882; the Draka had saved Britain from ignominious defeat, an important step in their progress to Great Power status.

"See the inset gold notches? Kills. Duels only of course, not countin' war. The last one was the one he remembered best. An Englishman, durin' the stalemate on the Danube. Damn fool thought a duel was a game fired in the air." Karl smiled, the warm smile of a man remembering his childhood. "Pa always laughed when he told us how *surprised* the Brit looked when he gut-shot him . . . Honor makin' you acquaintance, sir." He replaced the pistol. "Best ever . . . still take them ovah anythin' but a submachine gun . . ."

A liveried servant took stance by the doors that led into the palaestra wing and the stairs to the terrace.

"My Masters!" she cried, sharply rapping the staff she carried on the flags. "The banquet awaits you."

"Oh, Poppa, are you sure you can't come?" Solange said, stepping back and turning her head a little to examine herself in the mirror.

How lovely, Jules Lebrun thought. *How much like her mother.* The image twisted with a pain worse than the growing lumps under his ribs, and he smiled to cover it and the tears that threatened his eyes. His daughter was dressed in a long form-fitting gown of platinum sequins, burnished until they glittered in a blinking, continuous shimmering ripple. Her hair hung loose down the length of her back, and thrown over it was a net of gossamer silver wire, the joinings of the mesh marked with tiny blue-white diamonds.

Solange turned to view herself from a different angle her hands moving down from below her breasts and over her hips. "I look like a *princess,*" she said happily, with a smile that highlighted the slight flush on her cheeks.

No, my child, you look like a very expensive toy, Lebrun thought with an aching sadness. The chamber that had been set aside as a dressing room was crowded: the quartet and their instruments, Solange and Yasmin, their friends. It smelled of cigarette smoke, clothes, brandy from the flask one of the musicians was handing around, faintly of the singer's jasmine perfume.

"Ernst is an old friend, child," he said. "Mr. Kenston will be leaving tomorrow"—*actually rather sooner*—"and we will never meet again, probably. I must spend some time with him, while his duties allow."

Solange sighed. He could tell why—only a few privileged house serfs would be allowed to listen to the entertainment, from below in the courtyard, and she must have wheedled to get him included. Then he saw her cast off the shadow. *Determined to be happy, and allowing nothing to stand in her way,* he knew. She came over and embraced him lightly and he put his arms around her scented and bird-delicate shoulders.

"I love you, Poppa," she said, brushing her cheek against his. "Wish me luck—this could be the most important performance of my career!"

Career? he thought. "I love you too, my child," he whispered. *And it is true. We love our children as we love our country, not because they deserve it but because they are ours, and we must.* Angrily, he felt his weakened body betray him and the tears spill over his eyelids.

"Oh, Father, don't be *that* sad, you will have *hundreds* of times to hear me sing!" She straightened, and gave her makeup a last check. "Yasmin, are you ready?"

The other serf girl looked up from her mirror. "Hold you horses, Solange sweet," she said placidly. "Plenty of time." She was dressed in a white-silk fantasia loosely based on an Arab burnoose, a color that set off her creme-caramel looks. Satisfied, she nodded, rose, hummed an experimental note and opened the neck of her garment a trifle more.

"Goin' be some hungry eyes on us tonight," she said complacently, linking arms companionably with Solange. "Only until we sing. Then they will be lost, and afterwards, it will drive them mad."

They made for the door, the musicians trailing, but it opened before they reached it and Chantal stepped through, followed by Marya.

"Why, hello!" Yasmin said to Chantal, then looked more closely. "You lookin' bettah, honeybunch!" The Frenchwoman flushed at the faces turned toward her, but it was true; she was still haggard, but neatly groomed and holding herself erect.

Chantal's eyes passed over the serf with blank indifference, fastened feverishly on Jules Lebrun. Yasmin pursed her lips and turned to Solange with a shrug and roll of the eyes that said what-can-I-do more eloquently than words.

Solange's smile and nod to the nun had a trace of good-natured mockery, looking her up and down. "You are also looking . . . well . . . Sister," she said as the two singers passed through the door. "Good night."

Lebrun remained silent after the door closed, glancing warily from the flushed excitement on the young woman's face to the worried concern of his Resistance commander's.

"Well?" he said at last.

"Chantal . . . Chantal, unfortunately, has stumbled across our . . . enterprise, Professor Lebrun. Specifically, she has deduced that Frederi— Mr. Kenston is not what he seems."

"I saw him with you, last night," Chantal said triumphantly. "But I wouldn't have been fooled; I saw you all day when you thought you'd have to lie down for him. You hid it but you were looking into the grave. I'm not stupid enough to think you would change so quickly. He is an American, an *ami* agent, is he not? And that 'servant' of his, he is from the nuclear facility—"

"Quiet!" Lebrun said. Marya opened the door again and looked quickly up and down the corridor.

"And I know something that *you* perhaps do not. Master Edward mentioned it to that slut Yasmin, while he was violating me the other night. An Alliance submarine was spotted off Nantes just the day before yesterday, and the Draka cannot find it. *That* is how the American and the Boche are to escape. Well, *I am going too!* You thought you could keep me in ignorance, I who was arrested and tortured for Resistance work as well, leave me here to be a beaten drudge and whore, *I am going too.*"

"Oh, Chantal," Marya said softly. There was mourning in her voice, and Lebrun met her eyes with a like sadness. They nodded slightly at each other, one thought in their minds. *She knows too much.*

"Chantal, child of God, believe me, only the American and the scientist are leaving," Marya said. "I swear it by Father, Son and Holy Ghost, on my hope of salvation."

Chantal's fists clenched. "You may stay and be a martyr, I have done enough."

The nun closed her eyes in pain. "As you wish it, Chantal," she said. "We are to send a radio message, then you will come with us to the shelter in Bourgueil, where the . . . courier from the coast will take you to a boating dock, upriver."

Lebrun stiffened in shock, then looked at the sickened, weary face of the Pole and understood; away from the Great House, to where the armed Resistance fighters were. Amid rubble where one more hidden body would be a little matter. Marya crossed herself and spoke softly in Latin. Which he understood and Chantal did not, although he knew he was not the Person she addressed:

"And Caiaphas said, is it not expedient that one man should die for the people?"

Lebrun replied sharply, in the same language: *"And if your eye offends you, pluck it out."*

"Truly," she sighed, crossed and took Chantal's hands with a smile. "It would be better if you had not tried to force our hand so, Chantal. So much better. But I understand, truly, and with all my heart I forgive you."

There was absolute sincerity in her voice, on the square homely face. Lebrun looked at it and shivered, knowing it was true, knowing it would be equally true in the moment Marya pulled the trigger. *God protect me from the truly righteous,* he thought, then almost laughed to himself at the unintentional irony. There were times when he congratulated himself on the sheer convenience of skepticism.

"Do you understand, *Sister?*" Chantal said, the anger still in her tone. She disengaged her hands. "What you were afraid of *happened* to me, over and over, for weeks, I had to . . . to do . . . and now I'm *pregnant,*" she spat. "Pregnant by that swine, but I'll never bear it, never stay here to be a sow farrowing little slaves. Never."

For a moment Lebrun felt only a detached sympathy. Then his eyes flashed to Marya's face, appalled, and saw her go pasty-white beneath her tan. Inwardly he was cursing himself for the quotation he had chosen, remembering the first lines of it: "Whoso shall offend one of these little ones . . . it were better for him that a millstone were hanged about his neck and that he were drowned in the depths of the sea . . ." Knowing that she would have thought of it herself, that no argument on earth short of a direct pronouncement by the Pope speaking *ex cathedra* would convince her that Chantal was not carrying a human soul beneath her heart. And that she was as incapable of harming what she considered a blameless child as she was of defiling the Host or committing necrophilia.

Well, the one-time professor of anthropology and ex-soldier thought. His eyes rested on Chantal's triumphant form with detached appraisal. *She's stronger than I am in this state. It will have to be from behind, and quick, before the Sister can intervene. She'll accept it once done.*

Kustaa found himself surprised at how mild the banquet's entertainment was, nothing like the propaganda; of course, this was an important occasion, and a conservative family. The food was good enough that his first concern, how to force enough into a tension-tight belly to avoid being conspicuous, turned out to be misplaced. *Watch it, old son,* he told himself. Not good to be stuffed before action. He looked around the hollow square of tables, snowy linen, the glitter of crystal and silverware and bone china. More formal than the afternoon; the men in dark evening suits with lace stocks or uniforms, the women out of uniform, all in draped classical-style gowns that left one shoulder bare.

Light from the globes, and from burning cressets hung between, as well; the Draka liked to see what they were eating, not grope by candlelight. Seafood, appetizers, soup, fish, a main course of roast suckling pig, salads, vegetables, while the chamber group played soft Mozart and he listened to the conversations; Andrew and Vashon rehashing their efforts to track him down, the female aeronautical engineer at his side explaining the long-term potential of hydrogen-fueled ramjets and lamenting the difficulty of modeling high-speed airflows; the Landholders and their close kin discussing weather and crops in words that might almost have been the ones he grew up among in the rural Midwest.

He raised a glass of wine and pretended to sample the bouquet; an act, it all smelled and tasted like spoiled grape juice to him. He was strictly a beer-whiskey-and-aquavit man. He noticed nobody was getting more than mildly tipsy, or stoned on the kif that was also on tap. *Well, they are health fanatics to a man,* he mused. It might almost have been a very tony Long Island gathering at home, except for the costumed mime-dancers who enacted the legend of Leda and the Swan. They were dark women, with the bodies of ballerinas; professionals from the older territories, considering the length of time those skills must take to learn. The swan wings and mask of the one playing Zeus transformed were really lovely—feathers and jewels and delicate gold work—but then, this was not a society that went in for mass-production of anything but weapons and the cheapest consumer goods; it could afford artisanship.

The dance ended behind a covering of downswept ten-foot wings; the whole done with delicacy rather than gross explicitness, even erotic in a sort of eerie way. He noticed that Vashon had fallen silent to watch it with a burning intensity, and stacked away the datum for the OSS files. The mimes rose, bowed low, ran off in a flutter of feathers and long hair. That was after the tables had been cleared, set with coffee and liqueurs and nuts. Kustaa recognized the singers who came forward next, but was surprised by the sudden silence that fell as they stepped out before the musicians. He did not think it was for their looks, or not mostly; it was simply that they saw no point in having fine music unless they were going to listen.

Tasteful bastards, he thought, inhaling the aroma of the Kenya coffee, this time with genuine appreciation. *May they rot in hell.*

"My Masters," Solange said with a graceful curtsy. "For your pleasure, we shall present a duet from the opera *Lakme,* by Delibes, with modified string and woodwind accompaniment of my own adaptation."

Kustaa had never enjoyed classical opera much: too many fat ladies in odd clothes screeching, despite the valiant attempts of his mother, who had a dogged self-improving Scandinavian regard for capital-C culture, and Aino, who had dragged him to a fair number in New York after they moved to the capital. The Frenchwoman stepped forward and opened her mouth, and the OSS agent prepared for yet another run-through of the thousand ways the extraction could go wrong. Sound wove its way through the threads of his mind, unraveling. His eyes opened in shock, to see a face transformed into something beyond beauty, a purity of self-absorption as complete as the music that poured effortlessly from that quivering throat, wove around the deeper notes of the other voice, returned . . .

He blinked himself back to awareness as Solange and Yasmin walked the circuit of the table, hand in hand, bowing and flushing at the long sharp ripple of applause. Some of the guests even rose to clap as they went by, and a standing ovation was not something Draka did casually. At last the two came to the head table before their owners; there they sank gracefully to their knees and made the full bow, palms before eyes. The clapping continued, louder, directed to the Landholders now, congratulating them on possessions beyond price. *What a waste,* Kustaa thought angrily as the singers and musicians withdrew. *What a total, fucking waste.* It was obscene, far more than the unclothed dancers.

A deep breath, and another; he would have to listen to the first of the after-dinner speakers, at least. It was the retired Field-Marshal who rose, propping a cane against his chair. There was a murmur from the tables, then silence once more. He stood for a moment scanning them thoughtfully, a steady appraising stare.

"I am the eldest von Shrakenberg present," he said abruptly. "As we're here to celebrate the reinforcement of the Race by two of the youngest, it's appropriate that I speak." A smile. "Although I can't promise to be as melodious as what we've just heard." There was laughter, and a general settling-in rustle.

"I was born," the elderly Draka continued, "in 1882. This would be a good occasion to reflect on the changes my lifetime has seen. When I received my commission, the Domination was still officially the *Dominion* of the Draka, part of the British Empire. We ruled all of Africa, but no more; the British still thought of us as a subject-ally. Europe," he added with a shark's smile, "was just beginnin' to worry about us. Many of the institutions you're all familiar with were in their infancy; I can remember when the thought of women bearin' arms would have seemed fantastical. Why, I can remember old men usin' 'white' and 'black' as synonyms fo' Citizen and serf. A different world."

The scored eagle face swept around the tables. "Now everythin' since seems . . . inevitable. I can tell you, we didn't think so at the time! We were afraid of the Europeans, fo' example. No, don't look shocked, it's fact. They were all openly set on subvertin' our institutions, *and they were stronger than us.* We were afraid." A grin. "The Yankees were just a cloud on the horizon. There were those, Draka among them, who thought our overthrow was just a matter of time. And they had a good case, on purely logical grounds.

"We all know what happened in the Great War; I was blown up over Constantinople, makin' it happen." He slapped the stiffened leg. "We saw our enemies' weakness, and we struck. *Then* words like 'world conquest' and 'Final Society' started to look more credible. The mo' sober worried that we'd be drunk with success, with victory disease. Europe was still the stronger, if only it would unite against us, despite the vast conquests we made. Japan, Germany, Russia threatened our new northern and eastern borders.

"And"—he held up his hands—"here we stand, in the heart of Europe, here in France. Where are the children of the men who befo' 1914 calmly sat to debate how 'enlightenment' and 'reform' would be forced on the primitive Draka, how they could bring us 'democracy'? In graves from here to China, workin' in our fields and kitchens, laborin' in mines and factories to build our power, singin' fo' our pleasure after this excellent dinner, and"—he crooked a sardonic eyebrow at the owners of the plantation—"servin' pleasure in other capacities. Soon enough, fightin' and dyin' fo' us. Doesn't this seem like the unfoldin' of Destiny, the sacred destiny of the Race?

"*Horseshit!*" The speaker's fist crashed down, and Kustaa saw startlement replace bored agreement on many faces. "We won because we were tough, and prepared . . . because we were *lucky* enough to have enemies who'd fight each other—rather than us. This land here is already a breedin' ground fo' Draka; I won't make the usual tiresome references to the reproductive habits of digger wasps. If you young people plan to extend *their* Domination, you'll have to be *twice* as tough, *twice* as disciplined as we were. *We can still lose it all.* Never forget that, *never.* Every day we live, we live on the edge of oblivion. It's up to you, the young. Rule or die, kill or be killed, *crush or be crushed.* Always on guard fo' opportunity, takin' what we can, never relinquishin' an inch.

"Destiny is what we make it. *Service to the State!*"

The guests came to their feet in a sustained roar.

"Glory to the Race!" It crashed out like thunder, broke into a spontaneous chant that lasted for minutes before dying out into self-conscious laughter and a rising buzz of conversation once more.

Short and to the point, Kustaa thought behind his grin, looking up at the lights in the upper room of the tower. *Let's see how you like being on the receiving end, you evil old bastard.* He had a perfect excuse, too. One hour more, and he could call. He rose, bowed to the center of the head table. Tanya von Shrakenberg's head came up, and returned the gesture with a wave.

"A good evenin' to you, Mr. Kenston," she said. "Just tellin' Uncle Karl here that he should go into politics, but some things are even mo' urgent, eh?" Slyly: "And don't let her convert you."

Good-natured laughter followed him. He smiled, nodded as he walked toward the glass wall on the inner side of the terrace. For a moment he halted beneath, stared up at the glowing backlit shape of the Drakon. *Fuck you, snake,* he thought, and pushed through. Behind him, the lambent yellow eyes stared sightlessly out over the darkened fields.

The sounds of the waters outside her hull were the loudest things that could be heard in the control center of the *Benito Juarez.* Whale song, mysterious clicks and pings and creaks. Occasionally the distant throbbing of engines, once or twice the hard ringing of a sound-detection scanner.

"2100," the horse-faced OSS controller said.

The captain nodded to a tech-5 at a console. "Up buoy, stand by to monitor," he said softly. Theoretically a normal speaking voice was no threat, but pigboaters had a superstitious reverence for "silent running," and the attitude of mind was one valuable enough to encourage. The man nodded, depressed a switch.

Guzman strained his ears, but only imagination could supply the sound of the float inflating, rising out through the flooded hatchcover, with its spool of wire playing out carefully behind. Breaking surface with an inaudible splash, invisibly black against black water, no more metal than the cable itself and so near-invisible to electrodetectors, nothing for their microwaves to reflect from. Not much risk. The quick throbbing of destroyer screws had not been heard since they settled to the bottom.

The radio operator clamped on his headset, twisted dials. Time passed; Guzman brought out a stick of mint-flavored chicle, offered it to the agent, grinned to himself as the man refused with a repressed shudder. Not a *gringo* custom, but more comfortable for a submariner than tobacco; although he had to admire the way the *yanqui* waited without a twitch as the minutes dragged: most of the bridge watch were fidgeting and glaring at the unfortunate able seaman like buzzards around a dying donkey. The captain himself planned to turn in as usual when his watch ended; this would be the first vigil of many.

Time passed. Guzman looked at his watch: 2115. Ten more minutes until—

"Contact," the radioman whispered. "Contact on the assigned frequency, sir."

The OSS man crossed to the radioman's seat in two strides, took the headphones and listened; his face was still impassive, but the blue lights glistened across the wet skin of his forehead. His right hand went out, and the operator shoved the pad and pencil beneath it. He jotted without looking down, waited.

"They're repeating," he said. "Prepare to send confirmation."

The operator looked up at Guzman, unconsciously touching his tongue to his lip. The dark officer took the wad of chicle out between thumb and forefinger, considered it for an instant. Now the danger began. *The jaguar is in the jungle,* he thought.

"Do it, sailor," he said calmly, and replaced it, chewing stolidly.

The OSS man took the microphone, spoke slowly and distinctly. "The caa is in the paaak," he said, just once. A slow smile spread over his mouth as he looked up at Guzman.

"Two men and a treasure chest coming back, Captain," he said in his nasal Bay State twang.

Guzman surprised himself; he saluted, and took the agent's hand. "He is a man, that one," he said quietly; then thought of this dry stick of a spy flying low and slow up the Loire, over the Domination's defenses, landing with nothing more than a sidearm and risking capture by a people to whom mercy was scarcely even a word. "And so are you."

To the exec: "Number two, maintain silent running drill; all hands to action stations, prepare to take her up." Ten minutes on the surface, to unpack and launch the bird. Two hours waiting at periscope depth for the return, and then the hideous risk of a radio beacon. *We're all going to be,* he thought. *Or dead.*

"Nobody here!" Solange sang, as she and Yasmin came out onto the terrace. The lights had been extinguished and the tables stripped, shadows washed across the yellow marble of the floor, and the air had begun to take on the cool spicy smell of late night in the dog days of summer. The Frenchwoman sang again, a wordless trill, and danced out into the open space, whirling the other serf by the hands until she pulled them to a halt, laughing herself in dizzy protest.

"They *loved* us, me, wheee!" Solange sang again, giggling. "Did you *hear* them applaud, did you see their *faces*? Mistress says I'll be in demand for appearances all up and down the *river*; maybe she'll even send me to the *city* for more training, maybe even to *Archona*, and they'll make *recordings.*" She spun, arms high. "And I'll perform before the Archon, and people will offer Mistress *millions* for me and she'll laugh at them!"

"Solange, honeybunch, you drunk an' on more than wine 'n' smoke. Calm down, maybeso it happen that way an' maybeso no—mmph!"

Solange had stopped her mouth with a kiss, and when she released her, Yasmin was laughing again herself.

"That nice," she said. "But I've got anothah engagement, Solange darlin', an' he impatient. See you t'morrow, and doan' dance the *whole* night away."

Yasmin left, and Solange laughed more quietly; she began dancing by herself, singing wordlessly under her breath, until she saw the glow of a cigarette tip by the far end of the terrace, froze for a moment, then walked forward, swaying toward the white outline of Tanya's gown.

"Don't let me stop the celebratin'," the Draka said. "You deserved it, Solange." She was leaning back against the angle where the head table met its neighbors, one hand under the other arm and the free fingers holding the cigarette. "I really may look into that trainin', that voice deserves to live."

"It was all for you, Mistress," Solange crooned softly when they were at arm's length. "I was doing it all for you, couldn't you see it? I could feel your eyes on me warm like hands." Her own eyes were wide, the pupils swollen until the violet color was a rim around pools of black, her voice slurred and husky. "Everything I am and do is yours, Mistress. Everything."

Very true, Tanya thought happily. *But still nice to have it so enthusiastically volunteered.* The serf's swaying made her platinum sheath quiver in the night like a candle flame of moonlight. *You are a treasure Solange, an absolute treasure.* She smiled, shivering slightly at the expression in the other's eyes, abasement and exaltation. *So much beauty, so much intelligence and talent and skill, and you are* mine.

"Oh, Mistress, you give me so much, make me so happy," the serf said. "How can I thank—*oh!*" She giggled again. "Don't move, Mistress, stay right there, I know just the thing." She skittered off, returned in an instant with a cushion from one of the chairs, dropped it at Tanya's feet.

"A cushion?" Tanya said. Solange was playfully crazy even when sober, but wild on wine and kif . . .

"*Mais non,* the cushion is for me, Mistress, these flags are hard." Her open mouth was moist as she leaned forward to press a quick kiss on her owner's lips, and she smiled slyly as she dropped to her knees on the padded cloth. "I am for you, Tanya."

The Draka looked around for a moment to make sure they were truly private; it was dark . . . *Hell with it,* she decided. *Why not?* The cigarette made a minor meteor as she flicked it away over the railing and leaned back, resting her weight on her palms. *There goes my little half-hour chat with Tante Sannie about the trials of childbirth; oh well, tomorrow.* She let her head loll upward; that brought the dim light of the tower's highest room to view.

Damnation, she thought with a frown, as Solange lifted the fabric of her skirt and tucked the front hem neatly into her belt. *We are visible from the radio room.* Not that that would bother her normally; serfs did not count much when it came to privacy, but Jules Lebrun was up there tonight, and making him watch this would be the sort of pointless cruelty she despised.

Tanya looked down; Solange was rolling down her left stocking with elaborate slowness, planting light kisses on the leg as it was exposed. The soft moist sensation was unbearable, and the singer was humming as she worked. *On the other hand, he can always look out the other window at the pavilions.*

"God, I thought I'd never get away," Kustaa muttered as he pushed in from the tubelike spiral stairwell; the efforts of the other partygoers to make the cripple feel wanted had been as entangling as glue-covered bungee cords. The radio-room door was a blank steel sheet like the armory one story below, but not locked in the normal course of things. He halted outside the panel; there was a murmur of voices from within. According to plan, then.

The American halted, drew his automatic and took in a deep breath. A glance at his watch: 2330, right after the plantation's scheduled call-in, no alarm until the next was missed in four hours. The stairwell was redolent of old stone, with a faint underlying tang of ozone from the electronic equipment within; cables in metal conduits ran up the walls beside him, new metal and brackets drilled and bolted to the ancient tufa ashlars. This was the turning point, the step that could not be taken back. He shook his head; that was cowardice speaking, as stupidly as it always did, the desire to buy safety for a few more hours or days at the expense of real escape after a brief risk. He firmed his lips and pushed open the door.

A square room, the size of his bedroom. Brightly lit, naked overhead fluorescent tubes. Small square windows facing east and north. Metal tables bolted to the walls, and banks of equipment: telephone switchboard, shortwave set, teletype. Five people: Ernst and Jules sitting stony-faced over a chessboard, Sister Marya, Chantal—*what in God's name is she doing here*—a nameless ordinary-looking serf with his back to the door, sitting in a swivel chair and speaking to the nun.

"I know the visitor's boy is authorized up here to play chess with Jules, Sister, but you and the other lady will have to—"

"Don't look around," Kustaa said in French, in the flat emotionless voice that intimidated so much better than screaming. His hand had locked in the serf's hair, drawing his head to one side until the muscles creaked. The agent reached around to waggle the muzzle of the automatic in front of his eyes, just in case, then put it in his ear.

"One sound and you're all dead," he said for the watch-stander's benefit. "Down on the floor, hands behind your heads, *move.* Not you," he added, checking a scrambling movement to exit the chair with the hard cold metal grinding into an ear.

"Don't kill me," the man blubbered, but enough in control not to shout. "Please, Master, I'll—"

"This is the Resistance," Kustaa said.

The man started violently."Oh, God, no. Please *go away*, you'll get us all killed. They'll impale us all, our families, *please—*"

"Shut up." You never knew what twisted paths courage might take, even in a rabbit like this. "I'm going to let go of your hair. Keep your head pointed the same way or I'll blow your brains all over the wall."

Trembling silence, while Kustaa unclenched his left hand from the man's scalp and used it to pull the hypodermic from his pocket. The serf started once when the American plunged it home, then slumped.

"Out for hours," he said, as Marya rose and scrambled across to lay the man straight and peel back an eyelid for a check. The agent tossed her a roll of adhesive tape, and she began to bind the unconscious form, hands and ankles, strips across mouth and eyes. Kustaa dropped the hypo by his side. It was Domination-standard with his own fingerprints on it. All that *should* spare the bystander from anything too gruesome; serfs were expected to surrender meekly to force. If not . . .

Toughski shitski, as they say in the Polish Marines, Kustaa thought, gleeful under the hammering pulse of action. His movements were crisp and controlled as he sat before the shortwave set.

"What the hell is *she* doing here, Sister?" he asked as he turned the dials, calling up the settings before the eye of memory. His head jerked towards Chantal, as he set the pistol by his right hand and propped the battle shotgun by the chair.

"She is with us," the nun said, rising and coming to lean beside him. Swiftly and very quietly, in German: "She is the communist from my cell, she saw us together and guessed what you are. Be careful, we must get her to the cave. The master has been forcing her and she is pregnant and it has driven her . . . wild. She thinks you can take her out and will not listen to reason."

"English or French!" Chantal hissed. "Don't think I'm stupid. If I suspect you, I will scream."

The settings were as correct as he could make them and this was a big military-issue set, powerful enough to punch messages across continents. He took up the microphone, giving the young Frenchwoman a single hard glance. *Par for the course. Always something to fuck up at the last minute,* he thought. There was a certain detached pity in his glance. *The girl looked close to the edge, but . . . Mission first, buddies second, your own ass third and bystanders a distant fourth,* he quoted to himself, the unofficial rule-of-engagement the Marine assault battalions had operated by.

"Break, four-seven, four-seven," he began, repeating it half a dozen times. You had to believe they were listening, that no electromagnetic freak was damping it out so that they got static and a ham operator in Patagonia was picking it up loud and clear.

"This is loganberry"—Donovan's perverse sense of humor again—"loganberry, with a friend, repeat, with a friend and a Christmas package. A package as big as two loganberries." The extraction aircraft wasn't very fast but at least they'd factored in a wide margin on lift. "Coordinates follow." He read them off. "A grassy path bordered by light, repeat, a grassy path bordered by light." Let whoever they'd sent wonder how he'd gotten a marked runway for them. "Over."

He lifted his thumb from the send button and waited, suddenly conscious of sweat soaking his cotton jacket beneath the arms, crawling greasily out from around the rim of his hair; a hand squeezing up under his lungs. One broadcast might not catch some monitor's attention, but . . .

Hiss. Crackle. Wavering hints of words, spillover, this was close to a commercial frequency, an unused bit of bandwidth in a crowded neighborhood. Then: "The caa is in the paaak."

Kustaa grunted in sheer relief, suppressed euphoria; this was no time for it. He pulled out the yellow-edged Pan-Domination map for the region, confirmed his earlier estimate. "ETA, not long, it's a good little aircraft," he said. "Hit that light."

He looked up, saw that the northern window that overlooked the terrace was shuttered, the one the Resistance people could see through the periscope. "What the fuck—sorry, Sister."

"I have heard soldiers before, Frederick," she said, rising to open it and giving Jules Lebrun's shoulder a silent squeeze on the way. "This is a battle."

The lights flickered three times, three times again. "Now, let's go—" he began, rising.

And there was a scream from the door, long and loud. Kustaa whipped around so quickly that the swivel chair nearly dumped him on the floor, time slowing like treacle as he clawed up the pistol and staggered into some imitation of a crouch. The singer, the one from the banquet, standing in the doorway in some sort of pajama outfit, eyes wide and drawing breath to scream again. Chantal directly in his line of fire. His own legs driving, throwing him to one side, left hand slapping out for a breakfall, *too late too late*—

"Get the fuck out of the way!" he yelled, trying to get off one shot, but the girl was collapsing backwards; Chantal was standing with her mouth an O of surprise.

The face vanished as the girl threw herself back; there had been only the single scream, but he could hear the sound of tumbling and running footsteps going down that narrow stone corkscrew. *God, a single woman's scream is nothing here, if she just goes to ground we can still make it*—

"Quickly," Marya said. "Quickly, she will go straight to the mistress, *quickly.*"

"Three lights!" Henri said, and slapped up the handles of the periscope. Ybarra and Jean sprang to their feet and snatched up their sacks. "You two, down to the cars; I'll get the lights. *Allons, mes enfants!*"

There was a smile on Henri's face as he led the charge out the opened door of the shelter, up the short length of tunnel, and hurdled the green steel box they had placed on the lip where excavation met pavement. It would be quicker to load that way, and besides, being in the same room with it made even Henri nervous.

✧   ✧   ✧

Moaning, Solange tumbled out of the stairwell into a main corridor; it was dimly lit, and for a moment she nearly screamed again, in panic at not knowing where she was. Blood was trickling salt-musky from her nose, and one eye was almost swollen shut where her fall had driven her face against the stone. She moaned again, seeing the horror of the room, the man bound, the gun coming up toward her, its black pit turning toward *her*, and her father sitting there, looking at her, doing nothing while the gun came up to kill her, kill *her* . . .

She shook her head, whimpered at the pain but almost welcomed it as her thoughts cleared. Tanya, she must get to Tanya at once, get out of this nightmare, get to safety. Hugging her bruised arm to her side, she limped down the corridor, tears of pain running down through the sheeted blood on her face, not conscious of speaking aloud.

"My God, Poppa, how could you, how could you betray me again, Poppa, Tanya help me, everything was so nice, Poppa, why did you spoil it—"

Figures, looking at her, jumping aside. House servants, common ones, asking questions. She ignored them, they could not help her, nobody but Tanya could help her. The door, the dear familiar bedroom, her pallet and nook, nobody there. *It isn't fair, it isn't fair, where is she, she must be here, she said she had to get to bed, the hunt tomorrow—* For a full minute Solange could only stand and stare, willing the empty bed full, seeing Tanya rising with concern and comfort, making the whole nightmare go *away*.

The Master. She must be with the Master. Panting through her mouth, Solange turned and plunged back into the corridor. *She must be.*

"Keep up, damn you!" Ybarra hissed. *That damned Jean, falls on his ass without a pavement under his feet,* she thought. There was ample moonlight for running here, with nice clear tracks between the vine trellises. Easy compared with darkness in the hills above the Ebro, waiting to ambush the Fascist supply convoys. Her hand gripped the knife hilt more tightly. It had been amazing how soft, how coopera- tive, how eager to please the toughest Fascist prisoner had become, when she showed him what she could do with the knife.

Jean got to his feet, brushing at the machine pistol across his chest, clearing the sandy dirt from the action; he was still panting from the run down the long slope. Ybarra jerked him down into a crouch.

"The car park is just beyond those trees," she said. It was actually a pasture, pressed into service for the celebration. "We'll go down to the end of the vineyard, low and quick. Through together to the first vehicle, they're parked in rows. You cover me, three cars behind, and I'll plant the little bomblets." A thumb-sized piece of plastique and a chemical detonator for each, not precision timers but reliable and good enough for this work. She sniffed the air; nothing but the rich damp earth smell of this place, so dif- ferent from the hard dry odors of her native Asturias, the bleak arid hills and the mining towns. A moment's fierce nostalgia seized her, fueled her rage again. Asturias was no more, all the blood spilled in the uprisings against the mine owners and the victorious war against the Fascist generals, wasted.

No sounds, except for night birds and those accursed rasping crickets. No lights, except from the manor and the tents on its immediate grounds.

"Forward, Jean," she said.

"Why not you?" he replied. There was an unpleasant note in his voice, and her eyes narrowed. Perhaps his nerve had broken; that happened sometimes, men just ran out of whatever it was that kept them going. As well to remind him that there was no retirement from the Resistance.

"Because I have an uneasy feeling you might drop too far behind, *maricon*," she said, letting the honed edge of the knife show for a second; it was not blackened, like the rest of the metal. She could see his Adam's apple bob up and down. "And if this behind you makes you uneasy, Jean, *comrade*, remember I've never yet cut a man's throat unless I intended to."

Kill her now? Jean thought, fingering the trigger of the machine pistol. *No, she's too close.* He shuddered, remembering again the sound the overseer had made. This one had eyes like a master, hard and flat and you were nothing, not even a cockroach . . . no, among the cars would be better.

Tanya sighed, and squeezed her husband's hand. *How nice just to lie here and talk over the day,* she thought drowsily. *Just the two of us, no distractions—*

The door to Edward von Shrakenberg's bedroom burst open, and Solange stumbled through. Tanya shot bolt upright—the serf's face was a mask of blood and bruise all down the left side, one eye a slit in the blue-shining swelling, and she was clutching at an arm whose fingers were limp. A low moaning trickled from her lips, turning to a sob of relief as she wavered toward the bed.

"Shit," Edward said with quiet anger and rolled out of bed and onto his feet, reaching for clothes and gunbelt. A flick turned the lights from dim to bright, and the serf looked even more ghastly then; Tanya was by her side immediately, an arm supporting, guiding her to a chair.

"Who did this?" she said, with low deadliness. *Somebody's going to die for this,* ran through her with cold conviction. Her fingers probed gently but irresistibly. No broken bones, the arm was just badly bruised; painful, but it looked worse than it was. Solange's arms shot up with an anaconda grip around the Draka's shoulders, and she began to cry hysterically.

"Who *did* this?" Tanya asked more firmly, nostrils flaring at the scent of blood and fear-sweat, overpowering the familiar cologne and musk of Edward's room. Solange gave a muffled cry, raised her head, jerked back a little in involuntary terror at the expression on the face of the Draka who held her.

"I'm not angry at you, sweetlin'. Now, *tell* me." Firm but not loud . . . *Wotan's spear, if it's that swine Vashon, I'll call him out and gut-shoot the serf-born bastard.* Solange was far too well trained to have offered any provocation that would remotely justify this; even if somebody had the gall to ignore courtesy and take her, she would have submitted and complained later. This was wanton brutality for its own sake. "I don't let anybody treat my own like this, Solange. Was it Vashon?"

"No!" The serf shook her head, winced, continued. "It was that Kenston, the mute."

Tanya felt her face go slack with surprise. *Kenston,* she thought incredulously. You could tell a serf abuser, they showed it by a thousand mannerisms, Kenston she would have pegged as the type to spoil with sentimentality.

"He . . . he tried to kill me, Mistress. I went up to say good night to Poppa, to tell him how beautiful it was when I sang, and . . . and Raoul, they had him *tied up,* Chantal and . . . and Master Kenston, I screamed and . . . and Master Kenston tried to take his gun and, and shoot me and, and—"

"*Chantal?*" Edward bellowed, halting in the middle of stamping his foot into a boot.

Solange flinched, closed her good eye and continued in a breathless gabble. "Oh, it was horrible; there were Chantal and Marya and Poppa and the German and Master Kenston and they had Raoul tied up and they were talking—" She stopped, took a deep shuddering breath, visibly forced control. The eye came open again, and when she spoke her voice was shaking but coherent.

"Master Kenston was talking. Really talking. Like . . . like an American."

"Shit." This time it was Tanya who spoke. Edward's hand was flashing to the glass-covered alarm plate above the bed. There was a crunch, but not the expected shrilling of bells. Tanya lowered the bedside telephone in the same instant. "Out," she said. "Not even a tone." Which meant the lines were cut.

"Uprisin'?" Edward said bleakly.

"No. Smells wrong. Somethin' we weren't even meant to know about fo' a while." Aside: "Solange, you did well. Very well. Now, shut up." To her husband. "All right, twenty adults here overnight. Fifteen arms bearers." That was not counting the crippled, very aged or severely pregnant. "Personal arms only." A hard mutual grin: the armory was just below the radio room, presumably in enemy hands. "It's night." Edward nodded; that made her commander, a one-eyed man was at a serious disadvantage without light.

Tanya had been pulling on trousers and shirt from a wardrobe as she spoke; several of her outfits were always here. "Edward, you collect the guests. We've got to collect an' guard the youngsters." Too much of the future of the Race was at stake, their own blood not least. "Once that's done, able-bodied an' any licensed armed servants assemble *inside the main gates.*" Sheltered from possible snipers in upper windows. "Tom was in the armory, right? I'll scout there first, try an' make contact." The ex-Janissary's loyalty also went without saying. "Let's *do* it, love, let's *go.*"

Tanya hit the door running, ignoring the man behind her: she would not have married one she did not trust. A break-roll, looking both ways, painfully conscious of the light weight of the little 9mm Togren in her hand; it was the sort of token gun a city dweller in the Police Zone kept . . . down the corridor, vision hopping in a methodical skitter, another bubble of rage at having to go combat-mode in her own *home*, suppress it, count doors, *this* was Issac's. She wrenched it open and slapped the light plaque without ceremony. The narrow cubicle lit, and Issac rolled off his wife, reaching automatically with his good arm for the pistol he had been issued after the ambush this spring crippled a shoulder.

"Bushman trouble," she said.

"*Scheisse!*" he said, reaching for his clothes, throwing a rapid stream of Yiddish over his shoulder to the girl who sat with growing alarm on her face, pulling the sheet up around her as if that was a defense.

" 'Zactly. Main entranceway, *fast.*"

Back into the hall, swift cautious zigzag from cover to cover. Tom was in the armory; a good man, but he'd've been drinking tonight, it was traditional . . . *Freya, I hope he's all right,* she thought, then ground the words out of her brain. No time for words, hope, fear, anything but the automatic reflexes of war—she had a household to defend.

Behind her, unseen, Solange hesitated in the doorway, staggered, put her hand to her head. It *hurt*; somewhere she was conscious that she must have a concussion, things were showing double. She wavered again; she could shut the door, back there in the room. Shut it and wait for it to swing open again, the gun, like before, smashing glass and laughter and pain . . . *no. The mistress, I must follow her. There is safety.*

"*Fuck it!*" Kustaa hissed in frustration. The radio room had turned from a fortress into a killing box in a few seconds. His hands were on the levers of the junction box, slamming them down into the "off" positions, insurance, a few extra seconds. "Come on, let's go."

"No," Jules Lebrun said. "I will stay, and disable the equipment." A smile. "There is no time to argue, and I am a dying man anyway. Cancer will give me pain even the Security Directorate cannot rival, and I will not be taken alive. Go!"

" . . . an' then we pulled back to th' mosque," Tom rumbled, pleasantly aware of the glow of admiration on the face of Yasmin as she sat at his feet, arms wrapped around her knees. His wife Annette was a good wench, but she didn't appreciate a good story the way his daughter did. "Jus' five o' us lef', no officers, ragheads a' yellin' an' screamin', hundreds of 'em. They din' know we wuz five *devil dogs*, 'n' pissed as hell."

The armory about him was dim, the racked weapons and boxes of ammunition shadowy backdrops to his memory; the honest smell of his own sweat staining the thin cotton undershirt across his chest, beer and gun oil and steel. Memories of warm nights in barracks and the casern, all his old friends, strong young men, laughter and dice, drink and the laughing friendly whores. He took another pull at the beer and belched, feeling a familiar humming in his ears. *How many?* Twenty, or only ten? Fuck it. 'Nuff storytellin', time to get back home and give Annette another young un'. He wasn't *that* old.

He dropped his hand to Yasmin's curls, opened his mouth to speak. A scream interrupted him, loud even through the steel door, and *close*.

"Wha'?" he said, his chin rising from his chest. "Wha' that?"

Yasmin was on her feet. "Poppa!" she said urgently. "That Solange, it came from that-there radio room." Puzzlement fought with alarm on her slender features.

Tom lurched to his feet, waving her vaguely back. "Y' pretty fren'?" he said with bewilderment. "Wha' she doin' here?"

He walked to the door and pushed it open, glancing around. A slight hint of light and voices from upstairs, but nothing out of the ordinary. Tom shook his head, rubbed his hard-callused palms across his face. There was something wet on the step, at chest level, too dark to see color, only a blackness that glistened. He touched, raised his fingers to nose, lips. Utterly familiar, in a way that began to wash the fumes of alcohol out of his brain.

"Blood," he said wonderingly. "Gots ta' see whut happenin'," he muttered, and began to climb.

This place is turning into a shitty railroad station, Kustaa thought disgustedly as the door swung open again. A conscious effort kept his trigger finger loose. The last thing they needed was the sound of a firefight breaking out. Worth the time to gag and tie whoever it was.

A black. Big man, bigger than Kustaa, fifties, balding. Heavy muscle well padded with fat, beer belly and a bottle of beer clutched like a miniature in one ham-sized fist. Stained white T-shirt and baggy olive-green pants, splayed bare feet . . . eyes bloodshot and puzzled and mild in the heavy-featured African face.

"Silence," Kustaa barked. "Come in, lie down, put your hands behind your head."

The other great hand slowly squeezed shut into a fist and the eyes were still bloodshot yet anything but mild, thick lips drawn back from strong yellow teeth. "Yaz no Mastah!" he said in wonderment, glance darting to the bound form of Raoul.

"Janissary, *kill him!*" Chantal shouted, but Kustaa had seen too many fighting men to need the warning; his finger was tightening even before the man finished speaking. The 10mm bucked in his hand, three shots merging into one, echoes in the small stone room, three soft-nosed slugs blasting into the black's solar plexus no more than a hand's width apart. The last so close the thin fabric of his shirt was crisped and singed, and that was the one that stopped him, stopped the bull bellow and huge hands reaching to kill.

Yasmin followed, and stood looking with utter disbelief at the heavy body lying jerking at her feet, blood pouring from overlapping exit wounds in the small of his back, a raw cavity bigger than her paired fists full of shattered bone splinters and things that glistened and moved. The dark girl's hands came up, one on either side of her face, pressing palm-in as if to drive the knowledge out of her skull.

"Poppa?" she said in a tiny voice, sinking down by his side. "Poppa?" A small shriek, and she was tearing at her clothing, shoving the scraps into the impossible gaping wound.

"Poppa, doan' die, doan' die, Poppa, *please*, I love you, Poppa, doan' die, *please*—" She abandoned the hopeless effort and threw herself on his chest, clutching at his shoulders. "No, Poppa, no!"

Kustaa turned his head; one of the others would know how to quiet her. That shift saved his life, Yasmin's clumsy thrust with her father's belt knife scoring along the American's ribs down to the bone rather than sinking into his belly. Then she was a blur of white cloth and brown arms and heavy razor-edged steel, hacking with a berserker frenzy that lacked only knowledge to make it instantly deadly. Kustaa shouted again as the edge jammed into his shoulder, clubbing frantically with the pistol as he tried to bring it round close enough to bear point-blank.

"You killed my poppa! You killed my poppa!" Intolerably shrill, almost a squeal.

Christ, she's going to kill me! ran through him as he blocked and struck with elbows, knees; bone-shattering strikes but she would not stop, *It's my own bloody fault shitshitshit—*

The muzzle of his battle shotgun reached around him and shoved itself into Yasmin's stomach. Chantal pulled the trigger, and the explosion was muffled by flesh and cloth. The result was not; the slender body of the serf girl catapulted back over the swivel chair and struck the ground already limp. The Frenchwoman stepped over to the dead serf, looked down into the blood-spattered face frozen in eternal surprise.

"Bitch," she said in a voice that cracked, and retched dryly. The floor was running-wet, like a bathroom where the sink has overflowed— or the toilet, for it stank of salt, shit, the raw chemical smell of burnt propellant.

The scent of glory, Kustaa thought as he forced himself straight, vision returning after the grayness of shock; he felt the same brief irrational disbelief that always came after being wounded, compounded of *so fast!* and *I was all right just a second ago!* Neither ever helped . . . a long cut on the ribs, stab in the shoulder, superficial slashes, bleeding but no arteries cut, he could keep going for a little longer, he *had* to keep going.

"Come on," he said, and plunged down the stairwell. The others followed, all but Lebrun stone-faced before the radio and the bound and unconscious Raoul. Into the armory, across to the window that latched from the inside, only three feet down onto the low-pitched slate roof. He and Ernst helped the women through, and he gave the Austrian a tight smile.

"Not doing badly," he said.

"I fought on the Italian front in the Great War," Ernst said. "It is nothing I have not seen before." He helped Kustaa through in turn.

Whore, filthy whore, Jean thought, frantically. There had been no opportunity, not down all the dozen cars and vans, not until now. The fuel tanks of the last two autosteamers were underslung, and Ybarra had to drop to her back and crawl beneath. *Now!* His finger began to close on the trigger, he could feel the cool metal against his skin and the tiny slack and the muscle would not close. It was very surprising, the way his head and body did not work the way they should, why couldn't he pull the trigger, he hated her, she was going to put him back in the chair with his father screaming around the gag, pleading and—

whitenoisenothoughtnothought

Kill her, kill her, the Master will reward you. But the finger would not close, and if he did not then it would be Marie-Claire, bending over the block while the giant—

whitenoisenothoughtnothought and he could feel his arms and legs start to shake, and tears were running down his face. The clicking started again behind his eyes, but this time there was no sharp clarity of thought, nothing but the noise inside his head growing louder and louder, hissing like the sea. It reached a peak and he thought he would have to scream, to cry out to God for pity, for relief, but he knew that was nonsense. There was no pity and no mercy and pain was the only thing that was forever.

Jean turned, the machine pistol dangling in his hand, turned and walked south. Not running until he was too far away for even Ybarra to catch, then at a shambling pounding trot; white noise was almost continuous now, but that was good, it kept the visions from his eyes, memories and fears, all too terrible to be borne. Vision came in glimpses, and thought; the Schmeisser dropping from his nerveless fingers in a field—they would shoot him down on sight, a strange serf with a for-bidden weapon. The gardens at last, he was too far east of the house; everything was quiet, and he almost ran into the man standing fifty meters from the great tents.

"*Halt,*" the man said, in bad French. "No serfs past here. I'm the bossboy; give me your name."

Jean leaned against him, hands pawing weakly for support as the knowledge of his own exhaustion came through the white noise. He made gobbling noises as his mouth tried to speak while his lungs could spare no wind for it, none, they were dry and tight and aching, and the gasping breaths did him no good.

"Drunk?" the bossboy asked. Short and dark and thin, with a long willow switch in his hand. He prodded Jean with it, as the French-man bent over and leaned his hands on his knees, rasping for air. "You drunk? You got drink with you? Our party's not until Wednes-day. Nobody here but masters and the wenches to pleasure them. That bastard Arab fieldboss posted me here where I can listen and do nothing."

"Vashon," Jean wheezed.

"What? What you say, boy? You belong who? Who your master?"

"Vashon, Master Vashon, Strategos Vashon, I have news, now, *hurry.*"

"The greencoat?" Even in darkness Jean could see the fear on the serf foreman's face, the little start of recoil; he stood up, heartened. Even the Master's *name* was a thing of power. "Third door, he have wenches in there." The switch trembled as it pointed. "You lie, he kill you. Not Erast's business."

Jean walked forward, stumbling, pushed through the heavy flap, into the dimly lit shadows. He could see the Master's face. At first he thought it was floating, all amid a froth of feathers and giant wings and the limp head of a great golden swan that lay and stared at him with eyes of tourmaline. Then his brain made sense of the pattern of line and movement before him, Vashon was on a woman, kneeling with her legs over his shoulders, embracing another who leaned back from her position astride the first's head. The Frenchman's mouth dropped open; the women were darkly beautiful, lithe as cats, the Master a study in power, his skin rippling, bunching, the whole human pyramid shaking with the power of his thrusts. There was another clicking behind his eyes and Jean fell to his knees, a vague wash of awe and terror and worship submerging consciousness.

"Who the Eblis—" Vashon's roar cut off, and Jean's eyes jerked open. Only seconds could have passed, for the Master was just rising. His green eyes were like jewels in the gloom, narrowed as he recognized the double agent, came to stand before him like a squat minotaur statue gleaming with sweat and fluids.

"Jean," he said. The voice was soothing, deep, all that Jean remembered from—

whitenoisenothoughtnothought

"Master," he said, a choking in his voice. "Master."

"I am very pleased with you, Jean," the voice said, and the serf felt an uprushing of joy. "Now, tell me. Tell me everything."

A moment to marshal his thoughts. They seemed so clear, once again, as if the noise in his head and the shaking were all gone. *He is strong, he bears the burdens of my sins,* Jean thought, and began, rapid and precise: "At the cave to the north, Master. Three of us. Here, the American who calls himself Kenston, the nun, the Boche; there is a box of the poison dust, and . . ."

Afterward nothing could bother him, not the shouting or the noises or the shots, the darkness or the cramping of his muscles as he knelt, nor the whimpers of uncomprehending terror from the dancers, who clung together and stared at him with white rims around their eyes. His strong lord was pleased with him, and all was well.

Tanya heard the distance-muffled shots a dozen meters before the stairwell entrance. She took the stairs in a rush and flipped the gun into her left hand, leading with it as she went up the steep spiral treads in a silent crouching bound. The open door of the armory drew her in like a magnet, coming up in a knee-roll and quartering the empty room. Nothing, racked weapons and drained beer bottles beside a cooler and an open window . . . she darted over, noticing the fresh blood trail without focusing on it. All her attention was out on the slate roof, on the figures at the far end of it, over a hundred meters, impossible distance with the snub-nosed toy she carried. A careful brace of the elbows against the windowsill, and all but one of them were gone, squeeze—*crack-crack-crack*, and did he stagger or was that a wish and the distance and the starlight? *No time,* she thought, spinning back to the stairwell. No time for pursuit, she couldn't go haring off on her own. No telling how many there were, either. The stairs above the armory were wet, slow congealing trickles that were an old story to her, of the astonishing amount of blood a human body carries and the swiftness with which it can escape through massive wound trauma as the heart itself shoots the pulse of life out to scatter and cool.

Jules Lebrun sat before the ruined equipment, watching it spark and refusing to turn. Even when he heard the pistol snap below, the light *tick . . . tick . . .* sound of bootsoles pulling free from what coated the floor stones outside. Instead his lips moved; surprising himself with the first genuine prayers since he had been an earnest middle-class chorister in Paris, all those years ago. Prayers for another.

"Ah, Tom," he heard Tanya's voice say behind him. The feet moved to the dead girl's side. "Yasmin, sweetlin', I should . . ."

They stopped behind him, and he waited for the bullet, wondering whether he would hear the click of the action first, and at how the pains in his chest seemed further away, almost unimportant.

Even then the small hairs along his spine seemed to crawl and struggle to stand erect when he heard her voice. "Well, well, what have we heah?"

"A man who would rather die than be a slave," he said quietly, proud of the fact that his voice did not quaver.

"No." The word was calm and even, but suddenly a hand spun him around and wrenched him upright with a force that jerked his limbs loose as a puppet's. The pistol was under his chin as Tanya held him off the ground, his eyes level with her own. She spoke, and now the killing was naked in the guttural snarl: "*No.* That choice you made three years ago, Lebrun, it's too *late.* So what we have heah is a fuckin' rabid *mad dog*, that turned on its owners, an' now will be put *down* like one."

There was a faint sound from the Janissary, a mixture of grunt and sigh. Lebrun felt himself thrown backward over the desk and against the dials and hanging severed wires of the radio, felt them gouge into his back. The pistol remained unwavering on his face as she knelt beside the man who was incredibly not quite dead.

"Yas . . . min?" Tom said in a breathy whisper. His head had fallen turned away from her; Tanya looked up at the corpse, rested her free hand on his forehead, leaned close and spoke with clear conviction as the man's eyes wandered unseeing.

"She goin' be fine, Tom. Hurt, but not bad."

Another sigh, and a catch in the faint breathing. The next words were fainter still, almost a suggestion: "Reportin' 's ordered . . . suh."

Tanya closed the lids with thumb and forefinger, rose, and gripped Lebrun by the back of the neck, until he could hear the tooth-grating sound of protesting vertebrae through the bones of his skull.

"No," she said. "Not quite like a dog, even at the risk of a few seconds, wouldn't be fitting. We were discussin' what we have?" Suddenly she pulled him over to Yasmin's body in a slithering rush that sent him banging and twisting against unseen hard objects as they passed. The man found his face pushed down to within inches of the dead girl's.

"What we *had* here," she said, "was Yasmin. A pretty, happy little wench, who loved music an' babies an' wanted most of all never to hurt anyone, anyone at all. What we have now is fuckin' *dog meat*."

Another rush, over to the Janissary's body. Again the thrust nose to nose with the dead flesh. "What we have here, is a brave man an' a good soldier who died loyal to his salt. Who *should* have died thirty years from now, in his sleep, surrounded by grandchildren."

She spun him around, tapping the pistol barrel against the bridge of his nose. "An' what we have here—here—here is the last thing you'll ever see, yo piece of vomit."

"Please," Solange said.

Tanya's head jerked around so quickly that her hair lashed across Lebrun's eyes before he could blink them closed, starring them with tears. His daughter was standing in the doorway, staring at the bodies with the backs of her hands pressed to her mouth.

"Oh, Poppa, what have you *done?*" she mumbled. Then her hands dropped, and she walked to the Draka. "Please," she said again, knelt. Pressed her cheek to her owner's foot. "It is your right, it is your right, we are yours . . . but he is my father, I beg, *please.*"

"No," Lebrun said, and looked up into the Draka's eyes. *She must know, know I am dying*, he thought. She smiled.

"I give you life, on her plea," she said. Her hand held his head while the pistol came down with precisely calculated force. "Solange . . . Solange! He'll be out fo' a couple of hours, *tie him up* and then go back to my room and *wait.*"

Ah, the peace and quiet of the country, Andrew von Shrakenberg thought. The leaves of the vineyard rustled as he strolled down the rows, enjoying the cool contrast of the air and soil still carrying fragments of the day's heat. *Am I being ironic, or not?* It was certainly more peaceful than the pavilion, now mostly occupied by the noises of vigorous fornication. Fresher, too, dew-damp leaves and turned earth.

Which is not displeasing in itself, but not conducive to thought either. Perhaps it was time to take his sister's advice and settle down. He looked up at the stars, smiling and remembering the night when he had first seen them with *depth*, not as lights in a dome but as tiny fires suspended in infinite space, feeling an echo of that elating, terrifying rush of vertigo. Wondering if somewhere out among the frosted scattering of light something was looking skyward at him.

And to them, all our loves and hates, wars and passions are so insignificant that they can't be seen, not even as a shadow on the sun.

"Jean? Is that you?" a voice said. French, accented . . . a woman's voice.

Peace held his mind in its embrace a moment longer. "No," he said, chuckling. "But if it's a man you lookin' fo', wench, I'm willin' to volunteer."

Starlight glittered on the blade of the knife as it drove toward his belly.

Smack. The edge of his left palm hit her wrist, and he felt the familiar jolt as the small bones of the joint crushed under an impact that would have broken pine boards. It was the measure of his bewilderment that his follow-through was completely automatic, a strike upward with the heel of his right hand that sent the woman flipping back with her nasal bone driven into her brain and neck snapped. The knife flew off, tinkling, but his fingers touched the piano wire garrote coiled within her belt before the body stopped twitching.

He stood, and the first of the vehicles blew with a huge muffled *thump* that struck his face like a soft warm hand. Light blossomed beyond the line of trees that screened the vehicle park, and explosions followed like a string of giant fuzz-edged firecrackers.

"I think," he said quietly to himself, "that a serious mistake has been made." Turning, he drove for the laneway at a steady loping run.

There was a bristle of guns under the arched entranceway to the central court of Chateau Retour. They lowered as the figure approaching halted and grunted out her name.

"Tanya," she said, shifting the body to a more comfortable fireman's carry over her shoulders, then dropping it in the midst of the crowd. "This one's neck number was dye, not tattooin'."

The face sprawled upward as the body rolled, a small black hole between its brows. Tanya stretched, looked around, estimating numbers and weapons. Sixteen Draka, pistols, three submachine guns, two battle shotguns, two assault rifles. More in the armory, of course . . . Five armed serfs who would do to stand guard. The scouts had all reported back, and there was no sign of bushman activity beyond the one small band. *Which is enough, enough,* she thought sourly.

"Oerbach," Vashon was saying, "by Loki and the soul of the White Christ, Oerbach." He looked up at her. "Congratulations." Back down at the body, and a murmur. "Because you may have just saved me from the Aral Sea."

"Dumb luck," she replied. "Hundred meters with a Tolgren, pure fluke." To her husband. "Situation?"

"Transport gone," he said calmly. "Power out. Communication out. Runners to the neighbors." Draka runners, nearly as fast as horses, but still a half hour there, more time to organize, transit time back . . . three quarters of an hour to an hour. "Children, sick an' bearin' mothers down on the yacht, Uncle Karl presidin'." A weight lifted from the back of her neck, a thing she had not been conscious of until that moment.

"Information from the Strategos here," Edward went on. "Three bushmen from Lyon, one a double who reported in to warn us. Two mo—"

Andrew interrupted: "One, if the second was a woman with a knife," he said bluntly. "She's fertilizin' you vineyard, sister."

"One mo' up at the winery, with the Yankee callin' hisself Kenston, an' the wenches Chantal an' Marya. Yankee plane comin' in, soon."

"And many, many kilograms of plutonium oxide," Andrew said.

"Bad?" Tanya asked as a fist clenched under her gut. She had seen the fallout-victim wards, the ones caught in the plume from the Ruhr strikes toward the end of the war. An image welled up in her mind—Gudrun, Tim, the newborns, their ulcerated skins sloughing away—

"The radiation isn't that severe," Vashon began.

"It doesn't have to be," Andrew cut in decisively. "Garbage is so toxic chemically you don't have *time* to die of the radiation sickness an' cancer that would kill you in days to weeks. It's worse than nerve gas, submicroscopic particles deadly almost immediately; the amount they've got could kill everythin' within light-artillery range of here, or *worse*. Dependin' on how it's scattered." He jerked his head toward the kilometer-distant glow of the vehicle park. "We *know* they've got explosives, and imagine how an updraft like that would scatter a finely divided powder."

"Shitfire." Hushed awe in the word.

A thick silence fell. "We've got to attack," someone said.

"Sho'ly do! And quick. Befo' they can loose that stuff."

Tanya held up her hand, and silence fell. This was her land, and Draka were soldiers; they understood the need for teamwork down in their bones. She looked around, at steel and fugitive gleams from eyes and teeth.

"We can't just roll over them," she said slowly. "We may have to talk them out."

"No!" That was Vashon. "The Race doesn't back down from a threat! We take that plutonium back, and—"

Tanya nodded, and there was a multiple click and rattle. Vashon froze as the cold muzzles of weapons touched lightly on his skin. She walked close, held her face inches from his.

"Strategos . . . let us say, I'm not very *impressed* with the quality of you security work. Seein' as the position we're in."

Someone behind him spoke. "The *hell* we don't back down from threats, how do you think we got this far, by bein' bull-stupid like so you?"

Another: "It's our land and children, Vashon. I think the von Shrakenbergs are senior here . . . Hell, we *are* the Race."

Tanya continued, never taking her eyes from the man's. "Nobody here will do anythin' prejudicial to the interests of the Race or the State," she said. "Andrew, run it down fo' me."

"Bad if"—he kicked Oerbach's body—"had gotten away to the Yankees; he is, was, a genuine thinker, an experimenter an' theoretician in one. Unfortunate if they were to get his research to date, but no disaster, we've got it too. Mildly unfortunate to let them have the plutonium, it's rare an' expensive, but still just matériel."

Tanya nodded. "Against which we have to balance risk to the lives of two-score members of the Race. We're not a numerous people, Strategos, never start imaginin' you can spend our lives the way you might do serfs'. That's not the way we've operated, ever." A pause. "I think it might be bettah if somebody else took care of this mastah's gun; the gleam in his eyes is a touch too fanatical fo' my taste." Hands reached out. Green eyes met gray, nodded. There would be feud, but not now.

Tanya looked around. "You, Sofie. Down to the dock and tell Karl to cast off with the kids, downstream as fast as he can an' not run aground. The rest of you . . . *follow me.*"

They turned and ran toward the north, to the caves, toward the waiting poison.

"No, no, *no*," Kustaa said, pounding his fist into the turf.

"He is with God," Marya said quietly. They were resting in the shadow of one of the disabled Draka aircraft, with the winking rectangle of the landing strip stretching away.

"That isn't going to do any good to the fucking Taos Weapons Research Lab!" Kustaa shouted, then mumbled apology as pain lanced through his wounds.

Marya examined them again, frowning; there had been bandages, iodine, sulfa powder in the aircraft first-aid kit, she had cleaned and bound as best she could, but he needed stitching and plasma, and complete bed-rest. Instead he had insisted on a stimulant, and he was right, but it made it so difficult for him to lie still. "Quiet, Frederick. We have done what human hands can do, the rest is with God."

Her eyes went doubtfully to the steel box. It had been transformed into a lumpy gray mass by the ten kilos of plastique they had wrapped around it. The batteries and improvised switch rested atop it, wires spindling down to the detonator. *Such a simple thing,* she thought with a shiver. Their insurance. A deadman switch, so just a name. Grip, *so.* Press down sharply and now you must *keep* pressing or the contact will be made, contact, current through the detonator, detonator explodes, rapid-propagating shock wave provokes sympathetic reaction in the plastique.

And all this dies, she thought, looking around at the night countryside with another shudder. *Like the wrath of God upon the cities of the plain, only this wrath is man's.* It all dies, the beasts and the humans, innocent and guilty, fathers and mothers and babes in arms for leagues around.

She signed herself, knelt by the box and began to pray; first seeking the intercession of the Saints, that they might stand between her and the terrible necessities that God seemed to demand of her. Then asking mercy of Mary, the Mother that was the pattern of all mothers, human flesh united in nine months' inconceivable communion with the Word. Then at last to the heart of Mystery. The words ordained, and then her own.

Lord God, she begged, *let there be mercy in this hour. As you would have spared Sodom for ten upright men, spare those poor souls dwelling here, whose lives are humble and full of suffering yet still precious to them, as You intended. For indeed Your world is good, where we have not marred it. And if only through blood may there be remission of sin, let the sword fall upon me alone.* Wordless for long minutes. Then: *Lord, I am unworthy, full of pride and sin and conceit of my own righteousness, yet ever willing to be Your instrument. Give unto me not that which I ask, but what is best for me, though it be the thing I fear most. Not my will, but Thine be done.*

"Amen," she murmured and took the switch in her hand, pressing down sharply.

The others looked up at the hard clicking sound. "It will not become

easier to do if we wait," she said. "If we are successful, I can disconnect one of the wires."

Chantal glanced aside, then laid her head back on her knees,
muttering under her breath. From this position, the nun could hear
clearly what she had only suspected.

"I had to do it. She deserved it. I *had* to. She deserved it."

"Chantal!" Marya snapped. "I am losing patience with you!" The
other's head came up, with anger in her eyes. "That is half a lie, worse
than a whole one. It was necessary, to save Frederick's life. And she
did *not* deserve it; the poor girl had been mistaught, grievously, since
she was a little child. But of herself she was a gentle soul who only
acted from natural grief. You are trying to blame her because it eases
your conscience, aren't you? So that you won't see her face and what
you did to her? Remember it! Don't lie to yourself, and don't lie to
me, either."

Chantal turned her back, but silently. Marya looked down at the
bundle of steel and explosive again. *And it makes my temper still worse
than it usually is,* she thought.

"By God, the plane," Kustaa said quietly. "The plane!" he shouted,
half rose, sank down again with a grunt. Marya strained her eyes
and ears: nothing. Then a hint of something, a shadow against the
stars, a muffled purring drone. Circling, returning toward them, falling
feather light in a steep slope out of the sky, and the nun felt her
eyes prickle with tears for the first time that night. It landed, bounced,
trundled toward them, a flat complex wing with two engines buried in the structure and thickly wrapped in shrouding cowl, a teardrop fuselage.

"That's it, that's the Spector," Kustaa was saying in what was almost
a babble. "Isn't she a beauty, takes off on a postage stamp, lands on
a balcony, noisy as a scooter, seats four with cargo—" He stopped,
looked at her. "And Ernst is dead," he finished in something closer
to his normal tone.

"But Henri is alive," she replied sharply, turning to find the darker
shadow that was the sole survivor of the Resistance team. He was
walking up the slope in a crouch that rose toward a full stride, his
impassive stubbled face finally breaking into a grin of unbelieving
triumph as the cockpit window of the aircraft folded back and an arm
emerged, waving.

Marya smiled at the Frenchman in return, watching as he grew solid
in the darkness, as his grin went fixed, his stride stiff-legged, as he
toppled forward with the glint of the throwing knife's hilt winking from
his back. *Thump* went the body. Limp as sleep, limp as death, kicked
twice, lay still.

"Down!" Kustaa yelled.

"Deadman switch, deadman switch," Marya shouted out into the
night, at the full stretch of her lungs. "The plutonium is sitting on
ten kilos of high explosive, and we have a deadman switch. Think
about that and hold your fire!"

There was another shout of pain, mingled with rage this time, from
the encircling shadows. Then a brief burst of fire, a Holbars on full

automatic, a dozen rounds that chewed into the left engine of the American aircraft, followed by whapping thuds and sparks and a sudden metallic screeching as the internal parts seized hard. The prop slowed from its silent blur, froze into four paddle-shaped metal blades. Then the stream of tracer waggled crazily up into the sky, went out, more thuds and grappling sounds.

"Wait, wait!" Tanya's voice. "That was a rogue . . . *no, don't kill him, you fools!*" The latter seemed directed at her own people. The hailing voice again: "There are twenty of us out here; we have enough firepower to cut that paper airplane into confetti—think about that!"

Silence, until Kustaa crawled to the airplane's landing struts; the effort left him gasping.

"No closer," Tanya called. "No packages!"

They were close enough for words, murmured too low for the nun to hear. He crawled again, to her side, and lay for a moment with fresh blood seeping through her careful bandages, his fingers digging into the soil as if it were his mother's body to which he clung.

"We're fu— We're in trouble, Sister. One engine completely out." The voice had the hard flatness she had come to know meant his deepest effort at control.

"It can fly. It can even carry a passenger . . . one passenger, preferably a very light one."

Marya prayed again, this time an utterly wordless appeal. She gasped sharply.

"What is it?" Kustaa asked.

"I think . . . I think I see what I must do," she said grayly. "Oh, Frederick, I had hoped . . . hoped so much you might return to your wife and daughter."

To the Draka: "We have no time, and nothing left to lose. Will you talk, or do we all die?"

"I'll talk. Shall I come closer?" Tanya again.

"Agreed."

The Draka strolled into the dim glimmer of the landing lights, elaborately insouciant, her hands on her hips. Dark clothing, bright hair, the eyes throwing back the light like ice; she stood waiting for the nun to speak.

She is playing for time, Marya thought. Then: *Of course. They have sent their children to safety; the longer we wait the better. And the authorities will arrive at any moment.*

"No games," the Pole said. "The plane can take one of us out, only."

"Not the plutonium, of course . . . and not the Yankee. He stays; that's a matter of honor."

The OSS agent sighed, then looked up at Marya with a smile more relaxed than any she had seen him wear before. *There is a relief in acknowledging the race is lost,* she thought. *But there are more important things than life.*

"I won't let myself be taken alive," Kustaa said.

"Well, obviously," Tanya said with cool contempt. "You a treacherous bastard abuses hospitality, but not a fool. You have that gun, don't you?" She grinned with bared teeth. "The one that you kill drunk old men an' harmless serf girls with?"

"Enough," Marya said. "If you let the plane go with one of us, we will promise not to detonate this weapon."

"I made the mistake of underestimatin' you, but please don't reciprocate with an insult to my intelligence," Tanya replied evenly. "Once it's out of sight, you'd simply set it off anyway."

"To spare myself pain?" Marya asked. "Have you sent your children away?" Tanya nodded warily. "And those of your serfs?"

"Ahh, I see," the Draka said. "Then you will surrender anyhows?"

"No," Marya replied, meeting her owner's eyes in a steady glare as hard as the Draka's own. "Frederick knows too much. We will take it below, into the shelter. That can be sealed, and I will promise not to release the switch until it is. Quickly, decide, there is no time."

Tanya nodded, turned. "The terms are these," she said in a clear carrying voice. "We let the Yankee plane take off, with my wench Chantal on board. My wench Marya an' the Yankee go into the shelter an' we seal them in with they little hellbomb, after one hour's grace." There was a protesting murmur, and she held up one hand. "Listen! We lose nothin' by allowin' the plane back. Chantal's also nothin', unless the Yankees are perishin' fo' want of a so-so bookkeeper and bed wench." A mutter of unwilling laughter. "We keep the plutonium, it can be recovered, an' they lose their agent an' all his knowledge. I'd call that victory! An' I take full responsiblity fo' any repercussions from the State. Objections?"

"It's agreed," she said, turning to the American and the nun and raising her hand. "Word of a von Shrakenberg, by our honor."

Chantal had turned back to them, and watched Marya's face with an expression of thoughtful wonder. "No," she said, on the heels of Tanya's oath.

Marya looked over at her and laughed with a catch in her voice. "What a collection of martyrs we are . . . of course you must, Chantal."

"I . . . can't take your life!" the Frenchwoman said. "I want to, God, I want to, but how could I live with myself, remembering this? How could I owe you this, and never be able to repay?"

Marya sighed. "Chantal, nobody can give you their life. Only your own." More softly: "If you feel you owe me a debt, choose another and pay it to them, and I will be repaid in full and to overflowing." Chantal's face cleared, she touched her stomach involuntarily, then gave the nun an ashen nod.

"Will you give me the kiss of peace, Chantal?" Marya said, brushing her free hand across her face. The younger woman stood with sudden decisiveness, bent to offer her cheek, met the Pole's lips instead. Her eyes widened, and she swallowed convulsively.

"Kustaa reached inside his jacket. "And would you take this to—" he began.

"No!" A voice from the darkness. "No papers, no chance to pass along microfilm, Yankee."

Suddenly Kustaa was on his feet, a big man bristling with rage, the lumberjack strength of his shoulders showing despite wounds and weariness. *"It's a letter to my wife, you bastard!"* he roared.

"Mah heart bleeds fo' you. Verbal only!" A dozen lights speared out to trap Chantal. "An' the wench has to shuck and bend, so's we can see she's not carryin'"

Kustaa turned to the Frenchwoman, who stood blinking and shading her eyes with a palm. "Tell Aino I love her," he said. "And Maila. Say"—he glanced back at the nun—"say she can be proud of the way her father died, and the company he kept. Tell her . . . tell her everything."

"I will. Rest assured, I will." When the cockpit door of the airplane closed on her, the nakedness was a lack of clothes only.

The single engine whined, stressed beyond its limit.

Kustaa sank to the ground beside Marya, the shotgun clenched white-knuckled in his lap as the Spector took off.

"I know," she said. "I want to run after it shouting, 'Come back, come back' myself."

"Good," he sighed. "I was beginning to think saints were too perfect to live around."

"Mr. . . . Frederick," she said, and he glanced around in shock at the cold anger in her voice. "You will *never* call me that again. Never!"

"Sorry, Sister," he said.

"I too . . . my temper was always bad . . ." To Tanya: "Mistress, it would be a courtesy if someone would fetch the radio for us, from the shelter."

The Draka nodded, and signaled with one hand; the parcel came, and Kustaa busied himself with dials and antennae, tuned to the Draka Forces emergency network. Time passed, and the night grew colder and more silent; in the distance, the fires of the burning vehicles guttered low. The headlights of a high-speed convoy flickered up to the main gates of Chateau Retour, and a runner went at Tanya's order to halt them. Another returned with a radiation detector, pointed it at the box with its leprous covering, and paled as the needle swung; there was a rustle from the darkness as the besieger's circle drew back.

Kustaa looked up, squeezed his eyes shut. "They missed it," he said softly. "It's full time, and they're going crazy looking for it. We won." A sour laugh. "In a sense, I suppose."

Tanya shifted her stance, the first movement in half an hour. "The Security people will be here soon," she said. "I've got influence, but not enough to stand off their rankin' people. My oath; I'm not answerable for them."

"It is time," Marya said. "Just one more thing." She raised her voice. "We need someone to carry this box; Frederick is wounded and cannot possibly do so."

Tanya snorted. "We'll send for a strong serf."

"No! Someone here, immediately. No time for tricks." *And I will not condemn an innocent. Any adult Draka is a murderer, fornicator, blasphemer.*

Another slight rustle in the darkness. "I can't order anyone to—" Then a voice "I volunteer."

"No," Tanya snapped, as her brother Andrew strolled up, paused to lay his weapon on the grass, walked toward the American's shotgun, which tracked him with a smooth turret motion.

"But yes, mah sister," Andrew continued gently. "Be logical, as you usually are. Here I am, thirty-two, unmarried, no children of the Race, a middlin' good Merarch among thousands . . . The Race can spare me."

"It can't, and neither can I!" Tanya said, and Marya heard open pain in her voice for the first time that night.

"Yes, you can," he said, stopping to confront her. "Mo' than I could you. Furthermo' it's a risk of death, not certainty. Furthermo' to that, it's my choice. Service to the State, sister mine." Matter-of-factly: "If'n I'm unlucky, would you see to my girls and my valet?" She nodded wordlessly. "Glory to the Race, then."

"Yes, indeed," she said thickly. "I love you brother."

"And I you, Tannie." Two more strides brought him to Marya's side, and he crouched smoothly.

"Watch it, you son of a bitch," Kustaa said, holding his weapon close. "Slow and careful."

"Yankee, don't be mo' of an imbecile than nature intended," Andrew said dryly, running his hands around the box. "I'm squattin' next a live bomb, with enough poison inside to destroy Archona, an' you puts a *shotgun* in mah ear an' tells me to be *careful*?"

Kustaa flushed slightly, but kept the weapon pressed against the Draka's back. "I know how you snakes train by snatching flies out of the air without hurting them," he said. "You still can't grab her hand faster than I can pull this trigger. Like I said, slow and careful."

Andrew's face went blank as he drew a deep breath. "Now," he said, and exhaled with a long sustained grunt as he stood. A seam parted along the rear of his jacket, and they could feel the ground shake slightly as he took the first step toward the shelter door. Tanya stood to one side, eyes hooded. As they passed, her hand came up in salute, held there. "I'll see there's a priest to bless the ground," she murmured.

"Thank you," Marya replied. Their eyes met, but there were no more words.

The shelter lights seemed painfully bright; Kustaa blinked against them and the ringing in his ears that was growing worse. Andrew was whistling under his breath as he bolted home the steel covers over the ventilators, checking carefully to make sure the sealing rings seated square. Almost, the American missed the quiet sobbing sound.

"Sister, what is it?" he said anxiously, dropping down beside her with the shotgun trained across the room. Tears were dropping into her lap, onto the clenched knuckles of her right hand on the switch, onto the steel and dough-gray explosive.

"Fear, Frederick," she said, between catches of breath. A laugh through the sobbing, as she saw his face.

"Frederick, I fear death, so much . . . pain even more. You know what they can do, would do if they took me. They can make a hell on earth, less than Satan's only because it is not eternal. They would never believe I knew nothing of consequence . . . oh, Frederick, I have had nightmares of that, ever since . . ." A shake of her head. "But if there was a way, I would walk out that door and right now and let them take me to the place of torment."

"*What?*" he said.

"Thank you for listening, my friend, when you too must need to speak . . . Frederick, I am in such fear that I cannot bear it, that this thing I am doing is self-murder. I tell myself it is not, it is as a soldier does when he charges the machine gun or throws himself on a grenade to save his comrades, but . . . self-murder, murder of the soul, damnation." The tears became softer, and her voice thickened. "Damnation . . . not the pains of hell, but never to see God in the face . . . never . . . never to see the other Sisters of St. Cyril again, and Frederick, I am the last. They are all with Him in Glory, they were saints and martyrs, but sisters in truth, dearer than any earthly thing to me. Never to see them, never to share their joy, oh, I cannot bear it!"

I have gone crazy, Kustaa thought, as he heard himself speak. *But it's a pleasanter madness than the one before.* "I'll do it then," he said. "Here, give me the switch."

"No! Frederick, no! You may not believe suicide is mortal sin, but it is for you as well. How could I buy Paradise at the cost of your damnation? This is my *fault*, Frederick, my weakness; if I were more worthy God would have called to my heart, shown me a better way . . ." The control and serenity were cracking out of the nun's voice, leaving only raw pain and will.

Kustaa turned and drove a fist against the wall. "Dammit," he swore. "If only we could have gotten the microfilm out. If only that, at least!"

"Oh, we did, Frederick," Marya said, half listlessly. "Did you not notice—" She halted in mid-sentence, and both their heads swung to the Draka. He completed the last bolt and dropped lightly to the floor, dusting his hands on the black uniform trousers.

"Feh," he said, an exhalation of disgust. "I don't suppose you'd believe a promise not to tell . . . No, I don't suppose so." There was no need to mention that the Draka would mobilize every keel and wing to hunt the Alliance submarine if they knew. He walked lightly to the outer door, stood with one hand on the wheel. "I could refuse to close it," he said.

"Your friends and relatives, snake," Kustaa said with a grin of jovial hatred. "Much more limited spread, from here."

"Yes, there is that," Andrew said, pulled the door home with a clang, spun the wheel until the bolts went *shhnnnk-click* into their slots, and pushed the locking bar. "Shit," he said meditatively. "Suddenly a long, dull life becomes so much less wearisome in prospect." Suddenly he was laughing as he strode back to stand before them, a low wicked snicker.

"What the fuck are you laughing at?" Kustaa glared, glancing from the weeping nun to the scarred aquiline face and the earring that jiggled in time with his mirth.

"Everything an' nothing, Yankee. You bourgeois have such a tiresome gravity about serious mattahs, takes a gentleman to bring the proper levity to the grave. If it's one thing I've learned in thirty-two years, it's that the only thing mo' amusin' than this farce we call life is the even more absurd farce known as death. If there was an afterlife, the sheer comedy of it would be too much to bear!"

"Have some respect," Kustaa said, raising the shotgun despite his own sense of its futility.

"Oh, I do, an' that's the most comical thing of all, Yankee." His voice dropped. "Sister." She raised her head, startled to hear the title on a Draka's voice. "Sister, pardon me fo' listenin' to you, ah, confession. But it occurs to me that while you belief is as absurd as anythin' else, you belief in it, is not." He spread his hands. "So, since if one is goin' anyway, one might as well go with a grand gesture—"

Kustaa screamed and fired, but he was too late—the fluid Draka speed had outmatched him, the boot heel struck the nun with needle precision and pickax force directly above the nose. Sound merged, the snap of bone, the shot, the beginnings of a roaring blast as dead fingers unfolded like the petals of a rose.

Chapter Sixteen

"All victories are ephemeral. Only our defeats are final."
Secret journals of Professor Jules Lebrun, Last Entry
Chateau Retour Plantation infirmary

Epilogue I

CHATEAU RETOUR PLANTATION,
TOURAINE PROVINCE
OCTOBER 1947

"Am I bein' sentimental, love?" Tanya von Shrakenberg asked, as they watched the captive priest bless the earth. It was a raw autumn day, they were the only Draka present, sitting their horses behind a screen of drab-coated serfs, while the world spread around them in gray cloud, wet earth, faded brightness of vine leaves that whirled away down the wind like messages to yesterday.

"Yes," her husband replied. The gaping hole had been refilled, where the decontamination crews had pumped the shelter full of liquid concrete and taken out the block entire. Filled with good earth, and now consecrated as a graveyard. The vestments of the priest were a splash of color against the raw brown earth and the simple granite tombstone; but even before the ceremony, the serfs had begun to come with flowers and ribbons for the resting place of the one who had died for them.

"Yes," he said. "But we can afford a little, now and then." A squeeze of their gloved hands. "Andrew has his memorial, and it's mo' showy; let them have theirs." He took up the reins. "C'mon, love, dinner's waitin'."

They reined about and heeled their horses. The serfs bowed as they passed, but remained kneeling to pray for her whose spirit surely abided to guard this place.

475

Epilogue II

HOSPITAL OF THE SACRED HEART
NEW YORK CITY
FEBRUARY 1948

"Names?" The woman who looked up at the nursing sister was exhausted with the long labor, triumphant, but she had no slightest trace of the furtiveness the staff had come to expect of unwed mothers. Of course, there was some mystery involved; the nurse looked over at the godparents, a short Indian-looking man in naval blue with commander's stripes on his arm and his blond wife with the soft Carolina accent. They visited often, and the quiet widow with her daughter, and the horse-faced man who your eyes never really seemed to rest on.

"Of course I've got names," the young woman was saying, in the French accent that had been considered exotic before the War and the refugee influx. She looked over to the cradle, the two sleeping pink forms still with their golden-blond birth fuzz.

"Frederick Kustaa and Marya Sokolowska Lefarge," she said, closing her eyes with a sigh. "I don't believe in making it easy for children. *That'll* give them something to live up to."

LOW EARTH ORBIT
JULY 1ST, 2014
INGOLFSSON INCURSION TIMELINE
EARTH/2B

"Yet there must have been some disaster?" Nomura said. "Some . . . weakness, some . . ."

Carmaggio shook his head. "Son, one of the scariest things about this multiple-worlds shit is that it reminds you just how much depends on people—and that's to say, on something *utterly* unpredictable." He looked out at the starscape. "After that, things moved more quickly . . ."

BOOK THREE

Prologue

VIRUNGA BIOCONTROL INSTITUTE
WEAPONS RESEARCH DIVISION
WEST RIFT PROVINCE
MARCH 1, 1964

"This is the first series," the project manager, a stocky brown-haired woman in her thirties, said. The wall lit up with a three-dimensional rendering of a virus molecule. It was color-coded, black and scarlet. "You see how we've replaced—"

"Doctor Melford," the Senator said, with soft courtesy. The other members of the audience turned slightly to catch his words. "We've all absorbed as much technical information as possible from the prep files, and while I'm sure the computer projections would be very interesting, perhaps . . . ?"

He was a tall man, eagle-faced, with silver-streaked blond hair and mustache, conservatively dressed in indigo velvet and white lace. There was no impatience in his posture, leaning back at his ease in one of the two dozen swivel chairs that lined the little auditorium. Still, the woman in the white lab coat flushed slightly, coughed to cover it; her fingers moved on the controls.

"Well," she said. Her vowels had a rather crisp tone, an East African accent; she had been born in these highlands. "Well, here are the recordings of the chimp results."

The screen blanked for a moment and split. "The left is our control sample, an' the right is the Series 24D group." The Senator watched, stony-faced amid his silent aides, as the dance of madness and death ran to its close. The plainly clad woman at the heart of the other clump laughed aloud. A minute passed, and nothing living remained on the right-hand screen. To the left the chimps might have been a picture of the innocence before the birth of man.

"It seems," he said, "that you've been makin' progress, Doctor."

She nodded eagerly. " 'Specially since you got us the new computer," she said, one hand caressing the row of pens in her breast pocket with a nervous gesture.

The Senator smiled for the first time. "Thank the Yankees; it was the best we could steal," he said dryly. "How confident are you that these-here results can be transferred to humans?"

"Very, yes," the geneticist nodded. "Chimps are the best possible test subjects, they're so close to us. Ninety-eight percent genetic congruence, only five million years since the last common ancestor, which . . . Yes. The endorphin response is modified into a feedback loop. That still needs work."

The woman to the Senator's left spoke, in a flat Angolan accent: "What's y're success rate?" She was younger than the Senator, perhaps forty-five, head of a committee in the House of Representatives that attracted little public attention.

Melford nodded at the right-hand screen. "Ovah ninety-nine percent, no point in finin' it down further until we moves to human subjects."

"In y' professional opinion, is this project go or no-go?"

"Go." A decisive nod. "Provided we get the necessary fundin' an' personnel. Mo' work on the vector—we're still relyin' on blood to blood—and the secondary keyin' sequence. Four years, eight maximum, an' we'll have it on spec."

"Ah." The Senator dropped his chin onto the steepled fingers of both hands, and the lids drooped over his narrow gray eyes. "Doctor, what about keepin' it from the Yankees when we deploy it against the Alliance?"

"Well." A frown. "Well, they're not as, um, sophisticated at biotech as we are. Those Luddite fanatics of theirs who keep protestin' every time they try to use somethin', and then again they can't test humans to destruction the way we can. Sloppy. Still, they've got some good people."

The Senator looked across to his colleague; she nodded and spoke: "What'll you need?"

"Um, more funding. More personnel, as Ah said. An' experimental subjects, of course. Several hundred humans, assorted gender an' age in the postpubescent range, pref'rably the same ethnic mix as the target population. Very delicate, to get it contagious but with a fail-safe turnoff. Don't want it becomin' a global pandemic, do we?"

"Wotan, no," the Senator said. "Well, Doctor Melford, certain othahs will have to be consulted, but unofficially I think you can take it that the project will be approved fo' further development." He rose. "Service to the State."

"Glory to the Race," the scientist answered absentmindedly as the audience left; she was keying the machine again, reviewing the additional resources that would be needed.

"Well, how do y'like it?"

"Nice view," the Senator said, nodding down from the terrace toward the lake and drawing on his cigarette.

The Virunga Biocontrol Institute was built in the hills overlooking Lake Kivu, at the southern edge of the Virunga range. A century old now, almost as old as Draka settlement in these volcanic highlands. Low whitewashed buildings of stone block, roofs of plum-colored tile, almost lost among the vegetation; the gardens were flamboyantly lovely even by the Domination's standards, fertile lava soils and abundant rain and a climate of eternal spring. National park stretched north and west, to the Ituri lowlands: haunt of gorilla and chimp, elephant and hippo and leopard; of the Bambuti pygmies also, left to their Old Stone Age existence.

Plantations stretched widely elsewhere across the steep slopes, green coffee and tea and sheets of flowers grown for air-freighting elsewhere; the air was scented with them, cool and sweet. The city of Arjunanda lay two thousand feet below by the waters, turned to a model by distance: buildings white and blue and violet with marble and tile, avenues bordered with jacaranda and colonnades roofed in climbing rose and frangipani. Even the factories and labor compounds that ringed it were comely, bordered by hedge and garden. Sails speckled the waves, and they could see the pleasure boats beating back toward the docks, and dirigibles lying silvery in the waterfront haven.

"It's a famous beauty spot," the woman said with elaborate sarcasm, indicating the sun setting behind the mountains to their right, amid clouds turned to the colors of brass and blood. "No mo' games, man."

He flicked the butt of the cigarette over the railing. *It's just like her, to be cold even when she's angry. You can see why our enemies nicknamed us "snakes," looking at her.* The burning speck fell like a tiny meteor, to lie winking for a second before one of the Institute outdoor serfs arrived to sweep it up.

"It might work," he said quietly.

"It *will* work. This time you suspicions of biotech don't wash. And this project was mah price fo' supportin' *you* pet schemes."

"Granted."

They gave each other a glance of cool mutual hatred and turned again to the view beneath. Shadow was falling across the city and the lake as the first stars appeared above. The streetlights of Arjunanda flicked on in a curving tracery, and the lamps of the plantation manors scattered down the hills. An airship had cast off from the haven, and the thousand-meter teardrop rose from darkness into light as it circled, bound northward with cut flowers and electrowafers, strawberries and heavengrape wine.

"Have you ever wondered," the Senator said meditatively, "why we Draka love flowers so?"

The woman blinked, her fox-sharp face shadowed in the dim glow. "No, can't say as I have," she said neutrally. "Why?"

"They're safer to love than human bein's," he said thoughtfully. "An' unlike humans, they deserve it." He turned. "I'll be in contact after I speak to the Archon."

Chapter One

It's too crowded in here, Yolande Ingolfsson thought irritably.

The crowding was not physical. The van was an Angers-Kellerman autosteamer from the Trevithick Combine's works in Milan, a big six-wheeler plantation sedan like a slope-fronted box with slab sides. There were five serfs and one young lady of landholding Citizen family in the roomy cabin; the muted sound of the engine was lost in the rush of wind and whine of the tires. None of them had been this way before.

Young Marco the driver was chattering with excitement, with stolid Deng sitting beside him giving an occasional snarl when the Italian's hands swooped off the wheel. The Oriental was a stocky grizzle-haired man of fifty, his face round and ruddy. He had been the House foreman since forever; Father had brought him from China when he and Mother came to set up the plantation, after the War. Saved him from an impaling stake, the rebel's fate, or so the rumor went, but neither of them would talk about it. Bianca and Lele were bouncing about on the benches running along either side of the vehicle, giggling and pointing out the sights to each other.

Not to me, Yolande thought with a slight sadness. Well, she was fourteen, that was getting far too grown-up to talk that way with servants.

The van had the highway mostly to itself on the drive down from Tuscany, past Rome and through the plantations of Campania; Italy was something of a backwater these days, and what industry there was clustered in the north. There was the odd passenger steamer, a few electric runabouts, drags hauling linked flats of produce or goods. Nevertheless the road was just as every other Class II way in the Domination of the Draka, an asphalt surface eight meters broad with a graveled verge and rows of trees on either side; cypress or eucalyptus here, but that varied with the climate.

Fields passed, seen through a flicker of trunks and latticed shadow slanting back from the westering sun, big square plots edged with shaggy hedges of multiflora. Fields of trellised vines, purple grapes peering out from the tattered autumnal lushness of their leaves; orchards of silvery gray olives, fruit trees, hard glossy citrus, and sere yellow-brown grain stubble. Fields of alfalfa under whirling sprinklers, circles of spray that filled the air with miniature rainbows and a heavy green smell that cut the hot dust scent. Melons lying like ruins of streaked green-and-white marble tumbled among vines, and strawberries starred red through the velvet plush of their beds.

Arch-and-pillar gateways marked the turnoffs to the estate manors, hints of colored roofs amid the treetops of their gardens. Yolande felt what she always did when she saw a gate: an impulse to open it. Like an itch in the head, to follow and see what was there, who the people were, and what their lives were like. Make up stories about them, or poems.

Silly, she thought. People were people; plantations were plantations, not much different from the one she grew up on.

Words and surfaces, hard shiny shells, that was all you could know of people. Yet the itch would not go away. You thought that you knew what they were like, especially when you were little; then a thing would happen that showed you were wrong . . . she shivered at certain memories.

The Draka girl leaned back with a sigh, feeling heavy and a little tired from the going-away party last night. She had the rear of the autosteamer—a semicircle couch like the fantail of a small yacht—nearly to herself: her Persian cat, Machiavelli, was curled up beside her. He always tried to sleep through an auto drive; at least he didn't hide under a seat and puke anymore. . . . The windows slanted over her head, up to the roof of the auto, open a little to let in a rush of warm dry afternoon air. She let her head fall back, looking through the glass up into the cloudless bowl of the sky, just beginning to darken at the zenith. Her face looked back at her, transparent against the sky, centered in a fan of pale silky hair that rippled in the breeze.

Like a ghost, she thought. Her mind could fill in the tinting, summer's olive tan, hair and brows faded to white-gold, Mother's coloring. Eyes the shade of granulated silver, rimmed with dark blue, a mixture from both her parents. Face her own, oval, high cheekbones and a short straight nose, wide full-lipped mouth, squared chin with a cleft; Pa was always saying there must be elf somewhere in the bloodlines. She turned her head and sucked in her cheeks; the puppy fat was definitely going, at long last. She was still obstinately short and slightly built, however much she tried to force growth with willpower.

At least I don't have spots, she mused with relief. It was her first year at the new school, and her first in the Senior Section, as well.

"Bianca, get me a drink, please," Yolande said, shifting restlessly and stretching. The drive had been a long one, and she felt grubby and dusty and sticky; the silk of her blouse was clinging to her back, and she could feel how it had wrinkled.

The air had a spicy-dry scent, like the idea of a sneeze. Yolande sipped moodily at the orange juice and watched as the auto turned south and east to skirt the fringe of Naples. Her mouth was dry despite the cold drink. She handed the glass back to the servant girl and wiped her palms down the sides of her jodhpurs, hitched at her gunbelt, ran fingers through the tangled mass of her hair, adjusted her cravat.

"Bianca, Lele, my hair's a mess," she said. "Fix it." There was a sour taste at the back of her mouth, and a feeling like hard fluttering in her stomach.

Don't fidget, she told herself as the tense muscles of her shoulders and neck eased at the familiar feel of fingers and hairbrush. *It's serfish.* It was emotional to be frightened of going to a new school; they weren't going to hurt her, after all. Children and serfs were expected to be emotional; a Citizen ruled herself with the mind. Bianca was humming as she used the pick on the end of her comb to untangle a knot. Yolande's hair had always been feather-soft and flyaway.

The school was on the bay itself, surrounded by a thousand hectares of grounds. A herd of ibex raised their scimitar-horned heads from a pool, muzzles trailing drops that sparkled as they fell among the purple-and-white bowls of the water lilies.

"Turn right," Yolande said, unnecessarily; there was a servant in the checkered livery of the school directing traffic.

The sun had sunk until it nearly touched the horizon, and the light-wand in the serf's hand glowed translucent white. More servants waited at the brick-paved parking lot, a broad expanse of tessellated red and black divided by stone planters with miniature trees. The van eased into place, guided by a wench with a light-wand who walked backwards before them, and stopped; Yolande felt the dryness suddenly return to her mouth as she rose.

"Well," she said into air that felt somehow motionless after the unvarying rush of wind on the road. "Let's go."

Deng pushed the driver back into his seat. "Not you, Marco," he said.

The younger man gave him a resentful glare but sank down again. Deng was not like some bossboys; he did not use the strap or rubber hose all the time, but he was obeyed just the same.

Yolande ignored the stairs, stepping out and taking the chest-high drop with a flex of her knees. An eight-wheeler articulated steamer was unloading a stream of girls; that must be a shuttle from Naples, the ones coming in from the train and dirigible havens.

They were all dressed in the school uniform, a knee-length belted tunic of Egyptian linen dyed indigo blue, and sandals that strapped up the calf. She felt suddenly self-conscious in her young-planter outfit, even with the Tolgren 10mm and fighting knife she had been so proud of. They were mostly older than her; all the Junior Section would have arrived yesterday. Their friends were there to greet them, hugs and wristshakes and flower wreaths for their hair . . .

Yolande swallowed and forced herself to ignore them, the laughter and the shouts, ignored a tiltrotor taking off and turning north. She blinked; in half an hour it would be past Sienna. Past Badesse, past home. Over the tiny hilltop lights of Claestum; her parents might look up from the dining terrace at the sound of engines. Tantie Rahksan with her eternal piece of embroidery . . . Moths would be battering against the globes, and there would be a damp smell from the pools and fountains. Warm window-glow coming on in the Quarters down in the valley, and the sleepy evening sounds of the rambling Great House. Her own bedroom in the west tower would be dark, only moonlight making shadows on the comforter, her desk, airplane models, old dolls and posters . . .

This is ridiculous, she scolded herself, working at the knot of misery beneath her breastbone. The quarrel at the old school had *not* been her fault; even if somebody had to leave, it should have been Irene, not her. Would have been, if they had not valued peace over justice.

"Hello."

She looked down with a start; a girl her own age was standing nearby, hands on hips and a smile on her face.

"You're Yolande Ingolfsson, the one from up Tuscany way?"

She nodded, and grasped the offered wrist. Then blinked a little with surprise, feeling a shock as of recognition.

I must know someone who looks like her, she thought.

"Myfwany Venders," she was saying. "Leontini, Sicily. I'm in you year, and from out-of-district, too, so I thought I'd help you get settled."

The other girl was a centimeter taller, with brick-red hair and dark freckles on skin so white it had a bluish tinge, high cheekbones, and a snub nose; big hands and feet and long limbs that hinted at future growth. She grinned: "I know how it is. They pitched me in here last year and I went around bleating like a lost lamb. It's not bad, really, once y' get to know some people."

"Thank you," Yolande replied, a little more fervently than she would have liked. Myfwany shrugged, turned and put thumb and forefinger in her mouth to whistle sharply.

"It's nothing, *veramente*. Let's get the matron."

"Missy."

Yolande stretched and turned over, burrowing into the coverlet.

"Missy. Time to get up."

That was Lele with the morning tray. She was wrapped in a robe, her own half-Asian face still cloudy with sleep.

"Thank you." The Draka yawned and stretched, rolled out of bed, and drank down the glasses of juice and milk.

The other score or so of girls in her year and section were already gathering in the courtyard, dressed like her in rough cotton exercise tunics and openwork runner's sandals, talking and yawning and helping each other stretch. Baiae School was laid out in rectangular blocks running inland from the water's edge; it was slightly chilly in the shade of the colonnade that ran around three sides of the open space, and the sun was just rising over the higher two-story block at the east end. The low-peaked roof was black against the rose-pale sky, and the sound of birds was louder than the human chatter. In the center of the court was a long pool; water spouted from a marble dolphin, and she could feel a faint trailing of mist as she walked out into the garden.

A few heads turned her way as she rummaged among the equipment on a table—weights for the ankles, and to strap around her

wrists—she bound back her hair with a sweatband, and sniffed longingly at the smells of coffee and cooking that drifted over the odor
of dew-wet grass and roses. No food for an hour or two yet.

"Ingolfsson!" It was Myfwany Venders, the redheaded one who had
greeted her at the parking lot. "Come on over here, meet the crew."
The girl from Sicily continued to her knot of friends: "This is Yolande
Ingolfsson, down from the wilds of Tuscany." She turned to the newcomer.

The introductions ended when the teacher came to lead them on
their morning run. They inclined their heads respectfully. "Now, it's
six kilometers befo' breakfast, and I'm hungry. Let's *go*."

Yolande hesitated at the entrance to the refectory, one of several
scattered throughout the complex. There were seven hundred students
at Baiae School, half of them in the senior years, and Draka did not
believe in crowding their children. In theory you could pick the dining area you wanted from among half a dozen. In practice it was not
a good idea to try pushing in where you were not wanted, and she
had tagged along with Myfwany's group from the baths where they
had all showered and swum after the run.

I feel like a lost puppy following somebody home, she thought resentfully. Back at the old school she had had her recognized set, her own
territory. Here . . . *Oh, gods, don't let me end up a goat*, she thought.
Yolande knew her own faults; enough adults had told her she was
dreamy, impractical, hot tempered. School was a matter of cliques, and
an outcast's life was just barely worth living.

The dining room was in the shape of a T, a long glass-fronted room
overlooking the bay with an unroofed terrace carried out over the water
on arches. Yolande hesitated at the colonnade at the base of the terrace, then closed the distance at a wave from one of Myfwany's friends.
There were four of them, five with her, and they settled into one of
the half-moon stone tables out at the end of the pier. It was after seven
and the sun was well up, turning the rippled surface of the bay to a
silver-blue glitter that flung eye-hurting hints of brightness back at her
like a moving mirror, or mica rocks in sunlight.

There was shade over the table, an umbrella shape of wrought-iron
openwork with a vine of Arabian jasmine trained through it. The long
flowers hung above their heads translucent white, stirring gently in
the breeze that moved the leaves and flickered dapples of dark and
bright across the white marble and tableware. Yolande stood for a
moment, looking back at the shore. You could see most of the main
building from here, stretching back north. It was a long two-story
rectangle like a comb with the back facing Vesuvius; the teeth were
enclosed courtyards running down toward the sea. The walls were pale
stone half overgrown with climbing vines, ivy or bougainvillea in sheets
of hot pink, burgundy, and purple.

Formal gardens framed the courts and the white-sand beach. At the
north end of the main block another pier ran out into the water from
a low stone boathouse; little single-masted pleasure ketches were moored
to it, and a small fishing boat that supplied the kitchens with fresh

seafood. Beyond that she could see a pair of riders galloping along the sea's edge, their horses' hooves throwing sheets of spray higher than their manes.

"Pretty," she said as she seated herself.

"Hmmm? Oh, yes, I suppose it is," Myfwany said, pressing a button in the center of the table. "Everyone know what they want?"

"Coffee, gods, coffee," one of the others said as the serving wench brought up a wheeled cart.

Yolande sniffed deeply, sighing with pleasure. The scent of the brewing pot mingled with the delicate sweetness of the flowers over their heads and the hot breads under their covers, iodine and seaweed from the ocean beneath their feet, and suddenly she was hungry. For food, for the day, for things that she could not know or name, except that they made her happy. She looked around at the faces of the others, and everything seemed clear and beautiful, everyone her friend. Even the serf, a swarthy thickset woman with a long coil of strong black hair; the identity number tattoo below her ear showed orange as she bent to fill the cup, and the coffee made an arc of dark brown from the silver spout to the pure cream color of the porcelain.

"Thank you," she said to the servant, with a bright smile. "I'll have some of those"—she pointed to a mound of biscuits, brown-topped and baked with walnuts—"and the fruit, and some of those egg pies."

"Grapefruit," Muriel said sourly, watching with envy as the others gave their orders and Yolande broke a roll. It steamed gently, and the soft yellow butter melted and sank in as soon as it was off the knife. The plump girl had lagged badly when they sprinted the last half-kilometer of the run, and bruised herself doing a front flip over one of the obstacles. The wench put two neatly sectioned halves before her. "I loathe grapefruit."

"Then don't be such a slug, Muri," Myfwany said ruthlessly, looking up from a clipboard. "You were doing quite well last year, and then spent all summer lolling about stuffin' youself with ricotta and noodle pie."

Somebody else giggled, and Muriel's face went scarlet; her expression went from sullen to angry, and then her eyes starred with unshed tears.

"Honest, Muri, everyone's just tryin' to help—" one girl began.

There was a rattle of crockery as Muriel pushed her half-eaten plate away, rose, and left at a quick walk that was almost a run. Myfwany scowled at the girl who had tittered.

"Veronica Adams, that was *mean*."

"Well, I didn't call her a *slug*, anyway."

"An' I didn't laugh at her. Are we friends, or not? I thought you two were close."

Veronica frowned and pushed strips of chicken breast and orange around her plate. "Oh, all right," she muttered. A moment later: "I'll tell her I'm sorry." A sigh. "It's just . . . all the trouble we went to, an' she slides back down the hill when we stop pushin'."

"Things aren't easy fo' her," Myfwany continued, expertly filleting her grilled trout. Aside, to Yolande: "Her parents are religious."

Yolande kept silent for a moment, biting into the biscuit and catching a crumble beneath her chin with her hand. Myfwany was obviously the leader of the group, and it would not do to offend . . . not while she was on probation.

There was a slight taste of honey and cinnamon to the pastry, blending with the richness of the butter and the hot morsels of nut. The egg pies looked good, too, baked in fluffy pastry shells with bits of bacon and scallion; she ate one in three swallows, feeling virtuous satisfaction. Her body felt good and strong and loose, warmed from the run and the swim, relaxed by the masseur's fingers.

It would not do to look tongue-tied, either. She swallowed, looked up and raised a brow. Religious . . . That *was* unusual, these days. "Aesirtru?" she asked. You still found a scattering of neopagans about, though even in her grandfather's time it had been mostly a fad.

"No, worse. Christians."

Yolande made a small shocked sound, one hand going unconsciously to her mouth. *Very* unusual, and not altogether safe. Not forbidden, precisely. After all, only a few generations ago most Draka had been at least nominal Christians. But now . . . It was enough to attract the attention of the Security Directorate. Believers were tolerated, no more, provided they kept quiet and out of the way and gave no whisper of socially dangerous opinions. The secret police took the implications of the New Testament seriously, more so than most of its followers ever had; and it could kill any chances of a commission when you did your military service, even if the *Krypteia* could do no more to you than that.

She felt the eyes of the others on her. "Well, she's a Citizen," she said with renewed calm, undoing her hair and shaking it out over her shoulders. The sea breeze caught it and threw it back, trailing ends across her eyes. "She's got a right to it, if she wants to."

Myfwany smiled with approval. "Oh, it didn't take," she said waving her fork. "That's part of the problem, we talked her out of it last year—partly us, some of the teachers helped—and then when she went home it was one quarrel with her parents after another, and she was gloomin' all the time. She'll snap out of it." Another hard look at Veronica. "*If* we help her."

"I *said* I'd say I was sorry," the girl snapped back, then bridled herself with a visible effort. Softly: "I *am* sorry." She was broad-shouldered, with a mane of curly dark-brown hair and the sharp flat accent of Alexandria and the Egyptian provinces. "What's today?"

"Intro Secondary Math 0800 to 1030," Myfwany said, glancing back at the clipboard. "Classical Lit from 1045 to 1215. Historical Geography till lunch, rest period, and then we're back to Bruiser and The Beak. Shouldn't be too bad, Beak's givin' us a familiarization lecture on rocket-launchers today."

"Moo," the third girl said. "Secondary Math." Yolande fought to remember the name. Mandy Slauter. Tall and lanky and with hair sun-faded to white, pointed chin propped in one hand. "Tensor calculus, an' Ah had trouble enough with basic. Euurg, yuk, *moo*."

"Y'can't make flying school without good math," Myfwany said, reaching for a bunch of grapes from the bowl in the center of the table. She stripped one free, flicked it up between finger and thumb and caught it out of the air with a flash of white teeth. To Yolande: "You've fallen in among a nest of would-be spacers."

They all gave an unconscious glance upward. It had only been a few years since the first flights to orbit, but that was a strong dream. Only a few thousand Draka had made the journey beyond Earth's atmosphere as yet, and rather more Americans, but it was obvious that the two power blocs who dominated the planet were moving their rivalry into space. There would be thousands needed when the time came for their call-up in half a decade.

Yolande flushed. "Me, too," she said. "Both my parents were pilots in the War." With shy pride: "Pa was an ace. Twelve kills." Some of the others looked impressed. *Thank you, Pa,* she thought. Well, it was impressive.

Mandy shrugged. "But tensor calculus . . . sometimes Ah'd rather just settle fo' the infantry. Not so much like school, anyway." She reached for a passion fruit, cracked the mottled egg-shaped shell, and dumped the speckled grayish contents into her mouth.

"How can you eat those things with your eyes open?" Veronica said. "They look like a double tablespoon of tadpoles glued together with snot." In an aside to Yolande: "Mandy's boy-crazy already, that's why she's considerin' the infantry." The pilot corps was two-thirds female, while the ground combat arms had a slight majority of men.

Mandy laughed and raised the fruit rind threateningly. "Ah am not boy-crazy—"

"Aren't we all a little old fo' food fights?" Myfwany said, looking at her watch. "Class time."

Chapter Two

BAIAE SCHOOL
DISTRICT OF CAMPANIA
PROVINCE OF ITALY
DOMINATION OF THE DRAKA
SEPTEMBER 18, 1968

It was full dark now on the beach, and the driftwood fire crackled, sending sparks flying up with sharp popping sounds. The flames were blue and red and orange, a white-crimson over the bed of coals below; the smell was dry and hot. Inland, the trees and shrubs rustled, shadows dark and moving against the lesser dark of the sky. The waves were breaking in a foam of cream, glittering in starlight and moonlight, surge and retreat. The sound of them was like heartbeat in her ears, like lying beside some huge and friendly beast. Out beyond, her friends were still diving and playing, flashes of white bodies otter-sleek among the water. Their voices dropped into the warm night, no louder than the cicadas and night birds.

Yolande laid her head on her knees and wiggled her toes over the edge of the blanket. The powdery white clung to them like frosting; she tapped her feet together and felt the grains trickle down her insteps, tickling or clinging where the skin was still damp from her swim. Looking up, the moon path lay on the water like silver, almost painfully bright. The stars were sparse around the moon, abundant elsewhere; the lights of men were far too few to dim them. A faint glow west across the bay was Naples, and she could make out the long curve of the coast by the wide-scattered jewels that marked the towns and manors of her people.

She lay back on the striped wool and smiled, stretching her arms above her head. Stars . . . there was a trick to that. A mental effort, and the velvet backdrop with its glowing colored lights vanished; instead there was *depth*, an endless dark where great fires hung burning forever amid the slow-fading hydrogen roar of creation. Her lips parted, and she felt a sensation that might have been delight, or a loneliness too great to bear; she forced herself to hold the wordless moment, mind suspended in pure experience. Moisture gathered slowly around her eyes, trickling in warm salt streaks down the wind-cooled skin of her temples.

"Woof!" Mandy's voice. "I'm turning into a *prune*. Come on!"

Yolande started as the others dashed out of the ocean, wiping away the not-quite tears with the back of her wrist. They ran past her to the freshwater fountain at the edge of the beach, laughing and splashing each other around as they sluiced off the salt. The darkness closed around as they threw themselves down on the blankets about the fire; now it was a hearth, the tribe's fortress against the night. Myfwany sat cross-legged beside her, leaning back on braced palms. She was still breathing deeply from the swim; from Yolande's position her face was shadowed against the backlit dark-red curtain of her hair. The drops of water that ran down her flanks glistened with the rise and fall of her chest, changing from blood-crimson to lemon-yellow.

"You're quiet, 'Landa," she said. "Head still troublin'?"

"Mmm . . . no. Hammerin' great headache yesterday, couldn't hardly move this mornin'. Now it's just a bit stiff all ovah. No, I's just lookin' at the stars and thinkin'."

Myfwany probed at her neck, tracing the cords down to her shoulders; she shivered slightly at the touch, still cold and wet. " 'S right, stiff," Myfwany said definitely. "Maybe swimmin' wasn't such a good idea. Muriel, give me a hand? Roll ovah, 'Landa."

Yolande turned onto her stomach and laid her cheek on her crossed hands, feeling a painful warmth in her stomach. "Thanks," she muttered. Massage was usually serf's work, although everybody learned it; it was something you did for close friends, a sign that status was put aside. Two pairs of hands began to work on her, one starting on the soles of her feet, the other where the neck muscles anchored on the base of her skull. She felt uncomfortable for an instant, as the pressure made her aware of soreness she had been ignoring, then surrendered to the sensation.

"Y'all bein' mighty nice," she said sincerely. Myfwany snorted, and Muriel laughed and slapped her lightly on the calf.

"You the one bruised the Bruiser," Mandy said. She was kneeling by a basket across the fire, rummaging within. "Never seen her move so fast; mean of her to thump you head, though."

"No, that's the point," Myfwany said. "Bruiser *had* to move fast, an' react automatic-like."

"Jus' so—*Veronica, watch where you puttin' that dirt!* I's got *scallops* in heah!"

The stocky girl had been raising the fine sand in double handfuls, letting it trickle down over her body. She laughed and bent backward from her kneeling position until her head touched the blanket behind her, a perfect bow, stretching.

" 'Salright," she said as she rose. A sigh. "Ah jus' *love* this time of year. Perfect, just cool enough fo' a fire, but not cold. Look! There it is!"

She raised a hand. They followed the gesture, and saw a moving star crawling slowly across the southern horizon.

"That our'n or their'n?" Mandy asked. The Domination and the Alliance had both put up another dozen orbital platforms in the last few years; the rivalry was pushing development hard.

"Ours," Myfwany said, sinking back on her elbows. "Oh, ours." Her voice became dreamy. "I wonder . . . how do the stars look from *there*?" To Yolande: "What were you thinkin' of, starwatcher?"

"Lots of things," Yolande said abstractedly. "How we can't see the stars, jus' the light they sent long ago. Like readin' a book, hey? An' . . . how far away, an' how perfect."

"Perfect?"

"There's no right or wrong with them," Yolande continued, almost singsong, whispering. "No lovin' or hatin'; they just . . . *are*."

They were silent for long minutes, each staring upward past the fire glow and the dancing sparks.

"Well," Mandy said, her hands moving again in the basket. "Who's fo' lemonade, and who's fo' wine?"

"Mm, I'll take the wine," Yolande said.

"Lemonade first, I'm too thirsty fo' drinkin'," Myfwany said. "That enough, 'Landa?"

"Feels nice," she replied.

Veronica and Mandy were making skewers from a pile of willow switches, sharpening the ends and threading on pieces of scallop and shrimp wrapped in bacon; they handed the limber sticks around, with wicker platters of soft flat Arab bread, and glasses. The five girls drew closer to the fire. Yolande sat up, watching the flames. The breeze had picked up slightly, and gusts of it blew the tongues of colored flame toward her. She sipped at the wine as the bacon sizzled and dropped fat to pop and flare on the white coals; it was cool from the earthenware jug, rather light, slightly acidic. A southern vintage, she thought, probably from Latium.

"Strange," Muriel said, hugging her knees and leaning back, letting her head fall against Veronica's shoulder.

"What?" Mandy asked.

"I was thinkin' . . . here we are. In twenty-odd years our own daughters will be here, or someplace like here. Maybeso raaht here; maybeso doin' and thinkin' just what we are. Strange."

"What brought that on?" Myfwany said. She brought the skewer close, examined the seafood critically, and used a piece of the flatbread to pull it off. "Mmm, these are *good*."

"I was . . . I was thinkin' about history class. An' about the things Ma and Pa used to tell me, you know, those religion things." Muriel stuck the butt end of her skewer into the sand and rolled the wine cup between her hands. "I mean . . . if you believes all that, the God stuff, then"—she frowned—"then it would all look different. It would be *comin'* from somewheres, and *goin'* to somewheres. Like-so a story, hey? An' if you don't believe it, then it's . . . all sort of, well, it just *happens*."

"If'n yo believes it, we're all goin' straight to hell," Veronica laughed, giving a light tug on Muriel's brown curls.

"Pass the wine, will you, hey?" Yolande said. There was a clink of stoneware. "Thanks, Mandy. Well, the way Harris says it, it's the story of the Race; where we came from an' where we're goin'."

Muriel rested her chin on the edge of the cup. "That sort of depends, don't it? I mean, the *Race* didn't have to happen; Harris says so herself. History's a story leadin' up to *us*, but only on account we happened. If the Yankees killed us all off, then it'd be a story about *them*, an' we'd just be part of their history."

"But we did happen, an' the Yankees aren't goin' to win; we are," Myfwany said definitely.

Yolande chuckled. "So the story has an endin' and a meanin' because we're tellin' it." A pause. "Us here, too. It's . . . true because we make it true, eh? So we tell history like ouah own story, like we was writin' it. Like God."

The others looked at her. "Say, that's really pretty clever," Myfwany said.

Yolande flushed and looked down into her wine cup, continuing hastily. "Speakin' of which, what *are* we goin' to do once we've conquered the Yankees?"

Myfwany laughed. "My brothah, Billy? He likes the Yankee movies; says the girls look nice. Says he's goin' buy a dozen when we put the Yoke on them."

"Euuu, yuk, *boys*," Mandy said. "Oops, this is overdone. . . ."

"Ah thought you *liked* boys," Veronica said. She bent her head to whisper something in Muriel's ear, and the other girl giggled and worked her eyebrows.

Yolande looked at Veronica and flushed again; the Alexandrian girl was no older, but she had definite breasts, and the dark-brown hair between her legs was thick and abundant. It made her conscious of her own undeveloped form again. And . . . *strange about sex and things*, she mused. *When you young, you know about it an' it isn't all that interestin', an' all of a sudden it's scary an' important*. She shook her head; at least there was a while before she had to worry about that sort of thing. *Freya's curse, I hate being shy!*

"I do like boys," Mandy said. "At least I sort of like the *idea* of 'em. But they still sort of yucky, too. You know, my brothah Manfred, he only a year older than me, an' he's got ouah cook pregnant? Ma found him ridin' her in the pantry, an' cook's *thirty*, with a bottom a meter across an' a mustache. I mean, we're not planters, we've only got a dozen house serfs, but Pa bought him a regular concubine when he turned thirteen, and still he goes an' does things like that." She brooded for a moment. "Yucky."

"My ma," Yolande began, "says it's on account of they don't have enough blood." She grinned at their blank looks and held out a hand, palm-up, then slowly curled up her index finger. "You know, all the blood rushes to they crotch, their brains shut down fo' lack of oxygen, an' they stop thinkin'?"

There was a moment of silence, and Yolande felt a flash of fear that her joke had fallen flat. Then the laughter began and ran for a full half-minute, before trailing off into teary giggles.

"Aii, that's a good one," Muriel said. She glanced up at the stars again. "When we've beaten the Yankees, we'll put up mo' of those power satellites my pa's workin' on."

"Build cities on the moon!"

"Turn Venus into anothah Earth!"

"Give Mars an atmosphere!"

"Hollow out asteroids an' fly 'em to Alpha Centauri!" The comments flew faster and faster, more and more outrageous, until everyone collapsed into giggles again. Myfwany rose, and pulled out a velvet case from their bundles.

"This is your'n, isn't it, 'Landa?"

"Yes—careful!" Yolande took the long shape in her hands; they moved toward it with unconscious gentleness. "It's a mandolin."

Muriel whistled between her teeth. "An' Archona's a city. Old one, hey?"

"My great grandma's," Yolande said. She put the pick between her teeth while she arranged the case across her lap, then settled the instrument and slipped it onto her hand. "On my ma's side, she Confederate-born. Had it fancied up some . . ." She tuned it quickly; the strings sounded, plangent under the fire crackle and *shhhhh* of the waves. The wood was smooth as satin under her fingers, the running leopards inlaid in ivory around the soundbox as familiar as her own hands.

"Well, give's a song, then," Myfwany said.

"I don't sing all that well—"

"C'mon," Mandy said. "We'll all join in."

"Oh, all right." Yolande bent her head, then tossed it as the long pale ripple of her hair fell across the strings. She swept through the opening bars, a rapid flourish, and began to sing: an alto, pure but not especially strong.

> " 'Twas in the merry month of May
> When green buds all were swellin'
> Sweet William on his deathbed lay
> Fo' love of Bar'bra Allen—"

The ancient words echoed out along the lonely beach; everyone knew *that* one, at least. They all had well-trained voices as well, of course; that was part of schooling. Myfwany's sounded as if it would be a soprano, rich and rather husky. Muriel's was a bit reedy, and Veronica's had an alarming tendency to quaver; Mandy's was like her own, but with more volume. They finished, gaining confidence, and swung into "Lord Randal" and "The Wester Witch."

"What next?" Veronica said. "How about something modern?"

"Alison Ghoze?" Muriel said.

Mandy made a face.

"Oh, moo. Call that modern? It's a hundred years old; modern if'n you count anythin' after the land-takin'."

"I—" Yolande strummed, forced the stammer out of her voice. "I've got somethin' new, care to hear it?"

The others nodded, leaning back. *Calm. Breathe deep. Out slow.* She began the opening bars, and felt the silence deepen; a few seconds later and she was conscious of nothing at all but the music and the strings.

It ended, and there was a long sigh.

"Now, *that* was good," Myfwany said. She half-sang the last verse to herself again:

> "An' we are scatterin's of
> Dragon seed
> On a journey to the stars!
> Far below we leave—forever
> All dreams of what we were."

"Who *wrote* that, anyways?"

"I—" Yolande coughed. "I did."

They clapped, and she grinned back at them. Mandy laughed and jumped to her feet.

"C'mon, let's dance—Muriel, get you flute out!"

The silver-bound bamboo sounded, a wild trilling, cold and plangent and sweet. Yolande cased her mandolin and joined the others in a clap-and-hum accompaniment. The tall girl danced around the outer circle of the firelight, whirling, the colored driftwood flames painting streaks of green and blue across the even matte tan of her skin and the long wheat-blond hair. She spun, cartwheeled, backflipped, leaped high in an impossible pirouette, feet seeming to barely touch the sand.

"C'mon, you slugs, *dance!*" she cried.

> " . . . as we dance beneath the moon
> As we dance beneath the moon!"

Myfwany came to her feet and seized Yolande's hand in her right, Muriel's in her left. "Ring dance!" she said. "Let's dance the moon to sleep!"

"Oh, wake up, Pietro," Veronica said, kicking the serf lightly in the side. He started up from the grass beside the little electric runabout and loaded the parcels as they pulled on their tunics and found seats.

"Do y'know," Mandy said, tying off her belt, "that the Yankees wear *clothes* to go swimmin'?"

Veronica made a rude noise. "And go' takin' baths, too."

"No, it's true, darlin'," Muriel said. "My pa visited there, an' they do." She outlined the shape of a bikini. "Like underwear."

"Strange," Myfwany said. They settled in for the kilometer ride back to the main buildings; nothing else moved on the narrow asphalt ribbon of the road, save once an antelope caught in the headlights for an instant with mirror-shining eyes. It was much darker now after moonset, and they rode with an air of satisfied quiet.

"Go into Naples tomorrow?" Veronica said. Tomorrow was a Sunday, their only completely free day.

"Fine with me," Mandy said; Muriel nodded agreement, and Myfwany nudged Yolande with an elbow.

"How 'bout it?" she said casually.

"Why—" Yolande smiled shyly; this was acceptance no longer tentative. "Why, sho'ly."

The runabout ghosted to a silent halt by the east side entrance. They made their farewells and scattered; Yolande blinked as she walked into the brighter lights of the halls and colonnades. It was after twelve and there were not many about; twice she had to skirt areas where the house serfs were at their nightly scrubbing and polishing.

"Missy?" That was Bianca, yawning and blinking up from a mat by the entrance—Yolande's own door, looking more familiar now somehow. Machiavelli yowled and circled until she picked him up; the cat settled in to purr as she rubbed behind his ears, sniffing with interest at the shrimp scent on her fingers.

"Jus' turn down the bed, put this stuff away, then go to sleep," Yolande said, padding through to her bedroom. *How do I feel?* she asked herself, with relaxed curiosity. Tingly from the swim, tired from that and the dancing. Relaxed . . . *Happy*, she decided. *Maybe that's part of growin'.* When you were a child, happiness was part of the day, like sadness over a skinned knee or sunlight on your face. Till one day you *knew* you were happy, and knew that it would pass.

"Tomorrow's also a day," she muttered to herself, setting the cat down on the coverlet. She yawned hugely, enjoying the ready-to-sleep sensation; that was odd, how it felt good when you knew you could rest, and hurt if you had to stay up. The bed was soft and warm; she nuzzled into the pillow and felt the cat arranging itself against the back of her knees. "Tomorrow . . ."

Chapter Three

CLAESTUM PLANTATION
DISTRICT OF TUSCANY
PROVINCE OF ITALY
APRIL 1969

The aircar was a Trevithick Meerkat, a little crowded with six. Shiny new and smelling of fresh paint and synthetics; civilian production had just gotten under way, and they were still expensive enough that only the more affluent Citizens could afford them. Yolande, Myfwany, and Mandy were squeezed into the backseat, with Muriel in the front and Veronica on her lap, careful not to jostle the driver. He was a serious-looking young serf, thin and very black, flying cautiously, trained at the Trevithick Combine's works in Diskarapur in the far south. A pilot and two mechanics had come with the aircraft.

"Oh, hurry up, boy," Yolande said irritably as he banked the car into a circle at a thousand meters and began a slow descent, the ducted-fan engines turning down for lift. They had been slow getting away; the eight-month academic year was ending, and the Baiae landing fields had been crowded. Of course, an aircar like this could be driven by road and take off from any convenient open space, but serfs operated machinery by the book. Her hands itched to take the controls; this was all fly-by-wire, you *couldn't* redline it, the computers wouldn't let you. . . .

"Just you parents to home?" Veronica asked, turning her head and resting it on Muriel's shoulder.

"Mmm-hm," Yolande replied. "Edwina and Dionysia both turned eighteen last year; they in Third Airborne, stationed near Shanghai. John would've been out but they picked him fo' officer's trainin'." That meant an extra year's active service beyond the usual three, or possibly more. "He might be back on leave soon, though. . . . Ma said her cousin Alicia's up from the south; she's in textiles, Shahnapur. Just got divorced, up here restin' like. May move up."

The sound of the fans altered as they came to a halt a hundred meters up and lowered with a smooth elevator sensation.

497

"Oooo, woof, nice," Mandy said from her right, as their descent gave a slow panorama of Claestum Manor. "I like it when they use the old things."

There were admiring murmurs as the aircar extended its wheels with a cling-*chung*, and Yolande felt a warm glow of pride like sun on bare skin. They had landed at the southern entrance of the main building, where the road widened into a small plaza after its winding journey up from the Quarters and through the gardens. Ahead was the house complex, and the tall oaks and chestnuts that crowned the hill and tumbled down the northern slope.

It is *pretty*, she thought, trying to look at it as a stranger might. Her parents had laid out the Great House in the shape of a U along the south-facing slope, with its apex open to the woods at the crest. Both flanks were old Tuscan work from the pre-War town, each ending in a tower; weathered red tiles and sienna-colored stone overgrown with flowering vines. The newer buildings knitted them together, and the southern end of the U was closed by a curved block in classic Draka style; two stories of ferroconcrete sheathed in jade-green African marble. Fluted pillars of white Carrara ran from the veranda past the second-story gallery to end in golden acanthus leaves at the roof, and the windows behind were etched glass and silver.

"Oh, it's all right," Yolande said casually, as the gullwing doors of the aircar soughed open. She put a hand on the rim of the passenger compartment and vaulted out.

Home, she thought, swallowing. *It smells like home*. Green, after the filtered pressurized atmosphere of the aircraft; the mildly warm fresh-green scent of a Tuscan spring. Odors of stone, dust, flowers, water from the two fountains that flanked the wrought-iron gates into the central courtyard. The piazza of checkered brick beneath her feet was where she had learned to ride a bicycle, the trees flanking it were ones she had watched grow. Her parents had been waiting beneath the gate, out of reach of the miniature duststorm an aircar made in landing. They came forward as their daughter's friends clambered out of the Meerkat. Yolande swallowed again and drew herself up calmly, cleared her throat.

"Hello, Mother, Father," she said. One of the house girls behind the Landholders was coming forward with a curtsy, bearing a courtesy tray with a carafe and glasses. Yolande smiled with a flush of pleasure. There would be a formal greeting; her parents were treating her friends as adults, not casually as children.

"Service to the State," her father said. He was a stocky man and rather short for a Draka, no more than 175 centimeters, dressed in planter's working clothes: boots and loose chamois trousers, cotton shirt and gunbelt, and a broad-brimmed hat in one hand. Hazel eyes and gray streaks through seal-brown hair and mustache. "Thomas Ingolfsson, Landholder, pilot, retired," he continued.

"Johanna Ingolfsson," her mother took up, handing out the glasses and raising her own. "Landholder, pilot, retired. Glory to the Race." She was a finger's breadth taller than her husband: a wiry-slender blond woman in her forties with a handsome hatchet face and scarring around her left eye, dressed in a long black robe with bands of silver mesh at neck and throat. They all poured out the ceremonial drops and sipped, murmuring the formula. The wine was a light, slightly sweet white; not the *classico* vintage that was Claestum's pride, but that was a red dinner wine and unsuitable as an aperitif. "Well, do the honors, daughter."

"Myfwany Venders, Arethustra Plantation, Sicily." she said. Myfwany clasped forearms with both the elder Ingolfssons. "Mandy Slauter, from Naples; Veronica Adams, Two Oaks Plantation, Lusitanica; Muriel Quintellan, Haraldsdal Plantation, Campania."

Her parents went through the ritual gravely. Then her mother turned to her and smiled, spreading her arms. "But *you* are still my baby 'Landa, hey?"

Yolande flung herself forward, and felt the familiar slender strength of her mother's arms around her, pressed her face into the hard curve of neck and shoulder. It smelled of soap and a faint rose perfume and the clean summery odor of Johanna's body, the scent of comfort and belonging. "Hello, Mama," she whispered. "Thanks awfully." Her mother held her out at arm's length.

"You *are* fillin' out," she said. Yolande grinned with pride, then gave a whoop of surprise as hands gripped her under the arms and swung her in a circle.

"Y'are indeed, but still bird-light," her father said, laughing up into her indignant face.

"Daddy! Put me *down!*" He laughed again, giving her a toss; she felt the strength in his hands as he lowered her, gently controlled and as irresistible as a machine.

"Greetin's, child," he said. To the others: "Y'all will fo'give me, ladies; I've got an overseer gone and broke her leg, and fo' hundred hectares of vines to finish prunin', while my wife lazes about." He nodded and strode down the plaza, where a groom led a horse forward.

"If he thinks wrestlin' with that accountin' computer and those League bureaucrats—" Johanna shook her head. "Well. Friends of my daughter, y'all are to consider Claestum you own, and make youselves to home. Veronica an' Muriel, I'm puttin' you together?" The friends were standing hand in hand; they exchanged a glance and nodded, smiling. "East tower, then; you servants an' baggage arrived safe last sundown. Or pick another if it doesn't suit; one thing this stone barn's not anyhow short of, it's space. 'Landa, I'm puttin' y'other two friends directly either side of you old rooms over t' the west tower. Rahksan heah will settle you in, and see y'all at lunch."

"Oh, it *is* good to be home," Yolande said, throwing her gunbelt on a table and sinking into a wicker chair. "Shut up, cat, if'n I'd taken you by air, you'd have puked."

Machiavelli looked up from the cushions of the chair opposite, giving her a cool green-eyed stare of resentment before ostentatiously grooming. He had been sent ahead by train with her luggage and maids, and would be a while forgiving her. The Draka girl shed her boots with a push of instep against heel, and let them drop; she peeled off her socks with her toes and rubbed the sole of each foot down the drill fabric of the opposite pants leg.

Rahksan laughed, scooping up the holstered pistol and racking it neatly on the stand beside the door before picking up the boots. "Good to have yaz back, Mistis 'Landa," she replied, examining the scuffed heels. " 'T cat Ah could do without."

Yolande sighed, linked her fingers behind her head and stretched, wiggling bare toes against the edge of the reading table as she watched the serf drop the footwear outside the entranceway to the corridor and begin unpacking the hand case Yolande had brought with her in the aircar. She could feel her mind settling into the familiar spaces, at rest with every cranny of the rooms that had been hers since she moved down from the nursery. There was the old tower above, with its spiral staircase; the rooftop aerie, a private study below, then her bedroom. This lounging room on the ground floor, lined with bookcases and the tapestries Uncle Eric had looted from Florence during the War and given for her naming feast. Her desk, over there in the corner; a video screen, her own retrieval terminal to the House computer, the new digital sound system she had gotten for her thirteenth birthday. Chinese rugs on the gray-marble tiles of the floor, glowing in the bright morning light that streamed through the glass doors of the terrace.

Rahksan came back from taking her toiletries through into the bathing rooms. Yolande looked at her more closely. The Afghan had been a fixture of her life as long as she could remember. Ma had been given her as a present by an uncle when they were both five, to raise as she might a puppy or a kitten, a ragged girl-child pulled out of the rubble of a gassed village during the conquest of her wild and mountainous homeland. She was a short woman, round-faced and curve-nosed and slightly plump, big-breasted and -hipped, with curling dark hair still glossy despite the silver streaks.

"You lookin' good," the young Draka said affectionately. Rahksan had done much of the day-to-day rearing of the Ingolfsson children, and supervised the serf nursemaids. "Younger, or at least thinner."

"Tanks kindly, Mistis," Rahksan said, running a complacent hand down from silk blouse to pleated cream-colored skirt. With a slight grimace: "Had to live on rabbit food, an' swim ever' day till I thought mebbeso I'd grow fins, but I shed five kilos." A sly wink. "Certain person said it'd be all lonely nights if'n I didn't."

Yolande smiled and closed her eyes, surprised at her own brief embarrassment. She had always known that her mother slept with Rahksan occasionally, at least since she was old enough to be conscious of such things at all. It was nothing unusual. For that matter her father had probably sired Rahksan's own son; he had the look. *But it's sort of uncomfortable to imagine Ma and her actually . . .* doing *it,* she thought. And it still sounded a bit strange to hear "Mistis" instead of the child's title of "Missy."

"How's Ali?" she asked, changing the subject. "Drink, please. Youself, too."

Rahksan slapped her forehead. "Ali! That boy!"

There was a sideboard near the stairs with a recessed chilling unit, the usual. The serf poured two glasses of lemonade, handed one to Yolande, and sank gracefully to her knees, sitting back on her heels; it would not have been fitting for her to use the chair, of course.

"Ah *swear* he do things jus' t'grieve his ma—" She shrugged. "Do mah best fo' him, and what do Ah get? Trouble an' gray hairs. He workin' in the House stables now." A sniff, and grudging admission. "Doin' right well. Mastah say he natural with horses, mebbeso head groom somedays. Still, he doin' field-hand work when he coulda lived clean an' been clerk o' somethin' here in t' House."

She drank, and rolled the cup between her palms. "I tell him you 'quires, Mistis, tank y'kindly."

Yolande cleared her throat. "Did Myf . . . did my friends like they rooms?" she asked.

"Why, sho'ly," Rahksan said blandly, finishing her juice and rising to replace the etched-glass tumbler on the counter; her back was to Yolande for a moment. "They all settled in good." A pause. "That Mistis Myfwany, she a fine young lady," she continued. "Mos' particulah interested in you, Mistis, ask questions an' all." Another pause. "Powerful pretty, too."

"We're good friends!" Yolande snapped. "All of us," she added.

"Did Ah says different? A body'd thinks mebbeso you was sweet on somebody . . ." She turned, a wide grin flashing white against her olive face.

"Oooh—!" Yolande half rose, flushed with anger, then sank back, joining helplessly in Rahksan's laughter. "You *impossible*, Rahksan!" she said, throwing a pillow.

"No, jus' impudent an' triflin'; comes a' havin' wiped you butt an' changed you diapers . . ." The smile softened. "Didn' mean hurt you feelings, sweetlin'," she said warmly, laying a hand on her shoulder.

"You didn't," the girl said, throwing her arms around the short woman's waist and laying her head on the comforting softness of her bosom. "Oh, Tantie Rahksan, maybe I am sweet on her, a little . . . I don't know, it's all mixed up, don't know *what* I want." A sniffle that broke into a sob. "Why can't everything be simple, like it used to?"

"There, chile, there," Rahksan replied, stroking her hair. "My little 'Landa growin' up, is all." She hummed softly in her throat, rocking the Draka girl for quiet minutes. "Some day you looks back on *this* as y' happy an' simple time. Be happy in it; growin' is painful sometime, but believe me, bettah than agin'." A rueful chuckle. "T'ings works that way, sweetlin'. Wait fo', five years an' you starts gettin' interested in boys, now *that* complicated. They a lot mo' different."

Yolande giggled tearily and made a mock-retching sound. The serf bent and kissed the top of her head. "Y'change y'mind somedays, girl. They necessary, an' mighty nice in they own way. Anyways, take things as they come. Here."

The serf produced a handkerchief, and proceeded to wipe Yolande's face. The girl surrendered to the childlike sensation, but reclaimed the linen to blow her own nose. She was grown-up, or almost, after all.

"Thanks, Rahksan," she muttered. "Sorry I was so silly." Looking up, she saw the blotch her tears had made on the front of the other's blouse, and winced with embarrassment. "Didn't mean to be such a waterin' pot." That prompted remembrance: she felt in her pocket. "Got somethin' fo' you in Palermo last month."

Rahksan unwrapped the tissue and opened the small blue jeweler's box. "Why, Mistis 'Landa!" she exclaimed, lifting out the locket. It was a slim oval of pale gold rimmed in pearls, on a slender platinum chain. She opened it, holding the cameo up to the light; a classical piece in the modern setting, translucent white against indigo blue glass, a woman's head wreathed in a spray of tiny gold olive leaves. "That beautiful, sweetlin'; nice to remember y' ol' Tantie Rahksan."

"I'll nevah fo'get you, Rahksan," she said quietly.

"Well." The serf put the chain around her neck, then bent to kiss Yolande on the forehead. "Whenevah y'needs somebodies t' talk to . . . o' cry on, Mistis . . . Ah'm theah." A glance at her watch. "Bettah get goin'. Mastah John's rooms need a check; them useless bedwenches of his neglects things somethin' awful. That Colette, particular."

Yolande watched her leave and finished the lemonade, vaguely ashamed of the display of emotion. *I'm too old for tears, really. . . .* The sadness was gone, though. Now she felt truly relaxed; this was her home ground, after all. She undid her cravat and pulled it loose to finish wiping her face, then tossed it aside, undid the top button of her shirt, and held the Egyptian linen away from her skin. *I am filling out*, she thought with satisfaction. Not much, but then Ma wasn't much bigger, and she was the most beautiful person in the world. What had she said? "Anything more than a handful is a waste." Curious, she touched the smooth shallow curve with the pads of her fingers. In biology class the teacher said breasts were mostly an ornament, like a peacock's tail. The touch had a sort of shivery feel to it, almost like an itch.

Her fingertips brushed across the pointed pink cone of the nipple, and she jerked the hand away; it was the sort of sensation that could feel good or bad, depending. Too strong, anyway.

She rose to her feet and paced, letting her hand trail across the bookshelves. Good friends here: *Gulliver's Travels,* her *Alice Underland* and *Looking-Glass World*, family heirlooms in smooth leather and stamped-gilt titles. Some she could remember her mother reading to her at bedtimes; others she had discovered herself. The old books had a rich scent all their own, leather and the glue of their bindings and a slight hint of dust that reminded her of summer afternoons. She opened one and smiled to herself; there was a vine leaf still pressed where she remembered, brown and gossamer-fragile. They had seemed so big, then, filling her lap, the smooth paper with the dyed edges transparent gateways to wonder. Verne, Stevenson, Lalique, Halgelstein, Dobson. Illustrated histories, and the *Thousand and One Nights*; most of all horse books: riding, breeding, showing.

There were models on the shelves as well, from the time when flying had won co-equal place in her heart with the stables. Early machines: Pa had gotten the model of the *Ahriman* for her; it was nearly a hundred years old and had been made when the first war dirigible was launched. An odd looking machine, cigar-shaped with the spiral wooden framework dimpling the fabric covering, and big room-fan type propellers jutting out from the gondola. Miniatures of her parents' Eagle fighters, from the Eurasian War. Pencil-slim twin-engined planes, perfect down to the blackened exhaust trails behind the big prop engines and the kill-marks on the wings; they had been going-away gifts from their ground crews. A plastic suborb missile she had put together herself from a kit: a slender sinister black dart. And a scramjet fighter, long slim delta shape banking in frozen motion on its stand. She touched that, symbol of freedom from earth's bounds and gravity's pull.

There were data-plaques piled beside her terminal. Yolande grimaced at the size of the stack of the palm-sized wafers, in school colors; enough to keep her busy several hours a day. She put her palm against the screen for the identity check and pushed a wafer into the slot beside it. The machine chimed: *Introduction to Evolutionary Ecology.* Text and pictures flickered by, moving diagrams showing energy flows, reconstructions. Feathered dinosaurs and ground apes from Olduvai—and space for the data she would be entering, answers, and essays. That would be interesting, at least, but mind and body rebelled at the thought of more study now.

She turned through the open glass doors to the ground-level terrace instead, and reached overhead to grip the steel bar just outside. Moodily she began a series of chin-lifts, stopping at fifty to hang with her knees curled close to her chest and controlling her breathing to a deep steady rhythm. Bruiser said it was the best way to clear your mind for thinking: let the muscles soak up and burn the hormonal juices the body tried to cloud your mind with. *It's a good remedy for confusion,* she thought wryly. *If I could be sure what I'm confused* about.

"Hio, 'Landa." The terrace outside her rooms ran all along the west front of the building, but her section was separated by a carved-stone screen that ran out to the low balustrade. Myfwany's face leaned around it, smiling. "Want company, or you set on devolvin' into a gibbon?"

"C'mon ovah," Yolande said. She raised herself to chest-height against the bar, counting twenty slow breaths, then dropped to the ground, acutely conscious of her rumpled state. "Everythin' all right?"

"Better than that," Myfwany said, swinging around the balustrade. "Been lookin' forward to seein' you homeplace quite some time, now. Can't know a person till you've seen where they come from, hey?"

The other girl had shot up these last six months, and standing flat-footed on the tile pavement, Yolande's eyes were level with her nose. She had changed already, into a round-necked cream-silk sleeveless shirt and fawn trousers; there were bracelets in the form of curled snakes pushed up on her upper arms, and a fillet of the same silvery metal holding back the red curls that fell to her neck. They walked to the balustrade together, leaning on the stone and looking down. Yolande cast a covert eye to her side, admiring the way the platinum snakes seemed to ripple as the muscle moved beneath the freckled skin of Myfwany's arms.

"Utilities an' such?" the redhead asked, nodding downslope.

The hill fell away gently to the northwest. There was a strip of lawn three meters below them, then terraces behind low brick retaining walls, flowerbanks and cypresses, fountains and stairways. At the base of the slope the buildings began, two rows of them built back into the slope so that the pale yellow tile of their roofs made steps leading down to the pool at the bottom. They were half-hidden from here by the trees planted about them, chestnuts and oaks.

"House stables, toolsheds, garages, some sleepin' quarters," Yolande
answered. Most of the house girls bunked in the attics, but not the garden
staff. The plantation's transformer was down there, too; electricity came
in by underground cable, brought down from the hydro plants in the
mountains. She laid a hand on Myfwany's. "Thanks . . . thanks fo' comin'
along, Myf. Missin' goin' to you home, and all. Would've been lonely,
without."

Myfwany turned her hand palm-up and squeezed for a moment before
releasing the other girl's fingers. "No great sacrifice," she said quietly,
not looking around; she smoothed the wind-tossed hair back from her
face. "Got to get it cut . . . My stepmother an' me don't get on so
well, anyhows."

Yolande tried to imagine what it would be like, for her mother to
die and a stranger take her place, and shivered. "Come on, there's
time for a swim befo' lunch."

There was a shout from the pool. Johanna Ingolfsson looked up from
her papers, and saw her daughter balanced on her red-haired friend's
shoulders. The other girl reached up; they clasped wrists and Yolande
did a slow handstand, grinning downward through dangling strands
of wet blond hair.

"Now!" she said.

Myfwany pushed up and Yolande twisted, doing a complete three
hundred and sixty degree turn before arrowing into the water headfirst.
Johanna nodded approvingly as the sleek body eeled along the bottom of the pool for a dozen meters before breaking surface and crawl-
stroking for the far end. Myfwany followed. They paused for a moment,
treading water and hyperventilating, then dove for a game of subsur-
face tag. Johanna quirked a lip. *Not the only type of touching friend
Myfwany has in mind, if I can still read the signs,* she thought.

"Looks like my youngest might make a pilot; got the reflexes, at
least," she said musingly. "About time, the first three bein' in the ever-
lovin' *infantry* of all things."

Rahksan chuckled; she was sitting on a cushion at the bottom of
the lounger, embroidering a circle of silk held in a wicker frame.
"Mebbeso she pick the Navy, eh, Mistis?"

Johanna snorted and reached for the glass of cooler. The outdoor
pool was set along the eastern flank of the Great House, along the
outer rim of the terrace built up and out from the hillside. It had been
convenient; the space beneath provided room for things best tucked
away, the heat-pump system, the fuel cell for the war shelter deep in
the rock beneath the manor, the armory, a laundry . . . a pleasant
place for an outdoor lunch, as well. One hundred meters by twenty-
five, with a basic pavement of black onyx marble they had gotten cheap
after the War, stripped from ruined *palazzi* in Sienna. The rough stone
of the wall behind them was overgrown with bougainvillea, bright now
with pink-purple garlands; low limestone troughs held banks of clematis,
pearl rhododendrons, azaleas; there were stone bowls with topiaries
and small trees, or lilac bushes for the scent.

The older Draka returned her attention to the documents. There had been *another* change in the League accounting procedures for olive-oil delivery, specifically the extra-virgin first pressing Tuscan that Claestum produced for the restaurant trade. The Landholders' League bureaucrats never seemed to tire of searching for the perfect paper-work solution.

"Lady Freya bless," she muttered. "Some day the civil service will grow right over the Domination like-so coral on a reef, an' we'll all freeze in place." She made a notation, signed, and snapped her fingers. "Guido, take these an' give them to the bookkeeper; we have to have *written acknowledgment* from the Florence office, tell her that." Next thing would be to do a check on the irrigation piping in the orchards, hands-on work, but that could wait until after lunch.

Stretching, she looked back at the pool. Yolande was sitting on the edge of the little island at its center; there was a two-meter-high alabaster vase in the center of that, with water cascading down from a spout in its center. She was smiling and swinging her legs, talking to Myfwany as she floated nearby; Johanna could hear their laughter over the sound of the fountain. Her mother turned her head to the other lounger where . . . Mandy Slauter, that was her name. Lying up on one elbow under the dappled shade of the pergola, fanning herself with her hat; a nice enough girl, a bit citified, but it was good that Yolande was making friends outside Landholder circles. Some people liked to pretend it was still 1860, but the Domination had changed; unless you were prepared to rusticate all your life, connections in the urban classes were essential.

Johanna nodded in the direction of the pool. "They two seem to get on very well," she said. Mandy nodded. "Are they sleepin' together yet?" she continued casually.

Mandy blinked and coughed, would have squirmed if etiquette permitted. "Ah, Miz Ingolfsson, they, ah, that is—"

Johanna's cousin spoke without raising her eyes from the book in her lap. "Gods, Jo, y'always were as subtle as a steam truck. Spare the girl's feelin's, hey?"

Johanna chuckled; adolescent affairs were a long-standing tradition for Citizen-class women, but there was an ancient convention of not mentioning them before adults. Probably a survival from times when such things were strongly frowned upon, but it had been silly even in her youth. "Younger generation's less discreet than we was, Alicia," she said. To Mandy: "Hard though it is to imagine, girl, I went to school, too. Jus' inquirin'."

"Ah, no. I don't think so," Mandy said. Under her breath: "Moo."

"Well, as they please," Johanna said contentedly.

Yolande had never been very popular at school in her younger years: too much the loner and dreamer. It was reassuring to see her fitting in so well and making friends. A lover was only to be expected given her age, although Johanna had never thought much of the hothouse-romance atmosphere of Senior School herself. In theory it was supposed to be emotional training for adulthood, but she had never seen the point in falling in love with someone you couldn't marry. Not that school sweethearts necessarily drifted out of touch; ex-lovers who were godmothers and unofficial aunts to each other's children were a staple of Draka life . . . But it was all no preparation for how *different* men were.

Well, I was always eccentric, she mused comfortably. Deciding who you were going to marry at sixteen was decidedly unusual, even if he was a neighbor's son. She smiled down at Rahksan; that was an entirely different matter, of course. As the Roman poet had said, it was pleasant to have it friendly, easy, and close at hand . . . friendly especially, otherwise it just wasn't worth the trouble, usually.

Rahksan smiled back, laying aside her embroidery. "You got anythin' fo' me to do, next hour or two, Mistis?" she asked.

"No, not particular, Rahksi. Why?"

"That boy of mine," she said. "Wants particulah to have a talk with me, says it impo'tant. Allah, most of the time he don' give me the time of day, an' now he jus' *has* to have a chat."

Johanna pursed her lips; Rahksan's son was a classic pain in the fundament. Spoiled from house-rearing, restless as a cat on hot tiles, and sullen; a lot of young serfs went through a stage like that, particularly the males, but he was considerably worse than average. It was no help that Ali had been sired by Tom. Contraception had been more difficult then, and Rahksan careless about it; the three of them had been play-pleasuring, and the Afghan had decided to keep it on impulse. Not that half-Draka bastards were uncommon, but mostly they grew up in Quarters and it made no particular difference. Ali had run tame in the manor; looking at it from his point of view, she supposed it was natural enough for him to be more discontented than most. To make it worse, he was completely besotted with Colette, her son John's new French concubine.

Who is a gorgeous mantrap and a teasing bitch of the first water, Johanna thought sourly. The wench had been a present from her cousins Tanya and Edward, who had a plantation west of Tours in the Loire valley; John certainly hadn't complained—he indulged the wench—but his mother was beginning to think her kin had unloaded a trouble-maker. *Tanya's bloody sense of humor,* she mused.

"Rahksi, that boy needs some serious talkin'-to," she said. "Half a dozen times I've talked Tom out of kickin' his butt good an' proper. Fightin', drinkin'; he's first-rate with the horses, but he's back-talked the head groom enough to get anyone else triced up to the frame fo' ten-strokes-an'-one. Freya, honeybunch, I cain't let him ruin discipline." Bending the rules too far for a favorite was an invitation to trouble.

"Ah knows, Mistis." A deep sigh, and the serf's brows drew together. "Blames myself, really do. Too easy on that chile; I get set to rake him down, an' then remembers him so little an' sweet. He too kind treated, never reminded strong of his place; it better if'n y'learns that young."

Rahksan looked suddenly older, Johanna sat up and gave her a gentle squeeze on the shoulder. "Isn't easy bein' a mother, Rahksi. Don't worry, we'll straighten him out."

The Afghan shrugged and smiled ruefully. "I'll tells him you threatenin' to sell him to the mines," she said.

Johanna snorted. "Bettah use somethin' he'll believe," she replied.

The Ingolfssons and her own von Shrakenberg clan had definite ideas about managing their serfs; they did *not* sell them to strangers, except as punishment for some gross crime like child abuse. Such extreme measures had not been necessary on Claestum since the brutal days of the settlement, right after the War. Besides which it would break Rahksan's heart, which was not to be contemplated.

"Say we might send him down to the boats fo' a year," she continued. Claestum had a part-share in a tuna-fishing business on the coast, run in cooperation with a half-dozen neighboring estates. The Landholders oversaw their hired managers carefully, but it was rough work.

Rahksan winced slightly and made a palms-up gesture. "Tell you true, Mistis, I've thought on that. Might do him good t'see how soft he's had it, an' get him away from his momma's skirts. But—"

"I know, he's you own and you'd miss him." Johanna rested one of her own hands on the serf's. "Look, Rahksi, this just an idea. Tom was sayin' Ali makes a terrible house boy but might do well as a soldier; we could get him a Janissary postin' if he volunteered."

And it would be just what he needs to make something of himself, she thought. *The boy's strong an' smart enough, it's the attitude's the problem.* An induction camp's hard-bitten master sergeants had no interest in the anguished sensitivities of the adolescent soul, or anything else beside results.

Rahksan bit her lip. "That generous, but they mighty rough an' he ain't no how used to it." A talented serf could rise far in the military. Not just to noncommissioned rank in the subject-race legions; Janissaries had opportunities for education, training of every sort. There were ex-Janissaries throughout the serf-manned bureaucracies that ran the Domination, below the level of the Citizen aristocracy. "Though . . . I wouldn't see him much that way," she finished softly.

"Rahksi," Johanna said seriously. "He's not you little boy no' mo'. Ali's a grown buck, an' he has to learn to look his fate in the eye. He cain't hide behind you fo'ever. Else he'll do somethin' we can't overlook, an' . . ." She shrugged. "Ahh, well, run along an' try reasonin' with him. But think about it. We'll talk it ovah mo' tonight."

Johanna put the matter out of her mind as Rahksan left; time enough later. She could hear Olietta directing the wenches setting the table behind her, and glanced at her watch—1258 hours, Tom would be in from the fields any time now. It was a house rule that the family ate together; otherwise you might as well be living in a hotel.

"C'mon, you two!" she called to the girls in the pool.

"That was fun," Yolande said, as they slid out of the water. The verge was covered in the same blue-and-green New Carthage tiles as the pool; they felt warm and slick under her feet, and the dry air cooling on her wet skin. It had turned out to be a not-quite-hot day, just right for outdoors.

" 'Twas," Myfwany agreed. "I'm *nevah* goin' be able do that circle-flip like you can, 'Landa."

Yolande grinned with pride as the servants came forward with towels; Bianca and Lele, her own. The deep pile of the cotton was a pleasure in itself, smelling crisply fresh and slightly of the cherry blossoms they had been laid on in the warming cupboard. She had always rather enjoyed being dried; there was less distraction than when you had to do it yourself, and after a swim it made you feel tingly and extra clean. Like wearing new-laundered underwear, only it was your own skin. She reached down and absently patted Lele's head as the Eurasian serf worked over her feet.

"How's Deng?" she said.

"Still poorly, Mistis. Gives many tanks fo' the crystallized ginger you sent up last month." Lele looked up and grimaced. "Says he hasn't seen any since China. I tried it. I kin see why." Yolande laughed and held up her arms for the serf to slide the Moorish-style striped *djellaba* over her head. The fine-textured wool settled against her skin like a caress, and she ran her fingers through the damp mass of her hair to spread it over her shoulders.

The serfs gathered up their towels and left; Myfwany looked up, adjusting her belt-tie. "You've got wonderful servants," she said sincerely, shaking back the wide sleeves. Disciplined obedience could be bought from any good labor agent, but enthusiasm was not as common. "Spirited but not spoiled."

"My parents' doin'," Yolande said in disclaimer. "They had problems, back right after the War. Had to kill a few, even; but now we go six months without so much as a floggin'. Pa doesn't hold with whippin' much, says it's the last resort of stupidity an' failure."

"Good teacher still needs a good pupil," the other girl replied with a slow smile. "You've got the nature, like Marsala wine: strong but sweet."

Yolande smiled back, and then the expression faded. There was a feeling of cold under her breastbone, yet it was hot as well, cramping her breathing. She could feel her lips paling, and her arms and legs wanted to tremble; her vision grayed at the edges until Myfwany's face loomed in a tunnel of darkness. There was a moment when the whole surface of her skin seemed to prickle, drum-tight, then the world snapped back to normal. Or almost—the hot-chill sensation in her stomach settled lower and faded to warmth, and she put her hand to the side of her head, gasping for breath.

"You all right? *'Landa?'*" Myfwany's voice was sharp with concern, as she gripped her friend by the shoulders.

"I—yes, just felt funny fo' a second." She shook her head. "Little scary . . . must've held my breath too long underwatah. Anyways, let's go eat; I'm starvin'." She had suddenly a bottomless hollow feeling almost like nausea. It was worrying, even if they had only had rolls and fruit with their coffee that morning. No run, after all, and only a couple of hours in the water . . .

A serf struck with quiet precision at a tiny bronze gong by the table. Another seated herself at a harp nearby and began to play softly as the Draka assembled. The table was near the house wall, the usual rectangular slab of polished stone on curved wrought-iron supports, shaded by oleanders. Yolande dropped into her wicker chair and grabbed at a roll from a basket, breaking the soft fresh bread and eating it without benefit of butter. The taste was intoxicating and she finished it off and took another, more slowly. Muriel and Veronica had arrived, looking sleekly content; they nodded around the table as they drew their chairs closer.

"Where *is* you father?" Johanna asked, as the serfs handed around the first course; it was iced beet-and-cucumber soup, for a warm day. "And are they starvin' you down at school, child?"

"Mmph," Yolande said, then swallowed to clear her mouth. "No, I just had a . . . really strange sensation. It's funny, I was lookin' at Myfwany an' thinkin' on how nice she is, then all of a sudden my head was swimming and my knees felt watery and my skin went cold an' I broke out in a sweat, and then my stomach felt strange. Figured I must've not noticed how hungry I was . . . What are y'all laughing at?" she concluded with bewildered resentment.

Her mother had put fingertips to brow and her shoulders shook. Aunt Alicia was coughing into a napkin; Myfwany looked back and forth between them, blinked in understanding, and then focused on carefully pouring herself a glass of white Procanico wine.

Mandy looked at her owl-eyed. "Y'are joshing 'Landa?" she asked, and turned to Veronica and Muriel. "She is joshing isn't she? Please, tell me, nobody could be that ignor—"

"Johanna!"

It was her father's voice, from the French doors that gave onto the terrace from the main house.

"Look-see who *I've* brought to lunch!"

" . . . so it turned out they were just Keren tribesfolk who wandered across the border," her brother was saying. "It's pretty wild there in south Yunnan, mountain jungle. Of course, they could have been Alliance operatives *pretending* to be tribesfolk, so we turned them over to the headhunters." He grinned and buffed his fingernails. "And my tetrarchy got extra leave fo' stumblin' across them. Scramjet shuttle to Vienna, overnight dirigible to Milan, caught the train to Florence an' so forth."

The soup was removed and the next course arrived: seared sea-scallions with asparagus, stuffed Roman artichokes and truffled walnut oil, *insalata* in cumin vinaigrette and a paella salad on the side. Plain country food. Her parents disapproved of the modern Orientalizing fashion of bits and pieces of this and that, saying it was bad for digestion and distracted the attention from the real pleasures of dining and conversation. Hunger satisfied, she touched a finger to her wine glass for a refill and watched the others. John was getting respectful attention in his description of an impromptu tiger hunt in the rhododendron thickets of the Yunnan mountains, up on the Nepalese border. Mandy was drinking it in, with her chin resting on her hands.

Well, he is pretty dashin', Yolande thought critically, glancing at her brother. Tall and long-limbed, which showed to advantage in garrison blacks. Russet-colored hair and close-cropped beard, straight high-cheeked features and gray eyes against brown-tanned skin, set off by tasteful ruby ear studs and the silver-niello First Airborne Legion thumb ring.

" . . . so I ought to be able to squeeze in a week here to home," he finished.

Johanna signed for the serf to remove her plate and lit a cigarette. "We'll be havin' some people over next Tuesday, if you haven't lost the taste fo' countryside jollifications. . . . I'm goin' over the orchards this afternoon. They're in bloom; why don't you come along and help show Yolande's friends about?"

"Hmmm." The serfs were bringing coffee and desserts, blueberry lemonade sorbets and almond flan with fruits and cheeses. "Actually, Mother, I had somethin' else planned fo' this afternoon. Glad to, tomorrow. Sorry." He grinned unrepentantly.

Yolande looked up at the harpist. Colette, her name was. A gift to John on his twenty-first birthday from the von Shrakenbergs of Chateau Retour, over in what had been France; they were kin, first cousins on her mother's side and more remotely on her father's, as well. The wench's mother was a serf artist of note, a singer trained pre-War at the Paris Conservatoire. Colette had inherited some of the talent, and her looks as well. Tall, slender, dancer-graceful; softly curled hair the color of dark honey to her waist, and huge eyes of an almost purple violet. Priceless, and faultlessly trained, but Yolande had never liked her; conceited, given to dumb insolence, and unpopular with the other servants, which was always a bad sign. Except for a few of the bucks hopelessly infatuated with her, of course.

The serf met the Draka girl's eyes for a moment, smiled with an almost imperceptible curve of the lips, then dropped her gaze to the instrument. Sunlight worked in flecks through the flowers overhead and patterned the white of her gown.

Yolande's father laughed. "Give the boy a few hours to . . . settle in, darlin'," he said. Johanna smiled and slapped her son on the shoulder.

"Don' wear youself out. See you at dinner then," she said as he rose.

"If there's anythin' left of you tomorrow, you might help with a problem, son." Thomas Ingolfsson said. "We've been losin' sheep, over to Castelvecchi."

"Ah." His son turned back, alert. "Wolves? Wildcats?"

"Leopard, from the sign." Yolande saw her father's eyes narrow in amusement at the sudden prickle of interest around the table. "Yes, they must finally be breedin' enough that they're spreading out of the Apennines."

The upper hill country had been stripped bare of population after the War; that was standard practice, for security reasons and because such areas were seldom worth the trouble of cultivation by Draka standards. The Conservancy Directorate had reforested most of the abandoned lands and introduced appropriate wildlife. The Italian reserves were still not as rich as North Africa's, where a hundred and fifty years of care had left the mountains green and teeming with game, but there was enough to allow limited culling. Draka loved hunting with a savage passion, and were preservationists accordingly, but letting the big cats into densely populated farming country was excessive even by their standards.

"In fact, the Conservancy people said go ahead an' take them, not worth the trouble of trappin'."

John sat down again; behind him, Yolande noticed Colette playing with an irritated vehemence.

"I could ride over tomorrow morning with the dogs; take Menchino and Alfredo . . . Join me, Pa?" he said eagerly. "Ma?"

His parents shook their heads reluctantly. "Winnifred went and broke her arm, can't spare myself," Thomas Ingolfsson said.

At John's frown, Johanna added: "Can't come myself either; we're sortin' the yearling colts fo' the Siena show. Tell yo what, though, Johnny, why don't you take Yolande and her friend Myfwany?"

"Thanks—" Myfwany and Yolande began in chorus, then broke off with a giggle. John opened his mouth to say what he thought of taking his baby sister and an unknown teenager along on a leopard hunt, caught his mother's eye, and nodded.

"Glad to, sprout. An' you too, Miz Venders," he added.

"Thanks awfully," Myfwany said. "No leopards on Sicily yet, an' my elder sister got one down in Kenya last year an' she's always on about it."

Johanna turned smoothly to the other girls. "Best not to cluttah up a huntin' party too much; I'd be honored if y'all would come with me and assist at selectin' the yearlings—we're rather proud of our ridin' stock here at Claestum—an' to be sure, pickin' out one each fo' youselfs, as well."

Mandy smiled with delight. *John-boy, you still can't compete with horses,* Yolande thought satirically. Muriel and Veronica were enthusiastic as well: *of course, they like anything they can do together.* She suppressed envy and hunted a last blueberry around her plate.

"I'm sure there'll be one left you'll find suitable, Miz Venders," Johanna continued. "'Landa's been half-livin' in the stables since she was knee-high, she can help you pick."

"That was beautiful," Myfwany said.

They were riding their horses through the Quarters, but blossoms from the orchards still clung to their shoulders and hair. Yolande could see them starring the other's dark-red mane, pink cherry and white of apple and peach; the blossom season had overlapped this year, which was a little unusual.

"Y—" Yolande cleared the stammer from her throat with an effort. "You are beautiful."

"No," Myfwany said fondly, looking around. Side by side with their boots touching, they were just close enough for private talk. "I'm good-lookin', just. You are beautiful." A smile quirked her mouth as the other girl shook her head in a spray of flowers.

A companionable silence fell, and Yolande enjoyed the feeling of communicating without speech. The roofs of the Great House were just visible on the distant hilltop, over the cypresses and the outer wall of the gardens; some plantations tucked the serf village away out of sight, but the Ingolfssons were Old Domination and not shy about the foundations of their wealth. The cottages were native stone, tile-roofed and closely spaced along brick-paved streets; shade trees flanked the lanes, and each four-room house stood in a small patch of garden, vegetables and often enough a few flowers. It was getting on toward evening, and the quarters were noisy enough to drown the clop-clatter of hooves and the occasional metallic kiss of stirrup irons.

Heads bowed toward the riders from passing serfs, dutiful routine deference to the Landholder and her daughter, curiosity toward the guests. Folk were back from the fields and the compulsory evening shower, work-gnarled older men in shapeless overalls, short thickset women brown as berries and seemingly built of solid muscle. Younger ones with enough energy left to throw jokes and snatches of song at each other as they scattered to their homes. Children played run-and-shout games along the sidewalks, or helped their mothers carry home baskets of round loaves that gave off the tantalizing scent of fresh baking. Cooking-smells came from the cottages, tomato and garlic and hot olive oil. They reined in to the little plaza where the lane joined the main road to the manor, and Yolande called to her mother: "Ma!"

Johanna Ingolfsson reined up.

"Ma, Myfwany and I'll go right around to the stables an' walk up." The Landholder raised one brow; the grooms could take their mounts from the Great House steps just as well. A touch at her stirrup made her look down; Rahksan was there, gripping her ankle. She frowned slightly at the lapse in decorum and bent low to listen to an agitated whisper.

"Please youselfs, girls," Yolande's mother said after a moment. She extended a hand; the serf gripped her wrist, put a foot on the toe of Johanna's boot and swung up pillion behind her owner. The Landholder looked around, abstracted. "Two hours to dinner," she finished, and touched heels to her horse. There was an iron clatter of hooves as Johanna spurred up the road.

Myfwany and Yolande walked their horses across the square. There was a small fountain in the center, Renaissance work salvaged from some forgotten hill town. The public buildings of the Quarters lined the pavement, the larger houses of the Headman and senior gang-drivers, the school, the infirmary, the bakery, and baths. There was a church as well, a pleasant little example of Tuscan baroque reassembled here at some little expense, and another building that served as a public-house with tables set outside; a few workers sat there over a glass of wine or game of chess. Serfs never touched money, of course, but Claestum had an incentive scheme that paid in minor luxuries or tokens accepted at the inn. *Farming is skilled work,* Yolande remembered her father saying. *Difficult, and easily spoiled. Needs the carrot as well as the stick.* She nodded to the priest in his long black gown and odd little hat as they passed, and he signed the air.

"Funny," Yolande said, as they turned their mounts left to the laneway that skirted the base of the hill. "Nothin' much has happened today, but it feels special, somehow."

"Know what you mean, 'Landa." Myfwany ran her hands through her hair and rubbed them together, shedding bits of petal. "Smell."

Yolande leaned her head to the other's extended hand; it carried hints of soap and leather, overlain by the spring-silvery scent. Like a ghost memory of the orchard, tunnels of white froth against black branches, sun-starred with water diamonds and rainbows from the sprays.

Her heart clenched beneath her ribs and she felt suspended, floating in a moment of decision like the arch above the high-dive board. She bent to kiss the soft spot inside the wrist, and felt cool fingers brush across her lips. Glanced up, and their eyes met.

The moment passed and they laughed uneasily, looking around. The garden wall was still on their right, whitewashed stone along the gravel of the road. The lawns were a vivid green beyond it, trees and flowerbanks, groves and summer-houses, ponds and statues. Hedges and onyx-jade cypresses gave glimpses of the workaday area to their left, barns and pens, round granaries and the sunken complex of the winery, smithies and machine-shops. The sun was sinking behind the Great House and they lay in the shadow of its hill, an amber light that turned the dust-puffs around their horses' hooves to glinting honey-mist. They passed under an arched gate and Yolande waved her riding crop to the one-armed man who bowed from the veranda of the cottage next to it.

"Evenin', Guido," she said, as they passed. A boy had run ahead, and they turned downslope into an area of low stucco-coated stables and paddocks fenced in white board. The horses side-danced a little at the smell of home and feed, eager for their evening grooming and mash. Yolande smoothed a hand down the neck of her mount as stablehands came up to take the reins.

"Nena, Tonyo," Yolande said as they swung down.

"Mistis Yolande," they replied. "*Buono* ride, Mistis?" Tonyo continued, with a flash of white teeth against olive-tanned skin.

"Tolerable good," Yolande said, grinning back. Both Draka gave their mounts a quick once-over before turning over the reins, and Yolande slipped a piece of hard sugar to hers. Slipping into local dialect: "Did that barn cat have its kittens?"

The young man shrugged and spread his hands apologetically, but his sister dipped her head "Stable four, Mistis," she said. "Up in the loft, I heard it." Myfwany looked at her with raised brows; the patois on her family's Sicilian estate was different enough to be a distinct language.

"Cats?" she said.

"Kittens," Yolande replied. "Have a look?"

"Meeeroeuuw!" the cat said warningly. It had been reasonably polite, but it was *not* going to tolerate strange fingers touching the squirming, squeaking mass of offspring along its flank.

The two young Draka backed away on hands and knees across the loft's carpeting of deep-packed clover hay. It had a sweet smell, still green after a winter's storage. They flopped back on the resilient prickly softness; the long loft of the stable was almost night-dark, the last westering rays slanting in through the louvered openings above them. Yolande stretched, feeling the breathless heat as a prickle along her upper lip. There were soft sounds of shifting hooves through the slatted boards beneath, and the clean smells of well-cared-for horses. There were a dozen of the long two-story stables here below the hill: personal mounts for the Landholders and their retainers, used for the routine work of supervision, or the hunt or pleasure riding.

Yolande turned on her side, watching her friend's face and probing at her own feelings. *Happy,* she decided. Myfwany's face was a
pale glimmer in the darkness, her eyes bright amber-green. *Scared.*

"Yes," she said, to a question not spoken in words.

They moved together, embraced. Yolande gave a small sigh as their
lips met; a shock went over her skin, like the touch of the ocean when
you dove into an incoming wave. Their arms pulled tighter, and her
mouth opened. She tasted sweat-salt and mint.

"Gods," she murmured, after an eternity. "Why did we wait so long?
I'd've said yes months ago. Didn't you want to?"

Myfwany chuckled softly. "Almost from the first," she said, and laid
her hands lightly on the other's flanks. "Beautiful, muscle knitted to
you ribs like livin' steel . . . Waited because the time wasn't right."
Yolande shivered as the hands traced lightly up to her breasts.

Voices from below, jarring. Yolande fought down a surge of anger;
what did they have to do for some privacy, go check into a hotel? A
dim light shone up through the floorboards; the voices of serfs, angry
and quarreling.

"Send them away," Myfwany breathed into her ear.

Yolande controlled her breathing and crawled toward the big square
hatchway that overlooked the tack-room; a little light was coming up
from below, a hand-lantern's worth. Not that it was any serf's business what she did or with whom or where, but she was suddenly tooth-
gratingly conscious that the estate rumor mill would passing news of
every straw in her hair and undone button before morning. Whoever
it was—sundown was after plantation curfew—there had better be a
good excuse for this, or somebody was going to be sorry and sore.
She recognized the voices as her head peered over the timber frame
of the trapdoor, and the anger left her like a gasping breath: Rakhsan,
and her son Ali. She was five meters above their heads; it was unlikely
in the extreme that they would look up. Myfwany caught her tension
and froze beside her.

Ali's voice, speaking Tuscan. A tall young buck, in groom's breeches
and shirt and boots, tousled brown hair. A friend of his beside him in driver's
livery; she hunted for the name: Marco, understudy pilot for the aircar.

Rahksan put the lantern down and stood with her arms crossed.
Underlighting should have flattered the well-kept prettiness of the serf's
face, but somehow brought out the High Asian cast of the strong bones.
The voice was as familiar as her own mother's to Yolande, but the
tone was one she had never heard the Afghan use. Flat, level,
uninflected, she replied in the Old Territory serf-dialect.

"Ali," she said. "This isn't trouble you in. We not talkin' whippin'
here, we not talkin' sniffy around Mastah John's bedwench an' havin'
her laugh at yaz." She leaned forward, and her clenched fists quivered by her sides with throttled intensity. "Goin' bushman means *death,*
boy. The greencoats ties you to a wheel an' breaks you bones slow
with an iron rod, an then they rams a stake up you ass an yaz *dies,*
it kin take *days,* the crows pick out you eyes an'—" Her voice broke
and she grasped for control, panting. "Oh, Ali, my baby, my chile,
please listen to me."

Ali jerked; Yolande could sense threads of argument reaching into the past, like walking into a play halfway through. "I—it's worth the risk, to be free."

"Free." Then there was emotion in the woman's voice, an anger and hopeless compassion. She pressed her fists to her forehead for a moment, then looked up. "Ali," she said, her voice calmly serious. "We beyond gamin' an' twistin' words to make points. This the time fo' truth."

Marco made an impatient sound; Ali cast him an appealing glance and gestured before returning his gaze to his mother and nodding gravely.

"Did I have a magic stick, I'd wave it an' send you to England. Break my heart to lose you, son, but I'd do it. You happiness that important to me. Does you believe me?"

"Yes, Momma," he said, with warmth in his voice.

"But I don' have no magic stick!" She buried her hands in her hair. "Allah be merciful, whats can I say to a boy of nineteen? You doan' believe yaz can die. . . ." Rahksan stepped to her son and reached up to take his face between her palms. "Ali, my sweet, my joy, I knows you full of pride an' shame. What you think, I says cast them out 'count it makes trouble fo' me?"

She kissed his brow. "Son, that sort o' hard pride, that fo' Draka; an' I wouldn't be Draka if'n I could, I seen what it make them into. It ain' no shame to be serf! We not serf 'count of bein' bad, or worthless it just . . . kismet, our fate." She paused, licked her lips, continued. "Mebbeso the mastahs take the world, like they dreams. Mebbeso they loses, an' then they dies, on 'count they don' accept they can ever lose—win or die, every one. Think on it, boy, does yaz see strength or weakness in that? Whatevah happen, *we* still be here. That the honor an' pride of serfs; to *live*. We is *life*, boy. You wants pride . . . *Look* at this place. Who built it? We did, our folk. Who builds everythin', grows everythin'? Our folk. We *is* the world. *That* cause fo' pride."

"Momma . . ." Ali gestured helplessly. "Momma, maybe . . . you could be right, but I *can't, I* just can't. Please, come with us. I want you with me there, Momma; I want to see you free, too. I know it's risky, but maybe they *won't* catch us."

"Oh, son," she said, in a voice thick with unshed tears. "They caught me long ago. I'm bound with chains softer an' stronger than iron. I'd send you if I could, but my life is here."

"Don't listen to her, Ali!" Marco burst in. "She's a Draka-lover. Be a man!"

Rahksan straightened and glared at Marco, glanced him up and down. "Man?" she said with slow contempt, and the Italian flushed. "Big man, makes his momma an' poppa stand an' watch while the headhunters break his bones, an' they gots to watch and cain' do nothing."

Her voice went whip-sharp. "Yaz poppa, Marco, *he* a man. Live through the War, an' help you momma live. Right afterwards, they was times, plenty folks dyin'; you poppa keep othahs from gettin' theyselves killed, riskin' a nighttime knife in t'back to do it. I hears him myself, talkin' to the mastahs, respectful an' firm, askin' fo' let-up so's the

rest don' do nothin' foolish. There're Draka who'd've skinned him fo'
that. Ours wouldn't, but how he know that? He settle down with yaz
ma, t'make the best of what fate give him; doan' think that take a
man? Works hard, helps her raise their chillen. *That* a man. You? Yaz
not even much of a *boy.*"

Marco clenched a fist, would have swung it at the beginning of any
movement. "Julia and I can never have children of our own," he rasped,
and his flush of anger faded to white around his mouth. "Is a *man*
supposed to lie down for that?"

Rahksan touched her stomach. "You don't have chillen, boy. We do.
Julia, she can go down t' the clinic ever' six months, same as any
wench on the plantation, an' get a shot. I does, regular. She fo'get
o' don' care, have her two while she a house girl, so they ties her
tubes. Mebbeso you wants to get six mo' with her to prove yaz a *man*,
then see them sold off to the serf traders when they turn fourteen?
The Ingolfssons don' breed us fo' market. An' I notice *Julia* ain't here,
hm?"

Rahksan extended a finger toward him and he flinched. "Marco, like
I said, I'm no Draka; so I won' take no pleasure in seein' you die.
But I savin' my sorrow fo' you folks. My boy Ali here, he bein' bull-
stupid, but it honest stupid. You doin' this outa bent spite, lyin' to
youself an' draggin' my son in to make youself feel bettah about it.
Mebbeso yaz got cock, balls, an' voice likeso a jackass, but that don'
make you much of a *man* t' my way a' thinkin'."

She turned back to Ali. "Tell me honest, son. Bring it out. You
agreein' with his opinion of you momma what bore you?"

"I—" The boy's eyes hunted back and forth between them. "You—"
He stopped, then the words burst free. "You love *her* children, you always
have, better than you love me; it was smiles and stories for them, and
lectures for me! Isn't that being a Draka-lover?"

"Ali." Rahksan forced her son's head back toward her. "You my son.
Nine months beneath my heart, inside my body. Blood an' pain when
I bore you, an' the midwife laid yaz on my belly. My milk fed you.
You the dearest thing in all the world to me! If'n I been hard on you
sometimes, that love, too, tryin' to teach yaz how to live. Loves you
mo' than life."

She took a deep breath. "No, I'm not a Draka-lover. Yes, I love the
Mistis' children. They *children,* Ali." She put her hands beneath her
breasts for a moment. "One I gives suck to. All I cleans, an' picks
up when they cries. Holds they hands when they learnin' walkin'. Plays
with. Hears they babblin' an' first words. Comforts when they skins
they knees o' they pet rabbit dies, same's I did with you. Woman who
don' love a chile aftah all that, she *don' have no lovin' in her heart!*"
A wry smile. "There some othah Draka I likes, o' anyway respects;
that not 'lovin' the Draka.' As fo' the Mistis"—a shrug—"we best friends,
always have been."

Ali spoke with ragged calm. "How can you say that, say that you're
the *friend* of someone who owns you, uses you, who—" He paused,
continued almost in a mumble. "I can't . . . can't stand to see them
touch you. It makes me feel ashamed."

"Oh, chile," she sighed. "How can she and I be friends? It ain't easy, is how. I a serf, Ali; I cain' change that, neither can she. She own me; law say she can sell me, whup me, kill me. Forty years in t' same house, same room mostly, how often you thinks we gets riled with each othah? How often she work to hold her hand? How often I make myself not use that to hurt her? She still a Draka, chile, an' that mean arrogant as a cat an' near as cruel, sometime, 'thout even' knowin' it."

She paused, made a sound halfway between laughter and pain. "As to touchin' . . . Ali, I knows it shockin' to every boy t' learn this, but mothers don' stop wantin' and needin' when they has they sons. Fo' the rest—look at me, Ali. No, *look* at me."

He obeyed. "I is forty an' four, Ali. Still right comely, but they are dozens, mebbeso hundreds, younger an' better-lookin' would dearly like to get on right side with the mastahs by lyin' down with them. Why you think Mistis still want me? An' I her, Ali? 'Cause we has *likin'* fo' each other; knows each other to the bone. The pleasurin' nice, but it comfort, too and bein' with someones you shares memories with." Rahksan crossed her arms on her chest and continued calmly. "Love you, son. Give my life fo' yaz, but I won't lie about what I is, o' pretend to bein' ashamed of it. Nevah did find a man I wanted full-time; wish I had, might have been bettah fo' you to have a pa. But I didn't, an' there nothin' wrong with takin' what's available along the way.

"Now, Ali," she continued. "It's time, son. Fo' my sake . . . an' fo' yourn . . . give this up. *Please.* It madness. I wants to see you happy, see you give me grandchildren. If'n you cain' be happy here, there other places; we can work somethin' out, *but I can't let you go kill youself, Ali.*"

Marco stiffened in suspicion. "She's betrayed us, turned informer!" he snapped. "Quick, get the ropes! We can get her to the car, it's two hours until that bastard Nyami is back, I've got the keys, *hurry!*"

Rahksan hurled herself forward, gripped her son in a fierce embrace. "Allah, be merciful—Ali, Ali, I'd die fo' you; I'd give you up an' never see you again if'n you had a chance to do this crazy thing. *Ah, god, you crackin' my heart in two!*" The last was a wail, and tears were running down the face she raised to her son. "Even kill you love fo' me, my chile. Even that I'll do fo' you."

Marco grabbed for her. Ali's arms were around his mother, uncertain whether to comfort or confine. Rahksan struggled against both of them, or shuddered in her weeping. Above them the two Draka girls tensed as one, ready for movement, but Yolande's hand pressed her friend back. There was someone at the door of the stable.

"Well." The serfs froze, the footsteps halted by the stable doors, and a hand flicked on the lights. The horses stirred, whickering and stamping in their stalls. Yolande slitted her eyes to make out the figure in the entranceway: her mother, still in the black riding leathers. The silver rondelles on her gunbelt shone like stars against night, and her face seemed to float detached as she skimmed the broad-brimmed hat aside. The boots went *tk-tk* across the brown tile as she walked to within arm's reach of the serfs. There was a cigarette in her left hand; the other stayed near her gunbelt, the fingers working slightly.

The Draka spoke again, in a tone of flat deadliness. "*Take—those—hands off—her.*" The two young men released Rahksan and stepped back reflexively. Ali's eyes followed his mother as she moved to the side, tears running down a face that might have been carved in olive wood. Then back to the Landholder, standing stock-still with explosive movement packed ready beneath her skin. Johanna spoke to Rahksan, with infinite gentleness. "You don't have to watch this, Rahksi."

"Yes, I do, Jo. It my fault. This my punishment."

Johanna nodded. Even then, Yolande felt shocked at Rahksan's use of the first name without honorific; a privilege that could only be exercised in strict privacy. Her eyes turned back toward the two serf males. Evidently they were no longer considered witnesses.

The Landholder blew meditative smoke from her nostrils as she stared at Marco. When she spoke, the tone was almost conversational.

"Buck, you are just too stupid to live. Plannin' to take that lumberin' cow of an aircar to England? Yes?" Marco gave a frozen nod. "Across the heaviest air defenses in the world? Boy, they can see a *bird* movin'. England? You'd be lucky to make it halfway to Florence. Lucky to be blown out of the air, mo' likely forced down. Free out of Ingolfsson hands then, into Security's."

The serfs flinched at the mention of the secret police, and Johanna nodded. "Try convincin' them you don't know anythin' political. Talk to the scalpels, an' the wires, an' the drugs. Three weeks, maybe they'd believe you and send you to the Turk." They flinched again at the obscene nickname for the impaling stake. Marco was shaking now, white showing around the rims of his eyes.

The Draka sighed. "Haven't had to have a killin' on Claestum since befo' you birth, boy. I really regret this." Her voice became more formal. "One choice that can never be taken away, an' that's to die rathah than live beneath the Yoke. Marco, as you owner an' an arm of the State, I hereby judge you a threat to the welfare of the Race and so, unfit to live," she said. The serf made the beginnings of a motion, perhaps an attack, perhaps only an attempt to flee.

Even to the Draka watching from the loft what followed was a blur, a dull smack of impact and Marco was sinking to the floor clutching his groin, face working soundlessly.

She pulled it, some reflexive corner of Yolande's mind thought. Otherwise there was no room for thought, for movement, scarcely even for breath. Heartbeat hammered in her ears. "You should listen to you momma, boy," she said quietly to Ali with a voice full of calm, considered anger. " 'Stead of to Marco, who can't even commit suicide on his ownsome without takin' his friends with him. Gods preserve me from friendship like that-there. Understand me, boy? Louder, I cain't hear you."

"Yes, Mistis." A breathy whisper.

"Are yo *listenin'* to me, boy?"

"Yes, Mistis."

"Nineteen years old, Freya . . . Forty years you mothah and I've been together, Lord, forty years. Youth an' age, night an' day, war an' peace . . ." She touched the scars around her left eye where the ridges stood out under the overhead floodlights. "She helped put me togethah again aftah this. Helped midwife my children, an' I was there when you were born. Incidental, I was there when you were conceived, too." A shake of her head. "You momma worth ten of you, buck. Mo' guts, mo' brains, mo' *heart.*" Very softly: "Times was, when she was the only thing kept me from freezin' solid."

She leaned forward, and her index finger tapped him on the nose; from above, Yolande could see him jerk at the touch, and the sheen of sweat on his skin. Her mother's voice became calmer still.

"So she's what's kept Old Snake off you back, many a time. She's why I'm bendin' strict law, accordin' to which the Order Police should be here now. Bendin' it enough that I'd be in some considerable shit myself if it came out. But we comin' to the hard place, boy, between wish and will and duty, the place where I got no choices left. Rahksan dear to my heart, but I live here; my children do, my husband, my kin. I can't keep a mad dog in my household, or sell it into someone else's. Are you an Ingolfsson serf, or a wild bushman? No, don't look at her, or him. This is the narrow passage; here there's no brothah, no friend. *Decide.*"

A long pause.

"Yes, Mistis."

"Louder, boy."

His voice cracked. "I am yours, Mistis. Mercy, please!"

Johanna nodded, and her mouth twisted as at the taste of some bitterness. "Gods damn you Ali, why couldn't you have thought on that befo' things come to this? I nevah asked fo' you likin', just obedience. Now I have to kill part of you to save the rest." More kindly: "I know you sorry now, Ali. I know you frightened. It's enough, now; you a brave boy, an' stubborn. Fear isn't enough, because it don't last. You has to show me, and show youself, right down where you soul lives, who and what you are." Her face nodded toward the wall "Pick up that shovel, an' come back here."

Ali's face had gone gray-pale with understanding; he stumbled to the wall, took the long-handled shovel from the rack. Marco had risen to his feet, still clutching at himself. His breath whooped between clenched teeth. Johanna moved again, kicking twice with delicate precision. The point of her boot drove into Marco's solar plexus and straightened his body up in paralytic shock. The edge flicked up into his throat, and he dropped to the floor bulge-eyed, jerking and twitching.

"Kill him, Ali." The Draka drew her pistol; the chunky shape of crackle-finished steel glittered blue-black. "If not, I'll make it quick."

Rahksan turned her back, hands over her face. The shovel went up, hesitated. Ali was shaking almost as much as his friend, who strained to draw air through a half-crushed windpipe and made noises that were part pleading, part choking. Strengthless hands rose from the floor to ward off the iron.

"No!" Ali screamed. The shovel swung down and struck, clanged. Marco's body jerked across the floor like a broken-backed snake. Rahksan twitched where she stood, as if the impact had been in her. "No! No! No!" Another blow, and another; it took six until the other man stopped moving and Ali was able to drop to his knees in the blood and vomit himself empty.

"Serf." Johanna's voice cut through the spasms, and Ali looked up, wiping at tears and blood and vomit on his chin. Horses moved and whinnied in the stalls, frightened by the scent of death. There were voices in the distance, and other lights coming on. The Draka's face might have been carved from some pale wood; she gripped the side of his head, hair and ear, and jerked him close.

"You bright enough to understand that you've found the way to compel me, to hurt me; by makin' me hurt you mothah through you. *Look.*" She jerked his head around, forcing him to face Rahksan. "Is it worth it? That's you doin'." Another twist, toward Marco. "So is that." Back eye-to-eye.

"Now. This is what happened. Marco went crazy, and attacked you momma. You had to hit him, an' it was all ovah by the time I got here. Nobody will say otherwise; go get Deng, an' the priest. They'll fetch the mastah and do what's needful. Get out of here, boy. *Remember, don't you ever make me do this again.*"

He stumbled out into the awakening night. Johanna's calm evaporated. She threw the cigarette down with a gesture of savage frustration and ground it out beneath her heel as she slammed the pistol back into its holster.

"Shit, shit, *shit!*" she swore venomously. Then, gently: "Rahksan."

The other woman turned from the wall and let her hands fall. Her face had crumpled, and there were fresh lines beside her mouth. "Did we have to?" she asked, in a thin small voice. "Oh, Allah, Jo, did we have to?"

"Rahksi—" Johanna held up her hands, a helpless motion. "There wasn't time . . . another hour, an' too many would have known. I'm sorry, I'm truly, truly sorry. There was nothin'—he had to learn, Rahksi, it was that or kill him."

Rahksan nodded as the tears spilled quietly down her cheeks. "I know, Jo. I should've taught—" Then she was moving, stumbling forward into the outstretched arms.

"Oh, Jo!" They clung fiercely, and Rahksan's gray-shot head was pressed against Johanna's throat. She was sobbing, a harsh raw sound of grief that shook her like a marionette in the puppeteer's fist.

"It'll be all right, Rahksi, my pretty, shhh, shhh," Johanna said, stroking her hair. "Cry fo' him, Rahksi. Cry fo' all of us. I wish I could."

"My baby, Jo, my baby!"

"I won't let anyone hurt him, I promise. Shhh, shhh."

Yolande felt an overwhelming guilt and grief, sensed Myfwany stirring likewise beside her. Her skin crawled; this was something they were never meant to see, something that was *wrong* to see, something that could never be forgotten. They shared a single appalled glance and began cat-crawling backward, using the growing clamor to fade into the welcoming night. Behind and below them the two figures remained locked together, the Landholder's cheek resting atop the serf's head as she crooned wordless comfort.

Chapter Four

CLAESTUM PLANTATION
DISTRICT OF TUSCANY
PROVINCE OF ITALY
DOMINATION OF THE DRAKA
APRIL 1969

"Mistis." Yolande stirred and blinked her eyes; Lele was at the foot of her bed, touching the mattress to wake her. Machiavelli was there, too. The cat rolled, flexed its feet in the air and tucked itself into a circle on the other side, tail over nose.

I wish I could do that, Yolande thought, swinging her feet out and taking the juice, yawning and stretching.

"Mornin', Lele," she said, rising and walking over to the eastern window and leaning through the thickness of the stone wall. There was just a touch of light over the trees, and the last stars were fading above. The air was cool enough to raise bumps on her skin, but there were no clouds. It would be a warm day, and sunny.

"Terrible about Marco, Mistis," Lele said. News spread fast on a plantation. "Whatevah could he want to hurt Rahksan fo'?" She began laying out Yolande's hunting clothes. There was indignation in her voice; violent crime was very rare in the countryside. And Rahksan was very much a mother-figure to the younger house girls, which said a good deal. Favorites were not always so popular.

"Who knows?" Yolande said, forcing the memory out of her mind and starting her stretching exercises; she felt sluggish this morning, and sleep had come hard in the dark loneliness. She lay down on the padded massage table, and felt the blood begin to flow under the serf's impersonally skillful hands.

"Ali quite the hero, Mistis," Lele continued in a dreamy tone, patting a little scented oil into her palms. Rahksan's son was popular with the wenches, too, for entirely different reasons.

"Lele, *be quiet,*" Yolande snapped. The serf subsided, quelled as much by the sudden tension in the young Draka's muscles as by the tone. "Is Mistis Venders up yet?"

521

"Yes, Mistis," the serf replied. "She—" There were footsteps, and Yolande turned her head to watch as her friend climbed the stairs. She was already dressed in hunting clothes, boots and chamois pants, pocketed jacket of cotton duck with leather pads at the elbows, wrist guards and a curl-brimmed hat.

"How y'feelin', sweet?" Myfwany said softly.

"Pretty good," Yolande replied, and realized it was true, suddenly. The achy feeling was gone, and her body was rested and loose. She arched her back against the masseuse's fingers, sighing with contentment as her friend perched one hip on the table by her shoulder and began braiding her hair with swift deft motions.

"Ever taken the big cats befo'?" Myfwany said.

"No," Yolande replied. "Little harder there on the small of the back, Lele. . . . No, just wildcat. Foxes, of course, an' wolves now and then. Plenty of deer. John has, though, lion an' tiger an' leopard, gun an' steel huntin' both." Her people usually took game smaller than Cape buffalo on horseback, with javelins or lances, terrain permitting.

Lele finished the massage, carefully rotating knees and ankles to ensure suppleness, and brought the clothes. Yolande turned to look over one shoulder—Myfwany was watching her dress with frank pleasure, still half-sitting on the table with one leg swinging. Draka had little body modesty—the nudity taboo had been dying in her grandmother's day—but the feeling of being watched with desire was strange. *I like it,* Yolande decided. It was like being stroked all over with a heated mink glove, tingly and comforting and exciting at the same time.

"Ready fo' some huntin'?" she asked, buckling the broad studded belt and holstering her pistol. Automatically, her hands checked it, ejected the magazine, pressed a thumb on the last round to make sure it was feeding smoothly, worked the action, reloaded, snicked on the safety, and dropped it back into the holster, clipping the restraining strap across behind the hammer.

"Ready fo' that, too," Myfwany said. "Where's that brothah of yours?"

"C'mon, let's go roust him out; much longer and the sun will dry out the scent."

They clattered down the stairs, jumping four or five at a time with exuberant grace. Out through her rooms and down the corridors, past the sleepy early-morning greetings of the House staff, up and about their sweeping and polishing. They passed through the library complex, a series of chambers grouped around an indoor pool, two stories under a glass dome roof; galleries ran back from it, lined shoulder-high with books, statuary, paintings. This had always been one of her favorite indoor parts of the manor, for reading or music or screening a movie; last year they had gotten a Yankee wall-size crystal-sandwich unit, the first in the region.

Off to one side a group of serfs was sitting about a table littered with papers, printouts, coffee cups, and trays: the senior Authorized Literates, managerial staff at their morning conference.

"Hio, Marcello," Yolande said, waving them down as they made to rise. That still felt a little strange. "No, go on with you breakfasts, everybody."

Marcello was Chief Librarian, a lean white-haired man in his sixties who had been a university professor before the War. Normally that meant Category 3m71, deportation to a destructive-labor camp, but her mother had thoughtfully snapped him up from a holding pen while scouting out the estate on recovery leave in '42. Yolande returned his smile; he had been an unofficial tutor of sorts when she was younger. Not that she was under House-staff direction anymore—no Draka child was, once he turned thirteen and carried weapons—but there were fond memories. She nodded to the others she recognized: the paramedic from the infirmary, the schoolteacher—these days, even a plantation taught one child in five or so their letters—and the librarian's son and daughter, understudying as replacements in the usual way.

"We're off huntin'," she said to the elderly Italian serf. "Tell the Lodge we'll be there in 'bout half an hour, an' have somethin' sent to the armory, coffee an' a snack, will you?"

"Gladly, Mistis," he said. "I'll see to it." His accent was odd, much crisper than the usual serf slur, and as much British as Draka in intonation; she remembered some of the neighbors saying he talked too much like a freeman for their taste. He hesitated, then continued: "Will, ah, any of the Family be at the funeral, Mistis?"

Yolande scowled, then forced her features straight and her mood back to where she wished it. "No. I wouldn't think so, all things considered."

Usually the Landholders of Claestum put in a brief appearance at such affairs, as a token of respect. The other serfs at the table exchanged glances, then returned their eyes to their plates and documents. Some estates would have hung an attempted murderer's body up in the Quarters for the birds to eat, as an example.

"John's through here," she continued, as they came out an arched doorway and into a long arcade. Cool air and dew from the gardens to their right; they cut through, and into her brother's rooms. "Hio, Johnny?" she called.

The lounging room was empty, with only the sound of moving water and music playing. A Gerraldson piece, quiet and crystal-eerie, the *Conquest Cantata*. Yolande had never liked it, it always made her think of the way serf women cried at gravesides, which was odd since the sound wasn't anything like that. But somehow there was laughter in it, too. . . . The outer room of John's suite was larger than hers, since he used it for entertaining, and surfaced on three sides with screens of Coromandel sandalwood inset in jade, mother of pearl, ivory, and lapis; they could be folded back to reveal the cabinets, chiller, and displays. The furniture scattered around the lavender-marble floor was mostly Oriental as well; there were a few head-high jade pieces, Turkestan rugs, and a familiar bronze Buddha in the ornamental fish pond that ran through the glass wall into the garden beyond.

"Slugabed!" Yolande said indignantly. "An' there he was, goin' on about how we should make an early start. Come on, Myfwany, we'll tip him out an' throw him in with those ugly carp."

There was a colonnade through the garden, which was mostly pools and lilies. "Ah, 'Landa, maybe we should call ahead—" Myfwany said as they pushed through carved teak doors and down a hallway.

"Johnny!" Yolande chorused, clapping her hands as they turned past the den into the bedroom. "C'mon, you big baby, sun's shinin' and we got an appointment with a kitty-cat! Oh."

John Ingolfsson was sitting half dressed in one of the big black-leather lounging chairs. Colette was kneeling across his lap, and wearing nothing but anklets sewn with silver bells. They chimed softly as her feet moved. Her owner's mouth was on her breasts, and her hands kneaded his shoulders, the tousled blond hair fell backward to her heels as she bent, shuddering.

She gave a sharp cry of protest and opened her eyes as John raised his head and looked at his sister with an ironical lift of eyebrows.

"You might knock, sprout," he said dryly, lifting the wench aside and setting her on her feet as he rose. "Or even, if'n it isn't askin' too much, use the House interphone."

Yolande tossed her head, snorted and set her hands on her hips. "All afternoon, all night an' you *still* can't think of anythin' else?"

She eyed the huge circular bed. John's other two regular wenches, Su-ling and Bea, were there in the tangled sheets. Bea was sitting, yawning and rubbing her face, smiling and making the slight courtesy bow to the two Draka girls. She was a big black woman, Junoesque, older than John, a present from relatives in the southlands given when he turned twelve. Yolande nodded back. She had always rather liked Bea, the wench was unassuming and cheerful and unsulky about turning her hand to ordinary work. Su-ling made a muffled sound and burrowed back into the sheets. Well, who could blame her?

"Should see what wezuns had to make do with in those border camps," John said. He stretched, naked to the waist, showing the classic V-shape of his torso. Smooth curves of rounded muscle hard as tile moved under tanned skin, like a statue in oiled beechwood. Not heavy or gross, the way an over-muscled serf who could lift boulders might be; graceful as a racehorse in motion. She felt a glow of pride. Even by Citizen standards, he was beautiful.

"Men," Yolande continued. "Hmmmph. It's a wonder we let you vote."

Colette was standing, panting and ignored, sweat sheening on her long taut dancer's body. Yolande caught a glare of resentment from the huge violet eyes, frowned absently at her. The serf glanced deliberately from Myfwany to Yolande and back, smiled ironically and made the full obeisance from the waist, palms to eyes and fingers to brow. The Draka girl gritted her teeth. The wench needed a good switching; John spoiled her.

"Colette did sort of distract me," he was saying mildly. "Meet you in the armory in, oh, no mo' than five minutes."

"Sho'ly, John," Myfwany said, touching Yolande on the arm. She giggled as they left the bedroom, flapping one hand up and down in a burnt-finger gesture. "Oh, hoo, hoo, quite a sight!" she said.

Yolande blinked surprise at her. "Who, Colette?" she asked. "Needs a belt taken to her rump."

"That might be interestin', but I was thinkin' of you brother, sweet, in an aesthetic sort of way," Myfwany said, twitching at the other's braid. "You a good-lookin' family."

"I'll tell him you thinks so," she said, grinning slyly. "I mean, seein' as Mandy's makin' moon eyes at him already . . ."

Myfwany laughed and slapped her shoulder. "Don't you dare; swelled heads runs in you family, too."

The armory was a single long room on the lower level, a twenty-by-ten rectangle smelling of metal and gun-oil and of coffee and hot breads and fruit from the trays on the central table. The kitchen wench had put it down and scuttled out; ordinary serfs were not allowed past the blank steel door with its old combination lock and new palm-recognition screen. There were no windows, only a row of glowsticks along the ceiling. Military-model assault rifles along the left wall, a light machine gun, machine pistols, helmets, body armor, ammunition, communications gear and night-sight goggles. Benches at the rear held the tools of a repair shop. Ismet sat there: a big balding ex-Janissary, the plantation's gun-smith and one of the four licensed armed serfs on Claestum, although he was technically state property, rented rather than owned.

The hunting gear was on the other wall. Broad-headed boar spears, javelins, crossbows, shotguns. And rifles of the type Draka thought suitable for game when cold steel was impractical, double-barreled models.

"Here," Yolande said. "This is my other Beaufort style . . . unless you'd like somethin' heavier?"

"No, 8.5mm's fine fo' cat, I think," Myfwany said, popping a roll of melon and prosciutto into her mouth and dusting her hands together. She accepted the weapon and looked it over with an approving nod, thumbing the catch that released the breech; it folded open to reveal the empty chambers. The barrels were damascened, the side plates inlaid with hunting scenes in gold and silver wire, the rosewood stock set with figures in ivory and electrum.

"Nice piece of work, really nice. Sherrinford of Archona?"

"Mm, yes," Yolande said, taking down her other rifle. They were part of a matched set, and Sherrinford worked only by appointment; you had to be born a client. Over-and-under style, like a vertical fig-ure eight; her parents thought that made for better aim than the more usual side-by-side. She watched as her friend snapped the weapon closed and swung it up to dry-fire a few times. *How graceful she is.*

Her brother finished taking down three bandoliers. "I'm usin' the 9mm, but 8.5's fine as long as you've got the right cartridge. A big male leopard can go full manweight, an' we're talkin' close bush country here. These're 180-grain hollowpoint express, ought to do it. There's a range with backstop at the lodge, Myfwany, so you can shoot in on that gun."

"Lovely," Myfwany said.

The balloon tires of the open-topped Shangaan hummed on the pavement as they wound east from the manor. The road was like the broad-base terraces on the hills, and the stock dams that starred the countryside with ponds: a legacy of the Land Settlement Directorate and the period when the estate had been gazetted, right after the War.

The labor camps were long gone, and the work of the engineers had had time to mellow into the Tuscan countryside. Babylonica willows trailed their fierce green osiers into the water, and huge white-coated cattle dreamed beneath them with the mist curling around their bellies. Roadside poplars cast dappled shade, and the low stone walls of the terraces were overgrown with Virginia creeper.

"I like this time of year," Yolande said. "It's . . . like waking up on a holiday morning."

She inhaled deeply; the air was still a little cool as the sun rose over Monti del Chianti to the east. The olives shone silver-gray, and the vines curved in snaking contour rows of black root and green shoots along the sides of the hills; shaggy bush-rose hedges were in bloom, kilometer upon kilometer of tiny white flowers against the lacy thornstalks. Their scent tinted the air, joining smells of dust, dew, the blue genista and red poppies that starred the long silky grass by the roadside verge, the scarlet cornflowers spangled through the undulating fields of wheat and clover. The air was loud with wings and birdsong, plovers and wood doves, hoopoes and rollers. The white storks were making their annual migration southward, and the sky was never empty of them in this season.

"It's beautiful any time of year," John said; he was at the rear of the fantail-shaped passenger section of the steamer. Yolande looked up. His voice was completely serious, different from the bantering tone he usually used with his youngest sister.

"You love this place, don't you, John?" she said.

He smiled, shrugged, looked away. "Yes," he replied musingly. "Yes, I do. All of it."

They were passing through the lower portion of the estate, as close to flat as any part of Claestum, planted in fruit orchard, dairy pasture, and truck gardens. A score of three-mule plow teams were at work, sixteen-hand giants with silvery coats and Roman noses, leaning into the traces with an immemorial patience. The earth behind the disk-tillers was a deep chocolate color, reddish-brown, smelling as good as new bread. The work gangs were there already, unloading flats of seedlings from steam drags, pitchforking down the huge piles of pale-gold wheat straw used for mulch, spreading manure and sewage sludge from the methane plant, or wrestling with lengths of extruded-aluminum irrigation pipe. Some of them looked up and waved their conical straw hats as the car passed; the mounted foremen bowed in the saddle.

"Y'know," he continued, and shifted the rifle in the crook of his arm, "we say 'Claestum,' and think we've summed it up. It all depends who's doin' the lookin'. A League accountant looks at the entry in her ledgers and sees forty-five-hundred hectares, yieldin' so-and-so many tonnes of wheat and fodder, x hundred hectoliters of wine and y of olive oil per year. Security District Officer down t'Siena calls up the specs on a thousand-odd serfs an' checks fo' reported disorders. An ecologist from the Conservancy people thinks in terms of"—a flight of bustards soared up from a sloping grain field and glided down to a hedgerow—"that sort of thing."

"Ma and Pa?" Yolande said. *Damn, can't get to know your own brother until you grow up,* she thought.

"They see it as something they made," he replied. "Almost as somethin' they fought and broke. I can understand it; every time they look out they can say, 'we planted these trees,' or 'it took five years of green-manurin' to get those upper fields in decent tilth.' Pa told me once it was like breakin' a horse; you had to love the beast or you'd kill it in sheer exasperation."

"And you, Johnny?" she continued softly, careful not to break the mood.

"It's . . . home," he said. "Some people need that feelin' of creation. I don't. I love . . . it all; sights and smells and sounds, the people an' the animals and the plants and . . . oh, the way the sun comes over the east tower every mornin', the church bell soundin'— Shit, I'm no poet, sprout; you're the only one in the family with ambitions in that direction."

He smiled ruefully. "I suspect I love this place mo' than any individual, which may say somethin' about yours truly. At least, a community an' place is longer-lived than a person. I won't change anythin' much, when it's mine. A bit of tidyin' up here and there, maybe bring in a herd of eland, it'd do well . . ."

"Mr. Ingolfsson?" Myfwany asked.

"John," he said.

"Thanks, John . . . I was wonderin', don't mean to pry, but if you like it here so much, why did you volunteer fo' officer trainin'?" Everyone started equal in the Citizen Force, three years minimum and a month a year until forty, but not everyone wanted to prolong their spell in uniform.

"Payback," John said, opening a thermos of *caffé latte* and passing it around. Myfwany made an inquiring sound as she accepted a cup of the coffee.

"I pay my debts," he amplified. The road was winding upwards again, through fig orchards and rocky sheep pasture dotted with sweet chestnut trees.

"Down at that school, they're probably fillin' y'all up with you debt to the Race and the State." He shrugged. "True enough. I likes to think of it on a mo' personal level. A plantation can feel like a world to its own self, but it isn't. It only exists as part of the Domination. The Race makes possible the only way of life I know, the only world I feel at home in, the only contentment I can ever have."

He laughed. "Not least, by controllin' change. It must be powerful lonely to be a Yankee; by the time one of *them* is middle-aged, everythin' they grew up with is gone. Like havin' the earth always dissolvin' away beneath you feet. Cut off from you ancestors an' you descendants both. Here, barrin' catastrophe, I can be reasonable sure that in a thousand years, what I value will still exist.

"It's here because Ma and Pa an' others like them fought fo' it, bled fo' it. A decade of my life is cheap payment. I wouldn't *deserve* this unless I was ready to die fo' it, to kill fo' it." He blinked back to the present, and the gray eyes turned warm as he smiled at his sister. "It'll always be here fo' you, too, sprout, when you come back from that space travellin'."

The lodge was pre-War Italian work, only slightly modified. The plantations fronting the hill nature reserve maintained it jointly, part of their contract with the Conservancy Directorate to manage the forest. Vine-grown, it nestled back into the shadow of the hill, flanked by outbuildings and stables and a few paddocks surrounded by stone walls. The huntsmen were waiting in the forecourt, with the horses and dogs, beside a spring-fed pool. A dozen lion dogs, the type the Draka had bred to hunt the big cats in the old African provinces: black-coated, with thick ruffs around their necks and down their spines. Massive beasts, over a meter at the shoulder and heavier than a man, thick-boned, with broad blunt muzzles and canines that showed over the lower lip. They rose and milled as the car stopped, straw-yellow eyes bright with anticipation, until a word from the handlers set them sinking back on their haunches in disciplined silence.

"Menchino, Alfredo," John said, nodding. The huntsmen were brothers in their early thirties, one fair and one dark, with the slab-sided, high-cheeked faces of the Tuscan peasantry.

"Master John," Menchino said, making the half-bow as the Draka stepped down from the car and the driver pulled away in a *chuff* of steam and sough of pneumatics. There was a smile on his face; hunting was the brothers' religion, and John Ingolfsson had been a devout fellow-worshiper since he was old enough to carry a rifle.

"Missy—" Alfredo began. "Mistis," he corrected, as she frowned and tapped her gunbelt in reminder of her adult status. Adult as far as serfs were concerned, at least. A slight glance out of the corner of his eye to the other serf, the hint of a shrug; she suspected it was the thought of two young females going after a dangerous beast. Italian serfs were funny about things like that, and Ma said it would take another generation or two to really break them of it.

They had learned not to let it *show* some time ago, of course.

"We'll probably be back fo' lunch," Yolande said to the middle-aged house girl on the veranda. "Myfwany, you pick y' mount?"

The serfs led the horses over, and the Draka checked their tack. Light pad-saddles, with molded-leather scabbards for their rifles; the huntsmen had much the same, though without the tooling and studs. The two Ingolfssons and their guest slid their weapons into the sheaths and fastened the restraining straps. Their pack was sitting quiet, but the dogs knew what that meant; tails began to beat at the gravel of the drive, and deep chests rumbled eagerness.

"I'll have the dapple," Myfwany said reaching for the bridle of a spotted gray mare. It blew inquisitively at her, and politely accepted a lump of brown sugar. She turned eyes bright with excitement to her friend. "Less'n you'd rather?"

" 'S fine," Yolande said, gathering her own reins and vaulting easily into the saddle one-handed. The brown gelding sidestepped, then quieted as she gathered it in and pressed her knees. She ran a critical hand down its neck, checking the muscle tone, and turned an eye on the others. They were fresh but not rambunctious, which meant the lodge staff had been exercising them properly.

"Keep the dogs well in hand," John said to the huntsmen. "They not used to anythin' bigger an' meaner than they are."

"That's it!" John said, reining in on the bank of the little stream. The sound of the pack had changed, the deep *gerrr-whuff!* barking giving way to a higher belling sound. "They've sighted."

"Less'n they've taken out after a deer." Myfwany grinned, reached down beyond her right knee. The rifle came out of the scabbard with an easy flip, and she rested the butt on one thigh. The other Draka followed suit.

One of the Italian serfs snorted, and the other coughed to cover it. John laughed. "Not this pack," he said. "Not when we gave them a clear scent."

They heeled their horses down the slope in a shower of gravel and dust. A two-hour chase had brought them deep into the high hills; the Monte del Chianti were mountains only by courtesy, more like steep ridges, few more than a thousand meters high. It was just enough to keep the air comfortably crisp as the morning turned clear and brilliant. The forest was shaggy and uneven, part old growth, much new since the conquest, you could see the traces of old terracing, or the tumbled stones of peasant houses. Oak and chestnut covered the lower slopes, with darker beech and pine and silver fir above; feral grapevines wound around many, and there were slashes of color from the blossom of abandoned orchards.

This spot was cool under tall black pines, full of their chill scent. There were poplars along the stream; the mounts stepped through cautiously, raising their feet high as horseshoes clattered on the smooth brown rocks. Spring rains and sun had brought a brief intense flowering where sun reached through the trees; the far slope was too thin-soiled to carry timber, and it blazed with wild field lilies, grape hyacinths, and sheets of purple-and-yellow crocus. Yolande rose slightly in the stirrups as the gelding's muscles bunched to push it up the hillside in a series of bounds. The bruised herbs raised a sharp aromatic smell, of sage and rosemary and sweet minty hyssop that shed anthrophora bees and golden butterflies in clouds before the horses' hooves.

"Hi*yaaa*," Yolande shouted, as they broke onto an open ridgeline and swung into a loping canter. One of the serfs sounded a horn, *taaa-brrrt*, and the sound of the dogs rose to a deep baying roar; the prey was treed or at bay. She could feel the blood pounding in her ears, and the wind cool after them; it tugged her hat down and blew streamers of pale hair free of her braid, flickering at the corners of her vision. The horse moved between her knees like a beating heart, a long weightless rocking and then the rhythmic thumping of hooves, snort of breath, a creak of leather, and rattle of iron.

"Whoa-*hey*," John said. The dogs were raving, just out of sight ahead, and then the voice of one rose to a shrill scream of pain, cut off sharp as a knife. Another sound, a wild saw-edged snarling shriek that never came from a canine mouth, and the cries were echoed and reechoed as if from stony walls, fading to a harsh far-distant clamor. Yolande's horse laid back its ears and shook its head slightly, and she tightened her legs to reassure it.

The horses slowed to a fast walk as they went under the shade of a stand of tall fir, then again as they emerged into a semicircle of open space surrounded on three sides by trees. The ridgeline was broken here, with a steep slope that turned into a cliff ten meters high. The spot had been improved slightly, the sort of thing the Conservancy Directorate did to encourage the game: a spring had been dug out halfway up the cliff and funneled through a stone lion's mouth, leaping out to feed a pool and the trickle that drained down toward the creek. A big maple grew out of the cliff near the spring, thick twisted roots gripping at the rocks like frozen snakes, the trunk sweeping out almost horizontally and then flaring upward. Six of the lion dogs were leaping and calling beneath the trunk; five more were clustered around the base of the tree.

"*Merda!*" Alfredo swore. One of the pack was lying at the base of the slope, still twitching but with its intestines hanging gray and pink out of its rent belly. It was plain enough what had happened. The five dogs at the tree were barking frantically toward the dense foliage farther out, making short dashes out the broad sloping surface of the trunk and then retreating, as if daring each other. Through the leaves the hunting party could see a flash of brown and orange, and hear the yowling screech of the leopard. Only one dog could approach at a time. A lion dog might outweigh a leopard, but its jaws alone were no match for the big cat's claws and speed.

"Call them in, Alfredo," John said, without taking his eyes off the tree.

The Draka all dropped their reins, and the horses froze into well-trained immobility; nervous, though, and sweating, their eyes rolling at the scent of carnivore so close. Alfredo blew a series of notes on his horn, and his brother rode among the dogs snapping his whip. They milled, bellowing, then drew back with a rush, standing in a clot with their muzzles raised toward the tree. Discipline kept them motionless and quiet, but there was a straining eagerness in their posture, and they shifted weight from foot to foot as unconscious whines of frustration slipped between their fangs.

Yolande worked her mouth, suddenly conscious of its dryness. The glade grew quiet; there was the soft background surf-sound of air through the trees, and the incongruously soothing rush of water into the pool, the small noises of the horses and dogs, and for a moment the fading echoes of Alfredo's horn. *Gods, this is exciting*, she thought. The branches shook as the leopard moved restlessly, then settled, and she could see its amber eyes peering through the leaves. *Exciting.* Quiet outside, inside a torrent of feelings: pity for the dead lion-hound, awe and pity for the great deadly beast seventy meters away. The peculiar combination of sorrow and deep happiness she always felt hunting, but raised to a new level, an aliveness that seemed to reach out to encompass every speck of dust in the slanting beams of light, every movement of leaf and shadow. As if she could track the bees by their humming, or know every rock and crevice of the cliff . . .

"Fist fo' it," John said easily. He drew his binoculars left-handed and focused. "Hooo, lordy, that's a big one. He-cat, old an' mean. He *not* happy at all." Her brother laughed softly with pure pleasure as he returned the glasses to their case at his saddlebow. "Sprout, you first."

They both beat their left fists through the air, then opened them simultaneously.

"Scissors beats paper, tow-hair," John said. "Miz Venders?"

"Myfwany," she corrected, raising her hand. "One, two, three—" The girl's hand came out closed: rock. The young man's was scissors again; he swore good-naturedly.

"You win, Myfwany. Remember, he'll come down fast; that's, oh, thirty meters. Ten in the leap from the tree, then a couple bounds to us. Got it?"

"Mm-hm," the redhead said. There were two spots of crimson high on her freckled cheeks as she kicked one leg over the neck of her horse and slid down, then went to one knee. The muzzle of the rifle stayed pointed half-down, and rock steady. The breeding pairs for the Italian leopards had been imported in the late '40s from the Atlas and Kayble mountains, and not much hunted since; they would have little fear of men. Still it was possible this one knew what a gun meant; if nothing else, the scientists used dart guns for tagging specimens. She was equally careful not to stare directly at their prey.

"You next, sprout."

Yolande brought her right leg over the low horn of her saddle, rested her left hand behind her and eased herself down to the ground. The springy turf gave beneath her boots; it was a long way down, a fifteen-hand horse and a short person. She dropped the reins, which meant "stand still" to a gun-trained mount, and brought her Sherrinford to high port. Her brother waited a few seconds and then dismounted, careful to make no abrupt movements.

"Menchino," he said, in the same soft, conversational voice. "Take you rifle, circle around and come up behind that tree. Don't shoot less'n you has to. If'n you has to, don't hesitate."

"*Grazie,* Mastah," the serf said; some Draka might have sent him up there unarmed. He drew his own plain single-shot hunting weapon and dropped back to follow the edge of the trees around the clearing and approach the maple from behind.

"Spread out," John continued. The two Draka fanned out from Myfwany, leaving her directly facing the tree. Alfredo snapped leashes to the collars of the lead dog and bitch, drawing them to one side to anchor the pack. They could all hear the leopard moving restlessly in the branches, a coughing grunt and an occasional snarl, glimpses of patterned hide.

"Mastah, there's a cave back here," Menchino called from the dense scrub at the base of the slope. The soil was thin there, but the rock was damp with seepage and carried dense thorny maquis, rock rose and broom. "Sign and scat."

"Lair," John called. "Ignore it." He waited until the huntsman was well-positioned at the base of the tree. "Can you see him?"

"Yes." There was a tight quality to the serf's voice. "Jesu and Maria, Mastah, he's a big one. Two and a half meters long, easy."

"Good. Now send him down."

Menchino shouted and began kicking the underbrush around the base of the tree; he roared insults, waved his arms, skated rocks out toward the thicker branches. Yolande wiped her hand on her jacket and took a firmer grip on the rifle. To a cat, noise and motion were threat; it would probably break forward. And predators were more sensible than humans, they were dangerous when cornered or where their young were concerned, but they rarely attacked something except in self-defense or to eat. Leopards were an exception sometimes, though. . . .

The serf fired his rifle into the air; then she could hear the hasty sounds of his reloading. Again.

That brought the cat out into the open, out along a thigh-thick branch that had only a tuft of leaves at the end. Flowing out, then halting blinking in the sun. The light seemed to catch fire on its coat, hot spotted gold rippling like living metal, and the tawny pools of its eyes with the pupils slitted against the sun. *Wotan, it* is *a big one,* she thought delightedly. The North African breed were larger than the sub-Saharan variety, but this was exceptional, even so. An old male, one ear chewed to a stump. Not a happy one, either; the head was forward and the ears laid back, the tail lashing. Menchino fired again, into the upper branches of the tree, and cut twigs pattered down.

That's decided him, Yolande thought, with a pins-and-needles sensation that ran down to the small of her back The long body froze, tail extended and rigid, and then the haunches moved, settling and gripping. She could see the muscles bunch, the claws extend and dig into the rough pale bark. The leopard screamed.

And leapt. An impossible distance out from the branch, soaring as if in flight. Myfwany's rifle came up, seeming to drift, with the deceptive calm of a motion that is fast but very smooth. The muzzle halted, steady, and the flat *crack* of the heavy game round broke the air with a startling suddenness. The yellow grace recoiled in midair and fell, hitting the tall grass with an audible thump; it thrashed, sending stalks and wildflowers and divots of turf flying amid a wild squalling that set the horses shuddering and the lion dogs growling like thunder. Then it was up again, flowing like swift water across the open ground, stretching and bunching. Yolande brought her own weapon up, and saw the fangs bared in the V of the backsight. Myfwany fired again, and the predator seemed to stumble with a grunt, fall, sliding into the ground shoulder-first, tumbling end-for-end, then lying still. Time began again.

"Wait fo' it!" John called. They waited, in a moment that seemed forever. Yolande met her friend's eyes, bright in a flushed face, and felt a shock that seemed to run down to the pit of her stomach.

Myfwany glanced away. "He's not breathin'," she said, slightly hoarse. Yolande looked at the leopard; it was smaller, somehow. The eyes and mouth were open, the tongue lolling like a pink flag; blood pooled out, and there were flies on it already. She walked over to Myfwany, putting a hand on her shoulder, and together they looked down at the dead leopard. It was a little past its prime, marked with the scars of its prey and of mating fights, but still sleek and strong. Triumph and a huge sorrow mixed to make a feeling that was wholly pleasure; she took a deep breath and let it out in a sigh, letting the moment pass with it.

John came up and clapped Myfwany on the back. "Nice shooting," he said heartily. "'Cross the loins with the first round, and right through the lungs with the second," he continued, pointing out the grounds with his toe. "Want to skin him out?"

"No," the redhead said, breaking open her rifle and letting the spent brass tinkle down to ping on rock and bounce off the warm skin of the cat. Loosening the sling, she hung it muzzle-down across her back. "I'll water the horses, if'n you don't mind."

The young man nodded, slung his own weapon and drew the long clip-pointed Jamieson from its sheath along his leg. The honed edge glinted in the morning sunlight, a line of silver along the blackened steel of the narrow blade.

"Alfredo, give me a hand," he said, kneeling and holding the hilt in his mouth while he rolled back the sleeves of his hunting jacket.

Yolande let the barrel of her rifle fall back onto her right shoulder, reaching left-handed for the reins of her mount. Myfwany collected the other horses, soothing them with words and a firm stroking band on nose and neck, leading them carefully around the bloody bodies of dog and leopard. They shied slightly at the smell as they passed, then quieted a little; the wind was from the hillside, and she thought it must still carry the dead cat's scent, if it had been denning here. She gathered the reins and pulled her horse's head around, following her friend.

"Mastah! Look out!" Menchino shouted.

She looked up, and for a second perception warred with knowledge; the leopard was dead, but a leopard was charging toward her from the shrub beyond the pool. Running in long low bounds, the tail swinging to balance it, fluid and sure. Menchino fired from above, and his bullet kicked dust and spanged off stone by the animal's side. It swerved slightly, the platter-sized feet spreading and gripping in automatic adjustment; swerved toward Myfwany. The horses were rearing and neighing. Myfwany's hand was tangled in their reins; she was fighting to free it, clawing with her other for the pistol by her side. Alfredo's rifle was still in its scabbard on his saddle; John's was across his back, and his hands busy with the skinning.

Yolande felt the reins burn through her left palm. The Sherrinford's muzzle came forward as she yanked at the stock with her right hand, but slowly, so slowly, caught in air thick as honey. Only the leopard was moving at normal speed, the bounds lengthening. Myfwany's face was chalk-pale, the green eyes enormous. *Slap* and the forestock of her rifle hit her palm, *hold* the breath *squeeze* the trigger. *Bam!* and recoil hammered at her shoulder, another spurt of dust by the cat's forefeet, and now it was rising in the final leap, head high, Yolande let the muzzle drop again—*straight-on shot* ran through her head—and *bam!*

Then she was running toward the tangled figures on the ground, rifle held high by the barrel, shouting wordlessly. She swore as she ran, every muscle tensing for the single blow, then froze. The leopard was not moving, but neither was Myfwany. . . . Yolande dropped the rifle heedlessly, buried her hands in the cat's ruff and strained backward, heaving at a limp unresisting weight that was like a roll of damp canvas; the animal's bones and sinew moved in their natural courses, but flopping loose without a directing mind, hampering. She heaved it half off the other girl and dropped to her knees, hands smoothing blood-matted hair back from blood-slicked skin.

"*Myfwany!*" she said frantically. "Oh, gods, Myfwany, are you all right, *please* be all right, I tried, oh please, I love you, *please!*"

"Phffth," Myfwany said, spitting blood to one side. The matted lashes fluttered open. "It's—*pfhth*—not my blood, an' get this thing *off* me!" She kicked and shoved, freeing herself, then sat up and caught at Yolande's shoulders. "And I love you, too." Suddenly they were laughing, embracing, with kisses that tasted of rank blood and fear and joy.

"Touchin'," John said, dryly and a trifle breathlessly. The girls broke apart and rose, leaning on each other. Yolande's brother heaved the animal over on its back. "Female, nursin'." The teats along its belly were enlarged. "In through the lung, an' a perfect heart-shot," he continued. "Dead in the air."

Myfwany gripped Yolande harder, and gave way to a single deep shudder. "Felt like someone fired it at me like a cannonball, an' it was sprayin' blood." Yolande felt her stomach knot with fear-nausea, and pushed it down; there had been no time before, and now it would be foolish. She slipped her arm down to rest around Myfwany's waist, unwilling to break contact, unwilling to let go the concrete feeling of life.

"Bet there's kits in that-there cave," she said.

The leopard cub mewled, and Machiavelli danced back from the box that held his fascinated regard, hissed, then turned tail and bolted up the tower stairs. Yolande heard Myfwany laugh, and gripped harder at the stone of the balustrade, biting at her lip and choking back a sob.

"Sweet, what is it?" Myfwany asked.

Yolande turned to see her framed by the opened French doors of the lounging room; behind her the servants were scurrying out. The afternoon wind blew up from the gardens, cuffing with warm soft hands at red hair still damp and dark from the baths, plastering the thin cloth of the robe to her body.

"I—" She breathed deeply, winning back control. Her head felt light, only vaguely connected to the rest of her. "I just realized again. Yo— might have *died*, Myfwany. You might be *gone*, right now."

"So." The other smiled, warm and fond; then her expression grew serious, and she stretched out her hands toward the other, palms up. "Come to me. I'm here."

The cub was looking doubtfully at the bottle. Yolande looked up from fastening her eardrops as it hissed.

"Come on, *eat*, you little moron," Myfwany said, pushing the bottle toward the spotted form. It tumbled backward in the blankets, crowding toward the back of the improvised cage the plantation carpenter had knocked together for them. The huge amber eyes were opened wide, and it made a pathetic gesture of menace with the too-large paws.

"Oh, the poor thing!" That was Sofia, Myfwany's maid. She reached toward the leopard and yanked her hand back, sucking at the scratches and spitting curses in Sicilian.

"Here," Yolande said, laughing. She picked up the comforter from the rumpled sheets of her bed and threw it over the cub, then clamped the wriggling form through the thick fabric while the others tucked it into a bundle.

"Now, let's get the head free . . . right. Give me the bottle, darlin' . . ." The cub was glaring and hissing again; she waited until it quieted a little, then dribbled milk on its muzzle. It squalled, but licked its fur as well, and she could almost see it pause mentally at the warm almost-familiar taste. "There, little tiger, that's bettah, isn't it?" Yolande moved the rubber teat closer, then gently brushed it against the cub's lips. It hesitated, then began to suck strongly; she let it feed for a moment, then brought the fingers of her other hand close enough for it to smell, rubbing along its jaw.

"Lele, Sofia, *that's* how y'all does it," she said. "Ready to go down to dinner, darlin'?"

"Sho'ly, love," Myfwany replied. The word was still new enough to send a stab of pleasure. "How do I look?" She stood and turned, holding out her arms.

They were both dressed in evening wear, the neo-Grecian gowns that had been standard formal dress for Citizen women since the Classic Revival a century and more ago. The draped and folded chiton still felt a little strange, children did not wear such. The right shoulder was bare, and the end-fold hung over the left elbow. Myfwany's was a warm bronze color, edged in a turquoise that matched her eyes. Yolande had decided to stick with ivory-cream; ash-blondes tended to look washed-out in anything lighter.

"You look wonderful," Yolande said, running her fingers gently down the other's neck. "Ready to face the music?"

"I didn't know you meant it literally," Myfwany said. Dinner was indoors today, it being still a little cold for dining on the terrace after sunset. The two girls had halted in the corridor outside the lounge where the family gathered before the evening meal, and they could hear the sound of harp and flute through the tall carved-ebony doors.

"Oh, you," Yolande said. Then: "Oh, *you*." She made a few last-minute adjustments to the hairpin in the psyche-knot above her left ear. "I'm nervous. I mean, I feel, you know, *different.*"

"Love, you didn't have a big 'V' fo' 'virgin' stamped on y'forehead, anyhows." Myfwany smiled heavy-lidded, and leaned forward to plant a gentle kiss on the skin between Yolande's breasts, above the drape of her gown. "Besides, it's only fifty percent deflowerin'."

"No fair, I cain't grab when we're all dressed up!" Yolande whispered, then chuckled.

"What's so funny?"

"Well . . . it wasn't like I expected. I mean, I knew it was a *plea-sure*, everyone's always goin' on about it, but I didn't expect it to be so much, oh, *fun*. Like a tickle-fight, hey? An' I feel so much *bettah*."

Myfwany joined in her laughter. "I think that depends on who, sweet," she said, and held out a hand. "Shall we go in?"

Yolande took the hand in both of hers. "Myfwany, I want you to know something. As long as our names are spoken together, I'll never do anythin' to make you ashamed of me."

"Nor will I," Myfwany said, equally grave. They linked arms and turned.

The door swung open easily with a hand push against one of the silver lion's heads that studded the night-black Coromandel wood, into a space more dimly lit than the corridor. The room within was a long L-shape. The inner wall held bookshelves and a huge fireplace; the outer, Flemish tapestries between tall windows. Cedar logs burned with an aromatic crackle, their light ruddy on the couches, settees, and low tables. The serf musicians were gathered unobtrusively in a corner, the Draka grouped around the hearth: her father and mother and brother, of course. and Aunt Alicia; her friends from school; the three overseers. This was a semi-formal occasion, to celebrate the successful hunt.

"Greetin's," her father said with a slight bow, raising his brandy snifter. "Honor to our leopard killers." He was smiling, but there was real pride in the gesture.

Yolande nodded back to the stocky figure in the dark velvet jacket and lace cravat, feeling a rush of love. The others raised a polite murmur and joined the toast before resuming their conversations. A house girl brought round a tray of aperitifs, and the girls accepted glasses of chilled white wine with their free hands as they joined the loose grouping around the fire. She sipped, marveling at the tart refreshing taste, the sensual pleasure of fire-warmth on her skin; everything seemed new, everyone sharing her joy.

"Congratulations again," John said, taking a wafer dabbed with beluga from a passing servant. He looked at their linked hands. "On all counts."

Her mother looked up from a lounger; she had been talking to Rahksan, who sat beside her on a stool working listlessly at her inevitable embroidery.

"Well, here's a cat that's found its way into the dairy," she said dryly. "Took long enough."

"*Mother!*" Yolande said, with a sound halfway between affection and exasperation.

Veronica had been leaning against the mantelpiece. "An' about time," she added, grinning.

Myfwany leaned closer to give Yolande a kiss on the cheek. "My sentiments exactly," she said aloud. In a whisper: "They just teasing, sweet."

"Don't I know it," Yolande replied, and realized that this time at least she did not mind, her heart knew as well as her head did that the words were without intent to hurt. Today nothing could diminish happiness, except the knowledge that today must end.

She looked down at Rahksan; the serf's face was drawn tight around the eyes and mouth, a look of suffering. *Poor Tantie.* She gave her friend's arm a squeeze.

"Just a second, love," she murmured, then crossed to sit on the lounger. "Y'all right, Tantie?" she asked softly, putting a hand on her shoulder. The official story was that Rahksan had been attacked, which would account for her being shaken. The Draka girl grimaced mentally at the memory of the scene in the stable, then put it aside with adolescent ruthlessness; nothing seemed strong enough to cast a shadow on the changing of her life. "Anythin' I can do fo' you?"

"No, thank y' kindly, Mistis 'Landa," Rahksan said. Some life returned to her face, and she reached up to pat the girl's hand. "I jes' need a little time, is all."

"Which reminds me, time fo' an announcement," Johanna said casually. "In recognition of his quick and decisive action, Rahksan's son Ali is bein' recommended as a candidate fo' State service, an' will be leavin' in two months fo' preliminary testin' at the Janissary base in Nova Cartago."

There were raised eyebrows among some of the Draka. The number of recruits needed was limited in these days of peace, and there was fierce competition for the available slots among the one and a half billion of the serf population. Recommendation was a privilege usually only given to exceptionally deserving cases, and Ali had been notorious as a troublemaker, aside from this latest incident. Of course, the Janissaries were not house serfs or field hands, and qualities which made a man unsatisfactory on a plantation could be valuable in the armed services. . . .

Rahksan nodded deferentially to the congratulations, murmuring thanks. "I jes' hope he do well, Mistis," she said to Johanna. "He never goin' be happy here, that sure. Maybeso this the makin' of him." She blinked, her lashes wet. "But I don' see much of him now, that sure too."

"Hey, don' be sad, Tantie," Yolande said, concerned. "He get leave now an' then, you sees him as often as Ma sees me or Edwina or Dionysia or John."

A sigh. "That true." The Afghan smiled wearily, but with genuine warmth. "Congratulations fo' yaz an' y'friend, Mistis 'Landa. Good to see m'other chile's growin' strong an' happy."

"Thank you, Tantie," Yolande said, touched.

Her mother reached out a finger and touched Rahksan's cheek, taking up a teardrop. "Speakin' of children, why don't you go an' talk to y' boy some, Rahksi?" Johanna looked up to meet her husband's eye; he nodded slightly, smiling. "See you later this evenin'."

The Landholders and their guests walked through into the dining room—one of the smaller ones; there would be no point in eight people losing themselves in the halls meant for entertainment. This was spacious enough but cozy, a round rosewood table and sideboards; the white linen and burnished silverware shone beneath the chandelier, and the house girls were laying out the appetizers: smoked salmon and foie gras and oysters nestling in beds of crushed ice. Yolande found herself and Myfwany seated to the right of her parents, the senior positions.

The smells suddenly made her mouth water; it had been a long day, and she had skipped lunch.

"My, that looks good," she said, as the serf laid salmon and capers on her plate. Another poured the first wine, a Valpolicella the color of straw. She sniffed, sipped.

"Fifteen an' hollow legs," Johanna said. "Children . . . oh, speakin' of which, Tom an' I have *anothah* announcement." She reached across and took her husband's hand. "We're havin' some mo'."

Yolande choked on her wine. Myfwany thumped her back but she could still hear John's glass hit the table with a heavy *chunk* as she coughed.

"You *what*, Ma?" she gasped. She was the youngest of the four, and had had fifteen years of hearing Johanna's fervid relief that that particular duty to the Race was complete.

"Loki you say!" her brother added, with a snort. "That's a surprise."

Her father laughed, deep and rich. "Soul of the White Christ, everyone's Methuselah to their offspring," he said leaning back and grinning at their discomfiture. "Frig and Freya, boy, you going so slow on the grandchildren, we thought we'd show you how."

"An' we're not exactly too old yet," Johanna said, raising a brow. Then, relenting: "You youngsters do tease easy. Oh, we not doin' it *personal;* that would be too risky at my age, certain-sure. Not to mention barbaric an' uncomfortable. We had a couple dozen frozen ova stored by the Eugenics people, just goin' have them warmed up and borne by host mothers, brooders. *Finally* they figured a way of havin' the unpleasant part done by the serfs." A bland look at Yolande. "Provided you approves, of course."

"Certai—oh, *Mother*," Yolande said, casting an appealing eye at her friends. It was bad enough being teased by your contemporaries, but parents were much worse. She saw suppressed laughter, as her schoolmates examined their plates or the ceiling.

"It'll be nice to have babies around again," she said. That was true enough; babies were even more fun than kittens. "An' they're no bother, after all."

"Sho'ly will be nice," Johanna agreed, nodding. "The Eugenics people talkin' about improvements, as well. Now, about the party next week—"

Chapter Five

PROVINCE OF SARMATIA
DOMINATION OF THE DRAKA
CRIMEAN MILITARY RESERVE
AIR TRAINING SECTION
15,000 METERS
MARCH 10, 1973

"Beep. Beep. Beep." The missile lock-on warning repeated itself with idiot persistence, a drone in the silenced cave-world of the pilot's helmet, sharper than the subliminal moan of the engines.

"Shit," Yolande muttered to herself, throwing the aircraft into a series of wild jinks and swerves, just enough to keep the beeps from merging into the continuous drone of launch.

She was half-reclining in the narrow cockpit of the Falcon VI turboram fighter, immobile in a hydraulic suit that cushioned her against acceleration and a clamshell couch that left nothing mobile but fingers and head. The sky above her was blue-black through the near-invisible canopy, here on the fringes of space; ahead was the smooth semicircle of crystal-sandwich screen, the virtual control panel with its multiple information displays. Mach 3.5 and climbing, and *nothing* on the fucking screens, nothing at all.

It was a testing exercise, another name for sadistic mental torture. They might have programmed an error into her machine. Or simply cut the input from its electrodetectors; it was resentfully acknowledged that the Alliance was ahead in ECM and sensor technology, and this could be a test of how she would deal with that in combat. Her lips curled away from her teeth behind the face mask. The Domination was *not* behind in engines and materials, so use that. . . .

Her hands moved on the pressure-sensitive pads inside the restrainers. The Falcon pitched forward and power-dove straight down. Something soft and heavy and strong gripped her and *pushed,* pushed until she could feel the soft tissues trying to spread away from her bones and gray crept in at the corners of her eyes. The suit squeezed, fighting the G's and pressing the blood back toward her brain, but nothing could make it easier to breathe or stop the feeling that her ribs were about to break back into her chest. Mach 4, and the altimeter unreeled; 15,000 meters was *not* far at these speeds. The indicator hesitated in its maddening beep, then resumed.

"Now!" she yelled to herself, and yanked at the pads, pulling the Falcon up in a wrenching curve that stressed it to ten-tenths of capacity. The pressure grew worse, crushing, vision fading, hands immobile but the AI would continue the curve. *Hold Wotan damn it hold don't grayout not* now *you stupid cow—* The red telltales blinked back to amber: Mach 3.8, 6,000 meters; half the altitude gone in seconds. The orthodox maneuver, and not good enough, the lock-on was still sounding and altitude was so much easier to lose than regain. Air brakes. Dump velocity, emergency mode, cycle the vent. The high-pitched roar of the ramjet faltered, stopped.

The airplane shuddered, thrumming, rattling her teeth, ramming her body forward against the clamshell as it slowed; not as good a fit as a body-tailored squadron unit would be. Might be, if she passed. Her mind drew a picture of how it would look from outside: the long oval of the fighter's fuselage, the stubby forward-swept wings, edges flexing and thuttering as the spoilers popped open along the trailing edge.

Far below, serfs in the plantations of the Kuban Valley paused for an instant at the flash of silver overhead, the rolling *crack-crack* as the fighters passed, then bent again to the immemorial rhythm of their hoes; it was a familiar thing, and the bossboys were watching.

Mach 1 and dropping. *Lost him—shitshitshit!* The scanning warning started up again, the beeps coming closer and closer together. The rubber taste of the mouthpiece was bitter against her tongue; he must be *close* now, very close. Still nothing on the detectors.

"Override stops," she said. The computer acknowledged with a patterned light, releasing its control of maneuvers that threatened the integrity of the aircraft. *Threatened to leave me as a long greasy smear on the landscape*, she thought, and pushed it away.

Fingers moved, like an artist's on the piano. Left-two-right-one-one. Fractional seconds, time floating by so calm, so leisurely. Touch, touch, crack the vent and bleed air into the turbines for low-altitude boost. Bring the vectored-thrust louvers online, still closed. *Now.*

The fighter flipped up, presenting its belly to the axis of flight. In the same moment the underside jets cut in, super-heated air pumping out like retrorocket thrust. Shock struck, like hitting a brick wall, and this time she did gray out, felt the jolt of the medicomp pushing stimulant into her veins. Something in the airframe *pinged* audibly, and a warning light began strobing crimson. And something flashed by outside, above, a streak from one side of the sky to the other. *"Eeeeehaaa!"* she shrieked exultantly, and pushed at the throttle. Speed crawled back up, then the ram cut in, building to maximum thrust, and the giant was back on her chest. Too low for optimum burn, too rich a mixture, the ramjet sound was wrong, thready. But the enemy was on her screens now, the thermal signature of a ramscoop engine centered in the weapons section. He had still been decelerating when she did the kick-up; Yolande's Falcon must have disappeared from his board as if teleported out.

The release of tension was like neat brandy on an empty stomach, like orgasm after a long teasing tumble.

"Die, you shit, fuckin' *die!*" she screamed happily. Closing, closing; the rearward sensors were less powerful than the ones in the nose, and her own ECM would help. Visual range, nothing fooled the ol' Eyeball Mark 1, they were both accelerating fast but she had the edge. A touch and the gun sight sprang out on the weapons screen, with the green blips at the lower corners; a Falcon had two 30mm Gatlings at the wing-roots, a concession to the dogfighting days. *Not going to give him a lock-on warning,* she thought. Closer still, and she remembered her mother's advice: *an ace is someone who climbs right up the enemy's asshole before they shoot.*

He dodged, too late and too point-blank now. Her fingers danced on the pads, and the slim form of the fighter was one with her, dancing in sky. The triple line of the vents filled the sight, and she fired. *Ping-ping-ppng,* and the computer stitched a line of hit marks across the instructor's fuselage; his own machine went rock-steady and began a careful circle back to base, a sign that the AI had acknowledged defeat and taken control for landing. Yolande pulled her own plane back and drove for the upper levels. She was halfway through the second victory roll when the weakened vanes blew.

"That was, without any shadow of a doubt, the most stupid, arrogant, purely *moronic* thing you've done, in a course of study marked by mo' than its share of fuckups, Ingolfsson."

Yolande swallowed. The ejection had produced instant unconsciousness; the next thing she remembered was the murmur of Russian as the field hands lifted her out of the pod, their broad weathered faces whirling against a nauseatingly mobile sky. A day in the infirmary had taken the worst of the sting and ache away, but her neck still felt as if it had been wrenched all the way around twice and every vertebra in her back seemed to have been squashed into its neighbor. The medicomp weighing down her right forearm clicked and dribbled something into her veins, and the pain behind her eyes eased—the physical pain. Her stomach twisted, and she could taste acid at the back of her throat. Clammy sweat ran down her flanks from the armpits, and the light fabric of her garrison blacks was a clinging burden.

"Yes, ma'am," she said, bracing to attention and staring over the head of the seated Chief Instructor; she fixed her eyes on the crossed flags behind the desk. The national flag, the Drakon, a crimson bat-winged dragon on a black background, clutching the slave-fetter of mastery and the sword of death in its claws, a green-silver-gold sunburst on the shield across its chest. The Air Corps banner, the skull of an eagle in a circle of gold on black, with flames in its eye-sockets.

The Chief Instructor's office was a plain white room in what had once been the Livadiya Palace, here in Yalta, looking out over the garden and with a view down to the Black Sea. The Livadiya was more than a century old, once a resort for Russian nobles. The time of the Tzars had passed, and it had been a playground for the more exalted of the Soviet *nomenklatura*. The Eurasian War came, and now for thirty years, the Crimean peninsula had been a training reserve of the Directorate of War.

"Well, have you anythin' mo' to say fo' y'self?" Merarch Corinne Monragon was a small woman, no taller than Yolande; in her fifties, with an ugly beak nose and a receding chin and gray hair streaked with an indeterminate mousy color. There was an impressive array of ribbons over the left breast of her garrison blacks: the Flying Cross, for more than six confirmed kills in air-to-air combat, and the Anti-Partisan medal.

Freya, not a washout. Disgrace, at this stage. Everyone carefully avoiding talking about it, not-friends commiserating. Two years driving some lumbering gun-truck groundstrike monstrosity with damn-all chance of space training. No chance of being posted to the same base as Myfwany. Black edged in around her sight.

"Ah . . ." Yolande pulled on her training, clamping inwardly on the tremors that threatened to make her voice shake. Her face was expressionless, save for the beads of moisture along her hairline, and that could have been the crash trauma. The windows behind the big desk were slightly open on a pale winter noon gray with cloud, and chill damp air, which cuffed at the heavy silk of the banners, slid across her face.

"Ah, I *won*, ma'am."

The officer sighed and touched a screen on the desk before her. "Records: Ingolfsson, Yolande, pilot-trainee." She examined it in silence for a moment, then looked up.

"There *is* that, Ingolfsson. There is also *this*." Her hand tapped the screen. "Which contains good news an' bad, apart from the good-to-passable academics." She folded her fingers and leaned forward, the nose with its pearl stud like the beak of a bird of prey. "The good is that when you good, you very, very good indeed, a shit-eatin', bird-stompin' wonder of a pilot." The merarch's voice rose slightly. "And when you bad, *you is fuckin' awful!*"

Another sigh. "So this time, you suckered the best pilot instructor we got. Wonderful. Then you turned a 1,750,000-auric trainer into a large, smokin' hole in a cherry orchard outside o' Krasnodar by doin' acerobatics—just didn't *notice* the air-frame alarm, eh? We have an *enemy* to shoot down our aircraft, lngolfsson, but you've decided they don't deserve the privilege, eh? Well."

Wotan, Yolande thought, impressed despite herself. That was half the price of a fully-stocked plantation. Some imp of the perverse spoke in her ear: *They aren't going to dock it out of my pay, are they, ma'am?*

The instructor took a deep breath. "Well, you application fo' scramjet or deep-space trainin' is, of course, denied." Those postings were reserved for people with squadron experience.

"I suspect if it weren't fo' you friend Venders's steadyin' influence, you'd have washed out into ground-support work, or even the infantry, a while ago." A pause which grew long. The five friends who had entered pilot-selection training were down to three now; Muriel and Veronica had transferred out. "As it is, you've made it. Just. Barely. See the adjutant fo' you orders; the usual two months' leave, then report fo' squadron service."

"Yes, *ma'am!*" Yolande threw a cracking salute, right fist to chest. *Calm. Why do I feel so calm?*

"An' Ingolfsson?"

"Ma'am?"

"Flyin' fighters isn't a game, Ingolfsson. I know there's a killer instinct somewheres inside of you; find it. Or it may turn out to be a *very* good thing fo' the Race that we have a deposit of you frozen ova, understand?" She rose and came around the table. "Congratulations," she said, and they exchanged the wrist-grip Draka handshake. In her other hand was a box with pilot's rank-tabs.

"Thank you, ma'am." The ruby bars clipped onto the epaulets, and she tucked the old silver cadet's pins into a pocket of the tunic. Yolande forced her face to gravity as she pulled the peak-billed cap from her shoulder strap, unfolded it, and settled it home on the regulation recruit's inch-long haircut.

Now I can grow it long enough to comb, she thought gleefully as she did a smart about-face and marched into the outer office, past the desks and the gray-uniformed serf Auxiliaries. Out into the corridor, past the two motionless Janissaries, like giant insects in segmented impact armor and visored sensor helmets. She looked down; her hands were shaking. *I didn't even notice*, she thought. She concentrated a moment; the floating feeling at the back of her skull diminished. Down the arched colonnade, thin rain falling on tiles and potted trees on her left, bas-reliefs of the Eurasian War on her right. Through more offices, into a waiting room.

Her pace picked up as she saw Mandy and Myfwany, turned to a jog as they saw her grin and wave. Then she was running, dodging tables and people in uniform, and flinging herself into the air, heedless of the jar to her bruises.

"*Wuff!*" Myfwany caught her in midleap; Yolande wound her legs tight around her friend's waist and propped her elbows on the hard muscle of her shoulders. "Why, Cadet Ingolfsson, someone might think you'd had good news."

Yolande clasped hands behind the red head, as close-shaven as her own, and kissed her. It turned long and passionate, until she felt herself as breathless as in a high-G turn, lost in touch and scent and taste. Taste of salt as two tears slid down her cheeks to the meeting of their lips. She turned her head aside and buried it in the collar of the other's uniform.

"You hurting, love?" Myfwany whispered into her ear.

"No. Happy. We'll be together." Her hug turned fierce.

"Oh, *moo*," Mandy said. "Y'all are always at it. Good news, you make out. Bad news, you make out. Nothin' else to do, you make out. C'mon fellas, we've all gotten through Selection, let's go *celebrate.*"

Yolande unlocked her legs and slid down to stand. "Well," she said huskily, smiling up into Myfwany's turquoise-green eyes. "Myfwany an' I could celebrate by goin' back to our room an' fuckin' our brains out—*oof.*" She broke off as the blonde jabbed her under the ribs with her fingertips. Myfwany laughed. "Do we complain at the boys y' always dragging in?" she said.

"No, y'all steal 'em," Mandy said.

"That's not fair, we just *borrowed* a few; they are reusable, you knows," Myfwany replied. "Anyways, you know what they say: 'Men fo' amusement, women fo' pleasure, cucumbers fo' ecstasy.'"

Yolande sighed, closed her eyes, and leaned into her friend's side; they were just the right height for that, about a handspan's difference. As far as she was concerned, Mandy could keep the men—it was as often uncomfortable as enjoyable—but she supposed Myfwany was right, you had to broaden your experience. *I guess I'm just a prude,* she thought regretfully. For that matter, she didn't much like sleeping with serfs, either; it was always difficult to tell whether they really wanted to, and if they didn't, why bother?

"There's always the Flamingo Feather," Mandy said.

The Crimea had been taken by amphibious assault in the fall of '42, early in the War, and had become a major base area for the drive west, since the harbors had fallen relatively intact. Between the Germans and the Draka and the general chaos, there had been little of the native population left; when the European section of the Eurasian War wound down in '45, it had seemed sensible to make it a military reservation, and the remaining locals were moved out to provide labor on the wheat plantations of the Ukraine. There were mountains, plains, seashore, forest, and steppe, a reasonable facsimile of a Mediterranean climate along the southern shore for barracks, and every other type of weather and terrain within easy reach. Recruit training became the major occupation as the settlement of the lands west of the Volga proceeded, and the Citizen population built up.

So the Crimea was not really part of the Province of Sarmatia, not really of any specific location. It was Army, an island in the archipelago, a way station in the Domination's largest institution, and a cog in the slaughterous efficiency that had conquered two-thirds of the human race. That meant more than barracks and armories.

"Hoppin' tonight," Mandy said, as they pushed through the bead curtain. The Flamingo Feather was an aviators' hangout, a dozen linked public rooms with the usual facilities, palaestra and baths and bedrooms.

"Everybody glad to be off restriction," Myfwany replied. Few Draka used enough of anything to endanger their health; it was stupid, and illegal besides. Pilot-trainees were on an altogether stricter regimen, enforced by the medical monitors they wore at all times; there were even restrictions on sex, leading to a good deal of resentful graffiti about the Orgasm Police.

Yolande looked down on the sunken room. There was a haze of blue smoke under the rooftop lights, a little tobacco, considerably more Kenya Crown *ganja*. Tables scattered around the edges, a dais for the musicians and singer; dancers going through their paces in the center. Big murals on the walls, holograph copies. She recognized one: it had been done by her mother's uncle's daughter Tanya, who had been a cohortarch in the Archonal Guard until '45. Gray shattered buildings under gray sky, with a column of tanks going through, mud squelching up from under their treads. Hond III, mid-Eurasian War models. The hatches were open, and the Draka crews showed head-and-shoulders out of the turrets. Wrapped and muffled against the cold, looking with a weary and disgusted boredom at the skeletal corpses lying rat-gnawed along the avenue.

"Eeugh," she said, as they handed their rain cloaks to the serf and walked down the stairs. She had seen her share of bodies—Draka children were taken to public executions fairly early to cure them of squeamishness—but this was just purely ugly. "I like that one bettah." The other side was a picture holo. A tropical beach, palm-fringed, backed by jade-green sugar cane and dark-green mountains beyond; the sun was setting over a stretch of purple sea speckled with white foam-crests, in a riotous banner of clouds in cream, gold, and rose. "Nosy-Be, isn't it?"

They found an unoccupied table in a nook, settled back in against the cushioned settees. The attendants had seen their new-minted pilot's bars; this was Graduation Week, after all. A bucket of ice with a bottle of champagne appeared, and finger food, grilled spiced prawns and crawfish.

"I think so," Myfwany said. "Which raises the interestin' point, where do we go after the Great Escape?" The next two months would be the longest leave they would have before they mustered out on their twenty-second birthdays.

Yolande halted with the glass halfway to her lips and set it down again on the smooth stone of the table. "It's real," she said dazedly. "It just hit me, *we're adults.*" Her eyes were wide, and she felt a slight tug of alarm. The speeches and parades would come later that week, but it was official enough now. "We can . . . oh, we can vote. Get elected Archon." She took a gulp of the wine, then slowed down as the chill piquant sweetness hit her mouth.

"Watch the sacrilege there, that's Old Klik," Myfwany said, and took up the game as she sipped at her own. "Or we can get called out in a duel. At least while we're not Active Service."

"Apply fo' land grant. Or get married," Mandy said, propping chin on a hand with a distant look.

The other two exchanged glances; their friend *had* been getting an awful lot of letters from Yolande's brother John. It was a bit May-September, but the difference in ages mattered less as they grew older.

"Well, not much point in that," Yolande said. "You've got to live in barracks fo' the next twenty-six months at least. Not really practical to have children, either."

"Oh, I don't know," Myfwany said. "Use a brooder fo' the children. These days, no need to incubate you own eggs. But it's true there's no point in marryin' until you can set up house together; I wouldn't consider it fo' another three, five years, myself."

Yolande felt a chill that ran down her spine and settled under her ribcage. With a too-familiar effort of will she shoved it aside and sprang up. "C'mon, love, let's dance," she said. "Shadowdance."

Myfwany grinned back at her; the strong-boned young face was the most beautiful thing in the world. "Sure, sweet," she said.

They rose and threaded their way hand in hand to the dance floor, their soft boots rutching on the tessellated mosaic of the surface. The band was just setting up for a new number: Hungarian Gypsies by their look, and in native costume, playing violin and flute and something like a hammer dulcimer. Except as horse handlers, Gypsies made poor workers, but they were fine entertainers and the leisure industries had bought up a good many of them. The lights dimmed. The music began low and sweet, with a swinging lilt; then it grew wilder, sorrowful, and with a hint of dark empty places and wind through faded grass. The singer stepped up to the edge of the dais and began a soft throaty lament; the hoop earrings bobbed against the toffee-colored skin of her neck, and the multicolored silk flounces of her dress glittered.

The two Draka stood face to face and extended their arms until their hands touched, very lightly, at the fingertips. Shadowdancing was a development of the martial arts, originally a method of training in anticipating another's movements. Yolande half-closed her eyes and let the music take her, the gentle pressure on her fingertips, the whole-body *sense* of the other. They turned, circling, swooping, bending, the lead passing from Myfwany to Yolande and back with each dozen heartbeats. She felt the boundaries of her self blur; motion was uncaused, unthought, total control merging into total abandonment of will. The tempo picked up, and they were whirling, leaping, then suddenly slowing to half-time and a languorous drifting. It was a pleasure halfway between flying and making love, and like both it translated you outside yourself. They slowed almost to a halt, palm against palm on either side of their faces, feet skimming the tile with cat-soft precision.

The music stopped, and Yolande returned to herself with an inner walking down a step that wasn't there. Sensation returned, and she knew she was breathing deeply, felt the prickle of sweat on her skin. The other dancers had emptied a circle around them, and a few were applauding. Myfwany was close enough for her to watch the pupils contract from their concentration flare, close enough to smell the clean warm scent of her body, like summer grass and fresh sheets.

> "I watched you, not the teacher, all that long summer's noon
> Though he taught Leonardo, with loving respect
> I was blinded by knowledge of where we'd be soon
> And my eyes wandered dazed on the curve of your neck
> Oh, statues and portraits, now to me you're a part
> Of my golden Myfwany; kisses and art."

AIRCAR
100 KM SOUTH OF NANTES LOIRE DISTRICT
TOURAINE PROVINCE
DOMINATION OF THE DRAKA
APRIL 5, 1973

Nantes in ten minutes, Yolande thought, banking the aircar north toward the Loire estuary and beginning the descent. *Chateau Retour in another fifteen after that.*

The little aircraft dipped smoothly; the whole top was set transparent down to waist-height, crystal-sandwich luxury. Poitou wheeled beneath them, broad squares of plowland and vineyard and straight dusty roads, patterned with the shadows of a few fleecy white clouds on this bright spring morning. She had a temptation to swoop down and barnstorm—the aircar was as responsive as a fighter at low altitude—but resisted it with a caressing motion on the sidestick that waggled the wings. *She is a honey,* the Draka thought happily. A six-seater Bambara, Archona-made by Dos Santos Aerospatial. The very latest, twin ceramic axial flow turbines, vectored-thrust VTOL, variable-geometry wings that could fold right into the oval fuselage. Supersonic, just barely, though she ate fuel like a stone bitch if you tried to cruise above .9 Mach; obscenely comfortable by comparison to any sort of military issue. The four rear seats were recliners, swivel-mounted around a table-console and bar. Myfwany's parents and hers had clubbed together to buy it for them, as a graduation present.

Myfwany and she had spent the first month of their furlough travelling in the Bambara. Money was no problem; they had the basic Citizen stipend now, their pilot's pay, and their families had put them on an adult's allowance from the joint enterprises, about as much again. Yolande looked over her shoulder at her lover, curled asleep on one of the rear seats with her hand under one cheek. It had been like school holidays again, only better, with nobody to tell them what to do. They had rented a little island for a week. Sleeping during the hot days, watching impossibly lurid sunsets, spearfishing, grilling their catch on the long empty white beach while the surf hissed phosphorescent under the huge soft stars, making love by moonlight and lying entangled under the palms until dawn. Visiting distant relatives had been fun, too: the parties and sports, the cities and museums and galleries and plays. Giving each other presents—Myfwany had found her a signed first edition of *Ravens in a Morning Sky* in Damascus, and Yolande had dug up a Muramachi blade someone had left in a dusty shop in Shanghai.

The serf sitting behind her craned to see the semicircle of the control panel, smiling a little uncertainly as the Draka caught her eye. *Jolene, dammit, remember the name,* Yolande told herself. Jolene had been their latest impulse buy. They had picked her up at an auction in Apollonaris, on the coast of western Africa, two days ago. Yolande frowned a little; it had been Myfwany's idea, and in her opinion it was a bit reckless just to buy a serf like that. Ingolfssons did not sell their human chattel except for gross and deliberate fault, which meant you had to be careful. Mind you, travelling from base to base, they *would* need at least one literate bodyservant, someone in Category IV or V, trained to handle communications equipment and secretarial business. Jolene was well educated and beautifully trained, crèche reared and certified by Domarre & Ledermann, who specialized in high-skilled and fancy items. Very pretty besides, in a broad-nosed, high-cheeked Mandingo fashion—and pilots had a certain status to maintain in their personal gear. Skin the shade of ripe eggplant, almost purple-black, with natural yellow-blond hair and eyes like hot brass, the result of some sport of wandering genes. Yolande rather liked her; she was eager to please without being fawning, glad to be in good hands, and charmingly agog at seeing the world beyond the strait confines of the crèche.

"Nantes control, this is A7SD24 approachin', requestin' clearance fo' in-district release," the Draka said, touching the smooth surface of the control panel. "Headin' upstream to Chateau Retour Plantation."

"Is that—" the voice hesitated, as the ground-sensor computers queried the machine's. "Greetings, Citizen." A French accent, some serf technician. "Feeding clearance data for approach routes, central control under two thousand meters."

"Ovah to AI," Yolande said, lifting her hand from the stick. The aircraft turned east and then north to enter the in-city approach path, sliding down an invisible line in the sky and weaving its way among the busy low-level traffic over the Loire estuary. A Bambara did not extend to that sort of computer, but Nantes ground control would be handling it from here. She nodded toward the other forward seat. "C'mon up front, if'n you like," she added.

"Thanks kindly, Mistis," Jolene said, sliding forward and buttoning her blouse; she and Myfwany had been necking in a desultory sort of way until a little while ago. Alertly, the serf studied the controls. She was a Category V Literate, authorized to operate powered vehicles, but this board was all-virtual, touch-sensitive simulations of dials and screens, and that was just now coming in for the top-line civilian market. "May I?"

At Yolande's nod, a slender black finger touched the upper quadrant screen. She ran through the menu quickly until a map of Nantes appeared; the Loire valley as far east as Trous. A light flicked on the bank of the river.

"This where we stayin', Mistis?"

"Fo' a few days. Meetin' my second cousin Alexandra an' my brothah John, a friend name of Mandy—family gatherin'," Yolande said. "Then up east a ways, boar hunt."

The aircar was slowing down to 500 kph and banking in for the approach path; you could always tell when a computer was flying. . . . Jolene touched the screen again and hesitated until the Draka signed permission with a flick of her wrist. The sale contract from Domarre & Ledermann scrolled up.

"Eight hundred aurics?" Jolene said, disappointment in her voice. Ten times what a prime unskilled laborer cost, but less than might be expected for a special item like her.

"Notice," Yolande said, indicating two clauses. "We suckered them. See, a buy-back option fo' you, and a first-purchase option on any of you children." At the serf's questioning look, she continued: "We're . . . my family doesn't sell, 'cept in-house."

"Oh." The serf looked relieved.

Probably afraid we'd just picked her up for the holiday, Yolande thought.

Then, after a pause: "You don't intends to breed me, either, Mistis?"

"Not fo' sale, anyhows, or if you don't want. Like children?"

"Oh, yes." Jolene said, with a shy smile. "I helped out in the nursery a lot at the crèche. I—" another hesitation "—I was sort of hopin' to be a nurse, had some of the trainin' but . . ." She made a gesture toward herself. The startling hair hung halfway down her back in a mass of loose curls; she had the long-limbed African build, slender neck, high firm breasts, buttocks that were rounded but showed the clench of muscle in the tight trousers. Carefully exercised, with a pleasant glow of youthful health.

Yolande nodded; not much chance the Agency would sell her at three hundred aurics as a medical technician when they could get two or three times that for a fancy.

"Well," she said, "we might find you work in a plantation infirmary, later. Plannin' on keeping you with us, while we're in the Service."

"Thanks, Mistis, I was . . . hmm, I was afraid I hadn't been pleasin'.'"

"Oh, that," Yolande shrugged. "Don't worry, that's my fault. I'm sort of inhibited that way. Need to get to know you better befo' it works proper fo' me. Myfwany certainly enjoyed you. Not the main reason we bought you, anyhows."

Reassured, the serf smiled. "Glad to hear it, Mistis. I's lucky." At Yolande's questioning look: "Nightclubs and such-like were biddin' on me, too." She made a slight face. "Rather belong to folks I can get to know personal. . . . Glad to get the auction an' such ovah with 's well, I mean, the waitin' once you passes eighteen an' all. . . . We meeting you old servants down theres, Mistis?"

The Draka nodded; the other staff were nearly as important to a fresh purchase's life as the owners, and just as much a matter of potluck. She thought for a moment; as Pa used to say, a little consideration went a long way in getting first-rate service. Besides that, as Ma always said, serfs were inferiors, but inferior people, not machinery; there was no point in making their lives more difficult than necessary.

"Lele, my maid, she won't give you any trouble," Yolande said judiciously. "Sensible wench. Sofia, she's Myfwany's, she gets, ah, a little jealous sometimes." In fact, Yolande thought that deep down there were times when Sofia got jealous of her, which was ridiculous beyond words. Pitiful, in fact. "Don't stand any nonsense, and I'm sure you'll make friends soon enough." That prompted another thought. "Oh, remind me when we get in, I'll have you cleared with Central Communication to call back to you crèche, talk to you friends there when you've a mind to."

"Oh, thank you, Mistis," Jolene said, her face lighting.

There was a stirring behind them. "Thanks fo' what?" Myfwany asked. The serf rose and slid back into the body of the aircar; Yolande heard a brief yelp-giggle before her friend sank down in the bucket seat, yawning and rubbing her hands over her face and hair, the red locks now just long enough to curl. They exchanged a brief kiss before the other Draka turned to run a quick eye over the displays.

"Damn, down to twenty-five percent, need to refuel again," she said.

"Could be worse; they could have made this thing run on hydride 'stead of kerosene," Yolande said, and laughed. Turboram and scramjets ran on hydrogen compounds.

"Not until they build 'em orbit-capable. . . . What's so funny?"

"Oh, nothin'. Just happy, is all. Wishin' this holiday could last fo'ever." She stretched with her hands over her head, watching the other's green eyes narrow in a silent grin. Myfwany's face had more freckles now, and a faint golden bloom that was as much of a tan as her complexion and SolaScreen would allow, much lighter than Yolande's toast-gold. The flight-school pallor and gauntness were gone; she looked relaxed, fit, sleeker.

"Know how you feel, love," Myfwany said gently, brushing the back of her hand on the other's cheek. "Though we'd get bored with it, soon enough."

A beep from the machine, and they looked back to the board. The middle of the main screen had switched automatically to an under-belly shot, showing a city center of garden-green interspersed with roofs of umber tile and black slate. It shifted as the aircar banked, and then a message flashed: MANUAL CONTROL BELOW ONE THOUSAND.

"Jolene, number between one and ten," Myfwany said, and looked at Yolande. "I'm six."

"Fo'," Yolande said.

"Mistis Yolande wins," Jolene said; her voice slightly muffled, as she pressed her face against the side of the canopy.

"Shit," Myfwany replied good-naturedly, and sat back. Yolande let her hand fall on the sidestick. "Initiatin' sequence," she said, and touched the console. "Manual."

"Cleared, Citizen," the Nantes control answered; a trifle grumpily, she thought. *Probably prefer me to let the computer do it. Fuck that.*

She throttled back to 400 kph, and the wings slid forward to right angles with the fuselage. The river wound below them, blue shimmer marked with the gold teardrop shapes of sandbars and the metallic silver of shallow water. Levees flanked the wandering braided stream, although the level was down from the wintertime floods; Yolande brought the aircar down to three hundred meters, close enough to see details. Much greener than Tuscany, where you could sense the earth's dry hard bones even in the rains. They passed over Samur on its white cliffs, the pale stone of the castle blinding in the morning light; then the banks sank lower, only subtle changes in crop and growth show-ing where the sandy flood plain gave way to upland *gatine*.

"This it?" Myfwany asked.

"Mmm-hmm," Yolande replied.

Unmistakable, an old chateau built in a checkerboard of white stone and red brick, with black Angers-slate roofs; four towers, and a big pool-reservoir behind the Great House with landscaped banks. The Quarters were to the east, the cottage roofs almost lost among the trees. Around the manor grounds were blocks of orchard, pink and white froth of apple and apricot and peach; dairy pasture down by the river, green-blue wheat and dark-green corn farther north, and long low slopes of vineyard black-shaggy with new growth. A hoe gang looked up as they passed, faces white under the conical straw hats, then bent again to their work.

"There's the House landin' field," she continued. A square of asphalt among trees, on the border between the manor gardens and the crop-lands. She touched the transmitter control.

"Chateau Retour, Yolande here," she said.

"Mistress Ingolfsson." A serf's voice, the plantation radio watch. "Please—"

"Hiyo." A Citizen . . . yes, Aunt Tanya. A courtesy aunt, Yolande's mother's first cousin technically. "Y'all cleared. You stuff arrived yes-terday."

"Thanks, Tanya. See you in a bit."

The near-inaudible whine of the turbines altered, as the slotted louvers beneath the aircar's body cycled open. Motion slowed, turned slug-gish as the Bambara dropped below aerodynamic stall speed and shifted to direct vertical lift. The inship systems balanced it effortlessly, and Yolande began to relax her grip on the pistol-trigger throttle built into the control column. It didn't require much in the way of piloting, really, just a steady hand. . . .

And memory, she thought, reaching out to touch the bypass fan initiator. There was a *chung* sound from behind the compartment, and a lower-pitched toning as the engines transferred some of their energy to pumping cool air through the nozzles. Ceramic turbines were adia-batic: they ran *hot*, hot enough to melt metal; that was what made them efficient. Also hot enough for the exhaust to damage an asphalt landing stage, and Edward and Tanya von Shrakenberg would best appreciate that. *Sometimes I think I need a computer just to keep the relations straight*, she thought idly.

The altimeter unreeled. She touched another part of the smooth glassy surface before her, and the wings folded back and in, disappearing in their slots as the wheels lowered. Engine noise mounted, and wisps of dust flew off the smooth pebbled surface of the stage. An indica-tor blinked as the wheels touched down. Yolande touched the ground mode button and the console rearranged itself; Bambaras were theo-retically road and surface-water capable, although she felt that was a needless flourish.

The canopy above them split into three segments and half retracted to the rear. Air poured in, spring-chill and fresh, smelling intensely of blossom, greenery, very faintly of burnt fuel. Quiet struck, the ears ringing with the engines' silence after so many hours. Nothing was louder than the *ping* of cooling metal; there was the murmur of wind in trees, bird sounds, no background city sound of engines. She had missed that country quiet, these last few days.

The landing field had a low hangar at one end, overshadowed with trees and vine-grown; Yolande could see a twin-engine winged tiltrotor craft within, a couple of ducted-fan aircars. Plantation servants were already loading a dolly with the suitcases from the Bambara's luggage compartment. She and Myfwany rose, buckling their gunbelts and donning the Shantung silk jackets they had picked up in China. That prompted a thought; Yolande looked back and saw Jolene standing and staring about with an expression of half delight and half bewildered terror, the small carrying case that held all her kit in one hand.

And getting goosebumps. Yolande snapped her fingers for the serf's attention, then took her hand and laid the palm against the screen. "Scan, identify," she said. That would access the personal file from the Labor Directorate net. "We'll have to have the plantation seamstress run you up a few outfits, Jolene."

The two Draka vaulted out of the aircar; the compartment was only chest-high above the pavement, not worth the effort of opening the door, and Jolene clambered down more slowly to where Myfwany could grip her at the waist and swing her to the ground. Yolande could feel the residual heat of the jets on her legs through the linen of her trousers as she flipped up an access plate and touched the panel within. The canopy slid back above the passenger compartment and flashed from clear to mirror to a dull nonreflective black.

"Thumb here, Jolene," Yolande said, and keyed. "All right, you've got vehicular access." Not to the controls, of course. Raising her voice, she called one of the porters: "You, boy." The stocky middle-aged French buck looked up from laying a cylindrical leather case of hunting javelins on top of the pile of baggage and bowed. "See this wench to our rooms along with the rest of our things."

"Yolande Ingolfsson, kitten adopter, small birds rescued to order," Myfwany said fondly, as they strolled arm in arm to the pathway that lead to the manor.

"I'll spoil my half an' you can flog the othah," Yolande replied dryly.

"Nothin' wrong with a kindly heart, love," Myfwany said, and yawned again, stretching. "Now let's lunch."

Chapter Six

BOMBS AWAY TAVERN
ALLIANCE SPACE FORCE ACADEMY
SANTA FE, NEW MEXICO
UNITED STATES OF AMERICA
ALLIANCE FOR DEMOCRACY
AUGUST 25, 1969
0100 HOURS

"Hey, Freddie! I say, Freddie old man!"

The voice bellowed inches from Frederick Lefarge's ear, and was barely audible. The Bombs Away was the trainees' watering hole of choice, and the graduation party was still going strong; the quieter spirits had mostly left with their families in the afternoon. Every table was full, and the bar was packed six deep; smoke drifted under the piñon-pine rafters, about half tobacco, and the air was solid with the Yipsatucky Sound music roaring from the speakers, the noise of several hundred strong young male voices. Speaking every language of the Alliance, though English and Spanish predominated. . . .

"What?" Lefarge screamed back, halting in his forward-tackle drive toward the beer taps. The air was solid with smell, too, sweat and sawdust and liquor.

It was "Randy Andy" McLean, a transfer student from the British national military, and a few years older than the run of students; it was common for candidates to take lateral transfers into the direct Alliance service. Short, slight, unbelievably freckled, and newly assigned Junior Power Systems Engineer on the *Emancipator*. That was the first and to date only example of the second generation of pulsedrive spaceships, a plum posting for a new-minted Academy graduate; McLean had been celebrating his success ever since the assignments were announced, or drowning his sorrows at the prospect of joining an all-male branch of the Service. The pulsedrive ships were opening the area beyond Luna to Alliance exploration and development, and the cruises tended to be long.

"I say, who are those two stunners waving at you, you dog?" he

continued. The Scot's nickname was not undeserved, and represented a real achievement in Santa Fe, with its heavy surplus of young men.

Stunners? Lefarge thought. He had a few friends among the female tenth of the Academy's student body, but he wouldn't consider any of them worthy of that particular appraisal; besides, they were supervised like Carmelites, and none of them would be here tonight. Santa Fe was a government-research-military town, families and young single men mostly. . . .

"Excuse me!" he bellowed at his two nearest neighbors, putting his hands on their shoulders and levering his feet to knee-height off the ground. There were two young women waving at the cantina's courtyard door.

"Well?" McLean said. Lefarge began to laugh, and pulled his friend closer by the high collar of his uniform jacket. "It's my sister," he shouted into the other man's ear.

"You lie!" A pause for thought. "Well, who's her friend, then?"

"My godfather's daughter, we grew up together!"

The redhead's face fell, and the native burr showed under his carefully cultivated Queen's English. "Yer a fookin' traitor to the Class of '69 and men in general, ye know," he said with mock bitterness. They worked their way steadily toward the door, and the trace of cooler air that found its way in.

"Well, I can still introduce you," he said in a more normal tone. "Just watch your step, Randy, or I'll break the offending hand."

"That bloody Unarmed Combat prize went to your head," McLean said, pausing to adjust his jacket and pull the white gloves from his belt. "Lead on, old chum, and fear not: once a McLean, always a gentleman."

"Meaning you never pay your tailor. *Marya! Cindy!*"

His sister gave him a quick strong embrace and a kiss on the cheek. They were twins, and looked it, the same high-cheeked oval face, straight nose, dark-gray eyes, black hair, long-limbed build. She was three inches shorter than his six feet, with a graceful tautness that suggested dance classes and gymnastics; her hair was in a plain ponytail, and she wore a sneakers-jeans-windbreaker outfit that made her look far younger than her twenty-one years.

He turned to Cindy Guzman and put his hands on her shoulders. "How's Mexico City?" he said softly. She was nineteen and . . . *McLean's right*, he thought breathlessly. *Stunner*. Anglo-Mayan looks, olive skin and greenish hazel eyes, hair the color of darkest mahogany. Figure curved like—*down, boy!* he told himself sternly. *Remember Don Guzman and his machete*. Cindy's father had been a submariner in the Eurasian War and after had retired a commodore . . . and had never abandoned certain of the attitudes he learned as a farmboy in Yucatan.

Not that my intentions aren't of the most honorable, he thought dismally. *Lieutenants just can't marry*. Not if they had any concern for their careers, and while he would be willing to risk it, Cindy would not. Captains could marry, of course. That had been a considerable element in his academic success. A good report never hurt.

She hugged him and exchanged a long but frustratingly chaste kiss.

"Mexico City's still as crowded and nasty as ever," she said. It was the fourth-largest city in the United States, after all, and the postwar growth had been badly handled. "Luckily, I don't have to leave campus very often. Who's your friend?"

"The Honorable Andrew McLean of McLean, fifth of that ilk," Lefarge said. McLean bowed with his best suave smile, somehow suggesting a kilt, with gillies and pipers in the background. Cindy and Marya extended their hands, found them bowed over and kissed rather than shaken.

"Och aye, an' my friend Frederick, he wasna joking when he said that here would be two flowers fairer than any the Highlands bear," he said.

Lefarge smiled, remembering his friend's description of the family's seldom-visited ancestral hall, late one night after a few beers:

Built by cattle thieves for protection against other cattle thieves. Och, it's this ghastly great drafty stone barn, uglier than Balmoral if that's possible, and if y' ken Balmoral . . . the land? Bluidy pure. Heather, beautiful and useless. Great-great-great-gran'ther drove out all the crofters and tacksmen in the Clearances and then found it wouldn't even feed sheep to any purpose. We've lived off renting the deer shooting and the odd bit of loot ever since.

"Shall we find a table?" Lefarge said. The Bombs Away had several outdoor patios.

"Ah, Fred, Cindy wanted to go back to the hotel. She's staying with Maman, and doesn't want to be out late." Marya made a slight shooing sign with her fingers as she spoke. There was something puzzling in her face as she looked at McLean, as well, it was too smoothly friendly. His sister was not a naturally outgoing girl. . . . Well, it had been nearly a year, and people changed.

"Andy," he said, slapping the smaller man on the shoulder. "Be a brick, would you, and see Cindy back to her room. She's staying with my mother"—*who you know is a dragon*—"and I'm sure she'd appreciate it." *And I know where you live, you cream-stealing pirate.*

"A pleasure and an honor," the other graduate said, extending his arm and sweeping a bow to Marya. "Until we meet again."

Brother and sister watched them go, then moved out onto the patio. This was an old building, Spanish-Mexican in its core; the original had been built in adobe brick around a courtyard, then extended to an H-shape later.

"Uncle Nate's here," Marya said quietly. "With his working hat."

"Oh." Lefarge felt a chill shock run into his belly, like the moment before you went out the door on a parachute drop. Nathaniel Stoddard had taken turns with Commodore Guzman in being the father they had never known; he was also *General* Nathaniel Stoddard, Office of Strategic Services . . . and now their commanding officer as well. "Let's go."

The older man was sitting at a table in the outer courtyard, hard up against the wrought-iron fence; it was dark there, with only candles in glass bubbles on the tables. Stoddard rose with old-world courtesy as they approached, a lanky figure in a conservative houndstooth-tweed suit and dark blue cravat; as Eastern as his Bay State accent. The face was pure New England as well, long and bony, with faded blue eyes and gray-streaked sandy hair; the face of an extremely mournful horse. There was an attaché case with a combination lock on the table before him, half-open; Lefarge caught sight of equipment he recognized, a detector set that would beep an alarm if any of the active long-range snooper systems were trained on them. The younger man glanced up quickly at the parking lot visible through the grillwork: It was full of Academy student steamcars, battered Stanley Jackrabbits and cheap Monterey Motors Burros; also a few very quiet, systematically inconspicuous men.

"Marya, Fred," Stoddard said, shaking hands with them both. They sat. A waitress in synthetic-fabric pseudo-Southwestern cowgirl costume brought coffee for the younger pair.

"Anytheek for you, sir?"

"Nh-huh," Stoddard said, touching his glass of water. "Fine, thank you."

"Mike's not here?" Lefarge asked. Stoddard's only son was Air Force, stationed in Asia, but he had been planning to take leave. Marya's face froze, and Lefarge looked up in sharp alarm.

"There was a brush over the South China Sea," Stoddard said. He was staring at his water, voice flat. "Trawler out of Hainan lost its engine, drifted into Draka-claimed waters; one of their hovercraft gunboats came out after it. We sent in fighters, so did they. Mike's wingman reported him hit." A pause. "Missing, presumed dead. Hopefully dead." The enemy recognized no laws regarding treatment of prisoners; their own military were expected to fight to the death.

"Oh, Jesus, Uncle Nate," Lefarge said, crossing himself.

His sister followed suit. "Jesus."

Stoddard raised the glass to his lips, the hand was steady. The homely face was emotionless as he sipped, but there was an infinite weariness in it.

"How's Janice?" His daughter-in-law.

"In Hawaii with the baby, waiting for news," Stoddard said, and sighed slightly. "So, Fred, you'll see I couldn't make the graduation ceremony."

Lefarge nodded slightly, groping within for a reaction; grief, anger, hatred. *Nothing*, he thought. *I must be dazed.* There were continual border skirmishes along the line that divided the Domination from the Alliance; even in space recently. But that was like traffic accidents or cancer; you never thought of it as something with a relation to *you*, you and the people you knew.

He was a good joe, Lefarge thought. *Bit too solemn, but he always put up with me.* He remembered the older boy patiently explaining to the visiting New Yorker how to use a fly rod, and letting him hold a safely unloaded bird gun. Later Mike and Uncle Nate and he had gone on long hunting trips up to the Maine woods, and—

"Jesus," he said again, shaking his head.

The sky above was clear and full of stars; this city was at seven thousand feet, and far too small for the lights to dim the sky the way they did at home, in New York. When he had lain in the hammock on the veranda at the Maine cottage, Mike and his father had taught him constellations. There was a far-off growl like thunder, only it did not end; another star was rising, from the mountains to the northeast. Rising on a pillar of light, laser light, into the sky: a cargo pod from the launcher at Los Alamos. He followed it with his eyes, up toward the moving stars. Space platforms, and these days weapons platforms armored in lunar regolith. Suddenly the stars were very cold; reptile eyes, staring down with ageless hunger.

"Ayuh," Stoddard said. "To work."

Only someone who had known him all their lives could have seen through the mask of calm; Lefarge did, and now anger flushed warmth into his skin. Stoddard would grieve in the manner of his kind, with a silent reserve that encysted the pain, preserving it like a fly in amber.

His hands were sliding a file out of the attaché case. "First, one thing, Fred. Do you still want the Service?"

Lefarge nodded, slightly surprised; that commitment had been made long ago. Not that the OSS recruited openly; to his classmates and most of his instructors, he was just one more astronaut-in-training, with a specialty in cryptography and information systems. One who went somewhere else for the holidays, most of the time. Plus a more-than-fair halfback . . . *Concentrate*, he reminded himself. An astronaut could not afford to let anything break his mind's grip on a problem, and neither could an Intelligence agent.

"Then look at this," Stoddard continued.

He pushed an eight-by-eleven glossy across to Lefarge. The younger man took it up and inclined it toward the candle, then accepted a pencil flashlight. His lips shaped a soundless whistle. Ultra-chic, somewhere between twenty and thirty. In a strapless black evening gown, a diamond necklace emphasizing the long slender neck without distracting from the high breasts beneath. Smooth, classic-straight features, dark blue eyes, glossy brown hair piled high; one elegant leg exposed to the knee by the slit gown, with a daring jeweled anklet. Holding a champagne glass in one gloved hand, gesturing with the other, laughing. At some sort of function: black suits, very expensive dresses. An old-looking building, with a Georgian interior.

"European?" he said. She had that look. Millions had made it out of Western Europe during the last phases of the Eurasian War; his own mother had, in 1947, although that had been a special case. The Draka serf identity-tattoo on the neck could be surgically removed. "In London, recently?"

Stoddard nodded with bleak satisfaction.

Marya spoke: "Marie-Claire Arondin: that's actually her name. Elder brother is Jean-Claude Arondin, refugee from Lyon. Got out in '48, officially stowaways in a cargo container aboard a dirigible. Established a machine-parts business in London, and made a fair go of it, despite occasional alcohol problems. The sister went to English schools, latterly a fairly expensive boarding establishment. Did her National Service as an assistant nurse in a West End hospital; the alcohol-rehabilitation ward, where she made some . . . interesting contacts." His sister's voice had a dry tone he recognized; someone reciting from a file.

"Set up a small dressmaking concern after studying design at the University of London; soon, not so small, due to discreet gifts from several prominent men with whom she became quietly involved." Her right hand was resting in her lap; the fingers of the left tapped the table. "A very classy and high-priced courtesan, if you examine the record."

"Agent?"

Stoddard nodded. "Ayuh. Her brother was a sleeper—he died in '66 and she was trained in London. Financed very carefully from the Security Directorate's cover-assets in the Alliance." The British capital was the world center of espionage and fashion, if of little else these days. "The usual thing, pillow talk leading to compromise, then blackmail to keep it coming."

"How did—?" he stopped; if there was a need-to-know, he would be told the method of discovery.

"Her mother was still in the Domination; that was their lever. She died. We started suspecting one of Marie-Claire's . . . clients, when one of our sources on the other side turned up data only he could have leaked."

Stoddard slid another package across the table. Lefarge broke the seals and pulled out the first envelope. It was a set of assignment orders, in his name.

"Assistant Compsystems Officer on the *Emancipator*!" His eyes narrowed. "This had to come from the Service, right?"

The general nodded wearily. "Because she told us the latest of her conquests, Fred," he said, with a tired disgust in his voice. "Open the next package."

Lefarge obeyed with fingers suddenly gone clumsy. There had to be a reason he, of all people . . .

Lieutenant Andrew McLean, RN, Alliance Space Force. "Oh, shit, God, Andy would never sell out!"

"He didn't," Marya said, an impersonal pity in her tone. "She met him at some social affair when he was on leave from Portsmouth, before he transferred here, and hit him like a ton of cement. Far too expensive for him, and she guided him to some of the best clip joints and casinos in Britain. Then found 'friends' to tide him over with loans, then . . . By the time she let the hook show, he was in over his head." She hesitated. "She told the debriefers she's convinced he's in love with her, as well. Gave him a long story about the threats the Security Directorate were holding over her family, that sort of thing."

"It doesn't matter," Stoddard said quietly. "For money, for a promise of Draka Citizenship, for love . . . it's treason, Fred."

"Why hasn't he been arrested?" Lefarge said, but felt the knowledge growing in his gut, a cancer of nausea.

Stoddard nodded. "We turned Arondin, and the Security Directorate doesn't know it. Won't for several years, during which we'll feed them a careful mixture of accurate data and disinformation . . . but the stuff she's been getting from McLean has a short half-life, Fred.

Nothing too important yet, but the *Emancipator* is the best we have. He can't return from that cruise, and it has to look like an accident. You're the best-placed operative."

Lefarge opened the rest of the sealed packages. An Execution Order. "I . . . don't like it," he said hoarsely.

"I don't like it either," Stoddard said. "The personal approval of the Alliance Chairman and a quorum of the High Court . . . It's still a secret trial, and that wasn't what this country was founded for." More gently: "And I know he was your friend, Fred."

"He was." Lefarge slammed his fist into the wall beside him, then looked in shock down at his own bleeding knuckles. "The bastard, the stupid, stupid brains-in-balls *bastard*."

Marya looked away. Stoddard continued. "Can you do it?" Lefarge pressed his fingertips into his forehead. Could he kill a friend, a man who trusted him? Another thought twisted the knot below his stomach tighter. He would have to live at close quarters with him. Laugh at his jokes, pass the salt, never let show that anything was different. . . .

"I can," he said. And that was a bitter thing to know about himself, as well.

Marya relaxed, and brought her right hand up from under the table. Lefarge's eyes widened; there was a gun in his sister's hand, an ugly stubby little silenced custom job. For the first time in his life, he felt his jaw drop with surprise; she flushed and looked down. Stoddard reached out and slipped the weapon into his own hand, pointed it out into the night and pulled the trigger.

Nothing. The young woman's head whipped around, and she gave the general an accusing stare. "You claimed there was evidence he might be involved!" she said.

"Circumstantial evidence," the general replied. He snapped the clip out of the weapon and thumbed the square rounds of caseless ammunition out. "He was a close friend of someone we *knew* had gone over. Actually, I never doubted him."

He smiled bitterly. "Fred, you just passed a test. Your test is willingness to eliminate McLean. This little charade was hers. Marya was lucky; the information we gave her about *you* wasn't real. We just needed to see how she would react if it *was* real." The expression lost any resemblance to good humor. "This is what I told you, long ago. This business of ours, it takes . . . a different sort of courage from a soldier's. A soldier"—his voice stumbled for a moment—"may have to sacrifice his life. More is asked of us; we get the danger without the glory, such as that is. For us, there's the dirty business that has to be done; we may have to sacrifice a friend, a brother . . . our own sense of honor." He slid the material back into the attaché case, stood. "I'll be in touch."

Stoddard left by the back gate, walking toward an inconspicuous steamer. Two of the silent men followed, one taking the wheel. There was an almost imperceptible *whump* of water hitting a flashboiler, and the vehicle slid away.

"Shit, what a night," Lefarge said, a shakiness in his voice. "Shit."

A hand fell on his, and he looked up to meet his sister's eyes. "Would you have shot me?"

"If I thought you were a traitor?" she said, gaze level. "Yes." The eyes glimmered suddenly, in starlight and moonlight. "I'd have cried for you after . . . but yes."

The moment stretched. "Thank you," he replied. Their fingers met and intertwined. *"Merci, ma soeur,"* he said again, in their mother's native tongue.

Presently he sighed. "Look . . . can you drop me back at Maman's hotel? I'd . . . like to see Cindy again."

"I understand. It's not far from mine."

"But not the same hotel as Maman?" he said, with a faint smile.

His sister's was more wry. "Maman's never going to accept that I don't have a vocation, Fred," she said.

"Christ, when the Sisters sent that bloody *delegation* around to explain you were a perfectly good Catholic, just not suited—!" It was an old anger, a relief to slip into it.

Marya shrugged. "Hell, I might as *well* be a nun, the chances I'm going to get in this line of work . . . Fred, Uncle Nate told me a little bit more about how he got Maman out of France, back in '47."

"Oh?" *Thank you for changing the subject,* he thought. *I need something to calm me down first.* "Her Resistance work and so forth?"

"Fred . . . Maman was in the Resistance, all right. But she wasn't Uncle Nate's contact. She wasn't supposed to come out at all."

"What? Look, I know there was an agent in place, I'm *named* after the man, but—"

"Shh. That nun that Maman told us about, Sister Marya? She was the Resistance contact. Maman just got dumped in the same place, bought out of a Security Directorate pen in Lyon by a planter. She . . . found out about the operation they were on—you can guess it was weapons research—and . . . well, threatened to blow the cover unless she was pulled out of there. The whole extraction phase went sour, your namesake was killed, so was the nun . . . Had to kill themselves, rather. Maman's considered it her fault, ever since."

"Mary mother. No *wonder* she was so set on getting you into the Order!"

"Expiation, and more than that, Fred. There wasn't any husband killed by the Snakes."

"You mean she wasn't pregnant then?" He blinked bewilderment. *Maman? Maman had an* affair *after she got to New York?* He had never seen his mother miss Mass or confession in all his life; and he still remembered the thrashing she had given him when she caught him with that women's underwear catalog under the bed.

"Yes, she was . . . We're half-Draka, brother."

For a moment Frederick Lefarge saw gray at the corner of his vision, and then his skin crawled as if his body were trying to shed it. Oh, it made no legal difference; by Domination law, only those born of Citizens on both sides were of the ruling caste. But—he made a wordless sound.

"I know," Marya replied. "I threw up when I heard; I've had a week or so to get used to the idea now. But you can see why, why she's never looked at another man, why she was so dead set against me going into intelligence work. Any sort of field where there was a chance I might be captured." She pressed the button for the waitress. "I think you need a stiff one; then I'll drive you over."

"Cindy, Cindy!"
"Honey, what is it?" Shock and concern, and fear of what could have harrowed him so.
"Hold me, will you? Just hold me."

Chapter Seven

NEW YORK CITY
FEDERAL CAPITAL DISTRICT
DONOVAN HOUSE
NOVEMBER 20, 1972

"Not going to the Inauguration, General?"

Nathaniel Stoddard snorted without turning from the window and brushed at his mustache. It was nearly solid gray now, only streaked with sandy brown, like the rather untidy mop of hair he kept in an academic's shag-cut. *Getting older*, he thought. *Older and creakier and more weary . . . Is it time to retire?* He probed at himself, with the same ruthless analysis he might have used on an agent under strain. *No. Still flexible, not making too many mistakes.* You couldn't overvalue yourself either; if you were indispensable, you weren't doing your job properly.

"Work to do," he said, in a voice that earned the flat vowels and drawl of Boston. "The OSS never sleeps."

Frederick and Marya Lefarge were waiting patiently in their seats, still in tropical kit, looking a little rumpled from the two-hour flight from India, a little worn from tension and sleeplessness. Looking harder than they had once, after the work he had put them through these past four years. Easy with each other, and that was important; this had been their first mission together. There were jobs a team like this had an advantage in.

"And its agents don't get any sleep either," Fred was saying. "Here we are, just off the Calcutta shuttle, and you don't even give us time to stop off at O'Toole's for a beer."

Donovan House was at the northern edge of the Federal District, the series of interlinked squares and parks that occupied the center of Manhattan Island. More and more of the capital's swelling bureaucracy was being moved out to Long Island or the Jersey shore, but the Office of Strategic Services preferred staying close to the centers of executive power. This office was twelve stories up, overlooking Jefferson Avenue; from here you could see north and south to the Hudson and

East rivers. The parade was still moving down the six-lane avenue, between sidewalks and buildings black with the crowds. Paper confetti spun through the air, and the noise was loud even through the sealed double-glazed panes. Another flight of fighters went by ten thousand feet up—contrails and a brief silvery flash—and their sonic booms rattled the furniture.

My, aren't we noisy today, Stoddard thought.

The marching youth groups were past, the cheerleaders and bands, the cowboys and *vaqueros* and Hibernians . . . Troops now. Squat tanks with their long cannon swiveling in hydraulic pods above the decks, APCs, huge eighteen-wheeler tractors drawing suborb missiles on mobile launchers.

It's a good thing the infantry aren't marching, he thought dryly. *Messy, after all those horses.*

He took a sip from the coffee cup in his hands, thankful for the warmth. Thankful that he was inside, and not out there in the raw weather; it was damp and cold, the sky stark blue with streamers of cloud. An aircar went slowly by outside the window, down the length of the procession: a light open-topped model with ABS markings, and six ducted-fan propellers in swivel mounts spaced around the flattish oval body. The drone of its engines hummed through the air between them, and he could see the blue tinge to the faces of the televid crew in the little four-seater.

"Better you than me, friends," he said.

"Sir?" Marya's voice, cool and neutral. *In a more just world, maybe she would be my successor*, Stoddard thought. *She's . . . not harder than Fred. Cooler, less of a closet romantic. This line of work will do that for a woman. But then, in a more just world she wouldn't have had the extra toughening.*

Stoddard grinned at his protégés. "Just feeling each and every one of my sixty-eight years, Fred, Marya," he said. "And glad I'm not out there courting arthritis." The use of the first name had become a signal between them to drop formality.

They were all in the wolf-gray uniforms of the Alliance military today: high green collars and epaulets and the American eagle on their cuffs. Frederick Lefarge had a captain's bars, his sister Marya a lieutenant's; the older man, a general's oak-leaf clusters, although his position here made his authority nearly equal to that of a member of the Alliance Combined Staff.

"Not missing the distinguished company?" Frederick had a little more accent than his sister's, Academy mid-American, with a slight trace of East Coast in the vowels; Stoddard noted absently that a linguist would immediately place him somewhere between New York and Baltimore. "The Pope's there."

"And all sixty-two State governors," Stoddard said, turning back to his desk.

It was severely plain, like the rest of the office. Plain dark wood, in-out baskets marked HATE and LOVE, a telephone, a scriber, the screen and keyboard of a retriever terminal. There was a table and settees for guests, bookshelves that held a mixture of mementos, leather-bound volumes and color-coded ring binders. Two paintings on the walls, New Hampshire landscapes by Parrish, the chilly perfection of his late period. And two photographs on the desk: one of a plain middle-aged woman and three children standing beside a weathered saltbox home, the other of a young man in a flight suit. That was bordered in black.

Stoddard gave it a glance as he sank into the swivel chair and filled his pipe. "And the College of Cardinals," he continued between puffs. "The Chief Rabbi, Her Honor the Mayor, half the Alliance Grand Council, the Combined Chiefs, His Majesty Georgie the Fifth, the Prime Minister of Australasia . . . bit of a dog's breakfast. Not to mention the speeches."

"Bilingual, yet," the other man said, sitting by the table and reaching for a manila folder. "It would make more sense to have them in French or Yiddish, in this town. Or deep Yorkshire."

Stoddard nodded, blowing a cloud of aromatic blue smoke. A fifth of the United States was Spanish-speaking, but that was mostly in the states carved out of Old Mexico. New York had always been a polyglot city; the great magnet during the immigrant waves of the 1890s and 1920s, then the primary center for the millions of European refugees just after the War, the lucky ones who made it out before the Draka had the coasts of Western Europe under firm control. The English were the latest wave all along the Atlantic coast; the British Isles were the Alliance's easternmost outpost, and not a very comfortable place to live, these days. It was a little embarrassing, for an old-stock Yankee. He could remember when a British surname was an elite rarity here; now every second waiter, hairdresser, and ditchdigger was a new-landed Anglo-Saxon. Not to mention prostitutes, pimps, street thugs, and the gangs who were pushing the Mexicans and Sicilians out of organized crime . . .

"Well, India's patched up for the moment," Frederick Lefarge said, riffling the folder. "That little scandal about Rashidi and the hamburger killed the Hindi Raj Party deader than Gandhi." He laughed sourly. "Why didn't he smuggle something safe, like heroin? For a Hindi nationalist, running a clandestine beef trade . . ."

Marya frowned. "Well, I was mostly working with the Indra Samla people," she said. "They were ready enough to believe the bad about Rashidi. Too many Moslems in his background, besides him being their main rival. Still and all, a lot of them had trouble believing he could make a blunder that big."

"Double-blind," Stoddard said. "He didn't. We framed him."

The captain sat bolt upright. "Jesus! If *that* ever gets out—"

Stoddard took another draw on his pipe. "You were the test, Fred. You took a first-rate team there for the investigation; if you couldn't find our sticky finger marks, who could?"

The younger man shook his head and pursed his lips slightly. "I don't . . . It's not what we're supposed to do."

"What's the alternative?"

"He would have won the election. And left the Alliance." A long pause. "How could he be so . . . stupid's an inadequate word. Are the Snakes bribing him?"

The general gestured with the stem of his pipe. "Fred, Marya, when you've been in harness as long as I have, you'll learn two things: first, human beings don't have to be stupid to act stupidly, they just need to feel strongly about something. Second, conscious evil is actually quite rare, even rarer than deliberate hypocrisy."

He cradled the bowl of his pipe between the heels of his hands. "Rashidi is no fool, he's just convinced that American influences are sapping and undermining Hindu culture." A shrug. "He's right, too."

"Did he think the Snakes would be better?"

Stoddard smiled sourly. "Actually, there are some similarities between their system and the old Indian caste setup, and the doctrine of *karma* is the most diabolically effective mechanism for keeping the lower classes in order ever invented . . . No, the Hindi Raj people certainly didn't want a Draka conquest—they weren't insane. They thought a neutral India could stand off the Domination by itself—with unacknowledged help from us—and successfully industrialize behind tariff barriers without having to accept the, hmmm, 'culture of individualist rationalism,' isn't that the way Rashidi used to put it?"

"That's insane."

"No, just wishful thinking. Actually, there are only two possible alternatives for human beings on this planet now. Us and the Domination. One is going to utterly destroy the other and incorporate everything else. It's one of the truths everybody knows and nobody says. The nationalists in India simply refuse to believe it, because believing that would mean that they *cannot* have what they most want."

"Stupidity."

Marya had leaned back in her chair and closed her eyes; now she opened one and chuckled. "Brother, while you were out playing astronaut"—he winced slightly—"I've been doing more straight political work. Your training's made you overestimate the role of rationality." A wry grin. "Also, you've never had an observer's chance to see how stupid most men are with their pants down."

Stoddard nodded. "Not stupidity, humanity. Which means this is a battle won, not a war. The discontents continue, and they will find another vehicle."

Lefarge shook his head. "Hindi Raj is a dozen quarreling fragments, the Progressives will win the next three elections without trouble." A wolf's grin. "And some of those fragments *were* being paid off by the Snakes. We can use that if they start building momentum again. So much for deliberate evil."

"A rather petty evil. I've got the reports, and none of them were selling anything vital." He leaned back and blew a smoke ring at the ceiling. "Grafters like that are the political equivalent of tax frauds. They cheat, relying on the fact that most people don't, so they keep their money and get the benefit of the services, too . . . The Draka lose there by their own racial prejudices. They may not care about the color of the people they enslave, but they do when it comes to granting Citizen status. Best bribe they have. That's the way they got Ekstein."

"The filthy little traitor," Frederick Lefarge said, flushing with anger.

"Even so . . . I've never understood how he could do it. Why would anyone want to become a *Snake*?"

"Captain, now you're allowing prejudice to blind *you*." A gentle laugh. "If you don't mind me asking, when did you lose your virginity, Fred?"

He blinked in surprise, then smiled reminiscently. "Junior high. I was fifteen."

"Ekstein never did."

"I'm not surprised."

Stoddard nodded. "He was an obnoxious, ugly, sweaty little toad with all the inherent appeal of a skunk and an overcompensated inferiority complex as big as all outdoors. Smelled like a skunk at times, too. No friends, and no female in her right mind would have touched him without being paid, which he was too terrified to do. Also one of the most unhappy and lonely young men I've ever met. It's the reason he went into electronics design; that was something he could do without face-to-face contact and get a certain degree of respect for. It was our fault the Draka were able to contact him, they gave him a palace in France and a harem. Not your idea of paradise or mine, but Ekstein's happy."

Marya made a *tsk* sound. "We should have fixed him up. I would have, if I'd been his case officer . . . even have volunteered myself, which shows you my devotion to duty." She raised an eyebrow at her sibling's discomfort. "Tool of the trade, Captain Brother Sir . . . Who *did* we have working on him?"

"A Sector Chief, ex-Sector Chief now, domestic surveillance. Very sincere fellow. Baptist." They all winced. "It was slick, I must admit. Off to England for a design conference, and the next thing we know his bed hasn't been slept in."

"I suppose it's too much to hope he stopped producing over there in the Snake farm," Fred muttered.

"Ayuh. Tapered off a mite at first, then better than ever. The Maxwell and Faraday Combines are rushing his latest microwafer designs into production on a maximum-priority basis, or so our sources tell us."

"Damn!" The younger man shook his head again. "It was our job to prevent it . . . and I always hate to see them get their hands on our technical secrets. Technology's our big advantage over them, after all."

"Particularly the sapphire-silicon and gallium-arsenide stuff they're doing up on the orbital platforms," Marya put in. "And Ekstein was in that up to the zits on his earlobes."

Stoddard shrugged. "We're ahead in some respects. Those tanks out there"—he pointed with the stem of his pipe toward the window— "*we* copied from Draka designs. Same with our small arms. They're ahead in mining, ferrous metals, some machining, basic transport equipment. About equal in aeronautic power systems. Way ahead in biotechnology. We've got a commanding lead in agricultural machinery, synthetics, electronics, particularly circuit wafers." He smiled sourly. "And in household appliances."

Fred flushed, opened his mouth to speak and paused, after a glance at his sister's relaxed form. "Wait a minute, General. I know your methods; you're trying to get me to think through something by pretending to defend the Snakes."

"Draka. That's one part of the lesson, son: calling them 'Snakes' is a way of denying that they're human beings. Which leads to under-estimating them, which is fatal."

"They don't *act* like human beings."

"They don't act like *us*." Stoddard dug at the bowl of his pipe with a wire. Meditatively, he continued: "Ayuh. It's a handicap for you in the younger generations, growing up in so . . . uniform a world." He shook his head. "Just the fact that you can go anywhere on the globe and get by in English makes it a different planet from the one I grew up on. It's made us, hm, not less tolerant, but less used to the concept of difference. One of the reasons I sent you to India was to meet people who were genuinely *alien* in the way they thought and believed, seeing as the rest of Free Asia's gotten so Westernized. . . ."

Fred ran a hand over his crewcut. "It did that, general. Do you know, some of those Muslim types wanted to secede from the Alliance so they could declare a jihad against the Sna . . . against the Domina-tion? Crazy."

"Just different; when you really believe that dying in battle gains you instant admission to Paradise, it gives you a different perspective. Also, they're quite right that nobody in the Western countries gave a . . . rat's ass—isn't that the younger generation's expression?—about them until the Draka attacked Europe. As long as it was niggers and wogs and chinks and ragheads going under the Yoke. . . ."

The other man winced. "Ancient history, though try convincing those stupid bastards of that."

"Fred, Fred . . . historical amnesia is an American weakness. Most people have a longer collective memory. The Draka certainly do."

"Quite true," Marya put in, without opening her eyes. "I spent more time with Maman and the refugees, Fred, while you were out prov-ing how assimilated you were. You wouldn't believe some of the things they raked up and threw at each other; stuff nobody but history professors knows here."

"Don't Draka have any weaknesses?"

Angry, but controlling it well, even tired as he is, Stoddard decided. *Good.*

"Certainly," he said. "They don't understand us, not even as well as we—some of us—understand them." He laid the pipe down and leaned forward, laying his hands on the blotter. "They could have lulled us to sleep so easily, so easily . . . Fred, the great American public doesn't like being confronted with evil, or with a protracted struggle. We're not a people who believe in tragedy; history's been too good to us. Evil is something we conquer in a crusade, and then every-body goes home a hero."

Lefarge snorted, and his mentor nodded. "Yes, I know, but we're professionals, Fred. And you have personal reasons to keep the truth fresh. All the Draka would have to do is ease up, tell some convincing lies, and we'd have our work cut out for us keeping even a minimal guard up."

A sour twist of the mouth. "You wouldn't remember it, but there were substantial numbers who refused to believe the truth about Stalin, until Hitler and the Draka between them released the pictures and records of his death camps. The Draka could have railroaded our credulous types just as easily. Instead they've virtually flaunted what they are, and pushed at us every chance they got. Trying to scare us, but Americans don't scare easily. It's the flip side of our weakness; we're the Good Guys, and therefore have to win in the end. All the stories and the movies and the patriotic pablum the schools dish out instead of history prove it. God help us if we ever lose a big one; we'd probably start doubting we were the Good Guys after all."

"I thought you said the Draka were smart?"

"Ayuh. Very smart, and very, very tough. But they don't *understand* us; some of them do, intellectually, but not down here." He touched his stomach. "Our reactions don't make sense to them, emotionally, any more than theirs do to us, and they're . . . a little less flexible. They know it, they repeat it to themselves, but it's . . . hard . . . for them to really believe anyone could fudge a power contest, could *want* to fudge one. For them, life is lived by the knife. That's reality for them. They believe in enemies; they don't have our compulsive need to be liked. For a Draka, if you've got an enemy you destroy or subjugate them; it's their lifework. Subconsciously, they assume that everybody else is the same, only weaker and less cunning."

Fred grinned wolfishly. "The way we assume that deep-down everyone is just plain folks, and you can always make a deal and square the differences, and the guy in the black hat either repents or gets shot five minutes before the hero's wedding? That's the point of these Socratic dialogues you've been putting us through?"

"More like Socratic monologues, I'm afraid," Stoddard said. "Also the temptation is, when we realize somebody isn't like that, to hate them. Which interferes with the task at hand."

"Elucidate, as you Ivy League types would say."

"The task of wiping every last Draka off the face of the Earth," Stoddard said calmly, and touched a control on the surface of his desk. A printer began to hum, and pages spat out into a tray with a rapid *shft-shft* sound.

The younger man snorted. "Glad to hear you say it, Uncle Nate; the sweet reason was beginning to wear a little."

The general paused with his finger on the control. "Ayuh, not so sweet, Fred." A pause. "I grew up in a world where the Draka were a blot, not a menace. I've had to watch the Domination grow like a cancer, metastasizing. Watch my children"—he paused again, face like something carved out of maple—"nieces and nephews and *their* children grow up in the shadow of it."

His eyes met the younger man's. Frederick Lefarge had seen danger. Leading an incursion team ashore in Korea, to snatch a fallen reconnaissance drone from the coastal hills. Once on the surface of an asteroid, when a friend turned around and saw his hands reaching for the air controls of the skinsuit. Never quite so strongly as now, in the gentle horsey face of the New Englander. There had been Stoddards who signed the Mayflower Compact, stood at Bunker Hill, helped break the charge of the Confederate armor at Shiloh. *Certain things you shouldn't forget about Uncle Nate*, he reminded himself. The memories were real, visiting the New Hampshire farmhouse, snowball fights and tree forts and sitting in the kitchen with Uncle Nat and Aunt Debra . . . and this was real, too. Every man had his god; Stoddard's was Duty, and he would sacrifice both the Lefarges to it with an unhesitating sorrow, as he had his own son, as he would himself.

Stoddard blinked, and the moment passed. "It doesn't pay to get emotional about it, is all. You'll be happy to know the Ekstein problem is what I want you working on. He has to go."

"I thought you were sorry for him, General."

"I am. What's that got to do with the barn chores? I've selected a partner for you, too; Captain Lefarge will be your backup on this one."

"*Captain* Lefarge?" Marya sat bolt upright at that.

"You deserved it," Stoddard said. He pulled a small box out of a drawer. "This job has a few compensations, anyway.

"And here's the Ekstein file," he continued. "All but the eyes-only portion. Marya, you covered this before you left for India."

"Yes, sir, partially." Marya said. "Need to know," she added to her brother. "He's really quite formidably good. And I attended a few lectures of his at the Institute."

Frederick looked a question at the general.

"MIT, their Reserve Training Program." Fred nodded; he had known *that* much. "We wanted her to qualify as an electronics specialist, microwafer design and comp instruction both." Fred blinked surprise; it was not at all common to be an expert in designing computers and in the instructional sets that ran them as well.

"We put the captain through MIT under an assumed name, and fudged the physical records on her military service; enough to keep the Security Directorate from tagging her with a routine border scan."

"You *have* been a close-mouthed little sister," Fred said.

"Need—"

"I know, I know. Why do you think I never asked where you were, when you dropped out of sight for three months at a time?" The general's last words sank home. "We're going *in*?" he asked sharply.

"Certainly." Stoddard rose and walked to the window again. "You'll both be in for intensive briefing, starting Monday. Take the next few days off, rest. This may get messy, but we certainly can't afford to let them keep Ekstein much longer." The general looked aside at the black-bordered portrait of his son whose P-91 had taken a seeker missile over the Pacific. Just a skirmish, border tension . . . and a valuable indication that the Alliance electronic countermeasures were not as good as they had hoped. "Not much longer at all."

✧　✧　✧

VON SHRAKENBERG TOWNHOUSE
ARCHONA, ASSEGAI BOULEVARD
ARCHONA PROVINCE
DOMINATION OF THE DRAKA
NOVEMBER 21, 1972

"Gayner's next," the assistant said.

Senator Eric von Shrakenberg tipped his chair back from the desk. "Spare me," he muttered, rising and pacing with a smooth graceful stride.

It was a warm summer's afternoon, and the windows of the office were open on the sloping gardens that overlooked the city below. The von Shrakenberg townhouse was old; the core of it had been built around 1807, in the time of his great-great-grandfather, when Archona had been new. He tried to imagine it as it had been then, a vast rocky bowl on the northern edge of the great plateau; olive-green scrub, dense thickets of silverleaf trees around the springs and the Honeyhive River. A chaos of muddy streets and buildings going up by fits and starts, mansions and hovels and forced labor compounds, bars and brothels and fitting-out shops for the miners and planters, the hunters and slavers and prospectors pushing north into the great bulk of Africa.

"Why exactly do you detest Gayner, suh?" the assistant asked. She was just back from the yearly Reserve maneuvers of her legion in the Kalahari, bronzed and fit with rusty sun streaks through her black hair. "Apart from her bein' a political enemy."

"Why?" Eric stroked a finger over his mustache in an unconscious gesture of thought. "Because she's totally ruthless, insanely ambitious—personally, as much as for the Race—and has no more scruples than a crocodile."

"Yes, but what does she *want*? And . . . we're idealists?"

"No, Shirley. We're utterly unscrupulous for the greater good," Eric said, smiling without turning. At fifty, he was a generation older than his assistant, dressed in a gentleman's day suit: jacket and trousers of loose cream silk brocade trimmed in gold, ruffled shirt and indigo sash, boots and a conservative ruby stud in the right ear. The clothing brought out the lean shape of his body: broad shoulders tapering to slim hips. The long narrow skull bore faded blond hair worn in an officer's crop, short at the sides and back, slightly longer on top. His eyes were gray, set over high cheekbones in a face that was handsome in a bony beak-nosed fashion.

"What does Gayner want? I suspect she doesn't know herself; at a minimum, all this."

He nodded out the windows. The reception office was on the second story, and beyond lay Archona. It had long outgrown the original site; there were twelve million dwellers now, Earth's greatest city. Hereabouts were mansions and gardens, like the townhouses of country gentry, used when business or politics brought them in from their plantations for a few weeks; for the whirl of social life in season as well. Tile roofs set amid green on the low slopes below him, red- and plum-colored, the flash of sunlight on water or marble. Quiet residential streets, lined with jacaranda trees as municipal law required. A mist of purple-blue in this blossom-time, spreading down over the hills and into the valley below and up the far slope, kilometer after kilometer. There were few tall buildings, and those were for public use.

The blue haze of the flowers sank into the languorous sienna-umber tint of the high-summer air, giving a translucent undersea look, as if the Domination's capital were Plato's lost Atlantis still living beneath the waves. At the center, the House of Assembly loomed, a two-hundred-meter dome of stained glass on thin steel struts, glowing like an impossible jewel amid its grounds. From there, the Way of the Armies ran east to Castle Tarleton, west to the Archon's Palace, each set on the bordering rim overlooking the old city. He could recognize other landmarks: the cool white colonnades of the University, the libraries and theaters, pedestrian arcades lined with shops and restaurants . . . . gardens everywhere, small parks, streets lined with marble-and-tile low-rise office structures. More parks beneath the tall pillars of the monorail. A train slashed by with the smooth speed of magnetic induction.

There was little noise, a vague murmur under the nearer sound of children playing. Draka hated blaring sound still more than crowding, and even in the central streets voices and feet would be louder than traffic. The air smelled freshly of garden, hot stone, water; there was only the faintest underlying tint of the vast factory complexes that sprawled north of the freemen's city, the world of the Combines and their labor compounds. Decently hidden away, so that nobody need visit it except when business took them there. His mind filled in the other hidden things: the vast engineering works that brought in water from the Maluti mountains and the headwaters of the Zambezi a thousand kilometers away, the nuclear power units buried thousands of feet below in living granite. . . . He had known this city all his life, and still the sight was enough to catch at the breath.

"What wonders we've built and dreamed," he said softly. The aide leaned closer to listen. "Wonders and horrors . . ." Above the horizon tall summer clouds were piling, cream-white and hot gold in the fierce sunlight. Aircraft made contrails high overhead, and the long teardrop shapes of dirigibles drifted below. "Gayner . . . it's a melodramatic word, but she *lusts* for control over the Race. And she'll never have it, because to rule them she would have to . . . love this world we've built. And to do that she'd have to understand it, understand how beautified and how utterly evil it is . . ."

"Suh?"

"Forget it," Eric said. "Just keepin' up my reputation as a heretic." He turned, and his face went as cold as the flat gray eyes. "At seventh and last, I hate Gayner because she's a distillation of our bad qualities without our savin' graces; like a mirror held up to the secret madness of our hearts." A pause. "And if she and hers had their way, there'd be nothing human on this earth in a hundred years. Things that walked on two legs and talked, but nothin' we'd recognize."

Louise Gayner snapped the box file shut and sank down in the rear seat of the runabout. It was a hired vehicle rented by the month. She preferred them: less bother than maintaining your own. Her house was temporary, too, a modest four-bedroom rental in the eastern suburbs. Archona was not her home; she was city-bred, but from the west coast, Luanda. And not interested in luxury for its own sake.

Unlike some I could name, she thought sardonically as the car turned under the tall wrought-iron gates of the mansion. The wheels rumbled on the tessellated brick of the drive, a louder sound than the quiet hiss on asphalt.

Five hectares: the von Shrakenbergs had arrived early, and kept wealth and power enough to preserve what they took. A slope, on the southern side of the basin that had sheltered the original city. Generations of labor had turned the stony ground into a fantasia of terraces and tiled pools, fountains, patios. Native silverleaf and yellowwood, imported oaks and paper birch towered to give shade, and the high wall that surrounded the estate was a shape beneath mounds of rose and wisteria. The car soughed to a halt before the main entrance.

"Why are we bothering?" her assistant said, as they emerged into the dazzle of sunlight, then gratefully forward into the shade of a huge oak.

Gayner flicked her wrists forward to settle the lace, adjusted her gunbelt. "It's like dancin', Charlie," she said flatly. "You have t' git through the steps. Speakin' a' which—"

The half-moon of the drive was fronted by a last stretch of rock garden, with topiaries in pots. The stairway ran up the middle of it, polished native granite casting sun flecks back at them; dark foreshortened strips of shade lay slanting across it, from the Lombardy poplars along the edges. Servants came forward as they disembarked, one to show the driver the way to the garages; two more knelt smoothly to offer glasses on trays.

Gayner looked down at them, holding her gloves in her right hand and tapping them into her left. Wenches, a matched set; about nineteen, their movements as gracefully polished as the silver and crystal in their hands. One an ash-blond Baltic type, the other the gunmetal black of a Ceylonese Tamil, both in tunics of colorful *dashiki*, hand-embroidered cotton from the Zanzibar coasts.

The two Draka took the wine and poured out ceremonial drops before sipping. The aide's eyebrows rose. "Constantia," he said.

Sweet, with a lingering aroma as of flowers. Priceless; there was only one estate which produced it, down in the Western Cape province, and that was preserved as a historical landmark by the Land Settlement Directorate. Gayner smiled grimly as she replaced the glass; it was all faultless Old Domination manners, emphasizing that they were guests of the house. The finest of welcoming cups, presented with art . . . but no Citizen to greet them, subtly reminding her of status. Von Shrakenberg was a senator, she merely a committee head of the House of Assembly. He a retired Strategos, a paratrooper four times decorated, while her military service had been with the Security Directorate. Her family moderately obscure Combine execs and bureaucrats, descended from rank-and-file Confederate refugees, his among the oldest in the Domination. The von Shrakenbergs had been mercenaries in

British service during the American Revolution, and they had arrived in the then-Crown Colony of Drakia with the first wave of Loyalist refugees. And every generation since had produced a leader, in war or politics or the arts.

"Up," she said to the serfs. They rose with boneless grace and led the way, up the steps and into the colonnaded veranda, into the cool shade past the ebony doors. A house steward bowed them in; he was elderly, a dark-brown man with a staff of office that he had probably borne for thirty years. Estate-bred, she decided; he had the look common in the southern Police Zone.

"Mistis, Mastah," he said, with a deferential smile. "My Mastah bids youz free of his house. Does you wish to be shown to the reception room at once, oah is there anythin' you desire first? Rest, refreshments?"

"No," she said dryly. "It's excellent wine, but we didn't come here to drink." Tempting to keep the senator waiting, but childish. Nor did she wish more conversation with this relentlessly polite serf, who spoke far too much like a Citizen for her taste.

He bowed again. "A case has been sent to you cah, Mistis. . . . This way, if it please."

Through rooms and courtyards, up a spiral staircase. Portrait busts in niches, von Shrakenberg ancestors from the time of the Land-Taking on.

Dead men, she thought flatly. *All long dead; as useful as a plantation hand's fetish.*

Or perhaps not. Dead as human beings able to help or harm; powerfully alive as myths. *The question being, is von Shrakenberg using the myths or being used?*

The upper corridor ran the length of the building, glassed at both ends, with a strip of skylight above. The steward swung the door wide, stepped in to announce them.

"My Mastah, the Honorable Louise Gayner, Representative for Boma-North," he said. "Centurion Charles McReady of the Directorate of Security."

"Gayner," Eric said.

They had met often enough at official functions that no more was necessary. She was a slight woman, a decade younger than he. Reddish-brown hair, hazel eyes, a sharp-featured foxy face, freckled and with a pallor that spoke of a life spent indoors. Nothing soft in her stance, though; she had the sort of wiry build that always seemed to quiver on the brink of motion. Dressed with almost ostentatious plainness in pale-green linen, no more than a single stickpin in her cravat. A statement, in a way: so was the gun. Not an ornamental dress weapon. A Virkin custom job, worn higher-slung than usual and canted forward in a cutaway holster, the molded grip polished with use. A duelist's weapon, and the four tiny gold stars set into the crackle-finished black metal of the slide were a reminder of the ultimate argument in Draka politics.

Well, I'm not the only one who can deliver a hint, he thought with self-mockery, rising to grip forearms.

"Von Shrakenberg," she replied. "Kind of you t' make time fo' me, Senator."

Did I always dislike that Angolan accent? It was ugly, a nasal rasp under the usual soft-mouth drawl of the Domination's dialect of English . . . but that might be subconscious transference from the decade they had spent in political sparring.

"No trouble at all," he said, which was true enough; VTOL aircars cut the commuting time to his family's plantation to less than an hour. Not like the old days . . . ox wagons then, a once-a-year trip. Moving the capital here from Capetown had been the first of the notorious Draka *faits accomplis*; the British governor-general had protested all the long wagon journey through the mountains of the Cape and across the high-veldt plateau. Unavailing protests, since the local Legislative Assembly held the power of the purse, a purse England needed desperately while locked in its death struggle with Napoleon.

The two leaders' aides were laying out papers, treating each other with rather less courtesy than their elders. Eric watched in amusement as they bristled; his assistant was visibly looking down her well-bred nose, and the Security officer responded . . . *exactly as you'd expect*, the senator thought. He looked to be the sort of thug-intellectual the headhunters usually recruited, anyway.

"About the legislative docket—" Eric began, and halted as the doors swung open again.

"Oh, sorry, Pa." A group of Draka adolescents in tennis whites or the loose bright-colored fashions the younger generation favored. Eric's smile turned warm as he greeted his eldest.

"A last-minute appointment, Karl," he said. Turning to Gayner: "My son, Karl. His aunt Natalia"—the politician blinked at the teeneged girl until she remembered that Eric's father had remarried late in life—"my sister's daughter Yolande and her friend Myfwany, down from Italy." Eric's eyes swung back to Gayner, narrowed slightly.

"Karl," he continued, "Miz Gayner and I were just about to discuss somethin' private. Why don't you and you friends show Centurion McReady an' Shirley around fo' about an hour or two? We should be through by then, and we can be down to Oakenwald by dinnertime."

Gayner stared back at him for an instant, then gave an imperceptible nod to her subordinate, waiting until the door shut before speaking.

"What's y' game, von Shrakenberg?"

"An end to games," Eric replied. He walked to the desk, pressed a switch beside the retriever screen. "Private; my word on it."

Gayner inclined her head: "I believe you," she said neutrally. *Fool* was left unspoken.

"Gayner, between us we command the largest single voting blocs in the Party. . . . That's our power, and that's our danger."

"Party unity's an overworked phrase," she said.

"Because the Front has been in power too long; the other parties are shadows. Which means that everyone who wants office or powah crowds in, which undermines unity. But contemplate the consequences of an open split, and an electoral contest."

She nodded warily. At the very least several years of uncertainty, while the factions settled who had most backing among the Citizen population. And it might not be her own group who came out ahead. . . .

"What do y' propose?" Gayner said.

Eric seated himself across from her and leaned forward, tapping one finger on the papers. "On the budget and the next six-year plan, we can compromise easily enough. It's all technical, after all. I still think you radicals are too ready to approve megaprojects. The Gibraltar dam worked out, but we're *still* patchin' and fittin' on the Ob-Yenisey diversion to the Aral Sea. . . . Still, we'll let it pass. We agree on shiftin' mo' of the military appropriations to the Aerospace Command; we can compromise on the *amount*. Let's get on to the real matters, an' start the horse tradin'."

She tapped paired thumbs and looked aside for a moment. "Y' right, dammit." A long pause. "Of the truly difficult . . . the new Section fo' serf education an' selection."

"You don't think it'll work?"

"Too well. We're concerned with the long-term implications."

Eric sighed and rubbed a hand across his face. "Look, Gayner, the pilot program has been yieldin' excellent results; *that's* why we got the votes to put it through. We *need* mo' Specialists, we *can't* raise them all from childhood in crèches, an' psychological testing is a crude tool at best. Competition an' selection are necessary if we're to get results; we can only substitute quantity fo' quality so far and no further." A hard smile. "Or do you really think we can point to this one or that an' say: 'Drop the hoe, lay down that jackhammer, now go an' write comp instructions fo' our missile computers'?" He shrugged. "We've always picked out the mo' promisin' serfs for further training. This just systematizes it a little mo' than the Classed Literate system."

"What about those who get some trainin' and then aren't selected? What about 'rousin' expectations we can't satisfy?"

"That's what the Security Directorate is fo'; let the headhunters cut off a few mo' heads, then. Thor's *balls*, woman, *we need those serfs trained!* If fo' nothin' else, to increase automation. We've always tried to keep the urban workin' class small as possible, here's our chance."

"Reducin' total numbers at the cost of buildin' up the most dangerous section. The fields we're talkin' shouldn't be serf work at all, nohow. We Citizens're producing too many architects, too many so-called artists who sit an' draw their stipends and 'create.'"

Eric raised his hands, palms up. "This is an aristocratic republic, not a despotism," he said dryly. "Citizens are free to pick they own careers, providin' they do their military service. We get enough career soldiers, enough administrators. Even enough scientists, usin' the term strictly. It's *routine* skullwork that's unpopular, and which we're short of. A matter of choice . . . unless you were plannin' on makin' some changes?"

"That'd be electoral suicide." *Fo' now*, she continued to herself with a tight smile of hatred.

Eric nodded. "Which is why that program has solid backin' among the independents," he said. "Not much of a concession t' you faction to drop their opposition. Brings us to the court reforms.

"An' *that's* a matter of principle," she said. "That proposal *isn't* popular. Citizens have rights, serfs do not—at most, privileges revocable at will. If administrative changes are necessary, let the owners an' Combines make them."

"Well," Eric said softly. "Nobody's proposin' to let the serfs have access to our courts, or to limit the power of owners. Or to limit the rights of Citizens in general." The Code of 1797 had given the free Draka as a body power of life and death over every individual of the subject races; the privilege was jealously guarded. "All that we're askin' fo' is a set of tribunals to regulate ordinary administrative punishments by serf supervisors. *Not* fo' convicts or labor-camp inmates; just fo' the labor force in general."

"Why?"

"*Because as it stands every little strawboss can do as they fuckin' please!*" He gathered control of himself. "An' if you thinks *that* don't impact on productivity and worker morale, talk to somebody in any of the industrial branches." Eric's finger brushed at his mustache in a quick left-right gesture. "Harsh regulations can be lived with, harsh enforcement, but there has to be some *regularity* to it."

"It still sounds like rights to me," Gayner said with soft stubbornness, watching him closely. "An' it sets up mo' classes within the serf caste; we've got too many as it is. I can see why Janissaries an' Orpos need special treatment, but extendin' it beyond that is bad policy, whatevah the payoff." She waited, still as a coiled mamba, before proceeding silken-voiced. "That's what I believe . . . an' on *this* issue, *I've* got the independents behind me, I'm thinkin'."

Her paired thumbs tapped together. "It's quid pro quo time, von Shrakenberg. What're you givin' me, to take back to my people when they ask why we're not fightin' you in caucus?" Silence stretched. "I want the Stone Dogs, an' I want the trial run on the psychoconditionin'."

"No." His voice was quiet, a calm that matched his face and the relaxed stillness of his body. "I'm willin' to have you new toy used as an alternative to the traditional drugs-an'-lobotomy fo' incorrigibles, but no mass application an' no accelerated research."

Her palm cracked down on the teakwood. "Gods *damn*, von Shrakenberg, you the one always goin' on about catchin' up technologically; biochemicals an' genetics are ouah strengths, an' you fight every time we try to apply them!"

"Incorrect. I pushed as hard as you fo' eugenic improvement of the Race, and fo' the reproductive techniques. I'd've thought that would count fo' something especially fo' those not inclined to the traditional methods."

Eric watched with satisfaction as Gayner flushed. She had never married, or borne children herself—which was odd, since according to his reports she was heterosexual to the point of eccentricity for a Draka woman. . . . As little as a decade ago voluntary childlessness would have ruled out a serious political career, but now one's duty to the Race could be done by proxy, via a deposit of frozen ova with the Eugenics Board.

"An' as far as the long-term genetics projects fo' the serfs are concerned, I'm all fo' them *as long as they're selectin' from within the normal range*. Wotan knows we've been scatterin' Draka genes among the wenches fo' generations; breedin' the serfs for bidability might make . . . harsher measures . . . less necessary. But I say *no* to lowerin' general intelligence, an' no to direct intervention to remove the will."

"Why?" she asked; he thought he heard genuine curiosity in her voice, beside the hard suspicion.

"Well." He inclined his head toward the obligatory bust of Elvira Naldorssen, the Domination's philosophical synthesist, and the copy of her *Meditations* that rested beside it. "What did she say? That it was the mark of humanity to domesticate subsapient animals, and of the Race to domesticate humanity? We rule our human cattle—though they outnumber us forty to one, though even most of our soldiers an' police are serf Janissaries—by dominatin' their wills with ours. Where's the pride of the Race, if they're not human beings, with potential wills of their own?"

Gayner rose and walked to the opposite wall, looking at the pictures hanging there. Portraits of Eric's parents, of his wife and children. One of a serf wench, a Circassian in a long white dress.

"You know," she said slowly, without turning, "that argument goes ovah well with the dinosaurs in you group; even with some of my people . . . Tickles their vanity. You and I both know it's bullshit. Which leaves me with the question, why do you use it? I think you soft, von Shrakenberg. Weak-stomached. The serfs are organic machinery, no mo', and runnin' them all through a conditionin' process would eliminate major problems an' costs. I know, I know"—she waved an unstated objection aside—"there's still unacceptable side effects on ability. But those are just technical problems. Genetic manipulation to remove the personality is even mo' promising. Y' real objection is squeamishness. Soft, I say."

Eric rose, too. "You not the first to think that, Gayner," he said flatly. "Those that did, mostly found I could be as hard as was necessary."

"P'haps so," Gayner said. Her gaze had gone to a battle scene beyond the portraits. It showed the ruined mountain-pass village Eric's Century of paratroops had held against two days of German counterattacks, back in the opening stages of the Eurasian War. "This-heah certainly covered up you earlier peccadilloes." She jerked a thumb at the picture of the Circassian. Eric winced inwardly; she had been his boyhood concubine, and he had sent the child she died bearing out of the Domination. To America, to freedom . . . to the hereditary foe of the Race.

It hasn't helped that little Anna grew up to be a prominent novelist, he thought between irritation and pride. He had had works of his own win prizes; it seemed to run in the blood.

"I hope you not threatenin' to bringin' *that* up again," he said dryly. The Archon of the time had publicly said his action in the pass had saved the Domination ten thousand Citizen lives; and the Draka were a practical people.

"Oh, no, I'm makin' no threats," she said. She turned, and her eyes slid over him from head to toe. "There's an old rumor, that the Security Directorate tried to have you arrested by administrative procedure right after that there battle. Befo' yo' became the untouchable hero with the *corna aurea*, of course. Even sent an officer to do it."

"His mission was classified," Eric said with the ease of long practice. There were very few left who knew the truth of what had happened . . . *By the White Christ, was it really twenty-six years ago?* "In any case, moot; he shouldn't have wandered about an unsecured combat zone."

"Two Walther 9mm slugs," Gayner agreed. Another pause. "I used to wonder about how my brother died," she continued, approaching with steps that were soundless, leaning on the table until her face was inches from his. "But yo' know, fo' the last fifteen years I haven't wondered who fired that pistol, at all."

Eric kept his face motionless. Inwardly he felt a chill wariness that reminded him of going into close bush country after leopard.

"I presume," she continued, moistening her lips, "that this means you'll agree to the Stone Dogs project, von Shrakenberg?"

With an effort of will Eric forced himself to clear his throat and speak.

"Quite right, Gayner. It's still insanely risky, but it does oppose our strength to Alliance weakness, an' if war *does* come, it'd be invaluable. I was hesitatin' because I thought it might provoke the conflict itself, if they discovered it."

She nodded, still without taking her eyes from his face; the intentness of it was akin to love, a total focusing of attention on another human being. Her pupils expanded, filling the light hazel of her eyes with pools of black, and the small hairs along his spine struggled to stand.

"That's agreement in outline, then. I'll get my people to drop their opposition to the trainin' and tribunal motions; you agree to puttin' the Stone Dogs through the Strategic Plannin' committee; we shelve the chemoconditionin' trials. Agreed?" He nodded. "Let's have our subordinates draw up the draft proposals, then. I'll be goin'."

"Wait." She turned; he was standing at unconscious parade rest, with his hands clasped behind his back. "You think I'm soft. What's more, you think the Domination's gone soft, don't you, Gayner? Not like the hard, pure days back in the '50s?"

"In danger of it," she said, with her hand on the handle of the door.

"You should read some history, Gayner; about what things were like just befo' the Great War, when we'd had two generations of peace. But think on this, Gayner: Let's do a best possible case heah; let's say the Stone Dogs work, an' we destroy the Yankees. Cast you mind forward of that, say we've pacified them; say the Domination is coterminous with the human race, as we've always dreamed. *Whose policies do you think the Race will find most agreeable then?*"

She blinked at him in surprise for a moment, then relaxed. "Well, then, we'd have only our *personal* matters to attend to, wouldn't we? In any case, by then other . . . hands may be at the tiller. A very fond, an' very anticipatory farewell, von Shrakenberg."

She swept out the door, and Eric went to his desk, sat, thumbed the record switch and dictated a digest of the legislation to be drafted. He flicked it off, thought for a moment, then thumbed it again:

"Note to Shirley. We've won, two out of three," he said, "Why is it that I don't feel too happy about this?"

Chapter Eight

CHATEAU MOULIN
PROVINCE OF TOURAINE
DOMINATION OF THE DRAKA
FEBRUARY 8, 1973

The chateau was south of the Loire, in the Sologne. A nobleman by the name of Philippe du Moulin had built it five centuries before. Most of the time since, it had been a hunting seat, for the Sologne was an area of poor acid soils, of marsh and forest. When the Draka came they decided that the effort of reclamation was not worth the cost. Too many richer lands lay desolate, their tillers dead in the slaughterhouse madness of the Eurasian War; the remaining French peasants were deported elsewhere, or set to planting oak trees. For two decades the mansion lay empty, until the Security Directorate needed a place of refuge for a defector with very specific tastes.

"Here he is," the Farraday Combine representative muttered with throttled impatience. "At last."

The Tetrarch from the Directorate of Security shrugged and raised her hands in a gesture of helplessness, then let them fall back to the surface of the table. There were three terminals and keyboards built into it, the only outward sign of modernity in the room with its tapestries and suits of plate armor.

"Hi!" David Ekstein said, as he bounded in. The Security officer winced and looked away. *Not quite so disgusting as he was*, she thought resignedly.

"Dave, it's really *impo'tant* not to keep people waiting," the officer said.

"Oh, gee, sorry, Cathy," Ekstein replied. He was in his mid-twenties but already the wiry black hair was thinning on top: a short man with a sticklike figure that turned pudgy at face and waist and buttocks. Acne scars, and his skin was still wet from the pool, mottled brown from the sunlamps. Bitterly, she told herself that the defector probably thought he was fitting in with Draka custom by coming to the business meeting in a black pool robe . . .

Tetrarch Catherine Duchamp Bennington gritted her teeth and smiled back at him. Officially she was Security liaison here. *Actually, I'm bearleader to this little shit,* she thought. Much of her effort was spent keeping him away from Draka. He was officially an honorary Citizen, but half an hour in normal society would have left him with a round dozen challenges to pistols at dawn.

Not that he was nasty, just . . . *like a damned smelly fat puppy,* she thought. Providential that a castle in France had been his private daydream, so they could immure him in the middle of this hunting preserve. Even better if they could have stuck him in an SD property in Africa or Russia, but the orders were for soft hand treatment. You could see why. Creativity was so delicate a quality, and this slug was a hothouse flower of the first order.

"Mei-ling was playing handball with me, and I really wanted to win," he continued.

At least that was going well. The Directorate had bought him two dozen concubines, every one of them from the top crèches and with special training to boot. The Domination wanted full value from David Ekstein, and the wenches were leading him with patient subtlety into healthier habits. He had already lost a good deal of weight. It was unlikely that Ekstein would ever be anything remotely resembling what a Citizen should be, but with luck, in a few years and fully dressed he could avoid arousing actual disgust. His social skills had been marginal at home and were nonexistent here, but with careful management that could be handled. The Eugenics people had a sperm deposit in their banks, anyway.

"So, what's your problem?" he continued, rubbing his hands and turning to the Combine exec. "I thought those designs were pretty good, really." Servants bustled in with trays of coffee, fruit, and breakfast pastries.

"Ah," the exec began. The electrowafers were excellent, and had opened up a whole new range of near-space applications, not to mention the eventual civilian uses. "Well, we're havin' real quality problems. Seventy percent rejection rate, even on our best fabricators, an' we *needs* those wafers." He caught himself just in time, not mentioning the use to which the sensor-effector systems would be put. The American—the *ex*-American, he reminded himself—was a defector, after all, and quite startlingly naive politically, but it was better not to remind him of certain things without need.

Ekstein frowned, took the data cartridge from the man and slipped it into the table unit. His hands skittered over the keyboard and the ball-shaped directional control; Bennington noted how their clumsiness vanished, turning to fluid skill. "Hey, no problem," he said after a minute. "It's the amorphous layer that's causing it. You're getting uneven deposition. How do you—"

Tetrarch Bennington tuned out the technical discussion and stared moodily out the mullioned windows of the salon. It was a cold bright morning outside; the courtyard's brick pavement was new-swept; white snow in the mortar grooves between herringbone red brick. Gardens laced with white-ice hoarfrost, fairy-silver grass, and black tree trunks beneath hammered-metal branches, flowerbeds pruned back and dormant beneath their coats of mulch straw. The edge of the forest was a black wall, and the surface of the moat clear gray ice. It would be warming soon, though. She was a banana-lander from Natalia, born in Virconium, and the clear freshness of the northern spring never failed to enthrall.

"Oh," the exec was saying. She glanced up with a start. Her coffee had gone cold, and she signed for the serf to bring another.

"Oh, well . . . Why didn't we think of that?" He looked down at the screen, rubbing his brow in puzzlement.

The American grinned. "Hey, man, it always looks that way. That should get you down to, hm, fifteen percent rejections, easy. Null-G applications of amorphous silicon deposition are tricky; it's not my specialty, you know, but I think that's the way to go. Especially with EV channels and particle-stream etching, you know."

"Many thanks, suh," the exec continued, as the terminal downloaded the details into his attaché case and clicked completion. He shook hands with the ex-American. "Service to the State."

"Have a nice d—, Glory to the Race," Ekstein replied.

The room fell silent as the exec left. There was a crackle from the big fireplace, a glimmer of flamelight, and pale winter sun on polished stone and wood. Ekstein sighed, shifting restlessly and then moodily taking another croissant. The serf moved in deftly to sweep up the crumbs around his plates. She was a pert little thing, in a uniform of short skirt and white cap and bib apron that had been another of Ekstein's eccentricities. He ran a hand up her thigh, but half-heartedly, even when she leaned into the clumsy caress and smiled.

That's a bad sign, Bennington thought. *He's not screwing anything that moves, anymore.*

"What's the matter, Dave?" she said quietly as the serfs left.

He slumped in the chair, hands resting loosely between his knees.

"Oh, I don't know," he said, frowning. "I . . . I feel lonely, I guess."

"Hm, I thought you were lonely befo'," she replied. Every word and gesture was going down on record for the SD psychs to mull over, but you had to get a personal gestalt to really know an individual. Besides, he *was* like a puppy; you wanted to see him wag his tail. "You girls not givin' satisfaction?"

"No, no, they're great!" he said. "Mei-ling and Bernadette especially." His face puckered a little. "Yeah, I was real lonely. Only . . . well, sometimes Bernie and Izzy and Pedro would come over, and we'd have beer and peanut-butter-and-jelly sandwiches, and play Knights and Sorcerers on my old Pacifica. I sort of miss it, I guess. I can play against myself here, but it's not the same."

He looked up, and his eyes were misty. "Say, Cathy, maybe you could get me an online terminal, and I could patch into PanNet? Then I could play them remote."

Bennington sighed inwardly; you had to swat a puppy if it piddled on the rug, but it wasn't pleasant. She forced a warm smile. "Mm, Dave, I don't think we could do that. I mean, the other end wouldn't allow it." Probably true, and no *way* the SD would let an OSS op get a line on this prize.

He blinked. "Look," she continued, "you've been workin' too hard, Dave. What say, in a month o' two, we fly down to Nova Cartago or Alexandria. We'll go out to some of the nightspots, meet a few"—*carefully selected*—"people, relax, hey?"

He nodded, halfway between interest and listlessness. She crossed around the desk, put an arm about his shoulders. "An' in the meantime, we'll have cook make us up some peanut-butter-and-jelly sandwiches"—*Mother Freya, the things I do for the Race*—"an' you can teach me how to play Knights and Sorcerers. Mei-ling and Bernadette will sit in."

OSS SAFEHOUSE
STATE OF VIRGINIA
UNITED STATES OF AMERICA
JANUARY 1973

"Goddammit, my brains are going to run out my nose!" Marya said, and grunted as she bench-pressed the weights again. "Ninety-nine, *one hundred.*" The link rod fell back into its rest with a clang. She took a deep breath; the room smelled of sweat, hers and others, of oil and machinery and the straw matting on the floor. The lights were sunlamps, to give them the appropriate tan, and the walls were lined with mirrors.

"That's, '*Gods curse it* mah *brains is* goin' *run out* mah *nose,*' " the instructor said. "Repeat it, Lefarge."

She lay back on the padded exercise bench and repeated the sentence in Draka dialect, turning her head to watch the instructor. He was a defector from the Domination, about twice her age: an unremarkable man, medium-brown hair and eyes and an outdoorsman's weathered face. He was doing one-handed chin-ups while he listened with a slight frown of concentration on his face.

"Bettah," he said. "But remembah, don't drawl *too* much. Brains is *buh'rains*, not *braaains*. The dialect has roots here-abouts, but it's changed in different directions since the 1780s. Over to the cycle."

She groaned and swung herself up, walking over to the fixed exercise cycle. Her sweatsuit was soaked and chafing; she wiped her face on the corner of the towel around her neck. Her brother was using the Unitorso machine beside it, with his forearms against the vertical spring-loaded bars, pressing them in to his chest, holding, then slowly out again. The muscles of his chest and stomach stood out, moving fluidly beneath the fair skin. Marya felt a sudden sharp stab of affection, oddly mixed with the sort of aesthetic admiration you might feel for a statue or a sunset.

Damnation, she thought dismally. The number of eligible males around was small, and seemed either gentlemanly or disinterested. A man could marry outside the field, as long as the wife didn't mind not being told a lot of things. For a female agent, another agent was about the only game in town. *It's like being tall*, she thought. *You have to go for the tall boys, but the short girls poach on them, too.*

Of course, she could start asking them herself. . . . Her mouth twisted wryly. Sex was a tool of the trade, and she was sure enough she could do anything required in that line, but somehow it was different in a social setting. *Benefits of a Catholic upbringing. Shit.*

The instructor had finished his second sequence of fifty and dropped lightly to the ground, landing silently on the balls of his feet. He was dressed as they were, in loose felted cotton exercise clothing and soft shoes, but he seemed to flow as he walked.

"Get to it," the Draka said. "You wind needs it." He stopped by Fred, looked him up and down appraisingly. Then he seemed to blur, and his fist struck the man low in the belly. Marya winced at the hard *smack*, and her brother doubled over with a grunt. His hand had come down to block and stayed suspended three-quarters of the way to completion.

"Bettah," the Draka said, then chuckled. "Back home they'd envy me mah chances, gettin' to beat up on Yankees fo' a livin'."

Marya pedaled grimly. "If you loves us so much, why're you heah?" she enunciated carefully.

The Draka looked at her. "Good. Treatin' yo' r's right, now."

It isn't a lack of expression, she thought, puzzled. Like most Draka she had seen, the instructor somehow gave an impression of still-ness even when he was moving. *Ah. No unintentional gestures*, she decided. The hands moved only when he wanted them to, and the body stayed rock-still unless ordered to move. No twitches, jerks, shifts.

"It was a mattah of circumstances, luck an' opportunity," he con-tinued. "I's an only chile, and mah mothah died early. Pa away most all the time, no relatives near. Raised by serfs mo' than most, didn't fit in well at school. Eventually realized that all the people I really cared about had numbahs on they necks, and that I was spendin' my life grindin' them down." He grinned, a gaunt expression. "Had an opportunity to get out, took it. Doesn't mean I've got any par-ticular affection fo' Yankees or Yankeeland. The air stinks, everythin's ugly, there's no decent huntin' an' the people are soft an' contempt-ible."

He checked the medical readouts built into the cycle: heartbeat, respiration, neurological profile. "Good enough. Two of you are gettin' as near passable as you ever will in the time available; toward the top of the bottom one-fifth of Citizens. Pity, you've both got good potential. Bettah than average."

Fred was using the Unitorso again, the mark of knuckles a fad-ing red splotch on his stomach below the solar plexus. "If . . . that's . . . so . . . why're we . . . so . . . god damned . . . rotten?" he asked, careful to keep his tone neutral.

The Draka looked up at him. "Time," he said. "Y'all didn't start early enough; that affects y'whole system. Bone-density, fo' example, basic body-fat ratios, metabolic rate an' so forth. Mah genes is no more than middlin', athletics-wise, but y'all will never catch up. If you'd been in the *agoge* from age five, you'd be notable excellent."

❖   ❖   ❖

ABOARD AIRSHIP *DOULOS*
APPROACHING NANTES AIRHAVEN
LOIRE DISTRICT, TOURAINE PROVINCE
DOMINATION OF THE DRAKA
APRIL 3, 1973

Frederick Lefarge had not flown by airship since he was a child; in the Alliance countries lighter-than-air was used mainly for freight, these days. The Domination had its own turbojets and scramjets, but simply attached less importance to haste, and neither of the Powers allowed overflights by aircraft of the other. London to Nantes was the sole passenger link between the Alliance and Europe, maintained by the Transportation Directorate; the Alliance had accepted the arrangement, but insisted that only slow and easy-to-monitor dirigibles be used.

"Welcome home, Mastah, Mistis," the serf customs clerk said, handing him and Marya the forms.

The ferry dirigible was still at five thousand feet, more than time enough to complete the paperwork, but the American agents had come early to the lounge. That was in character for their personas, Draka eager to be home.

It is a comfortable way to travel, he mused. *But it gives you too much time to think.* He had been learning something of the nature of fear, this trip. Swift flashes, like the moment they passed the barricades in London and stepped onto territory that was Draka by treaty. The first green Security Directorate uniform, with the skull patches on the collar. Watching the Channel dwindling away below. A slow gnawing; every moment increased the danger, and there were a *lot* of moments to come.

Still, dirigibles are comfortable. Particularly compared with being strapped into a windowless hypersonic tin can, boring through the stratosphere at Mach 12 with the leading edges cherry-red. The *Doulos* was a teardrop of fiber-matrix composite five hundred meters long; near the bow a semicircular strip of the lower hull had been made transparent, as windows for the main lounge. The clear synthetic curved sharply outward for nearly two stories above his head, and from his seat at the edge of the deck he had a view straight down that would have made an agoraphobe cringe. Countryside for the last few hours, and now the broad greenbelt that always surrounded a major Draka city. There were a quarter million people in Nantes.

None of the jumbled mixed-use fringe you saw in the Alliance; plantation fields, then parks and public gardens and manicured forest. Transport corridors, more rail and less highway than he was used to. The industrial sector was to the east, along a section of the river that had been dredged for shipping. Anonymous factories with their labor compounds of three-story flats grouped around paved courts. Shipyards bristling with overhead cranes, warehouses, all along an orderly gridwork of paved streets and rail sidings. Some of the streets were tree-lined; that grew more numerous toward the west, in residential districts reserved for the serf elite of technicians and bureaucrats.

Then the Citizen quarter, a cluster of public buildings and a scatter of homes wide-spaced amid gardens.

He turned his attention to the paper:

Name. Antony Verman.

Place and Date of Birth. Archona, 1947: a Citizen population of over two million, which cut down the chance of meeting someone who should know a personality that existed solely as pits and spots in a read-only optical memory bank. Quite a good cover; they had worked hard to slip it into the files.

"Flagged," the instructor had said. "If the Security Directorate checks it, they'll get a warning you're War Directorate Military Intelligence; the War Directorate will be told you're a Krypteia hotshot."

The Domination's two armed services liked each other only marginally more than either loved the Alliance, and talked no more than they had to. Of course, the cover would still not stand up to detailed investigation; there were too many records, in too many separate files.

Military Service. Infantry, XXI Airmobile; as close to anonymous as you could get.

Occupation. Ceramic design consultant, luxury manufactures like that were generally handled by small businesses, not the omnipresent Combines. A designer was doubly independent, was more free to be a rolling stone with no connections. Better still to have no occupation, but without a good excuse a person who just lived on their Citizen stipend was a figure of some suspicion and contempt, and would attract attention when travelling.

Purpose of visit abroad. Reviewing samples of American ceramics, of course. There was an interesting collection in the memory of the impeccably Draka Helot-IV analogue/digital personal comp in his attaché case, and anyone making inquiries would find a string of design studios and shops with perfectly genuine memories of the two young Draka. That had been the beginning of their assignment, seeing if they could fool Americans first. And pass the critical gaze of the Draka defectors who had been their final instructors, in everything from etiquette and gossip to fighting style and sexual technique.

He glanced aside at his sister. *Tradecraft's good enough to fool me,* he thought. They had both had minor cosmetic implants to make their faces unrecognizable to anyone who knew their genuine identities, hormone treatments to change their body-fat ratios, but it was more than that. Most of all the look, the hard-edged glossy feel of one of the Domination's elite. Not even just Draka; looking at her with his persona's eyes he could place her, city-born, probably from the southern provinces.

He finished the form and snapped his fingers for the serf. The lounge was growing a little crowded. Two hundred or more; thirty or so Draka, settling in around them, and the rest from the Alliance, mostly Americans and English. Some on business, others well-heeled tourists prepared to pay highly for sights and experiences only the Domination could offer; Fred looked at them with a distaste most of the Citizens around him seemed to share. The Domination allowed a trickle of closely supervised visitors, as much for the Intelligence opportunities as for the Alliance dollars they brought.

There was a subliminal change in the vibration of the hull; he looked back and saw the big turbocompound engine pods swiveling. Distant pumps went chunk-*whir*, compressing hydrogen to liquid and draining it into the insulated tanks along the keel. Fred's mouth was dry as he felt the slight falling-elevator sensation of descent; he sipped at his glass of sparkling mineral water. They were over the airhaven now, passing rows of dirigibles in their cradles, acres of concrete and rail. The tall cylinder of the docking tower was ahead of them, and the *Doulos* slid toward it with the calm precision of computer piloting.

Contact, and a dying of machine noise that had been imperceptible before. More movement but with a different feel, heavier than the cushiony grace of lighter-than-air, as the airship established negative buoyancy and sank into its cradle; more chunking noises, as the fuel and gas lines connected. The scene outside sank to four stories above ground level, then pivoted slowly as the cradle turned the airship and drew it toward the waiting terminal. There were three others with their noses locked into the huge cone-shaped depressions in the giant building's wall. The *Doulos* glided into the fourth docking bay and halted; there was a whine as a ten-meter-broad section of the forward window slid up.

"Let's go," he said.

Home—in a way, Marya thought, as they walked through the gate into the terminal. *France. The country where we were conceived.*

This terminal was post-War, pure Domination. Probably built in the early '50s to a standard pattern. A huge barrel-vaulted passenger terminal, the coffered ceiling in pale blue and silver-gilt tiles; the walls were murals, landscapes, the floor streaked gray marble. Pillars around the walls, trained over with climbing plants. The Citizens' section of the great building was relatively small; most of the traffic was over the other side of the low stone balustrade. *There* it was busy, swarming even. Most of the serfs there were in overalls of varying cut, livery, color-coded Combine suits with identifying logos on the backs. Or uniforms, green for SD internal-security, dove-gray for the serf component of the Directorate of War. Management level, authorized to travel alone.

And a coffle, forty or fifty people crouched within a rope barrier. Young adults with children, and a few ranging up to middle age, in cheap cotton overalls or blouses and skirts. They were mostly dark, with high cheeks and slant eyes: Asians, brought in from the main reservoir of surplus labor in the Far East. Nantes was a shipbuilding center, and Intelligence said that the submarine yards were being adapted to produce components for the second generation of Draka pulsedrive spaceships. The nuclear-powered deep-space vessels were more like ships than aircraft; no need to shave ounces when total payloads were well over five thousand tonnes.

Enough. Not your mission. She forced herself not to notice how a woman grabbed her child and winced as a guard walked by with a shockrod. They walked across to an information kiosk. The clerk covered his eyes and bowed, then smiled.

"You will, Masters?" He pronounced it *mastahire*, a Frenchman. A little overweight, unremarkable. The number stood out below his ear, glaring. His fingers hovered over a keyboard below the stone-slab counter; there was a screen on their side as well.

"Hotel Mirabelle," Fred said. "And a car, please. Four-seater, suitable fo' country drivin'. And a weapons store."

"Phew," Fred muttered. His sister could read his thought: *Made it.* Another milestone: nothing flagged on the Security net attached to their identities.

Marya stopped with him at the bottom of the stairs, and took two glasses of mineral water from a refreshment stand. They drank, hardly noticing the taste except that it wet dry throats, looked about. They were in a broad corridor, open to the roadway in front and lined by shops at their back. The serfs who moved about them mostly looked to be personal servants on errands, or airship haven staff. Steamcars were pulling up and leaving, parcel-delivery trucks, boxy little electric town runabouts. The Draka they saw were largely travellers, intent on their destinations.

Safe, she thought—or as safe as they could be on enemy soil. That had been something it took the OSS a long time to learn: that an agent was safer and more effective posing as a Citizen than as a serf. It went against common sense. There were so *many* more serfs, but most of them were plantation hands, or compounded workers; they just didn't *move* very much. Most of the ones who did travel were tightly integrated into some organization, known faces, and for a serf the Domination was a bureaucratized labyrinth, with monsters waiting at every corner to eat you if you made a wrong step. . . .

Whereas a Citizen had fewer day-to-day constraints than the average American, if you didn't count things like the right to open a newspaper. Once that had mattered little, when the Domination and its ruling caste were smaller. But the Citizen population was no longer the tiny tight-knit band it had once been. Seventy-odd million was more than enough to be anonymous if you kept moving and avoided your supposed hometown.

They returned the glasses and walked into Sanderton's Arms and Hunt Supplies. "Donal Green," the man said, gripping their wrists. "Trooper, Special Tasks, Long-Range Reconaissance, retired. Late of Mobaye-North."

That was a province north of the Congo river, thinly settled. Probably a hunter; it would go with the military specialty. There was an interval for the usual pleasantries. A black came up behind the Draka, and waited with something of the same relaxed patience.

"What can I do fo' y'all, Citizens? Sidearms?"

Fred had an uncomfortable feeling that the remote brown eyes were recording them both inch by inch. It prickled between his shoulder-blades; machinery was tireless, but it only asked the obvious questions, and it had no intuition. Every contact with a potential informant risked bringing those uniquely human facilities into play.

"Yes, please. Just back from a trip outside the State." To Draka, there was only one. "We're doin' some huntin' as well," he said.

"Ah." Genuine interest in the Draka's eyes. "Local? We've got some fine boar, deer, wolf, and leopard territory here abouts. Or if y'all're interested, my family runs a wild-country outfit down in Mobaye-North."

"Sorry. We're booked, fo' the Archangel Reserve."

More than a little interest now. "Tiger?"

"No, bushmen." The ideal cover story, for someone buying what they needed.

There were still bands of partisans, Finnish and a few Russians, in the great taiga forests that stretched from the northeastern Baltic up into the Arctic Circle: *bushmen*, in Draka dialect. The OSS even had contacts with them, few and sporadic, when a submarine could elude the ever-improving surveillance. Few Draka had ever wished to settle in those remote and desolately cold regions, and even the timber Combines worked only the most accessible parts. The military had hunted down the most dangerous bands in the early '50s, and as for the rest . . . a Citizen who wanted game more exciting than any on four legs could book a tour. It even made sense, for a people who hunted lion with cold steel. One of the many ways used to keep the edge from rusting in an era of peace.

Not peace, he told himself. *Just an interval between battles.* To the Draka, there would be no peace until they ruled the human universe. *Or until we kill the last one.*

"Lucky you," Donal Green said. "Y'all be wantin' somethin' special, then. Price range?"

"Show us what you've got," Fred replied.

A wide grin. "As it just so happens . . . Bokassa, fetch the new models." He led them to one of the examination tables. "Now, we've gotten a shipment of the latest stuff. They're retirin' the Improved Model Holbars now, you've probably heard, replacin' it with a caseless round? Well, the prototype production run got sold, and bought up an' customized down in Herakulopolis." That was the city by the dam across the straits of Gibraltar. The black man arrived with a case, folded it back. His master lifted the weapon within free.

"Lot of it's space-made," he said. In appearance it was a virtually featureless rectangular box; there was a barrel at one end, with a thinner rod above, and a cushioned buttplate at the other; a pistol grip below, and a stubby telescopic sight above.

"Loads from a cassette, two hundred rounds," Donal continued, and slid a long box through an opening just above the buttplate. "Three-point-five-millimeter, but hypervelocity, prefragmented tungsten slug; designers say it'll only come apart in a soft target. Barrel's a refractory superalloy, an' it has a linin' of single-crystal diamond."

A smile. "They tryin' to use that fo' spaceships, thrust plates, but even in vacuum and microgravity it's stone tricky. Thissere's an intermediate use. Charge the first round by turnin' this knob in a complete circle. The slide here sets cyclic rate, up to two thousand rpm; at that, you gets a three-round groupin' less than twenty-five-millimeter apart at eight hundred meters. Max effective range 'bout one thousand. Here," he continued, unloading the weapon, "sight on somethin'."

Fred took the weapon in his hands; it was superbly balanced, although it felt a little odd to have the action right by his ear and the grip halfway down the rifle. No heavier than the Springfield-12s he had trained on, lighter than the IM Holbars-7's the Domination was using now. The sight lit as his eye came into line, with the peculiar glassy brightness of electro-optical imaging . . . and a red dot in the center of the field. The Draka heard his surprised grunt.

"Laser sightin'," he said. "Where it falls, there you hit. Frequency filter in the sight, you can see it an' the target can't. Adjusts fo' range, as you up the magnification."

"Excellent, we'll take two," the American said calmly, fighting down his glee. *This* was an advantage a Draka agent wouldn't have anywhere in the Alliance.

"Ah . . . I'm afraid they're six thousand aurics each."

He pretended a wince; quite a sum, by Draka standards. A little more than the basic Citizen stipend. A standard low-skilled serf could be bought for a hundred and seventy-five.

"Hmm . . . well, yo want the best, goin' after bushmen. They do have rifles, aftah all. Yes, two. An' the usual; nightsight goggles, some light body armor."

"Well, the measurin' rooms are this way—"

"Jesus, I just can't believe it was that *easy*," Marya said.

Her brother laughed, guiding the Bushmaster down the access ramp and onto the road marked City Center. That tone meant she had completed the sweep; the instruments in their perscomps were swift and thorough. For the moment he felt good, relaxed and strong and confident. The air rushing in through the opened window was cool, smelling of brackish river and warm asphalt pavement; the greenery and bright-colored buildings of the freemen's city showed ahead.

"No . . . Did you know, there was a time when you could get guns like that back home?"

The road was four-lane and raised on a five-meter embankment, narrower than a limited-access route in the US; more steamdrags, more buses, fewer private cars. And the Domination used rail transport more than his people. A checkerboard of streets was passing on either side, residential from the look of them. Brick-built walkups, patterns of red and white, an occasional square of decorative tile. Elite housing, individual family apartments for the literate class of industrial serf. Sidewalks, trees lining the streets. He could see the odd building that looked like a church, others that might be schools or stores . . . No, ration centers, the goods would be distributed rather than sold. It might almost have been an older suburb of an American city . . .

Marya touched his arm. There was an iron cage hanging at one of the intersections below, with a man in it, almost level with them. The sign wired to the bars read SABOTEUR, there was a crowd of children gathered below, watching or throwing rocks. At first he thought the man inside was dead—nothing so skeletal could be alive—but then one of the stones bounced through the bars and a stick-arm waved.

"Shit," he said softly. Pictures were not like the real thing. Something prickled at his eyes, and he turned them back into the windstream as the car went past. *His head just rolled on his shoulders. He couldn't have been watching us.*

"You were saying?" Marya continued. He glanced aside at her: flawlessly composed. Of course he couldn't see past the dark sunglasses. . . .

"You're a cool one," he said.

She turned her head to look at him, smiled. He felt a slight chill wash away the nausea. "I'm saving it up," she said.

"Yes . . . oh, the guns. Back before the War, you could buy military-style rifles, handguns, the lot. The Constitution, you know: 'A well-regulated militia . . . ,' the right-to-bear-arms clause."

She frowned in puzzlement. "Oh, you mean the Army Reserve? Well, even these days, a lot of them keep the personal weapons at home."

"No, nothing to do with the military. Those are under seal and inspected pretty often, anyway. Not just people in hunting clubs, either. *Anybody.* Cheap pistols, sawed-off shotguns, the lot."

She shook her head. "Live and learn . . . I know why the *Draka* always carry iron, they want to be able to kill at any time. What possible use could—" A shrug. "Never mind. Let's check in, and then we'll start working magic on the hotel infosystem." She pulled off the sunglasses and chewed meditatively on one earpiece. "Because I suspect magic is what we'll need."

Chapter Nine

HOTEL MIRABELLE, NANTES
LOIRE DISTRICT, TOURAINE PROVINCE
DOMINATION OF THE DRAKA
APRIL 4, 1973

God that thing's ugly, Marya thought, looking at the ghouloon. The transgene animal was *big*, for one thing, about three times her brother's weight. Basically a giant dog-headed baboon, four-footed most of the time but able to walk or sprint on its hind legs. The thumbs on feet and hands were fully opposable, and the forehead was high and rounded. The biocontrollers of Virunga had started with Simien mountain baboons, then added something from leopard and gorilla and the *jag hond* . . . but there was more than an animal's intelligence behind those eyes. Human genes as well, a mind that knew itself to be aware and could think in words. It wore a belt, and a long knife and pouch.

They were in one of the dining courtyards of the hotel, out under the mild midmorning sun; little fleecy clouds went by overhead, like something out of a Fragonard painting. Her brother and her and the Draka they had met: Alexandra Clearmount, a woman in her thirties, nearly their own age—a geneticist. The ghouloon was of the first "production batch." It had attracted a good deal of attention, although Draka considered it ill-bred to stare; the serfs were frankly terrified of it.

" . . . mass production," she was saying. "So costs ought to come down pretty steadily. The War and Security Directorates've got large orders in already."

"They can be used in combat?" Fred sounded politely skeptical. A waitress brought their platter of shrimp and *crudités*.

"Fo' some things. Not much technical aptitude, not intelligent enough, but they'll make killer infantry. Eh, Wofor?" She laughed and tossed a shrimp.

The ghouloon caught it out of the air with one hand, holding it between finger and thumb, sniffing curiously. Then he ate it, exposing intimidating fangs, and a long pink tongue washed the black muzzle.

"Wofor *good* fighter," he said. The voice was blurred but understandable. "Wofor brave. Wofor smart." He slapped at his chest with his hands, a drumlike sound.

For a moment Marya's eyes met the bronze-gold slit-pupilled gaze of the transgene; she could see the lids blink and the wet black nose ruffle slightly to take her scent. *Abomination*, she thought. That was what the Church taught, and for once she agreed wholeheartedly. The Draka woman was talking to Fred again, leaning forward with interest.

Lucky, Marya thought. Lucky that they had stumbled on someone heading for the Sologne Forest Preserve. The Conservancy Directorate usually rented out the hunting rights to the smaller preserves to groups of neighboring Landholders, in return for maintenance work. Very economical, but it made it difficult for an outsider to get a permit, and Draka law and custom were not easy on poachers. This Clearmount had connections with the local planters—*She might even be a relative*, Marya thought ironically—and could get them into a hunting party. *Even more lucky that she's interested in Fred and not his sister*. Not that she wasn't prepared to make the supreme sacrifice, but . . . *Better him than me.*

Citizen sexual mores were a tricky subject. Their instructors had gone into detail, tracing it back to child-rearing patterns . . . One thing Draka had never been was puritanical: sadomasochistic hedonists, that was the term the psychs used. The boys had concubines from puberty on, or casual sex with any serf woman they wanted; that was a tradition dating back to their Caribbean origins and beyond. Not many pious middle-class Protestants in the bloodlines of *this* nation. Citizen women had been legally barred from any contact with serf males until quite recently, though, and it was still socially unacceptable. Given the sex-segregated boarding schools, the Draka neoclassicism and the near-total lack of erotic inhibition otherwise, she supposed a tradition of homoeroticism was natural enough. For that matter, young women generally wanted more romance in the mixture; that didn't seem to hit men until true adulthood. So young Draka women faced a perpetual shortage of interested men. Marya's mouth quirked, remembering her own teenage years.

I always suspected courtship was something adolescent males put up with because it was the only way to get laid, she thought. *This more or less confirms it.*

Draka teenage boys got all they wanted, and tended to be profoundly indifferent to females of their own caste, who could say no. So girls were thrown back on each other; they were supposed to grow out of it in their early twenties, theoretically. Most did, to the extent of marrying and bearing children; granted, there was really strong social pressure to do that, as well. The agent grinned to herself. The Draka woman's come-on to Fred had been disconcertingly blunt. *That's logical, too.* In the Alliance countries sex was something that women had and men wanted, and men had to conform to the indirect approaches women preferred. Here, precisely the opposite.

I wonder what hunting boar with a spear is like? she thought meditatively.

✧　✧　✧

SOLOGNE FOREST PRESERVE
PROVINCE OF TOURAINE
DOMINATION OF THE DRAKA
APRIL 10, 1973
1030 HOURS

"Shit!" Myfwany said, reining in her horse. "What a complete cockup!"

Yolande nodded agreement, switching her reins to the spear hand and wiping her hair back from her forehead with the other. The rain had given way to a steady drizzle, just enough to keep them soaked and replenish the low mist drifting through the trees. They had halted in a clearing, a hectare or so of knee-high purple heather amid old-growth oak; the chill cut to the bone beneath the leather and wool of their hunting clothes. Discomfort could be ignored; they were also lost, which was rather more frustrating. She reached for her hunting horn and blew, a dull *rooo-rooo-rooo* sound through the endless patter of rain on leaf. The air was raw and full of the smell of marsh, vegetable decay, and wet horse.

"Hear that?" she asked, standing in the stirrups and cupping a hand to an ear. Their mounts stamped and blew, shaking their heads in a jingle of bridle and bit. Far away came the belling of hounds.

"Sa," Myfwany said, her head coming up. "Think they caught the scent again?"

"We can hope. C'mon, this way." The Sologne was a half-million hectares of wilderness, but the keepers tended to the paths at least.

SOLOGNE FOREST PRESERVE
CHATEAU MOULIN
PROVINCE OF TOURAINE
DOMINATION OF THE DRAKA
APRIL 4, 1973
1000 HOURS

"Out!" the Security Tetrarch said. The serf flinched back from the deadly quiet of the tone. "You brainless slut, you supposed to keep *track* of him!"

Mei-ling swallowed and straightened. "Mistis, Mastah Dave doan' like it, when we keeps him too close. We supposed to make him happy, aren't we? Anyways, Bernadette with him."

The green-coated secret police agent looked down at her control board and keyed a sequence. "Then why isn't she carryin' her transponder? Oh, hell." Another touch on the board. "Decurion, turn out the ghouloons, let's see them earn their keep. No alarms, our little electronics wizard don't like the bars of the cage showin'." She stood, shrugging into a waterproof jacket. "Come on, wench. *Show* me where they might have gone."

"Where the hell have you *been*?" Mandy asked, as Yolande and Myfwany reined in. John looked up from overseeing the serf huntsmen who were rigging the nets between the big beech trees, waved, went back to work.

"Where have *we* been?" Myfwany grinned and waved at the surrounding forest. "Y'all were supposed to keep everyone in sight or hearin' of the dogs. Fo' that matter, where the hell are we *now*?"

A faint shout came from the woods ahead. The trees were tall here, thirty meters or more, but widely enough spaced that patches of underbrush flourished, spiny thorn and witch hazel. They all swung down, dropping their reins. Yolande swallowed and took a firmer grip on her boar spear; it was a head taller than she, with an oval point as broad as her hand and a steel crossbar beneath to prevent a tusker from driving itself up the shaft to gore a hunter. The nets made a deep funnel, with them at the apex . . . it was a slightly disconsolate feeling, as the servants led the mounts away to safety.

Damn, but I'm still light for this, she thought. No more than a hundred fifty tall; strong for her weight, but wild pig had *heft*. "Shut up, you crybaby," she whispered to herself under her breath, inaudibly. Aloud: "Where are those city-bred, the ones Alexandra picked up?" There was a slightly patronizing note to her voice; the pair had seemed nice enough, but she thought her cousin could do better . . . and had been a little undiscriminating, since her divorce. *Oh, well, not everybody can find the right one*, she thought charitably, sparing a quick glance for Myfwany. They all faced the gap in the net, spreading out to twice arm's length, just close enough to give support. A horn blew ahead of them, and John came trotting back toward them.

"Don't know," Mandy said with a shrug. John stopped to give her a brief hug before taking center position; Yolande noted how they were almost of a height, now. *Mandy's really filled out*, she thought, with a slight envy. *I'm always going to be like a sylph beside her.* And it looked as if she might be a sister-in-law. . . .

"Alexandra lost track of them herself, an' said she was goin' lookin'."

"Shit. Oh, well, could be worse. Could be rainin'."

The wind picked up, blowing into their faces, and the cold drops came more thickly.

Myfwany laughed. "You had to say it, eh, sweetlin'?"

"Sign!" John said sharply.

They fell quiet, leveling their weapons in a two-handed grip. The boarhound pack was in full cry not two hundred meters ahead, and then there was an enraged squealing sound. The dogs stopped. *No fools they*, Yolande thought, as the squeal sounded again, closer. No way of telling which way the boar would go, either. Wild pigs were omnivores, like people; much more likely to go looking for trouble than a meat eater like wolf or lion. She stamped the rough-soled boots deeper into the slippery leaf mold and emptied her mind, letting her vision flow. The tips of the bushes quivered against the wind.

"He's breakin'," she called.

"Got him," John said, grin white against his tan.

He moved slightly forward from the line. The bushes tossed again, and the pig came out. He stood motionless, three-quarters on, watching them with tiny red eyes. The massive head was held close to the ground,

and the curved tusks stood up like daggers of wet ivory. Bulky and
bristling, the shoulders moved behind as weight shifted from one cloven
hoof to another. The pink snout wrinkled as the animal tried to take
their scent; an organic battering ram twice the weight of a heavy man,
knife-armed, faster than a horse and many times as intelligent. The
dogs bayed again, nearer; the shouts of the huntsmen ran beneath that
harsh music, and the sound of their horns racketed from the trees.
John leveled his spear and moved forward, dancer-light.

"Come on, you ugly son-of-a-bitch," he crooned. "Get past me and
you home free. Come *on*."

The boar seemed to sink lower against the wet grass and heather
of the forest edge. Then it moved, springing forward as if shot from
a catapult, stumpy legs churning the leaf mold, and nose down to
present nothing but weapon and heavy bone. Yolande's breath caught
as her brother took two swift strides forward, poised the spear, thrust.
Another squeal, louder, full of pain and rage, blood bright under the
wan sun and John was pushed back two bodylengths before he could
brace the iron butt of the boar spear against the ground. The animal
stumbled, and she could see its mouth wide open in a spray of blood
and saliva; then it went to its knees for a second, but the hind legs
were still pumping it forward. Mandy closed in to the side. Her spear
lifted, body and weapon a perfect X across raised arms, braced legs.
Yolande saw the point dip, then vanish into the boar's ribs with a
precise snapping thrust.

"Hola!" Yolande cried, and saw her friend's rapt smile as she and
the man pushed the beast backward, still fighting. Words formed in
her mind; half-consciously she began to work them into form. *Arms
together/blood and love*—

"'Ware!" Myfwany shouted.

Another boar had followed in the footsteps of the first; it broke cover,
grunted uncertainly at the scent of blood, then angled around the
struggle. Myfwany sidled off, and Yolande moved away from her, closing
the beast's escape route. She could see its eyes roll from one of them
to the other, and a hoof pawed at the ground. *Is it a little smaller
than the other one?* she thought. *Maybe. Wotan, I hope so.* Myfwany
was beside her; unthinkable to flinch. Yolande could feel the coiled
vitality of it, like raw flame. Then it was coming at her, bouncing off
tensed hindquarters, and there was no time for thought of anything.

Keep low. From above a boar was all bone and leather and gristle
armor over its vitals. She stooped, crouching, spear held underhand.
The ashwood shaft was smooth on the sharkskin palms of her gloves,
and the broad point seemed to follow a scribed curve to the juncture
of neck and shoulder.

"Haaa!" she hawk-screamed, and the point bit. Then the weight of
it struck her through the leverage of the spear, and it was like running into a wall at speed, like trying to stop a steamcar. "Ufff!" she
grunted, and found herself scrambling backward. Then she went over
on her tailbone, white pain flowing warm-chill across the small of her
back. The spearhead was half-buried in the tough muscle, and blood
welled around it, but the beast was pushing her backward with her

backside dragging, squealing ear-hurting shrill and hooking savagely at her feet as they dangled within striking distance of the tusks.

"Hold him, hold him!" Myfwany shouted, racing alongside and trying to find a target for a lunge.

"*You fuckin' try it!*" Yolande was half-conscious of screaming.

The spearshaft wrenched her from side to side as the boar lunged and twisted, it was as if she was on the end of a ruler somebody was pounding against trees and dirt with negligent flicks of the wrist. With a supreme effort she threw her weight down on it, using the impetus to draw her feet back and up; the tusk clipped her heel, sending her body sprawling sideways. At the same instant the butt of the spear dug into the turf, caught in the crook of a root. The boar staggered, squealed again as its own momentum drove the razor-edged steel deeper into its body. Instinct brought its head around, as it tried to gore this thing that bit it. She could smell it, heavy and rank.

Myfwany moved up beside her, throwing herself forward. The wet metal gleam of her spearhead met the taut curve of the animal's neck. The Draka went to her knees as jugular blood spurted down over the bar of the weapon and along the shaft, and the boar seemed to grow lighter. Yolande panted with a sudden joint-loosening rush of unacknowledged terror as the beast's death tremor shuddered up the spear. It sprawled, toppled over on its side; the little savage eyes grew misted. She rose, feeling exhaustion and bruises for the first time, braced her foot on the animal's body and tugged the spear free. There was blood speckled on her lips.

"Wuff." Yolande leaned on the spear and hugged Myfwany one-armed. "*Woof!*" Her friend returned the embrace.

"You had me frightened for a moment, there, Yolande-sweet," she said.

"I had *me* frightened," Yolande replied, laughing with relief. Suddenly she broke free with a whoop and tossed the spear up into the air, then rammed it point-first in the earth and kissed the other heartily. "Makes you feel alive, don't it?" she asked, when they broke free. She looked over to her brother. "Shouldn't we be about findin' the others? I could use a nice long soak an' dinner in front of the fire."

Frederick Lefarge swung a hand behind himself, palm down. *Stop.* Marya halted, then eased forward to follow the pointing muzzle of his assault rifle.

Ah, she thought. Barely perceptible at waist-height, a line of light. Laser light, only showing because of the mist; modern systems were selective enough to take that and not trip until interrupted by something more substantial. And beyond that at ankle height a camouflaged sensor clipped to a tree, capacitor detector. She went to one knee and swung her backpack around before her; it had been her responsibility to come ahead and cache their equipment. Not difficult to "lose" themselves in the woods, not when everyone else was following the sound of the dogs.

This would be the difficult part. She stripped off her gloves and flexed her fingers to limber them before assembling the apparatus. A light-metal frame to hold the clamps, *so*. Close the circles of wire around the beams, *so*. Her finger hesitated on the switch, then pressed. A modest green light flashed once on the black-box governor. Marya exhaled shakily, letting her palms rest on the cold damp leaves. She looked up, and the cold drizzle was grateful on her cheeks.

Her brother slapped her once on the shoulder, and they nodded. Marya caught up her rifle and followed as he hurdled the gap in the sensor chain she had created.

The two OSS agents froze in unison at the hoarse cries from the path ahead. Then voices, a man and a woman's, laughing. These woods were more open than those outside the guarded perimeter; they had had to halt half a dozen times to identify and disarm sensors. Marya slowly drew a map from a pocket on the side of her leather hunting trousers and glanced at it, nodded to the other American. They were right on target . . . if the information they had received from the underground was correct. If not, there might be nothing waiting for them but a Security Directorate capture team.

Frederick Lefarge stepped through the last screen of brush. The rain had stopped, but there were puddles on the flagstones of the pathway; beyond it he could see banks of flowers, and then a screen of hedge marking a pavilion. It was obvious enough what the pair had been at; the woman had mud on her knees and was still adjusting her underwear, the man fastening his belt. For a moment Lefarge felt a surge of panic—this did *not* look like David Ekstein. Too thin, too tanned, the complexion too clear . . . then the bone structure showed through. The other man's face was liquid with surprise as he stared at the two figures in hunting leathers.

"Hey," he said, drawing himself up. "This is *my* place!" A neutral Californian accent. Then, as if remembering a lesson: "Uh, Service to the State, Citizens."

Lefarge felt himself smile, and saw the other man flinch.

"Glory to the Race," he said, and the smile grew into a grin.

The serf girl nodded to the two agents, then stepped back. He stepped up to Ekstein, pushed the muzzle of the rifle into the defector's stomach and fired twice. Recoil hammered the weapon into his hand, augmented by the gases cushioned in flesh. Ekstein catapulted backward, jack-knifing, the leather of his jacket smoldering. Back and spine fountained out in a spray of bone, blood, and internal organs; the air stank of burned flesh and excrement. The body fell to the earth and twitched, was still.

So simple, he thought. Always a surprise. So different from the viewer, rarely any dramatic thrashing around, no last-gasp curses, not with a wound like this. The body fell down and died, and it was over. A whole universe within a human skull, and then nothing. *Jesus, I hate this job*. It was done. Now they must escape; the easy way, if they could get back to the hunting party, or the hard way, switching identities and oozing out through the underground net.

"*Merci*." That was the serf woman. "*Et moi aussi*."

"What?" he said sharply in French, looking up. She was young, barely in her late teens; cool brunette good looks, face unreadable as she looked down into Ekstein's final expression of bewilderment.

"Now me," she said, looking up at him. "Surely you were told, monsieur? If you do not I must contrive it, and they will suspect everyone if I suicide. Most are blameless—I am the underground contact here—but that will not spare them interrogation, and I know too much."

He felt his mouth open and the muzzle of the rifle drooped. "*Merde!* Nobody said a word about that to us!"

She swallowed, and he saw a slight tremor in the hands that smoothed back her disordered hair. "Please, quickly." She turned her back, looked up into the wet sky with fists clenched by her side. "There is not much time before he is missed."

"I—" Lefarge felt himself lock. There was white noise in his mind, caught between *must* and *cannot*. Marya stepped past him with a soft touch on his arm.

"As you wish," she said to the serf girl, an infinite tenderness in her voice. "As you wish."

"I wish we hadn't had to drop the rifles," Marya said. The rain was lifting, finally this time by the rifts in the clouds. Their horses had been waiting where they were left, damp and restless and turning large brown eyes full of reproach on the humans.

Frederick Lefarge shrugged, guiding the big animal with the pressure of his knees; Draka used a pad-saddle and an almost token bit. It would be like carrying a "guilty" sign to have the weapons when the police came around. Not that either of them could stand a close questioning, but if they *could* slip back into the hunting party . . . They walked the mounts out into the open, out of the continual patter of moisture from the wet canopy above, but the air was colder where the wind could play. Six cars, parked along the verge. Two big steam trucks for the horses and dogs, two vans for the huntsmen, two tilt-rotor dual-purpose jobs for the people . . . *Draka*, he told himself. *Don't get* too *much in character.*

The tall fair young woman was leaning against the open door of one aircar: Mandy, the just-graduated pilot. And his Draka persona's lady love, Alexandra, supervising the loading of two dead boar; her ghouloon attendant lifted one under each arm and slung them casually into the bed of the truck. The van jounced on its springs under the impact, and the American felt a slight crawling sensation across his shoulders and down the spine. *That thing's as strong as a gorilla*, he reminded himself. Rather stronger, in fact, and much faster. It snuffled at its hands, licking away the blood and turned to its owner; standing erect it was easily two meters tall.

"Eat?" it said, in that blurred gravelly tone. "Eat?"

Alexandra laughed and slapped it on one massive shoulder. The sound was like a palm hitting oak wood. "Later," she said, and the transgene bobbed its head in obedience, tongue lolling and eyes turning longingly toward the meat; drops of rain spilled from the coarse black fur of its lionlike mane.

He turned a grimace into a smile as she looked up at him and waved.

It would not do to appear unenthusiastic. Actually, it had been interesting, at least the sex had. *That* was like coupling with a demented
anaconda. The smile turned into a rueful chuckle; it was also the first
time he had been called "charmingly shy" in bed.

"Hiyo!" he called, as he and Marya handed their boar spears down
to the servants. "Sorry we got separated."

"Whole damn party did, Tony," Alexandra said. "John's out gatherin'
them all up, with Yolande and her girlfriend. Ah'm gettin' hungry as
Wofor."

"Wofor *eat*," the ghouloon said.

"I—" Mandy began, and was interrupted by a chiming note. She
leaned in to take the microphone of the aircar's com unit. "Wonder
what the headhunters're sayin'?" she said curiously.

The American felt a sensation like an ice drill boring through the
bottom of his stomach. That was the Security override alarm. Casually, he whistled the first bar of "Dixie," the code signal. Marya swung
down from her horse and turned toward the aircar; he slid the pistol
from his gunbelt and checked it. A late-model Tolgren, 5mm prefragmented bullets, caseless ammunition and a thirty-round horizontal cassette magazine above the barrel. He slipped the selector to three rounds
and set the positions of the Draka in his mind: the youngster leaning into the lead aircar; Alexandra ten meters back, by the steam truck.
The serfs could be ignored, they would hit the ground at the first sign
of violence and stay there.

"Not bushman trouble 'round here?" he said, with a skeptical tone.

"Gods, no," Alexandra replied. Her hand had gone to the butt of
her sidearm automatically, but it dropped away again as she twisted
around to look toward Mandy. "I's born not a hundred clicks from
here"—*news to me*, the American thought—"and the last incident was
the year I was born."

Time went rubbery, stretching. His body felt light, almost like zero-
G, every movement achingly precise, the outlines of things cut in crystal.

Mandy was speaking again.

"Oh, *moo*. Some sort of escape or somethin' from a headhunter
facility. Everyone's to stay put an' report movement until further notice.
Erg, mo' waitin' in the rain."

"Damn," the American said. "And I's real anxious to get out of here."

Wofor gave a growl, and Alexandra began to turn back, a casual
movement that turned blinding-fast as her peripheral vision caught the
muzzle of his Tolgren. Even then, it cleared the holster before the flat
brak of his weapon stitched a line of fist-sized craters from breastbone to throat. *Falling*, she was falling away in a mist of blood and
roar; the ghouloon leapt from the rear of the steam truck, its great
hands outstretched and jaws opened to nearly ninety degrees. *Flying*
toward him, the huge white-and-red gape, and two pistols fired in the
background and he was levering himself backward off the horse. Inertia
fought him like water in the simulator tank, back at the Academy. Then
he was toppling, kicking his foot free of the stirrup.

The horse shied violently at the ghouloon's roar and the crack of
the firearms, enough to throw him a dozen paces further as he fell.

Damp gravel pounded into his back, jarring, but he scarcely noticed. Not when the transgene struck the horse at the end of its flight; the big gelding went over with a scream of fear, and for a moment the two animals were a thrashing pile on the surface of the road. Just long enough to flick the selector on his pistol to full-automatic and brace it with both hands. Wofor rose over the prostrate body of the horse, looming like a black mountain of muscle and fur, yellow eyes and bone-spike teeth.

Even with a muzzle brake, the Tolgren was difficult to control on full-automatic. The American solved the problem by starting low enough that the first round shattered a knee, letting the torque empty the magazine upward into the transgene's center of mass. Wofor's own weight slewed him around when the knee buckled, and the massive animal slammed into the ground at full tilt, a diagonal line across his torso sawn open by the shrapnel effect of the prefragmented bullets. The earth shook with the impact. Lefarge yelled relief as the pistol emptied itself, screamed again as the ghouloon's one good hand clamped on his ankle. Dying, it still gripped like a pneumatic press, crushing the bone beneath the boot leather and dragging his leg toward the open jaws. The human twisted, raised his other leg and hacked down on the transgene's thumb with the metal-shod heel of the boot; once, twice and then there was a crackling sound. He rolled, pulled free, came to his feet with a stab of pain up the injured limb.

Boot will hold it, he thought with savage concentration, as his hands slapped another cassette into the weapon.

Marya was running down the line of cars; the blond Draka lay on the ground, her hands to her belly. Lefarge hobbled forward, felt a stab of concern at the spreading red stain on the side of his sister's jacket.

"Just a graze, first car in the row, go, go, *go!*" she shouted. At each car she paused just long enough to pump three rounds into the communicator; even so, she was in time to help him into the first as he hop-stepped to safety.

"Let's *go*," he snarled, wrenching at the controls as she tumbled through the entrance on the other side. The turbines shrieked and the aircar rose on fan thrust, just high enough to clear the treetops before he rammed the throttles forward. The SD would not shoot down a planter's car, not until they got confirmation, and Marya had delayed that a vital fifteen minutes. At worst, a clean death when a heatseeker blew their craft out of the sky; at best, they would make it.

"We did it," he breathed. Something slackened in the center of his body, and pain shot up the leg from the savaged ankle.

"We—did," Marya replied. She was fumbling in the first aid box. "We . . . *did.*"

"I didn't know that," Yolande said, looking down at the body of her cousin.

The eyes stared empty upwards into the rain, and the steady silver fall washed the blood pale-pink out of the sodden cloth. The ambulance took off with a scream of fans; Mandy would be in that, and John riding beside her. Myfwany put an arm about her shoulders.

"You couldn't, sweet," she said. "If'n Alexandra couldn't tell, how could you? Y'hardly met them."

"Oh?" Yolande shook her head, and indicated the ghouloon; Wofor was not quite dead, though far beyond help. He had crawled the ten yards from the broken-backed horse with one good arm and one leg, trailing the shattered limbs and most of his blood. Now he lay with his head at Alexandra's feet, and Yolande crouched to shelter his head from the rain.

"Not that," she said softly, as the last trickle of sound escaped the fanged mouth and the labored breathing stopped. Her hand indicated the ghouloon, touched its muzzle. A bubble of blood burst at the back of its throat. "I didn't know these could cry, is all."

Chapter Ten

NEW YORK CITY
FEDERAL CAPITAL DISTRICT
UNITED STATES OF AMERICA
DECEMBER 31, 1975

"Should auld acquaintance be forgooot—"

"I hate that bloody song," Frederick Lefarge muttered, taking another sip of his drink. The room was hazy with smoke, and flickering light and music came through the door from the dance floor; the room smelled of tobacco and beer. More and more of the patrons at the bar were linking arms and swaying, attempting a Scottish accent as they sang.

It reminds me of Andy. Forget that.

O'Grady's was supposed to be picturesque, a real Old New York hangout and Irish as all hell. The wainscotting was dark oak, and the walls of the booths were padded in dark leather as well; there were hunting prints and landscapes on the walls. It was *crowded* as all hell tonight, and noisy, but Cindy had swung a private booth just for them; some noncom friend of her dad's ran the place. The food was better than passable, and the sides of the booth made conversation possible. There was a viewscreen on the opposite wall, showing the crowds outside in Jefferson Square, and the big display clock on the Hartmann Tower. Ten minutes to midnight, and the screen began flashing between views. Different cities all over the Alliance, Sao Paulo, London, Djakarta, Sydney. The Lunar colonies—they could almost be called cities themselves, now—and the cramped corridors of the asteroid settlements. A shot from low orbit, the great curve of Earth rolling blue and lovely.

"Don't be such a grouch, honey," Cindy said, and nibbled at his ear. Lefarge laughed and put an arm around her waist, always a pleasant experience. "You were happy enough after dinner."

"There were just the two of us then," he said.

"Grrr, tiger!" Another nibble on his ear. "And I've got some news for you, darling."

"What?" he asked, raising the glass to his lips.

603

Cindy Guzman had had only two glasses of white wine with seltzer, but there was a gleam in her eye he knew of old. She was sitting in a corner of the booth, looking cool and chic in the long black dress with the pearl-and-gold belt. Her legs were curled up under her; the glossy dark-red hair fell in waves over her shoulder, and the diamond-shaped cutout below the yoke neck showed the upper curve of her breasts. The glass in his hand halted and he sat motionless, utterly contented just to look. She gave off an air of . . . *wholesomeness*, he thought, which was strange; you expected that word to go along with some thick-ankled corn-fed maiden from the boonies, not the brightest and sexiest woman he had ever known. It was like a draught of cool water, like . . . coming home.

"Miss?" Lefarge started slightly. It was old Terrance Gilbert, the proprietor, a CPO on one of Cindy's dad's pigboats back when. He gave the young woman a look of fond pride and Lefarge one of grudging approval. "Will there be anything else, Miss?"

"Not right now, Chief," Cindy said. "Happy New Year."

"And to you, Miss. Sir." Lefarge was in uniform tonight, the major's leaves on his shoulders; the owner nodded before he disappeared into the throng.

"Finish your drink, darling," Cindy said.

He sipped. "What was the news, honey?" he asked.

"I'm pregnant."

He coughed, sending a spray of brandy out his nose; Cindy thumped him on the back with one hand and offered a handkerchief with the other.

"The devil you say!"

"Dr. Blaine's sure," she said tranquilly. "Aren't you happy? We *will* have to move up the wedding, of course."

She flowed into his arms, and they kissed. Noise and smoke vanished; so did time, until someone blew a tin horn into his ear. Cindy and he broke from their clinch and turned, he scowling and she laughing. It was Marya and her current boyfriend—*cursed if I can remember his name . . . yeah, Steve. Wish she'd pick a steady*—in party hats and a dusting of confetti.

"It isn't 2400 yet," Marya said, sliding into the other side of the booth. Her face was flushed, but only he could have told she had been drinking; there was no slur in her voice, and the movements were quick and graceful.

She's a damned attractive woman, Lefarge thought. In a strong-featured athletic way, but there were plenty of men who liked that. Plenty who liked her intelligence and sardonic humor, as well, but she seemed to sheer off from anything lasting. *Hell, this isn't the time to worry.*

They all turned to watch the screen again; it was coming around to time for the countdown to midnight. It blanked, and there was a roar of protest from the crowd, redoubled when an NPS newscaster appeared. Sheila Gilbert, he remembered; something of a star of serious news analysis, a hook-nosed woman with a patented smile. She looked . . . *frightened out of her wits*, he thought suddenly. And it took something fairly hairy to do that to a professional like Gilbert. There was a sudden feeling like a trickle of ice down his stomach to his crotch: fear. Lefarge and Marya glanced at each other and back at the screen.

" . . . President Gupta Rao of the Progressive Party has committed suicide."

"Shit!" Lefarge whispered.

"I repeat, the President of the Indian Republic has shot himself; the body was found in his office only two hours ago. The suicide note contains a confession, confirmed by other sources in the Indian capital . . ." More shouting from the customers, but less noisy; Lefarge strained to hear, and then the volume went up. " . . . Hindi Raj militants have documentary proof that OSS agents were responsible for planting the information which led to the Hamburger Scandal and the disgrace of late presidential candidate Rashidi. Riots have been reported in Allahabad and—"

It was a full ten seconds before Lefarge felt Cindy's tugging on his arm. Gently, he laid a finger over her mouth and looked at his sister.

"We'd better—"

"Attention!" The civil-defense sigil came on the viewer, cutting into the newscast. "Alliance Defense Forces announcement. All military personnel Category Seven and above please report to your duty stations. I repeat—"

DRAKA FORCES BASE ANTINOOUS
PROVINCE OF BACTRIA
DOMINATION OF THE DRAKA
JANUARY 14, 1976
1500 HOURS

" 'Tent-*hut!*"

The briefing room was in the oldest section of the base, built fifty years before, when this had been part of newly conquered northern Afghanistan. Built for biplanes, ground-support craft dropping fragmentation bombs and poison gas on the last *badmashi* rebels in the hills, when the Janissary riflemen had flushed them out. Yolande blinked at the thought: two generations . . . her own parents squalling infants, way down in the Old Territories. Her birthplace still outside the Domination . . . A few banners and trophies on the walls, otherwise plain whitewash and brown tile.

Fifty years from biplanes to the planets, Yolande thought as she saluted. *Not bad.*

"Service to the State!"

"Glory to the Race!" A crisp chorus from every throat.

"At ease." The hundred-odd pilots sank back into their chairs.

The hooting of the wind came faintly through the thick concrete walls, and the air was crackling dry. There was very little outside that you would want to see. Pancake-flat irrigated farmland hereabouts, near the Amu Darya, and the climate was nearly Siberian in winter; even

more of a backwater than Italy, unless you were interested in archae-
ology. The hunting was not bad, some tiger in the marshes along the
river, and snow leopard in the mountains. Quite beautiful up there,
in an awesome sort of way; the Hindu Kush made the Alps look like
pimples. Otherwise nothing to do but fly and study, almost like being
back at the Academy. She and Myfwany had both passed their Astronautical Institute finals last month, and could expect transfer soon. Now
that would be something. . . .

"The balloon's going up day after tomorrow."

The squadron commander grinned at them with genial savagery. Her
nickname among the pilots was *Mother Kali*, and not without reason.
There was a collective rustle of attention. Yolande felt a lurch below
the breastbone, and reached out to squeeze her lover's hand.

"Here's the basic situation." The wall behind her lit with a map
of the Indian subcontinent; the Domination flanked it to the north and
west, the Indian Ocean and the ancient Draka possession of Ceylon
to the south.

"The Indians pulled out of the Alliance last week, aftah the headhunters revealed the little nasty the Alliance OSS pulled on they last
election . . . but it's almighty confused. Burma"—an area in the lower
right corner shaded from white to gray—"counterseceded back to the
Alliance, and there was fightin' in Rangoon. Alliance seems to have
won, worse luck. We've stayed conspicuously peaceful"—a snicker of
laughter ran through the room—"which put the secessionists firmly in
power in New Delhi. Just long enough fo' the ground an' air units
the Indians were contributin' to the Alliance to transfer their allegiance
to the new Indian Republic, but *not* long enough fo' them to settle
their share of the orbital assets. We've recognized the new government, an' they've reciprocated. Nice of them."

Another wave of chuckles. "Which means as of the present *everybody* has recognized the new government as sovereign. *But.*" The squadron commander tapped her pointer into a gloved hand. "But, the Alliance
hasn't yet signed a defense treaty with the Republic, which has no
credible nuclear strike force *or* defenses. We've got a window of
opportunity; now we're goin' jump through, shootin'. Calculation is
that the Alliance will run around screamin' and shoutin' and do fuck-
all fo' the week or so we need to overrun India. We'll carefully avoid
any provocation elsewhere, or in space. Now, befo' I proceed to the
tactical situation, any questions?"

"Ma'am?" A man's voice, from the seat on the other side of Myfwany.

Yolande turned to look at him. Pilot Officer Timothy Wellington; a
slim man of middle height, with a conservative side-crop and a seal-
brown mustache, a jaunty white scarf tucked into his black flight overall.
She gritted her teeth and fought back a flush. Not that he was a *bad*
sort. City boy from Peking; knowledgeable about the visual arts, worth
talking to on poetry. She had even quite enjoyed the several occasions
when Myfwany had invited him over for the night. *I just wish he'd
learn not to presume on acquaintance,* she thought. *Also that Myfwany
would slap him down more often*. He had been hanging around entirely
too much lately.

"What if the Alliance treat it as an attack on they own territory?" Wellington said.

The commander shrugged. "Everybody dies," she answered. "Any other questions?"

He sat down and leaned over to whisper in Myfwany's ear; she turned a laugh into a cough. Yolande keyed her notebook and poised to record, elbowing her friend surreptitiously in the ribs: *This is important.*

"Our role will be to interdict the medium-high altitudes. We're doin' this invasion from a standin' start, can't mobilize without scaring the prey back into the Yankee camp. We expect the Alliance to continue feedin' the Indians operational intelligence. No way we can complain of that as hostile activity. Our preliminary sweep will be—"

"Woof," Myfwany said, as they cleared the doorway. "And to think, only yesterday I was complainin' on how dull everythin' is around here!"

Yolande nodded, standing closer for the comfort of body warmth. "Some of that schedulin' looks tricky; we're dependin' hard-like on the groundpounders takin' the forward bases."

She stretched. "Well, let's go catch dinner." Their squadron had always been theoretically tasked with neutralizing Alliance turboram assets in India . . . in the Final War nobody had been expecting. *This won't be the Final*, she told herself firmly. Images of thermonuclear fire blossoming across Claestum painted themselves on the inside of her eyelids, and she shivered slightly. *Nobody's that crazy, not even us. I hope.*

"Ah—" Myfwany hesitated, then leaned against the corridor wall. "Ah, actually, sweetlin', Tim sort of invited me ovah to his quarters fo' the evenin' and night. You don't mind, do you?"

"Oh." Yolande swallowed. A pulse beat in her neck. "Mmm, was I included in the invite?"

"I'm sure Tim wouldn't mind 'tall, if'n you wants to, sweet."

"I—" Yolande looked aside for a moment. "Let's go, then."

CENTRAL INDIAN FRONT
15,000 METERS
JANUARY 16, 1976
1400 HOURS

"Shitshitshit," Yolande muttered to herself. *Myself and the flight recorder*, thought some remote corner of her mind.

The canopy of the Falcon VI-a went black above her for an instant. Automatic shielding against optical-frequency lasers—the Alliance platforms in LEO had decided that that did not constitute intervention, and all the Draka orbital battle stations could do was to respond in kind. She banked, and acceleration slammed her against the edge of the clamshell, vision graying. The Indian P-70 was still dodging, banking; they were at Mach 3, and if he went over the border into Alliance airspace the battle stations would not let him back in. There was no way to dodge orbital free-electron lasers; they could slash you out of the sky in seconds . . . as the Alliance platforms would do to *her* if she followed the Indian too far.

"*Bing!*" Positive lock on her Skorpion AAM.

"Away!" she barked. The computer fired, and the Falcon shuddered; on the verge of tumbling as the brief change in airflow struck. The canopy cleared, and she had a glimpse of the missile streaking away. Then her fingers were moving on the pressure pads, cut thrust, bank-turn-dive, and the red line on the console map coming closer and closer. Closer, too close.

The squadron override sounded. "*Ingolfsson, watch it.*"

"I am, I am," she grunted, feeling the aircraft judder. Blood surged under the centrifugal pull, and she could feel a sudden sharp pain at the corner of one eye, a warm trickle; a blood vessel had burst. *Fuckin' insane, these things aren't designed for this limited airspace.* Like playing tackleball on a field of frictionless ice, with instant cremation the penalty for touching the sides. A turboram could cross India from edge to edge in thirty seconds or less.

The calm voice of the machine. "Impact on target. Kill."

There was no time even for exultation. "Myfwany, you pickin' up anythin'?"

"Not in our envelope." Her voice was adrenaline-hoarse. "You getting too low, 'Landa."

"Tell me."

The edges of the wing body were starting to glow cherry-red, and the sensors told the same story. Ionization was fouling up her electrodetectors, too; she might be too fast for the low-altitude tur-bojet fighters, but anything optimized for the thicker layers that happened to be in the right position would eat her.

"Come on, you cow," she muttered to the aircraft. "Up we go."

The ground was shockingly close, and she was still far too fast. *All right, double Immelman and up.* Her fingers cut thrust, and the aircraft flipped. G-force snapped her head back, and for an instant she was staring at the maplike view of the subcontinent below. A point of blue-white light blinked against the brown-green land, and the console confirmed it. *Five kiloton.* A blast of charged particles. *Radiation bomb.* A nuke warhead designed to maximize personnel damage, wouldn't want to mess up the new property. *Shitfire, I'm glad I'm not down there* . . .

Pulling up, six G's, seven. Nose to the sky, open throttle and here we go, fangs out and hair on fire, *heee-aah*. Feed thrust, overmax; speed bottoming out at Mach 1.7 and climbing, 2.1, 2.2, 2.8. The screens showed Myfwany closing in to wing guard position. And *damn*. The canopy went black. *Pretty. Very pretty*.

The squadron commander broke in again. "No bogies, I repeat, no bogies our quadrant. Good work. Check fungibles."

Her eyes went back to the console. "Fuel .17, no Skorpions. Full 30mm drums." Close combat was proving to be something of an anachronism.

"All MK units, all MK units, squadron is cleared fo' alternate E-17, mark an' acknowledge."

The exterior temperatures were not falling the way they should, they must be tweaking the laser up there. Yolande spared a moment's snarl for the invulnerable enemies above. *Your day will come, pigs.* E-17 came up on the landscape director, down by her left knee; northern Punjab, enemy base. Status showed heavily cratered runways, fires, no actual fighting and low radiation count, but massive damage to the facilities. *No runways, vertical landing,* she thought unhappily. Which meant no takeoff at all, until the unit support caught up with them; that would burn the last of the fuel. The follow-up waves would be using their base back in Bactria, logical but unpleasant.

"All MK, take you birds in," the commander's voice continued.

Yolande felt a vast stomach-loosening rush of relief and pushed it back with a savage effort. "It isn't ovah till it's ovah," she told herself. Aloud: "Acknowledged."

CRACK.

Marya Lefarge threw herself flat and rolled, over the edge of the wall. The ditch was two meters down, but soft mud. She leopard-crawled, did a sprint and forward roll over a bank of shrubs, fell to her belly again, rolled down a short slope and raised her pencil periscope to look back. Smoke, smoke rising against the far blue-white line of the Himalayas that towered over the Punjab plains. Sunset already beginning to tinge the snowpeaks with crimson. The line of the retaining wall, and . . . helmets. Enemy, ridged fore-and-aft and with two short antennae at the rear. Their IV and millimetric scanners would be looking for movement, for human-band temperature points.

Two Draka troopers had vaulted down from the terrace. The building above it had been the HQ offices of Chandragupta Base; now it was burning rubble, after the cluster-shell hits. The troopers were bulky and sexless, visored helmets and articulated cermet armor; they went to their stomachs and scanned back and forth across the flat runway before them. Nothing moved on it, nothing except the smoke and flames from smashed aircraft that had been caught on launch. One had gotten into the air before the homing missile hit, and its ruins sprawled across half a kilometer. The air was heavy with the oily smell of burning fuel and scorched earth.

There were smashed revetment hangars across the way. Something was moving there. A trio of low beetling shapes moved out onto the pavement, their gun pods swiveling: light tanks. The two Draka infantrymen rose and trotted toward them, and more followed over the retaining wall. They moved with impressive ease under their burdens of armor and equipment, spreading out into a dispersed formation. *Good,* Marya thought. *They'll be concentrating on the link-up.* She waited a hundred heartbeats, then a hundred more. Waiting was the worst. Running and shooting you didn't have time to be frightened . . . *Mission first,* she reminded herself. A bollixed-up mission to save remnants from the worst disaster in decades. There was data in the base computers which must *not* be allowed into enemy hands.

Marya rose into a crouch. She was wearing a standard Alliance base-personnel gray coverall, with Indian markings. That fitted her cover identity; the bomblet launcher in her hands did not. . . . Runway to her left and rear, hectares of it, swarming with enemy troops now. HQ complex ahead, and she would just have to take her chances. A deep breath, and *now*. She sprinted back along her path, leapt, caught the lip of the wall and rolled over it. Nothing on the way back, nothing but a steamcar in the middle of the gardens, bullet-riddled and . . . not empty. A body lying half-out the driver's door, a pistol in one hand. She moved quickly from one cover to the next, feeling lungs hot and taut despite the dry-season cool of the air.

In through the front doors, and there were more bodies, enough to make the air heavy with the burnt-pork-and-shit stink of close combat. Past the front offices, and the light level sank to a dim gloom, shadows moving with uneven flamelight. She stopped in a doorway long enough to pull the filter over her nose and mouth, then froze. Steps coming down the hall, booted feet.

Sorry if you're a friendly, she thought, and plunged out into the corridor with her finger already tightening.

Schoop. The launcher kicked against her shoulder, and the 35mm projectile was on its way as the Draka assault rifle came up. Marya went boneless and dropped, as the round impacted on the center of the soldier's breastplate. That was a ceramic-fiber-metal-synthetic sandwich . . . but her bomblet was a shaped charge. The finger of superheated plasma speared through the armor, through vaporizing flesh, splashed against the backplate. Body fluids turned to steam and blew outwards through the soft resistance. Marya threw herself upright and ran forward; she tried to leap the corpse and the spreading puddle around it, but her boots went *tack-tack* on the linoleum for a minute afterwards.

Nothing moved as she tracked through toward the command center. *Critical window*, she thought; the moments between the assault landing and the arrival of the Intelligence teams. Soldiers had a natural preference for dealing with the things that might shoot back at them, and so might leave an area already swept lightly guarded. She turned another corridor, came to a makeshift barricade. The bodies beyond were Indian, a scratch squad of office workers and one perimeter guard in infantry kit; they bore no wounds, but lay as if they had died in convulsions. Marya's skin itched, as if insects were crawling under it. *Contact nerve agent*, she thought, and put an antidote tab between her back teeth. That might work. . . .

The stairs that led down into the control center were ahead. It would be guarded, but . . . She turned aside, into an office. It was empty, with a cup of tea still on the desk and the screen of the terminal flickering, as if the occupant—Ranjit Singh, from the nameplate on the door—might return any second. A quick wrench with her knife opened the ventilation shaft. The American pulled a pair of lightmag goggles out of a pocket and slipped them over her head. Darkness vanished, replaced by a peculiar silvery flatness. Marya slung the bomblet launcher down her back, took a deep breath, and chinned herself on the edge of the ventilator.

Just wide enough, she thought. *Just.*

✧　✧　✧

The Draka working over the base computer had the gear-wheel emblem of Technical Section on her shoulder; so did the two gray-uniformed serf Auxiliaries helping her. They were all in battle armor, though, a technical commando unit tasked with front-line electronic reconnaissance. Marya could see them all, down the short section of vertical shaft; she was lying full-length in the horizontal passageway above, with only her head out. That ought to make her nearly invisible from below, with the wire grille in the ceiling between her and them. And . . . yes, movement just out of sight. Probably troopers, guarding the tech. The peripheral units of the Alliance computer were open, and boxes of crackle-finished Draka electronics set up about it, a spiderweb of plug-in lines and cross-connections.

The OSS agent strained to hear.

"Careful, careful!" the Draka was saying. "Up ten . . . Fo' mo'. Right, now keep the feed modulated within ten percent of those parameters, and she won't blow when Ah open the casing."

Another figure, a middle-aged Indian in uniform, with his arms secured behind his back. A bayoneted rifle rested between his shoulder blades, jabbed lightly.

"Yes, indeed," he babbled in singsong English. "That is the way of it."

Too bad. The black-uniformed TechSec specialist pulled the visor of her helmet down and took up a miniature cutting torch. *Cracking the core unit,* Marya thought grimly. The embedded instruction sets of a central computer and the crucial hard memory were physically confined in its core, even on civilian models. This was a maximum-security military Phoebos, and it would be set to slag down unless you were *very* careful.

Careful is a word, Marya thought. This mission was important enough to make her expendable . . . but there was no point in being reckless. Her lips moved back from her teeth behind the mask. What was it Uncle Nate used to say? "A good soldier has to be ready to die. A suicidal one just leaves you with another damned empty slot to train someone for."

If I push the launcher over the edge at arm's length, she thought, *and then drop the satchel charge right away, the ceiling should shelter me from most of the blast.* That would certainly take care of the mission, now that the Draka had conveniently opened up the armored protection around the core. *Then I can go back up the shaft, and try to make it out.*

Soundlessly, she mouthed: "And maybe the horse *will* learn to sing."

Millimeter by millimeter, she inched backward until only the end of the launcher tube was over the lip of the vertical shaft. Her other hand brought the explosive charge up, plastique and metal and soft padded overcase. It scraped gently against the tube wall in the narrow space between hip and panel, and the sound seemed roaringly loud. No louder than the beat of blood in her ears. *Stupid, stupid,* a voice called at the back of her mind. *You volunteered, you're too stupid to live, you could be* home *now.*

"Fuck it," she said, and pulled the trigger.

✧   ✧   ✧

"Mistis—" the Janissary decurion began, as the canopy of Yolande's fighter slid back and she rose from the opening clamshell restraints. The cool air of the Indian night poured in, lit by a swollen moon and the lingering fires. Then eye-drying warmth as the inflow crackled across the fuselage of her aircraft. The Draka picked up her ground kit, machine pistol, and helmet. There were a half-dozen figures in infantry armor, with a flat cart of some sort.

Then the serf soldier's voice altered. "Mistis Yolande!" He saluted and flipped up the faceplate of his helmet.

Yolande stared for a moment; it was an unremarkable face, heavy beak nose and olive complexion . . . then memory awoke.

"Ali?" she said. "Rahksan's Ali?"

His grin showed white as she stepped up onto the rim of the cockpit and jumped down, careful to avoid the savage residual heat of the leading edges.

"The same, Mistis. Swears it like home leave to see you."

"Freya bless, small world," she continued, and gave him a light punch on one shoulder. Her gloved fist rang on the lobster-tail plates of his armguard. The legion blazon on it showed a hyena's skull biting down on a human thighbone; that was the Devil Dogs, one of the better subject-race units. "An' you comin' up in it, Ali. I tells yo ma, first thing."

His fist rang on the breastplate as he saluted again, then noticed his squad glancing at each other. Myfwany's Falcon lifted its canopy.

"Ah, Mistis, we got field shelters set up over to there." He pointed, and she saw prefabricated revetments on an uncratered stretch of runway. Two big winged tilt-rotor transports, as well; one began revving for takeoff as she looked. "We's gotta get y' plane towed ovah there. You support team's comin' through, later tonight. We's got perimeter guard."

"Myfwany, you remembers Ali, from Claestum?" The redhead came up, with a bounce in her stride, despite the sweat that plastered the curls to her forehead. "Coincidence, hey?" The squad was hooking the cart's towing hitch to the nose of her aircraft. "Carry on, Decurion; nice to know mah bird's in good hands."

"Eurrch," Yolande said. "C'mon, love, why don't we turn in?" Most of the squadron was there, but it would be a day or two before they had anything to do but stay out of the way. In the meantime, they had been assigned quarters. The original occupants certainly had no need of them. . . .

The prisoners were being held in a mess hall; sorted in groups by rank and age, in squares marked off by colored rope. The guards were Security Directorate, Intervention Squad specialists, but there were a fair number of Draka making inspection; Citizen officers of the Janissary legion, pilots from their outfit, others. She looked at the captives with mild distaste; they had been stripped of their uniforms as a precautionary measure, and secured with the old-style restraints, chain and rod links that bound elbows and wrists together behind the back. Indians, mostly. Base techs, the sort of work that was done by unarmed Auxiliaries in the Domination's armed forces. A few had the glazed look of shock, or docilizing drugs; most were openly terrified, even *crying*.

"You can turn in if'n you wants to, 'Landa," Myfwany said. She was smiling, and there was a glitter to her eyes; Yolande swallowed past a hollow feeling. *I love you dearly, but there are times when you make me angry enough to* spit, *sweetheart*, she thought resignedly.

"Oh, all right," Yolande said. "Let's take a look."

They walked down the edge of one of the green-rope enclosures. Green for lowest priority, younger specimens. She supposed they would be sold off, after the fighting, or sent to work camps, something of that sort. Her nose wrinkled from the pungency; they stank of fear, and some had pissed themselves. Across the room there was a high scream. Yolande looked up and saw the Security troopers dragging an older prisoner out of the red-corded pen for interrogation. A paunchy type in his fifties, already babbling. *Glad they're not doin' it in public*, she thought idly. *Headhunters, eurgh*. Necessary work, she supposed, but disgusting.

"This one looks interestin'," Myfwany was saying. "On you feet, wench."

Yolande looked back. The prisoner had risen easily despite the restraints. In her late twenties, she estimated; much lighter-skinned than most of the others. Good figure, very nice muscle tone for a serf; cropped black hair, expressionless dark eyes . . . The neck was number-bare, that looked unnatural. *Sixty aurics basic*, Yolande thought. *Depending on where she's sold, of course*.

"Who're you?" Myfwany asked the serf. Silence, and then the Draka struck. *Crack*. The open-handed blow rocked the prisoner's head back; Yolande was surprised she kept her feet. Sighing, she glanced aside. *Myfwany gets too rough with them, sometimes*, she thought unhappily. Of course, this one was feral and had to be taught submission, but still . . .

"Marya Lenson." *Crack*. A backhanded blow this time.

"That's Marya Lenson, *Mistis*, serf." The Security guard glanced up, came over idly twirling the rubber truncheon by the thong around his wrist.

"Mistis." The serf's voice stayed toneless, flat.

"Indian?" Myfwany put a finger under the serf's chin, turned her head sideways. "Europoid, I'd swear."

"My parents were from California, Mistis."

Myfwany turned to Yolande. "A Yank! What say we sign this'n out and play with it, 'Landa?" she said.

Yolande sighed. "Oh, come on, sweet," she said exasperatedly. *I hope we're not going to have a fight, like we did when you wanted Lele*. It had taken two days of not speaking to each other before Myfwany realized she was serious about letting the servant say no. "Where's the fun in that?"

"We can use aphrodizine," Myfwany said impatiently.

"Eurg." Not that the aphrodisiac didn't *work* but . . . "Look, sweet, you just got after-fight jitters. You don't really want to—"

Myfwany released the serf and spun to confront her friend. "Look youself," she hissed. "I'm not you keeper, Ingolfsson, and you not mine.

You've got somethin' better to do, go do it." The green eyes turned heavy-lidded. "Tim or someone be glad to help me out."

Yolande felt shock close her throat. This was fear, not the hot sensation of life danger up in the clouds, but dread coiling at the pit of her stomach. She forced a smile.

"Oh, don't get so heavy 'bout it, love!" A glance aside at the serf. *Myfwany'll probably get tired fairly soon.* "If'n you's set on it, certainly." *Not as if there was anything actually wrong with it, after all. You have to compromise on differing tastes.* "Let's . . . let's take a walk an' check on the birds, first, hey? Get some fresh air."

"Sure, 'Landa-sweet," Myfwany said. She smiled and took the other Draka's hand. Yolande felt the knot in her stomach melt. *Or most of it*, she thought. *Oh, well.* "I've got a rotten temper. Don't know why you puts up with me, sometimes."

She called the guard over, palmed the identifier clipped to his belt. "Send this one ovah to our quarters, would you?"

Frederick Lefarge felt the sweat trickle down from the rim of his helmet, itching under the armor and camouflage smock. He glanced at his watch: 2000 hours. The pickup squad was in a stand of tall pale-barked trees not far from what had been the perimeter wire of Chandragupta Base. A dozen of them, with nothing but their fieldcraft and two boxes of very sophisticated electronics to keep them out of the tightening Draka net. Two were wounded, and he didn't think Smythe was going to make it, he'd been far too close to a radiation bomb yesterday, when the rest of them had been sheltered in the cellar. Vomiting blood was not a good sign, either.

"Sor." Winters, the Englishman. Professional NCO in the Cumberland Borderers before transfer to the OSS special forces. Very reliable. "Sor, it's past time."

She isn't going to make it, he thought. *Either she's dead or she should be.* He fought down the hot flash of rage, let it mingle with fear until it became something cold and leaden in his gut. Something that would not interfere with the job at hand. . . . He remembered a moment in Santa Fe, and the pistol in Marya's hand unwavering upon him. *We always knew the price*, he thought. *Go with God, ma soeur.*

And *her* mission accomplished—the explosion in the base HQ proved that—but nothing beyond. He raised the visor of his helmet and bent to the eyepiece of the spyglass. There were pickups all over the operational area, where his men had left their optical-thread connectors. The fires were mostly out now. Those had been from the initial blitz, suborb missiles with precision-guided conventional explosives. Dibblers for the runways, earth piercers for the hardened weapons points, then a rolling surf of antipersonnel submunitions. The assault troops—1st Airborne Legion, Citizen Force elite—had come on the heels of those, but they had moved out once the area was secured, now there was a brigade of Janissaries doing clear-and-hold. And support personnel, Intelligence, transports, two squadrons of low-altitude VTOL gunboats, another of Falcons.

And now they think it's secured, he thought grimly. *Time to disabuse them.*

"Hit it, Jock," he said.

"And we—" Myfwany stopped. "What the fuck was *that,* Ali?"

They and the Janissaries were standing outside a dugout. The explosion was a kilometer away, across the base. A flash, and the muffled *whump* a second later, a ball of orange flame rising into the soft Indian night. The troopers went into an instinctive crouch, and Ali cursed, rolling back into the sandbagged slit and reaching for the groundline com.

"Suh?" he said. "Post Six, second tetrarchy—shit, it out!"

Another explosion, and another; a rippling line in an arc along the perimeter opposite them. Yolande and Myfwany exchanged a glance and pulled on their ground helmets, slipping down the visors and turning the night to a pale imitation of day. Each had a tiny dot of strobing red light at the lower left-hand corner; jamming. Then a *real* explosion. The two Draka threw themselves flat at the harsh white glare. Even reflected around the edges of their visors it was enough to dazzle, and the shockwave lifted them up and slammed them down again hard enough to stun and bruise on the unyielding pavement.

Yolande heard one of the Janissaries shouting. "Nuke? Dec, was that a nuke?" Her eyes darted down to the readout on the sleeve of her flight suit. No radiation above the nervous-making background already there, and a spear of blue-white flame was already rising from behind the broken hangars. Secondary explosions bellowed, like echoes of that world-numbing blast.

"No, it ain't," Ali was saying. "That the fuel store."

Liquid hydrogen and methane, Yolande realized. High-energy fuels for high-performance craft, difficult to transport. One of the reasons the attack plan had made this base a priority target in the first place. And—

"The birds!" she shouted to Myfwany. Fatigue and worry vanished in the rush of adrenaline, at the thought of the turboram fighters caught helpless on the ground. The Falcons were two thousand meters distant, behind the parked assault transports.

Myfwany nodded. "Ali, you tasked with that?"

The burly Janissary was climbing back out of the revetment. He hesitated for a moment; he was, but having two Citizens along out of the regular chain of command was *not* a good idea. . . . The two Draka women saw him shrug and nod, accepting what could not be changed.

"Let's go," he said. "Marcel, Ching, Mustafa, come with me. Brigitte, Nils, Vlachec, hold the position an' report when the com comes back up."

"Now!" Frederick Lefarge kept to one knee and watched the dozen OSS special-ops troopers scurry by. In *toward* the base that now swarmed like a kicked-open termite mound. Their only chance . . .

He rose to his feet and followed. There they were, ten *Buffel* tilt-rotor assault transports, standing ready with their turbines warm. Nobody around them but unarmed ground crew. The Alliance soldiers could charge on board and take off in ten different directions; the Draka IFF would hesitate crucial seconds before overriding their own electronic identification . . . and the battle was still a chaos of Draka and Indian-held pockets from here to Burma. Just insane enough to have some chance of success. The Springfield-15 seemed light as a twig in his hands; his gaze hopped across the flat expanses of the airbase, watching for movement. *There.* Light armor, moving out of laager in the vehicle park, coasting toward them with air-cushion speed. His hand slapped a switch at his waist.

"Down!" Yolande shouted, when the lines of fire erupted upward out of the stand of trees to their right. She and Myfwany threw themselves apart and forward without breaking stride; she could hear the light impact of her lover's body on the concrete, and seconds later the pounding slam of the Janissary heavy infantry hitting the pavement.

The weapon that had fired was some sort of rocket automortar; she watched the trajectories arch and then plunge back down. Down toward the trio of Cheetah hovertanks that had been approaching them; a hundred meters up, the self-forging warheads exploded in disks of fire, sending arrowheads of incandescent metal streaking for the thin deck armor of the Draka tanks. The impacts were flashes that would have been dazzling without the guard functions of her visor. The air-cushion vehicles bounced down as if slapped by the hand of an invisible giant, then exploded in gouts of fuel fire and ammunition glare. Hot warm air struck her like a pillow, and a pattering rain of cermet armor and body parts began to fall around the soldiers of the Domination.

"'Landa!" Myfwany called. "Look right, are those hostiles?" Yolande halted and went to ground conscious of the others following the pilot's extended arm.

Frederick Lefarge threw himself to the ground and rolled to one side as the group running on an intercept vector with his opened fire. Muzzle flashes strobed before the silvery light-enhanced shapes of enemy soldiers. Shrapnel flicked at his exposed legs and arms, nothing serious, but he could feel the blood trickle behind the sharp sting. *Can't stop for a slugfest,* went through him. His special-forces unit were only lightly armored, and there was no cover on this artificial concrete desert.

"Eat this!" the OSS trooper beside Lefarge cried, flipping up to his knees and firing a grenade from the launcher beneath the barrel of his S17. It burst with an orange flash behind the enemy firing line; one of the rifles stopped, and there was a scream of pain. Then a chattering flash from directly ahead; machine pistol, not the louder growl of a T-7. The trooper who had fired pitched backward, torn open. Lefarge snapped off a burst toward the source and began crawling forward. Another sound came from near where he had fired, a scream that raised the tiny hairs along the back of his neck.

"Keep them occupied!" he shouted to his men, heading for the cockpit ladder of the *Buffel*. It had a 25mm Gatling in its chin turret; if he could reach that . . .

"Keep them occupied!" a voice shouted. Yolande ignored it, braced behind an overturned supply cart.

"Myfwany?" she called, looking over to where the other Draka had snap-fired last. "Hey, Myfwany?"

There was no movement. A long shape lying motionless on the concrete, impossible to see detail at this distance. Machine pistol resting on the ground, no movement.

"Myfwany?" Yolande said, this time a whisper. Then she was moving, a sprint that leaned her almost horizontal to the ground. She forward-rolled the last five meters, rolling in beside her friend. "Myfwany?"

The body moved into her hands, infinitely familiar, utterly strange. Moving loosely, slack. Blood flowing down her hands from the band of black wetness across Myfwany's chest. Bits of soft armor, bits of bone and flesh; something bubbling and wheezing. Yolande tore off her own helmet, to see by natural light. There was enough to show the lashes flutter across the amber eyes, focus on her. The lips below moved, beneath the rills of blood that covered them. Perhaps to say a name, but there was no breath left for it. She slumped, with a total relaxation as the wheezing stopped. Yolande felt a sound building in her throat, and she knew that everything would end when she uttered it.

The firefight hammered through the darkness; Lefarge flipped his visor up for better depth perception and ran crouching. He was almost on the two Draka before he saw them. Lying on the pavement, one with the utter limpness of the newly dead, the other holding her. His rifle swung round, clicked empty; the magazine ejected itself and dropped to the runway with a hollow plastic clatter. For a moment only the eyes held him. Huge, completely dark in a stark-white elfin face daubed with blood, framed in hair turned silver by the moon-light. They saw him; somehow he knew they were recording every detail, but it was as if no active mind lived behind them. Then he was past, his feet pounding up the aluminum treads of the transport's gangway.

"Hunh!" Marya jerked awake, surprised that she had slept at all. Dawn was showing rosy through the window; the air smelled of cool earth, explosives and fire and dead humans. And the door had swung open.

A Draka stood there. One of the ones who had looked her over in the prisoner pen earlier. Short, slender, and blond. Different; her uniform was smoke-stained, grimy; there were speckles of dried blood across her face. The face . . . the eyes were huge, pupils distended with shock. The American felt a clammy sensation—not quite fear, although that was in it. As if she was in the presence of something that should not be seen . . . The dead-alive eyes focused on her, and Marya saw a spray injector in the other's hand.

"It's you fault." The words came in a light, soft voice. Almost a whisper, and in utter monotone. "I was weak, squeamish. She wanted to play with you, and I didn't, so I got her to go fo' a walk, thought she'd forget the idea. She's dead. I saw his face . . . he's not here. They got some of the planes, but she's dd—" A brief stutter, and the marble perfection of the face writhed for an instant, then settled back. "Dead."

The Draka touched the controls of the injector, held it to her own neck and pulled the trigger. Shuddered. A degree of life returned to the locked muscles of her face as she lowered it and changed the controls.

"This is fo' you," she said, her voice slightly thick now. "Relaxant, muscle weakener, maximum safe dosage of aphrodizine." The cold metal touched Marya on the arm, but she scarcely felt the sting of the injection. It was impossible even to look away from those eyes, like windows into a wound. Something flowed across her mind, warm and sticky, pushing consciousness back into a room at the rear of her head. Fingers as strong as wire flipped her onto her stomach and began to unfasten the restraints.

"We're goin' to have a sort of celebration in memory of her, just this once," the Draka said. "And then I can think up somethin' else for you to do."

Chapter Eleven

About three hundred of us, Marya estimated. It had taken an hour for the big room to fill; this one was square, under the same warehouse roof. Absolutely blank, except for a waist-high dais and comp terminal at one end. Four of the big steel-mesh doors, one in each wall. No chairs, of course. No talking allowed; one prisoner had persisted, and the guards had picked her up and thrown her into the wall, just hard enough to stun, and the shockrods were always there. There was another white line around them on the floor; the prisoners had learned enough to treat it like a minefield. Marya had worked her way to the second line from the front with slow, careful movements. *They're going to give us some sort of information*, she decided. *I'll get it all, and make my own use of it.*

This place had the depressing regularity of a factory; it was designed to make you feel like sausage meat. *That is information, too.* The door behind the dais opened, and two more Orpos stepped up on it, one going to the terminal; she laid a hand on the screen, then made a few keystrokes. A tall woman, hard to tell age with the shaven head. The uniform was a little more elaborate, with a sidearm and complicated equipment on a webbing belt; she had the traditional metal gorget around her neck on a chain. *Chain-dog*, Marya remembered. *That's what the serfs call the Order Police. Appropriate.*

"All of them supposed to understand talk," Marya heard her say to her companion. *Talk must mean English.* She filed the datum away.

"Right." The voice, amplified now, boomed out over the huddled crowd. "Listen up, cattle." The face scanned them; tight shin stretched over bone, a white smile. "Y'all are serfs. I'm a serf. There are serfs and serfs; y'all are cattle, I'm you god, understand?" An uneasy silence. "Yaz all from India. Yaz here because our noble mastahs—" Marya's ears pricked. Was that a note of sarcasm? *Listen. Wait.* "—are souvenir

619

hunters. That what yaz are. Trinkets. We shippin' yaz fo' that. Sometimes, trinkets get broke."

The Orpo jerked a thumb toward one of the crowd. Marya recognized the young man she had helped earlier, with dried blood caked on his lower face and the nose swollen. A Bengali, slight and dark and with a nervous handsomeness apart from the injury, about twenty. A junior officer in the Indian ground forces, from his mannerisms. The crowd parted to leave him in a bubble of space as the guards closed in, shoved him roughly to the edge of the dais. The Orpo noncom had lit a cigarette; now she flicked ash off the end and looked down at the Indian.

"Just in case yaz thinkin' y'all too valuable to hurt," she said, and nodded.

The guards moved in; Marya could see their elbows moving, hear the heavy thuds of fists striking flesh. A moment, and the young man was hunched over when they parted, dazed. The Orpo with the cigarette nodded again, and her companion on the dais stepped forward, pulled a wire loop from his belt and bent to throw it around the man's neck. Marya drove her teeth into her lower lip and made herself watch.

The greencoat grunted and lifted the slight Bengali youth without perceptible effort, holding the toggles of the strangling wire out with elbows slightly bent. The youth bucked, heels drumming against the dais, made sounds. His face purpled under the brown, tongue and eyes bulging, sounds coming from him. From behind her, too, she could hear vomiting. A stain spread down the front of the Bengali's overall, and she could smell the hard shit-stink as his sphincter released; see the thin smile on the executioner's face as he jerked the wire free of the man's neck and cleaned it lovingly with a handkerchief. Blood trickled down Marya's chin.

I will remember you, too, my friend, she thought grimly.

"Yaz nothin'," the amplified voice continued. Gray-suited attendants came in, threw the corpse on a wheeled dolly and took it away. The door slid shut behind them with an echoing clang. "Y'all barely worth the trouble of keeping alive. Yaz cattle, meat, dogshit. Understand?"

The man who had used the wire noose bellowed: "That's *Yes, thank you, ma'am,* apeturds!"

Marya opened her mouth and shouted with the others. *Words are nothing,* she told herself.

"One lesson an' it all yaz need. *Do what y' told.* Anything y' told, anythin' at all. Right now yaz total worthless; with hard work an' tryin' mebbeso yaz work up to just worthless. Understand?"

"*YES, THANK YOU, MA'AM!*" the prisoners screamed. Someone behind Marya was crying again, slow racking sobs.

"Oh, one mo' thing." The Orpo noncom pulled a flat crackle-finished box from a pouch at her waist; it was roughly the size of a pocket novel, and a miniature keyboard showed when she opened it. "Them pretty-pretty bracelets. They new. Space research, monitors. Trace yaz anywheres, identify yaz to the comps. Take readin's heartbeat. And a little nerve hookup, inductor. Right to a center in yaz brains, if y' got any." Her fingers stabbed down on the controller.

PAIN. Marya fell limp and boneless to the floor and her head cracked on the concrete and the skin splitting was wonderful because for a single fractional second it blocked the *PAIN* but then there was nothing but the *PAIN* and there had never been anything but *PAIN* and her heart and lungs were frozen and death would be wonderful but there was no death only *PAIN*onandonandonandonandon—

It stopped. Marya drew breath, screamed, blood and tears and mucus covering her face, and then she curled around herself and hugged the hand with the controller bracelet and laughed because it *stopped* and the bleeding from her cheek was heaven and the stabbing behind her eyes was better than orgasm and the sensual delight that it had *stopped* and she knew she could never feel pain again because that had been *pain* not the pain of anything not surgery without anesthetic not grief not longing not fear, it had been everything and nothing and pure, purest simple *pain*.

"Up and quiet, or I give yaz anothah five seconds. Now, wasn't that wonderful!" A shriek. "*Understand?*"

"YES, THANK YOU, MA'AM!"

They were all up, quiveringly silent. All except for one woman who lay motionless while the serfs with the dolly came and removed the body, and some of the others looked at it with envy.

"Most places, it's bettah to live than to die. Here, we can make it bettah to die than to live. Remembah that, cattle."

The van doors opened. "Out," the serf guard said. Marya slid forward and looked around; they were in the Citizen section of Mashad. Startling after five days in the blank steel and concrete of the Transit station. The guard pushed her ahead, through a revolving door into a hotel lobby. Warm. The first real warmth since Kabul, and a fear worse than the gnawing anxiety of the cell came with it. Across the ornate marble-and-tile splendors of the lobby, the walls were sections from the mosques that had once made this city a wonder of Islamic architecture. An elevator, bronze rails and fretwork, that took them up five stories. Down a corridor, through a teakwood door. Her mouth was paper-dry again; she called up strength from the reservoir within.

But what do I do when it's empty? she thought for a moment. Then: *Never.*

A serf came to meet them in the vestibule, a room of pale glossy stone walls and floors covered in rugs of incredible colors. She was odd enough to snap Marya's attention aside for a moment; a black woman with yellow eyes and a flamboyant mane of butter-blond hair, in a white robe. There was pity in the brass-colored eyes, and in her soft voice.

"I'm sorry," she said, after signing the invoice the driver presented. "I'm really sorry. I . . . tried."

More corridors, then out into a double-storied lounging room, massive inlaid furniture and a glass wall looking out over a cityscape coming alive with evening lights, reflected on the falling snow. A Draka waiting in a reclining chair, smoking a water pipe, dressed in a striped *djellaba* with the hood thrown back. The face from Chandragupta Base. Thinner, with dark circles under the huge mad gray eyes; Marya lowered her own to hide the sudden stab of fury she felt. *Looks older.* Marya knew the lines that grief drew. *Good.*

"Stop," the Draka said. "Look at me, serf." Marya looked up. "I'm Yolande Ingolfsson. Remember me?"

"Yes, Mistis," Marya said with equal softness. A smile twitched at the Draka's lips. The American swallowed a sour bubble at the back of her throat.

The black serf spoke hesitantly. "Mistis—"

"Jolene," Yolande said, "I heard you out. I said no. Now if you don't want to watch, get out. I'm not angry with you. Yet."

The African bowed silently and left; Marya could hear her steps quickening to a run.

"Take off the overall, and stand ovah there," Yolande continued. Marya moved to obey, found herself in the middle of a three-meter rectangle of clear plastic sheeting; the rug scrutched underneath it, feeling bristly-soft to her bare feet.

"Oh, it's good to see you again. Took a while, gettin' leave, and I don't have long until I have to report to the Astronautical, but it's good to see yo, Yank. You fault, it is."

"Now," the Draka continued. "There's somethin' I want from you. Guess?"

Marya looked up sharply. The other's eyes were fixed on her with a curiously impersonal avidness.

"Are you . . . going to abuse me again, Mistis?" she asked flatly. There was no sign of a drug injector.

Yolande chuckled; it had a grating sound. "Oh, not that way. That was a special occasion. . . . No, there's something else I want you to do fo' me. It was you fault, aftah all."

Her free hand pulled something out of a pocket in her robe. Crackle-finished in black, the size of a small book. Opened it. Marya felt herself begin to tremble, heard a moan. Knew that in a moment she would beg, and felt a brief stab of shame that she felt no shame, because *nothing* was worse than that.

"What—" she choked, swallowed to clear her mouth of saliva. "What do you want me to do?" she asked, clamping her hands together to halt the shaking.

Yolande opened the controller and poised her finger. Her eyes met the American's, and Marya could feel them drinking.

"I want you to scream," she said, and pressed down.

NEW YORK CITY
FEDERAL CAPITAL DISTRICT
DONOVAN HOUSE
JANUARY 21, 1977

"I still say it stinks, General," Frederick Lefarge said. His body somehow gave the impression of tension, even when he sat relaxed in the stiff government-issue office chair.

Nathaniel Stoddard nodded, considering the man who sat across from him. *Thinner*, he thought. *And not just in body.* Pale as well, with the pallor that comes from long months inside a submarine, or a spaceship.

"I agree, but . . ." He pressed a spot on the desk screen, and a thin-film rectangle slid up along one wall.

"India hurt us," he said quietly. "Not so much physically—it was the sinkhole of the Alliance—but in our souls. Our first major brush with the Domination, and we lost. Granted it was the Indians' own damn fault, that disinformation campaign wouldn't have produced secession if they hadn't been completely irrational about it. Granted, but we still *lost*, and another three hundred million went under the Yoke."

He rapped the desk with his knuckles. "First, we needed a victory and the asteroid agreement is that. What we have to guard against is not treason, that's the enemy's problem. What we have to fear is *defeatism*; the turning-away from useful work into hedonism, because people don't think there *is* a future. That's the real danger, in the short term."

"I'd rather have kicked the Snakes out of the belt and everything outward."

Stoddard shook his head. "Not feasible, Colonel. It was turning into a struggle of attrition, and they outnumber us." He produced his pipe, took comfort from the ritual of lighting it. "Nor can we fight full-scale near Earth, not anymore. India took us to the brink of that, and it's only the sheer insanity of Draka ruthlessness that let it get that far." He puffed. "Now, list for me the *positive* aspects of these miserable few years."

Lefarge shrugged. "The Alliance will stand, now."

Stoddard nodded; the constituent nations had agreed to a full merger of sovereignty. A pity in a way—he had always regretted the increasing uniformity of life in the Alliance—but necessary.

"And not just among the electorate, either." His expression became wholly blank. "Now, I'm about to tell you something that requires complete commitment. If I'm not satisfied by your reactions from this point on, then the only way you will leave this building is as a corpse."

Lefarge sat upright, a slow uncoiling motion. His eyes met the other man's for a long moment.

"You're serious," he said flatly.

"Never more so. Want me to continue?"

The moment stretched. "Yes."

Stoddard cupped the bowl of the pipe. "We—that is, the permanent staff just below the political level—we've become convinced that if things go on as they are, we're headed for the Final War. If only because the limits of the Domination's ability to adapt to technical progress are on the horizon, and they'll bring everything down in wreckage rather than see us reduce them to irrelevance."

Lefarge smiled. "Then the only alternatives are annihilation or surrender?"

"Surrender *is* annihilation, certainly for freedom, probably for

humanity," he said, nodding agreement. "And the Final War is annihilation, too; it's the seeping realization of that that's been paralyzing our leadership echelons." He touched another spot on the screen,
and a starfield lit the rectangle that hung from the ceiling.

"Tell me, Fred, what do you know about fusion power?"

Lefarge blinked narrow-eyed at the older man. "Controlled? Still a
ways off. Plasma confinement, we just reached break-even, possibly
a workable reactor by the turn of the century. Inertial confinement shows
some promise. Solid-state tunneling reactions are tricky and we still
don't understand them: much longer."

"Look at this, then." A schematic appeared, a huge sphere with a
tube protruding from each end, like a straw through an orange. "Build
a big sphere; doesn't matter much of what, as long as it's thick enough.
Throw fusion bombs in through this magnetic catapult. Set them off;
we've got an electron-beam system that looks likely to work, but
uranium's cheap off-planet these days. Bomb goes off, vacuum, no blast.
Just radiant energy; shell absorbs the energy, you *extract* the energy,
then beam it anywhere you want via microwave. Simple, robust, nearly
as cheap as solar past Mars . . ."

"Useful," the younger man said without relaxing his lynx stare.
"Particularly in the Belt. With that, we could really set up a self-
sustaining system, and *fast*. But that isn't what you had in mind."

"No. Incidentally, we think the Draka are using a much cruder form
of this to mine ice from Sinope or Himalia, off Jupiter." Another tap
on the screen. The artifact that appeared this time was a simple tube
of coils and large-scale industrial magnets floating free in space, contained by the outline of an enormous box. "What's buried in New
Mexico and eats power?"

"Linear accelerator . . ." His hands gripped the rests of his chair.
"*Antimatter*, by God!"

"Right the first time, give the man a cigar." The stem of the pipe
pointed. "And that's the *first* of the secrets you'll be expected to guard.
You think, Fred. *Think.*"

Slowly. "It can't be for bombs. We've *already* got bigger weapons
than we can use." A pause. "Spaceship drives?"

A nod. "Paahtly. The ultimate reaction drive. We've tested models
with the minute amounts we've made here Earthside. A great advantage, even over the improved pulsedrive models we're working on. Even
over the fusion models that we'll have in a decade."

"But not *enough*," Lefarge said. "It'll never be enough, a better
weapon, more weapons, even when we've got a lead we're too gutless to use it."

The general frowned. "Fred, the price of open war is *too high*. And
getting higher! They can at least copy what we do." He shook his head,
waited for a second, then summoned up another image. "All right, look
at this."

This was a spaceship, with an outline he recognized beside it for
comparison; a Hero-class deep-space cruiser, the type he had been
operating out of in the Belt. Those had a 7,000-tonne payload . . .
and this one was dwarfed by the model beside it. A huge cylinder,

basically; a wheel and a ball at one end, at the other a long stalk and a cup.

Awareness struck him. "Judas Priest!" he wheezed. "A starship!" For a moment he was a boy again, watching Bat Markam, Alliance Future Patrol, planting the blue-and-gold on a planet of green-tentacled aliens. . . . Then his teeth skinned back. "Shit." A *bolthole*.

"How do you feel about the idea, Fred?"

"Jesus . . ." He ran a hand over his face. "General, could we do it?"

A shrug. "Ayuh. Theory's all right, the engineering is big but nothing radical. Have to test the drive, but the math works. Alpha Centauri in forty years. And, Fred, they've been looking that way with the Big Eye." That was the fifty-kilometer reflector at the L-5 beyond Lunar farside. "There's a planet there."

The excitement surged again, mixed sourly with bitterness at the back of his throat. "Inhabitable?"

"Mebbe. Mebbe not. It's got an oxygen-nitrogen atmosphere, water vapor, continents and oceans . . . Yes, the definition's that good. A little smaller than Earth and further out, and the orbit's funny, what you'd expect." The Centauri system had three stars, that *must* be complex. "A Mars-type as well, subjovian gas giants, moons, asteroids we *think* from the orbital data. A planet by itself isn't enough these days." More slowly: "How do you *feel* about it, Fred?"

Unconscious of the general's stare, the younger man rose and paced, running a hand through his close-cropped black hair. "Christ. I love it; that's something I've dreamed since I was a kid. When the news flash came through about the *Conestoga* reaching orbit, I was on my first date, you know? Sheila Washansky. Her folks were away for the afternoon, we were on the couch upstairs, I had my hand up her skirt and the TV on downstairs—and I dumped her on the floor, I got up so fast. Never even noticed her walking out the door. Thirteen, my first chance to score, and I never noticed: that shows you how I feel."

He stopped and drove a fist into one palm. "And I hate it, the idea of running away. Even as a last resort—" He swung toward the general. "It *is* a last resort, isn't it?"

"Ayuh."

"Just to get a few hundred clear—"

"More like a hundred thousand, Fred."

At his surprise, Stoddard continued: "The other side aren't the only ones who do technological espionage. They've about perfected a reduced-metabolism system that works; down to less than one percent of normal. Our biology people say they can work out the remaining bugs without using their methods." They both grimaced slightly; one reason the Domination made faster progress in the life sciences was its willingness to expend humans.

"So the passengers age less than a year. Crew in rotation; no more than five years each. Seeds, animals, frozen animal ova, tools, knowledge, fabricators . . . all the art and history and philosophy the human race has produced. Enough to restart civilization—*our* civilization. America was started by refugees, son. What's your say?"

Lefarge nodded once, then again. "Yes. As a last resort, because too much is at stake. It's not as if the resources were crucial. The Protracted Struggle isn't going to be tipped by a percent here or there."

Stoddard sighed with relief, and his smile was warm.

Hell, that's Uncle Nate's smile, Lefarge noted with surprise.

"Fred, you just passed the test," he said, coming around the desk to lay a hand on his shoulder. "And I can't tell you how glad I am."

"Test?"

"Yes. Look, Fred, we've got *lots* of anti-Draka fanatics, the Domination produces them like a junkyard dog does fleas. They're useful; that's one reason India cost the Draka the way it did. But fanatics are limited; they can't really think all that well, not where their obsession is concerned, and *they aren't reliable*. They've got their private agendas, which is fine if they happen to coincide with the command's, and if not—" He shrugged. "This is too big to risk."

Lefarge nodded slowly. "And I've just shown I'm not a fanatic? General, don't bet on it."

"Mebbe there's a difference between that and a good hate." He made a production of refilling the pipe. "Well, that was a big enough secret?"

"Oh, sure." Lefarge grinned like a wolf. "Out with it." *Another secret*, went through him. *And this one has to be a weapon. Something that can well and truly upset the balance.*

"Nh-huh. You *are* going out there. With a promotion to lieutenant colonel. Security chief, overall command with War Emergency Regulation powers. The rank will go up as the project builds up."

Lefarge whistled silently. War Emergency Regulation. Power of summary execution!

"You see, Fred, you're perfect. Good technical background; good record with the OSS. Known to be space-trained. But not prominent enough to make the Security Directorate flag you, particularly. Not more than they watch fifty, a hundred thousand other officers." There were twenty million in the Alliance military.

"Just the right type to be put in charge of a middling-important project. Like a fusion-power network for the asteroid belt; like an antimatter production facility. Like a fleet of antimatter-powered warships. Layers like an onion; by the time, which God forbid should ever happen, they come to the *New America*"—Lefarge nodded at the name—"you'll be senior enough to oversee security work on that."

"And?"

Stoddard leaned backward against the desk, cupped an elbow in a hand. "And that's as much as anyone on Earth knows, except me, thee, and a few technical people. Damned few know *that* much. The technical people will be going out with you; they'll brief you when you get there. All the Chairman and the President know is we're doing something, and the appropriations are in the Black Fund."

"Yeah. Everyone's feeling rich these days." Even with the military burden, taxes had been cut and cut again in recent years, as wealth flowed in from new industries and from space. Economists kept warning that the budget surplus would wreck the economy if prices went on falling the way they had. "They won't miss it."

"You'll get everything you need. We're encouraging development of the Belt, you may have noticed, and doing it *hard*. That'll give more background to camouflage you, and more local resources to draw on in the later stages. This project is going to be a black hole, and you're the guardian at the event horizon. Nobody comes back. Nobody and *nothing*. Except you, occasionally, and you report verbally to me or my successor. I don't tell anyone anything. Not until it's ready."

For a moment, for the first time in a year, Lefarge felt pure happiness. Then he hesitated, reached into his uniform jacket for a cigarette. *Have to give this up again*, he thought. *At least until whatever habitat we build gets big enough.*

"Any news?" he asked softly. They both knew he could only mean his sister.

"Fred—" Stoddard returned to his chair, fiddled with the controls. "All we've been able to learn is that she's alive, they haven't penetrated her cover and she's been bought up by a pilot officer who was there." He leaned forward, sorrowful and inexorable. "No, Fred, no. We will *not* expend assets—people!—trying to pull her out. And we won't try to trade for her, because we have to keep what bargaining power we have for situations where it's really needed."

There was more emotion in the old man's voice than Lefarge had heard in many years. "Fred, I love you both as if you were my own, you know that. Marya's tough and smart. It's not inconceivable she could get out. Or die trying. Until then, the only help, the only protection she has is that cover story. You will not endanger it, understood?"

"Yes. Yes, sir." Lefarge straightened, set his beret on his head. "I'm to report in a week? Well, if you'll excuse me, sir, I intend to go take advantage of the time. First, by getting very drunk. Safely, alone."

Stoddard sighed and dropped his face into his hands as the door closed. *I cannot weep*, he thought. *For if I do, will never stop.*

**CLAESTUM PLANTATION
DISTRICT OF TUSCANY
PROVINCE OF ITALY
MAY 1976**

"Yolande?"

She stopped, caught between impatience and sick relief at the excuse for delay. It was John, looking grimmer than she had seen him in a long time, since Mandy got back from the last operation, in fact. Galena was behind him, trying to make herself invisible. Yolande stopped, sighed, rubbed a hand over her forehead.

"Yes, John?"

He faced her, looked aside for a moment, then directly into her eyes.

"There's somethin' I'd like to discuss with you, sister," he said. A nod in the direction of the plain door ahead; they were in a little-used section of the manor, only sketchily finished at all, suited for the use she had put it to. "That serf of yours, in particular."

The day was warm, but Yolande felt her skin roughen under her field jacket. "That's . . . not somethin' I care to discuss, brother," she said carefully, eyes on his face. The dappled sun-shadow patterns from the tall window at her back fell across the hard tanned planes of it, bleak and angry.

"I care to discuss it," he said. "Not just fo' myself. Fo' our parents, you sisters, for Mandy."

She opened her mouth to reply, then hesitated. The look on his face was enough to bring her out of self-absorption, with a prickle of feeling that it took a moment for her to recognize. *Danger.* This was the wrong context, the wrong person; this was her brother, Johnnie . . . and a very dangerous man, an extremely angry one. A cold-water feeling, a draft of rationality through the hot, tight obsession these rooms had come to represent.

"All right," she said, impatiently. "Say you say."

"Not here. In there."

Yolande blinked, conscious of her lips peeling back. Unconscious of her hand dropping to the butt of her sidearm, until she saw him copy her motion with flat wariness.

"If that's the way you want to discuss it, 'Landa."

"I—gods, Johnnie!" She shook her hand loose. "All *right*, then." Her back went rigid at the thought of another seeing this with her. She pushed open the door.

The American serf had been sitting at a table, picking listlessly at the wood. She looked up at the sound of the door opening, and scuttled to the far corner of the room; her hands caught up the tablecloth in passing, held it tented out in front of her as she scrabbled to push herself back into the stone.

"Noo," she said. They could see her mouth through the thin fabric, open in an O as round as her eyes. "Nooo. Ahhhhh. Nooo." The serf's face looked fallen in, as if something had been subtracted from it, and her arms were wasted.

Yolande swallowed and turned her back, it was different seeing it with John there. Suddenly she felt herself seized, the back of her neck taken in a grip as irresistible as a machine, turning her about.

"Look at that!" John said. "That is what I wanted to . . . This can't go on, 'Landa, it cannot. I will not allow it. None of us will."

The serf was making a thin whine, clutching the tablecloth to her with arms and legs, rocking. Yolande reached back, used a breakhold on the thumb to free herself, spun to face her brother, panting.

"You disputin' my right to do as I will with my own?" she grated.

"*Not on my land!*" he roared, the sound shockingly loud. "*Not in my family's home!*" John reached over and pulled her pistol free, grabbed her hand, pressed it into her palm.

"Kill her, if that's what you want. Or get rid of her. Or if you want to keep actin' like a hyena, *get you gone.*"

Yolande looked at the weapon, up at her brother, her eyes hunting for a chink in his rage. "Are—" She fumbled the weapon back into its holster. "Are you tellin' me I'm not welcome in my family's home?" she said, in a small high voice.

"My sister Yolande is always welcome here," he said flatly. "My sister wouldn't do that"—he jerked his head at the moaning serf—"to a mad dog. It's your property . . . Don't you understand, 'Landa, you doin' this to *youself*. Every time you think of Myfwany, you takes it out on that poor bitch. Does that ease you pain? Does it? Is *that*"—he pointed again—"what you want your memories attached to? You've got to start livin' again. Not just goin' through the motions."

Yolande turned, braced her hands against the wall. Something inside her seemed to crumble, and she felt an overwhelming panic. *Gods, he's right. I'm poisoning all I have left.* That couldn't be right. *It's her fault . . . or is it my fault?*

"All right," she said dully. "All right." His hand touched her shoulder gently, and she turned into his embrace. "All right." Her neck muscles were quivering-rigid, but her eyes stayed dry.

"You want me to handle gettin' rid of her?" he asked.

She straightened, wiped her hands down her trouser legs, looked over at the serf. Appraisingly, this time. "No," she said calmly. "You're right. I won't use the controller on her any more. I'll try and have her patched up . . . but I'm not lettin' her go. Lettin' go isn't my strong point, brother. But thank you. Thank you all." A nervous gesture smoothed back her hair. "If'n she recovers, I'll . . . Oh, I don't know. Find somethin' else fo' her to do. That enough."

He nodded. "Welcome back."

She laughed, quietly bitter. "Not yet. Just startin', maybe." A glance at the sunlight. "I've got the afternoon, befo' I have to take the car in." She was on short-leave. "See you at dinner."

I am Marya.

"Oh, y'poor hurt thing."

Gentle hands were lifting her, holding a glass to her lips. She recognized the hands, the scent; they were surcease from pain. Black hands, sweet voice.

I am Marya Lefarge.

"C'mon, honey, we gets y' to the doctor. Give y' somethin' to sleep. Mistis isn't goin' do that no mo', she was just crazy, honest, no more."

I am Captain Marya Lefarge.

She was walking into a place that smelled half medicinal, half of country air, warmth. Children were playing outside, she could hear them. She was lifted into a soft bed; a pill was between her lips. Drowsy.

"No more painmaker, no mo'."

I am Captain Marya Lefarge, and nothing can hurt me. Because beside *that* there was no pain. She had felt the worst thing in the world, and she was still alive. *Nothing can hurt me.* I will remake myself. However long it takes, I will.

"Ah, Myfwany." The turf had healed over the grave, on the hill across from the manor. It was lonely here, not many graves in the Ingolfssons' burying ground yet. . . . She looked up to the next space, that would be hers.

"I wanted to die, Myfwany, for . . . it seemed like a long time. Or to go away, go away from it all. And I had to . . . keep goin', keep on doin' things. The things we talked about, the Astronautical Academy, qualifyin'. So . . . *dry*, it was like I *was* dead, dead on my feet and rottin', and nobody could notice. They say it heals . . . oh, do I *want* it to?"

Yolande hugged her knees to her and laid her head on them; one hand smoothed the short damp grass. Somewhere she could feel a pair of warm green eyes open, somewhere in the back of her mind.

"Yes, love, I know. I takes things too much to heart." A rough laugh. "You wouldn't have gone . . . hog-wild with that Yankee, the way I did. It should've been you that lived that night, love."

The Draka rose, dusting off her trousers. "I promise it'll do bettah now, Myfwany-sweet. Somehow I'll find a true revenge fo' you. And . . ." Her eyes rested on the far hills. *I think it would be better if I could weep, at least alone*, she thought. "I'll live, as you'd have said. Make the memories live, somehow." Her eyes closed, and she felt scar tissue inside herself. *Scars don't bleed, but they don't feel as well, either.* "Good-bye fo' now, my love. Till we meet again."

EUGENICS BOARD NATALITY CLINIC
FLORENCE
DISTRICT OF TUSCANY
PROVINCE OF ITALY
DOMINATION OF THE DRAKA
SEPTEMBER 1, 1976

"Now, shall we proceed, Citizen?" the doctor asked politely. He had glanced at the medal ribbons as she came into the office, and Yolande suspected he would look up her record again as soon as she left. A tall thin wiry man with cropped graying dark hair and brown eyes, with a Ground Command thumb ring. *Technical Section*, she decided.

The office was a large room near the roofline of a converted Renaissance *palazzo* down near the Arno; the windows looked away from the river, out to the cathedral with its red-and-white candy-stripe Giotto bell tower and the green mountains beyond. It was cheerfully light, white-painted with a good tapestry on the inner wall, bright patterned tile floors, rugs, modern inlaid Draka-style furniture. There was a smell of river and clean warm air from outside, faint traffic noises, the fainter sound of a group of brooders counting cadence as they went through their exercises.

"The brooder I sent in is satisfactory?" she said.

The doctor kept his eyes steady on hers as she turned back from the window, but could not prevent an inward flinch. You saw suffering in his line of work, but not like *that*.

"A little underweight, but otherwise fine," he replied, calling up the report. "The psych report indicates stabilized trauma, surprisin' recovery. Hmm, prima gravida . . . good pelvic structure, but are you sure a licensed Clinic brooder wouldn't do?" Yolande shook her head wordlessly.

"The technicians report she's . . . hm, seems to have been under *very* severe stress. Good recovery, as I said, no biological agent; still, I'd swear she's been sufferin' from *somethin'.*"

"She has," Yolande said, with a flat smile.

"What?"

"Me."

The doctor opened his mouth, shut it again with a shrug. It was the owner's business, after all. "Well," he said after another consultation with the screen. "We adjusted her hormone level, so she's ready fo' seeding anytime. Now, as to the clone." He paused delicately.

Yolande lit a cigarette, disregarding his frown. The new gene-engineered varieties of tobacco had virtually no carcinogens or lung contaminants, and the soothing was worth the slight risk.

"I'd think it was simple enough," she said. The glassy feeling was back, a detachment deeper than any she had ever achieved in meditation. "My lover was killed in India. I want a clone-child, with *this* wench as brooder."

"Tetrarch Ingolfsson . . . you do understand, a clone is not a reproduction? All the same genes, yes, but—"

"Personality is an interaction of genetics an' environment, yes, I *am* familiar with the facts, Doctor." She sank into a chair. It was odd, how the same physical sensation could carry such different *meanings*. The smooth competence of her own body: a year ago, it had been a delight. Now . . . just machinery, that you would be annoyed with if it did not function according to spec. "I realize that I'm not getting Myfwany back." Something surged beneath the glass, something huge and dark that would shatter her if she let it. *Breathe. Breathe. Calm.*

The medico steepled his fingers. "Then there's the matter of the Eugenics Code."

She stubbed out the cigarette and lit another. "I'm askin' fo' a *clone*, Doctor. Not a superbeing."

"Yes, yes . . . are you aware of the advances we've made in biocontrol in the last decade?"

Yolande shrugged. "I've seen ghouloons," she said. "Bought a modified cat awhiles ago."

He smiled with professional warmth. "If you'll examine that-there screen by you chair, Citizen." It lit. "Now, we've had the whole human genome fo' some time now, identified the keyin' and activation sequences." His face lit with a more genuine warmth, the passion of a man in love with his work. "Naturally, we're bein' cautious. The mistakes they made with that ghouloon project, befo' they got it right! We're certainly not talkin' about introducing transgenetic material or even many modified genes. Or makin' a standard product."

Double-helix figures came to three-dimensional life on the screen. "You see, that's chimp DNA on the left, human on the right. Ninety-eight percent identical, or better! So a *few* changes can do a great deal, a great deal indeed." Seriously: "And those changes are bein' . . . *strongly encouraged*. Not least, think of how handicapped a child without them would be!"

"Tell me," Yolande said, leaning forward, feeling a stirring of unwilling interest beneath the irritation.

"Well. What we do is run analysis against the suggested norm, an' modify the original as needed. Saves the genetic diversity, hey? With you friend—"

His hands moved on the keyboard, and Myfwany's form appeared on the screen; it split, and gene-coding columns ran down beside it. Yolande's hands clenched on the arms of the chair, unnoticed despite the force that pressed the fingernails white.

"See, on personality, we're still not *sure* about much of the finer tuning. We can set the gross limits—aggressive versus passive, fo' example, or the general level of libido. Beyond that, the interactions with the environment are too complex. With you friend, most of the parameters are well within the guidelines anyway. So the heritable elements of character will be identical to an unmodified clone.

"Next, we eliminate a number of faults. Fo' example"—he paused to reference the computer—"you friend had allergies. We get rid of that. Likewise, potential back trouble . . . would've been farsighted in old age . . . menstrual cramps . . . any problems?"

"No." Even with feedback and meditation, those times had been terrible for Myfwany; Yolande had only been able to suffer in sympathy. The child—*Gwen*, she reminded herself—Gwen would never know that useless pain.

"Next, we come to a number of physical improvements. Mostly by selectin' within the normal range of variation. Fo' example, we know the gene groups involved with general intelligence . . . Genius is mo' elusive, but we can raise the testable IQ to an average of 143 with the methods available. Fo' your clone, that would mean about fifteen percent up; also, we've been able to map fo' complete memory control, autistic *idiot savant* mathematical concentration, and so forth. On the athletic side, we build up the heart-lung system, tweak the hemoglobin ratios, alter some of the muscle groups and their attachments, thicken an' strengthen the bones, eliminate the weaknesses of ligaments—no mo' knee injuries—and so fo'th."

"The result?" Yolande said.

"Well, you know, a chimp is smaller than a man . . . and many times stronger. After the 'tweaking,' the average strength will increase by a factor of four, endurance by three, reflexes by two, twenty-five-percent increase in sensory effectiveness. Greater resistance to disease, almost total, faster healin', no heart attacks . . . slightly lower body-fat ratio . . . perfect pitch, photographic memory, things like that."

"So," Yolande's chin sank on her chest. She had wanted . . . *He's right. Gwen has to have the best. As I'd have wanted for Myfwany.* "And?"

"Well, this is the most advanced part. We've been able to transfer a number of the autonomic functions to conscious control. . . . Not all at once! Imagine a baby bein' able to control its heartbeat! No, we're keyin' them to the hormonal changes accompanyin' puberty, fo' the most part. Like any Citizen child learns, with meditation an' feedback, only it'll be *easy* fo' them, natural, able to go much further.

Control of the reproductive cycle. Heartbeat, skin tension, circulation, pupil dilation, pain . . ."

He looked at the screen. "You friend was in fine condition, but she had to fight fo' it, a lot of the time, didn't she? Your . . . Gwen, she'll be able to set her metabolic rate at will. Eat anythin', and it'll be *easy* to stay in prime shape."

Yolande remembered Myfwany sighing and turning the dessert menu facedown. A wave that was dark and bitter surged up, closing her throat. *This is absurd*, she thought, squeezing her eyes shut for a moment before nodding to the man to continue.

"A lot of human communication's by pheromones: sex, dominance, anger, fear. We increase the *conscious* awareness of 'em, an' make the subjects able to deliberately govern their own output." He grinned. "Ought to make social life real interestin'. That's about it, 'cept fo' one thing." A weighty pause, Yolande endured it.

"We've been lookin' into agin', of course. No magic cures, I'm afraid. The whole *system* isn't designed to last. Normal unimproved variety, you and me, Tetrarch; we wear out at a hundred an' twenty absolute maximum. Modern medicine can keep us goin' longer, maybe right out to the limit by the time you're my age, but that's it. Then"—he shrugged—"you know that Yankee story, about the steamcar made so well everythin' wore out at once?"

Yolande felt herself snarl at the name of the enemy, hid it with a cough, nodded.

"Best we can do is stretch it. To about two hundred fifty years fo' the next generation."

Her eyes opened wide; that *was* something worth boasting about. "Show me," she said.

The column of data beside the figure of Myfwany disappeared; a baby's form replaced it. The infant grew, aged; limbs lengthening, face firming. Yolande stared, caught her breath as it paused at fourteen, eighteen, twenty. *Oh, my darlin'!* something wailed within her.

No. Not *quite* the same; the computer could not show the marks experience laid on a human's face. A few other minor changes, fewer freckles, slightly lighter hair. If you looked *very* closely, something different about the joints, in the way the muscles grouped beneath the skin.

"Gwen," she whispered to herself. For a moment the responsibility daunted her; this was a twenty-year duty she was undertaking, not a whim. A person, a Draka, someone she would have to play parent to as long as they lived. Give love, teach honor. Then: "Yes. I understand, Doctor; that's entirely satisfactory." She paused. "Just out of curiosity, what's planned fo' the serfs along these lines?"

He relaxed. "Oh, much less. That was debated at the highest levels of authority, an' they decided to do very little beyond selectin' within the normal human range. Same sort of cleanup on things like hereditary diseases. Average the height about 50 millimeters lower than ours. No IQ's below 90, which'll bring the average up to 110. No improvements or increase in lifespan, beyond that, so they'll be closer to the original norm than the Race. Some selection within the personality spectrum;

toward gentle, emotional, nonaggressive types. About what you'd expect."
He laughed. "An' a chromosome change, so that they're not interfer-
tile with us any mo'; the boys can run rampant among the wenches
as always without messin' up our plans."

"Yes," she said again, interest drifting elsewhere. "When can we do
it?"

"Tomorrow would be fine, Tetrarch. The process of modifyin' the
ova is mostly automatic. Viral an' enzymic, actually . . . Tomorrow
at 1000 hours?"

Yolande looked up as the serf walked into the room. Marya was
dressed in a disposable paper shirt; the medical technician pulled
it off and pushed her toward the couch. It was at the center of the
room, surrounded like a dentist's chair with incomprehensible machinery, near a curved console with multiple display screens. The room
was deep within the Clinic, far from the morning sun; the American captive's eyes blinked at the harsh overhead lights, reflected from
gleaming white tile and synthetic. Her eyes darted from the doctor,
busy at the console, to the other serf meditech in white who waited
by the table.

She started uncontrollably as she saw Yolande rise from the corner.

"Nhhh!" she gasped, then clenched her teeth, staring at the palm-
sized controller clipped to the Draka's belt. Her left hand hugged the
left wrist to her stomach, as if she could bury the controller cuff on
it into her flesh, away from the radio commands.

Yolande forced herself to watch the flinch, the eyes gone wide and
white around the iris. *I should be enjoying this*, she thought, hating
her weakness, remembering the American's stubbornness. Instead it
made her faintly nauseated, like a wounded dog. The faint medicinal-
ozone smell of the Clinic was a sourness at the back of her mouth.

"Marya!" she said sharply. "You won't be punished, as long as you
obey. Do as these people tell you."

"M-mistis," the serf stammered. Docile but quivering-tense, she waited
while the other technician laid a paper sheet on the table, then climbed
onto it and lay back.

"Feet in the stirrups," the serf technician said. "That's aright, little
momma, this no hurt ata-all." She buckled the restraints at neck, arms,
waist, knees, and thighs. "Now, we get a you ready for the visitor."
She began to rig a visual barrier below the serf's neck.

"No," Yolande said, walking closer. The serf looked up with a
respectful dip of the head. "No, I want her to see it all."

The meditech looked toward the doctor, mimicked his slight shrug.
"*Si*, Mistis." She touched controls instead, and the equipment moved.
The couch bent into a shallow curve, raising Marya's shoulders and
buttocks. The stirrups moved apart and back with a slight hydraulic
whine, presenting the serf's genitals.

"Thisa no hurt," the meditech repeated. She pulled down a dangling line, attached it to Marya's throat.

The doctor looked up from his screens. "She's hyperventilatin' and
on the edge of adrenaline blackout," he said dryly, giving Yolande a

resentful look. "One cc dociline." She could read his thought: *Damned amateurs messing up a medical procedure.*

Fuck you, she thought back.

Marya's straining relaxed a fraction, and sanity returned to her eyes. *Good*, Yolande thought. *It would be terrible if she went mad.*

"W-what—?" the serf shook her head angrily, as if trying to fling the stammer out of her mouth. "What are you doing to me?"

Yolande rested a hand on her stomach. "Seeding you womb," she said quietly, looking into the other's eyes. "Myfwany left me her ova. They don't have the egg-mergin' technique mastered yet, or I'd do that. So we're clonin' her; you're to bear the egg."

The serf froze for a moment, then began to throw herself against the restraints, hard enough to make them rattle; it took Yolande a moment to place the sound she was making. *A growl.* The two meditechs frowned without looking up from their instruments, and the doctor swore aloud.

"Frey's *prick*, Tetrarch!" His hand touched the controls. "*Two* cc dociline, an' if you don't stop interferin', I won't be responsible fo' the procedure!"

Yolande nodded, but spoke once more to the serf. "Marya." She raised the controller box; the anger drained out of the serf and she whimpered. "If the pregnancy an' nursin' go well, I won't use this on you again. *If they don't, I'll lock it on until you die!* Understand me, wench?"

A frantic nod. Then Marya's eyes darted down as the meditech touched her.

"Dona you worry, little momma," the meditech was saying from between the serf's legs. "This just take a *momento*." She had an aerosol can in her hand; with careful, swift movements she applied a thick pink foam to the genital area and lower stomach. "Now just wait a minute."

"N-no!" Marya bit at the corner of her lip. Yolande looked up; the other meditech had rolled her sleeves back to the elbow and thrust both hands into a claver. There was a flash and hum, and when the technician withdrew them they were covered in a thin film that glistened like solidified water where the highlights caught it.

"All right, Antonia," she said.

"Hnnn!" from the serf on the table. Yolande followed her eyes; the meditech was wiping off the foam with cloths that had a sharp medicinal smell, moving down from belly to anus; the hair came with it. The Draka could see the muscles of Marya's belly and thighs jerk as the tech followed with a clear sharp-smelling spray. The pinkly naked flesh gleamed.

The serf with the molecular-film gloves replaced her coworker. "Whata you think we win the bridge tournament?" she said casually, spreading the subject's vulva with her left hand. With her right she ran an experimental finger into Marya's vagina. "If that crazy Giuseppe no— Jesus-Mary-Joseph, she tight like stone!"

Yolande pushed down with the flat of her hand. "Marya, relax," she said in a clean clipped tone. After a long moment she felt the serf loosen into obedience.

"Thank you, Mistis, thata better," the meditech said. Her companion handed her an instrument like a speculum, giving it a quick spray of lubricating oil from another aerosol.

"Agg. Nhhhhnng." Marya's voice, as the meditech inserted it with a series of deft, steady pushes. She gave the threaded dilator at the base two turns and hooked fold-out supports over Marya's thighs to hold it in place.

"Please! God, please!"

The doctor whistled through his teeth. "Catheter now, Angelica," he said.

"Giuseppe, he crazy like fox," the other tech said, unreeling the end of a spool of what looked like black thread from a machine on casters. It rolled near. "Here. He say you play too cautious, you lose alla time."

The gloved meditech threaded the tip of the catheter through the instrument and into Marya. "Master Doctore?"

"Good, anothah ten millimeters. Careful now. Very slowly." Yolande stroked Marya's stomach and watched the wild, set eyes that stared down between her legs. "Good, that's it. Hmmm. Acidity balance good, uterine wall looks good . . . getting a reading . . . let's boost . . . All right, here we go."

Yolande looked down at the shuddering body on the couch, imagining a tiny form with red birth fuzz lying in her arms; she smiled, and for a moment the weight of hatred lifted.

"Blastocyst's in the uterus. That's the egg in the womb to you lay people," the doctor chuckled. "All right, Tetrarch, one seeded brooder. Virtually certain to take, anyway. Leave her here until tomorrow; she ought to be immobile. Intend to bring her back fo' the bearin'?"

"No," Yolande said, with a slight smile. "We've got a perfectly good midwife on our plantation. Look at me, Marya." The serf looked up, licked her lips. Wisps of hair were plastered to her brow, and Yolande pushed them back with one finger, and touched her navel with the other hand. "You're going to bear Gwen fo' me, Marya, an' suckle her. That's how you serves me and the Race, now. Understand?"

The serf jerked slightly. The meditech had withdrawn the speculum and catheter; the two technicians laid a cloth over Marya's crotch and adjusted the stirrups so that her legs were together with knees up. One waited patiently with a blanket, while the other stripped the thin film gloves from her hands. The doctor rose.

"You can pick her up tomorrow. Unless you'd care to sit with her."

"No," Yolande said. The meditechs draped the blanket over the serf, tucking it around her neatly and freeing one hand next to a plastic cup of water. "No, I've got a date." This was better than inflicting pain, but she did not want to stay and watch. "And Marya here needs to be alone with her thoughts, hey?"

Chapter Twelve

SOUTH WING WAITING ROOM
CASTLE TARLETON
ARCHONA
ARCHONA PROVINCE
DOMINATION OF THE DRAKA

The family was waiting for her in the ring-road plaza by the south side of the Castle Tarleton grounds. Her brother John and Mandy, sitting at a table under an umbrella and talking. Looking exactly what they were, Landholders in from the provinces, down to the broad-brimmed hats and conservative Tolgren 5mm's . . . David, their latest infant, cooing and gurgling in the arms of stout Delores, his brooder-nurse; Jolene, Adele . . . and Marya, with Gwen. Gwen.

"Momma! Momma!" The small red-headed form bounced erect and ran toward her, toddler's tunic flying. "Momma!" She leaped up.

"Ooof." She was heavy for a five-year-old; that was the denser bones. Incredibly strong. Yolande grabbed her under the armpits and swung her in a wide circle, laughing up into the face that smiled back at her.

"Zero-G!" the child cried. "Zero-G, Momma!"

Yolande darted a look of apology at her brother, and tossed her daughter up with a swoop-catch. "There you go, spacer! And—*one* and *two* and *three* and *dockin' maneuver.*" She gave the child a smacking kiss and hugged her.

Gwen's arms tightened around her neck, and she pressed her head against her mother's. "Love you, Momma," she said.

"Love you, too, my baby Gwennie," she said.

"I am *not* a baby! I'm *Gwen*," she replied firmly.

"Indeed you are, light of my life." Yolande signed to Marya. "Here, now stay with you Tantie-ma fo' a minute, an' hush."

John and Mandy were smiling indulgently at her, hands linked.

"I gathah the news is good," her brother chuckled. Mandy was using her belt phone to call for the car; the family had rented the latest for their stay in Archona, a superconductor-electric with maglev capacity on the few stretches of road relaid for that luxury.

"You are lookin'," Yolande said, buffing her nails, "at the *newest* Cohortarch in the Directorate of War."

"Well, well, *well*, we Ingolfssons are movin' up in the world," he said, with a swift hard embrace. John had never been more than a tetrarch, or wanted to be. He and Mandy did their Territorial Reserve duty, and that was enough distraction from Claestum and its folk. "Even as I dragged you appalling offspring through the zoo and amusement park. Wotan's stomach, the things they do with rides these days! While Mandy shopped the estate into bankruptcy; we'll need a Logistics Lifter to get the loot—"

He winced theatrically as the tall blond woman dug him in the ribs. "Gwen didn't enjoy those rides half as much as you did," she said. "Do I quarrel with you gettin' every toy Biocontrol dreams up fo' the credulous planter? Like those steakberries?" John winced more sincerely; the high-protein meat-mimicking fruit had proven a beacon for every vermin, pest, scavenger, and grub in Italy. Their son began to cry softly. "I could scarcely take Davie along with you and Gwen, now could I?"

They glanced over to the nurses. Delores was just lifting a full breast out of her blouse and brushing the engorged brown nipple across the infant's mouth; she rocked the child and crooned, smiling, as he suckled.

"That reminds me, you-know-who dropped a broad hint it'd be appreciated if I had anothah befo' shippin' out. Hm, Gwen? You likes a little brothah or sistah to play with you?"

The girl had been seated on Marya's lap, watching the adults and ignoring her cousin with five-year-old disdain. "Can't play with a baby," she said practically. "They just makes messes an' sleeps."

Yolande laughed, and glanced an inquiry at her brother and sister-in-law. Mandy nodded. "One more's no problem, 'Landa. Freya knows, what with ours and the two new ones ma an' pa are having, we gettin' to be more of a tribe than a family."

Yolande's mother had borne four children naturally, but seemed to prefer the new method wholeheartedly.

"I'll have to pick a brooder," she said.

"No problem . . . 'Ship out'?" her schoolfriend said.

Yolande shrugged, spread her hands and looked from side to side in the universal Draka gesture for secrecy. Not that the Security Directorate needed to have spies hiding behind bushes these days.

"Be gone fo' quite some time. Months, leastways."

Gwen made a protesting sound, frowning and pouting, blinking back tears. Yolande moved over toward her on the stone bench, smoothing the copper hair back from her brow.

"Now, where's my big brave girl?" she said gently. "Momma has her work, an' I'll bring you back another piece of a star, sweetie." Gwen had been just old enough after the last voyage to understand that the light pointed out in the sky was where her mother had been, and the lump of rock from Ganymede was her most precious possession.

"I don' want a star. I want Momma!" She tugged on Marya's hair. "Tantie-ma, tell Momma she cain' go!"

"Hush, Missy Gwen. You know I can't tell your mother what to do." The serf wrapped her arms around the child and made soothing noises.

"Now, don't be a baby, Gwen," Yolande said. "Momma doesn't have to leave fo' a week yet"—which was forever to a child this age—"and when I go, you can come up to the station with me, how's that? Right up above the sky." No more risky than an ordinary scramjet flight, these days, and she could probably swing it.

"And you'll have Uncle John and Auntie Mandy and Tantie-ma, too, and all the friends you makes at school next year. Oh," she continued, looking up at Marya. "I meant to tell you. I've posted bond, you're moved up to Class III Literate." That meant nontechnical and nonpolitical literature, and limited computer access to menu-driven databanks; the classics, as well, most of them.

Marya looked down, flushing. "Thank you, Mistis," she whispered. For an instant Yolande thought she caught something strange and fierce in the wench's expression, then dismissed it. *Must have been boring, nothing much to read*, she thought. *Should have done this before.* Gwen subsided, looking up with nervous delight at the thought of flying to orbit.

"Well, what have we planned?" Yolande asked.

"Lunch," John said. "Then the Athenaeum, then dinner at Saparison's. Then there's a Gerraldson revival at the Amphitheater, the *Fireborn Resurrection*, and Uncle Eric used some pull to get us a box. We'll drop the children off first, of course."

"Nnoo, I think Gwen might enjoy it," Yolande said, considering. "The dancin' at least. Marya can keep her quiet, or take her out in the gardens if not." And it would be a treat for Marya as well; she had been behaving well of late. Gwen was certainly devoted to her, which was a good sign.

The electrocar had hissed up on the smooth black roadway a dozen meters away. The main processional streets of Archona had been the first public places in the solar system to be fitted with superconductor grids, just last year. Their car floated by the curb, motionless and a quarter meter above the roadway as the gull-wing doors folded up; it still looked a little unnatural to Yolande for something to hover so on Earth, without jets or fans. She reached out for Gwen's hand and the child took it in one of hers and offered the other to Marya. Their eyes met for a moment over the child's head, before they turned to walk behind the others.

Strange, Yolande thought. *Life is strange, really.*

"I *did* it! Cohortarch, independent command, I *did* it!"

Jolene looked up smiling as Yolande collapsed backward onto the bed in her undertunic, the formal gown strewn in yards of fabric toward the door. The room was part of a guest suite in the von Shrakenberg townhouse, beautiful in an extremely old-fashioned way; inlaid Coromandel sandalwood screens in pearl and lapis, round water-cushioned bed on a marble dais with a canopy, a wall of balcony doors in frosted glass etched over with delicate traceries of fern and water fowl. They were opened slightly, letting in a soft diffuse glow of city light cut into fragments by the wind-stirred leaves of ancient trees; it smelled of water, stone, and frangipani blossoms, and the air was just warm enough to make nakedness comfortable.

"Congratulations, Mistis . . . again," the serf said.

Yolande shook her head wordlessly; it had been a perfect evening, after a stone bitch of a week shuttling from one debriefer to the next and wondering what the Board would say. Her mind still glowed from the impossible beauty of Gerraldson's music . . . *Why* had he killed himself, at the height of his talent? Why had Mozart, for that matter? And this mission, it was the *perfect* opportunity, for so many things. She rolled onto one elbow and watched Jolene. The serf was sitting on a stool before the armoire, brushing out her long loose-curled blond mane, dressed in a cream silk peignoir that set off the fine-grained ebony of her skin. And also showed off the spectacular lushness of her figure; the black serf had filled out a little without sagging at all. The Draka grinned.

"You pick out a father fo' the new baby, Mistis?" Jolene asked. "That nice Mastah Markman?"

Yolande chuckled. "No, not this time. We're giving it a raincheck fo' a while, different postin's." Teller had been a good choice for an affair; interesting and friendly without trying to get *too* close. "Myfwany's brother agreed to release sperm from the Eugenics banks when I asked. As fo' you, wench, you just miss the variety." She and Teller had tumbled Jolene together a few times, and the wench had been enthusiastic.

"Mmmh." Jolene said, meeting her owner's eyes in the mirror as her hands brushed methodically. "It was nice." More seriously: "Nice to see yo' smilin' agin, Mistis."

Yolande shrugged, sighed. "Ah, well . . . You can only grieve so long. Gwen deserved better, little enough she sees of me." Work could keep you busy, hold the pain at bay until it faded naturally; work and the things of daytime. Nights were worst, and the moments when the protective tissue seemed to fall away and everything came back raw and fresh. "Grief dies, like everythin' else." For a moment, her mind was beyond the walls, under the unwinking stars. *Except hate. Hatred is forever, like love.*

Jolene rose, arranged the armoire table, bent to pick up the gown and fold it, swaying and glancing occasionally at the Draka out of the corner of her eyes. Yolande watched with amusement, lying on her stomach with her feet up and her chin in her hands.

"Oh, fo'get the play-actin' and come here, wench," she said. "I know what you want." Jolene sank down on the padded edge of the bed and Yolande knelt up behind her, reaching around to open the buttons of the silk shift and take the serf's breasts in her hands; she traced her fingers over the smooth warmth of them and up to Jolene's neck, down again to tease at the pointed nipples. Her own desire was increasing, a soothing-tingling whole-body warmth.

"Mmmm feels nice . . . Mistis? *Mmm—*" as Yolande ran her tongue into the other's ear. "Mistis, you picked the brooder yet?"

"Freya, you feel good. Up fo' a second." She drew the garment over the serf's head and tossed it aside. "You first. The brooder? No, I'll look at the short list when we get back to Claestum." There were always plenty of volunteers to carry a Draka child; it meant a year of no work and first-rate rations at the least, often the chance of promotion to the Great House, personal-servant work or education beyond birth-status. Being a child-nurse as well as brooder was a virtual guarantee of becoming a pampered Old Retainer later. "Lie down."

The serf lay back and Yolande straddled her, running her hands from the black woman's knees up over thighs and hips, circling on the breasts and starting over. Jolene arched into it, squirming and making small relaxed sounds of pleasure. Yolande savored the contrasting sensations, the firm muscle overlaid with a soft resilient layer of fat. *Not flabby, but so different from a Draka*, she thought.

"You do this with the brooder, Mistis?" Jolene asked through a breathy chuckle.

"Maybe," Yolande said, running her fingernails up the other's ribs. That brought a protesting tickle-shiver. "If she's pretty an' willing'. I'm goin' pick her for hips, health, an' milk, not fuckability."

She leaned herself forward slowly, until they were in contact, hips and stomach and breasts, then kissed her. *Mint and wine*, she thought languidly. There were times when this was *exactly* what you wanted: friendly, slow and easy. It might be the crèche training, but with Jolene she always felt affection without the risk of the wench getting excessively attached, which was embarrassing and forced you to hurt them, eventually.

"Mhhh . . . I'd . . . I'd like to do it, Mistis," Jolene said. "Have you baby."

Startled, Yolande rose up on her hands and looked down into the other's face. "Why on earth?" she said. The movement had brought her mound of Venus into contact with the serf's, and she began a gentle rocking motion with her hips; the other slipped into rhythm.

"I . . . like babies, Mistis."

"Hmmm. Up a little harder. You can have you own, anytimes; take a lover or a husband, I don't mind."

"Thanks kindly, Mistis, not yet. I hopes to travel with you sometimes, see them faraway places. But you away lots next little while. An' . . . well, you knows I gets friendly with Marya? No, not like this, just she don' have many to talk to. Other Literates at Claestum sort of standoffish, 'specially with her." Yolande winced slightly, remembering her early treatment of the wench. It would mark Marya with dangerous misfortune, in the eyes of most.

"Then, she don't have much to talk about *with*, with the unClassed." The vast majority on a plantation, illiterate and forbidden even the most limited contact with information systems.

"Marya good with babies, but Gwen gettin' to be a holy terror; we kin"—she ran her hands down her owner's flanks, gripped her hips to increase the friction of the slow grind—"kin help each othah. 'Sides," she said, raising her mouth to the Draka's breasts, "I like the idea."

"Mmmm. All right, I'll take you in to the Clinic and have you seeded. Now shut up an' keep doin' that."

✧   ✧   ✧

Bing. The bedside phone. Yolande raised her mouth from Jolene's. "Shit." *Bing. Bing. Bing.* "It isn't goin' away." Not that it was all *that* late, she had only been back from the Amphitheater two hours.

Her left hand went to the touchplate, keying voice-only. Her right stayed busy; not fair to stop now. "Yes?" she said coldly.

"Uncle Eric here." An older man's voice, warm and assured. "If I'm not interrupt—"

Jolene shuddered and stiffened, crying out sharply once and then again.

"Ah, even if I am, niece, I've got a gentleman here I think you'd like to meet an' some matters to discuss. Half an hour in the study? Strictly informal."

"Certainly, Uncle Eric," Yolande said, breaking the connection. "Senator, possibly Archon-to-Be, war hero, Party bigwig, darlin' of the Aerospace Command, he-who-must-be-obeyed by new-minted Cohortarchs, *shit*," she muttered, looking down. Jolene was smiling as she lay with her eyes closed, panting slightly. "Got to go fo' a while, sweet wench," the Draka said.

Jolene's eyes opened. "Half an hour, the bossman said," she husked, swallowing. "Five-minute shower, five minutes fo' a loungin' robe and sandals. Ten-minute walk; that leaves ten minutes. No time to waste, Mistis-sweet, you just lie back there an' put you legs over my shoulders."

Yolande threw herself back and began to laugh. *I wonder*, she thought in the brief moment while thought was possible, *I wonder what he has to say?*

The study was book-lined, with the leather odor of an old well-kept library; there was a long table with buffel-hide chairs, and another set of loungers around the unlit hearth. A few pictures on the wall: old landscapes; one priceless Joden Foggard oil of Archona in 1830 with a smoke-belching steamcar in front of this townhouse, a nude by Tanya von Shrakenberg. A few modern spacescapes. The doors to the patio had been closed, and the room was dim; a house girl was just setting a tray with coffee and liqueurs on the table amid the chairs. There were three men waiting for her. Uncle Eric; nearly sixty now, and looking . . . not younger, just like a very fit sixty: the hatchet-faced von Shrakenberg looks aged well. His eldest, Karl, thirty-six and a Merarch already, like a junior version of his father with a touch of his mother's rounder face and stocky build; also with more humor around his eyes.

They rose, and she saw the third man was still in evening dress rather than the hooded *djellaba* robes she and her hosts were wearing. A rather unfashionable outfit, brown velvet with silver embroidery on the seams and cuffs, and a very conservative lace cravat. An unfashionable man, only fifty millimeters taller than she, broad-built and bear-strong; you could see that he might turn pear-shaped in middle age among any people but Draka. A hooked nose, balding brow, and a brush of dark-brown beard.

"Greetings," she said politely, gripping his wrist. "Service to the State."

"Glory to the Race," he replied; the return grip was like a precisely controlled machine. His accent was Alexandrian, like the Board chairman this morning, but with a human pitch and timbre. And a hint of something else, unplaceable.

"Doctor Harry Snappdove, my niece, Cohortarch Yolande Ingolfsson," Eric said, with a smile at her well-concealed surprise. "I am on the Strategic Planning Board, Yolande," he said.

They all sank into the chairs; the house girl arranged the refreshments and left on soundless feet.

"I felt," her uncle continued, "that it was time you and I started . . . talkin' occasionally on matters of importance, beyond the purely social."

His voice was genial as they sipped at the chocolate-almond liqueur, and the other two turned politely toward her, but for a moment Yolande felt as tense as she had before the Appointments Board. Then the mellow contentment of her body forced relaxation on her mind, and she sent a thought of silent gratitude to Jolene.

"Hmmm. Ah, Uncle . . . am I to presume I'm bein' invited into the infamous von Shrakenberg Mafia?" The factional struggles within the Party had been getting fiercer these last few years, and it was well-known who led the controlling circle of the Conservative wing.

Eric laughed soundlessly. "Wotan, are they still callin' it that?" Seriously: "You're reaching the point where political commitments become necessary." Yolande nodded slightly; that was *almost* true. The Domination had never been able to afford real nepotism; you had to have plenty of raw talent to get promoted. Still, it had never *hurt* to have family and Party connections.

"The Party is going to split soon," he continued. Yolande felt a cold-water shock at the casual tone, the equally casual nods of the other two. The Draka League had always been there in the background of her life, like the atmosphere.

"How?" she asked.

"Oh, along the present factional lines. About thirty percent to my Conservatives, maybe twenty to twenty-five to Gayner and her Militants, the rest to the Center group; the Center will pick up what's left of the other parties, the Rationalists and so forth. Melinda"—she thought for a moment before realizing he must mean Melinda Shaversham, the present Archon—"hates the idea; she'll probably end up with the rump, the Center, and try to hold things together. The Center have the largest numbers, but they're short on organization an' leadership. We'll prob'ly have an unofficial Center-Conservative coalition, for a while at least. The long-term struggle will be fo' the Center's constituency."

"Well, if you lookin' fo' my vote, Uncle Eric," she began dubiously. He shook his head.

"Somethin' far mo' fundamental, Yolande." He paused, looking down into his glass for a moment. "One thing the Militants *don't* lack, it's leadership: McLaren, Terreblanche, and Gayner. A thug, a loon, and a loony thug, but *smart*."

"Call themselves Naldorists, don't they?" she said.

Karl's snort matched his father's. "Naldorssen's been dead since 1952," he said decisively. "The Militants just wave her name, since we've all had her Will-to-Power philosophizing shoved down our throats in school."

"Well, son, she did put it mo' coherently than Nietzsche, even the formulations he made after he migrated to the Domination and calmed down," Eric said charitably. "And the Militants do have a point. All that *trans-human* stage of evolution thing was mystical drivel when Naldorssen made it up, back when. With modern biocontrol, it could happen." His mouth twisted slightly. "Under the *adjustment to circumstances* mealymouthin', what the Militants have in mind is reorganizin' the human race on a hive-insect specialization model."

"Gahh," Yolande said. *Maybe I should have been following public affairs more carefully.*

"Bad biology, too," the professor said. "The hive insects haven't changed an iota in seventy million years."

Karl laughed sourly. "Precisely Gayner's definition of success. Not surprisin'; the ice bitch's never had an original idea of her own, anyways."

"But we live in a more challenging environment than insects do," Snappdove mused. "And . . . intelligence doesn't necessarily imply a self-conscious individual mind, y'know. Let the Militants get in control for three, four generations, and it'd be a positive disadvantage, even for the Race. We'd end up as empty of selfhood as ants."

"Loki on ice," Yolande said, alarmed. "I *have* been out of touch. Well, off Earth an' busy. Don't tell me the electorate is buyin' this?"

"Not directly, but then the Militant inner circle aren't spellin' it out in those terms," Eric said. "And it appeals to our national love of unchanging stasis, and the basic Draka emotion." Yolande looked a question. "Fear."

"Oh, come now, Uncle—"

"Why else would we have backed ourselves into this social cul-de-sac?" He rolled the liqueur glass between his hands. "Ever since the Landtaking, we've been in the position of a man runnin' downhill on a slope too steep to stop; got to keep going, or we fall on our face an' break our necks. Individual relationships aside, don't delude youself that the serfs as a group like us as a group. They don't. Why should they? We enslave them, drive them like cattle; because if we did any different, they'd overrun and butcher us."

Yolande looked from side to side, not a conventional gesture but genuine alarm.

"Don't worry," her uncle said dryly. "This place is swept daily by technicians personally loyal to me. It works, or I'd be dead."

"Well . . ." Yolande gathered her thoughts. "It's true, some aspects of the way serfs are treated is . . . unfo'tunate." She remembered deeds of her own. "I gathah you'd like to increase the scope of those reforms you've introduced, the serf tribunals an' such?"

Eric nodded. "Yes; but those are strictly limited. Administrative measures, really. They regularize the way serfs treat serfs . . . perhaps not so minor a mattah, since we use serfs fo' most of our supervisory work. It's certainly improved morale and efficiency, among the Literates . . . and they *still* provide the headhunters with the most of they work. An ex-slave in America once said that a badly-treated slave longed fo' a good master, and a slave with a good master longed to be free . . . Not *entirely* true, thank Baldur the Good, or even mostly, but often enough to be worrisome. No, the *long-term* solution is to eliminate or reduce the fear. Do that, make the Citizen caste absolutely sure they're not in danger from the serfs, an' genuine reform becomes possible.

"You see," he continued, leaning forward with hands on knees. The dim glowlight outlined the craggy bones of his face. "You see, an outright slave society like ours is a high-tension solution to a social problem. Extreme social forms are inherently unstable; ours is as unviable as actual democracy, because it's as unnatural. It's too far up the entropy gradient. We have to *push*, continually, to keep it there. Remove the motive of fear and necessity an' the inherent human tendency to take the path of least resistance will modify it. Eventually—perhaps in a thousand years—we'd have . . . oh, a caste society, certainly, an authoritarian one, perhaps. But somethin' mo' livable fo' everybody than this wolf-sheep relationship we have now. A better way out than Gayner's bee-hive, fo' certain. That's almost as bad as annihilation."

"Leavin' us Citizens as sheepdogs instead?" Karl asked rhetorically.

Eric grinned at his son. "Don't quote me back at mahself, boy. But yes, the human race will always need warriors and explorers, leaders even."

Yolande paused, picked up a brandied chocolate truffle and nibbled on it. "Uncle, with all due respect, Ah don't see *how* you could remove the necessity fo' strict control. It's been . . . well, the root of everythin'. Except by turnin' the serfs into machinery o' ghouloons."

Eric's grin became almost boyish. "We use *go-with*, on the Militants," he said. Yolande frowned in puzzlement; that was an unarmed-combat term, a deception ploy which used an opponent's weight and strength against themselves.

"You've been in contact with the Eugenics people, fo' your daughter?" She nodded.

"The Militants thought they'd fought through a favorable compromise, a first step. We suckered them. Look—what are the biocontrollers removin' from the serf population? It'll take centuries more than the changes they're making in the Race, but what? Not intelligence; they're *increasin'* that, by eliminatin' the subnormal. Not creativity; Loki's tits, we don't *know* what causes that an' I suspects we never will, same as we'll never have a computer that does mo' than mimic consciousness. We're just removin' . . . that extra edge of aggressiveness that makes a warrior, from the subject races. We all know serfs that be no menace however free we let them run, right?"

"And Draka who aren't much mo' dangerous," Karl laughed.

Eric acknowledged it with a nod. "So, eventually . . . no fear. Not that the serfs would be without bargainin' power; they'll still outnumber us by eighty to one, and we'll still be dependent on them . . . but we could let the balance shift *without bein' terrified it'd shift all the way.* And *think* of what we could do if we didn't have to keep such tight clamps on their education an' such!"

Snappdove made a vigorous gesture of assent. "Better evolutionary strategy than Gayner's," he said. "More flexible. Couldn't count the number of species that've hit extinction by being overspecialized. Not that specialization's altogether bad, have to strike a balance."

She sipped at the drink again. Silence stretched into minutes. "Uncle Eric . . . Senator . . . you've always been good to me, and honest with me. I'll be honest with you; it sounds good, and mo' or less what I've been thinkin', though I haven't articulated it. I've Gwen's future to think of, and my other children. But on foreign policy, as I understand it, the Militants stand fo' absolute, well, *militancy.* And that's my position, too. I . . . have reasons." She stopped, feeling her own fragility.

"Oh, so do we," Karl said.

"Absolutely. Political equations don't figure as long as the Alliance is in it," Snappdove rumbled, combing his beard with his fingers. "Adds too much tension and anxiety."

"Yes, I'm afraid so," Eric sighed. "I wish . . . well, we live as we must, and do what is necessary. Our prim'ry obligation is to our descendants, aftah all. As to the Yankees . . . we'll probably have to kill most of them." He set his glass down. "Gods, how sick I am of killin'!"

"I'm not," Yolande said grimly. To herself: *Is there anything I value more than revenge?* Gwen, perhaps . . . A ghost opened green eyes at the back of her mind and whispered. *Don't borrow trouble, 'Landa-sweet. Or torment yourself with decisions you don't need to make.*

"Which brings us to the secondary mattah of Task Force Telmark IV," Eric said. "Incidentally, Arch-Strategos Welber is one of us."

Us, Yolande thought. *So we make irrevocable decisions, without a spot you could stop and say—"Here. Here I did it."* She shivered slightly; the trip to Archona had been difficult enough when only an Appointment Board was at stake. Now she had joined a political cabal, and Draka politics was a game played by only one rule: rule or die.

"We—the inner circle of the Conservatives, that is—want to win the Protracted Struggle very, very badly. In the interim, we've got to be seen to *wage* it effectively; one hint of softness an' the Militants will be over us like flies on horseshit. This *is* an impo'tant mission. I think you can handle it. Wouldn't have recommended you fo' it, otherwise."

A wolf's expression. "Doesn't hurt that you a von Shrakenberg relation, from the Landholder class . . . and have been seen extensively in my company these past days. Politically profitable glory fo' all. If you win, that is. Fail, and it's a setback fo' me." *And a disaster for you, girl,* went unspoken between them.

"M-ha," Snappdove said. "Very important. If that object's what we think, our materials problems in the Earth-Moon area will be solved for the better part of a decade, *without* having to cut back on anything. By which time the outer-system projects will be on-line. Finally."

"We were over hasty," Karl agreed. "Whole space effort has been.

Those early scramjets, they were deathtraps." He shook his head. "Both sides. The Yankees kept trying to model the airflows with inadequate computers, and *we*, we built a gigawatt of nuclear power stations, used the whole Dniester for cooling, to get that damned Mach-18 quarter scale wind tunnel. And we *still* had disasters."

Snappdove spread his hands. The gesture triggered something in Yolande's memory, and suddenly she could place the overtone to his accent—East European. His family must be one of the rare elite given Citizen status after the conquest. Scientists, mostly; that would explain a good deal.

"We needed the lift capacity, if we were to develop near-space in time," he said ruthlessly. "The only other way to orbit was rockets, and they are toys. Even those first scramjets could carry six tonnes to orbit; now they're up to fifty."

"The early pulsedrives were almost as bad," Yolande said. "We lost a lot of brave people, using them in the outer system."

Snappdove smiled at her, and to her astonishment began quoting poetry. Hers: *The Lament for the Fallen who Fall Forever*, part of the *Colder Than the Moon* collection. It had used a literary conceit, a fantasy, that the quick-frozen bodies retained a trickle of consciousness in their supercooled brains:

> "And those graveless dead drift restless
> In the emptiness of space
> Who died so far from love and home
> And the blue world's warm embrace . . ."

"But now those problems are largely solved," he continued. "What remains is engineering. Wonderful engineering, though!" He warmed, eyes lighting. "Perhaps that is why we of Technical Section support the good senator . . . Did you know we have funding for the first Beanstalk project, now?"

"Ah?" Yolande said. That *was* news. "Where?"

"Titan!" He made the spreading-hands gesture again at her raised eyebrows. That was a cutting-edge project, lowering a cable from geosynchronous orbit and using it to run elevators to the surface. Daring, to put it on one of the moons of Saturn. . . .

"Logical," the professor insisted. "The gravity there, that is nothing, only .14 G, but the atmosphere is thicker than Earth's, and the problems of operating on the surface horrendous—lasers or mass-drivers out of the question. But a Beanstalk that gives us even *cheaper* transit, and once we do—nitrogen, methane, ethane, hydrogen cyanide, all types of organic condensates! It will take nearly a decade, but even so, once completed we can pump any desired quantity of materials downhill to sunward. Better we had concentrated on Saturn's moons in any case; the distance is greater but the environment less troublesome than Jupiter." The giant planet had radiation belts that were ferociously difficult even with superconductor-magnetic shielding.

"Energy would be a problem, wouldn't it?" Yolande speculated. *This is part of the bait*, she thought without resentment, looking at her uncle sidelong. *They know my dreams.* That was politics, and the dream was shared.

"Well," Eric said easily, "there we've taken a tip from the Yankees. Here, look at this."

He slid a folder of glossy prints across the table to her. She flicked through them rapidly. They were schematic prints for some large construction; zero-G, or it would have collapsed. Circular, with two—large railguns?—at either side.

"What is it?" she said.

"Somethin' the Yankees fondly believe is secret," Eric said, then glanced at his son. "Need to know," he added.

The younger man rose. "Goodnight, all," he said cheerfully. "I've got company waitin', anyhows. Less intellectual but mo' entertainin'.'"

Eric waited, then continued. "Example of how it's easier to do things in space," he said. "We *still* haven't got a workin' fusion reactor here on Earth. This is one—in a sense. Big empty sphere with heat exchangers an' superconductor coils in the shell. Throw two pellets of isotopic hydrogen in through the railguns, *splat*. Beam heat at the same time. Hai, wingo, fusion."

"Ahmmm," Yolande said thoughtfully. "Sounds like what we're plannin' fo' the next-generation pulsedrive." A pause. "Crude, though, as a power source. Mo' like what we'd do. And why do they need nonsolar power sources in the Belt?"

"Yes," Snappdove said. "Patented brute-force-and-massive-ignorance method, very Draka . . . but it will work. Even useful for industry—the sun is fainter out there, microwave relay stations for the power . . . also typical of our methods. Here." He pulled out another of the prints, showing a long rectangle of some thin sheet floating against the stars. "And what our sources in the Belt say is being subcontracted for."

She read the list. "Superconductor coils . . . wire . . . *tungsten?*"

"Linear accelerators," Snappdove said. "Not for mass-driving, not for research. Antimatter production."

Yolande blinked. "Is it possible?" she said. "I thought . . . wasn't there an accident, a whiles back?"

"TechSec facility in the Urals." Eric nodded. "Equivalent of a megatonne sunbomb. Discouraged us no end. Engineerin' problems in laser coolin' and magnetic confinement, but antimatter is an old discovery on a laboratory scale, back as far as the 1930s. Mo' sensible to do it in space, though. Question is, why so secret?"

"Weapons?" she thought aloud.

"What point? We've *already* got weapons mo' powerful than we dare use here on Earth. Oh, yes, tactically useful in deep space. Even better as a propulsion system, if'n it can be managed, the ultimate rocket, yes. Still, it's puzzlin'. This has to be a long-term project, an' expensive as hell. The maximum security approach makes it even *mo'* expensive an' slow. Fifteen years even to start on large-scale production. Probably mo'; it's doable but all sorts of problems. They'd put it in the Belt, certainly." The Alliance was encouraging "homesteading" there by every means possible. "We're goin' to deuterium-tritium fusion pellets fo' pulsedrives soon, then deuterium-boron 11. That's almost as efficient, all charged particles. They can't be goin' to this much trouble just to build a better pulsedrive fo' warships."

Snappdove snorted. "We have a pilot project, at the Mercury-Shield Platform." That was a research settlement orbiting in the innermost planet's shadow. "Developing a plan to mass-produce solar power farms for near-sun use. Easily adaptable to powering antimatter production, perhaps early next century. We do the usual, wait for the Yankees to solve the tricky problems, steal their development, rejig it for our needs. They get a little ahead but not much."

"So it *can't* be just what it seems," Eric said grimly. "Not just a power source for Belt settlement, not just a try fo' better drives. There's a *big* secret here. The sort that I have nightmares about, knowin' some of our big secrets."

"Well . . . yes, Uncle Eric, but what's *my* part in it? Thought the High Command was sendin' me to grab a rock?"

"Aha," Eric said, with a mirthless laugh. "A rock comin' from fairly close to where a lot of Alliance personnel have been *goin'*. And not comin' back, never. Now, we have information on a launch . . ."

Chapter Thirteen

EARTH ORBIT
PLATFORM FRONTIER FIVE
ALLIANCE SPACE FORCE
MAY 6, 1982

Earth turned beyond the dome like a giant blue shield streaked with the white of clouds, glowing softly with an intense pale light. The western coast of North America was on the edge of vision, turning toward night, and the sunlight glittered on the ocean through a scattering of cirrus. There were scattered spots of light across the surface, above the last azure haze of atmosphere, moving or drifting in orbit. Spidery cages of aluminum beam extended in every direction in a latticework that linked powersails, broadcast rectennae, machinery of less obvious purpose. Further out were docking arms of tubing connected to the main pressure modules behind them; two held passenger scramjets, long melted-looking delta aircraft, featureless save for the big squarish ramjet intakes under the rear of their lifting-body shapes.

It was an old story to Frederick Lefarge. He twisted in the air to watch his wife's face instead. *How did I ever luck out like this?* he thought. The pale chill-blue light washed across the hazel-green of her eyes, the mahogany hair and olive-bronze skin. Tears glistened at the corners of her eyes.

"Listen," she said softly. Her voice had an accent that was a blend of her mother's South Carolina drawl and her father's Spanish-Mayan; soft and lilting at the same time. "You can hear it."

"What?" he said.

"The music of the spheres," she answered, then scrubbed the back of her hand across her eyes.

A bell pinged. "All passengers, flight Hermes 17A, forty minutes to final call. Forty minutes to final call."

"Damn, I wish you'd change your mind," he said fiercely.

"Honey," she replied, smiling. "How many times have we been over this? I wouldn't be anything but a burden for the next month; need-to-know, remember?"

650

She nodded to the scattering of people on the floor and sides of the domed lounge. Lefarge felt the familiar vertigo-inducing twist of perception, and now he was looking *down* with the great curve of Earth above his head. A ground ape's fear of falling passed through him unnoticed, and he studied the others. Several dozen. You could tell the Space Forcers and old stationjacks, and not just by their clothing; to them a floor was just another wall, and they used the ripstick pads on feet and knees and elbows to negotiate their way with innocent disregard for orientation. You never saw them drifting free without a handhold, either, like that hapless woman wearing a sari of all things, thrashing in midair until a crewman anchored a line from the reel at his belt and leaped out to her.

Most of the rest were those who would be leaving on the *Pathfinder*. Forty of the eighty, come for a last look at the home that none would see again for years, many never again. The majority were young, more than half men, technical workers of every type. He saw tears, laughter, raucous good humor, nervous excitement among the handful of children. There was a scattering of older folk, married couples solemn with the thought of what this meant. His own two daughters were already aboard the *Pathfinder*, sleeping in their cocoon-cribs in Cindy's cabin. His stomach twisted at the thought.

"You'd be aboard a warship, if you waited," he said.

Cindy sighed. "Honey, it's important I get to know some of the project people without . . . well, without you around." There were a dozen recruits for the New America project aboard, the rest were leaving at Ceres. *But only one who has any inkling of the* real *project*, he thought. *In time, in time. Patience.*

His wife was continuing: "Free people don't like living under War Emergency Regulations, Fred. For things to work right, they've got to *want* them to work right, and for that they've got to see you as a human being, not some all-powerful bureaucrat. What better way than to get to know your wife and children, on a three-month voyage? There's only a few thousand people in the whole *Belt*, darling, and a few hundred on the Project. We're going to be a *real* small town for a long while." Quietly. "Let me do my part for this too, Fred."

Cindy was cleared for the third-level version of the Project, but he suspected she had guessed more.

"It isn't *safe*," he said.

"Darling, it's *safer* than coming out on the cruiser. It's been years since there was a clash in the Belt, isn't it? And the only incidents have been between warships."

He ran a hand through his hair, sighed. "Okay, okay, you convinced me before. The only thing the Snakes have scheduled is an expedition out to Jupiter, anyway." Pulsedrive warships were still not common, and mostly very fully occupied.

"And we *will* get to Ceres about the same time," she continued with gentle ruthlessness. His ship would be leaving much later, but the *Ethan Allen* was a new-launched pulsedrive cruiser, vastly more powerful. This would be her shakedown trip, in fact.

"All right, Cindy! I just hope Captain Hayakawa understands how important a cargo he's hauling."

They linked hands, and she pulled herself closer, putting an arm around his waist and her head on his shoulder. The hair that drifted up around his nose was short-cropped (nothing else was practical in zero-G), but it shone in the Earth-light, smelling faintly of Colorado Mist shampoo and flowers. Her gaze went back out to the curve of the planet above.

"Well," she said, "he *is* carrying part of something precious." At his glance, she added: "Hope, for our tired old mother there. Up here, where there's room to breathe." She dimpled. "Even if there isn't much air . . ."

"You're a romantic," he laughed. Somberly. "And the Snakes are here, too."

She nodded. "Like our shadows," she said, sadly. "Or like an ancient set of armor with nothing inside but a corpse that's rotting and pitiful and thinks it's alive, walking and clanking and killing and trying to eat . . ."

"For a nice person, you've got a way with images," he said, shivering slightly at the thought. It was appropriate, though. The Domination was something that *should* have died a century ago. *And it's my job to bury it*, he thought as they turned and braced their feet against the crosswire.

"Gently does it, honey," he said.

They pushed off, floating down the ten meters to the deck; he kept his arm around Cindy's waist as they twisted end-for-end and landed. The ripstick on their slippers touched down on the catch-surface of the floor, with a *tack* sound as the miniature plastic hooks and loops engaged. The crew supervisors from the *Pathfinder* were shepherding their passengers into one of the radial exitways. As they passed the dogged-open pressure door, he had another flash of twisted perspective, and now they were at the bottom of a long well five meters broad, lit by strips, with handholds in regular receding rows. It was lined with close-cropped green vines, part of the air system, and a contribution to the eternal rabbit protein of the spacer's diet. The joke was that you shouldn't leave gravity if you couldn't face rodent.

Or there was fish, of course. Frontier Five had a *big* watertank, like most industrial-transit stations with a population over a thousand; all you had to do was take a multitonne lump of Lunar silicon and point mirrors at it, inject some gas and continue to heat. *Voila*, as Maman would say. An aquarium, a convenient heat-sink regulator and fuel store. You could rent a facegill and go swimming there, if you didn't mind sharing the water with trout and carp . . . the *other* inevitabilities of life in space . . .

Why am I thinking about this? he asked himself as they passed a junction and caught a main-tube beltway. Cindy snuggled closer as they rode the strip of conveyor. Incoming traffic passed them on the left, and there was another set above. They could see the heads of the passengers whipping by three meters beyond. *Because it's a distraction, that's why*, he thought.

The departure lounge was thronged. Most of the exit docking tubes led to the thrice-daily Luna shuttles, off to the moon settlements of Freetown and Britannia, and New Edo. One of the larger tubes had a rosette of four MPs in Space Force blues hanging around it; they snapped his colonel's bars a salute, and the three men eyed Cindy with respectful appreciation.

Washington and *Simon Bolivar* were in, he remembered, downlined with skeletal crews for new thrust plates and repairs to their drive feed systems. The *Ethan Allen* was up at one of the L-5 battle stations, doing final calibrations on her drive and getting the auxiliary comps burned in; it was policy to keep as much of the deep-space fleet as possible away from Earth. Too many heavy lasers and beam weapons between here and the moon, too many missiles and hardened launchers, too many sensors. A warship needed room to be effective . . .

Another exit, with the circular railing guard and a crewwoman in Trans-American silver. Briefly, his mouth quirked; the early skinsuits had been that color, for insulation. Someone had wanted to call the Space Force the Silver Service, back then, until a tabloid came up with the inevitable "Teapots in Space" headline. The display beside her was flashing: FLIGHT HERMES 17A—TRANS-AM SHIP PATHFINDER—NOW BOARDING FOR CERES.

"This is it," he husked.

Cindy stood for a moment, then seized him in a grip that nearly tore him loose from the deck. "I'll miss you, honey," she whispered, her forehead pressed into his chest. "*Vaya con dios, mi corazon.*" Tears drifted loose, glinting like minor jewels; one landed on his lips, tasting of salt.

"I'll miss you and the tykes, too," he said, his own voice a little husky. Stepping back, he held her hands for a moment. "Go on then, have them all charmed silly by the time I get to Ceres!" he said.

"Will do, Colonel, sir," she said, smiling and wiping at her eyes with a tissue. She put a hand on the rail and stepped over, pulling herself down the access tube feet-first to keep him in view a moment longer.

"Shit," he whispered to himself, as she passed out of sight.

CLAESTUM PLANTATION
DISTRICT OF TUSCANY
PROVINCE OF ITALY
DOMINATION OF THE DRAKA
MAY 7, 1982

"Well, Myfwany," Yolande began.

The graveyard was empty now, save for the dead and her. Gwen had come, to solemnly lay her handful of wildflowers on the turf; she was down by the bottom of the hill now, playing with Wulda, their new ghouloon. He had been expensive, but her daughter was entranced; she could hear the happy high-pitched shrieks from up here, see the girl-doll tiny with distance and perched on the transgene animal's shoulders as they romped by the car. For the rest there was silence, and the warm sweet smells of early summer in Italy: clover, wild strawberries from the hedgerows. Bees hummed among the banks of trembling iris that lined the flagstone pathways.

"Gwen's growin' like a weed," Yolande continued quietly. She was kneeling by the headstone, a simple black basalt rectangle with name and dates inlaid in Lunar titanium; she thought Myfwany would have liked that. "And gods, she's smart. I love her mo' than I can tell, sweet. Goin' to be tough and fast like you, but sunnier, I think."

She paused for a minute. You could see a long way from here, between the trunks of the big oaks and cypresses. Over the vale and the morning mist, past the terraced vineyards to the Great House shining in its gardens, into the blue-green haze of the hills beyond.

"I'm havin' a baby, by you brother Billy," she said. "Took Jolene in fo' the seeding yesterday . . . don't know exactly why she volunteered, maybe she misses you, too, darlin'." Suddenly Yolande pressed the heels of her hands to her eyes. "Oh, gods, I miss you so! I try, sweet, I try but I'm not strong like you . . . I wish you could tell me what to do." A shaky laugh, and she lowered her hands. "I know, darlin' I'm being soppy again like you used to say. Hated hearin' it then, and now I'd give mah soul to hear you rake me over the coals again. I've gotten a new command, though, love."

She rose to her feet. Her voice whispered. "And I swear, by you blood below my feet, Myfwany, I'll make them pay fo' you. Pay, and pay, and pay, and it'll still never be enough." Aloud: "Good-bye fo' now, my love. Till we meet again."

She turned to walk down the hill; there was the flight to catch. *Why don't I cry?* she thought. *Never, here. Why?*

LOW EARTH ORBIT
NEAR LAUNCH PLATFORM SKYLORD SIX
ABOARD DASCS *SUBOTAI*
MAY 23, 1982

" . . . drive systems at one hundred percent," a voice was saying in the background—the last of the checklist.

Yolande leaned back in the big crashcouch. Only the elastic belts were buckled across her skinsuit; the massive petal-like sections of the combat cocoon had folded back into the sides. The bridge of *Subotai* was dark, lit mainly by the screens spaced around the perimeter of the eight-meter circle. A dozen stations, horseshoes standing out from the walls with a crashcouch in the center, all occupied. Her own in the center portside of the axial tube, surrounded by sections of console like wedge-shaped portions of a disk. Dozens of separate screens—physical separation rather than virtual, for redundancy's sake. Light blue and green from data read-outs, pickups, graphs, and schematics.

"*Subotai* on standby," said the First Officer, Warden Fermore; she had voyaged with him before.

A screen before her flicked to the face of Philia Garren, captain of the other warship. "*Batu* on standby," she said.

"*Marius* on standby."

"*Sappho* on standby."

"*Crassus* on standby."

"*Alcibiades*, on standby."

Cargo carriers: the heart of this mission. A substantial proportion of the Domination's fast heavy-lift capacity, originally built for work around the gas-giant moons. She tapped for an exterior view. The Telmark IV flotilla was stationary a bare kilometer from SkyLord Six and perhaps ten from each other, touching distance in these terms. The armored globe of the launch station swung before her, with the 200-meter tubes of the free-electron lasers around it like the arms of a spider. The other ships . . . Yolande allowed herself a moment of cold pride at the power beneath her fingertips.

"Status, report," she said. And there was a certain queasy feeling, before any mission. Like having eaten a little too much oily food— and it was worse this time. This time *everything* was her responsibility . . .

"Time to boost, three minutes and counting," the First Officer said.

She looked at the other ships. The *Batu* was a twin of her own. Two hundred and fifty meters from the bell of the thrust plate to the hemisphere dome of the forward shield; most of that machinery space open behind a latticework stretched between the four main keel beams. The heat dumpers, running the length of the keels and the drive lasers; the long bundles that held the plutonium fuel pellets; the jagged asymmetric shapes of rectennae, railgun pods, Gatling turrets, launch tubes. And the cylindrical armored bulk of the reaction-mass tank, with the smaller cylinder of the pressurized crew zone half embedded in it. The transports were blockier, squat, similar propulsion systems but without the weapons, more reaction mass . . . A pulsedrive *could* run on just the fission reaction and the byproducts, but that was bad for the thrust plates and squanderous of fuel.

All of them clamped to strap-on boost packs, of course. It was not very nice to fire off a pulsedrive just outside the atmosphere; the EMP would destroy electronics over half a continent.

"Cleared for boost, SkyLord Six," she said

"Guidance lasers locked. All locked. Excitement phase beginning."

An amplified voice that would sound throughout the flotilla: "STAND BY FOR ACCELERATION. STAND BY FOR ACCELERATION. FIVE THOUSAND SECONDS, MAX AT ONE-POINT-SEVEN-EIGHT G. TEN SECONDS TO BURN. COUNTING."

She gripped the rests, let the fluid resilience of the couch enfold her. Far behind her back the supercooled oxygen in the strap-on booster would be subliming under the first teasing feathertouch of the station's lasers. A pulse to vaporize—

Whump. The *Subotai* massed 14,000 tonnes with full tanks; now that moved with a faint surge, growing as the magnetic equalizers between thrust plate and hull frame absorbed the energy. And another pulse to turn vapor to plasma—

WHAM*whump*WHAM—too fast to sense, building to hundreds of times per second as the lasers flickered. The exterior view showed long leaf-shaped cones of white flame below the strap-ons, and the ships were beginning to move. Weight pressed down on her chest, building; the acceleration would increase as mass diminished. It was nothing compared to flying atmosphere fighters, but it went on much longer . . . 5,000 seconds of burn. Very economical, to save their own onboard reaction mass. It was liquid O_2 and dirt-cheap here near Luna where the mines produced it as a byproduct; more precious than rubies out where you needed it, at the other end of the trajectory. Even more economical to save on the tiny plutonium-beryllium-plastic pellets that powered a pulsedrive. Full load for a Great Khan cruiser was half a million pellets, which meant *six tonnes* of plutonium.

The world had been mass-producing breeder reactors for twenty years, to fuel ships like this.

Minutes stretched, and the pressure on her chest increased. She breathed against it, watching the time blinking on half a dozen screens and remembering. Other launches; her first . . . only six years ago? Assistant Pilot Officer, then. Not *quite* a record for promotion. There had been casualties, and a massive expansion program, and not everyone wanted space assignments . . . Uncle Eric had pulled strings to get Gwen allowed up for the launch, and she had actually been quiet when they showed her the ships through the viewport; there was one who was *definitely* going to go spacer herself.

The stars were unmoving in the exterior view, but the station was dwindling. Dwindling to a point of light, against the curved shield of Earth; that shrinking to a globe. Other spots of light around it, some things large enough to be seen: station powersails, then a real solar sail half-deployed near a construction station. Ten minutes, and the planet was much smaller. The terminator was sweeping over the eastern Mediterranean. Dusk soon at Claestum. Jolene was there, with Yolande's child below her heart; she remembered holding the serf's hand in the Clinic. Pinpoint lights from the darkness over Central Asia, possibly launches from the laserlift stations in the Tien Shan. City lights. Very faint straight lines on the northern and southern edges of the Sahara; one of the few things you could see from this distance were the reclamation projects.

The moon was swelling; they would use it for slingshot effect, about an hour after the burn stopped. Back in . . . '62, it had been, she remembered how exciting, the first moon landings. Going out with Ma and Pa on the terrace at home, the servants unfolding the 150mm telescope, Ma showing her how to spot the tiny flame. The Yankees ahead—*may they rot*—but only by a few months. Strange-looking clunky little ships, hand-assembled around those first primitive orbital platforms. A dozen figures in black skinsuits and bubble helmets climbing down the ladders in dreamlike slowness to plant the Drakon banner on the moon; she had stayed up past her bedtime, glued to the viewer, and no one had objected.

"How far we've come," she murmured. *Only a single generation. Of course, we had incentive.* Ten percent of GNP for decades could accomplish a great deal.

The First Officer responded to her words rather than the meaning. "Making eight kps relative, Cohortarch," Fermore said. "Twelve hundred seconds of burn to go; then a quick whip 'round and it's a month to Mars." *Minimum burn, for pulsedrives.* And you could pick up reaction mass, at the Draka station on Phobos.

She felt the weight of the sealed data plaque over her breast. Sealed orders, and there were only six others in the flotilla who knew, of more than six hundred; she would tightbeam the course change when they were a week out. A profligate trajectory, since it was necessary to deceive the enemy until the last minute, burning fuel and mass recklessly, but the prize was worth it.

BETWEEN THE ORBITS OF EARTH AND MARS
ABOARD DASCS *SUBOTAI*
JUNE 18, 1982

The wardroom of the *Subotai* was small and cluttered; it doubled as an exercise chamber, up here just below the bowcap of the cruiser. They would be a long time in zero-G and the hormone treatments did only so much to slow calcium loss. Just now Yolande and Snappdove had it to themselves, their feet tucked into straps under a table. There was a lingering smell of sweat in the air under the chill freshness the life-support system imposed.

"Your health," Yolande said, raising her bulb and sipping lemonade through the straw. Flat, but carbonated beverages in zero-G were an invitation to perpetual flatulence. *Such are the trials we face pushing back the frontiers of the Race,* she thought dryly.

Snappdove's beard had been clipped closer, for convenience in the helmet ring of his skinsuit. "Our success!" he said, clinking his bulb against hers with a dull *tamp* of plastic. "Not to mention our wealth."

"The news good as all that?" Yolande said.

"The core samples are all in now," the scientist said. "Definitely an ex-comet, somewhat larger and less dense than we thought . . . ah, there is so much we do not know! Always we discover theory-breaking facts faster than we can make plausible theories, out here." He shook his head ruefully. "Ex-comet, or at least something that came from the outer system, sometime. Complex orbital perturbations, collisions . . . Comet, asteroid—we impose definitions on nature, but nature does not always agree."

Yolande sighed inwardly. She had not had much time to get to know the head of the expedition's Technical Section crew—they had only been here five days and he had been madly busy, but it had been enough to know that he was unstoppable. *A true natural philosopher, out of time,* she thought. *The facts entrance him because he can think about them, not necessarily because they're of any use.*

"You have a theory?" she asked.

"Hm-mm. Crude, but . . . several passes into the zone between Earth and Mars resulted in the loss of the outer layer of volatiles, various ices. The process was fairly gentle—I doubt if the object ever came within 1.1 AU of the sun—and the solid material, the organics and silicates, were not thrown off. Instead it formed a protective crust; there must have been a truly unusual amount of such heavier materials. This was through many passes, you understand. Perhaps asteroidal material was incorporated. Now, though, we have a fairly complete crust, there may be some sublimation still, but nothing drastic." The slight foreign overtone to his accent became stronger as his animation grew. "We will have to be careful; ammonia or methane could still be present."

"The composition?" she asked, reigning in impatience.

"As favorable as could be hoped!" He spread his hands. "Carbonaceous outer layer, rock and organic compounds. Under that . . . ice! Over a *billion* tonnes of ice. Dirty ice at that, many complex hydrogenated compounds. And—an additional bonus—rocky core with high concentrations of platinum-group metals. At a guess, the object *did* encounter asteroidal material. At some time, the ice softened enough that . . . well, never mind." He chuckled, and parked the drink in the air to rub his palms. "My so-aristocratic colleague, has it occurred to you that we are now very, very rich?"

Yolande blinked. *Why no, it hadn't*, she thought. "Point-oh-one percent of the value divided by . . . two hundred and thirty Citizens is that much?" A moment's pause. "Oh, I see what you means."

"Yes, indeed. This discovery will power our space-based development for half a decade."

The commander of the flotilla nodded, mildly pleased. Not that she had ever wanted for money; few Citizens did, and she less than most. Still, it would be pleasant; she was of Landholding family but not landed . . . A land grant was free, but that meant raw territory you had to spend a generation licking into shape. Nothing like the opportunities her parents had had in Europe after the Eurasian War. With *enough* money you could get one of the rare plantations for sale, or pay for someone else to oversee development. A heritage for her children; and then, it would be useful to have an Archona townhouse . . .

"Can we move it?" she added practically.

"If it is possible, my crew can do it," Snappdove said with another chuckle. "They are well motivated, even the serfs."

Glory, she supposed, as well as wealth, for the Citizens. The serfs would get the satisfaction of exercising their specialties; these would be mostly Class V-a Literates already, many crèche-trained for the military. And privileges, apartments, guarantees of education for their children. They would be eager for success, too.

"It is my ambition to get through a project without a single execution," Snappdove said, echoing her thoughts. "And yes we can move it, I think. Monomolecular coating, reflective to decrease the heat absorption. Single-crystal cable webbing. Then we set up that thrust plate—beautiful piece of work, astounding things they do with cermet composites these days—and it only has to last a month. Then *boom!* and *boom!*—we use our bombs. Earth orbit, very eccentric one but the details after that are not our concern."

She nodded. "Sounds good," she said. "Very good."

He sighed happily. "Yes, every year the size of project we can accomplish increases. Geometrically. Did I tell you, we have nearly completed the long-range feasibility study for terraforming Mars?"

Her ears pricked. For a moment, she was back on the dark beach below Baiae School, lying around the campfire and watching the moving stars and dreaming of what they would do. Myfwany . . .

"No," she said hastily. *Gods, how it sneaks up on you*, she thought dismally. *Work, more work. That's what I need.*

"Oh, yes. We float big mirrors near Mars, melt the icecaps. Much water and CO_2 there. More mirrors, increase the solar heating. Then we blow up Callisto—"

"Wotan and the White Christ!" she blurted. That was one of the major moons of Jupiter. "That's biggah than Luna!"

He nodded, and ran fingers through his beard. "But ice, only ice; much more than we need for Mars. And there is no limit to how big we may make our bombs. We drop pieces on Mars . . . comets also, if convenient. Already the atmosphere will be thicker and warmer. Water vapor increases the greenhouse effect; tailored bacteria and algae go to work cracking the oxides, the sun splits water vapor. An ozone layer. Nitrogen we get from various places, Titan . . . In a long lifetime, there is breathable air, thinner than Earth, higher percentage of oxygen. Then we build the Beanstalks, and work begins on the ecology; not my field. Many small seas and lakes, about half the surface."

His eyes stared out beyond the bulkhead. "And then we bring in serfs to till the fields . . . strange, is it not?"

"No," she said frankly. "Should it be?" For a moment she imagined condors nesting on the slopes of Martian canyons longer than continents, forests five hundred meters tall . . .

He snorted. "A matter of perspective. Me, I will buy an estate in perhaps South China, for my children. And a block in the Trans-Solar Combine, they have contracts in the project." Another shrug of the massive shoulders. "All this is moot. We must finish with the Alliance, first."

Yolande grinned. It was a much less pleasant expression than the intellectual interest of a moment before. "To business, then. Can you get me retanked on reaction mass? I ran it down somethin' fierce, matchin' velocities here."

"Oh, yes. Trivial. Do you wish water or liquid oxygen?"

"Hmm. No, we're rigged fo' O_2, we'll go with that. How long?"

"Two days for your ship, and one to rig the stills. A week for the rest of the fleet."

"Do it, then. First priority. We need the intelligence data on that Yankee ship." *And an installment payment on the debt they owe me,* she thought. *A small, small payment on a very large account.*

❖   ❖   ❖

ABOARD TRANS-AMERICAN SHIP *PATHFINDER*
EARTH–CERES
JUNE 12, 1982

The lounge of the *Pathfinder* had acquired a certain homeyness
in the month and a half of transit, Cindy decided. It was on the
second-highest of the eight decks in the pressure section, a semicircle on one side of the core tube, across from the galley and stores.
One corner was posted with drawings and projects; she and several
of the other mothers held classes for the children there, around the
terminal they had appropriated. Young Alishia Merkowitz showed real
talent in biology; she really should talk to the girl's parents . . .
There was a big viewer, but the passengers generally only screened
movies or documentaries; the sort who moved to the Belt didn't go
in for passive entertainment.

There was a group mastering the delicate art of zero-G darts, another
arguing politics. The coffee machine was going, scenting the air; it
looked odd, but you did have to *push* the water through here. A courting
couple were perched by the sole exterior viewport, but they were holding
hands, oblivious to the spectacle of the stars. Two young men were
building a model habitat from bits of plastic—scarcely a hobby, they
were engineers and had a terminal beside them for references. She could
catch snatches of their conversation: " . . . no, no, you don't have
to use a frame and plating! Just boil out the silicates, inject water,
heat and spin and the outer shell will . . ."

Dr. Takashi moved his piece. Cindy Guzman Lefarge started and
returned her attention to the *go* board.

"Oh, lordy, Doctor," she said. "You're never going to make a *go* player
of me."

"You show native talent," he said, considering the board. It was
electronic, and they were using light-pencils to move the pieces; the
traditional stones were a floating nuisance in space.

"I'm surprised you don't play the captain," she said, frowning. A
quarter of her pieces were gone . . . which still left her with more
than her opponent, who had started with a substantial handicap. But
far too many were nearly surrounded.

"Ah." He smiled; Professor of Cybernetic Systems Analysis Manfred
Takashi was a slim man, fifty, with dark-brown skin and short wiry
hair. "Captain Hayakawa is impeccably polite, but I doubt that he would
welcome social contact. Not from me."

Cindy raised her brows. "Well, he is fairly reserved. I would have
thought, though, you being Japanese—"

The professor laughed. "*Half* Japanese, my dear Mrs. Lefarge, *half*
Japanese. Even worse, half *black*."

The woman winced, embarrassed. Overt racial prejudice was rare
these days in the cities of North America, even more so in space. Of
course, some of the family in the South Carolina low country were
still unhappy about her mother's marriage to a Maya from Yucatan,
even a much-decorated naval veteran of the Pacific campaigns back
in the Eurasian War.

"Actually," the man continued, "it is an interesting change. In Hawaii it was the *Japanese* side of my heritage which created problems."

She nodded. The Imperial occupation in the early '40s had been brutal, and the angers had taken a long time to dissipate. Even now some of the older generation found it difficult to accept how important Japan had become in the councils of the Alliance.

"You must be eager to get to work, on"—she lowered her voice— "the Project." Best to change the subject.

"Indeed." He turned the light-pencil in his hands. "I—"

Tchannnng. The sound went through the hull, like an enormous steel bucket struck with a fingernail. Conversation died, and the passengers looked up.

"*Attention!*" the captain's voice. "We have suffered a meteorite impact. There is no danger; the hull was not breached. I repeat, there is no danger. All passengers will please return to their cabins until further notice."

"I must get back to Janet and Iris," Cindy said, rising briskly. She forced down a bubble of anxiety; a meteor strike was very rare—odd that the close-in radars had not detected it. "Continue the game after dinner, Doctor?"

"I hope so," he said quietly, folding the board as he stood. "I sincerely hope so."

"Distance and bearing," Yolande said.

"One hundred k-klicks, closing at point-one kps relative," the sensor officer said.

Yolande could feel the strait tension in the ship, a taste like ozone in the air. A week's travel. Overcrowded, since she had dropped off most of the ship's Auxiliaries who handled routine maintenance and taken on another score of Citizen crew from *Batu.* The main problem with Draka was keeping them from ripping at each other. Constant drill in the arcane art of zero-G combat had helped. And now action. Not that the pathetic plasma-drive soupcan out there was any menace to a cruiser, but they had to *capture*, not destroy. Much more difficult.

"Bring up the schematic," she said. They would not detect the *Subotai* for a while yet; her stealthing was constructed to deceive military sensors.

Two screens to her left blanked and then showed 360-degree views of the Alliance vessel, *Pathfinder.* A ferrous-alloy barrel, basically, the aft section holding a reaction-mass tank and a simple engine. An arc broke the mass into plasma, and magnetic coils accelerated it out the nozzle, power from solar receptors or a big storage coil. Thrown out of Earth orbit much as the *Subotai* had been, then additional boost from a solar sail. That was still deployed, square kilometers of .05-micron aluminum foil, rigged on lines of sapphire filament; but soon they would furl it and begin velocity matching for Ceres. A long slow burn; plasma drives were efficient but low-thrust.

Would have begun their burn, she corrected herself. It was odd, how vengeance always felt better beforehand than after . . . Sternly, she pushed down weakness. There was a duty to the Race here, and to her dead. If she was too fainthearted to long for it, then nobody else need know.

Yolande reached out a hand; that was all that could move, with the cradle extended and locked about her. The couch turned on its heavy circular base to put her hand over the controls. The schematic altered: command and communication circuits outlined in color-coded light. *Provided this is up-to-date—*

"When's their next check-in call?' she said.

"Five minutes."

There were no Alliance warships nearby or in favorable launch windows, but it was important not to give them more warning time than was needful. She wanted to have *Subotai* back with the flotilla long before anything could arrive; this was direct provocation, and it could escalate into anything up to a minor fleet action. Probably not. Still . . .

Her fingers played across the controls. "Here. See this rectenna? Throw a rock at it first. Time it to arrive just after they report everything normal."

"Making it so," the Weapons Officer said, keying. "Careless of them, all the com routed though that dish." A low chuckle from some of the nearer workstations.

"They like to mass-produce," Yolande said. A light blinked on one of her monitor screens, echoing the Weapons Officer's. On the outer hull a long thin pod would be swiveling.

"Monitoring call," the Sensor Officer said. "Standard garbage, messages to relatives." She paused. "Coded blip. Recordin' fo' future reference." A minute passed. "End message."

"Fire," Yolande said. A cold-flame feeling settled beneath her breastbone. The first attack on Alliance civilians since the Belt clashes.

The light blinked red. "Away," the Weapons Officer said. In the pod, two charged rails slammed together. A fifty-gram slug rode the pulse of electromagnetic force, accelerated to ninety kilometers per second. "Hit." The target would have vanished in a puff of vapor and fragments.

"No transmission from target, monitoring internal systems."

"With all due respect to ouah colleagues of the Directorate of Security," Yolande said, "I'm not takin' any chances that they got the plans exactly right. We'll cripple her first on a quick fly-by, *then* get within kissin' range. Drive, prepare fo' boost; pass at one kps relative, then decelerate an' match at five klicks. Weapons, cut the sail loose, hole the control compartment, wreck the drive." A plasma jet could be a nasty weapon in determined hands. "Cut the connections to the main power coil." There were megawatts stored in that, and if it went nonsuperconducting all of it would be converted to heat—*rapidly.* "Then we'll see."

"Odd they don' have no suicide bomb," the assistant weapons officer said, as she and her superior worked their controls.

"Too gutless," the man replied. "Ready to execute."

"Drive ready to execute."

"Make it so," Yolande said.

The speakers roared: "PREPARE FOR ACCELERATION. ALL HANDS SECURE FOR ACCELERATION. TEN-SECOND BURN. FIVE SECONDS TO BURN. COUNTING."

Somewhere deep within the *Subotai* pumps whirred. Precisely aligned railguns charged as fuel pellets were stripped from the magazines, ten-gram bundles of plutonium-239 and their reflector-absorber coatings.

"BURN."

The pellets flicked out behind the cruiser. Her lasers struck and the coating sublimed explosively, squeezing. Fission flame loomed, flickering at ten times per second. Nozzles slammed liquid oxygen into the carbon-carbon lined hemisphere of the thrust plate to meet the fire, and the gas exploded into plasma. The superconductor field coils in the plate swept out magnetic fingers, cupping and guiding the blaze of charged particles into a sword of light and energy, stripping out power for the next pulse. The thrust plate surged forward against its magnetic buffers. And the multi-thousand-tonne mass of the warship *moved*.

"Burn normal. Flow normal at fifty-seven-percent capacity. Point-nine-eight G."

"Comin' up on target. Closin'. Preparin' fo' fire mission. *Execute*."

Needles of coherent light raked across the lines that held the sail to the *Pathfinder*. The single-crystal sapphire filaments sublimed and parted in tiny puffs of vapor, but no change showed in the giant bedsheet of the sail; it would be hours before the vast slow pressure of the photon wind made a noticeable difference. It was otherwise with the *Pathfinder* itself. A dozen railgun slugs sleeted through the control chamber, and the steel-alloy outer hull rang like a tin roof under hail. The missiles punched through and out the other side without slowing perceptibly, leaving plate-sized holes; the edges shone red as air rushed past, turning to a mist of crystals that glittered in the unwavering light of the sun. Light flickered briefly within as systems shorted and arced.

Other slugs impacted the nozzle of the plasma drive, turning the titanium alloy to twisted shards. A finger of neutral particles stabbed, cut across the lines that connected the arc to the main power torus. *Pathfinder* tumbled.

"STAND BY FOR ZERO GRAVITY." The subliminal thuttering roar of the drive ceased, leaving only the quiet drone of the ventilators. "STAND BY FOR MANEUVER." Attitude jets slammed with twisting force, and the cruiser switched end for end. "STAND BY FOR ACCELERATION. EIGHTEEN-SECOND BURN. THREE SECONDS TO BURN. BURN." Longer and harder this time; they were killing part of their initial speed and matching trajectories as well. The sound was duller, more mass going onto the thrust plate.

"Matched, closin'," the Drive Officer said. The attitude jets fired again, briefly. "Stable in matchin' orbit, five-point-two klicks."

Yolande keyed the exterior visual display, switching to a magnification that put her at an apparent ten meters from the Alliance vessel. "Well done," she said to the bridge; it looked precisely as she had specified. "Ah." Flames were stabbing out from parts of the can-shaped transport, and the tumbling slowed and stopped. "Nice of him." She hit the control, and the combat braces folded away from her with a sigh of hydraulics. "Number One, boardin' party to the forward lock. Sensors?"

"She's dead in space, apart from those attitude jets. Internal pressure normal except on the control deck; that's vacuum. Doan' think much damage to internal systems."

"Weapons, connectors away."

"Makin' it so. Off."

Two of her screens slaved to the Weapons station showed a rushing telemetered view of the enemy vessel, as the tiny rockets carried the connectors. Their heads held pickups and sundry other equipment; mostly, they were very powerful electromagnets. The cables themselves were no mere ropes: optical fibers, superconductor power lines, ultrapure metal and boron and carbon, armored sheathing, the whole strong enough to support many times the cruiser's weight in a one-G field.

"Ah, human-level heat sources in the control chamber. Three, suited. Multiple elsewhere in the hull."

"Very well," Yolande said. "Maintain position, prepare to grapple when the target's secured." That was doctrine, and only sensible. The *Subotai* and her crew represented an unthinkable investment of the resources of the Race.

She rose, secured her boots to the floor. "Number Two, carry on. Boardin' party, I'll be with you shortly."

Janet had been squealing with excitement when Cindy returned to the cabin, Iris solemn and earnestly trying to remember what she had been told about emergency drills. It was still hard to believe, how different twins were; or how complete and yet alien a personality could be at five . . .

Then they both quieted, sensing her seriousness. She zipped them quickly into their skinsuits; Fred had paid out-of-pocket for those luxuries, rather than rely on bubble cocoons, and now she blessed the extravagance as she worked her way into her own. These were civilian models, little changed from the original porous-plastic leotards the first astronauts had worn. The fabric was cool and tight against her flesh, with a little chafing at groin and armpits where the pads completed the seal. She helped her daughters on with the backpacks, then checked her own; the helmets could be left off but close to hand, for now. God forbid they should have to use them, but if they did every minute could count.

"Come on, punkins," she said, guiding them to the pallet that occupied most of the sternside wall of their cubicle and strapping them in. "Mommy's going to tell you a story."

They settled in on either side of her; she had just begun to search her memory when the sound came. A monstrous ringing hail, like trip hammers in a forging mill, toning through the metal beneath and around them, like being *inside* a bell. The *Pathfinder* was seized and wrenched, the unfamiliar sensation of weight pulling at them from a dozen different directions, inside a steel shell sent bounding downhill. The locking bolts on the door shot home with a metallic clangor and even over the ringing of the hull she could hear the wailing of the alarm klaxon and the slamming of airtight doors throughout the ship. Her skin prickled.

"Mom! Mommeee!" Janet shrieked. Iris had gone chalk-pale, her eyes full circles, and her panting was rapid and breathy.

"Meteor swarm, O sweet mercy of God, let it be a meteor swarm!" she whispered under her breath. Their stateroom was the first-class model, with a porthole. The light that stabbed through it into her eyes was like mocking laughter; there was only one thing in the human universe that made that actinic blue-white light, that spearhead-shaped scar across the stars. A nuclear pulsedrive.

"Shhh, shhh, Mommy's here, darlings." She used hands and voice and quieted them to whimpering by the time the reaction jets fired and the ship shuddered back to stability. *Just in time*, she found a moment to think. *I'm feeling sick and Iris looks green.* They were all on antinausea drugs, and it took some powerful tinkering with the inner ear to override those.

The *Pathfinder* drifted and steadied. Cindy looked out the port again, blinking against the afterimage of fire that strobed across her sight, against the tears of pain. Then she jammed her knuckles into her mouth and bit down, welcoming pain to beat down the stab of desperation, the whining sound that threatened to break free of her throat. The shape that drifted model-tiny there was familiar, very familiar from the lectures she had attended before signing on with the Project—she was the Commandant's wife as well as a biologist. A Draka cruiser, the third-generation type. A Great Khan, and the only things in the solar system which could match it were a month's journey away.

Cindy Lefarge felt the world graying away from the corners of her eyes, a rippling on her shin as the hairs struggled to stand erect. Bile shot into the back of her throat, acrid and stinging as she remembered other things from those lectures. *No.* A voice spoke in the back of her mind, a voice like her grandmother's. *Y' got yore duty, gal, so do it!* She had the children to protect.

"Jannie, Iris, listen to me." The small faces turned toward her, pale blue eyes and freckles and the floating wisps of black hair. "You girls are going to have to be very brave for Mommy. Just like real grown-up people, so Daddy will be proud of you. This is really, really important, you understand?"

They looked up from where her arms cradled them against her shoulders. Iris nodded, swallowing and clenching trembling lips. Janet bobbed her head vigorously. "You bet, Mom," she said. "I'm gonna be a soldier like Dad, someday. So I gotta be brave, right?"

She pulled them closer. Twin lights sparkled from the Draka cruiser, seeming to drift toward her and then rush apart in a V. She closed her eyes, waiting for the final wash of nuclear flame, but all that came was two deep-toned *chunnng* sounds. The *Pathfinder* jerked again, rotating so that the Domination warship was out of her view. The overhead speaker came to life with a series of gurgles and squawks, then settled into the voice of Captain Hayakawa; calm as ever, but a little tinny, as if he was speaking from inside a skinsuit helmet.

"Attention, please. We have been attacked by a Draka deep-space warship. The engines have been disabled, our communications are down, and the sail has been cut loose. The main passenger compartment has not been holed, I repeat, *not* been holed. Please remain calm, and stay in your cabins. This is the safest place for all civilians at the moment. Ceres and Earth will soon detect what has happened and *SKREEKKKKAAWWK*—" The noise built to an ear-hurting squeal and then died.

Cindy Guzman Lefarge bent her head over those of her children and prayed.

"Assault party ready," the Centurion from *Batu* said.

Yolande nodded assent as she secured the straps on the last of her body armor. It was fairly light (weight didn't matter here but mass certainly did), segmented sandwiches of ablative antiradar, optically perfect flexmirror, sapphire thread, synthetics. Not quite as much protection as the massive cermet stuff heavy infantry wore on dirtside, but easier to handle. She settled the helmet on her shoulders, checked the seal to the neck ring, and swiveled her eyes to read the various displays. She could slave them to the pickups in any warrior's pack, call up information—the usual data overload.

The boarding commandos were grouped in Hangar B, the portside half of the chamber just below the nosecap of the cruiser. The Great Khans carried one eighty-tonne auxiliary, but it was stored in vacuum on the starboard, leaving B free as a workspace where systems could be brought up and overhauled in shirt-sleeve conditions. Both hangars connected with the big axial workway that ran through the center of the vessel right down to the thrust equalizers, nine-tenths the length of the ship. Now this one was crowded with the score of Draka who would put this particular piece of Yankeedom under the Yoke.

Her lips drew back behind the visor, and she slid her hand into the sleeve of the reaction gun clipped to her thigh. A faint translucent red bead sprang into being on the inside of her faceplate as she wrapped her fingers around the pistol grip, framed by aiming lines. The bulk of the chunky weapon lay rightside on her arm, connected to her backpack by an armored conduit. It was dual-purpose: a jet for short-range maneuvering and a weapon that fired glass-tungsten bullets and balanced them with a shower of plastic confetti backwards.

"Right," she said, over the command push. "Listen, people." There were certain things that had to be repeated, even with Citizen troops. "This is a raid; we want intelligence data, not bodies or loot. Go in, immobilize whoever you find, get theys up to the big compartment just rearward of the control deck. Then we'll sweep up everythin' of interest, and get out. Make it fast, make it clean, do not kill anyone lessen you have to, do *not* waste any time. Service to the State!"

"Glory to the Race!"

"Execute." There was a prickling feeling all over her skin as the pressure in the hangar dropped; nothing between her flesh and vacuum but the layer of elastic material that kept her blood from boiling—*except the woven superconductor radiation shield and the armor and the thermal layer and—oh, shut up, Yolande*, she told herself. An eagerness awoke, like having her hands on the controls of a fighter back in the old days.

The pads inside her suit inflated. Combat-feeling: a little like being horny, a little like nausea, a lot like wanting to piss. The surroundings took on the bleak sharpness of vacuum, but she knew the unnatural clarity would be there even if there was air. *Donar, I could have the suit monitor my bloodstream and* tell *me how hopped-up I am*, she thought.

The Centurion's voice. "By lochoi!"

Hers was first. "Follow me," she said, taking a long shallow dive through the hangar door. Out into the access tunnel, three meters across, a geometric tube of blue striplights and handholds two hundred meters sternward of her feet. She pointed her reaction gun toward the open docking ring over her head and pressed once. Heated gas pulsed backward; she stopped herself with a reverse jolt at the exit and swung around to face the enemy ship, adjusting perception until it was below her. The dark, slug-dented surface of the control deck swam before her eyes, jiggling with the distance and magnification. She fixed the red aiming spot on the surface and reached across to key the reaction gun.

LOCKED strobed across her vision. "Slave your rg's to mine," she told the others, crouching. It would adjust the thrust nozzle to compensate for any movement short of turning ninety degrees out of line, now. Yolande took a deep breath. "Let's—*go*."

The hull of the Alliance ship thunked dully under their boots, sound vibrating up her bones for lack of air.

"Let's take a look," she said.

"Yo." A crewman slid a long limber rod through one of the impact holes.

She called up a miniature rectangle of vision keyed to the fiber-optic periscope, fisheye distorted but it would do. Dark, with the chilly silver look of light enhancement. A drifting corpse, legs missing at the knee where flesh and skinsuit had fought a hypervelocity missile and lost badly. Grains of freeze-dried blood still drifted brown nearby. Wrecked equipment, a very elementary-looking control system, none of the fabled Alliance high technology. *Of course, they want to build these cheap and quick,* she thought. The Domination had no equivalent class of vessel; the closest were unmanned freighters. The Draka economy did not produce the same set of incentives as the Alliance's nearly laissez-faire system.

"Patch to their com," she said. A sound of voices in some Asian-sounding language; well, everybody who could have gotten a ship command would speak English. "Y'all in there," she said. "Surrender. Last chance."

Silence. She shrugged, looked up at the warrior who was preparing their entranceway, made a hand signal. That one finished drawing the applicator around the shallow dome of the spacecraft's nose.

It had left a thick trail of something that looked very much like mint toothpaste.

"Secure." They backed off, tagged lines to protuberances on the surface. The *Pathfinder* was built smooth-hulled because that eased fabrication, but there were fittings aplenty. "On the three."

"One. Two. Three."

A flash of soundless light, and the hull flexed slightly to push her up to the limit of the line. Then the cap of steel was floating away, dark against the mirror-bright surface of the sail; it would strike it, before the film could sweep away on the breeze from the Sun. The warrior nearest the giant circular hole freed a grenade from her belt and tossed it in, a flat straight line like nothing that could be done planetside. There was another pulse of light.

"Storm!" Yolande shouted, and the Draka slid forward, throwing themselves into the hole.

Thung. Yolande twirled in midleap to land feet first on the deck. A figure in a foil-covered skinsuit was thrashing, ripped by the shards from the grenade; his blood sprayed out, and she could see the scream behind his transparent bubble helmet. Her eyes skipped, jittering. Another Alliance suit, rising from behind a spindly crashcouch, something gripped in both hands. The red dot pivoted toward him, but before she could fire the man's torso exploded in a corona of red and pinkish white. The bullets from a reaction gun were tungsten monofilament in a glass sabot; they punched through hard targets, but underwent explosive deformation in soft.

"Shit," she swore, seeing the rank-tabs on the man's shoulders. "That was the captain." Yolande batted a lump of floating *something* away from her faceplate with a grimace; zero-G combat was *messy*. Two others were zipping the wounded man into an airbag and doing what crude first aid they could.

"Labushange, Melder, stay here. Pull the compcore and see if y' can patch through to log memory. Anderson, take the door." That was a hatch in the middle of the floor. "Pressure-lock it."

The warrior knelt and focused on the door, calling up a schematic to show the vulnerable spots in his faceplate. Two others peeled the covering off the base ring of a plastic tent and slapped it adhesive-down on the deck around the hatch. The lochos stepped inside, zipping it over their heads.

"Got it," Anderson grunted. "Ready?"

"Go," she snapped.

He locked his boots to the deck and pointed the gauntlet gun. It flashed twice, and translucent confetti drifted back to join the particles already rising out of the hole above their head, mixed with a haze of blood. The deck sparked with impact and glittered with a new plating of molten glass, and there was the blue flicker of discharge. Yolande kicked the lockbar of the door; it slammed down with blurring speed, and air roared in to bulge the tent over their heads.

"*Bulala!*" she shrieked, and dove through the opening into light.

✧   ✧   ✧

"Shhh," Cindy said again.

There had been sounds, clanging, shouts, screams, a sharp *ptank-tank* rapping she could not identify, even pistol shots. *I wish I had taken the gun*, she thought desperately. She had had the usual personal-defense training in school, though her National Service had been in the research branch; even the worn old high school submachine gun would have been *something* . . .

Probably just enough to get us all killed, she thought bleakly. Even worse was the knowledge that that might be the best thing.

The locking bar of the door moved a half-inch back and forth. She started, then unstraped the children and pushed them back into the farthest corner of the cabin, bracing herself in front of them with her arms across the angle of the wall. There was silence for a second, then a bright needle of flame spat from beside the door. It swung open; she had a brief glimpse of the boot that kicked it, before a thin black stick poked in. A figure bounced through two seconds afterward and stopped itself with one expert footblow against the far wall. The fluted muzzle of a weapon fastened to the right arm pointed at her; she crowded her daughters farther behind her body.

Another head came through the doorway, then a body likewise strapped around with pieces of equipment. They were both in skinsuits and some sort of flexible armor that was a dull matte black, but a line of silver brightness showed along a scratch on one's chest. She swallowed through a mouth the consistency of dry rice paper and tried to keep her face from twisting. Then they unlatched their helmets and pushed them back against their backpacks.

The first Draka she had ever seen in the flesh. For a moment she was surprised that they looked so much like the pictures. These two were both men, young, hair cropped close at the sides and slightly longer on top. One had a stud earring, the other a rayed sunburst painted about an eye—hard faces, scarcely affected by the usual zero-G puffiness, all slabs and angles, almost gaunt. The first one spoke, in a purring drawl hurtfully reminiscent of her mother's . . . No, more archaic sounding, with a guttural undertone.

"All cleah." That into the thread-and-dot microphone that curved up from the neck ring of his suit. "Yes, suh, these're the last. We'll get 'em secured an' up to the lounge."

"You," he said. "Out of the skinsuit. The picknins, too."

The words flowed over her mind without meaning. *Can't be, can't be*, was sounding somewhere inside her. *Bad movie.*

"Shit," the man said in a tired voice; it sounded more like "shaay't." He reached across to do something to the weapon, and a red dot sprang out on the wall beside her head. It settled on her forehead for a moment, then shifted to the outer surface.

Bang-ptank! A hole the breadth of her thumb flashed into existence in the steel, and there was a shower of something flakey and glittering from behind his elbow. A brief whistling of air, before the self-sealing layer in the hull blocked it off. The red dot settled between her eyes again.

"To t' count a' three, wench: One. Two—"

Trembling slightly, her hands went to the seals of her suit, then hesitated. *My god, I'm only wearing briefs under this.* The Draka made a gesture of savage impatience, and she stripped out of the clinging elastomer. "Help the picknin," he snapped.

"Come on, punkins," she said. The girls were staring enormous-eyed at the two Draka; Iris's lips were caught between her teeth as she fought rhythmically against her sobs. "We have to do what the man says."

"Mom!" Janet said, scandalized. "Those—those are *strangers!*"

The red dot settled on her daughter's face. Shoulder blades crawling, Cindy put herself between the gun and Janet, taking her by the shoulders and shaking her. "Come on, you silly girl," she forced herself to say, harshly. "Quickly."

The Draka in the doorway held up what looked like a medical injector. "Docilize?" he said to the other.

"Na, quicker if we let her handle the sprats," he said. "Don' have time to fuck around." He looked at her, up and down, and grinned. "Pity. Maybe latah." Reached out, quite casually, and grabbed her crotch.

Cindy closed her eyes and gritted teeth. Then something windmilled by her and struck the Draka with a *thump*. It was Janet.

"You bad man! Leggo my mom! Leggo!" The five-year-old was clinging to the man's harness with one hand and trying earnestly to punch him with the other, while her feet flailed at his stomach. "You let go, or I'll kill you!" Iris started to scream, shrill high-pitched sounds like an animal in a trap.

The Draka snarled, rearing his head back and raising the arm with the gun to club at Janet. Cindy felt a great calm descend as she readied herself; reach down and immobilize the left hand, strike up with the palm under his nose . . .

A hand snaked in with the injector and pressed it against Janet's side. It hissed, and the girl slumped; not unconscious, just drifting with her eyes half-closed. The Draka with the drug gun laughed and reached around her to plant the muzzle against Iris's neck.

"Dociline," he said to her as the screaming stopped. "Trank. Haa'mless." To his companion: "Let's get on with it."

She huddled back with her children as they ransacked the cabin, giving the comfort of skin against skin that was all she had to offer. The two warriors went systematically through the tiny closet and the bulkhead containers. Cindy noticed what they took: books, letters, data plaques, her new Persimmon 5 portable perscomp that Fred had got from the PX, all stuffed into a transparent holder. One of them came across her jewelry, but that went into a pouch at his belt.

"Right," the one with the face painting said when they had finished. "You. Hold out y'arms. Togethah." A loop went around her elbows, painfully tight; she could use her hands, but awkwardly. "Now, listen good. You take the picknins, an' we're goin' up to the top level. An' wench—any trouble an' we kill you spawn. Understand?" She gave a tight nod. "Go."

Cindy gathered her daughters with slow care; they had curled into fetal positions floating near her, and it would be easy to bruise them if she moved too quickly. She kicked her feet into the ripstick slippers on the floor and began to step out into the corridor. The man who had groped her earlier reached out one hand and stripped the briefs off her with a wrench as she went by.

"Later," he said.

"Is that the last of them?" Yolande asked, as the woman steered the two children into the lounge.

"Yes, ma'am," the Centurion said. "'Cept fo' the one who gave us trouble."

"Number Two," she said, "target secured. Reel her in an' run a tube over to the airlock on this level."

"Makin' it so, Cohortarch. Twenty seconds to commencement."

"Silence!" she called to the crowd of prisoners through the exterior speaker on her helmet. "Everybody brace themselfs."

There were about eighty of them, milling about at the far end of the grubby lounge. Most had been wearing skinsuits, and so were nearly stripped; she looked at them with disgust. *This is the enemy? Flabby, soft-gutted rubbish*, she thought. A few had been docilized. Those thumped painfully against the wall when the ship lurched again, and so did a few of the fully conscious ones. *Sheep.* There was an almost imperceptible feeling of sideways acceleration for a few minutes, and then the cables went slack; the *Subotai* would be backing off with her attitude jets, to reestablish zero relative motion.

"Line them up," she continued.

Her troopers moved in, prodding with their gauntlet guns. A moment of trouble from two young men, stocky-muscular; they looked like they played—what was that absurd Yankee sport? Football? A flurry of dull thudding sounds and they were against the wall with the others, one clutching his groin, the other a flattened nose that leaked blood in drifting red globules. Three more figures floated up through the central batch. A wounded Draka with a long cut through the belly section of her armor, hands to a pad over the wound, helped by a comrade. Then a prisoner trussed hand and foot. Hand and elbows, rather; one forearm ended in a frayed stump covered in glistening sprayseal, typical gauntlet-gun wound.

"What happened with *him?*" the Centurion asked.

"Had a fukkin' *sword*," the wounded Draka said, between clenched teeth. Soft impact armor gave excellent protection against projectiles, but very little against something sharp and low-velocity. "Under his pallet covers. I blew his hand off on the backswing."

"Careless," the Centurion said. There were clanging noises and voices from the background, as the tube was secured and the airlock opened on the temporary seal between the two vessels. "McReady, get her back to sickbay. Bring up the rest of the bodies."

Yolande reached up to remove her helmet, wrinkling her nose at the proof that some of the prisoners had lost control of their bowels. She looked at the one-handed man. Black-Asian, she guessed, about fifty. Wiry and strong, stone-faced under her gaze. Shock, part of that calm, but that was one with a hard soul. It would not do to underestimate them all; few of the Alliance peoples were natural warriors, but they could learn, and the Americans in particular had a damnable trader's cunning that made them capable of all manner of surprises. *I wish they hadn't brought the picknins.* She pushed the children's sobbing below the surface of her mind. Now—

Cindy forced herself to take her eyes off the raw stump of Professor Takashi's hand. She tried to imagine what that would feel like, failed, raised her eyes to his face. He was smiling; that was almost as shocking as the wound.

The Draka commander was removing her helmet. A woman, she saw without surprise. The face was huge-eyed, triangular, delicately feminine, haloed in short platinum-colored hair. Then the eyes met hers, and she shivered slightly.

"This one?" the Draka said, to the man holding Takashi.

"Cybernetic Systems Analysis," the guard said.

"Lucky fo' us you didn't get killed," the woman said genially.

The dark man shook his head, smiling more broadly. "Not so—*ah!*" he shook once, slumped. The guard cursed, felt for his pulse.

"Dead," he spat. "Must've taken something."

The commander turned back toward the prisoners. "Listen," she said, and all fidgeting died away. The voice was deliberately pitched rather low, so that they would have to strain to hear it; it was soft, naturally light, Cindy thought.

"Yo will, starting at the right, go one by one to that table." She pointed to one where a group of Draka were going through the identity documents of the passengers. "You will state you name and profession, and answer *all* other questions. Then go *back* to *that* end of the line. Understood, serfs?"

There was a rustling, and they glanced at each other. The Draka waited for a moment, then continued in a tone of weary distaste.

"Stubborn. Fools. All right . . . Who's a Yankee heah? I have a special and particular dislike of Yankees." The big eyes slid down the line. Gray, with a rim of blue. *Colder than any I've ever seen,* Cindy thought. She could almost have preferred a sadist's glazed sickness; it would be less intelligent.

The eyes settled on the Merkowitz family. A gloved finger pointed. "They two slugs look repulsive enough to be Yankees. Fetch me the pretty little bull beside them, an' make a steer of him."

A dozen of the Draka had been hanging ready by the opposite wall. Two crouched and sprang, blurring across the lounge, twisting end-for-end and landing one on either side of young David Merkowitz with balletic gracefulness; they grabbed his arms and leaped again, releasing him just before they touched down. The warriors let their legs cushion impact like springs, coiling; the teenager from Newark landed against the wall with a soggy impact. Stunned, he floated for an instant until they spreadeagled him on a table. Others moved in to hold and secure; one of the Draka reached over her shoulder and drew something as long as her forearm.

Cindy felt a glassy sense of unreality as she recognized the tool. It was a cutter bar, a thin film of vacuum-deposited diamond between two layers of crystal iron-chrome. Alliance models had the same back-ward-sloping saw teeth, although they did not come to the sort of wicked point this one did. The Draka spun the tool in the air, a blurring circle, then reached in. The hilt slapped into her palm—bravado; that edge would go through fingers as if they were boiled carrots. She raised it in mocking salute to the prisoners and swaggered over to the boy; one of those holding him had stuffed a cloth into his mouth to muffle his screams, and was holding up his head so that he could not help but see.

The Draka with the cutter bar paused, turned, slashed the edge down on a metal table frame. The steel tube parted with a ringing sound, and the woman smiled. She smiled more broadly as she pulled off the undersuit briefs, wet one finger and drew it up young Merkowitz's scrotum and penis. He convulsed and made a sound that was aston-ishingly loud; she gripped the testicles in her left and raised the knife with taunting slowness.

"No." That from the man at the head of the line. He moved for-ward toward the table with the interrogators. Cindy looked at the Draka commander, who had been hanging relaxed, smoking a cigarette and looking up at the ceiling; the American saw a slight tension go out of the enemy commander's shoulders.

"Very well," the short blond woman said. "Hold it there, cut him if any of the rest make trouble." The Draka with the cutter bar low-ered the weapon and waited, loose but alert as she faced the prison-ers. Her other hand stayed on the teenager, stroking lightly. He began to weep.

"Name."

Yolande looked aside at the prisoner. A wench in her late twenties, with two picknins floating near; the children had been shot with dociline and were just coming to, still muzzy and vague. She was ruddy-olive, quite good looking in a slimmish sort of way, spirited from the calm tone she used, which was a relief. The sniveling from some of the others had been nauseating, even for feral serfs—especially when you considered that she had not *done* anything of note to them yet. Not that this whole business was very pleasant, at all; necessary, but distasteful. *Find it easier to kill them from a distance, eh?* she thought, mocking herself. *To desire the end is to desire the means.*

"Cynthia Guzman Lefarge," the wench was saying. She was the last of them. "My daughters Janet Mary and Iris Dawn. Master's degree in Applied Biosystems from the University of Anahuac in Mexico City. Going out to meet my husband on Ceres; that's his picture there."

Yolande looked at the timer display on the sleeve of her suit. Less than an hour from boarding, good time. A disappointment that the compcore had been slagged, but only to be expected. Still . . . She looked down at the picture in the booklet.

"Wait." Her hand slashed down. *Impossible.* She could feel herself start to shake as she looked at it. Impossible. With an effort greater than any she could recall, she took a deep breath. One. Another. The shaking receded to an almost imperceptible tremor in her fingers as she lifted the record book. Square face. Dark eyes. Dress uniform, not the mottled night fatigues. Same face, the *same face,* the Indian night and its hot scents, the smell of Myfwany's blood. The broken body in her arms, jerking, mumbling the final words around a mouth filled with red. Gone. Gone forever, dead, not there, *gone*. The face in the night.

"Sttt—" She cleared her throat. "Stop." Her voice sounded strange in her ears. She leaned toward the wench, seeing with unnatural clarity every pore and feature and hair. There was a sensation behind her eyes, like a taut steel wire snapping.

"That's enough," she said. The tone of her voice had a high note in it, but it was steady. Somewhere, a part of her not involved in this was proud of it.

"Separate the prisoners," she said, without taking her eyes off the picture. "The aft section is cleared out? All the children, put them down there. Decurion, get a working party, transfer supplies from the foodstore; it's on this level. Enough, then weld the door shut, get the picknins down there and weld the hatch to *this* level shut. Wait, that wench and that wench"—she pointed at two of the mothers, ones who had listed no occupation—"with the children. *Move*. No, not these two picknins, leave them with the wench here."

There was a shift, movement, kicks and thuds and shuffling, wailing. A bit of confusion, before the prisoners realized that to Draka serfs were only children up to puberty. Yolande turned to consider them, the booklet gripped tight in one hand. "Docilize the adults," she said. Breathe. In. Out. "Shift them across." She keyed her microphone. "Number Two, how's the mass transfer goin'?"

"Should have the last of it in our tanks in 'bout ten minutes," he said. "Back up to sixty percent. Everythin' all right?" That in a worried tone; he must be able to sense something. Later.

"Good," she replied. "I'm sendin' ovah the prisoners, docilized. Repressurize Hangar B, secure them to the floor. Make arrangements fo' minimal maintenance until we get back to the task fo'ce." There would be plenty of room there; inflatable habitats had been brought along. "Set up fo' a minimum-detection burn."

She turned to the Centurion. "Get those bodies," she said. "Transfer them to the cold-storage locker on this level. Strip everythin' else out, 'cept cookin' utensils, water an' salt, understand?" He nodded, impassive; she had a reputation for successful eccentricity.

Yolande reached back over her shoulder and drew the cutter bar, handling it with slow care. She walked toward the American woman, and held the booklet up beneath her face.

"I know you husband, wench," she said, almost whispering. "It's a hereditary trust to hate all Americans," she continued. "But he . . . took somethin' . . . that I valued very much. So much so that if'n I had him in my hands, not a lifetime's pain could pay fo' it." She halted, and waited immobile until the sounds of movement had died away behind her. The last of the work party shoved the mass of cans and boxes through the main hatch and into the cabin area beneath, then welded the hatch with a sharp *tack* of arc heaters. Then there were only she and the Yankee and the two drugged children. Forget them, they were *his*.

"So tell you husband, tell him my name. Yolande Ingolfsson, tell him that. Tell him to remember the red-haired Draka he killed in India; tell him he'll curse that day as I've cursed it, and mo'. Because befo' I come fo' him, I'm goin' to take everythin' he values and loves, and destroy it befo' his eyes; his ideals, his cause, his nation, his family. And then I'm not goin' to kill him, because . . . Do you know what the problem is, with killin' people, slut? Do you know?"

Silence that rang and stretched, with her eyes locked to the honey brown of the prisoner's. "*Answer me!*" Yolande touched the cutter bar to the other's cheek. Skin and flesh parted, a long shallow cut; blood rilled out, misting across her eyes. *Carefully, carefully.* The other woman gasped, but did not move. "Answer me."

"I don't know."

Yolande moved the cutter to the other cheek, sliced the same controlled depth. "Because being dead doesn't hurt. It's in livin' that there's pain, wench." Another silence. "Do you understand? I'm leavin' you here. Lots of space. Plenty of water. Air system's good fo' two months, easy, an' they should be here, so' you in, oh, minimum three weeks, maximum seven. You can even leave, if'n walkin' buck naked in vacuum doesn't bother you."

"But, but, how shall I feed my children?" the other asked.

Yolande forced herself not to look at the slight drifting forms, pushed the image of Gwen's face aside. Instead she smiled, and saw the American flinch as she had not at the touch of the knife.

"*Try the meat locker!*" she shouted, and leapt for the exit.

Twenty-nine days later, Colonel Frederick Lefarge was the first of the boarding party from the *Ethan Allen* through the airlock of the *Pathfinder*. His eyes met those of his wife.

They screamed.

Chapter Fourteen

BETWEEN THE ORBITS OF EARTH AND MARS
ABOARD DASCS *SUBOTAI*
JUNE 30, 1982

"Makin' remarkable progress, Merarch-Professor," Yolande said. They were teleconferencing, and the astroengineer was suited up; she could see segments of construction material behind him.

He waved a dismissive hand. "These are the heat dispersers," he said. Composite honeycomb sandwich, laced with superconductor on the interior, the same system that pulsedrive ships used; superconductors had the additional useful property of maintaining a uniform temperature throughout. Of course, this *was* a pulsedrive, it just used fusion bombs instead of ten-gram pellets. "We should start assembling the thrust plate soon."

Yolande linked through a view of Hangar B; the near-motionless forms of the prisoners were arranged in neat rows around the shrouded equipment. Skinsuited Auxiliaries were hosing the area down and hauling off the inert bodies; it had gotten quite noisome, with sixty drugged humans and a week's worth of high-G boost.

"We got you some additional labor," she said. "I know they don't look like much, but most of them have trainin' in zero-G construction an' so forth. We'll have to give a few to the headhunter to disassemble, of course."

"Good, perhaps it will keep him away from me," the scientist said, with an obscene gesture for any possible monitors.

"We'll put controller cuffs on them, maybe minimal-dosage dociline," Yolande continued. "You'll have to supervise them closely, but it ought to come out positive."

"Certainly. Hmmm, what to do with them when the project is completed?"

"Oh . . . take them back to Luna, I suppose. Maybe the political people can trade them off fo' somethin', or we can just sell them." Alliance-born serfs had a substantial curiosity value, for their rarity. "Hand them out as souvenirs, whatevah."

676

"Not to mention hostage value," her executive officer said. "Too much Yankee heavy iron in the Belt, fo' my taste."

Yolande chuckled. "Well, there are enough of *our* units further out," she said.

"Long ways off."

"Not so far as you might think," she said, and laid a finger along her nose. "Between you, me an' the Strategic Planning Board, there are a few surprises fo' the damnyanks in this. Fo' one, we've got high-impulse orbital boost lasers in the Jovian system, which we're pretty sure they don't know 'bout. Multiple strap-ons, hey? If'n the damnyanks move, our cruisers can leave station around Himalia, boost on strap-ons with low mass." A pulsedrive ship could make much better acceleration with less reaction mass in her tanks—while the fuel lasted. "Do a quick-and-dirty burn to Mars orbit, arrivin' with dry tanks."

She called up a map of orbital positions. "An' notice, just right fo' a quick stopover at Phobos to fill up? So unless the damnyanks is willin' to get here empty, leavin' them between us and the outer fleet, with nothin' to maneuver with—in which case we'd wipe them, then proceed to mop up the Belt piece by piece—they just naturally have to keep their iron floatin' out there by Ceres and Pallas."

"Ah," the exec mused. "Nice. That still leaves them with three Hero-class here in the inner system, though."

"Update?"

"*Ethan Allen* still boostin' fo' the *Pathfinder* like there was no tomorrow." He frowned. "Faster than we could, unless they're burnin' out their thrust plates."

"Well, the Heros have the legs on a Great Khan, but we've got mo' firepower. Anyways, that'll put her out of the picture fo' a whiles. The two in Earth orbit, we may have to see off. Note we're floatin' next to a fuel depot, though. Also, I've got a few ideas 'bout usin' some of our industrial equipment. Reminds me, staff conference fo' 1200 tomorrow, we'll go ovah it. Three weeks to encounter, minimum. Wants you there, too, Professor."

"Service to the State," he said formally.

"Glory to the Race," the two officers answered.

Yolande yawned. "Time to turn in, Number Two," she said rising from the crashcouch.

"Just one thing, ma'am," he murmured as she passed his station; the offwatch was handling the bridge, minimum staff.

"Yes?"

"Back there . . . when you saw those bodies come out the airlock, I was set up for a minimal-burn boost back to the flotilla. You took us on a max speed trajectory, got us here dry. That was like hangin' up a big sign ovah the whole system pointin' to the *Pathfinder*. Why do it that way, ma'am?"

Yolande glanced at her fingernails. "Oh, better tactics. Impo'tant not to leave the object unguarded." She thought again of the sleeping faces of the two children. *Yankee* children, she reminded herself again, but . . . "Or call it as close as I could get to changin' my mind."

✧   ✧   ✧

"Status," Yolande said.

"Unchanged," the Sensor Officer said. "No relative motion."

"Good." *An odd situation to describe as static,* she thought ironically. *Bass-ackwards to the end of beyond.*

Not too untypical of a space-warship action, though. She looked at the screens again. An exterior view would have shown nothing but bright dots moving against the fixed stars, if that . . . The battle schematic was much more accurate. A fixed dot, the asteroid; the regular five-minute pulses of its monstrous drive flaring back toward Earth. The flame was only partly shaped by the magnetic fields of the thrust plate; those forces were still too vast and wild for Earth's children, and it hid a good deal behind it from most sensors. An excellent place for her to conceal the vulnerable transports.

Yolande grinned like a shark in the darkness of the command center. *Subotai* and *Batu* were falling back toward the flotilla, with the two Alliance cruisers in pursuit; all on free-fall trajectories, with their thrust plates presented to the enemy. That was the most heavily armored portion of a pulsedrive ship, *built* to withstand near-miss nuclear explosions. And the drive was the most dangerous weapon in itself; chasing a deep-space warship was a chancy proposition, since getting too close would mean self-incineration. Once you got within a certain distance, in a one-on-one there was virtually no choice but to flip end for end and coast until something changed the situation. You could disengage, of course, but that meant backing off and freeing your opponent from the menace of the nuclear sword.

Perfect, she thought. The Draka warships had drawn the Alliance craft on just enough; the enemy vessels were slightly faster than hers, and more nimble, but they were farther from base and so obliged to be sparing with their burns. A perfect matching-velocity flip, which meant they must pursue or quit, and pursue precisely in line with the Draka ships for fear of presenting a vulnerable flank. The asteroid was coming up rapidly; the fog of energetic particles around it negated her enemy's superior sensors, too; she did not *need* to detect much, here.

"Distance," she said.

"Two-hundred-twenty klicks. Transit of asteroid in seventy-one seconds, ten klicks clearage." Just enough to avoid the worst of the fusion-bomb explosions.

Nothing for it but to wait; all the orders were given, the personnel ready. Sweat soaked into the permeable fabric of her skinsuit, under the armpits and down the flanks, chill in the moving air the ventilators sent across her body. Sixty seconds. Life or death decided in one minute; victory and glory, or eternal shame. *Genius, or a goat. Which I wouldn't be there to see. Bones of the White Christ, this sort of thing sounds better in retrospect. Adventure is somebody else in deep shit far, far away.*

Fifty seconds. Snappdove had thought she was insane, for a while. *Maybe I was. Dammit, they* are *pressing home their pursuit.* The Alliance wanted to damage her; the only way to do it was to chase her cruisers off far enough that they could do a firing pass at the asteroid and its work force as they turned and fled themselves. *A two-body problem with only one solution.*

Ten. Five. The pursuers maintaining position with beautiful precision; those were good ships and well-trained crews. Three. Two. Past.

"Now!" she shouted, superfluously.

"DECELERATION," the speakers sounded. It wrenched at her, throwing her forward against the combat cocoon. Reaction mass was being vented from the forward ports, run through the heat dumpers to vaporize. Not nearly so powerful as the drive, but enough to check their headlong flight. The main drives of the Alliance craft lit in a brief blossom of flame, just enough to match.

And the asteroid was *turning.* A mass of billions of tonnes is very difficult indeed to move out of its accustomed orbit; it had taken dozens of fusion weapons to spend that much energy. It is much easier to pivot such a mass about its center of gravity; while the hydrogen-bomb flare had hidden them, the cargo vessels had nestled their bows into holes excavated in the rock and ice of the asteroid's crust. A cruiser could not have done it without self-destruction, but the haulers had been modified to act as pusher tugs at need. Now four drives flared, and the lumpy dark potato shape pivoted with elephantine delicacy. Toward *Subotai*'s pursuer, blinded by its own drive for the crucial seconds. Fusion blossomed behind the rock's assigned stern, and the products of it washed out tens of kilometers; charged particles, gamma radiation striking metal and sleeting through as secondary radiation and heat. Through shielding, through the reaction-mass baffles around the command center; tripping relays, overloading circuits, ripping the nervous systems of the human crew as well.

"MANEUVER." *Subotai* flipped end over end. "DECELERATION." The main drive roared, a deeper thrumming note as it poured reaction mass onto the plate and spat out fission pellets at twice the normal rate. The cruiser slowed with a violence that stressed the frame to its limits, as if the ship were sinking into some yielding but elastic substance. Crippled, the Alliance vessel overshot. Weapons flashed out at ranges so short that response time was minimal, from both directions, for the wounded ship was not yet dead.

"Overheat, disperser three."

"Gatling six not reporting."

"Penetration! Pressure loss in reaction baffle nine."

"Wotan, get that missile, get it, *get it.*" Rising tension, until the close-in gatlings sprayed the homing rocket's path with high-velocity metal. It exploded in a flower of nuclear flame, and the radiation alarms shrilled.

Yolande felt the cruiser shake and tone around her, like a vast mechanical beast crying out in pain. Sectors flicked from green to amber to red on the screens; but the Alliance ship was suffering worse, its defenses shattered.

"Hit!" Railgun slugs sleeted into the *Washington*'s heat dispersers. "Hit!" Parasite bombs dropped away from the *Subotai*'s stern, into the neutron flux of the drive; their own small bomblets detonated, and the long metal bundles converted energy into X-ray laser spikes.

"She's losing air," the Sensor Officer reported. "Overheat in her reaction mass tanks—pressure burst—losing longitudinal stability—she's tumbling!"

Lasers raked across the enemy; armor sublimed into vapor and the computers held the beams on, chewing deeper. The particle guns snapped; sparks flickered along the cartwheeling form of the Alliance cruiser. Then the exterior screens darkened.

"Something got through," the Weapons Officer said softly, and consulted his screens. "Secondary effects . . . her fuel pellets just went."

A cheer went through the *Subotai*, a moment's savage howl of triumph.

"Stow that!" Yolande snapped. "Sensors, report."

"The *Bolivar*'s breaking and runnin' fo' it, ma'am." Only sensible; with two ships to her one, the Draka could bracket and overwhelm her.

"Damage Control?"

"Ship fully functional. Missin' one gatling turret. Three dead, seven injured." Yolande winced inwardly. *Shit*. "Slow leaks in two sectors of the reaction mass tank. Seventy-one percent nominal. Drive full, remainder weapons systems full."

"Number Two, shape fo' pursuit." There was a momentary pause in the drive, and it resumed at normal high-burn rates. Stars crawled across the screens as the attitude jets adjusted their bearing. "If *Bolivar* gets back within the orbit of Luna, they'll do it with dry tanks an' scratches on that shiny new thrust plate." A pulsedrive ship could move on fuel pellets alone; the first generation had, using vaporized graphite from the lining of the plate as reaction mass. It was neither recommended, good for the frame, nor safe.

"Oh, and all hands," she said, switching to the command push, "well done."

Chapter Fifteen

SPIN HABITAT SEVEN, CENTRAL BELT
BETWEEN THE ORBITS OF MARS AND JUPITER
JANUARY 4, 1983

Habitat Seven was the latest and largest of the Project's constructs, half a kilometer across and two long; nickel-iron was cheap, and easy to work with big enough mirrors. Now the former lump of metal-rich rock was a spinning tube, closed at either end, with a glowing cylinder of woven glass filament running down its center. There was atmosphere inside, and part of the inner surface had already been transformed; gravity was .5 G, as much as was practical or necessary. Grass grew in squares of nutrient-rich dust, and hopeful flowers. Individual houses were going up, foamed rock poured into molds; there were dozens of different floor plans.

"Goddamn circus," Frederick Lefarge said. "We're running this like the bloody Los Alamos bomb project, back in the '40s. Everything and the kitchen sink."

"Not really," the man beside him on the polished-slag bench said. "In the long run, the actual construction will go faster if we spend the time to get the infrastructure in place." A sigh. "And even the . . . fourth Project will require a good deal of preliminary groundwork. We are going to miss Dr. Takashi very badly, as the years go by. I am more for the crystals and wafers and wires, me; he was the instruction set genius."

"Yes." He looked aside at Professor Pedro de Ribeiro: a vigorous-looking forty-five, with the usual Imperial Brazilian goatee in pepper-and-salt and an impeccable white linen suit; the cane and gloves were, the American thought, a little much. Very competent man, but . . . "I'd have thought that was less so for the final Project than for the rest of the New America enterprises. It's basically a set of compin-structions, isn't it?"

"Não." De Ribeiro's English was impeccable, but it slipped now and then. "I have been thinking much on this matter, since I was contacted . . . and have concluded that we must almost reinvent the art

681

of information systems here, if we are to accomplish what we wish."
He rested his hands on the silver head of his cane and leaned forward. "Abandon our assumption that because we have always done
things one way, that is the inevitable path. Another legacy of the struggle
with the Domination . . . Tell me, Senhor Lieutenant Colonel, what
would you say to the idea of writing compinstruction procedures on
a perscomp?"

Lefarge blinked, taken aback. "That's . . . well, it would be like
using a shovel as a machine tool, wouldn't it?"

"Bim, but only because we have made it so." He tapped the ferrule of the cane on the ground. "Perhaps computers could only have
started as they did, large machines used for cryptography, for the
handling of statistics. Precious assets, jealously guarded. They have
grown immensely faster, immensely more capable, even rather smaller—
that first all-transistor model in 1942 was the size of a house!—but
not different in nature."

"Well, how could they be?"

"For example . . . it is certainly technically possible to build central processing units small enough to power a perscomp. Yes, yes, quite
difficult, but the micromachining processes we have developed for other
purposes would do . . . if there were a strong development incentive.
But our computers were always, hmm, how shall I say, *limited* in access.
Perscomps were developed from the other end up, from the machinery intended to run machine tools, simulations, deal with the real world;
only their instruction storage and the interfacers are digital, and the
rest is analog. We build them for a range of specific uses, and then
develop the instruction sets on larger machines; they are loaded into
the smaller in cartridges. Complicated machines such as space warcraft
have a maze of subsystems like that, linked to a central brain."

Wild speculation combined with restatement of the obvious, Lefarge
thought. Then: *No, wait a minute. We've been too narrowly focused
on immediate problems. The Project's going to need real ingenuity,
not just engineering.* "But if we'd gone the other way . . . Jesus,
Doctor, it'd be a security nightmare! Even as it is, we have to throw
dozens of people in the slammer every year for illegal comping.
There might be . . . oh, *thousands* of amateurs out there screwing around with vital instruction sets. The Draka could scoop it
up off the market! Then think of the problems if you could copy
embedded corepaths and instruction sets over the wires between
perscomps. Lord . . ."

The Brazilian nodded. "Exactly! And who would find it more difficult to adjust to such a world, us or them? We must be radical, on
our Project. That is an example."

He laughed as the younger man rocked under the question's impact.
"Also, one of the reasons I have come here. Here we will be relatively
free of the security restrictions—if only because we are already imprisoned, in a sense! For the first time, a completely free exchange of
ideas and data."

Another tap at the metallic pebbles of the walkway. "The thing we
wish to devise, it must be more than a set of hidden compinstructions.

It must be a self-replicating, self-adjusting pattern of information, a . . . a *virus*, if you will. One able to overcome all the safeguards the Draka place on their machines; the redundant systems, the physical blocks, the many interfaces. We will have to reinvent many aspects of our art. Takashi agreed with me; it is better to start with a majority of younger men . . . and women, to be sure—ones free of the rather bureaucratized, specialized approach of other research institutes. And less dominated by us old men, who are so sure what is possible and what impossible! The *New America*, the starship, that is engineering. Wonderful engineering, many tests, unfamiliar challenges, but development work. In our Project, we must learn new ways to *think*. Ah, the senhora, your wife."

She was walking now, with care and in this half-gravity. The forgetfulness was diminishing, and the crying fits; there would be no need for more transplants. The doctors were quite pleased. . . . Something squeezed inside his gut, as he looked at her. She looked. . . a well-preserved forty, and moved with slow, painful care. Her face had filled out, a little, and she had gained back some of the weight, if not the muscle tone. The hair was cropped close, and only half gray; her teeth were the too-even white of implanted synthetic. Professor de Ribeiro rose and bowed over her hand.

"A salute to one so lovely and so brave," he said formally, bowing farewell to them both.

Cindy sank down with a sigh, and leaned her head against Fred's shoulder. He put his arm around hers, feeling the slight tremor of exhaustion.

"Should you be up, honey?" he asked gently.

"I'll never get any better if I don't push it a little. I was with the girls," she said. "God, they're doing great, darling. Just . . . I get so *tired* all the time." He looked down, and saw that slow tears were leaking from under closed lids, made wordless sounds of comfort. "And I feel so old, and useless and *ugly*."

"You're the most beautiful thing in the solar system, Cindy," he said with utter sincerity. "I've never doubted it for a single instant."

She sighed again. "I like the professor. He's on whatever-it-is that's being hidden behind the *New America*, isn't he?"

Cindy laughed quietly, without stirring, as he tried to conceal his start of alarm. "Don't worry, sweetheart, I haven't been steaming open your letters . . . Honestly, I'm *sick*, not *stupid*. And I've had plenty of time to think, and anyway we're all here for the duration. I do like the professor; he reminds me of Dr. Takashi—"

Suddenly she began to shake, and he turned to hold her in the circle of his arms. "Oh God, oh God, the end of his *hand* was gone and, and, *uhhh*—"

"Shhh, shhh," he said. "I'm here, honey, I'll always be here, I'll never let them hurt you again. Never again." The taste of helplessness was in his mouth, like burning ash.

At last she was still again. "Sorry. Sorry to be such a . . . baby," she said, gripping the breast of his uniform.

"God, honey, you're stronger than I could ever be."

She shook her head. "I get angry, and then I start feeling so sorry for everyone." A long pause. "Even her."

"Now, that's going a bit too far," he said, trying for humor. *Funny, hatred is actually a cold feeling. Like an old-fashioned injection at the dentist's.*

"No, darling. I tried to think how it would be, if somebody killed *you*, you know, what she said . . ."

"That filthy—" He bit off the words. "Sorry, honey."

"They can't help what their . . . way of life does to them. You know," she continued, "I think she really didn't want to hurt any of us, until she recognized your picture. It was as if she just . . . had a blind spot, couldn't *understand* why we weren't doing what she wanted, as if we were *making* her fight us. She . . . had them put all the other children in safely, with enough to . . . to eat."

He held her tighter. "Try not to think of it," he said. "And, honey, I'd do almost anything for you, except forgive the people who did this to you."

"I wouldn't want you to," she said unexpectedly, looking up at him bleakly. "I don't want you to become like that, eaten up with hate. But I don't want those people in the same universe as my children, either. Kill them all, Fred. Whatever you're doing here, *do* it."

The tension went out of her. "I really do feel sorry for them, though. What a life it must be, without a real home, without love—without even natural children. That's the first love of all, for the baby in your arms." Cindy yawned. "I feel sort of sleepy, Fred sweetheart," she whispered. "Take me home."

He bent and lifted her with infinite gentleness.

CLAESTUM PLANTATION
DISTRICT OF TUSCANY
PROVINCE OF ITALY
JANUARY 5, 1983

"Shit, I hope I'm in time," Yolande muttered to herself. She keyed the console and spoke: "Central Mediterranean Control, Ingolfsson 55Z-4, here. Mach one-point-one at 9,985 meters, permission to commence descent."

"CMC here," an amused voice replied; one of the Citizen supervisors who had been following her dash from the orbital scramjet port in Alexandria. Being a national hero was proving more trying than she had expected, but it had its compensations. "Permission granted, we've cleared it."

"I'm not goin' need much room," she replied. Her hand hit the safety overrides—*Not designed for fighter pilots anyway*—and kept the wings at maximum sweep-back; the Meercat turned on its side and dove.

"Right," she said. "Remember, this fuckin' *aircar* wasn't built fo' fighter jocks either." The ground swelled with frightening speed; she pulled the nose up in a half-Immelmann, vectored the bellyjets to lose speed, grunted as the craft seemed to hit a brick wall in the air. "Aaaaand again." The sonic boom must have rattled windows for kilometers around. She shoved the wings forward and hit the spoilers; the speed wound down toward aerodynamic stall. "A little too much." That was the Monte del Chianti ahead; she banked again, giving a touch to the throttle and hedgehopping. That was almost a forgotten sensation; amazing how much *faster* everything seemed with an atmosphere and planetary surface to reference from.

The Great House lay below her, like a model spread out on its hilltop. Nothing in the front court, and to *hell* with the pavement. Yolande rolled the craft in a final circuit of the hill, brought the vectored thrust fully vertical; the wings folded into their slots, and she could hear the landing gear extend as she let the aircar fall at maximum safe descent.

"God, I hope I'm in time," she said to herself. The canopy retracted and she vaulted out, hit the ground running, paused at the main stairs.

"Hiyo, Ma, Pa, I'm home. Am I in time?"

Her parents glanced at each other. "Everyone from here to Florence knows you home, after that approach, and yes. Only just. Run fo' it, girl!" her father said.

Yolande ran. Through corridors, hurdling furniture, once over a startled housegirl on her hands and knees scrubbing a floor. *Wotan and Thunor, I'm like lead, I should have worked out in the high-G spinner more*, she thought dazedly as she arrived at the birthroom door, breathing deeply. A voice stopped her.

"Clean up! Youa clean up before you come in!"

Middy Gianelli, no mistaking that bleak voice. Compelling herself not to fidget, Yolande hurriedly stripped off her uniform jacket and her boots, slipped on a sterile robe and slippers and stood under the UV cleanser until the buzzer sounded. Proper procedure, after all. Almost certainly unnecessary, modern antibacterials being what they were, but there was no sense in taking chances with her baby. Suddenly nervous, she stepped through the door.

"Ma!" Gwen was on the other side of the table. "Ma, the baby's comin'!"

"Hiyo, dumplin'," Yolande said, distracted. "I know . . . How's it going, Jolene?" she continued, stepping to the serf's side.

"Fine, M—*nnnnng*," she grunted. The black woman was resting on the birthing table; it was cranked up to support her upper body at a quarter from the horizontal, with a brace for her hips, raised pedestals for her feet; her hands were clenched on grips behind her head.

"You shoulda be asking me that, Mistis," the midwife said. She was an Italian serf, spare and severe; expensively trained, in her late fifties, much in demand on neighboring plantations. The Draka had never considered pregnancy an illness, and used doctors only when something seemed to be going wrong. "Dilation is complete, the water's justa broke; position normal, like the scanner said. Nexta time, use this wench again or picka one who's had her own *bambino*, it go easier."

"Glad . . . you . . . here," Jolene panted.

"No more talk, I been telling you what to do these six months now. Breath *in*, bear *down*. Yell if it helps."

The door opened again; Yolande's mother and father came in, and her brother John and Mandy; none of her brother's children were old enough to be here, of course; that would not be fitting until they were near adult. The serf midwife scowled at the newcomers, snapped at her assistant-apprentice. Jolene filled her lungs and bore down with a long straining grunt, again. Again. Again. Her face and body shone with sweat, and her face contorted with her effort. Yolande laid a hand on her swollen belly, feeling the contractions through the palm. Time passed; Yolande looked up with a start and realized it had been nearly an hour. The other adults waited quietly; Gwen left her seat and stood, craning her neck to see around the two serf attendants.

"Oh, wow, Ma," she said. "I can see the head."

"Quiet, Gwen," Yolande said gently. "Come on, Jolene, you can do it." The contractions were almost continuous now, and there was pain in the grunting cries. She saw the crown of the head slide free of the distended birth canal, red and crumpled and slick with fluids. The stomach convulsed under her hand, and Jolene screamed three times, high and shrill. The baby slid free into the midwife's filmgloved hands. She cleaned the mouth and nose, then lifted it and slapped it sharply on the behind; it gave a wail as she laid it down on the platform, tied and severed the cord, began wiping the birth bloom, dipping the child in the basin of warm water her assistant held near. The crying continued as she dried and wrapped the child and handed it to Yolande.

"Ah," the Draka breathed, looking down at the tiny wrinkled form that quieted and peered around with mild, unfocused blue eyes. "My own sweet Nicholas; I'm goin' call you Nikki, hear?"

Gwen was tugging at her elbow. "Ma, can I see?" Yolande went down on one knee. "Why do they look so . . . rumpled up, Ma? Did I look like that?"

"Just about, honeybunch. They have to squeeze through a pretty tight place, gettin' out. Here, see how perfect his hands are? Isn't it wonderful?"

The girl nodded, then looked aside where Jolene was shuddering and wincing as she worked to expel the afterbirth. "That looks like it really hurts, doin' all that. I'll never have to do that, will I, Ma?"

Yolande spared a hard glance at Marya; what had the wench been saying to the child?

"No, of course not," she said to her daughter.

"No, Missy Gwen," Marya said, in her usual cool tone. "Your serf brooders will bear your eggs for you, just like this."

Gwen nodded, and Yolande rose and bent over Jolene. The serf was still panting, exhausted. She flinched slightly as the attendants cleaned her, slid a fresh sheet beneath her and wiped away the sweat before drawing up a coverlet and setting the controls to convert the birthing table into a bed; she would be moved later. Still, she smiled broadly as Yolande brought the small bundle near, reaching out her arms. "Can I?" she said.

"Of course," her owner replied, laying the infant gently on her abdomen. Yolande kissed her brow, then looked up to meet Gwen's eyes. "Remember we owe Jolene a lot, daughter. We have to look after her always."

Gwen nodded solemnly, then gave her mother's hand a squeeze before she ran over to Marya; standing, her head was nearly level with the seated serf's.

How swiftly they grow, Yolande thought. Her daughter reached forward and hugged the American.

"Thank *you*, Tantie-ma Marya," she said earnestly. "1 didn't realize how hard you worked, havin' me. Thank you."

Marya returned the embrace, the other Draka were smiling at the entirely proper show of sentiment. The serf stroked the red head resting on her bosom.

"You are welcome, Missy Gwen," she said. Then looked up, met Yolande's gaze, looked down at the child. "*You* are welcome."

Yolande felt a slight chill, then cast it aside. *Hearing things*, she decided, looking down at her son. A rush of warmth spread up from belly to throat, so overwhelming that her head swam with it. She was conscious of her family gathering around her, her father and mother's arms over her shoulders. John was popping a champagne bottle in the background, and someone pushed a glass into her hand. She sipped without tasting, watching the baby lying quietly with the dozing serf. Wondering, she stroked his cheek, and his head turned toward the touch, mouth working. "Why, he's an eager little one," Jolene said. "Mistis, help me?"

Yolande pulled down the sheet to bare the swollen breasts, and curled the infant into the curve of her arm so that he could take the nipple. He sucked eagerly, and Jolene closed her eyes with a sigh. "They been so sore an' tender. That feels good."

There was more quiet conversation as the infant nursed, and then the midwife cleared her throat. "Mastahs, Mistis, this not a good place for a party. An' this wench and the bambino, they needa their rest."

Thomas Ingolfsson rumbled a laugh. "True enough. Out, my children."

Chapter Sixteen

CENTRAL OFFICE, ARCHONAL PALACE
ARCHONA
DOMINATION OF THE DRAKA
NOVEMBER 10, 1991

"That will be all," Eric von Shrakenberg said.

"Excellence," his aide replied, bowing and leaving.

Damned insolence of office, he thought with amusement. The Domination's chief executive was selected for a seven-year term, with no limits on reelection. Hence the Archonate staff tended to become used to an incumbent, set in their ways; he was still running into problems with that, except with the people he had brought in himself last year. The serf cadre were even worse . . .

"Five minutes," the desk said.

He sighed and seated himself, feeling a little out of place. This shape of carved yellowwood and Zambezi teak . . . how many Occupation Day addresses had he seen it in, from the other side? On film back during the Eurasian War, on screens of gradually increasing clarity since. *Wotan, fifty years!* he thought, looking around the big room. Not overwhelming, although the view was spectacular, when the curtains were open; the dome of the House of Assembly was about half a kilometer away. History-drenched enough for anybody, he supposed, thinking of the decisions made here.

And now I sit here and hold the fate of the human race in my hands, he thought. *If anyone's listening at the other end of these communicators.* Having people obey when he spoke was the difference between being a leader and an old man in a room. *A fact not commonly known, and it's better so.*

"Incoming signal," the speaker said.

"Receive."

A spot of light appeared at head-height beyond the desk. A line framed it, expanding outward until it outlined a rectangle three meters by three; the central spot faded, and then the rectangle blinked out of existence. Replacing it was a holographic window into the interior

688

of Donovan House. Eric knew it was an arrangement of photons, as insubstantial as moonbeams, but still wondered at the sheer *solidity* of it. *Genuine progress, for a change,* he thought. You could get the true measure of an opponent this way, the total-sensory gestalt read from every minute clue of stance, expression, movement. The same applied in reverse.

"Madam President," he said, inclining his head.

"Excellence," she replied, with meticulous courtesy.

She may have been added to balance the ticket, but I don't think the Yankees lost when Liedermann slipped on the soap, Eric decided. President Carmen Hiero was the second Hispanic and the first woman to sit in the same chair as Jefferson and Douglas; before that she had been a Republican *jefe politico* in Sonora, still very unusual for a woman in the States carved out of Old Mexico. Fiftyish, graying, *criolla* blueblood by descent, mixed with Irish from a line of silver-mine magnates: that much he knew from the briefing papers. Old *haciendado* family, but not a shellback by Yankee standards; degrees in classics, history, and some odd American specialty known as political science, whatever that was. *A contradiction in terms, from the title.*

"I regret that I can't offer hospitality," he continued.

She shrugged. "Debatable whether it would be appropriate, under the circumstances. I hope you realize how much trouble with my OSS people I had to go through to allow Domination equipment here."

"And the political capital *I* must expend to let Yankee electronics in here," he added dryly. "Our Security people are still more paranoid than yours, not least because it is a field in which your nation excels us. Still, we can now be reasonably sure nobody is recording or tapping these conversations." He paused. "Why *did* you agree, Señora?"

The black eyes met his calmly. *Almost as much body-language control as a Draka,* he thought with interest. *Better than some of us do, actually. I wonder how deep it runs.*

"I suspect my reasoning was much like yours, von Shrakenberg. The convenience of dealing with essential issues without the circumlocutions essential where things are said in public, without the necessary lies of party politics. In addition, the chance of gaining personal insight into my enemy, set against the risk of him doing likewise. Well worth that risk. Always it is better to act from knowledge than ignorance." Eric nodded, spread his hands in silent acknowledgment as she continued. "Although, *por favor,* why did you not request such a link with the Alliance Chairman?"

Eric chuckled. "For much the same reason that you would not have agreed, had Representative Gayner's nominee been sittin' in this chair."

Her eyebrows rose slightly. "I would not compare Chairman Allsworthy to your Militants," she said.

"Not in terms of policy . . . a certain structural similarity in position on our relative political spectra. Perhaps a similarity in believin' too strongly in our respective national mythologies. Besides, the American President is still rather mo' than first among equals."

It was Hiero's turn to spread her hands silently. *Certain necessary fictions must be maintained even here,* he read the gesture.

"Turnin' to business," Eric continued, "was it really necessary to tow those-there gold-rich asteroids into Earth orbit? I admit it's industrially convenient havin' gold fall to the same value as tin, but the financial problems!"

A thin smile; the Alliance currency was fiat money, while the Domination's auric had always been gold-backed. "You could refuse to trade for gold, and maintain an arbitrary value," she said in a tone of sweet reason.

He snorted. "Thus sacrificin' the industrial advantages, and endin' up with all the disadvantages of a metallic standard, all the problems of a paper-money system, and none of the compensatin' flexibility," he said. "Between me and thee, we're movin' to a basket of commodities, although with the general fall in prices—"

An hour later, Hiero leaned back. "Well," she said, "all this indicates several areas of potential agreement." They both nodded; technical discussions were easy, once the top-echelon political decisions had been made. "Perhaps we can move on to others, at later meetings. Certainly we have more of a meeting of minds than I could with your Militants."

Or I with Allsworthy, Eric inferred. Quite true; the Chairman had what amounted to a physical phobia toward Draka, taking the nickname "Snake" quite literally.

"Please, don't misinterpret," he said softly. "On some issues of purely . . . pragmatic impo'tance, perhaps. On mo' fundamental issues of foreign policy, my Conservatives will follow an essentially Militant line."

"Why? If I may ask."

"Because . . . Madam President, the internal politics of the Domination can no way be interpreted in terms of what you familiar with; a word to the wise, to prevent misunderstandin'. The universe of discourse is too different. To call my faction paternalistic conservatives an' Gayner's biotechnocrats is a very crude approximation. Our real differences are on issues of domestic policy—very long-term domestic policy at that, arisin' after we dispose of you. Or you dispose of us, in which case it all becomes moot, eh? It's extremely impo'tant that we try to understand the parameters of each other's operations, otherwise things could get completely irrational."

"I see your point." A hesitation. "May I ask you a personal question, Excellence?" At his nod, she proceeded: "I've got the usual Intelligence summaries on you . . . and I've read your novels. Within limits, I received the impression of an intelligent and empathetic man. Which leads to certain questions."

Eric turned in his swivel chair and poured a measure of brandy into a balloon snifter, turned back, paused to swirl the liquid and sniff, sip.

"I assure you, they've occurred to me as well," he said meditatively. "Why, in essence, don't I retire to my estate and let the world rave as it will?" He felt his lips twist into the semblance of a smile. "Well, in all honesty, Madam President, why don't you? It's in the nature of an ambitious politician to imagine all alternatives to himself are disaster. I flatter mahself I'm right."

"Duty," she said. "I'm . . . not indispensable, but there are worse people to occupy this chair. For my children, my nation, and for the cause of freedom, if that doesn't sound too pompous."

Eric laughed harshly. "You Americans have been a lucky people, on the whole . . . what convenience, to have national interest an' high-soundin' ideals so congruent." He made agesture with the glass. "Forgive a slight bitterness. Leavin' aside the question of whether morals are objective reality or cultural artifacts, I'm left with some similar motivations. I have children, grandchildren. And my people. As my fathah once said to me, you nation is like you children; loved because they are yours, not necessarily because they deserve it. Moral judgment—that has to be made in the context of political and historical reality, not some imaginary situation where we start with a *tabula rasa*."

"Even in polities, surely moral choices are an individual's responsibility?"

"A true difference of national temperament, I think. If'n a Draka thinks of choice at all, it's as constrained within narrow bonds; human beings make history, but they don't make it just as they choose." He laughed again, this time with more genuine humor. "Interestin' question, whether perception is the result or cause of social reality . . ." He set the snifter down and leaned forward. "One thing is sure. Either of us would start the Final War *if we thought it was the right choice*. And neither of us wants to be forced into that decision prematurely. Which leaves us with certain common difficulties."

"*Bueno*, I am glad you realize this. This conflict—it has gone on so long, both sides, they have accumulated serious vested interests with a stake in waging it. Organizations, bureaucracies, careers are invested in it; power, vast profits. Always these push toward its intensification. We have a common interest then, in not allowing the instruments of policy to set our policy."

"True." He nodded decisively. "Very true. Although, hmmm." He rubbed his chin meditatively, then decided to speak. It was no secret, after all. "Madam President, remember always that there is no true symmetry between our positions, here. There is an element in the Alliance which seeks to simply grow around and beyond us, reduce us to an irrelevance." She nodded. "This is precisely what much of our strategy has been designed to prevent. The border tensions, the convention we have allowed to grow up that there is no peace beyond Luna . . . It is you dynamism we fear. The tension inhibits it, forces you into military an' security measures where we can compete mo' easily."

Hiero's mouth clamped in a grim line. "*Sí.* So my analysts tell me. Let me warn you then, Excellence. This policy has its own dangers. Firstly, it makes the task you have, of restraining your military, more difficult. Secondly, both our societies are becoming dependent on resources and manufactures from space; this entails massive activities and investments beyond the Earth–Moon system. In turn, these create interests whose voices cannot be ignored. Also . . . when only explorers and pioneers were at risk, nothing vital was threatened by clashes in deep space. Now we are approaching the point where *vital matters of national security* are endangered in the heavens. We would not tolerate an invasion of Burma or England. Should we then regard Ceres as less?"

"Correct," Eric said, with soft precision. "As you point out, my task of control is mo' than yours; nor would I modify our tradition of decentralized decision making even if I could." He sighed. "A world bound in chains of adamant, that's our legacy. The stalemate becomes ever less stable. If nothin' else, inaction would give my opponents too much opportunity. The fact that I'm presented with an insoluble dilemma, and they know it, will not restrain them from takin' political advantage of it."

Hiero tapped a finger to her lip in polite skepticism. "I am to endure provocation from you, because if I do not, another even less restrained would take your place?" She continued with heavy irony: " 'The whip is not so bad; fear instead, my brother, who will use scorpions?' "

"I see you point. So both of us looks for a means to *break* the stalemate; I don't suppose it's much consolation that I would use it with regret, while anothah in my shoes might do it with Naldorssenian glee and invocations of the Will to Power. But be careful, be very careful, Madam President. Neither of us wishes to destroy the planet. Don't rely too much on secrets—such as you New America project, out there in the asteroids. Conveniently on the opposite side of the sun from Earth, most of the time, eh?"

She was shaken for a moment, he was sure of it: a thousand tiny signs said so. Then she rallied. "Or your Stone Dogs, *sí?*"

It was his turn to feel a hand squeezing at the arteries in his chest. *Control yourself, you fool,* he said behind a smiling mask. *Ah . . . she didn't match my disclosure of* her *project's location.* Only a half-dozen knew the full to most of those charged with implementation. *And don't start flailing about to discover her source. The effort itself could tell them too much. Overwhelmingly probable they have discovered only that it is a secret, and important.*

He glanced polite inquiry. "Stone Dogs . . . an old nickname fo' our Janissary infantrymen. Perhaps a code name? I can't very well follow every project, of course." Their eyes met in perfect understanding of the game of bluff and double-bluff. "Well, we all have our little surprises," he said. "Tell me, do you ever suspect what you subordinates aren't tellin' you?"

She gave him a glance that was half ironic, half a reflection of shared fear. He remembered times when he had lain awake sweating with that particular horror, the worst of which was that there was no way to disprove it. A successful deception ploy was invisible by definition, and thinking of it too much—that was the road to paranoia and madness.

"It has been, ah, interesting," the president said at last.

"At least that. Perhaps in another few months."

"Of a certainty. Excellence."

"Madam President."

The holo vanished, and Eric waited a long moment with the heels of his palms to his eyes before he touched a control on the desk. "Shirley," he said. "Send in the estimates, would you?"

His eyes sought the curtains. The sun had fallen . . . Perhaps next week there would be time for a visit home. *Stop reaching for the carrot, donkey*, he told himself brutally. *Bend your neck to the traces and pull.*

President Carmen Hiero shook her head thoughtfully as the aides bustled about, rearranging the room.

"The poor man," she murmured, in her mother's language.

"Ma'am?" the Secret Service agent said.

"Nothing, Lindholm," she said, standing. It had been a long day, and there was a dull pain in her lower back. *And more dull pains to be endured at dinner*, she thought wryly. For a moment she looked again at the air the transmission had occupied. "Nothing that matters . . . in the end."

NOVA VIRCONIUM
COMMAND CENTRAL
HELLAS PLANTITIA, MARS
DOMINATION OF THE DRAKA
NOVEMBER 17, 1991

"Here she comes!"

The Martian orbital shuttle was like nothing else in the solar system. Delta-shaped, but with huge slender wings that could only have flown under this light gravity and tenuous wisp of atmosphere. It swelled from the east, out of sky already gone purple and starlit, its riding lights bright against the dark ceramic of the heatshield. Just then the outline lights of the pathways blinked on, like a great glowing circuit diagram across the plain, stretching out to the horizon. Daggers of brighter light appeared beneath and about the shuttle: steering jets and final braking. The flat belly and underwing surface drifted down to maglev distance, fields meshing with those of the runway, and it slid frictionless at half a meter until the gentle magnetic tugging brought it to a halt.

Yolande rose, straightened her uniform. The others in the party bustled likewise as the windowless arrowhead slid its nose into the terminal docking collar. The band made a few preliminary tootles . . .

"Marya," Yolande said. The serf had been standing at the railing; she turned silently and faded into the background of the welcoming party. The doors below cycled open, and the passengers came through. A big clot of children, which dissolved like sugar under hot water as they scattered to the waiting families. A small group that hung uncertainly near the doors. Yolande recognized Jolene's blond mane first, then Gwen. Another girl next to her, and a smaller form next to Jolene . . . Nikki.

"Let's do it," she said.

The Martian Rangers decurion saluted with a grin, and called to his guard party. They were ghouloons, of course; in surface suits and armor, but with faceguards swung back. Their muzzles dipped in unison as they wheeled, split into two lines of fifteen, and trotted down to take station in four-footed parade rest up the broad stairway that ran from the upper lounge to the lower. Yolande moved to the head of the stairs; the band struck up the *Warrior's Saraband*, and the decurion turned to the double line of inhuman fighters.

"Commandant-Governor's . . . *salute!*" he barked, as Yolande walked down the stairs. The ghouloon troopers threw back their heads and gave a short barking howl.

She was close enough to see her daughter's face now, flushed with a combination of delight and terminal embarrassment, as the crowd in the main terminal parted. There were cheers and claps; Yolande had come to the Commandant-Governor's post with a good reputation, and was popular enough . . .

"Ma. Ah, Service to the State."

"Glory to the Race." *Oh, Freya, she looks so much like her*, Yolande thought, with a brief twisting pain inside her chest. For a moment the years and light-minutes slipped away, and she was a rumpled teenager alone and lonely on her first evening at Baiae School. *Like that first time I saw her*. Gwen was fourteen now—a little taller than Myfwany had been, a little slimmer. Perhaps more relaxed about the eyes. *My own Gwendolyn*, Yolande thought.

"Hello, daughter," she said and opened her arms.

The hug was brief but bruising-strong, the New Race muscles squeezing her ribs. Yolande released the girl and held her at arm's length. "You lookin' good, child of my heart." Nikki had been jittering at Jolene's side; now he tore free and threw his arms around Yolande's waist, smiling up gap-toothed. She ruffled the sandy hair and closed her own eyes for a moment: they were rare, these instants of true happiness. Best to seize them while you could.

Nikki was looking sideways at the Rangers. "Decurion Kang," Yolande said, "I think my son might like to review you guard party."

"You *bet*, Ma!" the seven-year-old said enthusiastically.

Yolande nodded to her aide, saluted. "I think we can carry on from here, Tetrarch," she said, and turned back to her daughter.

"Ah, Ma?" Gwen was pulling her companion forward. "This is my friend Winnifred Makers, I told you about?"

Wide blue eyes, a sharp-featured New Race face, dark-blond hair. Swallowing a little, but bearing up under the stress of meeting the planetary-governor mother of her schoolfriend. *Good*, thought Yolande, sizing her up. *All in order. I don't care what the younger generation says, it's unnatural to get involved with boys before you're eighteen. More than good.* They exchanged formal wrist grips.

"Don't be too intimidated, Miz Makers," Yolande said kindly. "It isn't a very big planet, and there aren't many people on it yet." The girl gave a charming smile.

They turned to walk up the stairs. The ghouloons were keeping eyes front, but their pointed ears had swivelled toward the officer and the boy with his earnest questions.

"Imp," his mother said fondly. "Ah, Gwen, here's you Tantie-ma." Yolande watched, was gratified to see her daughter give the serf an affectionate peck on the cheek.

"Glad to see you again, Tantie-ma," she said.

"I'm . . . glad to see you, too, Missy Gwen," Marya said. There was a smile on her face, slight but genuine.

Gwen slapped a hand to her forehead. "Oh, here, I brought you somethin'. Those books you wanted, from that store in Archona? Here's the plaque."

SPIN HABITAT SEVEN
CENTRAL BELT
BETWEEN THE ORBITS OF MARS AND JUPITER
DECEMBER 28, 1991

"Aw, Dad!"

Frederick Lefarge looked over at his wife. She was mixing them martinis, at the cabinet on the other side of the living room. Dinner was a pleasant memory and a lingering smell of guinea-chile and avocado salad—*God, what did I do to deserve a good cook, on top of looks and brains?*—and he wanted that drink, and his feet up, and more quiet than two teenaged daughters promised. On the other hand . . .

He glanced sternly at Janet and Iris. "Homework done?" he said. *Gods, they're getting to be young women*, he thought. *Halter tops, yet.* And those fashionable hip-huggers . . . the damned things looked as if they had been sprayed on.

"Yeah," Janet said. Well, her marks had been excellent, particularly the math. It looked as if there *was* going to be at least one spacer in the family, if this kept up. Iris nodded. *Her* current fancy was composing. Well, at least she was still working at that, not like the other fads.

"It's a nice group," Cindy said. She finished shaking the cocktail pitcher, broke it open deftly and filled the chilled martini glasses. "From school, and a bunch over from Habitat Three. You know, the Martins and the Merkowitz kids?"

Lefarge pushed his chair back. "All right," he said, glancing at the viewer; it was set on landscape, with a time readout down near the lower righthand corner. "But be back by 0100, latest, or I'll shut the airlock on you for a week, understand?"

"Thanks, Dad!" Janet gave him a quick hug.

"We'll be back on time, Daddy." Iris kissed his cheek. "And they're playing one of my dance tunes," she whispered into his ear, giggling.

He sighed as he watched them fling themselves down the hall with an effortless feet-off-the-ground twist; they adjusted to the varying gravity of the habitat's shell decks the way he and Marya had to the streets of New York.

"Next thing you know, I'll be beating off boyfriends with a club," he grumbled, accepting the drink. "Ah, nice and dry."

Cindy put hers on the table and went behind the chair. Her fingers probed at his neck. "Rock. Don't worry, they're sensible girls, and we've got a nice family town here." He closed his eyes and rolled his head slightly as she kneaded the taut muscles. "At least we don't have to worry about juviegroups and trashing or having them go into orbit over Ironbelly Bootstomper bands," she continued.

Lefarge shuddered. "No, thank God. Sometimes I think the spirit that made America great hasn't died—just emigrated."

Cindy laughed and leaned over him; he felt a sudden sharp pain at the base of his cropped hair.

"Hey, cut that out!"

She held an almost-invisible something close to his eye on the tip of one finger: a gray hair. "You don't have enough of these to be an old fogey yet, honey," she said, and kissed him upside-down. Her face sobered. "Something's really bothering you, isn't it?"

He reached up to run his hand through her hair, streaked with silver against the mahogany color, shining and resilient. "You're too old to be so indecently beautiful," he murmured. Then: "I have to take a trip back dirtside," he said.

"Oh. That chair big enough for two?"

She picked up her drink and settled in against him, curving into the arm he laid about her shoulders. The silk of her blouse and skirt rustled, and he smelled a pleasant clean odor of shampoo and perfume and Cindy. "Uncle Nate?"

"He's sharp as ever, but not getting any younger," Lefarge said grudgingly. "You know how it is, anyone in his position so long makes enemies." The executive positions two or three steps down from the top in an agency like the OSS were coveted prizes. Not high enough to be political appointments, but they set policy. "Those who want his job, if nothing else; the problem is they're all disasters waiting to happen."

He paused to take another sip of the martini. "I have to blather to a couple of select committees. On top of that, Nate's afraid the new people in charge over in Archona are foxy enough to let up the pressure. That von Shrakenberg's a cunning devil; he knows how quickly some of us will go to sleep if they're not prodded." A frown. "I don't like it, when the Snakes get quiet. They're planning something. Maybe not now, maybe in a decade; something big."

Cindy shivered against him, and he held her closer. "No more raids, at least," she said. "Oh God, honey, I was so frightened."

And when the raid sirens turned on, went straight from your office to your emergency station and had the rest of them singsonging and playing bridge, he thought with a rush of warmth. *Jesus H. Christ, I'm a lucky man.* Grimly: *And we took out a major warship, too. They may be pulling back their fingers because we singed them.*

"There's something else, isn't there?" she went on.

"Witch." He sighed. "In the latest courier package from Uncle Nate." The Project was on the AI-3 distribution list; this was as secure an OSS station as anywhere in the Alliance, if only because so little went out. "They're in contact with Marya again."

"Bad?" Cindy said softly.

"No worse than before. That Ingolfsson creature's spawn . . ." He turned his head aside for a moment, then continued. "Anyway, Marya's been taken to their main Martian settlement. Working in household accounts, but even better, she's made some social contacts with the HQ office workers . . . just rumor, gossip, but priceless stuff. Contact's a priest; Christ, it's dangerous, though!" More softly: "And I miss her, sweet, I really do."

"So do I. She was always like a big sister to me . . ."

The disk player came on, with a quiet Baroque piece that Cindy must have selected beforehand. The lights dimmed, turning the homey familiarity of the living room into romantic gloom, and a new scene played on the viewer. He recognized that beach with the full moon over the Pacific and the swaying palms. Surf hissed gently . . .

"Why, Mrs. Lefarge," he said, looking down at her face. She grinned. "If I didn't know better, I'd say that a respectable matron was trying to seduce her husband again."

She wiggled into his lap. "Why, Mr. Lefarge," she whispered, twining her arms around his neck. "Why do you think I was so eager to get the girls out of the house?" She nibbled at his ear. "And if *you* are too young to be a fogey, *I'm* too young to be a matron. So there."

Chapter Seventeen

DRAKA FORCES BASE ARESOPOLIS
MARE SERENITATIS, LUNA
MARCH 25, 1998
2000 HOURS

Yolande turned her head to scan the other side of the Wasp-class stingfighter. *This is what it's like to be a ghost*, she thought. She ran her hand through the solid-seeming bulk of a crashcouch, looked down to see her shins disappear into the deck. A Wasp had room for exactly two crew, clamped into their couches for most of the trip. *Or what it's like to be a time traveller.* The events she was experiencing were nearly a thousand hours in the past. She watched the movements of the pilot's gloved fingers on the rests.

"Coming up on pod," the pilot said. "Twelve kay clicks and closing. Status." The wall ahead mapped trajectories and ran digital displays.

"Locked," her Weapons Officer said, his voice tight but steady.

So young, Yolande thought. *Gwen will be that old in a few years. So young . . .*

"Unauthorized craft, identify yourself." That from a resonator film somewhere in the cabin. Flat, grating Yankee accent with the mechanical overlay of a simple AI-interactive system. "You are on an intercept trajectory to within prohibited distance. Identify yourself or alter course."

"Visual," the pilot said.

"Acquisition," the Weapons Officer replied, and called it up on the screen.

A rough cylinder of slag-surfaced metal, pocked with bubbles and lumps from the vacuum-condensation refining process. A pod at one end with sensors and the guidance system, and rings of low-velocity hydrazine steering jets, a minimal course-correction system to send a hundred thousand tonnes of whatever from the asteroid belt to the Alliances melters and factories, here on the Moon and points inward. These days, a good deal of it might end up on Earth, headed for splashdown sites in the Sea of Cortés or the Cook Strait or the Inland Sea.

"Composition," the pilot was saying.

There was a second's pause and the Wasp's computer replied: "Iron, fifty percent, nickel twenty-one percent, chromium group, sixteen percent, tungsten ten percent, fissionables three percent, volatiles and trace elements."

Valuable, Yolande thought. The Yankees were stronger in the asteroid belt; their initial lead in deep-space pulsedrives had given them an opening they had never relinquished. Much cheaper to drop heavy elements down into the solar gravity well than boost them out of Earth's pull and atmosphere, even now that freight costs were coming down so low. The Alliance would trade metals for the water and chemicals the Draka took from the Jovian and Saturnian moons, of course, but it was cheaper to hijack where you could. Better strategy, too, since it hampered their operations and forced them to divert resources to guarding their slingshot modules and scavenging the asteroids for scarce volatiles . . . She had had a hand in formulating that policy.

At least it's been better strategy until now. A rectangle appeared in the "air" in front of her, an exterior simulation of the two spacecraft. The Wasp drifted, a blunt pyramid tapering from the shockplate at the rear to the crew compartment at the apex. Slim tubes rose from each corner of the plate, linked to the pyramid with a tracing of spars; asymmetric spikes flared out to guide the parasite bombs riding in station around the gunboat. The simulation limned the outlines, since like any warcraft this was armored in an absorptive synthetic that mimicked the background spectra.

"Closing," the pilot said. The outside view showed a needle-bright flicker behind the gunboat, deuterium-tritium pellets squeezed into explosion by the lasers. Yolande started, almost surprised not to feel the deceleration that pushed the crew back into their cradles. "One-ninah kay clicks, matchin'."

"Unidentified craft, this is your last warning," the robot voice droned.

"Eddie, shut that fuckah up, will you?" the pilot said, exasperated. The man grunted, touched a control surface.

The control chamber vanished, leaving a blackness lit only by the face of the investigating officer in the central portion. "That's it, Strategos," he said, shrugging. "End datalink. The fighter went pure ballistic from then until we grappled what was left." Yolande gestured, and the black went to gray, then faded into her office. She motioned again.

"All right," she said, as the rectangle expanded to occupy a square meter above the surface of her desk. "Give me the record of the recov'ry action."

"Well, the Yanks scrambled once they'uns realized what was happenin'," the Intelligence Section merarch said. The three-dimensional image lifted a cigarette to its lips. "Two Jefferson-class patrollers, with six and four gunboats respectively, in position to do somethin'. Thirty personnel, all told."

Yolande nodded: Yankee gunboats were single-crew, and the Jeffersons had ten apiece. The Alliance military relied more on cybernetics than the Draka did. "That was all they had within range."

Space was *large*, and even with constant-boost pulsedrive units it took a *long* time to get from anywhere to anywhere, compared with on-planet applications. There were times when she thought it was more like the situation back in her great-grandfather's time, when it could still take weeks to cross an ocean, months to traverse a continent. Then trouble blew up, and the soldier on the spot was left with his ass hanging in the breeze and no way to call for mama.

"Luckily, we'n's had three Iron Limper corvettes on, ah, patrol." *Corsair duty*, her mind added sardonically, using the crew slang. "This's what happened."

The view shifted to points and data columns, a schematic of the corvettes and their twelve—*no, eleven*—gunboat outriders, and the machinery's best guess on the Yankees. The usual thing for space combat, a long gingerly waiting before a brief flurry of action. A pulsedrive was sort of hard to hide anywhere in the solar system unless you had something the size of a planet to shelter it, but that told you very little except the past position and a fan of possible vectors. Spaceships were another matter; between stealthing and datamimic decoys, long-range detection had always run a little behind the countermeasures.

"Well, both parties knew they'd have to intersect somewhere along the trajectory of the cargo pod and the stingray." A section of the curve that looped in from beyond the orbit of Mars turned red, the area where either set of warships could match velocities. "The Yankees went into constant-boost, figurin' to overrun us on the pass, then go back fo' it. We went silent, coastin'; had the advantage, comin' out-system from sunward."

"Ah." She could guess what came next. You could think of a pulsedrive as a series of microfusion bombs and field-shielding and reaction mass heated to plasma—or as a sword of radiation and high-energy particles tens of kilometers long. That was the Staff way of seeing it. Her imagination flashed other images on the inner screen of her consciousness. The matte-black shapes of the Limpers falling outward. A shallow disk perched on a witch's maze of tubing like some mad oil refinery, all atop the great convex soup plate of the pusher. The dozen crewfolk locked into their cocoons of armor and sensors, decision-making units in a dance of photonics. Units that sweated with fears driven down below consciousness; the ripping impact of crystal tesseract mines scattering their high-V shrapnel through hulls and bodies, blood boiling into vacuum. The pulse of a near-miss and secondary gamma sleeting invisibly through the body, wrecking the infinitely complex balances of the cells. Tumbling in a wrecked ship, puking and delirious and dying slowly of thirst . . .

Fears carried down from the ground ape; hindbrain reflexes that twitched muscles in desperate need to flee or fight, pumped juices into the blood, roiling minds that must stay as calm as the machines that were master and slave both. Yolande swallowed past dryness, and used the inward disciplines taught by those who had trained her for war. The slamming impact of deceleration; railguns, lightguns, mine showers, missile and countermissile, the parasite bombs driving their one-megaton

X-ray beams like the icepicks of gods. The drives punching irresistibly through fields and shieldings, perhaps a single second for the stricken to know their fate as plasma boiled through the corridors.

Silence. Long slow zero-G fading past, waiting for the sensors to tell you if you were already dead . . .

She shook her head. "*Hugin* totalled." Sheer bad luck, a parasite-bomb impact just as her drive was cycling out a new pellet. Twelve dead. "*Lothbrok* mostly made it." If the biotechs could repair tissues so riddled. "*Ragnar*, no losses."

"A successful engagement," the Intelligence Officer said. "But . . ."

"But we still don't know what the *shit* happened with that-there original intercept."

"Strategos . . ." The merarch hesitated, then continued. "Strategos, admitted all we've got is what downloaded to optical storage befo' they bought it . . . but *somethin'* catastrophic *did* happen. If'n I didn't know better, I'd say point-blank parasite bomb hit, with a chain fire in the feed tubes fo' the drive. But there weren't no parasite bombs travellin' with that cargo pod."

"Incorrect, Merarch. There were five."

For a moment the man looked blank, then his eyes widened slightly in shock. Their gaze met in agreement: *With the fighter, its own weapons.* "This is speculation, an' not to go on record. Understood?"

He nodded. They were silent for a moment; his voice was slow and musing when he continued: " 'Bout the prisoners . . . we kept them in filterable-virus isolation an' did a complete scan, as per usual." Security had gotten even more paranoid of late, now that Alliance nanosabotage capacities were approaching the size level of Draka gene-engineering skills. Not to mention the ever-present nightmare of data plaque contamination; the Alliance's superiority in compinstruction was indisputable. The Domination took what precautions it could—offline backup systems for all essential functions, manual overrides, physical separation—but there were limits to what could be done in an environment as dependent on computer technology as space.

"Well, somethin' sort of odd came up. *Very* damn odd. The biotechs *found* somethin' on six of the seven livin' prisoners, some sort of latent . . . weeell, virus or *somethin'* back in the central nervous an' limbic systems. Very tricky, very; they only found it on 'count the discrepancy in the neural DNA analysis was the same on each. Wouldn't have found it, say, two years ago; it would have come out as the usual noise garbage." The cellular codes of any mammal have far more information capacity than they need.

"So we blipped the info to Biocontrol Central." Yolande waited while the man moistened his lips. "Order came back, freeze in place. Then about two hours latah, a priority-one command to wait fo' a courier. One came direct, with orders to turn them ovah to the headhunters. That an' wipe the data an' forget we'd ever seen it."

"Castle Tarleton?"

"No, from the Palace. From the Archon's office, an' under his personal code." They exchanged another glance; he had placed his life in her hands with those words. A calculated risk; that Eric von Shrakenberg was her uncle was widely known. That she met regularly with him on more than family matters was not.

"Well." For the first time in the interview, Yolande smiled, a slow cold turning of the lips. "Well, we can't argue with *that*." Normally there would have been a bureaucratic gunfight; Aresopolis was War Directorate territory, after all. "Not that I don't love to trip our esteemed colleagues up as much as anyone, but in *this* case . . ."

She grinned at the thought of the slow disassembling the Security Directorate would use on the prisoners, and the other officer turned his eyes aside slightly. Yolande Ingolfsson's feelings concerning the enemy in general and Americans in particular were well-known, but still a little disconcerting to meet in practice.

The grin faded, to be replaced with something resembling a human expression. "And, Thomas . . ." The first name was a signal, and he leaned forward, an unconscious expression of attention. " . . . I have an odd feelin' about this. That data had better *really* disappear. Or I think *we* might."

"What data?" he said.

She nodded. "Ovah. Service to the State."

"Glory to the Race," he replied formally, and the rectangle went blank.

"Fade," she said, and the lights dimmed. "Review, casualties."

Her mouth thinned; this was a disagreeable chore. Theoretically, the unit commander . . . No, she had ordered the action. The general policy was set higher up, but she made the operational decisions. It was her responsibility. A figure in the form-fitting vacuum skinsuit blinked into existence before her, turning toward the pickup and laughing, bubble helmet in one hand. A cat hanging in midair beside it, obviously unused to low-G and falling in spraddle-legged panic. The figure was young, with fair hair cropped close. Data unreeled below: Julian Torbogen, born . . . Very young, only a year older than her oldest. A face with the chiseled, sculpted look the Eugenics Board was moving the Race toward, but an individual for all that. The dossier listed it all: pets, hobbies, grade evaluations, favorite foods, friends, love affairs, hopes (*habitat design is so* complete *an art!*), hates.

Yolande called up the medical image and placed it beside the laughing youth. Explosive decompression is not a pleasant way to die, especially combined with a wash of radiant heat that melts equipment into flesh across half the body. Two-thirds of the face was still there, enough for the final expression to survive.

A long moment, and then she closed her eyes and began to dictate. "Dear Citizens. As your son's commanding officer, I . . ."

It took an hour to complete the messages: they were brief but it was crucial to give each one the individual attention it was due. These were Citizens, the hope of the Race. *Cells must die for the whole to live. But we must mourn them, because we are cells who* know *what we are. That is our immortality.*

She shook off the mood and rose, calling the lights back to normal. *Coming home*, she thought wryly. Half her existence these days seemed to be spent in illusion and shadows, riding the silica threads and photon pulses, until she could hardly tell waking from sleeping.

"Call Tina," she said to the machines that always listened. "Brandied coffee, please." Absurd to use a form of courtesy with a computer, but it was another connection to real life.

This outer room of her sanctum—was this home? *As much as anyplace, the last five years.* A long box-rectangle, her desk at one end. Lunar-basalt tiles, covered by fur rugs from animals created by biotech. Leather-spined books, and shelves of real wood, expensive on Luna, but Loki knew there were *some* compensations for this job. The outer wall was set to a soft neutral gray for concentration's sake; it was a single blank sheet five meters by ten, a thin-film sandwich holding several hundred thousand thermovalves per square centimeter. It could be set to display anything at all, well enough to fool even an expert's eye until you touched it, but she was suddenly weary of vicarious experience. And of the fresh clean recycled air.

"Transparent and open," she said. It blinked clear and slid up with a minor *shhhh* as she walked out onto the balcony.

That was near the top of the ring wall, a lacy construction of twisted vitryl, filaments of monocrystal titanium-chromium-vanadium alloy and glass braided together. Those were words; the reality was smooth curves of jade-green ice, thin as gossamer, stronger than steel. The sky above was of the same material, a shallow ribbed dome across the hundred-kilometer bowl of the crater. A thousand meters over her head one of its great anchor cables sprang out, soaring up and away until it dwindled into a thread and disappeared into the distance; the sky was set to a long twilight now, and she could just make out the blue-white disk of Earth. She walked to the waist-high balustrade, looked out and down.

The crater was in natural terrace steps to either side and sheer cliff below, nothing but air and haze three kilometers to the tumbled jungle-shaggy hills at the base. To her right a river sprang out of the rock, fell with unearthly slowness in a long bright-blue arc until it misted away into rain; a lake gathered underneath, and the river flowed like silver off through the mottled greens of the landscape below. Clouds drifted in layers, silver and dappled with Earth light; they cast shadows over fields, meadows, forest, roads. There was no horizon, only a vast arch that melted green into blue. Lights were appearing here and there; far and far, she could just make out the high spike of the mountain at the crater's center, bright-lit, with the thin illuminated streak of the elevator tower rising to the landing platform on the airless side of the dome.

"Mistis."

A presence at her elbow; she took the cup without glancing around, murmured abstracted thanks, propped one haunch on the balustrade, sipped. Kenya Mountain Best, diluted with a quarter of hot cream and a tenth of Thieuniskraal. Warmth and richness flowed over her tongue, with a hint of bite at the back of her mouth and down her throat. It was very quiet, the thunder of the falling water far enough away to be a muted background. The soft wind that flickered ends of her gray-blond hair about her face was louder; she ignored their tickling caress. All about the balcony, rock that had lain lifeless since the forming of the Earth was covered in rustling vines that bore sheets of pale-pink blossoms; they smelled of mint and lavender.

As they had been designed to do. So had the multicolored birds that flitted through the flowers been designed for the intricate flute-like songs they trilled; farther out a yellow-feathered hawk banked on four-meter wings and called, a long mournful wailing. Yolande sipped again, feeling a sensation that was half contentment, half the reple-tion that followed the end of a poem. This *was* a composition, and she one of its manifold creators; part of what she had dreamed, as a child looking up at the new lights in the sky over Claestum. The Glory of the Race was more than power; that was just the beginning. It was accomplishment, it was to *do*.

She closed her eyes, squeezing them against a flash of old remem-bered pain. *Myfwany, darlin', if only you could be here to see it with me,* she thought. Then somewhere far back in her mind a ghost met her gaze with sardonic green: *Freya, what a sentimentalist you are, Yolande-sweet, to let me haunt you so. One thing I never aspired to be was the drop of fall in your cup; you alive, so live, girl.*

"Such good advice, and as always easier to give than to follow," she murmured to herself.

"Mistis?"

"Nothin', Tina," Yolande said to the serf who squatted at her feet and peered through the finger-thick rods of the balustrade.

The wench rose. Tina had a glass of milk in one hand, and a white mustache of it on her upper lip that she licked away with unself-conscious relish; then drank more, taking the slow care needful in one-sixth gravity. Eighteen and softly pretty in a doe-eyed Italian way, big-hipped, the four-month belly just starting to show. Yolande smiled and laid a hand on it; the serf smiled shyly back and put her hand over the Draka's in turn. For a moment Yolande wondered what it must feel like, to bear a living child beneath the heart. She was too old herself, of course, even if there had ever been time, and bearing your own eggs was eccentric to the point of suspiciousness now, anyway. Strange to think that she herself was of the last generation of the Race born of their mothers' wombs.

She rubbed her serf's stomach affectionately. "Time to get you home to Claestum, Tina," she said.

The later stages of pregnancy did not do well below .3 G; in theory, regular centrifuge was enough to compensate, but she did not intend to take any chances at all. Strictly speaking, there was no need to get involved in the process to this extent; a lot of people just sent the fertilized ova in to the Clinic and picked up the baby nine months later. Yolande had always found that too impersonal; she insisted on being present at the implantation and the birthing, and used only family servants as brood-ers, volunteers from the plantation. It seemed more . . . more *fitting*, somehow. Birth was no less a miracle because the Race had mastered its secrets, after all. And this was the most important of all, truly hers and Myfwany's, now that the ova-merging technique was perfected.

"Yes, time to get home Mistis," Tina said with a sigh, leaning into the caress and looking out over the crater. "I will miss this. It so pretty."

And such a vanity, Yolande thought. Oh, not *so* difficult, not when you could use fusion bombs and bomb-pumped lasers for excavation; not when energy poured down in vacuum, to be stored as pressurized water or liquid metal or in superconducting rings . . . Anything local and not too complex was cheap, given autofabricators, and the whole construct was basically titanium and glass. Oxygen and silica and light metals were abundant on the moon; launch lasers and magnetic catapults at Gibraltar and Kilimanjaro and in the Tien Shan were part of the War effort, and might as well be kept to capacity with cargo loads; an abundance of water and volatiles was coming in from the outer system. Also, a closed ecosystem was a tricky thing; the bigger you made it the easier it was to manage.

Also a chance to put the Drakon's eye up here on the Moon, she thought. *And wouldn't the Yankees love to stick a thumb in it.*

Which was why the bulk of Aresopolis was burrowed kilometers deep into the lunar crust—factories and dormitories, refineries and chemosynthesis plants, the far-down caverns with their stores of liquid hydrogen, oxygen, methane, ammonia, metals, a Fafnir's horde gathered from as far out as Saturn. The orbital battle stations clustering about Earth were largely armed and built from here; so were the outposts at the L-5 points, the far-flung bases, Mercury, the Venus study project, Mars, a scattering of outposts in the Alliance-dominated asteroids. Half the two million souls the Domination had sent into space lived here, in this strange city of warriors and warriors' servants; a third of them free Citizens, the highest ratio of any city in the Domination.

All of there beneath her command—and able, in their leisure, to come out here to walk naked under living green, swim in water that bore silver-speckled trout, to fly with muscle-powered wings as no humans before them had ever done. She flicked the last droplets from the cup out into the void, watching the long dreamy slowness of the fall.

"They say the neoredwoods we've planted down there will grow a thousand meters tall in another fifty years," Yolande said, softly. "I'll bring the children here, and we'll rent wings and fly off the highest branches like eagles." She should still be hale, then, with modern biotech.

"Will you bring me to watch?" Tina asked, and snuggled another question.

"Yes," Yolande said. "That's a promise. And no, get you off to a nice quiet bed, wench; mind you health."

The serf left with the long glide-bounce of an experienced Aresopolite. Yolande lingered for a moment, yawning and rolling the still-warm porcelain of the cup between her palms. The sky had gone true dark, and the hard bright stars were out; the clouds below reflected blue-silver Earth light back into her eyes. Moving stars, many of them, and she could see another rising swiftly to join them from beyond the crater rim, a laser-boost capsule from one of the emplacements that studded the mountains around the city. That was one

of their functions; another might be to rip targets as far away as
Earth, one day.

Suddenly she was on her feet, shaken with a wild anger. The flung
cup arched out into emptiness with maddening slowness; there was
nothing on the planets or between that could express the wash of
loathing she felt. *They* were there, too, the Yankees, the destroyers of
all happiness, the oaf-lump impediment that stood always in the Race's
path. This single city, an ornament above a fortress, when the Moon
might be laced with them like living jewels. Scorched meat made of
lordly golden boys who should be here playing tag with eagles, or going
out to make green paradise of frozen Mars and burning Venus. Always
intriguing, threatening with their sly greasy-souled merchant cunning,
menacing the future of her blood. Gwen, Nikki, Holden, Johanna still
unborn, whose years ought to stretch out before them like diamonds
in the sun . . .

"I *will* be back with them, in you despite," she said in tones quiet
and even and measured. "Everythin' you are, we'll bring to nothin';
we'll grind you bones to make our bread, and you children will serve
mine until the end of days."

With an effort she turned back into the office. *A consummation
devoutly to be wished*, she thought. *To which end, I'm going to get
Uncle Eric to tell me* precisely *what's been goin' on here.*

"Message," she said to the sensors. "Strategos Alman Witter, Vice-
Commandant; Allie, I'm droppin' down to HQ fo' the week. You step
in as per, stay on top of the patrol incident an' keep me posted soonest.
Message: Transport, Aresopolis to Archona"—she looked at her desk:
2140—"departin' 1100 to 1200 tomorrow. Message: private, code fol-
lows—"

"*One-hundred-forty*-nine, *one-hundred*-fifty," Marya Lefarge gasped as
she finished the series of situps, and sank back on the exercise table,
panting.

No more. That finished her daily three-hour program, but there was
a druglike pleasure to exhaustion as hard to fight as sloth. The 1-G
exercise chamber was crowded and close, a slight smell of sweat among
the machinery that glistened in the overhead sunlamps. The floor had
a slight but perceptible curve; it was a wedge section of a giant wheel
spinning deep beneath Aresopolis. Dual purpose like most things
offplanet, a flywheel storing energy for burst use, but time here was
still limited and rationed. Most of the occupants were pregnant brooders,
wearily putting in their minimum on exercise bicycles, with a scattering of others whose owner's credits allowed or tasks required high-
gravity maintenance. Mostly they leafed through picture books, listened
to music on ear plugs or chattered among themselves, leaving her in
a bubble of silence.

Cows, she thought bitterly, looking at them as she swung her legs
off the table. Then: *That's unfair. Not their fault.* Some of them looked
back at her out of the corners of their eyes, then away again. She
felt the slight ever-present tug of the controller cuff on her right wrist,
more than enough reason to shun her; who knew what she had done,

to need an instant pain paralyzer? Guilt was contagious, especially here, where every word and gesture was observed by the never-sleeping senses of the computers and the endless probing vigilance of the AI programs.

There was a man working with spring weights near her who did not look away. Handsome, younger than she, a Eurasian with smooth olive skin and bright blue eyes; he smiled, lifted his brows. Lithe-bodied and strong, he could be anything from a dancer to a Janissary . . . *Why not*, she thought, hesitating a second, then shook her head as she smiled and left, towel thrown over one shoulder. She felt his eyes on her neck, memorizing her number. Probably he could reference it through Records; probably he would sheer off when he learned who owned her.

And it would be too easy, too easy to make yourself comfortable with little compromises until there was nothing left. Better not to start, just as it was better not to talk too much. When every word could kill, talk meant fear. Fear until you censored the words, then the dangerous thoughts to make that easier, then stopped *having* the thoughts. Better to talk to yourself in the safety of your head.

Marya walked inward toward the hub, up steps that gradually flattened into floor as the centrifugal force weakened and lunar gravity took over. She ignored the faint ferris-wheel feeling of disorientation from her inner ears and halted before the gate; it slid open, and she stepped into the narrow chamber and pressed her back against the antispinward wall. There was a brief pressure as the inner ring of the wheel slowed and stopped; the inner door opened, and she walked through into the hub.

Showers and sauna were crowded, too, but at least they were not open-plan. She stripped off the exercise shorts and threw the disposable fabric into a hamper, nodding to a few persons she knew as she waited in line for a cubicle, studying herself in the mirrored walls. *Not bad*, she decided. Especially for fifty; not much sagging, although of course the light gravity helped, and the daily exercise she had kept up as a silent gesture of self-respect . . . and the fact that Strategos Yolande Ingolfsson bought her personal servants top-flight Citizen Level medical care, which meant the best in the solar system. Viral DNA repair, cellular waste removal, synthormone implants, calcium boost, the works. There were strands of silver in her long black hair, crow's-feet beside her eyes, but for the rest she could have passed for mid-thirties.

A woman in her mid-thirties who had borne a child and breast-fed it. Her fingers traced lightly over the cracked-eggshell pattern on the taut muscle of her stomach.

"Not now," she murmured to herself, her eyelids drooping down as she turned attention within, finding the pattern of calm. Her gaze was cool as she raised it back to the mirror. *Yes, not bad. That could be important*, she thought with cold realism. *Things are moving to a crisis; you've got to know*. Clandestine-ops mode. *Think of yourself as a sleeper*. She grinned sardonically at the joke as she stepped into the vacated cubicle.

❖   ❖   ❖

"Sector Three, level two," the transporter capsule said.

The lid hissed open, and Yolande stepped out into the station, past the unmoving guards. Probably unnecessary; the machinery would simply not obey unauthorized personnel. On the other hand, there were ways to fool machinery, and it was not in the Draka nature to trust too completely to cybernetics. The Orpos were the regular pair, and saluted briskly; she blinked back to awareness of her surroundings and returned it. Downside there might have been actual physical checks.

Lucky we're not quite *settled enough to start importing surplus bureaucrats*, she thought wearily. Sector Three was command residence country; Civil, War Directorate, Security and Combines both; status was being close to the main transport station. Yolande sighed slightly as she palmed the lock of her outer door; the inner slid open as the corridor portal cycled shut, another emergency airlock system. It might have been more efficient to pack everything close together in one spot, but this *was* supposed to be a fortress. Carving rock was no problem either, not when the original function of Aresopolis had been to throw material into Earth orbit to armor battle stations. So the city beneath was a series of redundantly-linked modules, any of which could function independently for a long, long time.

"Hiyo, Mistis," Jolene said, waiting with a hot lemonade. The entranceway was a circular room ten meters in diameter, with a domed roof over a central pool and fountain. The walls were holo panels between half-columns, right now set to show a steppe landscape: rolling green hills fading into a huge sky, wind rippling the grass, distant antelope.

"'Lo, Jo," Yolande said, accepting the glass.

Machiavelli IV came bounding into the room and raced around the wall to reach her, running with innocent unconcern across what looked to be empty space and soaring to land on the foam-lava floor by her feet. Two housegirls followed more sedately with her lounging robe and slippers; Yolande sipped moodily at the hot sweet-tart liquid while they removed her uniform and redressed her, moving only to transfer the glass from hand to hand.

"We're leavin' tomorrow," she said abruptly. Then, to the apartment: "Walls, blank." The holo panels dimmed to a neutral pearl-gray color. Yolande spared them a moment's irritation, she would have preferred mosaic, but the necessary skills were still scarce on Luna, and anyway this *was* the Commandant's quarters. Furnished rooms, in a sense.

"Tomorrow, Mistis?" Jolene asked, puzzled. It was a month before leave was scheduled.

"I said so, didn't I?" Yolande snapped, then sighed and drew a hand across her face. "Sorry, Jo. Somethin' came up. Down to Archona, stayin' with Uncle Eric, then a quick trip up to Claestum to drop off Tina with John an' Mandy, then back here. Call it fo' days; just pack an overnight bag an' Tina's things."

She looked down at the housegirls, kneeling with hands folded in their laps and eyes downcast; both rather new, and still a little shy, especially at hearing the Archon referred to as "Uncle." "Run along, there's good wenches . . . I'll take Lele, none of the other staff." No point in carting a dozen servants along for a visit, and Jolene hated space travel. "Light supper, an' . . ."

The inner door sighed open and shut. Yolande looked over her shoulder; it was Marya. " . . . An' set up the chess game fo' after, Marya."

King's pawn to knight four, Yolande decided. She moved the carved-ebony Janissary and leaned back in the lounger, sipping at the white wine; it was Vernaccia. *Checkmate in, hmmm, seven moves.* She was not doing as well as usual tonight, and it was getting a little late. *Damn, I'm not sleepy, either,* she thought.

The lounging room was arch-roofed, a relic of excavating techniques in the early days, back in the mid-1960s; the Commandant's quarters had been enlarged but not moved as the city grew. There were a few pictures, some hangings, but she had had most of the walls left in the natural white-streaked black rock interspersed with hand-painted *azulejos* tile; the furniture eras modern and local, spindly shapes of lacquered bamboo and puff pillows. The room seemed cavernous and dim now, yet somehow cramped despite space enough to guest a hundred. Perhaps it was subliminal knowledge of all those kilometers of rock above. Yolande stirred restlessly.

What was it Michelangelo said about Vernaccia? she thought, sipping again. It *"kisses, licks, bites, thrusts, and stings."* There's *my subconscious telling me what I want.* That was a little awkward; she had told Tina no . . . She was not in the mood for Jolene's friendly complaisance, and the rest of the staff were unsuitable or too new, too much in awe, to be very interesting. *Maybe a man?* That was nice occasionally; unfortunately, no Citizen she knew well enough was available, probably. Well, she could have a nightspot send a buck around—perfectly legal nowadays; the Race Purity laws had been updated back in the '70s.

No, maybe I'm old-fashioned, but no. Ah well, there's always the headset. That brought sleep without chemical hangovers.

"Mistis." Yolande blinked out of her reverie and saw the serf's next move.

"Thought so. You shouldn't be so . . . schematic about you pieces. See." She took the other's last bishop and indicated the alternatives. "Neither of us's up to scratch tonight."

"Ah, Mistis. There was an unusual note in the serf's voice. Yolande looked up, saw that she was studying a piece held in one hand. A pawn in ivory, in the shape of a German soldier of the Eurasian War. "Ah, can I ask you a question?" The fall of her hair hid most of her face, and the tops of her ears were pink.

The Draka blinked puzzlement. "Certainly."

"Were, ah, were you planning on going to bed alone tonight, Mistis?"

Yolande's eyebrows rose, and she spoke with a chuckle in her voice. "Is that an invitation, Marya?" *I hope so. Have for years; wonder what changed her mind?*

A nod. "Well, well, that *is* a surprise." She cleared her mind and looked. *Rather nice. Not young, but then, neither am I anymore.* It was getting to be a little embarrassing, bedding teenagers. Granted they were only serfs, still . . . *And I've wanted you for a while.*

She rose and extended a hand. "Shall we?"

"Ah!"

Yolande went rigid as the orgasm flowed over her like waves of warmth, felt the world swim blue before her eyes. She was straddled, kneeling across the other's shoulders, arched back on her heels with her shoulders resting on the serf's upraised knees. Now she leaned forward and sank lower, linking her hands behind her neck and smiling down at the face between her thighs. "One mo' time, pretty pony," she said softly, moving her hips in languid rhythm to the sweet wet friction of tongue and lips. The serf's eyes were closed below a frown of concentration; her head moved with the arching of Yolande's pelvis, and she gripped the Draka's hips with a clench that whitened her fingernails.

"Ah. Mmm*mm.*" Yolande moved more quickly, shuddered, locked immobile with a long hiss between clenched teeth. This time the color went beyond blue to indigo, shot through with veins of red. She nearly collapsed forward—would have in normal gravity.

"Wonderful," she sighed as she eased herself down beside the other and reached up for the wine glass. Blood pounded in her ears like retreating drums, and the dreamy relaxation was like flying in dreams. Marya's eyes fluttered open, dark and unreadable. Yolande poured the last of the wine on her lips and kissed her, savoring the pleasant mixture of tastes. The room was dark except for a wall set to show a landscape of lunar mountains jagged across the three-quarters Earth; that cast a pale silver glow over the circular bed. The air was lightly warm, and she could smell the roses in planters around the walls, musk, a slight tang of sweat and warm flesh.

Marya turned on her side and laid her head on her owner's shoulder; Yolande stroked her back. *At least the third-arm problem is less up here*, she thought drowsily. *Gods, I haven't felt this relaxed in months.*

"I'm glad you liked it, Mistis," the serf said, yawning into the curve where neck met deltoid.

"Freya, yes. I's so tense without knowin' it, I went off like a sunbomb. That damn stingfighter's got me tied in knots . . . *can't* figure out how the damnyanks did it." She was muttering, half thinking aloud; absently, she set the glass down on the fused stone of the headboard and began stroking down Marya's flank. "And on *top* of that, those fuckin' prisoners. Why is *Biocontrol* gettin' into the decision-makin' loop? They're just a research institute, even if they're so almighty impo'tant these days . . ."

She paused, hand lingering on the firmness of the other's hip. "Lift you knee . . . Did *you* like it, Marya?" Her fingers trailed down the inside of the serf's leg and lightly cupped her groin.

"Couldn't you tell, Mistis?" the other said. She smiled and rolled onto her back, raising and spreading her legs.

"Hmm, I could tell when you came; that isn't the same thing." Yolande slipped her free hand under the serf's neck while she kneaded softly with the other, rising on one elbow and bending her head to Marya's breasts. The nipples were dark and taut, the large aureoles around them crinkled, ridged smoothness under her tongue.

"I . . ." Marya caught her breath as Yolande bit gently. "I volunteered. This time."

There was quiet for a few minutes, broken only by the increasing sound of the serf's panting. Yolande leaned closer, studying the other's face. The dark eyes were wide, iris swallowed in the pupil. *Ah, nearly*, she thought, laughing and increasing the feather-light pressure of her fingers. Marya's arms went back, gripping the headboard, as her knees pulled up and wide; the cords in her neck stood out as she gave a series of gasps and then a sharp cry.

"I think maybe you *do* like it," Yolande said. "Pity you don't like me; it increases the pleasure." She wiped her hand on the sheet.

Marya sighed. "You've been . . . You haven't been as . . . strict with me these last few years, Mistis."

Embarrassed, Yolande lay back. "Oh . . . Well, I wasn't thinkin' straight, fo' a while after Myfwany was killed. You sort of stood fo' the Yankees, in my mind. But that isn't fair, of course; you aren't a Yankee anymore, you my serf. Not fittin' to abuse you. Besides"—she patted the other's stomach for a second, then took her hand—"you bore Gwen. Not willingly, of course, but you still carried an' nursed Myfwany's clone-child; I couldn't keep up the hatin' after I saw her at you breast, could I?"

She was silent for a moment, letting drowsy thoughts sift through her mind. "Still . . . playin' chess, you get to know a person somewhats." She yawned. "You strange to me. As different as two bein's of the same species can be. Draka I understand. An' serfs. Yankees I meet in structured situations, like battle; logic of objective conditions forces a certain amount of similarity to they behavior. Most of my serfs like me well enough; I'm a good owner. You . . ." She shrugged. "You wasn't raised to think that way." *I think I'm still the enemy, in your heart*, she thought. *What do they taste of, the kisses of an enemy?*

"Mistis, take me with you, on this visit?"

"Why so?"

"I . . ." Marya turned her head away from the one on the pillow beside her. "You're right, everyone here is still strange to me, even after all these years; but you less than the born-serfs."

"'Kay," Yolande muttered. She turned on her side and threw an arm and leg across Marya's body. "Sleep now." Her eyelids fluttered closed.

Marya's right arm was free; she raised it in the dim light of the reflected Earth, letting it shine on the imperishable metal of the controller. Then she brought it to her lips, opening them to the cool neutral taste, slightly bitter. She lay so, motionless except for an occasional slow blink, as the hours crept by and the sweat cooled on her skin.

Chapter Eighteen

NEW YORK CITY
HOSPITAL OF THE SACRED HEART
FEDERAL CAPITAL DISTRICT
UNITED STATES OF AMERICA
APRIL 7, 1998

Nathaniel Stoddard grinned like a death's-head at the shock in Lefarge's eyes.

"Happens to us all, boy," he said slowly. "Ayuh. And never at a convenient time."

Lefarge swallowed and looked away from the wasted figure, the liver-spotted hands that never stopped trembling on the coverlet. *I've always hated the way hospitals smelled,* he thought. Medicinal, antiseptic, with an underlying tang of misery. The private room was crowded with the medical-monitoring machines, smooth cabinets hooked to the ancient figure on the bed through a dozen tubes and wires; their screens blinked, and he knew that they were pumping data to the central intensive-care computer. Doling out microdoses of chemicals, hormones, enzymes . . .

"I'd have told them to stop trying two years ago, if I hadn't been needed," Stoddard said. The faded blue eyes looked at Lefarge with an infinite weariness, pouched in their loose folds of skin. "But if I'm indispensable, the nation's doomed anyway, son."

Lefarge looked up sharply; that was the first time the old man had ever used the word to him. He reached out and clasped the brittle-boned hand with careful gentleness.

"My only regret is that you couldn't take over my post," Stoddard said. "But what you're doing is more important. Janice and the boy all right?"

Lefarge smiled, an expression that felt as if it would crack his cheeks. "Janice is fine. Nate Junior is a strapping rockjack of thirty now, Uncle Nate. Courting, too, and this time it looks serious. We'll have the Belt full of Stoddards yet."

The general sighed, and closed his eyes for a moment. "The Project? What do your tame scientists say about the trans-Luna incident?"

Well, at least the information's still getting through, Lefarge thought. *I might have known Uncle Nate would arrange to keep a tap into channels.*

"They . . . " He ran a hand through his hair, and caught a glimpse of himself in the polished surface of a cabinet. *Goddam. I show more of Maman every year.* His cropped hair was as much gray as black, now; no receding hairline, though. "Well, the consensus is that it . . . mutated. They had to make it so that it could modify itself, anyway. The trigger is multiply redundant, but it's just data, and if something knocks out a crucial piece . . . " He shrugged and raised his hands. "No estimate on spread, either. Slow. Maybe ten percent penetration by now, if we're lucky. Two years to critical mass. Absolutely no way of telling if there'll be more, ah, mutations. Or if they'll figure it out." He shrugged again. "The Team says de Ribeiro was right; we took a . . . less than optimum path in computer development, way back when. Too much crash research, too much security. Though they practically end up beating each other over the head about what we *should* have done! Anyway, even the Project can't redevelop an entire technology. They've pushed the present pretty well to its limits, and what we're using is the product."

Stoddard's eyes opened again. "Fred . . ." He fought for breath, forced calm on himself and began again. "Fred, don't let them throw it away. We can't . . . The Militants will win the next Archonal election in the Domination. Coalition . . . we're pretty sure. War . . . soon after. Inevitable . . . fanatics. Think of the damage if they attack . . . first. Remember . . . Nelson's eyepatch."

Fred felt the hair crawl on the back of his neck. Admiral Nelson had been signaled to halt an attack; he put the telescope to his blind eye, announced that he had seen no signal, and continued.

A red light began to beep on one of the monitors. Seconds later a nurse burst into the room.

"Brigadier Lefarge!" she said severely, moving quickly to the bedside. "You were allowed to see the patient on condition he not be stressed in any way!"

He leaned over Stoddard, caught the faded blue eyes, nodded. "Don't worry, Uncle Nate," he said softly. "I'll take care of it."

"Brigadier—" the nurse began. Then her tone changed to one he recognized immediately: a good professional faced with an emergency. "Dr. Suharto to room A17! Dr. Suharto to room A17!" Her hands were flying over the controls, and the old man's body jerked. More green-and-white-coated figures were rushing into the room; Lefarge stepped back to the angle of the door, saluted quietly, wheeled out.

The office in Donovan House was much the same, missing only the few keepsakes Nathaniel Stoddard had allowed himself, even the Parrish landscapes were still on the wall. Something indefinable was different, perhaps the smell of pipe tobacco, perhaps . . . *I'm imagining things*, Frederick Lefarge thought, as he saluted the new incumbent.

Anton Donati was holding down Stoddard's desk now. Lefarge had worked with him often over the years; less so since the New America project got well underway and he was seldom on Earth. About his own age, thin and dark and precise, with a mustache that looked as if it had been drawn on. Competent record in the field, even better once he was back at headquarters. But a by-the-book man, a through-channels operator. The other man in the room was a stranger, a civilian in a blue-trimmed gray suit and natty silver-buckled shoes; the curl-brimmed hat on the stand by the door had a snakeskin band and one peacock feather. A whiff of expensive cologne; just the overall ensemble that a moderately prosperous man-about-town was wearing this season.

"Anton," Lefarge nodded. He continued the gesture to the civilian, raised an eyebrow. His superior caught the unspoken question: *Who's the suit?*

"Brigadier, this is Operative Edward Forsymmes, Alliance Central Intelligence."

Fucking joy. He is *a suit.* Still, this was no time to let the rivalry with the newer central-government agency interfere with business. San Francisco was capital of the Alliance, and the Alliance was sovereign. The OSS had been founded as an agency of the old American government; it was only natural that the Grand Senate wanted an intelligence source of its own. *And the suits still couldn't find their own arses with both hands on a dark night.*

Lefarge extended his hand; the ACI agent rose and shook with a polished smile. There was strength in the grip; the man had a smooth, even tan, and no spare weight that the American could see; thinning blond hair combed over the bald spot, gray eyes.

"Jolly good to meet you," he said pleasantly. *British?* Lefarge asked himself. *No. Australasian; South Island, at a guess. Probably Tasmanian.* A quarter of the British Isles had moved to the Australasian Federation over the past century, and the accents had not diverged all that much, especially in the Outer Islands. "Shall we proceed?"

The ACI man sat and clicked open his attaché case, pulling out a folder. It had an indigo border, Most Secret. An OSS code group for title; the New America designation. Lefarge shot an unbelieving glance at his commanding officer.

Donati shrugged, with a very Italian gesture. "The Chairman's Office thought the Agency should be involved," he said in a neutral tone.

Christ, Lefarge thought with well-hidden disgust. Not enough that San Francisco was getting involved, but the Agency and the Chairman's office. The Chairman was all armchair bomb-them-aller, and the Agency was a band of would-be Machiavellis, and the two never agreed on *anything*—except to distrust the OSS.

"Well," he said. "What's the latest on the hijacking incident?"

Donati waved a hand to the civilians.

"Really, quite unfortunate," the ACI man said. "Your boffins did say that this would be a *controllable* weapon, did they not?"

Lefarge flicked a cigarette out of his uniform jacket and glanced a question at Donati. "Sir?"

"Go ahead, Brigadier."

"It's *largely* controllable," Lefarge explained patiently, thumbing his lighter. "Christ, though, look at what it has to penetrate! We're trying to paralyze the whole Snake defensive *system*, not just one installation, you know. That means we have to get into the compinstruction sets when they're embedded in the cores of central-brain units; then it has to jump the binary-analogue barrier repeatedly to spread to the other manufacturing centers where they burn-in cores. Talking *sets* here, not just data. *Plus* the continual checks they run against just this sort of thing; they're not stupid." He drew on the tobacco, snorted smoke from his nostrils. "One replication went a little off, and responded to a specific-applications attack command instead of the general-emergency one. If we could get more *original* copies into fabrication plants . . . What've we got on reaction?"

The Australasian tapped his finger on the file. "The SD are running around chopping off heads," he said thoughtfully. "But rather less than we expected. It seems they had the beginnings of a tussle over those prisoners of ours they took in the hijacking, the usual War-Security thing they amuse themselves with . . . and then their top politicals stepped in. Closed everything down; shut off all investigation; had the core from the stingfighter they lost, *and* the prisoners, *and* the bodies, all shipped to Virunga Biocontrol. We did catch an unfamiliar code group; all we could crack was the outer title. *Stone dogs*, whatever that means." He smiled at the two OSS officers. "You chappies wouldn't be holding out on us, would you?"

Lefarge and Donati exchanged a glance.

"We've never gotten a handle on it," Donati admitted. "The name's cropped up"—he paused to consult the terminal in the desk—"five times, first time in 1973. Again in '75, '78, '82. Then now, which is the first time in nearly a decade. It's about the most closely held thing they've got, and all we can say firmly is that it's fed to Virunga . . . which *might* mean something biological. Or might not."

"Those damned Luddites!" the ACI man exclaimed. Donati and Lefarge nodded in a moment of perfect agreement; the antibiotech movement had crippled Alliance research for a generation. It was understandable, considering the uses to which the Draka had put the capabilities, but a weakness nonetheless.

"Still," he went on musingly. "*Why* is *that* involved . . . when we know that it was our little surprise that caused the incident with the stingfighter?"

"Let's put it this way," Lefarge said grimly. "The Stone Dogs, whatever they are, are as closely held as . . . the Project. What's the Project? Our ace in the hole. Now, what's wrong with this picture?"

The agent winced slightly. "I say, bad show. Well, not our affair, what? There's no compromise of the Project; they'll go over that stingfighter's core, but their standard search models won't find a thing." He thumbed through the file. "We *are* getting some interesting data, from the deep-cover agent with the Commandant of Aresopolis." He laughed. "A deep-cover agent between the covers, eh? From the pillow talk, she must be fantastic—"

Lefarge was dimly aware of Donati wrestling him to a standstill, of the ACI man scrambling backward, snarling, with a hand inside his jacket.

"That's my sister you're talking about, you son of a bitch!" he shouted. Coming back to himself, shuddering, smelling the sudden reek of his own sweat.

Inch by inch, they relaxed. "Look, Fred," Donati said. "He didn't know, all he saw was a code description; he's got no *need* to know, he *wouldn't* know if you hadn't blown up!"

"Right," Lefarge said, shaking off the arm and straightening his jacket. *Breathe. In. Out.* He pulled a handkerchief out of his pocket and split the package, wiping his face down with the scented cloth and sinking back into his chair.

"I apologize, Brigadier," the ACI agent said.

"Accepted. You had any experience inside, Operative Forsymmes?" The other man shook his head. "Then don't make comments about those who have to operate in the Snake farm. For your information, my sister was missing-in-action in India in '75. She contacted the OSS again, on her own initiative. *Twenty-four years in there!*"

"I apologize again, Brigadier," the man said patiently. "The fact remains, the New America Project is not compromised, as far as we know. Time to saturation remains on-schedule and then we will be in an unassailable bargaining position."

Lefarge smiled with a carnivore's expression. "Certainly we will. After we've pounded their strategic installations into glowing rubble and destroyed everything they have off Earth—" He paused at something sensed between the other two. "There's been a change of plan?" he said, in an even tone.

Donati looked down at his linked fingers. The agent spoke in the same smooth tone.

"No, of course not. Your Project will finally give us the top hand, and we'll use it, never fear. Not in an all-out surprise attack, of course. That was '70s strategy. We'll demonstrate it; with the balls cut off their space defense capacity, they'll have no choice effectively but to surrender. With guarantees for the personal safety of their top people, of course."

"Ah." Lefarge glanced over at the other OSS officer. "General Donati, is it just this suit, or are they all fucking insane out there on the West Coast?" He glanced back at Forsymmes. "Are you? Completely fucking insane, that is?"

The agent's tone grew slightly frosty. "Brigadier Lefarge, I'm going to charitably assume that your personal . . . background and losses have made you somewhat unbalanced on this subject. Are you aware, my dear sir, of what even *one* hypersonic surface skimmer could do to a major city? Even given the most optimistic possible projections, the Project could only disable eighty percent of their space-based systems, less on Earth. That's primarily the defensive systems, at that. The Project's little photonic bug can't *fit* into anything smaller than a shipcomp core, and the enemy use more distributed systems than we do, which can be decoupled from their core computers. They would still have some capacity to operate their ships by manual linkage, and their installations. Furthermore, even if we wait *three* years, some of the older backup cores would be uninfected. They are not, as you pointed out, fools. We will show them they can't win an exchange, and offer terms."

Lefarge shook his head in sheer wonderment. "You . . . *somebody* thinks the Snakes are going to be deterred by *casualties*? You look old enough to remember the fall of India, even if you haven't read any history. Perhaps you recall them shooting the top fifteen thousand officials of the Indian Republic's government in batches, on the steps of the goddamn Archonal Palace, and broadcasting it worldwide? How many millions more were slaughtered or chemically brainscrubbed?"

"There's no need to spout propaganda at me, Lefarge!" Forsymmes snapped.

"Oh. Then maybe you've tuned in to their public execution channel? Impalements in living color; I'm told the breaking-on-the-wheel is—"

The agent sighed with elaborate patience. "Brigadier, I'm fully aware of the enemy's contempt for *other people's* lives. We are talking about putting their *own* lives at risk."

"And maybe you think it's a myth their troops commit suicide rather than surrender? What about Fenris?"

"The so-called doomsday bomb? Nobody's ever been able to prove that it's active; evidently a bluff."

Donati intervened. "In any case, we're talking in a vacuum, here," he said mildly. "None of us are exactly at policy-making level, are we?"

"No, that's true," Lefarge said calmly. The discussion became technical.

"Lefarge, do you really want to be taken off the Project?" Donati asked, turning to his subordinate as the door closed behind Forsymmes.

"No, sir, I do not," Lefarge answered.

The black eyes probed him. "If you don't, I'd better not see another performance like that," the general warned. "Stoddard's protégé could get away with things because Stoddard had been here longer than God and knew where all the skeletons were buried. They were terrified of him, from the chairman and the president on down . . . at least the chairman was; I don't know if Hiero's scared of anything. Herself, probably, like all the rest of us. But—and this is the important *but*— her attitude to the constitutional relations between the Presidency and the Alliance is correct to a fault. Hell, Fred, the president knows Allsworthy's a horse's ass as well as you or I do. But he's the boss man."

"We're neither of us a General Stoddard," Lefarge agreed. "Does that mean we have to swallow this horseshit?"

Donati shrugged and lit a thin black cheroot in an ivory holder. "As far as it goes. You know the ACI, they like to use scalpels where a sledgehammer's needed."

"Christ, Anton, that so-called strategy of theirs could lose us a dozen cities—if we're *lucky*. Fenris is as real as this table." He rapped his knuckles on the wood.

"You know that. *I* know that. The people in San Fran, they don't believe it because it's . . . 'fucking insane,' to their way of thinking."

"Not to a Snake . . . Yeah, Anton, I know—" He shook his head. "Of course, we could be in a use-it-or-lose-it situation before that. If the cover goes, or they spring *their* surprise on us, whatever it is. What do you think our Great Leaders will do then?"

"If the Project's cover's blown? Back off, if it's before saturation point. Dither a little and then use it, after that. If the Snakes attack first, everything gets used."

"I wish Stoddard were here. You going to the funeral?"

"Yes." Donati drew on the cheroot, his hollowed cheeks giving a skull cast to the thin face. "I never thought he'd die, you know?" There was compassion in his voice as he continued. Everyone had known Lefarge and the old man were close. "I'm glad you made it back before the end; it was so sudden . . . What did you talk about?"

"Nothing. Personal things." *And Nelson's eyepatch*, Lefarge thought with chill satisfaction, as the other man nodded agreement. A soldier's duty was obedience, but there were other duties. *I'm glad Uncle Nate reminded me of that*, he thought. It would have been a lonely burden to bear alone.

"And, Fred, remember you've gotten out of touch with the institutional balance while you had your head up there in the clouds all these years. Stoddard kept the wolves off your back while you pushed the Project through." He rose and crossed to the sideboard. "Scotch?" Lefarge accepted the glass. "Here's to him." They clinked glasses. "You're going to have to walk a little smaller, for safety's sake. The view's great, but there *are* disadvantages to having your head in the clouds, you know."

It's still better than having it rammed up your ass, Lefarge reflected, as he raised the glass in bland acknowledgment.

"We'll all do our jobs," he said. *Whether the suits want me to or not.*

DRAKA FORCES BASE ARESOPOLIS
MARE SERENITATIS, LUNA
MARCH 26, 1998
1100 HOURS

There were dozens of launch sites around Aresopolis, and swift linear-induction subtunnels to all of them. Yolande chose to exercise a Commandant's privilege and use the central dome exit when possible, and to travel aboveground. They left from another of those privileges, a small private villa on the lip of one of the natural terraces that rimmed the crater. It was daywatch, and the sky was set to a bright blue-green that dimmed everything but a ghost outline of the three-quarter Earth, and the unwinking fire of the sun. The house gleamed white and blue and its roofs russet-red; the walled hectare of garden smelled of damp earth and plants from the nightwatch rain.

The staff were lined up before the round doorway; they bowed with hands before eyes as she drew on her gloves, this being a formal occasion.

"Good-bye," she said. "You've served well, and while I'm gone, y'all can stay here in the villa servants' quarters an' grounds." They brightened; it was a rare treat, they were usually only here when the Mistress was in residence.

"Maintenance work only, an' Jolene's authorized to draw supplies fo' an entertainment, youselves and a guest each." Cheers at that. She nodded at Jolene. "Keep 'em in order, hey?"

"You command, Mistis," Jolene said, bending to kiss the Draka's hand.

Yolande put the palm under her chin and raised her to meet her lips. "Be seeing you."

Marya sank back on the cushioned seat beside Tina and watched the Draka board the airsled. Yolande ignored the steps, vaulting over the side in a complete feet-uppermost turn that looked slow motion in the .16 G, landing neatly in the bucket seat; she turned and smiled broadly at Marya, with a wink.

The serf smiled back. *It's like method acting*, she told herself in some cold inner pocket of her mind. You had to construct a part of you that actually was what you portrayed; only here, you had to write the role as you went along. Impossible to do consciously—there was no way to concentrate long or hard enough; eventually you would slip up fatally. More a matter of creating and living in a persona. She suspected most born-serfs did the same from infancy, less consciously; it was impossible to tell how many retained anything beneath the role, how many *became* it.

Careful, she doesn't expect you to fawn, Marya reminded herself. Yolande turned to the controls and stretched, cracking her fingers together over her head before dropping them to the sidestick. *Just keep her happy and relaxed, and she'll keep talking. Why not? You're only a serf.*

Knowing people was useful in ordinary life, the margin of survival for a spy, life itself to a serf. Yourself most of all. *She isn't cruel by their standards*, Marya told herself. *Nor stupid. As for last night . . .* The shame was less than she had expected; decades spent in the Domination could not help but rub off on your attitudes. *It wasn't rape. You asked her.* And while it was not something she would have otherwise chosen to do . . . *Face it, it was physically pleasant.* Yolande had been gentle, and took pleasure in giving pleasure as much as in receiving it—from what she knew, not something a serf could count on. The irritating part had been remembering always to let the other take the lead. *Oh well, call it waltzing.*

No, not unpleasant, she thought, letting her tired body relax into the cushions. Apart from the lack of sleep, she felt fine; the body had its own logic. Expecting it, she could handle the irrational rush of friendliness. That was a common pattern as well; hopefully, her owner would see no reason to suppress it. Yolande liked to be liked, even by her chattel, when possible.

She's not evil, Marya thought with analytical dispassion. Neither was an apple full of cyanide.

It was simply too dangerous to be allowed to exist.

Yolande took the airsled straight up from the courtyard. It was basically a shallow dish of aluminum alloy built around a superconductor storage ring, with seats and windshields and small noiseless fans. Lift and drive were from pivoting vents on the rim, a dozen of them making the little craft superbly responsive. She glanced up into the rearview mirror.

Not the only thing that's superbly responsive, she thought happily. *Freya, but I needed my clock cleaned. That was different, not as bland as most serfs. More push-back.*

A sensor went *ping* at three hundred meters: echo sounder, of course. Air pressure here was uniform right up until you ran into the sky. The aircraft slid forward at sixty kph, beneath a light scattering of fleecy pancake-shaped clouds.

There were times when you had to step back from a problem, turn your mind to something else, before you could see it plainly. She had climbed the command chain faster than anyone before her—native ability, connections, luck, and sustained drive—that because she had seen that the deadlock on Earth would squeeze resources into space, where they could at least accomplish *something*. For more than a decade, ever since Telmark IV, the knowledge that there could be nothing better here than a stalemate at a higher level of violence had eaten at her. Her mind prompted a list.

Item: Uncle Eric and the others aren't stupid. They must realize that as well as I.

Item: Only something on the order of technological surprise could break the stalemate. And if it went on long enough, it would be the Alliance that came up with the winning card. She grinned at the thought, not an expression of pleasure, but the outward sign of a hunter's excitement. So the Final War had to come before then—but it would be a disaster, as things stood. *Seemed* to stand.

Item: The Supreme Command knew that, too.

Item: Commandant of Aresopolis was high enough up the command structure to be on the verge of the circles that made policy, political decisions. High enough that she would get hints of purpose, not just code-verified orders.

So. Perhaps the incident with the Yankee prisoners was something significant, perhaps not. There were a thousand clandestine programs going on, everything from espionage to cultural disinformation. But perhaps this was different, and they had promoted her to the level where they had either to bring her into the picture or shoot her. Nor could her appointment be an accident.

I'm competent, she told herself judiciously. *More than competent; but even so, there are dozens of others with qualifications as good.*

Uncle Eric and his Conservatives knew where she stood; foursquare with them on domestic policy. She was a planter and an Ingolfsson and a von Shrakenberg connection, after all, and besides that, she agreed with them. On the other hand, in foreign policy nobody could doubt she followed the Militant line; nobody at all.

Yolande began to hum softly under her breath. This promised to be interesting, very interesting indeed, when she got some data to work with. Her mind felt as good as her body, loose and light and flexible, ready to the hand of her will like a well-made and practiced tool. Quite true what the alienists said: celibacy was extremely bad for you, as bad as going without proper diet or exercise or meditation, and as likely to upset your mental equilibrium.

I must do something nice for Marya, she thought as the crater slid by below.

This view always heartened her. Most of the Domination off-Earth was like being inside a building all the time at best, or more commonly imprisonment on a submarine. Efficient, necessary, even comely in the way that well-designed machinery could be, but not beautiful; difficult to love. Space and the planets *were* lovely, but they were unhuman, beyond and apart from humankind and its needs, too big and too remote. Here were reminders of what she was fighting for.

There was a river beneath them, meandering in from the rim, weaving between broad shallow lakes that had been subcraters once. Reeds fringed the banks, brown-green, except for a few horseshoe shapes of beach. The water was intensely clear, speckled with lotus and water lily, and she could see a fish jump in a long, slow arc that soared like an athlete's leap. Trees grew along the shores, quick-growing gene-engineered cottonwood, eucalyptus, and Monterrey pine, with a dense undergrowth of passionflower and wild rose.

Beyond was a rolling plain of bright-green neokikuyu grass, the plant of choice for first establishment, rolling in long thigh-high waves beneath the warm dry air. Beneath that, earthworms, bacteria, fungi helping grind dead soil into life with millennial patience.

Yolande grinned and sideslipped down to ten meters over the grasslands. A herd of springbok fled, scattering like drops of mercury on dry ice, their leaps taking them nearly as high as the belly of the car. Two grass-green cats a meter long raised implausible ear tufts and yowled at her with their forepaws resting on a rabbit the size of a dog. She banked around them, skimmed over a boulder-piled hillock planted in flat-topped thorn trees that exploded with birds.

"*Mistis*." She looked back as her hands straightened the aircraft and put it on an upward path. Tina was looking green and swallowing hard.

"Sorry, Tina," she said. Morning sickness had struck the brooder hard, and she was still easily upset.

They flew more sedately across tree-studded plain, then a section of still mostly bare whitish-brown soil—*regolith*, she reminded herself. Vehicles and laborers moved over it in clouds of dust, spraying and seeding. Then over another waterway, a stretch of forested hills beyond that curved out of sight on either hand. The area within was more closely settled, networked with maglev roads and scattered with buildings: lodges, inns, experimental plots, landscaped gardens. Ahead lay the central mountain.

Long ago an asteroid had struck here, carving the crater in a multi-gigatonne fireball; a central spike half as high as the walls had been left, when the rock cooled again. For three billion years it had lain so, with only the micrometeorite hail to smooth the sides; then the Draka engineers had come. The dome they built required an anchor point and cross-bracing; the mountain was bored hollow, and a tube of fiber-reinforced metal sunk home in it. That rose from the huge machinery spaces below through the ten-meter thickness of the dome itself, and the long monofilament cables that ran in from the circumference melded into a huge ring kilometers overhead. Yolande looked up, tracing their pathway. Thread-thin in the distance, like streamers of fine hair floating in a breeze; swelling, until they bulked like the chariot spokes of a god.

The slopes below had been carved as well, into stairs and curving roadways, platforms and bases for the buildings, or left rugged for the plantings and waterfalls that splashed it with swathes of crimson and green and slow-moving silver-blue. The buildings were traceries of stone and vitryl and metal, like an attenuated dream of Olympus, slender fluted columns and bright domes. Yolande brought the airsled in toward the main landing field, a construct that jutted out in a hectare of flange from a cliffside. She sighed at the sight of the reception waiting; *some* ceremony was inevitable. *I am Commandant, after all*, she thought reluctantly, and let the sled sink until it touched the gold-leaf tiles.

She touched down. Waiting Auxiliaries pushed up two sets of stairs, one for her and another for the servants. She stepped onto the red carpet of the first, and a band struck up "Follow Me," the anthem of the Directorate of War. A cohort in dress blacks snapped to attention: human troops, Citizen Force. Her own Guard merarchy. Bayoneted rifles flashed, drums rolled, feet crashed to the tiles in unison. *Not easy to do without kicking yourself into the air, here,* she thought ironically as she saluted in turn, right fist snapped to left breast.

"Service to the State!" she called.

"Glory to the Race!"

The Section heads were waiting, with their aides and assistants. Aresopolis was still organized like a War Directorate hostile-territory base, although that was growing a little obsolete. Commandant, herself. Vice Commandant and Operations Chief, Alman Witter. Weapons, Power, Lifesystems, Construction, Civil Administration. The Security commander, in headhunter green—a surprisingly reasonable sort, she had found, with a weakness for terrible puns. The Aerospace Command chief. The civil administrators. In four years she had come to know them all quite well; twelve-hour office days were something they all had in common. Except during emergencies, when it was rather more.

There's irony for you, she thought. Yolande Ingolfsson was niece to the Archon, an Arch-Strategos, and scion of two of the oldest Landholder families in the Domination. Wealthy in her own right even by Landholder standards, owner of several dozen human beings directly, and of thousands if you counted interests in Combine shares and other enterprises. And she actually had less leisure than a State-chattel serf clerk toiling away in one of the anonymous offices below her feet, and not much more in the way of personal freedom. *Well, a little more. I have all sorts of choices. Who I go to bed with, and what clothes I wear.* She looked down at her uniform. *Sometimes.*

"For this we conquered the world," she muttered under her breath, then looked up. The Earth was in its invariant place on the horizon, and she could make out the shield shape of North America. *Not all the world; it will be better once we have.* Her teeth bared for a moment, and then she forced relaxation. *Ah, well, it would get boring with nothing more to do than swim, hunt, and make love.*

"Strategos Witter," she said formally to her second in command. "Citizens," to the others, "I expect to be back in about a week."

There was the usual exchange of civilities, but only Witter stayed with her as the metal rectangle rose a handspan and floated off into the three-story arch in the cliff; there was a mesh of superconductor laid below the tiles.

"Thomas was notably uncommunicative about the patrol incident," he said.

The skid was moving through a long corridor cleared for her use into a great circular hall, overlooked by ramps and walkways. The hall stretched out of sight in either direction, encircling the launch stations; crowds thronged it, away from the Orpo-cordoned path to her gate. Arches were traced on the walls, covered in brilliant mosaics; the sights of the solar system, mostly. Jupiter banded in orange and white, or the rings of Saturn against the impossible skystalk rising out of the hazy atmosphere of Titan. A few landscapes from Earth. And endlessly repeated above, the Drakon with its wings spread over all. She heard murmurs, foot slithers: a troop of new-landed ghouloons following their officer, peering about and hooting softly in amazement. One forgot himself and bounced two meters in the air, slapping at his chest and shoulders for emphasis as he spoke.

"Ooh," he burbled. "Big big. *Big.*"

"Merarch Irwine had his orders," she said.

"Meaning, shut up?" the other Draka replied.

"Not quite. But all is not as it appears, Alman. I'm goin' down to find out. I may find out something; I may not. In any case—"

"There are Things We Were Not Meant To Know," he replied. The skid stopped before a final door. "Exactly," she said, stepping off the platform as it sank to the floor. "See you next Thursday."

"Service to the State."

"Glory to the Race." She turned to the door guards. "Scan."

One of them touched a control; something blinked at her eyes, like a light flashing too quickly to be noticed.

"Arch-Strategos?" the tetrarch said. "Ah, ma'am. You serf, the tall one." Yolande turned; he was indicating Marya. "She's cuffed, but you don't have the controller activator on you."

"Thank, you, Tetrarch, but I think I'm safe from my housegirls," she said dryly, tapping her fingers on her belt. He flushed and stepped back with a salute.

"Yes, ma'am," he said. "Straight through, Arch-Strategos."

✧   ✧   ✧

"Tell you the truth, I'd forgotten the bloody thing," Yolande said, as they seated themselves.

"I . . . never have, Mistis," Marya said, touching the cuff with the fingers of the other hand.

The capsule was the standard passenger form, a steel-alloy tube five decks high. There was an axial passageway with a lift platform, a control bubble at the bow and a thrust nozzle and reaction-mass tank at the other. There were the usual facilities, and a small galley. Nothing elaborate—cargo versions didn't even have a live pilot—but quick and comfortable. The usual load was several hundred passengers, although this flight would be hers alone; a seven-hour flight, under 1 G.

She sighed and looked around the lounge, empty save for herself and Marya; Tina had gone to lie down in water-cushioned comfort. This was a wedge-shaped section of the topmost passenger deck, set with chairs and loungers and tables. A long section of the wall was crystal-sandwich screen. Yolande touched a control, and the wall disappeared. Smooth metal showed a half-meter away. Clanking sounds, and it began to move; magnetic fields were gripping the capsule. They slid sideways with ponderous delicacy, then into a vertical shaft. A slight feeling of acceleration, like an elevator. That lasted five minutes, past more blank metal; they were rising through one of the many passages that honeycombed the central lift shaft.

"Ah." They were out, on the hectare-broad pentagonal metal cap; flat and empty now, no other launches just now. The dome stretched around them, and dimly through it she could see the landscape below. From above and close-by the structure of the dome was more apparent, the layers of gold foil and conductor sheathing.

"Stand by for boost, please."

She swung the lounger to near-horizontal. Not that the acceleration would be anything to note. Below her lasers would be building to excitation phase, mirrors aligning. A rumble, as the pumps began pushing liquid oxygen into the nozzle. *Whump.* Thrust, pushing her back into the cushions, building to Earth-normal. She sighed again, glanced over at Marya.

"Marya," she said. The other woman looked up. "What am I to do with you?"

"What you will, Mistis."

Yolande laughed with soft bitterness. "What I *will?* Now there's a joke." She brooded, watching the lunar landscape grow and shrink behind the windowscreen, the ancient pale rock and dust, the roads and installations her people had built. "Duty . . . I was raised to do what is right; duty to the State, to the Race, to my family and my friends and to my servants. For the State and the Race, I've helped preside over a useless nonwar that shows no signs of endin' except in an even mo' useless *real* war that will destroy civilization, if not humanity. My best friend I failed . . . not least, by failure to let go of grief. My family?"

She sighed and stretched. "Well, my children have turned out well. And I've been a good owner to my serfs, with one exception. You, of course. It was wrong to torture you, hurt you beyond what was necessary to compel obedience. Actin' like a weasel, to assuage my own hurt."

"Are . . . " Marya hesitated. "Are you *apologizing* to me, Mistis?" There was an overtone of shock in her voice.

Yolande opened one eye and grinned. "It's rare but not unknown," she said. More seriously: "Marya, I know you've never accepted the Yoke, not in you heart. But you behavior's been impeccable for more than twenty years, which means my obligation is to treat you as a good serf. I . . . seriously violated that, back when." Her smile turned rueful. "I'd consider letting you go, were it practical. Or just giving you a cottage on the Island and letting you live out y' years." She owned one of the Seychelles islands outright, but seldom visited it.

"Mistis? May I speak frankly?" Yolande nodded, and the serf continued. "You don't feel in the least, ah, disturbed about enslaving me, but using this"—she raised the controller cuff—"makes you feel, mmm, guilty?"

Yolande linked her hands behind her neck. "Slightly *ashamed*, not guilty; such a bourgeois emotion, guilt." She frowned. "Not about— yes, enslavin' is the correct term, I suppose—no. You not of the Race; I am. My destiny to rule, yours to obey and serve. Obedience and submission: protection and guidance. Perfectly proper."

The Draka studied the serf's face, which had taken on the careful blankness of suppressed expression. "One reason besides Gwen I've kept yo around, not off somewheres clerkin' or something. You so *different*. It's refreshin', keeps me on my toes mentally, like doin' unarmed practice against different opponents. Here." She snapped open a case on the table beside her, brought out two pair of reader goggles. "I'm promotin' you to Literate V-a." That gave unlimited access to the datastores. Except for information under War or Security lock, of course, and Citizen personal files; it was the classification for top-level civilian-sector serfs. Very rare for someone not born in the Domination. Yolande tossed the other pair to Marya and put on her own; they had laser and micromirror sets in the earpieces so that you saw the presentation on an adjustable "screen" before your eyes.

She sighed again. *One more time at the data, and maybe I can make sense of it.*

Chapter Nineteen

CENTRAL OFFICE, ARCHONAL PALACE
ARCHONA
DOMINATION OF THE DRAKA
MARCH 27, 1998
1700 HOURS

"Sweet—mother—Freya," Yolande said, looking wide-eyed at her uncle. Rank and station, the slight residual awe this office evoked, all vanished. "Shitfire!"

"Both appropriate," he said, rising stiffly and walking to the sideboard. "So is a drink . . . Arch-Strategos."

For a moment even the news she had just heard could not block a stab of concern. *He looks so much older.* Nearly eighty, but with modern medicine that was only late middle age. Still straight, but he moved with care, and the lines were graven deeper into the starved-eagle face, below the thick white hair. It was a killing job, this; his pallor was highlighted by the dark indigo of his jacket and the black lace of his cravat. Then the immensity of what she had heard swept back, and she felt her stomach swoop again. *My teeth want to chatter.*

She accepted the glass and knocked half of it back: eau de vie. The warmth spread in her belly, and she closed her eyes to let the information sink in.

"Uncle, this is the best news I've had since . . . Loki, I don't know."

"Is it?" He sank down behind the desk. "Is it really?"

Yolande looked up, met the cold gray eyes, and refused to be daunted. "Uncle Eric—Excellence—I've spent the past decade dead-certain convinced that we were headin fo' the Final War without a *prayer* of comin' out on top. You just gave me hope—fo' myself, not so important; for my children and the Race, rather more so!"

He nodded and rested his face in his hands for a moment before raising his drink.

"Now you know, daughter of my sister, what only a dozen other people outside Virunga Biocontrol know—and we've kept the ones who worked on the project locked up tighter than a headhunter's heart."

For an instant his voice went flat-soft. "Yo realize, even the *suspicion* that yo *might* reveal this would mean a pill?"

Yolande held one hand in a gesture of acceptance. A bullet in the back of the head was an occupational risk at the highest levels of command and power. "And when is acceptable saturation?" she continued.

"Well . . ." Uncle Eric seemed oddly reluctant. "This year, accordin' to projections. No way to be absolutely sure, so they put a large margin of error in. Didn't want a wholesale infection; that would increase the chance of detection too much. We coded a stop; it replicates a certain number of times and then goes noninfectious. Then we used unknowin' vectors for the various targets: their command an' control echelons, Space Force and so forth. There may be some spillover to the bulk of their military, even civilians, but not much. You little brush beyond Luna gave us a random sample that fitted right in with our best-case hypothesis."

"Trigger?" she said.

"Coded microwave; resonates, activates it. Irregular period beyond that, but once it starts, stress accelerates the process."

"No way of shieldin'?"

"Not unless yo know. Heavy tranquilizers an' psychotropics can mitigate the effects, until the thing cycles itself out; takes about four, five days iff'n the subject is restrained that way. But even so, you not worth much in that condition. Questionin' the test subject indicates it's like . . . a combination of *Berserkergang* and paranoid schizophrenia, with some mighty nasty hallucinations thrown in. Works best on the highly intelligent."

Yolande sipped again at the fiery liquid, imagining the consequences. In the crowded workstations of a battle platform, in the tight-knit choreography of a warship's control center. A hard grin fought its way toward her face, was pressed back.

"Effectiveness?" she asked.

"Depends . . . they're more automated than we are, but they still haven't cut humans out of their action loops, not at the initiation stage. Given surprise, an' an all-out attack along with it, the projections indicate we could take out their Earth-orbit capacity to about ninety percent, and still come through with enough of our own to block what little of their offensive strength survived. We've built redundant, fo' exactly that purpose."

"Ah," Yolande exclaimed. "The Militants, they must know, too! *That's* why they're confident enough to talk openly about startin' the Final War."

"Their top triumvirate. Gayner was in on it from the beginnin'. The rest, no, of course not. They're just the bloodthirsty nihilistic loons they come across as."

"Shitfire," Yolande whispered again. The alcohol seemed to slide down her throat without effect. "Gayner nearly lost it right there on the viewer when you got the reelection vote, back in '97," she said.

Eric smiled thinly. "One of my mo' pleasant memories. She was wild to be in this chair when we reached go-level." A harsh laughter. "What immortality, fo' the Archon who led the Race to victory in the Final

War? Someone in that position could do anythin', get any program put through. Trouble would be to keep the Citizenry from electin' him—or her—to godhood."

"When do we attack?" Yolande said.

"You, too," the Archon said with resigned bitterness. "I've been hearin' that question with increasin' frequency fo' six months now. Accompanied by thinly veiled threats, from Gayner and her cutthroats."

She looked at him bewildered for a moment, then felt her eyes narrow. "Why *not*, fo' Wotan's sake?" she said. "Every moment we hesitate longer than we have to is deadly dangerous. Use it or we risk losin' it."

Eric gave a jerk of his chin. "Oh, yes. They behind in biotech, but makin' slow progress . . . and computer analysis is basic to that, too. The rate of increase in computer technology is slowin'—the experts say it's pushin' the theoretical limits with known architectures—but it hasn't *stopped*. Sooner or later, they'll get a clue; if nothin' else, from the strategic deployment choices we've been makin'. On the other hand . . ." He looked up at her and tapped his fingers on the desk. "This incident of yourn, it wasn't the bioanalysis of the prisoners that got you interested initially, was it?"

"No. *Somethin'* destroyed that stingfighter. Some sort of interference with they infosystems."

"*Our* nightmare. And they've been *matchin'* our deployments. Increasin' the proportion of orbit-to-ground weapons. Exactly the sort of thing you'd put in, if you expected to be in a position to hammer Earth from space with impunity."

"Wait," Yolande said with alarm. "They *could* just be matchin' us tit fo' tat. Their buildup didn't start until well after our current six-year plan."

"But it points to *somethin'* they are doin' to *us*. And . . ." he hesitated. "I saw the results of nuclear weapons, in Europe, back at the end of the last war. Stoppin' *almost* everythin' isn't the same as stoppin' *everythin'*." He looked out through the wall, at the lights of the city winking on below, and continued very softly. "Not to mention how many of them we'd have to kill. Not to mention . . ." He looked up. "Arch-Strategos, the final decision in these matters is mine; the responsibility comes with the office. We will move when I authorize."

Yolande rose and set the peaked cap on her head. "Understood, Excellence," she said, saluting. Then: "I'm takin' a week's leave, Uncle Eric. That all right?"

"Oh, yes. We won't begin the war without you, niece," he said. "Besides, it'll keep the enemy from wonderin' what you doin' back on Earth."

Yolande grinned at the sarcasm, it was just like Uncle Eric. *A little too squeamish*, she thought. *But basically a good man.*

"Service to the State," she said.

"Glory to the Race," he replied.

She left, and he turned down the lights, watching the multicolored glow of Archona below. Minutes stretched, and he sat motionless. "Glory indeed," he said. His mouth twisted. "Glory."

❖ ❖ ❖

SPIN HABITAT SEVEN
NEW AMERICA PROJECT
CENTRAL BELT, ALLIANCE INTERDICTED ZONE
BETWEEN THE ORBITS OF MARS AND JUPITER
MARCH 31, 1998

"First-rate dinner," Manuel Obregon said.

Cindy Lefarge nodded thanks and finished loading the dishes into the washer. She touched a control and the cylindrical hopper sank into the countertop. A quiet hum sounded through the serving window. The Lefarge living-dining area was open-plan in the manner that had become fashionable in the '70s, when the price of live-in help rose beyond the budgets of the upper middle class. *It always was, here in the Belt*, she thought with slight cynicism. *Amazing how fast domestic gadgets got invented when it was really necessary.* The thought was a welcome distraction from what would be said tonight. She picked up the tray with the coffee and carried it around to set on the table.

There were six others dining at Brigadier Lefarge's house that night, four men and two women. Department heads, or in two cases shockingly *not*, a few steps further down the chain of command. They shifted uneasily, buying a few more minutes passing sugar and cream around until everyone was settled; these were people of authority, but not military, not conspirators. Scientists for the most part, or scientific administrators at least, engineers, used to hard-material problems and juggling workers and resources. This smelled political, and not office politics either.

"All right," Fred said abruptly. Cindy could feel a harshness behind the tone, the same force that had been hag-riding him since his return from Earth. There were new lines graven in the heavy-boned face, down from nose to mouth. "First, let me say you're all here because I trust you. Your intentions, and your ability to keep your mouths shut. We've all worked together for . . . at least a decade now. You've all shown that you are willing to cut yourselves off from the outside world to work on the Project in its various phases." He paused, looked down at his hands for a moment. "I think most of you who haven't been told have guessed; the *New America* is not the only purpose of this installation."

Ali Harahap nodded. "Indeed so," he said in his singsong Sumatran accent, lighting a cigarette that smelled sharply of cloves. "But what is not said, cannot be betrayed." There were more nods around the table.

"Good man." Fred nodded, satisfied. "That was the right attitude. It isn't anymore. Before I go on, I want to make clear that what I'm about to say is unauthorized. If this ever gets out, I could be shot." A slight intake of breath among the others. "And all of you could be ruined, your careers ended. Does anyone want to leave?"

Colin McKenzie laughed shakily and wiped at the sweat on his high forehead; he was Quebec-Scots, a heavy-construction man. "Wouldn't do any good, would it, unless we finked? And you're the OSS rep here, Fred."

The security chief waited. When a minute had gone by, he turned to de Ribeiro. "Fill them in, Professor."

"We all know we have been building a starship," he began stroking his goatee, "with surprising success—although the only way to test it is to undertake the voyage. Scarcely a low-risk method! Many of you have suspected that the reason for this is as a last-ditch guarantee against defeat, to preserve something if the Alliance falls."

Patricia Hayato nodded. "We've all gotten used to secret projects," she said. "Since the war, every five years another group of scientists drops out of sight. The Los Alamos Project pattern. Mistaken, in my opinion. It sacrifices long-term to short-term; more suitable for wartime than the Protracted Struggle."

De Ribeiro inclined his head graciously. "What is the best disguise? A disguise that is no disguise at all. Here we hid the *New America* within a series of concentric shells of secret projects, each one genuine. Within the *New America*, the ultimate secret. A weapon."

Hayato threw up her hands. "Oh, no, not some superbomb!" Everyone else winced slightly; the rain of fission weapons that had brought down the Japanese Empire toward the end of the Eurasian War was still a sensitive subject. "Just what we need, more firepower. What have you discovered, a way to make the sun go nova?"

Lefarge rapped sharply on the table. "Ladies, gentlemen, we've all been cooped up with each other so long our arguments have gotten repetitive. Let the professor speak, please."

The Brazilian examined his fingertips. "We've developed a weapon that is no weapon—which should appeal to you, my dear colleague." Hayato flushed, she took neo-Zen more seriously than the founders of that remarkably playful philosophy might have wished. "You were quite right; bigger and better means of destruction have reached a point of self-defeating futility. But consider what *controls* those weapons."

"Data plague," Henry Wasser said. He was head of the antimatter drive systems, and worked most closely with the Infosystems Division de Ribeiro directed. "I always did think you had too much facility for what we needed."

De Ribeiro beamed; he had always had something of the teacher about him, and enjoyed a sharp student. "Exactly." A sip of coffee. "To be more precise, contamination of the embedded compinstruction sets of mainbrain computers, the cores." The white-haired Brazilian sighed. "Their complexity has reached a point barely comprehensible even to us, and the Domination's people are somewhat behind." He brooded for a moment. "The paranoia both sides labor under has been a terrible handicap. Both in designing our little infovirus, and in spreading it. The absolute barrier between data storage and compinstruction . . ." Another silence. "Still, perhaps our errors in design have spared us certain temptations, certain risks. Often I feel that computers might have been as much a snare, a means of subverting our basic humanity, as the Draka biocontrol. As it is, we have reached a limit and will probably go no further—" Lefarge rapped on the table again, and he started.

"Sí. In any case, it was unleashed perhaps a year ago. It spreads slowly, from one manufacturing center to another, as improved instruction-sets are handed out. In the event of war"—he grinned—"the Draka will find their machines . . . rebellious."

"And when enough are infected, the Alliance would move. That was the original plan." Lefarge looked around the table. "We're cut off here. Not from the latest fashions or slang; we get those coming in. But from the movement of thought, opinion, the climate of feeling. They've relaxed, down there, this past decade. They've started to think there might be some alternative to kill-or-be-killed. Fewer and fewer clashes, no big incidents. The Draka have been cutting back on their ground forces; these so-called 'reforms' . . ."

His fist thumped the boards. "They know enough to see that tanks aren't going to win them any more wars. And a better-treated slave is still a slave . . . Hell, I don't have to tell *you* all this. The crux of it is, they've changed the plans, there in San Fran. They're thinking in terms of an ultimatum; demonstrating our capacity, then demanding that the Draka back down, accept disarmament as a prelude to"—his mouth twisted—"*gradual reform.*"

Their eyes turned to Hayato. The lifesystems specialist fiddled with her cup. "No," she said. "It wouldn't work." Meeting their regard: "Yes, I know I've made myself unpopular by saying Japan would have surrendered without cities being destroyed by nuclear weapons. I still think so. The Domination is a different case entirely. The old militarist caste in Japan, they could surrender, sacrifice themselves for the benefit of the nation. The Draka, the Citizens, their caste *is* their nation. If that's destroyed, everything worthwhile in the universe is gone, and they'd bring the world down with them out of sheer spite."

Lefarge turned his hands palm-up. "Anyone think different?"

McKenzie hesitated, then spoke. "Fred . . . look, I'm just a glorified high-iron man. What the hell do I know? That's what we've got spooks like you for, and a government we elected, come to that. Policy's their department."

Lefarge opened his mouth to speak. Hayato cut in: "That's bullshit, Colin, and you know it. We've got the power; that means we have the responsibility to make a decision, one way or another. And it *is* a decision, either way."

He slumped. "I've got kin back on Earth," he said.

"We all do," Lefarge said. "Every indication of the way they've configured their off-Earth forces, every intuition I've built up about Draka behavior, tells me that the Snakes have some sort of ace in the hole comparable to us. It's a race, and we know for a fact that they won't hesitate a moment once they're ready; *they* aren't going to suffer from divided counsels. That's why we've got to act. Right, let's have a show of hands."

One by one, they went up. McKenzie's last of all, but definitely.

"I hope everybody realizes we're committed? Good, here's what we do. First, we make *multiple* insertions of the infovirus; we're set up for it. Next—"

Cindy Lefarge held her husband's hand. The grip was strong enough to be painful, but she squeezed back patiently, waiting in the silence of the emptied room.

"Am I doing the right thing?" he asked at last, in a haunted voice.

"It's what Uncle Nate wanted, honey," she whispered back.

"Yes, but . . . he was an old, *old* man by that time."

"And he'd taught you to think for yourself," she replied sharply. He looked up, startled, as she continued.

"You wouldn't be doing this if you didn't think it was right," Cindy went on. "For what it's worth, I agree . . . but you know what Uncle Nate always said: 'You take the choice, you bear the responsibility.'" More gently: "I can't be sure that what you're doing is right, Fred. But I'm behind you, and I always will be."

"I know," he said, and raised her hand to his cheek. His shoulders were still slumped, as if under an invisible weight. "I'm left with another question. Is what I'm doing *enough*?"

INGOLFSSON ISLAND PRESERVE
SEYCHELLES DISTRICT
ZANJ COAST PROVINCE
DOMINATION OF THE DRAKA
APRIL 2, 1998

Marya Lefarge shaded her eyes and looked out over the waves. It was a clear day, and the afternoon sun was white light on the hammered indigo metal of the ocean; there was enough wind to ruffle it, throwing foam crests on the waves and up the talc-fine powder sand of the beach. The endless background hiss of the light surf was the loudest sound; above her the wicker sunshade thuttered, and the fronds of the coconut palms rustled over that.

Out in the water the three Draka were playing, and she could see their bodies flashing through the surface layers. Then they were in the shallows, and Gwen and her young man swept Yolande up between them. They came trotting up the beach with an effortless stride; New Race muscles could do on Earth what ordinary humans did in low gravity.

She studied them as they washed off the salt under a worked-bronze waterspout and walked over to the blanket and deck chairs. You could see the differences better nude and wet; slight variances in the way the joints moved, the pattern of muscles sliding under tight brown skin. It was natural; they could secrete melanin until they were at home under this equatorial sun or pale to cream white at will; tablets had done that for Yolande and herself. No body hair, save for the scalp and the pubic bush. They walked unconcerned over sand that had made the elder Draka slip on thong sandals, Yolande moved with the studied grace of an athlete in hard training; the younger pair had the fluid suppleness of leopards.

Oh, Gwen, she thought. *It was easier when you were a child.* A saddening thing, not to be able to wish luck and happiness to one you loved.

"Remind me not to play tag with you New Race types," Yolande was saying, her hands resting on their shoulders. "I wonder that you puts up with us fossils."

"Oh, we've got time," the man chuckled. He was a handspan past six feet, with a head of loose white-gold ringlets.

That they do, Marya thought with a slight shiver in the warm tropical day. They were in their early twenties, and it would be two centuries before they showed much sign of age. *How can even a Draka bear to cut themselves off from their descendants so?*

Gwen gave her companion a good-natured thump on the ribs. "A little mo' respect for my momma, there," she said. "See you up at the house, Alois."

"Gwen. Miz Ingolfsson," he nodded to the two.

Yolande threw herself down on the blanket and stretched. "Nice boy," she said. "Drink, please, Marya."

Marya smiled to herself as she opened the basket and took the pitcher from the cooler. Yolande regarded her daughter's newfound enthusiasm for the opposite sex with tolerant indulgence, as appropriate for her age. To the elder Ingolfsson, Marya suspected, men were nice enough in their way, often pleasing, but with some exceptions basically rather stupid and prisoner to their emotions. Not an uncommon attitude among female Citizens . . . She glanced up and met Gwen's eyes, for a moment they shared amusement.

"Ma," Gwen said, taking one of the chairs. "Do me a favor?"

"Anythin', child of my heart," Yolande said, accepting the chilled papaya juice. "Thank you, Marya. Have what you like."

"It's that damned controller cuff," Gwen was saying. Marya froze for a moment, with a feeling of insects crawling on her skin, then made her hands busy themselves in the basket. "Tantie-ma's never said much about it, but it makes my backbone crawl. Take it off her, would you?"

"Ah." Yolande rose on one elbow and considered the serf, "As a matter of fact . . . Hand me that case from the bottom of the basket, would yo, Marya?"

There was a thin leather binder about the size of a small book; the serf's hands shook slightly as she handed it to her owner, kneeling beside her. She had not noticed it, slipped in among the bowls and packages and softcover volumes of poetry brought along for a day by the ocean. Yolande opened it and took out a slim jack on the end of a coil cord.

"Hold out you hand, wench," Yolande said.

It was shaking worse as the Draka took it and slid the jack into an opening on the front edge of the thin metal circlet. The bright sun darkened and the world blurred before Marya's eyes. She saw Yolande's fingers touching controls within the opened binder. There was a tingling in her wrist, and a subdued *click*. Marya heard herself whimper slightly as the metal unclasped; the skin beneath it was very white. Angry, she caught her lower lip in her teeth as Yolande turned her palm up and dropped the cuff into it. The metal was still warm from her skin.

"Do what you want with it," the Draka said.

Marya looked at it, feeling the tears cutting tracks down her cheeks, and making herself remember the *pain*. It had been twenty-four years, and not a day had passed when she had not suppressed that memory;

now she let the holds crack. The two Draka were looking politely aside as she rose unsteadily to her feet and walked out into the light, down to the edge of the water. The sand was scorching through the thin sandals, the waves cool as she walked into their knee-high curling. There was an intense smell of ocean, of iodine from the seaweed along the high-water mark. A gull went by overhead, shadow against dazzle, *grawk-grawk-grawk*. Her arm went back, seeming to drift. Forward with an elastic snap, and the cuff was soaring until it was a dot. Hesitating at the top of its arc, then dropping down at gathering speed. A last *plek* as it broke the smooth curve of a wave in a tiny eruption of white.

Gone. She dropped to her knees and bent forward, heedless of the ends of her hair trailing in the foam. *Gone.*

Yolande looked back to her daughter with a smile. "That seemed to go well, honeychile," she said.

Gwen nodded and lay back on the deckchair to spare the serf intrusive eyes. "Thank you, Ma," she said.

Yolande shrugged. *How strong and beautiful, and how sweet with it,* she thought. It was an ache in the chest, pride and love beyond bearing. *Me and Myfwany—you have the best of us both,* she thought. *Of both your mothers.* Marya was still down by the water's edge. *Or all three.*

Gwen took a fig from the basket and nibbled. "Almost a shame to be leavin'," she said happily. "It's been a good three days, just you and the sibs, Ma."

"Liar," Yolande said amiably. "Y'all are indulgin' me, and I know it. You thoughts are divided about equal between the new ship an' dancin' the mattress gavotte with Alois; he's likewise, and polite to me because he's got long-term designs on you. Holden is bored in the manner of six-year-olds, and Nikki"—she shrugged again; her oldest son was fifteen—"likes it here because there are a whole new set of housegirls to lay. Plus good spearfishing."

Gwen laughed, turning her eyes skyward. "*Lionheart*'s a real beauty, though, Ma," she said musingly. "Gods, when we took her out fo' the shakedown! Deuterium-boron drives've got it all ovah the older types, the exhaust's *all* charged particles." Her voice took on a dreamy tone. "Fifty thousand tonnes payload, she's fitted out like a liner! Even a spin-deck at one G. Only—"

"Gwen."

"—two months to Pluto! Granted we'll be there a year settin' up the base, but—"

"Gwen, honeychile, *I was on the design committee.*"

Her daughter laughed and waved acknowledgment. "Sorry, Ma."

"You've been noble not talkin' shop, Gwen. I recognize true love when I hears it."

"And, well, I *am* sorry to be leaven' you. And not . . . Know what I mean?"

"Oh, yes, child of my heart, I know *exactly.*" A long laugh, and she reached up to squeeze a shoulder. "Fo' reasons too numerous to state, I'm feeling first-rate just now. But you are always a . . . string of lights around my heart, child. Ah, here comes Marya."

Gwen rose. The serf stopped at arm's length and threw back her head; she had never stooped, but Yolande thought she saw a different curve to the neck. "Thank you, Missy Gwen," she said.

The young Draka embraced her. "Always welcome, Tantie-ma," she said. "Well—"

Her mother made scooting motions. "Alois and you have notions on how to spend the afternoon. Honestly, with an eighteen-month cruise ahead of you—"

"Ma!"

"But youth will be served. Or serviced—"

"*Ma!*" Mock indignation.

"Run along, you, Tantie-ma and I will find *some* way to pass the time." Yolande winked, and thought she caught a hint of real embarrassment on her daughter's face. *One thing that hardly changes*, she thought. *It never seems quite natural when the older generation doesn't lose interest.*

"Strange, Mistis," Marya said, watching the child she had borne walk away into the palms and oleander and hibiscus.

"How so?" Yolande turned her attention back to the serf. Her half-hour by the waves seemed to have composed her, at least. The coffee-brown synthtan suited her, as well.

"When . . . when she was little, she was so helpless as I held her. Now I can feel how gentle she's being hugging me, and she could crush me like an eggshell. Strange to remember her so tiny."

"True enough. Lie down here."

Marya sat beside the Draka, wrapping her arms around her shins and laying her head on her knees.

"You want me?" she said, smiling faintly.

"You and a snack and a nap befo' dinner," Yolande said. "Settle for the snack and nap if you tuckered out."

"Not yet," Marya said, with the same slight curve of her lips. "You have been very . . . energetic, since Archona."

"Good news does that to me, and no, I can't tell you what."

CLAESTUM PLANTATION
DISTRICT OF TUSCANY
PROVINCE OF ITALY
DOMINATION OF THE DRAKA
APRIL 4, 1998

"Hello, Myfwany," Yolande said, sitting by the grave with her elbows on her knees. Wind cuffed at the spray of roses.

There was another nearby, now, her father's. There were a few clouds today, white and fluffy. The air was just warm enough to be comfortable sitting still, with an undertone of freshness that was like a cool drink after the tropical heat.

"Tina's coming along well," she continued. "Gods, it'll be interestin' to see what a merger of my genes and yourn comes out to! With all the little improvements they puttin' in these days."

The wind ruffled the outer leaves of the flowers. They were still a little damp from the sprayer in the arbor where she had picked them. Yolande leaned forward to smell the intense wild scent.

"And Gwen . . . ah, love, you'd be proud of her. Assistant com officer on this new ship, the *Lionheart*. Exploration voyage, really; establishin' a study base for the outer system and the Oort clouds. Cold out there . . . Hope it works out for her. Hope she settles with Alois, he's a good sort."

She smiled and touched the flowers and the short dense grass. "And there's somethin' else. Wotan and the White Christ, it's so secret I hardly dare tell *you*, sweet! Gods witness, I'd begun to despair of the whole Domination, we seemed to be goin' nowhere, until Uncle Eric let me in on the secret. Been in the plannin' since"—she swallowed—"since befo' India. A chance to put an end to the struggle, once and fo' all."

Yolande stopped for a moment. *This is the most painful pleasure of my life*, she thought. "I'm . . . worried, though. About Uncle Eric. He's . . . not frightened—it's just so *easy* to be indecisive at these levels, love! Always easier not to decide. He hates the idea of usin' it, takin' the risk. Even of the killin' involved." Slowly: "I admit it, love, I don't like the idea either. The fighters . . . they take the chances, same as I. Always hated hurtin' the helpless, and as fo' throwin' sunfire across the land . . ." She made a grimace of disgust, looking out across the hills of her birth country. Birds went overhead, a flock almost enough to hide the sky for an instant.

She hammered a fist on her knee. "But what can we *do*, love? I could live with the thought of everythin' bein' destroyed, when there was no choice. Now there *is*. And the longer we wait, the worse. Ah, Myfwany, it's so hard to know what's *right*."

Shaking her head, she rose and dusted her uniform. "I wish you were here, honeysweet," she said. "I promise . . . I'll do my best fo' the children. Good-bye fo' now, my love. Till we meet again."

"What the hell is *that*?" Marya exclaimed. "Mistis," she added hastily.

"That," Yolande replied, "is the most expensive toy evah built."

She had managed to shake most of the crowd of officials at Florence Airhaven; even the officer from TechSec, who was reasonably interesting when he got onto the yacht's construction. *Enough of crowding back on Luna*, she thought, and besides, she had checked out fairly thoroughly on the simulators. They were almost alone on the floater; even this backwater had modernized maglev runways, now. The craft before them was *not* something it had seen before, or most other airhavens in the Domination, either. Ninety meters long, a slender tapering wedge; the bottom of the hull curved up at the rear into the slanted control fins. There were control-cabin windows at the bow, scramjet intakes below the rear edge. And what looked like a huge four-meter bell pointing backward at the stern.

"It's from the test program fo' the fifth generation pulsedrives, the Rex class." A sliver of afternoon light fell within the thrust plate, and glittered off the lining. "Synthetic single-crystal thrust plate, stressed-matrix/mag equalizers, deuterium-boron-11 reaction. They had two of the first units left ovah. Decided to try matin' them to a heavy scramjet assault transport; first Earth-surface to deep-space craft ever built, is the result." A Yankee might have junked the test units, but Draka engineers had a rooted abhorrence of throwing anything that still worked away.

"The power-to-weight's good enough you could take off on the pulsedrive," Yolande continued, as they came to the lift and stepped on board. It hummed quietly and swept them past the black undersurface heatshield; the top of the craft was dark as well, but the texture was subtly different. "Though that wouldn't be neighborly. Actually it's a waddlin' monster in atmosphere, and mostly fuel tank inside; liquid hydrogen, of course. Got good legs, though; that reaction is *energetic*. You could make it to Mars or even the Belt, iff'n you didn't mind arrivin' dry."

They stepped through the open door. It swung shut behind them, and she took a deep breath. Filtered air, the subliminal hum of life-support systems; pale glow-panel light, and the neutral surfaces of synthetic and alloy. *Space*, Yolande thought. Even though they were still on the surface, it had an environment all its own. She ducked her head through the connecting door into the control cabin. There were comfortable quarters aft; it was essentially a very expensive yacht. *Not that they're likely to become a hot item anytime soon,* she thought wryly. Even discounting the cost of the drive as part of the research overhead, the *Mamba* would price in at about the combined family worth of the Ingolfssons and the von Shrakenbergs. For now, the Archon and the Commandant of Aresopolis were assigned one each.

She returned the pilot's salute. The control deck was horseshoe shaped, with pilot and copilot forward, Weapons and Sensors to either side on the rear. Only the two pilots were here now, of course.

"Pilot Breytenbach," she said to the number two. "You can go aft; I'll sit in on this." Yolande grew conscious of her servant hovering behind. "Well, come in, wench." Marya flinched slightly, fingering the bare strip on her wrist; the controller cuff would have shocked her away from activated military comp systems like this. Yolande saw her take a deep breath and step forward. *Good wench*, she thought.

"That crashcouch," she said, indicating the Sensor station. She swung herself into the copilot's seat and pulled the restraints down. "All yourn, Pilot," she said. He nodded briefly, running his eyes in a last check over the screens.

"Highly cybered," Yolande said, indicating the control panels. " 'Less you has to fight her"—*in which case you bumfucked, because those lasers are a joke*—"menu commands to take you anywheres within range."

She settled back happily. "I'll take ovah out of atmosphere," she said. They would be back to the world of the Commandant's office soon enough. *TechSec designs a toy, I might as well use it*, she reflected. The big vehicle lifted off the runway with the peculiar greasy feel of maglev and turned toward the long reach.

Chapter Twenty

DRAKA FORCES BASE ARESOPOLIS
MARE SERENITATIS, LUNA
NOVEMBER 11, 1998
0930 HOURS

"Sector Seven, level twelve," the transporter capsule said. The lid hissed open, and Marya stepped out.

"Ident," the guard said. The room was a narrow box with only one exit, brightly lit and completely bare, smelling of cold rock. The guard was in Security Directorate green, battle-armored and carrying a gauntlet gun; his head turned toward her like a mirrored globe, her own distorted face reflecting off the helmet shield.

She stepped up to the exit and laid her hand against the screen set in the wall beside it. "Marya E77A1422, property of Arch-Strategos Ingolfsson, Commandant, on personal errand."

Her mouth was tissue paper, and the pulsebeat in her ears roared louder than trumpets. This was action, covert action. It was impossible to disguise, impossible to cover, no matter her skill on the infonet. Recognition sets were embedded in the central brains, and flagging from a station with this priority was direct-routed down to read-only memory. It would stand out, stand *out*, the minute anyone did a search on her activities today. Even the most dimwitted Orpo would notice someone being in two places at once.

Only for you, my brother, she thought, controlling the impulse to shudder. The message had been like none she ever received. Far longer. Not just instructions on a new drop, a new contact code; orders to *do*. The thing she carried at her belt. *Something is very wrong here. Fred's never been in the loop before, neither of us would dare.*

The screen flicked light at her eyes. A laser read the pattern of her retina; the information sped away as modulated light. Another scanned her palmprint, the abstract of her voice. Information flowed into a central computer's ready-storage peripheral; embedded instruction sets were tripped. Data from deep storage was copied, run through a translator into analog form, compared. Another code phrase tripped a set in the response machine.

"Confirmed. Marya E77A1422, property of Arch-Strategos Ingolfsson, Commandant. Literate Class V-a. Delay, query." The idiot-savant routines would be calling her owner's private quarters. Marya breathed in, calmly. That was where the interception loop she had established would work; or not. The machine spoke again: "Query, confirmed. E77A1422, proceed."

The guard nodded. "Confirmed. Present, wench," he said. Marya turned and bent back her head to bare the serf-tattoo beneath her right ear. There was a box clipped to the serf policeman's waist; he pulled free a light-pencil on a coil cord and ran the tip down her tattoo. The box chirped, encoding her ident on a data plaque within: another footprint.

With a slight hiss, the door opened. Marya noted the thickness of it, featureless sandwich-armor alloy. The corridor beyond was plain, but there would be instruments and weapons in the walls. Another door, and she was out into a vestibule of the factory; more guards, crewing control desks. They waved her through. She walked on, past color-coded doors and more corridors. Through a transparent tube, over a long room where workers bent to their micromanipulators and screens. They were assembling circular electrowafers in tubes, building the precoded stacks that contained the instruction sets for major computers and their closed-access internal memories. Others fitted the pillars of wafers into the rectangular platforms of the logic decks; she could imagine the submicroscopic tools soldering their gold-wire and optical-thread connections.

All familiar enough; the basic technology had not changed in a generation, despite vast improvements in detail. *And I've heard Draka complain the Alliance isn't introducing as many refinements for them to steal lately*, she recalled. Exterior data storage, translator/interfacer unit, memory, instruction sets, logic deck. And beyond this complex, the most crucial area of all, where the design teams' compinstruction data was turned into physical patterns for embedding in the cores . . .

"Hello," she said to the receptionist in the office area. Polite but not servile; she was a command-level officer's personal servant. Not as formally high-status as this expensively trained technical secretary, but they were both Class V-a's, and her owner outranked the Faraday Combine exec who ran this facility. "Is Master MacGregor in? The plant manager?"

The receptionist looked up from his keyboard, looked Marya up and down. "Your message?" he said. "Master MacGregor can't be interrupted, he's in conference." *He's checking my clothes*, Marya thought. Silk shirt, pleated trousers, jeweled clasps on the sandals and belt. Obviously a houseserf, equally obvious from someone not to be offended.

"It's an invitation," she said. "From the Commandant." Marya held out a folded parchment sealed in gold with the Drakon signet, then pulled it back when the man reached for it. "Personal service." That *was* one of her duties, keeping track of the obligatory social functions Yolande hated, and seeing that the invitations were in harmony with the relative status of each participant. A personal hand-delivery to a Commandatura reception was just slightly more than MacGregor rated; just enough that no underling of sense would endanger it.

"Oh, excuse me." The serf's heavy Arab features knotted. "Ahh . . ." There was a waiting area behind the desk, but that was for Citizens. "Here, I'll take you to his office. You can wait there, and give the invitation."

"Will he be long?" Marya said, with a frown of concern. "Mistress, the Arch-Strategos Ingolfsson, expects me back." *Sometime this evening, probably, but the rank ought to make you sweat.* Marya's owner took her lunches at her office, and it was vanishingly unlikely that her absence would be noted. Even less likely that anything would be made of it. Marya was authorized to leave the household and entitled to do so at discretion, so long as her work was done. *But every minute is another chance to be missed.*

"It's right this way," he continued. She followed; there was carpet here, muffling even the light sound feet made under lunar gravity. He touched the wall, and a section slid upwards; *that's right, lay on the courtesy.* He *could* have made her wait in the hall, but it was never wise to antagonize one who had the ear of your superior's superior. She stepped through. A typical office chamber, big enough for pacing, with a holowall landscape, desk, workstation. That was activated, notes and papers left carelessly around the terminal. The release of tension was like nausea or orgasm. She turned that into a one-two-kneel motion, sinking down on her heels and closing her eyes, hands and invitation folded in her lap. The Perfect Servant, concentrating on the task in hand. *Go away*, she thought with deadly concentration at the receptionist. *Don't make polite conversation, don't offer me refreshment, go away.*

He did; she waited until the door closed, and sixty heartbeats beyond. When she rose, it was with a smooth economy of motion that wasted no second of time, time that she was buying with her life. There was no turning back; it could be months before she might have to use the pills carefully hoarded in her room, even years, but the clock was running from this moment.

Exec MacGregor had been careless, leaving his terminal up. A violation of procedure, even here in the heart of a guarded facility. Even behind a door only those with authorization could access. She took the dataplaques from the pouch at her waist and touched the keyboard.

-*Work in progress*-, she typed.

[Core memories. Actuation sequences.] A long string of codes; she picked out the ones she knew, the ones on the plaque she should have wiped but could not bear to, the one with her brother's image.

[Cr-ex 5-5 Btstation orbital: launch sequence. IFF.] There.

Her fingers moved. -*Halt. Memcheck, active*-. Then the only time embedded sets were held in access memory. While they were being *transferred* to the cores. Feverishly, she checked the work-in-progress table on the status of the sets; they were finished, ready to be templated for the master pattern in the assembly hall.

-*Modification*,- she typed.

[Delay.] Seconds of white terror. [Accepted. Load sequence.]

Marya stared at her hand until the slight tremor disappeared. She pushed the first of the palm-sized synthetic rectangles into the receptor.

-Create parallel file temp:1-

[File standing.]

-Load receptor D: seq-

An almost inaudible whine, as the reader/translator loaded the contents of the plaque into the virtual space she had created. Another. Another. There were five of the plaques. Three minutes in all; now for the difficult part. She gave silent thanks that the Domination used a standard working compinstruction language. There were three in the Alliance, not to mention illegals.

*-Run temp:*1 *comparison* workfile: *Cr-ex 5-5 keyphrase com; master-*

The screen flickered, as the computer matched the sets.

[Congruence sector core: code exe.] The master recognition commands, friend-foe.

-Mergeset: modify workfile *Cr-ex 5-5 keyphrase com: master-*

[Merging.] Long seconds, while the machine knitted the new symbols with the old, matching smoothly where the coded ends fitted the set. [Complete. Workfile 2temp:1.]

Shit, she thought. It was making duplicate drafts, not substituting.

-Compare workfile / workfile 2temp:1-

[Congruence 99.73 abs.]

-Wipe workfile-

[Query?]

-Wipe workfile-

[Query?]

"Oh, shit, shit, shit!" she said. *Think. Think, damn you, wench. What are you, Draka cattle or a human being?* The station and table around it were littered with paper notes; this MacGregor was a worrier. Hated to do anything irrevocable. *Calmly. There are only a few ways you can alter the procedures.* Designer compinstruction sets were embedded as well, after all. A single note at the bottom of a stack, old and faded, in pencil.

Marya gave a shark grin and returned her hands to the keyboard.

-Wipe workfile-

[Query?]

-coverass-

[Execute *-wipe* workfile-]

-Load workfile *seq all mainmem-*

[Unfind: query? namefile.]

"I got it, I got it!" Quickly now, but carefully.

-dename workfile 2temp:1/ *rename* workfile-

[Execute *-dename* workfile 2temp:1/ *rename* workfile-all. Wipe workfile 2temp:1?]

-command aff-

[Execute-*wipe* workfile 2temp:1-]

Now to check; only an anal retentive of the first order would log under a code like this, but . . .

-time/work log coverass *perscode/master-*

[Query? coverass unrec Logtime/work MG-A1?]

Marya looked at the time display in the lower right corner of the screen; 09:41, exactly eleven minutes since she entered the fabrication complex.

-time/work log thisdate MG-A1-

[Inlog 0800 01/07/98 lastsrk 0929 dto MG-A1]

"Exactly why only designers get these free-access memories," she muttered to herself. "Too easy to cheat a little." Her handkerchief dusted across the keyboard, no use making it easy for the greencoats if things blew soon. A quick pass across her face left it damp; nothing she could do about the trickles from her armpits down her flanks.

I have just condemned myself to death, she thought, as she settled back on the floor—*Can't pollute the Race's holy chair with my serf ass*—and folded her hands. "And I haven't felt this alive in decades."

"No, I don't want anything," Yolande snapped, then forced herself to calm. *The housegirl isn't to blame,* she thought. It would be alarming enough that she was back here at the Commandant's quarters at 1200, only four hours after she left. The serf was looking at her wide-eyed. *Be gentle. They're frightened when the routine is upset.* "Run along, Belinda. I'll call later if I want lunch."

The memory of the message from Archona was a sour taste at the back of her mouth as she stalked past the fountain into a lounging room. *No party planned. Invitation superfluous.*

"He isn't going to do a fuckin' *thing,*" she told herself, lost in rage and wonder. Months past saturation point on the Stone Dogs, and no action whatsoever. *Be honest with yourself,* she thought, flinging herself down on a couch and staring at the ceiling. Throwing yourself down was curiously unsatisfying on the Moon; like punching pillows, there was no thump.

It's two months into Gwen's voyage. She's out of the inner system, out of any possible combat. And Gwen was the only one of her children old enough for military service. Short of a catastrophe that wrecked the planet, the others would be safe. The Draka prided themselves on being a foresighted people; since before her birth they had been building deep shelters, every plantation and school, city and town in the Domination was *ready.* And the facilities had been improved constantly. They would work, provided there was a living world to return to.

"All right." She asked herself, coldly realistic, "What can you do, Yolande?"

Very little. It was bitter knowledge. She knew of the Stone Dogs, now; perhaps two dozen others did. *Could I get in touch . . .* No. The only others she knew of for certain were Gayner and the two Militant leaders; they would not trust a niece of the Conservative bossman. *And it would be like shooting Uncle Eric in the back.* Morally unthinkable, and . . . you did *not* betray Eric von Shrakenberg and enjoy the consequences. Perhaps it would be worthwhile, if there was no alternative. Not *until* there was no alternative. She had a year until the *Lionheart* returned from the edge of the system. For that matter, Gwen would not thank her for being sheltered from danger. *So she's as stupid as anyone else that age. No more essential to the State than a hundred thousand other junior officers*. A fine balance, duty to the Race and to family, but clear in this case.

"I'll have to fuckin' *wait*," she hissed to herself, and then clamped down on her own mind. *The Will is Master*, she repeated. Breathe . . . Presently she won a degree of calm.

"Belinda," she said to the air; the housecomp would relay it. "Lay out a fresh uniform in my changin' room."

"Marya!" she said, pushing open the door. It had no lock, of course. "Yo—"

The room was empty, and there was no sound from the others. Yolande stopped, blinking slightly in surprise. *Could have sworn the comp said all servants present*, she thought in puzzlement, looking around. It was a fairly standard upper-servant's suite, bedroom, sitter opening off the corridor through a nook, and a bathroom at the rear. The lights had come on as she entered, but the air had the slightly dead feel of space not used for several hours. *I wonder where she is?* It was annoying; grabbing a quick nooner was not something she did all that often, and there was nobody else in the household right now she would feel that relaxed with; Jolene was down dirtside, visiting her daughter and Nikki back at Claestum.

Oh, well. It was no great matter; she turned to go, and then hesitated. *I've never actually been in here*, she thought.

No reason to visit the servants' quarters, really, except a sudden impulse to surprise . . . Nothing in the bedroom but a bed with a quilt coverlet; there was a signed holo of Gwen by the bed, and a book open beside it. The sitter was a room about four meters by three, lit by a glowceiling, walls of foam rock and tile floor covered by throw rugs. A couch along one wall, a couple of spindly low-G chairs, cushions. The viewer screen, and a bookshelf with a dozen titles, mostly classics; a row of dataplaques beside it, with the garish covers of serf entertainment. The new perscomp on a table, with a chair still pushed back as if in haste; the screen was dark, but the indicator was on, something running.

"Careless," Yolande chuckled, and walked over to it. There was a wrap-robe on the back of the chair. The Draka picked it up and brought the cloth to her face; there was a faint scent of Marya on it. *Damn, I wish she* was *here*, Yolande thought, sitting and picking up the dataplaque lying on the table.

"'Serving Pleasure #15,'" she read, and laughed again. An erotic-instruction sequence. *No wonder she's getting so imaginative*, she thought, flattered. *Wonder what's on it*. Impulsively, she snapped it into the port and hit the DIVIDE command on the keyboard. The perscomp was a fairly capable one, the type midlevel serf bureaucrats were issued. Embedded accounting, datalink and display functions. A million-transistor logic deck, two hundred thousand bits of core storage besides, and a plaque receptor.

The screen blanked to light gray, then lit. Yolande watched in growing bewilderment. *Sodomy? Basic Passive Sodomy?* she thought, watching as the instructor showed the young buck how to brace his elbows on his knees before stepping behind. *What in Freya's name is Marya doing with—*

The screen blanked again, the grunting figures replaced by a man's face. In an Alliance uniform, with brigadier's shoulderboards. American eagle, OSS flashes. Unremarkable face, square, rather dark, big-nosed; in his fifties, plenty of gray in the flat-topped black hair, eyes black too, so that the pupil didn't show. Deep grooves, ridged fore-head, the face of a man hagridden for many years. Yolande heard her own breath freeze in a strangled gasp, felt a sheet of ice lock her diaphragm.

Him.

"Marya, my sister, you must realize from this how desperate the situation is."

Him. India. The cool Punjab night, and the missiles arching up from the trees. *Psssft*-thud, and Myfwany's graceful stride turning to a tumbling fall.

"This plaque must be wiped as soon as you've read it. Likewise the others. *Those most of all*. Here are your instructions."

Him. The face, under the upraised visor. That single glimpse.

" . . . je t'aime, ma soeur," the voice concluded. A moment of blank screen, and the instruction sequence cut back in. She touched the controls. Her own face reflected dimly in the darkened screen. Eyes gone enormous, lips peeled back until the gums showed. A trickle of hoarse sound escaped her throat.

"His *sister*. *His* sister. I've had his *sister* in my own household fo' *twenty-five years*!" A bubble of laughter escaped her, and she ground her teeth closed on it, feeling something thin and hot stabbing between her eyes.

I'm dead. The thought was almost welcome. *I'm a walking corpse.* Nothing and nobody could save her from Security after *this*. The message had mentioned previous drops; even if nothing vital—*there couldn't be, I hardly talked to her for years until*— "Until she volunteered to play pony, gods damn me for a *fool*, why else would she suddenly decide she wants to lie down with me," she said. And now a sabo-tage operation.

I could kill her, Yolande thought. Just one quick bullet, and call disposal. Or apply for some drugs, get the information, *then* kill her. Perfectly legal—*no, the headhunters would smell something immedi-ately*. The Directorate of Security was an unofficial arm of the Mili-tants, or vice versa. They watched the von Shrakenberg connections like vultures around a dying camel. For an Ingolfsson to kill a houseserf was a break in the pattern, a red flag that something unusual was going on. They would ferret it out if it took them a decade.

No, it was her duty to report this. Put down everything she knew and suspected, write up a report, then one quick bullet of apology to the temple. *The family will be involved*, tolled through her with dreadful knowledge. A knot like the claws of something insectile hooked under her ribs. *Gwen will be disgraced.*

Duty—

"Oh," she breathed. There was a way to use this. *A spy you know about is an asset, not a liability*, she reminded herself. A slow, calm smile touched her lips. *It's even personally fitting*, she reflected. *He's known I had his sister as my serf. Used her for a brooder, probably knows she's been serving pleasure. Torture, to a Yankee.* Her hands touched the keys; she would have to find out what the perscomp was running. *Carefully, Yolande, carefully. She can't suspect, not for a moment.*

This evening . . .

"You *bit* me, Mistis," Marya said.

Yolande bent and kissed the U-shaped bruise on the inside of the serf's thigh. The bedroom was dark, and she had set the wall for a winter landscape in Tuscany.

"I was excited," she said, lying back. *True, by Loki, lord of lies. I didn't expect that.* It was odd, she felt no hatred. *I suppose I burned all that out long ago, for her.*

"It usually doesn't take you like that, Mistis."

"It's the news," Yolande said. "Here, rub my back." She rolled on her stomach, felt the serf's breath warm on the damp skin of her neck as her fingers kneaded at the muscles along her spine.

"What news, Mistis?"

Yolande made herself hesitate. "Well, it can't hurt now. No point in bein' overcorrect. Remember the good news I got back when, in Archona?"

"I thought it must be important," Marya said calmly, with a hint of a wink. "Certainly set you at me, Mistis."

Are her fingers trembling? Yolande thought. *Good. Sweat a little. Don't stop to think.*

The Draka laughed. "It's our secret weapon," she said. "There really *is* one. I always knew they must have somethin' planned . . . A biological, to disable the Yankee crews in near-orbit. Really nice piece of work; code name *Stone Dogs*. It's a stone killer, too! Delicate trigger, modulated microwave emission. We go to War-Condition Alpha tomorrow."

The serf's hands *were* shaking now. Yolande put a raised eyebrow into her voice. "What's the matter, Marya? Don't worry, yo aren't in any danger. Should be a cakewalk, and anyways, this is the best-defended place on Luna." She pulled the other close and kissed her. "Think I'll get a land grant in California, after," she continued. "Anyways, stay close to the quarters, the tubeways'll be closed down." The lights dimmed toward sleepset.

"On second thought, I've got a few things fo' you to do. There may be some surface damage, worst-case. That crate of Constantia '87 Uncle Eric sent, fo' that cruise on the *Mamba*." She felt the serf jerk slightly at the mention of the yacht. "Be a shame to lose it, even if that damned toy's not here when Gwen gets back fo' the victory party. Go on out tomorrow, and supervise strippin' all the personal effects out, bring them back to quarters. No droppin' hints, now!"

✧　✧　✧

"What?" Yolande looked up from her desk at the holo image of Transportation Central, the traffic control nexus for Aresopolis.

"The *Mamba*, Commandant, we would have appreciated notification of a lift!"

Yolande felt a cold pride at the expression of mild surprise on her face. *Of course, it's a good thing they don't have a medical sensor going on me*, she thought stonily. The face in the screen was New Race; they *could* control their heartbeats. She wondered how it felt . . .

"So would I," she replied drily. "Since I am *here*, and have authorized no such mission. Where is the pilot?"

"I . . ." The hawk-featured young face took on an imperceptible air of desperation. She knew the feeling; the sinking sensation of bearing very bad news to someone far up the chain of command. "You pilot is in his quarters, Arch-Strategos. That was why we assumed, ah—"

"Don't assume, Tetrarch, *do*. I presume you've hailed?"

"Of cou—Yes, ma'am. No response."

There wouldn't be, Yolande thought. She had very carefully had all the com systems decommissioned for preventative maintenance. An investigation would find that significant, but far too late.

"Well, we'll have to assume an unauthorized lift," she said, frowning with the expression of a high-ranking officer forced to intervene in trivial matters. "Issue a warnin' to the *Mamba* and whoever's aboard, to surrender or be fired upon. Alert the orbital platforms."

"Ma'am, it's, ah, the trajectory indicates a boost for translunar space. Mars is, well—"

"I'm familiar with orbital mechanics, Tetrarch," she said. *Stop tormenting the poor boy.* Her fingers touched the desktop. "On that burn, the Belt would be the logical destination. Hmmm. The *Mamba*'s fairly valuable, but there's nothin' on board we'd be all that embarrassed fo' the Yankees to get . . . Worth a chance on not scrubbin' it. Dependin' on who's aboard. Get Merarch Tomlins on the screen, we'll see if we can set up an intercept."

"*You what?* You pillow-talked a bedwench *that*, and then let her *escape*?"

The Archon's image was alone before her. For a moment Yolande felt a sensation she had not known for many years: raw, physical fear.

He looked down at the copy of her report, and the fury on his face went cold and blank. "This had to be deliberate on you part. Usurpation of command prerogative as well as treasonous incompetence."

"She was an agent, Excellence," Yolande continued expressionlessly. "If you'll examine the appendix to that report, you'll see we found clear evidence of dataplague sabotage. No way of knowin' how long this has been goin' on, either." A skull grin split her face, below eyes that were edged in red. "We went aftah the Yankee personnel. They planted a, a virus in our comps. Typical, isn't it?" Her hand twitched slightly as she reached for the glass of water. "The fact remains, Excellence, that we no longer have an intercept or strike option on the *Mamba*. Inside of three days, the Alliance craft *will* intercept, and shortly thereafter they'll know about the Stone Dogs."

She waited the seconds it took for light to reach Earth and return, on this most secure of links.

Eric von Shrakenberg rose behind his desk, and she felt his will beating on her like waves on a granite headland. "I will have you *shot*. I will have you fuckin' *shot!*"

"That is you prerogative, Excellence," Yolande said. *And I don't care nearly as much as I thought I would,* she realized. Yes, the body reacted: sweat rolling down from her armpits, muscles tensing in millennial fight-flight reflex. But somewhere deep in her soul, she would accept it. "If you wishes to relieve the Commandant of this installation just befo' the . . . outbreak of hostilities."

She saw that ram home. "Use it, or lose it," she continued.

Silence, for long minutes. At last he looked up again, older than she remembered. "Why?"

"I—" A pause, while she considered how it could be said. "I disagreed with you hesitation, but I would have accepted that. On a professional level. But you gave me a weapon, Uncle Eric. And I decided to use it. Fo' . . . personal reasons. Love and hate." Another pause. "And afterward—if there is an afterward"—she laid her sidearm on the desk, in range of the receptor—"I'll save you the trouble, iff'n it's still important."

The ancient, weary eyes stared into hers. "The fate of worlds, fo' *personal* reasons?" he said wonderingly.

"Are there any other kind?" she answered.

At last: "Go to Force Condition Seven, and await further orders, Arch-Strategos." With a touch of ironic malice: "Service to the State."

"Glory to the Race, Excellence."

Chapter Twenty-one

DRAKA FORCES BASE ARESOPOLIS
MARE SERENITATIS, LUNA
NOVEMBER 2, 1998
0600 HOURS

"Whew." Yolande collapsed into the chair. For a few minutes she forced herself to sit quietly, breathing, letting the wash of cool air from the vents help her body flush out the hormonal poisons. Then she reached for the communicator.

"Staff conference, immediate," she said. "Forcecon 7."

" . . . . And all nonessential traffic between sectors has been closed down," the civilian administrator was saying.

Yolande looked around the table. "Mark?" she said.

The Aerospace Command Strategos shrugged. "We've moved all the available units into sheltered orbits," he said. If there was one thing that a generation of skirmishing in space had shown, it was that ships were helpless in confined quarters with high-powered energy weapons.

"Move them out further," Yolande said. "Outer-shell orbits fo' the Cislunar Command zone. Sannie, start pumpin' down the bulk water in the dome habitat, fill the reservoirs."

"That'll play hell with the Ecology people's projects," she warned.

"Don't matter none." The other officers around the table glanced sidelong at each other. Yolande saw carefully controlled fear. This was the nightmare that had haunted them all from their births. "And yes, that means I knows somethin' y'all don't. Somethin' bad—and somethin' good, too."

"Now, and this is crucial"—she paused for effect—"startin' *immediately*, and *while* you moving to full mobilization, bring you redundant compunits on-net. Then do a *physical separation* of the main battle units, and run simulations of actual operations—everythin' but the final connections to the weapons units." She held up a hand to still the protests. "Y'all will find malfunctions, I guarantee it. Report the make an' number of the malfunctionin' cores, *immediate*, to Merarch Willard here, who's now Infosystems Officer fo' Aresopolis. We'll patch across to maintain capacity. Believe me, it's necessary."

CLAESTUM PLANTATION
DISTRICT OF TUSCANY
PROVINCE OF ITALY
NOVEMBER 2, 1998

"*Vene, vene*, keep movin'!" The serf foreman reached out to stop a field-hand family; one of the children was cradling a kitten. "No livestock in the shelter, drop it." The girl began to cry in bewildered terror.

The bossboys were as ignorant as the rest of the serfs, but they had caught the master's nervousness. John Ingolfsson whistled sharply to catch the man's attention and jerked his head; the foreman's rubber hose fell, and the line began moving again as he waved the serf girl through with her pet.

Makes no nevermind, the master of Claestum thought, watching the long column disappearing into the hillside. He swallowed to moisten a dry throat, pushed back his floppy-brimmed leather hat, and wiped at the sweat on his forehead. It was a clear fall day, and still a little hot here in the valley below the Great House. The shelter was burrowed under that hill, quite deep; begun in the '50s, and refined and extended in every year since. This entrance was disguised as a warehouse, but behind the broad door and the façade was a long concrete ramp into the rock. The elevators were freight-type, and the thousand-odd serfs would be in their emergency quarters in another hour or so. Armorplate doors, and thousands of feet of granite—

It should be enough, if we have an hour, he thought. There was hatred in the glance he shot upward. Nothing but the coded messages over the official net, but you could tell . . . *I always grudged the money and effort.* Full shelter for all the serfs, sustainable if crowded; fuel cells, air filters, water recyclers, and food enough for three years on strait rations.

He had had just time enough to put most of the farming equipment under wraps; the sealed warehouses held seed grain. There was even room for basic breeding stock, on the upper level.

The last of the field hands passed through, and the overseer looked up from the comp screen by the door. "That's the last of them," she called. Rumbling sounded within, as thick metal sighed home into slots.

Silence fell, eerie and complete. Nothing but the hot dry wind through the trees, and the tinkle of water from one of the village fountains. He stood in the stirrups and looked around; the land lay sere as it did with autumn, rolling away in slopes of yellow stubble, silver-green olives, dusty-green pasture and the lush foliage of the vineyards. Commonplace infinitely dear. Yesterday his only worry had been the falling price of wheat and the vintage.

"Run one mo' check," he said. "Wouldn't want to leave one of they brats out by mistake." The overseer was taut-nervous herself, but her fingers were steady on the keyboard.

"All of 'em."

"Right." He ran a soothing hand down the neck of his horse as it side-danced with the tension. "Sooo, boy, easy. Now, let's go jump in a hole and pull it in aftah us."

DONOVAN HOUSE
NEW YORK CITY
FEDERAL CAPITAL DISTRICT
UNITED STATES OF AMERICA
NOVEMBER 3, 1998
0700 HOURS

"Could it be a drill of some sort?" one of the figures in the screen said.

The Conference Room was nearly empty; just the president, and a few of her chief aides there. The Alliance Chairman was in the center of the holoscreen, with the military chiefs and some of the most crucial administrators. In theory the other Alliance heads of government were coequal, but this was a time for practicalities, and the American head of state was still much more than *primus inter pares*.

Carmen Hiero forced herself not to sigh in exasperation. "*Amigo*, they've started closing down factories and evacuating the population to the deep shelters," she said. "Look at the reports; there are abandoned dogs walking through the streets of Alexandria! You think they're doing this—it must be costing them astronomically—for a *drill*?"

Allsworthy tapped his fingers together and looked to one side, toward his pickup of the ACI chief. Hiero frowned slightly; she thought the chairman tended to rely on his Intelligence people rather too much. *Enough*, she thought. *Listen*.

"Anything congruent? Any reason for it to start *now*?" the chairman said.

The ACI man licked his lips slightly. "Nothing we can spot on short notice, Mr. Chairman," he said. His face was calm, but the tendons stood out in the hands that twisted an ivory cigarette-holder. His Australasian accent had turned slightly nasal.

You too, my friend, Hiero thought.

"But . . ." he continued. "Well, something jolly odd *did* happen yesterday, up on Luna. The *Mamba*—that's the personal yacht of their Commandant of Aresopolis—did an unauthorized takeoff and is running for the Belt. Continuous boost trajectory for Ceres; should be there in about ten days."

"That quickly?" Johannsen, the Space Force CINC.

"Well, it's got one of their new fifth-generation pulsedrives," the ACI commander said. "And whoever's piloting it isn't leaving any reserve for deceleration, we think. They've got two Imperator-class cruisers trying to catch it, and they've been beaming a series of demands that the *Mamba* stop, and warnings to everyone else to stay clear. We've no earthly idea what it's about, really. The yacht is either unwilling or unable to communicate."

Hiero leaned forward and touched the query button on her desk. "Can they catch it? Can we?"

"No, and yes, if we have something start matching velocities *now*. Considerably sooner than it might reach Ceres, if we use one of the *New America*'s auxiliaries." A collective wince, that would mean blowing the Project's last line of cover. "Under the circumstances, I'd say it's justified."

"I say we do it," Hiero said.

"Sir?" The ACI man looked to the chairman, who nodded abstractedly.

"Ah, sir?" That was Donati, the OSS chief of staff; he was looking off-screen, and his fingers were busy. "We do have—yes, we do have something significant, just now. They're . . . ah, yes. Trying very hard to keep it quiet, but our ELINT is picking it up. They're pulling up their backup comps on . . . hell, one sector after another. Running some sort of check program on the central comps. Then—they've just put out an all-points to their military, to downline the AV-122 series. That's their most recent battle-management comp."

Hiero's own fingers moved; yes, everyone here was cleared for the fourth layer of the New America Project.

"Is that one of the ones we managed to infect?" she said. Chairman Allsworthy's question came on the heels of theirs.

There was a long moment of silence. "*Mierda*," she whispered. "A leak."

Allsworthy grunted, as if someone had hit him in the belly. "We . . ." He looked down at his hands. Hiero felt herself touched with sympathy, and a moment's gratitude that the final decision was not hers. The life of the planet lay in those palms. "Recommendations?" he continued.

"Attack immediately; we're already at Defcon 4," Hiero said.

"Attack." Donati, more decisive than usual.

"With all due respect, Mr. Chairman, that would be premature." The ACI commander's balding head shone. "If . . . a leak in the Project security would not be enough to put them up to this level of alert. They'd know it would focus our attention; they'd try and isolate the infected comps clandestinely, so that we wouldn't know it's been done. There's another factor here, one we haven't grasped . . . Maybe the *Mamba* has the answer. Whatever it is, *God*, sir, even if we *win* with the present inadequate level of infection in their infosystems, we're talking *hundreds of millions* of dead. *Everybody*, if they use Fenris. We have to play for time."

Hiero sat silent, listening to the debate. This was not a committee, could not be, and she had said what she believed . . . At last the chairman raised a hand for silence.

"We'll present an ultimatum," he said. "How long until the *Mamba* is intercepted?"

"Twenty-four to thirty hours, sir."

"I authorize immediate interception. Take whatever measures are necessary. Secretary Ferriera, draft an immediate note to the Domination; their mobilization is an intolerable provocation and threat, and we will consider ourselves in a state of war unless they begin withdrawal by exactly"—his eyes went to a clock—"1000 hours tomorrow. General Mashutomo, all Alliance forces to Defcon 5 and proceed on the assumption that hostilities begin as of the expiration of the ultimatum." He looked around. "Any questions?"

Hiero waited until she was sure there would be none, before she spoke. "No. I disagree with this course of action, but we must have discipline or we are truly lost." A weary smile. "And I very much hope I am wrong and you are right, *Señor* Chairman."

"Roderigo," she said, as the last of the president's council were leaving. "Wait a moment." When they were alone. "Miguel and the grandchildren are still on Ceres. Send a message, tightbeam, priority: *Stay*. He will understand."

EAST TENNESSEE
UNITED STATES OF AMERICA
NOVEMBER 3, 1998
1500 HOURS

"Captain, what the hell *is* this place?"

The trooper was nervous. They all were, after the sudden Defcon 5 and the scramble of orders that had sent them barging off into the hills, away from any news of what was going on.

The Ranger officer looked up from his maps; they had walked the last half-mile, up into the hills. The air was cool here in the high Appalachians even in summer, chill with winter now the steep mountain ridges were thick with oak and maple and fir, the scars of the mines long healed. He had been born not far away, and he remembered the deep woodland smell of it, a little damp and musty, deeply alive. There were few enough left who could call the mountains home. Unforgiving hard country to scratch a living out of, once the pioneers had taken the first richness; the timber companies and the coal miners had passed through, and then the people had followed, down to the warm cities and the sun.

"It's a disused coal mine, son," the captain said. *They're supposed to be independent-minded*, he reminded himself. *And they're feeling lost, yanked out of their regular units*. Most of the Rangers were helping with the last crates, up from the disused road and through the carefully rundown entrance. The shielding started a little way beyond that, and then the storerooms and armories. "You married, son? Close relatives?"

"No, sir," the soldier answered. He was in his late teens, with a fluffy yellow attempt at a mustache standing out amid the eye-blurring distortions of a chameleon suit that covered his armor. "Not really."

"Nobody here does," the officer continued. "And in that cave there's everything we'd need for a long, long time."

The soldier swallowed. "Yessir. I get the picture." The officer noted with pleasure that he did not ask if there were other refuges like this. *I suspect so*, the captain thought. *But neither of us needs to know*. One of the noncoms below called with a quietly menacing displeasure, and the young Ranger saluted and turned to go. That gave him a glimpse of the last contingent, looking unaccustomed to their fatigues and carrying various items of black-boxed electronics.

"*Girls?*" he squeaked, then remembered himself and saluted again.

"Technicians," the captain said softly to himself, looking up. "Edited out of the comps, like all the rest of us. Unlikely to be missed. Not on paper either, anywhere."

The last chameleon-suited troopers were following up the trail, replacing bent branches and disturbed leaves, spraying pheromone neutralizers. He folded the map and tucked it into a shoulder pouch. It was going to create the biggest administrative hassle of all time, getting this set up again when they had been stood down.

"I hope," he murmured. "I sincerely hope."

NORFOLK, VIRGINIA
UNITED STATES OF AMERICA
MALVINA SSN-44
NOVEMBER 3, 1998
1700 HOURS

"Take her down to a hundred meters," the captain of the submarine said. "All ahead full."

Commodore Wanda Jackson glanced around the command center. It was up forward, near the bows of the metal teardrop. Only half a dozen in the bridge crew, a score more in the rest of the vessel. The drive was magnetic, superconductor coils along the length of the hull; most of that was filled with the nuclear power plant, essential life support, and thirty torps. Hypervelocity sea skimmers with multiple warheads, on a ship that could do better than fifty knots, or dive as deep as the water went, in most places. The finest class of submarine the Alliance had ever built, and the last, nearly obsolete.

"Well, they seem to have found *some* use for us," she said. "Number Two." The Executive Officer came to stand by her chair. "We'll open the sealed orders now." Their squadron was spraying out from Norfolk like a fan of titanium-matrix minnows, each with its own packet of deadly instructions.

"Yes, ma'am."

Her thumbnail hesitated for a moment on the wax of the seal. *I'm glad we never had kids,* she thought; her husband was in Naval Air, out of Portsmouth. The paper sprang free with a slight *tock* sound.

The commodore's eyebrows rose. "Make course for the Angolan Abyssal Plain," she said. "Down to the bottom, and wait."

✧ ✧ ✧

ABOARD DASCS *MAMBA*
TRANSLUNAR SPACE
NOVEMBER 4, 1998
0500 HOURS

"God," Marya muttered. The new trace on the screen was matching velocities fast.

She was in the pilot's couch of the yacht, where she had been since the takeoff. Never leaving it, except for a few dashes to the head. The floor around her was littered with the wrappers of ration bars; it was important to keep up the blood sugar. Sleep you could avoid, by popping stim, even when you were accelerating at a continuous 1.3 G. Over forty hours now since the last sleep, and things were beginning to scuttle around the edges of her peripheral vision. The icy clarity of her senses was growing disconcerting, a taunting, on-edge twisting that left you wondering if the information coming in to the brain was accurate. Could she really smell so sour already? *Am I thinking straight?* The dimmed lights still seemed hurting-bright.

Her eyes flicked back to the board. The Draka cruisers were still there behind her, three of them. Not gaining much; this ship was *fast*. Grotesquely overpowered, and the deuterium-boron-11 reaction was fantastically efficient. The first drive that really didn't need reaction mass; all it produced was charged particles for the coils to squeeze aft . . . Those cruisers were fourth-generation, deuterium-tritium fusion. This much continuous boost was probably doing their thrustplates no good at all, they must be using just enough water mass to protect the diamond films. Still, eventually they *would* get close enough to get parallax and bring their beam weapons to bear.

An alarm chimed, one of the warships' lasers was impinging on the *Mamba*'s thrustplate. Marya's fingers touched the board, and the magnetic fields twisted slightly against the fusion flame. The *Mamba* skittered sideways . . . The Draka craft were still light-seconds away, enough to make dodging easy. Missiles and slugs were out of the question without matching or intersecting vectors; not enough sustained boost.

"Oh, shit, no *way* I can fight this thing," she muttered, looking over to the vacant couches. One untrained person could just barely pilot it, on an idiot-proof minimum time, maximum thrust boost, if they knew the theory and how to stroke computers. A quarter of the screens were dead anyway, the com systems, *all* of them down, and no time to check why without getting sliced into dog meat by the pursuit. In the meantime she was half-delirious and wholly terrified.

She laughed. "And I feel *great*. Fucking wonderful!" Because she was doing, accomplishing; perhaps only her own death in a quick flare of plasma, but that would be something. It was helplessness that was the worst thing about being a slave. Not abuse, not privation, not the ritualized humiliation; it was not being able to *do* anything except what they wanted. This was the most alive she had felt in twenty years.

The new trace was still closing. Marya blinked and recalibrated. Her eyes felt dry, but the lids slid up and down as if lubricated with mercury.

Whatever it was was boosting at 2G to match velocities, and had been for the better part of a day. Better than the *Mamba* herself could do. Again she looked in acid frustration at the dead com screens; there was probably enough information flying back and forth, threats and warnings and demands, to tell her everything she needed to know. *I might as well put a message in a bloody bottle and throw it out the airlock*, she thought. *3K klicks and closing at 1k per second relative.* Soon they would be in visual distance, as something more than a point of light . . .

"Visual," she muttered to herself, unconscious of speaking aloud. "Maybe, if they're looking—"

Impatiently, she called up the maximum magnification and waited. Presently it appeared, no class of vessel she was familiar with. For a chill moment she thought it might be another like the craft she was flying; the tapered-wedge shape was plainly meant to transit atmosphere. Then she saw the Alliance colors, the Space Force blazon. Even the name *Sacajawea*. It was bigger than the *Mamba* as well, corvette-sized, a couple of thousand tonnes payload. Her hand touched a section of the console.

-Airflight mode-

[CURRENTLY IN VACUUM], the computer replied with electronic idiot-savant indifference to circumstances.

-Airflight mode, landing lights, exterior.-

[OPERATIONAL: ON/OFF (Y.N)?]

She touched on. Off. On . . .

"Sir."

Frederick Lefarge looked up from the plotting console. The *Sacajawea* was one of a dozen shuttlecraft the *New America* would carry, mirror-matter powered, equally suited to atmosphere or deep-space work. That was easy enough with a power supply as energetic as antihydrogen. If the *New America* ever sailed, it would be a one-way trip with not much hope of return, and a long time before a functioning economy could be established at the target star. Her auxiliaries had been designed to last a century, and do everything from lifting kilotonne-mass loads out of a terrestrial-sized gravity well to interplanetary freighting. This one could cross the solar system and back in forty days, without refueling.

And it could fight an Imperator-class cruiser quite handily; hence the large bridge crew. Lefarge looked hungrily at the spread of trajectories on the board before him. Those Snakes were going to get a *very* unpleasant surprise, if push came to shove.

"Sir?" That was the *Sacajawea*'s captain, Ibrahim Kurasaka.

"Sir?" Lefarge said in turn. He outranked the other man but there was only one commander on a bridge. For that matter, his manning a board here was irregular, but there were times when the book didn't matter all that much.

"Ab . . . Brigadier Lefarge, I'm getting a damned odd pattern of visuals from that Snake pleasure barge."

"I'll be glad to take a look," Lefarge said. An image blinked into

the center of his screens, and he narrowed his eyes. Not a random
pattern . . . Suddenly, he chuckled harshly.

"You didn't go through the National Scouts, did you, Captain?"

"No, Brigadier, I didn't," Kurasaka said. He was Javanese-Nippon-
ese, and the Indonesian Federation had not been advanced enough for
a universal youth movement back then.

"That's an antique system; Morse, it used to be called. Probably in
the datastore; let me . . . yes." He raised one hand with enormous
effort against the drag of acceleration and began keying. After a moment:
"Oh, my God."

"Marya, Marya! *Ma soeur, ma petite soeur—"*

For a moment she was lost, content simply to hold him. Then she
pushed herself to arm's length. There was shock in his eyes, enough
that she was startled. *Do I look that bad?* Forty hours of stim, but
still—

"Fffff—" Appalled, she stopped. The stammer she had overcome so
long ago was back. *Not now, not now!* A medical corpsman was floating
down the connecting tube behind her brother, crowding along the wall
to let the squads of Intelligence types past as they headed for the quick
ransacking of the *Mamba* that was all the available time would allow.
She had an injector in her hand, and the single-mindedness that went
with the winged staff that blazoned her elbow. Antistim and trank.

"NNnnnnno!" Marya stuttered, pointing. Her brother half-turned, cut
off the medic's protest with an angry gesture.

"You need rest," he said. The words were banal, not the tone, and
there were . . . yes, tears at the corners of his eyes.

Tears are for later, she thought, and felt a flat calm return. A deep
breath in.

"Liii-sten," she said slowly. "Therrre is a bbbbiological . . ."

CENTRAL OFFICE, ARCHONAL PALACE
ARCHONA
DOMINATION OF THE DRAKA
NOVEMBER 4, 1998
0500 HOURS

"So." Eric von Shrakenberg looked around the circle of the table.
"Is that the consensus?"

Louise Gayner snorted and snapped a thumbnail against the crackle
finish of her perscomp. The others glanced sidelong at each other;
the Supreme General Staff representatives, the Directors of War and
Security, the Council members. No teleconferencing, not for this. A
dozen human beings, and they were all those who must be consulted in this matter.

Silence. Nods. At last the head of the Staff spoke:

"Excellence, we've *already* lost twenty percent of our capacity to
this damned comp-plague, and there'll be mo'. *Must* be mo'. The Stone

Dogs are our only hope. If we lose that there's nothin'. There's no *time*, Excellence; every moment we wait is a nail in our coffin."

The Archon looked down at his fingers. *They're waiting for my decision, my choice.* The thought was hilarious, enough so that he did not know whether laughter or nausea would be more fitting. *All my life I've wanted to set us free,* he thought. *Free from a way of life based on death. Now my only chance of it is to inflict more death than the combined totals of every despot and warlord in the whole mad-dog slaughterhouse we call human history.* Could it be Yolande's fault? Could it be *anyone's* fault that it had come to this, the whole of human history narrowing down to this point? Ten thousand generations, living, rearing their children, working, dreaming, going down to dust, and now . . . He would say the words, and they would lie like a sword across all time, no matter the outcome. If there were humans at all, a generation hence, they would call this the decisive moment. The ultimate power, and in his hands.

A leader is someone who manages to keep ahead of the pack, he knew bitterly, feeling the cold carnivore eyes on him. There was exactly one practical choice he could make, within the iron framework of the Domination's logic, and the Draka were nothing if not a practical people. Or he could refuse it, and the only difference would be that he would be safely dead in twenty minutes. For a second's brief temptation he wished he could; it would spare him the consequences, at least.

No. At seventh and last, I am a von Shrakenberg, and I have my duty. Besides that, if nothing else it would give Gayner too much pleasure.

"Activate the Stone Dogs," he said; his voice had the blank dispassion of a recording. "Force Condition Eight. Service to the State."

"Glory to the Race," came the reply. There was another brief pause, as if the men and women gathered around the table were caught in the huge inertia of history, the avalanche they were about to unloose. Then they rose and left, one by one.

Gayner was the last. Eric watched her with hooded eyes as she snapped the perscomp shut; time had scored his old enemy more heavily than he, for all his extra years. Only traces of red in the gray-white hair, and there were spots on her hands.

"Happy?" he said, at last. There was a curious intimacy to a perfect hatred, like a long marriage.

"Not particularly," she replied, straightening her cravat. Their eyes met. "The Yankees . . . that's not personal. They're cattle." Then she smiled. "You, on the other hand. Ahhh, come the day, *that* will make me happy."

"Nice to know Ah can afford anothah human being such satisfaction," he said. There was no particular hurry now; neither of them was much involved in implementation. The snow was moving down the slope. Still glacial slow, but there was no stopping it. "Headin' fo' y' bunker?"

"No." She looked up at the wall. "I've got a trans-sonic waitin'. I'll sit this one out in Luanda. Home." Gayner looked at him again. "But don't worry. *I'll be back.*"

✧　✧　✧

DOMINATION SPACE COMMAND PLATFORM MOURNBLADE
LOW EARTH ORBIT
NOVEMBER 4, 1998
0900 HOURS

The commander of the battle platform looked up sharply. "That's the code," he said. His second nodded, confirming. They were in the center of the platform, and the Chiliarch allowed himself a moment's pride; this was the newest and best of Space Command's orbital fists.

"Initiate Zebra," he said.

There was heavy tension on the command bridge, but no confusion, no panic. This was what they had trained long years for; if any of the operators at their consoles were thinking of homes and families below, it made no difference to the cool professionalism of their teamwork.

"Preparin' fo' launch," the Weapons Officer said.

The commander touched his screen.

[Detonation sequence activated]

"What the *fuck*—that's not the launch protocol." There was controlled alarm in his voice. "Weapons, pull that sequence!"

Frantic activity. "Suh, it's not responding. The central comp's not acceptin' input."

[Ten seconds]

A warning sent through Security crept into the Chiliarch's mind. "Dump the core, over to dispersed operation." A sound of protest from the Infosystems Officer; that would reduce their combat capacity by nine-tenths. "Do it, do it *now*."

"Initiatin' . . . suh, it won't respond. Null board."

"Get in there and slag the core, physically, now."

[Seven seconds]

Fingers were prying at access panels. Hands tore bunches of wire free, and sparks flickered blue.

[Five seconds]

Sections of screen were going dark. He could see globes of fire rising and flattening against the upper atmosphere, down below on Earth. Vortexes of black cloud were gathering.

[Three seconds]

Even now there was no panic. Desperate effort . . . *Impossible*, he decided. The Chiliarch closed his eyes, called up a certain day. He was small again, and his father was lifting him . . .

[Two seconds]

. . . up so high toward the tree . . .

[One second]

. . . with Mother smiling, and . . .

[Detonation]

◇   ◇   ◇

DONOVAN HOUSE DEEP SHELTER
FEDERAL CAPITAL DISTRICT
NEW YORK CITY
UNITED STATES OF AMERICA
NOVEMBER 4, 1998

"This had better be worth it, *compadre*," Carmen Hiero said, fastening her robe. It was the early hours of the morning, and she reached grumpily for the coffee. Then she saw her aide's face, and gulped without tasting. "Something more about those broadcasts?"

"No, still just harmless modulated signals," the aide said. "But there's something else . . . Madam President, the chairman's gone to the Denver War Room." Thousands of feet under a mountain; she felt something clutch at her windpipe. That was where the real decisions would be made, as was right and proper; the Alliance was sovereign, not the member states. "Please, the briefing's being prepared." It was a short walk to the War Room; even after all these years, she still found the salutes a little incongruous for an elderly Sonoran lady in a housecoat.

"What's the status?" she asked, sinking into the command chair. There was a tired smell of cigarettes and stale coffee, under the artificial freshness.

"They've gone to Force Condition Eight," the general said. "Full mobilization. Evacuations in progress; nearly complete, in fact. Nothing overt, not yet; we're matching, of course. No panic . . ." Unspoken, the knowledge that the civil defense measures were inadequate passed between them. *Yes, yes, General. I did my best. Pray that we will not see how far short of enough that is.*

"And they're continuing that crazy broadcasting. The experts say the only thing it's going to affect is the homing sense of pigeons. Evidently that's in the same range, planetary magnetism or some such. And . . . yes, Denver says the Project people in the *Sacajawea* did match velocities with the *Mamba*."

Hiero nodded. She had always felt that name was a little ill-omened; Sacajawea had led Lewis and Clark on their expedition to the northwest. Heroic, if you looked at it from a Euro-American perspective, but even if the family did not talk about it, there were *indios* in the Hiero background. And from their point of view, of course—she forced her mind back to the present. Best not to think too much of the past, here and now. That way lay thinking that somehow she could have prevented this.

"They're—" He frowned. "That's odd, they're making a Priority A broadcast, *from the shuttle.*"

She snorted. "Get me Orbital One. Split screen, and call up the *Sacajawea* broadcast."

Reason fought with sick dread. It made no *sense*; the balance had not changed. Von Shrakenberg was still in power over there, and still a rational man, for a Draka. They had been counting on that, on him keeping the Militants out until the Alliance was ready . . .

How could they have found out about the Project? she thought; *that* was enough to send a stab of pain from the incipient ulcer through her stomach. "Milk," she said. *No. It must be more. They would know we are not ready.*

"Madam President, we're having a little trouble with the link to Orbital One," the comtech said, puzzled. "The signal's odd. Here's the Project broadcast."

It was Brigadier Lefarge. She sat bolt-upright at the sight of his expression. "To all Alliance bases and personnel. To all Alliance bases and personnel. The Domination has engaged in a"—his voice paused, as if searching for words—"an act of biopsychological—"

She felt a sudden quietness spread from the tech's desk, rippling out. "Put them on central screen and *get Orbital One*," she said. *Oh, my children.* "Now. *Vamous* . . ."

The communications desk of the orbital battle station came on, but there was no one behind it. Silence, then a flicker. Then the image on the screen jumped, to the command deck. A man turned to look at them, and Carmen Hiero crossed herself reflexively. There were screams, and one of the techs started vomiting on her console. The man on the screen wore the uniform of an Alliance general; there were deep nail gouges down the side of his face, and an eye hung loose on a stalk along his cheek.

"*Urr*," he said, advancing on the screen pickup. They could see the body behind him, broken and floating in the zero-G chamber. Little else, too much blood was coming from the throat. More floated around the general's mouth. "*Aaaaa.*" The mouth swelled enormous, and a slick grating sound came through the speakers; the sound of teeth on crystal sandwich. The general was trying to gnaw his way to the command room on Earth. Wet mouth on the screen, and the teeth were splintering now. Chewing, with shreds of tongue hanging between the jagged ends. "Ah. Ah. Gggggg."

Below her in the War Room the tech was screaming again, but now he was standing, tearing out handfuls of his hair. The president lifted her hands against the sight, and the fingers turned on her. They smiled, showing their fangs. Burrowed toward her face and began to feed, smiling.

Pain. That was the first thought. Then, absurdly: *So this is what madness is.*

She stood, floated upward, landed on feet that rooted themselves deeper than the world. That was terrible, because she must run, she must hide. The *Anglo* girls at Mount Holyoke had sprinkled brown sugar over her sheets again and—

—She was walking down the corridor toward the elevators, and the wall kissed her shoulder wetly. A tech was kneeling in a corner, hands locked around her feet, shivering with a tremor that sent waves of blue into the air in time with her whimper. Hiero pulled her own hands away from her face, feeling the tendrils stretch and pulse. A man stumbled toward the tech and squatted before her. He had a fire ax in one hand, and a mass of bloody tissue in the other; the spurting wound between his legs showed what it was. He held it out to her, and Hiero wanted to weep with the numinous beauty of the motion that smelled of pomegranates.

Instead she walked into the elevator and keyed for the surface. It shot upward and inward, compressing her into a fetal curl. Bones snapped and flesh tore as it masticated her, rolling her into a ball that it spat out into the corridor. Tissue and fragments flowed together and she crawled along a carpet that moaned in pain and writhed away from her. Something grabbed her and jerked her upright. Insect-stick limbs, oval body, buzzing wings, centered in a face she knew. *What is this monster doing with Roderigo's face?* she thought, and felt rage seep wetly out her stomach. Words spattered around her, heavy with evil oils. She lunged forward and it ran, ran before her out onto a balcony beneath a sky that shivered and thundered.

Light blossomed, and there was a moment of total clarity as her melted eyeballs ran down her cheeks. Then—

SEABED, ANGOLAN ABYSSAL PLAIN
MALVINA SSN-44
NOVEMBER 4, 1998
1005 HOURS

"Damned fragmentary, Captain," the Exec said. The lines scrolling up the screen were the longwave relay from Hawaii. "What the hell does that mean?"

"The first part's an all-points from some Space Force johnny," Jackson replied, rubbing one hand across the other. She felt a little off, as if things were blurring at the edges. *Christ, I can't be coming down with the flu* now *of all times.* "The stuff after that is completely garbled. Rerun the first, the comp ought to have decoded it by now." That was NavCommand for you, nothing better to do than cryptography.

Wanda Jackson read the report over once and then again, then turned her head to look at the Exec. Her hand reached for the controls, and she keyed the general circuit.

"Now hear this," she said. "All hands. This is the captain speaking. All hands will proceed to the nearest medicomp and take the maximum waking trank dose, *immediately*. Remain calm. Once you have taken the medication, report to sickbay by watches."

The Exec handed her an injector; she pressed it against her neck and felt a cool bite. A wall of glass came down between her and the world, imposing an absolute calm. *That was close.* The sick feeling at the edge of her vision was still there, but now she could feel it as something apart from her. The captain touched another control, this time to sickbay.

"Dr. Fuentes?" she asked.

"*Sí*, Capitan," he answered. Dull, heavy tone. Good.

"Have your psychotropic basket of tricks ready. You understand?"

"*Sí.*"

Still with the flat lack of caring; trained reflex would take over, when motivation was gone. That would be enough, until they took the counteractants. Paranoia and schizophrenia were reasonably well understood, and you could suppress the symptoms quite readily, for a while.

It would reduce their efficiency, of course. But they could do the job. *Good thing I don't care much what must be happening*, she thought idly, and rose to head down the corridor.

OFF THE COAST OF NORTH ANGOLA
2,500 METERS ALTITUDE
NOVEMBER 4, 1998
1035 HOURS

"Oh, shit, oh, shit," the pilot of Louise Gayner's aircar was saying as he fought the controls.

"Pull yourself together, man," she snapped, and looked down at her wrist. 1035, November 4; not a day she was going to forget very soon. *Perhaps that was a little unfair* she thought, as he quieted. The aircraft was down low, no more than two thousand meters, and doing better than Mach 2; not bad, considering the turbulence since the blast front hit. That had probably been Lobito, considering their position on the coast; a medium-sized port city. *Pity. Thought they'd stick to counterforce.* The weather outside was turning strange, with cloud patterns she had never seen before. Nothing on the standard channels, nothing but the roaring static bred by the monstrous electromagnetic pulses that were rolling around the Earth. High-altitude detonations. Her aircar was EMP hardened, of course . . .

Nothing but cloud above, choppy blue-gray ocean below, visually. The radar was crawling with images, higher up: hypersonic craft, decoys, suborb missiles, bits and pieces of this and that. She swallowed, and realized with a start that her throat was dry; her flask was steady as she raised it to her lips. Wine and orange juice; to hell with the doctors. Two more traces, lower down, *fast*. From off to the west, only a few kilometers ahead of them. Something lanced down out of the sky, a pale finger that touched one of the traces. The explosion was a bright *blink* against the sea; the other trace was gone away, over the horizon.

"I don't think . . ." Gayner began. Another dagger from the sky, this time brighter and more ragged. *Ablation track*, she thought, and sipped at the flask again. *Missile, trying for the submarine.* As if to punctuate the identification, the sea erupted in a dome of shocked white, kilometers across. A low-yield fission weapon, tactical type. "I don't think there's much point in continuing on to Luanda," she continued.

The canopy went dark, and showed only the blossoming sunrise in the east. For a moment there were two suns; Gayner braced herself, and felt the automatic shock bars clamp down around her body. "Not much point in trying to reach home," she whispered. "We'll divert east and land in the Kasai." *If we make it.*

A fist struck.

❖   ❖   ❖

DRAKA FORCES BASE ARESOPOLIS
MARE SERENITATIS, LUNA
NOVEMBER 4, 1998
1200 HOURS

Yolande Ingolfsson felt the rock tremor beneath her. "What was that?" she asked sharply. For an instant she felt bitter envy of the operators crouched over their screens. They had no *time* to think.

"Sector Ten," one replied. "Levels one through eight not reportin'. Penetrator." That was serf housing, she remembered. The breakthroughs seemed almost random; the last hit had been a fabrication plant. This would mean heavy casualties, ten thousand or better. Crushed, burned, explosive decompression. *Probably fairly quick, at least.* It was a good thing that grief was not cumulative; impossible to really feel more than you did for an individual. If you could pile one up on top of another, human existence would be impossible.

"Incoming." Yolande looked up from her warship-style crashcouch to the main screen. Another spray was coming into sight over the mountains, fanning out in blinking tracks. Some vanished even as she watched, but that quadrant's main battlecomps were down, the weapons reaching for the warheads were under individual control.

"Those three are going to—" The faint vibration again, then a louder, duller sound. "That's the dome gone."

A hand closed on her throat. *Don't be ridiculous, it's only an artifact,* she told herself.

"Outside com?" she asked.

"Very irregular, from Earth," the officer replied. Yolande looked over to the main view of the mother planet, routed in from a pickup well out. Cloud reached unbroken around the northern hemisphere, and large patches of the south. Even as she watched a light blinked blue-white against the night quadrant. Decision firmed.

"Order to Ground Command," she said. That was the Army CINC here in Aresopolis—*what's left of it,* her mind japed at her. The Damage Control board's schematic of the city showed nearly half red; the residential sectors were mostly still blue, but much more of this and there wouldn't be enough afterwards to maintain the people. And there would probably be very little help from Earth. "Activate Contingency Horde-Two."

"Ma'am?" The Tac officer looked up from his board. *"Now?"*

Yolande keyed the releases of her combat cradle and stood, pushing herself up with a brief shove of one hand. "The troops will be safer dispersed on the surface," she said dispassionately.

Her chin jerked toward an overview of this area of Luna. "Most of this garbage is comin' from New Edo. It must be civilians or reservists, takin' over from incapacitated military personnel; we didn't get complete exposure fo' this Stone Dogs thing. That's why it's so irregular an' uncoordinated; we can *almost* handle it even crippled up as we are. That bein' so, they can't noways be in a position to stop us if we go in, dig out their perimeter on the surface, an' then blast down to get at the inhabited levels."

She thought of forests frozen dead in the dome, and then of ghouloons hunting the enemy through their own tunnels. There was a certain comfort in it, dry and chill though it was.

"Oh, and please to info'm Strategos Witter that I'll be with the assault brigade." The Tac officer made to protest, shrugged, fell silent. "Don't worry, Merarch, he'll object, too, but all the policy-level decisions've been taken. This is our last throw. I'm certain-sure not needed here."

CENTRAL OFFICE, ARCHONAL PALACE
ARCHONA
DOMINATION OF THE DRAKA
NOVEMBER 4, 1998
1700 HOURS

"Excellence, they're getting some of the birds away," the liaison officer said pleadingly. "Please, it's important that you get to the shelter."

Eric von Shrakenberg shook his head. "We didn't expect to disable all the submarine launchers," he said quietly. "But if they get Archona, then it's pointless anyway. I'll live or die with my city . . . Call it an old man's fancy. Status report."

The Palace infosystem was excellent. Not that he was in the command loop, of course. Today he was a spectator.

Have I ever been anything else? he thought wearily. The lines traced over the globe. Somewhere outside there was a mammoth *crack*, like thunder. Manmade thunder, a laser burning a trail of ionization through the atmosphere, and a particle beam following it.

"We got the sub!" someone shouted. Lines were spearing out from somewhere off the Cape of Good Hope. "Four skimmers away." Hypervelocity, low level. "Sweet mercy of the White Christ, that's Mournblade's sector."

"The close-in will stop it . . . One down. Two. Three. Come on, baby, come on—"

The voices cut off, as if sliced. An awed voice spoke. "That's Cape Town gone."

The mother city, Eric thought. *Cradle of the nation. Taste victory, old fool. Savor it.*

"Status," he said, without opening eyelids that felt heavier than worlds.

"Excellence, we've lost . . . Wotan, we've lost nearly half the discrete platforms out to L-5. Alliance, ninety percent down an' falling fast. Freya bless, Excellence, if it hadn't been fo' the Stone Dogs"—a quaver, hastily suppressed—"there wouldn't be anythin' *left*, Excellence."

Another stone-shaking roar of manmade thunder through the walls. Eyes darted to the screens, relaxed; the last salvo had been at low-orbit targets, ones that were unlikely to respond. Eric forced his eyes open, onto the screens. Forced his mind to paint the full picture of what the bloodless schematics meant, through the hour that followed. *Your doing. Your responsibility.*

A man was cursing softly. "Oh, shit, oh, shit, that's Shanghai. Penetrator. Two. Another."

"Northern hemisphere stations report high-incidence cloud cover—"

"I don't believe it," somebody said. Eric looked up; that had been soft awe, not the hard control that had settled on most. "London's gone."

Eric slammed a hand down on the arm of his chair. "Who ordered that? Get me their name!"

"Excellence—" the operator looked back over his shoulder; the New Race control of hormone levels must have slipped, inattention, because there was a sheen of moisture across his forehead. "Excellence, they did it themselves."

Eric sighed and sat back, reluctantly letting go the balm of anger. "It'll happen, if you inflict insanity on those in charge of nuclear weapons," he said quietly.

"Multiple detonation, Japan." A toneless voice, lost in procedure. "High-yield groundbursts. Sublevel." A pause. "Jacketed bombs. Prelim'nry sensor data indicate radioactivity—"

The Archon listened through the figures. "Schematic on distribution, given projected wind patterns," he said. "Give me an intensity cline, geography an' timewise." The deep lines beside his beak nose sank a little deeper as the maps twisted themselves. "Note to Plannin' Board: We'll probably have to evacuate the survivin' shelters from the Korean Peninsula up through the Amur Valley, minimum. Draw up estimates." The Japanese had been true to their tradition, and had taken a good deal more with them to the land of the *kami* than their home islands. *They never liked the Koreans, anyhow,* he thought.

Minutes stretched into hours, as the quiet voices and screens reported. The thunder spoke less often now, outside; more of it was being directed offensively, into space, to make up for battle stations left derelict. More and more often his eyes went to the screens that showed the cumulative effects, graphs rising steadily toward the red lines that represented estimates of what the mother planet's biosphere could stand. *Conservative estimates . . . we think,* he reflected.

At last he spoke. "Strategos, a directive to the Supreme General Staff. No mo' fusion weapons within the atmosphere. Kinetic energy bombardment only, on Priority Three targets and above." Active military installations. "Throw rocks at them."

"Excellence—" A glance of protest from the Staff's representative.

Suddenly Eric felt life return, salt-bitter but strong. "Gods damn yo, that's *our planet* you fuckin' over, woman!" A dot expanded over the Hawaiian Islands. "There goes twenty-five percent of Earth's launch capacity! Do it. Get them on the blower, do it!" *What's a few million lives in this charnel house?* he asked himself mockingly. *Go on, finish the job.*

"If only it were that easy," he muttered to himself. "If only." Aloud: "I'm goin' to catch some sleep." Chemicals would ensure that, and these days they could bring true rest. *Whether you deserve it or not.*

"Wake me immediately if we get any substantial info'mation on the translunar situation."

Even this day had to end, sometime.

BEYOND THE ORBIT OF MARS
ABOARD DASCS *DIOCLETIAN*
NOVEMBER 5, 1998

The bridge was still chaotic, but it was a more orderly confusion now. Merarch Gudrun von Shrakenberg took another suck at the waterbulb and glanced over at the console that had housed the main compcore; there was an ozone and scorched-plastic stink from it even hours after they had crashed it with two clips from a gauntlet gun. A bit drastic, but it had worked . . . Now the circular command chamber was festooned with jury-rigged fiberoptic cables, and a daisy chain of linked perscomps floated in the center.

"Ready?" The Infosystems Officer looked up from his task. *Goddam New Race bastard* still *doesn't look tired*, she thought, then caught herself. It was amazing how habits of mind stayed with you, long after the circumstances had made them irrelevant. *Now everything is irrelevant, with two exceptions*, she mused.

"Ready," he affirmed, and looked down, flexing his hands.

"Sensor Officer?"

That one spoke without taking her eyes from screens that had to be manually controlled. "They're still matching at what they think is a safe distance." There was a vindictive satisfaction in the tone, and Gudrun nodded in agreement. Safe distance from the standard suicide bomb, but not from everything on the cruiser rigged to go at once.

She felt very tired, herself. "The rest of the squadron?"

"Still acceleratin', Cohortarch; looks like they'll be able to break contact."

The Stone Dogs had scourged the enemy fleet even more drastically than the comp-plague had crippled the Draka; it was the Alliance's civilian jackals who were closing in on the helpless *Diocletian* now. Miners and haulers and prospectors, fitted with a few haphazard weapons and crewed by irregulars . . . gathering like buzzards around a prey they would not dare to approach if it were hale.

"Cleon," she said conversationally, "you were at Chateau Retour last leave, weren't you? Met my mothah?"

"Yes, Cohortarch," he said, making a final adjustment. "Always admired her paintings." And he was probably sincere, considering what they were about to do.

That had been a good leave. *It would be good to see home again*, she thought. The vintage would be in; the fruity red of Bourgeuil, the Loire Valley Pinot Noir that smelled ever so faintly of violets.

"Actually, I was thinkin' of somethin' she told me about the Eurasian War. She was in tanks then, the Archonal Guard."

"Oh?"

"Yes, they had a sayin' . . . Is that damn fool still comin' in to board?"

The Sensor Officer nodded. "Makes sense, actually. We've been givin' a pretty good imitation of a dead ship. Be quite a prize if they could get it."

The Infosystems Officer made an affirmative sound, then asked: "About that saying, Cohortarch?"

"Oh. 'If you tank is out of fuel, you becomes a pillbox.'" Her hand closed on an improvised switch, and her eyes went to the screen. Nothing fancy, someone had chalked a line on the surface. When the blip crossed it . . . "'If you out of ammunition, become a bunker. Out of hope, then become a hero.' Service to the State!"

Her finger clenched.

"Glory to the R—"

CENTRAL OFFICE, ARCHONAL PALACE
ARCHONA
DOMINATION OF THE DRAKA
NOVEMBER 14, 1998

"So," Eric said, looking at the head of Technical Section. The table was more crowded for this conference than it had been for the final one on the Stone Dogs. "Strategos Snappdove, what you sayin' is basically that we in the position of a man in a desert with a bucket of water. There's enough to get us to safety, but we got a dozen holes in the bucket and only one patch." Somebody actually managed to laugh, until Eric stared at her for a moment with red-circled eyes.

The Militant Party's man frowned. "None of the problems seem insoluble, on the figures," he said suspiciously.

Eric kept his face impassive; somewhere within him, teeth were bared. *You'll be dancing to our tune for some time, headhunter*, he thought coldly. The wall-screens were set to a number of channels; one showed the streets outside. Rain was falling out of season, mixed with frozen slush . . . *We humans may have earned this*, went through him. *The plants and the beasts did not.* His hand gestured to the scientist.

"Ah." Snappdove tugged at his graying beard. He looked as if he had not slept for a week, and then in his uniform, but that was common enough here today.

"Hmm," he continued. "Strategos, you are missing the, ah, the *synergies* between these problems." His hands moved on the table before him, calling up data. They scrolled across one wall, next to a view of Draka infantry advancing cautiously through a shattered town. The troops were in full environment suits, ghosting forward across rubble that glistened with rain. It was raining in most places, right now.

"We lost some fifteen percent of our Citizen population," he went on.

Unbelievable, Eric thought. *Worse than our worst predictions.*

"And twenty-two percent of the serfs. Three hundred million in all. But these losses are concentrated in the most highly skilled, educated components, you see? Then again, half our Earth-based manufacturin' capacity is still operable. But crucial components are badly hit. And to rebuild, we need items that can only come from zero-G fabricators: exemplia, superconductors and high-quality bearings. Not to mention the electronics, of course."

"Ghost in the machine," the Faraday exec half-mumbled. They all glanced over at her. "We *still* haven't gotten certain-sure tracers on that comp-plague," she went on, and returned her gaze to her hands. "May have to close down all the fabricators commissioned in the last decade—what's left of them—an' start from scratch."

Snappdove nodded. "So we need the orbital fabricators. But we lost mo' than *eighty percent of those*. And of our launch capacity. We must rapidly increase our launch capacity, but"—he spread his hands—"much of the material needed for all forms of Earth-to-orbit launch is space-made. And so it goes."

"Not to mention mo' elemental problems. Miz Lauwrence?"

The Conservancy Directorate chief raised her head from her hands. "We stopped short of killing the planet," she said dully. *There's someone who looks worse than I do,* Eric thought with mild astonishment. "Just. Lucky the worst effects were in the northern hemisphere, where it was winter anyways. Even so"—she waved a hand to the screen that showed freezing rain dripping on the jacarandas and orange groves—"damn-all crops this year from *anywheres*. Not much in the north fo' one, maybeso two years. Oceanic productivity will be way down, we got ice formin' in the *Adriatic*, fo' Freya's sake. Even half normal will take a decade; it'll be a *century* befo' general levels are back to normal." A death's-head smile. "That's assuming some beautiful synergism doesn't kick us right ovah the edge."

Eric looked over to the Agriculture Directorate's representative. "We can make it," he said. "*If* the transport system can get back to some-where like thirty percent of normal in a year or two. And *if* there's no more excess demands, and we impose the strictest rationing. We'll have just enough in the stockpiles to tide us ovah without we have to eat the serfs." A few hollow chuckles. "We're already freezin' down the livestock that died. Best we get control of the enemy territory's grain-surplus areas as quick as may be."

The Archon nodded to the Dominarch, the head of the Supreme General Staff. He was coolly professional as he took over control of the infosystem.

"Well, we made a mistake tryin' fo' immediate landings in North America," he said. Casualty figures and losses in equipment flashed on the wall; his tone became slightly defensive at the slight but perceptible wince. On the screen beside the schematic a firefight was stabbing bright tongues of orange-red through the gray drizzle.

"Too much of our orbital capacity is out: reconnaissance and inter-diction we don't have. Not all that many organized fo'mations to oppose us, but we're hurt badly, too; also, we've had to keep back a lot of troops to maintain order an' help with relief efforts." He paused. "An' they had a damn good fallback force waitin'," he said grimly. "Couple of cases, it was like stickin' our dicks into a meatgrinder. It goin' be a *long* time befo' we get that area pacified. 'Specially if'n we have to give priority to economic uses of our launch capacity. We're occupyin' a few strategic areas, stompin' on any major concentrations, an' otherwise pullin' back. Fo' one thing, we still haven't gotten the last of those subs."

Snappdove joined in the general nod; Trincomalee had taken a hypersonic at short range only yesterday. "In any case, the survivors in North America would be almost as much trouble in labor camps," he said. "Making better progress in some other areas we are, but . . . these are territories dependent on a mechanized agriculture. We cannot support it, and the industries that did we have smashed. Also, ground combat devours resources we need elsewhere, not so much of matériel as of trained personnel."

"Aerospace?" Eric said.

A nod from another of the Arch-Strategoi. "Well," she said, "in Cis-Lunar space, we won—if'n you consider bein' *almost* wiped out as opposed to *completely* wiped out in those terms. Only Alliance installations survivin' are in Britannia an' New Edo, with our people from Aresopolis sittin' on them. Aresopolis came off surprisin' well, which is a good thing because fuck-all help *we* goin' give them these next few years."

"Outer system."

A shrug. "Excellence, Mars is pretty safe, not least because what's left of the Fleet is mostly in orbit around it. A lot of them with their compcores blown. Not much direct damage to the Martian installations; the comp-plague hit them bad, wors'n here, but they on a planet, which makes the life support easier. Trouble is, the Fleet units down are our best, the most modern." Another shrug. "As fo' the gas-giant moons, we be lucky just to keep them *supplied*, and that's assumin' no hostile action."

"And in the Belt?"

"We lost. They whupped our ass, Excellence. We hurt them bad, totaled Ceres, but they've got pretty well complete control in there now. No offensive capability to speak of, but plenty of defense, all those tin cans with popguns an' station-based weapons. And that starship. We don't know much of its capacity, but we do know its auxiliaries are Loki on wheels; roughly equivalent to what's left of our Fleet. Less the *Lionheart*, but they're out of the picture and runnin' their systems on the research computers."

"Dominarch," Eric said formally, "is it you opinion that, as matters stand, we can break the remainin' enemy resistance?"

The head of the Domination's military looked to either side at his peers, then nodded. "Depends on you definitions, Excellence. In Cis-Lunar space, not much of a problem, for what it's worth. On Earth, we can prevent any organized military challenge, yes. Dependin' on the resources made available"—he inclined his head toward Snappdove—"we can pacify the last of the Alliance territories in twenty to fifty years. Pacify to the point of bein' open fo' settlement. I expect some partisan activity fo' a long, long time."

He bit his lower lip and tapped at the table with a stylus. "Problem is Trans-Lunar space. There's may be half a million ferals still left in the Belt, an' they have that starship and the facility that built it. We have our own antimatter production, just comin' on stream near Mercury, but the transport an' guardin' problems . . . And they are standin' above us on the gravity well." A long pause. "All factors considered, yes. We'll have to devote everythin' we can spare to it beyond survival, but yes. Certain advantages to bein' nearer the sun, and we do grossly outnumber them, in production as well. Long, long war of attrition, though. Possibility of technological surprise, although I doubt it; rate of innovation was slowin' down even befo' this, and they won't have nearly as much to spare fo' research now."

Eric tapped his fingers together, looking around the table. The Draka were not a squeamish people, nor easily frightened—but the magnitude of this was enough to daunt anyone. *Myself included*, he thought, and surprised them with a harsh laugh.

"Come now, brothers and sisters of the Race," he said. "These are the problems of *victory*. Think how our enemies must be feelin'!" He turned to the Dominarch again.

"Consider as an alternative that we get a year's grace," he said. "In addition, that that starship actually *leaves*."

"Oh. Much better. Same prediction here on Earth; then . . . oh, say forty years to mop up the Belt. Still difficult an' expensive, but it would give us some margin."

Eric tapped the table lightly. "Here is my proposal. We offer terms to the remainin' enemies in Trans-Lunar space. The, ah, *New America* to be allowed to leave; we can guarantee that with exchange of hostages an' so forth. They turn ovah the complete schematics on the compplague. In addition, we offer Metic Citizenship to any who surrender on Luna an' beyond." That meant civil rights but not the franchise, with full Citizenship for their children. "Between the ones who leave, and the ones who take our offer, we cut the problem down to size."

Shock, almost an audible gasp. The Militants' spokesman burst out: "Inconceivable!"

Thank you, Eric thought. *Gayner would have been more subtle.* "There's ample precedent, aftah the Eurasian War, fo' example." Everyone there would be conscious that Snappdove was the child of such.

"No precedent fo' that *scale*. And many of them would be racially totally unsuitable."

Eric smiled thinly. "Is there any precedent fo' the size of this *war*? Fo' the extent of our *losses*? Fo' the *situation*? We need those skills, fo' sheer survival's sake. War to the knife now might bring down the Domination." He paused at that, for the political implications to seep home. *That's right, think on the fact that I'm the Archon who's winning the Final War. Who'll be seen as the prudent one, and who the reckless, if you push this issue.* "As to the cosmetic problem, the Eugenics Board can see that their children have suitable exteriors." *And they will know which party to throw their support behind, a factor not to be dismissed.*

"But—letting them establish a colony, on the nearest star; an insane risk!"

"Nearest? With a forty-year transit time?" Eric said mordantly. Heads nodded; most of those here had a reasonably good idea of the sheer immensity 4.5 light-years represented. The whole solar system was a flyspeck by comparison. "Strategos Snappdove?" The Militant flushed, knowing this was collusion and unable to use the fact.

"Ah. Well, we estimate that they could take no more than a hundred thousand, assuming they use our Low-Met process. No matter how well equipped, this is a very small figure to maintain a technological civilization, the specialists required . . . The Belt itself is not self-sufficient, not really; it is almost impossible to fully duplicate a terrestroid ecology without a terrestroid planet . . . Using worst-case analysis, that is best-case fo' them, a century after arrival befo' they are established firmly enough to think of anything beyond bare survival. Therefo' we can expect no hostile action for a century an' a half, at an absolute minimum. Mo' probably a century beyond that.

"Besides which," he went on, "our studies indicate conclusively that attackin' a defended planetary system is virtually impossible. Interstellar war at sublight speeds is an absurdity; so is interstellar government. In two centuries, we'll be fully recovered, mo' powerful than a strugglin' colony could possibly be, and I'll stake my life and soul *we* wouldn't have the slightest chance of successfully attackin' *them*. If they did attack us, we could swat them like mosquitoes. Far mo' rational to put a fraction of that effort into colonizin' stars further out; which, incidentally, we'd be doin' as well."

Eric waited until the expressions showed the argument had been assimilated, the balance of doubt weighed, and acceptance.

"And finally," he said, "a meta-political point. We Draka have always lived fo'—not necessarily war—but to excel, to dominate, to prove ourselves. As far as we can tell, there's no other sophont race within reach. Leastways, none with a technological civilization. The universe isn't enough of a challenge, it isn't conscious; without some rival, even if it's a rival we can't fight directly, what is the Race to measure itself against?"

He cleared his throat. That was a good concluding note; he had shown them just how grim the situation really was, and a way to simplify it considerably. And besides the practical reasons, a philosophical one squarely in line with tradition.

"We'll need to study this in far mo' detail, of course," he went on. "And a number of factors depend on the enemy's reaction. But I take it we have a preliminary consensus to present to the Senate and Assembly?"

CENTRAL OFFICE, ARCHONAL PALACE
ARCHONA
DOMINATION OF THE DRAKA
JANUARY 14, 1999

The face of the man in the screen was haggard-blank. Eric suspected that that was more than the psychotropic drugs thwarting the viral saboteurs at the base of the American's brain; it would be enough, to see a world perish while you stood helpless. *There is something worse than these ashes of victory*, he thought, moved. *Defeat.*

"You are a son of a bitch even for a Snake, you know that?" the American said.

"Those are the best terms you can expect," Eric said, making his voice gentle. The minutes of relay time were an advantage; his brain felt gritty with lack of sleep. "Oh, you mean my little offer of Citizenship?" He raised an eyebrow. "Well, you can scarcely blame you compatriots—ex-compatriots—on Luna for mostly fallin' in with it. Considerin' the alternatives."

"It's not altogether over," the voice from the screen grated. "We . . . hold the Belt. We're standing over your head, Snake."

"The war is ovah. Was over befo' it began, or the human race would be dead. It couldn't be fought, only finessed. We both knew that; you lost, General Lefarge." *For reasons you'll never know.* "Even assumin' you support in the Belt stays rock-firm, all you can do is hurt us befo' we drag you down. Which we will in the end; to kill the Race you'd have to kill Earth. Meanin' two billion innocents; any one of whom, of course, can exercise the option of dyin' on they own initiative any time they wants. In terms of you own ethic, sacrificin' them for victory is one thing. Deprivin' them all of they personal choice just to make the Draka suffer mo' is a little questionable, isn't it?"

"Not as questionable as trusting a Draka's word on allowing the *New America* to leave peacefully."

I've won, Eric thought. It brought a workman's satisfaction, if no joy. "We don't expect that. What I'm asking is fo' you and I to work out a way which doesn't *require* that you trust us." He spread his hands. "To be absolutely frank, we don't really have the capacity to stop y'all, only to make the best departure orbit unworkable and slow you down. Which you can send observers to verify. In any case, my offer *has* split you community. To the brink of civil war, if you refuse this option."

Slow minutes of waiting. He felt the chill; it was colder than it should be, here in Archona, much colder. *Not too much. Near the edge, but we pulled back in time. Our Mother is wounded, but she'll recover, if I can buy her time.* Eric used the opportunity to study the other's face while the message arrived. *That is a dangerous man*, he decided. *Am I doing the right thing?*

"We accept, pending the details," Lefarge spat. "And your sympathy isn't worth shit, Snake." He recovered an icy possession. "Tell me, though. Why not just offer admission to the Snake farm to our traitors?"

Eric spread his hands in concession. "Two . . . no, three reasons, Brigadier Lefarge. First, many mo' will take the offer, if they can salve they consciences by knowin' y'all have a place to go." He smiled.

"Sun Tzu said that one should never totally block an enemy's retreat; retreatin' refugees are less troublesome than a last stand, at the moment. Second, and this I used with my colleagues, what are the Draka without an enemy, however distant? We won't be able to follow y'all anytime soon—that's anothah thing we can arrange to verify—but we'll *know* that you there. Third, fo' my private consumption . . . Well, let's say that the Domination . . . forecloses certain options, as a path of human development. Better that not all the eggs be in one basket fo' Earth's children."

A curt nod and the screen blanked. Eric sat in thought, watching the chill non-summer rains beat against the window. Then he keyed the office com again.

"Put Arch-Strategos Ingolfsson on," he continued. There was work yet, before he could sleep. "Secured Channel Seventeen, and leave me, please."

Yolande looked up from her desk, her hand shaking as she took another stim and swallowed it dry. *Got to watch these,* she thought.

"Excellence." *Wotan, he looks worse than I do. Of course, he's eighty.*

"Arch-Strategos. This is on Channel Seventeen, you can speak freely. In brief, you are relieved and ordered to return to Archona." The starved eagle face leaned closer to the pickup. "Seven hundred million dead," he continued quietly. "Includin' millions of our own people. How does it feel, bein' the greatest mass murderer in human history?"

Yolande squeezed thumb and forefinger to the bridge of her nose. "If this is victory, perhaps defeat is preferable," she said. "I'm ready fo' you firin' squads, Excellence."

"I've seen defeat just recently, and you're wrong," Eric said and laughed; she shivered slightly. It was the laugh a hanged man might make. "And I'm not lettin' you off so easy as that."

She looked up, and he was grinning at her.

"A third of the human species dies, and *Louise Gayner* survived; accordingly, I can't spare the 'Hero of the Tunnels.' And y'are kin, aftah all . . . I *ought* to send you to Australasia to pacify it."

A pause. "No, I'm givin' Gayner that joy; it's butcher's work, she'll enjoy it. And hopefully do it badly enough to give me an axe-swing at her neck . . . No, you, dear niece, are comin' home to put the remnants of our space capacities together. We need them, if we're to get this planet back on its feet."

Another corpse smile. "Just to help, I'm goin' to be sendin' you lots of qualified personnel. We're goin' to be handin' out Citizenship fairly liberal; some millions, as many as I can swing. Awkward to have them around here—off to you. Now you can *really* learn how to handle Yankees." Flatly: "And that firin' squad is in abeyance, not dismissed."

She looked up sharply. "Think about it, niece. I just 'won' the Final War. I've got a decade at least in which to use that, politically, and I intend to *use* it. And you . . . you troubles are just gettin' under way."

Yolande nodded. It was difficult to care, when you were this tired. "Was that smart, lettin' the *New America* go?" she said. *And are the Lefarges escaping me, or have I taken the most complete vengeance any human being has ever achieved?*

"I think so," he said, nodding heavily. "Keeps us on our toes, makes sure the Race goes to the stars as well. And . . . maybe this *victory*"—

his mouth twisted at the word—"means Earth is goin' down a dead end, much as we try to see otherwise. The *New America* means an insurance policy fo' our species, at least. See you soon, partner in crime."

Chapter Twenty-two

"Could things have turned out otherwise? My father went to his grave blaming himself for the Fall. Some others who should have known better still do so. Yet how far can any individual be blamed or praised for a historical event so large and complex? Here on Samothrace we have developed an exaggerated idea of what one person can do, perhaps. An entire solar system with less than a quarter-million inhabitants will do that. We are on our own, on a frontier whose homeland has been eaten by time and history. And our heritage is one of belief in individual responsibility, the sacredness of choice, in the human being as the embodiment of humanity. Rightly so: even to the extent of renouncing the temptations of the trans-human, whether electronic or biological. We make our own destiny here.

So we see our history-become-myth in terms of heroes and villains. My father was a very great man; the New America's completion is his monument, for without his driving will it might well never have been ready to carry our saving remnant. This world is his monument, as much as any single man's, for his leadership in the first terrible years of the Settlement. Yet in those final months around Sol the lovely and the lost, how many separate acts—of cowardice, heroism, treachery, honor, love, hate, stupidity, inspiration—went into the making of the Fall? The past we do not know, the future we cannot. I knew the living man, and know he never did less than his utmost. Perhaps that should be added to our new Republic's proud motto: Ad Astra et Libertas."

A Heritage of Liberty
by Iris Lefarge Stoddard
Adams University Press
New Jerusalem, Planetary Republic of Samothrace
Alpha Centauri
2107 AD (109 Dispersal)

EPILOGUE I

CLAESTUM PLANTATION
DISTRICT OF TUSCANY
PROVINCE OF ITALY
DOMINATION OF THE DRAKA
JUNE 1, 2000

Yolande Ingolfsson paused and looked back from the entrance of the graveyard. The hills looked raw, without the ancient olives; the new plantings were tiny shoots of green, and she could see the workers still piling the black stumps and branches together for burning. There were gaps in the fruit orchards as well, despite all the anticold bacteria, and the sheep were few and sickly. The winds out of the west had been cold, these past winters; cold and full of death. But the land would recover, if not fully in her lifetime; the grass stood green, and the thin rumpled grainfields were beginning to show yellow with promise. She shivered slightly, pulling the collar of her coat closer about her; it would be a long time before Italy was as warm as it had been.

The grave was a little ragged, neglected when so much else needed every pair of hands. She knelt and laid the roses on the shaggy grass. *That's all right,* she thought, smoothing it with her hands. There were small white flowers blooming in it; they smelled of peppermint. *It's life, is all.*

"Myfwany," she said, and found herself empty of words for a long time. The sun moved, and her shadow crept across the living flowers and the ones she had brought.

"Myfwany, sweet," she whispered at last. "I don't know what to say. They're calling me a hero, now. Even Uncle Eric, in public." She shook her head again. "The world is so full of mourning, it should make my own griefs seem small. And yet . . . I'm lucky, I suppose. Gwen's safe; our children are safe. There's no war hangin' over they heads now. But—" she beat her fists together. "Oh, love, did I do right, or did I fuck it all up?"

Warm wet slid down her cheeks, into the corners of her mouth. She raised her hand to her face, reached out to lay the teardrop on the roses. It slid onto the crimson petal, lay glittering.

"Oh, honeysweet," she said, her voice shaking with the sobs. "All the tears I never cried, would they have made a difference? My love, rest you well. Rest ever well. Till we meet again, forever."

EPILOGUE II

CONTROL DECK
ALLIANCE SHIP *NEW AMERICA*
PAST THE ORBIT OF PLUTO
OCTOBER 1, 2000

"That's it," Captain Anderson said with a sigh. "If we needed any more confirmation." He eased the earphones from his wiry black hair;

a stocky pug-faced Minnesotan of Danish descent, and a physicist of note as well as a Space Forcer. "Over to you, JB," he continued formally.

The Second Officer nodded and touched a control. Anderson turned to the gaunt man who stood behind him, watching the receding light of Sol in the main tank-screen in the center of the control deck. It was set to show what an unaided eye would see from this distance: no more than an unusually bright star.

"So they're keeping their word, for once," Lefarge said softly. "Not that we left them any choice, the way we had it set up." It was surprising enough that von Shrakenberg had trusted *him* to broadcast the final specs on the comp-plague . . . He pushed the complexities out of his mind. It was difficult; that was something he was going to have to learn all over again, to live for the future. Cindy would help, and they would both offer what they could to Marya.

"They couldn't touch us at this range, anyway," Anderson said meditatively.

"That's true," Lefarge agreed. His voice had an empty tone, to match his eyes. "They'll probably follow, one day. If not to Alpha Centauri, to other places."

"We'll be ready," Anderson said, coming up beside him. There was no other sound besides the ventilators, and the subliminal tremor of the drive. That would continue for months yet . . . "Or we . . . our descendants could go back, first."

"No. No, not if they have any sense. There'll be nothing here worth coming back for; we're taking all the valuables with us. All that's left."

The ship's commander cleared his throat. His authority was theoretically absolute, until they reached the *New America*'s destination, and he knew Lefarge would obey as readily as any crewman. But there was something in that lined face that made him reluctant to order; it would be an intrusion, somehow.

"Brigadier—" he began.

Lefarge looked up and smiled; it even seemed to touch his eyes, somehow. "Fred," he said. "While we're off duty, Captain."

"Fred. Look, man, there's no real need for you to stand watches; yes, you're qualified, and it'll be only five years total." The bulk of the colonists would be in Low-Met all the way; there were five active-duty crews, who would work in rotation. "But it's at the other end we're *really* going to need you. Hell, why waste your lifespan? You're going to have a life's work there, and barring catastrophe the crew's doing routine. For that matter, I'm going to have time to finish that novel at last."

"I think I am going to have a life job, when we get there," Lefarge said, nodding. "And to do it properly, I'm going to have to be looking forward." He met the captain's eyes again, and his were like raw wounds. The other man had seen more than enough of grief these last few months, but it was still shocking. "So I need time for . . . thinking. And to get the saddest words in the English language out of my system." He laughed bleakly at Anderson's silent question. "If only. If only."

EPILOGUE III

OBSERVATORY DECK
DASCS *LIONHEART*
NEAR PLUTO
OCTOBER 5, 2000

The bright dot of the *New America*'s drive was another star among many, in the screen that fronted the darkened chamber. Gwendolyn Ingolfsson hung before it, lost and rapt, unconscious even of the man whose arm was linked with hers.

"Oh, gods," she whispered; starlight broke on tears. "How I envy them!"

LOW EARTH ORBIT
JULY 1, 2014
INGOLFSSON INCURSION TIMELINE
EARTH/2B

Nomura sat silent for a long time. "Obviously, that was not the end of the story," he said quietly.

"Yeah." Carmaggio nodded, running a hand over jowls that rasped with blue-black stubble. "You've been working on the physics parts of IngolfTech. What else do we sell?"

Nomura looked down, to where an Australia whose deserts were turning green passed by, and up—to his employer, a man in his sixties who looked and probably felt younger than he had in the last year of the old century.

"Biology," he whispered. "Genetic technology."

"The New Race they created replaced them—ironic justice, but it doesn't do shit to help us. *Homo Drakensis*; and *homo servus* to serve them. One of them came here."

The physicist's ears perked up. "Cross . . . temporal travel?"

"Time travel *and* cross-temporal travel; they were working on using wormholes for FTL, and something went wrong."

"Wrong?"

Carmaggio nodded. "You're going to be among about twenty people who know the truth, about the one specimen of *homo drakensis* we got handed by accident." He smiled wryly at the eagerness behind the younger man's poker face. "And you're going to regret knowing it," he said. "Welcome to the Nightmare Club. Because somewhere out there"—his nod indicated a direction beyond the universe that turned outside the windows—"they're still waiting. They know about us. They're trying to find us. And they're hungry."